THE
DRAGON'S
BLADE
TRILOGY

MICHAEL R. MILLER

CONTENTS

BOOK 2 - VEILED INTENTIONS

BOOK 3 - THE LAST GUARDIAN

Foreword

If you have found this series via reading *Songs of Chaos* then it's worth noting that this was the first series I wrote, and at that time I wrote it in UK english.

Naturally there will be many words spelt differently to the US system and there may be turns of phrase you are unfamiliar with. I'd ask my US readers to please bear that in mind as they read.

This omnibus print edition of the trilogy was made primarily 'to be cool'. The series also found its feet as a completed edition in ebook and even more so in audio. Creating a massive hardback edition of the full trilogy seemed the natural swan song now the capacity is there to create it. I hoped to make it as stunning as possible to be a fine addition to any fantasy collection.

Given it's size it's hard to fit this many pages into one tome, so the side margins are narrower and the font a bit small. If you are reading the series this way anyway, I commend you!

The Dragon's Blade was born out of a childhood love of this genre; from the seed of an idea for an amazingly cool sword, its powers, and who might be the one to hold it. When nine-year-old me emerged from seeing *The Fellowship of the Ring* at the cinema, I was hooked for life. The idea for what would become this story did then not leave me alone until I at last completed it.

I threw myself into writing this series as a release valve of sorts during what I can only describe as a 'quarter life crisis'. I was 22 when I started *The Reborn King* and 25 when I finished the first draft of *The Last Guardian*. For a first outing it was an ambitious idea, and felt like a real apprenticeship in writing. Completing the series was cathartic enough after a lifetime of thinking about it. For it to find the success it did is, with hindsight, staggering. Few are so fortunate and I'll never take that for granted.

So whether this is your first time opening The Dragon's Blade or you're an existing fan picking up this set as the capstone of the series, I'd like to say thank you. Thank you so so much for helping me live my dream of being an author.

Happy Reading!
Michael R . Miller, 2023

P.S. To chat to me and like minded readers join my Discord server here https://discord.gg/C7zEJXgFSc

P.P.S - You can grab two FREE Novellas from my worlds by signing up to my mailing list here https://www.michaelrmiller.co.uk/signup

THE
ARGENT
TREE

RIVER AVVORN

RIVER DORAIN

TU

HINTE

VAL'TARRA

INVERDORN

BREVIA

LOCH MINIAN

CROWNLANDS

SU

SPLINTERING

THE GOLDEN
CRESCENT

TORRIDON

CAIRLAV MARSHES

COLD POINT

SOUTHERN

TH

THE BOREAC
MOUNTAINS

THE REALM OF
TENALP

MICHAEL R. MILLER

THE
DRAGON'S
BLADE
THE REBORN KING

PROLOGUE

Sixty Years Ago

In the void between worlds, where infinity had already gone on for too long, a voice called out.

"Come," it said. It echoed on through the nothingness, commanding, "Come."

And he answered it. He did not have a choice.

Green light filled his vision and the only thing he heard was screaming. Perhaps it wasn't screaming? It might have been the sound he made as he sped towards the voice.

He existed because the voice beckoned him. That was all he understood.

The green light turned to darkness and he felt heat all around him. There was a silence, brief but complete, until the voice boomed once more.

"Rise and obey. You shall be named Dukoona."

The heat intensified until flames leapt up around Dukoona and he rose, as he had been bidden. He looked down at his forming body. Fire and shadow swirled greedily around white bones, thickening and weaving until a pair of dark purple hands took shape. He twitched his fingers and they danced to his commands. The rest of his body assembled from the shadows, becoming so dense it might have been flesh. His feet touched stone, which was cold despite the fires.

And the voice spoke once more.

"You will obey. Answer me, Dukoona."

"Who are you?" Dukoona said, and he found his voice was deep. "What do you want with me?"

"You will lead my armies," it said, rumbling through the endless cavern.

"And who are you? Whose armies am I to lead?"

The voice did not answer.

There was a snapping sound and then Dukoona was not alone. In front of him appeared two small creatures, gnashing and biting at the air.

"These are the demons you will command," the voice said.

Dukoona inspected them. Their flesh was like his own but less dense, the shadows closer to a black mist with bones still visible beneath. They were twisted, hunched and far shorter than Dukoona. Each bore a long shard of rusted metal in one hand.

"Now," the voice continued, "reach out to one, order it to kill."

To kill what? There was only himself and the small demons present. Yet the voice was compelling and, on instinct, Dukoona cast his mind towards the demon on his right and thought, clearly, 'Kill.'

The demon did as instructed. It spun to face its brother and pierced its body with its crooked blade. Smoking blood gushed from the wound and the murdering demon howled manically in delight.

There was another great crack and three more demons joined the survivor.

"Again," the voice ordered. "But reach out to three this time."

Dukoona cast his thoughts forward more widely and gave another clear order to kill. At first, the demons responded to his wishes, turning on the one that had so recently murdered its own brother, but before their weapons fell, they halted, turned and faced Dukoona instead.

All four began to march slowly towards him.

He tried to reach out to their feeble minds, to tell them to stop, to regain control. His thoughts met an immovable force and he could not break through. The demons drew closer, their rusted blades raised. Dukoona had no time to think. Desperately, he tried to take hold of them again, but whatever controlled the demons threw him back. They were on him, shrieking in their guttural tongue.

Their weapons paused inches from his body. Falling silent, the demons went languid and backed off.

"Good," the voice said.

"I lost control—"

"Because I took command of them," the voice said. "Consider this your greatest lesson. You cannot hope to turn my servants against me."

"Yes, Master," Dukoona said. He fell to one knee. "What would you have me do?"

Dukoona received his answer in the form of images, burning into his mind. Information flooded him, showing him this world and the creatures that inhabited it. One image lingered for longer than the others. There was a pale-skinned creature, with two arms and legs, and hair on its face. Dukoona was imbued with the knowledge that this was a human. Besides the human was a similar-looking creature, though its skin was blue, its hair was silver, and folded, transparent wings rested on its back. This, he learned, was a fairy.

"Those creatures will not be of use," the voice said. "Kill them if they stand in your way."

A final image was then forced into Dukoona's mind: a creature very much like a human, but with a beardless face, a hardened expression, and a thickset body in golden armour. Dukoona learned this was a dragon.

"Capture them," the voice told him. "Bring as many to me as you can. Kill only if you must."

Dukoona's frustration grew. "And who are you?"

In answer, a figure of purest darkness appeared. It might have been one of those humans or dragons, but looking at it was like staring into the void. The figure hung in the air, a little off the ground, its faceless head peering down upon Dukoona. It was more of a force than a physical being.

His master raised a dark arm and waved it. Where once the cavern had been empty, some invisible veil was lifted to reveal a horde of cackling demons. The noise was overpowering. Their numbers were beyond counting.

"To you and this world, I am Rectar." The voice was beyond mere power and beyond resistance. "Now, Dukoona, we have much work to do."

1

THE PRINCE

Present Day
Brackendon – City of Aurisha – The Royal Tower

In a high room in the tallest tower upon the plateau of the dragon capital, Brackendon put the prince through his paces. Drawing upon magic, he had tested Darnuir all morning and it always surprised him how well the dragon could keep up. The superior strength and constitution of his race explained this, of course, yet Brackendon couldn't help but marvel at the dragon's stamina all the same.

With a silent jerk of his head, Darnuir indicated he would now train with his bow. Brackendon obliged, pulling the shades down over the windows and setting the target dummies into position; all with a flick of his fingers. The burn of magic, of Cascade energy, warmed his veins, running from his head, through his shoulder, down to the hand gripping his silver-wood staff. There the power would be processed, the poison removed. Such trifling uses of magic did not run the risk of addiction, of breaking, but they carried the same pleasure that could lead to those terrible ends.

Restraint still had to be exercised.

Darnuir had retrieved his bow and quiver. He stood now with an arrow nocked, taking careful aim. The reduced light in the room would hurt the aim of a human, but not Darnuir. His eyes glowed gently, like a cat's in the darkness. Yet in every other respect, to look upon Darnuir, or any dragon, would be to see a human.

The prince's chestnut hair fell loosely around his face, obscuring his sharp jaw and aquiline nose. Golden plate mail encased his lean, muscular frame, a figure no human of his age could hope to maintain. Even at sixty years old, Darnuir could outrun and outmuscle any human at their peak.

Brackendon himself could not hope to match such physical strength. Tall and slim, the young wizard wore sapphire robes over a scholar's body. His advantage was his magic, marked by the silver spark in his eyes. But magic had its costs. As currency, it had to be spent frugally, if at all. Despite his youth, Brackendon's short hair already suffered a grey tinge, one small indicator of the toll that magic was already taking on his body.

Darnuir released his arrow. It sliced through the air to bury itself in the centre of the target. He quickly drew and released more arrows, his aim so true that the bullseye quickly ran out of space.

When the quiver ran dry, Brackendon rewarded the prince with a token clap.

"Hard to imagine where you could improve," he said.

Darnuir growled deeply, stomping over to retrieve the arrows. He pulled each one out of the target with undue force, ripping the lining and spilling straw as he went.

Brackendon suppressed a pained sigh. When the time eventually came for Darnuir to inherit the Dragon's Blade and gain access to magic, their demon enemies would suffer greatly, yet Brackendon doubted the prince would control the flow of magic well. The thought gave Brackendon sleepless nights.

"Again," Darnuir said.

Brackendon bit his lip. "Perhaps you ought to visit your father before the meeting this afternoon. King Arkus and Queen Kasselle will be arriving soo—"

"There is still time. Again."

Brackendon looked to a fresh target dummy that was slumped against the wall and nearly pulled it over. But he stopped himself. He had to hold his ground. He was one of the few who could.

"Your skill with a bow alone will not win the war."

He flicked his hand, this time to pull up the shades over the windows, allowing light to flood in once more. The golden stone of the room glistened and Darnuir blew a frustrated breath through his nose.

"You know I am right," Brackendon said.

"Perhaps if my father trained more, fought more, we wouldn't need the humans or the fairies," Darnuir said, a bite in his voice. "I won't let myself go like he has."

"Even Draconess cannot turn the tide alone."

Darnuir rounded on him. "How do we know? When was the last time he took to the battlefield?"

"You overestimate the power of the Dragon's Blade."

"You encourage his weakness." Darnuir clenched his fist, snapping the bow in it like a twig. Snorting, he threw the broken pieces across the room and then hung his head. He squeezed his eyes shut for a moment, a flicker of pain running across his face. "You cannot understand. This war has raged for too long, decades of death before you were even born."

Brackendon held his tongue. He'd always considered himself a learned man, but he'd also come to learn that some things could only be taught by experience. Recent events with his wizarding kin had imparted it painfully.

"More evacuees arrived yesterday," Darnuir went on, "fleeing the oncoming demons. Our outrunners say it is a force greater than we have ever encountered. Rectar has reclaimed last year's hard-won gains. Now we have only the city left." He spat out these last words, as though just admitting it caused him great pain.

Almost in a trance, Darnuir unslung his quiver and unsheathed his sword, running a practised finger along the metal of the blade. Brackendon had noticed Darnuir did this when he sought comfort.

"Lost in thought again, wizard?"

"Not so much lost as… exploring."

"You think too much."

And you don't think enough, Darnuir.

Picking a fight would be pointless. If the prince was to change, it would have to come from within. Brackendon's calm countenance appeared to frustrate Darnuir.

"I only want what's best for my people. I hate to see them bleed out like this. Hate that I can do little to prevent it."

Brackendon nodded. "I know. I don't envy your position."

A moment of quiet understanding passed between them before Brackendon opted to chuckle, an attempt at livening the mood.

"If you're quite finished telling me of our doom, I assume you would like to continue your training?" He pointed his staff at a barrel full of swords and lifted the contents into the air, directing them at Darnuir.

The prince's reflexes were altogether unhuman. They were too quick. Darnuir had the sort of speed that would snap the muscle and sinew of a human man. This was, of course, to be expected; yet it had always caused Brackendon unease to see dragons in action like this, unenhanced by magic. He had decided years past that this discomfort stemmed from some primal fear, like being around a predator, not knowing if it would strike. This fear was tempered by his own powers, but ordinary humans did not have such a luxury. When around dragons their fears would be piqued and it was doubtless a source of tension between the two races.

Darnuir made quick work of the swords and the six that Brackendon sent in as backup. The prince was neither sweating nor out of breath, but he was smiling.

"At least with you here we might stand a chance. Your magic will be sorely needed in the battle to come."

Brackendon's cheek twitched. "You shouldn't rely on me either."

"Why have power if not to use it?"

"You know fine well. My order holds back for a reason."

Darnuir swiped at the ground in frustration, the tip of his sword sparking against the stone. "The Cascade Conclave is gone," he said. "Literally a ruin. Now isn't the time for caution. Had your order contributed their full might before now we might not be in this situation. Castallan might still be on our si—"

Brackendon raised his hand. "Castallan betrayed my kind. Betrayed us all. All for his own selfless ends. You would have me act like him?"

"Of course not," Darnuir said through gritted teeth. "But surely it cannot be so black and white; surely you can fight while controlling your desires. Surely..." He trailed off, shaking his head.

Brackendon was glad for it. They must have had this fight half a hundred times already.

Darnuir sheathed his sword. "Do you think we can win this? Do you think we can hold the city?"

"That is not for me to decide," Brackendon said. "That is for your father and his council, of which you are a part. I have no voice there. If you wish to defend the city, then you must convince the council with the strength of your own words."

"How diplomatic of you. My father," Darnuir chewed heavily on the word, "and his wise council will not have the courage for it. Mark my words, we will evacuate this entire city next."

"If that is his decision then you must—"

"Must what?"

"Must respect his wishes," Brackendon said, stern now.

With another snort of fury, Darnuir tore from the room. Brackendon gave chase, pulling open the doorway in his mind to draw upon a little magic. He used the energy to empower his legs, granting him speed. Using magic to enhance movement like this was cheaply done and again he felt the euphoria as the power flowed through him, funnelling to his shoulder and then his staff.

He found Darnuir leaning against one of the many balconies that wrapped around the Royal Tower. Brackendon caught up with him, enjoying the refreshing breeze blowing in. From this vantage point, all the northern and western segments of the city of Aurisha could be seen.

"You don't have to say anything," Darnuir said. "I will always perform my duty to my father and my people. It is just... so hard at times. All my life we have been fighting. Sixty years of endless struggle. You are still young, but come back after another forty years and tell me you too are not tired of the stalemate. Of this lack of action."

Brackendon was lost for words. He often forgot how old Darnuir was, how long he had endured this conflict. Before he could marshal his thoughts, a tall figure appeared at the end of the corridor. It was none other than the king himself.

Although broad and powerful like most dragons, Draconess bore little resemblance to his son, aside from stature. His hair fell at the same length, yet it was lighter, almost golden in places. Pale blue eyes sat above a far softer jawline, while his face was strained with weary lines. Further signs of the king's burden were evident. His hair was unkempt, his eyes were sunken, and his shoulders drooped, as if his responsibility physically weighed upon him.

Draconess stopped just short of Darnuir and seemed to toy with the idea of embracing him, before fumbling with his hands.

"Darnuir," Draconess said softly.

The prince's expression remained frosty. "Father."

"We were just on our way to the docks," Brackendon offered, hoping that Darnuir would play along.

Draconess nodded, though his eyes seemed to stare off into the distance. "The wind has been poor. I doubt the ships will arrive on time."

Darnuir offered nothing.

Brackendon sensed that to remain would be unwise. Politely, he addressed the king.

"If it is possible, my lord Draconess, I wish to return to my study. Arkus has been pestering me to return to Brevia. He says I ought to be with my own people and I'd rather not suffer his childish pleas today."

"Of course, Brackendon," Draconess said. "He has been asking me to order you to return as well. I suspect he wants you to try and re-establish your order, but I don't think that would be wise at present."

"Indeed, it would not, my lord; I am pleased you take my counsel seriously." He gave Darnuir a knowing look before stepping away from the dragons. Drawing on a pinch of magic, he sped away from the pair of them. An indulgent use of the Cascade, perhaps, but some feuds were worth avoiding.

2

THE BRAVE, THE WISE AND THE YOUNG

Darnuir – The Royal Tower

He watched Brackendon stride away, resentment threatening to boil over. If the wizard would only lend his support, they might convince the council to defend the city. As it stood, Darnuir knew that his father would choose the coward's option.

He had chosen that path too often.

"We should head to the docks," Draconess sighed, nodding towards the corridor that Brackendon had taken.

Their short journey took them down the spiralling stairs of the Royal Tower until they descended the final grand staircase and passed under the great marble archway to the plaza beyond.

Warm morning air and a bright sun greeted them. Darnuir could see Brackendon ahead, making towards the switchback southern stairs which led from the plateau all the way down to the docks. The wizard's Arcane Sanctum was several levels down. He moved as though with the wind, his blue robes billowing behind him. Darnuir and Draconess were much slower by comparison as they followed behind.

The plaza spanned the top of the plateau of rock, around which and upon which the city of Aurisha had been built. Once a forum for the dragons of Aurisha, the plaza was a vast space, intended to hold thousands. Ornate villas and columned buildings lined the outer edges. Like much of the city, it was constructed from a resilient, dirty-gold stone-metal hybrid known as starium.

Some said the villas were designed to mimic the dragon nests of ancient times, back when they had scales and could fly. The thought amused Darnuir.

Aside from the Royal Tower, the other major landmark was the Basilica of Light – a domed tribute to a dying religion. It sat on the southern side of the plateau, overlooking the switchback road. Darnuir averted his eyes, angered by its mere presence.

His people were on their knees. If his father spent less time on his own knees praying, they wouldn't be in this sorry state.

As king and prince reached the top of the southern stairs, Darnuir savoured the view: the forest of tall homes they would navigate through, down the many layers of the switchback road, to the harbour and the long bay stretching off to the wider ocean. From the east, the sound of waves could be heard crashing against the plateau's cliff face.

Darnuir and Draconess began their descent. Around halfway, they passed a tower which leaned at a looming angle, as if threatening to fall over. This was the Arcane Sanctum, where wizards and witches would gather when staying in Aurisha. Only Brackendon used it now. Aside from Castallan, he was the last of his kind. Darnuir considered that it must be a very lonely place inside. He imagined the wizard in his solitude, walking along dark corridors and performing work that no one else could understand. He envied Brackendon for it. Being left alone would mean more time to train and less hours wasted on council meetings.

As Darnuir marched next to his father, he contemplated the future of Aurisha. It was yet to fall to an enemy. It had been attacked many times, but never taken.

How will history recall us, we who gave it up?

Most of the human and fairy armies were on the other side of the world, leaving dragons as Aurisha's only defenders. Yet to allow the demons to take the city would grant them full control of the east.

We cannot forfeit so easily if we are to survive.

Their whole journey had been in silence. Darnuir sensed that his father was unwilling to engage prematurely in the argument that he knew would come. Yet once they were down at the harbour, with the bustle of the port all around them, the beating sun intensifying the aromas of fish and seaweed, and the billowing flag of the human king's capital ship off on the horizon, Draconess broached the issue.

"Darnuir, you know fine well that Aurisha cannot be held." He spoke so quietly it was almost a whisper. "We have to evacuate the city. I gave the order this morning and every ship we have is being prepared to take our people across the sea as we speak. Kasselle won't be troubled to hear this; she is wise, and will understand that nothing can be done. Arkus, however, won't be pleased that we are abandoning Aurisha. I will need your help in persuading him otherwise." The king paused for a moment before putting a hand on Darnuir's shoulder. "Do not fight me on this."

Darnuir was not at all surprised to hear those words spill from his father's

mouth. "And what, Father, is the point of your councils if not to make collective decisions?" He shrugged the hand off his shoulder with a brusque jerk. "Why bother
with this sham? You know my feelings on this matter and you have decided that they
count for nothing."

"Given your other failed judgements, I assumed you would be more cowed,
Darnuir," Draconess said, quietly but sternly. "In this instance, there was no time for
discussion. Scouts returned before dawn: the enemy will be upon us tomorrow, if not
before. I had to make a decision in the moment."

"And you chose to flee."

"I chose to regroup, and give us a chance to gather our full strength."

"For what?" Darnuir snapped. "To assault our own city? To throw our men
against our own defences?"

"No," Draconess said simply. "As always, you see only through the lens of our
people."

"It is our people who will win this war."

"Since Castallan turned against us and took up residence in the Bastion, we face a
war on two fronts, Darnuir. It is not in our interests to have our allies tied up,
fighting that traitorous wizard in the west."

Darnuir's interest was piqued. "You mean to retake the Bastion?"

"That fortress was designed to repel dragons. Do you think you are capable of
taking it?"

His mind began to fill with plans for assaulting Castallan's fortress. Despite
himself, he also smiled. A chance at revenge to sweeten the bitter retreat. His father
was a decent diplomat, Darnuir could admit that much.

"If I am guaranteed the command, then yes, I will help convince Arkus to take
this course."

"It would be fitting for you to lead this one," Draconess said. "I hope Arkus will
also see the merit in my decision."

Arkus could be difficult to reason with; it had been troublesome for the dragons
to coordinate armies while he sat debating with his own courts. The Queen of
Fairies, Kasselle, on the other hand, was different. Darnuir admired her greatly, and
though he was a mere boy to her, she had always respected his position. At around
one hundred and twenty years old, she was perhaps the oldest being on Tenalp. If she
agreed to what Draconess was planning, then Arkus should fall into line.

The distant ships entered the harbour, draped in the silver and blue of the fairies,
as well as the white and black of humanity. Once moored, Darnuir and Draconess
moved to greet their guests at the gangway.

Arkus stood below Darnuir's height and was hardly an imposing figure. Yet there
was a sternness to him, and he radiated an aura over his men that Darnuir could
never quite interpret. Was it fear, or respect? The human king's black hair was slick

against his scalp, and his face was darkened with stubble, an unusual sight in a city where no dragon allowed their beard to grow. Shrewd eyes roved over his surroundings. His charcoal robes, trimmed in white, brushed the gangplank as he walked, and he received salutes from a score of fully armoured guards.

Kasselle, on the other hand, seemed content to bring only two bodyguards: blue-skinned fairy warriors with huge swords strapped to their backs under folded wings. Not the wings of a bird, but insect-like and translucent. Kasselle herself was not gifted with flight. She was taller than Darnuir and infinitely more elegant then Arkus. A gown of silver silk hung lightly over her slender frame, gently lifted up by the breeze to give the impression that she was floating. Her silver hair bounced lightly and the sky-blue hue of her skin might have been mixed by a master painter. Her eyes were a deep indigo and moved to observe Draconess and Darnuir in turn.

Draconess greeted them with all the dignity of the occasion. They then turned expectantly to Darnuir, who said, as politely as he could, "It is good to see you again, my lord, my lady." He gave a small bow to each of them.

They returned the favour, Kasselle smiling broadly, Arkus more reluctantly but lowering his head all the same.

"I'm only sorry that it is not under better circumstances," Kasselle responded in a soft, tuneful voice.

"When can there be good circumstances in war, my lady?" Draconess said.

"When you're winning!" barked Arkus. "I'm sure Rectar and his foul circle are quite joyful at present."

Everyone shifted uneasily.

"Shall we continue our conversation up in the war room?" Draconess said at last. "The docks are not an appropriate location for our discussions."

"Quite right," Arkus said, pivoting on the spot to get a better look at their surroundings. "What are all these people doing here?" He laughed. "You'd think the whole city was trying to get on a ship and leave."

"Like I said," Draconess beckoned, "we should continue our conversation in the war room. Please come."

Kasselle briskly followed. Arkus looked a little confused, as if trying to work out if he had been correct in his presumption. Darnuir was about to follow as well, when Arkus wheeled around and looked at Darnuir as if he was plucking up the courage to do something daring.

"I had wondered whether you would do me a favour?" he asked furtively.

Darnuir raised his eyebrows. This was bound to be rich.

"You see, ever since my son was lost to me, I've decided to take my daughter everywhere with me to keep an eye on her, you know." Darnuir kept his eyebrows raised, now out of shock. Arkus' wife, Ilana, had not long since given birth. The girl could not be more than a few months old. The thought of minding a baby, never mind a human one, was distasteful.

I will not play minder to your whelp. We are not equals, Arkus.

"Bringing an infant across open waters during a time of war doesn't seem the safest thing to do."

"Please don't question me, Darnuir." His tone implied that many had questioned his decision before. "I cannot bear to lose another child, another heir. I might be here in the city for weeks. It is my right."

It seemed like mild hysteria to Darnuir and he wondered briefly if he should raise this with his own father. The only thing worse than a slow human king would be a mad one.

"She's here now," Arkus went on. "It's done. I hope you can understand."

"I do understand," Darnuir said mechanically. "But what has she got to do with me?"

"Well, I was only wondering if you might personally oversee her protection."

"Don't you have soldiers who can do that?"

"Yes, but even a thousand men couldn't offer the protection you can," he pleaded, though the obvious flattery did not please Darnuir. "Not necessarily you personally. I mean, you have some sway over the Praetorian Guard, do you not?"

Darnuir narrowed his eyes. What possible threats did Arkus foresee befalling him while he was a guest in Aurisha?

"I would be honoured to watch over your daughter, Arkus," he lied, "but I think my presence is better served in this meeting. It is my right, after all," he added firmly. Arkus fumbled and looked as if he was going to speak again when Draconess called back to them.

"I hope there isn't a problem?"

"Not at all, Draconess," Arkus called back. Hastily, he made his way over to the small company of royals.

Darnuir followed behind the trio, trailing them like a ghost as they made their way west around the base of the plateau, through the lower city and towards the lift in the northern district of Aurisha. This great lift would allow them to make the ascent to the plaza far more quickly than walking the meandering switchback road.

Darnuir allowed his feet to carry him, his mind circling Arkus' request. The human king had attempted such transparent power moves before – poor efforts to assert his own position over Darnuir, a mere prince. Yet Darnuir was twenty years Arkus' senior and had fought in countless battles while Arkus sat upon his cushions. Neither Arkus nor his recent forebears had led their men in battle themselves. Too easy to kill, and too weak, like all the rest of his kin.

Before Darnuir knew it, they had reached the lift and began ascending the seven hundred feet to the plaza.

He continued to follow absentmindedly behind the others as they made for the Royal Tower, his thoughts drifting between anger at his father's decision and excitement for the assault on the Bastion. That fortress was designed to repel his kind, but he'd take great pleasure in breaking it apart. If the traitorous wizard thought himself secure, he was sorely mistaken.

Their feet echoed lightly off the marble as they entered the tower and approached the grand staircase, with those fierce, carved dragons forming the railings. The royals trudged up the spiral staircase to one of the highest levels. Arkus let loose a pained little yelp and clasped his hands over his ears. They must have finally popped due to the elevation. Darnuir smirked to himself.

When they arrived at the war room, the elderly tower steward and several attendees hastened to serve them.

"Some food and wine for our guests, please, Chelos," Draconess said to the steward.

Chelos bowed earnestly and his underlings followed him from the room.

The war room was cluttered, full of depictions and trophies of wars fought and won long ago. Most impressive was the table itself. Carved from starium, the table was a large crescent moon with two imposing stone seats side by side. One for the king and one for the guardian.

Draped atop the left chair was a carved dragon in all its bestial glory. Its wings spread outwards as if shielding the one who sat below, and its eyes were wrought in such a manner they seemed to follow the onlooker around the room. This was the seat of the king. The guardian's chair was entirely different. A severed sun was carved there, one half marked with criss-cross lines as though scorched, and the whole image was pierced by a sword. Whereas the king led the people in civic matters and in war, the guardian headed the faith.

Yet there was no longer a guardian. There had not been one since before the war, and the last was presumed dead.

Opposite the stone chairs, on the outer sweep of the table, were three smaller wooden ones. Despite the obvious inference of where he was to be seated, Darnuir made towards the guardian's chair but was halted by a piercing look from his father. They had often had this argument too.

Still, father clings on to this ghost of a protector. If he hopes that someone might share his burden, why does he not share it with me?

Reluctantly, he took his place alongside Arkus and Kasselle. Servants hurried in, carrying dishes of giant green olives, round loaves, thinly sliced boar meat, and Darnuir's favourite dipping sauce, garum. Heavily watered-down wine arrived as well in golden goblets. Darnuir avoided the wine; dragons found it hard to handle at the best of times. Rather than a weakness, he saw it as a strength; while humanity drank itself to death, dragons laboured to achieve greatness.

Kasselle, like most of her kin, was not overly fond of meat. She picked at the olives and bread, while Arkus took a bit of everything, bar the garum sauce, which he claimed gave him a stomach ache. Darnuir ripped off a piece of loaf and greedily dipped it in. Draconess piled boar meat onto his bread in a calculated manner before eating.

When they were all done with their refreshments, Draconess rubbed his eyes and then began his speech.

"As you are doubtless aware, Rectar has launched a fresh campaign against the dragons. A demon army is approaching this city; a far greater army than any we have encountered before. Since pouring out of Kar'drun, the demons have swept south and have trampled our defensive outposts along the Crucidal Road. We've had no choice but to evacuate what people we could from our outlying settlements to Aurisha."

"What of Castallan?" Kasselle asked.

"Castallan is still within the walls of the Bastion," Darnuir said. "So far as we know. He should not trouble us here."

"This blasted war was going poorly enough when we faced Rectar alone," Arkus said. "How are we to deal with both Rectar and Castallan? Especially now Castallan seems to have been instructed by Rectar to summon demons of his own."

"I admit things have never seemed so bleak," Draconess said. He looked longingly towards the seat of the guardian.

There is no guardian to help you, Father. You must help yourself.

"And yet," Draconess continued, "a turning point must come. The world does not move down a determined path. We may yet see a reversal in our fortunes. But for now, my people flee to Aurisha."

"You are preparing for a siege?" Arkus asked, leaning forward.

"Not quite. I've ordered an evacuation of the city as well."

"What?" Arkus said stiffly.

"Well," Darnuir said, "I thought my father made it perfectly clear. We're leaving."

Arkus shot him a dirty look. "I know perfectly well what he meant. I only mean to say, Draconess, why abandon the dragon capital – your capital – and the Three Races' strongest foothold in the east without a fight?"

"We do not have the strength to defend the city," Draconess began, "not against such a host; not alone. As strong as the dragons are, we cannot turn the tide, and this one will crash over these walls, manned or not."

"Surely there is something we can do?" Arkus asked. "This must be the bulk, if not all, of our enemy's strength. If we can counter him here, then we might—"

"Arkus," Draconess warned, "we cannot hope to hold the city with dragons alone. We're too spread out and, as I recall, you requested I send a considerable part of my army to aid in your capital's defence. Dragons now also guard your walls at Brevia in case Castallan attacks you there."

"Castallan wouldn't even be a threat if it weren't for Darn—"

"What's done is done," Kasselle interrupted.

Arkus glowered but changed course, chewing upon every word. "If it was troops you required, Draconess, why not send for them? We could have brought thousands with us."

"The attacks escalated while you were still at sea, so there was no way to inform you," Draconess said. He sniffed and carefully rubbed the bridge of his nose. "I thought it best to start the evacuation and inform you once you'd arrived."

"Why have these councils if you do not require our input?" Arkus said.

"Because it is his prerogative as commander-in-chief," Darnuir informed Arkus in a pleasurable hiss. "As my father often reminds me."

"I do not think we should dwell on rights and privileges," Kasselle interjected, "yet I must confess, Draconess, I do not understand. It does not seem wholly wise to abandon the east completely, unless you intend—"

"To secure the west, my lady," Draconess said boldly, in a tone that Darnuir had not heard from his father in years.

"And root out the wizard?" Arkus said.

"Uproot him and find out what he knows," Draconess stated. "We must learn everything we can from him about Rectar. I intend for Darnuir to lead the campaign. While he retakes the Bastion for us, we will consolidate the rest of our strength in and around Brevia."

"Rectar and his demons will only chase us across the ocean," Arkus sighed. "My vassal, Lord Imar of the Splintering Isles, will hardly be pleased when his waters become subject to unchecked demon ships and likely invasion. What is to happen to his people if we cannot protect them? Some might be evacuated to Brevia, but not all, and my city is not the stronghold Aurisha is. If Castallan does not fall swiftly and we end up fighting on two fronts, we will surely be defeated."

"The wizard has been permitted to secure his paltry domain in the south of your kingdom because we are spread thin," Draconess said. "If we hit him hard then his Bastion will crack and break."

"That fortress was designed to be impenetrable," Arkus said. "Designed specifically, I might add, to prevent dragons from taking it with ease. How can you be so sure of victory?"

"I am sure we will find a way," Draconess said. "I have my faith. I believe the gods will not abandon us, even if others have."

Darnuir couldn't be certain but it seemed his father's gaze lingered for a moment upon Kasselle. The queen looked away, uncharacteristically sheepish. Arkus appeared oblivious to this exchange and took another sip of wine.

"Have they ever been on our side, these... gods?" he said, as though the wine in his mouth had turned sour. He smiled at Draconess. "Well, it is your prerogative to choose our path, isn't it?"

Draconess smiled graciously back.

The meeting continued for hours, largely discussing the logistics of bringing the dragons across the sea to stay for an undetermined amount of time. In the end, Draconess rose to his feet. He surveyed those around the table one last time.

"This is a most dangerous time for the Three Races. It could be the end of us or it could be the beginning of a renewed effort against Rectar, Castallan and the demons who serve them. I'd rather it be the latter."

"As would we," Arkus said.

"We have yet to give in," Kasselle assured him.

Draconess nodded at the pair of them then took his leave. Etiquette made Kasselle and Arkus wait before they too left. Arkus was greeted by the old steward, Chelos, who would take him to his quarters. Kasselle would make her way back to her ship and sleep there. She never stayed in the Royal Tower a moment longer than she had to.

Darnuir, however, remained where he was.

Now it came to it, he didn't want to get up; he didn't want to leave this room, this city, and his home behind. Assaulting the Bastion be damned, this was where he belonged.

Give me ten thousand dragons and I swear I'll hold the walls.

Yet he had no choice in the matter. Darnuir was to Draconess what Arkus was to him: measly and insignificant. His temper taking over, Darnuir backhanded the remaining wine goblet, sending its contents flowing like thin blood across the crescent table. Some of it splashed onto the chair of the king. Darnuir met the eyes of the carved dragon above it and felt judged.

If only he could turn into his people's true form of old. If only they still had a shred of the power they once held.

Rubbing fiercely at his eyes, Darnuir at last rose and left the room, the dragon, and this painful day behind him.

3

JUDGEMENT

Darnuir – The Royal Tower

Later that same evening, Darnuir stalked the hallways of the tower. He was in two minds, wishing dearly to confront his father but knowing full well the futility of such a move. Paying little attention to his surroundings, he stumbled into one of the guest wings and came upon Arkus.

The human king was outside his chambers, his face harder than normal. In his wake was a line of several guards carrying a crib into the room. Darnuir presumed it was his daughter but did not get a chance to confirm this theory before the guards entered and closed the door behind them. Arkus, seeing Darnuir, lingered in the hallway.

"Oh… what a pleasant surprise," he said with an attempt at indifference, though his hesitant start gave him away.

"Do you think that's wise?" Darnuir asked him, carefully approaching Arkus for maximum intimidation. "Leaving her up here?"

"She was sick during the last days at sea. I think it best if she sleeps on solid ground tonight. I'll be returning to the harbour shortly. We'll need to work through the night if we are to prepare this evacuation."

Darnuir was taken aback. It was not like Arkus to get his hands dirty.

Even he will act when father does not.

"There is much work to be done, after all," Arkus added.

This shook Darnuir from his reverie. "Much and more."

Arkus took this as his signal to leave and retreated into his room, his charcoal robes brushing the floor.

Darnuir continued his aimless wandering, deciding to get some fresh air after a time. When he exited the Royal Tower, he noticed a dim light emanating from the Basilica of Light. Its great dome rose like a half-moon, glinting under the starlight. A colonnaded entrance sat atop a severe set of marble stairs.

It had been years since he last entered that place. Draconess, on the other hand, was a more devout believer in the Way of the Light.

Are you there now, Father? Praying? Rather than helping in our darkest hour?

Of course Draconess would be there. Only a minority of dragons bothered with the dying faith, but his father and the Praetorian Guard were all vehement believers. But where had it got them?

Resentment towards his father flared hotly. Darnuir strode towards the Basilica, fully intending upon a confrontation.

Inside the cavernous temple, it took Darnuir a moment to gain his bearings. Torches and candles flickered along the walls, growing smaller in the distance. At the far end of this disconsolate setting, under the dome, was a lone figure upon his knees.

This space was designed to match the curvature of the dome with walls running downwards into the floor like enormous waves. Three reliefs adorned these walls, equally spaced from each other. Three gods, and not one of them ever came to answer Draconess' pleas. At the centre of all this stood three carved, plain stone swords, hilt up and spaced out in a triangle. Draconess knelt between these stone swords.

Darnuir took his time approaching, ensuring every one of his footsteps echoed loudly off the bare marble floor. Once closer, he observed that his father faced the relief of the god N'weer, deity of rejuvenation. Three spiralling lines spun out from a central point to create the symbol of N'weer, signifying the never-ending cycle of all things.

Draconess did not stir until Darnuir was right behind him.

"Come to argue with me more, my son?" His voice was heavy with exhaustion and perhaps sadness. "Or have you come to pay respect to N'weer, so that the dawn will come again?"

"And then, at daybreak, thank Dwna for giving us the light back?" Darnuir scorned. "No, Father, I will not plead with a god to bring the dawn. I haven't prayed in years, and still the sun rises."

"When you were a young hatchling, you used to pray with me."

"When I was a *child*, I believed in everything you said. Everything you did."

"Tell me, when was it that you grew so bitter towards me? When was it that you began to hate me?"

"Hate is a strong word, Father."

"And yet..." The accusation hung like a dead weight between them. Draconess kept his eyes closed.

"You cling on to this dead religion, Father, as if it will save us. Like you cling on to your notions of a guardian who will come again. These are dead things from an irrelevant past. Both are gone."

"Yet still the temple remains. As does my faith. I know these things will rise again."

Always the same fight. The same unfaltering argument. He has 'faith'.

"Our people once believed strongly in the Light," Draconess said, "and in those days, we were strong. We had purpose. We had a cause. Now our faith is all but extinguished, and we are weak. Do you not see?"

"Perhaps things would change if you stopped spending time on your knees and got out there." Darnuir pointed forcefully towards the arched doorway. "Keep your faith if you will, but act, Father; act rather than flee to your empty sanctuary."

"Act," Draconess said, still quite calmly. "And do what?"

"Kill demons? Lead our armies? At least help pack the ships tonight!"

"One demon or a thousand, it makes no difference so long as their master lives."

"Then kill him!" His voice reverberated around the temple. "You have the Dragon's Blade; you're supposed to have the power. If not you, then who?"

"You?"

Darnuir's laugh was maddened. "I have asked you for the sword countless times and you refuse. But yes, I will do it. If I must."

Draconess shook his head. "I once hoped that you might be able to take it, but you have proven that granting you such power would not be wise."

"One mistake, Fathe—"

"Reckless, susceptible, blunt and without subtlety," Draconess interrupted, his voice rising now. He remained kneeling but turned to face Darnuir. "Good intentions do not change that. You'll recall that Dranus once had such good intentions. He sought power to serve the Light, and in doing so he splintered our race. We fought the Black Dragons for centuries."

"You would compare me to some ancient enemy, again long dead? Let go of the past, Father. Think about our future. Dranus is not the enemy now; Rectar is. He needs to die. I ask again, who will do it, if not you?"

"This is why I pray, for I am certain the answer will come."

"You've given up, haven't you? That's what all of this is about."

"I have faith."

"You have an empty hall and emptier promises."

"Leave me," Draconess said, returning to face N'weer. "Go and take action. Do what you think you must."

Darnuir tore from the Basilica. His blood was hot, and his hand itched for his sword. It was a shame the demons were not here now. How cathartic it would be to tear them apart. Perhaps he ought to do just that. Drive into the horde. Kill. Shred their wispy, bony bodies apart. He could create a river of their smoking blood. And if he died, he would have at least done something.

Heart thundering, he stopped. Long, deep breaths helped to calm him. A strong wind whipped through the plaza, cooling his skin along with his temper.

Yes, he could stay behind and fight the enemy, but he would die. Somehow, he might fight all the way to Rectar's feet, but he would die there just the same. Would that really be any better than kneeling on a cold temple floor?

He decided to pursue his original course and headed for the docks. He could lend his hands to the evacuation even if Draconess would not. His people needed action, but nothing reckless. On that account, his father was correct.

But Darnuir was not his father.

4

THE FALL OF AURISHA

Darnuir – The Harbour of Aurisha

Dawn came, and with it blasts from the city's war horn – a massive instrument that took three dragons to blow. It sounded like the bellow of the beasts they once had been. Darnuir dropped the crate of grain he was carrying as he heard it roar. Everyone around him froze as well.

They have come.

Silence followed the horn. A few heartbeats passed by.

Then hysteria took over.

Those still waiting to board a ship lost all sense of order, rushing towards the remaining vessels. Shrill screams of panic rose. Despite their might, his people were afraid. Every dragon here was afraid.

Darnuir found himself caught unprepared. It was truly fight or flight. He desired the fight, but as much as it pained him to admit, it would have to be flight. Yet something had to be done in order for the escape to happen. The demons had come too early.

Stuck at the harbour at the southern end of the city, Darnuir could not see the approaching horde. They would assault the walls of Aurisha by land on the northern side. If they got over them and into the city too quickly, they would have access to the great lift and then the plaza itself would be endangered.

"Darnuir!" a voice strained over the crowd. "Darnuir! I need you. Please!" Arkus was pushing through the chaos.

The sudden appearance of the human king was both the last thing Darnuir expected and the last thing he needed.

"Why are you here? I thought you would have returned to your chambers."

"Th-th-there was so much to do," Arkus stammered. "Please, Darnuir. My girl, she is still up there."

Darnuir closed his eyes in fury and frustration.

The sooner this child walks, the better.

"I'm sure your men are capable of bringing her down here."

"You're quicker – so much faster. Please, Darnuir. Please!" A sweetness filled the air, the smell of human fear; this was as strong as a pot of honey. Arkus was deadly afraid.

Darnuir searched around for a replacement for the task, yet most of Draconess' elite Praetorians were making their way towards the western side of the city. The streets there hugged the base of the plateau at ground level and might be defended more easily should the walls be breached.

Arkus was almost whimpering now. Darnuir looked upon him, feeling both pity and disdain. Dearly he wished to join the Praetorians and his father, but he knew Draconess would not have him refuse Arkus. They could not afford for humanity to break apart over a succession crisis.

"Back to your ship," Darnuir told him. "I'll fetch your daughter."

He sprinted off towards the switchback road. As he began the ascent, he saw his father in the distance rallying his Praetorians. Draconess drew out the Dragon's Blade, its golden metal gleaming in the dawn light, its red hilt unmistakable. Each Praetorian was heavily armoured, wearing red-plumed helmets and holding rectangular shields that stretched from neck to shin. They roared in unison at Draconess' words before surging on.

It took everything Darnuir had to tear his gaze away and continue his journey up to the plateau.

Such was his haste in reaching Arkus' chambers that he actually had to stop to catch his breath. A stitch burned across his midriff – a sensation he had not experienced in years. He should have gotten more sleep.

As he reached for the door, it opened seemingly of its own accord and six steel-armoured guards nearly collided with him in their haste to exit. There was little time to exchange words. Darnuir saw the baby in its crib and was satisfied.

"Fast as you can," he implored them. They ran as swiftly as humans could behind him, back down the Royal Tower. Several of his father's Praetorians passed them as they made their way out onto the plaza. Darnuir decided to conscript them into service and signalled them over.

"But the king," one Praetorian protested. "My prince, we must go to him."

They were loyal to a fault at times.

"The king will not miss a few of you, nor will he be pleased if our relationship with the humans unravels. See her? That's Arkus' little princess. We have to get her to the docks."

Before more words could be exchanged, the anxious human guard at the head of the crib party piped up, "My lord, Darnuir. Please, we must not tarry. The child—" he began, but the Praetorians had already relented and moved to wrest control of the crib.

He would have ordered them to pluck the girl from the crib and run more easily but he feared a dragon's strength might damage her accidentally. There was a cry of protest from the humans, but they ceased their squawking under the glare of the seasoned dragon warriors.

The small company hurried across the plaza. Near the western edge, Darnuir risked a glance down to the lower city. A black mass of demons swarmed over the walls, virtually unopposed. Flames already licked upwards, as if trying to reach the plateau's summit. Burning flesh and the demons' death-like odour raked his sensitive nostrils.

Darnuir directed the crib party down a narrow street at the plateau's edge, which would avoid the main thrum of the crowd spilling towards the switchback road.

Sails dotted the blue landscape stretching off to the horizon. Ships were still departing, yet demon war vessels were closing in from the east.

As their company descended, Darnuir's view became obscured by rising buildings on all sides. Next thing he knew, chunks of rock were hurtling through the sky, likely launched from the demon warships. At the turning of the third road, a deafening bang overrode all other sound. Boulder-sized debris began falling from the impact of the projectiles.

At the fourth turning down the switchback road, another group of steel-clad human guards and a black-robed man fought through the crowds towards them.

"Darnuir!" Arkus yelled. "Thank goodness you—"

"I told you to stay put!"

Arkus gasped for breath and Darnuir cursed him. They'd have to move slower with him here now, and Darnuir couldn't very well abandon the human king here in the streets.

He heaved Arkus by the arm. "Come on, we don't have time to stall. The demons are moving far too quickly."

"I think Castallan is with them," Arkus heaved.

"Impossible. He's in the west, in the Bastion."

"I thought the same, but I saw bolts of arcane light soaring from the western streets. I've only seen Brackendon do such things. When he was aboard my ship last, I saw—"

"Watch out!" Darnuir cried, pulling Arkus bodily aside as a roof's worth of slate came crashing down.

It didn't end there.

Walls on either side of them began to crumble under the weight of the bombardment. Darnuir leapt, losing sight of Arkus as a jagged lump of starium pierced the ground where he had been standing just moments before. An avalanche of stone was falling now, and he lost his footing, falling hard onto the stairs. Pain and light exploded behind his eyes.

Darnuir rose with a groan and turned to check on the rest of the party, only to see several of the men who had guarded the crib lying face down, pools of blood spilling under them. Two Praetorians lay crushed; one was only visible by an outstretched hand. The crib itself and the last Praetorians seemed unharmed, but upon turning back to face Arkus, Darnuir found an impenetrable wall of rubble. Worse still, the quickest route to the docks was now cut off.

He dashed to the wreckage and began to shift what he could.

"Arkus? Can you hear me?"

There was a muffled response, words that Darnuir couldn't make out above the din of the siege.

"Come help me move this," he cried to his fellow survivors. They hastened to him and all heaved at the heavy stones, but the damage was too great. The grim reality sunk in.

They would not get through it in time.

As one of the humans reached for a chunk of rock, he jerked awkwardly and haphazardly. An arrow pierced through the man's neck, the crooked barb wet with blood.

Darnuir looked back to the top of the plateau. Along the southern edge, hundreds of demons were firing arrows down at the stragglers upon the switchback road. With a jolt, he remembered the baby and bolted to the crib. He lifted her out as delicately as he could in a hurry, heaved one of the dead Praetorian's shields up to cover them, and felt the arrows bounce off it.

Desperately, he looked for an escape route. There was only one door close enough that he could reach. He got up, baby in his right arm, shield in his left, and sprinted to it. More arrows grazed the shield and whizzed past his ears. He heaved at the handle of the door, but it didn't budge. He tried again but still nothing happened. Roaring with rage, he stepped back, dropped the shield, and kicked the door with all his might. As the door caved in, a flash of black whipped past his face. His left cheek flared in pain as the arrow sliced his skin.

He clambered to his feet and ran up the staircase before him. He knew not where he was, nor where he was going. He just kept moving, and all the while the girl wailed in his arms.

Bursting onto the first floor he continued as fast as he could down the corridor, hoping to find some way to exit on the other side of the blocked road. On and on he ran until, out of the corner of his eye, he saw a large crystal orb resting on a plinth in the middle of one of the rooms.

I'm in the Arcane Sanctum.

This revelation didn't much help his predicament. He'd rarely visited the tower and didn't know his way around. At the end of this corridor, he found another closed door. This one would not budge. Kicking it did nothing. He pulled back, secured the girl under his right arm and hurled his left shoulder at the door. His own force was propelled back at him, blowing him off his feet and onto his back.

The girl gave a shriek of protest at this latest ill-treatment. Darnuir blinked at the ceiling, unable for a moment to think or move. He tried to rise but found his left arm was limp.

Then he saw it.

The plate mail that defended his left shoulder had caved inwards upon impact, piercing his body. Gripped by shock, he didn't feel the pain, but it was the greatest of efforts to haul himself to his feet.

Clanking and banging mixed with the girl's cries, and he turned to see the silhouettes of demons coming up the corridor.

There was no way out.

Holding the princess tightly under his remaining good arm, he doubled back until he found a small storage area containing crates of food, heavy bound books, stacks of parchment and an abundance of clay inkpots. He put the baby down behind the largest crate, so that she was out of sight, then hid behind the door.

He ripped off his chest piece and examined his shoulder, which was now a mangle of muscle and bone. The pain now came to him, pain like he had never felt in his life: it seemed as though his whole existence was now concentrated upon his injury. Thankfully, his sword arm could still be used, and he drew his weapon, ready to strike.

Darnuir cleaved the head off the first enemy who entered the room. Lurching forward, he kicked the next demon in the stomach before impaling it on his blade.

Demons were not as small as they appeared but were often stooped or misshapen. They had no flesh upon their bones, which were sometimes visible behind their swirling bodies of fire and shadow. Their blood, if it could be called that, was like bubbling lava, the colour of rust. Darnuir was not afraid of them, but he knew he could not last in this room forever. However, he wasn't about to just lay down his arms and die. He hacked and slashed until the demons who had been chasing him had either been killed or had fled.

His last foe slipped past him, perhaps hearing the cries of the princess. Darnuir caught the creature hard on its side with the flat of his blade, sending it crashing into the shelf of inkpots. The cascade of falling clay smothered the demon and flooded the room in ink as dark as its own shadowy flesh.

Darnuir checked the girl. She was as fine as she could be, but her cries would only give them away. Stumbling back out into the corridor, he tried the magically sealed door again but, of course, it didn't give in to his will.

His left side was useless, his breathing ragged. He'd never suffered an injury like this and wasn't sure if even magic would be able to heal it efficiently. And what fight was left in him nearly died when a fresh wave of demons approached.

Whatever advantage the dragons had in strength, the demons more than made up for in numbers. Their chief tactic was simple but effective: swarm the enemy.

Four approached him now.

Darnuir reacted instinctively as the closest demon lunged at him, barbed blade in hand. He dodged the blow and brought the hilt of his sword down to cave in the creature's skull. Another leapt through the air towards him, bringing its weapon down. As he raised his sword to block it, he noticed the remaining pair of demons break off to either side.

He was surrounded.

Jumping back, he hit the impenetrable door and could go no further. He elbowed the demon on his right, simultaneously blocking the assailant in front of him with his sword. It worked, but now his left side was left exposed and the fourth demon made it to him. The little abomination howled in triumph as it plunged its dirk into Darnuir's waist.

As before, he didn't feel the pain at first. Perhaps the shock of it numbed him. Yet when it came, it was beyond screaming. His breath caught in his throat.

Hunched over and bleeding, he rose with the last of his strength, ramming his sword through the offending demon, feeling hot gore cover his hand. In a continuous motion, he ripped the sword free and brought his elbow back to crush the demon on his right against the door. The last demon hesitated and Darnuir kicked it so hard that it flew up the corridor, turning in mid-air to land on its head and leave a smoking trail of bloodshed in its wake.

Darnuir staggered, swayed on the spot and fell to the cold floor, his vision going cloudy. The pain was paralysing. More demons were clanging up the corridor.

He tried to resist thinking that this would be his inglorious end. Such an end would not be worthy of one of Brackendon's books.

The crying of the girl briefly became his whole world. He'd failed her. Failed Arkus. Failed his father. In the end, he had done no better. His people were doomed.

He reached out, as though he could pick up the girl. Human or no, she hardly deserved this fate; to be killed by an unthinking servant of the enemy, in an anonymous room in a crumbling city.

His hand fell. He couldn't hold it up. The pain ebbed away. The sound of the girl's wailing seemed to lessen, as though his other senses were already shutting down. Slipping further out of consciousness, his eyelids became dead weights.

No. I won't have my eyes closed when the end comes.

But try as he may, he could not fight it.

A burst of purple energy like thick lightning came from the door which had been sealed. Only now, the door was open. A robed man walked through it and Darnuir felt a spurt of hope that he couldn't quite register. Before his sight faded, there came a brilliant flash of white light, and then nothing at all.

5

UNFORESEEN TROUBLES

Brackendon – Cold Point

Light illuminated the little house. For a moment, it seemed like a star had fallen from the heavens. Brackendon and Darnuir materialised within the unnatural shine and then, like a candle blown out, the light vanished. Darkness enveloped the room once more.

Brackendon found himself inside a grubby shack, with dust-covered furniture and an old wooden bed up against one of the windows. The place had a smell that reminded Brackendon of the drains of Brevia; mould and unwanted growth. Outside the window, he could see snow blowing around in the wind, visible in the starlight. Clearly, they were no longer in Aurisha.

The Prince of Dragons lay unconscious at his feet. Bleeding out.

Brackendon drew upon magic, lifting Darnuir gently onto the bed.

A chill came over him and he could barely see in this gloom. There was a small fireplace but no wood for a fire. That was when he spotted the gnarled cabinet.

Concentrating on it, he slowly curled his free hand into a fist and the cabinet broke apart. Using magic for destruction or movement was relatively cheap, but he nonetheless felt the poisonous surge flow to his shoulder, down towards his staff, and enjoyed the relief as it drained out of him. His staff would process the magic for him, but it could only deal with so much.

Brackendon stacked the wood and sent a few sparks to ignite it. With the fire crackling, he returned to Darnuir's side. He now felt better able to examine his charge.

Darnuir was a mess. His cheek had a long red gash, which trickled blood. His shoulder was a tangle of flesh and bone, and then there was the knife protruding from his side. That would not be so cheap to mend. He could easily remove the knife, but healing Darnuir's wound and fixing up his shoulder would take a great deal of power. Perhaps more than he could risk.

He attempted to draw out the dagger with his hand, to save using even that small amount of magic, but the blade was twisted in deep.

There will be blood when I pull it out. A lot of blood.

Resigning himself, Brackendon began to slowly edge the dagger out magically. It slid out neatly onto the bed and a torrent of dark blood followed it. Brackendon had no choice. He used enough of his power to knit up the skin and muscle, so that the bleeding would stop. As the Cascade energy washed through him, empowering him, he turned his attention to Darnuir's shoulder. With this injury, he also did the minimum required to stop Darnuir bleeding to death. The protruding bone snapped back into place and a thin veil of pink flesh formed over it. When he finished his work, Brackendon slammed the doorway shut to the magic in his mind.

There was a moment of brief euphoria, a moment in which he felt invincible, unstoppable; then the full force of the residue hit him.

His body convulsed. He gasped for air as his lungs tightened and he fell writhing to the floor. Whimpering, he thrashed around, like an insect missing too many legs, before curling up into a ball. Cascade residue raged agonisingly through his body before enough of it drained to his staff to end the shaking. He gripped the silver wood so tightly that he grazed the skin on his own hand.

At last, he lay still. His head might have burst from how hard it pounded, and a bitterness lay upon his tongue.

I must be careful. It would not do for me to break; not here, not now.

For a wizard to break was a terrible fate. The more one drew on the Cascade, the stronger one felt and the more one was tempted to consume it. When a wizard broke, it meant he had surpassed the limit that both his body and staff could process. A common consequence was total psychological breakdown.

Brackendon had seen a few of his colleagues break in their youth; men reduced to boys, and boys to babes. It wasn't necessarily permanent, but the recovery process was uncertain. For many, it took years; for some, a lifetime.

Brackendon had just drawn on a significant amount of Cascade energy to heal Darnuir. It required far more power to heal and create with magic than it did to simply destroy.

'Wood versus stone' was what he had been taught. A house might be built quickly and cheaply out of wood, but one of stone would endure. Building things properly took time, effort and resources. The magical comparison was almost too much for anyone to bear. The body took a long time to heal, for example, and it took a magic wielder the same amount of energy to speed up that process and do it instantaneously.

Destruction, on the other hand, was an easy thing by all accounts. A masterpiece tapestry might take the weaver months to sew, but any urchin with a torch could ruin it in seconds. That cabinet he had just destroyed would have taken time and energy to construct, while he'd smashed it in the span of a heartbeat.

A lamentable fact. If only the reverse were true; if only killing and destruction cost dearly while healing and growing were cheap.

All considered, he had called upon infinitely more Cascade energy to heal Darnuir's wounds than he had in crushing the cabinet. And he had only just stopped the bleeding. He hadn't even tried to heal what other internal damage Darnuir might have suffered.

Regaining himself, Brackendon staggered upright and went over to inspect his patient, and noticed, to his horror, a greenish tint of poison upon the jagged knife he had extracted from Darnuir. This made matters even worse. Dragons had a weakness to poison, hence their aversion to alcohol. Crude as demon toxin was, Darnuir might well perish from it. A long moment passed during which Brackendon found himself lost and unsure.

What am I to do?

Darnuir shivered. Brackendon found some old blankets in a wardrobe next to the door, along with an assortment of mismatched, ragged clothing. He quickly shook the dust from them and removed Darnuir's remaining armour. The thick plates were so heavy that he had to use a little magic to move them. He winced while doing so, feeling the build-up in his system. Cold sweat covered Darnuir's entire body. Brackendon wrapped the blankets around him and placed the clothes bunched up behind his head for a makeshift pillow.

Kneeling by the bedside, Brackendon put his head in his hands.

What am I to do?

It had only been a stroke of luck and good timing that had saved Darnuir. Brackendon had resolved to disembark from his ship and aid in the defence when Kasselle had stopped him, urging him to find Arkus and Darnuir instead. Something about the king's daughter. Brackendon had only made it to the beginning of the switchback road when he saw the collapsing buildings form the blockage halfway up. He had continued only to find a wounded and exhausted Arkus. The rubble had cut him off from Darnuir.

Knowing the Arcane Sanctum would provide a way around the blockage, Brackendon had hastened that way. As he was removing the spell on the enchanted door, he'd heard the skirmish from the other side. Once through, he had dispatched the advancing demons and found Darnuir wounded. More demons had been coming. He could not have fought them all whilst moving Darnuir at the same time.

In the heat of the moment, Brackendon had seen only one path. Taking hold of Darnuir, he'd brought him by portal to the one place in the world he could: a small settlement called Cold Point, high in the Boreac Mountains, on the opposite side of the world.

A wizard could only travel in this way to the place where his or her staff tree resided, and even when they did travel in such a manner, where they ended up was never exact. It could be anywhere within a mile's radius of their staff tree. Brackendon supposed they had been fortunate to land inside an abandoned house.

Yet he had no clue where in the town they were. His knowledge of Cold Point was limited, having little reason to portal there himself. He'd only done so once before.

And while Darnuir was now stable, Brackendon was in a true predicament.

Were Draconess, Arkus and Kasselle still alive? Anything could be happening across the world. Hopefully, they would all make it safely to sea, heading to Arkus' capital of Brevia. Brackendon and Darnuir, however, were in the Boreacs, and far to the southwest of the human capital. They were, in fact, closer to Castallan's sphere of influence from the Bastion than any stronghold of the Three Races.

He was jarred from his thoughts when Darnuir began to stir. Very slowly, and with evident effort, the prince half-opened his eyes. He tried to speak but his voice was weak and rasping.

"Where are we?"

"Cold Point."

"In the Boreac Mountains," Darnuir murmured. The prince knew his geography well at least. Anything that was useful for war, he tended to know.

"You must be in incredible pain," Brackendon said. "There is no need to—" He caught his breath as Darnuir wrenched in agony, opening his mouth in a silent scream. Dragons were tough and Darnuir was tougher still. Brackendon had never known him to show signs of suffering before. These gestures unnerved him more than the wound itself had.

Once the convulsions ended, Darnuir spoke again; this time his voice was not much more than a whisper.

"The girl..."

What is he talking about?

Then it hit him like a shock of magic. Darnuir had been going to save Arkus' daughter.

"Darnuir, I'm sorry. She must have been left behind. I—" Brackendon stopped his confession as Darnuir slipped into unconsciousness again. His chest and stomach barely rose from shallow breaths.

Brackendon was left once more with his unanswerable question.

What am I to do?

Time ticked by and snow fell heavily outside. It collected around the edges of the window pane, further obscuring the world beyond. Little could be seen, other than the spiky outlines of towering pine trees.

As Brackendon stared out into the night, he recalled his previous trip to Cold Point. He had been aiding a friend's escape from a life he detested. His name was Cosmo, a young man from Brevia, then only eighteen. He had desired to disappear. Wherever he ended up, his plan had been to join the regional hunters, an organisation in which he felt he could achieve some good.

Hunters and huntresses fulfilled many roles. They sometimes acted as an elite scouting force, sometimes as local law enforcement, and other times, they did just what their title suggested – they hunted. Larger wild beasts were their primary concern these days, especially here in the Boreac Mountains, where wolves were a known issue.

Yet wolves were not their original targets. Brackendon looked to Darnuir with apprehension. During the Second War between humanity and dragons, the hunters had been the last line of defence. Once the war was over, a huntress called Elsie the Green had shaped her brothers and sisters into a firmer fighting force. Arrows, stealth and ambushes would achieve what meeting the dragons toe to toe could not.

Thankfully, those days of open conflict were far in the past. These days the hunters aided the people of their region first and foremost. This was what had drawn Cosmo to them. With luck, he would still be alive and well. And in a position to return Brackendon's favour in his time of need.

Perhaps if proper aid could be brought to Darnuir, he would pull through, though Brackendon did not allow his hopes to rise. Hope could be a fragile thing and Darnuir's fate was all but decided. There was one potential spell that Brackendon could use, but it was little better than death.

Would it be right to perform it? To kill him so that he should live?

For now, at least, he would seek out Cosmo. It was a start. There was little more he could do for the prince presently.

Guilt and worry welling in him, Brackendon summoned his courage to stand and leave Darnuir behind. What else could he do?

He left the warmth of the fire behind as well, stepping out into the freezing air. It seemed his little shack was right on the edge of the town. A jumble of flickering lights in the distance gave him guidance through the night as he trudged the streets.

Built in the steep valley, the town followed the flow of the land to the valley's tipped point where the mountainsides met. The effect was to make the layout of the town seem misshapen, and many believed that, if it was seen from above, it would look, quite fittingly, like an icicle.

Cosy, squat log cabins surrounded Brackendon as he walked, each covered in a layer of snow. The road underfoot was little better than a dirt track turned to a muddy river under the snowfall. The light sandals he had worn to combat the heat of Aurisha afforded him no protection against the chill water or the biting wind.

Knowing it was unwise, he reached for the door to the Cascade, allowing a trickle in to warm his extremities. Even this small amount caused him pain, the build-up of residue feeling like burning wine in his veins. Gritting his teeth, he soldiered on.

He allowed the magic to boost his muscles as he hurried towards the square ahead where the lights were the strongest. When he reached the square, he felt cobbled stone beneath his feet and sighed in relief to no longer be walking through the icy water.

Then he saw it. Twenty feet of gnarled silver bark with criss-crossing branches that weaved throughout one another as if in a frenzied dance. Silver and white leaves sprouted in equal measure. Cut away from the trunk was a long, thin section of wood. The same length as the staff he held.

Being close to his staff tree filled Brackendon with a kind of primal energy. He felt bolstered; powerful. Perhaps it was just as well, considering what he may have to do.

Despite the urgency of the situation he felt compelled to draw closer to the tree, stepping up as far as the encircling stone wall.

"Who goes there?"

Brackendon froze, which was not a hard thing to do in this weather.

"Turn around."

He did so, slowly. A hunter with a drawn bow stood not far behind him. It was a testament to his skill that Brackendon had not heard him approach.

A hunter's leather armour was designed to blend into the terrain of their region. This man's leathers were white, interwoven with pieces that were stained oily black and grey; camouflage against dirty snow and mountain rocks. A fur-lined hood hung behind his neck and bulky leather pauldrons accentuated the breadth of his shoulders.

"Do not be alarmed," Brackendon said, worried by the shake in his own voice. Was it the cold or the magic doing that to him? "I am but a simple traveller who is an old friend of one of your own." The excuse was feeble but he could barely string a sentence together in his current state.

"Name him," the hunter replied, his bow still raised.

"Cosmo."

"Cosmo?" the hunter said in admiration. "He's in the tavern with the rest of the men. We killed a demon raiding party today with no casualties on our side."

His tone implied that he savoured the victory, and rightly he should. Since Castallan's betrayal, demons had been scourging the southern human kingdom almost with impunity.

Brackendon thought it a cruel thing that here were men celebrating their achievement, while across the ocean, the Three Races' most coveted city was now in the hands of Rectar. The revellers of the Boreac Mountains did not know the doom that lay before them.

Brackendon could not fail.

"Will you take me to him?"

The hunter did not lower his bow. "Not just yet. Clearly, you're no demon, but I don't know many 'simple travellers' who wear such robes or carry such fine staves."

Brackendon cursed himself and struggled for words. "A good walking stick serves well in these mountains."

"Most walking sticks are not so tall, nor so silver," the hunter said, creeping forward.

Brackendon could see him better now. He was surprisingly young for a voice that confident. Disorderly black hair topped his head, while a young man's patchy attempt at a beard covered his cheeks and chin. A skinny frame hinted he was to grow more and his eyes contained a youthfulness that made Brackendon suspect the boy was barely fifteen.

"I'm only young," the hunter said, a bite in his voice, "but I think I know a wizard when I see one. And I only know of one who'd be around these parts."

He thinks I am Castallan. This thought had barely passed through Brackendon's mind before the lad released his arrow.

Forced to act, Brackendon did as little as he could, magically pushing on the air to veer the arrow off course. Even this small use of power was a strain on him now and he became acutely aware of the build-up inside him. His staff had barely processed the Cascade he'd called upon to heal Darnuir. The heat in his veins roared into a bonfire. Unable to stand, he let out a cry that tore through the night and fell once more onto his knees.

His hand steadied himself on the snowy cobblestones, but he could not feel the cold now. He could not feel much at all.

With effort, Brackendon lifted his head.

The hunter nocked another arrow.

"Garon, lower your bow!"

The voice had thundered from the now open tavern door; a dark silhouette stood there framed against the warm light.

The young hunter hesitated, keeping his bow held high.

"It's a wizard, Cosmo!" Garon said. "It's Casta—"

"Don't be so foolish," Cosmo barked, running to Garon, pushing his bow down and grabbing him by the scruff of the neck. "Do you think Castallan would show up here? I know this man, and I'd be most upset if you killed him."

"I'm sorry, Cosmo, I just – I just—"

"You were a bit overzealous," Cosmo said. "Shooting first is for demons and enraged beasts."

"And dragons?" Garon said, laughing a little.

Cosmo did not join him.

"Not for hundreds of years," he said. "And I would pity you if you tried to fight a dragon. They could snap you in two."

"It's just a joke, sir," Garon said, shrugging off the older hunter. "I am sorry," he said to Brackendon. "Please, forgive my brashness."

"I already have." Brackendon winced as he staggered to his feet. Cosmo moved to brace him, throwing an arm around his waist as they began moving towards the tavern. "We must discuss something privately," Brackendon whispered.

Cosmo nodded. "My absence will be noted if I leave," he whispered back. "We can talk inside. No one will overhear us in there. They are all too merry to notice much."

The young hunter, Garon, was looking suspiciously over his shoulder at the pair of them.

"Will he be trouble?" Brackendon said.

"Garon? No, I'd trust him with my life."

"I dearly hope so. The fate of the world may now lie with us."

6

THE FATE OF THE WORLD

Brackendon – Cold Point

He allowed Cosmo to lead him inside the tavern and over to the bar. After a quiet word to Garon, Cosmo thumped his fist upon the counter. Two frothy drinks were produced by the barman, slopping messily as they were placed in front of them.

"I dare say I'll need the strength to hear what you are about to tell me," Cosmo said, polishing off most of his drink in one draught. Brackendon sipped tentatively at his own. It was surprisingly light, but it wouldn't serve his needs for now.

"I'd prefer water, and lots of it."

"Been using magic?" Cosmo asked, gesturing to the barman that he required another ale.

"Maybe too much." He winced from the pain again and glanced worriedly around at the crowd. "We really must talk in private."

"We will. I sent Garon upstairs to find us a spot. We'll be amongst this revelry but not that noticeable. No one will overhear us. Does that sound agreeable?"

Brackendon wasn't sure, but he was too achy and tired to protest. He nodded, and Cosmo gave him a half-smile in return. Now, in the light of the tavern, Brackendon appreciated just how worn Cosmo was. It had only been five years since they parted but Cosmo already had a weariness to him. His eyes carried heavy, dark bags, and his face showed the remnants of scratches and slashes. His beard was full, though far from bushy, and his matted hair needed a clean. Yet his grass-green eyes retained their warmth. The eyes of someone genuine and caring.

Garon returned to them shortly after Cosmo's second drink arrived. He led them up the stairs to a table near the balcony's edge on the second floor. As they took their seats, Cosmo grabbed Garon's arm.

"Go get water for our friend here. Good, clean water, and cold if you can manage." Garon nodded and began to weave back through the bodies.

There were fewer people upstairs but the noise in the tavern was still great. Such was the gaiety that Brackendon wondered whether anyone had even noticed his arrival.

"We started early," Cosmo explained, as if sensing Brackendon's thoughts. "It's rare that the hunters or townsfolk get the opportunity these days."

From their vantage point, Brackendon could see many people who were not garbed in white leathers. Young women sat giggling in the laps of grizzled-looking hunters. Other women were themselves in the white and grey armour, with dangerous knives at their waist. Huntresses – armed, trained and in uniform. Dragons would not approve.

Mixed groups of civilians and hunters played dice, and absolutely everyone had a drink to hand. The tavern was well lit and reasonably spacious. Tables, railings and chairs were carved and smoothed from yellowish-brown and muddy redwoods. Brackendon could see an additional level above them where still more merrymakers enjoyed themselves, some hanging precariously over the railings.

"I wouldn't want to be sleeping in one of the rooms upstairs tonight," Cosmo said as he drank heavily from his tankard. Brackendon only felt another stab of pain. He clenched his fists and gritted his teeth until it passed.

"What's happened?" Cosmo asked. "Your robes are dirtied with blood, and not all of it is from demons. Why are you here?"

Brackendon sighed heavily as the pain subsided. Unfortunately, his pounding head did not abate. "I'm not sure where to begin. The last twenty-four hours should suffice."

As best he could, Brackendon then explained the events of the previous day. He had reached the point at which the demons had begun their assault on the city when Garon reappeared. The young hunter carried a large jug and spilt some of its contents as he set it down on their table. With a flourish, Garon whipped out a small glass from behind his back and placed it before Brackendon.

"My thanks, Garon," Brackendon said. He ignored the small glass and lifted the heavy jug to his lips. He drank eagerly, for water would aid his body's recovery. When he set the jug back down, half its weight was gone. Garon looked stunned.

"On you go," Cosmo said, shooing him away. "But stay in sight in case we have need of you."

"Yes, sir," Garon said. If he was perplexed at these odd requests, he didn't show it.

Cosmo returned his attention to Brackendon, giving him a grave look. "Is that everything, or is there more ill news?"

"Oh, much more."

Cosmo eyed Brackendon's barely touched tankard. He reached for it and, when Brackendon didn't protest, he took it for himself.

"Go on."

Brackendon continued with his story. He recited everything: his rescue of Darnuir, why he brought him here, Darnuir's injuries, his need to use magic on him, and even the issue of Arkus' daughter. Cosmo's face stiffened at this last piece of news.

"Poor old sod," the hunter mumbled into his drink.

"He's lost both his children now," Brackendon said, "and it's my fault."

Cosmo gave him a sharp look. "Don't say that. You didn't know she was there."

"I should have taken more time to think."

"You reacted in the moment. Had you brought her here, we would have had an infant to care for as well as a dying prince. What good would that have done?"

Brackendon raised his eyebrows.

"Ah, I didn't mean it like that," Cosmo said. "It's a terrible thing. Likely she is dead." He choked and took another drink. "But you can't dwell on it. *We* can't dwell on it."

"Brevia will react poorly to the news. The succession will be in question again. I take it you haven't—"

"No," Cosmo said curtly. "I haven't heard anything about Arkus' son."

"I was only asking."

"Well, ask something else," Cosmo said, returning to his drink. "I'm tired of hearing about Arkus' bloody son."

"Very well," said Brackendon, changing course. "Tell me, friend, what am I to do? I've been turning it over in my mind."

"Can anything be done?" Cosmo had to shout over a group of hunters, who had started to sing. Down below, several instrumentalists trooped out and started playing near the bar. One held a lute, two had fiddles, and the fourth wore two small drums. The songs were pacey, full of mirth, and the crowd joined in with gusto.

"There is one way to save Darnuir," Brackendon began hesitantly, "but it is little better than death in truth. A spell, one of rebirth. If I use it on him, it will send him back to infancy and he'll be free of any fatal damage."

"I don't understand," Cosmo said. "I thought healing magic was extremely costly. You seem to be on the brink of breaking just from stitching up his side."

"Oh, I am far from that brink," Brackendon tried to assure him.

Yet I am still too close to it.

"But the rebirth spell is not healing, exactly. I would be essentially destroying him

– undoing his body and removing his memories in the process. I'd be killing this Darnuir and leaving a new one, like a book with words wiped from the pages. It's destruction, not healing, and destruction is cheap."

Cosmo didn't immediately react. He gazed intently at Brackendon. "I've never heard of such a thing before," he finally admitted.

"Well, it has little utility. As I say, you are essentially killing the person in the rebirthing process. Time is rewound upon the subject and they are left as a baby. It doesn't save the person it is used upon. If someone you loved was dying, the rebirth spell would still take them from you. While that person matured again, their surroundings, the experiences that shape them would be different. They would never be truly the same. But Darnuir must survive," Brackendon urged, leaning back over the table. "In one form or another, he must. The poison in his system will kill him soon regardless."

Cosmo finished off the last of his ale. He set the tankard down slowly and was about to speak when a call came out from somewhere in the crowd below.

"Play 'The Way of the Beast!'"

"Aye," someone else agreed, "give us 'The Way of the Beast!'"

A general murmuring of agreement followed. The musicians obliged, and the tempo of the music changed dramatically. Drumbeats thumped slowly, one at a time, sending deep reverberations around the room. Weeping strings came from the fiddlers, and every hunter present began a low humming in unison.

Cosmo did not join them.

"Why, Brackendon? Why *must* he live? What I hear of his character does not paint him favourably. Ill-tempered, ill-mannered, and he has no love for humanity. Why should we care?"

Brackendon's hesitation did not help his point. The humming hunters turned now to song, their words a slow tune in the background.

> *"The wolf may howl, the bear will growl,*
> *And our arrows shall sing."*

"He must live. Who else can lead the dragons after Draconess?"

"I'm sure they are capable of raising up a new king," Cosmo said.

> *"A wolf bounds fast, a bear has strength,*
> *A dragon is the same."*

"They will never follow anyone but their true king," Brackendon whispered fiercely.

"Never? You're telling me that across their entire history they have never been without a king from the same royal bloodline?"

> *"The stag has horns, dragons have claws,*
> *So just stay out of range."*

"As hard as that is to believe, yes," Brackendon said. "They have tough immune systems and live far longer than us. No naturally-arising crisis of succession comes to mind, and no king other than Aurisha himself has ever died in combat."

> *"When arrows fly, the wild beasts die,*
> *A dragon dies the same."*

"The dragons are stubborn," Brackendon continued. "They certainly won't follow Arkus."

"Well, I wouldn't." Cosmo snorted in agreement. "But he is well-respected enough in Brevia. Maybe the dragons will just have to—"

"They won't. And you know it."

> *"The wolf will bite, the bear will swipe,*
> *The stag will charge its foe."*

"You ask why we should care? We need the dragons if we are to have any chance of winning this war. You might want to run and bury your head in the snow, but I work for the good of humanity. Of the world."

The singing in the hall rose to a crescendo.

> *"Still we as men can counter them,*
> *A dragon dies the same.*
> *When arrows fly, the wild beasts die,*
> *A dragon dies the same."*

"I thought you wanted to do good, Cosmo? To help people. There is no greater good you could do than help Darnuir right now."

"We have done good," Cosmo said. "We're celebrating a victory. The Boreac Mountains are now safe—"

"This celebration is hollow compared to events outside of these mountains."

Cosmo was about to retort when the hunters returned to their antics; the music was now increasing in pace with the consumption of ale. The pause seemed to give Cosmo time to think and he slumped in his chair.

"It's not that I don't want to help," he said. "But I don't see the benefit of it all. Even if you succeed with this spell, Darnuir will still be an infant. Who will lead the dragons then?"

"I cannot account for that," Brackendon said. "But it's not just about who leads them." He flinched, his head pounding again. He reached for his water. "There is the Dragon's Blade to consider."

"Some magic sword?" Cosmo dismissed. "What good has that done? Draconess has had the sword for longer than I've been alive, and it hasn't helped him win the war."

"It does have power. Tremendous power. I could sense it whenever I was near." He took a few gulps of water, washing down the bitterness in his mouth. "I believe it can only be passed on down the true royal bloodline. If Darnuir dies, and Draconess is already dead, the sword's power will also diminish."

"And if Draconess is still alive?"

"Then nothing will happen where the sword is concerned," Brackendon said. "However, Draconess' fate is unknown to us, and we have to make a choice based on the worst-case scenario."

"Oh, is it 'we' already?"

"It is, because I will need someone to watch over him while I go for aid."

Cosmo placed his head in one hand and ran his free hand through his hair. "And you want me to mind a baby dragon?"

"If the spell doesn't break me, I'll still be left weak. I can't take him with me and hope to keep him warm, or fed, or safe if we should be attacked upon the journey north. No, he'll have to stay until I can send help, and who else would I trust him with? That song your brothers and sisters just sang doesn't fill me with confidence."

"Please," Cosmo said with a wave of his hand, "it's just a song. Traditional; goes back hundreds of years. None of us are going to start shooting dragons anytime soon."

"Cosmo," Brackendon said seriously, "this is a very dangerous situation. Perhaps Draconess is still alive, in which case the dragons will not be leaderless, and his sword will not lose power. But is it worth the risk?"

Cosmo looked towards the tankards on the table and seemed disappointed that they were dry.

"Aurisha has fallen," Brackendon said. "It won't be long before Rectar sends his armies west over the sea. What happens when Rectar's strength is added to Castallan's? What happens then if the dragons do not fight with us? What happens to all the small victories you have achieved here?"

"All right," Cosmo said reluctantly. "Bloody fine. But I am not going to Brevia. Under any circumstances."

"Is that what you were worried about?"

Does he hate the city so much he'd risk the world to avoid it?

"It's not just that," Cosmo said. "I want to help people, you are right. But I don't want to lead them. I don't want that responsibility. I just want to do my duty. Taking care of a dragon princeling; well, it's too close to responsible for comfort."

"Don't you lead men on patrol?"

"Only the younger recruits and only because Captain Tael insists. For some reason, he thinks I'm good at it. Anyway, that's different. We go out for a week, maybe two, so I'm just temporarily in charge. When we get back to the station, it all goes back to normal."

"I'm not asking you to be his father," Brackendon said. "Just keep him safe for a few months. Once I'm back in Brevia, I can have an entire army come to extract him. Our forces will be moving south anyway. Draconess intends to remove Castallan from the Bastion, or he intended to, at least."

They sat for a moment in silence. Brackendon could almost hear the battle raging within Cosmo: do the right thing, the selfless thing, or back away.

"I can't resent you for finding the task overwhelming. But I need you now and you're the only one I trust. This spell might break me, and if it does, then I need someone to be there. To slit my throat and end it, if nothing else."

"You're going to do it regardless, aren't you?"

"Yes." The answer came easily to Brackendon. "It is the only thing we can do. Can I take it that you are agreeing?"

Cosmo let out the greatest sigh Brackendon had ever heard a man make. "Yes." Then he whipped around and motioned to Garon to come over.

"What are you doing?" Brackendon hissed.

"Don't worry; this is a precaution we must take. He won't learn anything crucial."

Already the circle widens.

In a flash, Garon appeared dutifully by their table.

Cosmo looked at him seriously, all trace of doubt wiped from his face. "You told me once that you would do anything I asked of you."

"I did," Garon said.

"If I asked you to keep a secret, even from Captain Tael, would you do it?"

"Yes, sir! Wait, I mean no, sir. I mean—"

Cosmo raised a hand. "Thank you, Garon. There is something I require of you. My friend and I are about to leave. When we do, wait for half an hour and then leave as well. I want you to walk to the edge of town, stay there for a while and then come racing back as fast as you can, shouting for help. Say that you heard a woman screaming, say you heard it coming from outside the town gates, and have others come with you to search. Are you with me so far?"

Garon nodded earnestly.

Cosmo continued. "After the search has been given up, return to town. We should have completed our task by then. I'll inform the others that I too heard the cries for help and went myself. I'll tell them there was a young girl, carrying a baby boy. It won't matter whether they think it is her own. In fact, the vaguer the details, the better. You know yourself how many refugees have come stumbling through the mountains of late. Just last week, there was one poor woman who left a boy of her own; what was his name?"

"Balack, sir," Garon said stiffly. It seemed to cause the boy a measure of pain to remember the scene.

"Balack, yes. Poor kid," Cosmo said, he too lost in a sad memory. "In any case, if anyone checks in with Grace and Olive at the lodge later, they will find a baby boy there. I doubt anyone will pay his appearance too much attention, truth be told."

"Everyone is quite distracted, sir."

As though on cue, a hulking hunter stood on his chair, beat his chest, then collapsed as the chair legs gave out from under him. Laughter ensued while the fallen man merely grinned stupidly.

Cosmo looked upon the scene and smirked. "If even Griswald is this far gone then the rest of them won't wake up for days."

Brackendon might have laughed, were it not for the serious nature of the situation and the poison shuddering through his body. He felt cold sweat cling to his brow, pooling at the nape of his neck. His hands looked white as snow and so did his face, for Garon was looking at him in some concern.

"You didn't want to join in the fun?" Brackendon asked him, hoping to deflect the boy's attention.

"Cosmo told me to stay in sight in case I was needed. I wouldn't want to be a legless lout if I'm required."

"Quite right," Cosmo said in a businesslike manner. All that ale he'd drank didn't seem to have affected him much. "Then you know what you must do. You must also promise never to reveal the truth of this matter."

"Of course, sir," Garon confirmed, beaming with pride. Cosmo rose to his feet and clapped a hand on Garon's shoulder. Brackendon followed behind as they wove between the clustered hunters and townsfolk, down the stairs and out of the tavern.

Brackendon felt the chill engulf him as they stepped outside. The snow was falling thickly now, limiting his vision to the extent that he could no longer see his staff tree. His body convulsed again and his stomach reeled, as though from a fever. Cosmo offered a hand, but he waved it away. Regaining his composure, he retraced his steps through the square and Cosmo followed.

"You trust that boy a great deal," Brackendon said.

"I do. He may be young, but he is skilled and loyal. Two excellent qualities, both of which he has in abundance."

"And he is loyal to you? Someone who is not so much older than himself?"

"Don't misunderstand me; he will follow the captain's direct orders over mine, but he is willing to perform certain tasks for me. I helped Garon gain a place in our ranks, you see. We found him out on patrol one day down near Farlen. He had a nasty wound and limped with a sprained ankle for good measure. He's originally from the Cairlav Marshes, just beyond the mountains, but his village had been devastated by a demon raid."

"How long ago was this?"

"A year ago, maybe a year and a half, around when Castallan turned his cloak. Garon looked a wretched thing when we found him. Mother dead. Father killed in the war. We brought him back to the station, nursed him to full strength, and I convinced Captain Tael to take him on. He was barely fourteen and normally only fifteen-year-olds can join as recruits, but Tael knows potential when he sees it."

Yes; he sees it in you, too.

"You gave him purpose," Brackendon observed. "Something to work and live for. It's no surprise he looks up to you."

"If you say so, friend. If you say so."

As they rounded a corner, light from the centre of town dwindled and they were left in almost total darkness. Yet Cosmo seemed to know where he was going.

"From the way you described the place, it sounds like that squalid shack near the back of town. I've had a notion to tear it down but there are always better things to do."

"It's a good thing you refrained."

They walked in silence for a time, feet sloshing through the gathering snow, the wind moaning lowly through the valley. Brackendon ached to draw on some magic to stave off the cold but resisted. He would need every modicum of strength to handle his upcoming task. Little light made it out from the windows of the cabins as the snow fell even heavier, almost like a white mist. The whole world seemed to have turned white, and empty, and cold.

It was Cosmo who broke their silence.

"What is he really like? Darnuir, I mean. You hesitated back in the tavern."

Brackendon was unsure how to answer.

Arrogant, brusque and bullish. Still, Darnuir had also been loving in his own way.

"Most of what you heard is true," he said. "But, if this is to be his final hour, then the lesser-known side should be remembered too. He loves his people, Cosmo; loves them so fiercely, it pains him that they are being slowly ground out of existence. I haven't known him for long, but he has gotten worse of late. Rasher, angrier. I think all the setbacks in the war have eaten away at him. This is just what I have observed, of course. He'd never sit down for a heart to heart." Brackendon chuckled at the thought.

"Are you friends?"

"I call him that for want of a better word, but I would not say that we are close. Over the past few years, he has spent a lot of time visiting my colleagues at the Cascade Conclave. I think he was hoping to gain some magical solution to the war, but we could offer him none. Still, he liked to keep a few of our younger members close at hand. Since Castallan's treachery, I was the only one left he could keep close. Maybe it is simply a dragon's nature to be distant."

"I met him once. Well, saw him really. I was just a small lad then, maybe ten years old? I remember because everyone was making such a big fuss around him; but through all the commotion, I caught his eye. I think I must have looked frightened, for he smirked. Just smirked at me and then walked on."

"That's all?"

"If I knew more about him, I wouldn't need to depend on all the rumours, would I?"

"Maybe he will change," Brackendon said. "I hope he does."

They finally reached the exterior of the shack. Despite the cold numbing his body, Brackendon hesitated to enter, terrified to perform his awful task.

Cosmo was not so tentative and opened the door. The dingy two-room hut was warmer than Brackendon remembered it. The warmth was even more peculiar, given that the window had been smashed. Shards of glass lay scattered on the floor and over Darnuir. A menacing sword was nestled in Darnuir's right hand.

The realisation hit Brackendon with the force of a hammer blow. Glistening in the dying light of the fire, the sword seemed to be radiating heat of its own. Did it know its master required care?

Cosmo gasped. "Is that the—"

"Dragon's Blade? Yes, it is. That it is here means only one thing. Draconess is dead and Darnuir is now king."

"But how?"

"The Dragon's Blade will always find its master: that much I know. It can fly. I've seen Draconess launch it and it soar back into his hand. I had wondered whether the distance would matter, but—"

"Evidently not," Cosmo said, stepping closer.

"Careful, Cosmo," Brackendon snapped.

"I'm just looking. It's the deadliest work of art I've ever laid eyes upon."

Brackendon agreed. Its hilt was a dark ox-blood in colour and shaped in the head of a dragon, in their beastly form of ancient days. Carved scales covered the grip, leading up to the foreboding head. Two rows of pointed teeth stretched up the base of the blade itself. A forked tongue, wreathed in fire, slithered its way out of the dragon's mouth and up the body of the metal. The blade itself was a thick, dark gold; an extraordinary metal that even Brackendon did not know by name. A cross-guard in the form of dragon wings erupted from the edges of the dragon's head and curved down over the grip, where there was just enough space for two hands, if required. Every detail was exquisite: the raised scales above the eyebrows; the indent on the chin; the sinew and bones on the wings. Only the eye seemed strange. It looked as though something was missing from a small, cavernous socket.

Brackendon moved around to the other side of the bed and saw that the eye was complete on that side. A small red ruby sat neatly in place, glinting and giving the head of the dragon a sense of life.

He looked towards Darnuir's clenched left fist and saw the missing ruby between his fingers. Tentatively, he pried the fingers apart and picked up the gemstone. It was heavy, far heavier than anything its size should weigh. *What is this magic?* Sensing it would not be wise to continue holding it, he carefully placed it back into its allotted space on the sword. The blade glowed orange as if giving approval.

"Shall we do it?" Cosmo asked apprehensively.

"Yes. There is no reason to wait; not now," Brackendon said, moving around to the foot of the bed.

"It seems not all dragons die the same," Cosmo said. He stood awkwardly, unsure of what to do.

"Be on your guard," Brackendon warned, raising his staff. "I'm not sure what will happen."

Darnuir

He was neither asleep nor awake, hovering between waking and dream where sounds are muddled and more violent on the ear. Voices spoke nearby, enhanced tenfold by his exhaustion.

He had managed to open his eyes when the Dragon's Blade had come crashing through the window and forced itself into his hand. Yet he was still so weak, his limbs refused to answer his commands. The pain was less severe after the sword had arrived.

Is that all the power it has? Have I desired and dreamed for an empty promise?

The sword had done nothing to stop death creeping towards him. He knew he was dying; some instinct told him that.

The voices stopped, paused, and then he heard something song-like. In his exhaustion, the words were strange and unnerving, a twisted rhythm and rhyme that sounded alien to him. Ethereal lights flooded the room, bright even through his eyelids, and in colours he had never seen before. He noticed that the chill breeze from the window no longer reached him. The very air had halted.

For the first time in his life, Darnuir felt afraid, though he could not reason why.

He could barely think at all. Everything was instinct, and his mind was darkening. His body began to move again; it thrashed around out of his control.

"Hold him!"

Hands pressed down on his chest, but he continued to lash out. The hands left his body and a hard crash followed. More shouting and the hands returned; this time, they felt heavier. His muscles continued to jerk but the hands held him in place. His flesh writhed and convulsed under his skin. Then he was motionless; everything was still.

It was far too still.

Then came a new sensation. He was losing himself. Large chunks of his being were vanishing. There was no pain, just a sudden emptiness. Memories erased, leaving blank spaces in their wake. Like a smashed glass, the contents of his mind were flowing from him, and the remaining pieces were jagged and broken.

He tried to hold onto something, desperately, anything at all. Aurisha under attack; a baby in his arms; running through a hail of arrows; cornered, in pain and someone was crying.

There had been a light. But who had made it? A single word came to the forefront of his rapidly decreasing mind.

Brackendon!

His eyes burst open and the otherworldly light flooded his vision. He wanted to cry out, but nothing came. His eyes met those of the figure above him. They were silver and determined. This was his last thought, and there was something about the eyes that gave him comfort.

Then, there was nothing.

7

TIME FLIES PART 1: THE EARLY YEARS

Darnuir – Cold Point

He lay securely in the curve of an arm. The fabric around him was soft, warm, enveloping. He felt safe here.

"Swear to me, Cosmo. Swear you'll await my return before you move him."

"I promise."

"I will need to see how matters play out in Brevia and amongst the dragons. The sword won't reactivate for him until he is of age, but—"

The speaker stumbled, falling into an icy puddle. Darnuir swayed as the person holding him crouched down by the fallen man's side.

"You're weak. You should rest a while. Carrying that sword won't help."

"I only need a small amount of magic to lift it. Perhaps if I can get it to Val'tarra, I can—" There was a loud, forceful whoosh and something golden flashed by.

"Where is it going?"

"I don't... I don't..."

"Brackendon, stay here. I insist. If the sword has gone, then—"

"No. I must press on. Kasselle and Arkus must be informed."

"At least warm up first. Let me give you some supplies and proper clothing."

"That would be a kindness. But no one can know I was here."

"I'll be discreet."

Darnuir must have drifted off to sleep, for his eyes sprang open when the person holding him stopped moving.

"Wait here. I will signal to you when it is safe to come in."

There was a creak, and then he was moving again. His carrier's footsteps rapped against a harder surface. It felt much warmer in here. Darnuir approved.

"Cosmo? What are you doing here? Oh? Who is this?" The voice was light and motherly. Darnuir approved of that too. He felt himself being handed over and considered crying in protest. Before concluding on the matter, he blinked up at the face above him. It was a smiling face with bright eyes, rounded pink cheeks and bouncing brown curls. Darnuir decided not to cry after all.

She smiled and waggled a finger at him, but her voice sounded less joyful now. "Oh, not another one. Did the poor woman tell you her name?"

"Sadly not. It was all she could do to hand him over to me."

"Well, he's in safe hands now," she said, returning to smile at Darnuir. "I'll just check if we have enough sheets for him."

Darnuir was transferred again from one pair of arms to another.

There was a momentary pause before the person holding him swivelled to the door, opened it a crack and then hissed, "Come now. Quickly!"

Another face appeared, drained almost entirely of colour but with sparkling eyes.

"Head up to the third floor. Second door on the right should be free. Go. I'll bring you some needle brew."

The ashen-faced man hurried off.

"Good news!" rang the motherly voice. "There is space for him along with little Balack and Eve." The rosy-cheeked face reappeared above him.

Darnuir found himself passed yet again. Now he thought he should cry about it. He only wanted to sleep after all. Couldn't they leave him be?

"I'm afraid I've caught a chill from outside. I'll just boil some needle brew for myself and run upstairs to change my boots before I head off."

"Yes, I'm sure you have celebrations to get back to." The woman began scrunching her lips at Darnuir. She did this a few times, over and over. Abruptly, she stopped. "Oh, Cosmo. I think we are running low on the silver pine needles. You'll see yourself. Could you tell the next party heading out to gather more for us?"

"For you, Grace, I'll put it at the top of my list."

The rosy-cheeked woman turned an even brighter shade of red.

Feeling himself at last free to sleep, Darnuir closed his eyes, very much hoping to be undisturbed.

Two Weeks Later

. . .

On his back, in his crib, Darnuir gargled up at Olive. He knew she was Olive, as everyone always made that sound to get her attention. Her face was thinner than Grace's and she did not scrunch her lips at him as much, but he liked her well enough.

There was a lot of thudding from above them. Olive peered towards the ceiling, looking annoyed. Then the knocking came closer and Olive bustled off towards it, her thin frame disappearing briefly out of sight. The pounding feet grew closer and then a breathless Cosmo appeared over him.

"Are you really so doubtful that we can look after him?" Olive snarled. "You're here almost every day."

"There has been an urgent call to mobilise and retake the lower mountains," he panted. "Castallan's forces have withdrawn and we're going to seize the chance. I wanted to say goodbye first."

"His demons have withdrawn? Just like that?"

"It would seem so," Cosmo gasped. "Our scouts report that they were already well out of the mountains and heading north. We have teams stationed to keep watch over the situation. If the demons suddenly return, we'll know in plenty of time."

Six Months Later

Darnuir was being held by Grace as Olive changed his bedding. He liked the soft, swaying motions and the warmth from being pressed up against her. She was anxious, though. He could tell by the way her heart beat faster, how her words came out quicker.

"You would have thought after this much time that we might have heard some news."

"Normally, no news is good news, little sister."

"Yes, but for this long?"

Olive ignored her and busied herself lugging chunks of wood into the fireplace. "We'll need more soon. We're always running low these days."

"Oh, who cares about some silly wood."

Olive gave her sister a withering look and wiped her brow.

Grace bit her lip. "Sorry. I know I'm worked up. It's just, I... well—"

"I know who you are worried for," Olive said, exasperated. One of Darnuir's fellows began crying and Olive swooped down upon the crib, pulling him back up and rubbing his back. "There, there, Balack, nothing's wrong. Were we making too much noise? I'm sorry," she cooed, rocking him back and forth. "I feel safer holding this one than him," Olive added, nodding at Darnuir. "The other day he reached out and squeezed my finger. I didn't feel it at the time but look how bruised it is now."

Grace peered fondly down at Darnuir. "You must be stronger than you look," she said, tapping his nose affectionately. As she did, Darnuir heard loud cheering coming from outside.

"What in the world is going on?" Olive said.

Grace placed Darnuir back into his cradle. Olive did the same with Balack and both women ran eagerly to the window.

"It's them!" Grace squealed. "It's the hunters! They're back!"

Some of the crowd must have entered the lodge for the noise became deafening to Darnuir. He wiggled his head to better see what was happening and wailed loudly to indicate his displeasure.

"Such a story to tell you both!" one hunter yelled.

"You cleared out the lower mountains, then?" Olive asked, then yelped in surprise as she was lifted into the air.

"What, over half a year?" another voice asked incredulously. "No, we did much more than that!"

"What, then?" Grace shouted, half-laughing and half-crying with relief as a beaten-looking Cosmo stepped forward to embrace her.

"We shouldn't have to worry about demons for quite some time," Cosmo announced, releasing Grace and fighting his way through to Darnuir's side.

His face was haggard; a red line stretched across his withdrawn cheek. A rough beard had sprouted on his dirt-smeared face, but his smile and bright green eyes shone as warmly as ever. As he bent lower over Darnuir, he whispered something into his ear.

"Well, we certainly bought you some time."

Five Years Later

"Tell me again!" Darnuir demanded, swinging his head from side to side. He was perched on top of Cosmo's shoulders as they sauntered through one of the valleys close to town. A ragged and beaten-up target dummy was squished under Cosmo's left arm.

"You've heard this story too many times," Cosmo laughed. "I think you should be the one who tells me."

"Fine," Darnuir squeaked. "Basically, you and Garon and all the other hunters went down the mountains, and they were empty." He paused to think.

"A good start, Darnuir. Do carry on."

"Well, nobody was there. So, you all went out of the mountains to find out what was going on and you met lots of men on horses!"

Cosmo laughed. "A company of chevaliers reduced to such lowly terms? I don't think they'd like that."

"And then the men on horses told you that everyone was gathering to fight the demons in the north and then you, erm, you... erm, you went there. And there were fairies and dragons too, and you beat the demons!"

"I suppose that is a decent enough summary," Cosmo said. "And what is that battle's name?"

"Demons' Folly! That's easy to remember."

"Well, I'm glad of that."

"Cosmo, were there trolls there too? Grace tells us stories about frost trolls and how they have big pointy teeth and will eat you up."

"No, Darnuir," Cosmo sniggered. "There were no trolls. There are no such things as trolls."

"But Grace told us! She tells us stories just like you do. Eve gets scared of frost trolls, but I don't." He gallantly waved his wooden training sword in the air.

"I think Grace tells you about trolls so that the three of you will behave. You do behave with Grace and Olive, don't you? Remember, I won't take you out to train if you are naughty."

"I know," Darnuir said glumly.

They continued their leisurely pace through the valley until the ancient trees on the mountainside offered some variance to the otherwise white landscape. As Cold Point poked itself over the horizon, Darnuir saw Grace and Garon awaiting their arrival at the town gates.

Garon marched out to meet them. "Captain Tael has requested your presence to help organise the reinforcements from the Master Station."

"When did they arrive?" Cosmo asked, putting Darnuir back down on his feet. Darnuir hurried to wrap himself around Garon's leg, as was his custom.

"Earlier today, while you were training with Darnuir," Garon said. He shook Darnuir playfully, tousled his hair and winked at him. "They say their journey was demon-free."

"Thank you, Garon. Wait here for me while I return this one." Cosmo pulled Darnuir off Garon and scooped up his hand, leading him over to Grace. She did not come to meet them but stood coyly, twirling the ends of her hair around a fingertip. As they drew closer, Darnuir rushed forward and hugged her.

"Hello, Darnuir," she said, picking him up and kissing him on the cheek. "Did Cosmo have you whacking things again?"

Darnuir grinned.

"One little handful back. He's all yours," Cosmo said, stopping so close to Grace that Darnuir was the only thing between them.

"Thank you, Cosmo, although I do wish you would let Balack go as well. He gets terribly upset when Darnuir isn't around."

"Very well. Next time, I'll take them both out." And then he leaned closer to Grace and whispered something into her ear that Darnuir could not hear. The two drew apart and Cosmo walked back off to join Garon. Grace spun on the spot and strolled off into town with Darnuir, humming under her breath.

Four Years Later

Darnuir and Balack sparred with their training swords in the yard of the lodge. The weapons were new and thus deserved a proper bashing. The boys were joined by Eve, who sat fidgeting with her hands on the steps leading to the back door.

The yard was tightly rammed between the buildings on either side. A thin layer of snow had melted under the first summer rays and a few determined knots of grass could be seen. Today, there was the addition of a dismantled chair, which owed its destruction to Darnuir. How he had managed this just by kicking it was a mystery to him.

Mud-stained from head to toe, he jabbed at Balack. His auburn-haired friend, equally muddy, was giving him no quarter.

"I want to play too!" Eve demanded.

"You don't have a sword," Darnuir said as he slammed his own into Balack's side. Balack buckled for a moment, then pulled himself upright.

Clutching at his side, Balack gasped and pointed at the broken chair legs. "Let her play. She could use one of those." He ran over to pick one up and delivered the makeshift weapon to Eve.

"Thank you, Balack," she said very pointedly, keeping her gaze on Darnuir. "I think we should team up against Darnuir, don't you?"

"If you think so—" Balack began, but Eve did not wait for an answer. She bounded over to Darnuir, thrusting the chair leg amateurishly at him. Darnuir blocked her first strike easily. Balack stood awkwardly.

Eve's savage blows were soon undermined by her clumsy footwork. She stumbled, fell, and, on her way down, Darnuir was able to knock the piece of wood out of her hand.

"Ha!" he cried triumphantly. "Do you yiel—"

Balack took him by surprise, slamming into him. The pair tumbled on top of the remaining pieces of the broken chair and then the sodden ground.

"Darnuir," Eve squealed, "you're bleeding!"

He sat up and put his hand to his head. Upon retracting it, he found a warm red patch on his palm.

Balack looked horrified. "I'm sorry. I didn't mean to."

Eve shoved her would-be teammate aside to reach Darnuir, gruffly saying, "Move," as she did so. "Oooh, it looks bad." She produced a clean handkerchief and pressed it against Darnuir's head.

"I'm fine," Darnuir told them. "It's just a scratch."

"I'll be the judge of that," a stern adult voice informed them. Olive stood on the steps, looking harassed. "Now come inside, all of you. It's bad enough that Grace ran off all day with Cosmo. The last thing I need is a head injury." Following her lead, the three of them trooped back across the yard.

Two Years Later

Their campfire crackled, its heat a relief against the night, the smoke pleasantly scented from the wood.

"Grace seemed upset when we left," Darnuir said.

"She's just worried about you three, that's all," Cosmo said. "She thinks you're too young to be out like this."

"She's afraid a wild animal might come and eat you," Garon clarified.

"But you said there aren't any bears this close to town," Eve said, a tinge of fear in her voice.

"Or wolves," Balack added, his voice a touch high.

"Oh, none of them," said Garon. "But there are big mountain cats with teeth the size of your arm and—"

Eve gasped, clasping a hand over her mouth.

"Thanks for that," Cosmo said, frowning at Garon. "I'm certain we are quite safe here, Eve. We're only an hour from the gates of Cold Point. You all want to be hunters one day, right? Well, you need to get used to camping out in the snow."

"I imagine Grace is also afraid you'll get a nasty scar a week before your wedding," Garon added.

"Occupational hazard," Cosmo said, raising his skin of ale for a drink.

"I'm getting too cold," Eve shivered. She pulled her thick fur cloak around her.

Darnuir flexed his fingers over their slowly dying fire, pretending he was not in any discomfort. His teeth betrayed him by chattering.

"Well, then," Cosmo announced, "another aspect of camp life is collecting wood for the fire. I felled a tree a little way back." He pointed into the darkness. "Darnuir, why don't you go get some for us? Balack and Eve, you two can learn from Garon how to set up our cookpot."

"I hope one of you is more of a natural chef than I am," Garon said, opening one of his larger knapsacks and rummaging around.

"Anyone who doesn't burn the food is a more natural chef than you," Cosmo said.

"Charring adds flavour, kids," Garon said. "Don't listen to the city snob."

As the group fell into conversation, Cosmo nudged Darnuir to get a move on. He got up and faced the night. A gentle stream of falling snow obscured the way ahead, but he was getting used to such conditions.

It wasn't long before Darnuir could no longer hear the others. His breath steamed in the chill air and his feet sank into the snow. He stumbled upon the fallen tree long before he saw it, stubbing his toe. Groaning, he bent to pick up the first small branch, then another. Soon, he had a nice pile between his arms.

A powerful gust of wind whipped through the valley, catching him by surprise and sending him sliding to the ground.

Darnuir got to his feet, grumbling at his scattered branches. As he set about picking them back up, he heard another pair of feet crunching through the snow.

"Eve? What are you doing here?"

"The wind blew out our fire. Cosmo asked one of us to go help you, so I said I would." She smiled weakly.

They set about their task. It was harder than it ought to have been, for their heavy furs weighed them down. He even heard Eve breathing hard nearby.

"Are you all right?" Darnuir asked.

"Yes," Eve said, confused. "I'm fine. Why?"

"No need to pretend. I can hear you're out of breath. If you want to head back, then—"

"I thought that was you."

Snow crunched somewhere in the darkness.

"Balack?" Darnuir asked.

No one answered, but the heavy breathing increased to a pant.

He took a few steps back, dropping his new pile of wood in favour of holding the largest branch he could in two hands. His heart forgot to beat. He nearly screamed when Eve drew up beside him.

"We have to go back," she whispered.

"If we run, we'll only make it worse."

They backed away as quietly as they could. The heavy feet drew closer, the panting became a heave.

"Come on," Eve said, jerking at his arm. She bolted.

Darnuir turned just in time to see the white wolf bound out of the darkness at her. Eve screamed and fell as it padded up to her, sniffing at the air. It didn't seem as big as it ought to, but it would easily overpower them. Its jaws opened wide.

"No!" Darnuir cried, leaping over to Eve and swinging wildly with his branch. The wolf let loose a squeal, snapping at the wood. Eve got up and ran. The wolf bit into his makeshift weapon and yanked on it hard. Darnuir pulled back and found that he'd somehow won the contest, falling back with the force of his own heave. It only made matters worse.

The wolf was pulled closer to him and he lost his grip on the branch. A greedy tongue licked the air. Darnuir shut his eyes, not wanting to see the wolf sink its teeth into him. He could feel the beast's hot breath on his face. Fat tears welled; his heart worked so fast it would surely burst.

Then there was a thump, a muffled grunt, the sound of steel being unsheathed and a yelp of pain. Silence reigned.

"Darnuir," Cosmo said, "are you hurt?" Large hands brought Darnuir to a sitting position and felt around his body for injury.

"I'm fine," Darnuir sobbed, finally opening his eyes. "Eve. Where is—"

"She's back with Garon. She's safe. I doubt there are more. That looked like a pup. Must have been alone and starving to venture this close to Cold Point. Poor thing."

Darnuir shook violently, though it could not be from the cold. He was not cold; in fact, he could feel the sweat upon his face. He rocked uncontrollably, and Cosmo wrapped his arms around him.

"I'm sorry," he wailed.

"Sorry?" Cosmo said. "Whatever for?"

"I didn't know what to do," Darnuir said. "I was too afraid." He continued to cry and pressed his face into Cosmo's furs.

"Shhhh," Cosmo said, holding him tight. "It's okay to be afraid. It's only... well, it's only human."

Three Years Later

Darnuir, Eve and Balack joined Grace in a farewell to Olive as they awaited her hunter escort down to Farlen.

"Are you sure?" Grace asked her for perhaps the hundredth time that morning alone.

"Absolutely," she reassured her sister. "It's time I moved on. I've got a position working for Lord Boreac himself. I'll find a new life in Brevia."

"You have one here!" Grace reminded her.

Olive took her hand. "I'm not really needed anymore. Things are stable again; the children are all moving on to the hunters soon, and you have Cosmo." She choked a little on her words. "I'll send word when I reach the city. Maybe one day you will come visit me?"

Her tone was optimistic but they all knew that was unlikely to occur. Cosmo held some major grievance against the capital, and it would take a great deal of convincing to get him to travel there.

Grace sobbed in agreement and the sisters embraced in a long hug. As they parted, a band of hunters came into sight. Garon was leading them; this was to be his first command. He would see Olive safely out of the Boreac Mountains, where she would join other travellers and link up with hunters from the Southern Dales to take them further north towards the Crown Lands.

As Olive gave them all one last kiss on the cheek, Darnuir found it hard to decide what she meant to him. Neither of the two women was quite like a mother to him, for they had spread their care over many charges. Yet over the years, the older children had been taken in by the hunters until, one by one, it was just the three of them left. Their family was an unusual one, but a family nonetheless.

Unlike Eve, Darnuir resisted crying, although he felt that familiar hot and prickly sensation play on the tip of his nose. They stood silently and watched as Olive walked off with the hunters, disappearing from their lives.

Six Months Later

Their three-day journey down from Cold Point was almost at an end. The hunter station could only be accessed by a narrow road high above the town of Ascent. One of the few buildings in the Boreacs made of stone, it was a complex construction with observation decks overhanging the mountainside. Slated and angled roofs directed snowfall safely off it. Nestled high above the valley where the town of Ascent lay, legend had it that this was once the site of a dragon nest in ages past. Darnuir thought it was remote enough and large enough to have been the nest of some great creature.

He risked a glance down to the valley below. Ascent seemed miniscule in the distance, as did the crystalline loch near it.

At fifteen years old, Darnuir, Balack and Eve could now formally join the hunters. Darnuir and Balack were already well advanced in their martial skills, thanks to Cosmo and Garon. Eve was lousy with a sword and bow, so opted to become a healer instead. As they drew up to the station's entrance, Darnuir took note of the heaviness of the gate, the trapdoor above it, and the numerous slits in the front wall for arrow fire.

Cosmo greeted them as they entered, and took them straight to Captain Tael in the main hall. Braziers lined the hall and, at the far end, the captain stood in front of a wall adorned by the stuffed heads of the region's largest kills. The head of an enormous brown bear was the central piece. Its paws alongside it were outstretched, as if welcoming them all to a dinner of which they were the main course.

The captain was by no means an aged man, but he was the eldest of all the hunters. He was short and in no way aided by a wound to his right leg that had left him reliant on a walking stick. The colour was fast draining from his beard and thinning hair, but his eyes were as sharp as any and he had a kind heart. When he wasn't disciplining his men, of course.

"It is a particular delight to bring you three into our ranks this day," Tael said. "Through Cosmo and Garon, I feel like I already know you well and, I must say, I expect great things."

Darnuir grinned at Eve and Balack, feeling proud.

"Yet do not think you shall receive an easier time here because of it," Tael continued. "Becoming a fully trained hunter is no easy feat. We are no mere butchers and have not been since Elsie the Green laid down our values centuries ago. You will learn not only to fight but how to track, skin, cook, clean wounds on yourselves and heal injured beasts where you can. Not all creatures pose a threat and your compassion must extend beyond humans alone. You must learn discipline, how to cope with hard living; these days we even lend our hands to building homes. Perhaps you may even come to understand who you really are—"

"Apologies, Captain," a deep and assured voice said from a side door. The hunter was rather tall, with broad shoulders, cropped hair and a crooked nose.

Tael turned expectantly. "Yes, Rufus?"

"Garon has just returned from patrol in the lower hills. He claims they have encountered demons."

Tael swallowed hard and then quickly looked between Cosmo and Rufus. "Is anyone injured?"

"Garon has a nasty cut," Rufus said. "He went straight to the healers, else he would have delivered the message to you personally. His patrol was taken by surprise but, thankfully, there were no deaths."

Darnuir, Eve and Balack exchanged nervous looks. Darnuir's heart quickened. *What does this mean?*

"Cosmo—" Tael began.

"I'll go immediately."

"Take a group of our finest," Tael instructed. "We must know the extent of this. Take Griswald too, in case things get troublesome."

"I'm sorry," Cosmo said to the three would-be recruits. "I will see you when I return. Rufus, with me?"

"Of course," Rufus said, and the two veterans hurried off.

One Year Later

Darnuir and Balack were standing with their legs and arms spread awkwardly beside their beds in the barracks. This allowed Grace and Eve to attach pieces of white and grey leather around them, which would form the basis of perfectly fitting armour.

Eve angled her pin. "Try not to fidget so much, Balack," she said tersely.

Balack gulped and nodded. His eyes followed Eve's every move. Her movements became hastier, less precise.

"Ouch," he winced, rubbing at his leg where her needle had struck.

"Sorry," she grumbled. She set the needle and thread down and backed away, looking flushed.

Grace threw her a glance. "Everything all right, dear?"

Eve folded her arms. "I just wish I wasn't so useless with weapons. I hate the thought of staying behind while you're both out there."

Darnuir and Balack shared a look.

"Healers have a vital role," Darnuir said.

"If anything, we're short of them," Balack added.

Eve glared at them both. "That's not it."

Darnuir frowned. It was becoming ever more difficult to get a straight answer out of her as they got older.

Grace moved to wrap an arm around Eve, raising her brow at the boys to tell them to say no more.

"I understand, dear," Grace said. "When I was your age, I must have helped dozens of them prepare like this. I could never hold a sword properly either."

Eve sniffed. "It just doesn't feel like I'll be doing much to help. I'd rather stop the injuries in the first place than patch them up." She looked to Balack, and then to Darnuir, lingering on him. "I don't want to have to patch either of you up."

What might lie ahead finally dawned on Darnuir. He had never seen a demon before, let alone fought one. Balack was stony-faced. A second passed, which felt like an hour.

"Cosmo will look after them," Grace said. Her face then turned a shade paler, as though her mind had led her on to asking, 'Who will take care of Cosmo?' They all left the question unspoken.

"Come here, you three." Grace beckoned.

They embraced as a group, trying as they always had to forget the inevitable. War would break out again. It had always been a matter of time.

As Eve placed a teary face on Darnuir's shoulder, he noticed Balack's mouth twitch and his eyes harden.

8

TIME FLIES PART 2: A PRELUDE TO WAR

Three Years Later
Darnuir – East of Farlen – The Lower Passes

An arrow blurred past Darnuir's shoulder. He barely registered the near miss, his focus on the demon before him. Its attack went wildly to one side, leaving it exposed. Darnuir took advantage, thrusting forwards through its bony chest for a clean kill. Smoke issued from the sword's entry point, curling up in the cold air.

Before he could catch his breath, another demon was on him. He twisted violently to avoid its blade, feeling his shoulder pull painfully, and still suffered a cut for his trouble. The movement sent him off balance, while the demon raised its barbed sword for another attack—

An arrow stuck the creature through the neck. Darnuir spun round and saw Balack drawing a fresh arrow, nodding at him. Blessing Balack's incredible accuracy, Darnuir gathered himself and assessed the situation.

Of the thirty hunters that had set off from Farlen two days ago, perhaps twenty remained. The youngest recruits had suffered hardest in the ambush.

"To me!" Garon called.

Obediently, the surviving hunters clustered around him. Those with bows dispatched the remaining demons and the skirmish ended with the last twang of a bowstring.

"Stay alert," Garon told them. "There will be more."

"How do you know that?" a recruit squeaked in fear.

"That was too large a group to be ranging without spectre control," Garon answered. "And if there are no spectres with them then stay alert at any rate. Without spectres, they are unpredictable."

Darnuir darted his eyes around the vicinity, his heart missing a beat at the faintest sign of movement: a bush rustling in the breeze, a small stone rolling off the mountainside, the shadow of a tree undulating against the rock.

"Garon?" Darnuir murmured. "Over there, is that shadow writhing?"

"Let me see," Garon said, pushing his way through their ranks, his bow drawn. "Yes, I fear it is a spectre. Keep me covered until I say so." The rest of the men complied and kept tightly packed, hiding Garon from view. "Balack? With me."

Balack nodded and nocked an arrow.

"Now!" Garon ordered.

The men split. Garon and Balack rose, took aim and fired at the peculiar shadow. Moments before the arrows hit their mark, four large creatures leapt forth from the bulging shadow.

As tall as men, with flickering fire on their heads, and bodies composed of a swirling, dark substance so thick that it might have been flesh, spectres were the demons that Darnuir feared most. Spectral demons, better known as spectres, were stronger, smarter and far better fighters than regular demons. They could also merge themselves into shadows and move along them at will, vanishing and reappearing during battle. Common demons could not do this and seemed to lack sense. They were wild without spectres to guide them.

Of the spectres who had just sprung from the shadow of the tree, the straggler of the group was caught by one of the arrows. The remaining three glanced quickly around for another shadow to escape into. Finding none, they stood still, seemingly accepting their fate. By then, Darnuir and the rest were on them.

His first strike met only air as the spectre vanished before his eyes. From somewhere behind him came a death scream. Whirling around, he saw the elusive spectre cutting down one hunter, then another, before the other hunters descended upon it to avenge their fallen comrades.

"Spread out!" Garon cried. "Don't let our shadows touch or they will travel between us!"

Hastily, they spread out, and the remaining spectres found themselves trapped upon shadow-free ground. Arrows were loosed, cutting down the furthest spectre and forcing its last comrade to dive wildly to avoid the projectiles. It must have found a shadow in a crack in the mountainside, for it disappeared entirely.

Garon thrust his hand out to tell the company to stay back and went alone to where the spectre had disappeared. After a quick examination, Garon stabbed into a measly-sized spot, surely too small for even a bug to hide. His sword seemed to do the impossible. It entered the shadow, into the very rock itself. When he withdrew it, the body of the slain spectre was dragged out with it, its smoking blood dancing in the air around Garon.

Although it was over, and he should have been relieved, Darnuir couldn't help but feel it had ended too soon. The rush was incredible. Something burned inside him with every engagement, more so than it did for the others. He liked it. Really liked it. The blood, the sweat, the smoke – something about the way the air turned sweet. Although that last one worried him and he didn't feel like mentioning it to anyone.

He just... reacted differently than the others, he supposed.

Garon looked gravely upon the fallen. "Strip their bodies for equipment. We'll send a retrieval party for them if we can." His lower lip trembled. "Let's hope the wolves are deterred by the demons as well."

Five Months Later

What had begun as a peaceful day was now a snowstorm; an unusual occurrence in the town of Farlen, as it was one of the lowest lying areas of the Boreac Mountains. Save for a few feet, nothing of the outside world was visible from within Farlen's inn.

Darnuir, along with many of the hunters, had gathered there, anxiously awaiting word from Brevia. Messengers had been sent to the Cairlav Marshes, the Southern Dales, the Crown Lands, and the Master Station at Brevia itself, requesting information and aid.

Skirmishes were regular events now, with perhaps one in every three patrols meeting demons. Their bands had also steadily increased in size, which only meant more hunter casualties. The people of the lower Boreac Mountains had been told to seek refuge in Farlen until the situation improved, as outlying farms and lumber mills were too vulnerable, and many had already been raided. This had a knock-on effect that disrupted trade, which only made things worse.

The atmosphere in the inn was appropriately dour.

Balack placed an empty tankard gently upon their table. "I think I'll get another one. Anyone else?"

"Needle brew, if there is any," Darnuir said.

"Doubt it," said Garon. "Hard thing to harvest when demons are likely to be lurking up the same tree."

"Then nothing, thanks, Balack," Darnuir said. Ale always seemed to go straight to his head. The term 'lightweight' had been bandied about.

"Cosmo?" Balack asked, though it was more of a courtesy. Two empty tankards already sat before him and he clearly had a thirst today. He often had a thirst these days.

"Err, yes," Cosmo said absentmindedly before he slipped back into his pensive state.

"Are you all right?" Darnuir asked.

"Let him stew," Garon said. "Likely marital troubles." He shook his head at the thought. "Not for me, I tell you. Why settle for one arrow in the quiver?"

Darnuir laughed. "Not all men can be like you."

Garon hadn't heard him. He'd caught the attention of one of the barmaids, smirking. Darnuir coughed loudly.

Garon was shaken back to the conversation. "Oh, loosen up, Darnuir."

"Don't let me stop you. Go ahead and talk to her if you like."

Garon waved the notion away. "Not much in the mood tonight. Bit grim and all. Besides, plenty more wolves in the woods."

"Try telling that to Balack."

"Well, he wants what he wants. Gotta respect that in a way, like our mute here." He nodded at Cosmo. "But you, lad. What do you want?"

"I've thought about becoming a captain one day."

"That's not what I meant."

"Well, in *that* respect, I'm not sure."

It was the truth. Sword and battle lured him more. Something in him itched to get back out there. Having a home to return to would keep him away from the fighting... but if he was a captain, well, he could place himself at the front of things.

Garon eyed him knowingly. "Fancy yourself as a leader?"

Darnuir shrugged. "Maybe. I'm too young to think about that."

"Well, you're in good company for it. He'll be captain after Tael, even if he doesn't want it." He spoke as though Cosmo was not there. "Stick around and I'm sure he'll hand it over to you as soon as he can."

Balack returned, thudding their drinks on the table. Cosmo reached silently for his and took a good, long draught. At last, he spoke.

"Grace is pregnant," he said flatly, as if the prospect held no joy in it at all.

Garon winced.

"Congratulations?" Balack said.

"It's a terrible time for it," Cosmo said.

"Better than open war," Darnuir said. "Better than twenty years ago. Will there ever be a good time?"

"If war comes when the child is still a babe... Grace would need so much help during the best of times..." Cosmo mumbled into incoherence as he returned to his drink. Upon resurfacing, Darnuir saw that Cosmo had the look of one preparing to reveal ill news.

Garon must have seen it too. "You wouldn't abandon us, would you?"

"Not permanently, no," Cosmo admitted.

"But we'll need you," Darnuir insisted. "Few are more experienced."

"There are plenty of fine fighters," Cosmo said.

"But few leaders," Darnuir said.

Cosmo's eyes fell upon Garon.

"Me?" Garon said, astonished. "Come now, Cosmo. There are plenty of your own generation who would be better suited."

Cosmo smiled. "In any case, Tael is your captain. And I believe I see him waving me over. Excuse me. Come, Garon."

Darnuir felt a twang of jealousy as Garon left with Cosmo. Garon was always included in important matters. Garon was his real protégé.

So what does that make me?

"Heard from Eve recently?" Balack asked, taking a stab at nonchalance and failing miserably.

"Not by letter, and the last time I spoke to her was our check-in at the station last month."

"I received a letter today," Balack said smugly. "Apparently, Harris 'approached' her last week when his patrol went to check in."

"Oh, did he now?"

"Yes, he did. She turned him down though." Balack smirked. "Told him there was 'someone else'."

"Poor Harris. He must have been rather *brave* to be so forward with her," Darnuir said pointedly.

Balack did a double-take. "Well, I admire his courage, but it was always going to be a futile attempt."

"Was it?" Darnuir asked, toying with him.

"Oh, come on now! Eve is... well, you know Eve, and Harris is just, well, he is just Harris, isn't he?"

"A masterful argument as always," Darnuir said. He flicked his finger against one of Cosmo's empty tankards to give him something to do.

"If you are going to be difficult, I'll change topic."

"No, no," Darnuir said calmly, trying not to arouse his friend's defensiveness. "I think we should have it all out now, because it's obvious you want to discuss it. Why else bring it up?"

"What are you talking about, Darnuir?"

"Eve. How you are in love with her."

Balack choked on his drink. "How did you—"

"I'm not blind, Balack," Darnuir said wearily. "And don't try and pretend like we haven't had this exact same conversation in the past."

"But we haven't!"

Darnuir just held his gaze.

"Why are you so insistent I do something about it?" Balack moaned.

"Because if you don't tell her soon, it is evident that others will, and she might just respond in kind to one of them."

"A few demons harass us and suddenly everyone is making hasty decisions."

"The threat of war is doing that."

"We don't know that yet. We just don't. Besides, even if war does break out, we are hardly a priority target for Castallan."

"Maybe not, but we will be an easy one," Darnuir reminded him. "The Boreacs lie so close to the Bastion and a few hundred hunters will not last for long against a large force."

"Even so, we are no threat to his flank, and he would be dealing with our actual armies, surely?"

A thunderous bang ended all conversation. The doors to the inn were flung open, letting in the howling wind and snow along with it. Three hunters and two huntresses stood exhausted in the doorway, carrying something that was clearly a body wrapped up in one of their cloaks. Darnuir was not familiar with any of them.

They dragged themselves inside and stood there until another hunter thought it best to shut the doors behind them. Captain Tael was the first to break the silence. Despite his age and injuries, he rose determinedly and spoke with authority.

"If the news is ill, then be out with it, Ava."

"Sir," the closest huntress began, "we arrived at the checkpoint where poor Aelfric and his team should have met us, only to find his head mounted—" Her voice cracked. "His body was some way away. There was no sign of the others."

"Mounted on what? Demons don't have pikes or spears."

"They stuck his sword into the earth and then rammed his head onto the hilt."

A few seconds of mournful silence took over the men.

"Spectres having some fun," Tael said grimly. "I want patrol groups doubled in size from now on."

"Captain," Ava continued, "this was crammed into Aelfric's mouth." She held up a piece of grubby paper with a slanted scrawl upon it. "It only has your name on it, sir."

"Very well, then. Bring me this message."

As soon as Tael took the letter into his hand, Darnuir felt a strange sensation wash over him, of losing all energy. This was worse than fatigue. He'd barely even drank – what was this?

"To all who would stand against me, I bid that you halt your hopeless thoughts."

The voice was gravelly and theatrical. It seemed to ring throughout the whole tavern, but also from right beside Darnuir and from inside his head, all at once. It was intrusive. Unnerving.

Darnuir shifted uneasily in his seat, his exhaustion descending swiftly into despair.

"For too long have my desires gone unheeded."

The voice is right, Darnuir thought. *It is hopeless. Why even try?*

"I have only ever wanted what is best for humankind," the voice went on. "Capitulate and join me. Step into a new age for humanity. I send this message to all the provinces of men, to whom I offer the hand of friendship. Why fight for the fairies that look down on you, or the dragons who have long abandoned you? Why fight still for Brevia and a neglectful king who does not care about you? But I do. Lay down your weapons and my hand shall be extended. Gifts of power will be granted. Together, we can forge a greater human race."

No one was quick to stir and the deadly stillness within the tavern remained unbroken for a long minute. Those few who moved were slow and lethargic, as if their joints were thawing out from a freeze.

"Some things never change," Tael said. "For those of you too young to remember the last war, Castallan sent a similar message then. Well, I for one believe none of it!" His casual brushing aside of Castallan's intrusion did not seem to reassure everyone. Darnuir, for one, still had the uncanny feeling of depression and nausea.

"Cosmo!" Tael commanded.

"Yes, Captain?"

"I know you do not want this, but I see no one else as qualified or respected in our ranks." He looked imploringly. "I require you to take my place as captain while I travel to Brevia for reinforcements. If there is to be war, the Boreacs will need more men."

"Sir..." Cosmo began, his face turning pale. After a moment, he rallied. "I understand."

Three Months Later

Darnuir and Eve were out on one of the station's observation platforms. The lack of wind and snow made for a clear picture of the landscape and Ascent seemed oddly close. Eve was in her hunter's garb. Though she was not well trained enough for combat, it was still the required uniform.

"I still can't believe Tael is gone," she said.

"It's hard to stomach," Darnuir said. "It doesn't feel real somehow, but it's true. Our new captain is called Scythe. He is overseeing the defence of Farlen."

Eve pounded a fist on the railing as though to make it untrue. "What happened?"

"The details are vague. Tael made it to Brevia but it seems he passed away some-time after arriving. Perhaps the journey took it out of him. He was getting on."

"He wasn't so old that he couldn't travel," Eve said. "And aside from his leg, he was fit enough."

Darnuir threw up his hands. "You know as much as I do. Scythe turned up with three hundred reinforcements two weeks ago. He has a writ from the Master Station declaring him as captain. Lord Boreac himself nominated the man."

"Lord Boreac is a dithering oaf who hasn't visited these mountains since I had pigtails," Eve said. "What does he know? What do any of them know in Brevia? Why not Cosmo instead?"

"He was more than willing to step aside. You know he never wanted the command."

"Well, is this Scythe any good?"

"He seems like the right man for the job," Darnuir said. "He'd rather lead from the front. That's why he hasn't visited the station yet. And he's one of the best swordsmen I've seen."

"Better than you?"

He shrugged. "Maybe one day we can put that to the test."

"I'll have my bandages ready," she teased. "Wouldn't want you to bleed out when he beats you senseless." She rapped him on the shoulder when he did not respond. "Don't be sour. I barely see you as it is." She had come closer to hit him and did not move back afterwards. Her proximity made Darnuir uncomfortable.

He cleared his throat. "Have you heard from Balack?"

"I got a letter three days ago," she said offhandedly. "But he always writes."

"Anything interesting?"

"Nothing out of the ordinary. Why?"

Darnuir was disappointed. His hopes for Balack seemed poorly placed. He'd have to encourage him again.

"No news is good news," Darnuir said. "I just haven't seen him as much lately. Our patrols rarely cross paths."

She didn't seem to pay much attention to his answer. Her hand had somehow fallen lightly upon his own.

"I just want you to be safe," she said. "Both of you, I mean. Of course, both of you." Unsure of what to say, he carefully extracted his hand and gently patted hers, staring determinedly out at the valley below.

One Month Later

. . .

Farlen was on fire.

Darnuir watched the town burn and brushed away the stinging liquid streaming into his eyes; a mixture of sweat and snow that melted to rain in the air.

"Move it!" Scythe called. "I said move, Darnuir." The captain appeared at his side and hauled him away by the shoulder.

Scythe was sporting a nasty cut to his cheek but otherwise looked unharmed. Tall and sinewy, Scythe appeared almost gaunt but was far stronger than his build and forty-five years suggested. Thinning, oak-coloured hair receded up his forehead and his nose was sharp, as if worked by a whetstone.

The pair joined the remaining hunters retreating up one of the small mountain passes only the hunters knew of. All the main routes had been blocked long ago.

Darnuir saw Balack waiting for him up ahead, leaning breathlessly against one of the rare evergreen trees that had turned silver. Seeing such trees was usually a cause for joy; the chance to harvest its needles for brew was never missed. Yet now, not even the thought of bolstering needle brew could warm his spirit.

Balack was sporting the gore of battle but he seemed to have avoided injury. His quiver now contained only a handful of arrows. The pair embraced before returning to their solemn march higher into the mountains.

No one spoke.

Two Months Later

The town of Ascent braced itself for attack. The demons had been relentless in their campaign through the Boreac Mountains. Their numbers seemed limitless, as if there was a constant flow of reinforcements, which was surely out of all proportion to the importance of the region. Nobody understood it.

Despite Cosmo, Garon and Scythe making excellent decisions, the hunters were slowly bleeding men and women. One hundred had already perished, meaning their force now stood at seven hundred. If they became caught in open battle, the sheer number of demons would certainly overwhelm them.

This fight was a crucial one. If Ascent fell, then the resources and haven of the station would be cut off from Cold Point.

Balack and Darnuir stood side by side high on a rock shelf above the column of demons below. Across the chasm, other groups of hunters took shots at the demons, aiming near blind in the darkness.

Yet night offered some protection. Without as many shadows, the chances of a spectre attack were much reduced. Spectres seemed to require a true shadow to meld into, not merely darkness itself.

Darnuir's quiver was half empty already but the demons below seemed unconcerned about the arrows that rained upon them. They just gathered in the passage,
waiting for their brethren ahead to break down the town gates.

A screech like daggers on rock cut through the night and the demons finally
surged forwards.

"The gates must have fallen," Darnuir said. The clank of metal and the roar of
battle raged off in the distance.

"We can't help them by returning," Balack said. "Two more swords won't help."

"Then what do we do?"

"I don't know," Balack wailed, his voice cracking. He wheeled around, looking
helplessly for a solution.

"There," Darnuir said, pointing to a large boulder sitting precariously on the
ledge. "Block the path with that!"

"We tried moving that before, remember?"

"It was Griswald and Garon who tried to move it," Darnuir said.

"If Griswald can't nudge it then neither will we. It's an enormous hunk of rock!"

"We have to try, don't we?" Darnuir said. He ran to hack at a thick branch on a
nearby tree, unconcerned about blunting his weapon at this stage. Procuring himself
a lever, he thrust it in under a small crack in the boulder's underside and pressed
down on the end of the wood. Balack ran to join them. They pressed down with all
their might.

Nothing happened.

"Come on," Balack bellowed.

"I'm giving it all I've got," Darnuir assured him, but still the thing would not
budge.

Another concerted effort only snapped the branch. Balack gasped and stumbled
backwards, panting. "It's no use."

"Damn it," Darnuir cried, slamming his palms against the rock. "Move, move,
move!" And then, in a moment of complete foolishness, he struck out with his
booted foot. He was guaranteed to do himself an injury. This fleeting thought passed
through his mind, but he couldn't stop. He was too angry.

His foot connected with the boulder, but this time, the boulder moved. It crept
forward then crashed off the ledge, picking up speed as it went, gathering more
debris as it landed on the demons below. Stones rained like hail after it, and smaller
trees and snow were churned up in a mini avalanche, blocking off the narrowest
section of the passageway. It sent the demons into complete disarray.

Balack's mouth fell open in amazement. "Dranus' black hide. How did you do
that?"

"I haven't a clue," Darnuir answered honestly. He inspected his foot. Remarkably,
he seemed unharmed. He put his weight back on his foot and it took it.

My ankle should have bent backwards. That boulder must have begun to fall at the last moment, it must have.

Shaking and in shock, he sat down to save himself from collapsing. Balack lay down as well and Darnuir turned to face him. They looked intensely at each other and then began to laugh, quietly at first, then doubled over in hysteria.

The next evening, Darnuir, Eve and Balack were making circuits of the hall in the station. Eventually, they found an empty table. The party was in full swing, thrown in celebration of their victory at Ascent. Darnuir had been hailed as a hero when Balack told everyone about their story, but he still insisted that he could not explain it.

Which was the truth.

Balack and Darnuir were given first pick of the ale, which had been taken off ration for the occasion. Scouts sent out after the battle reported that the demons were still retreating and would take days to regroup.

At first, everyone seemed uneasy about enjoying themselves, but once the idea settled on their minds, it quickly became apparent that they all needed a night without worry or battle. Indeed, Balack appeared fresher than Darnuir had seen him in months, though perhaps that was the ale taking effect. Eve too looked more like her old self, with her blond hair hanging loose once more. It danced around her face and the nape of her neck in an enchanting rhythm. His eyes lingered on her for a moment and she caught him, giving him an earnest smile in return.

An empty tankard slammed onto the table.

"Would you like to dance?" Balack asked.

Eve seemed taken aback but quickly recovered. "Sure, why not!"

Balack seemed put out by her choice of words but took her hand all the same. The pair drifted off into the swirling mass of people, dancing to the pitchy tones of instruments that needed to be retuned long before the demons had come. A huntress called out the instructions for the next dance, which seemed to involve a lot of switching partners and ducking under other people's arms. The result was a lot of crashing bodies.

Darnuir was not left on his own for long. Cosmo and Garon quickly took up the empty seats. Cosmo looked the more battered of the pair; his black hair was matted, and a bloody bandage covered his upper arm. Yet he seemed strangely sober tonight, of all nights, unlike Garon, whose eyes were bloodshot and whose balance was less than graceful.

"I think he needs a sit down," Cosmo said.

"Damn, but this ale is poor," Garon slurred. "Tastes like Dranus himself spat in it."

"It seems fine to me," Darnuir said.

"Well, you barely... barely drink the stuff," Garon said. "You don't know any better."

"I like to keep my head clear," Darnuir said.

"You hear that, Garon?" Cosmo said. "The kid is more responsible than you."

"Look... it's not my – hic – fault that you're as uptight as a bear's arse in hibernation. Could be our last party ever, you know. Better make the – hic – most of it."

"That's cheerful," Darnuir said.

"We're not done yet," Cosmo said.

Garon swayed, narrowing his eyes at Cosmo before throwing them open wide in some realisation. He rounded on Darnuir.

"It is your birthday soon, isn't it?"

"Garon, no," Cosmo warned.

"What's that got to do with anything?" Darnuir said.

"Ahhhh," Garon said, tapping his nose.

"There's no point discussing what's not certain," Cosmo said. He stood and confiscated Garon's drink, who gave it a look of deep longing. "I think you've had enough. Come on, I'll throw you into your bunk."

"Mighty kind of you," Garon said. "Always looking – hic – out for me."

Cosmo winked and handed Garon's drink to Darnuir.

"Go on. No reason to hold back tonight. There might not be another chance."

With that, he began dragging Garon off.

Darnuir contemplated the tankard. He sniffed it and his stomach churned from the smell. *What's wrong with me?* He glanced around the hall; everyone else was enjoying themselves. If they were all going to be worse than useless in the morning, then it would hardly make a difference if he alone remained sober. And Cosmo had given him an order... sort of. He took a sip, blinking at the bitter taste he wasn't used to, and then threw back the rest in one long drink.

Several hours and many drinks later, his world had become a blur. Darnuir spoke to people but did not remember what they said. He moved to one side of the room and then the other but did not know why.

At some point, Eve tugged on his arm with an impressive strength.

"Come on," she moaned. "Just one dance?"

"What... what you saying?" Darnuir mumbled, his head positively swimming.

Eve led him off. Had he been aware of his jostling on the dance floor, he would have been mortified. It was all he could do to recognise the girl before him.

She propped herself up on her toes to shout something into his ear, but the din of the room drowned her out. He just nodded and smiled in response, hoping this would be the right answer. She drew back from his ear but remained on her toes; her face was now close to his.

Too close, was all he could think. *She is too close.*

Their lips met and then she grabbed him by the hand and hauled him off out of the main hall. It was evident from the way she walked that her head wasn't exactly clear either. She found an empty room and shoved him inside.

Freezing air from the open window bit at Darnuir's face. Eve dashed to close the shutters. When she turned to face him, she was flushed, her chest rising and falling heavily.

Darnuir knew that this wasn't right. Every fibre of his being urged him to leave the room, save for one tiny treacherous part of him that seemed determined to stay. Even as he moved one foot backwards, the other remained rooted to the floor.

Eve drew even closer to him.

Too close. She is far too close.

"I'm cold," she whispered, putting her arms around his neck.

Darnuir was speechless. His brain could not work fast enough, and he swallowed nervously. As he forced his protesting feet backwards, she remained anchored to him and they stumbled to the door. With what little control he had, he kept his eyes away from hers and, with his free hand, he grasped in vain for the handle. He struggled before her own hand fell delicately on his own and pulled it away. To his dismay, he found his hand did not resist.

"Do you want to leave?" she asked, her lips now finding his neck.

He wanted to blame it all on the playful poison that now ran through him, that small but powerful part of him that did not want to move. Eve wasn't much better. It was plain that she was hanging onto him, in part, to prevent herself from sliding to the floor. His eyes accidentally fell upon hers and their gaze held just a fraction too long.

Then that treacherous part of him asserted itself and their lips met again. Eve's grip on him tightened. They swayed first forward and then slammed back against the door, and Darnuir took both hands to embrace her. One of Eve's hands still searched for something on the door and, after a few moments, Darnuir heard the loud click of the bolt being pushed into place.

The next morning, everyone and everything was being moved from Ascent to Cold Point, the highest town in the mountain range. Scythe had judged that if Ascent was taken by the enemy, then Cold Point would be left wide open with the hunters trapped within their own station. It would be a three-day journey and the retreat was to take place in stages.

With the high of the party fading, the harsh reality was beginning to sink in. All told, with so many people taking refuge in Cold Point, they had maybe a month's food left. Outside aid was required. But no one was coming.

Darnuir turned this over in his aching mind as he marched.

Even more cruelly, Balack was by his side.

"You've been quiet. You all right?"

He couldn't look Balack in the eye. "Yes, I'm just suffering from last night, that's all."

Balack grumbled an agreement and rubbed at his own eyes. The pair didn't speak for the rest of that day.

Three Days Later – Cold Point

The only welcome they received was the familiar sight of the great wrought-iron gates, standing sentinel at the entrance to the town. Flakes of rust coated the metal. Darnuir doubted they would hold for long.

Passing through, Darnuir noticed how crowded the town now was. Refugees had been fleeing there since the fall of Farlen but he had not appreciated the scale of the issue. Wedged in the valley, Cold Point was much smaller than either Ascent or Farlen.

In the town square where the gnarled silver tree stood proudly, Darnuir and Balack were given instructions on where to drop off their supplies. They parted ways in silence. He didn't know what to say, or if he should say anything at all.

He hadn't seen Eve since that night. She'd been in one of the first groups sent to Cold Point.

Cosmo was amongst the very last to reach the town.

"What has happened?" Garon demanded, barely giving poor Cosmo a chance to catch his breath.

"Cut off as we left," Cosmo spluttered. "Demons came pouring in from the eastern gate. Ran. Everyone else had already left the town." He stopped to lean on Garon. The others with him showed signs of great hardship as well. Some simply fell to their knees.

"Did they not give pursuit?" Garon asked. "How were you able to make it?"

"Scythe and the rear guard took action. They loosed arrows to draw the demons' attention before making a run for the station. Bought us time."

"Are they dead?" Balack asked, horrified.

"If they made it to the station in time, they'll be in a far better position than us," Garon said.

"The spectres won't have them wait upon a fortified position for long," Cosmo said. "Not when a softer target is within reach. Either way, we will have a few days at best."

All the hunters that were nearby in the square looked to Cosmo. Whether he wished it or not, he was now their captain. The hunters of the Boreac Mountains were proud and defiant, but their time was running out now. No help seemed to be coming and there appeared to be no end to the enemy's attack. There was nowhere left to retreat to; no more passages to barricade, no more secret pathways from which to harry their foes. They were trapped at the highest and most remote region in the human kingdom.

For Darnuir's part, he stood quietly amidst the crowd, as though struck dumb, wondering which confrontation he feared the most. Eve? Balack? Or the demons?

9

A WIZARD IS NEVER LATE...

Darnuir – Cold Point

Two days had passed since Cosmo delivered his ominous news. Two days of worry. Two days of desperate planning, of hurriedly teaching the rudiments of swordplay to willing townsfolk. For Darnuir, it had also been two long days of avoidance and guilt.

In an effort to evade both Eve and Balack, he had volunteered for every task that needed doing. He had hauled logs from the mills to the square and helped lash them in stacks upon the roofs as traps. He had gathered furniture, smashed it up and heaped the pieces into high barricades. Once he had passed the point of initial weariness, he found he could keep going far longer than the others, and ignored Cosmo's suggestions to turn in.

He now stood atop his latest furniture mound, one of many they had erected around the town square. Each one was at least two storeys high, and only the tavern and the hunters' lodge loomed taller. Hunters and huntresses lingered around the square, examining their efforts. Some were still precariously balanced on rooftops, trying to keep the logs in check; a task made more difficult by working solely by torchlight.

Through a great effort, only one route remained free for the demons: the main avenue up from the town's gate. This would funnel the horde up to the square itself, where the defenders would make their stand.

"Looking good, lad!" Griswald boomed.

"Anything else to add?" Darnuir called back down.

"Nah, not unless we're gonnae start smashing up our beds as well."

"That is an excellent idea," Cosmo called from another barricade.

"Ach, see here, Cosmo, I wis joking," Griswald protested, waving a crutch threateningly. "Some of us still need a decent place tae lie doon."

Cosmo jogged closer to them. "We won't use them all. Just from those of us who are fit enough to go without. We could do with more to block the alleys behind the lodge."

"You can use mine," Darnuir offered.

"That's generous of you," Cosmo said. "But I was about to tell you to go and use yours."

"I'd prefer to be useful."

"I'd rather have one of my best swordsmen rested for the fight," Cosmo said. "Griswald, you go rest as well. Tell Rufus he's to come out and bring me another warm, spiced ale."

"Nae need to tell me twice," Griswald said, hobbling off.

"Honestly, Cosmo, I feel fine."

"Must I give an official order?" Cosmo said sternly. The father, the trainer and friend had gone. Cosmo the captain was before him.

All that spiced ale is likely adding an edge to his voice.

A soft bell began to ring around the square. The old innkeep made his round, clanking his little brass instrument. It signalled midnight and the third day of their wait for the demons.

A fact clicked into place in Darnuir's head. It was his birthday.

And a very happy one it won't be.

When Whiteleaf's bell fell silent, a blinding light emanated from near the silver tree in the town square. Darnuir cried out, shielding his eyes as it shone brighter. He caught Cosmo's eye, but Cosmo didn't look worried.

In fact, he was smiling.

As the glow died down, the outline of a man appeared. He wore long blue robes and held the largest walking stick he'd ever seen.

Darnuir reached for his sword. All around the square, the hunters drew back arrows, yelling out to each other that Castallan had emerged in their midst.

"Stand down," Cosmo shouted. "Stand down, I say!"

Slowly, everyone complied, though they looked confused. Cosmo waved at Darnuir to come join him. He picked his way down the barricade and hurried to Cosmo's side.

They moved together to greet this new arrival. Up close, Darnuir could see that his hair was short and flecked with grey, yet he did not seem to be much older than Cosmo. What unnerved Darnuir, however, was the man's hand. It appeared to be burnt, except it was as black as pitch and curled claw-like around the staff he bore.

"You have perfect timing, Brackendon," Cosmo said. Then he embraced the stranger in a fierce hug. His tone was happy, almost giddy. "I was beginning to worry you wouldn't come!"

"I very nearly did not," the stranger, Brackendon, said. "But here I am when Darnuir turns of age. And here he is. How convenient." He took a moment to examine his surroundings, peering quizzically around the square before raising his eyebrows. "I seem to have arrived at a troubled time."

"Demons will be upon us soon," Cosmo said.

"Demons? This far into the mountains?"

"We've been under attack for months," Cosmo said.

Brackendon looked apprehensively around the square. More of the hunters had started to approach, which clearly made him uncomfortable.

"Perhaps we could talk privately? It may be the wiser course. I can explain all."

"We'll speak in private," Cosmo said. "For all the good it will do. You've made quite an entrance and, in any case, they will all know soon enough."

"Yes, they shall."

Darnuir did not like the idea of Cosmo being alone with this man. "Shall I accompany you, sir?" he asked.

Brackendon chuckled. "Darnuir, referring to someone else as sir. Well, you do have him well trained, Cosmo. And is that some stubble I can see as well?"

"What does that mean?" Darnuir said. "And how do you know my name?"

"Come along now," Cosmo said. "And calm yourself, Darnuir, I will not be needing protection. Ah, Rufus, there you are!" Cosmo looked greatly relieved as he took a mug of hot cider from Rufus' outstretched hand. He took a long sip. "Dranus, but that is better. Rufus, please see to it that the beds from the lodge are added to these piles."

They entered the tavern and their presence did not cause quite the same fuss as it had outside. Garon was enjoying a tankard in the company of some of the huntresses and healers. As they passed, Cosmo grabbed Garon by the scruff of the neck and yanked upwards.

"What the—" Garon wiped desperately at the drink that had slopped down his front. When he saw Brackendon, his eyes widened, and he followed without protest.

Cosmo led them up the stairs to the third floor where the healers were preparing space for the wounded in the inevitable battle. He picked a room seemingly at random and gruffly removed its occupants.

"You'll have to vacate this area for a while," he told them.

As they trooped out of the room, Darnuir's heart skipped a beat. Eve was amongst them and he could not avoid her eye. He gave a half-hearted smile, unsure of what else to do. Mercifully, Cosmo called upon him, allowing him an excuse to get away.

Once the four of them were inside, Garon bolted the door shut. Cosmo slammed his already empty mug of cider down on the bedside table, alongside the bandages, needles and foul-smelling pastes used on wounds. Like most rooms in the tavern, it was simply furnished, with a squat log bed, an uneven desk and dirty mirror. A rickety chair sat beside the fireplace.

"Perhaps Darnuir should take a seat," Garon suggested. "He has a lot to hear."

Darnuir opted for the sturdier-looking bed.

"Let's get a fire going," the wizard said. He pointed his staff towards a pile of hewn logs and several lifted into the fireplace of their own accord. Brackendon opened the palm of his hand and blew gently. Sparks flew at the wood to ignite it.

Darnuir sat bolt upright and gasped. "What the— what did you just do?"

"I used magic," Brackendon said, as though it were as common as tying shoelaces. The wizard warmed his hands. "Oh, that's better," he said, and sat in the nearby chair. "I don't know how you can stand the cold without it."

"You get used to it," Cosmo said.

The wizard raised his eyebrows as though he didn't believe Cosmo, then sank lower into his seat. He might have been an elderly man, readying himself to recount some youthful tale. There was an uncomfortable silence; at least, it was uncomfortable for Darnuir. Brackendon seemed to be rather enjoying his distress.

"I do hope your years in these mountains haven't frozen your tongue?"

When Darnuir said nothing, he went on.

"I haven't been to Cold Point since the day I brought you here. I would have come back to see you, prepare you perhaps, or whisk you away, but it never seemed safe, and for a long time, I was quite incapable. For too long a time..."

"Your hand," Cosmo said, as though seeing it for the first time. "Brackendon, did you—"

"Yes, I am afraid so."

"I'm so sorry," Cosmo said.

"It is I who should be sorry," said Brackendon. "I pushed myself too hard during the battle at Demons' Folly and drew on far more magic than I ought to have risked. I had barely begun to recover from my efforts with Darnuir. I wasn't ready. Did you not wonder why I had not sent word after all this time?"

"Naturally," Cosmo said. "But I assumed it was best to wait, as you said. I didn't want to move on my own."

Darnuir was lost. He decided to interrupt their catch-up. "I'm sorry, but could someone explain what this is all about? What efforts did you have with me?" He did not much like the sound of that.

"You haven't told him?" Brackendon asked irritably.

"What would have been the point until he was of age?" Cosmo said. "Without the sword—"

"What sword?" Darnuir asked.

"Your sword," Garon said. He clapped his hands together. "Let's not dawdle. You are not really a human. You are a dragon, and no ordinary dragon either. You are the rightful King of Dragons, wielder of the Dragon's Blade."

Darnuir was not sure whether he wished to scream or laugh. Cosmo threw Garon an incredulous look.

"What?" exclaimed Garon. "If you have an arrowhead in your leg, best to rip it out."

"Does everyone know this, bar me?" Darnuir asked. "And also, there is just no way—"

"Only those present in this room know," Cosmo said. "Brackendon, I had to inform Garon of the full truth. Once Darnuir started venturing on patrols, I needed someone else to take extra care of him."

"But I am not a dragon," Darnuir said matter-of-factly.

They all looked at him patronisingly, as though he were an infant insisting it was not bedtime.

"I'm afraid you are," Cosmo said.

"You kicked a boulder down the mountainside, for goodness' sake," Garon said.

"It was already falling," Darnuir said, knowing full well that it wasn't.

"You can see farther in the dark than the rest of us," Cosmo said.

"And you might be surprised to hear that your eyes glow faintly yellow when you're out at night," Garon said. "Now don't look so shocked, it's not that noticeable. It's also why you were usually the first on night watch, I'm afraid."

"I just..." Darnuir was utterly without words.

This is madness. They are all mad. Or maybe I am?

"Perhaps if I tell my story, it may help ease you in to the notion," Brackendon said. "Hopefully, it won't be long until your sword arrives. That should put matters beyond doubt."

Brackendon's story was long, and yet Darnuir got the feeling he was telling the shortened version. Those parts that overlapped with Cosmo and Garon's side of things checked out, and Darnuir was forced to accept that nothing about this was a joke or a trick, though he still held out hope that it might all be a terrible dream.

As the wizard moved on to the events after he left Darnuir at Cold Point, Garon and Cosmo wondered why Brackendon had not contacted them following Demons' Folly.

"As I said, I pushed myself too hard in the battle."

"I'm sure I saw your magic at work," Cosmo said. "It may have been a stormy day, but those lightning bolts and waves sunk too many demon ships to be completely natural. You might have made all the difference."

"I am glad that my sacrifice was worthwhile," Brackendon said. "Nineteen years of one's life is a high toll to pay."

He rolled up his right sleeve. The sight of his hand and forearm made Darnuir's stomach lurch. The blackened skin looked burned but there was a shine to it as well, like fish scales.

"It broke me," the wizard said mournfully "When I was an apprentice, I swore I would never break. I swore it. But on that day, I drew on too much energy in order to keep the demons at bay. I might have gotten away with it, but I had not yet fully recovered from the immense amount of magic needed to revert time on you, Darnuir. Not that I am blaming you, by any means."

Garon leaned closer to inspect his arm. He gulped. "I have heard of what happens to a wizard who breaks. You have my utmost sympathy."

"Thank you," Brackendon said mechanically. "Now you know why nothing was done about Darnuir. I was the only one who knew – apart from yourselves, of course – where he was and that he was still alive. Breaking turned me mad for years and it took many more for me to return to normal. My memories were dim and my wits dimmer."

"How did you recover from this 'breaking'?" Darnuir asked, feeling he should try and say something.

"The fairies took me in. They are best equipped and most experienced to help those who have overindulged in magic."

"Could the Conclave not help you?" Cosmo asked.

"I'm afraid the Cascade Conclave no longer exists," said Brackendon. "Arkus never made the effort to rebuild the order. I am the last wizard. Well, apart from Castallan."

"From what I know of Arkus, that seems unusual," Cosmo mused.

"It puzzled me for a time," Brackendon said. "I remember him being quite persistent with me about rebuilding the Conclave prior to the fall of Aurisha. However, my prolonged absence from the world of the sane has excluded me from the machinations of Brevia. My recent return to the city was not as glorious as I had hoped. Arkus no longer places confidence in me and refused me an audience. My contacts in the Lords' Assembly now scorn me or have died of old age. All considered, I had an ill feeling about the place and dared not trust a soul with Darnuir's whereabouts."

"And the dragons?" Garon said.

"From what I have gathered, the dragons went into seclusion after Demons' Folly, scattering across the kingdom. Lately, there have been disturbances, large swathes of the population vanishing or moving. It may well be them."

"Not much use to us, though," Garon said.

"And the fairies?" Cosmo asked. "Did you tell them?"

"I believe the queen suspected for some time, but I only recently confided my great secret to her. Kasselle also assured me that the Dragon's Blade would return to Darnuir when he was of age."

"You mean you don't know where it is?" Cosmo asked. "You don't know where it travelled to that night it flew away?"

"I haven't the slightest idea," Brackendon said. "But I trust in Kasselle. She has promised to send support."

"Excellent!" Garon said. "When will it arrive?"

"I fear it will not come fast enough," Brackendon said. "If there is a demon host marching upon our doorstep then we are on our own."

"We've been under attack for months," Darnuir piped up. "Why have we been left on our own? You should have revealed my identity sooner." He said the words but still did not believe all this was true. "You could have had an army of fairies fly down here, or whatever it is they do."

"Hmmm," Brackendon said. "Still a little prickly, I see, though you lack the bite of your former self."

"The boy has a point, though," Cosmo said. "Perhaps you could explain why we have been seemingly left to die down here?"

"We thought the war must be dire because no relief force was sent south to aid us," Garon said.

"Truth be told, there is no war," Brackendon said. "After Castallan made his bold announcement across the kingdom, not much happened. There have been escalating raids into the Cairlav Marshes and the Crown Lands but little more. The 'Long Engagement', some have called it."

"And what of the fairies?" Darnuir asked. "We've been dying. Do Brevia and Val'-tarra not care?"

"I do not speak for Brevia or the fairies," Brackendon said defensively. "Kasselle is wary of entering open conflict again. Her people are not as prepared as they once were."

"Then what help did she promise to send?" Cosmo asked.

"All she promised was that help would come," Brackendon said. "The very best help, apparently."

"Well, I'm afraid I don't see how we are any better off," Darnuir said. "If I really am a king, should I not have armies to command? That would be useful. Whatever gamble it was you all took with my life, it doesn't seem to have paid off."

"With a wizard here, our odds have dramatically improved," Garon said.

Brackendon shifted in his chair. "I do not want to guarantee anything, but I will certainly do all I can. And you may be surprised by what you can contribute once you have your sword—"

Glass shattered, wood ripped apart and a chill breeze swept into the room. Darnuir ducked his head and scrunched his eyes shut, feeling shards of glass bounce off his back. Something tapped eagerly at his clenched hand. He opened it without thinking and felt the unmistakable grip of a sword slide into his grasp. Before he could open his eyes, the weight of it brought him off the bed. His arm collapsed like a dead weight to the floor and his eyes snapped open as his head struck hard wood.

The cursed wizard chortled from his chair.

Groaning, Darnuir picked himself up and tried to heave the sword out of the floor. It had bitten deeply into the wood and he could not budge it. Despite his annoyance, he found himself in awe of the weapon.

Sinewy wings descended over the grip from a scaly, beastly-looking head. The golden blade was thick and forged of a metal he did not recognise, for it had signs of granulations, as if it were made of stone. From the mouth of the dragon's head poured etched flames, licking all along the blade to the tip, and red rubies sparkled within the beast's eye sockets. It was these eyes that seemed to bore into Darnuir's own, testing him, measuring him. After a few heaving attempts, Darnuir gave up.

"It's impossible to lift," he grumbled, letting go of it. As he sat back on the bed, the sword extracted itself from the wood of its own accord and flipped itself up and into his free hand. The red rubies shone brightly, then settled as if satisfied. Pain swelled in his head then, thrashing like a smith's hammer. It flared intensely for a few moments, feeling like his skull was being cleaved in two. Then it died.

Groaning, he massaged his temple.

Cosmo came over to feel his scalp for injury. "Nasty bump you took there, but you seem fine."

Garon approached more carefully, as though the blade were a wild animal. "It is incredible. Such detail, such intricacy. It's beautiful."

"The Dragon's Blade," Brackendon proclaimed. "Beautiful and deadly, and one of the most powerful magical artefacts in Tenalp."

"In what way?" Darnuir said breathlessly, fighting against the weight of the sword.

"Suffice to say that my staff has as much capacity to process Cascade energy as a common stick in comparison to that sword."

"You mean that I can use magic like you?" Darnuir asked.

"No," Brackendon said flatly, "at least not to my knowledge. I know little about it in truth. Not even the library of the old Conclave had much to say on it. Though it is common knowledge that, in addition to flying to its master, the Dragon's Blade has the capacity to breathe fire, like a dragon of old."

Darnuir looked again at the weapon, searching for some clue as to how to activate this feature. Failing in his search, he asked the wizard how to do it.

"Again, I do not know," Brackendon said. "I imagine you will figure it out in due course."

Darnuir got to his feet and tried to swing the blade, but it was too heavy. He placed it down on the bed to relieve himself of it, but it zipped back into his hand.

"Well, I can't even lift it," he said crossly. "And I can't seem to put the damn thing down either."

"Ah, this might help," Brackendon said with a flourish and pulled from amongst his robes a scabbard. It was made of wood but painted light gold to match the blade, and similar flowing flames had been carved into it. He tossed it to Darnuir.

"A perfect fit," Darnuir said in astonishment.

"A gift from Kasselle to Darnuir, the King of Dragons," Brackendon said.

"Queen or no, how could she know the dimensions? The scale?" Darnuir said. Brackendon's look suggested that the question might well be impertinent, but his response was kindly enough.

"Kasselle and her people know more about magic than they'll ever share with the likes of us. The Hall of Memories at the heart of the forest contains a particularly fascinating collection of paintings on the matter. The entire hallway is actually one large and continuous—"

"Will it stay in its sheath?" Cosmo asked, cutting over the wizard.

Darnuir strapped his new scabbard around his waist and carefully manoeuvred the Dragon's Blade into it using both hands. Thankfully, it stayed in place, though it dragged him down on his left side.

"Right, well, as scary as that hilt looks, I doubt it alone will give the demons pause," Garon said. "If Darnuir can't wield the blade, then we're back to panicking, I suppose. What was your plan, Brackendon?"

"I had not anticipated facing demons upon arrival," Brackendon said. "I thought I could take Darnuir to the fairies in Val'tarra alone. With his stamina and my magic, we could have made a speedy journey. I fear stealth and secrecy are no longer options."

"Why Val'tarra?" Darnuir asked.

"Brevia is no longer as welcoming," Brackendon said. "Better to head to the forest of the fairies and journey to Brevia from there with their support."

"I agree," Cosmo said. "If nothing else, travelling directly to Brevia would bring us too close to Bastion."

"Yet, for now, we are trapped," Garon said.

"Then what are we to do?" Darnuir asked.

Brackendon looked crestfallen. Cosmo hung his head.

Garon puffed up his chest and moved for the door. "If it is just going to be all doom and death up here then I'd rather not partake in it. Those ladies downstairs were rather fine company and I'd prefer spending my last night with them than with you gentlemen."

He pulled the bolt to unlock it.

Cosmo slammed his fist against it. "You may go downstairs, but only to fetch us more drinks and food. We have battle plans to discuss. You included. Bring Rufus, and Griswald, if he can manage the stairs."

Garon sighed loudly. "Would that be a tall jug of water for the wizard?"

"Oh, yes." Brackendon smiled. "As much water as you can find."

10

THE BATTLE OF COLD POINT

On the top floor of the tavern, Darnuir waited anxiously. The moon and stars flooded Cold Point with an eerie light, glistening upon the silver leaves of what he now knew to be Brackendon's staff tree. Silence had enveloped the town.

Darnuir ran a finger down the length of his bow then slowly back up. For this fight, he would carry two swords: his regular blade, made of steel, and his newfound masterpiece. The Dragon's Blade hung at his right side, as heavy as ever. He would much rather fight without it, as he was sure the weight would slow him down, but the sword seemed to have a mind of its own and refused to leave. Being on his off-hand side, he had no intention of drawing it out. He'd heard that dragons had strength far beyond humans, but he seemed to lack it.

Then again, I never tried to do anything out of the ordinary. I never thought I was more than human.

For now, he would have to rely on the limits he had always known.

Beside him was Balack, fidgeting frantically, running his hand back and forth through his auburn hair.

"Nervous?" Darnuir asked.

"Aren't you? This isn't like before. We can't get away this time."

"I'm trying not to think on it." He ran his finger back down his bow.

"I wouldnae be too worried, lads," Griswald said. He was perched on a window ledge, his crutches resting beside his own oversized bow. "Plan's good," he barked, "and we have that wizard now, and yer magic sword in all, Darnuir."

"It won't do us much good if I can't even pick it up."

"Aye. Aye, that's true enough. But you'd be amazed what you can do when yer life depends on it."

"It's too heavy for me and I don't know how to use its powers."

"Now look," Griswald said, "you've never been in a real battle. Those wee patrols are nothing compared tae this. Ye haven't been surrounded by thousands of clashing blades, ye haven't heard a hundred arrows over yer head, ye haven't smelled the stench of it all. When you're down there in the heat of it, you'll either break or you'll act. And when you're just reacting, you'll not be thinking so damned much." He picked up his crutches and hobbled across to Darnuir. "And if you don't lift it, I'll tell anyone who'll listen that you wet yer britches the night before yer first battle." He clapped Darnuir on the back before hobbling back to his perch, hand pressed firmly against his wounded thigh.

Balack raised his eyebrows and nodded, as if to reinforce what Griswald had just said. Scowling, Darnuir sat up straighter and stared determinedly out of his window towards the entrance to the square.

Snow began to fall, dressing the town in a fresh coat of white.

Scouts returned, announcing that the demons would arrive at any moment. Darnuir began to get excited. Better to get out there. Better to face the creatures, Dragon's Blade or not.

Hunters within each building hastily extinguished their lights and darkness engulfed the battlefield. Every building now appeared, at a glance, to be deserted.

The demons arrived in a greater uproar than usual. He heard the gates clatter open in the distance, heard the shrill cries of the host as it scrambled through the night towards the town square. Soon the place was filled with them, clashing their weapons and stamping in confusion as they found their path blocked by the barricades.

Like water, the horde fanned out, searching for an easy route, but found none. The demons who encountered the blockages tried to turn around, but finding their way barred by their fellows, they became agitated. The army had by now become noticeably wild and Darnuir felt the time was surely nigh to begin their ambush, but their orders were to wait for the signal.

As the screeches of the demons grew, spectres emerged, attempting to restore order. Darnuir had never seen so many in one place before. Several of the spectres congregated under the silver tree, pointing up at the buildings.

Come on, Brackendon. Give the signal. We must strike now!

A cloud moved above, letting moonlight fall onto the tavern. Strands of cold blue light spilled in through the windows of the top floor. Darnuir heard a rasping wind behind him. He turned, finding a spectre emerging from the new shadow upon the wall, poised to stab Griswald in the back.

"Look out!"

Griswald spun. "Piss aff!"

He slammed the spectre against the wall and followed this up by bashing his meaty fist against its head. With a great heave, Griswald sent the spectre clean out of the window. As it hit the ground, an arrow buried into the spectre's neck, courtesy of Balack, who pulled back and hid behind the wall.

"So much for the signal," Darnuir said.

He raced to nock an arrow. Pulling back the string, he finally saw a small barrel descend from the hunters' lodge across the square, moving as if guided upon the wind. It glided down and nestled in amongst the demons. A ball of fire followed it.

The explosion was far larger than Darnuir would have thought possible with such a small amount of oil. Perhaps it was enhanced with the wizard's magic. Demons within a five-metre radius were blown up or away by the blast, and every spectre visible in the square turned to face the source of the explosion.

Darnuir released his arrow into the mass beneath him. Not stopping to see if he had hit a mark, he hastened to fire again.

Arrows skirted across the square from every building now, their shafts looking like black streaks against the falling snow. Lights sprang up as the hunters relit their torches and lanterns. It would grant the spectres shadows to move in, but the defenders needed to see to fight.

Darnuir loosed a third arrow but missed his target – a regular demon heading for the tavern – while Balack sniped the head of a spectre behind Darnuir's more fortunate foe.

The demons started doing what they did best: swarming. Splinter groups made for each building in sight. Darnuir was able to get off one last shot before demons were pounding on the tavern's barricaded door.

"Loose above!" Garon bellowed from somewhere below. The call was repeated throughout the tavern and axes on the rooftop thudded. Logs began to tumble, one after the other, past the window and down onto the demons. Around the rooftops of the square, dark figures were hacking at the other piles, sending a crushing wave against their foes.

Yet the demons pressed on.

Leaving Balack behind with the better archers, Darnuir ripped out his trusted old sword and bolted for the stairs to join a stream of fighters running for the ground floor. After descending one level, he heard his name being called and stopped dead in his tracks.

Eve stood in the doorway of one of the infirmary rooms, a manic look in her eyes. The rest of the hunters ran on but Darnuir paused, frozen in place by her stare.

"Don't die," was all she seemed able to say.

Darnuir could not think of any way to respond other than a curt nod.

He ran on, leaping down the last set of stairs to join the fray. One hunter already lay dead under a smashed window, with glass strewn around him. Demons scuttled in through the broken windows like beetles. The door itself still held. For now.

"Stop them at the windows!" Garon yelled, dispatching a demon from behind as it crawled inside.

By the door, two spectres rose up from the shadows on the boarded floor, enormous axes materialising into their hands in a swirl of purple-black light. One moved off to hack at the barricades, while the other cleaved a defensive area around itself, cutting down several hunters.

Caution abandoned Darnuir. The door could not fall. He dashed towards the hulking spectre, dodging the arc of its swipe by a hair's breadth. Its companion was making short work of the barricade. Desperate, Darnuir dove underneath the spectre's next swing, cutting its leg. Howling, the spectre crashed to one knee and Garon stepped up to relieve it of its head.

Yet it was too late. The remaining spectre clove through the last bars on the door.

Demons clamoured en masse into the tavern.

"Forward!" Garon bellowed.

Darnuir jumped to his feet and let loose a cry as the two sides collided. The melee was brutal and packed. Those behind Darnuir pressed him forward, pinning him in place. All he could do was keep himself alive. Smoky blood from the demons filled his lungs, choking him.

He was being crushed. He could hardly breathe.

A powerful wave of air rushed over him, blowing back the smoke. He gasped as the crush eased and the demons melted before them. At the tavern's doorway stood Brackendon, staff raised, taking measured breaths as demons scattered around him. A team of hunters with him picked off the stragglers

"Come," Brackendon yelled. "We must relieve the other buildings."

Charging with the others into the square, Darnuir saw the trouble for himself. Somehow, several of the thatched roofs around the square had caught fire, and the flames were spreading fast. A burning man, screaming his last, leapt from a high window into the enemy ranks.

Running with the others to relieve the next building, Darnuir caught the first demon he met in the back. The second proved a more tenacious foe. It parried his blow, dodged the next, and then slashed at his waist. Darnuir blocked the slash but suffered a cut to his arm. Grunting in pain as blood stained his white leathers, he swept his sword over his head and brought it hammering down. The demon crumpled, dead before it hit the snow.

Embers from the burning roofs sparked off, setting other rooftops on fire. Soon, the heat began to lick at Darnuir's face, even from across the square. Between that and the constant fighting, he was already breathless. When one demon fell, another took its place, and with every swing, his newly injured arm throbbed.

He reached the stone wall surrounding the silver tree and leaned on it to take respite. Cruelly, a spectre emerged before him like a slow nightmare, drawing itself out of the shadow cast by the tree. In its hand, a long blade formed and solidified out of swirling purple energy. Darnuir blocked weakly and the spectre's strength smashed his weapon against the wall. His sword snapped into two jagged pieces.

He froze.

The spectre's free arm punched into Darnuir's chest and he collapsed backwards over the wall. He had enough sense to roll to one side and heard a screech as the spectre struck the ground where he'd been. He stumbled to get up and his back found the tree.

The Dragon's Blade shook in its sheath. Its weight seemed to have lessened. Griswald was right – if he didn't draw it, he was dead.

He cursed as his inexperienced left hand fumbled at the hilt, and then dropped to his knees to avoid the spectre's weapon. The ghostly sword stuck fast into the silver trunk of the tree. Beneath the creature, Darnuir slammed his fist into the spectre's midriff. It doubled over and Darnuir took the chance to stagger to his feet. His untrained left hand floundered with the weight of the blade until it flew into his right hand instead, as if it knew how to help him.

That's a little better.

The spectre was still trying to retrieve its weapon from the gnarled bark when Darnuir drove the Dragon's Blade through it, using both hands to help with the weight. Smoking blood ran down his forearms.

As he drew back, the rubies in the eye sockets twinkled at him and a sharp pain stabbed at his head again. It felt as though something was pressing on his mind. He did all he could to ignore the pain. Wiping the sweat from his face, he turned his attention to the rest of the battle.

By now, the defenders of the burning buildings had either escaped out into the square or perished within them. It seemed more had made it out than not. The roofs had collapsed, and the bulk of the fighting had pushed towards the square's entrance. A wall of white and grey leather met a curtain of fiery shadows, cutting the square diagonally, and smaller skirmishes raged all around.

The ground by the tavern was clear of fighting, though arrows still sang through the night from the upper floors.

Darnuir joined the forming melee and spotted Cosmo at the centre. He was fighting with a fury that Darnuir had never seen before. Brackendon was holding down another portion of their line, using his staff as a weapon, blasting demons back as he struck. Demon blades were halted inches away from him, and the air around him rippled as the blows were stopped. But Brackendon could not keep it up forever and wove back through the ranks, out of breath, shaking, his skin sickly pale.

Over the battlefield, Griswald's roars reached his ears. "They've broken through! Behind!"

Spinning, Darnuir saw them. Demons were tearing out of a narrow alley close to the tavern, behind their main lines. Arrows met the first ones through but more were pouring forth from the breach in their barricades.

Being nearer the back of the crush, Darnuir and those near him darted to intercept. They leapt over impeding logs and hacked into the flanks of the demons. Amid the chaos, Darnuir glimpsed a flurry of blond hair running from the tavern.

"Eve, no!" he called to her.

She and her fellow healers were trying to carry back the injured. "I'm here now," she chided him, falling to the side of one hunter. "I can save him if I staunch the bleeding."

"Don't! You have to—"

"No, this is what I can do. This is all I can do!" She pressed down with her weight upon the man's gushing shoulder.

Darnuir had little time to think as a rusty blade appeared at the corner of his vision. He gutted the demon; the Dragon's Blade opened the creature with ease. The orange glow along the blade's length intensified and Darnuir thought he could feel heat coming off it. Or was it coming from inside him? He thought his throat felt hot, though he could not be sure with the blaze raging around the square.

Darnuir's comrades in the tavern's defence had dwindled, yet the demons kept coming. Brackendon joined them now to secure the alleyway. Guarded by his shield of air, he managed to stem the worst of the tide.

Darnuir readied to meet those who had slipped by the wizard. "Eve, go!"

But she would not run. She poured a silver liquid onto her charge's shoulder and the wound hissed and smoked as it cauterised. All the while a pack of demons drew closer.

Cursing, Darnuir stayed to defend her. Two demons were felled from above and once again he was grateful for Balack's aim. But there were so many. That was always the worst part. There were just so many.

Eve screamed.

Darnuir pivoted around, almost losing his footing on melted snow and blood underfoot. Two demons bounded towards Eve. Darnuir ran. An arrow ended one of them, but Darnuir and Balack were too slow to kill the second. Its jagged dirk cut at her stomach and she crumpled to her knees and scrambled towards the stone wall of the tree.

Darnuir bowled the creature down, smashing into it with a strength he would have thought impossible. The demon's body lay broken underneath him.

He found Eve on her knees, one arm upon the wall for support. Darnuir raced over and brought her to her feet. She beamed at him and drew her hand away from her stomach. Relief washed over him.

Her hand was crimson with blood but it wasn't hers. It was her patient's. The demon had torn through her leathers but nothing more. She smiled at him, almost laughing in her own relief. Sweat drenched her brow, plastering her hair to her face, yet her eyes shone brighter than ever, deep and brown. Darnuir lost himself for a moment, watching the colour of her cheeks flare as he held her.

Then his relief twisted into guilt.

"Go back."

She nodded. And then her smile turned to shock.

Her jaw dropped in horror, as did her gaze. Darnuir followed her eyes to see a ghost-like shaft jutting out from the middle of her chest, the tip inches away from Darnuir's own body. Behind her, the spectre fully materialised.

There was no expression on the creature's face. Only blank malice.

A cry cut through the night from the tavern, the sound of a wounded soul.

To Darnuir, sound lost all meaning. He felt like he had gone deaf. Instinct made him hack with all his force at the spectre, even as an arrow buried into its skull.

Eve's body slumped to the ground below him, but he could not look down. He wanted to retch. He wanted it all to end.

Biting back the sensation, he turned dizzily towards the fight. Despite what had just happened, the battle raged on. That seemed strange to him. That seemed wrong.

His hearing returned as Brackendon beckoned all nearby to back away, his free hand pointing towards the roof of the hunters' lodge. The roof and wall that over-looked the alleyway shook violently until it collapsed, resealing the route. A score of demons remained trapped on their side and the sight of them caused Darnuir to boil with rage.

Heat from the Dragon's Blade grew and the orange glow began to oscillate. The burning sensation he had felt in his throat returned anew and something pressed upon his mind again, this time more fiercely. Clutching his head in one hand, he felt as though his skull might break apart.

He thought of the demons enveloped in cruel flames and the heat in his throat grew more intense. No clean deaths for them. They ought to burn. The demons had almost closed the gap to the tavern's last defenders when his own throat burned. Then his blade lit up and fire leapt from its tip like a lashing, forked tongue. Abnormal flames, flowing with purpose. They wrapped the demons up in ribbons of red, yellow and orange, squeezing them tight, roasting them to white cinders.

Darnuir's throat felt like it was on fire, though no flames emitted from him. The blaze from the Dragon's Blade did not abate. It stretched out; eight feet, ten feet, twelve feet. The stream seemed to sniff the air, looking for prey. He flailed pathetically as he clung onto the weapon, and the hunters nearby dropped to the floor to avoid the branching tendrils of flame.

"Darnuir," Brackendon called, "you must control it!"

"How?" he cried in dismay, but if the wizard had any advice to give, Darnuir did not hear it. The prodding in his head became a pounding and he went deaf again. He fought against it this time, pushing back with all his might.

It was the most peculiar feeling he had ever experienced. How was he to fight a foe within his mind?

Darnuir thrashed his head in the attempt until, with a final effort, he lurched both his gaze and arms upwards. He held his breath as he struggled and finally, the pounding ebbed away. The fire had ceased, but how or why he couldn't say.

Does this sword have a mind of its own?

Another monstrous wail filled his ears. Darnuir opened his eyes to see the overhanging silver branches ablaze. He must have done it when he'd raised the sword. The sensation of wishing to retch rose strongly again.

Brackendon screamed in anguish. The wizard hastened to his staff tree with a crazed look. He attempted to break off the burning branches but it seemed his power was faltering. Soon, the whole tree was on fire, a pyre in the centre of the battlefield. Brackendon stood aghast as his staff vibrated then exploded into splinters.

It seemed as if the world was ending.

Darnuir staggered away from the inferno but did not have his wits about him. Over at the melee, the hunters were beginning to show signs of breaking. Their right flank beside the hunters' lodge was dangerously thin.

He noticed that the prodding in his head had returned, but this time it was gentle. He glanced down to the Dragon's Blade and the rubies twinkled at him.

Is it trying to speak to me?

Prod, prod, prod.

Can you help me?

Prod.

He took that as a 'yes'.

Perhaps it was the sight of their line finally breaking, or the thought of Eve lying slumped against the wall, but Darnuir gave up the fight within. His mind filled with a feeling both alien and familiar, his thoughts and yet not his thoughts. Changing his stance, his eyes drank in the battlefield with a newfound understanding.

Darnuir watched on as an observer. He watched as his own hand acted without him controlling it, as it threw the golden blade towards the breach in the line.

It was as though he were dreaming. The Dragon's Blade hurtled at the demons, skewering three of them, and then flew back to his hand. Darnuir caught it before he crashed into the demons' ranks. He watched on, not in control of himself, as he waded through the demons, fighting foes on all sides with a speed and strength he never knew he had. The movements felt dizzying.

Spectres appeared in force to face him or prevent their lesser brethren from fleeing before his wrath. Yet even they were wary of him now; their agility was matched by his own. Before long they too pulled back, allowing another to stride in to face him.

This challenger wore full plate mail, the colour of dried blood. Small spikes covered the joints of his armour. A thick helmet hid his face but burning red eyes could be seen through the visor.

Is that a spectre?

But he'd never known a spectre to wear armour.

Is it a man?

Whatever it was, whoever it was, the spectres seemed to answer to it, for they ducked their heads as it strode past; many vanished altogether, and the demons nearby began losing focus.

The red-eyed challenger was yelling at them but Darnuir could not make out his words. Whatever force controlled his body, it had only one thing in mind. He engaged the enemy. Yet this was a harder fight than any demon or spectre could muster. Darnuir blocked a blow and the force of it sent him reeling. It must have been very strong to make him recoil like that.

Darnuir charged him, knocking the blood-armoured figure over. Its helmet flew off, but before Darnuir could see its face, an armoured hand backhanded his own. He spun away, spitting blood. When Darnuir recovered his enemy had fled.

A mound of dead demons lay near Darnuir and now, with their champion gone, the demons frenzied. They broke. Those at the front crashed into those behind. In the confusion, the hunters cut them down.

Darnuir gave chase as well. Soon it was a rout. He carried on the pursuit long after the hunters fell behind.

He regained control of himself just past the town gates, which were bent and dangling off their battered hinges. The Dragon's Blade felt heavy in his hand again, so he sheathed it and picked his way back towards the square, stepping carefully over the corpses. The survivors looked to him in awe and some looked on with fear.

Darnuir rubbed gingerly at his injured arm.

This was the sword's work. It was not me.

Everywhere, the snow was red and the smoky blood of the demons rose to meet the smog of the fires. The silver tree had been reduced to ash; only a gnarled stump remained.

Cosmo was helping a shaking and moaning Brackendon to his feet, taking him back to the tavern. Had the wizard broken again? Lost his mind?

Darnuir found his own feet guiding him back towards the tavern as well.

He stopped when he saw her body.

Eve was sitting upright against the stone wall, as if relaxing. Her eyes, however, were still wide with the horror of her final moments. Dark crimson encrusted her chest.

She needn't have died. This was his fault. She had only been doing her duty, but she had gotten too close. He should have seen that spectre coming.

Too close. She was too close.

Balack appeared in the tavern's doorway. He made his way over to Eve's body with such delicacy, it was as if he did not wish to break the snow. He said nothing. Darnuir met his eyes and saw an emptiness there, grim and dead.

Words stuck in his own throat; words he should have said but couldn't bear to.

I'm sorry. I'm sorry for everything.

Finally, he allowed himself to bend over the low wall and retch.

11

THE KING IN THE SOUTH

Cassandra – The Bastion

In the space above the ceiling of the so-called throne room, Cassandra lay flat on her stomach and peered through the sliding grate. She could have crouched if she wanted to; she could even have stood to her full height. Whoever had designed these secret ways in the Bastion had clearly intended for people far larger than her to manoeuvre within them. Lying down was the most comfortable, however, for she might be there for some time.

Chatter around the Bastion suggested something important was happening or had happened. It was hard to tell from the whispers she overheard and no one fully in the know would just divulge the details. If there was to be news or a major meeting, it would take place below. The fact that the scrying orb had already been set out suggested this would be so. The crystal ball sat atop an iron plinth; a gentle mist swirled inside the orb while it was not in use.

Cassandra waited.

Her patience was rewarded when the doors swung open. Castallan strode imperiously inside. Ashen-tinged hair was swept artfully back off his forehead, and greying stubble coated his face. His silver eyes, crackling with energy, marked him as different from normal men. The robes he wore fitted him well, a regal purple trimmed in silver.

Cassandra's jailer sat down on his high-backed throne; an imposing construction with a fan of ten staffs at the back. Each varied in design, but all were made from a similar silver wood.

Castallan gazed into the scrying orb, waiting with what looked like bated breath. The side of his mouth twitched and he tapped his fingers against the arms of his throne.

Now, who or what would make you jittery, Castallan?

No sooner had she begun to speculate than the white swirl in the orb began to spiral violently. In the chaos, a dark silhouette of a man's torso took shape; faint at first, but then clearer, until it seemed as if he was physically there in the room alongside Castallan. Only, it was not a man.

To Cassandra's amazement, she beheld a spectre in the orb, though it was unlike any she had ever seen before. Its shadowy flesh appeared fully solid, its muscles well defined across its bare back and chest. Tendrils of blue flame draped down behind its ears, like hair, without causing it any sign of discomfort.

Castallan looked taken aback. Apparently, this wasn't who he had been expecting.

"Why don't you come closer, wizard?" the spectre's voice drawled out, deep and intelligent. "Or perhaps elevate me to your own height. I do so hate to crane my neck."

Castallan hesitated for a moment before rallying. "Am I to take it that you are playing messenger now, Dukoona?"

If the comment was designed to sting, it appeared only to prickle the spectre. "The Master has far more pressing priorities than conversing with you."

"As do you, it would seem. I haven't had the displeasure of your company in many years."

Dukoona tittered. "My dear wizard, it has been many years since you have been of use."

"I am not some dog to be brought to heel."

"Remember who your spectres belong to," Dukoona said. "Or would you prefer I recall them? I'd enjoy hearing of your demons tearing you limb from limb."

Castallan's face darkened. "Tell me my task and be done with it."

Dukoona smiled, his purple lips pulling apart to reveal an unnerving set of perfectly white teeth. Cassandra would have been less disturbed if the spectre had borne fangs.

"The Master has commanded me to prepare our fleet. Every ship in our power will descend upon the human realm and it will be up to you, dear Castallan, to prepare a beachhead for our forces. Maintaining control of the Southern Dales near that fortress of yours will suffice."

"Hoping to avoid a repeat of your last landing?"

"How very astute of you. Ready our landing and you might find yourself rewarded."

"Why now?" Castallan asked. "It's been twenty years. Why this wait?"

"It is not for you to question the Master's decision."

"But it is for you?"

Dukoona gave another unsettling smile. "Perhaps."

"Why today, Dukoona?"

"Because the Master has willed it," Dukoona drawled. "His choice of timing is not your concern. Now, as a courtesy for your past services, I shall impress this upon you." His voice soured and lost all traces of amusement. "Our armies will come whether you aid us or not. I would have the Bastion for my seat as I lead the campaign against Brevia and Val'tarra. Be hospitable, and you will share in more of our power and stand in the Master's court as the last of your kind. Resist, hinder or fail us… well, there are special halls under Kar'drun that even I will not visit."

His cruel eyes bored into Castallan, who returned the enmity.

"How long?" Castallan asked.

"Do you have other things to attend to? Forget them. This is now your only priority. See that you do not disappoint me." The spectre lord's terrible smile disappeared as he departed, the orb returning to swirling mist once more.

Castallan's face remained blank. He seemed lost in some deep, calculating thought before he finally rose. He was halfway to the door when the mist began to convulse once more. The figure took form with its back to Cassandra, yet she recognised the spiked, blood-red armour and the thick helm to match it.

You'd better have good news, Zarl. He doesn't seem in the mood for failure.

Castallan must have sensed the orb at work, for he turned around.

"Ah, there you are, Commander. Have you succeeded in your mission?"

"I'm afraid not," Zarl said carefully.

"Out with it, then."

"I can confirm that the boy is whom we were led to believe."

"But?"

"I was unable to capture him," said Zarl.

Castallan stepped slowly back towards the orb. "Did I not allow you to take as many demons as you felt fit? Was enchanting your body to be greater than a dragon's not enough?"

"My king, I am eternally grateful to you for freeing me from my weak shell—"

"How could you not overcome that rabble of hunters?"

"There was a complication," Zarl said through gritted teeth. "The wizard arrived to aid them."

"Brackendon…" Castallan said. "So, he has returned to the world of the sane."

"Perhaps not for long," Zarl said. "Darnuir burnt the ancient tree of the town to cinders. Flames poured forth from his sword and he seemed unable to control them. And then, he suddenly became competent with it. I cannot explain it."

"Did he best you?"

"I could have taken him," Zarl spat, "but the spectres abandoned the fight the moment they saw me duelling Darnuir. The demons went wild because of it and broke ranks."

Castallan chewed his lip. "Rectar was too clever in teaching me to summon demons but not the spectres to control them. Those on loan from Dukoona are a necessary evil. Take as many of our own enhanced men as you see fit in future. That ought to keep them in line."

Zarl bowed his head.

"Such a shame Brackendon's staff was lost," Castallan continued. "I would have preferred adding it to my collection. Alas. At least it is one less foe to contend with. Our attention must now turn to the Dragon's Blade."

"You are certain that you require it for your work?" Zarl asked. "You have accomplished so much without it."

"Then imagine what I might do with it. The time for secrecy is almost over. Dukoona has informed me that an invasion is coming. If we are to save humanity and free ourselves of the dragons' yoke then we must no longer take half-measures. I need that sword, Commander. There is no better conduit of Cascade energy."

"Better than ten staffs?"

"Eleven," Castallan corrected him, holding up his own tall stave. "And yes, far better than if I could reclaim every staff from the Conclave. Combining the sword with the staffs, I may even surpass Rectar himself." His eyes stared off into the distance, as though he was enraptured by the thought.

"Do you need him alive?"

"Prising it from his corpse may serve; however, I would rather not needlessly risk the sword losing its power until I can bend it to my will instead."

"I shall require fresh forces. Should the hunters take refuge in the station, it will be an arduous battle."

"I shall assemble all our forces for you," Castallan said. "No more half-measures, Zarl. Once again, Brevia has answered me with silence. We must take matters into our own hands. If Dukoona arrives before we are ready, humanity will fall. You know the stakes."

Zarl bowed again and began to dissolve away.

Castallan swept from the throne room, barking out orders to servants out of sight.

Cassandra remained where she was, stunned by the revelations. Castallan had mentioned the Dragon's Blade. That sword belonged to the King of Dragons. The name too was familiar to her. Chelos, her carer, mentioned this Darnuir in hallowed tones as if speaking of the dead. And now, it seemed he had returned. Chelos would be thrilled. She ought to tell him at once.

She scrambled to the exit of the passageway. There were two options: a lever, which would open the wall out into the corridor beyond, or a ladder leading up. She took the ladder, as it was the quickest route back to her chambers. She climbed several storeys, her impractical dress hampering her movements. She heard a rip as it caught on a section of the ladder.

Damn, how will I explain this?

Her dresses had always been of high quality but she found they were too restricting for spy work. Yet she could not wear more practical boots, trousers and shirts and still pass through the open corridors of the Bastion as an innocent prisoner. Questions would be raised.

She reached her intended floor and carefully checked the corridor on the other side of the false wall for guards. A patrol passed and she paused, waiting for them to get a good distance down the hallway. That done, she quietly emerged from the secret passage.

The guards turned but she smiled and waved, as though she'd just walked down the hall herself. Thankfully, they nodded in acknowledgement and moved on, unable to see the tear in her dress at that distance.

When she arrived back at her chambers, she called out for Chelos. The old dragon shuffled out to greet her, his face crinkled with age, though he was still very capable on his feet. Long years had taken their toll on him, but there was still a deal of strength in him, as Cassandra often discovered when they sparred. Not knowing other dragons, she found it hard to believe at times that he was over one hundred years old.

"I was beginning to get worried, my dear," Chelos said in his weakening voice. "You know you should not risk such long trips."

"Yes, yes," she said hurriedly. "You'll understand once I explain."

And she did, recounting the events that she'd just witnessed. Memorising details of conversations had become second nature over the years sneaking around the fortress. And when she wasn't doing that, she was reading. There wasn't a whole lot else to do in the Bastion at times.

When she finished her tale, the old dragon stood a little taller and his eyes regained a spark she had not seen in years.

"I always knew he was still alive," he said. "Yet why has it taken so long?"

"Zarl was confirming a rumour. I don't think they were sure themselves until recently."

Chelos took a seat on one of the plush loungers. He seemed to decide upon something and gazed at her intensely.

"Cassandra, you must go to him."

"Go to him?"

The thought was as exhilarating as it was nauseating. Leaving the Bastion would mean freedom; freedom she had yearned for her whole life. Yet it would be perilous. Chelos had always cautioned her against it.

And now he wants me to go?

"You've always told me it was impossible. Every plan I've cooked up, you've shot down. Even if I escape, we both know I won't make it far. You said Castallan will just hunt me down again, right? This fortress is supposed to be impenetrable from the outside; it seems it works both ways."

"I have one idea," Chelos said.

"Have you always had it?" Cassandra asked.

Chelos stared back at her guiltily.

He did know a way to get out. This whole time, he's had some plan...

A small ball of fury began to spin inside her. "And you never thought to tell me?"

"It was never the right time before..."

Cassandra closed her eyes, incredulous at the gall of the old dragon. "Never the right time? When would have been the right time? When I was as old as you and past the point of caring?"

"You might not be free, but you are at least alive and well. It would break my already worn heart to see you hurt. It pains me even to risk letting you go now. But go you must." His voice hardened. "You must try, Cassandra. If nothing else, Darnuir needs to be warned. The whole world needs to be warned."

A million problems sprang to her mind.

"Even if I make it out, how will I ever get to the Boreacs?"

"Have Trask help you," Chelos said, though he seemed apprehensive.

Cassandra felt little better about the notion. "Trask has half a hundred ideas, but that doesn't mean any of them will work."

"But it will be my idea, not his," Chelos said. "And he'll do it. You know he'd do anything for you."

Cassandra frowned, unsure of this plan.

Chelos sighed. "You spend your whole life trying to convince me to help you flee. Now I am giving you the chance and you seem unenthused."

"It feels like you aren't doing it for me," Cassandra said. "It seems like you are doing it for him. This Darnuir. Why does it matter if he is back or not?"

"He is the king," Chelos said simply, as if that were enough. "Darnuir gives you a purpose in going. He gives you somewhere and someone to seek refuge with. There has never been a better opportunity."

Cassandra rocked on her feet. This Darnuir, this supposed dragon king, was her route out. She would go because she wanted out of this prison, but she could not help but be afraid.

It's what I've always wanted. Why worry over the timing?

"Trask, then?" she said decisively.

"Indeed!" Chelos said, rising purposefully to the door. "I will go to him and arrange a meeting for you as usual. Make yourself ready to go at a moment's notice."

Cassandra did as she was bid and hastened to her bedchamber, which, as Trask had once commented, was as large as the stables he worked in. She tore off her gown and donned simpler clothes of rough-spun leggings, shirt and leather jerkin. She also snatched up the sword that Trask had once smuggled to her and strapped it around her waist.

Looking in her mirror, she pulled back her long, wavy black hair and scrunched it into a messy knot. With her hair lifted away, her green eyes seemed to bulge larger and she grimaced. Even the shape of her face seemed different somehow, more delicate than before. Soft and weak; she'd spent too much time cooped up. Her pale skin spoke that in volumes. She scowled at herself, then relaxed.

Just breathe. You're getting out. You're getting out.

She repeated this mantra to herself as she collected what else she needed. Close at hand was a small, carved figurine that Trask had given her when she was still a child.

"It's a little dragon warrior," he had proclaimed proudly when he had presented it. His father had stolen some during the war; they were used to represent armies on maps. It could fit in the palm of her hand and was beautifully detailed, though the gold paint had almost worn away entirely by now.

Yet she considered the carving. If she had the strength of a dragon, she would have escaped her prison long ago. She wouldn't need help. Still, the memory of a younger, arguably sweeter Trask was pleasant. Back before he had grown older, his views skewed and he started looking at her differently.

Thinking fondly of her dragon warrior at that moment, she pocketed it.

She drifted through to her library for one last visit before she had to go. Shelves of books and scrolls lined the walls, reaching so high that ladders were required to reach the top. Books of history, myths and stories; books on everything, each bound in rich leather or precious metal hoops.

She ambled slowly around the library, running her hands along the spines. For some unknown reason, Castallan had given her this extreme luxury.

Perhaps he knew I wouldn't be as bothersome if I were occupied.

Her favourite was Tiviar's *Histories of Tenalp*, and a copy of it always lay ready. She now picked it up, for perhaps the last time. For all her love of the author, he had died nearly one hundred years ago, and no one else had thought to write anything down since, so far as her collection was concerned. Many times, she had urged Chelos to jot down something – anything. Who else would be better? He had been the steward of the Royal Palace in Aurisha. He must have lived through and experienced so much, yet he told her very little.

She heard the main doors to the apartments slam, followed by heavy breathing.

"Chelos?" she called. The aged dragon stumbled into the library, uncharacteristically breathless.

"Trask says... now," he panted. "It must be now. I've never seen so much happening down below." Chelos clutched his side and Cassandra worried that his heart would burst in his chest.

She moved to his side. "Chelos, are you—"

"I'm fine. Trask said he would meet you at the bottom of the tower as usual, but you must go now!"

Cassandra wasted no time in bolting to Chelos' bedchambers, for that was where their most valuable secret passageway was hidden. She slammed her fist into the pressure plate in the wall above the four-poster bed and heard a satisfying thud as the trapdoor swung open underneath. As she began to push the bed aside, Chelos clambered into the room, using anything he could reach for support. With what seemed a tremendous effort, he came to her aid and the task of shifting the bed became easy.

"Wait," Chelos wheezed. "Cassandra, the tunnel... you must know..."

"Your private secret," she said, remembering his allusions to a plan. "Where is it? Where does it go?"

"There is an entrance to a passage that should take you out underneath the walls. A false opening under the staircase of the curtain wall by the western gate. You must use this. Trask says they are inspecting every wagon leaving through the main gates."

If Chelos had more to say, he seemed to lack the breath to say it.

"Have you always known about this? Why are you only telling me now?"

She saw the answer written on his face. His king. His precious Darnuir. *This would-be saviour had better be worth the wait.*

In her frustration with the old dragon, she descended a few rungs of the ladder without bidding him farewell.

"Be safe, my girl," he wheezed.

She stopped. She could not leave like this. Cassandra climbed back up and embraced Chelos tightly.

He squeezed back. "Do not hesitate to use that sword if you have to."

"I won't," she said and, despite herself, allowed a single pitiful tear to roll down her cheek. She sniffed a little as she drew away from him. "What will you do when he finds out?"

No. I mustn't think about it.

"It does not matter what happens to me," Chelos said. "I am old. Far too old. Promise me that you won't worry."

She nodded, though of course she would worry all the same.

"Goodbye." The word sounded so meaningless; so small, so inadequate. Sadness fully engulfed her as Chelos closed the trapdoor, extinguishing all light. The bed was scraped back into place above. She did not take the time to wipe away her tears. There was little time and she had to go on.

12

ESCAPE FROM THE BASTION

The shaft was utterly without light, but years of sneaking around the Bastion had made Cassandra accustomed to feeling her way around. Pegs protruded out of the ladder at intervals to mark which floor she was on. Some ways down, she felt one these pegs, reaching out beside it to feel the engraving. XI. She had reached the eleventh floor. It had not felt like four floors already.

She continued her descent with only the rhythmic tap of her feet on the ladder and her own quickening breath for company. When her feet finally found flat ground, she took a few moments to collect herself. Her hands felt numb, though whether this was from nerves or the chill of the shaft, she could not say.

Carefully, she turned around in the dark then knelt to push at the exit slab. She had made this trip enough times to know its position by heart. She pressed on the stone. A soft hiss followed and a small segment of the wall began sliding away. She shut her eyes so as not to be pained by the rush of sunlight.

She kept low to the ground as she exited the inner tower of the Bastion and, blinking furiously, closed the passage. The earth was dry, hot, and cracked. All land within one hundred feet of the Bastion's citadel was like this. She'd seen its radius expand over the years. In places, the brown earth had even begun to take on a dark red hue and some areas were pitch black, yet beyond this arbitrary line, the soil remained soft and lush. There, the first blossoming blue crocuses of spring were making their way into the world.

A towering five-sided outer wall surrounded the citadel tower, with crenellated battlements. At each corner, where the walls met, the stone crested out into defensive platforms shaped like arrowheads. A secondary inner wall of the same style wrapped closer around the tower. If viewed from above, it would have looked like a misshapen star. Humanity's mightiest fortress; designed to counter dragons. If Dukoona were to take it for his own, the Three Races would be hard pressed to repel his invasion.

A loaded cart was drawn up near her secret exit and an impatient horse beat its hooves on the dusty ground. It was Trask's, but she could not see him, so Cassandra dropped to her belly and slunk under the cart to avoid the thousands of eyes in the inner courtyard.

Her heart missed a beat as a pair of feet came into view. They approached the cart. After a pause, they crept around to the back, stopped, and then she saw the legs begin to bend. She reached for her sword but it was at completely the wrong angle. She fumbled as a man's hand reached in for her.

"Cass!" Trask's hissed. "It's me. Get up, we have to move fast."

He grabbed her shirt and near enough dragged her out from under the cart. She scrambled to her feet and glowered at him.

"What was the need in that?"

"Sorry. I'm jumpy. I'm sticking my neck on the line here."

"We can wait if it's too risky."

Trask shook his head. "There won't be a better time. I don't see how you'll avoid being seen by the lookouts on the walls, or even make it out in the first place without all this distraction."

Cassandra looked around. She'd never seen so many people packed into the inner courtyards. Clearly, nothing was being spared in preparing the armies to move out. Only humans were allowed inside the Bastion – the demons were encamped further afield.

"Sorry I grabbed you."

"It's fine. I did try drawing my sword on you, so that wouldn't have been pretty."

Trask smiled nervously but he looked relieved that she had no hard feelings. The smile helped his face; Cassandra reckoned he ought to do it more often. He'd been ravaged by the pox in his youth but his eyes remained big and bright.

"What's the plan?" he asked.

"You're asking me?"

"Chelos said you'd know what to do."

Cassandra's heart beat a little faster. This was already going south.

"I need to get to the western gate on the inner wall. Can you help with that?"

Trask rubbed his head then rummaged in the back of his cart. "Put these on at least." He thrust an apron and washerwoman's cowl into her hands. Cassandra awkwardly put them on over her clothes. The knot of the cowl pressed tightly under her chin. She smeared dirt and dust onto her face and clothes for good measure.

"Looking good," he said. She frowned deeply and he laughed, his eyes falling upon her sword next. "And give me that as well." He reached for it. Cassandra reacted like a startled cat, whipping her hand to the hilt, not allowing him to take it.

"Come on, Cass. How will it look if you have a sword on with that get-up?"

Reluctantly, she handed it over and he threw it on top of an open crate of weapons on his cart.

"I'll give it back," he said. "We can hardly go on an adventure without it, can we? You're the one who knows how to use it."

"You think this will be an adventure?"

"Of course," he said, bemused. "Taking on the king's enemies will be the most fun a stable hand like me is going to get. Maybe you can teach me some moves while we're on the road."

For a moment, Cassandra's mind ground to a halt, trying to process this. Little of it added up.

"Chelos didn't tell you why I was leaving, did he?"

"No," Trask said. "But we're all heading out to hunt down some powerful dragon lord, I hear. Castallan needs him brought here to take his power or some such. Thought you were joining us?"

Cassandra bit back a cry of shock. Since when had Trask been such a staunch supporter of Castallan? His father had been killed in the war by demons – demons Castallan now consorted with. It made no sense.

Her throat tightened. One wrong word and her escape might unravel.

"Yes, I am," she managed. "So, you're not worried about Castallan finding out I've left?"

Trask shrugged. "You're his guest. Bit overprotective of you, mind, but there you go. You should get out and see the world a bit." He was smiling again, although weakly, his desires laid bare. "We could see the world together."

Cassandra resisted biting her lip. What delusions had he concocted for himself? Perhaps she should have headed this off long ago. Yet it was too late to worry about that. Her priority was still to escape. Once out, she'd have to sneak off in the night somehow. Evading one more person wouldn't make much difference. Swallowing her trepidation, she smiled back.

"First you have to get me out," she said.

"Sadly, I can't just sneak you out on the cart. All inventory is being checked. Chelos said you would somehow be able to get right outside the fortress on your own, though. Is that right?"

"That's what he said. Trask, I—"

He cut her off, quickly piling dirtied leathers of white, mud red, yellow and dark green into her hands from the cart. He stacked the pile high enough so that it covered her face.

Booted feet crunched closer on the dry earth.

"Yes, that's right," Trask said loudly. "We'll need *all* these uniforms well cleaned."
The booted feet crunched away.

"Thank you," she said, her voice muffled beneath the clothes.

"Thank me once you are out," Trask said. "I'll need to get going before it looks too suspicious. We've stood here long enough."

He clambered up to the driving seat of his cart and tugged at the reins. His horse snorted loudly before clopping off. Still blinded by the messy hunter uniforms, Cassandra was left uncertainly in the middle of the vast inner courtyard of the Bastion.

Not the best situation. Trask could have taken the clothes back off her at least. She carefully tipped the top layers off the pile.

"What are you doing, dear?"

Gasping, Cassandra turned to see a matronly washerwoman bustling up to her.

"Oh, I was just... I was just..."

Damn, what am I 'just' doing?

"Not to worry," the woman said. Her accent was thick, like most folk brought up outside of Brevia and the larger towns. "They need scrubbing anyway." She stared at Cassandra expectantly. At least the disguise was proving effective.

"Well?" asked the matron. "What are you waiting for?"

"I'm afraid I don't know where to go," she said, rather stupidly. Trask had really left her in the lurch. "I'm new. One of the stable hands just dumped this on me and left!"

The matron nodded in a knowing fashion, as if she expected nothing else.

"Come along, dear," she said, beckoning Cassandra to follow her.

Cassandra did, not knowing what else she could do.

"Ruddy chaos around here," the woman blustered. "If Zarl keeps recruiting more people, we'll have half the Southern Dales living here before long. And what will that mean for the likes of old Winnie here? More damned work and even less gratitude, I tell you!"

"Oh?" Cassandra said, her mind desperately working to find a way out of her predicament.

The woman was taking her completely the wrong way, over to one of the barracks most likely. No solution presented itself. With the inner courtyard so rammed with people, horses and carts, it was hard enough just to maintain her footing with her bundle of leathers.

Winnie droned on. "Aye, nae thanks. Fighters are getting enchanted to be fast and strong, but not us. Think of the loads we'd get through," she added mournfully. "But so long as the demons are kept far away from here, I shan't complain too much. And where are you from, dear? I like to get to know all my girls, but I don't remember you arriving."

"Um, I—"

She was spared from answering by Winnie throwing out an arm in front of her, which Cassandra then bumped into. A couple of mounted men were shoving people aside as they plowed through the crowds, evidently in some terrible hurry.

"Pillocks!" Winnie called after them, shaking a fist. "Watch where you're going, eh? Some people." She tutted. "I'm sorry, dear, where did you say you were from?"

"I'm from Deas," Cassandra said. It was the largest town in the Southern Dales and so seemed like the safest option.

"Ah, yes," said Winnie. "Lots of youngsters coming in from Deas. Don't think Lord Annandale is even bothering to stop Castallan's agents recruiting anymore." They drew closer to the eastern barracks, as Cassandra had feared. A forge was burning beside it, a mixture of smoke and great bouts of steam rising in the air as smiths tempered the weapons. Cassandra had to get away, but Winnie seemed glued to her side.

"So, who brought you in?" she asked.

"Who?" Cassandra asked. *Is there really such secrecy to all of this?*

"Yes, dear, who brought you to the wizard's noble cause?"

It seemed Trask's attitude was a shared one. Cassandra knew that many in the south were joining Castallan freely, but she had assumed it was out of fear or necessity. To call him noble was another matter entirely.

Cassandra's silence was starting to cause concern. Winnie stopped in her tracks, raising an eyebrow.

Think of something, you idiot!

A scream tore through the crowd, supplemented by angry calls, then galloping hooves. A cart hauled by two horses charged into view, out of all control. The boy at the reins, far younger than Trask, looked too green to be handling such animals. It was heading in Cassandra's direction.

Everyone started jumping out of the way. Winnie leapt back in fright, but Cassandra stayed still, in fear of the woman discovering her weak deception. She saw the path the cart was taking and judged it to be her only chance. As it soared past, it cut Cassandra off from Winnie and she relieved herself of most of her bundle of dirtied leathers, tossing them high into the air. She kept hold of a few pieces of darkened green and brown leather, which the hunters of the Dales wore.

The stampeding cart upturned a short way ahead and the explosion of clothes only added to the furore. Jerkins and shirts landed on the heads of other nearby beasts of burden, sending them into a panic. As many collisions ensued, all eyes faced the chaos.

It was a perfect distraction.

Cassandra ducked and weaved through the madness, ripping off the cowl and apron, but keeping hold of them. Dropping them would only make it obvious that she was not meant to be there. With any luck, Winnie might think she had simply fled the danger of the enraged horses and go looking for her in the crowd.

Cassandra stopped near the forge. The smiths had ceased their rhythmic hammering to stare at the commotion. Guards with red eyes appeared amongst the confusion, wrestling with the beasts to bring them back under control. One horse kicked out, hitting a red-eyed woman square in the chest. She stumbled but was otherwise unharmed and caught the next flailing hoof in one hand to halt the horse.

That's not possible!

Cassandra had never seen these red-eyed servants show their true strength before. Zarl would have little issue keeping spectres in line with a force of such people.

Amidst the carnage, many crates and barrels had been upturned. Swords, tent pegs, hard cheese, hard biscuits and dried meats lay strewn across the eastern court-yard, and the smiths were called upon to help with the mess. Grunting, they thumped down the broad axes they were working on and moved off. Cassandra seized her chance.

She skirted the chaos to the forge, tossing the washerwoman clothes into the furnace, and used the containers of water nearby to wash the worst of the dirt and dust from her face. A small, plump coin purse lay unguarded, likely from a recent transaction. Cassandra swiped it. Coins would be better than panicked horses at causing a distraction. She scuttled away, moving behind the forge and making for the base of the inner wall.

Her breaths came in huge, laboured gulps as she tried to collect herself.

That was ridiculous. I'm better than that.

She had never come so close to being caught in all her years in the Bastion, although the passageways inside the citadel made it infinitely easier. She would have to approach this false gate more quietly.

She glanced down at the hunter leathers she still possessed. It was not a full set, only the tunic, gloves and bracers, but it would have to suffice. She put the items on and undid the knot of her hair to let it fall to her shoulders and obscure her face to anyone looking side-on. Ready as she'd ever be, she began to creep along the base of the wall, heading from east to south on her way to the western gate. If she could stay stay close to the wall behind the buildings and vendors' stalls, she could hopefully make the journey without interruption.

Yet as she approached the southern gate, the guards on the walls above, along with the activity around the gatehouse, made it impossible to continue to cling to the wall so tightly. To her relief, she saw a group of hunters from the Dales making their way west, loud in conversation. She walked casually to the edge of a stall, pretending to peruse the fruit while she waited for her moment. The vendor claimed to have ripe fruit from Val'tarra, though his pears were browning.

Cassandra drew in a deep breath.

This has to be perfect.

As the hunters passed, she walked out with purpose and fell in just behind them. They began laughing at a joke and Cassandra feigned a quiet laugh of her own, tossing her head back like they were all doing.

To everyone else around, it would seem as though she was part of their gang, but she stayed just quiet enough that they did not turn around. The ruse would not last for long. It did not need to. The group were heading for the western gate; she was in sight of it now. She trailed the hunters for as long as she dared, then, when her gut told her it was time to move, Cassandra did not hesitate. Her instincts on these things were normally correct.

Slowing slightly, she allowed herself to drift back from the group and then melt into the jostle of people. Cassandra kept her head up but made sure she did not look at anyone directly. Everyone was busy; everyone had a job to do. If someone glanced at her, they would see her leathers and think she was nothing out of the ordinary, just a huntress. So long as she did not draw attention, she might just make it.

'*A false opening under the staircase of the curtain wall by the western gate,*' she repeated in her head. Her heart sank as she saw how many guards swarmed around that area.

The bulk of the traffic moving out of the Bastion was trundling through the western gate, or at least attempting to. She was quickly closing the gap to her destination, but she could do nothing while those guards were there. Yet she could not stop to think. To stop dead would be to draw attention. By the gate, a new cart had fought its way through the knots of people. It was Trask's.

Cassandra had never been so pleased to catch sight of him. Desperately, she stared at him so intently that she might have been trying to see into his soul. Trask hopped onto the back of his wagon, apparently under instructions to unload his haul for inspection. He had his arms around a barrel when he finally caught her eye. He froze.

Cassandra mouthed urgently to him. "Please," she said silently. "Help."

Mercifully, he understood and did not hesitate. He dropped the barrel he had half-lifted and clutched his arm, feigning some discomfort. The guards below him puffed their lips in annoyance and turned to look for help. Cassandra could hardly believe her luck when three of the four guards at the curtain wall ran off in answer.

Just one left.

Cassandra pushed her way through the throng of people as gently as she could, making sure her bearing would keep her out of sight. As she neared the guard at the foot of the stairs, she loosened the knot on the bag of coins she had taken from the forge. She casually flung the bag, sending thin bronze coins clinking and rolling. Predictably, those nearby scrambled to collect what they could, causing heads to bash and tempers to flare. The final guard charged into the brawl to maintain order.

Now was her chance.

A false opening under the staircase. Where is it?

No marks were scratched upon the stone, no bricks of a different colour, nothing to indicate that there was some secret gateway there.

Mild panic set in. She only had a few moments. She reached the section of the wall and started to run her hands over it frantically.

From behind, the guard called out brusquely, "Enough of that. Calm down, the lot of you."

Where is it? Where?

Her flailing hand pushed at the stone in front of her, only the stone was not there at all. She stumbled forward several paces, seemingly into the wall itself. Her hand remained outstretched, meeting only air. Turning, she found herself staring back out at the crowd scrambling for coins. In the space she had just stepped through, the air seemed to shudder and light entered at a strange angle, as though bent by shaped glass. Surely this was some kind of magic, though whose magic she could not say. And how did Chelos know of it?

She hardly had the time to pause and consider these matters now, however. A few steps further into this hidden space and the way ahead seemed blocked again. Her probing hand found another opening on her left. She squeezed along a narrow run in the wall under the stairway and entered darkness. That was no matter; Cassandra was used to that.

Her racing heart began to slow down as the feeling of success sank in.

She had made it.

Feeling her way, the passage twisted deep into the thickness of the wall. Eventually, she hit what seemed to be a dead end. She found a lever, and as there was nothing else she could do, she yanked on it. The floor disappeared and she plummeted down. It was all she could do not to scream in shock as her head thudded off the rungs of a ladder until she hit the ground.

Dazed and pained, she groaned and struggled to her feet. Cassandra felt around and found there were four directions she could take. She could not be sure which way they went. She needed to head west to get out of the Bastion. One seemed to run behind her and back under the inner courtyard. Two branched off, presumably following the shape of the jagged wall. Only one stretched off ahead of her.

Well, I don't have many options.

She walked down the well-paved passage, which offered plenty of space to manoeuvre. After a time, she grew more confident in her pace and thought the tunnel must have been designed as some escape route that people could run down, albeit with a lantern in tow.

At the tunnel's end, she found a second lever. Two great sections of the roof caved in, bringing in earth, leaves, roots and other debris, as well as rays from a sinking sun. Her eyes burned from the sudden influx of light and she curled up to shield herself.

Emerging from her own cocoon, Cassandra hauled herself up onto the ledge and then outside. The trapdoors must have been on a timing mechanism for they closed behind her. She exhaled with relief.

For several long moments, she simply stared out at the world. The whole world beyond the walls of the Bastion lay before her now. She was out. She was free. She was no longer confined by those great walls and battlements. Despite her years of yearning for this moment, she realised she was horribly exposed and was without food or shelter. Somehow, she needed to find Trask.

Now what do I do?

From this distance, it seemed like she might scoop the fortress up in her hand. The rolling plains of the Southern Dales swept towards the outer walls like waves. Running west from the Bastion was the baggage train – a trail of wagons, horses and marching men stretching off for miles. Torches were already flickering to life along the line as the sky above reddened. Night would soon fall.

Her need to find Trask intensified.

Luckily, Casssandra had emerged in sight of a small wood which would offer her better cover. Moving lightly on her feet, she sped along to the outer edge of the wood, moving from trunk to trunk to close the gap between herself and the main column.

Groups of hunters were entering and leaving the treeline. Some were foraging for food amongst the wild forest while others were attending to calls of nature. One pair, a huntress and a red-eyed man, had abandoned their baskets to get more intimate among the ferns and shrubs. Cassandra inched forward, cringing at the woman's giggling, and silently lifted one of their wicker baskets.

She made her way towards the baggage train, head held high as if nothing was amiss. She hadn't noticed her hunger until she glimpsed the basket's contents: yellow smooth-capped mushrooms with gill-like ridges spoke of a meaty flavour. Dotted around were red and orange alderberries, and she could even see some silver ones. She picked out a silver one and ate it. A refreshing sweetness burst into her mouth and she felt a small kick to the back of her head. Energised by the magic-infused fruit, she pressed on.

Her ploy paid off when she approached the road. No one questioned Cassandra with her basket of goods, and the gathering darkness obscured her lack of a full uniform. She passed dozens of wagons before she found him.

"Trask," she hissed under her breath, sidling up beside him.

He nearly dropped his reins. "Cass? Bloody hell. How—"

"Hide me!"

Trask peered around anxiously then began to slow his steed. He jumped down, took the basket from her, led her round to the back and lifted the tarred waterproof canvas.

"Get in, quickly. I've never seen them so agitated. We've to travel through the night, for all the good it will do. It will take days to reach the Boreacs."

"Will the horses even manage for that long?" Cassandra asked, clambering into the back of the wagon.

"Probably not," Trask said. "But those red-eyed folks can take over if need be."

"You don't have to do this if you don't want to," she reassured him, though she cursed herself for doing so. If he did get cold feet then she might miss her chance.

"I made a promise I'd get you out one day, and I'm going to keep it. Besides, I—"

"Quickly, boy!" a voice rang out. "Get moving."

"Yes, sir," Trask said. "Right away, sir."

Cassandra heard footsteps leading off and breathed easier. Trask finished strapping the cover over the wagon.

"I sometimes wish they would just keep their normal eyes. Those red eyes are unnatural," he said with a little shiver. "Still, whatever Castallan does to them, it makes them bloody tough. They'll show the dragons that we're not pushovers anymore."

Cassandra nodded and smiled weakly. "Let's hope so!"

Trask beamed, then finished strapping the coverings back down, safely hiding her.

Cassandra was beginning to think she'd placed too much trust in Trask. Getting away from him to go and find this Darnuir and his allies would be difficult if he expected her to stay. And he wouldn't be convinced to change his mind.

Trask blamed the dragons for the south's misfortune after the last war, as so many in the Southern Dales did. They blamed Brevia, too, for doing little to alleviate their suffering. Now that time had worn on it seemed many were looking to Castallan as the better option.

Cassandra did not know enough about life beyond the Bastion to decide for herself. Trask might work for the wizard, but the matter was simple for her. Castallan consorted with demons and anyone who did so was not worth allying with.

They were the real enemy, surely? Not the dragons. Without the dragons, the demons would have swarmed over the world decades ago.

The wagon started moving. Under the heavy cloth, Cassandra's senses were dulled. The clop of the horse's hooves was muffled but she felt the full effect of the jarring bumps as the wagon rolled on. She ferreted around very carefully in the crate where Trask had placed her sword. She extracted it and managed to tie it back round her waist. Though the wagon ride was hardly pleasant, Cassandra couldn't help but smile.

She was out of the Bastion. One step closer to freedom.

13

VISIONS AND FEATHERS

Darnuir – Cold Point

His vision was blurry. There was a vague outline of a man with hair swept back in an arc before him. The man was speaking quickly, though his words were hard to hear. Darnuir had the sense of being amused at how the speaker occasionally tripped up over his words.

His vision did not clear but his hearing sharpened enough to catch a part of what the man was saying,

"… with that, and enough time, I will find the answer for you – for us!"

"You are sure?" Darnuir asked. "I seek answers. Not more questions."

"I am, though it will take a deal of secrecy…" The rest of his speech became jarred again. Darnuir's vision swirled and he felt like he was being sucked upwards and away from his own body.

He awoke with a start, heart pounding and head dotted with beads of sweat. In his sleep, he must have taken hold of his new sword, for the Dragon's Blade was halfway out of its sheath, the ruby eyes glowing intensely. Swallowing hard, he sheathed the blade, wondering if the magic also caused bad dreams.

Cool strands of dawn light ushered in the new day. He had slept on the hard floor of the lodge, which had largely survived the flames, and was amongst the first to rise.

He felt exhausted; his head ached and there was a nasty, bitter taste in his mouth. Breakfast had never seemed a more delightful prospect.

He trudged slowly across the ruined square to the tavern, his muscles unwilling to move with any haste. Ash and soot from last night's inferno gently trickled down in place of snowflakes. Blood, thinned with melted snow, squelched loudly with each step.

Inside the tavern, evidence of the battle was clear. Broken doors were laid up against the bar and a large pile of glass had been swept to one side. Everyone stopped what they were doing when he entered the tavern. Hunter and huntress alike gawked at him; some apprehensively, some in awe and some in fear.

Remembering how he had fought at the end made him uneasy. He had looked on from the back of his own mind as his body performed feats far beyond him. Something, or someone, had taken control of him, and he suspected the sword was to blame. Perhaps Brackendon might be able to explain it. His fate was still uncertain.

Eve's was not.

She was gone.

Not seeing her face here amongst the others made that clear. Yet, even with that stark fact, he couldn't process it. Not yet. Not fully. The image of her slumped against the wall was burnt into his mind.

I must not think about it. I must not think about it.

His mind did not obey but remained fixated on it as his body absentmindedly collected his ration of porridge and found a quiet spot on the floor to sit. There was no usable furniture left.

He spooned the food into his mouth mechanically. It was watery and wanted for milk. They must have run out of it. A pinch of salt or crushed alderberries wouldn't have gone amiss either, though he would have favoured the berries. It was not just the taste but the colour. Alder bushes grew fruit of many colours; small, perfect spheres in red, green, blue, orange, even silver, each type a touch sweeter or tangier than the others. Yes, he would have liked to have seen some colour, though not more red. Sadly, there were no berries to hand.

We must have run out of everything.

"Mind if I join you?" Cosmo said, his voice reaching Darnuir as if from afar. Cosmo sat beside him, waving a hand in front of Darnuir's face. His senses sharpened and only then did he realise he had dripped a spoonful of porridge down his front.

"No," Darnuir said hoarsely.

Cosmo patted his shoulder.

"You're like a son to me, you know that," Cosmo said. "Balack is too, in a way, and Eve was like family as well. It hurts. It aches. I don't think I have felt this empty after a victory in my whole life."

Darnuir nodded and took another spoonful of porridge to avoid a verbal response.

"I know that some of us will miss her even more," Cosmo continued, and he flicked his eyes towards the hunched form of Balack, sitting as far away from Darnuir as he could. "But the only thing that will help is time. Words won't. People try to comfort through words and it rarely helps. Just be there for him, okay? And I will be here for both of you."

Darnuir tried to speak but his throat felt dried out from grief. "I'll do what I can for him," he managed to say.

Can I ever tell Balack what happened now? Will it be worse or better now he cannot confront her?

A small part of him felt relieved that such an encounter could never occur again and he felt disgusted with himself for thinking it.

"How is Brackendon?" Darnuir asked, feeling it best to switch topics.

"Rather ill," Cosmo said sadly. "He writhed in his sleep, and after his wails had subsided, he curled up in a foetal position, muttering incoherently."

"Cosmo," Darnuir began in sorrow, "I am so sorry. I—"

"It is not your fault."

"But it was me who—"

"It was a battle, Darnuir," Cosmo said gently. "Brackendon knew the risks, and you hardly meant it."

Darnuir pushed his oats around his bowl. He'd lost his appetite.

"We'll be leaving today," Cosmo announced, his tone becoming more businesslike. "The civilians are making their way back from the edges of town and we'll leave as soon as possible."

Darnuir had guessed as much. *What else is there to do?*

"Where will we go?" he asked.

"I'm not sure," Cosmo admitted. "But technically, that isn't my decision."

"Well, if Scythe is still alive then he'll be able to—"

"No, Darnuir. It is not his decision either," Cosmo interrupted. "The truth is that you hold the most authority here, in theory."

Darnuir's mouth somehow felt even drier than it had before.

"There are no dragons here; I'm not your king, am I?" he said, not really believing he was king of anything.

"I thought you wanted to lead one day?"

"One day, maybe," Darnuir stressed. "Far off, I'd always assumed. When I had a lot more experience. And I saw myself as a captain, not as the king of a people whom I've never met. I don't even have the faintest idea where they are. Now, fancy that, a king who has misplaced his subjects."

Cosmo did not seem entirely in the mood to coddle him. "If that sword didn't just answer to one dragon, and if your kind were not so stubborn, then perhaps none of this would have happened. Brackendon and I might not have gone out of our way to keep you alive. You probably would have died that night. I saw you, hot and shaking from a poison in your veins." He leaned in so Darnuir was forced to look at him. "Whether you like it or not, you'll be in charge soon. They won't give you a choice."

"And do you think I am ready for that?"

"No, you're not. I am to blame for that, for not preparing you better. I knew it was coming, after all. And yet... I don't know what I might have done for you. I've never wanted to lead. I still don't. I'm hoping that Scythe survived in the station more than anything right now."

"You may not want it, but you do it well," Darnuir said. "The men respect you. They would follow you."

"The benefit of being one of the oldest and most experienced, Darnuir. Don't be mistaken; it is my years here, not me personally, that make them follow me."

Darnuir decided to silently disagree.

He is a born leader who does not wish to lead, whilst I was born to lead and have no choice about it.

The unfairness of it then struck him. Not the injustice experienced by those who found themselves in charge, but the injustice felt by those who did not choose their leader. His dragons were in for a rude awakening.

"I don't have years, Cosmo."

"Then you'll have to earn it. It won't be so hard. Your performance last night has gone a long way towards that, and you will be thoroughly involved in all major decisions henceforth. Whether you like it or not."

"That wasn't me out there. At the end, I lost control of myself. I don't know what happened."

"Well, lose control like that a few more times and the war will be won." Cosmo got to his feet. "Finish up and then come and help us outside. We could use a strong dragon to haul debris."

The survivors wasted no time in leaving Cold Point to begin their slog through the Boreac Mountains. When they reached Ascent, Scythe and his men rendezvoused with them. The captain had even darker rings under his eyes, adding further to his gauntness, but otherwise, he and his men were unharmed.

"What happened on your side, Captain?" Garon asked. "We thought the demons would surely finish you off."

"They clawed at the station's gate so much, I thought they would blunt their weapons and leave themselves unarmed," Scythe stated with his typical brusqueness. "After half a day, they relented and must have thrown themselves at Cold Point instead. We could barely believe it when the report came in from the southern observation deck that they were fleeing through the mountains a few days later."

"I can barely believe it either," Darnuir said.

Scythe grunted and turned to Cosmo for a report, although all present contributed to the tale. As the captain heard of the events at Cold Point, his lips drew into a thinner line with each new revelation.

"So be it," he sniffed. "I shall ensure you are involved in all decisions henceforth, my lord of dragons."

It was a courtesy that he showed no sign of revelling in.

Darnuir suspected that Scythe's annoyance was born out of the new, confusing chain of command. Leadership was now a fluid concept. Many looked to Cosmo, as they had always done; some to Garon, when Cosmo made it clear that his priority was to look after Grace; and some even directly to Darnuir, although he never felt sure what to say. These people were, after all, those he had lived, worked and fought alongside his whole life. To suddenly be thrust into a position of responsibility over them, many far older than he was, felt unnatural.

One week passed and they drew close to Farlen at the base of the mountain range. Each day had consisted of walking, more walking and then, mercifully, sleep. And every night, Darnuir watched the same dream play in his head. The cautious man, the request for things unknown, and his own perplexing demand: "I seek answers."

He hoped it would change soon, or at least that he would forget it like other dreams. Yet there was something different about this one; it was almost as if it was real.

Their column meandered solemnly, feeling nothing like the freshly liberated ought to. What few poor beasts of burden remained to them dragged laden carts, filled with their last provisions, the sick and those still wounded.

Grace was sitting in one of them, her pregnancy now heavy upon her. Cosmo walked alongside her, giving up his place at the head of the group alongside Darnuir, Scythe, Garon and even Brackendon, who had emerged shortly before they departed Cold Point, looking sallow and shaken. Despite appearing at death's door, the wizard insisted that he did not require aid. He had walked alongside Darnuir for the most part, though he had shivered noticeably in the cold. However, the air was palpably warmer now they were in the lower part of the range and the change in climate seemed to have done Brackendon some good.

"You seem steadier on your feet," Darnuir remarked.

"I'll survive," Brackendon said. "Compared to breaking, this feels like a pinprick."

"What will happen now?" Garon asked.

"Little until I acquire a new staff. Now I only have my own body to rely on, and it truly is a feeble thing." He raised his half-scaled hand to reinforce his point.

"Where can you get another staff?" Darnuir asked.

"Not from the markets in Brevia," Brackendon said, "no matter how articulate they are in their pitch. A smoothed, wooden branch is not enough. I shall have to rely on the fairies once again."

"Just as well you arrived when you did," said Scythe, a slight edge to his voice. "I assumed it was the end for us."

That same day, they entered Farlen.

As they picked their way through the debris, Darnuir stopped beside the surviving monument in town. A life-sized warrior, holding his sword forward in one hand and holding an oversized shield in the other, protecting a crouching child. Made from stone, it had endured the fires, though it was charred in places. A brief inscription was etched beneath the figures' feet.

In memory of Dronithir, Prince of Dragons. Mankind's greatest friend.

A hand gripped Darnuir's arm.

"I sense something here," Brackendon murmured. "There is some magic at work."

"In what way?" Darnuir asked, his own hand moving to the hilt of his sword.

"It is hard to say. It is just a feeling," Brackendon said. He began to twitch.

"Don't strain yourself."

"I must try," Brackendon said through gritted teeth. "What if it is something sent against us?"

"Would you be able to stop it?"

"No," the wizard said mournfully. "'Tis strange, Darnuir. It is two feelings; one familiar and one I have never encountered before."

"What is this familiar one?"

"I cannot be sure, but this unknown thing, it unnerves me more. I have felt it for days, only now it has grown stronger."

He let go of Darnuir's arm.

Darnuir felt a great sympathy for the wizard. *This man has done so much for me, and I barely know him.*

"Back at Cold Point," Darnuir began sheepishly, "before the battle began. Why were you late in giving the signal?"

"I was afraid," Brackendon said. "There is no good in denying it. The last time I fought with magic, I broke. I think you would hesitate as well."

Something snapped in Darnuir's mind. Words tumbled out from him before he could think past his overwhelming anger and frustration.

"Then how can I possibly rely on you?"

His head ached terribly again and he lifted his fingers to squeeze the bridge of his nose. *What was that? Why did I say that?*

Brackendon frowned and backed away from Darnuir at the outburst.

"I'm sorry," Darnuir apologised. "I don't know what came over me."

Brackendon grumbled and took his leave. Darnuir thought about going after him but then saw Scythe approaching.

"I suggest we rest here for now, *my lord*," Scythe said stiffly. "We ought to send scouts to check that the passage north to the Dales is clear."

Darnuir nodded in agreement. "You don't need to address me like that, Captain," he said.

"No?" Scythe mused. "Very well. I'd rather not in any case. There stands the only dragon I might have followed willingly." He wafted a hand towards the monument of the long-dead prince. "He was able to set aside his arrogance."

"Only after he was taken prisoner," Darnuir noted. "Or so the stories go. Before that, he had launched the Second War between humanity and dragons and killed many of us."

"Us?" Scythe questioned. "You are a dragon, not a human, are you not?"

"I suppose," Darnuir said, though the notion still felt absurd. He did not know what he was. "People always speak indifferently of the dragons, or with disdain, but aren't they on our side?"

Scythe snorted. "I fought in the last war. I was young, of course, not much older than yourself, stationed out east before the demons began rolling back our efforts. There was this one legionary legate; well, I would question his intent. We, dragons and humans alike, had pulled back from The Nest. It's a fortress at the fork of the Crucidal Road. Anyway, we'd retreated, or so I thought. The demons outnumbered us. Yet, rather than fall back further to Aurisha, we were thrown into battle. And guess who was placed on the front lines?"

"The humans?" Darnuir said, sensing where this was going.

"Indeed," Scythe said. A strange expression crossed his face that was part laughter and part madness. "He still had over a thousand heavily-armoured dragons and yet he put humanity on the front. I believe it was to lure the demons in and draw their lines thin so that his dragons could charge them."

"You must have won the day somehow. Else you would not be here."

"We were saved in the end by reinforcements from the prince. 'The prince! The prince! The prince!' I heard the dragons call. I assume that was you?"

"It must have been, though I have no memory of it," Darnuir said.

Scythe looked again at the statue in obvious disgust.

"What's wrong?" Darnuir asked.

"I hated this thing from the moment I arrived," Scythe said. "Look at how humanity portrayed itself. A cowering child in need of a strong protector. We should have more faith in ourselves. Yet here we are again. A broken people who needed a dragon to save us."

"If you have a problem with me, Scythe—"

"That's not it... Please do not think of me as purely bitter. I have lost much and for people like me, especially in the south, bitterness is often all we have left. Yet I have not forgotten Demons' Folly, Darnuir, nor how the legions held strong there. My only regret is that Brevia does not feel it has the strength to hold its own. At Demons' Folly, at Cold Point, and with Dronithir during the Second War, we needed a dragon to save us. I think it is time we helped ourselves."

"On that, captain, I quite agree."

Scythe gave a curt nod before carrying on.

Darnuir had not been prepared for such an outpouring, but was glad of it. He would need to get to know the captain better if they were to work closely together. He then realised how very useless he must look right now, seemingly admiring the monument for this length of time. Yet he was not sure what he should do. He had always been given tasks to do and now he was left to his own devices.

Through the gathering crowd, he saw Cosmo helping Grace down from her wagon while Balack unloaded it. He went to aid his friend but, when the task was done, Balack quietly left him without saying a word. Darnuir wished someone would tell him what he was supposed to do, with Balack and with everything.

He turned to examine the road out of the mountains; a dirt and gravel track that widened considerably as it left Farlen and sloped out of sight. The main road out of the mountains would take them too close to Castallan's territory for comfort, but it was the quickest way to leave. What route they would take then, Darnuir did not know. It had not been discussed at length yet.

I hope they are not relying on me to make this decision.

A rather uncomfortable feeling of being watched crept over him. He found the offending pair of eyes off in the distance, belonging to a tawny eagle perched on a tree branch hanging high over the road. Such birds were not uncommon in the mountains, but it was staring with an unnatural intensity. The eagle cocked its head as Darnuir looked back at it, and then it glided closer to him, landing on the burned shell of Farlen's tavern. It was not a large creature; its wingspan was perhaps about as wide as Darnuir could stretch his own arms. Now it was closer he could make out the white feather tips on its wings and tail. A sharp yellow beak snapped playfully at him.

"What do you want?" Darnuir found himself asking stupidly.

Its response was to move its gaze from his face down to his sword. He instinctively took hold of the hilt. The eagle continued gazing at the Dragon's Blade, stretching its neck forth as if it were trying to get a better look. Darnuir edged the sword out of its sheath just a little bit and the eagle threw its head back in a caw of approval. It stood up and extended its wings, flapping them madly. Finishing its bizarre show, the eagle twisted to face the road out of Farlen. It raised a wing and swept it back and forth whilst alternatively looking at him and the path.

"Are you telling me to follow you?"

It cawed loudly, then flew off down the road, landing on an outcrop of rock and making the same sweeping motion with its wing.

Was this the unknown presence that worried Brackendon? If it was, then he was better off not going after it. But he was intrigued. With the perplexing recurring dream and now this, Darnuir was beginning to fear for his sanity.

Recklessly, he chased after the bird.

People called after him as he ran but he didn't look back. He did not intend to follow the bird too far. It swooped forward, looking back to ensure he was following. As they neared the point where the road turned, he stopped to draw his sword and was pleased that he managed it in one stroke, even if it was still heavy. Ahead, he saw the eagle circling an area of fir trees with colourful alderberry bushes underneath. Darnuir approached more cautiously.

In the bushes, he found a body. A crumpled body, whose face was obscured by wavy black hair. Her hand had been reaching out for the silver berries.

14

THE GREAT DEBATE

Darnuir – Farlen

Scythe leaned over the splintered table. "She's a spy, clearly. The whole thing reeks of suspicion, Darnuir. You were foolish to be lured away like that."

Cosmo, Brackendon and Garon didn't seem to disagree. They were all sat in council inside what had been Farlen's tavern. It afforded little privacy; half the roof had been burnt away and one wall was missing. Still, it was better than right out in the open. A frayed map of western Tenalp lay before them upon the table.

"I didn't sense any danger," Darnuir lied.

"It hardly matters now," Cosmo intervened. "But in future, Darnuir, don't be so reckless."

"I can handle myself."

"Could you can handle a pack of spectres on your own?" Scythe sneered.

"Could you?" Darnuir retorted.

"Enough," Cosmo said in a fatherly warning.

"You didn't see him at Cold Point, Captain," Garon stated proudly. "I'm not sure a score of spectres would trouble him." He gave Darnuir a quick wink.

"I think we can all agree that his swordsmanship is of an acceptably high level," Brackendon said. "The real question before us is this girl. What was her name? Cassandra?"

Garon leaned back a little, hands behind his head. "Aye, that's what she said. Pretty girl, too." He shot Darnuir a knowing look.

She is beautiful, Darnuir had to admit. But, given that he was supposed to be a king, he felt it would be best not to respond with too much enthusiasm.

"I suppose so."

Garon raised an eyebrow at him.

"All the more evidence that she should not be trusted," Scythe said. "I doubt Castallan would send a homely agent to entice you into a trap."

"But there was no trap," Cosmo said. "Not that I am suggesting we shouldn't be cautious. I am merely being fair, Scythe."

"She was badly wounded," Darnuir added, "and she looked pale, drained, exhausted."

"Of course," Scythe said. "I forgot that Castallan is incapable of trickery. We should just take her completely at her word."

"She was armed, Darnuir," Garon added diplomatically. "Not the best sword in the world, I grant you. I wouldn't want to hunt a rabbit with it, but she had one all the same."

"She's obviously been in some fight," Brackendon said. "The gash on her arm was deep and she has lost a substantial amount of blood. I can't use magic to help her, but the healers believe she will make it. I sensed no sorcery at work and I believe her wound to be genuine."

Scythe grumbled at this stumbling block in his argument. "Her story is unconvincing."

"She was half-dead when she murmured it to me," Brackendon said.

"I may have to agree with Scythe," Cosmo said. "She claims to have been a prisoner at the Bastion, who's only recently broken out and just happened to head straight for us?"

"I thought you were being fair?" said Darnuir.

"I trust you. I trust Brackendon, I trust Garon, and I trust Scythe. But I do not trust her. That is fair."

"And what of this pet eagle of hers?" Garon asked.

"I don't think it is hers—" Darnuir began.

"Exactly!" Scythe said, slapping his hand upon the table. "It will be Castallan's pet creature."

"Ah," said Brackendon softly, bringing his fingers together in a steeple. "I do not think we need to worry about the bird."

"Know something, do you, wizard?" Scythe said.

"You say it had white feathers?" Brackendon asked Darnuir.

"At the tips of its wings and on its tail."

"Then it is not a concern."

"Are you going to enlighten us?" Scythe asked.

"When the time is right," Brackendon said. He smiled, as though that settled the matter. "The other information that Cassandra offered is more pressing. She claims Castallan is amassing all his forces outside the Boreac Mountains. If we leave by Farlen's road, we'll be slaughtered."

Scythe dismissed it with a wave of his hand. "A trick to slow our progress, to buy the enemy more time to truly block off all escape."

"Either way, what choice do we have?" Darnuir asked. "How else are we to leave the Boreacs?"

"There are many smaller, narrower and slower routes, of course," Cosmo said. "But patrols of hunters navigating them is one thing. We have over a thousand people and would be carrying a great deal of baggage, even if we did reduce it to the bare necessities."

"We wouldn't have much to get rid of," Garon observed. "Food dwindles with every meal and the demons seem to have either slaughtered or chased off all the game."

"Then we must make a decision and make it soon," said Brackendon. "I say we make for the other passages."

"This is a matter for the hunters, wizard," Scythe sneered. "You are here because our lord dragon wishes it."

Brackendon, who was normally so considered and congenial, twitched his nose and leaned towards Scythe. "And what would the captain advise?"

"Wait, send scouts and gain intelligence. If there is an army gathering then it won't be hard to find."

"Those passages lead out into the Cairlav Marshes," said Garon, tapping a finger on the appropriate place on the map. "We'd hardly be able to make a quick escape that way."

"What is our way?" Darnuir asked. He was beginning to feel this would only become an argument. "Well?" he asked of the table. "What is our plan? Where are we going? What is our destination? Maybe then we can better pick one of our options."

He was met with silence and then all four men answered at once. Garon and Scythe said, "Brevia," while Brackendon and Cosmo said, "Val'tarra." More silence followed, punctuated only by Darnuir's exasperated sigh.

Of course. I would have the casting vote.

"I'm curious, Brackendon," Scythe said. "What was the plan? Your plan, I mean. You make your grand return to Cold Point and boldly proclaim Darnuir to be King of Dragons. Then what was to happen?"

"As I said," Brackendon began calmly, "I planned for us to make for Val'tarra. Just Darnuir and myself, or as few others as possible. With Darnuir's stamina and my magic, we could have made excellent time, but fate has taken us down a different route."

"You said Kasselle was sending help?" Cosmo inquired.

"Indeed. That is why I say we make for Val'tarra. Close the distance between ourselves and whatever aid she has sent."

Scythe sniffed distastefully. "Tell me, had any fairy army or task force left Val'tarra prior to you leaving? What kind of help did she promise to send?"

"No to the first. And I am not certain about the second. She just said help would come. The very best." The wizard came across as a little deflated, as if the rashness of his move had suddenly hit him. "I trust her, Scythe," he added in his defence. "Kasselle will not abandon us."

"No, I fear you are right on that," Scythe said in his well-practised sneer. "The fairies are well trained in jumping to a dragon's roar."

Darnuir's cheeks felt hot at that remark. He had the sudden desire to reach across the table and haul Scythe bodily into the air. A wave of anger that was not fully his own swept through him. He pushed the sensation down, although his head began to throb lightly again. Pushing through the pain, he looked to Garon.

"We have heard the reasons for Val'tarra. Now, why Brevia?"

"Seems like the natural thing to do," Garon said. "Above all, we need to reach aid quickly, so I am not opposed to making for Val'tarra, if that will be better for us. I admit that getting to Brevia would be more dangerous. Making straight for the capital from here would mean drawing dangerously close to the Bastion."

"We would never have to enter Castallan's lands," Scythe said, tapping the map. "The extent of his control isn't so great."

"Not officially," said Brackendon. "But those borders were never clearly defined, and they will be particularly volatile now."

"I've patrolled those borders," Scythe said. "Have you? In any case, I place my faith in my own people. Humanity will help humanity. Why place so much stock in the fairies over our own kind?"

"And what of the dragons?" Darnuir asked. "Where are they?" He felt ridiculous in having to ask.

"Most likely scattered throughout human settlements," Scythe said. "Even more reason to make for the capital. It will be easier to send out the call from there."

"Brackendon said there had been a lot of movement throughout the kingdom," Garon said. "Can you add anything to that, Captain? Could it be the dragons?"

Scythe frowned. "No such reports reached me before I left Brevia."

They all looked to Brackendon. "From what I gathered, sections of the population were vanishing or moving. If it is the dragons, then it is curious. The whole reason they disappeared was they had no king to follow."

"So, if not Darnuir, who are they following?" Cosmo asked.

"Precisely," Brackendon said. "All the more reason to seek refuge in Val'tarra. There, we can assess the situation and gather the fairies as well. A dragon king has not set foot in their forest for generations. Darnuir's presence will be a welcome piece of diplomacy."

"Mankind has the greater strength," Scythe insisted. "Both in military power and wider resources. We can still appeal to the fairies from a place of strength and we may even get word from Lord Imar of the Isles. In fact," Scythe added, standing triumphantly and placing a long finger on the map, "we could find passage across Loch Minian. That would avoid Castallan's borders completely and save time in traversing the Crown Lands. We would reach Brevia that much quicker."

"No!" Cosmo said. They were all a little startled at the force of his reaction.

Does he hate the capital so much?

"Scythe, I'm sorry, but I must disagree," Cosmo continued more tactfully. "Aside from the unlikely event that there would be passage for everyone, taking ships across the loch would require reaching its southern shore. We would have to traverse the Cairlav Marshes instead; and if we are making that journey, we would do just as well to push further west, through the marshes, and make for Val'tarra."

Scythe made to say something but stopped himself. He seemed to know that he had been defeated. "What say you, Darnuir?"

Darnuir did not feel like there was a great deal of choice. Both paths seemed desperate. He had reservations about trusting the word of a fairy queen he knew nothing of, and his trust in Brackendon was largely based on Cosmo's word. Darnuir was sympathetic to Scythe's position; humanity would be more familiar to deal with.

The hulking form of Griswald saved him having to announce a decision.

"Beg yer pardon, but the girl has woken up."

"Well?" snapped Scythe. "Has she said anything?"

"Erm, no, Cap'n, not really. Just keeps asking to see Darnuir and won't talk to anyone else."

Secretly glad for the opportunity to leave, Darnuir rose. "I need some time to make my decision. Perhaps she will have some more precise information for us."

Scythe looked disapproving, Cosmo mentioned something about Grace and Brackendon tried to steady a shaking hand. He looked ill again.

"Well, don't take too long," Garon said. "We don't have much time."

15

BEAUTY AND THE WITCH

Darnuir – Farlen

He left the deadlocked council behind and followed Griswald. The town had become one large campsite, with barely a space of soft ground unused. As they made their way through the bustle, Darnuir felt the stares follow him.

Do they blame me for their hardship?

"Don't worry too much, lad," Griswald reassured him. "They're just waiting for the next move. Sitting around on yer arse rather than taking action can cause more anxiety."

Yet more reasons for him to feel guilty. The pressure on him was already mounting.

"I will make my decision before nightfall," Darnuir said. He hoped he'd make the right one.

Past more tents and more concerned faces, they approached a small hut that was miraculously unspoiled by the flames. As it still had four walls and a roof, it was the best jail cell they had. Two guards, a hunter and a huntress, stood by the door. Darnuir recognised the huntress as the one who had found the enchanted message from Castallan all those months ago.

"Ava, Mardin," Griswald said to them. "She been any trouble?"

"Not at all," Ava told him. "We gave her some food, but the only other thing she asks for is to see Darnuir."

"Do you wish us to join you, Darnuir... I mean, my lord?" the hunter called Mardin said awkwardly. He was not much older than Darnuir.

"There is really no need to call me..." Darnuir found himself saying, but stopped. It would not do in the long run to pretend that things weren't going to change. He'd have to get used to the titles. "Wait out here," he said firmly. "Entering with two guards doesn't show much trust."

"Good luck, lad," Griswald said.

Darnuir clapped him on the back, then entered the hut.

Grey light and chilled air crept in through two broken windows. Their prisoner sat upon a battered chair. Her hands were bound behind her and her legs were tied to the chair. At least her wound had been neatly patched up.

The ordeal had left her pale. Long hair crashed in dark waves around her neck, but her green eyes reminded him of Cosmo's. They looked him up and down, judging every inch of him. Then she saw his sword and offered him a smile.

"Finally."

Words failed him. His throat felt dry.

She tilted her head and raised an eyebrow at him.

He coughed. "Yes, I am Darnuir."

"I can see that. Or at least that you've got a very good replica of the Dragon's Blade. Why don't you prove you're really its owner?"

"Prove it? How?"

"Your sword can create fire." She sat expectantly.

Darnuir's stomach sank. He would not soon forget Brackendon's staff tree.

"It isn't that simple," he said, folding his arms. "And, in any case, how do you know that?"

"Never simple, is it?" she said wistfully. "I've read about it. It's quite a famous sword, after all. And Chelos told me about it."

"Am I supposed to know who that is?"

Cassandra blinked, evidently confused. "He was your steward in Aurisha, wasn't he? He must have known you and your family for decades. You must remember him."

"He may well have been, but I have no memories of my past life."

"Past life?"

"Sounds mad, doesn't it? Were it not for the sword, I would never have believed it either." He had an idea. "You want proof? Watch this." He took out his sword and threw it as far as the weight and confines of the hut would allow. The Dragon's Blade bounced on the floor then whizzed back to his waiting hand. "How's that for proof?" He'd hoped he might have gotten another smile out of her, but she did not react at all.

"Yes, quite impressive." She tossed her head to remove the hair from her face. "It is still a sword, though? Can you please cut me out of these ropes?"

"They say I shouldn't trust you."

She huffed. "What's an unarmed girl supposed to do against the mighty Dragon King?" Perhaps she realised that such an approach would get her nowhere for she quickly changed her tone. "I don't like being trapped," she said much more softly, almost like a plea.

"You're not dressed for this weather," Darnuir said. "Those scraps of hunter leather you have on are from the Dales, right? Dark green and brown."

She nodded.

"Well, hunter armour or no, it won't be designed for the cold like ours. The quicker we finish here, the quicker I'll get you some of our own gear and more food."

"Great... more mealy oatcakes."

"Hey, they're pretty good... well... if they're not stale."

She laughed lightly "The ones I just had must have left stale behind weeks ago. Even Castallan treated me better!"

"Well, if it was so comfortable there then why would you leave?" He meant it to be playful, but her expression went cold again.

"Would you want to be a prisoner?"

"And were you?"

"Of course I was!"

All right, so this is a touchy topic.

"You know I have to ask the obvious. Why?"

Her features darkened further. "I don't know why, but I've been there my entire life. All twenty years of it. Who would do that to a person without explanation? It was like some form of torture."

Darnuir took a few careful steps towards her and crouched down. "Cassandra, right now, I'm probably your only friend here, and that is based on a gut reaction. Everyone else thinks you are some agent of Castallan's and that you are here to trick us, spy on us or perhaps worse. You say you have some information for us. Tell me. Tell me it all, and if I feel that you're genuine, I'll untie you."

"How about you untie me first?" She stared him down, as tightly wound as any stalking lynx. "I don't like being trapped."

His head was aching again. He winced and dearly wanted to leave; maybe plunge his head into the cold snow. Hoping to speed things up, he decided to release her. One last show of good faith. He used his hunting knife to cut her bonds.

When freed, she brought her hands together to tend her aching wrists. He cut her legs free as well and Cassandra visibly relaxed. The tension in her seemed to uncoil as she stretched out, but a second later she had wrapped herself up on the chair, bringing her knees up to rest her chin on in a guarded fashion.

"Thank you for finding me. Probably saved me. It was you, wasn't it?"

"Yes, though I had some help," Darnuir said. He found himself still crouched awkwardly below her, so he stood back up and retreated a suitable distance. "I'll accept for now that you do not know why you were Castallan's prisoner, but why then did you decide to come to us? Why now? Was it all about delivering this message Brackendon mentioned; of an invasion?"

"Was he the man with the silver eyes? He seemed kind, for a wizard."

"Try not to avoid answers. It will only take longer."

"Yes, I was to warn you about the invasion but there was also something else, about you. Castallan wants your sword. He told Zarl to capture you alive, if possible."

"Who is Zarl?"

"He commands Castallan's armies. He said he fought you at Cold Point. Do you remember fighting a man covered head to foot in red armour?"

The pounding pain in his head amplified, the feeling of something pressing against his mind returning in earnest as it had during the battle.

"I do," Darnuir said through gritted teeth. "What was with his eyes?"

"Castallan has been enchanting some of his followers. More and more, as he's practised the magic. You can't tell anything has changed until their eyes flash red. It's like they can just switch it on and off at will."

"How do you know all of this? Does Castallan tell you all about his plans and battles?"

"I've spied on Castallan my whole life. Well, when I can get away with it."

He gave her another look of incredulity.

She shrugged. "What? There is nothing else to do all day when you are imprisoned."

"All right, all right," Darnuir said, squeezing the bridge of his nose again, wondering why the head pain had to return right now. "So why does Castallan want my sword?"

"Are you feeling unwell?" she asked. "You could sit down?" She stood, offering him the chair.

"No. I'm fine," he said a little abrasively.

Damn it, what is causing this?

Thankfully, she didn't seem offended by his outburst. She just looked concerned. "Look, your sword is powerfully magical. Castallan said it would surpass even his whole collection of staffs. If he gets it, I can't imagine anyone will be powerful enough to stop him. Zarl is regrouping. His full force is gathering outside of the mountain range. If you don't walk into his hands, he'll come and take you by force. He'll bring you to Castallan and likely kill everyone else."

"Doesn't sound like we have many options," Darnuir said. "And you mentioned something about an invasion too? Although we should probably deal with one crisis at a time."

"There's some hope there, I think. A spectre lord called Dukoona told Castallan he wanted to use the Bastion as his seat as he made war on Brevia and Val'tarra. They aren't on good terms. Castallan is pouring his resources into finding you, meaning there's a chance to deal with him first before the main demon army arrives. Combined, they might be too much."

Darnuir squinted at her through the pain. Despite shivering from the cold, probably half-starved and fighting for her life, she was remarkably calm.

"Why put yourself in harm's way by coming to tell me all of this?"

"I did it for Chelos," Cassandra said. "It was the whole reason he finally helped me to get out. I wasn't going to break my promise to him. Besides, I didn't exactly have anywhere else to go."

"You really must have been desperate." His head finally overwhelmed him and he slumped back against the wall, sliding down until he sat upon the floor.

She contemplated him. "The great Darnuir. Chelos described you very differently."

"Should I be taller?"

"He said you were fearsome and a true dragon."

Darnuir's spirits lifted.

"But," she continued, "he also said you could be brazen, reckless and arrogant." She smiled at him all the same and he felt considerably better for it. She came to sit on the floor in front of him, lifting her knees, crossing her feet and wrapping her arms around herself. Her hair swept out behind her like a black cloak.

"It was very loyal of him to insist you come and warn me."

"You're his king. Apparently, that is enough for them. For dragons, I mean."

"If all dragons follow me so blindly, then that will be their downfall. My past self sounds like a far more capable king."

A particularly painful stab shot across his temple. He winced, sucking in his breath.

"Are you sure you're okay?"

"Yes…" he groaned. "I think my mind is just protesting all of this."

"It must be hard, to have so many people relying on you."

Darnuir nodded slowly, then met her eye. "One last question, okay?"

She nodded.

"How did you manage to escape?"

The silence that followed drew out to an uncomfortable length.

Why is she so reluctant to tell me this part of the tale? He held his tongue, though, allowing the silence to become unbearable, not giving her chance to avoid it. The others would ask this question. They'd never trust her if her story sounded false.

"I had some help from a... from a friend."

"So, what went wrong?" Darnuir said, pointing to her injury.

Cassandra became visibly tenser. She curled up into a tighter ball and dipped her head.

"Were you attacked?" Darnuir asked. "You and your friend? Did they make it?"

She shook her head so slightly it was almost imperceptible. "No, he didn't make it." Her voice was muffled beneath her knees and hair.

Darnuir thought it best to let the matter be. She had been forthright about everything else. If the others questioned him, he'd just try and put his foot down on the matter. He trusted her. That should be enough. In theory.

"Thank you for the warnings, but I should go. Everyone is waiting for my decision on our next move."

"Wait!" Cassandra said. She got to her feet, her face flushed, and it looked as though she'd been fighting back tears when curled up in that ball. She extended her hand.

She's offering to help me stand up?

Darnuir's mind swam in pain again, which temporarily blurred his vision. Scrunching his eyes in discomfort, he curiously took her hand. The ache in his head went out like a candle flame in the wind. Relieved, he got to his feet, beaming at her and feeling infinitely better.

"See?" she said. "No tricks. Do you trust me now?"

"I'm beginning to."

They were close to each other now.

'She is too close,' a guilty voice whispered in his head.

"I should go," he added hastily.

When he let go of her hand, the pain in his head returned, although this time dull and distant. Hopefully, it wouldn't build up again so quickly. If only he knew what had banished it there in the first place.

Exiting the hut, he ordered Ava and Mardin to fetch Cassandra more suitable clothing and extra food, as promised. He then made his way back towards the ruined tavern and found Cosmo and Scythe sat in deep discussion over a new map, one detailing the Boreac Mountains in depth.

Scythe frowned at him. "Well?"

"We make for Val'tarra," Darnuir ordered.

Scythe pressed his lips together but gave a gracious nod. "Very well. So be it. Come, Darnuir. Let us discuss our route out of the mountains."

Progress through the narrow passages was painfully slow. At times, the space was barely wide enough for three people to stand side by side. They had to leave such luxuries as carts behind them and carried everything on their backs. Poor Grace was forced to travel by foot too. Cosmo was with her every step of the way, his face sickened with worry.

Growls and roars echoed through the passages at times, reminding them that demons were not their only concern. More eagles flew overhead, but one always stayed much closer – a tawny eagle with white tips to its feathers.

Two days passed and the crisp air of the mountains began to thicken. It clung to the skin, uncomfortable and sticky. Ominous granite clouds gathered above and stretched to the horizon.

Darnuir walked once more at the head of the column and was one of the first to glimpse the Cairlav Marshes. Garon had found a vantage point and Darnuir joined him. A vast wetland lay before them, dotted with specks of precarious, water-seeped land and tall reeds. The sky was grey, the pools were muddied, yet fauna in reds and startling pinks coloured an otherwise bleak landscape.

"There will be no blending in here in our white leathers," Darnuir said.

"It will make it easier for friends to find us as well as foes," Garon added optimistically.

Brackendon struggled up beside them, a little out of breath, as did Scythe, who wrinkled his nose at the distasteful smell upon the air.

The eagle joined them as well. It swooped silently down nearby, having nowhere high to land.

"This will be hard terrain to cover," Scythe said. "My only comfort is that it will be just as hard to move a horde of demons across it with any speed."

"With any luck, it will take time for them to even realise where we've gone," Garon said. "We ought to send our fastest men forward to try and make contact with the Cairlav Hunters."

"Agreed," Darnuir said.

Scythe nodded. "We should rest as soon as we find suitable ground to do so. It has been an onerous trip already."

The eagle flapped its wings and protested with a loud squawk. Scythe unslung his bow.

"Is this your winged friend, Darnuir? I've noticed it has been dogging our trail. Perhaps it would be best if we get rid of it. Having it flying over us will only give away our position."

He drew an arrow back.

"Stop," cried Brackendon, moving between Scythe and the bird. Darnuir placed a hand upon Scythe's bow and pushed it down, to the captain's great frustration.

"What is the meaning of this?" he demanded.

"Kymethra," Brackendon said softly to the eagle, turning to face it. "I think you ought to just reveal yourself."

The eagle snapped its beak and cocked its head, peering around at the group of men. Then, to Darnuir's astonishment, it began to grow. It grew larger and its frame distorted; its wings morphed into arms and the talons into feet. A short, slender woman now stood in the eagle's place, with white-tipped tawny hair that flicked upwards at the ends. Her pale green robes resembled Brackendon's own, though tied in at the waist to accentuate her figure. She smirked at Brackendon and there was a glint of mischief in her silver eyes.

"Do you prefer me like this, Brackers?"

Scythe's face was livid at this fresh, unannounced arrival. Garon was quietly laughing to himself. Brackendon's face turned pink.

Is he blushing? The thought made Darnuir snigger as well.

"Kymethra, you almost got yourself killed," Brackendon said. "How did you even find me?"

"Did you think you could slip away so easily?" Kymethra chided him. "Not even a hint at where you were going. But vanishing seemingly without anyone seeing you go made it rather obvious, Brackers."

"I was not aware there were witches left since the Conclave fell," Scythe said.

"Took me days and days to fly all the way here," Kymethra continued, as if she had not heard Scythe. "And the things I saw... well, they were quite interesting. Men marching this way and that in golden armour; that poor bleeding girl who was dragging herself along as if half-possessed." She took in the whole group, moving close to each of them in turn. When she came to Darnuir, she paused. "This is him, then? This is who you left me for?"

Brackendon looked at her imploringly. "What else have you seen? Why did you squawk at Scythe's suggestion of camp?"

"The demons are on the move," Kymethra said. "They are making their way westwards towards the marshes already."

"How is that possible?" Darnuir said, his heart sinking. "How could they have known of our movements?"

"Perhaps Cassandra was not so worthy of our trust after all?" Scythe said.

"There have been some spectres roaming the mountains," Kymethra said. "Men with red eyes as well. Some in armour, others in hunter gear. Might be they came across an empty Farlen and worked it out."

"Might be we have a traitor as well," Garon said. "Or maybe you tipped them off." His hand still lay on his sword hilt.

Kymethra shot him a dark look. "Might be, or maybe the men in Castallan's service are not fools."

A general argument ensued. Darnuir's throbbing head pain began to dangerously escalate once more. He felt heat ripple from the Dragon's Blade and he feared it would catch fire again. He wanted this resolved so he could leave them. Maybe then he could go bite down on a stick and scream the pain away.

"Stop it!"

All those that were gathered froze and looked at him. "Kymethra, how long do we have until Castallan's army reaches the marshes?"

"Little over a day, I reckon. I'll keep an eye on them but they are moving quickly. You're nearly halfway through the marshes already from here. If you keep moving, you might stay ahead of them."

"Then we should continue on," Darnuir said. "We can't risk stopping for long."

"The people are exhausted," Garon said. "Cosmo won't thank you either."

The pounding in Darnuir's head overcame him.

"Cursed humans, always dragging me down," he found himself saying.

No, no! What am I saying?

A whistling wind through the reeds cut through the silence.

Darnuir opened his mouth to apologise but quickly closed it. He didn't trust himself. He could barely think through this pain.

"Well... I'll leave you boys to it," Kymethra said, throwing Darnuir an uneasy glance. "Do what he says, though. You need to keep moving." She morphed into her eagle form and took off to the east.

Watching her go, Darnuir suddenly regained full control of his mind. It was the most peculiar sensation, as if he was being thrown against the side of his own being. The pain vanished and he gasped, drawing in shallow breaths as though winded.

"What is happening to me?"

None could answer him.

"To the swamps, then," Scythe said, clenching his fist in an attempt to bolster their spirits. It didn't work.

Darnuir trailed behind the others, feeling afraid and ashamed as the fleeing inhabitants of the Boreac Mountains descended into the marshes.

16

THE SHADOW OF AURISHA

Dukoona – Aurisha – The Royal Tower

Within the war room, the lord of the spectres lounged upon what had been the king's chair, while his feet rested upon the crescent moon table. Pensively, he envisioned his enemies – well, his master's enemies – gathered here in their last desperate hour.

He glanced up to the carved dragon in bestial form, taking in its roaring snout, the enmity somehow etched into its eyes. It looked down upon him.

Dukoona smirked. If the dragon was real, then those wings would cast very large shadows. Melding into those shadows to avoid that danger would be easy. Perhaps his master had this in mind when summoning the spectres here.

The chair beside him, that of the guardian, did not grant the same ease of mind. A scorched severed sun pierced by a sword. Three elongated rays emanated from the weapon's tip. This was light. Should this guardian ever arise, Dukoona was uncertain how his kind might fight him. If their shadows were banished, so too was their power.

Rectar, his master and jailer, did not seem concerned by this. Dukoona, in turn, tried to cast it from his mind.

In summoning him to this world, Rectar had bound Dukoona to him. So long as his master remained in Tenalp, Dukoona would as well. Unless, of course, he got himself killed, but he would not need to take such drastic steps. At least, that was what he hoped.

Dukoona's memories of a time before he was summoned were jarred and fleeting. He sometimes saw flashes, perhaps another world, perhaps his world. There was an ocean and green fields but the mountains were strange. They were red and cracked like dried clay, and as he peered up to their peaks, the sky would change in an instant from day to starless night. Fire reigned from somewhere in the night and a green light blinded him.

That was it. Everything else he knew came from after this summoning. It wasn't much, but he knew it meant one sure thing.

He was not supposed to be here.

A long shadow stretched across the war table now, for the sun's rays were blocked by the columns of the balcony. Dukoona lazily lifted a dark finger and pressed down into the shadow before him. Immediately, he felt his body fuse with it, and he raced along it. His short trip ended at the base of the column, and he emerged in one fluid motion, reforming his body, and stepped onto the balcony.

The view north looked towards his master's distant dwelling in the mountain of Kar'drun. *Out of sight, but I'd rather be further away.*

At least this far away, his master's touch had become light and fleeting. Yet it would be foolish to assume it was gone completely. Indeed, Rectar had recently given instructions for the fleet to be made ready. Fresh ships were to be built and every demon crammed on every vessel.

Some of this construction was occurring in the long-abandoned docks of the Forsaken City, to the east of Kar'drun. Yet the bulk of the work was taking place here in Aurisha, under Dukoona's watchful eye.

It was time he inspected the work.

Puffy clouds whisked by, casting fast-moving shadows over the city. Dukoona waited for one of these to pass close to the ground underneath the balcony. Closer and closer and closer, until he jumped.

Diving from the tower, he merged into the shadow on the ground far below him. Had he missed the shadow, he would have splattered onto the hard stone. A risky business, but it was one of the few thrills he was allowed.

As the cloud's shadow crossed the plaza, Dukoona stayed in his shadow form and let it carry him. When he neared the southern switchback road, his excitement grew. There were so many dark corners between the buildings on the southern slope, so many places where the sun would not reach.

He leapt from the cloud shadow into the larger one cast by the Basilica's dome. He jumped from darkness to darkness all the way down the switchback road, reforming and re-melding with each transition. Gleefully, he descended until he was dockside.

Rectar had imbued him with much knowledge of this world. For instance, he knew that the dragons used to fly, back when they looked like the creature carved above the king's chair. He wondered if true flight was as exhilarating as shadow leaping. Actual flight would be more useful, of course, and would mean he could travel over oceans as well. Spectres could not meld into a shadow over water. Attempting it would bring them back into their regular form, to swim in the water like any other creature.

A pity. If only they could do so, Dukoona could take his spectres and travel swiftly west, negating the need for these cumbersome ships. Yet their lesser demon brethren could not shadow meld, and the land passages north had proven impossible to traverse without incurring heavy losses. So, ships it would be.

Rectar had amassed so many demons that it would take years to build an effective fleet. Dukoona had been given a few months at best. To make matters worse, fresh demons swarmed from Kar'drun daily, something his master had not done in over twenty years.

Fifty fat galleys currently sat moored in the harbour of Aurisha in front of him, and others were anchored out at sea. They had been modified from dragon designs to cram in as many demons as possible. The dragons had kindly left behind schematics for such things when they fled the city.

Dukoona had no need to enforce discipline in his workers. The demons scurried over the ships like black ants, hammering, sawing, and lashing rope. Spectres walked among them, barking orders here or there, but largely, the demons went about their tasks without trouble. Their master had complete dominance over their weak minds. Yet obedience did not equate to competence.

Often, there were setbacks, despite the vigilance of his spectres. Dukoona considered it a blessing, really, that they had to take their time about it. Each day that passed was another chance for the wizard and the Three Races to bloody each other.

Let them weaken themselves. Less of my people will die if more of my enemies are dead. And yet, that word troubled him. Enemies. They were, ultimately, his master's enemies.

Who is my enemy?

He had asked this question decades ago, and his master had burned it into his thoughts: enemies are humans, fairies and any dragons who would defend them. With humans and fairies, Dukoona was to kill on sight; with dragons, he was to capture. For years, he had fulfilled this purpose. He and his spectres would emerge from the shadows quietly and take captives. But dragons were quick and strong, and taking them always involved the deaths of some of his brothers. When battles ensued, he'd been forced to kill dragons as well.

His master had not liked this. Dukoona had suffered for it. Yet those moments of rebellion had been so glorious; those moments when he had simply cut down dragons and deprived Rectar of the thing he wanted most. Nothing seemed to frustrate Rectar more.

Despite his efforts, however, some dragon prisoners were always captured alive to be sent to the mountain. What happened once they got there, Dukoona did not know. Any time it seemed that one of his spectres was close to the answer, they would vanish. And he counted them as a tragic loss.

He was smarter now and wiser in handling his master. Preventing Rectar from securing his spoils of war had been a long and tedious line of mutiny; satisfying in its own way, to be sure, but the victories were always small. Inconsequential. He had hoped that the wizard might prove a useful ally in countering Rectar's strength, but Castallan had proven unreliable. He seemed hell-bent on fighting dragons as well, in his own way. Yet, for some time now, Dukoona had decided that dragon slaying was not a productive means of resistance.

This realisation had first struck twenty years ago when he marched into Aurisha after the conquest. After thousands of prisoners had been taken by his spectres, Dukoona had been unsure of what to do. Hand them over to his master or kill them all? In the end, he had sent one in five to Kar'drun and had his men dispose of the rest.

He had never felt sympathy for his supposed enemies, but something about that day haunted him. The killings had occurred in the plaza and the blood had flowed in torrents down the southern stairs. For the first time in his existence, he had found that he could not look on.

The age of the prisoners had not mattered, nor had their sex. They would gather spectres and skewer them, given the chance. This is what he had told himself. This is what he had told his spectres. And yet, as the slaughter had unfolded, he heard the clanking of metal on stone. Spectres had thrown down their arms.

Normally, he would have disciplined them, but when they were hauled before him, he found himself lost for words. They never said anything in their defence. They had simply ceased following orders. In that, Dukoona recognised the same defiance as he gave to his master and found he could not reprimand them.

The sight of the corpses had not moved Dukoona to tears – for he could not cry. He could not feel much at all. He never felt hunger or sickness. His shadows were not like true flesh. Yet the memory of that massacre often drifted into his thoughts. It had made him feel... something. Unease? Discomfort? Foreboding? He had considered them all.

Doubt. He had felt doubt.

At first, he thought this was due to fear of his master discovering his actions.

But I do not fear my master. There is nothing more he can take from me.

If Rectar were to kill him in some fit of fury, then that would be a welcome release. So, no, it was not out of fear; yet he still felt it, that terrible doubt. And as the blood flowed and the dragons' flesh began to rot under the Aurishan sun, all his spectres had gathered on the plateau. One by one, they came to look upon their work and to him. They had added their own dead to the pile, then set it all ablaze in the most gruesome fire that ever burned in the world.

The plaza was charred red and black to this day. Seeing that blaze, Dukoona had thought the whole world might burn before this was over, including himself and his people along with it.

And he could not allow his people to suffer anymore.

All these memories returned to him as he contemplated the upcoming invasion of the west. Their numbers were immense. They would root out the Lord of the Isles and storm his seat upon the Nail Head. They would break the walls of Brevia and burn Val'tarra down.

And then what? What happens when Rectar controls the world and has no more need for spectres or their lord?

He felt it again as he strode along the harbourside of his supposed enemy's greatest city. Doubt clawed at him.

17

LIFE FOR LIFE

Darnuir – The Cairlav Marshes

Grace's screams ripped through the night. She had collapsed a day into their forced march across the swampy terrain, and so they had been forced to stop and make camp. Had Cosmo and Darnuir not been close by her at the time, she might have been swallowed up by one of the foul pools of water.

The healers were by her side, along with Cosmo, inside the larger captain's tent. Scythe had not begrudged their use of it.

Darnuir paced anxiously outside. There was nothing he could do. His skill was in swords and war and he barely understood his own new weapon. He had relied on the old methods to light their campfire; the very thought of calling on flames from the blade was too alarming to contemplate.

The campfire crackled now, keeping the worst of the damp and the midges at bay. Foul creatures they were, feasting on the refugees and their misery.

Frustrated, he ceased pacing and resigned himself to taking a seat on the soggy ground. Brackendon joined him, looking dejected as ever. Without his staff, he was just another man. Darnuir had heard the wizard curse beneath his breath as Grace was taken under canvas.

"I could ease her pain, I could... I..." he had mumbled. But he could do nothing to help and Darnuir sensed this struck a hard blow to him.

Another agonised scream came from the tent.

"Bite down on this!" a voice commanded. The next shriek was muffled but none-theless upsetting to hear.

Another cry hit Darnuir's ears, but this time it came from above him. An eagle swooped down in a flurry of wings and feathers, its body undulating before Kymethra landed in her human form.

"What is going on? I could hear that from a mile away. If the demons didn't know where you were—"

"She's giving birth!" Brackendon said.

Kymethra didn't miss a beat. "Not well. I'll go in." She rolled up the sleeves of her robes and strode into the tent.

Darnuir's hope must have shown on his face.

"I'm sorry. She cannot help in the way that I might have," Brackendon said. "Kymethra was never truly part of the Conclave. She did not complete her appren-ticeship. Nor does she possess a staff. Without one, her powers are limited."

Darnuir was crushed. "But I don't understand. She can use magic. How else can she turn into an animal?"

"Kymethra has an affinity with shape-shifting," Brackendon explained. "Had she the proper training and a staff, she might have been able to transform into some truly fearsome creatures. Leaving all that aside, drawing on Cascade energy to heal takes a lot of energy."

"Well, what can she do, then?" he asked, hearing his voice crack.

"She can trick Grace's mind into thinking the pain isn't there. It doesn't require much power, so she can keep it up for some time. It won't help Grace physically, but it may help her through the night."

Kymethra's soothing magic must have taken effect, for Grace quietened.

"She must be skilled at that spell," Darnuir said.

"She had a lot of time to practice when I was broken."

Darnuir wasn't sure what to say to that. He wasn't sure what to do about any of this. All he could think about was Grace's reddened, pained face as they carried her into the tent.

"It's my fault," he said. "All of this is happening because of me. If Grace—"

"You can't think like that," Brackendon implored. "No good can come of it."

Darnuir slumped further where he sat and ran his hands repeatedly through his hair.

"Were we ever in worse situations before, Brackendon? You and I? What adven-tures did the Prince of Dragons and his wizard friend have?"

Brackendon chuckled. "We weren't friends, Darnuir, not truly. Friendship requires a mutual liking and trust, does it not?"

Darnuir's thoughts turned to Balack. Trust; well, he had broken that.

"Did I not like you?"

Brackendon brought his fingers together. "I'm not sure you liked anyone, but I didn't know you well. You were always guarded, and you carried your anger openly."

Darnuir had felt that anger flare in him lately – sudden fleeting pangs of frustration and rage – yet they did not feel like his own. He had felt it recently when their march had halted for Grace. *'Slowed down by a human whelp,'* he had thought. Yet he had not meant to think it. The prodding pain returned to taunt his mind and made his eyes water.

"I might be going mad," Darnuir said, and he sniffed heavily. "Ever since I've had the sword, I fear I have not been myself."

"The blade is beyond my knowledge. Kasselle may know more."

Another wail from the tent sent them into minutes of solemn silence. The wind picked up, whistling through the long grass. Whether hours or only minutes passed on that patch of dank earth, Darnuir didn't know.

His quiet contemplation was interrupted by the arrival of Balack, who took up a patch of ground beside him without a word. Darnuir made to say something but the words stuck in his throat; however, the look that passed between them said much more. They took each other by the shoulder. Balack gave a pained wince.

"Sorry!" Darnuir exclaimed.

Balack massaged his shoulder. "You must be getting stronger, then."

"It seems so," Darnuir said, unsure of how to strike up further conversation with Balack after their weeks of silence.

"Dreadful weather, this," Balack said.

"The worst."

Silence descended again, awkward and all-encompassing.

"I don't think I can lose Grace too," Balack finally blurted. "Not after Eve."

"I know. I miss her too; I miss her so much it aches."

"I never thought anything could hurt like this. But I know, Darnuir. I know it was you she really loved."

Darnuir's insides churned furiously.

Does he know what happened? How could he know?

"I know it was you she really loved," Balack repeated, more to himself. "I just thought... I just thought that she would change her mind. I wasn't so blind. I could see it plainly every day, but I chose not to 'really' see it. Does that make sense?"

"Sort of," Darnuir said nervously, his innards still knotted. "Balack, if you knew that then why did you—"

"Delude myself? Can't explain it. I think I agonised over telling her for so long because I knew. And I knew that as soon as I told her then she would tell me no and it would have been over. All of it would have ended with a few words." He choked. "Did you know?" he managed to ask, his words thickened by heartbreak. "You must have. Is that why you were always trying to push me to say something? To do the right thing?"

The right thing... What would that be here? I cannot tell him...

"I did know," Darnuir said. It was not the whole truth. Not the whole and terrible truth, but it was true. This small piece was easy to give him. He hadn't known for a fact until that fateful night, but he had long suspected it. Like Balack, he had seen it plainly but had chosen not to 'really' see. Perhaps they were both cowards. Yet listening to Balack confess his darkest despairs, Darnuir knew that he was the real coward between them.

"I thought so," Balack said in a fierce, prideful whisper. "You knew and still you always supported me. You were always my friend first." He took Darnuir firmly by the shoulder once more. "You are a good friend, whereas I have not been of late. I have shut myself away when your whole world has been overturned, but I will be with you now. Forgive me?"

It was almost a plea.

Forgive me? He asks for my forgiveness? I should be the one begging.

This was cruel.

"You owe me no apology. Not ever."

"Thank you. I knew you would understand," Balack said. "When we find the chance, I'd like to show you the new archery technique I have been working on."

"I'd like that very much."

More wailing came from the tent, but it was not Grace's cries, nor any adult's. The bawling baby had been brought into the world.

Darnuir looked up expectantly, hopefully; but then he heard another cry. This one was not of a child, nor a woman. It was protracted, guttural and deep, as if heralding that time and everything in it had ceased. Cosmo's anguish drew the attention of those both far and near. Every creature in the marshes must have heard his cry and felt stricken by it.

Kymethra burst from the tent. Blood covered her hands and robes. She looked out to them, horrified, and could only shake her head.

"I'm sorry," was all she could mouth before returning.

Brackendon's face was desolate. Balack sat frozen. Darnuir felt as though his sorrow might consume him.

The demons are hunting me. This wasn't her journey to make.

His sorrow receded as the thrum of the headache grew. He didn't have the strength left to fight it this time. He allowed the second presence within him free rein again, as he had during the battle.

And then he felt nothing at all.

Why should I care? It was just some human.

18

BOGGED DOWN

Darnuir – The Cairlav Marshes

Days passed, but it was hard to keep count. Grey days ended in dark nights in the marshes, as the stars were unable to penetrate the gloom.

The demons, the host, still pursued them. They could not stop.

Darnuir slapped at his face in a futile effort to fend off midges. They would gather in black clouds over likely victims, anticipating when someone would pause for rest, then descend.

His mountain leathers, designed for icy winds, clung horribly to him here in the muggy, sticky air, and he frequently found himself drenched in water. If not water from the heavens, then the many pools around them, which did an equally good job. Placing one foot in the wrong place could lead to you sinking waist-deep into a murky bath. Fever had even found a foothold in some of their weakest: namely the elderly and the children.

To cap it all, Grace's death loomed overhead, darker, heavier and more foreboding than those granite-grey clouds.

Cosmo was a broken man. His newborn son lay cradled in a sleeve of cloth at his chest, though he had yet to give the child a name. Every time he looked at the baby boy, fresh tears flowed down his cheeks. Whatever energy had galvanised him and kept him fit, even into the middle years of his life, seemed now extinguished. He ate little and spoke less.

Darnuir found himself walking back through the lines of grim-faced exiles, searching for Cassandra out of instinct. His head pounded as ever but being with her seemed to calm it. He also wanted the company of someone who had not known Grace and did not know Cosmo, for that topic dominated discussion elsewhere.

He found her near the middle of the refugee train, her hands cuffed roughly with rope and her expression forlorn. She now wore a spare set of white leathers. Her jailers were with her – Mardin in front and Ava behind.

"Sir—" Mardin began dutifully but Darnuir waved him off.

"Let her go."

"But Darnuir, I mean, sir," Ava protested, "the captain told us we were not to let her out of sight."

"I believe I outrank Captain Scythe now." He dearly hoped no one would run to Scythe to double-check. "She doesn't like to be trapped," he added, looking to Cassandra for a response. She gave him a weak smile in return.

The two hunters exchanged nervous looks but quietly complied. Ava pulled her skinning knife from her belt and cut the bonds.

"We should stay close," Mardin insisted. "Captain Scythe—"

"Did you see me at Cold Point?"

"Yes, Darnuir, I mean, sir—" Ava began.

"Then you'll agree that I can handle myself?"

They nodded.

"If it helps your conscience any, the demons have been tracking us whilst she has been under your care. She cannot be feeding information to them."

The logic appeared to win out.

"Come," he said to Cassandra. She walked with him until they were almost back to the head of the column. Her silence troubled him.

"You're quiet."

"Hmmm," was all she said. They continued on. Every so often, he took her hand to help her ford a pool or patch of slimy earth. Each time, the background pain in his head dissipated. She was hesitant to accept his help, but took it all the same.

"That was…" she said eventually, searching for the correct word, "kingly; the way you bossed them around."

"Bossed them around?" he said, abashed. "Isn't that what I am supposed to do?"

"Yes, I suppose," she agreed, though it did not sound like it. "It was just surprising. You didn't seem that way when we first met. But then, I didn't see you around anyone else."

"I'm sorry you feel that way." He could tell she was still not pleased with the situation. "Has it upset you?"

"Upset me?" she said with a laugh. "If you think that would upset me then your mountain girls must be made of snow rather than rock."

Darnuir was rankled at the jibe. "Well, good," he said, not knowing what else to say.

"Who said I wanted to walk with you?" she asked.

Darnuir was crestfallen.

"No one. I just thought—"

"Thought I'd obviously want to be with you just because you 'saved' me from those two," she said, aiming a sweeping kick at an approaching puddle. The splash soaked his already damp feet.

"I only thought you might want your freedom," he said, in as steady a tone as he could.

What is happening here?

"Am I free?" she asked. "The first thing you do after cutting me loose is tell me to 'come with you'."

"I meant it as a request, but as it seems I have forced you here against your will, go!" His head pounded worse than ever and the rubies on the Dragon's Blade flared angrily at him.

"No!" She stopped to face him. Passersby started to take an interest in the pair. "No, I don't want to leave. I just, I just..." She trailed off as her face reddened. "Would you really just let me walk away?"

"I'd rather you didn't leave, Cassandra. But yes, if you want to, you may do so." He felt thoroughly confused and put out. All he'd wanted was to escape the misery around him and his own aching head for a moment. Was that too much to ask for?

"But don't go," he added.

She shuffled her feet, bit her lip and stared at a point somewhere past his shoulder. "I want to help, you know. Help fight Castallan, I mean. I don't think I will ever feel free until he's dead."

She strode off and Darnuir was forced to jog to catch up with her.

"We could always use an extra sword," he said. "If you know how to use one?"

"I was trained by a dragon," she stated, as though this was enough.

"Chelos?" Darnuir said, recalling the name.

"He taught me when we could risk it. Sometimes, I would accidentally cut some cushion or the curtains, and that was always harder to cover up." She sniggered at some fond memory.

"Isn't he an old dragon?"

"Still better than any human, I should think."

Darnuir shrugged. "I wouldn't know."

She stopped again, looking serious. "Chelos is still trapped in the Bastion and probably paying for my escape. I owe him."

"We'll rescue him when we storm the Bastion."

Cassandra laughed again. "Are all dragons so sure of themselves?" She swept her arms across the boggy landscape and at the drab scene of their fellow refugees. "You think you will take the Bastion soon, do you?"

"I'm just trying to be optimistic," he said, though he felt deflated in truth. "I think that's the only way we can think now, especially after last night."

The cries of the baby, Cosmo's howls, and the blood on Kymethra's hands filled his mind.

Cassandra softened. "I heard about what happened. I'm sorry."

"I fear it will only get worse before the end."

"What happened to being optimistic?" she chided.

He laughed. "I think it got lost in the bogs. Like we are."

"Dragons don't fare well here," Cassandra said.

Darnuir had an inkling as to what she was referring to. The Battle of the Bogs had been the final conflict of the Second War between dragons and humanity. It had been where Dronithir had led the humans in a stunning victory and secured a peace. Every human child was told that story.

But I am a dragon.

"So long as no hunters start shooting at me from the grass, I ought to make it," Darnuir said.

They continued until the clouds broke apart and the setting sun appeared in streaks of pink and orange. Perhaps optimism would win out after all. Smells of fish and salt mingled with the damp of the marsh, and the gentle sound of rolling water could be heard against a stony shore.

They had come within sight of Loch Minian.

Log buildings dotted the shoreline and even out onto the water itself. Large roundhouses sat above the water's surface on great wooden beams, as though they had sprouted up from the bottom of the loch.

Yet there wasn't a soul in sight. The scene was deserted, although the inhabitants had not long departed. Barrels of freshly caught fish lay upturned, their scaly contents littering the pebbles at the water's edge.

"Halt!" The voice's owner and direction remained a mystery. "Nae further for now."

It was Scythe who answered the threat. "Has the damp of the marsh drowned your eyes? Can't you see our leathers?"

No response came for perhaps half a minute and then, out of the long grass and fauna, men and women appeared, garbed in hardened leathers of muddy reds and greens. The man at their head was short and stocky, with a strong jaw and a thick neck.

"Aye, Scythe," the man said, "we saw them. But it's unusual for so many of our Boreac brothers tae pay us a visit at once."

"Captain Edwin," Scythe sneered, "had you not considered that we are on the run?"

"Slowest run I've ever seen," Edwin said. "Forgive us, but we had tae be sure you were not here on ill purpose. The last few weeks have been anarchy. Some of our own ranks, who we thought tae be friends, turned on us or made off east. Their eyes glowed red, Scythe. Never seen anything like it."

Cassandra and Darnuir exchanged knowing looks before he addressed Edwin himself.

"We don't have much time. The demons hunt us. Or, more precisely, they hunt me."

Edwin turned his sharp eyes upon him, frowning. "Do they, lad? Ye ought tae run tae them, then. You might save a lot of lives."

"Careful, Edwin," Scythe warned. "This is Darnuir, the King of Dragons. He might open his jaws and bathe you in flames."

"Ha!" barked Edwin. His eyes found the Dragon's Blade. "Aye, he has a pretty enough looking sword to be sure. Scythe, you bastard, you better not be have'n me on."

"Am I known for lies?"

"No. You've always been a straight shot. Barely even raise yer voice, do you?" The two embraced briefly. "You look thinner though; didnae think that wis possible."

"We are all half-starved," Garon said. He had been accompanying Scythe at the head of the column. "The civilians even more so. Can you help feed them?"

"Not want a fish for yer'self?" Edwin asked.

"I can do without, if need be," Garon said. "Though if you know how to ward these little black horrors away, I'll be eternally grateful."

"How noble," said Edwin. "Aye, we'll find you some food, but not here. We've been pulling everyone oot west fae weeks. Those crannogs," he said, pointing towards the large roundhouses out on the loch, "they're good tae hide in when the tide is high. Thing is, the tide retreats from the shore, but demons won't. As for the midges, you'll be wanting this." Edwin moved to a low-growing plant, which seemed to sprout tiny green acorns. "Bog-myrtle will dae the trick. Crush it up and rub a bit on yer skin."

All present rushed for the hard-looking plant, except Scythe, who seemed impatient. "What news from the rest of the kingdom? What is Arkus doing?"

Edwin gritted his teeth. "We know little, I'm afraid. Cannae send messages east because of the demons, and most of the ships that sailed north havenae returned. What we do hear makes it sound like chaos. Towns and villages lying half-empty. Streams of people fleeing tae the capital, others making for the forest, though whether the fairies let them in is another question. And now we've had reports of a sizeable force moving south through the Golden Crescent."

"Who are they?" asked Scythe.

"Word is they are wearing golden plate mail. If I didnae know better, I'd say it were dragons." Edwin gave Darnuir a wry smile. "Don't suppose ye would know anything about that, lad?"

"Does it look like I am in a position to know?" Darnuir said, with more bite in his voice than was customary.

"Ha!" Edwin barked again. "Is that all the fire ye have in yer belly? You'll need tae work up more than that to tame your lot." He shook his head, turning back to Scythe. "Total bloody chaos, like I said." The Cairlav captain sighed before turning and whistling to his people. Two huntresses stepped forward at this summons. "These two will take you and yours to Torridon. Follow the shore west and they will take you the safest way through the rest of the marshes. There, you can find some food and respite."

"You aren't coming with us?" Garon asked.

"We're waiting for patrols to return from the east with word of the demons. We'll follow soon enough."

"Thank you, Edwin," Scythe said. "Some rest will do us all good."

"Aye, that it will. Go on, now. We'll speak later." Edwin gave Darnuir a good look as if sizing him up, then he and his hunters dispersed into the tall grass.

19

THE GOLDEN ONE

Blaine – The Golden Crescent

Blaine, Guardian of Tenalp, arose at dawn's light. The sky was clear, the sun's virtuous rays unimpeded. A good omen. His tent lay near the heart of the Via Primacy, which cut the army camp from north to south. Running east to west through the camp was the second central road, the Via Secundi. These roads derived their meaning from where the king and his heir would respectively place their tents within the camp.

Soon, we will have our king once more.

Blaine had sent out the call and, thus far, six thousand dragons had answered; two legions' worth. Such was the prowess and efficiency of the dragon military that time did not erode their memory of how things were done. Every camp was set up in the same fashion, so far as was possible, and it mattered not that these men were likely to be a mixture of different former legions.

Even now, beside Blaine's own quarters, a tent had been erected for a king that was not there. After twenty years, his kind would welcome their monarch's return. It had been even longer since Blaine had gone to war.

Too long. I hid from the world for too long.

Having checked that there was sufficient activity about the camp, he returned inside his tent to prepare himself for the day ahead. The trappings were comfortable but simple. A stand of armour stood adjacent to a large basin-and-mirror combo resting atop a wooden pedestal. He caught his reflection in the mirror and nodded in satisfaction.

Tall and broad-shouldered, he'd maintained a torso of flawless definition even while in exile. Impressive for a one-hundred-and-fifty-year-old dragon.

I must be an example. I must appear perfect.

His hair was thick and well groomed. It was the sort of dark blond that resembled gold, especially when caught in the sunlight. His eyes too had a golden tinge to them, for flecks of amber streaked across his blue irises. And always, without exception, he was clean-shaven.

Two younger dragon boys entered the tent on schedule, carrying a steaming jug of water. They silently poured the contents into the basin, bowed in reverence to him, and quietly left.

Blaine took up the brush of fine boar hair and dipped it first into the water and then into the small bowl of paste, which he mixed to a foamy consistency before applying to his face. He carefully cleaned and replaced the brush before choosing from amongst his razors. He had a choice of three, neatly arranged by himself the night before. Despite having this choice, he always chose the same one: a blade of sharpened silver with a blue pearl handle he had received as a gift from Kasselle. Picking it up fondly, he set about his task.

There was one final ritual he had to perform before beginning his day. Throwing on a loose shirt of linen, he exited his tent and made towards the centre of the camp, at the intersection of the two roads. Here was the most important part of the camp for Blaine. It was here that dragons on campaign could practice the Way of Light and pay reverence to the gods, as it had been ever since the time of the First Flight many millennia ago.

It is hardly the Basilica of Aurisha, but it will suffice.

Blaine entered the tent and found it empty, bar three dutiful souls.

This is unacceptable. What have the years we've spent amongst humans done to our conviction?

There were not even the proper cushions laid out to kneel upon. A tattered-looking banner bearing the symbol of the faith – the severed sun pierced by a sword – was the only sign that this was the correct tent. There was at least a dais where he might give a sermon, though he would have preferred marble to wood.

The scene was crushingly disappointing to him. Such conditions were unfit for the divines. He had hoped that more of the men would come as the days passed and word of his return grew. It was not as if the gods of light demanded much of them; merely contemplation at dawn, noon and dusk would suffice, if one had little time.

"Thank you, friends," he said to those present and made his way towards the dais. He took hold of it with both hands. A few more worshippers trickled in until there was perhaps a score of men on their knees before him.

Better, but still unacceptable.

"My friends, each day brings a new dawn, and each dawn drives off the darkness. The light of this morn is clear and bright, meaning Dwna blesses us."

"Dwna shines upon us," the congregation chanted.

"Soon, we shall bring our king back into the fold. May his will be strong and his faith stronger."

Blaine suspected that the king would have no comprehension of the faith, having grown up with humans, though his story was one of great significance.

"Our lord king, Darnuir, had his life renewed so that he may live to lead us against the shadow. For his renewal, I thank N'weer."

"N'weer revitalises our strength," the crowd murmured.

Whether drawn by the chanting or merely late, more men entered the tent to join the flock.

Blaine smiled. "Like our Lord Dwl'or, we are now half-blinded by the shadow. The east of our world lies in darkness, but our journey to lift that shadow begins here."

Yet this time, there was no response from his audience where Dwl'or was concerned.

Have they forgotten the words? How could Draconess let things slip so far?

Given time, he would rebuild the faith. There was also the matter of restoring his order to some semblance of its past strength. And for that, he would need capable warriors.

"Of those gathered here today, were any among you members of the Praetorian Guard? Rise if so." To his delight, every member of his small congregation got to their feet.

Ah, Draconess. You did not completely fail, then.

"I am moved by your conviction, friends. But the Gods of Light require us to be active as well as devout. Henceforth, I would have you all as the first members of my newly-resurrected Light Bearers."

They nodded solemnly. Many bowed their heads.

"Very well. Please leave your names in my quarters."

"My Lord Guardian," one of the closest dragons said, "where have you been all these years? Why has the shadow been allowed to spread?"

Blaine did not know the answer himself.

Because I failed and I was afraid? Would telling the truth kill what little spark remains in them?

"Those are questions to which you all deserve answers. Yet unfortunately, a deserving explanation will take time, and we are pressed in our current state." Blaine felt a quick display of the light might help bolster the men's belief. Why ask someone to believe blindly when they could see it with their own eyes? He drew the Guardian's Blade from his side, a brother to the Dragon's Blade.

The body of the sword was constructed from the same material as its sibling. Its hilt, however, was very different and cast in the symbol of his order with half of the severed sun at the pommel and the other at the cross-guard. Yellow and orange rays extended downwards as a cross-guard. White gems adorned the grip of the sword, sparkling brilliantly in the smallest amount of light.

The very sight of the sword drew gasps from his audience.

Blaine opened the door in his mind, leaving it ajar, so a drop of the Cascade entered his body. He directed the power through the blade, producing a beam of pale light from it. The beam hit the roof of their tent and Blaine intensified it until it seared through the cloth and was lost in the day outside.

His audience was suitably enraptured.

Satisfied, Blaine closed the door and the light went out. *Enough for now. I may need all my strength later.* Even the residue from this small amount coursed through his shoulder and down towards his sword to be processed. *Best to keep to small doses and use it only when required.*

His minor display had already galvanised his men. With any luck, they would spread the story and it would grow larger in the telling. If the story grew large enough then his congregation might swell accordingly. Time would tell.

Blaine swept from the tent, keenly aware that the legions ought to move out as quickly as possible. All were up and readying themselves, though it appeared many were still at their breakfast and others struggled with the straps of their gear.

Is twenty years too long? Even for us?

Something crunched underfoot. Several stalks of wheat lay crushed into powder. Being in the middle of the Golden Crescent, they had had little choice but to camp in one field or another. The region was renowned for being the breadbasket of the west, and it even supplied Aurisha too, or at least it had. The local hunters had not been ecstatic at two legions trundling through the farmland.

We cut the grain and bundle it for them. If anything, they should be thanking us for the service.

Humans were entirely ungrateful.

"Lord Guardian," came a small voice from nearby. It was one of the boys who had earlier brought him his hot water. "One of the outrunners has returned. He says he must speak with you at once."

"Is he incapable of finding me himself? Why have messengers if not to bring the message?"

"Your pardon, Lord Guardian," the boy said nervously. "Damien, that's his name, sir, he's in a terrible way. His breath comes hard to him and he clutches at his side."

Gods, but he must have run hard to be so out of breath.

The child's confusion was likely due to never having felt breathless before: never having pushed his limits, even as a dragon.

"I shall go to him. Thank you, and spare a thought for N'weer so that Damien's strength might be rejuvenated."

"I will, sir," the boy said, and hurried off to perform his other duties.

Far older boys normally fulfilled the role of attendant. Eighteen, nineteen, even twenty-year-olds. Not true children. He watched the boy scamper off. He could not have been more than nine, maybe ten. No better than a hatchling. It was a sign of his race's decay. There were too few of them left now. Far too few.

Their king was little more than a child as well. Darnuir would have to learn fast. Blaine disliked the idea of having to rule in his stead – which would have to be subtly done – yet he also wished to avoid handling a king with whom he was at loggerheads. To rule was not Blaine's place, but their people needed guidance and a firm hand to lead them back home.

Remembering that urgent news from the outrunner awaited him, Blaine set off down the Via Primacy to the south end of the camp. On his short journey, he saw other signs of degeneration that years of inactivity had wrought. Rows of tents, which ought to be pristine white, were pitted with dirtied canvases. Men tended to rusted and neglected weapons, trying to recapture some of their former sharpness. Others were strapping on damaged armour, the golden plates chipped and cracked in places. Containers of javelins lay half-empty. Blaine would have been incensed, were it not for his own lethargy.

This must never happen again.

The most obvious omission was clear to see from all points, for the camp's perimeter was marked only by the last tent and not, as it should be, by high, slanting palisade walls. This final collection of tents housed the outrunners; dragons with prodigious speed, stamina and even keener eyes, who would run on scouting missions or relay messages to other legions on campaign.

Blaine reached the southern outrunner post on the perimeter. As he swept into view, the men snapped to attention. The 'post', such as it was, was a crudely-constructed platform raised ten feet above the ground. A single ladder granted access to it.

It should have been a small tower, granting an unhindered view of the landscape.

Blaine suppressed a sigh.

The men were all down below the platform, huddled over a map of Western Tenalp, spread out on a table before them. One was clearly winded. He wore loose-fitting clothes that granted maximum flexibility and went barefoot, as was customary amongst the runners. He and his fellows were lean and wiry, compared to a dragon's usual bulk.

"Damien, I presume?"

"Yes, Lord Guardian," Damien struggled.

"You must have run like few of our kind ever have. What news is so urgent? Is the king in danger?"

"Yes, Lord Guardian," repeated the runner. "He and his company have arrived at the town by the loch. Torridon is its name, according to the map." He indicated its position. "But demons fast approach them. I ran farther into the marsh to gauge how long the refugee train is and saw the black tide accelerating on the horizon."

"How long until the demons reach the town?"

"I would estimate a day, maybe a day and a half at most, sir."

"What sort of state were the humans in?"

"A wearied one, sir," Damien said. "More than half their numbers appeared to be civilians. All haggard and worn from their journey. How things are inside the town, I could not say."

"Anything else?" Blaine pressed him, bending low over the map himself to better appreciate the scenario.

"I did see countless human parties fleeing north towards Val'tarra as I made my return. Most had hunters from the Crescent with them, clad in their yellow and brown leathers. I also saw mounted men carrying the banner of Brevia, but they were heading south like us."

"Chevaliers? What are they doing here?" Blaine pondered aloud. *Is anyone in control?* "Where are we in relation to Torridon?"

"Here, Lord Guardian," another outrunner said, pointing to the map for him. "Still some way to the north, but a day's hard march should close the distance."

"Then it is imperative that we secure the king," said Blaine. "You have done well, Damien. Take your rest." Blaine knew it would take some time yet to break camp and march to Darnuir.

We must act sooner.

"You there," he barked at the helpful map-reading runner, "take a message to the camp prefect. The men are to continue south to Torridon immediately, but ensure they have the strength to fight if need be."

"Shouldn't I bring this to the legionary legates, sir?"

Blaine grunted in annoyance. "Ordinarily, yes. But as there are currently no legates in place, the prefect will suffice."

Proper command will have to be installed as well. Perhaps I have been too hasty in my endeavours.

"Inform the prefect that I shall be leading a vanguard mission to secure the king. You will rendezvous with us there."

"Yes, Lord Guardian." The fresh runner saluted then dashed off.

Blaine resolved himself to action. Hastily, he made his way back to his tent and was satisfied to find the collection of former Praetorians who had gathered for prayer that morning. They were scratching their names down onto a piece of parchment as requested. There were even more now. Likely word had spread amongst the former guard.

"Praetorians, today I granted you the chance to join me as my Light Bearers. I must warn you now that to become a Light Bearer is to dedicate yourself to the Way of Light; to forsake your duties, even to your king, for you will serve a higher power."

"Lord Guardian, we are ready," one of the men said intensely. "Draconess swore that you would return; that you had not abandoned us. He told us that we must keep our faith and be steadfast, even when so many lost their way."

The outburst pleased Blaine greatly but also gave him some reservations. Had there been divisions amongst Draconess' own guard?

"Thank you," he told the dragon. "Thank you all. Now you have a chance to prove your worth to me. An outrunner brings news that the king is in danger. I intend to run to him myself and secure his safety. A host of demons draw near and he is surrounded by the weakness of humanity. Will you join me?"

A satisfying chorus rose in response to his request.

"Lightly equip yourselves and assemble at the southern perimeter. Now!"

They all sprinted out without delay. Blaine moved for his armour. Freshly cleaned by his own hand only the night before, the gold glistened. The armour was unique, like his sword, and it too had a sibling set that he would one day present to the king.

The metal was thick, far thicker than any human could endure wearing, with large ornamental pauldrons representing the severed sun of the guardian. The full symbol was engraved on the chest piece. He donned it all.

Readying himself for battle lit a fire in him that had guttered lifelessly for too long.

This will be my first fight since... But he could not remember the exact details. He glanced down at the three white gems on the grip of his blade. There, the full memory resided.

He pressed a thumb gently on the gem closest to the pommel and it popped out of its socket. The gem was heavy in his hand, laden with memories.

Dare he revisit his greatest failure? He had kept the memory in the gem so it would be stored perfectly. Inside the jewel, it would not fade with time or be altered by himself. *Consciously or not, everyone on occasion twists their own memories. If we alter it just enough for long enough then that becomes the truth of it.* It was a guardian's duty to preserve. Some memories should not be forgotten, however painful.

Another time, he decided, depositing the gemstone back into the sword.

He was not yet ready.

20

TORRIDON

Darnuir – The Cairlav Marshes - Torridon

The robed man materialised before him once more. As always, his vision was jarred and the familiar conversation played out.

"… with that, and enough time, I will find the answer for you – for us!"

"You are sure?" Darnuir asked. "I seek answers. Not more questions."

"I am, though it will take a deal of secrecy to begin my work without interruption or suspicion. Few are as open-minded or understanding as you, Darnuir."

"Few share my passion to preserve my race. Even my father lacks that most basic instinct of survival. I feel he has resigned himself."

"We shall turn the tide," the stranger assured him.

Darnuir felt as though he had more to say, even more to feel, but vision and sound swirled as the scene transformed in front of him. The next vision was far clearer. He found himself in a room high above a golden city, with a crescent moon table before him. Maps were strewn across it, along with plates of half-eaten food and goblets of untouched wine. He shared the room with a man who wore the Dragon's Blade at his waist. Resentment filled him.

"Father," he implored, "I see the strain you are under, but there is no need to continue if you can longer bear it."

Draconess shook his head. "You would ask me to abdicate? To grant you the power?"

"I would. Not for my sake but for the sake of our people. We both know I am the more natural warrior. With the blade, I could—"

"Storm Kar'drun?" Draconess said, his temper rising. "Cut your way through a hundred thousand demons and slay our foe yourself? Do you believe it is so simple?"

"I would win us more battles. I would retake lost ground; I would turn defeat into victory; and yes, I would kill him if I could reach him."

"Such arrogance. It pains me to see how little you have listened. How little you have learned."

Darnuir's frustration hit boiling point. "Father, give me the sword! It cannot make matters worse."

"Could it not?" Draconess said, unsheathing the Dragon's Blade with a flourish. The tip of the blade caught a nearby glass, sending its contents across the table. A map was left with a bloodlike stain.

Darnuir drank in the sight of the Dragon's Blade. The carved head of the dragon, the descending wings and the thick blade etched with a forked tongue. A hunger gripped him, along with a great desire to raise his hand towards it. Yet before any more could be said or done, Darnuir was jerked away from the scene and away from his body.

He awoke as he did most mornings now: heart pounding and chest heaving. His dreams were becoming increasingly vivid. The first one, the one he had most frequently, had expanded a little since his initial viewing. The second one had been new to him and even more disturbing.

I called him Father... so why did I feel so bitter in his company?

He was beginning to suspect that these dreams were flashbacks from his past life. That, or his imagination had become both twisted and stale. As to why they were appearing now, the reason eluded him, though, as with the headaches, he suspected that his new sword was to blame.

If they were memories, they were worrying.

What did I promise to the stranger? Why does that dream never appear fully formed?

He had a lot of questions and there was no one who could answer them. Brackendon had told him that Kasselle might have insight. He hoped she would.

As sleep was no longer an option, Darnuir decided to get some fresh air. First, he had to navigate his way over the other hunters inside the stuffy crannog. Their sleeping bodies lined the inner hall of the Great Crannog in a circle, following the shape of the cavernous space. He quietly stepped over his fellows and felt relief when he emerged out onto the decking. The cool wind woke him fully and he took in the scene in the pre-dawn dark.

The Great Crannog served as a hunter station for the Cairlav Marshes. Despite its impressive size, it was now quite full, swelled in population by the survivors of the Boreac Mountains and fleeing marsh dwellers. The town of Torridon at the water's edge had much the same problem.

Looking towards the town, Darnuir saw many rowboats and trading ships moored along the pebbled shore. Water lapped against the hulls, the stones and the columns of the crannog. A soothing sound upon his aching head.

Beyond the shore was the town itself, a blip of civilisation amongst the muddy pools, tall grass and bright fauna, separated by a simple wooden wall. He recognised pine from the Boreac Mountains. At least one thing was familiar.

The height of the town was raised several storeys by sizeable smokehouses, releasing a steady stream of fish-infused mist. The smell was intense. There was smoke, salt, and fish flesh, but perhaps something more? His nose twitched under the strain of the fumes. The strength of it led him to cough and splutter. In his convulsion, he only heard the footsteps approaching once they were right behind him.

"Are you okay?" Balack asked.

"Yes, I'm... I'm fine. Can't you smell it?"

"A little fishy. Nothing too strong. Why, what do you smell?

"I can't describe it. It feels like one of those smoked fish has been rammed up my nose."

"A disturbing image." Balack yawned. He stretched, sighed and looked to Darnuir with a frown. "I worry about you. You've not been sleeping right. Always muttering and reaching for your sword half the time."

"How do you know that?"

"Because I'm not sleeping well either. Though likely for different reasons."

"I'm all right," Darnuir lied. "I think I am just going through some kind of... adjustment period."

"It's not just me who has noticed, you know. You haven't quite been yourself at times. These strange moments that come over you, what are they?"

Darnuir looked down to the glassy surface of the loch. "I don't know. It frightens me a little, I must admit."

Almost on cue, the dull prodding returned.

"Does something bring it on? Do they just come out of nowhere? Have you noticed anything that eases it? Have you—"

"I told you, human. I don't know!" Darnuir said, rounding on a stunned Balack.

No! I didn't even have any warning that time.

"I'm sorry!"

Balack just looked concerned. "It's fine. I know you don't mean it." He stretched again. "I was going to practice with my bow. Care to join me? There wasn't a chance to stop in the marshes."

Guilt welled in him again at his friend's generosity, his understanding. He bit his lip, wondering again if he should just tell him right here. But things were so much better now. He didn't want them to revert to silence again. A silence that could last a lifetime.

So he chose the cowardly path and beamed. "Of course. I'd love to see what you've been working on."

Although the marshland hunters took quarters in their Great Crannog, the area they used for target practice was outside the town walls. It was necessary for archery, lest they lose countless arrows to the water.

Quivers slung across their backs and bows over their shoulders, Darnuir and Balack picked their way through the crowds. Their trip through the town was brief but awkward. The volume of refugees meant that the streets were packed. Darnuir's newly-enhanced sense of smell registered the pungent scents of sweat and grime. Like before, the intensity of it gave him the uncanny feeling that he was smelling something else entirely. Through it all, he smelled something strangely sweet, as though the people had lined their clothes with cake. The sensation was alien to him. Unnerving.

At the practice range, Balack warmed up by emptying his quiver into a stuffed sack that was dressed as a spectre. Darnuir took a few shots at a target himself but was more interested in watching Balack. After retrieving his arrows, Balack refilled his quiver but kept three arrows in hand.

"Is this what you wanted to show me?" Darnuir asked.

"I've been working on it for a while now. Mainly back at the station, when we were on leave. I think I'm ready to try it out for real now."

"As in combat?"

"What's the use otherwise? It should help. I found it hard to make good shots during our battles with the demons."

"What?" Darnuir said incredulously. "You always made excellent shots, a few I would have thought impossible."

"But that's just it. I only made a few. What are a few kills worth in a battle?" He paused, perhaps waiting for Darnuir to respond. "I felt useless at Cold Point. I mean... I couldn't do much from so far back."

"Balack, you must have taken out dozens of them."

"I was stuck behind a window. If I had been down there, I might have... I might have..." He trailed off.

"I was down there," Darnuir said, "and the spectre still got to her from the shadow of the tree. Nothing would have saved her."

"Even so," Balack said resolutely, "I don't want to be trapped behind a wall again. I don't want to be stuck at the back while everyone else is at the front. This will help."

"Holding three arrows in your draw hand will help?"

Balack shuffled his feet into position, readying himself. "Remember having to practice running and shooting at the same time?"

"Not fondly. I never got the hang of that."

"Few have mastered it. The first shot is easy. The trouble is reaching behind yourself for the next arrow, drawing it and firing, whilst maintaining your eye on the target, which is also moving in a real battle."

"That's why archers tend to stand still."

"Which is to our detriment. Think how deadly the hunters could be if we could all pursue our foes and fire rapidly after them."

"Show me, then."

Balack beamed at him, steadied himself with a few good breaths, then loosed. He immediately flicked one of his spare arrows up to the string, drew and fired again. He repeated this for a third time, each arrow slicing into the head of the fake spectre. It all took place in a matter of seconds.

Balack turned to him with an expectant look. Darnuir's stunned silence seemed to satisfy him.

"Now I'll show it to you on the move!" He drew another three arrows. This time, Balack advanced slowly while launching his arrows in quick succession. He sent each one at a different target. They weren't all perfect shots but they all hit. *Chest, midriff or head, the target is still dead.* Darnuir was beginning to see the power of this technique.

"Can you do it while you're running?" Darnuir asked. "I'm impressed, but walking in a fight isn't wise."

"I'm working on it," Balack said. He performed his display for a third time, stepping faster this time. "Damn. Missed one."

"In a packed fight, you'd likely still hit something. Just hopefully not a friend."

"Do you want to try it?"

Darnuir pondered. A bow had never felt as comfortable to him as a sword and this art seemed particularly delicate. He lifted out three arrows like Balack had, but struggled to even draw one without the others falling out of his grip.

"It's all in the finger-work," Balack said. "It will just take time."

Darnuir struggled a few more times. "This is really not my strong point."

Still, he tried again. And again. And again.

This was meant to take the edge off, not make me more frustrated.

He tried one last time, managing to get off the shot without dropping the shafts, but they slipped immediately after.

Why am I even doing this? I have a flying sword.

He dropped the bow and unstrapped his quiver.

"What are you doing?" Balack said. "You've only just started. Just firing one shot took me weeks."

Darnuir paid him no heed. He unsheathed the Dragon's Blade with a clarity of mind he had not felt in a long time. He focused on the target ahead, drew back his arm and launched the sword forwards. The blade whistled through the air, lopped off the dummy's head and soared back to Darnuir's waiting hand. He caught it and twirled the sword, satisfied.

Balack's open mouth was equally satisfying. "Well... that also works."

They laughed and Darnuir's head pain eased. It felt like they had not laughed at all in months, maybe longer. They continued at their new exercises, Balack running increasingly faster and attempting to hold ever more arrows in his draw hand. Darnuir also experimented with throwing his sword while moving. It seemed that no matter how far he ran or how bizarrely he weaved, the sword found its way back to his hand. If he veered suddenly to one side, the sword would adjust its path.

Time passed pleasantly and, as the morning sun rose, the town began to stir. A bustling could be heard on the other side of the town wall and they would have to relent soon to resume their true duties.

The days of being young hunters training together were over.

Reluctantly, Darnuir decided he ought to return and discuss their plans with Scythe and Cosmo. *If Cosmo will even emerge from his room. I need him.*

Deciding he could try one more test before headin back, he launched the Dragon's Blade out over the loch with all his might. He turned his back upon it, wondering if it would verr around him to return to his hand. Facing his new direction, he saw two mounted men approaching Torridon. Preoccupied by these men, Darnuir forgot about his sword. A powerful thump knocked him flat on his face. Dazed, he lifted his head from the lichen and wiped the worst of the mud off.

"Lose your footing?" Balack sniggered.

"If only. Maybe I have to concentrate on it coming back to me or have my hand open and ready for it to work?"

Balack shrugged. "Maybe? Sort of adds something to 'falling on your own sword'."

"Did you see those riders?" Darnuir asked.

"Yes," Balack said more seriously. "They looked like chevaliers. We should head back."

Suddenly, the wounded cry of an eagle cut through the air. Darnuir looked up and saw the bird descending, although it moved ungracefully with what looked like an injured wing. Kymethra landed inelegantly near them in her human form, clutching at her upper arm. Her robe was ripped and the muscle beneath was torn deeply. Blood poured from the wound.

They rushed to her side.

"I'm all right," she hissed through clenched teeth. "Edwin shot me. Clumsy bastard will be sorry when he gets back."

"It looks bad," Balack said. "You'll need to—"

"Shh, boy," Kymethra interrupted. "I can stop the worst of it." She placed a hand over her wound and fell to her knees, shaking and jerking. When she pulled her hand away, the skin had healed over but looked raw and rough. She let out a groan as she collapsed. Darnuir elevated her head. She looked so ill. A few strands of her hair turned white from the roots and her skin matched its pallor. "Sometimes, healing just makes you feel worse," she struggled to say. "Well, then, carry me back."

Darnuir lifted her without thinking and found she was quite light. Even for a small woman, she was far lighter than she ought to be. She wrapped an arm weakly around his neck and he found he could run while carrying her. This dragon strength was something he could get used to. Balack followed in their wake.

As they hurtled through the town gates, he passed the two riders but only caught a glimpse of them. They were covered in shining steel from head to toe and wore jet cloaks laced with white.

Kymethra groaned in his arms. "Brackendon... Get me... get me..."

"Hold on," Darnuir told her.

The last he'd seen of Brackendon was in the Great Crannog. They wasted no time in forcing their way through the busy town to the shore of the loch. The bridge out to the crannog was another matter. Darnuir had to employ some artful footwork to navigate the hunters and piled supplies there. Many shouts and calls of shock or surprise followed them, but they ran on.

"What happened?" Brackendon said gruffly when they found him in the inner hall.

"She was injured," Darnuir said. "She used magic to heal herself."

The need for action seemed to snap Brackendon out of the stupor he had been in of late. "Follow me, Darnuir. Balack, go find water and bread to soak up the residual magic in her. Quickly now!"

Balack did as he was bid. Darnuir shadowed Brackendon as he searched for a room with some privacy. There were many side rooms to check, most of which were only blocked off by thick curtains. Brackendon pushed back several hangings before announcing, "This looks suitable."

The room contained a single hard-looking bed, several quivers of arrows and multiple reed baskets of varying size. A squat-looking table bore some scattered ink bottles and parchment, underneath a small opening overlooking the loch.

"I think this might be Edwin's room," Brackendon commented, examining some of the paperwork.

"I'm sure he won't mind," Darnuir said, setting Kymethra down on the bed.

"The bastard... shot me," Kymethra mumbled. "So he better not make a fuss."

Brackendon bent down to her side and examined her in some wizardly fashion. He pressed his hand gently on her stomach and let out a coarse sigh.

"It's not so bad. You'll be fine."

"I know that, Brackers," she whispered.

"Why did you do it?"

"Was losing a lot of blood. Had to."

"You didn't try making more to replace—"

"Maybe," she said with the flicker of a smile. "Just a tiny bit. Got carried away."

"Fool," Brackendon said kindly, but stroked her hair all the same.

Darnuir began to feel incredibly in the way and unnecessary.

"How's my hair?" she asked.

"A few new whites," Brackendon told her. "Just a few strands."

She groaned.

"But I think I like it better like this," he said reassuringly.

Darnuir definitely felt it was time to depart. "If you have need of me then don't hesitate..." He trailed off as he slunk out of the room.

Balack appeared in a hurry, carrying a jug of water and a heel of crusty bread. Darnuir nodded towards the room and Balack dashed inside.

Re-entering the main hall, Darnuir found a harassed-looking Scythe.

"What has happened?" he asked.

"Kymethra is injured," Darnuir said. "She tried to heal herself but overdid it."

"Very well," Scythe said brusquely. "I need you to come with me. Riders have appeared at the gate demanding Edwin's presence. Chevaliers from Brevia, I am told. It seems you're drawing the world to us."

He'd never met a chevalier before, only heard about them from Cosmo's stories. They had ridden across the kingdom to assemble the armies for what became the battle of Demons' Folly.

"Do you think they are here to—"

"I think it would be best for us to simply go and find out," Scythe said. "I'd bring Cosmo along too, but I feel his manners might escape him around such people. Not that I can blame him." He seemed lost for a moment in contemplation. "I never truly appreciated how much work he did for me. Cosmo, that is. Since, well, you know, he has been so absent. For the men's sake, I hope he returns to us soon. Currently, he is asleep. Passed out from the drink."

"He needs our help now more than we need him," Darnuir said. He had been of little comfort to Cosmo so far. The pain was still too near. Approaching Cosmo would only make Darnuir feel worse. Yet he knew it was especially selfish of him to stay away. Cosmo had sat and talked with him the morning after Eve died, just to let Darnuir know he was there.

Since Grace's death, Cosmo had walked in silence, breaking his muteness only to forage their dwindling supplies of mountain-goat milk for his son. Every day, the smell of it had grown a little fouler, but the crying boy had sucked gratefully on the soaked cloth all the same. There had been little choice.

"And I would help him if I could," Scythe said. "But I have hundreds of hunters to care for and thousands of people, even just here in this one town." His brow developed a fresh crease.

Darnuir felt a lurch of respect for the man. Scythe was still leading, while all he'd done that morning was play with his new sword. He had to do better than this.

Perhaps Scythe noticed his dilemma for he smiled and took Darnuir by the shoulder. "Come, let us see what these chevaliers from Brevia have to say. I know I have a few choice things I'd like to say to them."

21

FRIENDS AND FOES

Darnuir – The Cairlav Marshes – Torridon

He travelled with Scythe back to Torridon's gates to meet the chevaliers. As they crossed the long bridge from the Great Crannog to the shore, Darnuir noticed Garon dishing out portions of porridge from a pewter pot to the youngest and sickest. The oats were watery but graciously accepted all the same. Slung over his spooning arm was a basket of the dried, smoked fish from the town. Garon broke up pieces of the trout and salmon and handed them out as well.

Darnuir felt compelled to join Garon, to make amends for his selfishness that morning, but Scythe needed him too. He could not be everywhere at once and Darnuir supposed that he would have to get used to that as well.

Fumes from the smokehouses hung thickly over the town, seeming to shrink the space and make the crowding even worse. Near the gates at the far end of town, the chevaliers had cleared a space free from the bedraggled. They were the most heavily-armoured men Darnuir had ever encountered. They remained mounted upon their enormous horses and towered above the refugees. Darnuir had seen few enough horses in his time but they had been less than half the size of these creatures.

One chevalier's face was hidden behind his visor, while his companion had deigned to lift his, holding a silk handkerchief under his nose. It was this one who appeared to be their leader.

"Ah, it's about time," the chevalier snapped haughtily. He looked to Scythe. "I was hoping to speak to Captain Edwin?"

"Captain Edwin is yet to return from the marshes. I'd have thought this would have been explained to you."

"We have been told a great many things," the chevalier said. "And none of them have been told the same way twice. Who are you, then? Your leathers give you both away as hunters of the Boreac Mountains. When leaving Brevia, we had word that the mountains had succumbed to the demons."

"I am Scythe, captain of the Boreac hunters. The mountains were under siege, but we who survived have escaped and are fleeing still. My companion here is Darnuir, King of Dragons."

"A king, you say? And of dragons, no less? Yes, that was one of the tales we heard while we waited here." The man examined Darnuir intently. "Darnuir? Could it be true? I have rarely seen a dragon with a burgeoning beard. My name is Raymond, for what it is worth."

"I shall not waste your time, Raymond," Darnuir said. He brought out the Dragon's Blade for the men to see. Raymond lowered his kerchief and momentarily forgot the odour in the air.

I'm beginning to like having that effect on people.

Raymond's companion, however, was unstirred.

"Yes, Darnuir is my name, and here is the Dragon's Blade."

"It looks impressively dragonish," Raymond said. "But can you fly? Breathe fire? Is your skin as hard as thick steel?"

"Has any dragon flown since the transformation?" Scythe sneered. "I can attest to Darnuir's authenticity. I have seen the blade launch fire and him singlehandedly beat off a demon horde."

He lied, of course, for he had not been at the battle, yet he spoke so convincingly that Darnuir felt no one would deny it. Darnuir smiled at Scythe, and he gave a quick nod back.

"It would not bode well to provoke a dragon with idle demands," Scythe warned. "We are but cowering children in comparison, are we not?"

"Far be it for me to deny a king of beasts," Raymond said pompously. "It has been so long since the dragons contributed to the world that it seems I have forgotten what they can and cannot do. Perhaps provoking the dragons would finally awaken them from whatever slumber they have dwelt in."

"I have done nothing to you," Darnuir said. "Why hold this anger towards me?"

"Oh, it's not just you, don't worry. You are but a representative of your leeching race. For twenty years your kind has taken from human lands, from human tables, and when our time of need arises, once more they vanish."

"Our time of need was great for months," Darnuir said. "Where was Brevia when the Boreacs burned and bled?"

"Struggling to cope with the chaos left by the sudden departure of your kind," Raymond said. "Good King Arkus sends a call to arms to counter Castallan's threats, and swathes of the men registered on the rolls leave his lands. Whole regiments depleted; any sense of order gone. Refugees from the Dales and Marshes scurrying north and demons roaming freely in the south. What help was the king to send in haste?"

"I am not in control of the dragons," Darnuir said curtly.

Raymond scoffed. "Clearly!"

"Stop it," Scythe said, for once the voice of reason. "Raymond, I have no great love for his kind, but this will get us nowhere. Now state your purpose. I can think of only one reason for chevaliers to roam so far from the capital."

"Indeed, and a far-flung place from the civilised world this is. As I said, King Arkus has called all able-bodied men and women to assemble in Brevia. Now that some semblance of order has been restored in the Crown Lands, there is a chance to gather in force."

"Are you not aware that Castallan's army crosses the marshlands as we speak?" Darnuir said.

His thrumming head took over again. *I am growing weary craning my neck to speak to you, human.* Another thought came to him: of the Dragon's Blade spinning gracefully and relieving the man of his head.

Darnuir shook his own head to clear it. *Why do I have these thoughts?*

"We are not aware," Raymond said. "We have been riding hard for weeks. We travelled west to the border of the forest, and down to the tip of the loch. After acquiring passage at Inverdorn, we have been progressing through the Golden Crescent, informing all we meet. So no, we have not heard of the movements of Castallan's army."

"Did droves of refugees fleeing north to the forest not seem suspicious?" Scythe asked.

"As I said, Captain, chaos is the word of the present. We are merely following orders."

"We will be happy to pass along your message to the people here," Darnuir said. "Perhaps you ought to leave and go get help, instead?"

Raymond tittered. "I do not take orders from you, dragon. King or no."

"We are fleeing for our lives," Darnuir implored. "Castallan's army hounds us. Go back to Brevia and tell Arkus to send his army west to aid us."

"Or south to the Bastion," Scythe suggested. "A distraction would be welcome. Whichever Arkus deems fit."

"You would speak of your king in such tones?" Raymond asked.

"I was always told that a good captain looks after his hunters and the people he is charged with," Scythe said. "Arkus is captain of us all, yet look around you, Chevalier.

Look at the state of his people. Brevia does nothing. We must take matters into our own hands."

"The consequence of following a dragon," Raymond said tersely. "They care nothing for us."

"Well, I do!" Darnuir said passionately. "These are my people too. They have suffered due to my existence and I will see them made safe."

"Then run to the demons," Raymond said. "Let them have their prize. Save your 'people' if you mean your words."

"Edwin suggested the same thing," Darnuir said bitterly.

"This Edwin sounds like a reasonable man," Raymond said. "And officially, we are to relay our message to him, so if you don't mind us waiting...?"

Darnuir felt his temper rising hotly in him; that same anger that caused him to lose control. *I must contain it this time.* He fought against it but the prodding on his mind quickened and it felt as if some invisible force were yanking at him from behind his eyes. Perhaps Scythe had an inkling of the signs of these episodes, for he answered Raymond on Darnuir's behalf.

"As we said, Captain Edwin is yet to return from patrol. He might be some time."

It seemed almost mocking that, at that very moment, the gates of the town swung inward and a band of bloodied and bruised hunters in mud-red leathers stumbled inside. A short, stocky, man with a strong but now swollen jaw led the pack.

"Ah," Scythe said. "That would be him now."

"Bleedin' spectres," Edwin mumbled by way of explanation. "Well, isn't this quite the gathering?"

"Captain Edwin?" Raymond asked.

"Aye, that'll be me. One moment, Chevalier." He turned to the hunters that had followed him through the gates. "You lot, go patch yerselves up." The men and women trotted by looking exhausted. Some had escaped whatever skirmish they had been in with only a few cuts, while others held limp arms, or leaned heavily on their bows for support.

Once they had passed, Edwin faced Raymond once more. "Must've been a spectre vanguard that found us. None o' the men I sent east returned. We would have come away even worse, or not at all, if we hadnae been alert. Some blasted bird kept swooping overhead, likely geeing us away."

"That eagle was a friend of ours," Darnuir said. "She's a shape-shifter. You wounded her badly."

Edwin blinked, seeming dazed. "What? Ach, I'm sorry, lad. I didn't know. She all right?"

"She should pull through."

Raymond coughed from above and sniffed loudly.

Edwin did not seem to hear him. "Glad tae hear it. Look, we have tae pick ourselves up and get going at once. We cannae stay here a moment longer."

Raymond coughed again.

"Can I help?" Edwin asked, spitting a glob of blood onto the ground.

Raymond eyed the saliva distastefully. "Captain Edwin, by order of King Arkus, you are to send every able-bodied fighter to Brevia. Half of your hunters are exempt, but they must maintain order in the region."

Edwin massaged his jaw for a few long seconds. "Didn't catch yer name there, Chevalier."

"Raymond. Raymond of House Tarquill."

"Ah, that's a nice name. We don't have nice names like that oot here. Can I ask ye something else, Raymond of House Tarquill?"

Raymond seemed confused but leaned in closer.

"Are ye deaf?"

The chevalier's expression hardened. "I beg your pardon?"

"Or simple? Maybe yer both?"

"I beg your pardon?" Raymond said again through gritted teeth.

"Pardon?" laughed Edwin. "No, you won't get that. Did ye not hear what I just said? There's a great big army of demons swarming all over the south, moving so fast you'd think Dranus himself is whipping their fiery wee arses!"

A clap of thunder rolled somewhere from the east. Darnuir saw dark grey clouds assembling, heavy with water and jagged in shape. As they edged closer, they began to block out the sun, casting long shadows. The horses grew restless and their riders fought at the reins to keep them under control.

Darnuir looked again at the faceless chevalier and felt uneasy. Instinct told him something was wrong. Other than settling his horse, he had not moved at all. Darnuir cautiously tightened his grip on the Dragon's Blade.

"So I'll ask ye again," Edwin said. "Are you deaf, or simple?"

Raymond's temper seemed to be reaching its limit. His hand drifted towards his own sword.

"Stop this," Darnuir said as sternly as he could. This was quickly getting out of hand.

"Edwin, you're exhausted," Scythe said. "You should take some rest while we prepare to move out."

"And I think you'd better leave now," Darnuir told Raymond. "Go tell Arkus to send aid. Tell him the King of Dragons has returned. A word from one of his chevaliers should be proof enough to satisfy the rumours that reach him."

The tension was palpable and broken only by the gatekeeper scurrying towards them.

"Sir!" the gatekeeper called.

Darnuir wasn't sure who the man was speaking to. One chevalier, two captains and a dragon king. 'Sir' just about covered them all.

"Sir!" he said again. "Men at the gate."

"What?" Scythe snapped, looking visibly stressed by the news. "Who are they?"

"I dunno, sir. But there's maybe thirty of them and they are wearing armour of gold."

Gold? Could it be dragons? Here? Darnuir had considered that meeting other dragons was still something far off. *I'm not ready for this.*

"By order of the Guardian of Tenalp, open this door!" The voice roared even above the wind, far louder than anyone could project naturally. "Open this door so that we may come to our king."

"This is turning into quite the farce," Raymond commented.

Scythe rounded on Edwin, as though for all the world he had caused all of this. "I thought you said they were far off."

"I said I heard they were. Nowt but rumours and hearsay, remember?"

"Open this door!" the dragon roared. "Very well. Light Bearers, prepare to break it down."

The poor gatekeeper looked aghast.

"Well, go and open the door before they charge," Darnuir said. It seemed to bring the man to his senses and he scarpered off.

The gates were opened peacefully and in marched the promised collection of gold-clad dragons, each one looking severe. They all carried rectangular shields, large enough to cover their bodies from shin to neck. The exception was the dark blond-haired dragon at the head of the group, quietly radiating confidence. His armour was either the most magnificent or the most ludicrous that Darnuir had ever seen. His pauldrons were gigantic and appeared to be ornamental suns.

I hope I never have to wear anything like that. That is far too cumbersome.

"Greetings, Darnuir," the dragon said. "May Dwna shine upon our first meeting. My name is Blaine, Guardian of Tenalp, at your service."

"Hello?" Darnuir said hesitantly.

"We are here to escort you to safety," he said. "A host of demons approaches and you must leave at once."

"We were just discussing that," Darnuir said. "I fear that if there are any more interruptions, we will never get going."

"We?" Blaine said curiously. His amber-flecked eyes lingered on the two chevaliers. "Darnuir, we cannot tarry. You must come at once. Many dragons await you in the forest of Val'tarra."

"Ah, so that's where you've all got to?" Raymond said. He had attempted his usual haughtiness but this time it contained a pinch of fear. Darnuir sensed a strange sweetness brush under his nose, as if it was coming from the chevalier.

Why would I be smelling that?

"Hiding once more," Raymond droned on. "Seeking the blueskins for protection."

"Careful, human," Blaine said. "Refrain from such condescending remarks of our fairy allies. That looks like fine armour. I'd regret having to prove how soft it really is."

Another clap of thunder, this time louder, and Darnuir did not fail to notice the shadows upon the ground grow larger as the jagged clouds crept closer.

Screwing up his courage, he looked this Blaine directly in the eye. "I'm not leaving. Not on my own, at least. Val'tarra is our destination, so we can make our way there together. All of us."

"Darnuir," Blaine began, as if speaking to a child. "My outrunners tell me that the demons number well into the tens of thousands. We cannot hope to defeat them in battle. Not here. We can only outrun them if you join us now. Your people—"

"Are right here. I will not leave them to die."

It was the one thing he was certain of. He was not going to leave them all, not now.

Not Cosmo. He needs me, I'm sure. Not Balack. Not Brackendon or even Kymethra. Not Cassandra either. I promised her she would be free, not condemned to death in the swamps. Even Garon — Garon?

The man himself appeared on the scene. He joined the gathering crowd, looking perplexed. His pewter pot was empty, as was his basket of fish.

"Is something wrong?" he asked.

Scythe threw out an arm. "Stay out of it. There are too many opinions here already."

"Yet only one that matters," Blaine said. "Darnuir, you will come with—"

"Can naebody use their ears today?" Edwin asked. "The boy said he ain't going. Isn't he supposed to be yer king? Shouldn't ye do what he says?"

"I have neither the time nor the desire to explain the minutiae of my position to you," Blaine said. "In short, I do not 'have' to. Darnuir, you will come with me now or we will take you."

"I wouldn't worry about his insolence, Lord Guardian," Raymond said. "These southerners have yet to learn how to address their betters."

Darnuir felt it then. Some instinct took over him. Something bestial. He raised the Dragon's Blade ready. Edwin drew his sword as well, brandishing it at Raymond. The chevaliers both unsheathed their weapons and kicked their steeds forward. Raymond pointed his sword threateningly towards the hunter. From his elevated position, he could take Edwin's head off if he had the notion.

Edwin spat. "Go on then, Raymond of House Tarquill. Prove yer man enough to use that thing. I dare you."

"Edwin," Darnuir pleaded. "Let it go. He'll be on his way now, right, Raymond?"

Darnuir looked to Scythe for support but the wiry captain seemed unable to find words.

"Eighty years have I been absent," Blaine said, "yet petty bickering still leads men quick to naked steel. Do not draw your blades, humans, unless you intend to use them."

Raymond narrowed his eyes, but slowly lowered his sword. "Come, brother. We have outstayed our welcome."

Raymond's silent companion began to move, but not away. Face still hidden under his visor, the man urged his horse the few short steps towards Edwin.

"Got something to add?" Edwin said.

The chevalier lifted his sword.

Edwin tried to call out one last time. Perhaps a final jibe or a howl of shock, but the sound caught in his throat as the chevalier brought his sword down hard. The stroke fell with an inhuman force, cutting the marshland captain to his heart. Gore laced Darnuir's nostrils, fresh and bloody; it made his own blood run hot. His head thrummed worse than ever.

Edwin collapsed to the mud, gargling his last breath.

Darnuir felt the tension tear apart around him as everyone rushed for their weapons. Raymond seemed the most appalled of all and was even more surprised when his fellow chevalier turned against him. The two clashed atop their horses and Raymond managed to strike his fellow upon the head. Helmet dented, the offending chevalier removed it.

Beneath was a face that should have been unremarkable. The man was plain, his hair a common brown, but his eyes glowed a malevolent red.

One of the dragon warriors sprinted forward and dragged the man off his horse. Darnuir thought it would be over in seconds but the red-eyed stranger deflected the dragon's strike with a speed and strength that was surely beyond him. He slashed at the dragon's legs, cutting at the knees, then jumped to his feet and rammed his blade through the dragon's face.

Blaine cried out. A flash of light burst from the guardian's sword and Darnuir's vision become temporarily blurred. The other dragons roared their displeasure at their comrade's fall and bashed their shields against the ground.

Darnuir rubbed at his eyes and staggered backwards. Regaining his sight, he found the red-eyed man remained still and silent, so sure of himself, despite being outnumbered. He even edged towards another of the dragons.

Then screeches came from all around as spectres bounded from the shadows.

On his left, Darnuir saw Garon club a spectre with his pot and make off to engage another two. On his right, a spectre materialised in front of Scythe and placed a hand on the captain's shoulder. The spectre seemed surprised when Scythe pulled it closer to him, flicked out his long skinning knife and punctured the demon's back.

Movement flashed on Darnuir's periphery. He turned to the right and shoved his sword arm forwards to skewer the leaping spectre through the mouth. Rust-coloured blood spurted out and smoked as it hit the air.

Despite the ambush, the dragons were faring well. Two golden bodies lay still in the mud but the rest fought on, forming ranks to make a shield wall. Blaine was attempting to clash with the red-eyed chevalier but spectres were continually getting in his way, to their own detriment.

"Darnuir!" Garon called to him. "The dragons can handle themselves. Help the people!"

He did not need to be convinced. Together, they turned their backs on the dragons and Raymond and charged into the tumult of the streets. Spectres leapt from shadow to shadow, picking off easy targets. Ahead, Darnuir saw one emerge from the side of a smokehouse, three storeys up, and ravage its victim as it landed. Hunters of both regions battled fiercely in the slippery streets. Despite the savagery, Darnuir felt more relaxed than he had during the drama at the gates.

This, at least, I understand. Fight until it's done. Fight or die.

He saw Garon peel off to enter one of the smaller homes; Darnuir carried on. The difficulty was avoiding accidentally hitting a civilian or an ally as he fought. He came upon a terrified woman who had stumbled to the ground, screaming as her pursuer made to finish her. Darnuir cut upwards, severing the spectre's wrists, and ended it with a thrust through its chest.

The smokehouses continued to emit their smog. It mingled with the smoking blood of the demons, obscuring Darnuir's vision further. He could hear people fleeing towards the loch. Likely there would be a crush on the shore as everyone tried to cross to the Great Crannog. The spectres would not be able to meld across the water so they'd be bottlenecked at the bridge. Yet so would the civilians trying to flee in the first place. The spectres would cut them down easily there. Darnuir had to prevent that if he could.

He drove on towards the water's edge, carving his way through the press of humans and spectres. A weight landed upon his back and a barbed blade appeared at his throat. With his free hand, Darnuir caught the spectre's arm, trying to wrench it away, but the spectre managed a cut all the same.

His neck searing with pain, Darnuir tightened his grip on the demon with a new strength. A dragon's strength. Bones crunched and the demon howled. Darnuir flipped it off his back and brought his sword down through its belly. He brought his hand to his throat to check the wound. Warm blood oozed between his fingers, but the cut didn't feel too deep.

He pressed on and was about to pass the largest of the smokehouses when he saw a spectre flying limply from its doorway. The large forms of Griswald and Rufus followed it, careering down the steps into the fray.

"Never a bloody moment's peace," Griswald roared, swiping bear-like at the nearest spectre. "You'll be sorry me leg is feeling better!"

Darnuir fought with them for a while, the huge men and Darnuir presenting a challenge few spectres were willing to take on. Most melded away into the shadows instead. Darnuir craned his neck, expecting spectres to dive down from up high, but none came. The sound of the battle was now most prominent from the loch. Darnuir tore off in that direction.

The fight at the shoreline was already desperate. A throng of shoving people was attempting to cross the crannog's bridge. Many were falling into the water, splashing in panic, screaming or sinking. Hunters remained trapped along the crannog's outer decking, taking shots where they could, though most were hesitant to even try. The risk of hitting a fellow hunter or civilian was too high.

Close to the water's edge, Cassandra and Balack were doing more than their fair share. Cassandra could clearly handle herself with a sword and Balack was using his new rapid fire technique to devastating effect. Several spectres made for them and each fell in quick succession.

Darnuir sprinted towards them. Underfoot, the pebbles were slick with blood from both sides and he fought for balance.

Four spectres rose from the shadows ahead. Cassandra caught one as it was still half-emerging; Balack reached for another arrow, but his fingers met open air above an empty quiver.

Cassandra screamed and yanked on Balack's quiver to pull him away from the oncoming enemies. The two of them lost their footing and collapsed into the shallow water.

Still running, Darnuir launched the Dragon's Blade. The sword slammed into the furthest demon, carrying it into the loch. The remaining spectre advanced upon Balack and Cassandra, raising its ethereal sword high.

Darnuir lunged, tackling the demon. They landed in the shallows and wrestled for a time before Darnuir managed to bring his fist down on his enemy's skull. His burgeoning strength left the spectre's head in tatters. The water turned foul.

Darnuir rose, completely soaked, and wiped the water from his eyes. He held out an expectant hand and the Dragon's Blade obediently returned. Cassandra and Balack lay in a heap where they had fallen. Darnuir rushed to help them up.

"Please don't die, you two," he shouted over the noise of the battle. "If you see a man with red eyes, just run."

"Why run?" Balack asked.

"He is very fast and strong," Darnuir explained. "Just like you said, Cass. He took down one of the dragons easily."

"Wait, there are dragons too?" she said.

"This is hardly the time," Darnuir said. "Just stay alive, please? Both of you."

They both rolled their eyes, clearly having no intention to keep out of the danger. He was hardly surprised.

The trio hastened to rejoin the battle at the crannog's causeway. Darnuir thought that the spectres' numbers were dwindling, that victory might be close at hand, and then his heart sank at the sight of the red-eyed man. He emerged from the smoking battlefield of Torridon, his sword dripping blood.

Many of the hunters who saw the red-eyed man were confused, taking him at a glance to be a chevalier. Their mistake cost them their lives.

"Stay back!" Darnuir yelled. "Stay away from him."

I'll have to do this. I'm the only one who can.

He was already rushing towards him when he remembered how this man had so easily bested that experienced dragon warrior. His heart beat quicker than Balack could fire arrows. *Now would be a good time to lose control again.*

"Chevalier!" he called out. "Yes, you, Red Eyes. Come here. Fight me!"

Red Eyes obliged, still as silent as before. They circled each other briefly then the man struck like a viper. Darnuir blocked him but the force sent him staggering backwards. Red Eyes followed with another blow that caught the Dragon's Blade near the cross-guard. The twinkling ruby eyes of the dragon's head were knocked from their sockets, falling to the stony shore.

In the ensuing duel, nothing Darnuir could do was good enough; all his usual steps and moves felt clumsy or slow compared to those of his foe. Remaining alive was his only achievement.

Nothing tugged at him from behind his eyes. Nothing prodded at his mind.

Come on! If there was ever a time for it…

Red Eyes made no errors but did slip momentarily on the bloody stones, dropping to one knee. Seeing his chance, Darnuir threw all his weight behind his next swing, bringing his sword down like a hammer. Red Eyes raised his own. The swords met and locked. The strength required to make a block like that would have been beyond most men. Red Eyes made it look easy.

Darnuir pressed down as hard as he could. He pushed himself to his limit and then, somehow, went beyond it. A doorway in his mind seemed to burst open, and a surge of power shot through his body, leaving a bitter taste in his mouth. It made him feel powerful. Euphoric. Red Eyes' arms started to give.

He was going to win this.

Then more of the strange power coursed through his body, up to his shoulder and down towards the Dragon's Blade. He felt as though he were drawing water from a dam and allowed it to flow freely, filling him, drowning him.

Agony blazed and he cried out in anguish as the energy overpowered him. He could not maintain it. He could not control it.

Beneath him, Red Eyes rallied. He pushed back against Darnuir and rose to his feet with a bull's force. Darnuir was knocked to the ground, colour exploding behind his eyes. Blood trickled from his nose, and a putrid taste was in his mouth.

Red Eyes leered over him, eyes flashing, sword raised.

"To the king!" boomed a familiar voice.

"To the king!" a chorus replied.

A beam of intense light swept across Red Eyes' face. It charred his nose and sent him reeling. Blaine raced towards his target with the speed of a galloping horse and held the advantage from the first blow of the fight. His agility and ferocity were terrifying as Blaine made Red Eyes look like a clumsy child.

Is this how I looked at Cold Point?

The fight ended when Red Eyes lurched towards Blaine, aiming low. Blaine spun to avoid his swing, jumped and landed on the man's outstretched sword, trapping it underfoot. Blaine then removed Red Eyes' head from his shoulders with a smooth, clean strike.

The remaining spectres wasted no time in fleeing, many throwing themselves into the first shadows they could find.

Darnuir staggered to his feet, winded. There were many more dragons than there had been before. Hundreds were filing onto the shore. Then he remembered his fallen rubies. Darnuir quickly scurried to the ground in search of them.

He found one easily and snatched it up. It felt heavy in his hand, far heavier than he anticipated. He placed it carefully in one of the eye sockets of his sword. The other gem eluded him.

"Looking for this?" Blaine said. The guardian wasn't even short of breath.

"Thank you," Darnuir said. Blaine placed the ruby in his hand and again the weight of it took him by surprise. He placed it back in the Dragon's Blade. Almost immediately, the pain in his head and the prodding on his mind returned. The correlation was too obvious.

Why do the rubies cause this?

"Time to leave," Blaine said.

"I won't leave them," Darnuir insisted. "Not the people from the Boreacs and not those from the marshes either." Just a glance around revealed the slaughter they would suffer. "We all go."

"They won't make it," Blaine said. "They won't outrun the demons. They can't outrun them. I'm sorry." It sounded like he meant it.

"Carry them, then," Darnuir said. "We'll carry them." Kymethra had felt light and these others dragons were surely as strong, if not stronger than him.

Blaine's face was a study in astonishment. "What?"

"Carry them. You're right. They won't make it. They are exhausted and their lungs will give out after a few miles. But ours won't, will they, Blaine?"

"Darnuir, to run all the way to Val'tarra will be no easy task in itself. To make our warriors carry humans like beasts of burden—"

"How many dragons have you brought?" Darnuir demanded. He was not going to renege on this. There would be no more needless death on his account.

"Six thousand."

"We numbered far less than that before," Darnuir said, "and we'll be even fewer now." His voiced cracked thinking about the death toll. "Your men can take turns carrying the civilians and the hunters, although the hunters will run whenever they can." His eyes bored into Blaine's, beseeching him. He took hold of the dragon's armoured shoulders. "Carry them."

Blaine looked to the dragon ranks. Some of the dragons already carried survivors upon their backs or children in their arms.

So not all my kind are indifferent to human suffering.

"Very well," Blaine said. "But the consequences lie with you."

22

THE 'FOURTH FLIGHT'

Cassandra – The Golden Crescent

She cursed as the wagon shook violently. The baby boy in her arms wailed in protest. He'd only just nodded off to sleep as well. Groaning, she tried to comfort him, but such a journey was not well suited for rest, be you baby, child or adult.

It could be worse, though. She could be out there. Running.

Five dragons hauled the wagon. The team had only rotated once since departing Torridon. Had it been three days now or only two? It had been hard to keep track. The running had continued long into the nights and often started before dawn, but the exertion had not proved too much for any of the dragons. At least, not yet.

Perhaps they are too proud to admit it? Chelos never admitted hardship, even when I knew something pained him.

Across the Golden Crescent they ran, demons trailing their every step. The invariably flat and wide landscape was ideal for such a chase. Thousands of stampeding feet kicked up dust and dry dirt, chopped and churned broken crops underfoot, and cut a swathe through blossoming field after blossoming field. Hunters from the Crescent had joined them at intervals, adding leathers of citron yellow and copper to the mix.

Now that Cassandra was surrounded by dragons, the differences between Darnuir and the rest of his kin were clear. At their first meeting, she had thought him softer than Chelos had described. His insistence that the dragons carry everyone else with them to safety suggested this was genuine. Though there were moments in which he was not himself; in which he appeared more like the dragon that Chelos had described.

In the Great Crannog, before the spectre attack, Balack had told her that Darnuir was worried by these occurrences. He was fiercely loyal to Darnuir, that much was plain, but she had not failed to notice that Darnuir did not always meet his friend's eye. Had the two fallen out over something? No, that did not seem right. Balack never spoke of a disagreement.

Perhaps Darnuir held a secret from Balack. But was that really such a crime? She kept her secret from them both as well.

Her mind drifted to Trask and her escape. How his eyes had lit up when they'd slipped away from the camp; how much of the wine he'd drunk at her encouragement. How pained he looked when he caught her leaving. She thought he'd passed out by then.

What came after was the worst.

Her nose prickled and the beginnings of tears gathered in her eyes. *I shouldn't think about that.* Her free hand rummaged in the pocket of her white leather jerkin and found the dragon figurine that Trask had given her years before. She squeezed on it until her knuckles turned white. But the memory would not let her be.

The tight grip on her shoulder; ringing metal; screaming—

"Cassandra?" Brackendon said. He sat opposite her. "Are you okay? You seemed lost there."

She snapped back to the present. "Yes, I'm fine."

"Good, good. I thought I might have been left without conscious company." He looked warmly down to Kymethra curled up beside him. She was able to rest deeply, despite the discomfort of the journey. A sign of how exhausted she must have been.

"How is she?" Cassandra asked.

"She's a damned fool," Brackendon said affectionately. "But she'll be okay. Magic really is a curse at times. The temptation to just use that little bit more, to think you can handle it in the moment; well, it is very strong."

The wizard shuddered for several seconds and closed his eyes against some phantom pain.

"You don't seem much better," Cassandra said.

Brackendon coughed twice, sighed deeply, and finally reopened his eyes. "The withdrawal is beginning to get to me."

"You're addicted?"

"All who use magic become addicted to it," Brackendon said.

"Castallan too?"

"He will be, in his own way. Some people handle it better than others."

"I never saw him in outward pain."

"No, well, he has never had his staff broken," Brackendon said bitterly. "And I assume he has never *been* broken either." He massaged his head.

"Is there no way to ease the withdrawal?"

"Only drawing on more Cascade energy would ease it. But I have broken before and that is once too many. No matter how badly I shake, no matter how badly I sweat and crave it, I won't risk it."

The baby gargled and Cassandra glanced down at him. He smiled toothlessly at her and gazed up with his oversized infant's eyes, deep and green. They were a lot like her own. She enjoyed holding him. He was sweet and always gave her a smile without expecting anything in return; no favours, no secrets, just joy.

"You're very curious," Brackendon remarked.

"Oh, I'm sorry. I didn't mean to pry." But she was eager to hear more, to learn more. Some things could not be found in books. "How did you lose your staff?"

Brackendon smirked. "Darnuir never told you?"

"No…"

"Probably because he's the one who destroyed my staff tree. Oh, not intentionally, of course," Brackendon added. "He was having some… difficulty controlling the fire from that sword of his."

"So, if destroying the tree takes your power away, then why not destroy Castallan's staff tree? He'll just be a mess looking for another hit of magic. Not a threat to anybody."

That would bring him down a peg or two, back down from pretending he's a god.

She had the sense to quell her own excitement. It was too obvious. And if such a thing could be done, surely it would have been destroyed already.

Brackendon's forlorn face confirmed this sentiment. "The fairies won't allow their prized Argent Tree to be destroyed."

"Oh," Cassandra said in one long disappointed sigh.

This explained a lot. No book she'd read about the fairies could go a few pages without talking about the Argent Tree; the largest, purest silver tree in all of Val'-tarra. Of all the world. The queen herself resided there. If Castallan's staff wood originated from it then that helped to explain his raw power.

Another thundering bump in the road shook the wagon. A clump of mashed grass and wheat flew up, spraying strands into Cassandra's face. Brackendon righted himself, clutching at his side and groaning like a far older man.

She looked to him, feeling so sorry for all he'd been through. "Why did Castallan get such a staff, and you did not?"

Brackendon blinked, taken aback by the question. "There was a feeling that the Conclave ought to contribute more… directly to the war. Castallan's staff was an experiment, I believe."

"A shame they didn't give it to you."

He shrugged. "Castallan had ambitions that wouldn't have been stopped by a regular staff. It's the man, not the staff which is to blame. Though I admit, I do wish things had gone differently. Perhaps if I had the more powerful staff I might have—" He pinched the bridge of his nose. "But no. To dwell on what one cannot change only rots the soul."

Cassandra wished she could reach across the wagon and give the poor man a hug. Words would have to do.

"Well, it was a nice idea. Yet we can't ask the fairies to burn that tree any more than you could ask the dragons to demolish Aurisha."

"You have an understanding of fairy life and history? Most humans know little, and they haven't been trapped in a fortress their whole lives."

"I read a lot while I was there. There wasn't much else I was able to do."

"Well, this is a pleasant surprise."

She felt a bit embarrassed by this. A wizard would have far greater knowledge than her. "It was just *Jedvar's Journeying Journal*," she admitted. "More of a travelogue, really."

"Ah," Brackendon said, straightening. "Jedvar is a reliable enough writer, though he misses many subtleties, especially where the fairies are concerned. You're right, the Argent Tree is like their capital city, but it is... so much more as well."

"Please, go on," she encouraged.

Having an eager audience did wonders for the wizard's mood. His eyes brightened.

"Val'tarra lies at the western edge of the Highlands," he began, "and the Highlands are rich with latent Cascade energy. Five of the Principal Mountains of Tenalp lie there, after all. Much of this energy seeps into the River Avvorn, which feeds Val'tarra. But few living things can deal well with excessive magic. Val'tarra is thus a forest of three parts."

He began to count them off on his fingers.

"The trees that thrive on magic and turn silver. Those that are normal, with brown trunks and green leaves; these are the ones that haven't yet taken in enough magic to either turn silver or—"

"Burn and die?" Cassandra offered.

"In a sense," Brackendon said. He held out his blackened forearm. "Trees in the forest that appear burned or charred are actually the victims of the Cascade. The fairies try to save them. If they didn't, there might not be much of a forest left. Their greatest achievement was the Argent Tree itself. They believe it was once a sapling rotted through, and yet it grew to be a wonder."

Cassandra better understood now. "Burn that tree and you might as well burn the whole forest down."

Brackendon nodded solemnly.

Kymethra began to stir then, muttering and mumbling for water. Brackendon tended to her earnestly. Seeing such pure love and trust was warming. In time, Cassandra hoped she could trust like that. A lifetime of having few to trust in had taken its toll.

The dragons yelled at one another to swap runners. They managed to switch drivers one at a time without interrupting their pace. All around, thousands of feet pounded in rhythm and the ground quaked beneath their collective weight.

A different sound reached her ears then – hooves. On Cassandra's side of the wagon, the chevalier called Raymond weaved through the runners until he was close enough to speak to her. His steel armour was scratched and stained from the battle. His horse's own armour had been stripped to ease its burden. Despite this, the poor creature looked close to collapsing.

"Are you Cassandra?"

"I am. What is it to you?"

"Does everyone believe I am a villain too?" he said bitterly. "I told Darnuir and that guardian that I had no idea about my brother's misadventure. Had I known, I would not have hesitated to bring him to justice. A chevalier's honour is his life and Sanders has brought shame to the name of Tarquill." With a grim expression, he pushed back his woes. "I am to take my leave, but Darnuir said you might know more about this magic Castallan has placed upon his men."

"I only know it makes them stronger, as you saw."

"Is there any way of knowing they've been enchanted?"

"You can't tell until their eyes turn red. There's no way you could've known about your brother, Raymond."

He pursed his lips.

"Don't blame yourself," Brackendon said.

"My parents may see it differently," Raymond said. He rallied himself. "I shall take my leave."

"Where will you go?" Cassandra asked.

"Back to Brevia. I will take word of events to the king like a good messenger."

"The passage across the loch is likely treacherous," said Brackendon. "The path through Val'tarra is longer, but safer."

"Perhaps," Raymond said dismissively, "but my poor horse cannot take another day of this. If we can reach the shore then we can progress more slowly from there. Inverdorn should remain safe for a time."

"Good luck, then," Cassandra said.

"I fear it is you who will need the luck," Raymond said. The chevalier broke off from the wagon and rode east, weaving between a multitude of speeding carts and dragons.

Cosmo's son began to wail again.

"Here, give him this," Brackendon offered, dipping a hollowed ram's horn into a container of milk to fill it. The tip of the horn had been cut away and a nib of twisted cloth had been placed there for the baby to suck on. Brackendon passed the horn to Cassandra and she lowered it to the baby's mouth. The boy drew ravenously from the cloth.

Brackendon chuckled a little. "I think he much prefers this fresher variety to the stale goat's milk."

Cosmo himself was in the rear guard with Darnuir and the others. He had emerged from his stupor following the spectre ambush at Torridon. Events at the loch had shaken the man. Trapped in the Great Crannog, he had been unable to help in the battle. Guilt and shame seemed to spark him back to life.

Yet Cassandra didn't begrudge the man his grief. She had never felt love like he obviously had. *How would I react if Chelos died?* Then she looked down to Cosmo's son. She felt as much affection for the little boy in her arms as anyone else who had entered her life. What would become of him, dragged along in a war? Blaine had inquired about the babe and muttered something about it being "ill luck not to give birth in Dwna's morning light." He didn't mention who it was ill luck for.

"Why won't Cosmo name him?" she wondered aloud.

"Only he could tell you that," Brackendon said. "Though I suspect it's a form of self-defence. If the boy isn't named then perhaps he can pretend it never happened."

"Do you really think that?" Cassandra asked, tilting the horn a little to help the liquid flow.

"Maybe he just hasn't decided yet," Brackendon said. "Not everything is so complicated."

"You would know. You've known him longest here, right?"

"I've known him for the longest, yes, but that does not mean I know him the best."

"He must trust you, though. Darnuir said that you took Cosmo to Cold Point like you did with him. He must have trusted you enough for that?" Brackendon raised his eyebrows, as if this were the first time he had truly considered it.

"It was either trust, desperation, or a little of both. I wasn't surprised when he came to me with his request, though."

"Why?"

"We met while I was an apprentice at the Cascade Conclave, but I shall say no more on the subject," Brackendon said guardedly.

"Why?"

"So curious!" the wizard exclaimed. "Or nosy. Why, you ask, will I not divulge personal matters? Because Cosmo would not want me to say. Not even Darnuir knows."

"Darnuir says Cosmo hates Brevia," she said. "I'd ask you why but—"

"I wouldn't tell you," Brackendon finished for her. "Though he does have a particular dislike of the capital; that much he has made public. I'll only say that some people, like Raymond, thrive there, and others don't."

The cart rocked violently again. A dragon had leapt aboard whilst it was still in motion. Now he rummaged through baskets and satchels.

"Looking for this?" Cassandra said, passing over one of the reed baskets from Torridon. It contained a collection of dried fish. Food was normally the reason for these surprise visits. The dragon sniffed at the fish and his face soured. "I think there is some bread buried in there," she said, pointing at the pile of victuals beside her. "Not sure how fresh it will still be though."

"This will do," the dragon said in a low voice. He picked up one of the smaller fish and started eating with gusto, consuming it in three mouthfuls. "Pass up more."

"There isn't much left," Cassandra warned.

"Necessary," said the dragon, who ravenously devoured another fish. Baskets in hand, he jumped from the wagon and threw out portions of food to other dragons that he passed.

"Not a very talkative lot, are they?" she said.

"Reserved, is how I would describe them," said Brackendon. "And to be fair, it's likely they won't have any breath to spare. Not during this great flight of ours."

Flight? The word triggered something in her memory from her reading. "Maybe one day, people will call this the Fourth Flight."

"The Fourth Flight?" Brackendon considered. "Clever. I assume you have also read from Tiviar's *Histories*, then?"

"All twelve volumes."

"Excellent. Tiviar is one of the few scholars worth reading on the subject. I think being a fairy helps to keep him impartial. Human and dragon writers can be terribly biased."

"I doubt this could be called a true flight, though," Cassandra noted.

"Perhaps not, but who is to say?" Brackendon said. The wizard was now quite animated. "As Tiviar himself comments, the earlier flights are so obscured by myth, we cannot say what they might truly have been about. Sources from the Third Flight two thousand years ago are more readily available, if still questionable."

"The time of Aurisha, the Transformation, and the First War against Dranus and the Black Dragons," Cassandra said. "Tiviar devotes three of his volumes to it."

"As well he should," said Brackendon. "The Transformation of the dragons is perhaps the most important event in all Tenalp's history. Tiviar decided that a Flight was such when the whole dragon race moved en masse with a collective purpose. While we do not quite have the entire dragon race with us, I think it would work well as a chapter heading in a book one day."

"It's nice to discuss this with someone and not have them roll their eyes," Cassandra said. "The hunters don't seem too interested."

"Don't be quick to judge. Not everyone has endless time and access to a wizard's library. Books are rare, and the time and wit to enjoy them, rarer still. Hunters need to learn many other things."

"Like how to fight? I can fight as well."

"But can you pitch a tent, gather wood, and start a fire with flint and tinder?" His tone reminded her of Chelos when he became particularly preachy. "Can you skin a rabbit, a mountain goat, a wolf, a bear? Can you bring those creatures down with an arrow without being seen? Can you use a bow?"

Okay, I get your point.

"Can you clean a wound or set a broken bone? Could you find your way home with just a compass and then still make it back if it breaks?"

Cassandra frowned at him. "No. No, I can't do those things." She felt dispirited. She had been fighting against the fear that she had nothing real to offer. "Are you trying to make me feel useless? I know I'm only as good as my information on Castallan is, and it really isn't that helpful."

"Oh, Cassandra. I didn't mean it like that at all. I'm sorry."

She forgave him but remained silent.

"I only meant to illustrate that there are things we can all contribute. You have already contributed. You warned us of the demon army camped outside the Boreac Mountains and this impending invasion as well." He smiled at her. "If you hadn't, we might well have stumbled into the demons or been trapped. Likely, this invasion would have come without enough warning as well. Though it may seem like you have done little, you may have saved the world through your actions."

She couldn't help but grin. "Thank you, Brackendon."

Another voice reached her ears then, even over the noise of the dragons.

"I told you I don't need to rest!" Garon was yelling. "Put me down. Put me down."

He was being carried by a dragon, and his carrier jumped up into the wagon smoothly without threatening to lose balance. The dragon plonked Garon down in the gap between Kymethra and the piled baskets.

"My apologies, human. But the king has ordered—"

"He's not my bloody king," Garon said, struggling to get up. The dragon held him firmly in place. "Damn it. I'm not going to tell him if you let me go."

The dragon sighed. It was one of the few signs of weariness Cassandra had seen from them. "Are your legs not tired?"

"Aye, they ache and my lungs are on fire, but someone else will be hurting more."

"I picked you up from the ground."

"I tripped, all right…" Garon deflated, sensing defeat.

"Stay and rest here now. When it comes to the next rotation, I will come and get you first, if that is what you wish?"

This time, Garon sighed. "All right. Thanks, Damien."

The dragon called Damien gave Garon a tired smile then leapt back out of the cart.

"You're a poor liar," Brackendon said.

"Well, of course I'm in agony," Garon said. "We all are. Well, apart from Darnuir and that Blaine fellow. Honestly, you wouldn't think Darnuir was hu—" He caught himself. "Well, he isn't, is he?"

"How are they different from the other dragons?" Cassandra asked.

"They don't seem to be wearing out much. All the dragons are tiring now; you can hear it in their voices and their pace has dropped a little. But Darnuir, he just seems to keep going. I caught him stopping to catch his breath once or twice but that is about it, and he was involved in a lot of the fighting at the rear."

"And Blaine?" Brackendon inquired.

"His stamina is even more unnatural," Garon said. "He hasn't looked sore or worn out, not even a little. It's not natural, I tell you."

"You should probably rest," Cassandra said. "Why fight it?"

"I always feel like other people need it more. It's just who I am. Now I'm here, though, I think it might take a great deal of effort for me to get back up."

"You can't help everyone all the time," Cassandra said.

"I know," Garon said pointedly. "I blame Cosmo for instilling this self-sacrificing streak in me. I try to fight it, but sometimes…" He appeared to get fondly lost in thought, emerging with a smile. "Back when Cosmo first took me in, he'd always give me the bigger cut of the game when we were out on patrol, and he'd always eat last in a group. He'd always be the last one to escape danger and the first one to head into it. He did all he could to look out for us because he was supposed to care for us." Looking a touch embarrassed by this outpouring, he attempted to shrug it off. "I don't know if he really did care or was just good at his job, but he gave us all some hope. Even today, when he turned up at the rear guard, you should have heard the roar he received for being back."

"I'm certain he cares," Brackendon said. "I could tell that from our first meeting."

"We've had our differences, of course," Garon said. "Particularly over women… oh, no offence."

Cassandra narrowed her eyes.

"It's cruel that Grace was taken from him, though," Garon continued, casting a sympathetic eye over the baby in Cassandra's arms. "I suppose I'm trying to make up for his absence of late. I've tried to fill Cosmo's boots for Captain Scythe but it hasn't been easy."

"And what of Scythe?" Brackendon asked. "How does he fare on the run?"

"He's another one," Garon said. "He seems to be running on air as well. He's taken the least rest out of the hunters but he's also run the hardest." He peered around the wagon with hungry eyes. "Any food going?"

Cassandra passed over one of the baskets. The pile was dwindling fast. Garon tore into the fish and found a few stacks of oatcakes bundled up with them.

"Not sure anything has tasted so good," he said, smacking his lips. "Now, where was I? Oh yes, Scythe. Aye, he's a tough one, but I'll be damned if I let a city boy beat me."

Another dragon hopped on board, and the wagon lurched. Painful juddering shakes rang up her legs. *Couldn't they at least warn us?*

This time, Balack was carefully deposited beside her. Unlike Garon, he did not protest. The dragon bounded away before anyone could engage him in conversation, shouting to the drivers that he would find help to pull the additional load.

"Our 'king' order you to get some sleep, too?" Garon asked him.

Balack mumbled something non-committal and then yawned. His head swayed, his auburn hair slick with sweat, and his chin collapsed onto his chest. Clutching at his shoulder, he groaned, "I think I've pulled something."

Hands shaking, he made a fumbled attempt to unstrap his quiver. Cassandra tried to help him with her free hand.

"You shouldn't push yourself so hard," she said.

"You'd do the same, Cass," Balack said. He was right, of course. Were it not for her charge over the boy, she would rather be doing something useful.

"What else can we do?" said Garon. "If we don't run, we'll be left behind, and we can't expect the dragons to carry us all the way."

"It will be no good to anyone if you run yourselves to death," Cassandra said. Her left hand still worked at the clasp of the quiver's strap. Balack's hand fell upon her own as he reached up to make another attempt. This time, she whipped her hand back as though scalded.

The memory rushed before her again – the hard grip on her shoulder, the flash of steel, a scream, pain, blood.

Balack gave up with his quiver, looking at her in concern. "Everything all right?"

"Yes – sorry. I'm… not sure what came over me." She gave him a weak smile. He returned it, eyes dim with exhaustion. There was nothing else behind them, though. She saw no trace of the same look that Darnuir gave her. That Trask had given her. Perhaps she could trust him better.

Balack took some food and his eyelids began to droop. Despite the turbulence of the wagon, he drifted off.

"I think Balack has the right idea." Garon yawned. "Might as well sleep while I'm here." His eyes closed almost immediately.

Brackendon chuckled. "Well, we appear to have the wagon to ourselves agai—"
He winced and shook, far worse this time. He regained control with a gasp.

"Perhaps you should rest as well?"

"Sleep is something of a struggle for me now."

Kymethra stirred beside him. She let out a rasping wheeze as if her throat was
bone dry. Brackendon brought a skin of water to her mouth. Kymethra dribbled as
she drank, then settled back down.

Cassandra bit her lip. That had not sounded good.

"The worst is over," Brackendon said, as though sensing her concern. "I understand it
doesn't look like it, but sleeping it off is the best way for her body to process the poison."

"She just looks so weak," Cassandra said. "Her skin is as white as the tips of her
hair."

"Yes, well, that's what the Cascade does to us," he said. "As bad as she seems,
this is nothing compared to breaking, I assure you. I'll make sure she recovers. I owe
her much more."

"Did she care for you when you broke?"

"That fails to do her justice. She didn't just care for me. She brought me back.
Brought me back from the babbling, the seizures and the insanity."

"Why?" The question was simple, blunt and verged on accusatory, but Cassandra
asked it without pausing to think.

"Why? That is a difficult question. Why do we do anything? Was it a necessity?
No. She did not 'need' to help me. Fear can also be a strong motivator, but it did not
drive her. Perhaps she felt like she owed me, and perhaps we are simply in a cycle of
owing each other. I did ask her myself: 'Why did you help me through it? Why give
up so many years of your life when there was no guarantee I would recover?' The
answer came easily to her. She just said that she loved me."

Cassandra wasn't sure how she felt about that. "So, she had been trapped by her
own feelings? She couldn't leave you?"

Brackendon seemed bewildered by the question. "She could have left me whenever she wanted to; no one was making her stay. She just chose not to go."

Sounds more like she couldn't. The idea unsettled Cassandra.

Brackendon remained quiet for a time. For once, he seemed distant.

"She was part of the Conclave before Castallan tore it apart," he said after a
while, his tone wistful. "Being a few years my junior, she never reached the stage of
obtaining a staff of her own."

"You said she owed you?"

"I saved her life when the fighting started."

"That's the whole story?"

"Curiosity is a fine thing, but now you are prying."

She carried on regardless. "And do you love her?"

Brackendon sighed, a little annoyed. "How could I not?"

"It isn't just that you owe her?" she asked. *I owe Darnuir, in a sense.*

"I think this is hard to describe unless you already understand it," Brackendon said. "There aren't any conditions. She could wake up healthy tomorrow and fly away. Soar far into the north and never come back, and I'd still love her. Yes, a part of it is knowing she loves me, and knowing she was there for me, but love is made up of many pieces." Brackendon gave her a hard look. She could almost feel him studying her.

"What?"

"You have some demons, girl. I can read it in your eyes. What do you hide? What is it that troubles you? *Who* is it that troubles you?"

She fought off the encroaching memory. "Now it is you who is prying, wizard."

The remainder of that day passed in silence. Cassandra spent most of the time rocking Cosmo's son, feeding him milk from the horn and tickling at his face when he was awake. A crisp wind kept the heat of the early summer sun from overwhelming her. Later, the sun dropped down, bright red on the horizon and leading a pink twilight in its wake.

Balack and Garon remained sound asleep, no matter how many lurches the wagon took. Cassandra was accustomed to them now, along with the rhythmic thumping of the runners, and the rumbling of the hundreds of wagons and carts being hauled along.

Occasionally, dragons would run past, shouting orders for food or rotation. Sometimes, they called for the men to go faster, for the demons were always gaining; and every so often, they cried out for fighters to fall back to the rear guard to replace the wounded or the dead.

No word came of Darnuir, of Cosmo or Scythe.

She cared less about the latter. He would have had her bound up in enough rope to hold a dragon if he could. He always had his eye on her when they were in each other's company; not a friendly stare like Balack, and not the way Darnuir looked at her. Scythe's was distrustful, yet it went further than that. She could never hold his gaze, for it bored into her, almost menacing. Still, she could not judge him too harshly.

Would I believe my story if our places were reversed? Not likely.

She had also tried to imagine herself in Scythe's position. A simple human amongst wizards and dragon lords. Darnuir wanted him there because he was not yet ready to lead alone, and poor Scythe was being pulled at from all sides. And no matter how well he did, no matter how efficiently he handled things, the men still wanted Cosmo.

Already gaunt in appearance, Scythe had looked increasingly stretched and worn since Cassandra had met him. Yet he had still done all he could. He was trapped in a position he'd rather not be in but was making the best of it. For that, she could find admiration for him.

Ahead, the horizon began to change. No longer endlessly flat plains but rising gnarled shapes. Silver leaves sparkled in the fading light.

"Val'tarra is in sight!" one of the drivers yelled.

The news spread throughout the stampede, and soon a general cry of relief arose from every runner. Some yelled in joy, others with disbelief but they joined in the cheering all the same. It rose to such levels that it woke Cassandra's three sleeping companions.

Kymethra's eyes blinked open fully for the first time in days. She appeared confused but perked up when she caught a glimpse of the horizon. "We're almost there," she said weakly.

"What is that?" Balack asked, rubbing at his eyes, as though worried he was seeing apparitions. Above the treeline, hundreds of dark blots were rising upwards and seemed to be moving towards them.

"Looks like fairies," Garon said, fighting back a yawn.

"Flyers!" Cassandra said. She had been looking forward to seeing some. Only about one in ten fairies had the gift of flight.

The first wave of fairies flew towards them at speed, their blue bodies easily spotted against the pink sky. More waves of flyers emerged behind their leaders. Soon, hundreds of them were descending amongst the dragons and humans. Some had skin of such a deep blue it made them appear as dark as a sunless wood, while others were the turquoise of clean shallow waters. Insect-like translucent wings vibrated in blurs upon their backs.

They carried the children off to safety first. In pairs, they then lifted the weariest running hunters. Buzzing wings mixed with the pounding feet and the sky above became just as busy as the ground below. Still other fairies continued overhead, holding long spears and heading for the fight at the rear guard.

Next, she saw the wounded being flown back. Cassandra felt something land on the top of her head. It trickled down her face and she saw a glint of red at the end of her nose.

She looked down and saw that the baby's face had also been splashed. A bit seeped into his mouth and he objected loudly to the awful taste. She quickly wiped him clean, feeling sick.

The blood and gore of Torridon had been bearable in the adrenaline-fuelled moment, but having warm blood drip down on her like this was chilling. Her wagon companions were all brushing sticky blood from themselves as well.

"This can't be good," Garon said, peering upwards. Pairs of fairies returning from the fighting were carrying human and dragon bodies alike between them. "We need to get back there!" he said with bravado. "Come, Balack." He tried to get to his feet, but his legs refused to accept his commands. They buckled beneath him and he collapsed face-first into the remaining baskets. He brought his head up with a scowl, flakes of fish speared onto his stubble.

An explosion briefly drowned out the world.

Cassandra twisted to look behind. A wall of billowing smoke rose steadily higher in the distance, stretching out for miles.

23

DRAGONS DIE THE SAME

Blaine – Val'tarra – Southern Edge Of The Forest

He was one of the last to cross the divide between forest and plains. Shuddering to a halt, he felt breathless for the first time in eighty years.

The Cascade energy in his system flowed towards his blade, and a dull burning flowed through his blood. A bitterness lay thickly on his tongue and his head ached. He had drawn upon a lot of magic on that run, even for him. And he was severely out of practice.

Wingless fairies were running in amongst the refugees, helping the stragglers and picking up those who had collapsed. Wagons lay abandoned or upturned. Crying, wailing and the gentle thud of bodies upon the ground filled his ears.

Dragons were falling all around him. Many of his kindred hit the leaf-strewn earth without even raising their hands to cushion the fall. Others dropped to their knees, exhausted but still conscious.

Blaine moved to the closest soldier and bent to check his pulse. Dead. Blaine had never seen the like of it in all his long years.

Darnuir had better learn a valuable lesson from this. Our kind are far from invincible.

Blaine had intended a run of dragons; one where they could have taken longer rests and run faster without the burden of all those humans. He jumped to check on another fallen dragon. Dead as well. How many dragon lives had this boy king lost already? Blaine checked on a third dragon. There was a faint pulse.

"N'weer, revive this man's strength," he whispered. "Grant him life and spirit anew." Then he caught sight of Darnuir walking back to the treeline. "Where do you think you're going, boy?" He leapt over the bodies and restrained Darnuir with both arms.

"I really wish people would stop calling me boy," Darnuir growled. He was even more breathless than Blaine.

He doesn't know how to use his blade properly yet. That will need to be rectified soon.

Darnuir struggled, but Blaine called upon the Cascade and his muscles became iron.

"Let me go. I have to go back. We can still save—"

"He's dead!" Blaine said. "You know it. And Scythe knew the risk when he offered to set the line on fire."

"He didn't know that was going to happen! I've never seen anything like that. What was in those barrels?"

"Scythe still knew it was a risk. He knew he probably wouldn't make it back through. Let him go, Darnuir."

Darnuir roared in defiance then collapsed, his body limp in Blaine's arms.

"He was a good man," Blaine said mechanically. He had only known the captain for a few short days, after all, though he was the most driven human Blaine had ever seen. Scythe had performed remarkably well on their journey. It would have been very useful to know that such a man oversaw the hunters. But the hunters were not Blaine's primary concern.

Blaine let Darnuir go. The king – his king – dropped to his knees.

"He didn't deserve that," Darnuir sobbed.

Is he blubbering? This won't do.

"Get up, boy."

Darnuir rose. There were no tears, but his face was red. "What happened?"

"This is not the time to dwell on it."

Darnuir swayed and Blaine moved to support him. "Come on. We can't stop here." Darnuir half-limped alongside him, staring at the dragons lying amongst the fallen leaves.

"Are they—"

"Dead?" Blaine snapped. "Some are, and some might be dying. I warned you there would be consequences."

"We saved the people, though."

"And what of your own kind? Your first act as king is to have them run themselves to death."

"Blaine, we were exhausted and beat up at Torridon. We couldn't have—"

"We? We, Darnuir? You're a dragon. Not a human."

"The way I see it, we saved thousands of lives. Is that not worth it?"

Blaine grunted. He could not disagree with him outright. Still, their people could not afford to bleed needlessly. "I only meant you ought to put your own people first. You are a dragon, after all."

"I'm not sure what I am anymore," Darnuir said dejectedly.

You're not a dragon yet, that's for damned sure.

Perhaps there was simply too much human in the boy.

"Are you not tired, Blaine?"

"Oh, I am tired, Darnuir. In more ways than one."

"Not like the rest of us are, though. I'm not sure how I am even still standing."

"You ran well. I didn't think you would cope as easily as you did, considering you have never pushed yourself like that before."

"Hunters are used to hard living."

"Your sword will have helped you greatly," Blaine explained. "One of its purposes is to keep you alive and it will passively draw on small amounts of magic to help you."

"Really?" Darnuir said. "I didn't notice it and I don't feel very different."

"Do you have a bitter taste in your mouth?" Blaine asked. "Does your head throb? These are indicators that we have drawn on Cascade energy."

Darnuir smacked his lips. "There is something there, now I think about it, but it was far worse after the fight at Torridon. My head nearly always pounds regardless."

Blaine frowned. "All the time?"

"Since I got the Dragon's Blade. Sometimes it feels like something is pulling at my mind. I can't quite explain it."

The news disturbed Blaine. He had never heard of such symptoms of magic. Any initial adjustment to passively drawing Cascade energy should have settled within a week or so. But for now, the priority was to regroup and rest.

"We'll discuss this properly later."

They staggered onwards. Eventually, Darnuir stopped leaning on Blaine and they could continue with more dignity. Blaine kept scanning for the camp prefect, hoping he might have been able to set up some forward position amongst the trees. Darnuir was silent beside him and kept one hand pressed against his evidently sore head.

Blaine's own headache throbbed, though it was starting to ebb. He had not drawn on too much at any one point, which was the wisest thing to do. Every time Blaine reached for the Cascade, it was as if he were opening a door and letting the ocean pour in. If he didn't slam the door shut fast enough, he would drown. Such a delicate balance. At times, he questioned whether he should ever use it.

Why would the gods choose us as their champions if dragons are weak to poison? His sword could handle a lot of power, but Blaine's body could not, and the blade could only process it so fast. If he left that door open for too long, he would die.

Yet all life was left scarred by magic. Merely glancing around at some of the blackened and deadened trees was a testament to that. Perhaps the gods had chosen dragons because they had natural strength and didn't need to rely on such volatile power.

Why then have the blades at all? Why did the prophet, Aurisha, command them to be made before he died?

Such questions were dangerous things, for they might lead to doubt. It was said that dragons could handle magic once, back when they existed in their true form. But the truth of that would never be known. Blaine knew it in his heart.

A true dragon will never walk this earth again.

They passed another body, this one a huntress of the Crescent in her yellow leathers.

Darnuir looked at the corpse and paled further. "It should have been me. Scythe should not have had to die."

"Don't be so foolishly noble, boy," Blaine said, exasperated. "Taking his place would have served no one but the enemy."

"I don't mean killing myself. I mean I should have been able to use the sword; send fire from a distance. Then no one would have needed to die."

"I noticed you seem reluctant to use that aspect of your blade." *It would have certainly been useful.*

"I can't control it," Darnuir said. It looked like he had more to say but then thought better of it.

Blaine gave a hard sigh. "You need training, that is certain. We will make time for it here in Val'tarra."

"How much time will we have?"

"That, I cannot say. I doubt the demons will follow us into the forest. The army chasing us was substantial, but not enough to face the wrath of the entire fairy race, plus the rest of our dragons. Though they were rather determined."

"If there are more like Raymond's brother amongst them then I imagine that, along with the spectres, they can instil a great deal more discipline in the demons."

"Perhaps," Blaine said, "but I wonder what the link is between these new red-eyed servants of Castallan and the spectres? As far as I am aware, spectres maintain order amongst their lesser kin because they are more powerful demons. Yet, as strong as the red-eyed man was, he was still unmistakably human."

"Perhaps the spectres answer to Castallan's red-eyed men?" Darnuir said. "They disappeared in a hurry when you killed Raymond's brother."

"Whatever the case, and whatever the chain of command, they are extremely dangerous foes," Blaine said. "Castallan seems to have enhanced their strength to match that of a dragon. Perhaps even beyond a dragon's strength. And, disciplined or not, that army will have to occupy itself somehow. The surrounding areas will suffer greatly."

Darnuir gulped loudly.

"A lot of people are going to die before the end," Blaine told him.

Darnuir half-laughed. "What is the end? I feel like I am struggling even to begin. Everything has happened so quickly since Brackendon showed up and this thing," he grasped the hilt of the Dragon's Blade, "destroyed a part of Cold Point's tavern to reach me. Too many revelations in too short a time. That includes you."

"Oh?"

"If you're so important, where have you been all this time? Why was I left on my own?"

Because I failed.

As with his Light Bearers, he knew it would not be wise to show any weakness.

"Training and knowledge," Blaine said. "You shall have both. And I will answer what I can, but some things even I do not know."

Darnuir raised an eyebrow. "You don't know where you have been? You don't know what you have been doing, rather than 'guarding'?"

"It is… complicated."

Now is not the time for this. I'm not ready for this.

"Yet more things unanswered," Darnuir said. "I'm struggling to keep up with all the secrets."

"Secrets?" Blaine said. "You think I would hide things from you on purpose, as if I were your enemy? No, boy. We all keep things private on occasion; I imagine there are things even you would like to keep hidden." He felt satisfied when Darnuir grunted and turned away from him.

Touched a nerve there. Whatever it is, I will have to prise it out of him at some point.

"You must be old, Blaine. There aren't even stories about any guardians amongst humans or I'm sure I would have heard of them."

"I am one hundred and fifty years old, and the guardians were not an open organisation even when we were strong. I doubt humanity knew much about us." Stating his age felt strange in a way. He hadn't had to consider it in a long time. Were these trees even as old as him?

Darnuir looked shocked. "One hundred and fifty! But you look no older than Cosmo. How is that possible, even for a dragon?"

"To live to one hundred and twenty years would be considered exceptional," Blaine said. "My life has been extended through my position as guardian." He drew his own blade for Darnuir to see. "I mentioned that the swords help us passively, that they seek to keep us alive. The Guardian's Blade is particularly well-attuned to health. So long as I am guardian, I will appear to remain the same age as when I received it."

"Does that make you immortal? Does that mean I—"

"No, you are not immortal, Darnuir."

"But are you?"

"No guardian has ever sought to test it. I can die in battle like anyone else, but I don't remember what it is to be ill."

"Why the difference in the blades?"

"I don't know, Darnuir. I told you, I don't have all the answers."

But the boy continued to look at him expectantly. He looked so young, no better than a hatchling in truth.

Dwl'or, give me strength. I need your guidance now more than ever.

As ever, he didn't receive any reply.

"If I had to guess," Blaine said, "I would imagine it has to do with the different natures of our positions. The guardianship is passed down from the current guardian to the dragon he thinks is worthy to succeed him. Kingship, on the other hand, is hereditary."

Well, mostly hereditary…

"What if the guardian never gave up his power?"

"Ah, well, that is why it must be given to someone worthy enough," Blaine said. "No guardian has failed to pass on his sword."

"Except you."

"Yes," Blaine said coolly. "Except for me."

"What would happen if the guardian were to kill the king? Would he not hold all the power then? If our swords are as similar as you claim."

Is he afraid of me or merely curious? I'd rather have his veneration. That is far easier to predict and manage.

"If I were to kill you, Darnuir, then I would be crippling myself. The blades are linked. Without the Dragon's Blade, my own sword has no power."

"And vice versa?"

"Indeed," Blaine said. "It is quite an elegant system, really. Neither of us has power without the other, so we must ensure that we help each other."

"A balancing act."

"Quite. When you were rejuvenated by Brackendon, your sword lost most of its power, as you were not yet of age. The power was not extinguished because you were not dead. When the power of the Dragon's Blade dimmed, my own diminished. For the last twenty years, I was little more than an ordinary dragon."

"Did the Dragon's Blade come to you after Brackendon worked his magic upon me? I'm told it disappeared after I was turned back into a baby, and not even Brackendon knows where it went."

"The sword did not come to me. Even I do not know where it might have gone. The blades hold many secrets."

"But before all this, you must have been powerful. The war lasted for decades before my 'rebirth'. There was still a dragon king then. Draconess, my father, or so I'm told."

"Ah," Blaine said. "This is where we do enter the realm of complications, and of secrets. You will need to know in time, but it is too intricate to handle now."

Darnuir gave him another distrustful look.

"I promise you will be told," Blaine said. "But not here. Anyone could be listening in."

"Over this chaos?"

"A perfect way to remain unseen. By all accounts, you have traitors in your midst."

"It would appear so," Darnuir said cautiously, "and I admit the red-eyed chevalier has caused me unease. If he truly fooled his brother, any of the humans might be in Castallan's service. Any of them might be hiding their red eyes, waiting to strike."

"This information comes from the runaway girl?"

Darnuir puffed out his chest. "I trust her, Blaine."

You are taken in by her pretty face, boy.

"I assume you do not," Darnuir said.

"I think it wise to treat her with a healthy dose of distrust until the real traitor or traitors are caught. I agreed with Scythe on that point."

Darnuir looked disgruntled but remained silent. This particular battle with the king would be a hard one to win.

He has a very long way to go.

They carried on through the woods. Night had descended completely, and starlight was glistening through the canopy when they were approached by a bare-footed dragon in loose-fitting clothes.

"Lord Guardian. My king," Damien said, giving a small bow to each in turn. "I am glad I've found you both. The prefect has set up a basic command post not far from here. He awaits you both there."

"You've proven yourself invaluable, outrunner," Blaine commended him.

"Thank you, sir."

"Are any of the hunters there?" Darnuir asked.

"Not that I know of, sire," Damien said.

"We will need someone there," Darnuir said, more to Blaine than the outrunner.

There's that 'we' again.

"You mean 'they', Darnuir?" Blaine said.

"Yes, of course. I meant that," Darnuir said, flustered. "Sorry."

No! Don't apologise to me in front of one of the men.

"We can arrange for some of the hunters to join us," Blaine said. "Lead on, Damien."

The command post, for want of a better name, was little more than some wagons placed between the gaps of several trees, creating a semblance of a wall. Empty barrels had been upended to serve as tables, and dutiful scribes were scratching furiously at parchment as messages were relayed to them. Counting the dead, most likely.

The small clearing was layered with leaves of silver, green and nut-brown. Scattered around were occasional charred branches from those burnt trees. Blaine was pleased to find a handful of his Light Bearers were present as well. They nodded at him as he approached. Then he saw the camp prefect, distinguished by the red plume on his helmet.

The prefect saluted. "Lord Guardian, we have had word from Queen Kasselle. She says more dragons arriving at your summons have been assembling by the Argent Tree as you requested."

"Excellent," Blaine said. "We will need to make our way there as soon as possible. I do not think the demons will follow us. They will likely take the opportunity to pillage and burn the Golden Crescent, but we are still too close to the edge of the forest for my liking."

"I think we will all require a short break," Darnuir said. "We have only just made it into the forest. It still seems like chaos all around us. Should we not camp here for the night and take rest?"

"We should not linger, Darnuir."

The prefect stepped forward purposefully when he heard Darnuir's name. He dropped to one knee. "Sire, it is truly you. You look identical. N'weer really has blessed you. My faith is restored."

A tense moment passed in which Blaine saw the confusion on Darnuir's face.

He knows nothing of the gods, either. Still, it was intriguing to note that Darnuir's rejuvenation seemed to inspire faith in the prefect. *Perhaps I can use it as more than just rhetoric?*

Blaine responded to save Darnuir from losing face. "Our gods are strong, Prefect, as you can see. The Light will shine again and drive our foes back."

"Yes, Lord Guardian," the prefect said, getting to his feet. "We have an estimated casualty report, my lords, if you would like to hear it now?" Blaine nodded and Darnuir imitated him. The prefect reached for a frayed piece of parchment with some scrawled calculations on it. "At least two hundred dead, maybe more. Five hundred are said to be exhausted or wounded. We are receiving more news all the time, my lords. These figures may change."

Blaine closed his eyes and bowed his head at the news.

"What of the hunters and civilians?" Darnuir asked. Puzzled by the question, the prefect glanced to Blaine for help.

"The good prefect here is most concerned with our own people," Blaine said.

"So you have nothing to share on them?" Darnuir said angrily. "They need leadership. They've lost two captains in the space of a week."

"Three captains," one of the scribes said quietly. Blaine looked to the hunched figure, obscured in the half-light of the flickering torches. It was only then that Blaine saw the long ebony hair that was tucked into her garments of blue and green leather.

A girl? In hunter leathers? Here with the army?

Blaine narrowed his eyes. "Prefect!" he snapped. "By Dranus, what is the meaning of this?"

"Lord Guardian... I... I apologise, but we were stretched thin when we first arrived in the forest. The girl was sent by the queen to deliver her message and I needed someone to start taking down reports from the outrunners."

"This is most unorthodox," Blaine said in a pained voice. "She is a human, Prefect. Look at her leathers."

"I'm not a human!" the girl said defiantly. "I'm a dragon. Why else would I have already been in the forest?"

Blaine blew air through his nose like an enraged animal. "You will address me properly, girl, as Lord Guardian."

Darnuir took a careful step away. "I wear my hunter leathers as well, Blaine. Is it so inconceivable that another dragon might?"

"Do you want proof, Lord Guardian?" the girl said. Her voice was carefully measured, as if she strained to maintain an air of calm. Blaine sniffed furtively at the air but could not smell the sweet scent of human fear. She was either a dragon, incredibly brave, or foolish.

The girl jumped to her feet and rummaged for a nearby branch. She found one of a decent thickness and proceeded to snap it in half with ease. She tossed the pieces at Blaine's feet and stared determinedly at him. Her eyes were grey, lined by thin eyebrows and short lashes. Her features were plain on the whole but she had a soft mouth, chin and small nose that some might have found appealing. Out of the corner of his eye, Blaine saw Darnuir smirking.

"What is your name?" Darnuir asked the girl.

"Lira," she said. "Erm, sire," she hastened to add. She gave a quick and awkward attempt at a curtsy. "The queen sent me. She came to me personally. She also said I was to tell you that you ought not to leave good dragons like me behind." The girl had the good grace to relay this message in a timid fashion.

Oh, Kasselle. Must you only cause me torment now?

"You're a hunter, Lira?" Darnuir asked. "Blue and green are worn by those from the Hinterlands at the gateway to the Highlands, if I'm not mistaken."

"Yes on both points," Lira said. "Sire!" she added hastily.

Darnuir waved her stumbling etiquette aside. "What did you mean by a third death?"

"Captain of the Golden Crescent, Captain Morwen, is also dead."

"How could you know that?" barked the prefect.

"Because I listened when one of the Crescent hunters came looking for assistance," she said. "They're lost and leaderless. Half their numbers are scattered, helping people flee from the demons or left behind to defend their station."

"Do you usually ignore vital information like this?" Darnuir inquired of the prefect.

The prefect bristled, unsure how to respond.

Blaine pulled Darnuir closer to him and spoke quietly. "Do not offend one of your commanding officers over such a matter. Have some sense."

"If we are going to get through this then we have to work together, as a proper alliance. Or do you intend to work separately from humanity?"

It would be easier if we could.

But such a course was unfortunately impossible. Humanity had a fleet. Dragons would need those ships to cross the sea to Aurisha.

"I am sure our prefect did not neglect such information deliberately," Blaine said aloud for the rest to here. "Our arrival here has been chaotic; I'm sure it was simply lost amongst the flood of information coming in. Is that not so, Prefect?"

The prefect rallied. "Yes, Lord Guardian. I beg your pardon, sire, it shan't happen again."

"I hope not," Darnuir said. "I would hate to think there is prejudice amongst the officers you have selected, Blaine."

Careful, boy. Be very careful. Blaine would not reprimand him here, not publicly. It was vital they presented a united front. *There is too much human in him.*

Still, Darnuir was proving he had some authority about him when he was riled up, and that at least was promising. Blaine's lack of response seemed to bolster Darnuir's confidence.

"How did Captain Morwen die?" Darnuir asked.

"The hunter didn't say," Lira said. She avoided looking at either Blaine or the prefect. "But I got the impression she had been dead for some time."

"As useful as this is to know," Blaine began, "there is little we can do about it now. Lira, perhaps you could run back to the Argent Tree and tell the rest of our people to make ready for their king."

It was a flimsy reason to send the girl away, but she had to go. Women were not part of army life. It was not the way things were done.

Lira looked confused. "But I came to help. I'm not just a messenger."

"Not just a messenger, Lord Guardian!" the prefect corrected her.

"That is okay," Blaine allowed. "It is not necessary to repeat the courtesy every time. So long as she keeps her tone respectful."

"I'm a trained hunter," Lira said. "I'd rather fight than write."

"We can discuss that later," Blaine said, hoping to shelve the subject for another time. She could stay with her hunters, but she would not join a legion.

"I don't see the problem," Darnuir said, to the shock of the prefect. "The more pressing concern is who will lead the hunters. I say Cosmo."

Cosmo? The man with the motherless son? He did not seem special in any way but Darnuir was enamoured by him. The boy had perked up greatly when Cosmo had joined them at the rear guard.

"Damien," Darnuir demanded, whirling to locate the outrunner, "you remember who Cosmo is?"

"Yes, sire."

"Search for him and bring him here. He was carried off from the fighting by a pair of fairies."

"The flyers landed close by," Damien said. "I should not be long." He jogged off through the trees.

Blaine was quietly impressed. That had been quite commanding as well. Perhaps the boy would not need so much work after all, though Blaine was not sure if that was a blessing or not. The less moulding the boy needed, the better, given their circumstances; however, Blaine also hoped to sculpt him the way he desired.

"Why this Cosmo?" Blaine asked.

"Because he is the best man for the job, whether he wants it or not," Darnuir said. "He has stepped up before when he was needed."

"I understand that he has suffered a great loss. Perhaps he is not in the best frame of mind."

"Then who would you choose?" Darnuir asked.

"I wouldn't trouble myself with it, Darnuir. Let the hunters sort it out for themselves."

"Is that indifference, or active dislike?" Darnuir asked.

"I have no particular prejudice against hunters."

Darnuir raised his eyebrows.

"Why should I?" Blaine said. "Because hundreds of years ago, hunters used to score a few kills against our kind? Perhaps you think that dragons fear hunters? I'm sure that's what they told you growing up. Well, let me disabuse you of that notion. Dragons are not animals that flee at the sound of a snapping twig or the rustling of a bush. If a hunter were stalking me, Darnuir, he would need to hope that I do not smell him or see him, because when I close the distance, no amount of coloured leather would save him."

"That is why they would shoot you before you closed the distance," Darnuir said perfectly casually.

"Such dishonourable tactics do not frighten me."

"That is how I was trained," Darnuir said. "Do you think I am dishonourable?"

"You will not practice those ways anymore," Blaine said firmly. "And once we get you out of those leathers and into proper armour, all the better. And you, girl." He rounded on Lira. "Darnuir's ignorance of his true nature might forgive him, but you knew you were a dragon, yet you are sporting human hunting leathers. Why join an organisation that sings songs about killing your own people?"

Lira had the grace to look crestfallen and a little ashamed.

Good. Twenty years with humans is far too long. The youngest of us have had too much contact with them.

"I wanted to fight," she said. "I needed to fight. My father died when Aurisha fell or so my mother told me. I was only very young at the time, barely walking and talking. What were we to do, Your Guardianness?"

"Lord Guardian!" the prefect snapped. A vein bulged on his brow.

"What were we to do, Lord Guardian?" Lira continued. "The rest of the dragons just vanished; you all slithered away after Demons' Folly. No one was collecting the tithe for soldiers' widows. My mother had nothing. It was her idea, actually. When we ended up in the north, she joined the hunters there and trained to be a healer. She looked young to them, of course, and had little me with her, so she must have looked a sad sight. I grew up at their station and, when I was older, I trained alongside them; and here I am." Lira ended hurriedly and a little hesitantly. Whatever courage had bolstered her to speak seemed to have faltered under Blaine's ire.

"Is it necessary to resolve this now?" Darnuir asked.

The Light Bearers, who had stood sentinel, rustled and shifted uneasily. Blaine heard one grumble something to the other.

Forgive our young king, brothers.

"I agree," Blaine said. "We should press on towards the Argent Tree. Prefect, ensure our dead are brought along for proper burial." Darnuir predictably opened his mouth to add to this command. Blaine cut him off. "Ensure *all* the dead are brought, Prefect. The wounded too. They'll find rest at th Argent Tree."

"Yes, Lord Guardian," the prefect said. "Which human should I liaise with on this matter?"

"This hunter of the king's."

"Cosmo," Darnuir said.

"What?" another voice said hoarsely from behind one of the wagons. Blaine thought he recognised it. Cosmo and Damien emerged into their small camp. "What do you want, Darnuir?" Cosmo asked, exhausted. "I have yet to find my son. Can't this wait?"

Blaine understood why the man was used to addressing Darnuir like this but it would not work in the long-term. However, there had been enough damage done already with Lira. To rebuke the hunter now would only lead to another argument. Blaine let it pass.

"No," Darnuir said, "it cannot wait. I'm sure Cassandra is taking good care of him."

"Whatever it is," Cosmo protested, "I'm sure Scythe is more than capable of handling it."

"Scythe is dead," Darnuir said with an effort. "I need you to—"

"What? No... he was fine when I was taken away. What happened?"

"He insisted on setting the line that we built ablaze," Darnuir said. "Something went wrong. There was an enormous explosion, far bigger than pitch should have made."

Cosmo was visibly shaken by the news. He steadied himself with a hand on the nearby wagon. "Isn't any ale here, is there? I'd take wine if that's what you lot drink?"

"Cosmo," Darnuir said more sternly.

"Yes, I heard," the hunter said. "And I saw the smoke rising up when we landed. What caused that? I thought we were just creating a long strip to set alight and force the demons to go around. All we stacked at my section were hay bales, dried wheat stalks and a few of those barrels."

"What was in the barrels?" Lira asked, perking up again.

"Some sort of black powder," Cosmo said.

"And you don't know what it was?" Lira said, a little confused.

"No," Cosmo said. "Should we? I assumed it was something they put on the crops."

"That wouldn't be wise," Lira said. "It sounds like dragon powder to me."

Dragon — what? This girl was beginning to make Blaine's head ache without the need for magic. That was impressive in its own way.

"What by the gods is dragon powder?" he demanded. "I have never encountered such a thing. I, who have lived several lifetimes."

The girl shuffled, looking at Blaine's freshly-flared annoyance, Darnuir's curious eyes and Cosmo's fatigued and sweaty face. "Others call it blasting powder or just plain black powder, like you said. But many up north call it dragon powder. They say it is made of dragons, ground down, and explodes when you anger it."

Blaine scowled. "I do hope that is not a literal interpretation."

"Of course not," Lira said. "It is used up north in the quarries to blow the rock apart, though it is a recent thing. Only in the last few years has it been used, I think."

"But what was such a thing doing in the Golden Crescent?" Cosmo said.

No one answered. No one had any theories.

Blaine felt a pang of unease at the news of this powder. *If this substance can reduce stone, what else might it be used for?*

"Yet another mystery to uncover," Darnuir sighed. "But Cosmo, I need you now. The hunters need you. You resist and resist, but every time you have to lead, you do it well, and the men love you. You took Scythe's place at Cold Point. You must do so again."

"Oh, must I?"

"Yes," Darnuir insisted. "Grace would want you to—"

"Don't you dare. You don't get to—"

"She was the closest thing I had to a mother. I miss her too."

"But she wasn't your mother," Cosmo said. "Her real son will never know her. And I am not your father either. I didn't ask for the job and I wouldn't ask for this one."

Even Blaine considered this harsh.

Darnuir swallowed a lump in his throat, fighting back a trembling lower lip. "Cosmo—"

"Have Garon lead them," Cosmo carried on. "The Boreac men will follow him, I'm sure."

"I hoped that you would lead all hunter forces," Darnuir said.

"That has never been done," Cosmo grunted. "What about the Crescent captain? Morwen, I think her name is."

"She is dead," Lira chimed in helpfully.

"Of course," Cosmo said bitterly. He strode the few paces to stand eye to eye with Darnuir. "The answer is still no."

Darnuir winced in some pain. His cheek twitched and his expression and bearing changed entirely. He might have been a different person. "Listen to me, human. You will do as I command."

Something caught Blaine's eye, even in the hazy light of twilight. On the Dragon's Blade, the ruby eye facing Blaine twinkled and glowed faintly. *Ah,* Blaine thought, *but to have enough memories stored to actively overpower the carrier would be extreme. More than I have ever heard of.*

"Command? Human?" Cosmo blustered, moving as though to take hold of Darnuir.

The Light Bearers looked to Blaine, hands flashing to their swords. Blaine raised a fist to halt them.

"You have changed, Darnuir," Cosmo said.

Darnuir's eye twitched and he held his head in one hand, unable to meet Cosmo's glare.

The hunter stormed away. "Leave me be. I'm going to find my *real* son."

Darnuir faced those who were left at the command post. Once again, it was only dragons. Damien stood impassively, awaiting more orders, as though the scene had not occurred. The Light Bearers slowly loosened their grips on their weapons. The prefect looked confused, likely taken aback that a human had spoken to his king in such a manner. The remaining scribes kept their heads down as good scribes should, but Lira still stood in her insulting leathers, seemingly rooted to the spot.

"Well," Darnuir said, "at least he is talking again."

A more awkward silence followed Darnuir's failed attempt to save face. Blaine let it hang for as long as he could bear, hoping that Darnuir might regain himself. He didn't.

"Prefect," Blaine said slowly.

"Err, yes, Lord Guardian," the dragon said, seeming to snap out of some reverie.

"Prepare to move further into the forest. I think you can leave handling hunter affairs alone for the time being."

24

THE TRUSTED

Dukoona – Aurisha – The Throne Room

The throne of the Dragon King was hard and unforgiving. For the most important chair in Tenalp, it was remarkably plain; its back was high and straight, its armrests broad, and simple. Steps fanned down to a plain stone floor, rather than the marble used elsewhere in the Royal Tower. Raw strength might have hewn it from the very rock of the plateau.

Dukoona sat upon the throne, his head cradled in his hands, fingers twisting around the cold, fiery tendrils that were his hair. He thought the throne to be a sign that the King of Dragons had no need to assert his power, that his people followed without question or the need for ceremony.

But if Draconess had been so powerful, how had he fallen so easily?

Dukoona remembered that moment well, when he had plunged his shadow-blade through Draconess' chest. Castallan had been there at the end, though his eyes had been fixed on the king's sword.

Dukoona, however, only had eyes for his greatest kill, drinking in Draconess' expression. It had been so very sweet. Not the kill itself, but robbing Rectar of his greatest prize. It had been one of his finer acts of resistance.

But that had been before the massacre atop the plateau. Before his doubt. Before Rectar's renewed strength.

It was now quite undeniable.

He is strong once more.

After Aurisha fell, Rectar's voice had dropped to a whisper. Somehow, he had lost the best part of his power back then despite the victory. Something had crippled him, and so Dukoona could resist more easily. But now, somehow, he had regained his strength.

Rectar had spoken to him earlier that day. His voice had come as waves of a storm crashed against the plateau of Aurisha. Dukoona had crumbled and been forced to listen. "Come," Rectar had said. The command was simple, but not since he had been summoned into the world had it been so strong.

At first, Dukoona thought the impending invasion of the west must have stirred life back into his master. But upon reflection, Dukoona suspected a more direct cause of events. This invasion was being hastily put together because Rectar had regained his full power.

But why now? And how?

And what would it mean for the spectres?

Dukoona was being summoned to Kar'drun and he hoped it was to launch their new campaign. Any other reason was too dangerous to consider. None entered the mountain, save for the mindless demons who were so much easier to manipulate. It had been decades since Dukoona had been allowed entry.

Does he suspect disloyalty? Does he know of it?

Dukoona leaned forwards on the throne, almost rocking in thought. He had often shown signs of resistance in the past, but it had never been an issue. He assumed his master expected his more powerful minions to push back, if only a little. Yet the brevity of the communication was worrying.

Does he no longer have use for us? Once, the thought might have cheered him. However, its implications were severe for his kind. *If we are not needed, then what will be done with us? And what will take our place?*

Lost in thought, he did not notice spectres materialising from the floor at the centre of the room; springing up from a shadow cast from the open doorway. He looked up only when they stood gathered at the base of the stairs leading to the throne.

Quickly, he attempted to compose himself. He did not wish to worry them. These spectres were some of his Trusted – those who had proven to him that they shared his doubts about their master.

Kidrian, for example, had been with him since the start. Patches of guttering purple embers burned upon his black head.

Dukoona looked to him for the report. "What news from Kar'drun?"

"Troubling news, my lord," Kidrian said in his croaky voice. "As you instructed, my men and I watched the mountain as we ostensibly oversaw the construction of the fleet in the Forsaken City. For weeks, there was no unusual activity, until a fortnight ago, when something emerged from the mountain."

"You saw Him?" Dukoona asked. For Rectar to step out of his sanctum was unheard of, but nothing else ever came forth from the jaws of that burnt rock, other than demons.

"No, my lord. The Master remains secluded, as ever. None of us saw the incident ourselves but a witness states that he saw a creature running across the Lifeless Lands, being chased by demons. The creature appeared to have red skin and was human or dragon in shape."

"Why the uncertainty?" Dukoona asked.

"It might have been a human or a dragon but for its size," Kidrian said. "It was quite large, apparently. As I say, none of the Trusted actually saw the creature."

"Do you believe what you were told?"

Kidrian nodded towards one of the spectres on his flank. This spectre was smaller and weedier than the others. Its form was not as solid as a regular spectre but more so than a demon. A shadowy mist swirled lightly, whereas the other spectres had a denser, flesh-like shadow. The creature was clearly one of the Broken; poor wretches whom the Master had failed to summon properly into the world. Looking at this frail member of his kind, Dukoona's aversion to his master flared.

"Sonrid here witnessed the event," Kidrian said. "He was close to where the creature eventually fell and came to us afterwards in confidence. His tale is quite... disturbing."

Dukoona beckoned the Broken to step forward. Sonrid shuffled awkwardly, a malformed leg dragging him down. His shadows flickered from nerves.

"Speak freely, Sonrid," Dukoona said. "I am eager to hear from you."

"My lord Dukoona," Sonrid said in a strained voice, as though his throat had a fist clenched around it. "The creature was indeed red in colour, its skin shining like fish scales. I thought it almost seven feet tall, but it was gangly and uncoordinated. Its face was long and stretched, and it howled as though tormented. It managed to make it as far as the edge of the Forsaken City before—" Sonrid looked to Kidrian, clearly apprehensive.

"Go on," Kidrian told him. "Our lord will want to know. He will not be angry at you."

Dukoona leaned forward. "Sonrid, if Kidrian had any reason to doubt your loyalty, you would not be alive today. Speak, now."

"A great number of demons chased the creature. They fell upon it at the edge of the Forsaken City and, after a brief fight, it lay dead, although it took a score of demons down with it."

"Were there no spectres at hand to fight this creature?" Dukoona asked.

"This is the part you will find disturbing. When nearby spectres moved to investigate, the surviving demons… they…"

"Yes?" Dukoona growled, moving to the edge of the throne.

"They turned on them, my lord," Sonrid said. He flinched as if Dukoona had struck him. "The demons swarmed over those spectres and killed them all."

"But not you? You survived."

"My lord, I was afraid of the red creature. When it drew close, I melded into a shadow to hide and saw the whole thing. Please, forgive my cowardice."

"Cowardice? To live in the shadows is our nature, Sonrid. To strike from them, to travel by them and to learn by them. You have learned a great deal by hiding and I am grateful you were not killed. Though this information is most distressing."

Sonrid hung his head. "I wish I could have done more."

Dukoona rose from the throne and swept down the stairs to cradle his head. "It is no fault of yours. Only the Master's. Every spectre he tried to bind to this world after we took this city was malformed."

The other spectres around the room turned to get a better look at Sonrid, as if he were some spectacle. Many of the Broken perished after only a few years; to see one alive was quite rare.

"Broken struggle to control demons. What could you have done that day? You might be among the youngest of our kind, Sonrid, but have you ever known demons to turn against a spectre?"

"Never."

"Then you did exactly what you should have. You hid, and watched, and brought this crucial information to me."

He raised his head to look Dukoona in the eye. If his wispy eyes had been well enough formed, they might have been pleading.

"My lord, to exist as I do is to exist in pain. Will you end me?"

Dukoona was caught off guard. "End you?"

The other members of the Trusted looked equally shocked. Kidrian's eyes popped, but the decision was Dukoona's. His alone.

"Such a brave request. Why ask this of me when a moment ago you were afraid of punishment?"

"I thought we lived to serve," Sonrid said. "If the Master is killing our kind, I see no reason to continue to suffer."

Dukoona took the Broken seriously. Such a request would not be made upon a whim. He stroked the little spectre's face, running one finger from the tip of his head down to the point of his misshapen chin. With both hands, he could twist Sonrid's neck and it would be done. And yet, he saw in the poor spectre all there was to mistrust and fear about their master.

We are only his tools. He does not care to fix us if we are broken. He will simply reach for a fresh one, or seek something else. A better tool for his purpose.

"I will not kill you. Too many of us have died already." He ascended the stairs, turned and addressed the room at large. "Too many," he told them. "And ever since we took this city, our numbers have not been replenished. The Master gave up when he could only summon the Broken after his power diminished. For diminish it did."

The Trusted nodded in agreement.

"I felt it. Perhaps you did too? His voice, once as loud as the howling winds, became little more than a whisper. Years ago, when he sent us north in search of passage through the Highlands, I marched deliberately into dead ends; I allowed those grey-skinned beasts to believe they were repelling us. Each day, I thought the Master would punish me and yet nothing came."

No one answered him. Kidrian, Sonrid and the others were enthralled.

"I feared that our kind were being sent to die; that every battle and loss was of no concern to him. Each spectre killed requires less of his will to bind to this world. Did he require strength for something greater? Today, that fear has become a reality."

"Do you mean to say that the Master no longer needs us?" Kidrian asked.

"I fear so," Dukoona said. "Something has changed. His strength has returned in full. And now we have more unanswered questions. What was this red creature? Are there more of them? Are they to replace us? In short, have our people been sentenced to extinction? Is this invasion only for us to throw our lives away to spare his new servants?"

Around the room, the Trusted stared first at each other and then at Dukoona. Little Sonrid just kept his head bowed, seemingly disheartened.

"What are we to do?" Kidrian asked.

"We will do what we have always done," Dukoona said. "We will wait and watch and learn; and we shall do it from the shadows. Above all, we will resist." The Trusted nodded in agreement. To resist was what they had always done.

Sonrid kept his head low.

"I did not kill you, Sonrid, because I have far more use for you alive than dead."

"But the Master—"

"Is happy to throw our lives away. I'd rather resist that a little longer. Wouldn't you?"

"Death would free me," Sonrid said feebly.

"Death would end you. And if you are dead, you cannot work against he who has brought you into this world to suffer."

"My lord, we cannot act directly against the Master's will," Kidrian said.

"No, not directly. But we are not the only ones who resist him." He gave them one last knowing look. "It is time we worked at more than simply killing dragons. But we must tread carefully. Go now. I must consider our next move."

They all bowed and slowly made their way out of the throne room. Kidrian was at the back of the group. As an afterthought, Dukoona called after him.

"Kidrian, find our new friend a place amongst the Trusted." The purple embers on Kidrian's head flared at the command, a sign he was disgruntled at the recruitment, but he gave another curt nod all the same before exiting. Sonrid looked alarmed at being brought into the fold, but he too left without another word.

When Dukoona sat back on the throne, he heard it again, that loud and awful voice ringing through his mind.

"Come."

Dukoona knew he could not delay for long. He would have to travel to the burned mountain: to Kar'drun.

25

THE FIRST DUEL

Darnuir – Val'tarra – The Argent Tree

"I shall require gold and lots of it," said the familiar robed man who inhabited Darnuir's dreams. As always, the scene unfolded before him in a jarring combination, being both vivid and opaque at the same time.

"I shall require gold and lots of it."

"And what will you need that for?" Darnuir asked.

"To find sufficient volunteers. Do you really want to know the details?"

"What you do with humans is no concern of mine, but I must insist you refrain from approaching my own people."

"Of course, my lord," the stranger said, now a little nervous. "In any case, I do not think dragons would be suitable. All I need from you is gold and a safe environment to work in. With that, and enough time, I will find the answer for you – for us!"

"You are sure? I seek answers. Not more questions."

"I am, though it will take a deal of secrecy to begin my work without interruption or suspicion. Few are as open-minded or understanding as you, Darnuir."

"Few share my passion to preserve my race. Even my father lacks that most basic instinct of survival. I feel he has resigned himself."

"We shall turn the tide," the stranger assured him.

"I hope so, Castallan."

The scene dissolved.

· · ·

Darnuir awoke with a sudden jerk. His head swam from the sudden movement and his heart pounded. Cold sweat clung to him and had dampened the sheets beneath him.

He reached for the large glass of water at his bedside. He had taken to having one on hand every night to help wash away the bitter taste in his mouth.

I don't know how I'll ever get used to this.

Starlight filled his room within the Argent Tree. His bed was a soft and welcome comfort after the many weeks of rough living and the four-day struggle through the forest to the Argent Tree. Interrupted by these dreams every night, he'd long since learned that he could not fall back to sleep after them.

He rubbed at his tired eyes then got up, hoping fresh air would wake him. The room was carved out of the Argent Tree itself, as was everything within the giant tree. As such, everything in his room was connected as though the room had grown that way naturally. Gnarled silver wood was painted over in intricate patterns of cool blues and greens. The fairies were truly skilled with their brushwork. A balcony rested on a sturdy overhanging branch outside.

Darnuir stepped out into the starry light, which was reflected by thousands of silver leaves all around him. Some drifted downwards in a genteel dance, sparkling as they descended hundreds of feet to the ground. Looking down, the canopy of Val'-tarra swayed in the breeze – black, green, and silver – stretching to the horizon. The air was crisp and chilled at this height but Darnuir felt at ease.

He had grown up in the snow and mountains. To him, the cold felt like home.

Some of the dragons had told him that Aurisha was a hot and dry place. The thought of living there was as alien to him as were the people he was supposed to lead. It was fortunate that the dragons seemed to adhere to his commands without protest, although they often glanced to Blaine for confirmation.

They have not fully accepted me yet. And why should they?

Among the hunters, captains and leaders only gained respect through their deeds. Scythe had earned that when he had staved off the encroaching demons in the Bore-acs, allowing them to hold back the dark tide for months. Yet Scythe had not garnered the love of the hunters.

He deserved it, though. He did his best and gave everything for us.

Yet Darnuir was beginning to understand that love and respect were two distinct things. Growing up, he had both loved and greatly admired Cosmo, so that the feelings seemed entwined. From what he had observed with Blaine, it was evident that he commanded respect from the dragons, almost without question, but it did not seem that they loved him. Blaine deserved that esteem from his demeanour and his battle prowess, if nothing else.

And which do I want? Do I want love or respect?

Knowing he had either would be beneficial.

There was something else he had occasionally noticed from the dragons: a wariness that, for some, verged on fear. It was subtle, only noticeable in the tentative way they approached him or cautiously backed away. Perhaps it was simply natural behaviour towards someone in his position, but Darnuir suspected that his reputation preceded him – or, at least, his previous reputation. No one hid the fact that his past self had been less than admirable.

It only made the recurring dreams more disconcerting. The latest one had been the most extensive yet, and the most worrying. *At the end, I said his name – Castallan.* He hoped desperately that they were only dreams, but some instinct told him they were more than that. *What did I do? What were the answers I hoped that Castallan could provide?*

As a more forceful breeze hit him, he decided that a good bout of training might clear his head. Perhaps some of those Light Bearers Blaine was so fond of might be awake and willing to spar.

He returned to his room and grabbed his leathers, leaving off some of the fur-lined pieces so he wouldn't be uncomfortable. The fairies had given his clothing a deep cleaning and Darnuir's nose was grateful for the fragrance of crushed flowers, as opposed to sweat and dried blood. He was beginning to get used to his increasingly acute sense of smell, but some scents still took him by surprise. Chief of these unusual aromas was the sweet smell he picked up when around some of the hunters or other humans. Another question for Blaine.

Grabbing the Dragon's Blade and strapping it to his waist, he began the long descent through the Argent Tree.

Steel clashed on steel as the dragons trained in the clearing. Darnuir squinted in the dawn light as he lifted his dulled training sword to block a downward strike from Lira. Her instincts were good. Very good. Darnuir had not faced anyone who could match him except for Sanders, the red-eyed chevalier, and, of course, the foe in blood-red armour at Cold Point.

He threw Lira off, but she maintained her balance, despite the damp morning dew underfoot. She lunged forwards and he spun to one side. He took a swipe at her, hoping to regain the offensive, but she danced out of the way with incredible speed. At least, it seemed incredible. Darnuir had rarely met a real challenge when he was younger. In hindsight, he had always been just a little too quick to react, his blows a little too strong for his size.

He thought he had just been gifted. They all had.

Perhaps I am not that talented after all.

Lira came at him again, lashing out with her blunted blade. The sword tips clashed in a metallic screech that grew louder as Darnuir pushed, scraping the edges against each other. Lira pushed back, and for a moment, they stood locked, frozen in mid-action. Then she buckled, thrown back by Darnuir's greater strength.

Lira's head hit the ground hard. She cried out and rolled but Darnuir was standing over her, pointing his sword down towards her neck.

"I yield," she said bitterly.

Darnuir offered her a hand and heard clapping from the treeline.

"I think you might actually be getting quicker," Balack called. Cassandra was beside him, waving one of the blunt training swords casually around.

He had seen them together more often lately. Why was that?

"You were too slow, boy," another voice called.

Blaine approached, flanked by a retinue of Light Bearers. They now bore a peculiar-looking symbol, painted expertly in yellow onto the face of their shields: a scorched severed sun pierced by a sword.

Blaine drew up short and glared at them. "In fact, you were both too slow." He threw Lira an unfavourable look. "How will you ever learn from fighting her? She is little better than a human."

"She fought well," Darnuir said in her defence. Lira smiled at him but cowered before Blaine.

Blaine ignored this. "We missed you at prayer this morning, my king. Had you no words to say to Dwna?" His tone held no surprise. Darnuir had been actively avoiding these gatherings. The whole concept baffled him. It seemed like speaking to the air without any response. Perhaps Blaine received replies in his head? But, if that was true, that might just make him mad. Yet it must make sense to others, for Blaine's followers grew daily.

"I needed to clear my head," Darnuir said. "I'd hoped one of your Light Bearers would be willing to spar." He glanced around at Blaine's followers. They all met him with impassive eyes.

Am I supposed to rebuke them for scorning me? Or are they beyond my 'power' as Blaine's preferred men?

There were many subtleties of his role that Darnuir was in the dark about, and Blaine seemed intent on keeping things that way, feeding him morsels of information as he needed to know.

"If it is a duel you want, then I shall spar with you." Blaine smiled.

Darnuir was taken aback. "You?"

The Light Bearers began to fan out in a circle. "If you are going to improve, you should learn how far you have to go." He drew out the Guardian's Blade.

"Is this not best for training?" Darnuir asked, holding up the dulled practice sword.

"Would you use that in a real fight?"

"No," Darnuir said stiffly.

"Then you won't use it here. I won't hurt you if that is what you are concerned about."

Darnuir threw an apprehensive look around him. He was surrounded by the silent Light Bearer sentinels. Lira had shied out of the way to join Balack and Cassandra. His pride already smarting, Darnuir tossed the training sword aside and drew out the Dragon's Blade. Other sparring pairs stopped their fights as they noticed what was unfolding. Gradually, the circle grew larger, becoming a makeshift arena.

"What if I hurt you?" Darnuir asked.

"I'm not worried about that."

Then Blaine attacked.

It was all Darnuir could do to block Blaine's first assault. He charged Darnuir with the same ferocity he had used when battling Raymond's brother at Torridon. The force of the blow nearly knocked Darnuir over, but he remained on his feet, stumbling back. Blaine came at him again. Darnuir thought he had anticipated Blaine's strike to his right but, at the last second, Blaine whipped his arm around in a blur. Darnuir's exposed side stung harshly.

"Dead!" Blaine yelled.

Murmurs rose from the onlookers.

Darnuir felt the strange temper rise in him again and his head throbbed with renewed vigour. Somehow, it was not wholly his own. Drawing several short and furious breaths, he moved to attack Blaine. The guardian dodged his blow as though Darnuir was a clumsy child. Darnuir did not relent. He struck again, this time forcing Blaine to parry. He swung repeatedly, high and low, pressing forward and putting Blaine on the defensive. It seemed he had turned the momentum of the fight around too easily, a fear confirmed when a concentrated beam of light emanated from the Guardian's Blade. Blinded, Darnuir's final swings met air alone and he felt another hard slap at the back of his legs. The force of Blaine's strike buckled his knees and he fell.

"That time I would have had your legs off," Blaine said.

"The light—"

"Would you call out a man with a shield blocking your blow? No, because it is a tool he possesses."

"Spectres and demons can't play tricks like that," Darnuir growled.

"We don't know what we will face before the end."

I have my own trick as well. If only I could control it properly.

Blaine stood ready for a third round.

Darnuir got back to his feet and they began to slowly circle each other. The surrounding crowd had grown larger and now contained hunters as well. Civilians, fairy, human and dragon alike must have been attracted to the spectacle, for children sat upon the shoulders of their fathers or mothers.

This time, Blaine took the initiative, leaping through the air towards Darnuir, briefly blocking out the sun. Instinct told Darnuir to raise his sword but he had a better idea. He held until the last possible moment then rolled aside. Blaine collided with the ground in an impact that would have shattered the bones of a human. Darnuir rounded on the hunched figure, bringing the flat of his sword down. The word 'dead' died half-formed in his throat as Blaine, still crouched, brought his own sword over his head to bat the Dragon's Blade away. Darnuir tried to quickly bring another strike to bear but Blaine jumped to his feet and Darnuir was suddenly back-pedaling, parrying until the edge of the crowd had to part for them. With a great effort, Darnuir pushed against Blaine until the two became locked.

More light began to glow around Blaine's sword.

The same cheap trick?

Darnuir wanted nothing more than for the fire from his own sword to leap forth. He thought about it hard, concentrating entirely on the bright flames spilling from the dragon's mouth. Then he felt it. His throat felt like it was burning, but there was nothing there, and suddenly, real fire lit up the Dragon's Blade.

Blaine cursed as the heat bit at his face. He kicked and Darnuir spun from the blow. Winded, he gasped for air. His throat still burned, and the fire must have continued to pour forth as he twisted, for a ring of fire now encircled Blaine and himself. Screams rose from the spectators and the wall of bodies rushed away from the flames.

He could not control it. It was just like at Cold Point. *No, no, no,* Darnuir thought in a panic as he flapped the Dragon's Blade around helplessly, as though it was a rag on fire.

"Put it out!" Blaine yelled.

Darnuir tried. He failed.

"I can't!"

Blaine was on him then, grabbing him roughly and pushing a strong hand against his mouth. "Hold your breath, boy."

Darnuir did as he was told, seizing up his airways and not letting a breath of air in. It seemed to work. The burning sensation in his throat died and the flames on the sword guttered out. Blaine let go of him and he gulped in air.

He coughed and spluttered as he fought to regain his breath. "I didn't know I had to stop breathing."

"You should be able to turn it off as naturally as you ignite the blade but, as you seem to struggle, bear that in mind for the future."

"Why does holding my breath help?"

Blaine did not immediately answer. He was preoccupied with scanning around for casualties. Thankfully, the dampness of the ground had impeded the fire spreading. The crowds had dispersed a fair distance, and Darnuir saw some fleeing the glade. Satisfied that no damage had been done, Blaine rounded on him.

"Fires will go out if they are starved of air."

"But the fire was on the sword."

"Did your throat not feel hot? That's how it has been described to me."

"The heat wasn't really in me. I can't breathe fire."

Blaine shrugged. "That is just the way it works, Darnuir. I told you I don't have all the answers."

Darnuir let out an exasperated sigh. *You've given few enough of them so far.* Still, the new knowledge was extremely useful. If he could practice controlling the fire in this crude manner, it would be a start.

Blaine must have sensed his frustration. "The blades embody different things. The Dragon's Blade embodies the nature of a dragon, or what it once meant, and so it can fly and spew flames."

"And yours? What does the Guardian's Blade embody?"

"The Light," Blaine said, "and the power to carefully watch the world over many years; hence, the long life and the memory storage."

"What do you mean by the—"

"Darnuir, I don't think here is the place, but I do think it is the time. Come." Blaine gestured for him to follow then swept off.

Darnuir felt thoroughly exasperated with the guardian. *Always just these little pieces at a time. Nothing is ever solid.*

As they neared the exit of the clearing, Darnuir caught a glimpse of Cassandra duelling playfully with Balack. Lira watched them both carefully, shouting out tips and instructions. He found his attention captured by the tumbling locks of Cassandra's thick hair, her slender figure as she wove around Balack, and her brilliant smile as she slipped and fell on the slick grass. He noticed how her eyes matched the colour of the forest floor and were alight with a spark that he had not seen in them before. She seemed happy.

"Darnuir," Blaine said slowly, "she will still be here when we are finished. Come along."

"I wasn't..." Darnuir said stupidly. "I was just watching."

"I know you were. I'd caution you, but I imagine you will ignore me."

Darnuir remained silent, refusing to rise to the bait.

Blaine's expression darkened. "I will offer you my caution all the same."

26

SWEET AIR, BITTER NEWS

Darnuir – Val'tarra – Base Of The Argent Tree

Blaine led him from the duelling glade to the banks of the Avvorn, the river that ran down from the Highlands through the heart of Val'tarra. Tinged with magic, the surface of the water shone a delicate icy-blue. The river was too wide for even the strongest dragon to leap, so they took the bridge. As they crossed, Darnuir saw something strange. Not far downriver, a score of fairies was tending to one of the blackened and burned trees.

"What now?" Blaine asked impatiently.

"What are they doing?"

"They are arborists," Blaine said. "They are doing their job."

The team of fairies moved carefully around the tree, placing their hands upon it in a manner that must have held significance, but which left Darnuir none the wiser.

"They are attempting to heal the tree," Blaine explained. "It has not processed the Cascade energy within the water well."

"They don't seem to be making much of a difference."

"Right now, they are checking whether it can be saved. If it can't, they will tear it down."

Darnuir, who felt that was all he was going to get out of the guardian, did not ask further, but he was intrigued by Blaine's allusions to answers.

He followed Blaine over the bridge. Trees were sparse here, as they had to compete with the thirsty roots of the Argent Tree. Before them was a veritable city of tents, filled with both refugees and warriors. The pair began trudging down the route of trodden grass which acted as a road.

The wounded were lain out in long rows on the soft grass, making it easier for the fairy healers to move amongst their patients. Hundreds of them tended to their charges in elegant, silken gowns.

One healer dashed towards a man thrashing in his sleep. Her skin was teal and her fine white hair was tied back in a long braid. Judging by the patient's muddy red leathers, he was a human hunter from the Cairlav Marshes. The sick hunter awoke as the fairy reached him, the sweat visible on his brow. One of his arms ended in a bandaged stump just past the elbow. As the healer unwound the linens, the smell of something rotting reached Darnuir and his stomach twisted. Impulsively, he raised his hand to cover his nose.

"Putrid, isn't it?" Blaine said.

The fairy was speaking softly to the man and wiping his brow. She inspected the wound, then looked up and made a signal to a fellow healer, who began to approach with a clanking case.

"No," the man whimpered, trying to move. "No, no, please." He sounded terrified.

As he struggled, he nearly knocked the healer down. She caught Darnuir watching them and her eyes beseeched him. He hurriedly picked his way over to the pair and pressed down on the man to keep him from moving. Blaine called after him, but he ignored it. The hunter cried out in fresh pain and Darnuir eased the pressure he was putting on him.

"I'm sorry," he said. "I have yet to learn my own strength."

"My lord?" the hunter said in disbelief. "I lost my hand at Torridon, but the rest of the arm has been fine since. Please tell her... please." The fairy gave Darnuir another stern look and shook her head. Her companion arrived, and she began rummaging in the case.

"I'm no healer," Darnuir said, "but my nose tells me it is too far gone. I'm sorry."

The man gave up under Darnuir's superior strength. He began to sob instead, the tears mingling with the beads of sweat running down his face. His eyes widened as the fairy produced a surgical blade, long and razor-sharp. Another smell reached Darnuir then; it was powerfully sweet, so sweet it was nearly sickly.

Is that fear I am smelling? He hated that he found it pleasant.

The healer brought out more supplies and finally, a thick piece of clean silver bark, which she passed to Darnuir.

"Bite down on this," she told the hunter. "It will help you."

He accepted the bark between his teeth, his eyes locked on the healer's knife. She began. The hunter bit down on the bark, fresh tears streaming from his eyes. Worst of all were the sounds of cracking and crunching as she cut through the bone. Mercifully, it was over quickly. The healer's companion collected the discarded flesh and knife and carried them away, whilst she applied a silver paste to the wound and rebound it with efficiency.

"You can let go now," she said, and Darnuir released the poor soul. She raised a gentle hand to the man's brow and his whimpers died away. He closed his eyes and his chest began to rise and fall softly in sleep.

"What did you do to him?" Darnuir asked.

She was shaking as she withdrew her hand. "I took the pain away but I might have overdone it. I need water." She rose unsteadily to her feet and Darnuir helped to stabilise her. "Thank you, Lord Darnuir. And for him," she added.

"Are you able to walk?"

"I should be fine. There is plenty of food and water for us." She scurried off towards the largest tent within the city of canvas.

Blaine appeared at his side. "We don't have time to stop and help every man."

Darnuir looked down at the hunter, remembering the sweet scent he had inhaled, and twitched at his own perverse senses.

"Blaine... can we smell fear?" Even as he asked it, the question sounded absurd.

Blaine gave a cruel smirk. "Sweet, isn't it?"

"It's a revolting thought. But I liked it."

"It is who we are. Perhaps a wolf picks up a similar scent when it hunts down its prey. You will get used to it eventually."

"Does it only come from humans?"

"Humans hold the most fear."

Standing amongst the injured and sick, Darnuir felt a little fear was justified. They were brave, he considered, to fight and make it this far. Spectres and demons were one thing, but the unknown of the sick bed was quite another.

"Come along," Blaine said. "We should avoid any more distract—"

"Lord Guardian!" a voice called from the grassy path.

Darnuir whipped his head around and saw Damien approaching. Blaine's expression softened when he saw the outrunner.

"Is this important, Damien?" Blaine asked.

"A message from the chevalier, sir."

"From Raymond?" Darnuir said. "How did he manage to get word to us here?"

"One of our long-range runners was given the letter by a bargeman who was passing up the River Dorain," Damien said. "It is in the central command tent for you, my lords."

"Very well," Blaine said. "It may contain word of the enemy."

They traced the path of the fairy healer and entered the same massive tent. Darnuir saw the healer sipping at a tall glass of water. Hundreds of jugs were laid out upon long tables, and other fairies glided serenely around, carrying trays of freshly-baked bread.

At the centre of the tent was a collection of angled tables strewn with maps, stacks of parchment and half-eaten meals. Armoured dragons and burly fairy warriors consulted there, placing little carvings on the maps to represent the forces at play.

Darnuir found it curious that every fairy warrior he had seen had a very similar look, as though they were designed specifically for combat. They were taller than the rest, and so thickly set that they made the dragons seem scrawny. Yet others, the ones with wings, were far leaner and wirier.

All of those present deferred to one fairy in particular. His skin was such a dark shade of blue that it might have been ink, contrasting fiercely with his long silver hair, elaborately braided to the middle of his winged back. Strapped over his shoulder was a vicious double-ended spear. His navy tunic, emblazoned with a large silver tree, was pulled in tightly by a belt of silver rope.

Sitting alone, dour-faced and looking out of place, was Cosmo. He scratched away on a sheet of parchment with stacks of reports piled around him. His white leathers looked freshly cleaned and he held a steaming mug in one hand. A cradle rocked gently beside him with his sleeping son inside.

As Darnuir and Blaine approached, the dark-skinned fairy looked up, seeming pleased by their arrival.

"Lord Guardian," the fairy intoned deeply, "it is good you have come. There is much we must discuss."

"Darnuir, this is General Fidelm, commander-in-chief of all fairy forces."

The ink-skinned fairy bowed his head towards Darnuir. "It is good to see you again, Darnuir. You really do look the same, apart from the stubble, of course."

"Thank you," Darnuir said, not sure what else to say. It was still disconcerting to meet people who must feel like they already knew him. "I presume it is you we have to thank for the timely aid of the fairies near your forest's borders?"

"If only we could have done more," Fidelm said. "Yet mustering my warriors is taking a great deal of time." He picked up a sheet of parchment from the table and passed it to Blaine. "From someone named Raymond."

Blaine scanned the message, frowned, and then handed it to Darnuir.

'*My Lord Dragons,*

I write to you regarding the situation at Inverdorn, a city now gripped in the throes of siege. I secured passage out on one of the last barges but there is now no way in or out via land. The demons arrived two days ago, led by a figure in full plate mail the colour of blood. I suspect more human treachery is at work.

The city is well-stocked but was not built for such an attack. Were it not for a healthy contin-
gent of your own kind here, I imagine the city would have descended into panic already. I estimate
two to three thousand dragons are here, trapped on their way to Val'tarra. Together with the city
guard and hunters from the Crescent, I'd put the defence force at around five thousand. Yet all
accounts place the demons at forty thousand strong. I trust you find this intelligence of use.

I pray that a relief force can be sent from Brevia with all haste, but I fear the city will fall
soon. I have given this message into the hands of one bargeman, Grenn, who is sailing north along
the Dorain. He is a jumpy fellow, particularly around a certain collection of barrels he has on
board. I can only hope these words find their way into your hands.

Humbly and faithfully,

Raymond, son of Jasper, of House Tarquill.'

Darnuir took a deep breath. "At least we know where the demons are – Inverdorn."
He was about to put the letter down when Cosmo perked up from his chair.

"If I may, Darnuir," he said through a mouthful of his steaming drink, "can I have
a word?"

Blaine looked disapproving again but Darnuir waved him off. "Go on, Blaine, I'm
sure you can manage without me for a moment."

He had not seen Cosmo since their short but fierce fight at the edge of Val'tarra.
He hoped they could make amends. Yet as Cosmo had initiated things, Darnuir
looked to him expectantly.

Cosmo cleared his throat. "I... I... want to apologise for how I reacted before. It
was out of all proportion. I can only blame the fatigue."

"And I am sorry for putting you on the spot like that. Have you given it any more
thought?"

Cosmo's expression darkened. "Just because I am saying sorry does not mean I
have changed my mind."

"Then why are you here?"

"Am I not allowed? I've found sleep to be difficult lately. Besides, this young man
wasn't in much of a sleeping mood either." He gently rocked the cradle. "I thought
I'd try and make myself useful. Fidelm suggested I compile a full report on the
hunters."

Sounds like you have already begun the job. Tact would be the better course to take,
however.

"I couldn't sleep either," Darnuir said.

"Pressure getting to you?"

"I think it's only just beginning to build. Maybe it is already eating at me."

"I'd be concerned if it wasn't," said Cosmo, taking another sip from his mug.

"Hmmm, very good, this. They call it shimmer brew; it's like needle brew but much purer. Ground up from those silver leaves, I'm told. Keeps you going."

"Why do you need to keep going? You should be resting. The fairies are taking good care of us."

Cosmo shrugged. "It's not in my nature to sit idle, and I have been idle enough of late." A brief silence passed. It did not feel awkward, but too much had happened in too short a time to make conversation easy.

I wish things were different. I could use the old Cosmo again.

"Well, if that is all—"

"May I read Raymond's letter? Fidelm felt it was inappropriate for my eyes."

"That wouldn't be an issue if you were captain of our hunter forces," Darnuir said pointedly. "The captain would require access to such communication."

Cosmo's expression soured. "Just give me the damn letter." Darnuir handed it over and Cosmo scanned it attentively. "Now imagine a city full of people like that. They hide behind glib tongues."

"You are hardly rough-spoken," Darnuir said. "City life has left its mark on you."

Cosmo tapped his fingers on the table and screwed his face up in thought. "I can't help who I am or where I have come from, but far worse things have marked me now." Once more, he gently rocked his son's cradle. "Perhaps I should stop running."

"If we've learnt anything recently, it's that even a dragon cannot run forever."

Darnuir was careful not to press Cosmo too hard. Grace's death had affected him like a broken limb and it would only get worse if he was dragged back to normality too quickly. Yet Raymond's letter suggested they would have little time to lick their wounds.

"We cannot stay here for long, can we?"

"Not unless we want Inverdorn to burn," Cosmo said.

"Forty thousand…" Just saying it felt daunting.

Castallan's army had proven swift and powerful. Their own forces were scattered and disunited. Darnuir always considered he would fight in a war; he had just never expected to be leading it.

"Do we have a better grasp of our own strength yet?" Darnuir said.

"We won't know the exact picture until General Fidelm gives us an estimate on how many fairy warriors he can muster."

"And what of the dragons?"

Blaine had brought most of the dragons, who had already assembled in the forest to Torridon, but more were arriving all the time.

"Why do you assume I know?" Cosmo said. "I'm just a lowly hunter to everyone else. The better question is: why don't you know?"

"Blaine has been taking care of things so far."

"Are you not the king? I didn't know dragons deferred to anyone else. That's why they went into hiding for all those years."

"Blaine says we are equals, of a sort."

"Hmmmm," Cosmo mused. "I would be careful around him. As far as I am concerned, the guardian was a thing of the past. Now he just appears, apparently out of nowhere, and takes control? It doesn't feel right to me."

"I'm just grateful for his help. I feel overwhelmed as it is." He sighed heavily. "I know I am pushing you into a position that you don't want, but I'd like you to stay close as this unravels. It's a selfish reason, though I do believe you are the best man for the job. Scythe, Edwin and this other Captain Morwen are all dead. Frankly, there is no one else, and having one strong captain now makes more sense than having three."

Cosmo smiled warmly at him. It had been a long time since Darnuir had seen that.

"You are doing well enough, I think," Cosmo said, avoiding answering Darnuir's unasked question.

"I have done little in truth."

"Well, I wouldn't be alive if the dragons hadn't dragged us halfway across the kingdom. It might make me biased but, yes, you're doing well."

"Blaine doesn't feel the same way."

Cosmo shook his head. "It is behaviour like his that has fractured our people's relationship over the centuries. You know what they say about the merging of humanity into the Three Races?"

Darnuir did; it was a well-worn phrase. "Bodies bought and bled for dragon wars."

"It's what many believe. They think humanity was forced into the alliance, only to be sent to die against the Black Dragons, and there is resentment over it to this day. But you have a chance to change that."

"And you'll help me?"

"I will always be there to help you, in one way or another," Cosmo said affectionately. "You know, I've never really wanted power, of any kind, because a lot of that is merely about having power for its own sake. I've seen what it can do to people and I never saw the point of becoming captain just because it was expected of me, or because it was the 'natural' thing to do. I could do all that I wanted as a regular hunter, but if I had some purpose behind that power, well, I wouldn't feel so bad in helping you to make it a better world. Bringing dragons and humans closer together, to undo some of that animosity, I think that would be a very good purpose." He tickled his son's cheek. "I reckon I owe it to him to try."

The baby gurgled loudly from his crib, as though in agreement. Darnuir moved closer and looked down into those oversized infant eyes, bright and green.

"Cosmo," Darnuir began hesitantly, hoping not to shatter the fresh reconciliation. "He will need a name eventually. Why the wait?"

Cosmo raised one eyebrow and smirked at him. "Probably for the same reasons you haven't told Balack about Eve."

Darnuir's breath stuck in his throat in horror. "W-what?"

Cosmo continued as though Darnuir had not reacted. "I have not named him because it would be too painful to do so; to do it without Grace and admit that she is truly gone. More importantly, I simply have not decided upon a name. Though, just as he will need a name, you will have to confront Balack at some point."

"How did you—"

"I saw the two of you leave the festivities that night and I noticed how you have been avoiding him ever since."

Darnuir just stood there, rooted in his shame like a young child being chastised, having been caught red-handed at some misdemeanour. Only this crime was far worse than any childish insolence. Rather, he had fractured his relationship with his closest friend. And he had done it in the worst possible way.

He felt the crack between them still. He'd missed his chance to tell the truth back in the marshes, and if he told it now, he feared that crack would break into a fissure they would not cross.

"He doesn't even suspect," Darnuir said meekly.

"I think he knows deep down but isn't willing to confront it, and I doubt he ever will. He never told Eve how he felt, after all. Yet letting him maintain whatever delusion he has created for himself is not a kindness."

"But if he is happier like this—"

"It is not a question of happiness, but of right and wrong. If you really want to build bridges between humanity and dragons, you must begin with this small step. Right this wrong."

"I can't undo it."

"No, you cannot, but you can admit your error and learn from it. Learn that just because you can do something, does not mean you should."

"He'll hate me."

Cosmo contemplated him. "Could you live forever with the lie?"

"I wish I could take it back," Darnuir said.

She was too close.

"Then do it for your own sake, if nothing else. You are a dragon. You might live for another century and you will have burdens beyond measure. By then Balack, myself and everyone you've ever known will be dust. Will you still have the ghost of Eve haunt you then?"

Darnuir groaned softly. He was resisting, but he knew Cosmo had the right of it.

"I've been running my whole life, Darnuir... and, strangely, it has gotten me nowhere. Only back to confronting the thing I flew from in the first place. Take my advice: face your fears now."

A crash broke the gravity of their conversion. Darnuir faced the source of the commotion. Blaine's fist lay clenched on the map and many of the wooden carvings lay scattered. Dozens of healers stopped in their search for bread and water to get a better glimpse of what was happening.

"Move along," Fidelm called out to them.

"I should go," Darnuir said.

"Think on what I said," Cosmo told him.

"If you promise to think on my request as well?"

Cosmo gave a noncommittal nod, then returned to his report.

Darnuir sidled over to Blaine's table. "What's the matter?"

"Blaine was expressing his frustration that it will take at least three weeks before my warriors are ready," Fidelm said. "Meaning that—"

"Meaning it is likely we will lose Inverdorn," Blaine said.

Darnuir was surprised. Inverdorn was a human city; why would Blaine care? *The dragons*, he realised. There were thousands trapped there.

"How long can the city hold?" Darnuir asked. "Could we lift the siege?"

"With only ten thousand of us, it would be a risk," Blaine said.

"More of your people are still coming," Fidelm said. "My flyers report dragons are still trickling into Val'tarra."

"Trickling is the exact word," Blaine said angrily. "Too many have brought their families along with them. It's slowing them down."

"Can you blame them?" Darnuir asked.

"Speed would have been our advantage. If all the dragons had come as I expected, then we could have crushed this army of Castallan's."

"In the Boreacs, we faced terrible odds and still won. Surely ten thousand dragons can defeat this army?"

"We're rusty. I don't like admitting it, but it's true. A hundred years ago, there would have been no issue. But now... now we've been amongst humans for too long. It has made us soft."

Darnuir let Blaine seethe quietly over the map and turned to Fidelm, who was a head taller than him. "General, why will it take so long for your men to assemble?"

Like the prefect back at the forest's edge, Fidelm looked over at Blaine to check that Darnuir had really asked such an obvious question.

I am not the dragon I once was. People need to keep that in mind.

It struck him that, for the first time, he had just referred to himself as a dragon without making a conscious effort to do so.

"My king is not as familiar with your people as he once was," Blaine said.

"Of course," Fidelm said. "My kind do not live statically, Darnuir. Other than the

Argent Tree, there is no permanent area of Val'tarra that we inhabit. Our people prefer to travel around our vast forest, never impacting upon an area for too long. This makes sending word out to all our people difficult."

"So, three weeks is still only an estimate?" Darnuir said.

"At best," Blaine said. The guardian rallied himself, standing up and regaining his usual commanding air. "Fidelm, we shall have to go over this later. There are important matters I wish to discuss with Darnuir. Privately."

Darnuir tried to mouth an apology to Fidelm as Blaine swept past, grabbing him by the arm as he did so. He caught a look of amusement on Cosmo's face as he wrestled free from Blaine's grip. Darnuir followed him onto the grassy road, heading for the Argent Tree.

"Keep up," Blaine called over his shoulder, "and do not make eye contact with anybody. I don't want any more distractions."

27

THE HALL OF MEMORIES

Darnuir – The Argent Tree

The interior of the great tree was hollow. A winding railed path ascended hundreds of feet, lit by thousands of wispy lanterns floating of their own accord. The parchment stretched so thin he could see right through to the flames that twinkled in constant imitation of a clear night sky.

Blaine wasted no time and charged up the curved walkway. Corridors and rooms branched off the main path. Just over halfway up, Blaine veered off into one of the twisting corridors. It was significantly darker than the walkway, and it took a while for Darnuir's eyes to adjust.

"Where are we going?" he asked, half-blind. "What is so urgent?"

"We are here. The Hall of Memories."

As his eyes adjusted, Darnuir found he could see quite well. *Is this another dragon trait?* He saw Blaine's eyes in the darkness, faintly yellow like those of a mountain lynx, and assumed his own must appear similar.

The corridor sloped upwards, bending around the corner and out of sight, probably following the curve of the Argent Tree. Paintings ran the length of the wall, without breaks – it was just one never-ending masterpiece. And unlike the paintings in Darnuir's room, these images were far more than mere patterns.

Closest to him, where the mural began, were ten mountains, mighty and snow-capped.

"The Ten Principal Mountains of Tenalp," Blaine said.

"What is this place?" Darnuir asked.

"A dedication to our world's history, or what we know of it, or think we know of it. Everything starts with those mountains."

"Not these gods of yours?"

"They came later. Life had to come first. Here." He pointed to what looked like a map of the world, except it did not look right. There seemed to be more of it and the land was all connected in one large ring. A great mountain stood in the area where Aurisha was now built. "This map shows how our world once was. At some point, magic poured forth from the peaks of those great mountains, or at least we assume it did. This was the Cascade, and hence we call magic Cascade energy. With the Cascade came life."

Walking along, the depiction changed and now the Principal Mountains were erupting with a blue substance. It soared high before falling to ooze down the mountainsides. Further along, the artwork showed blossoming vegetation, rivers being carved out by the Cascade, then animals, then fairies and, finally, dragons.

Darnuir paused at this point. The dragons portrayed were the mythical, scaled monsters of old; those fire-breathing beasts that were used to scare young children in stories.

"Fairies came first?" Darnuir asked.

"We'll never know for sure, but it is of little consequence. Let them think it."

"What about humans?"

"Humans came later. Much later," Blaine said, leading him further down the corridor.

The lavish illustrations of the primordial world gave way to mountains again. A snowstorm raged against a black sky. Dragons perched on rocky outcrops, roaring and breathing their fire high into the night. Floating ethereally above them were three bright, luminous shapes, radiating light onto the scene below. Blaine placed his hand reverently upon it.

"What do you know of our history, Darnuir?"

"Little, I'm afraid. We learned many things as hunters that most men would not know, but history was not one of them."

"I'm not surprised."

"It's just not practical. What use is it to us? Cassandra is more interested in this."

"What use, you ask? To understand all of this is perhaps the most useful thing you could know."

Darnuir raised his eyebrows.

"You are not just a hunter anymore; you are a dragon and a king," Blaine continued. "Moreover, you are one of the most powerful beings in the world, even if you do not yet feel it; and you will have greater foes to face than merely wolves, demons or spectres."

"And knowing some history will prepare me for it?"

"It will lay a good foundation for your understanding. This scene before us is known as the First Flight. Tiviar suggests it occurred five thousand years before the Transformation but no one can be certain. Legend tells that this was when our race gathered as one for the first time and received our purpose."

"Our purpose? Meaning every dragon is supposed to be doing... something?"

"To cast out the Shadow! A task given to us by the gods themselves. Look, boy, and see them here."

Darnuir looked again at the three incandescent floating beings.

"They are just shapes of light," he said. "They have no bodies."

Blaine half-laughed. "And why should the gods appear like us? They are not made of flesh and blood. They are gods. Forces. And far beyond our comprehension."

"Then what are these... shapes?"

"Depictions, symbols – does it really matter what they look like? How will any of us ever know?"

"But if you cannot be certain, why do you have so much trust in them?" Darnuir asked, hoping to uncover the real reason behind Blaine's peculiar devotion.

"I have faith," Blaine said simply. "But it is more than that. My blade holds in it a portion of their power; it can bring forth the very light that the Shadow fears."

"The Dragon's Blade brings forth fire, yet I saw Brackendon bring the roof of a building down and manipulate the air around him. I've seen Kymethra turn into an eagle and fly away. These things work by magic; why would your sword be any different?"

Blaine stared long and hard at the images of his gods on the wall.

"I do not expect you will ever believe or feel the way that I do. You have grown up in a time and a place severed from the old ways. But you cannot deny me this, Darnuir. The Shadow is real, our enemy is real, and if the darkness exists then the Light must as well."

"Well, when you phrase it like that, it is hard to disagree. But dragons also warred amongst themselves for centuries, didn't they? That much is common knowledge."

"If you are referring to the Black Dragons, they turned to serve the Shadow. That is why we fought them. They weren't really dragons then."

"But their leader was Dranus, a dragon, not some Shadow god," Darnuir said. "Our enemy now is Rectar."

"And what do you really know of either of them beyond the hearsay and the legends?"

Darnuir had little to add. Dranus' name was used as a curse, an old enemy of the dragons, but he knew nothing that was more concrete. *Cassandra likely knows*, he thought. *She has delved into the past enough to please Blaine.* Of Rectar, Darnuir knew only his name.

Blaine smiled triumphantly at his lack of reply. "As I thought. No matter, it will still do you well to understand. It all starts with the First Flight." He cast a hand over the scene before them.

Blaine directed Darnuir to look at the luminescent being on the left. Three rays of light emanated from some undefined centre where their pointed tips met.

"Here is Dwna, the Light of Creation," Blaine said.

Next, he pointed to the middle god – a large sphere halved lengthways. The upper half was a bright yellow-gold, while the underside was scored in dark lines.

"This is Dwl'or, the Shades of Existence."

Blaine pointed to the third depiction. Here, three thick, bright lines spiralled out against the dark night sky.

"And this is N'weer, the Infinite."

He allowed Darnuir a moment to take this information in. Darnuir, for his part, tried to remember the names of the gods, but they were strange and already slipping from his mind.

"The Gods of Light chose us as their champions," Blaine continued. "Some believe that Dwna helped shape us to be their weapon against the Shadow; I'd like to believe it myself. Regardless, we were chosen, and so our people have scoured this earth to root out the Shadow in all its forms."

Darnuir nodded along, although he couldn't help but think his people hadn't been very successful in this sacred task.

Blaine led him further down the hall, away from the First Flight.

"Yet our kind could not reach all places in the world," Blaine said. "We were too large, too cumbersome. Fierce and powerful we were, but what use is that if your enemy skulks in caves and under rocks?"

The next scene that Blaine stopped beside showed several golden dragons with their scaly heads bowed low before an equal number of fairies. The lead fairy was reaching out to place her hand on the snout of the dragon in front of her.

"This is why our friendship with the fairies began. They lived in the lower regions of the world and could help track our enemies, and this great purge became the Second Flight. The fairies say it happened three thousand years before the Transformation. In exchange for their help, we flew the fairies up to the highest peaks of Tenalp, where the Cascade flowed the thickest. In those days, the fairies were eager to harvest as much energy as possible."

A variety of images followed: fairies riding on the backs of dragons; fairies gathering the raw Cascade energy; fairies performing wondrous displays of magic; and even fairies being stalked and attacked by strange grey-skinned creatures.

"What are they?" Darnuir asked.

"Those are frost trolls."

"They're real?" Darnuir said in shock.

Is nothing in this world the way I was brought up to believe?

"I have seen some," Blaine said. "Though they keep themselves to the Highlands, as they have always done."

"Why are they killing the fairies?"

"Perhaps they wanted the magical power for themselves. Perhaps they thought the fairies made good sport. For centuries, the fairies went north to gather the Cascade and, for centuries, the frost trolls hunted them. There is a terrible amount of bad blood between them."

"Even now?"

"Even now," Blaine said. "But the trolls are reclusive. Don't trouble yourself with them."

"Well, then, what do I need to know? What is the important part?"

"It is all important," Blaine scowled, "but we are pressed for time. There are a couple more things you ought to know before we proceed."

Proceed? The word had an ominous ring.

The guardian strode off, passing much of the mural as he did. "We go now to the aftermath of the Third Flight."

Blaine slowed down as they passed an extended scene of what appeared to be smiths at their forges. However, the smiths were not alone; fairies mingled amongst them. Symbols of the gods were frequent, and the forges were being filled with a strange variety of ingredients. At the end of this segment, three swords were shown in glorious detail.

Darnuir recognised the Dragon's Blade and the Guardian's Blade, but not the third. It had a simple design in comparison: a plain hilt and cross-guard of thick, glinting steel and a woven cloth grip in black and gold. The same unusual metal comprised the blade itself but it contained only an etched groove and nothing more.

"The forging of the Three Blades," Blaine announced, as though to a great audience. "The Dragon's Blade, the Guardian's Blade and the Champion's Blade. Forged after the Third Flight two and a half thousand years ago, using the very talons of Aurisha himself."

"What, from his claw?" Darnuir sniggered. "They are swords, not bones."

"They are a mixture of his talons, starium and steel," Blaine said. "So far as I am aware, they are indestructible."

"And this all happened before the dragons transformed?" Darnuir asked. "It seems strange that the dragons should forge swords when they had no need of them in their bestial form. Yet if Aurisha was still not a true dragon, how could they have used his talons?"

"The Transformation occurred shortly before the Third Flight," Blaine said. "With the aid of the fairies, dragons took the shape of humans, who were still rather primitive at the time. We did this so we could fight the Shadow in all places without the assistance of the fairies. Aurisha was one of the last dragons that had the power to transform at will. He was powerfully magical and his scales were a deep red, much like the head upon the Dragon's Blade is. Back there, you can find the depiction of his fight against the traitor, Dranus."

Darnuir trotted back out of interest. He found the scene easily enough. Two dragons were locked in horrific combat. One had scales of dark blood, much like the hilt of the Dragon's Blade. The other was a mismatch of gold and black scale, the black patches close to Brackendon's own charred hand. This must have been Dranus. A hundred more questions came to him but he wanted Blaine to reach the point of all this. He returned to Blaine, still stood at the scene of the forging of the Three Blades.

"This third blade," Darnuir said. "This Champion's Blade. Where is it?"

"Ah, now that is the question. The Champion's Blade is rather different from our own. It will only be found by those most worthy."

"And what does that mean?" Darnuir said, beginning to feel frustrated.

"If I knew that, I might have found it myself."

"You searched for it?"

"In vain. I sought it for many long years – not for its own sake, I stress, but to confirm a theory. Perhaps things would have turned out differently if I had I found it then. Alas, I fear that my theory is true, and our foe wields a power in this world as great as our own; perhaps even stronger."

"You think Rectar has it?" Darnuir asked incredulously.

Blaine nodded.

"But surely he is not 'worthy'," Darnuir said. "You said he is of the Shadow."

"It is only a theory. The Champion's Blade has only appeared once, so far as we can be sure."

"When did it appear before?"

"I could tell you, but I'd rather show you."

Blaine took out the Guardian's Blade and pressed against one of the white gems embedded in its grip. The gemstone came free of the sword and he held it out in his palm.

"Within these stones lie the memories of the guardians who came before me. Each guardian may add to them, but only so many memories can be held. It is a difficult task to decide which memories should stay and which should go."

"And there is a memory about the Champion's Blade in there?"

"About the Second War between dragons and humans specifically, seven hundred years ago. Those rubies in your sword hold memories as well."

"My dreams!" Darnuir thought aloud, and suddenly, his disturbed sleep of the past months made sense. "Blaine, I think they have been influencing me somehow."

"I concur, but it is unprecedented for memories in the gems to affect you in such a way, especially to the point of influencing your behaviour, which I suspect is also occurring. Hopefully, by delving into those memories, we can stop the symptoms."

"Sometimes, I feel as though I am having thoughts that are not my own. Yet they are still recognisably me, of my voice. Does that make sense?"

"It appears your old self put so much of himself into those rubies that his memories are now literally spilling out and into you."

"Do you have similar problems? With the memories in your gems, I mean?"

"No. There is not enough from any single guardian to influence me to the same degree," Blaine said. "The king who wields the Dragon's Blade is the only one who may place memories inside its gems, and they are wiped clean with each succession. Your case is, however, a unique one..."

"He, the old me, must have done it as he lay on his deathbed in Cold Point. Brackendon mentioned that the sword arrived there that night. It must have been his last act." Darnuir bit his lip, nervous as to Blaine's reaction about his most disturbing dream. "His memories worry me. I feel like I might have done something terrible."

"We will know soon enough and, with some luck, the memories of your past life might help you to remember what it is to be a dragon. To truly fight like us; to be one of us."

"You certainly made a fool of me earlier today."

"You did well, in truth, considering you are not used to utilising your full potential, and your lack of practice with the blade."

"Thank you, I suppose." It was the first time Blaine had said something bordering on complimentary.

"You can thank me once you are strong again," Blaine said. "However, I'm afraid we do not have the luxury of time. The war will not wait for us to prepare and so you must be ready."

"Then let's do it!"

Darnuir withdrew the Dragon's Blade. He gently pressed on one of the rubies, then the other, popping them out of their sockets. They were a great weight in his hand; as heavy as the Dragon's Blade once felt to him.

"How does it feel?" Blaine asked.

"Heavy," said Darnuir. "Heavier than any stones their size should be." His head began to pound again, more acutely and painfully than ever. He winced. "What magic is this?"

"It is not magic but memory."

"I was not aware that memories had a weight."

Blaine looked upon him sadly. "Oh, Darnuir, memory is the heaviest of all things. Even the strongest shoulders will be hunched by it in time. Nothing weighs upon us more, nor for longer, than memory."

Darnuir's treacherous thoughts wandered once more to that chilled room, briefly bathed in moonlight.

She was too close.

His expression must have betrayed him.

"I see something weighs on you," Blaine said. "Something lay heavily upon your old self as well."

"You have lived longer than any of us," Darnuir said. "How do you cope?"

Pensively, Blaine played with one of his white jewels, holding it up between his thumb and forefinger. "Some of the weightiest I hide away and some of the lightest and joyous I place in here as well. But those are just for me." He ended on a smile.

Was that an attempt at humour?

Either way, it was a tender moment that smoothed some of the roughness away from the old dragon.

"Show me how to see," Darnuir asked, holding out the rubies. Blaine closed his hand around Darnuir's. The jewels were now in their joint grasp. Blaine gasped, his cheek twitched.

"Have you been carrying this the entire time?" Blaine said, almost in awe.

"It's not as severe when placed inside the sword, but... yes."

Blaine drew in a long, shuddering breath through gritted teeth. "Then I'm sorry I did not do this sooner. Let us place some of our burden upon each other. I have carried my own for far too long."

28

THE MURKY PAST

Darnuir – The Argent Tree – Hall of Memories

"We'll enter the memory I have stored first," Blaine said. "It is important that you see it."

"Do I need to do anything?" Darnuir asked.

He considered that the two of them must look rather strange, hands clasped in the dim light of the Hall of Memories.

"Nothing for now," Blaine said. "Just brace yourself."

Brace myself? What does he mean by—

Something yanked at his consciousness, dragging him away. His vision left the real world behind. Blaine and the painted walls vanished, and a swirling spectrum of colours raced before him.

Darnuir lost control of his body because he no longer had one; instead, he was just a flying thought sucked through a blur. Then his vision began to sharpen. Tall grass and bright flora loomed above gloomy pools and mossy ground. As the sky came into focus, the recognisable granite-grey clouds confirmed his suspicions. They were somewhere in the Cairlav Marshes.

Figures began to form; hundreds of hardened warriors wearing riveted gold plate mail with the symbol of Blaine's gods upon their shields. Light Bearers. Clearly, they were dragons, which made sense. Blaine said this was the memory of an old guardian.

"*Darnuir?*"

He heard Blaine's voice but could not tell where it came from. He tried to turn but found he couldn't move.

"*Darnuir? You won't be able to move, but just answer me.*"

"Hello," Darnuir said, feeling ever-foolish around the guardian. "*This is disconcerting.*"

"*You'll get used to it,*" Blaine said. "*We are both inside the memory of my predecessor, the guardian Norbanus. We are not physically here, so we are only communicating via thought.*"

"*Will we get our bodies back?*"

"*We are in Norbanus' memory, so we are seeing things from his perspective.*"

"*You mean we are in his mind?*" Darnuir said – or rather thought – feeling thoroughly nauseated by the sensation.

"*Yes and no,*" Blaine said. "*We are witnessing events from his eyes, as he saw it; however, we cannot hear his thoughts, as we are not him. Were this your own memory, Darnuir, then you would experience it in full.*"

"*So, we will just be watching?*"

"*We will watch and learn,*" Blaine said.

Typical, he's always holding back.

"*I heard that, boy,*" Blaine said. "*Remember, we are communicating through thought. Keep quiet if you want to keep things secret.*" Darnuir restrained himself from his next choice thought. The silence seemed to amuse Blaine. "*Just focus on events here. If I recall, there should be a messenger coming out of the grass right about... now.*"

The tall grass in front of them rustled and parted, just as predicted, and a Light Bearer came into view.

"The humans are advancing, Lord Guardian. Legate Varus has led his legion against the enemy."

"Varus is an arrogant fool for going alone. Still, the humans are unwise to act so boldly, even with their newfound ally. Signal the rest of our forces to move into position." The voice felt like it came from Darnuir, and so he assumed it to be Norbanus. Their host's voice was a lot like Blaine's; deep, assured, measured, and dripping with superiority.

"As you command, Lord Guardian," the Light Bearer said. The dragon moved off out of sight but there was a cry of annoyance shortly afterwards and Norbanus turned to examine the commotion. The Light Bearer had gotten his foot stuck in a thick patch of mud and other nearby dragons had moved to help free him, taking care not to misstep themselves.

"Be careful here," Norbanus said. "That goes for all of you."

"*They should have known this was a mistake,*" Blaine said.

"*Why? What—*"

"Light Bearers!" Norbanus cried. He was met with a resounding cheer. "Today, we end the human menace. Like these bogs, they shall rot here forever more. With me!"

Another wave of cheering roared throughout the Light Bearers. Norbanus then strode forward with the Guardian's Blade in hand, cutting swathes through the long grass.

"*We can speak freely again,*" Blaine said.

"*You said this was during the Second War?*" Darnuir asked.

"*Correct.*"

"*Then this must be the Battle of the Bogs?*"

"*Ah,*" Blaine said, sounding pleased. "*So, you do know something?*"

"*Every human knows of that battle.*"

"*I don't doubt. What do you know of it, then?*"

"*Only that the dragons lost and it was Prince Dronithir who led humanity to victory.*"

"*Were it only that,*" Blaine said solemnly. "*It was a disaster, a crushing and humiliating defeat. You heard Norbanus call Legate Varus a fool? Well, I am afraid my predecessor was no better for allowing the battle to occur here.*"

Norbanus and his Light Bearers continued to cut through the tall grass. Green sprays of foliage mingled with pink flora flew around them. Several of his companions fell behind, presumably caught in some watery trap, but Norbanus continued single-mindedly.

"*This seems a terrible place for a battle,*" Darnuir said.

"*Depends which side you are on,*" Blaine said.

"*Small bands of lightly equipped hunters with knowledge of the land might be able to make use of it, but these dragons, in their armour—*"

"*Should never have fought here. I quite agree.*"

"*So why did they?*"

"*Norbanus thought he had the gods on his side.*"

"*I hope you wouldn't make such a blunder.*"

"*If all goes well, I won't have to. The guardian is not supposed to lead armies. That is the job of the king. He was in a similar position to ourselves, in a way. Drakon the Fourth was king in those days, but he was old and could no longer enter battle. He sent his son, Dronithir, west to secure a beachhead, and the prince went gladly, eager to subdue the barbarous humans.*"

"*But Dronithir turned against the dragons.*"

"*And he saved humanity in doing so. Dronithir was young and unblooded when he came west. He landed his forces near where the Bastion now stands and carved out territory with ease. All he had to do was await the main invasion force, but the brash, young prince did not sit idle. He decided he would conquer as much of the Southern Dales as he could before the full power of the dragons arrived. Humanity had bowed before his might, he thought; humanity was meek and disorganised. He did not stop to consider his own limits.*"

"It sounds like he thought of the war as a game or sport."

"History has remembered him kindly," Blaine said. "The humans see him as a hero, yet were it not for the compassion of one woman, he might never have changed. The tale goes that Dronithir was ambushed by hunters in the marshlands and nearly slain. He was saved by one of their own healers, the woman I mentioned. Her name was Elsha. I have often wondered whether she and her fellow healers knew who he was. Did they heal him in the hope that he would turn against his own people? It seems desperate at best. Did they believe that his father, or perhaps Norbanus, would be dissuaded from the war if they held the prince hostage? Alas, such things have been lost to time."

"Perhaps they saved him out of kindness?"

Blaine answered him with silence and so Darnuir refocused on the memory before him.

The endless grass finally abated as Norbanus emerged out onto the main field of battle. Long grass was absent here but the morass was creating chaos for the dragons. They struggled to form ranks properly, the broken land causing holes to appear in their formations.

Norbanus rushed to the head of the troops, their half-formed ranks parting to allow him to pass. He then had an unimpeded view of the unfolding battle.

Ahead, the human army was arranged into dense spear formations, as if imitating the long grass of the marshes, and advanced like creeping thorn bushes. The humans had placed themselves expertly on solid ground with many pools littered on either side. The effect was that the dragons were pushed into a choke point. A howling wind brought the clamour of battle along with it, buffeting the dragons, who were forced to try and march against it. Norbanus' eyes quickly took in the entirety of the scene.

It was rapidly deteriorating.

More dragons charged forward to join the fray, seemingly without instruction, and were greeted with a hail of arrows from behind the spear walls. The treacherous ground caught many of the advancing dragons, pinning them in place or causing them to stumble and fall.

"Forward!" Norbanus cried, and all those who were nearby charged with him.

"This is foolish," Darnuir said. *"Couldn't he see what was happening?"*

"Chaos is the greatest enemy of the commander," Blaine said. "In nearly all previous battles with humans, a ferocious charge was enough to break them. Dragons fell prey to hubris on this day."

Norbanus' great charge slowed with each step. He caught up with the dragons ahead and so had no more room to gain pace. Arrows continued to fall, and the collapsing bodies created further obstacles. Soon dragons began running in the opposite direction. Areas of the front must have broken, for what began as a trickle soon became a torrent of fleeing dragons.

The chaos was then complete.

Those charging forwards collided with those retreating, unable to alter their directions quickly enough on the crammed, slippery killing fields. Norbanus bellowed orders but none heeded him. Only his Light Bearers seemed to navigate the sea of bodies, some of them even knocking fellow dragons aside with their large shields in order to keep going.

At last, they reached the front.

Spears thrust in continuous motion from the human line, spraying blood, bone and limbs, grinding up everything in their path like teeth in a monstrous jaw.

At the centre of the human line was another compact group of fighters, only these wore plate mail and carried shields and swords. At their head was a figure in magnificent golden armour. Dragon-head pauldrons pinned a crimson cloak in place. In his hand, he held a sword wrought of grainy gold metal. Its hilt and cross-guard were made of plain steel and Darnuir was certain that the grip, though covered by Dronithir's hand, would be woven black and gold cloth.

"*The Champion's Blade!*" Darnuir said.

"*Indeed,*" Blaine said. Somehow, Darnuir could still hear him perfectly, despite the din of the battle.

"*But how did he find it?*"

"*Pay close attention and we shall discuss it afterwards.*"

"Norbanus!" Dronithir bellowed. "You murderer! You craven zealous worm!"

The guardian strode forwards in answer to the challenge. "Prince Dronithir, you have erred greatly but your corruption can be cleansed. Give up this foolishness and let me purge the Shadow from you."

"The only evil here is you, Norbanus! You and my father. How long have you whispered in his ear for this? How long have you desired to cut humanity's throat and watch the loch run red?"

Dronithir approached Norbanus in a fury that Darnuir had never seen. He might have been handsome, but rage contorted his features, igniting a savagery in his eyes. His cheeks and chin were hidden beneath thick stubble.

Norbanus seemed unperturbed by the advance. He drew the Guardian's Blade. "You even look like one of them now; your father will be ashamed. The humans have fought well but they will break when they see you fall."

"And your Light Bearers will lose faith when they see you lying in the marsh."

As the two dragons clashed on the moss-covered earth, those loyal on both sides smashed in a melee around them. Neither side attempted a shield wall, nor any strategy other than raw ferocity. Such was its intensity that the entire battle now seemed to hinge on this skirmish and it, in turn, depended upon the outcome of the duel raging at its heart.

Darnuir wished he could hear what Norbanus was thinking. The guardian's initial confidence had shown in his early steps, as he treated Dronithir like some novice, but a few slips here and there seemed to make Norbanus less sure.

He was quickly on the defensive, parrying and dodging, rather than taking the initiative. The speed of the fight was tremendous and might have been sickening had Darnuir not gained his own small measure of experience.

Dronithir was brilliant. His every move compensated for the terrain and seemed perfectly aimed, and yet no warrior was flawless and Norbanus eventually found an opening. The guardian took his opportunity and took a swipe at Dronithir's neck. He aimed to kill.

"N'weer save you!" Norbanus screamed, but his blow met only air. Dronithir had vanished, momentarily invisible to Norbanus' eyes. Then there was a flashing fist, and Norbanus must have been taken clean off his feet. Darnuir lost sight of the battle, looking up to the sky instead. Norbanus' eyelids quivered lightly.

Dronithir stepped over the guardian, brought his foot down upon Norbanus' right hand and then kicked the Guardian's Blade aside.

"He disarmed Norbanus?"

"A sound tactic. My weapon does not fly back to my hand like yours."

Norbanus grasped for his weapon but Dronithir's boot remained in place. Norbanus' movements seemed sluggish now, even clumsy, compared to only a few moments ago. The prince grabbed Norbanus' flailing hand and hoisted him into a crouch. A backhanded blow swept before Norbanus' vision and suddenly he was face-down in the muck and water.

Darnuir felt that one strike should not have been enough to remove the guardian from the fight, no matter how powerful. *"That cannot be the end of it."*

"At first, they fought as equals," Blaine said, *"but then Norbanus lost his blade. Dronithir's blow must have felt like it had all the strength of the gods behind it."*

"It's over!" Dronithir cried.

Norbanus attempted to rise to his feet. His movements were unsteady, and he tripped once as he tried to stand. In the end, he fell to his knees looking desperately around himself.

Light Bearers were throwing down their weapons, some wailing in anguish at the sight of their fallen Lord. Human troops swarmed forwards, and Norbanus became surrounded by bristling spears.

As the guardian hung his head, the scene began to dissolve.

Darnuir felt the familiar sensation that ended his dreams as he was tugged away. He was flying through a void of nothingness until his real eyes snapped open again and he found himself back in the Hall of Memories.

"Don't drop the rubies!" Blaine warned as their hands parted.

Darnuir kept a firm grasp on them as he took a step back. Disorientated, he swayed, clasping at his pounding head. If delving into his own memories didn't help, he considered just smashing the damned things himself. For now, he fought through the pain. He had more questions.

"What became of Norbanus and Dronithir after the battle?"

"Dronithir became king in due course, but as the rubies empty themselves with each new succession, we have no access to his memories. His own accounts are clearly biased and mostly focus on his hatred for Norbanus and our very gods by extension."

"He might have scorned your religion, Blaine, but you cannot deny he found the sword. He must have been 'worthy' in the eyes of your gods."

Blaine looked pained, unable to reconcile logic with emotion. "This I cannot deny."

"And if we can find the blade, we'll have the extra power to defeat the demons."

"Were it so simple," Blaine sighed. "My many years of fruitless searching has led me to conclude that the legends surrounding the blade are true. One must be worthy in order to discover it. It is said that Dronithir virtually stumbled upon it, somewhere in the Boreac Mountains."

"The monument in Farlen..." Darnuir said in quiet acknowledgement.

"I travelled there first during my exile, but nothing indicates anything special about the place. Perhaps the evidence has been lost in time as well; it has been seven hundred years after all, yet surely the rock that held the Champion's Blade would have been preserved. Those mountains have been inhabited since fairies began collecting Cascade energy; I find it hard to believe that no one would have come across it. I fear the Champion's Blade will only appear to its chosen master."

"But what made him worthy?" Darnuir said. Something did not seem to add up. "It cannot be simply for defending humanity. Arguably, I did the same thing at Torridon, and still the Champion's Blade has not appeared."

"I agree," Blaine said, gently touching the depiction of the third blade upon the wall. "There must be something else to the tale."

"Dronithir called Norbanus a murderer," Darnuir said, "and you mentioned there was a healer who nursed Dronithir back to health after he was wounded? Would it be a stretch to assume Norbanus killed her?"

"That's exactly what happened."

"Dronithir loved her," Darnuir said. It was a statement of fact. He had seen it in the ancient prince's eyes. A passion and a hurt that he recalled seeing in Balack on that bloody night, with Eve's body within arm's reach. Eve, who had been too close. It wasn't so long ago. Had it only been a couple of months?

Darnuir shook his head to clear it. "Why did Norbanus kill her? Doing that only gave Dronithir more reason to fight him."

"Norbanus believed, as many did back then, that humanity was the chosen race of the Shadow, just as dragons are the chosen race of the Light. Likely as not, he thought that Elsha had corrupted the Dragon Prince." Blaine snorted loudly at the thought. "Well, she corrupted him enough, I suppose. Norbanus was wrong to act the way he did, of course."

"And how is this all connected to Rectar? How does this help us?"

"He was not always Rectar," Blaine said, a deep resonating sadness in his voice. "Once, he was a dragon; once, he was known as Kroener, and he was no different than you or I. He might even have been my successor. Yet, like Dronithir, he too went to war when he was young and, like him, he did not return the same."

"And here I am now," Darnuir said. "Young and off to war."

Blaine tried a strained smile that was more of a grimace. "The more I look back, the more I consider it, the more I see the patterns repeating. History throws it up if you look closely; working in cycles, an infinite cycle, just like N'weer, repeating and rejuvenating."

Blaine stepped intently towards Darnuir, looking into him as though searching for some profound truth. Darnuir edged back, wary of the guardian.

"You were blessed by him, Darnuir. You were revived and born anew."

"It was Brackendon, not a god, who did this to me. And if Rectar truly has the Champion's Blade then how can your gods be real? How could the blade be found by one so evil?"

"Perhaps he found the sword and was later corrupted by the Shadow?" Blaine proffered. "Perhaps I am wrong and there is some other explanation. We dragons have continually been our own worst enemy. The Black Dragons fell to the Shadow long ago and we fought them for millennia. Norbanus was the very worst of my order: zealous to the point of blindness. He was a fool to think that humanity was the chosen race of the Shadow, as we are the champions of the Light; but humans do not dominate this world. We do."

Darnuir felt uneasy about this rhetoric of superiority; looking down on the very people who raised, loved and saved him. Darnuir could not help feeling it was plainly flawed.

"Dragons don't dominate anymore, Blaine."

"We have only ourselves to blame. Our position is our own fault. Not humanity's, not the fairies', not even the wretched demons'. It is ours, and largely mine, but no more."

"Then tell me what happened, Blaine!" Darnuir urged the aged dragon. "Tell me everything."

He gazed into Blaine's eyes. For all of the guardian's outward show of strength and resilience, there was a sadness there. In the dim hallway, Darnuir saw something similar to Cosmo's grief etched subtly but deeply into his features that had been smoothed with time.

"Before we delve into my past, we should unlock your own," Blaine said. He held out his hand for Darnuir to take.

Darnuir still had the rubies in his grasp. He reached out to take Blaine's hand and his pounding head seemed to quicken in anticipation.

"Don't resist it," Blaine said. "Let the memories in."

Darnuir gulped. "The last time I did that, I lost control of myself completely."

"Do as I tell you, boy. If it works, you won't lose control, but nor will I be able to speak to you. As it is your own memory – well, your old self's memory – you will experience it exactly as you felt it back then."

"Erm, right," Darnuir said, completely confused.

"It feels like a dream when I look back on my own memories," Blaine said. "Only more real. You will feel everything you felt, think everything you thought at the time."

"Will you be there as well? Like before?"

"I will be there but only as an observer, as we were with Norbanus. I won't be able to communicate with you."

"I see..." Darnuir said, still apprehensive. Yet there was no way to avoid it and he needed answers for his own sake. He let go.

Once more he was sucked through a blur of racing colour, leaving the real world behind.

This time, as his vision cleared, the man with the swept back hair materialised fully before him. His hair and stubble were jet-black and his robes purple. Silver irises marked him as a wizard. It was the familiar scene from his dreams but now it seemed real, as though he was truly there. Castallan sat before him, his face shadowed in the darkness of the room.

Weak light shone from three flickering lanterns, and the one small window behind the wizard was covered by thick drapes. In this dank room, it seemed nothing else mattered in the world but Darnuir and Castallan. They sat upon low, crooked stools, Castallan leaning forward expectantly while Darnuir kept his posture rigid and his arms tightly folded.

There was an excitement in this secrecy, and Darnuir felt it. He wasn't simply watching the memory; he was living it.

"The war does not fare well in the east, then?" Castallan said knowingly.

Darnuir raised an eyebrow. "What makes you say that? You know that we pushed the demons back along the Crucidal Road. The Forsaken City may even fall within the year."

Castallan smiled. "But you do not really believe that, do you? When has Rectar ever allowed such easy victories?"

"It could be that we are winning the war."

Castallan shook his head. The wizard almost seemed disheartened. "Come now, Darnuir, you would not be here if you truly felt that. Victories should be hard-won, and the demons have simply melted before you of late. It almost seems lazy of Rectar to not even feign a realistic retreat."

"You seem sure of this."

"As sure as I was about the enemy's latest manoeuvrings. And it was that information which allowed your last great 'victory'."

Is he finally going to reveal his secret? The wizard's predictions of where the demons would emerge was too accurate. *Some magic is at work, but why does he guard his method?*

"Darnuir, I believe that I can help end this war."

"If so, why not share this with the Conclave?" Darnuir asked pointedly.

"The Conclave would not be so understanding. They would consider my position too dangerous; Brackendon would especially speak out against me to the Archmage."

"Then perhaps it is too risky. If you are sure the Conclave will reject the practice then I ought to have no part in it."

"It is not what I do so much as whom I speak to," Castallan said furtively.

Darnuir tensed, waiting for the great reveal.

Castallan leaned even closer. "The enemy has chosen to contact me."

"Rectar speaks to you?" Darnuir said suspiciously. The idea of it was unnerving and extremely dangerous. On that, the wizard was quite right.

"Not as you might imagine. Not in words; that is not how it works... but there are thoughts... images, and sometimes a spectre lord. I reached out once with the scrying orbs, cast my mind to Kar'drun, and he found me there."

"The Conclave would deem this insanity."

"But there are things we must know," Castallan urged. "His power seems infinite. How does he process so much of it?"

"And what have you learned?" Darnuir demanded. "Have you learned of our impending doom? Is this why you are so certain that we stand on the brink of defeat?"

"Yes," Castallan said bluntly. "I have seen his armies. Fresh and vast, massing beneath the mountain."

"And why would he show you all of this?"

"He wants me to work against the Three Races," Castallan said. "To be his agent amongst the Conclave and your own councils."

"I hope you did not agree to serve him?"

"I did agree – I saw an opportunity."

"To die?"

"To offer us insight. To win the war!"

Darnuir clenched his fists, feeling he ought to draw his sword and end the wizard right there. However, he remained where he was. This knowledge placed him in a difficult position. If Darnuir left now, he would have no choice but to inform the Conclave, and yet there was a chance here. The slimmest, most distant of chances. Hope buried within further hope.

"Do you think you are capable of pulling off this double agency?"

"I have so far, have I not?"

"Why me? By telling me this, you are gambling everything."

"Because I do not think you will let this opportunity pass by, my lord," Castallan said. "We are not so different, you and I."

Darnuir remained stone-faced and silent in answer to that impertinent comment.

Castallan smiled again, sensing progress. "You seek answers as well. Why else would you have come to the Conclave? And you wish to save your people any further hardship, as do I. You must realise that this fight cannot be won through swords alone. The enemy showed me something by accident, I think. Something I was not supposed to see. If I can replicate it, then my magical solution will create soldiers of incredible power to aid us."

The wizard had that much right, at least. Something radical was required to bring this war to a conclusion.

Darnuir met his eyes. "My people have bled enough. What can I do to help?"

"I shall require gold and lots of it."

"And what will you need that for?"

"To find sufficient *volunteers*. Do you really want to know the details?"

"No," Darnuir said without hesitation. "What you do with humans is no concern of mine, but I must insist you refrain from approaching my own people."

"Of course, my lord," Castallan said, now a little nervous. "In any case, I do not think dragons would be... suitable. All I need from you is gold and a safe environment to work in. With that, and enough time, I will find the answer for you – for us!"

"You are sure? I seek answers. Not more questions."

"I am, though it will take a deal of secrecy to begin my work without interruption or suspicion. Few are as open-minded or understanding as you, Darnuir."

"Few share my passion to preserve my race. Even my father lacks that most basic instinct of survival. I feel he has resigned himself."

"We shall turn the tide."

"I hope so, Castallan."

As the memory ended, it began to unravel, just like it did in his dreams. Darnuir anticipated the familiar flying sensation that would return him to reality. However, this time was different.

The blur was not simply of whirring colour but of other memories. Scenes of battle, council and quiet seething flashed before him. Emotions and feelings flooded him as well: anger, frustration, desperation.

He saw the Dragon's Blade being lifted high above him, out of reach – oh, how he longed for it. Not for its own sake, he told himself, but in order to act, to fight, to do what was necessary.

He saw and felt years of training and battle in mere seconds. The information was overpowering. It crashed into his mind like an avalanche filling a valley. Before long, he found it hard to tell which memories were his own and which came from the rubies. Everything was vying for his attention and it felt as though he had two minds: one old, one new, both colliding and chafing against each other.

He felt pain. Greater than anything he had experienced before. A memory came to him of a shattered shoulder, a gouged side, and all the pain of it did not come close to the agony he felt now. His very being was ablaze and some menacing part of him seemed to roar savagely: bestial and hateful.

How long it lasted for, Darnuir could not say. Seconds, minutes, hours, even days might have passed in the world and he would have been stuck in this vortex of memory.

Trapped between two lives.

Then, in an instant, it ended. He saw Blaine standing over him, fear and concern stark across his face. Darnuir's ears rang and he could not hear what Blaine was saying. He felt exhausted. A tiredness engulfed him, even greater than the fatigue that had followed the run from Torridon. Darnuir closed his eyes and left the world for the comfort of sleep.

29

THE GUARDIAN'S BURDEN

Blaine – The Argent Tree

He rose at dawn, as was his custom. A bowl of piping-hot water was brought to his chambers as expected and he shaved the prickly hairs that had sprouted during the night. He donned fresh whites and only then noticed the single silver leaf beside the bowl. It was perfect in form, its body curving up to a pointed tip, and so pure in colour that it might have been a jewel.

It's been over two weeks since I returned and she waits until now to see me privately?

He could not help but suppress a pang of exhilaration. He pushed it back down, deep down, so it would not cloud his judgement. Things were not about to change.

His morning service could wait today.

He ran his fingers over his armour before opting for a lighter green tunic. Reinforced plate would not help him where he was going. He left the armour of the guardian on its stand but contemplated the heavy chest beneath it. The armour of the king rested within and had done so for eighty years.

Will Darnuir ever be ready to wear it?

It seemed a lifetime since he himself had looked upon the armour, with its roaring dragon pauldrons, lined thinly with starium to grant the wearer the greatest protection in all of Tenalp. So heavy and thick was the metal that without the support of one of the blades, it could not be worn. His own armour was similarly strong. It would be a relief not to wear it for a time.

He strapped the Guardian's Blade around his waist nonetheless and left his room for the interior of the Argent Tree. Being close to the top of the great tree, he could look down the hollow trunk onto the star-like lanterns, radiating their delicate light throughout the interior.

Blaine enjoyed the world at its best during this time of day. He had gotten used to the quiet of Val'tarra during his years here and realised shamefully that a part of him secretly yearned to revert to that state of restful nothingness. Returning to the fold had been swift and hard, and he was starting to feel his age. It ran deeper than muscle or blood or bone. The Guardian's Blade kept him fit enough, but he was so weary.

But I must go on. The boy is not ready.

Allowing one hand to run along the carved railing as he walked, Blaine took his time while making his journey upwards. He smiled kindly at the servants who hurried along in their tasks. They all knew him well by now, yet none would ever have spoken of his existence until recent months. Like all fairies, these servants had been handpicked at birth for their role by the queen. Their silence was expected, given their duties of serving at the uppermost levels of the Argent Tree.

He reached the final set of stairs leading up to the highest room amongst the canopy; a spiralling ascent that wove tightly upwards until the light of lanterns was replaced by that of the day. The wind whipped at his face, cool and pleasant on his skin. He still had the single silver leaf in hand as he knocked thrice upon the door.

"Come in," Kasselle said.

Blaine stepped inside the royal chambers. The foyer was stocked with comfy loungers, cushioned chairs and soft rugs. So dense was the canopy above that a true roof was not needed. Trodden silver leaves scattered the floor. Daylight crept in through the gaps here and there between branches as thickly set as the trunks of normal trees. Bowls of fruits and nuts were set out, along with jugs of icy water from the Avvorn. A pot of shimmer brew steamed over a small fire, filling the air with its enticing bitterness. There was even the luxury of an entire bowl of silver alderberries.

Kasselle, however, was not present.

"Up here, Blaine," she called.

Her songlike voice echoed from one of the upper rooms. There were four in total, lifted higher from his present position upon the branches, the steps to them forming out of the gnarled wood.

Cautiously he ascended, making for her. He felt the crunch of every leaf he trod upon as he passed. His heartbeat spiked painfully.

Kasselle sat serenely before her tall mirror, gliding a brush through her long silver hair. This was not her most private bedchamber but a glorified wardrobe, with all the trappings necessary for the queen to prepare her appearance each day. Not that she needed to work at it. Seeing her sitting there in an extraordinary magenta gown, plain yet regal, he momentarily forgot himself.

"You look especially beautiful today."

"That is not an appropriate thing for the Guardian of Tenalp to say to me," Kasselle said without looking at him. She continued to stroke her hair as though nothing was amiss.

"Nor is it appropriate for the guardian to be alone with you in your privy chambers, yet here the guardian stands."

"And standing is all he will do. He will not be here for long."

A dead weight seemed to fall from his heart through his stomach. It was all he could do to force out some words.

"I believe it was you who summoned me?"

"I did," Kasselle said, putting down her brush and scrutinising her work in the mirror.

"Then what would the Queen of Fairies have of the guardian?"

"I would know when you intend to leave."

Another twist in his stomach, sharp like a knife. "Just me?"

"Blaine, if I wanted you gone, I would have sent you away decades ago. I mean when will the army move out?"

"We are still awaiting around half of your forces. I'd rather not march without being at full strength. Fidelm must have informed you."

"He did," Kasselle said curtly, rising to her feet. "He also told me that much of the demon host at Inverdorn has split off and is now burning the east of my homeland."

News of the burning of northeastern Val'tarra had come as another hard blow. Days had passed since then, and even though it was a crude measure, the demons would soon force Blaine to act. The fairies would not abide the burning of their forest. The battered dragon and human forces would have to face Castallan's host before they were ready.

"We are monitoring the situation," was all Blaine could say in response.

Kasselle swept past him without so much as a glance, back down to her foyer where she poured herself a cup of brew.

Blaine followed gingerly. *What does she want me to do? We are not yet prepared.*

"Darnuir has still not woken," he told her.

"It has been over a week now," Kasselle said. "We cannot be certain when he will rise again, and we cannot afford to wait for weeks or months. My people cannot afford it, Blaine." She gestured to the food and drink. "I'm expecting Fidelm and his men soon," she said by way of explanation. "You may have something if you like. You must be hungry."

With the knot in his guts, he didn't feel like it. Still, he didn't want her to know this, so he picked up an apple, red, round and oversized, and bit into it. It was perfect, like all that grew near the Avvorn. That which survived, at least. He withheld from taking anything further, not wishing to overstay his already strained welcome.

"If we march without Darnuir, I fear my people will lose heart."

"Will they? You seem to be the one in control."

"That may be the case for now, but Darnuir is their true king and a symbol both for my followers and the dragons at large. We cannot march without him."

"You told me when you first arrived back that he was not ready."

"The boy is a decent warrior. If we are to rush to battle then he needs to be in the thick of the fighting, like the great kings of old."

"And as Draconess did not?" Kasselle noted, throwing Blaine a look that was steeped in knowing.

Blaine looked to the floor. "I'd rather we did not discuss Draconess. What's done is done."

"Very much so. A grand failure of a plan."

She reached for a handful of nuts and began to eat. Even her chewing seemed graceful.

"I kept the secret between the two of you," she said. "I even tried to convince Draconess at times that it must end; that he should grant the sword to Darnuir and revive your own power, so that together you might try to end the war. I did all you asked of me, but my kind have only ended up further from safety and peace. Now demons burn Val'tarra itself. No foe has ever dared to come so close in all the ages of the world, and so you must forgive me, Blaine, if I no longer place as much faith in you or your schemes as I once did."

Blaine's hurt began to heat into anger. He glared at her.

"It turned out we were right to do as we did. You said as much. The boy's temperament was all wrong; he even colluded with the enemy. I've seen the evidence for myself now. Irrefutable."

"Perhaps he turned out the way he did because of the shackles Draconess placed around him. Draconess was a fine dragon, Blaine, but he was always cautious; I think now to a fault. Darnuir may have been driven to help end the war by questionable means, but what choice did he have? Wouldn't you do anything you could to save your people?"

"I would not have been so reckless. Darnuir may or may not have known what Castallan had planned; one memory does not make that clear. But if Darnuir had access to the blade, then—"

"Everything would be worse, I'm sure," Kasselle interrupted. She was halfway through her brew now and the kick from it had flushed her cheeks indigo.

It sparked a memory that flashed into his mind: of a happier Kasselle; a younger and laughing girl, who squeezed his hand tightly as they sneaked through the markets of Brevia. She found a fairy merchant with a pot of brew and smiled at Blaine as she drank it down, a dazzling smile that held him and had him. They had pretended to be anyone but who they were back then. For a few weeks, they imagined time would not move on and they could stay as they were forever: together and free. In those days, he had been happy, as had she. It was a pure time, when her flushed cheeks and smile were all that mattered in the world.

His fingers curled at the memory, hoping to find her hand once more.

"The past cannot be changed now," Kasselle went on, unaware of his reverie. "Yet, in the here and now, my people are suffering. We cannot sustain all these humans, dragons and even our own kin in such a concentrated area. Dozens of my healers have already died from their exertions and many more have been taken seriously ill. When healers get sick from their own healing, something is desperately wrong."

Blaine swallowed hard. His mouth was terribly dry. "I told Fidelm that they were not to overexert themselves."

"And I told him they should work as effectively as they can. We need this army out of our forest. I need both the demons and the war taken away from my borders."

"You have made yourself quite clear, my queen." She wanted a time of departure from him. Nothing more. "The earliest we could leave would be in two days, if I give the order immediately."

Kasselle nodded.

"There should be a council beforehand—"

"I have already arranged one for this evening," Kasselle said. "Ensure everyone you require is in attendance."

Blaine nodded. "And Darnuir—"

"May remain here until he returns to the world. He will be with family, after all. I shall see to his every need. Then I will send him to join you, along with the rest of my forces."

"Very well," he said flatly.

Is this how we are to part?

The thought kept him frozen in place, halfway between Kasselle and the door. She took another handful of nuts, perhaps to keep her hands busy. She still refused to look at him.

Saying something further would clearly be unwise. But he had to.

"Is this how I am to leave you?"

"Two days, you said. You are not leaving yet."

"I doubt we will have a chance to be alone before then," he said, pressing determinedly on.

She twisted in her chair to look at him. Her eyes pierced into him as only hers could.

"What do you want, Blaine?"

"Something more than this. I am to march off to war, the last war I am ever likely to fight. I'd rather our last words together were not you telling me you want me gone."

Kasselle closed her eyes, her lower lip trembling. "What is it you want to hear? All these years, and still you look at me like that. Why?"

"Because I have not forgotten."

"And neither have I!" She surged to her feet, an accusatory finger pointed towards him, her poise and grace shattered. "I remember it all, Blaine. And I can hardly stand it—" Her voice cracked.

Blaine took a half-step forwards, intending to console her.

"No! Stop."

Blaine's outstretched hand froze in mid-air.

"I meant what I said," Blaine told her gently. "I do not expect anything. Not now. I'm not such a fool. Yet surely there is something you could say. 'Please come back', 'I will see you again', anything!"

A single tear ran down her cheek. "I don't think you should come back."

The knife in his stomach cut deeper. Yet a part of him, that which still had some sense, knew she was right.

Why do I do this to myself? What is it I want to hear?

"I expect I will have many matters to attend to once we are back in Aurisha," he said mechanically.

He turned. He was halfway to the door.

"Blaine," she called. He whirled around. "Every time I see you, I remember. And I remember her. I see our daughter, and every time I do, I want to walk off one of these branches and never need to think of her again."

Blaine squeezed his eyes shut, fighting back tears of his own. He had not thought of Arlandra in a very long time. He had hidden almost every memory of her away in his white gems. Locked them up so that they could never surface to hurt him. Kasselle did not have such a luxury.

There was a loud knock at the door.

"One moment," she called, suppressing the hurt in her voice. Then, more quietly, she told him, "I do care, Blaine, but just not the way I once did. I cannot go on like this and I am a different fairy from the young queen-to-be you first met."

"You were thirty years old when we first met."

"And now I am one hundred and forty. My people are my life now."

Another loud knock rang, more deliberate.

"I said one moment," Kasselle snapped, quite out of character.

"My lady, I'm afraid it is urgent," Fidelm said steadily from the other side of the door.

Kasselle quickly attempted to compose herself and Blaine flicked the water out of his eyes.

"Very well, General," Kasselle said.

The door opened and in stepped the tall, winged fairy, his dark face betraying some worry. In his wake were a group of healers, who seemed in equal parts afraid and ashamed.

"What is the matter?" Kasselle demanded. "I was not expecting you so soon."

"It is Darnuir, my queen, Lord Guardian," Fidelm said, bowing briefly to each in turn. "He is missing."

All present in the room looked between each other.

Blaine was the first to rally. "He'll be confused after what happened. I shall search for him."

He only noticed then that his hand remained stupidly hanging in mid-reach towards Kasselle. His fingers slowly curled inwards in their vain quest to find hers once more. He balled his hand into a fist to save face and strode from the room.

He did not dare look back.

30

FRIENDS FROM THE NORTH

Cassandra – Val'tarra – Base of the Argent Tree

Dawn broke as Cassandra quietly perched upon her chosen branch. It stretched out over the top of the command tent and granted her a sweeping view of life around the Argent Tree. Her instincts for climbing, moving in secret and seeking solitude had not left her. Yet with each day, she began to feel more at ease.

The forest was such a pleasant place and she had never slept half as well as she had since arriving in the fairies' homeland. Her frequent nightmare of the hand on her shoulder, the flash of steel, the blood and the screaming, had not plagued her dreams of late. There was a tranquillity here. It was no wonder the fairies were so well-collected, living in such a place. The waters of the Avvorn were sweet and invigorating, though they had all been warned not to drink too much, lest they become addicted.

This treasured peace of the fairies had been disturbed with their arrival, and the occasional anguished cry from the wounded was a reminder of the more pressing reality.

Still, Cassandra enjoyed being able to wake as she pleased, walk where she pleased, talk with whom she wished and eat when it suited her. Darnuir had fought for her freedom and he had promised her that she would have it. On that, he had not disappointed her. With Scythe's death, even those most suspicious of her had withdrawn to the periphery. Only the last measurements of precaution were in place. She was not allowed near ink or parchment, nor was she allowed to be seen too close to important conversations.

Not that it matters. I hear things all the same.

Rumours of a traitor or traitors had spread in abundance since Torridon. The Cairlav hunters blamed those from the Boreacs, and the Boreac men suffered fractures from within. Those from the Golden Crescent were the greatest in number and had suffered the fewest losses in battle but their forces had splintered in defending their people. Many had remained behind at their station on the western coast to protect the towns and villages there, while others had taken refugees to Inverdorn. News of the red-eyed chevalier who had fought so fiercely at Torridon was increasingly common knowledge and a terrible point of suspicion. If there were traitors among them, then they may also be as powerful, and there would be no way of telling friend from foe.

One morning, while collecting her breakfast, Cassandra had overheard a rather intriguing discussion between Crescent hunters.

"... and then there are those queer barrels to consider," an older female huntress had been saying. "Reckon they turned up at the station by mistake."

"How d'you mean?" a male colleague had asked.

"I mean that when the kitchen boys cracked open the first crate, it weren't what they were expecting! The barrels were marked as apples from Val'tarra but that's hardly what was in them."

"How would you know that, then?"

"'Cause I was there when the cap'n herself heard the news. Morwen became obsessed with finding out why there was some secret cargo being pushed around her territory. Perhaps a little too interested, if ye catch my meaning?"

"What you sayin', Gwen? You reckon old Morwen's death was no accident?"

Cassandra had then circled around carefully, picking casually at her chopped fruit and nuts, feigning trying to find a free spot to sit in.

"Alls I'm sayin' is that Morwen was escorting those barrels back to the loch when she was ambushed."

"By spectres, though. There were spectre corpses at the scene."

"Aye, so we've been told. Who knows what's happenin' these days? Dragons and demons roaming everywhere, trampling and burning our crops. Talk of magic swords and black powder that lights up a terrible blaze. I tell you, half of what we've heard is probably false and the other half played down!"

Instinct had told Cassandra that she ought to move on or risk being noticed, so she sat alongside Balack after easily picking him out amongst the crowd.

He had become her closest friend during their stay in the forest. She felt no qualms about confiding in him the information she overheard; information that would no doubt make its way from Balack to Garon to Cosmo. There it might find its way to Darnuir, though they had barely seen him since the great run. He was often with Blaine, training or somewhere high up in the Argent Tree where lowly people such as themselves were not permitted to venture.

And during the last week, he had apparently been out cold. The cause of this wasn't clear, for the whispers – from Blaine to Fidelm to Cosmo down to Balack – had become vaguer with each telling. Cosmo had at least made it clear, and angrily so, that he felt Blaine had something to do with it.

Being crammed into such a tight space around the Argent Tree was only aggravating the distrust in the ranks. Perched up on her branch, obscured by deftly chosen clumps of leaves, she could almost feel the tension thick in the air.

We will have to move on soon or begin releasing that tension on each other.

When the quiet routine of the morning suddenly broke below her, she thought that one or more party had finally snapped.

People were calling out to each other. "It's him!" they said. "He's back."

From her vantage point, Cassandra saw Darnuir striding out from the base of the Argent Tree, garbed in only the loose-fitting silks of the fairies. His march was determined but his face showed confusion. The Dragon's Blade hung from his waist, its red hilt a jarring shade against its surroundings. He disappeared into the command tent.

Cassandra scrambled back down the tree, landing in a forward roll and springing back to her feet in one fluid motion. A group of nearby children squealed their approval. She gave them a quick smile before pressing a finger to her lips to quieten them, then made to find Balack.

She tried the archers' range before finding him in the mess. He was rubbing his eyes, clutching at a mug of steaming brew as if his health depended on it. Brackendon sat opposite with Kymethra, who had recovered well. Though the magic wielders were accorded chambers within the tree, they seemed to spend most of their time within the camp.

Balack's eyes were half-closed when she reached him.

"Hey, wake up," she urged, giving him a shake.

His eyes blinked open and he made a grumbling noise by way of response.

"Balack, he's awake. He's up!"

"That's... great," he yawned.

"Leave him be, girl," Kymethra said, swatting away her hand. "The poor soul is clearly half asleep." Before the witch lay the remnants of a rather large meal. She claimed a large appetite was the key to recovery.

"I just thought he'd want to know."

Brackendon chuckled, his mood vastly improved since Kymethra had recovered. "Darnuir has been storming around looking for you, actually."

"Me?"

She considered he would have more important people to see upon breaking his slumber.

"Ask him yourself," Brackendon said.

"What do you..." She turned, already knowing who she would find.

"Cassandra, please come." Darnuir didn't wait for a response before stalking off. Cassandra shot the table a quick glance. Balack was unaware of who was around him, Kymethra just shrugged while reaching for a bread roll, and Brackendon merely nodded in Darnuir's direction. Confused, she followed.

Cassandra found herself breathlessly trying to keep up with Darnuir. He wove between the tents and bodies with an agility that far exceeded her own. Occasionally, he cast a glance back to check she was still following and, when satisfied, merely carried on. Frustrated, she jogged up to his side.

"What is going on?" she demanded. "Where are you taking me?"

He answered without slowing his pace. "Into the trees. I feel like I need to get away for a time."

She was naturally sceptical, although the need to seek solitude was one with which she was sympathetic. But if that was all, then why did he need her?

Their journey continued northwards until they left the bustle and the tents behind them, crossing over the threshold into the forest proper. The trees engulfed them. Even then, Darnuir continued at a brisk pace, leaping over felled, burnt trees rather than going around them.

At one such obstacle, his inhuman leap left her behind. She remained on the other side, irritated, attempting to clamber up the knobbly, blackened trunk until he reappeared at its precipice and lifted her up like a child. Dropping down, they continued to march on. When a strong gust swept a collection of multi-coloured damp leaves into her face and hair, Cassandra let her annoyance show.

"All right, stop," she insisted.

Darnuir, King of Dragons, turned slowly around. His gaze was part bewildered, part affronted, and the beginnings of a beard covered his face from the time he'd spent on his sick bed.

"I'm not taking one step more until you tell me what this is all about!"

"Such boldness to speak so towards a dragon lord," Darnuir said, his voice unmoved.

"Since when did you demand reverence? What happened to you? Did Blaine bring that big sword of his across the back of your head?"

"No... he showed me how to see."

"How to see?" Cassandra repeated, now concerned that he'd lost it. Perhaps he was still unwell? Her hand moved subtly towards her sword but she stopped herself. There would be no use in that if something went amiss; not against him. For the first time since she had met Darnuir, she felt afraid of him.

His nose twitched a little. "There is no need to fear, Cass," he said, sounding a bit more like himself. "I would never hurt you."

"Maybe you ought to return to the Argent Tree to rest? You don't seem like yourself."

He did not seem to hear her. "I don't feel exactly like I did, not then, nor even way back then. All those years ago…" He drifted off once more and remained silent for a time.

The forest around them was close, almost suffocating. The air was heavy and moist, and it felt dark, despite the brilliance of the morning. Arborists must have worked the area well for there was only one shrivelled, burnt shoot, not much more than a stump. Every third tree was a rich silver, dulled somewhat by moss and other growths. And though they were surely completely alone, Cassandra could not shake the feeling that she was being watched. She scanned the dense canopy but could see nothing. Not a leaf moved suspiciously, and yet the feeling was undeniably there.

Darnuir spoke again without warning. "I have his memories. The old me, I mean. Not all of them, just those he gave me, but I also have my own. They are both me, but they are also different people. I cannot describe the feeling."

"Sounds…" Cassandra searched for a word. "Messy."

"Hmmm," Darnuir mused, falling back against a nearby trunk. "I have some grave memories now. Mistakes I wish I could take back."

Still not knowing why she was here, Cassandra opted to play the sympathiser. "You cannot blame yourself for mistakes that your old self made."

"The mistakes do not all stem from him." He clutched his head in his hands.

"Does your head still hurt?"

"No. In fact, it has never felt clearer," he said, and then added, more to himself, "Cosmo was right. I must make amends for what I've done." He slumped further down until he was sitting on the damp leaves, his legs splayed out before him. It made him look small and ridiculous to be sitting in such a way. Cassandra couldn't resist laughing. When he looked up at her, she was thankful he grinned back.

"Laughing at me now?" he said, looking down at his outstretched legs. He half-laughed himself as he pulled his knees back in and the tension faded as Darnuir appeared to unwind.

Cassandra fell back against a silver tree opposite Darnuir. She slid down to the ground to join him and suddenly it felt like they were back in that battered little shack in Farlen. When he looked at her, his eyes were kinder again.

"I helped him, Cass. I allowed Castallan to become what he is. It seems I flooded him with gold and who knows what else," he said, his voice thick with regret. "I've wondered, in all your time at the Bastion, did he ever mention what I did for him?"

So this was why she was here? She was almost disappointed. Then again, this was why she was useful, wasn't it?

"From time to time, there was mention of a 'benefactor', though I could not say who that person was."

"Me, most likely," Darnuir said solemnly.

"The way he said it sounded like it was still ongoing."

"Perhaps I gave him so much gold it lasted him for years. Whatever I did, I helped him to reach his place now, alongside Rectar."

"I do not believe his allegiance to Rectar is strong. The spectre lord I overheard telling him of the invasion threatened him as much as informed him. He wants the Bastion to conduct his campaign and I think he would be happy enough to remove Castallan himself."

Darnuir nodded slowly. "This spectre lord has a name, if I recall?"

"Dukoona."

She would not soon forget that sinister face; the teeth too white and perfect, his hair a fiery blaze of blue strands. She grimaced at the thought of it.

"No matter," Darnuir said. "We'll take back the Bastion first. We always had to try."

"You sound more confident."

"My father felt assured we could take it. My father, Draconess. I never thought about having a father before, but I can see him now. I remember his face, his voice, the fights we had. Before Aurisha fell, he intended to root Castallan out."

He was quiet again for a time.

"Is there anything else you can think of that we might use to our advantage?"

She decided not to hold back any longer. He'd upheld his word so far.

"Well... I didn't just get away on the back of a cart."

"I assumed as much."

"There are passages within the fortress. I used them for years. That's how I got around unnoticed. The day I escaped, Chelos told me of one that led right out past the main gates from the inner courtyard. There might even be more for all I know."

"And he only told you about it then?"

"I think he always knew. He always said I would get out one day. He was just biding his time. Waiting for you."

"Could you find the entrance again?"

"I think so."

"Then don't you see? Chelos has sent me Castallan's downfall. If we can sneak past the walls, his Bastion means nothing."

"Does it not trouble you how he knew? I can't figure it out. How would the steward of the dragon Royal Tower know secret passages within a human-made fortress?"

Darnuir shrugged it off. "We can ask him when we rescue him." He seemed lost in his own thoughts, likely envisioning the conquest of the Bastion.

"Darnuir," Cassandra began tentatively, not wanting to ruin his good mood. "Why did you bring me out here?"

He clasped his hands upon his knees. "I wanted to be alone but not completely so. Being around you used to help my headaches, though I am not sure why. I suppose I just got into the habit; and I did want to ask you about Castallan, of course."

"What about Cosmo or Balack?"

"Cosmo would likely have lectured me or told me I should be resting, and Balack—"

"You do not feel comfortable around him anymore, do you?"

"What makes you say that?"

"He feels you have become distant. He thinks it is just due to your new responsibilities."

"But you see it as more?"

"Well, you did just allude to mistakes you regret."

"I did, didn't I?"

"Whatever it was, I am sure he would understand. It would be a shame for you to lose your friend."

Real friends were not to be taken for granted. The outline of Trask came to her then and she mentally scowled. Well, she should have known better.

"I am afraid he will feel betrayed either way," Darnuir said. He began sniffing furtively at the air again.

Cassandra's gut instinct that they were not alone intensified. She heard rustling above, but saw nothing amiss. *Probably just the wind.* As she returned to looking at Darnuir, she decided she'd had enough of tiptoeing around the issue. There he was. The King of Dragons. Strong by nature, more powerful for his magic sword, and supposedly the leader of the Three Races. Whatever this 'betrayal' was, she would have it out of him.

"Are you going to tell me?" She could not fathom what Darnuir could have done that was so wicked he would fear telling Balack about it.

"Has Balack mentioned a girl called Eve to you?"

"In passing. He tries to cover up how important she was to him, but you can glean it from his voice, his eyes; the way he drops her into conversation casually but often. It is clearly painful for him to discuss."

Despite herself, Cassandra had found Balack's openness quite endearing.

"We grew up with her, and Balack loved her since we were young. I knew, of course. He wasn't subtle about it, but then, why should he have been? Although he never actually told her, it was plain to see."

"Why didn't he?" Cassandra asked. It was a curious thing.

He cocked his head. "You've never loved someone like that, have you?"

She narrowed her eyes. "I haven't exactly had a normal life."

"I'm not calling you a bad person, Cass. I'm just saying that, if you'd ever felt like that, you wouldn't ask why he didn't tell her."

He was right. She didn't understand, didn't understand Balack's past nor Kymethra and Brackendon's present. Although she hoped one day she'd understand that trust.

"I just don't see what he had to lose?"

"I think he was afraid," Darnuir said. "He's confessed to me that he knew deep down she didn't share those feelings. I think he was afraid to turn his fears into reality."

He paused, probably hoping she would say something more. Yet, once again, Cassandra remained silent, letting Darnuir get there on his own. Not giving him a chance for deflection.

"I knew all of this, Cass, but shortly before she died, we... we—"

"I see," Cassandra said, indicating she required no further explanation. It wasn't quite what she had expected to hear.

"See, this is why I didn't want to say anything," Darnuir said. "Even you're uncomfortable just hearing me say it. How badly will Balack react?"

She pulled her knees up to her chest and wrapped her arms around them. Having done this, she wasn't exactly sure why. What he said wasn't so bad, but she felt a pang for Balack, who trusted him so much. To have that bond broken would be heartbreaking.

The memory came to her again, unbidden – the sword, the fight, the bitter glint in Trask's eye gone wild.

"Cass? Cass?"

With a yank she returned to the present, blinking and staring at him.

"You've gone pale," he said. He picked up a clump of leaves from the ground and let them fall. "Do you... think less of me?"

Cassandra gripped her knees more tightly. "It's not you." She buried her face into her legs, enjoying the darkness for a moment. When she emerged, she drew a deep breath and found herself unable to stop the words spilling out of her. "There is a little more to the story of my escape."

He was honest with me. I should be the same.

If Darnuir was perplexed at the sudden change of topic, he hid it well. "I'm listening."

She drew another steadying breath, then ploughed on.

"I had some more help in escaping. A friend of mine – well, sort of a friend – smuggled me in the back of his cart. If I'd had the chance to escape with supplies of my own, I might not have needed to – oh, but it doesn't matter now."

She sniffed.

"Trask was just a stable boy. His father was killed during the war. I don't know about his mother. But he resented Brevia's lack of support when Castallan rose, and then somehow decided that Castallan had the right idea. Many do. So many have joined him. Had I known how deeply it ran in him... well, as I said. It doesn't matter now."

Darnuir's entire focus was now on her. She spoke to the bark of the tree just over his shoulder, feeling that seeing his reaction full-on might tip her over the edge.

"When I went scurrying around the Bastion as a girl, he was the first person I bumped into. We were about the same age, so I could convince him to keep quiet. Chelos was angry at first but accepted that I needed someone else besides him to talk to." She pulled out the dragon figurine she still kept on her person and twirled it around with her fingers. "He gave me this, I think for my tenth birthday. I don't know why I still carry it around. Stupid little thing."

She rammed the figurine back into her pocket, and felt a hot tear well in her eye.

Darnuir got up at this, but she curled up into a tighter ball and that was enough to ward him off.

"What happened?" he asked kindly.

"Over the years I started to play along with his crazy ideas on Castallan. I didn't want – I didn't want to lose my only friend. But I shouldn't have. When it came to my escape, I kept it up. Finding out I didn't feel the same must have stung. I had been lying to him for a long time. At least that was partly it. I think he also got scared at the thought of them finding out it was him who'd helped me get away. He tried to stop me. So, I drew my sword on him."

She was fighting to control her breath now, her chest rising and falling in ever-quicker heaves.

"The idiot tried to fight me. He'd never been trained at all. What stable boy is? But he tried anyway. Even after I sent him flat on his back, he didn't leave it well enough alone. Clumsy git cut into my shoulder flailing that sword around as he grabbed me and tried again to haul me back. I think he had a little fantasy of us going off on this grand adventure together; maybe ending up in each other's arms. He didn't like it when I told him that wasn't happening. And just like that... he wasn't my friend anymore. He wasn't enchanted but I swore his eyes flashed red, and it's all a bit blurry but he said something about getting rewarded for turning me back in." She was rambling now, each word questing in the dark to find justification.

Darnuir moved to sit beside her now and she didn't care.

"I had to kill him."

The admission burst the dam.

A flood of tears began pouring as all the pain of that night rose to the surface: pain from the wound, and pain from the loss, the betrayal, the fact that he'd never really seen her for who she was. Cassandra was just some illusion he'd made for himself and couldn't deal with seeing shattered.

Darnuir placed an arm around her and she buried her face into his shoulder, grateful he was wearing soft silk, and grateful in that moment that he was there. She didn't want to be seen by him, or anyone else, as other than she really was or how she truly felt. Not again.

Time slipped by, with only the sad chirrup of small birds and the rustling of leaves to break their silence. She was glad of it. There wasn't much else left to say.

As she began to collect herself, a twig snapped. It came from overhead.

Darnuir started sniffing at the air again. He gently parted from her, got to his feet and placed a hand on the hilt of his blade.

"I can definitely smell something," he said. "I don't recognise it at all." He looked up. "Show yourself!"

Cassandra wiped her face, clambered to her feet and gripped the hilt of her own weapon. Another crack came from the canopy. She jerked her gaze upwards, darting along the branches, looking for its source. Some way off, the leaves rustled too much. Not the way the wind would blow them. And then there came a voice.

"No need for da swords, Dragon King. Ochnic comes as friend."

"Then show yourself, 'friend'," Darnuir said.

Something descended from above, falling with the grace of an acrobatic cat to crouch amongst the leaves. Its clothing was rudimentary at best: a loincloth and a crude covering for its torso, evidently made from thick white fur. The rest of its body was naked, its skin leathery and grey. Ice-blue eyes shone out like the Avvorn under a mop of frayed white hairs.

It stood upright, stretching out long, sinewy limbs, and though it settled into a hunch, it still towered over them. A large hide satchel was slung over its shoulder.

Cassandra looked on, amazed. The creature couldn't be what she thought it was. Frost trolls were just myths, hearsay, and yet the creature looked so like the descriptions.

As it bared its teeth, she noticed fang-like incisors, short, thick and pointed.

Darnuir drew the Dragon's Blade, holding it ready for a fight.

The creature waved its hands for peace. "Ochnic said der was no need for swords."

Darnuir edged forwards. "Why were you spying on us? Whom do you serve?"

"Wait," Cassandra said. "I think he is a frost troll. He is clearly no demon."

"As if it is only demons who work against us," Darnuir said. "We don't even know what this thing is."

"I told you," Cassandra insisted, moving to stay Darnuir's arm. "I believe he is a frost troll."

"A frost troll..." Darnuir said, mulling it over.

The creature looked confused. "Ochnic does not know of dees 'trolls'," it said, working carefully to try and replicate the word it did not know.

Darnuir still looked ready to gut the troll, breathing hard through his nose.

Cassandra stepped in. Her fascination was overwhelming. The depressive state brought on by talk of Trask was fast evaporating.

"Ochnic," she said clearly. "Is that your name?"

"Ochnic, I am." It thumped an oversized hand against its chest. Now she noticed it, his feet were oversized as well and appeared to have one toe much further apart from the others, almost like another pair of hairy hands.

"And what are you, Ochnic?"

The troll cocked its head quizzically at her.

She thumped a hand off her own chest, in imitation of Ochnic. "Cassandra, I am." She thumped a second time. "Human, I am." She turned to Darnuir, who did not seem to have caught on. She whacked his torso, saying, "Darnuir, he is. Dragon, he is."

At this, Ochnic seemed to understand. "Kazzek, I am."

She smirked with satisfaction at Darnuir.

"Okay, Ochnic," Darnuir said, sheathing his sword, but keeping one hand on the hilt. "How did you know who I was?"

Ochnic pointed to the Dragon's Blade. "Dey said da Dragon King would have weapon like dis." His words were slow and deliberate, though Cassandra sensed there was a great deal of intelligence behind them.

"And who are 'they'?"

"Kazzek chiefs."

"Not demons?" Cassandra asked, just to make sure. Ochnic growled deeply at that and stepped towards them. Darnuir was between them in a flash but his presence was unnecessary. Ochnic simply spat a large blob of thick spittle onto the leaves.

"De demons do not come as friends. Dey cut and bite and kill kazzek. They smash de stone men too when dey can. Der not many of dem left now."

"Demons or stone men?" Darnuir asked.

"Stone men," Ochnic grunted. "Of de demons, der are thousands and thousands, but not as many as before. Dey attacked our lands to da east. Made it hard to come and go. Den most left, but still many remain."

"And when was this?" Darnuir asked. He seemed more at ease than before.

"Two or dree moons ago."

"Dree?" Darnuir murmured in confusion.

"I think he means three," Cassandra whispered back.

"So, around the time the invasion of the west was conceived," Darnuir said.

"The timing seems to match up, even if it is a bit vague," Cassandra said. "Ochnic, why have you come? Your people have not been seen this far south before."

"Kazzek be needin help of Dragon King. We be dying. We be too few to fight da demons if dey return."

Darnuir suddenly became serious. "Is there a route through the Highlands? Would there be a way for the demons to reach us here, as you did?"

Ochnic nodded. "Always der is ways."

"Dranus' hide, but we have been fortunate," Darnuir said. "If these kazzek were the only thing preventing the demons from invading overland—"

Blaine's voice cut through the trees. "Darnuir! Darnuir! Fan out, men. Find the king. Something must be amiss. There is a foul smell in the air."

Darnuir rounded on Ochnic. "Try not to react brashly."

The kazzek cocked his head at him.

"Over here, Lord Guardian," someone called.

A Light Bearer was running towards them. Soon, a score more appeared from between the trees, Blaine amongst them, his heavy, golden armour glistening. All drew their swords when they saw Ochnic, encircling him. Ochnic leapt high into the branches above and was soon lost in the leaves. The Light Bearers arced their shields and eyes upwards.

"Careful," Blaine warned. "These frost trolls are crafty."

"I don't think he means us harm," Darnuir said.

"He is looking for help, not a fight," Cassandra implored.

Blaine shot her a disapproving look. "That you are out here alone with her is one thing, but to be so incautious is quite another. What if there had been more?"

Darnuir stepped towards Blaine. "I would have smelled them," he said fiercely. Blaine remained unmoving, considering Darnuir as one might a snarling dog. "It worked, Blaine," Darnuir said. "I have my old memories now. Well, at least those that were left behind. I would refrain from speaking to your king in such a way, Guardian."

The newfound tension broke as Ochnic re-emerged from above, dangling upside down and swaying slightly. The Light Bearers turned in unison to face the kazzek, slamming their shields into the ground.

"Ah!" Ochnic exclaimed, clearly delighted. "Dis one is dragon guardian?"

"I am, troll. What of it?"

Ochnic brought his satchel around to his front and began carefully rummaging through the bag. Seemingly frustrated in his search, he curled his torso upwards and stuck his head deeper inside. He did it all effortlessly and Cassandra wondered at how strong the troll must be to achieve such stability in the air. With a great flourish, Ochnic pulled out a beautiful silver necklace, its metal woven in an organic pattern that spoke of fairy design. In the centre of the chain was a recognisable letter 'A'.

Blaine's face drained of colour as Ochnic handed it to him. "How did you come by this?"

"Ochnic told to give dragon guardian dis by chieftains."

Blaine raised the necklace up in front of his disbelieving eyes. He looked as though he had seen the dead. It seemed to take a prodigious effort for Blaine to regain a measure of his usual bearing. He kept the necklace in his hand as he turned slowly away and began to trudge back towards the Argent Tree.

"Chieftains no say that it leave guardian tongueless," Ochnic said, baffled.

Well, there is a first, Cassandra thought.

Blaine marched off, kicking through the leaves. The Light Bearers seemed confused and, one by one, they turned to Darnuir instead.

"Come, my king!" Blaine shouted back. "We have a war to plan. Bring your new pet along too if you will."

31

TO PLAN A WAR

Darnuir – The Argent Tree

Word had been spread. The troops would leave on the morrow. Activity in the great tree was manic and Darnuir observed it as he descended the spiralling pathway of the hollow trunk, Lira at his side.

"I feel foolish 'guarding' you," she said.

"You're not a bodyguard. The Praetorians are my tool, like the Light Bearers are Blaine's. I shall wield the Dragon's Blade in one hand and the Guard in the other."

"And you trust me already?"

"More than most. I do not know my own kind well enough yet and they do not know me. You and I have been through similar circumstances; dragons raised by humans. I think you can understand my position."

"Perhaps. Still, I hardly have the experience needed."

"You're a hunter, Lira, like me. You have led teams of men, settled disputes and helped those in need. You are trained in both sword and bow and have acquired the skills of tracking and stealth that few dragons could hope to master now."

"They could be trained," Lira offered.

"The old are stuck in their ways," Darnuir said, slowing his pace. He did not want to be the first to arrive. His advisors could await his pleasure; the older Darnuir had always been insistent on that.

"So, what do you intend?" Lira asked.

"To make a guard worthy of the alliance that we claim is so important. An elite core of dragons, humans and fairies alike. I would even take some of these frost trolls if I could. If I am supposed to lead the Three Races, those around me should represent the best of each race. Stout dragons with thick armour and heavy shields might be good for fighting in the field but that is not the only arena of war."

"You sound different," Lira said, then added, "My lord. I mean, sire. I mean—"

"There is no need for such ingratiating titles in private. Though, in public, it would be good to observe expected courtesies, particularly around the guardian."

"He does not much care for me. It seems like he has a bad smell under his nose when he looks at me."

"I'm not sure he cares much for anyone. And he is tightly wound and secretive besides. He is keeping things from me; I am fully aware of that now."

"Such as?"

"This Guard, for one. He never deigned to tell me about the Praetorians and I only found out because of my unlocked memories. But there is much more beyond, though they are matters I do not desire to burden you with."

"As you wish."

"In answer to your question, I do feel different. I feel I am ready to start acting like a king. I have no desire to waste our time any longer. It is time to act."

"What would you have me do?" Lira asked, as willing to accept an order as Darnuir was now prepared to give it.

"Get out amongst the younger dragons. Find those akin to ourselves if you can; young and not yet hardened to the old ways. If they have enough talent with a blade, then consider recruiting them."

"Yes, sire," she said, a little unsure. "There are others like us out there – those who were so young when the Golden City fell that they cannot remember life before living amongst humans. They may be our best start."

They swapped hunter stories for the remainder of their journey. He enjoyed this lighter topic but was cautious of the stares he received from passersby. Most of the fairies recognised him now, as his white and grey leathers were not enough of a disguise to allow him to avoid detection. They saw the hilt of his sword and they knew what it was; who he was.

Ever since the Dragon's Blade had smashed through that window and placed itself in his hand, he had felt as though he was changing.

Am I now 'complete'? Is this who I am meant to be?

He was not fully human nor fully dragon; neither all of his old self nor all of the new. The old Darnuir's disdain for Blaine's religion had become enmeshed with his frustration for his father. It would be best to break cleanly from this bitter past. He would use his Praetorians to reflect what the Three Races ought to be: a true coming together. An amalgamation.

Just like me.

As they approached the war room, Lira veered off and continued down the winding walkway. Darnuir continued alone towards the grand old doors where a solitary Cosmo stood sentinel.

"Does this mean you are finally accepting my offer?" Darnuir asked.

But what was Cosmo to him now? Father, friend or instructor? As far as his father was concerned, the faces of Cosmo and Draconess now mingled together. It was unsettling.

"After a fashion," Cosmo said. "Though I was invited by the queen, regardless."

"Oh?" Darnuir said in some surprise. "Now why would she do that?"

"Because I have decided to stop running," he said with a touch of pride. He no longer seemed as weary as he had; only determined. "I have also decided upon a name for my son. He will be called Cullen."

"Cullen..." Darnuir mused. "A good name. A strong name."

"It was one Grace always favoured."

"He'll grow into it well, I'm sure," Darnuir said. "Shall we enter?"

"I see no reason to wait," said Cosmo, and together they pushed through the heavy doors.

A great table of silver wood sprouted up like a mushroom in the centre of the room, covered in a map of Tenalp. Painted figurines representing hunters from different regions along with fairies, dragons and demons were placed on the map as the council understood the current situation to be.

Castallan's armies were split. Demon figurines were positioned at the eastern edge of Val'tarra, with more further south outside of Inverdorn at the tip of Loch Minian. More demons were positioned in the northern Highlands, though these belonged to Rectar. They had no hard intelligence on their numbers or position there, however, only the vague words of Ochnic.

Their own forces – golden dragons, blue fairies and hunter carvings in red, yellow and white – were crammed in the area around the Argent Tree, deep in Val'tarra.

The air of the war room smelled oddly stale, as though the place had not been aired out in years. When the servants pulled back the curtains, clouds of dust burst into the air. A breeze drifted in through the windows, to Darnuir's relief. Other servants were busy hanging wispy lanterns upon the walls to combat the fading light of dusk.

Most of the attendees were already present.

Blaine, flanked by a handful of Light Bearers, sat near Kasselle, Fidelm and several other grim-faced fairies. Brackendon sat patiently with Kymethra beside him. Even Garon was there, as were Rufus, Griswald and two huntresses; one from the marshes and one from the Golden Crescent. Likely they were there at Cosmo's behest. Garon had an empty seat beside him, which Cosmo made for.

At a distance from the rest was Ochnic, sat on his own, looking uncomfortably crouched on a chair that was far too small for him. Several fairy guards stood at the wall behind him, their hands twitching over the hilts of their broadswords.

As there did not appear to be a set seating plan, Darnuir ambled to a spot not far from the troll. He had quickly developed a fondness for the creature after it had unnerved Blaine with such ease. Cassandra had been well taken with him too, conversing with the troll non-stop on their way back to the Argent Tree. Ochnic seemed most comfortable around her; there had been a snarling protest when they were separated. He was calm now, however, sitting thoughtfully, despite being in an alien land and amongst strange people.

After the last of the servants scurried off, Kasselle was the first to speak.

"Welcome, all. This council has been gathered to determine how we will deal with the threat posed to us by Rectar and Castallan. Each of you here is called upon to speak for your race, including our honoured guest." She directed everyone's attention to Ochnic. Darnuir was impressed at how effortlessly she granted the creature courtesy, despite the bloody history between their two peoples. Her own guards, however, still seemed to be sizing him up.

"Ochnic thanks de fairy queen."

Blaine shifted noticeably. "It seems a great shame that we have not heard from Brevia," he announced to the room at large, "when even such a reclusive race as the frost trolls sends an emissary."

Ochnic thumped his chest hard. "Kazzek, I am!"

"Yes... my apologies."

"Had we word from the humans, you would have been the first to know, Lord Guardian," Fidelm said. "It is unfortunate we have been left in the dark. Whilst these fine hunters here may vouch for their own, it is not quite sufficient to plan an effective strategy."

"Cosmo will speak on behalf of humanity," Brackendon said.

All eyes, bar Kasselle's, flicked towards Cosmo.

"That is quite a claim, wizard," Blaine said. "While we are all very grateful for his service, especially where Darnuir is concerned, I doubt a southern hunter can speak with humanity's voice."

"He is not merely a hunter," said Darnuir. "Cosmo is now captain of all our hunter forces."

"Encompassing only three companies, and those battered moreover," Blaine reminded him.

Cosmo spoke up. "I would agree with you, Lord Guardian, that a southern hunter would not normally be adequate for such an auspicious meeting. However, the son of Arkus would."

"We cannot speak to ghosts," Fidelm said. It looked as though he wanted to say more but Kasselle lightly touched his arm to stay him.

"There is no need," Brackendon said jovially, pointing to Cosmo. "You may speak with him now. Sitting before you is Brallor, son of Arkus, heir to the throne of Brevia."

A moment passed before the realisation struck home.

Darnuir froze in shock. Fidelm's stalwart jaw dropped, and even Blaine seemed utterly lost for words.

"Ah hah!" boomed Griswald, slapping a meaty hand upon the table. "That's put a stick in yer mud, eh, my Lord Guardian?"

"Quiet down, friend," Garon told him.

Blaine rounded on Kasselle. "My queen," he seemed to say with a hint of a struggle. "Did you... know of this?"

Kasselle didn't face him in return. "I was only recently informed myself."

"How recently?" Blaine asked pointedly.

Darnuir could not help but feel a glint of satisfaction. *Having secrets kept from you is not pleasant, is it, Blaine?*

"This afternoon," Kasselle answered, "when I informed Brackendon of the council."

"It was rather excellent timing," Brackendon chimed in. "Cosmo, I mean, Brallor—"

"Please just use Cosmo," said the self-proclaimed prince. "I am far more used to hearing that now. But yes, as Brackendon was about to say, I intended to step forward at any rate. This is merely convenient."

Blaine was not appeased. "Do you have any more members of Tenalp's royal families hiding in those mountains, wizard?"

"Not that I am aware of," Brackendon said, smiling.

"You might have said something," bristled Kymethra, more to herself than to the whole room.

"Cosmo," Darnuir found himself saying, gazing at the man he thought he knew so well. "Why?" was all he could add.

"For all the reasons I have ever given for leaving the city," Cosmo said. "I just neglected to mention who I really was. Please do not feel betrayed," he added, imploring his hunter colleagues and Darnuir. "Not even Grace knew."

"The main point is that we may count on Cosmo to bring humanity's forces to bear as we decide here," Kasselle said.

"I will not claim that I can guarantee anything," Cosmo warned. "I have long been absent. My father may well scorn me and hate me for what I put him through, but I will try my utmost."

Ochnic leaned forwards from his ill-sized chair, pointing a long grey finger at Cosmo. "So de white-furred hunter is de human prince?"

"I am," Cosmo said.

"Dis news is good!" the troll exclaimed. "Ochnic no need to go to da great human village now."

There was a short pause in which those around the table tried to comprehend the troll's meaning.

"We ought to begin by discussing the northern theatre," Darnuir suggested. "Ochnic here tells me that the demons have long been assaulting his people. They may have been attempting to cross through to the west for years."

"But no longer?" Fidelm inquired.

Darnuir looked to the troll to answer.

"De demons be going some moons ago, but not all of dem. Kazzek are weak now. If dey come again, we will not survive."

"If that is true, then it would seem Rectar has pulled the bulk of his forces back to Kar'drun, in preparation for his invasion," Blaine said. The guardian rose and picked up most of the demon carvings currently in the Highlands and moved them over, far to the east, to the mountain of Kar'drun. "If this armada against the west is imminent then the Highlands are not our primary concern."

"Perhaps not for the dragons," said Cosmo, "but for humanity and the fairies, it is another matter. The hearts of both our people nestle near the western edge of the Highlands. Should the north fall, Brevia and Val'tarra would soon follow."

"We have no reason to love the trolls," Fidelm muttered.

"What is long past should remain there, General," said Kasselle. "When history has passed from fact to legend, it is not worth remaining embittered."

"Are the tales true, troll?" Fidelm asked regardless.

Ochnic picked at his teeth with a long nail, eyeing Fidelm carefully. "What tales are dees?"

"When fairies used to brave the north, your kind hunted us. Killed us."

"Ah," Ochnic said, realisation passing over his grey face. "No. Da kazzek tell it differently. I dink the fairy queen is wise. Der should be no dwelling on dem tales. It has been seasons beyond de counting since blueskins came to our lands."

Darnuir was agitated by Fidelm's attitude. *Why must there always be fighting? Why do we begrudge each other so much?*

"Our guest has the right of it," Darnuir said. He then peered around the table, awaiting any challenge, lingering first on Fidelm and then on Blaine.

"You have a suggestion, then?" said Blaine.

"A joint force," Darnuir said. "Each race will send its own contingent. That way, no one will bear the full burden. We must ensure the Highlands are held."

"We have barely gathered our full strength as it is," Blaine protested. "How are we to fight a war on two fronts?"

"You would rather the Highlands fall?" Brackendon asked. "Cosmo is right. If that happens, the demons will simply march overland, leaving Val'tarra and Brevia exposed."

"This is a problem, Blaine," Kasselle said. "I want my homeland made safer, not vulnerable from a new direction."

"I am not suggesting we ignore the Highlands completely," Blaine said defensively. "To do so would be foolish. Yet it would be equally unwise to send too many troops there when we do not know the scale of the threat, nor the size of Rectar's armada."

"Our chief issue is that we are guessing blindly," Cosmo said.

Ochnic rapped his long fingers on the great silver table, clinking his nails off the wood, drawing attention to himself. "If you be fighting in da darkness, better to throw your spear dan not use it at all. You will hit nothing otherwise."

"Or keep your spear close," Fidelm noted, "so you have a weapon when your attacker finally reveals himself."

Ochnic shrugged, smiling slyly at the fairy general.

"The task force I have in mind would not be large," Darnuir said, hoping to put the conversation back on course. They needed to decide upon the Highlands and move on to the more pressing matter of Castallan's army on their doorstep. "I suggest sending three thousand dragons, a large contingent of our hunter forces, say a thousand, and a thousand additional fairies. Flyers might be preferable for the region."

"I cannot spare that many flyers," Fidelm said. "They are too valuable." He turned to Blaine, looking for support, yet Blaine did not seem as determined to resist.

"A whole legion…" Blaine said softly. "As much as I would rather have those troops to fight Castallan's horde and Rectar's fleet, sending less support to the kazzek would be fruitless, and sending more would leave us vulnerable. I believe Darnuir has the right of it, Fidelm. Though perhaps we should keep as many flyers with us as we can. Communication and intelligence are ever the keys to war."

"That, and supplies," Cosmo said. "Can we equip this expedition with enough food? How far are they travelling and for how long?"

The faces of the fairies around the room darkened.

"Give dem enough to make it to my homeland," Ochnic said. "Da kazzek have great stores."

"How long will it take, troll?" Fidelm asked. His eyes swept over the map. "Your people are so secretive that we do not know where your home actually is."

Darnuir looked to the Highlands as well. Fidelm was right; there was no indication of any civilisation there. The only marked features were five of the Principal

Mountains of Tenalp that resided there, and beyond them, at the northern shores of the world, lay a confusing strand titled only the Uncharted Wastes. Darnuir felt a pang of sympathy for the soldiers he was sending north. What dangers would await them there while he remained in the mapped and comfortable parts of Tenalp? The impending invasion notwithstanding, he knew he'd rather be on charted ground, in places where he could plan ahead and understand.

We do not have much choice. The Highlands must be held and the kazzek defended.

"A month of food will be enough, I dink," Ochnic said. The troll seemed reluctant to reveal the location of his people.

"Can this be done?" Cosmo asked.

Kasselle turned to some of her staff beside her and they nodded tersely, their lips pressed together in thin lines.

Darnuir looked to Ochnic. "And will those numbers be sufficient to help defend your people?"

Ochnic shrugged his great, gangling body. "Da chieftains will be pleased to have whatever help de dragon king will send. Ochnic knows you have your own fights."

This creature is more reasonable than half these council members. "I am glad to hear it."

"There is an issue of command," Blaine said. "I am happy to offer several choice candidates."

Doubtless, these would be from his Light Bearers. Darnuir, however, felt this was his idea – his expedition. He would have someone he could personally trust

"I already had someone in mind."

Blaine's cheek twitched.

"Garon!" Darnuir continued, catching the hunter's eye.

All turned towards the man. "Me, Darnuir?" Garon said, his eyes popping.

"The kazzek are in great peril," said Darnuir. "I have never known anyone so passionate in helping those in need. I intend to send the Boreac hunters on this mission as they are more used to the cold. They will know you, trust you, as I will. Crescent hunters and Cairlav hunters will also accompany you."

Garon was evidently unsure and looked to Cosmo.

"I'll be sorry to fight this war without you," Cosmo said, "but I agree with Darnuir. I'll feel better knowing as fine a hunter as you is holding our flanks. You've led men before."

"Not a small army..."

"Think of it like a very large patrol," Darnuir said. "Think of it however you choose, but I'm afraid I am giving you no choice."

The authority in his voice was clear.

"I, for one, am all for it," offered Griswald. "Can't stand all this sweating we've been doing since leaving the mountains. We'll be with you, lad."

"Cosmo always intended for you to take over from him if he was ever made captain," Rufus added encouragingly.

Garon nodded, gulped and placed his hands carefully upon the table as though for support. "Very well."

"Then it is settled," Darnuir said, relishing the achievement. He stood up and moved some of the dragon, fairy, and hunter figurines into the Highlands. He moved up all of the white and grey painted figures, representing the Boreac hunters, but kept around half of the red and yellow ones beside the Argent Tree for now.

Neither Blaine nor Fidelm protested any further but their expressions showed they held reservations. Three thousand dragons, supported by one thousand hunters and fairies. It would have to suffice.

"This may be a good opportunity to refresh ourselves," Kasselle said in her melodic voice. Without any further word or gesture, the doors opened and in poured fairies, carrying their customary food and chilled water.

An enticing smell reached Darnuir, more wonderful than any he had picked up in the forest. The fairies seemed to avoid meat for the most part, but his nose sensed it now. Along with the bread, nuts and fruit came three large, steaming trays of venison, roasted in pears and berries, and resting on beds of wilted spinach. The sauce was red and sweet. Darnuir had not eaten half so well since the demons had begun assaulting the Boreac Mountains.

Ochnic lunged forward for a handful of hard nuts and placed them before himself on the table. He sniffed curiously at them before mashing them down with his fist. He tried to scoop up the remnants with his fingers, but the pieces kept escaping him. Most of the table turned to watch the troll. Kasselle smiled politely and continued with her meal. Fidelm, on the other hand, was openly offended, staring incredulously at Ochnic.

Brackendon cleared his throat with a loud cough. "Ah, my friend," the wizard said, getting the troll's attention. Brackendon made a show of putting a whole nut into his mouth. Ochnic seized more to imitate but did not seem to like the taste very much. Nervous-looking servants dished up his share of the meat, which he attacked more greedily, ignoring the cutlery. He made a sound of disgust at the sweet sauce but scraped it off using a finger and began shovelling the venison away all the same.

Fidelm carefully but deliberately placed down his utensils in protest. Darnuir began to wonder about the general. What sort of hardened warrior was upset by loud chewing? How long had it been since he was bloodied in battle? Perhaps he would not have the general join his Praetorians after all, even in a ceremonial capacity.

After their food, silver shimmer brew was served, and even some small measure of plum wine. Cosmo declined drink for the first time in Darnuir's memory.

"I'd rather have my head clear," he claimed. Griswald gladly took Cosmo's share and the discourse began to circle around more immediate threats.

"The burning of eastern Val'tarra is a grave insult," Fidelm announced. "We must drive Castallan's demons away."

"How large is the force roaming at the edge of the forest?" Cosmo asked.

"Our outrunners suggest it is the bulk of Castallan's strength," Blaine said. "Raymond noted in his letter that the force initially besieging Inverdorn was forty thousand strong. My guess would be that at least ten thousand still remain at the city to keep it under threat, meaning we face thirty thousand in the field."

"Thirty thousand demons feels like too great a number to attack directly," Cosmo said. "However, if we relieve Inverdorn then we will gain access to some well-needed reinforcements. As the besieging force is smaller, we could be assured of victory."

"I'm afraid I must protest," said Kasselle, leaning forward and casting a hand over the demon carvings at the edge of her beloved forest. "With every pure tree that is burned, my people grow more restless and afraid. If you march south to Inverdorn instead of east, the demons will only have free rein to cause more destruction. Perhaps the Argent Tree itself will come under threat."

"There is no obvious option," Brackendon added. "We either leave Val'tarra vulnerable by moving to Inverdorn or, by marching to face the larger host, we risk the demons rejoining their forces to crush us in the field or destroy the city."

"But can we afford to lose Inverdorn?" Cosmo asked. "Besides the population, it has vast granary stores from the Crescent and the boats needed to move supplies easily. It also commands the loch."

"It is a hard decision," said Blaine. "There are dragons in peril there as well; maybe even more than Raymond estimated. Yet we cannot allow the forest to be freely attacked."

Darnuir scanned the map once more, losing track of the conversation around the table. He had a gut feeling on what they would have to do. Even before coming to the council, he had been sure there was only one path they could take. The older part of himself was sure at least and, in these matters, he trusted those old instincts.

He rose to his feet to command the room. "The demons have divided their forces. We should follow suit."

Everyone gawked at him.

"We are weak enough as it is," Fidelm said, straining to keep his voice respectful. "We just agreed to dispatch forces to the Highlands. You would have us divide our army again?"

Darnuir held Fidelm's gaze, knowing this was the right move to make.

"You would have us hit Castallan's army with everything we have and defend your homeland. I respect that and I understand. Yet even then there is no guarantee of victory with our numbers. We have to act with more cunning." He turned to Blaine. "Recently, you showed me what happened when one rashly charges a foe. A total victory in the field is unlikely, unless Brevia has already sent its army west, and that we do not know."

He moved to a better position over the map and figures.

"The commander who leads these demons – Zarl, I believe is his name – is careful. He took the Boreacs methodically, leaving nothing to chance. Were it not for Brackendon's arrival and my sword, we would certainly have lost. Zarl is being careful again now. He's created what should be an impossible situation for us. If we march to Inverdorn then we lose the forest. March to meet him openly and the city will certainly fall without relief."

"How bleak," Kymethra said, joining the conversation. "I have recovered well from my illness. I could fly with all speed to Brevia. At least then we might know if Arkus is sending aid."

"You cannot fly fast enough," Brackendon told her.

"My people cannot bear the drain on our resources for much longer, Kymethra," Kasselle said. "I'm afraid a decision must be made today."

"That is why I say we split our forces further," Darnuir continued. "The demons at Inverdorn number far less than those ravaging Val'tarra. If Fidelm takes the four thousand fairies we have to hand—"

"I would rather have my vengeance on those who are burning my homeland," the general announced.

"And you will," Darnuir assured him. "You will if we win. If we lose, and lose anywhere at this stage, we are all done." He picked up the remaining blue-painted carvings and moved them to Inverdorn. "Have flyers enter the city and tell the garrison to prepare for battle. The moment your own forces engage the besiegers, they are to open their gates and join you. You will have four thousand fairies with you; combined with those trapped in the city, it should be enough to crush the demons there if they are attacked from two sides." He optimistically removed the demon figures from Inverdorn.

"A fair strategy," Blaine said. "Yet without the support of the fairies, I fear our march east will be suicidal, if that is what you intend."

"I do intend it," Darnuir said, "but it will not be suicide. A headlong charge is surely doomed to fail and so we must not act like dragons usually do."

"Our greatest asset is our strength and speed."

"You can run hard and fast into the snowdrifts, Blaine, but eventually, they will envelop you. But there are other ways to take down a lumbering foe."

He picked up the remaining golden dragon figures and the bow carvings that represented the Cairlav and Crescent hunters. He moved them east of the Argent Tree over to where the demons were situated, the area now dubbed painfully by the fairies as the Charred Vale; the section of the forest the demons had burned.

"The remaining twelve thousand dragons and one thousand hunters will harass the main demon host. We will lure them into the trees where their numbers count for less, hit them hard and then run. We wheel elsewhere and do it again. Our speed will still be our strength. Hit a dire bear with enough arrows and it will flee or fall. If, by some miracle, we catch this leader of theirs, then we may even cut the head off the beast."

Cosmo was nodding, a smile playing at the corners of his lips. "Yes, use the forest to our advantage. Zarl hopes to draw us out. He wants us in the open, but we should not oblige him."

"Much more of the forest may burn before the end," Darnuir said to Fidelm, "but it is our best chance. If we can stall Zarl's main army, and you are able to relieve Inverdorn, our two forces will be able to manoeuvre freely and pincer the remaining demons between us."

"Hitting them from both sides," said Blaine, also rising and sweeping away the remaining demon figurines from the map.

"Zarl believes he has us cornered," Darnuir said. "He thinks that whichever way we act, he will win. I'd see that turned upon him."

"Now this is the Darnuir I remember," Brackendon said. "Only less foul-tempered. Should have reverted time on you long ago."

A little niggling voice crept up into Darnuir's thoughts. *Watch your tongue, wizard, or I will have it drawn.* Trying not to show anything was wrong, Darnuir shook his head and returned his attention to the table.

"It's hardly guaranteeing success," he added cautiously, "but I believe it is the best chance we have."

There was a silence that seemed to amount to assent. Everyone was drinking in the plan.

"Ochnic knows not de ways of dragon warriors but dis plan seems good. Break da demons into smaller chunks and dey will be easier to swallow." He bared his pointed teeth in a foreboding grin.

"Those who cannot fight may remain here," Kasselle said. "We are not so starved of resources as to turn away children and those in need. They will be safest here for now."

"Good," Darnuir said. "A large refugee train would only slow us down and be agonising to defend."

"What comes after?" Garon wondered aloud. "Even if this scheme works, Castallan will still remain at the Bastion, and then you will have Rectar's invasion fleet to contend with."

"We must hope that Arkus has assembled the full strength of humanity at Brevia and will be ready to join us," Kasselle said.

"The capital should be our first destination after relieving pressure on Val'tarra," Cosmo said. "We will soon know one way or the other."

"Raymond must have informed Arkus of the impending invasion by now," Darnuir said. "My memories of Arkus are not favourable, yet I imagine he has an instinct for survival like the rest of us. No offence," he added, turning to Cosmo with only the smallest hint of a smirk.

"None taken," Cosmo said. "Brevia's fleet will also be critical to our chances of halting this invasion, as will the ships of the Lord of the Isles."

"The war for Tenalp will soon be upon us," Blaine announced.

32

TO START A WAR

Brackendon – Base of The Argent Tree

The first columns of dragons and the remaining Cairlav, Crescent and Boreac hunters had already begun their long march east as Brackendon approached the Argent Tree. Twelve thousand dragons and one thousand hunters comprised this force. Fidelm was taking his fairies – a group nearly four thousand strong – south and then east towards Inverdorn. At the bottom of the enormous tree stood Darnuir, Garon, Cassandra and Ochnic.

Brackendon vowed to ask Cassandra more about her encounter with the troll and was desperately sorry that Ochnic would leave before he could make more inquiries. There was much to the north that remained shrouded in mystery. Cascade energy was thought to still pour forth raw up there, but few who ventured in search of it had ever returned; those who did were often broken or scarred in some other fashion.

It is for the best, he assured himself. Though he considered the lure of the magical springs of the north to be purely scholarly, he knew better than to fool himself. *I'd try it. I'd take it. The urge would be too great to resist.*

Addiction to Cascade energy was a hard battle to win. Few wizards were able to give it up completely. After all, what was the harm in drawing on a little here or there when you had a staff to handle trifling uses? Few had even been granted Brackendon's opportunity for a clean break. Time had limped on since. Yet the waters of the Avvorn had helped him through the final stages. The minute amounts of Cascade energy within it had helped him fend off the worst of his cravings. Now, he no longer needed it at all.

Kymethra too had thankfully made a speedy recovery once in the forest, though she had never felt the cruel sting of a long-term addiction. Without a staff and full training, she had always been more cautious. Having seen what breaking had done to him, Kymethra had no desire to go further. Death was preferable.

Brackendon's relief at the lifting of his addiction felt both a blessing and a curse, although he often wondered what his role was now. His place on the council the night before was due to his status as the last of the wizards. Yet, without a staff, he could offer no more than some advice on Castallan. Regrettably, he knew little on that topic as well. The man was a traitor, that was all he knew for certain. A murderous traitor; too hungry for power. Yet a small part of Brackendon felt sympathy for him as well. Castallan's own addiction must have grown greatly over the years; he might be as much a slave to it as the demons were to Rectar – a fate that Brackendon wouldn't wish on anyone.

If he, Brackendon – staffless and aimless – was the last wizard, then his order was finished.

It was a curious thing, for he could not fathom the road ahead of him now, nor indeed could he imagine what Kasselle would want with him personally. Or so he told himself. There could still be one reason why the Queen of Fairies would demand a private meeting at the eleventh hour. Her summons was clasped in the wizard's grip, his fingers thankful for something to hold on to. Occasionally, they itched to feel a staff between them. *And would I even want that now?* Fear flickered in the back of his mind, as did anticipation.

As he drew up beside the congregated party, he saw Darnuir handing a tightly-bound scroll to Garon.

"Your orders," Darnuir said.

"You are placing a lot of trust in me," Garon said.

"Cosmo always did," Darnuir said. "I trust you as much as I trust him. Unless you too have some secret identity?"

"Sorry to disappoint," said Garon, then added, more seriously, "I've known I would one day be taking orders from you, yet it feels as though it has come about all too suddenly."

"Part of me feels the same way," Darnuir said. "But another part sees it as only natural. One day, I will figure out how to reconcile myself." Darnuir leaned in closer to Garon to whisper something that Brackendon could not hear.

Brackendon continued inside the Argent Tree, only briefly glimpsing Cassandra trying to get Ochnic to shake her hand.

The journey up the walkway to the top was long and arduous. Before the end was in sight, he had to stop to catch his breath, and he yearned then for the power to quicken his pace. It was a relief to reach his destination.

Kasselle's throne room was a spacious but simple chamber, naturally well-lit. Like much of the fairy capital, everything in the room appeared to be carved out from the very wood of the tree in which it resided. The throne was no exception. It rose high, its carved silver roots weaving upwards into a fine stem and then a blooming flower, whose keenly detailed petals faced proudly out towards those approaching. A rich blue rug ran from the entranceway to the base of the throne where Kasselle sat waiting for him. In front of her, down on the floor, lay a long, thin crate. Brackendon's pulse quickened when he saw it.

"I will not insult your intelligence," Kasselle said by way of greeting. "I'm sure you are aware of why I have summoned you."

He could not tear his eyes away from the crate. "I have my suspicions, my lady. And I fear that those suspicions will come true."

"You fear I will give you a gift?" Kasselle said.

"Not if that gift is one of books or clothes. But if it is one of silver wood…"

"What are you afraid of?" the queen asked gently. "You have already suffered the worst a wizard can."

"Precisely, my lady. It is why I would avoid the risk of suffering it again."

"You were not afraid when you first recovered."

"I had a task to complete then. I had Darnuir to retrieve."

"And you performed it admirably," said Kasselle. "Yet there is one last charge that lies upon you."

Brackendon hesitated. "I will accompany Darnuir, Cosmo and the guardian as they attempt to put this world to right. I will give them my best counsel, but I do not see what more I alone can achieve."

"Please do not be so obtuse, Brackendon. You are not aware of what you might add as one who commands the Cascade?"

"Less than you might add, my lady, if you were to take this gift as your own."

Kasselle shook her head. "You know I cannot. My people long ago gave up magic in such forms. But there remains a wizard that must be dealt with, Brackendon. Who will fight him but you?"

"I'm certain that Darnuir and Blaine could—"

"You know that is not the answer."

He did.

"Do you not desire to see him fall?" Kasselle asked.

"Of course I do, but I am not driven by vengeance. Were it possible, I'd let the others wage the war without me. I wasted half my life as a broken man. I'd rather live what I have left in full without the burden of it. Only now that I am free of it do I understand how much it affected me."

Kasselle gazed down upon him, almost as a mother might. "You would let your kind, your order, fade into history? Assuming Castallan is stopped, there will be none like yourself left to carry on."

"The world may benefit from a lack of wizards," Brackendon said bitterly. "What good has our order ever done? Of late, it has only led to more woe."

"Had you not been there for Darnuir, he would have died, and without him, we would all be lost." She leaned forward. She gave him a radiant smile from her perfect face, appearing forever young, despite being more than thrice his own age. "It is not the power that corrupts, Brackendon. It is the fault of the one who wields it."

His gaze lingered again upon the crate. When he next spoke, his breath left him in a shuddering sigh. "Why must you tempt me?"

"Tempt you? Were you true in your conviction, you would have left the moment you saw what lies before you. I don't doubt the sincerity of your desires, but you know that you must take it. If not for your own sake, or for the sake of our cause, take it for me. My people will not be happy if word gets out what I have done."

"My lady?" Brackendon said, confused.

"Before you lies the most powerful staff ever created. I commissioned it to be made from the very core of the Argent Tree, kept safe since my people first hollowed it centuries ago. Castallan's own staff was taken only from a branch. Were it that, we could simply cut that branch away and have done with it..."

As Kasselle carried on speaking, Brackendon's world focused entirely upon the crate. He took several measured steps towards it.

He could not deny he was enticed. A new staff that was more powerful than his old one. It was one thing to believe he was over magic when the option of drawing on it was unavailable. Now the chance was literally within his reach, it seemed a lot harder to remember why he had not wanted this.

Had things really improved so much without his staff? He couldn't really be better off without it. And now that he was only a few paces away, his arms outstretched—

"No!" he said sharply, wrenching his hand back and twisting around.

Kymethra was there. How long had she been there? Shame filled him – he'd promised her he would never break again.

A lone tear fell as she spoke. "Neither of us will ever be free of it, Brackers. Take it. At least you might do some good."

"I thought you might need some extra persuasion," Kasselle said. Her voice was hard and flat, quite unlike her usual self.

In that moment, Brackendon hated her.

He moved to Kymethra, kissed her and held her tightly. "And what happens when all my hair turns white? When my skin begins to crinkle before its time? When my whole arm burns black?"

"Then I'll still love you," she whispered. "I swear."

Brackendon fought back tears of his own. He squeezed her, wishing never to let go, then pulled free. With a fierce, deep breath, he faced the crate; faced his fear.

An eerie silver light seemed to radiate out as he lifted the lid. The shaft was elegant and smooth, like his old staff had been. Lifting it, the wood felt sturdier yet lighter. Towards the top, the grain shone with such intensity that it might have been diamond. His itching fingers clasped around his new staff, gripping it so hard his knuckles turned white. Vigour flooded him like nothing he had ever experienced before.

The march east should have taken more than a week, even at a good pace. The dragons and those hunters with them had nearly traversed the distance now in only four days. Darnuir and Blaine had pressed them relentlessly.

For Brackendon, the journey had proved no issue. Movement and speed were cheap and required little Cascade energy, nothing taxing for his new staff. Kymethra soared high above them, ranging further out than the outrunners could, as they had to weave in amongst the trees.

Each day brought them closer to the demons. Their unremitting advance was spurred on in the hope that the demons would not notice they had divided their forces. This army of remaining hunters and dragons had to begin harassing the main demon host before Fidelm arrived within striking distance of Inverdorn.

Yet the effort was taking its toll and the hunters were beginning to flag. Even after getting the dragons to carry their gear, they simply couldn't keep going any longer.

On the fourth day, Cosmo made it clear that he could not force his hunters to go faster or they would be less than useless when battle came. Reports spoke of demon parties venturing west, deeper into Val'tarra, and at a considerable distance away from the body of the horde at the Charred Vale. Blaine had peeled off dragons to strike at them, while Darnuir remained behind as they made camp for the night.

Brackendon observed how Darnuir would move through the ranks – be they human or dragon – speaking with them, offering encouragement, helping to carry the hunters' heavy loads. He still wore his leathers. Was it a symbolic measure? With the Dragon's Blade at his side, bulky, red and menacing, and his white hunter garments, he certainly stood out clearly, no matter which race he was among.

Later, he found Darnuir overseeing a number of dragons duelling. Those practising seemed young and not as stony-faced as the elder generation. There were some hunters too, standing anxiously by, no doubt concerned about why they had been summoned. Lira was at Darnuir's side, pointing and gesturing as the pairs fought. The king noticed Brackendon and approached him.

"It is good to see you looking so lively, Brackendon. You must feel much more like your old self again?"

"Better than I have ever felt, in fact. Only time will tell if it is worth the trade-off."

"Trade-off?"

"Between freedom and the power to help. I wonder, Darnuir. Have you felt the effects of magic yet?"

"The bitter aftertaste is hardly pleasant."

Oh, my boy, what horrors may yet await you?

"I was referring more to its addictive quality," Brackendon said.

"I have barely drawn on it. In truth, I find it hard to control."

"Does it feel like a flood when you reach out for it?"

"Very much so. At Torridon especially, I felt as though I would drown in it. As if it were physically filling my lungs. I have not had the chance to learn much from Blaine in this regard."

"Perhaps I can offer some advice. Think of a door that holds back the sea of magic. It is a crude comparison but apt enough. Most apprentices describe the sensation as a 'flood', as did I when I first trained. All it means is that you cannot control the flow properly. Rather than throwing that door open, you must learn to hold it only slightly ajar; a little more when you require a fraction more energy, and so forth. Control the flow, Darnuir, and it should never overwhelm you."

"Blaine says the blades are second to none when it comes to processing Cascade energy."

"Having seen Blaine in action, I am inclined to agree. The danger lies in using so much energy that you poison yourself; go far enough and you break."

"Blaine has said nothing of either of us having to worry about that."

Brackendon considered this. He doubted Blaine was ignorant of such things, yet it would be unwise to fill Darnuir with disregard for the danger of his power.

"If you mainly call upon the Cascade for speed, strength and the flames from your blade, then it may be that Blaine is correct. Movement and destruction are cheap, after all."

Darnuir nodded intently. "Control the flow," he murmured. "Thank you, Brackendon. I shall try and master this."

"Take it easy at first," Brackendon warned. "If you don't build it up gradually, you will only succumb to the venom more quickly."

"I may not have the luxury of caution," Darnuir said. He looked as though he wanted to say more but many trainees had ceased duelling and pointed to the sky. Smoke crept above the treeline in the distance. "The demons must be close."

As it turned out, there was little to fear. Blaine's dragons had been on their way back from smashing the demons further afield and had soundly crushed this closer group as well. At Cosmo's request, they all met at once in his personal tent.

"A few hundred, perhaps," the guardian said. "No spectres though, as far as I could tell. We were vigilant. The last thing we need is them moving swiftly under cloud cover to discover our position."

"I'd say, as a first test of our strategy, things went well," Darnuir said.

"Well enough, though I also feel it was too easy," Cosmo said. "The lack of spectres is unusual, particularly for larger groups."

"If they were sent out to burn trees, it is unlikely that they need much direction," said Darnuir.

"Maybe…" Cosmo seemed on edge.

"Is something wrong?" Brackendon asked.

"Some of the hunters are unaccounted for," Cosmo said.

"Deserters?" said Blaine coldly.

"Could be," Cosmo said, "or it could be worse."

"Traitors?" Darnuir said.

"I wouldn't want to say for sure," Cosmo said. "But around sixty have gone missing since making camp this evening."

"Not being as familiar with the Cairlav or Crescent hunters is not likely to help the matter," Darnuir said, pinching the bridge of his nose.

Brackendon didn't fail to notice that. Was Darnuir's head hurting him again? Surely those symptoms had passed?

Cosmo looked to Darnuir, his expression wrought with anxiety. "I'm afraid most of those missing are Boreac men and women. Balack and Cassandra are also unaccounted for."

Blaine growled deeply. "I thought you trusted your own men entirely."

"I do, but those with us are the remnants of Scythe's men, and I never found the time to get to know them well. It is why Garon allowed them to stay behind."

"Balack is no traitor," Darnuir said.

"I'd find it impossible to believe as well," Cosmo agreed. "But Cassandra—"

"Is not either! You trusted her well enough yourself, Cosmo; you let her take care of your son!"

"As well I did not leave him with her today," Cosmo said. From his cot nearby, Cullen wailed in annoyance, woken from his nap.

"He would have made a prize hostage," Brackendon said. "The grandson of Arkus."

"I refuse to believe it," Darnuir said. "If Balack is missing too then they are likely off somewhere together—" This thought seemed to stick in the king's throat.

Brackendon didn't fail to notice this either. *He must still have a soft spot for the girl.*

"Often, it is those closest to us who disappoint us the most," Blaine added gravely. "We cannot feel as betrayed by strangers."

"We should find them," Darnuir said, making to leave the tent.

"Stop," said Blaine adamantly. "I have been impressed with you of late, boy. Do not ruin that."

Darnuir's cheeks flushed scarlet as he stalked towards the guardian. "You will not call me 'boy' again." His eyes were full of anger. Suddenly, Brackendon felt as though it were twenty years ago.

"I will refrain when you stop acting like one," Blaine said. "Clearly this girl has an effect on you. You cannot let some pretty human—"

"Oh, you think that is why I was about to go search for them?" Darnuir said defensively. "We have to look for all these missing people, surely?"

"If any are akin to Raymond's brother then they will be well out of our reach by now," Cosmo said.

Blaine grasped Darnuir by the shoulder. "We should break camp and continue east as soon as possible. Your plan is a good one but it requires us to strike before Zarl becomes aware of our motives. Have your hunters rested, Cosmo?"

"Barely, but needs must."

"Then we should march through the night," Blaine insisted.

"Go ahead," Darnuir said. "I can catch up easily enough." He stormed out of the tent.

The Guardian of Tenalp and the Prince of Humanity both looked to Brackendon.

"I may have rebirthed him, but I am not responsible for him!" They looked at him reproachfully. He sighed. "Very well, I shall go after him."

Darnuir must have torn off at some speed to escape him. Everyone Brackendon asked seemed to remember the king running in a different direction. Testimonials from the hunters were varied and Brackendon couldn't help but feel suspicious of every one of them.

As his frustration piqued, there came a scream through the trees. He faced its source and drew on a burst of speed. A taste like burned lemon gathered upon his tongue even with his new staff.

He found them not far from the northern edge of their camp. The situation was disquieting. Balack had suffered some head wound: dark blood mingled with his hair on one side. The hunter stood a touch too close to Darnuir, whose shoulders were squared aggressively. Cassandra stood back from the pair, her face stricken with worry.

"Darnuir," she begged, "he's not one of them. How could you think that?"

"I have to be sure," Darnuir said. "Faking an injury would be an ideal cover."

"D-Darnuir?" Balack stammered, half-dazed.

"Just tell me what you were doing out here," Darnuir demanded. "Tell me and we can put it to rest."

"I was… just… gathering firewood. Something hit me."

"It's true!" Cassandra exclaimed. "I came looking for him when he did not return."

"How can I be sure?"

"You trust me and not him?" Cassandra said incredulously. "He's nothing but loyal to you. Not that he should trust you as earnestly after what happened with Eve —" She slapped a hand over her mouth to stop herself. Her eyes bugged wide in horror, but the damage was done.

Brackendon drew closer, staff held before him. "We ought to get Balack aid; he is confused and hurt," he said, trying to bring a calm voice to the proceedings.

"What does she mean?" Balack said, an edge to his voice. The revelation seemed to have rallied his senses.

No, Balack, Brackendon thought desperately. *Leave it. Leave it! Whatever it is, just leave it be.*

"Nothing," Darnuir said, stepping away.

"What does she mean?" Balack demanded.

"Nothing!" Cassandra tried to say, but her look of guilt gave her away.

"Darnuir," Brackendon said slowly, "I think we should return."

"Yes. You're right." He turned, then Balack's hand fell upon Darnuir's shoulder.

"What does she mean?"

Darnuir wheeled around, a fire blazing in his eyes again. "I think you already know."

Balack's whole body began to quake as grief and rage fought for dominance. He looked upon Darnuir as though he was a stranger.

"I've been so understanding," Balack said, his voice now one of loathing. "Poor Darnuir, with your burden, your heavy sword, your headaches, all this change happening so quickly! But really, you were always like this, weren't you? Just an arrogant, selfish dragon."

Darnuir's backhand blow lifted Balack clean off his feet and sent him face down into the leaves. "And you are just some weak human."

Cassandra gasped.

"Enough!" Brackendon cried.

He blew Darnuir backwards, sending him crashing halfway up the trunk of a blackened tree. The king fell, tried to rise and Brackendon brought a vortex of leaves to contain him; twisting his staff to channel the wind, locking Darnuir in place. Over the howl of the air, Brackendon heard a faint "release me" but ignored it. He lifted Darnuir, encased in his leafy prison, high into the air, until he disappeared above the canopy.

The Cascade surged around his body, draining rapidly through his arm towards his shining staff, but there was too much of it and he could feel the burn within his veins already. He eased the door of his mind shut, stemming the flow of magic, enjoying the euphoric feeling before the inevitable bitter mouth and dry throat.

The wind died down, and Darnuir hurtled towards the ground. Brackendon caught him just before impact, manipulating the air beneath Darnuir to keep him afloat. He held him there for a second before letting go.

He shut the door in his mind completely.

Brackendon cricked his neck as his body contorted from the magic. He shook his free arm as if he could wring himself dry. The first moments after the high of releasing magic were always the worst.

"Enough," he said again.

Darnuir groaned as he picked himself up. His rage had cooled and he looked ashamed. He waded through the leaves to Balack's side. Cassandra was already crouched beside him and had propped Balack's head up onto her knees. Balack wheezed and coughed as Darnuir gently lifted him up, carrying him back to camp.

Two days later, the army set up camp at the foot of the northern hill of the newly-dubbed Charred Vale. More skirmishes along the way had bolstered their spirits, and morale was high as the late-afternoon sun beat down on the troops constructing their camps. By tradition, each legion of dragons would have its own camp; however, for reasons of space and security, Blaine had ordered that there be two camps with six thousand dragons in each.

Roll calls were more strictly conducted now and the hunters, especially, were checked four times daily. No bodies had been found in the woods, confirming their suspicions that those hunters who had departed must have deserted. So far, there had been no more, but Blaine and Cosmo were rightly concerned about the insurgents who might remain. Still, Blaine was satisfied with their progress and Kymethra had recently returned with favourable news.

This time, they gathered in Blaine's tent, the usual maps and figurines on the tables before them.

"Looks to me as though they are delving south but deeper into the forest," she had told them. "Might be they are trying to provoke a reaction from us, or perhaps they are just upping the amount of forest they want to clear. Either way, they have stretched themselves thin. I'd say they will crack quite easily if we shock them with several hard attacks."

"Show us precisely, please," Cosmo asked. Kymethra placed the black and red painted demon figures in a rough line, which – with the two hills of the vale – looked something like a smile.

"Obviously, with them being under the trees, I couldn't tell exactly where they were, but the smoke gave me a good enough indication."

Cosmo sucked his teeth. "It seems strange that they should arrange themselves like this. Potentially, they could surround us, and if those deserters were spies, they might know our intentions."

Blaine examined the map. "Our true plans have been closely guarded, yet that is no guarantee. Any one of us may have been overheard. So long as we have warning of their movements, we should be able to puncture a hole in any net that is sent to trap us."

"I'll stay in flight as much as I can," Kymethra offered.

"Are you sure?" Brackendon asked. "You seem worn out. Perhaps you should rest for now?"

"I'm all right, Brackers," she said, giving his hand a hard squeeze. "A short break and some food and I'll be all feathers and talons again."

"All for the good," Blaine said, "for I have need of you to take word to Fidelm with all haste." He handed her a sealed scroll. "Grant him permission to begin the relief of Inverdorn as soon as both his forces and those troops inside the city are ready to engage the enemy. We're close enough here to pursue the demons should they withdraw towards Inverdorn. More likely, we will make our own move soon."

"Has Darnuir been informed?" Cosmo asked.

"The boy is likely off sulking again," Blaine said.

Brackendon frowned. "He's distressed by what came over him, Blaine. Perhaps you ought to be helping him through this, rather than allowing him to self-soothe."

"And what do you want me to do?"

"I wouldn't know," Brackendon said. "Whatever you did to unlock his memories is your area of expertise and beyond my knowledge."

"His situation is unprecedented," Blaine grumbled, as if excusing himself.

"All the more reason to be there for him, I would think."

"Are you defending his actions?" Blaine asked.

"Of course not, yet ignoring the problem will not make it go away."

"I'll have a word with him," Cosmo said. "Blaine has enough on his plate."

Blaine gave Cosmo an approving look, then looked seriously to Kymethra. "Take the message to Fidelm. Battle draws near." His tone made it clear he wished to be alone.

The sun was making its descent west, marking the end of the day, when Kymethra was ready to leave.

"Fly high," Brackendon told her. "And fly back to me."

She kissed him. "Try not to kill too many demons. Leave some for the army."

He watched her go, soaring south towards the distant smoke trails of the demon host. He kept watching until she became a speck on the horizon and then finally vanished.

The sun had almost faded by then and torches were being lit. Sentries swapped their positions on makeshift towers, while others lined the edge of their perimeter ditch with sharpened stakes, hurriedly assembled at the insistence of Cosmo. His instincts were good. He might have been a hunter, but he knew when he was the hunted.

Brackendon was glad Cosmo had decided to take up his true mantle. He would never have fulfilled his true potential as a semi-alcoholic bear slayer. His grand return might even kick some life back into Arkus and spur humanity into proper action.

Brackendon had just crossed the threshold back into camp when he heard the cries.

"Fire! Fire!"

He pivoted, expecting to see the treeline ablaze and the demons emerging in droves. But nothing was out there. Swords screeched behind him. The cries of "Fire" morphed into the screams of battle. When he wheeled about, he saw smoke issuing up from near the centre of the camp. A horn blew loudly across the night.

A horn that sounded an attack.

33

WHEN PLANS GO WRONG

Cassandra – The Charred Vale

Dusk was gathering as Cassandra crested the top of the hill. A solitary tree grew at its peak, towering and natural in colour. Here, at the edge of the forest, silver trees were sparse, a situation aggravated by the recent burnings.

The vale to the south was now a smouldering landscape, sloping gradually into the River Dorain. Only recently, this hill had risen proudly from a sea of green. Now, half its side was burnt away and only a portion of its southwestern side remained untouched.

She drew in deep breaths, glad of the freshness of the air so high up. Guards had been posted to her tent and they had taken her sword but giving them the slip had been easy enough. Up here, she could feel free. There were no wandering eyes, no suspicious eyes, no judgement, no expectations. And no Darnuir.

His pursuit of her forgiveness was matched only by her reluctance to face him after what she had revealed to Balack. She hadn't meant it. It had just slipped out. But what he had done next had been frightening.

It occurred to her then that she might slip down the hillside, run into the trees and never come back.

And where would I go? Back to my room atop the Bastion?

She had felt at ease beneath the Argent Tree but that did not seem an option. The queen wanted everyone gone; she could send her away or keep her there as a 'guest'.

Cassandra knew full well what that would mean. Another room, another prison; more guards and less life.

It had been Darnuir who had deflected attention from her and allowed her to feel like she was living her life for the first time. Not even Cosmo trusted her anymore.

From dark thoughts to darker, her fingers wrapped around the dragon figurine that Trask had given her. She pulled it out and gazed at it. The yellow paint had nearly worn away entirely. Chips were missing in the wood. She was pleased to find that looking at it did not fill her with guilt or worry anymore. Cassandra clasped a hand tight around it, then brought her arm back before launching the figurine far out over the precipice of the hill.

She let loose a breath she wasn't aware she'd been holding. A tension unwound from between her shoulders.

Once more, she peered out over the steep slope into the forest below. In one step, she could be master of her own fate. One step and she could be free.

Instead, she pulled herself back and slumped against the lonely tree she had for company. If she vanished now, she would only validate the claims against her. She would forever be thought a spy or a traitor. Moreover, Balack was still here, and after what he had just been through it seemed cruel to abandon him as well.

And so she resolved to return to her tiny tent at the edge of the camp. She had no doubt been moved there so that she could not spy on anyone important. The cover of full darkness would be preferable for sneaking back in and, in any case, the fading sun caressing her face was most agreeable. It was warm and the grass was soft. Cassandra had almost reached a point of relaxation when she heard the footsteps.

She scrambled to her feet, grasping for a sword that was not there. When she saw who it was, she knew it would have been useless anyway.

"How did you find me?" she asked.

"You're good at sneaking around, Cass," Darnuir said, "but you need to learn to cover your tracks better."

She thought she had done a decent job of it. *Damn hunter.*

"Can't you take a hint? I'd rather be left alone."

"And I'd like to apologise."

"It's not me you need to apologise to. It's your friend you need to beg forgiveness from. Two broken ribs, Darnuir; he'll be out for weeks."

"Over a month, I'm told," Darnuir said painfully. "If healers can be spared then he may recover quicker but—"

"There will be more wounded soon," she answered for him.

"Can I not make amends with you at least?"

"Amends for what? I'm the one who let the secret slip."

"It can't have been easy, watching me lash out like that," he said. He stared off, perhaps collecting the courage to go on. He at least looked her in the eye when he found it. "Especially after someone you thought you could trust lost control before. I just wanted to say... to say it's not really me. I thought I was over this, but perhaps not..." He trailed off again, his courage waning.

She folded her arms tightly and considered him. "What I told you was difficult. But I don't want you to think of me as some brittle thing. I know what you're going through can't be easy, that you can't explain it. But it doesn't make it less scary."

What if you'd attacked me instead? she wanted to say.

His downcast, darkened expression suggested he knew exactly what she had just omitted. "Hearing you say that breaks my heart a little. When I first met you, I was so overwhelmed, but I felt better when I was with you. My head didn't hurt for some reason and I could forget for a while what was happening to me. With everything going wrong, I felt useless, but I could help you, and I did. It made me feel like I had done something worthwhile. I'd hate for that to be in vain because of one mistake. I promise I would never, ever hurt you. And as for what's happening to me, I'm scared as well. I don't know who I am anymore. I'm not the person you first met, yet I am not my old self. I am not even fully something new. When those outbursts come over me, it frightens me as well."

Cassandra nodded. "It's all right." And without knowing what more to say, she slumped back against the tree.

Tentatively, Darnuir joined her. They sat in silence for a while; her watching the sunset, him pulling up tufts of grass and letting them float away on the breeze.

"I thought about running away," she finally admitted.

He turned, a look of shock turning to a resigned understanding. "Do you wish to leave?"

"Am I still allowed to?"

"I'm sorry, Cass, but my hands are tied. I know you aren't a spy but if you go now... well, I hope you can understand Blaine's position."

"And Cosmo?"

Darnuir's silence said it all.

She shrugged. "Just as well I decided not to go in the end."

Darnuir perked up. "You don't want to leave?"

"Of course not. My friends are here," she said. "I've yet to discover from Brackendon whether there are any texts out there on recent history. Balack is wounded now; I want to keep learning swordplay from Lira, and I'd miss baby Cullen terribly, and—"

His hand fell upon her own, gently enough. She could have pulled away, but something stopped her. Darnuir rolled onto his knees, placing an arm against the trunk above her head.

Cassandra met his eyes. She'd suspected something like this might come, but not now – why now? Probably because of the looming battle, his turmoil over Balack,

Blaine constantly berating him. She couldn't decide in that moment how she felt. And it was a moment that passed too quickly. She knew that she didn't want to be this close but nor did she want to push him too far away.

Cassandra must have held his gaze for too long, for he moved even closer to her. The last moment to react passed. His kiss was gentle but unwanted, soft but still pressing. Her hands lay limp at her side, even as his drew up to her hair. Being trapped between tree and dragon, a prison of bark and white leather, was more restraining than all the walls of the Bastion.

It ended with a horn blast that ripped through the night.

Darnuir pulled away to peer back over the camp.

Cassandra stared at the blank space over his shoulder, not able to look at him.

More horn calls went out.

"We're under attack," Darnuir said. He jumped to his feet, drawing out his sword. "Come! It won't be safe up here."

Cassandra thought it may well be safer up here, but she would take this chance to prove she was no agent of Castallan. She was halfway to her feet when Darnuir grabbed her hand and dragged her up.

They careened back down the hill, less carefully than either of them had climbed. Darnuir still had her by the hand and she struggled to keep up. Cassandra's protests fell on deaf ears and on they flew until she tried to yank her hand free. She jerked her hand from his grip and lost her balance, tumbling backwards.

She plunged down the hillside as Darnuir's calls of horror faded away. Violently, she crashed through the undergrowth, thorns ripping at her face and arms. Her vision rolled as the slope tossed her.

Leaves, then stars; branches, then stars again; mud, then blackness.

A hard knock to the head caused an explosion of light behind her eyes but she only continued down; down and down and down, until she skidded to a halt upon the forest floor.

Aching all over, she wished to move but couldn't. She wanted to cry but even that seemed too difficult. Her eyes blinked open to the dark forest and her ears pricked up at the sound of voices.

"What was that?"

"Over here."

"White leather. She must be a Boreac lass."

Rough hands turned her over, but her vision swam. They were two men in grainy yellow leathers, but there was a third man standing behind them whose eyes were red. Everything seemed red. Something red oozed out from the mouth of the man who had turned her over. It slopped down over her, obscuring her sight. Then only the man with the red eyes remained, blood dripping from the blade he'd used to make the kill.

Another pair of red eyes appeared like burning coals in the night.

"It is her. Get word to Zarl. We have the princess!"

The newcomer dashed off.

The speaker remained and bent to pick Cassandra up as easily as if she were made of cloth. As he hoisted her onto his shoulder, her fingers brushed lightly against a hilt sticking up from his belt. Instinctively, she clutched it. He did not seem to notice as the knife punctured his neck. He only gave a gargled gasp of shock as he died, collapsing to the ground.

Once again, Cassandra found herself lying on the forest floor, but imminent danger sharpened her senses. The dead man's blood was warm and sticky, and she held back the urge to vomit as she rooted for his sword. She drew it out and was relieved that it was of a standard make. She could use it.

Disorientated, she staggered amongst the trees, her ears still ringing. A gnashing sound rattled from somewhere nearby. She caught the little demon's rusted sword only by accident as she turned. It reeled back, and she struck forward for the kill.

Her heart raced like a charging dragon as more enemies approached. She ran. She knew not which way she was going but she ran. They were chasing her; she could hear them coming. Arrows whistled by, but from friends or foes, she never knew. She only ran on.

Soon the very air grew stiflingly hot and her eyes slammed shut as an inferno blocked her way. She changed course, but they were on her then. Cackling demons leapt towards her and she skewered one in mid-air. The second tackled her legs but the weight of its companion on her sword brought her arm down hard on the demon below her.

They don't seem to want to kill me.

She kicked the remaining demon and then sprinted on. The fires were throwing up dancing shadows all around her. Even as she registered the danger, spectres emerged, three or maybe four. Her only advantage was their strange aversion to harming her.

One tried to knock her sword aside but she held on, screaming as she threw everything she had behind her counterblow. The next spectre that tried to touch her lost its arm but the remaining foe vanished. Dark hands grabbed her from behind, almost invisible in the night. She kicked and struggled but she could not break free. More spectres appeared, disarmed her, and dragged her off.

They must have been moving south, for the sounds of battle grew distant. The trees began to part until she saw a smouldering field before her. At the edge of the treeline, her party stopped.

"What are you doing?" a rasping voice croaked.

"We are to wait for Zarl."

"I'm tired of listening to that cursed human," the first one growled. "When Lord

Dukoona arrives with the fleet, things will work differently. Too much spectre blood has been needlessly spilled. We threw our lives away for nothing at Torridon."

"You disobey Zarl if you like," another said. "I won't weep for you when he rips your limbs away. The wizard has made them all too strong."

The first spectre spat, a ball of darkness which smoked upon the ground. "To Kar'drun with the wizard too. His tedious plans have held us up long enough. Like this one," it said, pointing a blade of coiled shadow at her. "I say just kill her and have done—"

An arrow cut the spectre off. It lodged in its head and its body fell limp. The one carrying Cassandra dropped her in alarm. She lay still. Getting up again seemed too much of a struggle.

"Cassandra!" a voice called from the treeline.

Cosmo?

She righted herself and saw him. Cosmo was dispatching the last of the spectres, a group of hunters, huntresses and dragons around him. The prince almost looked resplendent in his white leathers. He hurried over to her.

"Can you stand?"

"Yes," she said, still shaken and dazed.

"Good. On your feet now. Someone get me a sword."

As Cassandra steadied herself, Cosmo thrust a weapon into her grasp. Her free hand pushed her now matted hair off her face and picked out a twig. The wounds on her face stung fiercely.

The spectres were waiting for someone…

"Cosmo, we have to move now!"

"That was the idea," he said, signalling to the six dragons present. "Get her out of here as fast as you can."

"I can move myself," she insisted. "I'm not that hurt."

His look suggested otherwise. "They made straight for where you were supposed to be encamped. Castallan must want you back desperately."

"Take her!" a cruel voice yelled. "Kill the others."

They all spun to face the source of the threat. A man encased in plate mail as dark as blood stalked towards them. Flanking him were dozens of red-eyed men and women, as well as the odd spectre. They moved swiftly to encircle their small group.

The ensuing fight was bravely fought but done in vain. Those Cosmo had brought were quickly taken down. The prince himself fought so boldly, he might have been a dragon. A red-eyed hunter threw him onto his back but Cosmo cut at his legs then hammered his sword into the man's chest as he rolled to his feet.

"Cosmo?" the plated man sneered. "The rest of you, take her away. I'll handle him."

Cassandra was once again hoisted over a shoulder. Her body gave up struggling before her screaming ceased. A filthy cloth that tasted of bile was rammed into her mouth.

"Who are you?" Cosmo demanded. His voice faded as she was dragged away. "Why would you betray your own people?"

The plated man removed his helmet. At a distance now, Cassandra only caught a glimpse of him. His face was thin, gaunt even, with a razor-sharp nose and thinning oaken hair.

Scythe?

Darnuir

He sped through the trees as though he might end the war if he were fast enough. Upon his return to camp, he had gathered men to enter the woods with him after Cassandra, but he had now left them far behind in his haste.

It's my fault. My fault she fell. She might already be dead. Why was I so foolish? Why? It's my fault. She was too close.

He followed the trail of bodies leading south. Demons, spectres, humans and dragons alike were strewn along the bloody path. He thought he heard someone shouting an order up ahead but he could not be sure.

On and on he drove until the trees thinned and then parted, and before him lay the charred land that made up the vale. In the distance, and moving at an impressive pace, was a group of humans, half of whom were still in their hunter gear. He thought he saw a slung body over one of their shoulders. Not so far away, but still at some distance, was the mysterious plated man.

Darnuir froze, wondering whether he should give pursuit. He had taken one step forward when he heard it: a spluttering sound that sent a chill through him. Turning to face its source, his heart stopped dead; his stomach churned; his legs nearly gave way; he forgot how to breathe.

Cosmo had been lifted off the ground and pinned to a tree by a sword through his guts, a wound that would have meant a painful death even under normal circumstances. Cosmo grasped defiantly onto a low-hanging branch so as not to rip himself further.

Darnuir went to him, though there was nothing he could do. Cosmo's free hand reached for Darnuir and he took hold of it. His mouth was full of blood but it seemed he wanted to say something.

"Scythe," was all he managed.

It was the last thing he ever said.

Darnuir had no concept of how long he stood there. At some point, he removed the terrible sword that had held Cosmo in place and caught his body as he fell. Gently, he placed Cosmo down and closed over those grass-green eyes, which had always been so warm. He fell to his knees, cradling Cosmo against his chest. Eventually, others found them. They told him that they should return.

"I will carry him," he told them, whoever they were.

But first, he strode to where he had tossed the sword that had done the deed. It lay silently on the ashen earth as if feigning innocence. Darnuir took out the Dragon's Blade and chopped and smashed the sword into as many pieces as he could until they scattered beyond his reach.

"Scythe!" he roared. "Scythe!" he bellowed until all the breath had been forced from him. "I will kill you," he vowed quietly to the night.

34

TERRIBLE TRUTH

Darnuir – The Charred Vale

The traitor sat bound, dirt smeared across his face from being tackled to the ground. Darnuir did not know his name. It wasn't necessary. Yellow leathers suggested he was a Crescent hunter, or had been at any rate. The prisoner had extinguished his red eyes, perhaps in hope of garnering some pity. Darnuir would give him none.

"Who is Commander Zarl?"

"We never knew his real name."

"He lies," Blaine said. "I can smell the fear on him."

Darnuir couldn't pick up on it. His senses were swamped with the sweat, blood and smoke that clung to his clothes. Blaine called it true, though, for the man's eyes quickened in fright.

"We knew he was a hunter. A high-ranking hunter, too. From the Master Station."

"Anything else you would like to add?" Darnuir asked. He danced his fingers towards the man's hand, lying bare upon the table. He was well-restrained to his chair otherwise. As if running would do him any good now.

"N-nothing," he stammered.

"You seem quite afraid, for one of Castallan's pets," Darnuir said. He picked up the man's little finger with an exaggerated delicacy, making a show of holding it between thumb and forefinger. "I am only surprised because attacking a camp of trained dragon warriors, supported by hunters, is a bold act. Not one for those weak of stomach. You and your companions fought incredibly well."

"What are you doing?" the man asked.

"I am considering whether or not to crush your finger." These red-eyed men were as tough as dragons, perhaps tougher. Darnuir was sure the prisoner would not allow his finger to be mutilated. "There really is no reason to hold back on us. We have you."

He remained silent.

So be it, Darnuir thought and then squeezed on the man's finger.

Immediately, the man's eyes flared red and Darnuir found he could not succeed in his punishment.

"The arrogance of dragons," the man said, his voice dropping into a visceral rasp. "Castallan has freed us from your kind, beast." He spat at Darnuir. There was a smooth sound of a sword unsheathing.

"I'd like to see how those red eyes handle one of the blades," Blaine said. "Do you think you are strong enough to stop me sending you back to your master in pieces?"

"Humanity will be free!"

"Castallan is not a saviour but a traitor," came Brackendon's voice.

Darnuir hadn't even been aware of Brackendon entering the tent, so focused was he on the prisoner.

"A traitor to the dragons, perhaps," the man said. "Yet he never swore an oath to any dragon. What did he owe dragons?"

"He owes me some information," Darnuir said. "I bought it, after all." The man seemed confused. "I'm confused on one matter, though. How is it not treacherous to kill your own kind? Castallan has slaughtered humans in droves."

"Blood must be shed if a new order is to rise," the man said. "Those blessed by his magic try to kill only dragons where they can." He gave Darnuir and Blaine a twisted smile. "For dragons die the same, after all."

Darnuir searched his mind for that door to the Cascade. He tried to open it very carefully, as Brackendon had instructed, and let just a little bit of magic flow in. He pressed again on the man's finger. The prisoner screamed. Darnuir closed the door in his mind, feeling the peculiar rush down his arm.

"Scythe," the prisoner panted. "That was Zarl's real name."

The confirmation was a dead weight falling through Darnuir's stomach. Scythe's gaunt face floated into his mind. Where once there had been respect, even reverence, there was only anger.

"That wasn't so difficult, was it?"

"Darnuir," Blaine said, "perhaps you ought to relieve him of his thumb next?"

"Perhaps you ought to refrain," Brackendon protested.

"If you do not wish to see this, Brackendon, then leave," Darnuir said. He felt a hand upon his shoulder and turned to find the wizard looking upon him gravely.

"I hoped you would avoid becoming this," Brackendon said. "I hoped for a different man when I made my sacrifice."

Darnuir felt scolded. A war raged within him, shame and rage of equal measure. Before he could speak in his defence, Brackendon had stormed out of the tent. Breathing heavily, Darnuir rounded on the red-eyed man. At least he seemed cowed.

"What else do you want from me?"

"You attacked this camp deliberately," Blaine began. "You hit very specific sections, some of which were unimportant. Why?"

"We were looking for the girl."

"Cassandra?" Darnuir asked. The memory of their kiss still taunted him with its uncertainty.

"Is that her name?" the red-eyed man said lazily. "We were told to find a girl in white leathers, with long black wavy hair and green eyes. She was either to be in that tent at the edge of camp or near you, we were told," he said, looking to Darnuir. "Those men the commander had planted in the Boreacs knew her better."

"Do you know why Castallan wanted her back so badly?" Darnuir asked, taking up the man's thumb, this time to show he meant business.

"The girl is Arkus' daughter. The Princess of Humanity."

A memory jumped forth to Darnuir: a looming corridor, a shattered shoulder, and a crying baby lying not so far away.

"The princess died at the fall of Aurisha."

"Castallan was present for that assault," Blaine said. "It may well be the truth…"

"If it is true, it seems this information is too valuable to share with underlings," Darnuir said. "Why would you know?"

"I assure you, we were only recently informed," the man said. "The commander made it perfectly clear that if anyone killed the girl, they would find their face impaled upon one of the spikes on his armour."

The revelation impacted Darnuir physically. So many secrets were coming to light, he was not sure whether this might just be some bluff. Yet why else would the wizard have kept her imprisoned all these years? Why else, unless she was a hostage? Did this mean that Arkus knew? Is that why he had been so slow to move?

His silence seemed to amuse the prisoner. "The great king," he said tartly, his raspy voice wrapping itself around every word. "Such power you are supposed to have, and yet you know so little; unable to stand against a simple man from the Dales; unable—"

Darnuir flattened his thumb.

"Curse you, dragon," the prisoner howled. "Kill me, then, if you must. Though I suspect your kind gets a sick pleasure from playing with humans."

"You see now why I distrust this race," Blaine said. "They see us as monsters when we have only fought their enemies for them."

"For us?" the man cried, half in pain and half in indignation. "How much human blood has been spilled along the Crucidal Road? And what has it ever achieved for us? Dragon wars have only bled mankind."

"Cease your ramblings," Darnuir said. "There is one last thing we need of you. You were on the run from Torridon to Val'tarra, I presume?"

"I was," the man said bitterly.

"Then tell me what you know of this black powder."

The man blinked in confusion and a watery tear of pain dripped out. "Of what?"

"Dragon powder, some seem to name it," Blaine said.

"Ah, is that what caused the explosion?"

"What did I say about not being honest?" Darnuir said, selecting another finger.

"Seems you'll hurt me anyway," he scorned, "but I swear to you, oh mighty dragon king. I know nothing of it."

"Such a concoction reeks of the wizard," Darnuir said. "Who else might have produced such a thing?"

The man shrugged, his red eyes blank. "I tell you, I know nothing of it. Nor did I hear any mention of such a thing the last time I was at the Bastion. To my knowledge, Castallan has had no hand in it."

Blaine sniffed loudly. "I think he is telling the truth."

"Very well," Darnuir said, rising. "What will be done with him and the others?"

"If you are unwilling, Darnuir," Blaine said menacingly, "leave me to it. It shall be quick."

Darnuir was aghast. "Blaine, if you intend what I think you do—"

"It would take several guards to properly watch over each of them. We cannot spare the men."

"Find some way," Darnuir insisted. "We will not feed their cause, Blaine. Killing them will only strengthen the resolve of those like him who despise us."

"You seemed quick enough to harm him," Blaine said.

"They are not fully human anymore, I admit, but they are far from being demons. They are our prisoners. I will not allow them to be slaughtered."

"As before, the consequences lie with you."

"Like everything else is," Darnuir said. He stormed out of the tent and Blaine followed. Light Bearers moved in to secure the man.

Standing beside Darnuir, the guardian sighed at the ashes of his holy tent and symbol. Blaine went to stand in the middle of the wreck, knelt and placed his sword deep into the earth.

Darnuir watched him curiously. "It seems your gods are rather good at taking insults."

The guardian said nothing, his eyes closed in some silent vigil.

"We need to prepare for battle," Darnuir went on. "Scythe surely knows of our intentions. He will hit us hard with everything he has."

"We will be surrounded in a pitched battle. Their numbers are too great."

"Then we shall not meet him in the open," Darnuir said. "Scythe has granted us the hill. Let us hold it."

35

THE BATTLE OF THE CHARRED VALE

Darnuir

Their forces were deployed on and around the hill in an arc facing south. The hunters, some nine hundred in total now, would rain arrows from their elevated positions, aided by Brackendon, while the dragons would try and hold ground. They could only pray that there were no more agents of the enemy amongst them.

With Blaine's guidance, Darnuir had lined the dragons up traditionally, with some alterations given their situation. The javelin throwers were out front, ready to retreat behind their heavier units when the enemy closed in. Those dragons in the shield wall bore short swords for the crush of a melee. Time and exile had savaged the equipment of the legions. Those dragons without a shield stayed back as reserves, and small contingents were placed among the hunters in case of spectre attacks.

It was the best they could do.

A clear sky would have been preferable. Passing clouds offered the men some relief from the sun but it also allowed spectres to move amongst them, avoiding their shield wall as if it were not there.

Despite the early hour of the morning, the heat was uncomfortable. Mid-summer was searing into the world. Darnuir tugged at his collar, sparing a thought for the dragons kitted out in their plate mail today, although it would at least defend them well.

Darnuir stood now beside Blaine at the head of their army, overlooking the soon-to-be battlefield of the Charred Vale.

"Thirty thousand demons," Blaine muttered.

"Exactly what we hoped to avoid."

"The hill will give us some advantage."

"Not enough," Darnuir said dejectedly. "A valiant defence is only as good as the support you hope to receive. Out here, we are on our own, and four legions will not be enough. This is a last stand. And yet..." He remembered the fight that had raged at Cold Point. Remembered facing the red-armoured man. He had not defeated Scythe then, but he had forced him to withdraw. And when he'd fled, his forces had fled with him. "If I can kill him—"

"Scythe won't risk himself at the front," Blaine interrupted. "There's no need for him to do so."

"Then I must seek him out."

Blaine considered this for a moment. "Removing their leader might have an effect. Yet even if you manage to find him, manage to kill him, you would still be in the middle of the host. You would die."

Darnuir held Blaine's eye as a dark wave emerged from the distant treeline. The demons surged on, wasting no time in their advance. Zarl was eager for the kill.

It is Scythe, Darnuir reminded himself. *It is Scythe, and he betrayed us all.*

He clung to the freshest of Scythe's crimes, the better to fuel his own fires. He still wore the same leathers from the night before. The blood had dried in. He'd earn his place facing Scythe with Cosmo's blood still on him. Red leathers for red armour.

"I see no sign of him," Darnuir said.

"He must be conducting them from the back," Blaine said. "Are you sure you want to do this?"

"I feel I must. My old self did not pass on everything from his life. He was not what you would call a learned soul. Yet he devoured everything he could on war: every book or scroll or diary written by every general, king or soldier across the ages. He trained himself to master every weapon. I feel oddly comfortable with the thought of wielding a mace, an axe or spear, even though I have never grasped any of them in my life. He was obsessed with beating back the demons and he moulded himself into a weapon. That is all I might be: a machine of war."

"For now, that may be what we need most," Blaine said. "I forced you to absorb those memories, to become ready. Your first plan was a good one; were it not for the traitors amongst us, it might have worked."

"So you approve of what I intend to do?"

"I doubt I could convince you otherwise."

"No," Darnuir agreed.

"You know the risk and, whether you die out there or alongside your people, the result will be the same. One day, Darnuir, both of us – or just one of us alone – must face our true enemy. If you cannot win today, then we were always doomed."

With no more words, Darnuir unsheathed the Dragon's Blade. The golden metal caught in the morning light. He stepped towards the oncoming horde.

Darnuir started slowly at first, letting the demons close the gap. Blaine began shouting behind him but Darnuir soon lost track of it as the noise of the demons filled his ears. He picked up his pace before charging into a full sprint. It was madness, this, running head on against thirty thousand demons. A part of him was terrified, but another part – the older part – relished the chance. That side of him came to the fore as he allowed himself to be engulfed by the single-mindedness that only battle could bring.

The gap closed.

Darnuir increased his speed as he pounded on the smouldering earth. He reached out to that door in his mind, to the Cascade, taking great care to open it ajar. Extra power washed into him, like he had felt at Torridon, only this time it was controlled. The pace he reached would have shamed a galloping horse and he worked his legs harder still.

Closer, and closer, and closer.

Then he leapt.

The Cascade-fuelled jump hurtled him high over the demon ranks, flying far into the midst of their army. He landed, sending a shockwave around him and knocking nearby demons off their feet. Scythe was nowhere to be seen. Darnuir took to the air again, fuelling his jump with more magic from a standing start. Without momentum behind him, he did not travel quite so far, nor did his landing have the same impact. He whirled his sword around him as he rose to clear the area and found his mouth was bitter. He scanned again. No Scythe. He spat out the horrid taste in the face of one of the wretched creatures before leaping again.

Darnuir bounded through the demons. Leap, rise, cleave, look, spit. Leap, rise, cleave, look, spit.

Arrows flew at him. One clipped off his sword; one tore a neat cut in his side; most missed.

Leap, rise, cleave, look, spit.

Beneath him, the demons continued to surge forwards. During one flight, he glimpsed a figure encased in red. He adjusted his next jumps to find him.

Leap, rise, cleave, look, spit.

He almost took off again before realising he had found his quarry. Darnuir would soon be engulfed by foes and so concentrated upon making fire burst forth from his sword. His throat burned, the door to the Cascade shook on its hinges, but he maintained control. Thick lashing flames soon surrounded Scythe and himself, creating a small arena like the one in which he had fought Blaine.

Demons and red-eyed men alike howled in pain as the flames caught them. Smoke from demon blood rose with the smog of the fires.

Darnuir tried to turn the flames on Scythe next, but his foe streaked across the distance between them, clashing the Dragon's Blade aside with an inhuman blow. The force of it sent Darnuir to the ground. He scrambled along the earth, disarmed and panicked.

As he flipped onto his back, the Dragon's Blade returned to his grip just in time to block Scythe's next attack. Darnuir's eyes watered, perhaps from the smoke, perhaps from his use of magic. The effort it took to hold Scythe did not bode well. Caution aside, Darnuir heaved open the door to the Cascade and let it flood him. His next push threw Scythe aside like a rag doll.

Darnuir staggered upright, slamming the door shut, hoping he had not taken in too much. Something writhed down his arm towards the Dragon's Blade, as though thorns were in his blood. A putrid taste lay upon his parched tongue and he drew in laboured breaths.

"Overexerted yourself?" Scythe sneered. Even his sword had been cast in a malicious red, with a terrible serrated edge.

Darnuir did not deign to answer. He had no words for Scythe; the traitor would only receive his sword. The flames from the Dragon's Blade started to dwindle. With nothing around but charred earth, they had been kept up by magic alone.

I closed the door to their fuel. I don't have long.

Spinning his sword once in his hand, he advanced on Scythe with a two-handed strike. The fight became brutal. Scythe's enhanced physique made him akin to a dragon, perhaps even stronger.

Darnuir was brought to his knees again, then tried for Scythe's legs. The traitor jumped high to avoid it, landing his booted feet on the Dragon's Blade and pinning it in place. Darnuir caught Scythe's hands as he tried for the kill, using all his natural strength to hold him at bay. Scythe's sneering grin renewed Darnuir's rage and he lunged a knee forward, striking Scythe in the stomach, denting his armour and sending him reeling.

Doubled over, Scythe was vulnerable. Darnuir allowed the Dragon's Blade to flip up into his hand of its own accord and unleashed a flurry of blows. Darnuir pressed him back, nearly bowling him over, but it was a feint. Scythe let him in close and then whipped one of his slight and deadly hunter daggers from his belt, cutting at Darnuir's leg. The sharp blade slashed through his leathers effortlessly. Blood splattered.

Darnuir cried out, twisting his body away and smacking the dagger from Scythe's hand.

A metallic heel to the back of his knee sent Darnuir sprawling once more. He rolled along the charred earth to escape Scythe's next assault.

The glimpses he saw of his arena of flames were not promising; they would die out soon. Yet he was wary of opening the door again. Desperate, he rose after reaching the edge of their arena and threw the Dragon's Blade at Scythe with all his might. It almost worked, but Scythe placed a foot firmly in the ground and managed to deflect it. The effort cost Scythe the top third of his bloody red sword, but the Dragon's Blade went soaring off into the demon host.

Scythe charged. Darnuir could only attempt a tackle as he drew near. As they both fell, Scythe's now jagged sword was knocked out of his grip. Darnuir tried to find some purchase but the many small spikes on Scythe's shoulders made it too difficult. A fist slammed into Darnuir's head. Pain exploded across his skull. Dazed and unable to think or see, he found himself being lifted into the air. A hand was at the nape of his neck and the small of his back. Scythe was lifting him overhead.

"I'll bring you back dead after all. Castallan will have to forgive me if your sword does not—" Scythe's words were cut off by his own excruciating scream.

Darnuir fell limply to the ground. The Dragon's Blade nestled itself back in his palm. It must have clipped Scythe's arm as it had flown back. The traitor's wrist hung half-attached and cracked white bone protruded from the wound.

Spitting blood, Darnuir seized his chance. The fires around them guttered out as he opened the door to the Cascade again. He ignored the convulsions of his body as he felt his throat burn. The Dragon's Blade began to heat up, though he did not let the flames gush forth. He kept the heat contained and the metal of the blade glowed a blistering orange as he severed Scythe's wrist, cauterising the wound as he cut.

Scythe collapsed, utterly defenceless. Darnuir risked more magic to boost his strength. He picked Scythe up with his free hand and held him high, just as Scythe himself must have done to Cosmo before he pinned him to that tree.

All trace of menace vanished from Scythe's face. Fear shone in his eyes and Darnuir smelled it. It was ever so sweet.

He rammed the heated Dragon's Blade through Scythe's plated chest, the metal melting as he drove it through. Darnuir could not tell the blood from the armour. Scythe's gargled choking was lost over the sound of the distant battle and the demons around them.

He threw Scythe's body down and closed the door in his mind again, worried by his shaking arm. As the Dragon's Blade busied itself with draining out the poison, Darnuir's moment of elation swiftly turned to despair.

The demons were not fleeing. His gamble had been for nothing.

He found that he was leaning on the hilt of the Dragon's Blade for support, the blade stuck hard in the dry earth. His breath came in laboured gasps and he could barely stand the putrid taste in his mouth. The cut on his leg burned, his legs shook, and his knees demanded that he collapse.

Then he saw them.

Spectres surrounded him.

They were beyond count and beyond fighting. *This was a reckless move after all.*

Yet the spectres did not attack. They simply stood and formed an audience around him. Most of their eyes drifted over their fallen commander. One of the spectres stepped forwards and Darnuir raised his shaking sword arm. The spectre halted and threw out a hand as if to say he did not wish to fight. Its eyes wandered once more over Scythe's body, as if checking he were truly dead. Slowly, the spectre pulled back its lips in an unnerving smile.

Darnuir had never seen them do that before, nor seen how disturbingly white their teeth were. The spectre smiled broadly at him, then gave a little mock salute and the smallest of bows. After that, it melded away into nothingness, disappearing into a shadow cast by the clouds. All its fellows did the same, morphing into the shadows nearby. Darnuir was left stunned and exhausted.

Soon after the spectres left, the regular demons went wild. They ceased running towards the army around the hill and instead moved in every other direction. Some fought each other, some fled, and some simply stopped and stood still, as though they had lost all function. Others even turned on the red-eyed humans dotted throughout their ranks as they tried to flee. It was chaos.

His body aching, Darnuir marched slowly back towards the hill, the demons parting before him like a dark, cackling ocean. Closing the distance to him was a golden wedge, cutting through the demons and hunting them down.

It seemed the battle was won.

36

THE REBORN KING

Darnuir – The Charred Vale

The healers' tent was quiet now. The wounded had settled into a deep sleep and the dying had uttered their last breaths long ago.

Darnuir sat at Balack's side. He placed a tentative hand on Balack's own.

"I'm so sorry for what I did. For putting you in here. And for everything."

Balack said nothing, but slowly drew his hand away from Darnuir's.

"If you do not wish to forgive me yet, I understand."

I have yet to forgive myself.

Balack held his silence. He winced sharply and wrapped an arm around his battered chest. Bandages wove their way around most of his torso. He was sitting upright, propped up by several pillows at Darnuir's request so that he may speak with him. Likely, he'd rather just sleep and dream of simpler times.

Darnuir forced down the lump in his throat. "I will go, then. Take care, Balack. I won't be back for some time."

He got to his feet and turned his back upon his friend.

"I lost you both that night, didn't I?" Balack said with a quiet pain. "We won at Cold Point but I lost you both. You were right. I always knew. I always knew…"

For some reason, Darnuir's heart drummed in his chest, as if he had returned to battle. He struggled to find the courage to turn back, to find anything to say. Someone else stepped up close to them.

"My king," Damien said. "It is almost time."

"Thank you, Damien," Darnuir said, his mouth bone-dry. He managed to glance back to Balack on his way out, but his old friend refused to meet his eye.

Please come back to me, he thought. *Cosmo is gone, Cassandra is taken, and I've sent our Boreac brothers and sisters north.* Now only Brackendon remained whom he might call a friend, but those memories felt unsettling to him. *And there is Blaine, my 'equal', my 'partner', and yet I do not know him.*

"Lord Blaine has requested that you change first," Damien said, leading Darnuir to his pavilion. The king's tent at the centre of camp was an extravagance compared to its surroundings. Perhaps he ought to sleep more humbly like the rest. This large space would be better served as a mobile war room where he might take his meetings and conduct affairs. Such changes could be delayed for now.

"I shall wait for you here, sire," Damien said.

Darnuir entered the tent alone, feeling fatigued. The effects of the magic he had used to defeat Scythe were still wearing off. His arm shook and he grabbed the Dragon's Blade to let more of the poison drain away. He did nothing to alleviate the bitter taste still in his mouth. The victory was bitter enough. No other flavour would be suitable.

A heavy-looking chest lay in wait for him. A simple key rested atop a squat square of parchment. A short message was written on it in fine letters.

I believe you are now ready, my king. I recommend that you leave off the boots if you wish to move with any real speed.

Darnuir unlocked the box with a childlike eagerness. The armour inside was similar in material to the rough gold of his sword, though darker and heavier. He tried to lift out the largest piece and was so surprised by the weight of it, he almost dropped it. A breastplate? Then he recognised it. It was the armour he had seen Dronithir wear in the memory that Blaine had shown him. Roaring dragon pauldrons and riveted plate mail which looked like layered scales. When equipped, the set would cover his entire body. Underneath it all was a crimson cloak with clasps in the shape of talons.

He changed slowly out of his bloodied white leathers, carefully placing the pieces back on a stand as he detached them. He knew that he would miss the freedom of his hunter's garb, but he was no longer a hunter. The wound he had suffered from Scythe's dagger on his leg throbbed just then, reminding him of the disadvantages of the leather's minimal protection.

Old memories floated to the surface from decades past, telling him how to put the pieces of plate on and strap himself in. At first the pieces fitted horribly, as they had been designed for another dragon. Yet even as he considered removing them, the armour shrank and grew as needed, forming itself anew around his frame. A perfect fit. Still, it was heavy, almost beyond bearing.

I got used to the sword. I shall grow accustomed to this as well.

As he adjusted the pieces in the mirror, the tent's flap opened and several young boys entered, carrying a bowl of scalding water and a softly chinking pouch.

"What is this?" he asked them, recognising them as those who often tended to Blaine.

"From the Lord Guardian, sire," one of them said. "For your face, sire." They all scurried out.

Darnuir ran a hand through the burgeoning fuzz on his face. He did not shave as regularly as Blaine, but this rougher look, this human look, was not the way a dragon king should appear. His old self always had a clean face.

He soaked a cloth and brought the steaming water to his cheeks, chin and neck. The pouch was filled with bristly brushes, a tub of dry silver paste and a razor. The silvery paste foamed up into a thick cream as he worked it in, and as he removed the hairs, the skin underneath appeared the healthier for it. He tried to make his hair a little more presentable as well, tucking the ends back over his head and behind his ears. It had seemed to lighten of late, as though bleached by the sun that he rarely saw in the Boreacs.

Or perhaps I am becoming more like Blaine?

The thought was not entirely appealing.

Finally, he reached for his new gauntlets, delicate plates over crimson leather gloves. They morphed to fit his hands until they felt as natural as another layer of skin.

Now complete, he stood back to observe his new image in the mirror. His overriding feeling was that this seemed right. The Dragon's Blade hung casually from his side in a way that his old self could only dream of. With his magnificent armour and clean face, he at last looked the part. He looked like a king.

I will have to continue to look and act like a king. From this day forth, every day, until I die.

"My lord Darnuir?" Damien called from outside. "We should go soon." When Darnuir exited the pavilion, Damien seemed surprised. "Sire..." he said. "It is good to see you this way."

"Thank you. I finally feel the part. Are you fit enough for another long run?"

"That would depend how far I must go, sire. But yes. I can run. Do you need me to seek word from Inverdorn?"

"From Brevia, actually," Darnuir said. "But you will not be going alone."

In short order, they arrived at the burial service being held between the two legionary camps. Dragons had lined up on one side and humans on the other. Darnuir paced up the middle of the two races and stood awkwardly between Blaine and those hunters leading their own rites. Blaine was preaching something about his gods.

"In the beginning, this world was ours and Dwna shone upon it brightly. When the Shadow came, our world was cast in two. Like our Lord Dwl'or, we have existed for ages since in this duality."

The Light Bearers stood and many of the closest onlookers nodded in agreement, yet other dragons seemed unsure, and Darnuir saw them looking to him rather than the guardian. However, he had nothing to say about these gods. Darnuir was more inclined towards what the hunters said for their dead; the lament they chanted had always sounded simpler to him. Darnuir sang along ever so softly, barely moving his lips. Despite his inclinations, he knew it would not be good to be seen favouring one side.

"Yet now the time has come to lift the Shadow!" Blaine continued. "The power of N'weer will return our strength, our faith, and this world to us, as it used to be, just as he has blessed your king. See him now before you, rejuvenated and reborn!"

Ah, so that is why I am to look the part now. Because it suits you, Blaine.

"Hail Darnuir!" the dragons cried. "Hail! Hail! Hail!"

Cosmo was buried alongside the others. He would not have wanted any ceremony for his tomb. He would have wanted it simple, and therefore they had kept it so. Hours later, as the afternoon wore on, Darnuir knelt beside Cosmo's grave with Brackendon alongside him. The wizard had slept all day and even through the service to help recover from the battle.

"To Brevia, then?" Brackendon asked.

"To Brevia," Darnuir said. "Will you come with me?"

"I will. I think Blaine can handle things here on his own. And there is a matter in the city I must attend. Answers I must gain."

"Thank you, Brackendon. I should like to help you if I can. Find Lira for now. She is making the preparations."

"As for before, Darnuir, with that prisoner—"

"I'm not sorry for it. He was no longer human."

"I don't know whether that makes it right," Brackendon said. He seemed to consider whether he should say any more. Gripping his dazzling new staff more tightly, he pressed on. "I've mentioned before that the decision to save your life was one of necessity. Even Cosmo admitted it, though it took him longer to do so. But it wasn't you we were saving, but your position, your blade."

"Well, I am grateful that you thought me such a 'necessity'."

Brackendon knelt by the grave and placed his scarred hand on the soft soil. "My desperate hope was that you would not become the man you once were. For you to turn so easily to your old ways, that is not what I sacrificed so much for. What Cosmo sacrificed so much for. Even your own father was hard-pressed to love you."

"Yes, I was left some choice memories of him," Darnuir said. He felt numb. "I did not allow Blaine to kill that prisoner, nor the others."

"I know," Brackendon said. "I was tasked with binding them with magic, and it took a good deal of my strength."

"And was it worth it? To weaken yourself prior to a battle to save some traitors?"

"Oh, yes," Brackendon said without hesitation. "If you treat them with respect, how can they find cause to talk against you? Kill them, and sympathisers will only grow stronger in their conviction."

"That was my thinking also."

"Breaking fingers is not respectful, Darnuir."

"Nor is pinning a man to a tree with a sword," Darnuir said angrily. "I will do my best to bridge our people, but I am a dragon after all, and a king. I must look out for my own people first and foremost. If I find humans killing dragons, I cannot let that go unpunished. I hope you can understand that."

"I will find Lira," was all Brackendon said.

Left alone by the grave, Darnuir thought it unfitting for the man buried there. He deserved to be beside Grace at least, but fate had conspired to deny him even that.

After what felt like months, Darnuir found a moment of peace. No demands. No pressures. Allowed to finally grieve, he wept.

A part of him, his old self, felt disgusted at how he was behaving over a human. But that part was small. The Darnuir of the present was in control and all he wanted to do was weep and wet the earth. Perhaps it would cause some beautiful flower to bloom there. Perhaps it would only salt the soil.

"I will not chide you for this," Blaine muttered from behind. "The loss of one so dear is a pain worth hiding in your gems."

"I'd rather have the memories of him with me," Darnuir said.

"He wasn't such a hero. He ran from his duties his whole life. Some would call that cowardice."

"You ran away as well."

"I had my reasons."

Darnuir placed a hand on top of the soil. It was cool – peaceful. "As did he. You will tell me what your reasons were, I'm sure." Blaine had travelled in search of the Champion's Blade but that was clearly not the whole story. Darnuir got up and turned to face Blaine. "Tell me, Lord Guardian. What was that token the kazzek sent you and why did it affect you so?"

"It once belonged to someone very precious to me."

"And how did the trolls come to possess it?"

"I can only guess, Darnuir."

But you are sure, aren't you?

If Blaine had gone north in search of the sword, perhaps he had been following in the footsteps of another; the one he suspected had found it already, this Kroener, the dragon who had become Rectar. Blaine's shock at receiving the trinket suggested he did not know that the trolls had it in their possession. It must have belonged to someone precious indeed. A lover, perhaps? A friend? If the old dragon was even capable of making friends. Only Blaine knew the answers.

"I would have you tell me—"

"Darnuir, here and now is—"

"Not the time or place, I know. There will be time enough later. First, we have a wizard to handle, and the armies to gather. But you will tell me, Blaine. You will tell me everything. Even if I must prise those white jewels from you myself. I tire of secrets."

"I promise," Blaine said solemnly.

"I must also tell you what happened after I killed Scythe."

"The demons fled, as we suspected they might."

"Not quite," said Darnuir. "All the spectres gathered around me when I tossed Scythe's body on the earth. I thought they were going to kill me, there were so many of them. But one just gave me a smile and a bow, then they all left, melding away into the shadows. That's why the regular demons went berserk. Castallan's red-eyed minions must have no real control over them."

Blaine frowned. "Why would the spectres simply flee?"

"Perhaps they do not see eye to eye with Castallan? Cassandra mentioned that the spectre lord she witnessed at the Bastion threatened him."

"If our enemies are squabbling with each other, all the better."

"There may be a way we can use this to our advantage if we discover the true reasons behind it."

"What?" Blaine said sharply. "You would have us work with demons next?"

"No, Blaine. I just—" But he did not know quite how to finish. He did not yet understand, and so he could not know what he would do. All he could be certain of was that something was amiss within Castallan's ranks. If spectre dissent extended beyond just this one battle, if it went as far as Rectar's invasion fleet, then it could have enormous repercussions. He doubted Blaine would ever grasp this. He was too zealous in his war against the Shadow. Darnuir left the matter alone for now.

"One final thing," he said. "Before we unlocked my memories, my head pains always abated when I was close to Cassandra. Being around her made them disappear. Do you have any idea why that might be?"

"I haven't a clue," Blaine said. "As I have mentioned, your situation is unprecedented."

"I have a vivid memory now," Darnuir went on. "Of running through a golden city under siege with a baby girl in my arms. That girl was Arkus' daughter. That girl was Cassandra. After that, there is only pain and white light."

"Perhaps," Blaine began slowly, "if the girl was the last person you were connected to, in a fashion, it formed some kind of bond. When you reconnected, perhaps your old self in the rubies was tricked into thinking that all was as it should be."

"Whatever the case, we must bring her safe from the Bastion. I failed her at Aurisha and I failed her again here twenty years later. I don't intend to fail on the third attempt."

She was too close.

"As you will," Blaine said. "My king."

My king, Darnuir repeated in his head, thinking of the note Blaine had left along with the armour. *He means it now.*

"Take the army south and rendezvous with Fidelm, then head east to Brevia."

"You will not be joining us?"

"Speed will be essential. I will go ahead to the capital."

"You should not go alone," Blaine warned.

"I won't be alone."

Blaine's eyes narrowed. "I do not wish to cast aspersions on her abilities or loyalties, for I am sure she is dedicated to you. However, dragons are simply not used to female troops beside them, much less above them."

"Perhaps the older ones aren't, but these are not your dragons." Darnuir left Blaine with a firm shake, gripping him high up his forearm. Blaine returned the gesture. "Take care, Guardian."

South of the hill, he found Lira and Brackendon awaiting him. Two score dragons stood proudly behind her, handpicked, young; his to mould. It pained him that hunter members had not been recruited to the Guard, but facts were facts. Until Castallan was removed, the humans could not fully be trusted. Not that he would openly admit that to Blaine. Besides, this was to be another hard run and he had no desire to carry any humans on his back.

"You know why you are here," he told them. "You are the first of my new Praetorian Guard. You will be my elite. You will train in the ways of dragon, human and fairy. We will make a force that shows what this alliance should be – strong and loyal. If you would follow me, then do so now. If not, then return to camp and you will not be reprimanded." None of them moved. "Then run with me now; run to Brevia, and take our first steps in retaking our world!"

EPILOGUE

Dukoona – East of Kar'drun – The Forsaken City

He walked quietly through the ruined streets. The once-proud home of the Black Dragons had been reduced to rubble during their last war with their Aurishan cousins. Dukoona, of course, had not been there. He had never seen one of these 'other' dragons, though he suspected they were just the same. Though largely rubble, the style of the buildings was not dissimilar from Aurisha itself.

Crumbling towers must once have stood tall. Columned villas sat desolate, their pillars cracked or fallen. Forges rusted away behind collapsing shopfronts. There was even a rather large structure, perhaps as big as the Basilica atop Aurisha's plateau. Its roof had caved in but Dukoona sensed that it too had once been a dome.

He wondered what their quarrel had been about. There were no more dragons of this kind in the world now. He doubted whether the differences that existed between the two merited the destruction of the other.

He doubted most things now. He doubted whether his kind still had any value to their master. Investigations into the incident reported by Sonrid had not advanced. Dukoona and his Trusted were none the wiser about the red creature that had escaped from the mountain or why his people were killed for seeing it.

In the time since then, he had instructed his Trusted to tread with extreme caution. Spectres were no longer allowed into the mountain and his master's orders came only in powerful bursts before his presence faded out entirely. These instructions only concerned the invasion and the fleet. Dukoona was supposed to launch the eastern ships, and he would, eventually.

For now, he was meandering; taking his time; enjoying the rare novelty of walking for a change. The quiet streets made for a pleasurable stroll.

Dukoona was glad for the tranquillity. Demons after all made such a terrible noise –always snarling or gnashing or screaming. It became dreadfully difficult to think clearly around them, for a spectre would expend most of his energy keeping them in line. Even smaller groups in the hundreds were tricky to manage at once, and the size of the invasion horde was alarming.

Almost two hundred thousand in total. Not all were aboard their fleets here and at Aurisha; some would remain as reserves, but Rectar wanted to strike swift. And he wanted to strike hard.

The Three Races would be well occupied.

As Dukoona drew closer to the harbour of the Forsaken City, the noise inevitably escalated. There surely was no greater hell, other than perhaps his master's lair under Kar'drun. The ships stretched out far to sea, anchored until the last transport was full. They were fat vessels, overweighed with demons. It would take a deal of oar power to move them. Were it not for the fortunate fact that demons did not require food or rest, the whole endeavour might have failed.

The harbour itself was the one area that Rectar had deemed worthy of rebuilding and even expanding. It sprawled out fresh, strong and golden, in contrast to the decaying city all around it. As Dukoona strode along the bay, he found Kidrian awaiting him under the shadow of one of the great, fat hulls.

"Is all prepared?" Dukoona asked. Kidrian nodded; however, his eyes darted nervously around and his purple embers burned lower than usual. "Is something wrong?"

"It might be nothing," Kidrian croaked.

"Does it regard our *recent issues*?" Dukoona asked. They had to be careful how they spoke in the open.

"No, not that issue," Kidrian said. "I have been getting unsettling reports of missing starium from the city."

"Missing?" Dukoona said, surprised. "The whole place is a ruin, Kidrian. How could it be known whether some of the stone was missing or not?"

"Indeed, sir, a few bricks would go entirely unnoticed, but whole areas? I am told that whole sections of the city have been cleared."

"You trust these reports?"

"As I trust you, lord." This signalled that Kidrian had his information from members of the Trusted, ever watchful for unusual activity. "Additionally, a few of our closest brothers have not been seen in days."

More deaths? Rectar is not even trying to mask his movements. It is as though he only wishes to delay us...

"My lord?" Kidrian said.

Dukoona snapped back to the situation at hand. "Is there any indication where the material is being moved to?"

"None, sir, though there seems only one place it could have gone."

They exchanged a knowing look.

The mountain. What would Rectar need with such amounts of starium stone?

"The will of the Master is not for us to understand," Dukoona said, making a point of announcing it for any interlopers. "We have our instructions. Kidrian, pass along orders to all vessels from Lord Dukoona. The fleet is to set sail immediately."

Kidrian bowed low then melded away into the shadow they stood in. A thick rope stretched from the dock to the ship, allowing Kidrian to avoid the water below. He remerged on the brow of the ship's top deck and moved off, out of sight.

Dukoona watched the first ships depart, still as the dead city around him. He never suffered from aches in his body, he never felt tired, and he never had to sustain himself with food. There was nothing to do at times but to think, to battle his gnawing doubt, now more acute than ever. Yet, in launching the fleet, he was being deprived of time to contemplate. Events may soon get ahead of him and the fate of his kind lay in the balance.

The invasion of the west had begun.

MICHAEL R. MILLER

THE
DRAGON'S
BLADE

VEILED
INTENTIONS

PROLOGUE

Grigayne – Island of Eastguard – Splintering Isles

Eastguard had fallen.

From his longship out at sea, Grigayne watched the old fort upon the cliff burn. It had stood for centuries, keeping watch for dragon war galleys in ages past. Today, it had taken the demons mere hours to destroy it. The flames now licked towards the dense clouds, waving wildly in the wind.

We were undermanned, unprepared, and taken by surprise.

Grigayne rehearsed that line in his head. But no matter the reason, it was still a defeat. His father, Somerled Imar, the Lord of the Isles, would slump in disappointment all the same.

Grigayne tasted blood. It was trickling into his mouth and he dabbed at his injured head with a wad of cloth while the oarsmen around him heaved against the angry waves. Water splashed onboard, wetting his clothes, which were already damp from sweat. Some of it entered his mouth as well, mixing unpleasantly with the blood on his tongue: a salty, tangy, metallic taste. Foul. Though not as foul as their defeat had been.

"It wis hard fought," someone said from behind. Grigayne did not recognise the speaker. A coarse voice was a common trait amongst the inhabitants of the Splintering Isles. The salt was said to rub at a man's throat, a woman's as well.

"We should have sailed the moment we saw the demons approaching," Grigayne said. His own voice was lighter, his letters better enunciated. Lord Somerled had desired Grigayne to blend in at the Lords' Assembly in the capital of Brevia, and ensured he learned to speak properly.

"And gie up the fortress without a fight?"

"More lives would have been spared," Grigayne said.

"Most of the townsfolk in Errin got away. That's sumin'."

"I suppose."

Grigayne turned to get a look at the man. He must have been in his fifties, with a patchy brown beard and the gore of battle on him. His only noteworthy feature was the stump of his left wrist.

"Do I know you?" Grigayne asked.

"Doubt it."

"Well, who are you?" In the chaos, Grigayne had jumped aboard this boat without much thought.

"Oh, I'll be the captain. Name's Cayn."

"You don't sound certain, Cayn."

"Well, I'm sure I saw the last cap'n on fire during the attack. Then his first mate died with a spectre's blade in his belly, and then his closest mate died n'all. Seeing as it's only a small ship, that just leaves me in charge."

"And a fine captain you'll make."

Cayn shrugged. "Might do, though only reason I'm sat here is cause I cannae row." He waved his stump in demonstration.

Grigayne closed his eyes at that. More water splashed up and seeped through the cloth over his wound. It stung powerfully but he held the cloth in place, knowing the salt would help clean the cut.

"So, Captain Cayn, do you think you can take us to Dalridia?"

"I thought we would be stopping at Ullusay," Cayn said, giving his beard a good scratch. "Much closer than the capital. The weather is against us, and we don't have much in the way of food."

"Forget the weather. Every demon Rectar has at his command seems to be set against us, and we do not have time to stop. My father must be warned as soon as possible."

Cayn's expression was downcast, as if the aged man did not feel any amount of warning would suffice. "Aye, then. We'll make for Dalridia."

Grigayne took stock of the oarsmen he had left. Although many of them bore signs of the recent skirmish, thankfully they all looked experienced. Most had small axes or swords at their belts, but nothing compared to the larger war axe resting on Grigayne's own lap. He would have carried his strong round shield upon his back, but it had been cloven in two by the razor edge of a spectre's shadowy blade.

Grigayne would not call what had just unfolded a battle. The demons had come on so fast, there had been no warning.

"Ironic, really," Grigayne mused aloud, "that a fortress built to ward against dragons should fall so easily."

"Not enough men," Cayn said simply. "Place was a bit old too."

"Built at the same time as the Bastion," Grigayne said.

"Bastion has taller walls," Cayn said with another shrug. "And stone. We could've used more stone."

With the blazing fire in the distance, Grigayne could not disagree. The neighbouring islands were no better equipped to resist attack and would not last long. Ullusay, Ronra and the little island of Skelf would surely fall before he could return with aid. All the Splintering Isles were in peril.

All of Tenalp will be in danger from such a force. We'll merely be the first to fall.

He kept such thoughts to himself, however. Despair would hardly drive the men to Dalridia.

"Let us row with all our strength, Captain Cayn."

"Aye, milord. Hard at 'em oars now, lads. Heave 'n ho. There's a shark at yer arse, so heave and ho."

Grigayne settled in beside a rower who lacked a mate beside him. The man was shivering, though whether from fear or the cold Grigayne could not tell. He took the end of the oar and began to rock forward and back, forward and back, feeling the ocean resist his efforts. His head still rang from the blow he had taken, and his thoughts jumped from one uncertainty to the next. *Why now? Will Brevia send support in time? Will Brevia send support at all?* Grigayne didn't know the answers and so, for now, he focused on the rhythm of his arms.

Forward and back, forward and back, forward and back.

Will the dragons emerge to fight alongside us?

Forward and back, forward and back.

One thing, at least, was certain.

Eastguard had fallen.

Dukoona – The Island of Eastguard

A human was trying to scuttle away on a broken leg. When Dukoona reached him, he placed one of his shadowy feet upon the human's chest. His victim stopped squirming, then attempted to raise his small, round shield to cover his face. Now that Dukoona could see him, he seemed so young. Not much more than a boy. A crying boy.

Better a clean death.

A blade forged from the shadows swirled into Dukoona's open hand, ghostly purple and sharp enough to cut down through the wooden shield with ease. The boy lay still. He had been the last of the islanders left on Eastguard. The small band here had proven easy to remove. Dukoona's landing had surprised them, as he had intended. A few ships, however, had gotten away. Dukoona had intended that as well.

Kidrian appeared at his side, looking out to the longships heading south and west.

"They will alert the rest of the islanders," Kidrian croaked.

"As they should," Dukoona said. "Come, walk with me." He moved away from the boy's body and drew up short of the cliff edge facing south. Just beyond the horizon lay the island of Ullusay, and beyond that would be Dalridia, lying in the shadow of the Nail Head Mountain. If Dalridia fell, all the Splintering Isles would follow. Yet Dukoona was in no hurry to conquer it. Furtively, he checked his surroundings and then the sky. Dense clouds prevented any shadows from spreading across the land, so he needn't fear being overheard here. He could not place faith in all his spectres; only his Trusted.

"We may discuss matters here, I think," Dukoona said.

"What would you keep from the Master?"

"Most things, but right now, I'd withhold how easily Eastguard fell. Rectar may expect quick progress if he knows how quickly we took a foothold here."

"A foothold would require a more permanent base."

"I think you might be correct," Dukoona said, turning to face his companion. A wry smile crept up the side of Kidrian's face, starkly white against the dense flesh-like shadow of his body. The cold purple embers on Kidrian's head burned low. Somehow, the wind did not affect them as it would normal flames.

"A Shadow Spire should be constructed," Kidrian said.

"A wise move. One that would take a great deal of time, I'd imagine?"

"It may delay us by a month, maybe more."

"A necessary precaution."

"I quite agree, my lord."

My lord. He looks to me. I only wish I could do more for him, for all the spectres.

"Is there something more on your mind, Kidrian?"

The leader of the Trusted shifted uneasily. "The disappearances of some of our people at Kar'drun, my lord. They worry me still."

"I have not forgotten," Dukoona said. "But, as always, we can only be patient. Go now, before those we do not trust grow suspicious."

Kidrian bowed and took his leave. Dukoona lingered for a while, surveying Rectar's vast fleet as it swept along the ocean. He could not turn the demons back; only play for time. He needed that now – time to think, time to plan – but there was none. He did not know what he could do to save his spectres from extinction. They were caught between the Three Races and Rectar, as though exposed in a great expanse between two shadows.

Something stirred within his mind. In a split second, the endless presence of his master glanced towards him, then looked away. Rectar said nothing, perhaps satisfied to see the burning fort and dead humans sprawled around it. With the moment over, Dukoona relaxed.

He desperately needed time. But he could not delay for long.

1

A POOR START

Unlike previous eras, the Transformation of the dragons, the Third Flight and the forging of the Three Blades is the earliest period of what we can consider history, though it is still blurred heavily in legend. Sources from the time are scant but confirm just enough to allow us to speculate further.

From Tiviar's Histories

Garon – North of Val'tarra

A week had passed since Garon's expedition left the tranquillity of the Argent Tree, and two days since they left the forest of Val'tarra altogether. The Ninth Legion marched, three thousand dragons strong, along with a thousand hunters and as many fairies on their way northwards to safeguard the Highlands and aid the kazzek trolls.

Garon had kept their column close to the west bank of the River Avvorn. Its crystal water was clean and energising, laced with hints of Cascade energy from the Highland Mountains. Garon might have found it harmonious, had it not been for his gnawing fear.

He could still hear the pressing worry in Darnuir's voice when he had pulled Garon in close and whispered, "Be watchful for those with red eyes." The words had not been written among the orders on the scroll he had given to Garon, but it was an order nonetheless. He kept that scroll close. It was a reminder to Garon of who was counting on him. It reminded everyone else that he, a human, was in charge of this expedition. Garon thought it a bit of a joke that it had been left to him. The kind of joke that made you wince and suck in breath through clenched teeth. Yet he was in charge, and so long as that was the case, he intended to stay alive and keep it that way.

Beware the red-eyed men. Suppose I should beware the red-eyed women too.

The threat of these unknown red-eyed traitors loomed over him. He couldn't meet a strange hunter from the Cairlav Marshes or the Golden Crescent without staring awkwardly into their eyes, weighing them up, judging whether they had joined Castallan and been enchanted by his magic, as that red-eyed chevalier at Torridon had been.

Even those from the Boreac Mountains, he gave a second look; people he'd fought and bled alongside for years. All of them, apart from Griswald and Rufus. If he couldn't trust them, he couldn't trust anyone.

"Not like ye tae be so quiet," Griswald barked beside him. "Not seemed yerself since we left the forest."

"I'm mourning the loss of that sweet fairy girl," Garon said airily. He reached into a deep pocket of his leathers and pulled out a thin block of silver wood. "This is all I have to remember her by." He showed the block to Griswald – two painted patterned lines, one pink and one blue, wove halfway along the piece.

"Pretty. She forgot tae fill in the rest, though."

Garon tucked the wood away. "It's supposed to represent our time together. "Passionate, but cut short."

"Ha," Griswald laughed. "Young Pel better watch herself then."

"Wing Commander Pel," Garon said, strongly emphasising her rank, "is off limits."

"I won't hold my breath. If ye had a block like that for each of yer girls, you could build us a new station."

"Oh, come now, Griswald. A small hut perhaps, but not a whole station."

"Well, hold on tight tae that wee momento. I don't reckon there will be many more women where we're going."

"The Hinterlands aren't so far away. I'm sure there are women there."

"I hear they grow 'em tall and blond in the Hinterlands. I could be tempted. Sure I cannae persuade ye to change course?"

"I'm afraid I must dash your dreams of tall women to match your enormity. We'll be following the Avvorn northwards. That is how Ochnic came down. It is the fastest way into the Highlands, or so he says."

Griswald gave a loud tut of disappointment. "Where is the troll?"

"Further ahead with Rufus. They are scouting the best path for us to take."

"You trust that creature, lad?"

"Darnuir does," Garon said, tapping a finger against his scroll. "And so does Cosmo. That's enough for me."

"Aye, I'll take Cosmo's word for it. Even if the royal git hid who he was from us all these years."

"Would you call your prince that to his face?"

"Might be best to refrain when I next see him," Griswald admitted. "Expect he'll be wearing thick fancy robes by then, and a crown tae boot."

"I hear those girls in the court at Brevia grow very pretty."

"Aye? I'll march faster for that, lad."

And march they did.

At dusk, Garon called a halt. The warm amber light of a summer's eve was a perfect end to a far too affable day. *Something is bound to sour it.* Garon's thoughts immediately jumped to Legate Marus, Commander of the Ninth Legion, and the snide remarks he'd make for halting their march before they keeled over in exhaustion. For now, Garon had managed to avoid Marus, claiming he wished to sup in peace, though he had not protested when Griswald had taken up a space by the fire. A large space; it was Griswald, after all. The man's beard more closely resembled a thicket and a fair bit of cheese was tangled in it.

Griswald belched. "Woah, beg yer pardon."

"Denied," came the low voice of Rufus. Although not as large as Griswald, the cropped, black-haired hunter was still impressively broad.

"You're supposed to be scouting us a path with Ochnic," Garon said.

"The troll said I ought to return," Rufus said, taking a seat on the dry grass by the fire. "It wasn't looking promising, I'm afraid."

"So, where is he?" Garon said.

"Checking other routes," Rufus said. Garon eyed him, but Rufus just shrugged. "Apparently, he'd be quicker without me. Way that troll moves, I'm inclined to agree."

"I'm not sure if you've really earned your dinner, then," Garon said, pushing a basket of food over with one foot.

"Not a hot one, it seems," Rufus said, exaggerating a grimace. Garon rewarded him with a smirk. Whilst their fire was warm, their food, sadly, was not. Still, it was not without pleasure. Whatever the fairies did to their bread kept it tasting fresh for weeks. It even retained that fresh-baked smell. Garon picked at the small brown loaf, topped with seeds, and ripped chunks from his stash of cheese. As much as he had liked life at the Argent Tree, he could not have lived there forever. That venison served during the council had been his first bite of real meat for far too long. His mouth watered at the memory of it. His stomach knotted as well, though not entirely at the thought of slow-roasted deer.

I should have said no. I should have looked Darnuir squarely in the eye and told him, "No, bugger this, I'm staying."

He wasn't a leader. Sure, he had led hunter patrols, but that was different. And Cosmo had been there for him. He'd always been there. Garon had been so young when he had stumbled ragged into the Boreac Mountains, he had few memories intact from before that time. Perhaps his mind had blocked them out to save himself the ache. He remembered one thing though. The oozy black blood upon the door to his old home in the Dales; he remembered pushing it gently in. Remembered seeing the bodies—

He shook his head. *Why ruin a perfectly nice night thinking about that?*

He swallowed down the last of his sharp yet creamy cheese, oddly satisfied with his meal. A cup of shimmer brew to finish was tempting; the very thought of its bitter fragrance wafting in the air made him rummage into the supplies. It had to be rationed carefully, but one cup could be spared. He was on the verge of setting some water to boil, crouched over, his back to the rest of the camp, when he heard the footsteps.

"I thought I was clear," he said. "I do not wish to be disturbed."

"Unless it is these two, I see," came the irritated voice of Legate Marus.

"You will want to know dis, Garon pack leader," said Ochnic, discernible by his earthy voice.

"Something tells me I won't enjoy hearing it," Garon sighed. He turned to be greeted by a frowning Marus. The dragon had such thick dark-blond eyebrows that Garon was surprised he could see at all when frowning like that. Marus' red-plumed helmet was tucked under one arm.

"What is wrong, Ochnic?" Rufus asked.

"We cannot travel through da glens dis way," Ochnic said, his icy eyes piercing Garon's gaze.

"And why not?" Marus asked. "You made it down easily enough before, troll."

"Ochnic was alone before," Rufus said. "The terrain is winding and rough. It will slow us down considerably. Likely we'll be single file in places."

"Too slow," Ochnic said, drawing out the words in a long breath.

"And you had no idea of this beforehand?" said Garon.

"Do you know every rock of your own mountains?" Ochnic said.

"I was aware of spaces a bloody army might pass," Garon said. "Still, we must press on."

"It will take too long, Garon, pack leader," Ochnic said. "We must reach da kazzek before da rains come; before de lochs rise too high; before de winds blow us back."

"We are aware that autumn and winter approach," Rufus said, "but we still have plenty of time."

Ochnic seemed to ignore Rufus. He stepped closer to Garon, drawing himself up to his full and impressive height and Garon glanced apprehensively to the large dagger at the troll's side.

"I worry for da kazzek," was all Ochnic said, softly, almost pleading.

Garon relaxed and spoke softly in return. "I understand your concern for your people, but—"

"Last hope, I am," Ochnic said, thumping a hand against his white-furred chest. His thick grey skin wrinkled around his eyes as he fumed at Garon. One might have mistaken it for anger, as Marus seemed to do, reaching a hand for his sword. But not Garon. He'd developed an instinct for knowing when a person's anger was really directed elsewhere. Perhaps it came from years of hearing angry fathers curse his name.

"We'll get there, Ochnic," Garon said, reaching up to grasp the troll's callused elbow. Ochnic squinted down, perplexed at the gesture. "I don't intend to fail," Garon assured him.

"We must find a faster way," said Ochnic.

"And we shall," Garon said. He gave a friendly squeeze on the troll's arm.

"Thankful, I am," Ochnic said, taking Garon's upper arm in imitation and squeezing overly hard.

Garon winced. "You're welcome. Griswald, you've sat enough. Might you go fetch Wing Commander Pel? It seems we are in need of a change of course."

"That cheek will get ye intae trouble someday," Griswald said, but lumbered off all the same.

Garon, left uncertain of how to proceed, indicated that all should be seated around the campfire. An unpleasant silence followed. Marus removed his helmet and stared into the orange glow, Rufus fidgeted, and Garon half opened his mouth several times, trying to say something, but failing to think of anything. Ochnic didn't seem to mind. He just sat picking a strand of meat out of his teeth with a chipped nail.

"Shimmer brew, anyone?" Garon asked. The response was less than enthusiastic, but with little else to do he returned to his pot and dumped the silver leaves in. A tidal wave of sympathy for Darnuir crashed against any lingering annoyance he had for being given this job.

How much harder must his task be? This is just a mere taste of it and it's already going awry. He tapped his scroll again by way of tribute. *And if I fail, then we all fail. If I fail, the Highlands fall and Val'tarra and Brevia are vulnerable from the north. We'll be fighting outnumbered on two fronts. We'll lose. All if I fail to get this lot to work together.* He glanced around at each leading member of his expedition, who were all sitting grumpily, not looking at each other, arms folded, and was eternally thankful that Griswald returned promptly with Pel.

"I am told our mission may already be in jeopardy," said Pel. She was unable to hide the happiness in her youthful violet eyes, nor the flutter of excitement from her wings. Her silver hair was pulled back in a single long tail and a sleeveless blue tunic with an emblazoned silver tree revealed lean, muscular arms.

"A small snag, Wing Commander," Garon said.

"Perhaps we should return to the Argent Tree?" Pel said.

Ochnic growled.

"You would gie up so easily?" Griswald asked.

"There is a greater fight waging in the south," Pel said.

"We have been given a task and we shall see it through," said Garon. "I was at that council meeting, Pel. Your own queen approved of this mission."

"We have never been friends with the trolls, and General Fidelm —"

"Is outranked by Queen Kasselle," Marus said. "As is King Darnuir. I shall not return in disgrace having barely begun."

"One more interruption and I'll fly off," Pel said. "You, Legate, should treat me as an equal. And you, human," she scowled at Griswald, "I don't even know who you are."

"Griswald," the big man said with a nod of his great shaggy head.

"Griswald," Pel began. "Shut up."

Garon ran a hand through his hair. This was swiftly getting out of hand.

"How mature of you, Wing Commander," Marus said. "You are young, but that does not mean you should act your age."

"Marus, please," said Garon. "General Fidelm selected her for the mission. I'm sure he thinks her capable."

Pel laughed, an angry little titter of a laugh.

"What is it?" Garon said.

"Oh, I'll be blunt," Pel said. "Few of my kind wish to waste time wandering lost through the Highlands to save frost trolls. So few, in fact, that I was the only wing commander he could press into it, mostly by promoting me the day before we left." Marus and Griswald looked as stunned as Garon felt. Pel shrugged. "My people want to defend Val'tarra, our home. Not theirs." She flicked her hand at Ochnic.

Ochnic himself made a loud sucking noise as he finished picking at his teeth. He uncoiled his gangly body and began to slope off. "Call me when da fairy girl is more reasonable."

"Come back here, troll," Pel said. "You've even said it yourself, I'm told. We cannot go any further this way."

Ochnic stopped. "Always der is ways. Garon, pack leader, said so."

Garon smiled pleasantly at Pel. She did not return it.

"If the River Avvorn will not lead us, perhaps we could follow the Dorain instead," offered Rufus.

"Into the Hinterlands?" said Marus.

"The Bealach Pass is known to be wide," Garon said, drawing on old hunter lessons. "The town of Tuath lies at its end, or its beginning, depending on how you view it. Am I right, Griswald?"

Griswald scratched at his beard. "Rings a bell, but getting over to Tuath from here will take time, lad."

"How long exactly?" asked Marus.

"A week, maybe more," Garon said.

"Perhaps longer," Pel said. "We're on the wrong side of the Avvorn to reach the Hinterlands with ease. Doubling back or moving forward to find a crossing will take up yet more time."

"Den we should be movin'," Ochnic said.

"Is there an agreement?" Garon asked hopefully; too hopefully.

Pel snorted and Marus droned on. Twilight turned to night and still there was no decision.

I was a poor choice, Darnuir.

Garon knew he had been picked to lead this expedition because Darnuir trusted him, but that meant little out here. How could he make this fairy listen when her own general had admitted his resentment of this mission? How could he make a dragon listen to him when Marus could break him in two? How could he do any of it? Then he started to have dangerous thoughts. *Perhaps those who've gone over to Castallan have good reasons after all. That red-eyed chevalier at Torridon did more than stand up to the dragons. If I was that strong, I might make them listen...*

His thoughts were interrupted by a sudden silence. Ochnic was acting strange, creeping towards Marus and sniffing loudly.

"What's wrong?" Garon asked.

"Smoke," Ochnic said. "Burning." He leaned forwards a little more and gave the air another great sniff. "Fresh blood. Can you smell it, dragon legate?"

Marus' expression darkened. The legate sniffed the air as well, then reached for his sword and shoved his helmet back on.

A distinct crack of steel on steel reached them. A roar of a fight. Cries of pain.

"I don't think we need tae smell what's happenin'," Griswald said.

Be watchful for those with red eyes...

Pel flew off into the dark without a word. Marus and Ochnic bounded off at a speed Garon could never match. He joined Griswald and Rufus as they ran towards the noise of the skirmish. Hunters looked on, perplexed. They were all mixed together, a vibrant blend of white, grey, mud-red and grainy yellow leathers, illuminated by small pockets of light from campfires. Garon saw a glimmer of a larger fire to the south, towards their baggage train.

They ran into the dragons' camp, with all their white tents lined in neat rows. Most had removed their armour for the day. There was a surprising number of hunters here as well, mingling with the dragons, it seemed.

"Arm yourselves!" Garon cried to them.

Beware the red eyes…

And he began to see them; close by, in the semi-darkness, red eyes opened with a furious intent. Eyes like true predators. It was hard to believe that behind each pair was a human like him.

Knives were used to slit the throats of unsuspecting dragons. Some gouged at their bellies or backs from behind. Muffled screams barely left the dragons' throats.

A huntress in yellow leathers from the Golden Crescent weaved her way towards Garon. Her eyes flashed red as she whipped out her sword.

"I'm with ya, lad," Griswald said, hurtling his bulk at the huntress. Griswald was a bear of a man, but she knocked him back effortlessly and charged towards Garon. He dropped flat on his stomach and the huntress bawled in annoyance as her blade swished at empty air. Garon rolled to one side to avoid her stamping feet. Still prone, he cut at her ankles, then her shins, then her thighs as she was brought low. It wasn't sporting, but these traitors had changed the rules. She twisted around and Garon rolled again without thinking, hearing his leathers tear as her blade narrowly missed the skin on his back. Flipping onto one knee, he stabbed deep into her exposed side to end the fight. Then a broad figure was over him, grabbing him.

"Up you get," Rufus told him, blood running from his crooked nose. "They're popping up all over."

Griswald staggered over to them. He seemed winded but unharmed.

The camp of the Ninth Legion descended into chaos. The red-eyed men and women had taken the advantage with their surprise attack. In many places, it was hardly a fight. Half a minute passed, or half an hour, or half a heartbeat. Garon just tried to keep his head. Red eyes flashed in the night, running at him, as though he were their main target. He supposed he might be. He was the leader of this expedition, after all. Yet most were speeding southwards, towards their supplies where the fire grew brighter. He was only in the way.

A hard buzz grew overhead, a noise like a thousand murmuring people.

Fairies. About bloody time.

Some of the red eyes began to ascend, lifted by two or more fairies. They climbed higher and higher until the darkness swallowed them. Then they dropped and their eyes extinguished when they hit the ground. Garon stuck close to Rufus and Griswald; the three of them together offered a better fight to each traitor. Tents were aflame now too.

"We must reach the baggage carts," Garon spluttered, shielding his own face from the smoke. "Or we'll have nothing left to eat."

Griswald roared his displeasure at that, taking a swipe at an approaching red-eyed hunter. The traitor from the Golden Crescent avoided Griswald with ease, making the giant seem sluggish.

"Bastard," Griswald yelled as his quarry disappeared into the darkness and smoke. A moment later, the Golden Crescent hunter came flying back, clean off his feet. Legate Marus followed, his face red with fury, and buried his sword down through the man's stomach.

"Marus," Garon implored, "the supplies—"

"Come," Marus said. As they ran, the tide of the skirmish turned. Fewer red eyes could be seen in the night and many were taking flight.

By the time Garon reached the baggage train, the destruction of their supplies was already a full-blown nightmare. There was singed cloth and leather, ashes from burning shimmer brew leaves and the smell of burning bread – all that fresh fairy bread. Weapon carts were upended, swords and daggers stolen, arrows snapped or tossed into the fires. Dragons and fairies lay slumped against carts or strewn on the ground. Many had their throats slit.

Marus spat at Garon's feet. "I'd spit on your whole race if I could." The flames lit his face in fractured lines, giving him a maddened look. Garon had no words. Even if he could think of some, he was struggling for breath.

"This isnae our fault," Griswald said. "Naebody's but Castallan's."

"Be reasonable, Marus," Rufus said.

"We were sent north on a fool's errand," Marus bellowed, not listening to them. "Sent north to care for some backward race and get stabbed in the back by humans."

"Marus—" Garon began, but Rufus threw out an arm to stop him getting closer to the dragon. He crept closer in Garon's stead.

"Those who have joined Castallan have betrayed us all," Rufus said, stepping very delicately. "We have all suffered here." He stretched a hand out to Marus. The legate looked disgusted as it touched his shoulder.

"Get off, human." His heave sent Rufus reeling, staggering into the path of a red-eyed straggler; a Cairlav huntress with sword in hand. She ripped through Rufus' chest, through the muscle and the fat to chink off his ribs.

"No," Garon cried, but it was nothing on Griswald's howl.

Marus stood aghast, frozen, reacting slowly for a dragon as the huntress made to strike him next. All thought of her escape seemed forgotten. Marus parried but only just. Garon started forwards but before he could reach them, the huntress had her skinning knife in hand and was making quick work of the weak spots on the legate's upper thigh.

Marus crumpled.

Blood sprayed from the wound; colourful, scarlet blood that spoke of a cut artery. It splattered the huntress and her bright eyes turned on Garon. She advanced, wielding both sword and knife. Garon's block saved his life but the force behind her blow sent him crashing to the ground.

So, I've failed already. I'm sorry, Cosmo, Darnuir. Rufus is dead, likely Marus, and now me.

He didn't even think to shut his eyes.

Another figure rammed the huntress. It balled out of the night, all grey and white hair. Ochnic knocked her sword from her grip and spun in the air to land on his great hand-like feet, producing his own large dagger from his waist. For a moment, they circled each other. Then they wrestled; a savage brawl of scraping metal, tearing clothes and biting. They crashed and both lost their knives. The huntress was stronger but Ochnic was more agile, more flexible.

He got hold of her neck from behind.

He twisted hard —

And with a ringing crack it was over.

Griswald crawled over to Rufus's body. Garon didn't have the strength to look at their fallen friend. He groaned as he tried to stand and found a large grey hand helping him up.

"I was warned of such humans," Ochnic said. "But I did not think dey were dat strong."

"Marus is hurt," Garon said. His wits were just returning. He staggered the short distance to the legate. There was a lot of blood. "Hold him, Ochnic." He struggled with Marus' armour but managed to get the upper leg guard off, unstrapped his own belt and tied it around Marus' upper thigh. Garon buckled it and yanked down hard to clamp the blood flow.

"Ah," grunted Marus. "Get away, human. You too, troll." He thrashed, throwing Garon and Ochnic backwards. Garon landed on his back with a thud. He was getting fed up of that this evening.

"Do you want to die?" Garon said, getting up. He tore off layers of leather and pushed them down on Marus' wound. He lay most of his weight on the dragon to apply pressure. Ochnic joined him, gnashing his teeth angrily. Marus let loose a pained whimper like a wounded beast, too tough to let himself scream. He tossed again but Garon held on, hating dragons for their pride.

Would he rather die than admit a human saved him? But it dawned on Garon as he fought to save the legate's life: *he's more ashamed that a human has almost killed him.*

Something hummed nearby. "How bad is it?" asked Pel, landing beside them.

"Nicked an artery, I think," Garon said. Marus rustled again, knocking Garon on the chin. His tongue jolted in pain and he tasted blood.

"Lift the material," said Pel. She bent low and produced a small box like many fairy healers had carried at the Argent Tree. "This should stem the worst of it," she said, dabbing a generous portion of a thick silver paste to the wound. Marus stopped thrashing.

"Dat will still need fixin'," Ochnic said.

"He needs a surgeon," Garon said, rolling off Marus. "Griswald," he called, hoping the larger man could carry the dragon. "Griswald!"

But he did not respond. He did not even move.

"Griswald, da pack leader calls," Ochnic said. Some moments passed before Griswald reacted. Hunched over Rufus, he rolled back his great shoulders, which looked like small snowdrifts in his white leathers. At last, he walked mechanically over to them. One foot. Then the next. All in silence. He picked up Marus' limp body and trudged off.

Pel's face showed nothing; nothing that Garon could read, at least. Without a word, she took off, beating wind back into Garon's face with her wings. Then it was just himself and Ochnic. And the body. Poor Rufus lay as crooked as his nose.

"In da north, we burn our dead," Ochnic said. "Der is no tellin' what will happen if dey go into da ground."

"What?" Garon said, his head spinning. "No. We bury them here. I'll bury Ruf—" His voiced snapped. The word died. And then he felt a strong squeeze on his upper arm.

"Den I shall help you, Garon, pack leader."

2

HELPING HANDS

Aurisha and Dranus were brothers. Together they ruled the dragons, but discord arose. Dranus thought magic would better serve the gods while Aurisha thought they should serve through faith. While Aurisha dwelt in solitude in the Highlands, Dranus contrived to speak to the gods themselves. He flew to what was then the largest of the Principal Mountains, where the city of Aurisha now stands. There he called upon the Cascade in such strength he managed to touch their minds. In doing so, he brought down their wrath.

From Tiviar's Histories

Darnuir – The Crownlands

"Not even I could jump that," Darnuir said, gazing out across the breadth of the River Dorain.

"Be a shame to waste time finding a bridge," Brackendon said. "I'll make one."

"That won't be too much magic at once for you?"

"Not with this," Brackendon said, twirling his staff affectionately. Perhaps it was the magic in the silver wood, but its tip somehow shone diamond bright in the light. "Stand back," Brackendon added.

The ground around them began to shake. Darnuir stepped away as instructed, returning to the rest of their company. Forty young dragons, the beginnings of his new personal Praetorian Guard, were refilling their waterskins in the river. Beside him, Lira, prefect of the guard, splashed some water into her own face. She sighed in relief as the cooling water hit her and pushed her ebony hair off her face.

"Have you caught your breath?" Darnuir asked.

"Enough, my lord."

He smiled and said softly, "Lira, what have I told you?"

"Darnuir, sorry, sir," she said flustered. "I'm still not sure I feel right addressing you by name alone."

The vibrations in the ground intensified. Brackendon slowly raised his free hand and clumps of soil, grass, flowers, small stones and unfortunate insects orbited his extended palm. Then Brackendon brought his hand swooping down.

The earth fell into position, piece collapsing upon piece, creating a curving arch up and over the river. About halfway, Brackendon dropped his staff to raise his other hand, bringing in more earth to pad out the bridge to reach the opposite bank. When it was done, Brackendon swayed a little by the riverbank. His right arm shook and his knees wobbled.

Darnuir ran to his side. A lot of colour had left the wizard's skin.

Damn it. I should not have allowed this.

To Darnuir's relief, the wizard was fine. Brackendon snatched up his staff, and even chuckled lightly when he saw the look on Darnuir's face.

"No need to look so panicked. I just required both hands for a moment." His health was already returning to him. His skin brightened, his silver eyes sparkled, although his hair remained short and grey, and his blackened hand would forever be damaged.

"Is that staff truly so powerful?"

"I have yet to find its limits."

"Powerful enough to deal with Castallan?"

"That remains to be seen."

"Hmmm," Darnuir mused. "You won't be alone, at least. I'll—"

"Come nowhere near that fight. You'll recall what short work I made of you back in Val'tarra?" Darnuir did. The cage of wind and taste of damp leaves was still vivid in his mind. "We should move on," Brackendon added.

"Yes," said Darnuir. He faced his budding Guard. "Over the bridge." They hurried, three abreast, across the river. Once they were upon the other side, Darnuir heard a colossal splash. He glanced back to see Brackendon's earthen bridge had vanished. He looked to Brackendon, who gave him a wink.

"You didn't think that mud heap was stable on its own, did you? Eyes forward now."

Darnuir returned to facing the Crownlands before them. It was the most heavily populated region of the human kingdom and the capital city of Brevia lay on the

coast to the east. Darnuir had to get there with all haste. The sooner he got to King
Arkus, the sooner humanity's full strength could be summoned for the war to come.

*First, we deal with Castallan, and then we scramble to counter this invasion Rectar is send-
ing. We're always a step behind.*

He braced himself, sucked in a deep breath and yelled, "To Brevia," before settling
into a slightly uncomfortable run. Dragon or no, his new kingly golden armour,
trimmed with starium stone, was thick and heavy. The carved bestial dragon that
draped over his shoulders felt particularly heavy and made it sorely tempting to draw
on Cascade energy, to crack open the door in his mind and let a small current
through. A wandering hand inched towards the hilt of the Dragon's Blade and it was
with some effort that he withdrew it. He had drawn on plenty during his duel with
Scythe at the Charred Vale and his body had made him aware of it the following day.
The cut he had taken on his leg throbbed gently and the bitter aftertaste of the
Cascade still lingered in his mouth, no matter how many sips of water he took. He
settled for grunting loudly.

"Are you all right?" Brackendon asked.

"For now. Come, let us concentrate on running."

And run they did. On and on and on, across green fields, past towns and villages.
They generally tried to keep clear of people, but it wasn't easy to hide forty running
dragons; not when they hurtled by, scattering livestock and causing farmers' dogs to
bound after them, barking at their heels. They took what roads and paths they could
for the sake of speed. Hurried stops to take a bite of their limited food or fill up their
waterskins was all the rest they took. They ran some more. Even at night they
carried on, being able to see better in the dark; forty twinkling pairs of eyes picking
up the light that spilled from Brackendon's staff. They drove on until the earliest
signs of dawn came upon the world.

Dew-covered grass wet Darnuir's boots and a fresh day filled his nostrils. He
breathed it in deeply, as if the air could clean him from the inside out. At the first
sign of real light he heard the many feet behind him slow to a stop.

"Is something wrong, Damien?" came Lira's voice. Darnuir thought she sounded
more confident in front of her charges, which was good. He turned to see what the
matter was.

The outrunner Damien stood by Lira, looking a little anxious. Unlike the rest of
the dragons, he was barefoot, wore looser linens for comfort and was in better
control of his breathing. For an outrunner, a run like this was second nature.

"It is dawn, my king," Damien said. "Will we not stop in reverence to D'wna?"

Darnuir did not understand D'wna, nor any of the gods that Blaine held service
for. He hadn't in his past either. It was one of the few consistencies that spanned
both his lives.

"I do not follow the Way of Light," Darnuir said, keeping his tone neutral. He did not wish to offend Damien, but he had not known the outrunner was a believer in the old ways.

"You... don't?" Damien asked, looking around as if to check he had heard correctly. When Lira and the Praetorians did not look shocked, he turned back. "I only thought... as king... your father always—" But he stopped there, cautious perhaps of how far he should go.

"Draconess, yes, he did believe," Darnuir said. "I have some memory of that. My old self thought it was what brought the dragons such hardship. He – that is to say, I – felt my father spent too much time on his knees; saying words rather than taking action. I admit I am ignorant of the gods of our people. Yet my father spoke to them every day, and under him our kind were forced from our lands, our city and our homes; nearly wiped from the face of the world."

"There is truth in what you say, sire," Damien said.

"If you wish to take a moment, please do," Darnuir said, gesturing with open hands. "I will not rebuke those who follow Blaine's way. Who am I to judge? I've only known that I am a dragon for months, not even years. I don't want division, and I certainly do not want to cause one amongst my own people." He made sure to look over to his new Praetorians, catching a few in the eye. "But I am not going to start saying praise either, especially when these gods never seem to answer back." He was pleased to find that Damien did not look disheartened.

"I was never fully convinced by the old ways," Damien said. "Though some say it is our lack of faith that has gotten us here."

"Gotten us where? On the way to Brevia?" Darnuir said. "I believe that Brackendon saved me, not some god. I believe Blaine saved us at Torridon by gathering the dragons. I believe in everyone here and we cannot rely on a greater power to save us."

"If we abandon the gods, what will we do?" Damien asked.

"We must forge a new way. All of us. Dragon, fairy and human together. Will you help me, Damien?"

"I watched you charge into an entire demon army alone and come out alive. Of course I shall follow you."

Brackendon cleared his throat loudly. "I might point out that, apart from me, it is only dragons here."

"For now, that is how it must be," Darnuir said. "Humanity is divided. Castallan has poisoned the minds of many against dragons. With the memories I have now, and after seeing how our elders talk about humans, it is small wonder. How can we expect anything to change if we will not? You are not just my new guard. I hope you will be the new symbol of our people. A bright new future, free from old hatred and prejudice." He hadn't meant this to become a speech but it felt right.

"My father married a human," one called out.

"My mother and I were saved and taken in by humans," said another.

Lira spoke next. "I would never have been granted this position were it not for you. Humans allow their women to be captains and hunters. Why not us? We're all in your debt, Darnuir." The other young women amongst his Praetorians nodded along at that.

"There is no debt you owe me for that," Darnuir said. "Let's continue. We have paused for long enough."

They ran on.

By the second evening, Darnuir's lungs and legs were beginning to give. At least, he thought it was the second evening. His mind felt muddled and he blinked fiercely in the dying light. It felt like nails were driving into his feet and knees with each step. It was far worse than the run from Torridon, what with this armour and their lack of proper breaks. At least then they had taken shifts, and gotten food and sleep.

A large inviting barn lay on a quaint estate ahead. It looked warm, homely and big enough to house them all. As his thoughts drifted towards the comfort of sleep, his legs stopped moving of their own accord. His mouth was dry, yet he felt sweat under the armour of his arms and torso.

"Something the matter?" Brackendon asked. The wizard looked and sounded perfectly fine.

"I think I'm done," Darnuir said, a little breathless. A series of loud gasping and coughing came from behind them. "I think we're all done."

"We should rest for a while."

"Think anyone is in?" Darnuir asked, pointing towards the little farmhouse by the barn. "It looks quiet."

"I don't imagine the farmer will try to stop you."

"Unless he has a host of red-eyed men hidden in that barn."

Brackendon shrugged. "We'll find out. None of you can continue like this."

Feeling utterly spent, Darnuir agreed.

As Darnuir lead his Praetorians to the farmhouse, he caught sight of an old woman staring gormlessly at them. When spotted, her eyes popped and she snapped her wooden shutter across the window, as if this would make Darnuir forget she existed. He thought, therefore, that there would be no need to knock on the door with the chipped orange paint. But no one came to greet them.

Anger began to coil within him, gathering like a clot around that piece of his old self he had taken from the rubies of the Dragon's Blade. He pushed the feeling down.

Darnuir knocked lightly upon the door.

Nothing.

Huffing, he knocked again. This time a little harder.

No one answered but he heard voices this time.

"They're at the door, Walt."

"I gathered that, Belinda, dear."

"Don't open it!"

"If they're here to rob us or kill us then a door will hardly stop them." There was another muffled and hurried exchange. Then, at last, the door creaked open and half a face peered at Darnuir from the other side. The man's skin was brown and leathery – evidence of years toiling in the field. "Hello," he said.

"Please, there is no need to be afraid," said Darnuir.

"No?" gulped the man, presumably Walt. "Dragons, yes?"

"All of us except for my friend Brackendon here. Though he is a wizard."

"A wizard?" Walt said, rather high-pitched.

"My name is Darnuir, King of Dragons. We've run long and hard, and recently fought an army of demons. I'd like to speak with the owner of this estate, if you could point us—"

"I'm the owner," said Walt. "Foulis, is my name. Walter Foulis. You might have heard of my family?"

"I'm afraid I cannot say that I have," said Darnuir. "But if you would allow my Praetorians and I to take shelter in your barn for the night, you would be doing us a kindness."

"I… I err, well," Walt stammered. "I shall, um, just check with my wife." And he disappeared, leaving the door ajar. A squeak of a whisper soon followed.

"Check with me? No, no, no. Just say it's fine – it's fine and maybe they'll leave us—"

The door opened a fraction more and the full face of Walter Foulis appeared.

"The barn, you said? Yes, I think that should be fine."

"My thanks to you," Darnuir said.

"But it ain't perfect," Walt qualified. "Holes in the roof, and some of the bays are cluttered."

"That won't be an iss—" Darnuir tried to say.

"And part of the enclosure nearby is broken, so we had to move the sheep into the barn," Walt rambled on.

"It need not be luxurio—"

"I admit to not being able to afford the repairs, but it isn't the first shame brought on my family. It's been impossible to find extra manpower since the king called up all able-bodied men to fight."

"All of them?" Darnuir said. "King Arkus has taken every man?"

"Those who can hold a spear or pull a bow," Walt said.

"He has," came the voice of his wife. The door was jerked wider, the little woman seeming to have found her spirit. "All of them. All the boys from all our tenants and they've had it hard enough already, just like everyone. So many, called up to fight again. Fight your battles," she added, pointing a shaking finger at Darnuir.

"Belinda," Walt said, aghast.

Darnuir was unsure of the pair. As they had a family name and tenants, they must have been some minor nobility, although very, very lowly judging from their surroundings. Whoever they were, they were angry with both him and Arkus. That gave Darnuir an idea.

"What your own king does or does not do is no fault of mine," Darnuir said. "But perhaps a deal can be struck? I have many strong dragons with me. We could fix your barn, your enclosure and other small jobs in exchange for a place to rest and a hot meal, if you can spare the food?"

"You – what?" Belinda was evidently caught off guard by the offer.

"We shall earn our keep," said Darnuir.

"They are quite handy," added Brackendon.

"Oh, well, that's very generous of you, my lord dragon," Belinda said, completely taken aback, her cheeks growing a shade pinker.

"Very gracious indeed, my lord," said Walt. He made a clumsy bow. "We thought that... well, it doesn't matter."

Darnuir smiled at the couple. "Perhaps you could show us what needs doing?"

Despite their fatigue, the Praetorians set to work within the hour. Some hammered up on the barn's roof, others repositioned the stakes of the enclosure's fence, and the heavy clutter in the barn itself was cleared. The hardest task was given to Lira, who attempted to encourage the shorn sheep back into their pen, but the animals ran enthusiastically in any direction but the open gate.

"A good farm dog might have served better," Brackendon said.

"You could help," Darnuir said.

"As could you."

"Yes, but I want to speak to you about Castallan. You keep saying it is a fight I must stay out of. But there must be something I can do? Surely you cannot duel him alone."

Brackendon frowned. "Your kind aren't suited to magic. That sword of yours might process the Cascade quicker than a hundred staffs for all I know, but the energy is a poison, and dragons are made weak by it. There's a reason you can't handle your ale."

"I am aware of that," said Darnuir. "But what do you expect me to do? Wait as a bystander while you tackle him alone? I cannot let you do that. Besides, I feel I have yet to push myself to my real limits. Perhaps I would fare better than you think."

"I admit you seem capable of drawing on more power than I would have thought," Brackendon said. "Your battle against Scythe was impressive. But Castallan is leagues beyond—"

"If I cannot help you to fight Castallan, then how am I or Blaine or any of us going to tackle Rectar one day?"

"On that, I'm not certain." Brackendon sagged a little. "Tell me, why are you so insistent on this? One might almost think it was personal."

Darnuir had to wonder whether Brackendon was just observant or clairvoyant. The wizard couldn't know about how Darnuir had aided Castallan in his past life – could he?

Gold, and time, and volunteers… what a mess I made.

"Well?" Brackendon asked. Darnuir's mouth twitched involuntarily and he looked anywhere but at Brackendon. Over by the enclosure, Lira had resorted to simply picking up the poor sheep and dumping them over the fence. The noise of the animals' protests cut right through him in his wearied state. And then he felt hunger. Was that roasted meat he could smell, or was his imagination merely wandering as he looked at the huddled sheep?

"Darnuir?" Brackendon said.

He could take the Dragon's Blade, pour out flames, take a bite.

"Darnuir," Brackendon said more sternly. Finally, Darnuir looked towards him, still not quite able to meet the wizard's eye. "That silence has told me all I need to know. What did you do? It isn't about Cassandra, is it?"

"No, not her," Darnuir said, his throat suddenly dry. *Though I've been such a fool there as well. Why did I kiss her? Stupid of me. It's my fault she fell. She was too close…* He coughed. "My old self left me a memory of Castallan. In it, I helped him. I came to him, even, looking for a new way to fight Rectar and his demons." Brackendon blinked silently at him. "Castallan promised he had some solution to the war. Something he was working on. Clearly, I was wrong, duped, reckless," he said at a pace, hoping Brackendon might latch on to one excuse or another.

"Anything else?" Brackendon asked. "About Castallan. Anything about what happened at the Cascade Conclave?"

"Nothing. It was before he turned openly as a traitor. I don't think he'd attacked the Conclave yet."

"That's disappointing."

"Which part? What I did or the lack of information on your old order?"

"Both," said Brackendon, looking lost in his own thoughts. Further discussion was halted by the emergence of Walter Foulis, carrying steaming bowls in both hands.

"We've made supper for you," he announced. "If you want it. If you like this sort of thing." Belinda bustled out behind him, more bowls in hand. The Praetorians eagerly dashed over.

"Just a moment," Darnuir told them.

"Nothing fancy, I'm afraid," Walt said. "Just some of the stores we won't be able to eat through with just the two of us." Darnuir took one of the bowls and inspected it. A dark watery gravy swirling around chunks of meat, carrot, mushroom and onion. He sniffed deeply, practically tasting the lamb, searching for any poison. There was nothing untoward in it, so far as he could tell.

"Just a precaution," said Darnuir, handing the bowl back to the nearest Praetorian. She began wolfing it down with a grin. Darnuir turned to speak to the farmer but he had already dashed off, leaving his wife behind. "You have my thanks, Lady Foulis," Darnuir said.

"Least we could do," Belinda said curtly. "You're helping us, after all. A damn sight more than King Arkus ever has."

"You are not fond of your king?" Darnuir asked.

"My husband's family has been struggling for generations," Belinda said. "King Arkus cares not." She sniffed. "I have some bread baking. It should be ready soon." With that, she stalked off. Walt reappeared shortly after, struggling with a large steaming pot. Darnuir went to him.

"Let me take that."

Walt let go without protest. "Thank you, my lord."

"I hope we have not offended Lady Foulis?"

"Forgive her, my lord," said Walt. "Arkus calling up the army has brought up old memories. Terrible memories. We lost our eldest boys in the last war twenty years ago. They died in the east, we were told, but we never received their bodies."

"She blames me," Darnuir said.

"She blames dragons."

"Do you blame me?"

"It used to be all I thought about," said Walt. "But I'm getting on, I've nearly broken my body trying to keep this estate in order, and I've brooded for long enough. We have Ruth now, such a sweet girl, and my youngest boy, Ralph, is in Brevia with the hunters. Smart boy. A good boy. He'll rise up and make things right again. I won't ever love you or your kind, mind."

"We aren't perfect," said Darnuir.

"If I may say, my lord dragon, you're nothing like I expected."

"And what did you expect?"

Walt paused, weighing his words. "A bit more aggressive, I suppose."

A part of Darnuir yearned to say, "You have no idea, human", but he managed to ask for more bowls instead.

By the time everyone had a bit of food in them, the repairs completed and the sheep forcibly returned to their pen, night had fallen and eyes began to droop. The Praetorians threw down a thick layer of straw on the barn floor and curled up on their bedrolls. It was pleasantly warm with the lingering heat of day still thick in the air.

"We'll sleep until dawn," Darnuir said. "Then we must be on our way." He noticed that Brackendon was out on a bank of grass, staring blankly ahead of him, his staff lying to one side. Darnuir picked himself up and walked to join him. "You should get some sleep as well," he said as he slumped down beside the wizard.

"I'll live," said Brackendon.

"You've been through worse."

"A fate I would never wish on anyone."

"Even Castallan?"

"Even that bastard. Be careful how you use the Cascade, Darnuir. You must tackle early signs of addiction quickly. The longer you leave it, the more energy you may feel you need to satisfy your craving in one burst. The risk of breaking grows exponentially."

"Were you addicted, before you broke?"

"I was, in my own small way. We all are to some degree. We just have to keep it manageable."

Darnuir looked at Brackendon then. Really looked at him – at the crease lines of his face, at his prematurely grey hair, and finally at his blackened, scaly fingers. Despite the stark warning of what might come, Darnuir's hand twitched towards the hilt of the Dragon's Blade. He clenched his fist just above the pommel.

"I've never thanked you, Brackendon. Not properly. Not in the way you deserve." Brackendon raised an eyebrow. "I mean it," Darnuir said. "You sacrificed so much, and not just for me. For the whole world. And I'm sorry it had to be that way."

"I was glad to do it," said Brackendon.

"I probably didn't deserve to be saved," Darnuir said. "Even now. What I did to Balack… if you hadn't been there…"

"But I was there," said Brackendon. "On both occasions. Fate has a miraculous way of placing us where we are needed."

"I'm trying to apologise," Darnuir said. "For everything."

"Don't take the whole world and everything in it on your shoulders. Even for you, it's too much. Still, I appreciate the sentiment. It's always nice to know one's hardships have been recognised." He smiled more kindly.

"Would you still have saved me if you had known I helped Castallan?"

"I didn't save you out of affection. You're too important. That sword of yours is too important. So no, it wouldn't have changed my decision. In fact, knowing the truth might have been useful. All these years I thought Castallan had acted alone; one selfish, power-crazed man. But you helped him along. Perhaps others did as well, either voluntarily or through trickery. Perhaps I have been thinking about this too simply."

"What do you mean?"

"I mean, I have a nagging feeling there is more to this. In attacking and destroying the Cascade Conclave, Castallan took a great risk. Back then, he was one wizard with one staff. It makes no sense for him to have attacked the Inner Circle. So, why did he? And how did he manage to succeed?"

"We'll never know," Darnuir said. "Unless we take him alive, and then it's only his word."

"The Conclave tower is still in Brevia to this day," said Brackendon. "I kept my distance on my brief visit earlier this year. People say it's cursed along with all the land near it. They call the borough the Rotting Hill now, but if there is a chance I might learn anything, I should go, as painful as it might be to re-enter that place. If I can find some clue as to how Castallan succeeded in defeating the rest of my order, then perhaps I can use that against him in turn."

"I will come with you," Darnuir said.

"No. I feel this is something I must do alone."

Unsure of what more to say, Darnuir settled for, "I understand. Please, try to get some rest. We can't afford to stop like this again."

"I think I will sit a while longer," Brackendon said, and returned to gazing blankly across the estate grounds. A light was still on in the unadorned farmhouse and Belinda Foulis was peering out at them again through the lattice of the window. When Darnuir and Brackendon both caught her in the act, she slammed a shutter across.

"Good night, Brackendon."

Darnuir returned to his own straw pile and bedroll. He curled up, too tired to even bother removing his armour, but sleep eluded him. Beads of cold sweat clung to his brow and along his arms, his right arm especially. A thirst grew in him for more than water. *Brackendon would stop me if he saw me do it, but I just need a little – just enough to help me rest tonight. That won't be so terrible.* In silence, he reached for the hilt of his sword; in his mind, he pushed down on the handle of the door.

His sigh was soft and long. And then he fell asleep.

On the morning of the third day of their run, the vast city of Brevia loomed into view. Darnuir had never seen anything so massive; not in his current life at any rate. Brevia looked as though the entirety of Cold Point could fit inside it a hundred times over. It curved around the bay like a great horseshoe, enveloped by thick walls with tall towers like rolling black hills. Further off, closer to the mouth of the bay, an enormous white bridge spanned the banks of the city, its cresting peak visible even at this distance.

"Black limestone," Lira said, drawing up to him. "Nearly all of that will have come from the Hinterlands. Maybe even from quarries near Tuath."

"Imposing," noted Brackendon. "Though far from cheery. Used to be a light brown stone that made up the walls."

"So why the change?" Darnuir asked.

Lira shrugged. "The king's wishes. For nearly ten years, Arkus ordered all black stone hewn in the Hinterlands to be brought to Brevia. I saw them hauling it off in mile-long wagon trails."

Darnuir thought on the only other great city from his choppy memories: Aurisha, the city of gold. Brevia looked startlingly different from it.

"A statement, perhaps," Darnuir said. "One we must bear in mind. Arkus sets humanity apart from dragons, even in the colour of his city."

"And there is Arkus' army," said Brackendon. "Look southwards." He pointed. Another city lay in the distance, this one of tents, carts and ditches. Like Brevia, the human army's camp was the largest Darnuir had ever set eyes on. Yet there were more than just humans assembled there.

"Then we can march on Castallan that much sooner," Darnuir said. Something in the camps caught his eye. "Are those palisade walls?" he indicated with a waving finger, drawing a line around a portion of the camps in the air.

"I'd say so," said Lira. "I think we have found the rest of our dragons."

"There could be thousands still out there for all we know," Darnuir said. "Unsure where to go, lost, hunted by Castallan's red-eyed servants or perhaps oblivious to events. Everything has moved so quickly."

"I also think we've been spotted," said Brackendon. Darnuir looked out again, seeing many black-clad figures moving in and out of the main camp. A small group appeared to be coming straight for them.

"Hunters," said Darnuir and Lira together.

"They wear the black leather of the Crownlands," said Lira.

"And now I understand why," said Darnuir, glancing once more at the hulking walls of Brevia.

"Well, we must make ourselves known somehow," said Brackendon, tapping his staff on the hard earth. He took one step closer to the city then winced, taking his head in one hand.

"Brackendon?" Darnuir asked in concern.

"It is nothing," Brackendon said. "A fleeting pain. Lack of sleep." The wizard gave nothing away.

"Just a little further now," said Darnuir. He called the same back to the Praetorians. "We shall be comparing the food and lodgings to that of the Argent Tree soon." The Praetorians smiled gratefully through their fatigue and followed him and Lira towards the human capital.

3

EVENING BY THE LOCH

It is said Dranus angered the gods and they cursed many dragons for his sin, warping their bodies into a weaker, human form. The mountain shattered, breaking a corner of the world and leaving behind a bluff of rock crumbling into the sea. Dranus himself was left scarred, his once golden scales charred black from the Cascade.

From Tiviar's Histories

Blaine – Inverdorn

Blaine smelled Inverdorn before he saw it. A potent mix of smoke and fish, reminiscent of Torridon, with the added stench of a city suffering from siege. He had expected a faint aroma of sweetness to accompany it, but there was none.

They are no longer afraid. Fidelm must have succeeded.

The town itself soon came into view. Lying where the River Dorain entered Loch Minian, it might have looked serene in the late afternoon light were it not for the piles of bodies. Smoke rose from smouldering mounds of demon corpses. Inverdorn itself seemed relatively unscathed, but he could not account for its inhabitants. Blaine's concern lay with the dragons that had been trapped there. In the aftermath of the ambush at the Charred Vale by traitorous hunters, his concern for humans was limited.

His focus was on his dragons. The Second, Third, Fifth and Sixth Legions were with him. It had been from the Third Legion that the bulk of his new Light Bearers had come, and he favoured their company. Indeed, when they had searched Scythe's encampment after the battle it had been members of the Third who had brought him the scrying orb from Scythe's possessions. Sensible of them. Such a powerful instrument had to be held with caution.

The legions made camp outside of Inverdorn and Blaine approached the walls with a score of his Light Bearers in tow. A dark figure with inky skin stood on the parapet above the gate. Fidelm flew down gracefully before Blaine, a lean arm outstretched.

"It is good to see you safe, Guardian."

"And you," Blaine replied, taking Fidelm's arm. The fairy had a few small cuts but nothing serious. His long, braided silver hair had avoided harm.

"Your timing is not so good," said Fidelm.

"What's the matter?"

"You interrupted my painting," said Fidelm. "The light this afternoon has been exquisite. I fear I shall miss it."

"There will be other occasions," Blaine said. "I see the city is now ours."

Fidelm nodded. "To be fair to the boy, his plan worked remarkably well. Dragons and hunters from within Inverdorn joined us in our attack. The demons were taken from both sides." Fidelm cast his eyes around. "Where is Darnuir?"

"He runs to Brevia," Blaine said.

"Alone?"

"The wizard is with him," said Blaine, "as is that girl and those younger dragons she has been gathering." He didn't like speaking of Lira by name. Darnuir's disregard for tradition would be a dangerous combination with that hothead of his. Still, Darnuir had proved himself. He had killed Scythe, won the day, and Blaine had given him the king's armour. The rest, he prayed, would come in time. Fidelm seemed to be mulling it over. "I thought we might allow our men to rest here before moving to Brevia," Blaine continued. "This day is done at any rate."

"Rest would do everyone some good, particularly the humans," Fidelm said. Blaine clenched his jaw with a low growl. "Is something amiss, Blaine?"

"Are there many hunters within the city?"

"A few hundred," said Fidelm.

"Have them brought out to join their fellows," Blaine said, waving a hand behind him. All the hunters left after the battle of the Charred Vale were wedged together between the legions. If any of the wretches tried to betray them now, they'd be swiftly crushed.

"I do not underst—"

"I shall explain when we have more privacy."

Fidelm nodded again, though slowly. "Open the gate," he yelled. The sound of clinking chains and mechanisms followed, and the thick oak doors swung inwards. Blaine threw up a staying hand to the legates who were awaiting their orders. His

Light Bearers knew to follow, however, and walked with him and Fidelm into the city.

"Stay vigilant," Blaine told his Light Bearers. "Our enemies could be anywhere."

Fidelm shot him a wary look before muttering to some nearby fairies. They flew off and Fidelm spoke quietly to Blaine.

"I shall take you into the fairy quarter, Guardian. We may trust the ears there."

Blaine kept close to Fidelm, and his Light Bearers fanned out in an arc behind them. He took in the scene of Inverdorn. In his long life, he had travelled to most places in the world, even if only once. Inverdorn was no exception. On their way to the fairy quarter, they passed the shores of Loch Minian; a small harbour, although far larger than the rundown jetties of Torridon. It lay in silence.

Blaine remembered it as a bustling place, stuffed with fishing boats, merchant and passenger barges, taking goods and those with coin quickly across the loch. Now it seemed a watery graveyard of forgotten ships. The market strip at the harbour's edge was also dead. There ought to have been the smell of sweet or bitter shimmer brew stalls mixed with the pang of fish and their purveyors yelling about their freshness. He recalled the barges being loaded with grain from the Golden Crescent and the comforting smell from the bakeries nearby. There had even been a fairy painting market-goers for a few coins. She'd get her subjects to sit on a stool in front of her while she worked them up. It had been a very different place back then, whenever that had been. A slower time; a peaceful time.

Is it my fault the world has turned to this? Death and mistrust. War and more war. My failure; my fault?

"Many people escaped before the demons cut the town off," Fidelm said, as if sensing Blaine's morose thoughts.

"It is not the city I remember," Blaine noted. There was one easel set up at the edge of the embankment, half a picture of a glittering loch sketched out, as if it were a ghost of former times.

"Perhaps I will have a chance to finish this tomorrow," Fidelm said, collecting his equipment.

"I have not seen you paint in many years," Blaine said.

"I find it cathartic to create something after a battle." Fidelm held up his work to inspect it briefly. "A little rough. I might be out of practice." Yet the general did not seem perturbed and motioned to Blaine they should continue.

They veered off the shoreline and wove back through the narrower streets, where the shopfronts and homes steadily became more colourful. Painted patterns and trees had been brushed up; some silver, some burnt black, some brown and green, just like the forest of Val'tarra. Fairies had made this area of town feel a bit more like home. Val'tarra had been Blaine's home for so long now that he found himself feeling more comfortable as well.

Fidelm paused to let a band of Crescent hunters march by, with fairies at the front and the back of their column. The Crescent hunters were hunched and wide-eyed, and looked to Blaine as they passed. He saw their eyes take in his armour; thick, starium-reinforced plate, with pauldrons shaped into large halves of a radiant sun. Blaine lifted his chin and pursed his lips. These hunters could be friend or foe. Better to keep them afraid just in case. Best to show them the might of the dragons. They passed soon enough and Fidelm continued.

"Are you sure this is necessary, Blaine?"

"Quite sure. Have you known me to do things without reason?"

"No. But I know you can be... extreme with your feelings."

"Extreme?" Blaine said. Fidelm faced him, one eyebrow raised. "Keep it to yourself for now," Blaine told him. How much Fidelm knew, Blaine could not have said. Likely he knew too much. The general was confidant to his queen in many matters. Why not her past relationships as well?

Thinking of her was a mistake. Kasselle's voice drifted unbidden into his mind. *"I don't think you should come back."* Unbidden, Blaine's hand curled inwards, searching for hers.

"Let us talk here," Fidelm said, leading them into a cramped garden square. Grass replaced the dirt and cobbles underfoot, and in the centre of the space grew a lone silver tree.

"I was not aware this area was so strong with the Cascade," Blaine said.

"The Dorain runs from the Highlands as well," Fidelm said, walking up to place a hand upon the silver bark. "The waters aren't as potent as the River Avvorn but they still carry some energy. When fairies first took this area for our own, they carried water from the river and wet the earth, hoping a piece of home would grow."

"It is as good a place as any to talk. Light Bearers," Blaine said, rounding on his men, "watch the streets and alleys. I will not be disturbed."

"Yes, Lord Guardian," they chanted. Fidelm gave a silent nod to the fairies in the vicinity and they trotted off.

"Your men seem to be in good spirits after the battle," said Blaine.

"Casualties were low," Fidelm said. "Not much the demons could do. They fought hard, though, and something peculiar did occur."

"With the spectres?" Blaine said knowingly.

"Indeed. You experienced something similar, I assume?"

"If the spectres here also abandoned the battlefield, then yes."

"It was as well they did," said Fidelm. "During the battle, the number of spectres we were fighting suddenly swelled and I thought the demons might hold. Hundreds of spectres joined the battle at once, yelling at each other. Yet as quickly as they appeared, they left, every one of them. Victory came easily after that as the demons went wild."

"They also fled at the Charred Vale," Blaine said. "According to Darnuir they scarpered after he killed Scythe."

"Scythe?" asked Fidelm, perplexed. "The dead captain of the Boreac hunters?"

"Turned out he wasn't as dead as we'd assumed," Blaine said. "Stone cold now though, his red eyes extinguished."

"What happened up there?" Fidelm said. "I've not failed to notice that Cosmo, or should I say Prince Brallor, is not with you either. Has he run on to Brevia with Darnuir as well? Why would he leave his son behind with you? And what of this battle you speak of? I thought the plan was to harass the foe, not meet them in the open field."

"Cosmo is dead," Blaine said stiffly. "And I have his son. Cullen will be cared for well enough."

"He's dead?" Fidelm said, sounding crestfallen. "Of all the things to have gone wrong..."

"A lot went wrong," Blaine sighed. He explained everything as best he could; how the hunters, who had vanished as they marched east through Val'tarra, were red-eyed traitors in service to Castallan. He told Fidelm of their strength, their speed, their burning hatred for dragons. He left nothing out; not even Darnuir injuring that human boy, Balack. Cosmo's death was explained; pinned up against a tree by a sword. "There was even an incident with Cassandra," he added darkly.

"What of her?"

"She was taken by a group of those red-eyed hunters. Back to the Bastion, I assume."

"Why take her?" Fidelm asked. "To lure Darnuir? The boy has a soft spot for her, that is clear at a hundred paces, but Castallan must know we would come for him eventually."

"It transpires she is really a princess, sister to Cosmo—"

"Brallor," Fidelm corrected.

"Dead, either way," Blaine said. "Cassandra is Arkus' daughter. Taken by Castallan when Aurisha fell."

"For what purpose?" Fidelm said.

"Leverage, presumably."

"Perhaps once," said Fidelm. "Yet Arkus remarried. He has a new son; a new heir. I cannot imagine Arkus being held in place for fear of a daughter he never knew. Not after all these years."

"You'd know better than I," Blaine said.

"And you would know if you took a greater interest in the humans," Fidelm said.

Blaine ignored him. "Arkus cannot be the best of leaders if he has allowed his people to become so fractured, willing to turn to a traitorous wizard who fraternises with Rectar."

"Arkus has lasted this long. There must be something to him. Handling that Assembly is no easy feat. Takes both subtlety and a good measure of cunning." Fidelm stared at Blaine for a moment, then looked up. Blaine had heard it too. It sounded like something had landed in the branches, but he saw nothing other than a few silver leaves fluttering down.

"And you sent Darnuir to Brevia?" Fidelm continued. "On his own? Humanity will shut its gates to us."

"Of course, I didn't," Blaine said, snapping his eyes back from above. "He went of his own accord. Yet they might be more willing to listen to him, given his upbringing amongst humans. And I'm hopeful Brackendon will guide hi—"

There was a squawk from above and Kymethra descended from the upper branches in a storm of feathers, morphing from eagle to woman. Her green robes flapped around her from the force of the fall and her eyes bored into Blaine's "Brackendon? I've not seen him with you. Blaine, tell me. Is the man I love—"

"He was quite well last I saw him," Blaine said irritably. "This was meant to be a private discussion, Kymethra." She visibly sagged with relief.

"I'll leave you be," she said. "Just tell me where he went."

"To Brevia, with Darnuir," said Blaine.

"Then I'll go now," Kymethra said. She stood poised, ready to jump back into her eagle form. "Any message you'd like me to take?"

"Only that I have arrived at Inverdorn," said Blaine. "Tell Darnuir I will allow the men to rest, then rendezvous at Brevia as planned." With that, Kymethra leapt into the air. Her body transformed into the tawny eagle in one fluid motion, the white tips of her feathers shining brightly as she caught the setting sun.

"Well," Fidelm said with an air of finality. "The humans will be watched for now. I shall let you take your rest, Guardian."

"I need no rest. I rested for decades. It is time I made up for it. What of the dragons that were held up here before you lifted the siege? Were any injured or killed?"

"Yes, as often occurs in battles. We set up a field hospital at one of the larger dry docks."

"I shall visit them. Their faith is likely to be lacking after their ordeals."

Fidelm gave an exaggerated bow. "I shall have you escorted there. We shall speak later, I'm sure."

The fairy who led Blaine and his Light Bearers to the field hospital was quick and quiet. That suited Blaine just fine. The evening was nice enough after all. A clear sky meant the odds of a spectre attack were minimal, if the spectres were even coming back. The surface of Loch Minian was flat and glassy, reflecting Inverdorn like a mirror; each building, each boat and each pebble on the shore. And then he saw them, reflected on the water's surface: barrels.

So many of them. Scores of them, strung out in stacks along the wharfs. Blaine looked up and saw they ran up to the edge of the building his fairy guide was entering.

Blaine's heart missed one long beat.

"Wait," he called out to the fairy. "Do you know what is in these barrels?"

The fairy looked in the direction Blaine was pointing. "No, Lord Guardian," he said, sounding confused. "At least, not all. Many were scattered throughout the city. Some have fruit from Val'tarra, many grain from the Crescent. Some contain a strange black powder no one recognises."

Blaine felt a chill. Black powder; dragon powder; the substance that blazed a trail of destruction on their run from Torridon. He turned to his Light Bearers. All had been on that run. Their faces showed they understood. "We must separate the barrels of black powder," he told them quickly. "They mustn't be close to each other or the city. Take them out to the shore or into the loch itself. I don't want them anywhere near the army."

"Yes, Lord Guardian," they said in unison and hurried off.

"Take no risks," Blaine called after them. "No flame must come near the powder. Work fast to beat the dying sun." The fairy guide looked apprehensive. "Are there any more within the city?"

"Possibly, sir."

"Possibly?" said Blaine, his voice rising. "Return to General Fidelm at once. We must find every single barrel of black powder and move them to a safe location. I should have warned Fidelm of this danger, but how was I to know..." He trailed off, speaking more to himself. The fairy stood stock-still, unsure. "Well? Go!" Blaine told him and the wingless fairy scarpered. Blaine took a deep breath before entering the dry dock that doubled as a field hospital.

Cranes, pulleys, saws and other tools had been pushed against the walls to open out the space. Dragons, fairies and humans lay bedridden in various bloodied states. Fairy healers glided elegantly around, supported by some hunter colleagues. And was that one of his Light Bearers amongst the sick dragons? It was either that or another dragon had stolen one of their shields. He had his back to Blaine, leaning over a dragon whose head was covered in bandages soaked with dark blood.

"You there," Blaine called. "Light Bearer." The dragon turned, but his expression was not guilty. Blaine recognised those black curls; that olive skin; the presence Blaine could not quite explain, yet it was there. Irrefutably so. Blaine had been keeping his eye on Bacchus since the Charred Vale. The young Light Bearer was now one of the most enthusiastic in his duties.

As Bacchus stepped away from the bedside, the wounded dragon grabbed his hand. "No. Please," he said. "Don't leave — the pain..."

"I shall return shortly, brother," Bacchus said and gently kissed the injured dragon on the brow.

A little tender, perhaps. But it does have a comforting effect.

"Lord Guardian, I thought there would be dragons here in need of N'weer's blessing," Bacchus said. His voice was measured and steady.

"I would not have neglected them," Blaine said.

"I did not envision you would, Your Holiness. I only sought to serve while you attended other matters. Forgive me."

Blaine noticed that nearly every dragon was looking their way. More specifically, they were looking to Bacchus.

"You are forgiven, brother Bacchus," Blaine said. "But know that I trust my Light Bearers to many important tasks, not only in the work of the gods. You were on duty to guard Cullen for a reason."

"Four Light Bearers seemed sufficient for an infant human."

"An infant human that finds itself the heir to the throne of Brevia."

"I only wished to help our own people. Forgive me, Lord Guardian."

His earnestness cooled Blaine. "We defend our race's faith but we guard it in other ways as well. You acquitted yourself well in the battle. A talented warrior and devout believer such as yourself holds great promise. Trust in me and you will see the Light."

"How may I serve?" Bacchus asked.

"Return to comforting the wounded for now. I—"

"Lord Guardian," a voice said from behind. Blaine turned to see three Light Bearers.

"I thought I gave clear instructions?" he barked at them.

"We'll need more help to move all these barrels before sundown, sir," the leading Light Bearer said. That worried Blaine. Healers around the dry dock were lighting candles already.

"I shall aid you," Bacchus offered.

"Very well," said Blaine. "One of you run and fetch more of your brothers with all haste. As many as you see fit, but ensure a strong guard is kept on the child, Cullen. The rest of you go to help with the barrels." They all dashed off, drawing stares from the wounded and the healers. Blaine was on the verge of leaving to deal with the barrel issue when something stopped him – or rather, someone.

Though he was at some distance, one of the hunters seemed familiar. He was in white leathers from the waist down, but his torso was bare, revealing his bandaged chest. He favoured one side as he carefully got into a battered bed, helped along by a healer. Blaine was sure it was Balack.

Something came over Blaine when he saw him. It wasn't pity; not exactly. Darnuir had been brash and foolish in striking him, but all Blaine really knew was the two had once been firm friends. Likely, that was no longer the case. Still, Balack knew Darnuir in ways that Blaine did not, and if Blaine shared his secrets with Darnuir, he would get to know Darnuir's in turn. It would be painful enough for Blaine. His heart ached at the thought of Arlandra. How had he let such horrors befall his only daughter? Instinctively, he reached for the necklace and lightly touched the little A upon it, under the apple of his throat.

The crowd parted before him as he made his way towards Balack and the air grew sweet.

They are afraid of me. Good.

"Are you the hunter named Balack?" Blaine asked.

"I think you know that," Balack said. His voice was hoarse, as though it pained him to draw breath. He winced as the healer made a W shape with her hands and gently pushed her palms on the bruised area of his chest.

"Breathe in for me," she instructed, shooting an apprehensive look at Blaine. Balack breathed in, but gasped midway.

"Gah. I'm sorry."

"Don't be," said the healer. "A damaged rib is no minor thing." She pressed her palms on the healthy side of Balack's chest. "Again, if you can." Balack breathed in, slower than before, and managed to do so without stopping this time. Blaine saw the pain in the boy's bloodshot, watery eyes.

"You're doing well," the healer said. "Expansion is up from a few days ago. I just need a quick listen." She brought out a small brass device, like a horn. She pressed the larger end against Balack's injured side and her ear to the other.

Balack groaned again. "Strong, aren't you? You dragons. Could crush us all with your bare hands." Blaine looked the boy in the eye and Balack did not turn away. Blaine sniffed gently at the air. The sweetness had grown, but he doubted it was from Balack. "I'm as fine as I'm going to be today," Balack told the healer. "You should tend to people who need you more."

"Make sure you move as little as possible," the healer said. As she left, the potency of the sweet smell diminished.

"She's afraid of me," Blaine said.

"Of course she is," Balack wheezed. "You've treated every human at the Charred Vale like a criminal. We're not the enemy."

"How can I possibly know that," asked Blaine, "when your own Captain Scythe turned out to be a traitor? Not only a traitor but the leader of Castallan's forces, no less."

"People are good at hiding their true selves, I'll grant you that, Guardian."

"I've wondered where Darnuir got his insolence from. Maybe you were the bad influence on him."

Balack gave a pained smile. "What do you want?"

"To know why Darnuir struck you."

"Not out of concern for me, I'd wager," said Balack.

"I will be blunt with you. There are things about my past that Darnuir wishes to know. One day soon, I shall have to tell him. But I find it most unjust that he should have things hidden from me. We are linked, Balack. Darnuir and I," he unsheathed the Guardian's Blade, "our swords are linked. If he is to be at my side when we face Rectar, I'd know everything about him."

At last, Balack turned his gaze away from Blaine. The boy wasn't hesitant to speak; just saddened. "Why did he hit me? Well, a painful secret was revealed to me, and I said some rather nasty things to him in return. And then he lost his temper... all over something rather pathetic in the end." His gasping voice finally broke.

"There was a girl," Blaine said. It was a statement, not a question.

"He told you? Heh." Balack's laugh was blunted and pained. "Suppose he told everyone before me." Another gasp. "And he never even told me."

"He didn't tell me," said Blaine. "But I'm old, boy. When you've lived to see generation after generation grow, you see the same patterns repeating. A common way for two friends to come to blows."

Balack closed his eyes. "I loved her. She did not love me. Darnuir knew, but that did not stop him."

"Yes. I've heard that tale before."

Balack reopened his eyes, a colder fury in them now. "You want loyalty? Don't rely on him."

"I'm afraid I'll have to," said Blaine. He looked Balack over again and the pity he'd felt changed. Something in Blaine compelled him to say, "I understand the pain you're feeling."

"I don't need your false sympathy," Balack said.

"It's not false. I told you, I'm old. You don't get to my age without losing a lot. Like those you love the most." *What's come over me? Why am I talking about this with him?*

"Does it get any better?" Balack said.

"Barely, but you learn to soldier on anyway. You learn to throw yourself into your duty or find something to wake up for besides the person who's forever gone."

And I must learn to let Kasselle go. I have my purpose again. Prepare Darnuir, restore faith to the dragons. Defeat the Shadow. Enough to get on with. Despite this, his hand curled in. When it found only air, he had to fight back a tear. *Not in front of the human. Get a grip on your emotions.*

Balack rubbed at something in his eye. "Is there anything else you need, Guardian?"

"Not now. N'weer speed you to health, human."

"I thought your gods only —" He stopped, staring behind Blaine.

"What's wrong?" Blaine asked, spinning to see for himself. Not far away from them, at the main entranceway to the dry dock, fairies were moving equipment to make space. As Blaine watched he saw them uncover four dark barrels. One lifted the lid to see what was inside, waving at his fellow to come over. The companion held a torch.

Blaine's blood turned to ice.

His heart stopped.

Then came the flash.

It seemed to take forever for the bang to reach him, an ear-splitting roar.

Something in him reacted and he threw himself between the blast and Balack. He felt the impact on his back, his starium-reinforced armour absorbing the blows of debris. Intense heat followed and Blaine thought he would cook alive in his metal casing.

He looked down at the human he was shielding. Balack's eyes were white with shock. He'd curled up into a ball despite his broken rib.

Blaine held on.

He realised he was screaming but couldn't hear himself. Then he choked, gasping in pain as something hot and sharp pierced the back of his knee, between the joints in his armour. He buckled but kept low over Balack.

He just held on.

4

THE COURT OF BREVIA

When Dranus returned, he claimed the gods were using the dragons as tools in an endless fight against the Shadow. Furious, Aurisha dubbed his brother a heretic, exiling him and those who had been cursed into human bodies. Out of brotherly love, Aurisha allowed them to go in peace, thinking that they would wither and die in time.

From Tiviar's Histories

Darnuir – Brevia – The Throne Room

"Nervous?" Brackendon asked as they waited to enter King Arkus' throne room. The door in front of them was immense. Painted black, it was patterned with white gold and had sliding openings that allowed the attending servants to mutter quietly to colleagues on the other side.

"Not at all," Darnuir said. "Some rest would have been welcome, but it cannot be helped." He yawned and strained to keep his eyes open.

Arkus wouldn't have been difficult to deal with if Darnuir's memories of his former self had borne any accuracy, but he hadn't been left full memories of the human king so much as feelings and impressions he had of Arkus back then. All were laced with derision and scorn, making them far from intimidating.

"You seem half asleep," Lira said.

She's right. I need to be more alert than this.

Darnuir touched the blood-red hilt of the Dragon's Blade with the tips of his fingers, opening the door to the Cascade by a crack. Energy dripped into his system, staving off the worst aches of his muscles. He felt lighter, even glad, as the residue drained down his right arm.

"You shouldn't rely on that," Brackendon said so only Darnuir could hear.

Darnuir let go of the Dragon's Blade. "It was only a little."

"A little is how it begins. A lot is how you break."

"I am about to meet another king," Darnuir said. "I hope to show Arkus that I am a changed dragon. It won't do for me to fall asleep in the middle of the conversation."

"Being polite won't go amiss either. Mind your manners." Nearby, a servant wearing a black velvet doublet over a white shirt coughed loudly. "See, he knows what I mean," Brackendon said.

"Does Arkus usually keep guests waiting this long?" Darnuir said.

"His Majesty will call for you when he is ready," the servant said laboriously.

"He knows there is a war on, right?" Darnuir said. The servant provided no response, which irked Darnuir.

Is this some power play? Making me wait while an invasion looms upon us, while Castallan is still at large – while Cassandra is still hostage...

He breathed gently through his nose and calmed. He shouldn't get wound up before even entering the court.

"What about you, Lira?" Darnuir asked. "Nervous?"

She bit her lip, thinking for a moment. "As nervous as when I met you. Kings can have that effect."

"I feel that was due to Blaine's ever-soothing presence."

"The Lord Guardian was certainly intimidating," Lira said.

"Still, you held your ground," Darnuir said. "You won me over that day and this time you have the company of forty loyal dragons." The stony-faced servant, who had an ear against one of the openings, coughed again.

"Can we be of assistance?" Brackendon asked.

"Will all of your company be entering the throne room?" asked the servant.

"Certainly," said Darnuir. "I'm sure the court will not object to the presence of my Praetorian Guard." More muttering was exchanged at the door. To his side, Darnuir heard Brackendon groan again. "Are you sure you are all right?"

"It's not sore, it's..." But whatever it was Brackendon seemed reluctant to say. He held his head and scrunched his eyes shut. "It's nothing. I think I just need to sit for a moment," he said, dropping into a plush high-backed chair with a footstool. "We ran a long way after all." He sighed and stretched out luxuriously.

"You may enter, Lord Darnuir," announced the servant. Brackendon grumbled as he got back up.

"Form ranks," Darnuir ordered and the dragons snapped into place.

The huge throne room doors opened silently, revealing a long hall with polished benches facing each other in rows along the high walls. At the distant end sat a black throne on a raised white stone platform. On the upper benches the people were finely dressed, the extravagance of the garments diminishing with each level to those standing in attendance. Black walls continued high up into an arching roof, as though the throne room was draped in a dark cloak. Above, a system of shutters directed light to bathe the clean white floor before the throne.

"Announcing Lord Darnuir, King of Dragons," the servant called and audible murmuring swept through the court. "The Reborn King, wielder of the Dragon's Blade." The murmuring grew louder. "Also announcing," the servant went on, straining to be heard, "Brackendon, the Last Wizard."

"If only it wasn't so," muttered Brackendon.

"And the dragon Lira," the servant added, "Prefect of the Praetorian Guard."

Darnuir heard Lira gulp.

"Head up now," he told her, then took his first steps into the warm, stuffy throne room. Thick wafts of lavender and honey clogged his nose. He wondered whether the perfume was for his benefit or those on the benches. Such a sweetness would mask any sickly-sweet scent of human fear.

He focused on the great chair at the end of the hall, kept his face passive and walked with confidence. He was a dragon; the King of Dragons. In military matters, he held command of the Three Races. Even Arkus must answer to him.

But Arkus was not sitting on his throne.

Arkus wasn't there at all.

A line of guards stood before the steps to the throne's platform, but Darnuir struggled to see due to the angle of the light that was now shining into his eyes. Entering the pool of light made it worse. What lay at the top of the stairs was now a mystery. Yet the dark steel armour of the guards was familiar; their faces were hidden behind closed visors. Darnuir stopped as close as he dared to them, within arm's length.

All was still. He could hear the breath of the closest chevalier. Ahead, a door opened with a swish, followed by a pitter-patter of soft-soled shoes along the platform.

"Halt there, my Lord of Dragons," a voice announced. The speaker had a distinct pomposity about him.

I know that voice. It's the chevalier from Inverdorn.

"Raymond?" Darnuir said.

"Silence while you await His Majesty," said Raymond. Yes, it was most certainly the chevalier.

More time passed.

More silence.

Come along, Arkus. We do not have time to wait on games and posturing.

Yet more time drifted on and still the hall was silent.

Then, without warning, the light shifted.

Shutters over the windows were repositioned and the platform of the throne was thrown into relief. The black chair was simple but arresting, and a smaller version stood beside it. The change of light must have been a signal to the court because Darnuir heard everyone in the hall get to their feet.

Finally, a door at the back of the platform opened with a bang and King Arkus strode into view. His feet were hidden beneath his long black robes with white-trimmed edges. Darnuir's memory of Arkus was of a man with black hair to match his attire, yet the years had greyed him, his stubble was now a beard and his eyes, though small, were probing.

Arkus made a meal out of sitting down, sinking slowly into his throne. When at last he was settled, the shutters above snapped loudly, changing the direction of the light. A few faint rays converged just above Arkus' head, illuminating his crown. Arced and falling, like crashing waves, the crown looked to be pure white gold. It was a speck of radiance amongst the darkness of his robes, his throne and his expression.

The silence held a while longer.

Darnuir lost his patience and said, "How long must the King of Dragons wait? How long mus—" But Arkus threw out a hand towards him.

Darnuir felt a hot prickle on the back of his neck. A little heat even crept dangerously up his throat and he felt the Dragon's Blade warm at his waist.

No. I must show that I have changed.

"The court will remain standing for the *King's Lament*," Raymond said.

From the front of the crowd, two minstrels made their way onto the platform: one all in black, the other in white. The minstrel in white produced a flute and began to play sombrely at a high pitch, as though a deep and devouring sadness was whistling on the wind. The minstrel in black began to sing, his voice light yet tinged with melancholy:

> *There once was a black-haired beauty,*
> *With starlight in her eyes,*
> *There once was a black-haired beauty,*
> *Her smile was my demise,*
> *There once was a black-haired beauty,*
> *Whom I loved with all my soul,*
> *There once was a black-haired beauty,*

Now there's no one there —
At all.

The singer's voice cracked poignantly on the final words, as though the full weight of his grief had become unbearable. Both performers gave a small bow and then hurried off.

Two more people walked onto the platform. A pale woman came first, wearing a tiara of white gold on top of her elaborately tied blond hair. She took the smaller seat beside Arkus. Darnuir assumed she was the queen, although he had no memory of her.

Am I looking at Cosmo's mother? If so, she will be Cassandra's mother as well, although they look nothing alike.

Behind her came a man, and one singularly out of place. He had a wind-beaten, squashed face that was coated in a reddish fuzz. His figure was slender, his movements fox-like. Short in stature and short on adornments, his only jewellery was the longship brooch pinned to his chest. He stood on Arkus' left, between the king and Raymond.

Arkus, whose hand had remained outstretched for the whole song, finally brought his arm back in. He paused to cover his eyes, as if he were crying. Then, at last, it was done. Those gathered in the hall sat back down.

"My good king," Darnuir said, forcing down the heat in this throat. "We have run far and hard for days to reach you."

"No one asked you to." Each word Arkus said was well measured to ring throughout the hall. "You have come unannounced. You have come without invitation. You have come seeking the blood of my people."

"Bodies, bought and bled," came a soft echoing chant from around the room. It wasn't said by all but it was said by enough. *This isn't going to be easy.*

"It is Rectar who seeks to bleed your people dry," Darnuir said. "I only ask that some is spilled. All the Three Races will suffer before the end. I request that humanity's armies join me in destroying Castallan at the Bastion. I ask they join me to meet a demon invasion I have warning will come from the east."

"Yes, this invasion," Arkus said airily. "Raymond dutifully informed me." He waved a hand at the chevalier. It was only now that Darnuir realised Raymond was not in armour like the other chevaliers. Instead, he was in more courtly attire, a black velvet jerkin over a white shirt.

"I am glad to see you heeded his warning," said Darnuir. "Having your armies gathered will save precious time."

"Ha," squawked the man beside Arkus. "Time's oot, am afraid." He had a sharp voice, as though he was permanently biting into a lemon.

"My Lord Darnuir," Arkus began, with barely concealed bitterness. "May I introduce to you Somerled Imar, Lord of the Splintering Isles. He arrived not two days ago, with harrowing news."

Darnuir's stomach knotted, knowing fine well what that news would be. The Splintering Isles lay between east and west.

"A pleasure, Lord Darnuir," Somerled said, bowing. "The Splintering Isles are already under attack. My son, Grigayne, leads a desperate defence of our lands." A great deal of murmuring then rose in the hall.

"Silence," Raymond called.

The knot inside Darnuir tightened. "I am deeply troubled to hear that, Lord Somerled. My thoughts are with your son and your people."

"I'd rather have yer sword and yer dragons," Somerled said. "What good are thoughts?"

"My dragons are still scattered," Darnuir said. "Although many have arrived outside Brevia, I noticed. It grieves me to hear that the fight has already come on two fronts but Castallan has to be removed first before we can aid the Splinters."

"On that I agree," Arkus said. "The wizard has remained at large for too long. Yet I am hesitant to move, Darnuir. That fortress will not fall easily. You ask for some blood to be spilled, yet if we throw ourselves against the Bastion, then blood will surely gush."

"Nor will the Splinters last if ye have tae lay a siege," Somerled said.

"We'll be forced to assault the fortress," said Darnuir. "But I am hopeful it will fall without us wasting lives."

Darnuir knew that Cassandra had escaped through some secret tunnels. If they could be found again then countless lives would be spared. Arkus, of course, knew none of this, so he added, "I can explain this to you in private."

"Oh, can you?" Arkus said. "I'd listen more closely if you had more to offer than vague promises."

"Offer you?" Darnuir said, fighting down a fresh rage. *Calm. I must remain calm. This is just the exhaustion.*

Yet Arkus' smug look reignited the heat in his throat. Pressure built at the door to the Cascade in his mind, looking to fuel the fire.

I must be better than I was.

"Yes," said Arkus impatiently. "What do you offer me in return for my armies and my fleet? Dragons alone cannot win this fight. Dragons die the same, after all."

That did it.

"Offer, Arkus?" Darnuir roared. In doing so, he lost control of the door in his mind; it slipped ajar and a stream of Cascade energy surged into him. It magnified his voice to dominate the throne room. "I am the King of Dragons. Commander-in-Chief of the Three Races, am I not? I do not offer, Arkus. I demand." Outrage erupted from the audience. Hearing swords slide from sheaths behind him, Darnuir spun to reassure his Praetorians, gesturing they lower their weapons. Brackendon groaned, audible even over the outpouring from the crowd, but Darnuir knew what would quieten them. "What I will offer you is news," he yelled. "News of your son, and daughter." The crowd settled. The queen gasped, looking stricken.

"They are alive?" she said, half-shaking, though whether from fear or happiness Darnuir couldn't tell.

"Hush now, Oranna," Arkus said softly, offering her his hand. Oranna took it and seemed to settle. Then Arkus rounded on Darnuir. "My son is dead. My daughter was lost to me too, or do you not recall that?"

"My memories from my past life are few, but yes, I remember that," Darnuir said. His voice had returned to normal. He did not wish to mention that he had failed Cassandra a second time.

She was too close.

"Yet I promise you Cassandra is alive," Darnuir said. "Taken hostage by Castallan. I swear to you she lives." Arkus didn't even flinch at the words. He seemed unmoved. "I must also tell you of your son, Brallor, though I knew him as Cosmo." This time Arkus' features snapped into focus as he peered down at Darnuir.

"If you are here to open old wounds then I must caution you. The last time I laid eyes on you, Darnuir, you held my infant daughter in your arms. And the contempt I saw in your eyes panicked me. I feared you would simply dash her head upon the rocks that separated us. It worked out the same. You failed to make it through Aurisha to me and my daughter was lost."

The hall murmured once more, as though they had rehearsed this timing.

"And you were never to see my grief, my woe," Arkus went on. "As if you would have cared. It was almost too much to bear, to lose a second child. The pain – you cannot imagine. My first wife could not weather it. Her heart broke first and her body followed." Arkus paused. The queen beside him, his new queen, squeezed her husband's hand. "My son is dead," Arkus said flatly. "Do not think some memory of him will help me now."

"Arkus, painful though it is, you must hear this," Darnuir said. "It has bearing upon you all. Your son lived. Brallor lived. He spent his years in the Boreac Mountains as a hunter."

"It is true, Majesty," Brackendon interjected. "I must admit I was the one who took him from you. He asked me to take him away from the city, as far away as I could. I took him to Cold Point, where my staff tree once grew."

Arkus got up from his throne. "Will you make a mockery of my court with these stories? Demand your armies, Darnuir, and be gone!"

The crowd grew more restless, shouting, taunting and jeering.

"Sire," Lira cautioned Darnuir, but he pushed on. This wound Arkus bore still had poison in it. The man needed it drawn. He needed closure.

"He took a new name: Cosmo," Darnuir bellowed, "and he took a wife. They had a son."

This time the silence was so complete that Darnuir felt he had gone deaf. Arkus' face froze, his mouth half open. Queen Oranna paled even further, turning as white as the floor on which Darnuir stood.

"A son?" she said shrilly.

"Cullen is his name. Your grandson."

"How old is he?" snapped the queen.

"Mere months," Darnuir said. "Only a baby. But an heir all the same."

"Silence," Arkus cried, all his stiffness gone.

"My king and husband has an heir," Oranna said tartly. "Our son, Thane, a boy of eight years. A good and strong prince."

"And unlikely tae make it tae his ninth year if that cough keeps up," Somerled said. Oranna shot him a look of pure venom. "Oh, it's terrible sounding," Somerled added, a cunning smile playing on his lips.

"Enough," Arkus said, looking first to Somerled, then his wife, then Darnuir. "You dragons and your tempers. You have my full attention now, Dragon King. I hope that satisfies you. We shall speak later. The court is dismissed."

"You will rise for the king," cried Raymond, but his voice was drowned by the crowd.

"Bought and bled. Bought and bled. Bought and bled."

"Order," Raymond yelled but it had little effect. The chevaliers around the platform braced themselves, hands flying to the hilts of their weapons.

"Bought and bled. Bought and bled. Bought and bled."

Chevaliers were moving to encircle Arkus and Oranna, waving urgently, and attempting to take them away. Somerled Imar had quietly slipped away in the confusion.

"Bought and bled. Bought and bled. Bought and bled for dragon wars."

Darnuir felt something smash off his heavy pauldrons. Shards of glass littered the white stone at his feet and an amber liquid dripped off his armour. Soon more items were being thrown down on him and his Praetorians. They drew their swords in response. Darnuir didn't stop them. He'd just put an end to it.

Pulling forth the Dragon's Blade, Darnuir launched a blistering lance of fire into the air. He sent it up to the ceiling then split the flames and sent four strands arching against the roof of the hall. The noise of it covered even the shrieking crowd, and after holding it for a few moments, Darnuir killed it, bringing a silence once more. His throat felt hot and raw, but he barely even felt the residue from the Cascade flow down his arm. A gentle kick hit the back of his head and he felt very satisfied. A grin broke out across his face.

I must be getting more used to it. I can handle more.

In the eerie quiet, not a soul stirred in the hall other than Arkus.

The human king got back to his feet. "The court is dismissed."

5

THE CASCADE CONCLAVE

Despite their exile, Dranus and his Black Dragons flourished. They found a new home at Kar'drun, building the world's first great city on the eastern coast, and burrowed into the mountain itself for extra safety. Aurisha became concerned that Dranus would use the Cascade under Kar'drun to try and reach the gods again. More than that, he worried that Dranus had fallen to the Shadow. And so Aurisha convinced the fairies to aid him in transforming the rest of his true dragons into human form, in order that they might root out the Black Dragons from their mountain home. This was the Third Flight and the start of a long, devastating conflict.

From Tiviar's Histories

Brackendon – Brevia – The Rotting Hill

After the excitement of the throne room, Brackendon was more than happy to seek a little quiet, though whether that quiet would benefit him or not was another matter. While Darnuir had chased after Arkus, Brackendon had excused himself. He had some personal business to attend to. He was going to the Cascade Conclave.

The tower of the Conclave loomed upon a hill in the north-west of the city and could be seen from any point in Brevia. Only the enormous white bridge that spanned the far banks of the city could rival its height. From a street near the edge of the borough, Brackendon glanced at the tower and pulled up the hood of his cloak against the drizzling rain. The weather had turned foul since their entry to the capital that morning; it was now muggy and Brackendon's robes were sticking to his skin. No one paid him any attention as he walked; city dwellers hurried about their business or went indoors to escape the unpleasant weather.

As he approached the borough of the Conclave, he wondered what had become of the botany shops, bookmakers, and especially the bakers who made their living from the Conclave's existence. Within another street or so he saw his answer.

Closed.

Closed, boarded up or looted. And this was just one street a fair distance away.

There was something akin to mist before him, a blue and silver fog floating unnaturally at waist height. It halted abruptly halfway up this street, creating a border with the rest of the city. He looked once more towards the tower.

And he heard the whisper again.

Brraaaccck-eendon.

It was the feeblest of voices, but a voice nonetheless. He thought he had first heard it when he'd reached the outskirts of the city, and then again outside the throne room.

Brraaaccck-eendon.

It sounded uncertain, as though the speaker were learning a new language. Yet there was also an agony in it that chilled his blood more than any demon ever had. Whatever it was, his instincts told him it came from the tower.

He took his first steps into the swirling vapour.

"Wait," a small voice said. Brackendon turned slowly and found himself facing a group of young children, too young to be out on their own. A bold boy in baggy clothes spoke to him. "You can't go that way. It's haunted."

"Haunted by what?" Brackendon asked.

"A demon," said a little girl.

"No, it's a ghoul," another girl said. Both were shivering in the cold.

"It's a spirit of an ancient dragon," said the boy at the front. "My brother says it's what causes the smoke."

"I don't see any smoke," said Brackendon.

"Comes at night sometimes," said the boy. "Some nights there's lots and others there's none. Depends on how angry the spirit is, least that's what my brother says."

"Well, I'll keep an eye out for this spirit," Brackendon said. He stepped into the mist.

"You can't!" shrieked one of the girls.

"I know a dragon who can get especially angry," said Brackendon. "I can handle this... whatever it is. I can handle any ghoul or nasty thing." The children looked horrified. "Here, take this or you'll freeze." He unfastened his cloak and wrapped it around the two smallest girls. He then pulled out a plump coin purse and tossed it into the middle of the group. "You spend that on food now." Delighted, the children gathered up the money and ran off. Brackendon tried to clear them from his mind before continuing his journey towards the tower.

After a few more deserted streets he'd seen no sign of any evil spirit, but he could feel the Cascade energy in the air. Not pure energy, such as it was when he called upon it, but rougher, worked, stretched thin and worn: more dangerous. He smelled a faint trace of smoke. It was sulphuric, as though from a large wood fire. Presently, there was no smoke, but it was growing darker and the children said the smoke came at night. With so much twisted Cascade energy affecting the borough, he supposed that small wildfires could start and stop without much reason. For it to happen regularly enough to require an angry spirit as explanation would be surprising, but not impossible.

I should have returned long ago. I might have done something.

Though what he might have done to spare Brevia this magical fallout he didn't know. Witches or wizards of the Inner Circle might have known, yet the old order was dead. Literally. Only the tower remained. Only Brackendon remained.

And Castallan! I shouldn't have fled. I should have stayed to help when the fighting started.

But he hadn't. He'd run.

Not again. Never again.

As he trudged up the hill to the base of the Conclave tower, full of regret for his previous inaction, he saw that the earth between cracks in the paving slabs had turned a reddish colour and seemed dry.

Before long, the doors to the Conclave lay before him; broken, unlocked and yet entirely uninviting. Brackendon just stood there, staring at the entrance.

He didn't know how long he paused before the tower doors – long enough for the sky to darken and the rain to begin lashing down. He kept the rain off himself, manipulating the air around him. Guilt or fear rooted him in place, though he couldn't say which it was.

Then something took hold of his hand. It was quite wet.

"I hope you weren't thinking of going in there without me?" Kymethra said. Brackendon's heart, his entire being, warmed at her voice.

"You look drowned," he said, facing her and pushing back a sodden clump of hair. He kissed her. "And you're freezing."

"Heat," she managed through chattering teeth.

"One moment. Stay close."

As she hugged in closer, Brackendon took back possession of his hand and opened his palm. A moment's thought, a nudge more on the door to the Cascade, and a hot ball of fire appeared. He felt a flow of magic through him then, from shoulder to hand, yet it seared so low it was almost pleasant, like the warming feeling of a strong drink. Keeping the fire burning cost little energy, after all. Fire could destroy, and like movement, it was cheap; for destruction was far easier than creation.

"That's better," Kymethra said. She clung to him and after a while stopped shivering and began to breathe normally again. Her hair dried and fluffed up, the white tips curling upwards in their usual flick. "Ready?" she asked, nodding to the Conclave doors.

"I am now," he said, extinguishing the orb of fire in his hand. Together, they made their way inside.

The chill was the first thing Brackendon noticed as they entered. It was unnaturally cold for the season, miserable weather outside notwithstanding. His breath rose in great clouds before his eyes.

"I think you'll need to relight that fire," Kymethra said.

Brackendon took some tentative steps down the dark, dank corridor. "I don't think so. It's unbearably hot over here." He tugged at the collar of his robes.

Kymethra stepped to join him. "Ugh, we'll sweat to death like this. The Cascade is twisted here. Why come back?"

"I felt compelled... We don't know what really happened."

Brraaaccck-eendon, came the strange voice again, louder than outside the tower.

"What's there to know?" Kymethra crept past him. "All we'll come across are terrible memories. Bad memories, or likely something dangerous – ouch, my knee. I can't see a thing. Hurry up and light the way."

"Sorry," Brackendon said, distracted. "Can you hear anything?"

"All I'm hearing is you are not giving us some light."

"Like a voice," Brackendon said. "Like a whisper."

"No... Come on now, Brackers. Don't leave us in the dark."

Brackendon shook his head and lit up the end of his staff. The corridor was suddenly illuminated. Parchment was strewn everywhere, cushions lay ripped, furniture snapped, drawers pulled out of cabinets, and a trail of debris led into each room. He checked each one and found the shelves were completely bare, not a book or scroll left on them. He thought that perhaps some brave looters might have taken them along with items of more obvious value.

At the end of the hallway was a winding staircase that would take them nowhere. Navigating the Conclave wasn't obvious. You had to know your way.

Brraaaccck-eendon. Up...

"There it is again."

"Not that I'm jealous," Kymethra said, "but why is it speaking to you?"

"I have no idea. It is saying 'up'."

"Up?" Kymethra said, rolling her eyes upwards as if she could see through to the top of the tower. "Well, let's go." She took a few more steps down the corridor, as though heading for the stairs, and sighed with relief. "Oh, it's not so hot here, and mmm, it smells like alderberry pie."

"Kymethra, maybe we ought to turn back. I thought it would give me closure to come here; give us both closure. I thought I might find something to aid me against Castallan but there is no way he would have allowed anything valuable to be left behind."

Kymethra gave him that look that only she could. "Scared?"

"You're not the one hearing voices."

Up...

"I'm frightened too," Kymethra said. "This place used to be our whole lives. I'm terrified of what might be up there. We might even find your old hat." She shuddered at the thought. He smiled and then stepped towards her, happy to be out of the hot zone. Here the air really did smell deliciously tangy.

"That hat is what got your attention," Brackendon said. He kept on walking, veering into a side room that hid the real way to the higher levels of the tower.

"What got you my attention was my desperate need for help on elemental control."

"Shame you never really mastered it," said Brackendon. He twisted the inkwell at the special desk clockwise one full turn and a ramp descended from above. They began to ascend.

Up... up. Brackkkkkkkendon.

"Or maybe you were just a bad teacher," said Kymethra. "Good thing I make up for it with my mind tricks." She pressed three fingers over her ear in demonstration.

"Do you ever regret not completing your training?"

"A part of me does. I could be helping more than I am. But then—"

"You've seen what it did to me," Brackendon said. "I can't blame you for wishing to have nothing to do with the Cascade after that."

"Actually," she began, sounding slightly annoyed, "I was going to say that, had I completed my training, you might not have come for me that day."

"Of course I would have," Brackendon said. "How could you say such a thing?"

"Stop interrupting," said Kymethra. She halted before three doors. "Wait a moment. These are the shifting doorways, aren't they? There used to be a method to figure out which one is real."

"Yes, there was," Brackendon said, racking his mind.

Left... something hissed. Brackendon twitched his head around. *Left...* The voice seemed to be getting stronger.

"I think it's that one," he said, pointing at the left-hand door.

"What's the trick?"

"I'm getting some help."

"Or you could be being led into the void."

"I'll go first, then," said Brackendon. He pushed on it. "Stairs. I think we're safe. And I'm sorry for before. What were you trying to say?"

"That I'm glad I hadn't received my staff when it — when it happened. Otherwise, you wouldn't have come to take me away when the fighting started. And don't try to pretend like that isn't true. I could see it in your eyes. I remember. I've never seen you so torn."

"It wasn't an easy choice. But that doesn't mean I regret coming for you. Not one bit."

"I know," Kymethra said and this time it was she who kissed him. "Nor do I regret smashing Malik's face in with my alchemy tome when he tried to stick that glass dagger into you."

"Malik," Brackendon sighed, remembering the young apprentice. "He was only seventeen."

"He was trying to kill you," Kymethra said.

"It sickens me how Castallan twisted their minds. He must have been working on the youngest apprentices for a long time to get so many to join him."

"Didn't sway me."

Brackendon realised he had never asked before. "Did he ever approach you or try to persuade you to overthrow the Conclave?"

"Not directly," said Kymethra. "He came to speak to us all often though. A lot about how we should be using our powers to help humanity become stronger; about how we could end the war and make a better world for humans; a world where we weren't at the mercy or the whims of demons or dragons. I'll admit, he was charismatic."

"But you weren't convinced?"

"Many seemed to listen but it sounded like madness. He was talking about changing the whole world; overturning everything."

They emerged from the staircase into a new corridor where the wall turned sharply away, as if back on itself. Brackendon remembered this zigzagging set of hallways where their dormitories used to be. No room ever seemed like it would be large enough from the angles of the walls but they were always spacious once you entered.

Hurry... the voice urged, echoing as though a crowd of people were whispering all together. The air was thick with the Cascade. It looked clear to the naked eye but Brackendon could feel it as he began to walk. It was like wading through water – stinking, murky water that tried to pull him down. A noise followed him every step down the jagged hallway, like someone gargling their last breath.

"Can you feel this haze?" he said sluggishly.

"Y-Yes," Kymethra struggled.

The Inner Circle's council chamber... come...

"Would the fighting that day really have caused all this?" Kymethra asked.

"It's not just the Cascade at work here. We should go to the Inner Circle's council chamber. I think we'll find our answers there."

They fought through the quagmire of Cascade energy higher up the tower to the council chamber of the Conclave. This was where the Inner Circle, the eldest five members of the Cascade Conclave, used to meet. The door to the chamber lay in splinters against the opposite wall.

HURRY.

Brackendon steeled himself. He crept forward, Kymethra behind him, and they stood outside the room, backs to the wall. His breath came in short bursts, his heart beat a little quicker and the hairs on the back of his neck prickled.

"I do not know what we will find in there," he said.

"Come on," Kymethra said, squeezing his hand. Together they twisted around the corner as if bursting into battle. Brackendon held his staff forward and light flooded the room. He gasped as foul stale air caught in his throat and Kymethra shrieked. There, at the large round table, were five skeletons.

Some lay bent and broken; one of the skulls was pressed down upon the table itself, completely caved in. Another had a short dagger lodged in its eye socket. Another held its jaw open in an eternal silent scream.

"The Inner Circle," Brackendon said softly. "This is where it started."

"Why is there a dagger?" Kymethra said. "Brackendon, they look like they were killed with brute force, not magic. And what's with the rest of the place?"

He glanced around, tearing his eyes away from the bones. It was immaculate. Not a patch of dust or dirt could be seen.

You have come, the voice said.

"I can hear it now," Kymethra said hoarsely.

"What are you?" Brackendon called out.

We were the Inner Circle... five... now one. In the chamber, the voice was at its strongest, yet a distance remained to it. It was jarred and tangled, as if five voices were speaking in unison.

"Are you not dead?" Brackendon asked.

We wish we were, rattled the voice.

Brackendon felt a shiver run through him. "What dark magic did Castallan weave here?"

Full of anger. Full of fury...

"Castallan's going to answer for what he's done," Kymethra said. "For this and for everything."

Not his magic, not his anger... ours.

Brackendon looked to Kymethra. She looked as confused as he felt.

"This wasn't caused by Castallan?" Kymethra asked.

Impertinent, the voice rumbled. *Castallan would not listen. He would not accept our judgement.*

"So he attacked you?" Brackendon said.

Not him... us, hissed the voice.

"I don't understand," Brackendon said. He felt a dark cloud of doubt enter his mind.

We felt there was no other way. We demanded he hand over his staff. He refused. We had no choice...

"You attacked him?" Kymethra said, her voice high with surprise.

We had no choice... The voice moaned in terrible pain. *Even the apprentices would not listen. They tried to help him. Stepped between us... we cursed him more for that.*

"Y-you caused all of this?" Brackendon said. "You hurt the apprentices who got in the way?"

He was strong, stronger than we realised... And his experiments... scarlet eyes... such strength... such speed.

"So Castallan stood where I am now?" asked Brackendon. "Presenting his red-eyed men to you all? What did he want?"

Kill us.

"What did he want?" Brackendon asked again.

KILL US.

"Answer me," Brackendon demanded.

He wanted approval. He wanted our help. Said he needed more power to end the war. He wanted humanity to be strong. Through magic... the dragons would never have allowed... He was mad...

"And you reacted by attacking him?" Kymethra asked softly.

Too much change... he would not listen. KILL US.

Brackendon felt a chill in his heart. So Castallan had not conspired against the Conclave after all, not truly. He had intended for the whole order to join him. Brackendon wasn't sure if that changed things. He decided it didn't. Whatever injustice had been done to Castallan here, he had paid back tenfold to the world. He'd consorted with demons and used foul magic to enchant those whom he brainwashed in joining him...

Yet Brackendon was forced to stop this line of thought. The apprentices had stood in the way. They had believed enough in Castallan, more than just from coercion. Scythe must have truly believed as well.

"Are you all aware of what has happened since?" Brackendon said. "What Castallan has done?"

We are one... the voice croaked. *And we are aware of little beyond this room. The Cascade haze has prevented our spirits from departing the plane of this world. Trapped... trapped... KILL US.*

"Brackendon," Kymethra said, taking hold of his robes. "Do it. Free them. Please."

"If you know nothing beyond this room, how did you know I was in Brevia?"

Where the Cascade is strong, we can connect to the world. This tower... your staff... such power. Like lightning rods to the mortal realm. Pleeeeease – RELEASE US.

"I do not know if you deserve it," said Brackendon. "Castallan turned to Rectar after the Conclave fell. I thought it had been his plan, but perhaps he didn't have a choice. Your actions pushed him that way."

He had to be purged...

"The blood of thousands is on your hands. Fairy, human and dragon alike."

"Brackendon, please," Kymethra wailed. Then he felt her grip loosen. He turned away from the skeletons and found Kymethra with her head in her hands. "They're hurting me."

"Stop this!"

KILL US, the voice boomed and the whole tower quaked. *Trapped. Trapped. Torment and pain. KILL US.*

Kymethra screamed so hard that Brackendon thought her throat would rip.

Brackendon bellowed in turn, slashing his staff in an arc before the table. A thick purple light ripped from his staff and blew the skeletons to pieces. He felt the light residue from his destructive magic rush towards his staff and panted; not from the magic, but from the cry that had emptied his chest. "Kymethra, are you—" He froze in horror. Her eyes had rolled up into her head. Blood oozed from her nose and ears, and her skin had turned as pale as milk.

NOOOO, shrieked the voice. *It did not work. End us. END US.*

Brackendon ignored its pleas. Whatever hellish existence the Inner Circle were in was too good for them now. He reached out to the Cascade, yanking the door in his mind wide open. He filled his body with strength and speed and Kymethra felt lighter than a feather as he tore from the chamber with her. He streaked back down the Conclave tower, even as it began to collapse around him, trying to ensnare him.

The three trick doors appeared again.

Brackendon blasted them off their hinges and the correct way was revealed. He spat out a gob of bitterness building in his mouth.

Come back. Kill us or we'll kill her.

Brackendon did not listen. He ran on as fast as he could, not stopping, not even when a chunk of the floor gave way before him. He simply leapt, landing with bone-shattering force. His enhanced body shrugged it off.

The Cascade washed over him now, pulsing down his arm. Movement and strength were cheap in bursts but this was prolonged. He could have probably pulverised even Darnuir like this. Soon he was hurtling back down the ramp towards the tower exit, weaving between falling stones. He took a shortcut by shouldering his way through the walls of the ground floor.

KILL US.

Brackendon burst out of the Conclave into the pouring rain. Night had fully descended and the city flickered with torches. He could feel vibrations in the ground from the tower. Kymethra grunted in his arms and coughed blood.

He was enraged, angrier than he had ever been. He wanted revenge, he wanted the tower and everything to do with his old order erased from the world.

And he knew he could do just that.

He placed Kymethra down, praying she would last, and raised his staff high at the tower. After building up Cascade within his body, feeling the euphoria take him, feeling like he was a god, he began to close the fingers of his free hand into a fist. He did this slowly, for the tower offered some resistance. But piece by crumbling piece it fell.

He caught those pieces in the air so they would not fall into the rest of city and sent them hurtling back at the tower.

Rain lashed, stones cracked and Brackendon's fingers finally closed over. A small pile of gravel was all that remained.

Despite the din of the wind, the rain, and his own ragged breath, Brackendon thought he could hear an echoing sigh of relief, as though the voice was in ecstasy.

Thannnkkkkk youuuuuuuuuu…

Brackendon dropped to his knees. With a great effort, he closed the door to the Cascade. The pain of it felt like venom in his veins. Such levels of destruction would have been impossible without his new staff. It hummed loudly and the diamond-bright wood shone as it processed the magic. He clutched the staff desperately, his eyes shut against the rain.

"Brackendon. Brackendon," Kymethra said. He felt her hands take him by the shoulders. "Are you okay?"

His eyes blinked open. "Are you?"

"Yes, I'm all right. No harm done." She too was kneeling, right in front of him. Her bloody nose was gone and the colour had returned to her face. "You brought the whole tower down." She just stated it as fact. Brackendon fell forwards to lean on her and they knelt, embracing in the rain.

"The world is better off without it," Brackendon said. His throat was dry, his mouth was bitter. It took some time for his thundering heart to steady and the flow of magic down his arm to ebb.

"Are you going to be all right?" Kymethra asked.

"Oh, I think so," Brackendon said. "But perhaps we should head for the nearest bakery and kindly request a loaf or cheese roll to soak the magic up. Wherever that may be."

6

THE 'KING' IN THE SOUTH

Although our current Aurishan dragons will contend that they won the Third Flight, in truth it was a stalemate. As one of the last dragons still able to take their true form, Aurisha confronted his own brother in the final battle and both perished. The Black Dragons returned to Kar'drun and attempted to rebuild their lives. The followers of Aurisha moved south to build their own city on the site where their gods had spoken to one of their kind. It was holy to them, despite the actions of Dranus. Legend says they brought three of Aurisha's talons with them.

From Tiviar's Histories

Cassandra – The Bastion

When Cassandra caught sight of the Bastion, she felt sick. She would be a prisoner once more. Already she lacked freedom, being latched to this man's back as he ran at an inhuman pace alongside the other red-eyed hunters.

As the prospect of returning fully dawned on her, she emptied her stomach.

"Ugh," grunted the hunter carrying her.

"Are you ill, Princess?" Freya asked. She was a red-eyed huntress in yellow leathers.

"Extremely," Cassandra gasped. Her mouth tasted of bile. "If you want to cure me, you'd better take me far away from this place."

"Nonsense," said Freya. "The Bastion is strong and safe. Castallan can help you. He has helped all of us."

"You keep calling me Princess," Cassandra said. "Doesn't that mean you have to do as I say?"

"Castallan is our true ruler," Freya said. "We chose to follow him and—"

"Quiet," grumbled the hunter. "Clean her up and let's go. We're all exhausted."

Freya mopped Cassandra's face gently with a clean cloth. "That's better," Freya said and the group started to run again.

Cassandra closed her eyes to avoid having to look at the Bastion and those impossibly high walls. With any luck, she would fall asleep and not wake until Darnuir and his army had brought Castallan down. That was if Darnuir and the others were still alive. She had seen the demon horde moving towards their camps as she was sped away. But she tried not to think too much on Darnuir either. It made her too uncomfortable.

The incident atop the hill at the Charred Vale refused to leave her mind. He had half dragged her down the hillside afterwards; that had been how she'd fallen in the first place. She didn't want much to do with him after that.

Her captors began to cough loudly, then the smoke hit Cassandra as well. It was putrid and burnt. She opened her eyes to a mountain of demon bodies, piled high and burning.

"About time we did away with those creatures," the hunter carrying her said. "The spectres never kept them well enough in line."

"What will Scythe do with the army he took to the Charred Vale?" Freya asked.

"Who cares?" said another man who wore the dark green leathers of hunters from the Southern Dales. "We won't need them if he succeeds."

"And what if he hasn't?" Freya asked.

"If he was fool enough to fight the guardian and Darnuir, he won't have," Cassandra said. The hunter brought up his hand and slapped her. Her head snapped to the side at the blow, her cheek grazing the hardened leather on her bearer's shoulder.

"A dragon lover, eh? Might be literally for all we know." He spat on the ground. "Come on. We're almost at the main gates."

Cassandra assumed she'd be thrown in the dungeons of the Bastion, but she was wrong. After being hauled all the way to the top of the Bastion's inner tower, she was finally dumped into her old accommodation and left alone. Several juddering slams echoed as the door bolted over.

She glanced around. Her once lavish quarters had been roughly searched. Tables had been upended, heavy drapes torn down, drawers pulled out and their contents scattered. In her private chambers, her bed had been shoved against the wall, left battered in some fury. Sections of wall and floor had been hammered at or taken away. She dashed through to Chelos' room.

He wasn't there.

She had known he wouldn't be waiting for her – arms wide and smiling – but not seeing him still cut at her.

Hot tears rolled down her face. She sniffed, rubbed at her eyes and tried not to think about what might have happened to him. Something terrible, she imagined, for their great secret had been revealed. Chelos' bed lay broken and the trapdoor to the passageway beneath had been covered with iron bars. She backed slowly out of the room, as if a dead body lay there.

So here I am. Right back where I started.

Fresh tears began to well up, blurring her vision, but these were tears of rage. She was angry; angrier than she had ever been in her life. She screamed until she had no more breath. She kicked everything she thought she could break. A table leg buckled and then cracked on her third strike. She picked it up, wielding it like a mace, and began bludgeoning anything and everything she could.

Her makeshift club finally broke against an upturned chair, so she picked it up instead. Heart pounding, arms straining, she spun and lobbed the seat at one of the windows. It didn't go right through, but it smashed several panes, sending shards of glass and lead out onto the balcony. Cold wind blew in and she regretted her actions.

Cassandra stood panting, trying to collect herself. It had felt good, even if the temperature was now dropping. Then she noticed the library door was closed and unharmed. When she entered, she could hardly believe it. It was all there; everything – every book, every scroll, and every note – was just as she'd left it. A volume of Tiviar's *History of Tenalp* lay where she had last put it down. Old instinct made her reach towards it. When she placed her hand on it, she glanced over her shoulder, feeling this might be some cruel trick Castallan was playing on her. Cautiously, she picked up the weighty tome.

Nothing happened.

Tension unwound from her in relief. She ran a finger through the pages of the tome and suddenly felt a crippling fatigue come over her. Feeling defeated, exhausted and truly alone, Cassandra returned to her old bed. It had already been made. She'd been expected to return, it seemed. She reached the bed and fell limply on it.

Sleep eluded her.

Despite having closed her bedroom door, a chill was gathering from the broken window in the room beyond. She curled up against the cold under her sheets and propped up Tiviar's *History*. This was his volume on the Second War between humanity and dragons. She flicked it open to a random page and began to read.

· · ·

I have gathered over three hundred and twenty-two accounts of Dronithir's movements in and around the Boreac Mountains when he supposedly discovered the mythical Champion's Blade. Aside from vast contradictions in dates, locations, timings and spellings – the guardian at the time was not named "Noobano" – there is one constant element. It seems Dronithir spoke much about hearing a "guiding voice" within the mountain range. To my mind, the likeliest explanation is that Dronithir helped himself by claiming divine favour...

After a few pages, Cassandra began to lose focus. She blinked, trying to stay awake, but she was warmer now beneath the covers and tired. So tired. She tried to read one more line, but realised she was reading the same line over and over. And then, mercifully, sleep came.

She couldn't tell how long she lay curled up in that bed. She woke sporadically then drifted off again, never quite sinking into a deep, restful state. Food was brought to her regularly, delicious food, but she ate little of it. Bossy women with tubs, soap, hot water and brushes came to clean her but she lashed out at them until they left her. She would wake at dawn; she would wake in the darkest hours of night. She read a little, but mostly slept, trying to make time go faster.

Some days later, she couldn't say how many, she heard the bolts on the main door shift once more. Her stomach groaned loudly and she hopefully sniffed at the air. Smelling nothing, Cassandra braced herself for another row with the matrons, but paused as the chink of chainmail reached her ears.

"Princess Cassandra," called a man's voice. "Lord Castallan requests your presence in the throne room." Cassandra drew herself upright, her muscles protesting with lethargy. She gasped as her bare feet touched the cold floor and then slunk out of her bedroom on tiptoe.

"I deny him my presence."

The man's eyes flashed red. "He also requests that you wear this for the occasion." He stepped aside to reveal a red-eyed woman holding up a rich pale green gown with golden thread. "To match your eyes," he said indifferently. "Lord Castallan has been entertaining very important guests and requests you to appear as one, if seen. You'll find it is a perfect fit." The dress was handed to her. Cassandra looked down at the rough white and grey leathers she was wearing, ripped and dirtied in places. She dropped the ornate gown to the floor and ground it against the stone with her foot.

"No."

The man rolled his eyes. "Very well. Take her."

"I'll walk myself," Cassandra said, shrugging away as the woman moved towards her. "I've got enough bruises already." There was some muttering between the pair. Cassandra glared at them. "What?"

"Your face, Princess," the red-eyed woman said. "There is a mark—"

"Courtesy of the thug who carried me here."

"Perhaps we ought to cover it," the woman said, more to her companion than Cassandra.

"No time," said the man. "Come along now."

Cassandra followed without fuss. They kept close to her, but she had no inclination to try and flee. She was tired, hungry and worn. After years of being patient, waiting to be free, she had foolishly got caught up with warring wizards and kings. She really should have run and hid from the world. Yet she had made a promise to Chelos to warn Darnuir of what was to come. She'd done that at least.

Next time, I'm gone for good. I'll just need to figure out where to go...

A part of her was tired of wanting to run as well. She wanted a home. She wanted to feel as safe and happy and as part of something as she had during their weeks at the Argent Tree. With Balack, Brackendon, Kymethra, the occasional visit from Cosmo and his smiling son, it had almost felt like a family. She wanted that again. She wanted to belong. Where she might find that was another matter entirely. Her real family had abandoned her long ago.

Walking through the corridors of the Bastion she passed finely dressed guests, even some older hunters from the Southern Dales with grey stubble. Half were drunk, keeping one hand to the wall or stumbling. The rest were enjoying some natural high, smiling broadly, talking loudly and happily. Cassandra wasn't sure who to hate more – Castallan, for hosting a party while sending demon hordes to ravage the land, or these people who seemed perfectly at ease joining him.

Entering Castallan's so-called throne room was a strange experience. She had spied upon it from the passages above so often over the years, but had never stepped foot inside before. It seemed even larger in person. To her right was Castallan's self-proclaimed throne, raised on a newly built platform to look down on the hall. Ten silver staffs fanned out behind the chair: the source of Castallan's power.

The wizard himself was not up there. He sat alone at the head of a long table, big enough to accommodate fifty people. The table was laden with the remnants of a great feast: pickings of suckling pigs with cold grease stains, hollowed cheese wheels, whole fish that only had their bones sticking out, flagons of ale, pitchers of wine and heavy black pots of barley broth. Like Castallan's robes, the table was dressed in purple cloth trimmed in silver.

Cassandra was directed to the seat opposite Castallan and she dropped into it, making sure to scrape the floor with her chair as she dragged it in. Everyone left and she was alone with the wizard. Castallan looked especially smug as he lovingly eyed a piece of parchment before him. Then he looked to her.

"Did you not like my dress?"

"Where is Chelos?" she asked, ignoring his comment.

"Your dear old dragon is alive."

"I want to see him."

"Then you may go on wanting. He won't be seeing visitors."

"What did you do to him?" Cassandra asked, envisaging Chelos screaming on his knees before that throne.

"I had no need to harm him. Not as much as I thought."

"He's stronger than you think," Cassandra said with a sort of fierce pride. She noticed a sharp, serrated knife on the table by a breadboard, just within reach of her hand. With one finger, she caressed the base of it, feeling the cold metal against her skin, wondering if she would dare to take it.

"Strong, but old," Castallan said, "and I think he realised I wasn't going to believe anything except the truth. And what a truth it was. Secret tunnels throughout my fortress?"

"You'll have had them all caved in now," Cassandra said. "Is that why you're so pleased?"

"As a matter of fact, I've kept them intact. Does that surprise you?"

"Just tell me what you want."

Castallan breathed in through this nose and ran a hand through his swept-back, ashen-tinged hair. "I want what I've always wanted. A safe world. A better world. A strong humanity that can stand on its own feet."

"And what do I have to do with that?"

"No need to be so flustered, Cassandra. I have no intention of harming you. I never have. I am sorry my followers cannot always follow orders to the letter. Who did that to your face?"

"I wasn't saying nice things about Scythe."

"Ah. You know," he said solemnly, "it grieves me that he is dead. Slain in combat by Darnuir."

Cassandra perked up, and sat a little straighter. "Did you expect him to win?"

"He was one of the first to join me, and one of the strongest. My technique was not so refined back then, but Scythe survived it and was more powerful for it. He was a sly, cunning one, if a little cautious because of it. In the end, that might have been his downfall. He ought to have pushed matters at Cold Point before Darnuir could become stronger. My greatest regret is that he did not live to see our plans fulfilled." He tapped the piece of parchment.

"Did that involve slaughtering all your demons?"

"In part, though I hadn't planned on disposing of my demons so soon. However, I am told by my followers who fled the Charred Vale that the spectres took flight after Scythe fell. The demons went wild after that, completely useless. Before long the spectres closer to home abandoned me as well, and the regular demons left behind had to be put down. It's meant stepping up my plans, but Darnuir has forced my hand." He brandished the piece of parchment. Waxy seals dangled beneath a screed of minute text. "Signed by the Lords of the Southern Dales, including Lord Annandale himself. Their soldiers will arrive soon for enchantment."

"Why would they do that?" Cassandra asked, unable to keep the bite from her voice.

Why are so many swayed to him?

"Because many believe as I do," Castallan said. "Many want what I want. An end to Rectar; an end to war; and an end to human suffering."

"But not an end to my suffering?"

"I've never actively made your life hard, Cassandra. You really shouldn't feel all that special. You are just a piece to be played. An asset of value. And there is no point hiding who you really are now, Princess."

"Yes, I've heard," Cassandra said. It was unsettling all the same. "So it's true?"

"I carried you from Aurisha myself. I took part in that attack to acquire the Dragon's Blade. I failed in that regard, but the trip was not a complete waste."

"No one wanted to pay my ransom?" Cassandra said. Her stomach twisted a little. She blamed the hunger but her thoughts betrayed her, flitting to the idea of a mother and father she had never considered until recently. Yet they had left her here. With all the power of royalty, she had been left caged. *What good were they?*

"You act so brazen and strong but you cannot hide your pain from me. Sad, isn't it? To think you were so unloved. If it helps at all, I shall put your mind at ease. Your parents did pay handsomely, or rather, your father paid. Your mother, the once Queen Ilana, passed shortly after you were presumed dead." He paused for a moment, looking at Cassandra to gauge her reaction.

"So she's dead," Cassandra said, though her voice was oddly high. "I never knew her."

"Terribly tragic," Castallan said. "But in the aftermath of Demons' Folly, it proved advantageous to me. You see, the death of your mother placed Arkus in a very difficult position. Without an heir, stability was threatened. I informed him and enough of his lords quietly that I had you to avoid a civil war. All I wanted in return was a guarantee that Arkus would not bring an army down to take you. I threatened to kill you, of course, as I was not then strong enough to resist the might of Brevia, not even here. The threat of strife in the Assembly and potential bloodshed over succession kept him in line for a long time. I also got a little financing out of it, of course."

"I thought Darnuir gave you plenty of gold?"

"He remembers that, does he? I had wondered. The rebirthing spell had never been used practically before. I'm impressed, in truth, but then Brackendon was a great wizard."

"He still is," said Cassandra, thinking fondly of the man.

"His staff tree was burned."

"Queen Kasselle herself granted him a staff, carved from the heart of the Argent Tree."

Castallan raised his eyebrows. "Kasselle must be feeling desperate indeed to gift such a piece of her people's heritage. Well, I shall have to add this powerful new staff to my collection. Tell me, did Darnuir also remember trying to carry you to safety when Aurisha fell?"

"He does now. It seemed to take him some time. The guardian helped him to unlock those memories his old self had hidden away." Cassandra wasn't too sure if she fully understood it. "Something about the rubies on his sword."

"Ah, yes, the Dragon's Blade. I had forgotten the gems held that power," Castallan said. "Oh, how I have longed for that sword." He narrowed his eyes at Cassandra, studying her. "You ran to him when you escaped. Did you grow close to him?"

Cassandra narrowed her eyes right back but her insides squirmed. Castallan kept focusing on her eyes, smiling broadly at her discomfort.

"Hungry?" he asked. Without an answer, he clicked his fingers and servants hurried in carrying several fresh platters. The smell of roast chicken made her mouth water. The servants had barely taken the lids from the dishes before she lunged for the food.

"I'll take that as a yes," Castallan said lazily.

"Holding me hostage won't save you now," Cassandra said thickly through a mouthful of chicken.

Castallan laughed a cruel little laugh. "Oh, Cassandra, Arkus hasn't been deterred by the threat of losing you for many years. He took a new wife, the Lady Oranna, daughter of Lord Clachonn, chief family of the Hinterlands. And would you like to hear the sad circumstances of that marriage?"

Cassandra shook her head and thought she might now take the knife while he droned on. Her fingers gripped the steel, she raised it —

But something in her faltered and she excused her sudden motion by carving a thick slice of crusty bread instead.

"Arkus decided he was in need of a great deal of black limestone from the Hinterlands," Castallan was saying. "In some fit of grief, he chose to rebuild much of Brevia. He needed so much stone, in fact, that his treasury couldn't bear the cost of it. Yet Lord Clachonn agreed to supply enormous amounts at minimum cost, in return for Arkus marrying his daughter. The official story paints a more... romantic picture of our reigning royalty. But my, what a sad tale it is."

"You seem to know a lot about this."

"I have friends all over the kingdom," said Castallan. "While Arkus was busy building himself a black city to match his black heart, I was gathering those with sense to me."

Cassandra chewed more slowly, thinking that the best thing to do would be to let him ramble on, and maybe she would get her chance. She put the knife down but kept it close. He appeared to be enjoying himself, which seemed odd to her. He was a very relaxed man for one who must know his time was short.

Maybe he doesn't see Arkus as a real threat. Time to find out.

"So why keep me after all that?"

"It gets worse, I'm afraid," sighed Castallan with clear exaggeration. "Their only son is a sickly child – problems with his chest. Coughs so hard that his carers fear his ribs will break. So, while you are no longer the official direct heir, you are a likely spare."

Cassandra was about to tell him about Cosmo and his son Cullen, but managed to stop herself at the last moment. She half choked in doing so, coughing and spluttering into her sleeve.

"Could be it runs in the family," Castallan quipped. Cassandra continued to have difficulty and felt her face going hot with the blood rushing to it. "Now, calm down," Castallan said, waving a hand towards her. She stopped gasping at once and her airways felt clear.

"I admit, at times, I wondered whether I should keep you or not," Castallan said. "Marrying you myself would have lent me no extra legitimacy. My followers freely choose me and many think Arkus is a fool. Yet over the years he's become bolder; stopped sending me the gold I demanded. Then he got bolder still, telling me that my magic was not the only way humanity could become stronger, but he does not understand. It is the fastest way. It is the best way. To enhance ourselves; to become as strong as dragons; and once I take the blades, I will be able to reach out and destroy even Rectar himself!"

"Why don't you just admit you lust for the power?" Cassandra asked. "Why hide behind this façade of—"

"I do not," he said, banging his fist upon the table. When he spoke next, it was quieter, as if he were restraining years of anger. "Always, people have misunderstood my intentions, my vision. The only person I have tried to actively deceive is Darnuir, and then only in part. I doubted he would have agreed with my intentions to put humanity on an equal footing with dragons."

"Not the old Darnuir," Cassandra said, remembering the way Darnuir would sometimes snap in haughty orders, oozing superiority when he did so. "But I think he would listen now."

"It's far too late for that," Castallan said, in that same hushed tone. "So long as dragons remain more powerful than us, we are at their mercy, doing their bidding, fighting and dying in their wars. I said as much to the Conclave but they did not believe me. They were frightened of change too; I could see it in their eyes. I came to them with a proposition, a suggestion, and they answered me by trying to take my staff... my very life."

Cassandra looked into his radiant silver eyes and they did not lie. "You really do believe in what you are doing."

"Of course I do. I do not force people to follow me. It started back at the Conclave. I spoke to the apprentices first, those not so much younger than myself. Many felt I was right, and they paid the price for it: cut down trying to save me from being taken by the Inner Circle. The fools," Castallan added affectionately. "They died for me; for what they believed. They were the first martyrs of my cause. Of our cause. I'm glad the Conclave was destroyed for that. They hadn't counted on my volunteers being so strong, and that was before I perfected the magic. Now I have all the power of the Conclave at my disposal. I took their knowledge too, to keep it safe. I'm certain it would have been lost otherwise."

"My library..." Cassandra said, realising what he meant.

"My library, you mean. I'm not some monster, though I am sure many think I am."

"Not a monster?" Cassandra said indignantly. "Not a monster?" She could barely contain herself. Her hand searched for the serrated knife. "You kept me locked up. You kept me isolated. You tortured Chelos. You've killed people, hundreds if not thousands of humans whom you claim to want to help. You worked with demons and kill anyone who you think might stand in your way. What are you if not a monster? Do you think a few books can soak up all the blood you've spilled?"

"I kept you isolated for your own good, Princess. Do you think you would have been as safe if everyone in the Bastion had known who you are?" A portion of Cassandra's anger drained at those words.

Might there have been others like Trask? Is he right?

Her fingers touched the cold metal once more.

"I have worked with demons, yes, I admit it. But I had to learn everything I could from Rectar. I do regret some of the steps I've had to take, but what will it matter once he's defeated?"

Cassandra's fingers slowly curled around the hilt of the knife.

"Demons and spectres were a necessary deterrent until I was strong enough to move without them. I welcome their loss at the Charred Vale and their burning bodies outside."

Cassandra steadied herself.

"Sometimes deaths are necessary to build something great. I learned that at the Conclave. You must be prepared to fight for change. What's a few hundred lives, a few thousand, if Dukoona's invasion is thrown back, if Rectar is defeated and all of humanity made safe?"

Cassandra whipped the knife at Castallan, unleashing a lifetime of coiled fury. Castallan barely flinched as he blasted the knife across the long table. It skewered the remains of a ham as it crunched through it into the wood.

He sighed again, this time irritably. "Sit still, will you?" Cassandra felt an invisible force push her back down, holding her in place. She couldn't even wriggle.

"They'll come for you," she said softly, the fight leaving her once more. "Darnuir, the guardian, Brackendon – they'll come to kill you."

Castallan smiled then, as pure a smile as she had ever seen another person make. "I'm counting on them coming. I'm holed up in an impenetrable fortress, which will be garrisoned with all the troops and hunters the Southern Dales can muster. And so Darnuir and company will seek me out. They know there are passages throughout the Bastion, even one leading right under the walls."

"Darnuir might know how I got out, but I couldn't tell him exactly where the tunnel lies."

"Oh, don't fear. Chelos' information leaves me confident they will find it. And they will run to me, right into my arms. I shall take Brackendon's staff and graft a piece of it into my own, as I have done with all the others." He gestured proudly at his collection behind the throne. Now Cassandra looked at them more closely she could see small chunks were missing from each one. Castallan's own staff was whole but now she knew what to look for, and being so much closer, she could make out the faintest cracks running up the shaft like scars, as though it had been taken apart and stitched back together.

"I shall take the Dragon's Blade," Castallan continued in full swing, "and the Guardian's Blade for good measure. A new age shall begin, and when we are finally at peace, I shall destroy one staff every year until magic is no longer needed to make humanity strong. This I swear, Cassandra. This I swear."

"I still don't see why I am here."

"To lure Darnuir," Castallan said. "I needed to know if you had one last use, and you do. Your squirming at the mention of him told me enough. I want him to come to me, not fight out there on the walls. So, when the time comes, you will wait out the battle in this room with me. I'll make sure everyone knows where you are and Darnuir will bring me the Dragon's Blade. All I have to do now is wait. That, Cassandra, is why you are here."

7

TUATH

Three Talons for Three Blades, or so we are to believe. The Dragon's Blade is known across Tenalp. The second is the Guardian's Blade, held by the more secretive guardian. The third sword is the legendary Champion's Blade, often forgotten by many. Again, the rumours and stories are worthy of their own chapter, though I caution readers against thinking of it as anything other than a powerful myth. It holds allure because there is the chance that anyone might be bestowed great power if they are 'worthy'. However, it seems strange to me that the ancient dragons would make such a weapon when the other two are so specifically designed.

From Tiviar's Histories

Garon – The Hinterlands – near the town of Tuath

Things had gone from bad to worse for Garon.

First, there had been the attack of the red-eyed traitors. Second, Marus' injuries had made him no more amenable. He kept the dragons distant, communicating rarely and only through fairy go-betweens, who were themselves in a sour mood about continuing the mission. Thirdly, their journey eastwards into the Hinterlands and towards the town of Tuath had taken three days longer than expected, what with injuries and the need to hunt or forage for a lot more of their food. Those supplies were now running dangerously low. Fourthly, he now found himself at arrowpoint by about half a hundred blue- and green-clad hunters. It was a mark of the state of things that this did not immediately qualify as his greatest problem.

"We're not demons," Garon said. "There will be no need to shoot us." The hunters had emerged from the wood that hugged the base of the Highland range. Rugged heather-topped hills protruded to the left and grew into larger mountains in the distance.

"Just routine," a woman said, emerging from their ranks to greet him. She was curvaceous, he was sure, beneath all that leather. Her face was sharply defined by contrast and she managed to pull off close-cropped hair in a way that few other women would dare.

"Is it routine for a mixed army of humans, dragons and fairies to arrive in the Hinterlands?" Garon asked. He very much hoped that Ochnic would not make one of his surprise entrances and spook any hunter with a weak draw arm.

"Well, it's not everyday work, I grant you," she said, extending a hand. "I am Captain Romalla."

"Garon," he said, taking her hand delicately. "The pleasure is all mine."

"Oh please, let's not waste time. May I see the dragon in charge of this 'army'?"
Straight to business, is it? No fun for Garon anymore.

Something fun might have helped to distract him from things, from the lack of a certain crooked-nosed person.

"Legate Marus represents the dragons," he said. "But he is not in charge of our expedition. I am." He handed over Darnuir's orders. Romalla looked suspicious but took the scroll. Her eyes darted from left to right down the words. "I should warn you that there is a member of the kazzek race among our number. I'd be most grieved if one of your hunters shot him."

"What? Him?" Romalla asked, nodding to Garon's right.

Garon turned and gasped. "Ah, Ochnic, how do you do that? Twenty years of hunter training and I can't tell when a great big troll comes up behind me."

"I've trained for longer," Ochnic said with a toothy grin.

"You don't seem surprised, Captain?" Garon said.

"Hmm," Romalla said. She finished scanning the scroll and rolled it back up. "Surprised? No. You don't think this is the first kazzek that Hinterland hunters have ever seen, do you?"

"Our people do not wander so far," Ochnic said.

"Perhaps some get lost, then," Romalla said. "We send long-range patrols north to watch for dire wolves and bears coming down from the Highlands. Many on those patrols claim to spot a troll from time to time."

"Der senses must be keener than da pack leader's," Ochnic said, not unkindly.

"Romalla, we suffered a terrible attack from agents of Castallan," Garon said. "I ask that the injured take rest in Tuath, and we could do with supplies. My intention is to travel through the Bealach Pass as soon as possible."

"That would be my preference as well," said Romalla. "Come. We shall escort you to the outskirts of town. You'll set up camp a full mile from the walls, mind. No more than fifty of you lot inside at any one time."

"Perfectly understandable," Garon said.

The light lingered for a long time that night. Garon had never seen the sky turn lilac and slowly darken into purple, nor had he thought it would linger for so long. He longed to walk out underneath it and breathe in the fresh pine-scented air. Instead, he was perched at the windowsill in the captain's regular room at the Carter's Rest in Tuath, with a dragon, fairy and troll bickering with each other.

"What say you, Garon?" Romalla called to him.

With regret and an ache between his eyes, Garon tore his gaze away from the enticing sky. "There is no question. We go north as instructed. And we'll go with the forces left to us."

He saw fresh annoyance rise in Marus' face. The legate's leg was elevated on a chair while he sat. The fact that he was moving at all was impressive. Such an injury would have left any human in their beds, but through some stubborn dragon stamina, Marus was moving around; puffy eyed and evidently in pain, but still moving.

"I'll add again that I trust all my hunters," Romalla said.

"We cannot take the risk," Marus said.

"I understand," said Romalla. "From what you say, I could be in for a rude awakening. You'll have the supplies you need. That much I can grant you."

"That's very accommodating of you, Captain," Garon said.

"Then you may depart as soon as you feel ready," said Romalla. Her position was more than clear.

"And so, our short and thankfully amiable business is concluded," Garon said, with no small measure of sarcasm. Marus got up without a second thought, limping with a great swing of his foot towards the door and his dragons on the other side. Pel rose more slowly, her defeated gaze briefly lingering on Garon before turning to Romalla.

"Thank you, Captain," Pel said, "for being so helpful in our time of need. And thank you, troll, for your scintillating insights."

With his forehead resting upon the table, Ochnic groaned.

"Thank you, Wing Commander," Garon said, hoping to impress upon her that enough was enough. "You heard the captain. Our discussion is over. Go get some rest."

Pel traipsed out of the room, although her traipse was the graceful glide of a human after ten years of courtly training. Once she was clear of the room, Ochnic dragged himself upright. One of his tusks gouged a small chip in the wood along the way.

"I begin to regret dis great walk," Ochnic said. "Da cold waters of da river will freshen me. Night good, Romalla, hunter captain."

Romalla turned to Garon in confusion.

"It's 'good night', Ochnic," Garon said. "And thank you again for your patience." The troll flashed his fanged teeth in a gesture that Garon decided to interpret as a friendly salute, then he too lumbered off, ducking at the doorframe to avoid injury. With nothing else to do, Garon began to follow.

"Garon," Romalla called after him. "Come back."

Often, Garon had heard that phrase laced with a playful longing. Habit, therefore, prompted him to arrange his face into his best smoulder before turning, but a deep tiredness had come upon him with the evening's bout of arguing done and his lips and eyebrows felt unresponsive. In the end, it was all in vain. Romalla had her back to him, bustling with some papers at a desk she must have kept permanently in the room.

After a while, she turned to check on him. "Is something wrong or do you always look like that?"

Embarrassed, he returned his face to normal and moved to the desk. "Can I help you?"

"By succeeding in your mission," she said. "If this is all true then I will feel better knowing the Highland border is safe from demons."

"I wondered why you had accepted all of this so quickly."

"I accepted it because I have little choice. It's absurd in truth. You, some nobody in Boreac Mountain leathers, show up with a scrap of parchment with the signatures of two princes long thought dead – Darnuir, now King of Dragons, and countersigned by Prince Brallor, who supposedly died over twenty years ago as well."

"Both were very much alive when I left them."

"Not only that, but you – this nobody human – is leading this joint force. I can barely believe the dragons allow it."

"They do yearn to follow their king's instructions."

"Will you let me finish?" Romalla said. He smirked and threw up his hands in mock surrender. To his relief, she smiled back. "Look, it's all so utterly unbelievable that I have no choice but to believe it. Had you come alone with your piece of paper and a troll I'd have thrown you out of the Hinterlands with arrows on your heels. But you have the fairies, you have the dragons, and I don't believe this many people could be so sure of the circumstances unless it was true. That, and I can hardly prevent your little army taking anything it needs."

"Has Brevia sent no word?" Garon asked. "There has been chaos brewing in the south for about a year."

"Arkus called his army, and our Lord Clachonn dutifully summoned his vassals in the Hinterlands, and so on. Yet little solid information has filtered through. I had heard of the troubles in the Dales and Marshes affecting the Crownlands, but this business in the Golden Crescent, whole demon armies on the march — no, I had not heard. And if the hunters have been compromised, as you say, perhaps it runs to the core of the Master Station, or perhaps some of my own people have been selecting my communications very carefully. It is… troubling."

"You should enjoy the stability of your region," Garon said. "I feel it is the last one left in the kingdom."

"Stable, and drained," said Romalla. "Even before Arkus called us to war, I was sending many of my best hunters to Brevia for some unknown purpose. Lately, I've been loath to do so because none have ever come back."

"You're sending away your hunters without knowing why?"

"Indeed. Again, how can I prevent Arkus having what he wants? As for their purpose, you can take it up with Lord Clachonn if you wish. Arkus deals with him and then Clachonn deals with me, bypassing the Master Station altogether. The benefits of having your daughter as queen, I suppose. But enough of my woes. I'd like to know a bit about you."

"Me?"

"I don't see anyone else in the room."

"What does it matter? I'm just some nobody, after all."

"You're not anymore. Why you, Garon? Why were you given this task?"

"Darnuir didn't have many options, I imagine. That guardian fellow was hardly cooperative. I don't think he and Darnuir saw eye to eye."

"Guardian?" Romalla asked, her brow furrowing at this latest revelation.

"It's complicated," said Garon. He puffed out a breath and let it continue into a sigh. "Darnuir wanted someone in charge who he felt he could trust. Someone who would see the matter through to the end."

"And you're the best man for it?"

"I wouldn't have chosen me," Garon said. "But you've seen how they are, the dragons and the fairies. Pel was forced along because everyone senior refused to go. Marus gets on with it because the dragons want to kiss their king's boots, but he begrudges every step he takes. So no, I would not have asked for this. But I was given the job and I shall see it through. I've led patrols; this is just a big one. A great big, shambling, arguing one. In fact, it's worse. At least when the kids are being taken out for the first time they damned well do as you tell them."

"Did you lead Darnuir out on patrols?"

"I did," Garon said, remembering briefly more sane days, even if demons were involved towards the end. Things seemed to make sense back then. "He was a quick learner, fought well, and coped with the effort. Of course, it helped that he is a dragon."

"Lira was much the same," Romalla said. "Tell me, did she—"

"She made it to Val'tarra," Garon said. "She even made it to Darnuir's new Praetorian Guard."

"Really?" Romalla said, her eyes lighting up like a proud parent. "Well, her mother will be pleased to hear that. So you know Darnuir, is that it?"

"I was also trained by Cosmo – Prince Brallor, that is – during the years he stayed in the Boreacs. I didn't know who he really was. He kept that even from his own wife, poor woman. Grace deserved better than that." He saw Romalla was confused again. He hurried along. "Cosmo helped me when I had nothing. He gave me back my life and a purpose. In turn, I helped him to train Darnuir. My proximity to them is ultimately nothing more than coincidence, but it has led me here."

"So you act upon duty and friendship. Admirable, but hardly inspirational."

Garon shrugged. "What do you want to hear, Captain? I'm just a man. I'm not a prince nor a king nor a wizard, nor even a plain dragon; I don't have a magic staff or a magic sword. I have my bow and my wits, and I've only ever wanted to help people, the way Cosmo helped me. Foolish as that sounds, it's true. Going to save a whole race – well, that counts as a lot of help in my eyes, and I'll see it through, to whatever end."

"You realise this is all going into my report," Romalla said.

"Make me sound ten times as foolish if you like. All I need is those supplies."

"They won't last long," Romalla warned. "One region's spare rations and arrows can't see so many through a harsh Highland winter."

"Ochnic says his people will provide for us. I trust him."

"And even if you didn't, you wouldn't have much of a choice," Romalla said. She held out her hand again. "Take care, Garon, the nobody from the Boreac Mountains. And good luck." He took her hand with a firm shake. "I will be heading up the Bealach Pass tomorrow to return to our station. We shall escort your expedition that far. After that—"

"We'll be on our own. Thanks," Garon said. "I wish you a 'night good', Captain Romalla." He winked once then turned before she could say any more.

Out in the corridor and out of sight of Romalla, he took a moment to lean against the wall. His heart was beating quickly and his chest seized in pain. He strained for breath. *Am I having some sort of panic attack?* He hadn't had one of these since the last war, when he was fifteen at most. *Maybe this is too much for me to handle?*

He blew out his cheeks and shook his head to try and rally himself. After another deep breath he stood up straight and made his way downstairs towards the chatter of patrons in the Carter's Rest. At the top of the last staircase, the heat of the bar area hit Garon like a warm, damp cloth. Pulling at his collar, he descended. He hoped against hope that Griswald would be sitting at the bar. That he would be roaring with laughter at some mildly amusing joke, out of all proportion, just like the rest of him, and would call Garon over and slap his hand to order another mug of ale.

But Griswald was not there.

There were men covered in dust with hammers and chisels at their belts, but no Griswald. He would be back out at camp, grief still heavy upon him. Garon bit back a fresh wave of his own sorrow.

Don't think on it. You can't think on it. You need to hold up, be in one piece. You've lost men before. This isn't any different.

But this time it was different. Looking around this tavern, in this town he had never been to before, Garon knew no one. And of the two people he was closest to on this mission, one of them, Rufus – poor, poor Rufus – was dead. He had no desire to return to camp. Not right away. Perhaps a drink or two wouldn't hurt. Cosmo had always favoured that option and it seemed to work, in the main. It was then that he caught her eye.

A tall, blond huntress sat idly at the bar, well away from the quarry workers. Her blue-green leathers were loosened at her chest and her hair fell artfully inwards to cover the gap. She held his gaze for just a second too long to be accidental.

Oh Griswald, you really ought to be here. Just like you said.

Yes, he would stay for a drink, talk to this girl and – *well, who knows?* He'd take the chance to be away from it all again for one night. Just one night. Just like it had been before all this madness started. That wouldn't be so bad. The blond huntress at the bar glanced in his direction again. It would be an easy form of comfort, one that wouldn't help once the night was over, but he approached her all the same. No stool was free, so he leaned on the bar beside her casually, pushing an iron-topped miner's hat on the counter out of his way.

"Rough day?" he said, nodding to the tankard in her hand.

"Back from a two-week patrol on the Highland borders."

"Dangerous?"

"If you run into a silver dire bear."

"And did you?"

"Not this time," she said, taking another sip of her drink. "Doubt there are many left now. Think you could handle one?"

"Oh, it's not animals that frighten me anymore," Garon said.

"What does, then?" she asked.

Red eyes in the night, he thought. He saw the huntress rip Rufus' chest open again. Traitors could be anywhere.

"Let me see your eyes," he said, placing a finger gently but firmly under her chin. He searched them for some trace of red, for some sign of treachery. He thought if he stared into them long enough he'd find the truth, if it was there to be unearthed. Yet her eyes remained nut brown, with the tiniest flecks of green. Only her pupils changed, widening into onyx ponds.

"You're from the Boreac Mountains, aren't you?" she said. "I've always wanted to see the mountains there. I hear they are so much more beautiful than the Highlands."

"The Highlands hold a certain rugged charm."

"I'd like something a little easier on the eye," she said. Her hand brushed against his free one and a warm finger ran over his wrist. He could feel her breath on his skin. It smelled lightly of ale. He let her go, rummaged in a pouch for some silver then dropped it on the counter. He had some catching up to do.

He awoke the next morning before dawn. After the thrill and fun, Garon had hoped to rest undisturbed, but his sleep had been light and broken, and unrestful by most accounts.

The cold blue light of a pre-dawn Hinterland morning entered the small room. He felt too energetic and too exhausted to move all at once. Infuriated, he scrunched the edge of the woollen mattress in his fist, over and over, feeling every strand of muscle in his forearm strain. He rubbed his eyes enough to chafe the skin and realised it was no good. He edged himself out of the warm bed and winced as the chill of the morning bit at his skin. Gooseflesh appeared along his arms.

His companion muttered something. He had discovered her name was Jean. She was fully naked, delicately hidden under the sheets. She opened one eye. "It's not even dawn yet."

"I don't have the luxury of sleep, it seems." He finished strapping on his sword belt and grunted as he pulled it too tight. "Go back to sleep," he told her before taking his leave. Carefully, he trod through the tavern, cursed his fortune as each stair squeaked louder than the last on the way down, stepped over an abandoned crowbar on his way past the bar, pushed on the tavern's heavy door and stepped outside, where he was met by a scowling Marus.

"Stay for some fun, did you?" the legate asked. To Garon's surprise he was alone, propped up on a sturdy if roughly-hewn crutch.

"What of it, Marus?" Garon asked.

"I hoped to find our leader in camp to – now, what was it again? – lead."

Shame flared inside Garon and burned his cheeks. "I admit this isn't my finest hour."

"How can I be certain you won't be missing at a time of crisis?" Marus asked.

"I won't be missing again, I assure you."

"Can you swear to it?"

"Can you swear you won't be such a stubborn arse all the time?" Garon asked.

"To you?" Marus said. "No. I cannot." He smiled awkwardly, but whether it was in jest or to hide fresh pain Garon couldn't say. He wasn't sure if these older dragons were capable of humour.

"What was so urgent that you had to come into town to find me?"

"The troll wants a word," Marus said. "And as you asked him not to enter Tuath in case he terrifies the locals I have had to—"

"You could have sent an outrunner."

"I can manage just fine," Marus snapped.

"I see what this is," Garon said. "This is your pride killing you." He moved to Marus' left side, which was crutch-free. "Come, let me help you back to cam—" But Marus snorted and limped on, not giving Garon so much as a backwards glance or a thank you.

Damn you, Darnuir. Damn you for leaving me alone.

"You're going to have to learn to ask for help," Garon called to Marus' back. In the silent, smooth-paved streets of Tuath, his voice carried far and magnified off stone buildings.

"A dragon does not ask."

"Then a dragon may hobble in pain all the way into the Highlands," said Garon. The pre-dawn light had progressed to an orange haze, enough to see Marus by as he sped ahead. "Slow down. You'll damage that leg further."

Marus paused and turned, his chest rising and falling heavily. "Would you like me to slow down, human? Are you feeling weak after your exertions?"

"It's a sweet sort of weariness," Garon said more quietly as he caught up. "You might try it sometime." Though looking at the legate's dour expression, Garon felt no one would be interested.

"The only satisfaction I require is service to my king."

"Well, each to their own," Garon said. "But would it be of service to Darnuir to cripple yourself?" No response came from the legate. "I thought not," Garon added. "This whole mission was Darnuir's idea. He won't take it kindly if you ruin it. He might use some of that pent-up rage of his on you."

"How dare you speak about the king in such a fashion."

"I knew your king when he was in swaddling clothes," Garon said. "I held him. I even bloody changed him. He could make a right stink when he fancied."

Marus' nose was twitching unnervingly fast. "The troll awaits us," he said brusquely. Yet, in his haste to set off again, Marus twisted around too quickly, pressuring his injured leg. His knee buckled, the crutch slipped out from under his shoulder and Marus collapsed to the ground, armour ringing off the stone.

Garon swooped down to his side. "Damn it, Marus. Are you all right?" The legate clenched his teeth so hard that Garon worried his jaw would shake out from his skull. "No, of course you're not." Marus was struggling to rise, letting loose an unmistakable yelp when he attempted to bend his right leg. Garon offered him a hand but Marus swatted it aside.

"Oh, Dranus take you," Garon said. He got up and stalked away. If Marus would rather his leg fall off than admit he needed help, then so be it. Garon had a hard enough task. He didn't need to tiptoe around Marus' ridiculous need to be a good old tough dragon. He'd made it perhaps twenty yards up the street when Cosmo's voice entered his mind, as though he were sixteen again.

"On patrol, you never leave a squad-mate behind. Dead or dying, you bring them home, just as you would want to be. There is no room for heroes or pride, and wounded egos will heal into strong bonds in time."

Damn you as well, Cosmo, Garon thought. He turned back around. Marus was still squirming in silent pain on the ground. It was clear that he couldn't move. Garon spotted a worn wheelbarrow by the side of the road, loaded with tiny pieces of black gravel and propping up a glinting pickaxe. He went to it, shoved the pickaxe aside with a clatter, and was already moving the wheelbarrow over to the fallen dragon when Marus began to call, "Garon? Garon, please." His voice was so laced with pity and hurt that Garon couldn't help but feel a pang of guilt for leaving him.

"I'm here," Garon said, pushing the wheelbarrow, heavy as it was, into place behind Marus to support his back. "Sit up against that. It will give you some support." The legate sat himself up and leaned back against the edge of the wheelbarrow with an audible sigh. One of his hands remained protectively on his leg.

"Thank you," Marus said.

"You're welcome."

Garon sat down by the wheel near Marus, but not looking at him. For comfort, he raised one knee and put his arm over the wheel. He looked like he was tenderly embracing it. In his semi-delirious state of tiredness, the thought made him chuckle.

"Finding it hard to believe where you are and what you're doing?" Marus said, speaking low and slow as though on his deathbed.

"If I could travel back in time and stop this from happening, I would," Garon said. "Romalla was right to doubt me. I'm not cut out for this."

"I can sympathise."

"Come now, Legate Marus. Darnuir picked you. He must have thought you were capable."

"My king did not choose me," Marus mumbled.

"So who—"

"The Lord Guardian."

"And you didn't want to come?"

"I don't think Darnuir could remember who we all were," Marus said. "Not our names, not the legions we belonged to, not our — but I should not be bitter. Nor should I speak ill of my king."

"He's not infallible," Garon said. "That I assure you."

"Fallible or flawless, he wields the Dragon's Blade. None may challenge him. He is our leader and we must do as ordered."

"The guardian has one of those golden swords," Garon said. "Why not follow him?" For the second time Marus grunted something incoherent. "Why did Blaine pick on you?"

"I never believed much in the old religion, even before we fled Aurisha. My father did, but he died at the hands of three spectres, I am told, roaring how N'weer would return his soul to the world to fight on. Perhaps it's true, but I still lost a father. When the Lord Guardian came to select a legate for this expedition, I was doomed."

"He knew you were a non-believer just by looking at you?"

"Not quite. Some of us attended his services, so he recognised them. But when he gathered us all and announced there was a crucial mission to the Highlands, to lend our swords in service to the trolls, he asked, 'Who here lacks faith?' And I, being so foolish, thought by speaking out I might excuse myself from selection. I thought he would not want to send a non-believer. Turns out he wanted the exact opposite."

Garon felt a strange sense of calm wash over him. "I wasn't tricked into this, but I was pressured to some degree. I think we can understand how one another feels on the matter, especially considering Pel was also forced here against her will."

"I admit it seems unfair."

"Well, I for one say we begin to get along, just to spite them," Garon said. "What do you say to that?"

"I can't just forget the murders at the hands of humans."

"Humans died as well," Garon said. "As did fairies. Probably more will die in the south. I'm not asking you to forgive it all right away, but perhaps, for now, you could stretch to letting me help you to your feet?"

A pregnant pause followed and Garon prepared to sigh in supreme disappointment. But then—

"Very well," said Marus, and to Garon's shock the dragon lifted his right hand. Garon forced his own sore legs to work and stood up to take the dragon's proffered hand.

"You'll have to meet me halfway now," Garon said, panting as he tried to heave the legate up. With another groan of pain Marus managed to rise and wrapped an arm around Garon for support. And as they held each other up, the first rays of dawn broke, warming their faces from the east.

"Nothing makes the world quite as beautiful as a sunrise," Marus said. Though shocked to hear those words come from Marus, Garon couldn't help but agree. The stonework town suddenly looked fresh again in the pale light, even if the grey stone was drab and overused and each roof was slated in the same sharp black tiles. To the north there was fresh snow on the mountain peaks. It would only get colder now they were on the wrong side of midsummer but, to Garon, it felt a bit like going home.

"Thank you, Garon," Marus said. "Thank you for saving my life. It was remiss of me to wait this long to say it. It's not how a legate should behave."

"Don't mention it," said Garon. "Come, let's go find Ochnic." He scooped up Marus' crutch, handed it to him, and together they made their way to the camps outside of Tuath. Once outside the town walls, Marus let go of Garon to save face and they continued into the woodland beside the River Dorain. Ochnic had mentioned taking up residence there, favouring the trees, moss, ferns and general dampness.

To their surprise, they found Pel by the river, her azure skin clashing wildly with the green all around.

"Marus told me the troll wanted to speak to us," Pel said when they were near enough to hear her. "Though what would be so urgent he had to come ask before dawn, I don't know."

"Well, where is he?" Garon asked. Pel shrugged unhelpfully and Garon continued wandering through the wood. "Ochnic?" he called. But there was no answer.

"I hope their entire race doesn't hide from us like this," Marus said.

"There," Garon said. He'd spotted Ochnic's leather satchel at the root of a large hazel tree.

"Ochnic?" Garon called again, a little louder. This time there was snapping from above, like twigs breaking. Then the tall, long-limbed figure of Ochnic slid down from the trees and Garon, still walking, nearly collided with the troll's white-furred torso. Water dripped from the troll, rolling off his balding scalp and tusks. "I wasn't aware it had been raining," Garon noted.

Ochnic cocked his head curiously. "No rains have come, Garon pack leader."

"Then why are you wet?" Marus asked.

"Clll-eeening," Ochnic said awkwardly.

"So it bathes," Pel said quietly. "That's something." Thankfully, Ochnic didn't seem to hear her.

"Climbing da branches or rocks helps dry quicker but is better with more kazzek to chase."

"Naturally," Garon said. "Well, Marus says you wish to speak?"

"Da air from de north grows damper, pack leader," Ochnic said. He sniffed in demonstration. "Already da season changes. We must not delay."

"We'll move as soon as we have our supplies and the wounded have had a chance to rest," Garon said.

"Leave dem," Ochnic said and Garon thought he saw the troll's eyes flick towards Marus.

"We'll need every fighter we can get," Garon said. "We're already fewer in number than when we left Val'tarra and—"

"Leave dem," Ochnic insisted.

"I will not be left behind, Ochnic," Marus said. Garon was about to say something, but stopped himself, surprised at hearing Marus use Ochnic's name.

Promising, Garon thought. *Perhaps he is going to try.*

"We can hardly move faster," Pel said.

"You can try," Ochnic said. It was more of a plea.

"I understand your desire to reach your people quickly," Garon said, "but I promise you that we are moving as fast as we—"

"Last hope," Ochnic spluttered, darting forwards to Garon. Water sprayed from him like a wet dog. He took Garon by the shoulders as if to shake him. "Last hope, I am," he said repeatedly. Steel screeched as Marus half drew his sword, though he was unbalanced, and Pel's spear cut a swathe through the undergrowth as she swung it up to a guard position.

"Stand down, you two," Garon said. "Ochnic, stop." He grabbed the troll's rough leathery arms and tried to gently push him away, but he barely moved the towering kazzek. After a prolonged tussle, and much squirming on Garon's part, Ochnic finally released his grip to bury his great head in his hands. "Has something possessed you?" Garon asked, a little breathless.

"Sorry, I am, pack leader," Ochnic said. He hunched his shoulders and seemed to shrink a foot in height. "Eager, I am, to return. I have no news of Cadha."

"Your wife?" Marus asked.

Ochnic huffed, trying to think of the word. "No, not life mate. My girl." With one palm he pressed down through the air to his knees and with the other he waved at Pel.

"Your daughter?" Garon said. "Child?"

"Dat is da word," Ochnic said, scratching his head. "Da chieftains told me to travel to da silver tree before my clan reached de Great Glen. I had no news."

"I'm sure your clan and daughter made it, Ochnic," Garon said. He patted the troll on the back, his hand squelching against the troll's sodden fur.

"Maybe we could discuss this over breakfast?" Pel asked. "I'm starving."

"You want food?" Ochnic said, emerging from his hunched position. "Yes. You must have a hunger. I brought you here before you sleepy ones normally arise and forget. Sorry, I am."

Pel looked quite taken aback with this level of apology. "I don't... I mean to say... It's quite alri—"

But Ochnic began rooting through the bushes, along the embankment of the river, lifting fallen branches and scouring the earth. He moved around the area with such frantic haste that Garon could barely keep track as he darted between the trees. In what seemed a matter of seconds he had returned, carrying a collection of wild plants on a giant leaf that was larger than most roasting dishes. He presented it to Pel.

"Food," Ochnic explained. Garon braced himself for another outburst from her, but to his surprise she seemed to well up with emotion.

"You know what plants are edible?" Pel said. "I was never taught that like the other women. Just spear work for me." She reached out for a honey-coloured alder-berry, the only item on the flat leaf that Garon recognised.

"I know da wild."

"And you did it so quickly..." Pel chewed the berry with an open mouth, entirely forgetting her fairy etiquette.

"Always der is ways," said Ochnic. "Try this." He handed her a mushroom half the size of his hand with a thousand white strands sprouting up like a hedgehog and placed several delicate white flowers on top. Pel took it with only a small show of trepidation and took a bite.

"It's creamy, earthy and garlicky," she said.

"Feel better?" Ochnic asked.

"I'm starting to," Pel said. Then with some effort she added, "Thank you."

Garon sensed this was an opportunity to seize.

"So, are we all done having our moments?" he asked. "I ran away for the evening. I shall not do so again. Marus learned that sometimes you need help in life; Ochnic confessed his fears to us, and Pel has been fed. I've also learned that none of us wanted to be here. Marus offended the guardian; Fidelm forced Pel here; Ochnic would rather be back with his family, and who could blame him? And I, your sorry leader, would much rather be with Cosmo and Darnuir because I haven't been sepa-rated from them in twenty years and they are the only family I have." He surprised himself with the outpouring. The others were all gawking at him. Garon realised he had best carry on now that he'd started. "There have been deaths and traitors already, and we've each come out with some choice insults for everyone else, but I say it ends here. We're all in the shit, and none of us wanted it. Best thing we can do is come together and go help Ochnic's people and his daughter. Now, does that sound agreeable?"

"Yes," Marus said, bluntly but wholeheartedly.

"You speak true, Garon pack leader."

They looked to Pel.

"Fine," she said. "Yes, that's agreeable," she added with a little more enthusiasm. Then she took another greedy bite of the mushroom and flowers.

8

ON THE SHADOW SPIRE

After the Second War, the humans under Brevia's growing influence received help in constructing the mighty Bastion to help deter against future dragon aggression. One can understand why the humans of the Splintering Isles felt unfairly treated in this regard. The islanders received no such help from the new dragon king, Dronithir. A fortress on Eastguard was built, but it was no true barrier to dragons. That Dalridia and Brevia entered a form of rivalry is also understandable.

From Tiviar's Histories

Dukoona – Island of Eastguard – The former town of Errin

The island of Eastguard had been transformed. Dukoona had taken the town of Errin on the western coast and created a city for his demons. A sprawling mess of rickety shelters, stacked too high, too precariously and too close together; but what did those mindless runts care? Above it all loomed his Shadow Spire, facing outwards towards the rest of the Splintering Isles.

The Spire was a fortress built for spectres. As shadows gave spectres the most advantage, these were what the Spire created. Each wall had deliberately large gaps allowing light to enter at any time of day. Criss-crossing beams made from repurposed ship masts connected these walls, which would cast a web of shadows around the Spire and the surrounding lands. The Shadow Spire's twisting walls curled inwards at the top, as though a hand of broken fingers was grasping at the sky. Here, where the gnarled fingers of wood and metal met, was a viewing deck overlooking the grey sea. Dukoona stood there now surveying his fleet with Kidrian and little Sonrid at his side.

"We can delay no longer," Dukoona said. "If what you report is true, Kidrian?"

"I'm afraid so," Kidrian croaked. "I fear we might have lingered on Eastguard for longer than necessary."

"How heavily reinforced are the closest islands?" Dukoona said.

"Large forces on the islands of Ullusay, Skelf and Ronra, my lord, though the numbers on Skelf are the greatest, despite being the smallest. From what our Trusted could gather, young Grigayne Imar believes we will strike there first, as it is the weakest."

"Does he indeed?" Dukoona said. "Fortunate you discovered this information."

"We might have completed our missions sooner, my lord, but travelling by boat to each island is so slow; and then we had to be careful not to be intercepted."

"You are forgiven," said Dukoona. "Our inability to meld over water is a most inconvenient oversight by our master." He and Kidrian exchanged smiles of pure white teeth.

"Might we speak more openly?" Sonrid said in his half-formed voice. "Only I wish to make my own report and—"

Dukoona silenced him with a wave of his hand. "It is useful, Sonrid, to learn to understand beyond what one merely hears. Just as it is useful to see beyond what only your eyes can see." Yet Sonrid's half-closed eyes were a reminder that he was not as adept as the rest of the spectres. Poor Sonrid suffered daily. He was small and hunched, and his shadowy flesh was wispier than a normal spectre's. As one of the Broken, Sonrid had not been summoned properly to this world by their master, Rectar.

"I will try my best," Sonrid said.

"You have done well so far," Dukoona said and he meant it.

"I am rarely taken notice of. That is all."

"A trait I wish I had at times," Kidrian said. "Yet all the spectres know I am too close to Lord Dukoona. Those of our kind who are False watch me carefully."

"There have been murmurings," Sonrid said. "Some say the Master will not be happy about this delay."

"And what do others say?" asked Dukoona.

"Some are worried," said Sonrid. "They feel the Master ought to have done something by now. Forced us to move on. They are concerned about his indifference."

Yes, Rectar's indifference worries me greatly as well.

It was as if Rectar simply wanted his demons out of the way, putting a buffer between his lair at Kar'drun and the Three Races. Whilst adding to Dukoona's own unease, the news also offered some opportunity.

"Kidrian, perhaps we could seek out these troubled brothers and see if they are to be trusted?"

"You must be cautious," said Sonrid, and Dukoona was surprised to hear a sternness to his voice.

"I've been doing this for a rather long time," Kidrian said. "Don't concern yourself with me, Sonrid."

"You should be careful around Kraz," said Sonrid. "You say you are watched? Well, he watches most closely." Little Sonrid even jerked his misshapen head from side to side as if to check Kraz was not there with them.

"Kraz?" said Kidrian in disdain. "That flaunter can barely conjure a blunt sword from the shadows, never mind that double-headed axe he claims to use. Can't trust him with those bright yellow flames on his head."

Sonrid, however, appeared unconvinced.

"Do you fear him?" Dukoona asked.

"He talks of knowing how to better lead this invasion," said Sonrid. "To his own small band of spectres. And he's taken to keeping more demons near him of late."

"I didn't ask what you know of him," said Dukoona. "I asked whether you feared him." Sonrid shuffled awkwardly but nodded.

"He often threatens me, my lord. He speaks of hearing from the Master. That the Master would be glad to see the weakest of his servants culled."

"He boasts," Kidrian said offhandedly. "He exaggerates and he lies. None hear from the Master other than our Lord Dukoona."

Dukoona, however, was not so sure. "Many things have changed of late, Kidrian. Spectres are dying or disappearing. Great deposits of starium stone at the Forsaken City go missing to some unknown end. We should not dismiss claims like this on a whim. Not anymore. We must hear beyond what we hear," he reminded them both.

"I accept the possibility that the Master may speak to others now," Kidrian said. "Possibly. But surely not Kraz."

"He'd be ideal," Dukoona said. "A puffed-up, weak-willed spectre with little reason to question why he was suddenly being spoken to by the Master? A few words and some encouraging nudges and Kraz might really believe he was being singled out for extra power."

"My lord," Kidrian began, "do you truly—"

"I do not know what to believe anymore. I doubt everything. That is why we must work carefully. Still, there is no reason Kraz cannot be dealt with."

"Dealt with?" Sonrid asked, sounding both excited and terrified.

"Oh yes," said Dukoona. "If the Master truly speaks to Kraz then I fear how that might develop. If Kraz is merely lying, well… removing an insubordinate is my duty as Lord of the Spectres. I cannot have my spectres second-guessing me."

"What can I do?" Kidrian asked.

"You can prepare our ships to launch," Dukoona said. "I shall handle Kraz. Come, Sonrid." He leapt into the nearest shadow and felt the presence of Kidrian and Sonrid close by. A few masts down and Kidrian deviated down a different wall of the Spire. The shadows were so numerous and connected that there was no need to jump from one shadow to another. When they emerged at ground level, Dukoona strode with purpose towards the ramshackle town of Errin. He heard Sonrid pad up behind him.

"I haven't told you where Kraz can be found."

"You'll show me."

"Will we walk there?" Sonrid asked as they entered the chaos of the demon city. The shrieking was almost unbearable.

"I thought so. I know shadow jumping can be difficult for you."

"I am sorry to be a hindrance."

Dukoona swooped around to look at Sonrid. He cast a clear thought to the demons around: *Silence.* Those nearby stopped their howling. He got down on one knee to be at eye level with Sonrid.

"Never say sorry for being as you are. Rectar decided to summon you to this world. You didn't ask for it. He is the one who failed to do it properly; that is no fault of yours."

"My lord," Sonrid whispered, "anyone might hea—"

"This is something every spectre ought to hear and know. The weakest amongst us need our help, not our scorn. For our master will do nothing to help you."

Sonrid nodded firmly. "You have given me purpose again, my lord. I am grateful."

"Thank me by helping me fight back. Now, we must find Kraz. Lead the way." Sonrid shuffled on and Dukoona followed. The demons soon returned to their noise. Dukoona could sense their restlessness. It was well they would be shipped off to fight soon.

It was difficult to weave through the densely packed streets – if they could even be called streets. The entire demon town was becoming a mass grave. Human corpses lined the streets, left where they had fallen and exposed to the elements. Demons were not inclined to move them – they couldn't smell and weren't intelli-gent enough to care about blocked streets. Spectres could not smell either, but leaving the bodies had been an oversight. Now the Shadow Spire was built, Dukoona would have his spectres clear them.

He watched a crow fly down upon the soft, pulpy body of what had once been a
⌐ girl. The crow dove its beak into one of the girl's empty eye sockets and
    around for a scrap of meat that wasn't rotten. As Dukoona and Sonrid

passed by, the bird yanked up a strip of greying flesh and took flight. Dukoona looked away. Death just didn't please him anymore. Dragons, fairies, humans – they must all feel the same way about their own kind as he felt about his spectres. Every death was felt by someone. He thought of Kidrian lying dead, or even Sonrid, and felt as though a great weight was pressing against his chest.

I will not be able to save them all in this war, but I must do what I can.

Eventually, Sonrid stopped outside a tent-like structure made of a torn sail draped across the gap between two earthen houses. Under the canvas, a large hole burrowed into the ground with the entrance uncovered. This was not unusual. When the demons had found it too hard to build upwards they began to dig down instead. They were decent excavators, Dukoona would give them that.

Sonrid had no need to crouch to enter the tunnel; he slid in easily. Dukoona ducked and descended after him. Light soon vanished as they left the entranceway behind. The darkness was total and Dukoona heard Sonrid move closer to him. Spectres despised complete darkness, for without light there could be no shadows.

Patches of coloured fire flitted here and there from the flaming hair of passing spectres. They would be patrolling the tunnels, checking on the demons and keeping the peace. Fiery heads of green, orange and red flames bobbed by, muttering courtesies to Dukoona. All bright in the darkness, except for a Broken, such as Sonrid. The feeble grey embers on the little spectre's head were pitiful, like dying candles.

"It is just up here, my lord," Sonrid said.

"You go on. Let Kraz and his company see you first. I think you'll appreciate the look on his face when I appear shortly after you."

Dukoona followed close behind Sonrid for the rest of their journey, drawing back only when a luminous cavern shone ahead. Kraz and his fellows must have lit torches. Dukoona thought this an interesting choice; one that spoke volumes.

He let Sonrid continue alone and melded into the edge of a long shadow cast by a supporting beam. He travelled along the shadow and nestled in a finger's width of space. Dukoona stayed there, within sight and earshot of Sonrid entering the room.

"What do you want, scum?" came a voice.

"Apologies," Sonrid said. "I must have taken a wrong turn."

"Clear off, then."

"Wait," said a new voice, this one sharper than most spectres'. Another figure stepped into Dukoona's view. Yellow flames spiked in short sharp flames over his head.

There you are, Kraz.

"I know this one," Kraz said. "Come to take me up on my offer? Shall I end your miserable existence?" Shadows swirled around Kraz's hand and a long dark dagger materialised there.

"No," Sonrid said defiantly.

"What's that?" Kraz said. "He says no? Look, err, Sonrid, isn't it? The Master has spoken to me again. Told me that this war is to be won swiftly, and we can't have anything holding us back."

"I am not holding you back."

"No, that would be our mighty Lord Dukoona," said Kraz.

There were murmurs of agreement from around the cave.

"We've been stuck on this rock for too long," Kraz said. "There are humans close by that need killing."

More murmuring, louder this time.

Well, you have a point there, Kraz, but I can't stand your tone. Dukoona was about to emerge from his shadow and reveal himself but stopped as he heard Sonrid speak up.

"You're wrong."

The room fell silent.

"Did you croak something, wretch?" Kraz said.

"You heard me," Sonrid said. "You're wrong. Lord Dukoona is wise and vigilant."

"More like cowardly," said Kraz. "The Master does not appreciate wisdom. Only deaths." He stepped closer to Sonrid, raising his dagger.

Now was the time.

"What is happening here?" Dukoona asked, emerging from his shadow and sweeping into the room. Every dark set of eyes flicked frightfully between each other.

"Nothing, my lord," Kraz said, his dagger melting away into shadow. "Little Sonrid here was lost, weren't you?"

Sonrid remained silent. Dukoona made a show of looking thoughtfully around the room, letting his gaze linger on some of the torches. "Fire and light? An interesting choice. Did you anticipate needing shadows?" No one answered him. "You are all very quiet. I thought I heard conversation as I made my way here but I must have been mistaken. Were you lost, Sonrid?"

"I may have taken a wrong turn, my lord."

"I do hope that was the extent of it," said Dukoona, more to Kraz than anyone else. "We have too many battles ahead for our own to be divided. On that matter, Kraz, I have an important request to make of you."

"My lord?" Kraz said.

"I have been trying to decide upon a lead spectre for one of our landing forces. I thought you might be up to the task?"

"Absolutely, my lord," Kraz simpered. "I would be honoured."

"I am glad to hear it. You shall acquire for me the small island of Skelf."

"The smallest island, my lord?" Kraz said, unable to keep the disappointment out of this voice.

"A vital mission," said Dukoona. "Take Skelf for me. Then we will flank the humans on Ullusay and Ronra. Succeed, and I may grant you command of the assault on Dalridia."

Kraz could barely contain his idiotic grin. "I am thankful you realise my potential. I shall not fail."

Oh, you will, but that will be something which pleases me.

"I hope not," Dukoona said. "Come, Sonrid, let me help you find your way."

A day later, atop the Shadow Spire, Dukoona watched the assault force bound for Skelf set sail. The force tasked to take the island of Ronra to the north of Skelf had also sailed earlier that day, led by other spectres he knew to be False. From a deep shadow cast by the curving wall behind him, Kidrian emerged to join Dukoona. Hundreds followed, all Trusted; some of their most loyal. He was pleased that he could count on most of his people.

"I reduced the fleet heading to Skelf as you requested," Kidrian said.

"Poor Kraz," Dukoona said. "It seems he was not the Master's chosen after all." Although Dukoona had to admit to himself that sending Kraz to his doom wasn't conclusive proof either way. This stunt hadn't even drawn a passing glance from Rectar's enormous presence in the distant recesses of Dukoona's mind. Yet Rectar's disinterest could only last for so long.

"Will we take Ullusay, then?" Kidrian said. "Our forces here will overrun that island easily."

"No," Dukoona said. "Kraz is a fool, but he and those who sympathise with him have a point. We have lingered long enough. Whatever the Master's intentions, he will not be satisfied if we do not make progress." He summoned his favourite sword from the shadows. Long, curved, impossibly sharp, and a deep purple like the shade of his shadowy flesh. It had been a long time since he'd had a proper battle. Once, he would have been excited; now, he looked around his Trusted gathered there and felt only worry. Still, he had to encourage them.

"We will not go to Ullusay," he said, raising the shadow blade high. "We will go around it. We will cut to the heart of the islands. We sail for Dalridia!"

A MEETING OF KINGS

The oldest part of Brevia lies on the southern bank, where the Master Hunter Station now stands. Originally, it was a small port that was developed to begin trading surplus grain from the Golden Crescent to the expanding island centre of Dalridia. Since then it has grown, to say the least.

From Tiviar's Histories

Darnuir – Brevia – King Arkus' Palace

"Faster, Praetorians," Lira called. "You'll have to push yourselves to find where your true limits lie."

The young Praetorians repeated the exercises, quicker than before, but not quick enough. Darnuir thought it strange to think of them as young, for they were all close in age to himself; but he felt much older. Having the memories of a sixty-year-old dragon merge into his mind had altered his perception on a lot of things.

"I know how abnormal it will feel," Darnuir told them. "I found it hard to unlock my own strength. You've lived among humans all your lives; you're not used to it. But push. Come on, harder now." Each Praetorian drilled again, and again, and again. Their swords rang in the chevalier training hall that Raymond had kindly offered them. A few of the dragons were visibly breathless now. "That's it," Darnuir told them. "We dragons might be few now, but each of us is worth ten humans. You will all be worth far more than that."

Lira sidled up so only Darnuir could hear. "They weren't the most experienced but their attitudes aligned closest with ours. They'll be happy to work with humans."

"Skills, we can hone," Darnuir said. "Attitude is far harder to change. They'll need more practice with the bow. How good a shot are you?"

"Decent enough," Lira said. "Captain Romalla always said I was better with a sword."

"Captain Tael told me the same thing. Yet brute strength and extra stamina can do that when sparring with humans. Everyone thought I was gifted."

"You are skilled, sire."

"We fought briefly, Lira. You gave me too good a match for one who wields the Dragon's Blade. But I have learned a lot since then."

"We may have to be patient with them in learning the bow."

"I know," Darnuir said. "I don't expect them to master something that takes hunters years to learn. Although much of that is building their arm strength. These are dragons we're training."

Lira tilted her head thoughtfully, a little grin playing on her face. "Let's see how they do today."

Strength was a hindrance, as it transpired. Quite a few Praetorians whipped back their arms so hard the strings snapped, but eighteen broken bows later, a handful of them were beginning to hit the target more often than not.

"Focus on technique," Darnuir said, walking around each in turn to help. "Feet shoulder-width apart, left foot just in front with your toes facing the mark. Those left-handed will do the reverse."

"Find a comfortable position for your hand at full-draw," Lira told them. "This will be your anchor. Try to pull back to the same spot each time."

Darnuir saw one girl pull back her string too far. Her hand was past her ear, her string quivering with the tension. "Not so tense, now," he said, gently easing her hand back towards her face. "Do as Lira says. Find where it is comfortable. Perhaps where your thumb touches your ear or where your knuckles meet your cheek." The girl nodded, concentration etched into her expression. She loosed the arrow and it hit the secondary ring, a little off the centre.

"Yes," she cried, then reorganised her features more seriously after catching Darnuir's eye. "Sorry, sire."

"Don't be," he said, returning to patrolling around the group. "Just keep practising. Demons and red-eyed men aren't going to stand still for you. One day I want you to be able to run and shoot at the same time, as many experienced hunters can." Some of them looked to him as if this was insanity. "It's true. You forget that hunters were trained to kill dragons once. I know a hunter who can even loose three arrows within seconds... well, I knew a hunter..." he said to himself, trailing off. Balack was the greatest archer he knew but he doubted his once closest friend would ever help him in the archery yard again.

I don't deserve his friendship. Not after what I did. Not after dealing a blow to his heart and then his ribs.

"Lord Darnuir," a voice called to jar him out of his reverie. Darnuir turned to see Raymond at the entrance above them. Yet again he was without his dark steel armour and wore a black leather jerkin over a white shirt. "King Arkus will converse with you now."

About bloody time.

"Lira, continue with things here," said Darnuir.

"I am afraid I must ask your dragons to vacate the hall," Raymond said when Darnuir reached him.

"But why?"

"My superiors do not approve," Raymond said. "And I have had my privileges removed." He turned like a soldier to leave and Darnuir followed alongside him.

"I am sorry to hear that," Darnuir said. "Perhaps I could—"

"The White Seven feel I am already too close to you, my Lord of Dragons. If you were to intervene, that would only prove them right."

"Close?" Darnuir said, surprised. "I think you got over some of your prejudice at Torridon, but I would hardly call that close."

"That is close enough for many in Brevia," said Raymond, leading Darnuir through the black-carpeted corridors of the palace. Darnuir assumed they were going to Arkus' more private council chambers.

"I would have thought their more pressing concern would be your brother?" Darnuir said. "Castallan's agents and followers are clearly in high positions."

"That is exactly the issue. I should have realised before I opened my mouth to the White Seven."

"Your superiors?" asked Darnuir, not finding the term familiar.

"Yes, the White Seven," Raymond said, a touch of bitterness in his tone. "One for each region of the kingdom and one for Brevia itself. They have the king's ear in military matters. Telling them of events at Torridon, of Sanders' betrayal..." He gulped. "It did not go the way I envisaged."

"Tell me about it," Darnuir said. Something about this unsettled him. *Do such powerful men really work against me?*

"Some thought I was lying," Raymond said. "Told me it was safe to admit the dragons killed my brother. I said that was preposterous." His speech grew hotter as he continued. "I explained, Lord Darnuir, I did; that were it not for your decision and the great effort of the dragons, then all would have perished at Torridon. Alas, it did not help. Lord Boreac in particular—"

"Lord Boreac?" Darnuir said. "He's one of these Seven? What does he have to do with it?" Hearing that name only deepened Darnuir's disquiet. His thoughts raced, and then it came to him: a brief and painful memory of a conversation with Eve at the hunter station. She had asked why Scythe had been chosen as their new captain after Tael's death, and Darnuir had told her Lord Boreac had nominated Scythe for the job.

Could it simply be a coincidence?

"You seem distracted," Raymond said.

"I'm sorry. Continue."

"Certainly. Lord Boreac is one of the White Seven, but that is not unusual. About half of them are old lords who can afford the position. If not them then one of their sons often takes the region's post. I am told that was not the way things used to be, that once anyone could rise through the chevaliers with bravery, honour and skill, like the hunters. Now, I'm not so certain."

"How did you join, if I may ask?"

"My father asked King Arkus to grant my brother and I the honour," Raymond said. "He and my grandfather made a deal of money in new print methods – enough to aid Arkus in financing his reconstruction of Brevia; enough to make a name for our family. My father thought that Tarquill would be fitting. Yet we were always looked down upon, my brother and I."

"And you have been trying to prove yourself ever since," Darnuir said. "I sympathise, Raymond. I worried whether I could prove myself as a dragon and now as a king."

Raymond looked taken aback by Darnuir's honesty, but nodded. "I can see why Sanders would have been lured by the thought of some extra power. Perhaps he was sick of the jeers, of being given the second-rate tasks. But I'll never truly know why or how it happened..."

"You said you had your privileges stripped, but you were making announcements for Arkus in the throne room."

"If someone asked you to make announcements rather than don your sword and armour, how would you take it?"

"As a slight."

"Forgive me, Lord Darnuir," Raymond hastened to add. "You must think I'm grousing over trivial things."

"Your temper is nothing compared to mine," said Darnuir. "I'm sorry to hear all this, Raymond. You deserve better."

"The king has been kind to me in truth," said Raymond. "He helped keep me within the chevaliers when some called for my dismissal. He didn't just grant me my position as a repayment for a debt. Arkus has encouraged men like my father and grandfather – men with ideas, ambition and drive. I think they are jealous of the favour the king shows us."

Raymond slowed his pace and Darnuir matched it. Up ahead was a heavily guarded room, which Darnuir assumed to be Arkus' council chamber. Each man guarding the corridor was heavily armoured in dark steel.

"Are ten chevaliers necessary?" Darnuir asked.

"Arkus at least has taken my warnings seriously," said Raymond. "Yet I am ill at ease. Something does not seem right in the city anymore. The White Seven hand-picked these men but—"

"I understand," Darnuir said, more quietly as they drew ever closer to the group.

"Be wary, my Lord of Dragons," Raymond said in an equally hushed voice.

When they reached the guards, their leader stepped forward and removed his helmet. The chevalier was a little taller than Darnuir, with a mane of dark blond hair to his lower neck and marble-smooth skin. He smiled tauntingly at Raymond.

"Ah, that was quickly done. You'd make an excellent squire, Raymond."

"Gellick," Raymond said curtly.

"Please be seated, Lord Darnuir," Gellick said. "I shall inform King Arkus you have arrived."

"I had thought to tell the king myself—" Raymond began.

"You are dismissed, Raymond," Gellick said without looking at him.

"But, sir, I—"

"Dismissed," Gellick said. "Or must I ask you to brush our steeds next?"

Raymond's face was growing pink but he nodded to Gellick and bowed briefly to Darnuir before taking his leave.

"One moment," Gellick said. He entered the room, leaving Darnuir alone with the rest of the chevaliers. They still had their helmets on and visors down, making it impossible to see their eyes. Yet Darnuir had other methods.

Furtively, he sniffed the air, trying to find a trace of fear. There was a light sweetness but from which guard he could not tell. Nor was he truly more informed. *Are you afraid because you are worried about being caught or because of who I am, whoever you are?*

Frustrated that he was being forced to wait again, Darnuir dropped onto the plush bench, reaching to adjust the scabbard of the Dragon's Blade so that he could sit properly. The moment his hand touched his sword all the chevaliers had their own weapons out. Darnuir let go of his sword slowly and deliberately.

"I'm not here to fight," he said. The air was much sweeter now. That gave him some comfort. If they were afraid of him then they couldn't all be enhanced red-eyed men. As the chevaliers sheathed their swords, not saying a word to him, Darnuir wondered whether he could take all nine at once. He liked to think so. It might take a bit of Cascade energy, but he could do it. Ten humans, armour or no, couldn't hold up to him now. Just a little Cascade energy was all it would take. His hand twitched. He saw a mental image of the Dragon's Blade carving through their steel bodies like meat and could almost feel the rush of magical residue running hot down his arm.

What is the matter with me?

He breathed steadily through his nose to calm himself.

It was important to show Arkus he had changed. Sadly, those outbursts in the throne room wouldn't help matters. In the days since, Darnuir was sure that he had been kept at arm's length as a means of establishing the status quo. Arkus was saying "This is my city, my keep. We'll talk when I am ready."

Yet time was short and Blaine was still to show.

Darnuir had tried to get Kymethra to go scout out Blaine's movements, but she refused to leave Brackendon's side. The pair of them had become reclusive, holed up with heaps of old books and scrolls. Events at the Conclave tower had set a fire under Brackendon, although Darnuir was still unclear on what exactly had transpired that night. Arkus had been furious enough to deny seeing Darnuir that morning and now the days had rolled by.

What's Arkus waiting for? His armies are here. His fleet ready to sail. We do not have any time to lose.

Darnuir rose. "I am weary of this delay." He stepped forward, intending to push past the chevaliers if necessary. To their credit, they did not react brashly. Darnuir heard those to his flanks thump slowly in behind to surround him.

He reached for the door. The closest chevaliers reached for their swords.

"Yer as unreasonable as yer sluggish, Arkus," came a loud, sharp voice from inside the room. Then the doors swung inward. Somerled Imar stood there, his face red, arms wide from heaving the doors open. Up close, Darnuir noticed that Somerled was a good deal shorter than himself. "Do us a favour, Lord Darnuir, and knock some spirit intae him. Oot of ma way now." Somerled shoved past Darnuir and the chevaliers returned to their original posts.

"The king will see you now," Gellick said, as though nothing had happened.

The room was sparse and practical, the only real adornment being a life-sized portrait of a rather stunning woman, with long black hair and grass-green eyes, wearing a pale green dress. Her smile was dazzling.

Arkus stood stony-faced behind a large desk topped with maps, figurines and open books with minuscule text. A great steaming vat of shimmer brew rested by several thick mugs and a bowl containing heaped silver alderberries. Arkus' hair hung loosely due to the absence of his crown, which lay atop sheets of ragged old parchment like the most extravagant paperweight in the world.

"A little privacy please, Gellick," Arkus said, popping a few of the berries into his mouth. Arkus didn't acknowledge Darnuir. The King of Humans seemed preoccupied with his maps and accounts.

"Lord Imar appears displeased," Darnuir noted as he reached the other side of the laden table. The light fragrant bitterness of the brew was energising on its own.

"Somerled feels I ought to have sent reinforcements to his islands already," Arkus mumbled, not looking up from the map. The military figurines were mostly of humans, painted in black and white for Arkus' regular army. Most of them were outside Brevia but a collection stood farther south at the Bastion, along with bow and arrow carvings in dark green.

Has he already sent troops south? If so, why so few?

Arkus sniffed then finally looked up. "Somerled believes I am moving too slowly."

"Understandably so, but we must take the Bastion first, and for that we'll need to wait for Guardian Blaine to arrive."

"Why do you think I've called you?" Arkus said. "This guardian and his army should arrive at Brevia today."

"Today? Why wasn't I informed immediately?"

"Word arrived late last night and I am telling you now."

"That's hardly the level of communication I require," Darnuir said.

"I've had a lot to manage of late," Arkus said. He indicated the piles of parchment. "Brackendon's bit of vandalism hasn't helped either."

"He learned valuable information," Darnuir said.

"Did he?" Arkus asked. "So, we know it wasn't Castallan who struck first. It hardly helps us. I hope all this studying the pair of them are doing will produce results on how they can weaken him."

"Brackendon's never let me down before," Darnuir said. "I'd have thought you'd be pleased such a blemish as the Conclave tower was removed for you."

Arkus grunted. "It will be once the irregularity of the area clears, I suppose. The city's population could use more room. But enough of the damned Conclave. We have an impenetrable fortress to take."

"It might not be so hard," Darnuir said. "At the Charred Vale, we defeated Castallan's demon army. The Bastion will lie relatively unguarded, unless he has summoned thousands more in such a short space of time."

"Don't be so sure it is demons we will face," Arkus said. He pointed to the figurines around the Bastion. "It would seem Castallan has gathered fresh troops." He poured himself a fresh mug of shimmer brew and took his first sip loudly. "Those are no longer my forces," Arkus added, reaching for a large piece of parchment with a multitude of coloured seals at the bottom. He passed it to Darnuir to read.

To our former King Arkus, the Lords of Brevia and the kingdom, and every human drawing breath,

We, the Lords of the Southern Dales, and those lesser lords signed herein, do hereby renounce

*the overlordship of the City of Brevia and the king. We instead pledge ourselves to and proclaim
our king to be Castallan, Greatest of the Wizards. King Castallan even now burns his demons in
the embers of a renewed faith in humanity, while a resurgent dragon king attempts to restart a
conflict long since left in peace. Dragons thirst for war again and humanity shall suffer as we have
always done when dragons draw their swords. Only King Castallan, who wields the power of the
Conclave of old, may lead us to renewed security for evermore. We welcome all who feel the same
to join us. It is not a decision blithely made. It is not for power, nor for riches, nor the advancement of person, but for the benefit and defence of all mankind. It is a cause we believe in uphold-
ing, even with life itself.*

Chief Signatory,

Robert Annandale, Lord of the Southern Dales.

Scores of names followed, each with their own curly scrawl and lump of wax.
Darnuir's teeth scraped together as he clenched his jaw, the darker reality clawing up
from his gut.

'*Even with life itself*'... *more lives will end than will be saved with this madness,
Annandale.*

"I wished to confirm the truth of it before bringing it to your attention," Arkus
said. "If what Raymond says about these red-eyed men is true, then we will need
every dragon to take the Bastion now."

"His superiors did not believe him," Darnuir said.

"The White Seven are a conservative lot," Arkus said. "They can barely believe
that a book need not be copied by hand alone these days."

"And you?"

"If you can be reborn, then why not? Magic isn't something I claim to understand
and I've never wished to have much business with it."

"It is dangerous, yet it is the source of my strength, and we will need Brackendon
if we are to defeat Castallan."

"Brackendon's certainly a destructive force," Arkus said. "In any case, I believe I
have a tool equally as destructive. A substance of great power."

Darnuir raised his eyebrows. "Would this happen to be a powder? A black
powder?"

"Yes," Arkus said, deflating a little. "How do you know of it?" Darnuir proceeded
to tell him of the events of the run from Torridon, when they had piled a makeshift
wall across the land and set it ablaze, only to be greeted with explosions all along the
line.

"The head of my Praetorian Guard, Lira, also knew of it," Darnuir concluded.
"Told me it is used in the quarries of the Hinterlands. I don't think it is a great
secret."

"Few enough know just how strong it is, and given the circumstances, I'd be willing to use our stores in the fight to come."

"You plan on making a weapon of this powder?"

"A weapon," Arkus tittered. "My wife's dear father, Lord Clachonn, would baulk at that. He calls it a tool."

"A hammer is a tool, but it can smash your skull."

"A crude if effective method. Right now, the powder is crude but effective at blowing rock to pieces. Why not use it?" Arkus sounded quite jovial, reaching for another handful of silver berries.

Darnuir wasn't quite sure what to make of all this. The powder would give them a needed edge but it was dangerous, hard to wield. It might well explode on their own men. He felt uncomfortable but he couldn't say exactly why – it all seemed too straightforward; too open.

If only Blaine was so clear with me; my, wouldn't that be nice.

"You're being very honest with me, Arkus."

"Because I hope that we might be frank with each other, Darnuir. My people are divided on how they feel about your kind. Events in the Dales make that all too clear."

"The audience in your court seem to hold similar opinions," said Darnuir. "You as well, from what you said there."

"A small piece of theatre, Darnuir," Arkus said. "My rule is not like your own. I must strike a constant balance of having more of my lords and people on my side than against me. Since this chaos began, many have blamed the dragons and you for it. In the past, I too have had my issues; we have even had our issues, but you might not remember."

"I remember enough," Darnuir said. "Enough to want a fresh start, if that can be achieved."

"It gives me hope to hear you say that," said Arkus. "Hope that we might forge a more agreeable relationship after this war is over. Assuming we are still alive, that is."

"A stronger partnership is something I too seek," said Darnuir. "The Three Races should stand as equals."

"I had something else in mind," Arkus said. "Human autonomy."

"Break the alliance?" Darnuir asked, taken aback.

"Only in a sense," said Arkus. "Only to make it seem like I have removed the overbearing dragon lords from my back and, more importantly, from the Assembly. Besides, if we win, if Rectar is defeated, what need will there be for an alliance then?"

"Let us agree to discuss this matter seriously *if* the time comes," Darnuir said, extending a hand. It wouldn't be what Arkus wanted to hear, but Darnuir would not make important promises like this too hastily. It was all too quick and polite and smooth. After a moment, Arkus took his hand, if a little reluctantly.

"I'll agree to that for now. My people are the ones currently causing us the headache, after all." Arkus hovered a clenched hand over the figurines near the Bastion on the map, as though he meant to squash them.

"As you say, many blame the dragons. Castallan offers them an easy solution. It's disheartening how many believe in him."

"Castallan can be convincing, but there is something else he desires as well: power." Arkus bent to grasp his crown as he spoke. Picking it up, he balanced it delicately on his palms. He looked down on the white gold circlet with narrowed eyes. "He wants what's best for humanity, I don't doubt. But he also wants this. And I'm afraid I am not willing to give it up."

"Then what makes you so different from him?"

"Nothing, in truth. It is just self-preservation," Arkus said, tossing the crown unceremoniously back on the table. "Would you give up what you have?"

"I don't have a choice," Darnuir said. "The Dragon's Blade answers only to me."

"There is always a choice in these things," said Arkus. "Yet it simply isn't in our nature to make ourselves lesser. Annandale's words in his declaration are well put and inspiring, but they are false and mask his longing. Yet such is the way of words."

"People are capable of change," Darnuir said. "It seems you are. You are nothing like the memories I have of you."

"A shattered heart and a shattered people will do that to a king," Arkus said. "I have grown harder, less assuming; that may be the only way in which we can change. Those who don't will slip and fall. I did wonder whether you would be the same, when I heard you had been reborn. It did help to explain why you disappeared for all those years. The Darnuir I knew wouldn't have had the patience to wait for so long."

"I very nearly lost my patience waiting upon this meeting," Darnuir admitted, thinking of his frustration only minutes ago.

"And yet you did wait," Arkus said, giving Darnuir a quizzical look, as though he had done something singularly strange. "I confess, I expected you would burst into my chambers one day and make demands of me. But you didn't. In fact, you have shown a considerable deal of courtesy, apart from shouting sensitive information to my whole court."

"For that I am sorry," Darnuir said. "I ought to have shown more restraint, but—"

"You were being harassed and abused," Arkus said curtly. "Frankly, I'd have lost respect for you if you had simply taken it. You dealt a strong and deep blow with your words, more than I imagine you are aware of."

"I was simply stating the facts."

"And the facts are distressing to many of my noblemen," Arkus said. "My queen, in particular, is worried by them."

"You did not seem fazed to hear of Cassandra."

"No," Arkus said simply. He did not speak again for a moment or two, perhaps thinking hard on his words. "I had long been aware that she lived, and that Castallan had her."

Where does the honesty end with this man?

"You knew, and still you did nothing?"

"Precisely," said Arkus. "Marrying off politically important daughters requires more planning and strategy than any war. Having her as my sole heir created a tremendous issue for me, Darnuir. I was already staring down civil unrest at sword-point when she was lost to me. Nothing has been simple since Brallor ran off." Arkus' tone was dead, flat and cold. No emotion seemed to move him when speaking of his son.

"I am sorry, also, for bearing news of your son so crassly," Darnuir said. "I'm still reeling from the loss myself."

"Are you?" Arkus said more casually. "I am not. I presumed my son to be dead decades ago. That was the first wound and it has had the longest to heal."

"You have a grandson to love instead," Darnuir offered. "And Cassandra, when we save her."

"To love, you say? Perhaps," Arkus mused. "What is the boy's name again?"

"Cullen."

"I'll see he is well cared for, but for the sake of stability, Thane will remain my heir."

"Very well," Darnuir said. "My priority is defeating our enemies. So long as Cullen is cared for."

"He'll have an easier time of it than Cassandra, I'll wager," said Arkus. "Already the vultures circle overhead – Somerled for one. He wishes his son Grigayne to marry her."

Darnuir felt an involuntary twitch at his mouth at hearing that. "You refused him, I assume?"

"I said I would need to think on the matter. Something more favourable may yet turn up."

"I doubt Lord Imar believes anything is more favourable," said Darnuir.

"The Splintering Isles have always been a troubled region," Arkus said, taking another handful of silver alderberries. "I would hate for Somerled to believe he is getting what he wants. I judge you are not keen on the idea either, though I imagine for very different reasons."

"Why would it matter to me?" Darnuir said, cursing himself for his indiscretion.

"Why? Well, I only thought that you might also have been interested in her for her position," Arkus said. "I could be wrong, of course. You could just have feelings for her."

"You think I would?" Darnuir said, trying to feign some of the old scorn he knew his older self was capable of.

"My lord Darnuir, if she is anything like her mother, then I'd be shocked if you did not. Tell me, what is she like? Does she have green eyes full of warmth?"

"She is beautiful," Darnuir said, though warmth was not apt for her eyes. Cosmo's, yes, but not hers. "Beautiful but distant," he continued, "like the promise of spring in the middle of a long mountain winter." His gaze lingered on the portrait of the woman behind Arkus a little too long. It might have been Cassandra, had it not been for the flush on her cheeks and the brightness of her smile. He was certain that Arkus caught him staring. "Cosmo's eyes – I mean, Brallor's – his were warmer."

"His mother's eyes," Arkus said. He turned to face the portrait as well. "Does she really look so much like Ilana?"

"She does," was all Darnuir could say. A part of him felt ashamed at being affected in such a way by the mere thought of her. Cassandra seemed to keep most at arm's length. *But not me. She confided in me. We are close, right?* But he also knew that half of why he was drawn to her was based on the relief of his head pains; some intangible connection over his lives that had settled the memories trapped in the rubies of the Dragon's Blade before he unlocked them.

What was that kiss? Was any of it real, or was it all in my head?

Arkus let loose a shuddering, tired sigh. "I'm not sure whether my heart will leap or sink when I see her." His voice was suddenly hoarse. "Clever as well, I assume?"

"Of course," Darnuir said. "Intelligent and capable; she escaped from the Bastion, after all."

"I had wondered… I don't suppose you know how?"

"There are passages within the fortress," Darnuir said. "Though without Cassandra with us, I doubt we will be able to find the tunnel she used."

"Passages?" Arkus questioned. "Curious. I saw none when I inspected the old plans for the fortress earlier."

"You have the plans?" Darnuir said more eagerly. *Perhaps some other weakness can be found.*

"I do," Arkus said, reaching for the rather old and large sheets of parchment that his crown had been resting on before. "They were deep in the royal vaults, but we found them. However, you will see that there is no indication of any passages under the walls."

Darnuir studied each sheet carefully, noting with some trepidation the thickness and height of each wall, angled in such a way as to make it impossible to find a dead zone from defending archers. The detail was intricate, every measurement given, and each method of defence quantified. There was nothing, however, that looked remotely like passages either in the walls or the central tower.

"Are these the only plans?"

"They are. It is possible that later additions were added and the plans have since been lost. It is peculiar." Arkus looked more intensely to Darnuir then. "You only have Cassandra's word about these tunnels?"

"Well, yes," Darnuir said. "I believe her. And finding these passageways will be our best chance at success. I'll dig up half the Dales if that's what it takes to find them. Unless this powder of yours will bring down the walls."

Arkus glanced back at the plans. "My supply of powder isn't vast and these walls are thick, and there are two layers to contend with. We'll deploy it as best we can, but this will likely still be a job for swords and strength."

"And there are few enough dragons left now," said Darnuir.

"Enough to cause a panic when four legions of your kind arrived at the city gates."

"I'd be more concerned about the traitors surely lurking in your midst," Darnuir said. "The man I killed at the Charred Vale was called Scythe and he was one of your hunter captains. There ought to be investigations. Certainly into the hunters at the Master Station here in the city, if nothing more."

"No," Arkus said.

Darnuir half opened his mouth and then stopped, caught off guard by the blunt response. "No?" he said slowly.

"No," Arkus repeated.

"I do not think it to be an unreasonable request," Darnuir said. "Nor did I imagine you would wish such men to continue at large." Arkus swept aside to pour himself another mug of brew. Darnuir watched, perplexed, as Arkus threw back its contents in one extended gulp and his whole body shook a little with the injection of energy.

"I thought this point might be tough for you, Darnuir. If you truly have changed, as you say, then you will listen to me."

"Will I?" Darnuir said, his temper beginning to rise. "I can wait for an audience with you if needs be. I will leave you to run your affairs as you will. But this is a military matter and in that, until this alliance changes, I am not to be denied. These traitors revel in killing dragons. I would see them brought to justice."

"You would see their heads roll," Arkus said. "Don't deny it. I recognise that look about you, that much you have retained from your old life. The anger you turn to so easily. I urge you, however, to rethink. I urge caution."

"Caution? It is caution and planning and waiting that has gotten us into this position. Castallan should have been handled years ago. Blaine should have gathered the dragons years ago."

Arkus remained calm by comparison, staring Darnuir back down. "I find this bloodlust for traitors intriguing when you yourself helped Castallan get to where he is today."

Darnuir choked. "You know?"

"Now I do," Arkus said, a smile playing on his lips. "You just confirmed it. I only suspected before, though I was sure I was right."

"That was an error," growled Darnuir. "I'm not the same dragon anymore."

"Indeed," said Arkus. "A simple mistake of your past life, fuelled by misinformation and perhaps desperation. Could not the same be said of many of those who have joined Castallan?"

"It is hardly the same."

"But it very much is," Arkus said. "Annandale and Castallan have stirred up enough dissent in the south without us adding fuel to the fire. Your traitors are their brave new soldiers. You say you want justice for your people and I understand that. Believe me, I do. But I cannot have my kingdom torn worse than it already is just to satisfy you. They are humans and under my laws. That is why I plan to offer clemency."

"Clemency!" Darnuir's heart drummed at the thought. "You might not be so quick to forgive if you had seen your son pinned against a tree with a sword."

Arkus winced. "And I presume you have taken your vengeance already. Is that not enough for you? No, Darnuir," Arkus added sternly. "I won't do it. If I allow you to go carving your way through my city looking for traitors, it will cause us both irreparable harm."

"This is a military ma—" Darnuir began.

"This is my kingdom," Arkus said loudly, "and my people. Persecution will get us nowhere. Let us remove the leaders and allow the followers to return quietly to the fold."

There was a knock on the door followed by, "Do you need us, sire?"

"It is fine," Arkus called back, then to Darnuir more quietly, "if you seek a better relationship then trust me on this. Do not give them justification."

Darnuir seethed, snorting air like a bull. He was on the verge of continuing the argument when the door burst open.

"I did not say enter," barked Arkus.

"My king," Gellick said, ignoring Darnuir. "The dragon and fairy armies have been spotted."

"Then I think we can conclude matters here for now," said Arkus.

"We're done for now," Darnuir said. "But the matter is not." He stormed out of the room, letting his inflamed anger carry him back to the chevalier training hall. Lira and the Praetorians stood outside, their way barred by a group of dark steel-clad guards. "Back inside," Darnuir ordered.

"But Darnuir, the guards, Raymond told us—" Lira began.

"If they want to stop us, they are welcome to try," said Darnuir. "I want a fight." The air grew very sweet as he approached the closest chevalier on the door. "Well?" he asked, drawing close enough to the man to see his eyes widen behind the slots in his visor. The chevalier said nothing but moved to one side.

Right move, human.

He heard the footsteps follow him in, down the tiered room to the lowest level. It was like a small arena or pit this far down and an audience would doubtless form soon. Darnuir whipped out the Dragon's Blade, turning it over and over in his hand.

"We need to intensify your training," he told the assembling Praetorians. "Four of you, you'll fight me at once. The rest of you, pair up and spar. No exercises; fight like you mean it. Now."

They began. Darnuir's opponents were better than he anticipated; that was good. Each time he fought them off, he demanded they charge again. One managed to land a hit on him and that made him laugh. Soon he was lightly nudging on the door to the Cascade, letting a drop or two in.

That felt better than anything.

Soon he forgot why he was enraged. All he felt was the movement, all he saw was the eyes of those he trained with, all he heard was the thud of feet and the scrape of steel. He didn't stop. He just kept fighting.

It only ended when he saw what surrounded them. Hundreds of chevaliers, face-less behind their visors, stood silently around the hall. Had they snuck in? Had they crept in like mice scurrying around the feet of wolves? Darnuir looked to them. Raymond wasn't there but Gellick was, the only one to have removed his helmet. He looked down upon Darnuir with a blank, unreadable expression. With one hand, Gellick lightly tapped the pommel of his sword.

"We're done for the day," Darnuir said. His Praetorians were trying to calm their breathing around him. "Come. Let us go meet our kin."

10

THE END OF MAGIC

The wizards and witches of the Cascade Conclave are simultaneously remarkable and worth little attention. Their use of magic is extraordinary but their reserved nature – a necessity in handling magic in such a free manner – has dissuaded them from engaging in major events of the world. Had the order joined one war or another in full force, the course of history could well have been different.

From Tiviar's Histories

Brackendon – Brevia – King Arkus' Palace

"And there they go," Kymethra said. "Darnuir, Arkus, even Lira and enough guards to clog the streets. But not us."

"Not right now," Brackendon said. He didn't look up from his reading.

"Darnuir will want you down there." She rapped her knuckles on one of the tiny glass panes held within the lead lattice. The sharp tapping made Brackendon lose concentration on his page. He looked up and was met with Kymethra's frustrated expression.

"I'm busy," he said, his voice half a rasp. He glanced out of the window towards where Kymethra had gestured. The palace resided on higher ground than most of the city, and Brackendon's room was high within it. High enough to see beyond the black walls of Brevia and witness the dragon legions approach the city like a wave of molten gold. *And so we draw ever closer to the Bastion.*

His silence seemed to annoy Kymethra further. She was scowling. "You might help me rather than berate me," he said.

"We've been through all these books. There's nothing there. Too much was either stolen from the Conclave or lost."

"There might still be something—"

"But there isn't," she said, her voice half-cracking. His brooding was fatiguing her, Brackendon knew. But it was more. She was afraid, as was he, for each day drew them closer to the battle to come; each day drew him closer to Castallan.

Whatever it takes, it must end. We must end.

"Will you stop acting like this?" she said, a little desperately.

"Like what?" he said, returning to his reading.

"Like a child. It's not like you at all."

"I'm sorry if I've upse—"

"I'm worried, Brackendon. You've barely spoken since the Conclave. Each day you've fallen deeper into this mood. It's like a part of you died. I heard what those *things* had to say as well, but I'm not giving up on the world."

"The Inner Circle attacked him," Brackendon said. "Castallan was forced to act as he did."

"Maybe in that moment," said Kymethra. "But in every moment since? Everything he's done since? I don't see how this changes anything."

"It doesn't," he said morosely. *It doesn't, and yet it changes everything.*

"Are you just going to brood here?"

He nodded, closing his eyes.

"Rather than tell me what really troubles you?"

He continued to nod.

"Fine." She stormed towards the door. "I'll go. Hot-headed dragons sound more reasonable at present."

There was a slam and distant footsteps. Brackendon took in a breath, held it, and then let it go slowly through his nose. He opened his eyes and returned to the page he had been reading.

This one was Mallory's *On the Bitter Taste of Power*. So far it was proving a tedious read and wasn't offering any insight into the limitations Castallan might have. When Brackendon reached a section about the optimum diet for a cautious Cascade user – oddly, poppy seeds were the prime recommendation with most meals – Brackendon closed the book. He added it to one of the many discarded piles with a thud. Landing askew, Mallory's dense tome tipped the balance and sent the entire stack crashing off the desk.

Grumbling, his frustration mounting, Brackendon rose to tidy up the books that lay scattered beneath the window. In his haste, he bashed his hip into the desk corner. Groaning, he bent down to collect the fallen books. It was warmer beneath the window due to light angling in through the glass. One beam burned uncomfortably at the delicate skin around his eye. The vexing heat caused an itch and he jerked his head to escape it, only to slam against the underside of the desk.

This time he let loose a growl and tossed the book he had just retrieved back down. He gave up on the endeavour and stood, leaning his weight against the window and watching the dragons draw closer to Brevia. A blue mass crept into view behind them and behind the fairies marched hunters in red and yellow. *We're all gathering. Ready for the pointless slaughter.* It was a shame Kasselle did not join her forces. Brackendon could have used her advice and knowledge. But then, the toil of marching and war had never been Kasselle's way. She sent others in her stead. Brackendon had been granted a shiny staff and been sent to do the impossible.

For there had been no answers. Not then, nor now, on how he might actually win such a fight. Perhaps there might have been within the Conclave but he had brought that tower to dust.

He didn't regret it.

In the days since, he'd exhausted Arkus' limited vaults and found nothing. Like Darnuir's rebirth, the situation was the first of its kind. Castallan had possession of all the staffs of the Conclave, save for Brackendon's. As powerful as Brackendon's new staff was, surely it alone would not best such incredible processing power. And where once Brackendon had been fuelled by a sense of justice and revenge, driven by a belief that Castallan was the enemy, he now felt deflated. It was as if his previous conviction had acted as a barrier between him and the reality before him. Yet, since the Conclave, the full weight of the duel ahead had begun to crush down upon him. Slowly. A little more pressing each day. Slowly. Until Brackendon considered that they had all been fools.

Where had this infighting gotten them? To the precipice of disaster. It was too late now for either party to make amends. Brackendon wasn't sure why he ought to fight. He was simply on one side and was stuck there. It wasn't the 'right' side, not anymore, just a side. He supposed it had always been this way, but he had been blind to it.

It was only then that he noticed his hands had clenched into fists against the glass. They felt hot – too hot to be heated from sunlight alone.

Perhaps Castallan's intentions had once been noble, but Kymethra was right. His methods left him irredeemable. Brackendon would do his best against him, but not for the reasons he once had. It wasn't to avenge the Conclave; nor for humanity, for it seemed so many had joined Castallan, both then and now.

Something in Brackendon shook and the air around him grew even warmer. A tremor ran down his right arm, yet there was no staff in his grasp.

He wouldn't fight for Darnuir either, he decided, looking out at the massing dragons. He knew Darnuir hoped to rectify his own mistakes by killing Castallan. Brackendon reckoned all the dragons were paying for their past. Not even the memory of
Cosmo could move him. Yet Brackendon would fight. That was not in question.
Though what he would fight for would be very different.

I will fight to end magic.

If by some miracle he succeeded, then he'd break every staff that remained. He'd
burn his own as well, even if he risked breaking to do so. He'd pass on no teaching.

Magic will end with me.

The window shattered, breaking in a shockwave from his fists and pouring down
into the palace grounds. The tremor running down his right arm intensified, as did
the heat around him. He grabbed his staff and felt the stinging rush of the Cascade.

Loose sheets of paper were whipped towards the breach. Embarrassed, Brackendon tried to grab them out of the air but most of them made it past him and flitted
on the wind outside. Cooler air blew in and took the worst of the heat away, leaving
Brackendon ashamed of himself. He ought to go down. It was childish of him to lurk
up here when there was so much to do. There was nothing else that solitude and
books could offer him.

Sadly, Brackendon's mood did not dissipate on his journey down. There was a
restlessness within him, mixed with a reluctance to take part in whatever talks were
going on between Darnuir, Arkus, Blaine and the rest. The thought of standing in the
middle of that argument – for there was bound to be one – was enough to cause a
grating headache all on its own.

So he took his time, drifting slowly through the army camps outside the city. He
passed by the palisade wall of a legion encampment and saw a human with a cart
being barred entry by grim-faced dragon guards; that was, until he managed to
convey that he was delivering food. Then he was waved on through.

Dragons will take and take, and never give.

Fairies seemed allowed to fly in and out as they pleased, however. One shot overhead, drawing Brackendon's eye, speeding to some faraway section of the sprawling
tents above the rising strands of smoke and steam.

Soldiers laughed, soldiers wrestled in their boredom; some glanced inquisitively
at Brackendon as he walked by, while others ducked their heads to avoid eye contact.
Hunters and huntresses from the Crownlands patrolled in their black leathers,
setting those idle to work and bemoaning the quality of the men's equipment. One
pudgy fellow knocked into a stand of spears, nearly skewering passersby, and hastily
tried to pick them up before the hunters saw.

You might have called up many to fight, Arkus, but these are hardly soldiers.

As arrogant as the dragons were, Brackendon could not deny that humanity
would be at a woeful disadvantage in this war without them.

Somehow, Brackendon found himself before the hastily erected pavilion, positioned at the central point between the camps of the three races. There was a collection of chevaliers, Light Bearers and Darnuir's Praetorians outside, standing in an awkward silence. One amongst them was not armoured but seated by a crude-looking crib. Auburn hair and the favouring of one side signalled that it was Balack, a little hunched over in his white leathers – well, what passed for white under all that dirt.

Are those burn marks and singes?

"What happened to you?" Brackendon asked when he reached him.

"More of that dragon powder, or black powder, whichever it is," Balack said. He rolled up the clothing on one leg to reveal a series of burns.

"You must be in a lot of pain," Brackendon said.

"Could have been worse. The guardian shielded me, actually. Kept me in one piece, though I doubt I'll be battle-fit in time for the Bastion." He winced and gently put a hand to his chest. "What's wrong with you?" Balack asked.

"Nothing," Brackendon said, perhaps a little too tetchily. "Did you see Kymethra?" he added, attempting to sound more pleasant.

"She flew down a while back. I think she's inside. Are you not going in?"

"Darnuir can make his decisions without me. He always has."

"He's changed," Balack said simply. He didn't seem to want to add any more. Footsteps beat behind Brackendon, and both he and Balack were spared further talk of Darnuir by the arrival of the outrunner Damien.

"Milk for the child," said Damien. "Approved by Queen Oranna's trusted wet nurse."

"He'll be eternally thankful," Balack said, accepting the bottled milk.

"You didn't just bring the wet nurse?" Brackendon said, unable to resist despite his mood.

"She protested," said Damien. "Excuse me, I must return to the king." And he disappeared into the tent.

Brackendon observed as Balack prepared a horn for the milk and lowered it carefully towards Cullen. A wedge of good clean cloth stymied the flow of liquid.

"Why are you playing mother?" Brackendon asked.

"Well, I'm still injured and so won't be able to fight. If I am honest, I feel I lack the will as well."

"What do you mean?"

"It's difficult to put into words. I don't feel as strongly as I did before; a little empty, truth be told."

"Cosmo's death has hit us all hard," said Brackendon. "He and Grace were decent people. I find it cruel that they've been taken."

"Yes, that was hard. I still don't think I've grasped that he's gone. Darnuir seems fine, though. He just ran off. Barely even checked to see whether Cullen was alive, never mind being looked after by anyone who cares."

"That seems a touch harsh," Brackendon said. "He has been concerned about Cullen."

"Concerned, but not present. Not here... not the same."

Ah, so that is it. You miss your friend, even if you can't stomach the thought of him right now.

"It's not fair what happened to you either," Brackendon said. "None of this is fair."

"Back home, even when things got desperate, even before you arrived, I somehow didn't feel as bad as this," Balack said. He hadn't seemed to register Brackendon's words. "We were all together then. All fighting; fighting for each other. And now—" Balack stopped, as though something had stuck in his throat. He swallowed and then busied himself feeding Cullen.

"I feel like I've lost something too. Lost what was driving me, so to speak. I understand what you're going through, I think."

"Have you lost the ones closest to you?" Balack asked. "Were your friends sent far to the north while you stayed here? Did the man you might have called a father die without you being able to do anything? Did your closest friend betray you and crack your ribs?"

"I don't have many friends," Brackendon said, and it sounded strange to say it aloud. "Most of the people I cared for were lost to me when the Conclave fell or have died in some other fashion. Until recently, I thought I was fighting for their memories, to make things right. Now, I've discovered that many were not who I thought they were. Darnuir is far better than he was, but the only one I truly have is Kymethra..." *And I've been pushing her away.*

"I... I'm sorry," Balack said, looking guilty for his outburst. "I hadn't considered that. Still, I can do good by honouring Cosmo and helping Cullen. I'm glad to."

"You might be of more help in the war."

"What can one archer do?"

"What can you do for Cullen that all of Arkus' palace staff cannot?" Brackendon rebutted. Balack opened his mouth to say something, but then seemed to reconsider, burying his face into his hands instead. "We need to keep fighting," Brackendon urged him, kneeling beside the young man. "As hard as it seems, we must. You might not wish to go on for Darnuir, but you can still go on *with* him. We can both help. But in our own way. For our own reasons."

Balack lifted his head up slowly, looking Brackendon in the eye. "What are your reasons?"

"I'm going to kill that wizard, or break him, and I'm going to prevent anyone else ever having the power that we do. With more luck than I dare count on, I might live out my days as just a man. A recovering addict, sure, but just a man." Balack said nothing. "Is there nothing left to drive you?" Brackendon asked.

"Helping a friend is worthy," Balack said. "Cassandra is a prisoner again. Although she can take care of herself, and I think Darnuir will have the rest covered." He thought for a moment. "I'll fight for Cosmo. That can be my reason."

"All you need to do is help," Brackendon said. "And I can get you there. How many weeks have you been in recovery?"

"About three," Balack said. "I thought you couldn't heal with magic?"

"You can, it's just... ill-advised. May I?" He moved an inspecting hand towards Balack, who obligingly raised an arm. Brackendon hovered his hand above the injured rib, sensing the damage there.

"How is it?" Balack asked.

"Healing well already. About halfway there. Yes, this can be done."

"Are you sure?"

"Half the healing, half the magic," Brackendon said. "And I have a staff from the Argent Tree. I think I can handle one minor to moderate injury." He shut his eyes and reached out to the door to the Cascade. He twisted the ghostly handle, pushed it open and let it flow. That moment of euphoric joy infused him.

He held it.

Savoured it.

Then he set to work, fusing Balack's rib together and easing the swelling. He sensed a minuscule splinter of bone lodged in Balack's lungs and dissolved it. Finally, he reduced the burns enough so that they would no longer cause pain. When it was done, Brackendon felt a powerful rush down his arm as the poison was sucked towards his staff. He held his breath, believing for the length of a heartbeat that he had gotten away with it.

Then he doubled over in agony.

"Brackendon," Balack said in alarm, catching him as he swayed forwards.

"Well, it still hurt," Brackendon said through gritted teeth. "Did it work?"

Balack breathed in deep and fast. "I'd forgotten what it was like to not ache each time I draw breath. I feel better than ever."

"Oh, wonderful," Brackendon said, taking shallow breaths himself. He fixated on a trodden patch of grass, so as not to concentrate on anything too overwhelming. From somewhere behind him there came the sound of heavy footsteps on the hard earth, enough for several people.

"What is going on here?" came the unmistakable, disapproving voice of Blaine.

"Brackendon," Kymethra exclaimed. Suddenly, another pair of hands were pulling him off Balack. "What did you do? Your arm!"

"What about it?" Brackendon mumbled.

"There's another black streak," Darnuir said, stepping into Brackendon's shaky vision.

"What were you thinking?" Kymethra said.

"I was thinking that I might actually use my power to do some good," Brackendon said, getting to his feet. He felt a little off balance but nothing worse.

This staff truly is something.

"He healed me," Balack said. "Thank you."

"Thank me by not holding back at the Bastion."

"That was quite reckless," Darnuir said.

"I don't think you can comment on anyone's recklessness," Brackendon said. "Sorry, that was—"

"It's already forgotten," Darnuir said. "Are you all right?"

"I am," Brackendon said.

"Good," said Darnuir. "For we march to the Bastion on the morrow."

"Darnuir, if we may depart for a private word," Blaine said. He almost sounded hesitant. It was only now that Brackendon noticed Blaine was leaning his weight upon his left leg, and had bandages on his right calf instead of armour.

"Haven't you made things worse enough today?" Darnuir said. He only then seemed to notice that Balack was there. "Balack – it will be good to have you back as well. We'll be in need of your bow," he added, not quite looking at his old friend. A second passed before Darnuir scrunched his lips, unfurled them again, and opened his mouth to say, "Balack... I—"

"I hope that is the last controversy between us, Guardian," Arkus called from out of sight. Everyone turned to see chevaliers pouring out of the pavilion, and a pink-faced Arkus blustering through their ranks, his long black robes dragging on the earth. Darnuir didn't finish his thought. He glanced between Blaine and Arkus then swept off towards Brevia with Lira, Damien and the Praetorians filing in around him.

Blaine watched Darnuir go, looking disappointed at his departure before turning his attention to Arkus. "My treatment of the humans following the Charred Vale was—"

"Not appropriate," Arkus interrupted. "As I've had to explain to Darnuir. Those hunters are under my rule and my laws. Taking precautions is one thing. Making prisoners of humans out of mere suspicion is quite another. And as for the dragon powder—"

"Do not use that term," a Light Bearer with black curls said, drawing in closer.

"It's all right, Bacchus," said Blaine. "Allow me to handle this matter."

"I'll use what name I want, since it is mine," said Arkus, stepping even closer to the guardian. "I'm sorry about the accident at Inverdorn, more than you are, I dare say. That was one of my cities."

"If it is your powder then you seem to have lost a great deal of it," Blaine said.

"Barrels in the Golden Crescent, even more at Inverdorn. Where else might they turn up unaccounted for?"

"Clearly, mistakes have been made," growled Arkus. "And I will use all my power to investigate the matter."

"You'll forgive me if I do not feel the substance is safe in human hands for the time being. My Light Bearers will guard your stores as we transport it to the Bastion."

"Darnuir himself has agreed to my plans," Arkus snarled. "The powder is a human tool and should remain in human hands."

"Tell that to the dead of Inverdorn," said Blaine. "And you would do well to watch your tone with me. As guardian, I seek what's best for the world. This dangerous substance should not be trifled with."

"You guard the world?" Arkus asked, more quietly, stepping within an inch of Blaine. "Which world? This one soaked in blood? I remember Draconess used to mumble about a guardian; he revered you. Can't say I'm as impressed." It was only then that Arkus seemed to notice Brackendon. "Finished moping, wizard?"

Brackendon's stomach knotted. "I had come to join the discussion."

"There is little left to discuss," Arkus said. "Now, I will take my grandson back with me." Five chevaliers began to close in towards the crib at the king's words.

Balack stepped forward then. "Sire, if I may accompany Cullen, I'd like to see he is in good hands and say my farewells."

"And who are you, hunter?" Arkus said, scanning Balack with his shrewd black eyes. "Do you not feel my staff can attend to the needs of one baby? My own flesh and blood?"

"Excuse me, sire, I meant no offence," Balack said quickly. "My name is Balack. Your son, he meant a great deal to me. Something like a father, but also a friend and teacher. I'd like to part with Cullen properly; if only because I was robbed of the chance with Cosmo."

Arkus' expression softened. "A terrible name for a prince... Cosmo," he mused. "Very well, Balack. Walk with me."

"Thank you, sire," Balack said. "And to you," he added into Brackendon's ear as he set off with Arkus and the chevaliers carrying baby Cullen. Somehow there was just Kymethra, Blaine and himself left. An awkward grouping, Brackendon considered.

"Balack told me you saved him," Brackendon said to Blaine. "That was brave of you."

Blaine seemed to take a moment to decide what to say. "My armour could withstand the blast."

"But not your leg?" Brackendon said.

"A heated fragment of a barrel ring, blown apart," Blaine said, his face blank. "Slipped in the gap between the plates."

"You stood between the explosion and a human?" Kymethra asked.

"I felt no need to watch him die," Blaine said impatiently. "I must take my leave. The two of you will have matters to discuss."

At last, Brackendon and Kymethra were alone in the middle of the vast array of camps. He reached out for her hand, but she withdrew it. Her polite public demeanour changed into a disappointed frown.

"They want me to fly to Dalridia. To check on matters there for Lord Imar."

"Then you should not wait long."

"I can't leave again," Kymethra said. "Not now. We're too close to—"

"You must play your part," Brackendon said, "and I mine. I'm sorry for the way I have been acting. I have been afraid of what I must do." Kymethra nodded. She hit him hard on the shoulder, once, twice, then took a fistful of his robes and fell in against him.

"Everyone is ignoring it," she said. "All of them. They speak of marching to the Bastion and assaulting it, assuming it will all go well. But how can it?"

"For as long as I can remember, we've all spoken of defeating Rectar as well, and Castallan isn't as dangerous as him. We tell ourselves these things because to do anything less is to have already given up."

"These last days, I thought you had given up."

"I thought about it. Yet if Castallan and Rectar were truly invincible they would have no need for men, for demons, for flesh and blood, for walls or mountains. They need these things because they can be killed, even if it seems impossible. If I make it through this then we're done, Kymethra, I promise you. I'll snap my staff and we can quit playing our parts. We'll spend our days at the Argent Tree, eating fruit and walking barefoot through the forest."

"Don't you dare go into that fortress before I come back," Kymethra said. She kissed him. "I haven't quite forgiven you yet."

"Go on," Brackendon said. "Fly, and fly back to me."

11

HIGHLAND HUNGER

Of the Highlands, I have nothing to say. The frost trolls keep to themselves and I, a fairy, would certainly never be welcomed to journey there. I find it hard to imagine they have even kept records of their history. And there is some of that fairy scorn, so ingrained within me. I shall leave those words in this text, if only to serve the purpose of showing the effect of a lifetime's worth of prejudice.

From Tiviar's Histories

Garon – moving north through the Highlands

"Are we lost?" Pel demanded. "Where are all the kazzek?"

To avoid answering, Garon pretended to have a good look up the wide, deep valley, as though he wasn't sure it was totally empty. Jagged boulders dotted the landscape, poking out above the blooming heather; thatch-roofed homes sat beside long thin strips of farmland. But no kazzek could be seen. There hadn't been any in the last three glens either. Ochnic was on Garon's right, peering out at the landscape deep in thought.

"Well?" Pel asked again.

"Dey must have gone to da Great Glen," Ochnic said. "A place of refuge for kazzek in times of peril."

"And taken every scrap of food with them?" Pel said.

"Why would dey leave any behind? If we gather in da Great Glen, we don't know how long it will be for." Pel said nothing more but her wings fluttered in some agitation.

Garon bit his lip, unsure what they could do other than trudge on. *What choice do I have?* He gently placed a fingertip on Darnuir's scroll, though it offered him no answers. His stomach rumbled audibly and he found it hard to concentrate. Even the dim grey sky felt harsh against his eyes and he squinted to shield himself.

"Let's move on," Garon said. "Perhaps the kazzek will have left something behind." Ochnic's snort was not helpful. Pel visibly drooped and they walked a little slower. Their speed was not improved by the terrain. It had been arduous progressing through the Highlands. There were no roads, barely anything resembling a path; the wild land had proven a hindrance at every turn. Yet there was a rugged beauty to it that Garon could not deny. Heather bloomed brightly, ranging from amethyst to orange-yellow, but there were also clumps charred black with the poison of the Cascade, much like the trees in Val'tarra had suffered in places. Upon the mountainside, there was a large cluster of black heather like a scar slashed against the landscape. Garon noticed Pel looking up at it too.

"Do your people not remove those dead plants, Ochnic?"

"No," said Ochnic. "It is natural. Why remove dem?"

"That's what we do," Pel said.

"Da kazzek know de dangers of de blue poison. Burned bushes remind us to respect it." Pel looked confused but held her tongue. Garon smiled at her and nodded. He was thankful that she was at least making a concerted effort to be civil with Ochnic, despite their hunger.

They searched the homes of the kazzek. The trolls had cleared out anything useful, including tools. In one home a basket remained, its lid askew. Garon glimpsed orange as he strode by it and his mouth watered at the thought of one small carrot. Without daring to hope he pushed the lid clean off. It was, in fact, a bundle of carrots and even some onions. He grabbed for an orange delight and despaired at the blue mush where the root once had been. The onions were no better: black and rotten. The smell made him nauseous but he had nothing to throw up.

Giving up, Garon dragged himself back outside and sat down amongst the heather. Pel and Ochnic followed him; she began kicking at the undergrowth, wandering in a small circle, while Ochnic crouched low and brooding amongst the petals. Garon sighed and looked back on their expedition filing into the glen. The hunters and fairies came first, with groups of flyers already heading east to scout further. One dragon was already limping up to Garon, Pel and Ochnic.

"Nothing?" Marus said without hiding his bitterness. His thick eyebrows were furrowed into a single angry line.

"Ochnic believes the kazzek have fled to a refuge deeper into the Highlands," Garon said.

"How far is that?" Marus asked. "The extra supplies we picked up from Captain Romalla were only enough to help us reach the trolls."

"A week from here," Ochnic said. "Maybe a little more."

"We're already on half-rations," Marus grumbled. "Ochnic, I thought you promised—"

"I said da kazzek would help. Dey will. But I didn't know dey would have called to da Great Glen already... somethin' must be wrong."

"We still have some food," Garon said, trying to prevent any arguments. "And we can still hunt game, I'm sure. We have almost a thousand hunters, after all."

"Then where is our roast deer?" Marus asked.

"You'll struggle to find even a grouse once de clans have been summoned, dragon legate."

"The Ninth Legion marches on its stomach," Marus said.

"And humans and fairies are no different," Garon said. "We're all suffering here."

"Some more than others," Pel said. She brought out her spear and cut a swathe of heather in frustration. "At least your meat is cured. Food fit for fairies is running low."

"You're perfectly capable of eating meat," Marus said. "You'll just have to manage, Wing Commander. It's not our fault your stores got burned by Castallan's traitors."

"Stop it," Garon said. "We're all just hungry. Don't let it get to you."

Pel either ignored him or didn't hear him. "It's not our fault the trolls have all run off," she said, her voice rising. "Maybe they saw fairies coming and thought they'd take the chance to torture us while they feast up a mountain somewhere. Maybe—"

Ochnic rose a little out of his crouch, growling deeply.

"Pel, that's enough," Garon said, forcefully this time. He stepped between Pel and Ochnic, arms raised against the two.

"Dat won't be necessary, pack leader," Ochnic said, shoving his hand aside. "My daughter says things she does not mean when hungry. Let's hope she is feastin' and not facing a demon horde without me." He stalked off.

Pel's eyes widened. "Ochnic, wait. Please." But the kazzek kept on walking. Pel started forward, nearly taking off after him, but Garon stepped in to catch her arm.

"Let him go. You both need to cool off. We all do," he added, catching Marus' eye as well. The legate's face was unreadable.

"Very well," Pel said. She flew off in the direction of the other fairies. Garon's stomach ached from its emptiness and rumbled loudly again.

Marus, his gaze downcast, half turned to leave as well. "I am sorry for adding to that outburst, Garon. Let's hope we reach the kazzek sooner rather than later, and not only for the sake of our bellies. It might be best if we have a more natural figurehead in this Chief of Chiefs." He took his leave. Alone, Garon slumped back down into the heather.

Maybe he's right. Maybe I can't do this after all.

He thumbed the edge of Darnuir's scroll but it didn't help. It never really did.

12

THE BASTION BESIEGED

I am assured by military minds that the effort required to storm the Bastion would be incredible, even for the dragons. It is designed to repel them, after all. As a deterrent against future conflict between dragons and humans, the fortress works well enough. Yet should war ever come, I foresee this deterrent will decimate generations on both sides.

From Tiviar's Histories.

Blaine – Outside the Bastion – Camp of the Third Legion

It had been two weeks of ponderous marching south. They had followed the coast, enabling many of their supplies to be carried by Arkus' fleet. The humans made progress slow, and still Blaine had not found the chance to speak with Darnuir. The boy was giving him the cold shoulder since their less than cordial meeting with Arkus. In a way, Blaine was impressed by it. Darnuir was showing more backbone even if the timing wasn't ideal. And now they had arrived within siege range of the Bastion, time had truly run out.

Evening was fast approaching, so little would be done other than set up a perimeter to the west of the fortress. Troops would be sent to secure the woods a little south of their position. The trees ran until half a mile from the base of the

Bastion's south-west walls and would be an easy source of wood for siege engines and towers.

The colossal fortress could have been raised by gods during the world's creation, as though some power had left part of a mountain unfinished. Its mighty walls met at sharp angles like arrowheads to envelop the citadel tower in a star shape. Two sets of walls made two great stars if seen from above: two imposing grey, dead stars. An aura of challenge radiated from the Bastion, its very strength inviting foes to test it. To Blaine, it seemed inconceivable that humans could have made it – although it was with the aid of dragons, he reminded himself. Blaine knew that all too well.

Would Darnuir begin his search for the passageways of the fortress tonight? Blaine hoped not. He needed to speak with him about it, but a service to N'weer would need to be held first.

"Bacchus," Blaine called. The Light Bearer dutifully stepped forward from the entourage. "You have proven yourself trustworthy and diligent since the disaster at Inverdorn. I hope you do not mind me asking some small favours of you?"

"Never, Lord Guardian. I live to serve the gods, and you are their conduit."

"Find the king for me," Blaine said. "Tell him I request an urgent audience. Perhaps he won't be so scornful towards someone else."

"At once, Lord Guardian," Bacchus said, and he was away as light as a feather on the wind. Blaine was growing fond of the younger dragon. *If only more dragons that followed the Light were as dutiful, our race would fare far better*. Then again, Blaine had seen what had been done in the name of duty, in the name of the gods long ago. He tugged lightly on Arlandra's necklace.

"We should prepare for service," Blaine said to his remaining Light Bearers. "Multiple sermons across the legionary camps. More attend with each day, and we must not let the impending siege distract us."

"Yes, Lord Guardian," they said together.

Darnuir – Outside the Bastion

"We should begin searching for the passage under the fortress immediately," Darnuir said. A large, intricate map of the area had been found and the usual figurines placed upon it. With Darnuir was Arkus, Somerled and Fidelm, in a central command tent that was at the intersection between the camps of all three races outside the Bastion.

"It will be perilous searching blindly," said Arkus. "Trenches will be needed to protect our teams. It will need to be carefully done."

"Carefully sounds like it means time," Darnuir said. He wanted this fight to come swift and hard.

"It will take five days at least to assemble siege towers," Arkus said. "Maybe more."

"Can't it be done faster?" Darnuir said.

"Those walls are very high and we're hardly used to making such towers," said Arkus. "Few have been needed since the kingdom united. In any case, island aggression was always by sea, not land." He glanced to Somerled Imar. The Lord of the Isles was picking pieces of chicken from his teeth.

"Didnae need towers to sack Brevia back then, did we?" he said. "Shame the Bastion doesn't have a wide open bay."

"If there is any way to hasten the process..." Darnuir imagined the battle, the feel of the Cascade down his arm and the smell of fresh blood filling his nostrils.

"We should not rush our preparations, Lord Darnuir," Fidelm warned deeply.

"No, of course not," Darnuir said. His hand twitched and his thoughts drifted towards the door in his mind.

Fidelm narrowed his eyes. "Is anything amiss?"

"What?" Darnuir said. He shook his head. "No, I'm fine. We should prepare as best we can. My concern is for Lord Imar and the state of the Splinters should we take too long."

"I'm grateful for yer concern," said Somerled. "But what is a few more days now? I await my fleet from my southern islands before I can hope to ship reinforcements back north. I trust yer witch friend travels fast."

"She'll deliver your messages faster than anyone," said Darnuir.

"What of the Dales, General?" Arkus asked of Fidelm.

"My flyers report the lands are quiet. Castallan's forces are entirely holed up in the Bastion."

"So, he has left Deas exposed?" Darnuir said. "Perhaps if we placed pressure on their homes, your southern lords would forget their newfound loyalty to Castallan."

"I recall mentioning my displeasure at exacting harm on my people," Arkus said.

"I said pressure, not murder," Darnuir said. "The mere threat may cause some to lose faith."

"I will dispatch a force to cut Deas clean off from the Bastion if you wish," Arkus said. "I'll likely need a peacekeeping force present once the Bastion is taken."

"Yes, send a small force to threaten the idea of encirclement," said Darnuir. "But not enough men to weaken our chances here. The Bastion will be a terribly hard fight." A part of him was counting on it, hoping for it. He picked up the nearest wooden figurine, this one a dark green hunter carving of the Dales, and clenched it in his fist.

"Oh, Darnuir," Brackendon called from the tent's entrance.

"Coming to join us?" Darnuir asked.

"I was, but it appears you have a messenger," said Brackendon. The tent flaps opened seemingly of their own accord and Brackendon stepped in alongside a Light Bearer with curly black hair and a plain, unreadable expression. Darnuir recognised this one. Bacchus, he was sure, and he'd been with Blaine at the meeting outside Brevia. "He's very insistent," said Brackendon.

"My king," Bacchus said with a bow. He did not address the others. "The Lord Guardian wishes an audience with you."

"This again? He does realise I am busy with a war? I'd ask him to join us but I'd rather avoid insulting our human *allies*."

Arkus' face darkened at the very mention of Blaine.

Bacchus seemed unmoved. "The Lord Guardian requests you attend him. As the leader of the faithful—"

"Attend him?" Darnuir asked. In his anger, he crushed the figurine in his hand. The splinters and chunks of wood trickled from his grip onto the map below. Everyone looked to him.

That wound me up quickly, even for me – even for the old me. Am I truly angry with Blaine, or is it something else? He hadn't drawn on the Cascade since Brevia. He'd fought against it, but maybe it was time to surrender to it, else he might not make it through these war councils. *I shouldn't, I shouldn't, I can't.* Yet his hands shook at the very thought of the Cascade. *Just a bit,* some part of him urged. He opened his clenched fist, let the remains of the figurine fall, and dusted off his hands to excuse his fidgeting.

"Very well, I shall see Blaine. Forgive this interruption, my lords."

"We shall begin laying siege," Arkus said. "Good luck, Darnuir." And he smiled. Darnuir returned the gesture, glad for Arkus' understanding. There may well be a good future there after all. Bacchus fell in beside Darnuir as he left the command tent, as did the Praetorians with Lira at their head.

"Is something wrong?" she asked him.

"Just going to pay Blaine a visit," Darnuir said. "Bacchus here says I must 'attend him'. Tell me, Bacchus, how is Blaine's leg?"

"The Lord Guardian has recovered well from his injury," said Bacchus. "He has a slight discomfort, but moves as well as ever, sire."

"Yes, the Guardian's Blade is good at healing, or so he told me," said Darnuir.

"The Lord Guardian will be glad to hear of your concern," said Bacchus.

"I also hope he will be glad to take up my offer," said Darnuir.

"Offer?" Lira said.

"I'd like to challenge Blaine to another duel," said Darnuir. "It's been some time and it will be a good warm-up for the battle to come."

"I do not think the Lord Guardian intends to—"

"If Blaine wants to see me, it can be on my terms for once," said Darnuir. "Bit of a show for the troops as well. Surely he won't begrudge me?"

Bacchus took a moment to think. "I am certain he will oblige you, sire."

Blaine – Outside the Bastion – Camp of the Third Legion

Blaine made his way up the Via Primacy of the camp. He felt most comfortable here where there was a large majority of the faithful. He was almost at the central point of the camp when he spotted Darnuir approaching from the south with his Praetorians, Lira and even Bacchus in tow.

Well done, Bacchus. You've proven yourself again.

Now, if only Darnuir would keep his head long enough to hear him out. Sadly, from the expression on his face, that didn't look likely.

"Thank you for coming, Darnuir," Blaine said.

"Blaine," Darnuir said. Dragons nearby, especially those making their way to N'weer's service, were already beginning to stare.

"I'm afraid you've come just as service is to begin," said Blaine. "Will you await me in my tent?"

"I have another idea," said Darnuir. "What do you say to another duel?" That drew more eyes.

"Now?" Blaine asked.

"Now," Darnuir said.

"I wanted to talk."

"And I want to duel. We can talk after, though I am quite busy with the siege."

And have you ever thought I might have some important information in that regard?

"Your leg isn't ailing you, is it?" Darnuir said.

Blaine felt a twinge behind his left knee. "It is fine. But my service must come first."

"Lord Guardian, I could give the sermon tonight," Bacchus said. He stepped forward and all the onlookers now directed their attention to him.

"You?" Blaine said.

"Why not?" Darnuir said. "Other Light Bearers conduct your services elsewhere now."

"But this is the main congregation," said Blaine.

"You are the guardian," said Bacchus. "You should not have to trifle yourself with every matter. Allow me to free your time tonight."

Blaine pondered. The guardian Sulla never held service himself to increase his mystique, keeping himself hidden from the masses. But that was over a thousand years ago. Their faith was not so strong now. Blaine had to be the one to lead the way. Besides, his leg wasn't fully healed. A duel now would be painful and pointless. Why was Darnuir so insistent?

"I'll go easy on you," Darnuir called.

What is the matter with you, boy?

Then Blaine noticed it – an infinitesimal twitch of Darnuir's hand over the hilt of the Dragon's Blade.

Damned fool. He's seeking to use magic. This isn't good, but unless he gets a fix soon—

"Well?" Darnuir asked, interrupting Blaine's thoughts.

Perhaps if I make it quick, we can move past this and he'll be more inclined to listen.

"I think you've forgotten our last encounter too quickly, my king," Blaine said. "It is I who must go easy on you for the fight to be fair."

Darnuir's lips spread into a broad grin. "He accepts the challenge. All may come and watch. No holding back now, Guardian." To his right, Lira flicked her eyes between the two of them and shuffled one foot nervously.

"I won't," Blaine groaned. "And I shall follow you shortly." Darnuir and his Praetorians headed northwards up the Via Primacy, leaving Blaine with Bacchus.

"Thank you for believing in me, Lord Guardian," Bacchus said with a small bow.

Blaine stepped close and placed a hand on his shoulder. "This is a one-time thing," he said quietly. "You may hold sermons if you wish, but the Third Legion is mine."

"I understand," Bacchus said. "I meant no offence. I only thought to—"

"There has been no offence," said Blaine. "Go now. Our men require inspiration for the battle to come."

By the time Blaine reached Darnuir outside the camp walls, a small ring of spectators had already formed. The ground was soft underfoot, turning to sand at the far edge of the crowd nearest the coast. The smell of seaweed was thick in the air.

As Blaine passed through the ring of onlookers, he unsheathed the Guardian's Blade.

The audience drew a collective breath.

"Best of three strikes?" Darnuir asked. The Dragon's Blade was already in his hand, red and fierce. An orange tint lit the golden metal at the dragon's mouth.

"This won't take long," said Blaine. *I pray it doesn't,* he thought as his knee twinged again in pain.

Darnuir threw himself forward, twisting to Blaine's left in a blur. Blaine easily blocked the attack by pouring some magic into his own reflexes.

That eager to draw on the Cascade, Darnuir?

Blaine drove left with his shoulder, slamming into Darnuir's chest. Their heavy armour thudded dully and Blaine pushed them along the grass. Darnuir dug in his heels. They halted. A moment passed during which neither budged, then Blaine pulled back and the true sword fight began.

Darnuir had improved since their duel in Val'tarra. He was faster, stronger, and less obvious. Blaine recognised a feint and nearly had him but Darnuir lashed up at an impossible speed. The sheer force of it pushed Blaine's sword arm high, exposing him.

He saw the blow coming.

Blaine dropped to his knees, slamming his injured leg into the ground, and rolled. He heard the sword cut through the air above and struck at Darnuir's midriff with the flat of the Guardian's Blade as he rose.

The crowd remained tensely silent.

"One to me," Blaine said as he got up. His joints protested from manoeuvring in armour like that. His lower leg throbbed horribly and he bit his lip in pain. He risked opening the door to the Cascade to ease it. A trickle of power that warmed him, comforted him; then he slammed the door shut. Healing too often, even in bursts, would leave him much like Darnuir, Guardian's Blade or no.

Darnuir had already paced back to his starting position. "Ready?"

"I'm not the one losing," said Blaine. But he knew this round would turn sour.

The king came on a second time. He didn't feint. He didn't lunge suddenly to one side. He just came head-on.

There was a savagery behind the blows. With each block, with each narrow escape, Blaine felt his muscles burn hotter from the strain. He stepped back to the edge of the ring and unleashed a counterattack. He slashed down from shoulder to waist but Darnuir caught his sword on a wing of the Dragon's Blade. This time Blaine wasn't fast enough and Darnuir scored a hit on his upper arm.

"And one to me," Darnuir said. He gulped visibly as though he were swallowing an egg and winced at the taste.

Not spitting out that bitterness? Blaine thought. *At least you're trying to hide it.*

This time Blaine would not hold back. There was a large audience now and much more at stake than merely the next round. Blaine feared Darnuir would only drift further from him if he thought he was the more powerful. Blaine reassured himself he wouldn't lose. He had experience of fighting one such as Darnuir, after all. So he kicked the door open.

And he made the first move.

How long they fought for, he couldn't have said. Long enough that he heard Darnuir's breath come in ragged pants. Blaine too fought for air, his chest swelling within the confines of his breastplate. A Cascade-infused backflip left him dizzy but out of reach of Darnuir, and able to breathe. Then the Dragon's Blade came soaring towards him. He blocked it and it returned to its master's hand as Darnuir ran at him. Their fight raged on.

Blaine lost the feeling in his mouth as the harsh bitterness of the Cascade welled up. The rush to his blade threatened to pull his arm off.

But he would. Not. Lose.

"That's enough," Brackendon bellowed. As Blaine was in mid-swing, Brackendon whizzed in between him and Darnuir just as their swords would have met. There was a sound like fairy wings in flight, a whirring that was magnified a thousandfold, and Blaine was tossed backwards.

Face in the grass, he rolled over and blinked up at Brackendon. The wizard's staff shone like a star on the earth, crackling with sparks of blue and silver all along the wood.

"Call it a draw," Brackendon said, his voice returning to normal. "Don't ruin yourselves fighting each other." Blaine sheathed his sword, afraid he'd pushed it too far. "Go on now, all of you," Brackendon added to the spectators. After seeing what the wizard had just done, they didn't hesitate. Once the area was clear, Brackendon spoke again. "Kymethra has returned from the Splintering Isles. Lord Imar hopes you will join him in discussions."

"You go on, Darnuir," Blaine said. "As I'm not welcome on your councils anymore." And he left, exhausted, leg throbbing, all thoughts of speaking to Darnuir about the passageways of the Bastion forgotten. Blaine kept up a good show of strength until he returned to his private tent, where he collapsed onto the floor.

He lay in a heap for some time until he summoned a reserve of strength to unstrap his armour and take the weight off himself. He didn't even have the wits to place the pieces on their stand. He managed to wash his face then glug an entire jug of tepid water.

Gods, but I feel old now.

It was the last thought he had before he buried his head into a pillow and sleep took him.

Darnuir – Outside of the Bastion

As Darnuir watched Blaine go, he felt his body unwind after the battle. He was drenched in sweat, panting harder than a dog in summer, but he felt… good. Relief washed over him. The battle had released some pressure in him like water from a dam. His head felt clear, whereas before the duel it had been aggravated, almost fuzzy. In fact, he could barely remember the moments leading up to the fight: just the fight itself, and now this pleasantness. And what a fight it had been.

"You shouldn't have stopped us," Darnuir said.

"I should have stopped you half an hour ago," Brackendon said. He stepped in close to Darnuir. "I thought I told you to be careful with the Cascade," he hissed.

"You did," Darnuir said.

"Then what in Dranus' filthy long tail was that?"

"A duel," Darnuir said, feigning shock.

"It was the duel to end all duels. Do you want to break, Darnuir?"

"Of course not."

"Then don't needlessly waste your body pulling stunts like that," Brackendon said.

"I'm okay, Brackendon," Darnuir said, his voice rising higher than normal. "I'm not addicted," he added, trying to laugh it off. *But I am... or I will be. How can I possibly admit that to them and still have them follow me?*

"Denial is the first damned stage," Brackendon said. "You need help. Your fight with Scythe plus that run to Brevia must have affected you more than I realised. I should have known it would. Your body has hardly had a chance to build up a tolerance yet."

"Brackendon, I swear nothing is wrong. I actually feel great."

"You will leave Castallan to me. Understand?"

"You cannot be seriou—"

"Yes, I am," Brackendon said. "I didn't save your life all those years ago so you could break just months after getting your sword. I broke, remember? I wouldn't want to see anyone go through that, not even Castallan. Stay away from our fight."

"I will try."

"Try very hard," said Brackendon. "Magic truly is a curse. Now, let's move on."

Grumbling, Darnuir faced his Praetorians and was surprised to find Raymond standing sheepishly amongst them. The chevalier looked a little pale and he was still without his armour.

"It was I who came to deliver the message," Raymond said, sounding hoarse.

"Well, out with it, then," said Darnuir.

"You've had it, my Lord of Dragons," said Raymond. "About Lord Imar and Kymethra's return. I tried to get your attention but—"

"You did more than try," Lira said. "Nearly ripped your throat out shouting to them."

"Then why did Brackendon—"

"Lady Lira ran to fetch help," said Raymond. Lira blushed at the formality.

"And here I am, fetched," said Brackendon.

Darnuir looked around the group. None of his Praetorians gave anything away: they weren't afraid or disgusted, but they weren't admiring him either.

"I have acted inappropriately," said Darnuir. "Forgive me?" Silently, they nodded. Lira too, if a little stiffly. "Please, Raymond. Lead me to Somerled."

It turned out there wasn't much to discuss. Kymethra reported that demons had bypassed Ullusay and had landed east of the Nail Head Mountain, on the island where Dalridia was based. Every longship Grigayne Imar could spare was en route to the Bastion to pick up reinforcements as soon as the fortress was taken. Until that time there was little that could be done. Darnuir made his promises that Castallan would fall soon and took his leave. Night had fallen and, as always, Lira fell in beside him when he emerged from Somerled's tent.

"You're allowed to rest, you know," he told her.

"I think you should apologise to Raymond."

"I should. He's a good man."

She seemed to hesitate for a moment. "Are you… are you feeling okay, Darnuir?"

"Perfectly."

"As the Praetorian prefect, I feel it is my duty to—"

"I'm fine," Darnuir said irritably. She nodded quickly and cast her eyes to her toes. Then she yawned widely.

"If you intend to go see him now, I will leave you, if that is your wish."

"That's not what I meant," said Darnuir. "Come with me. You can send the rest of the Guard to bed, however. They will need to be well rested."

Minutes later they had made the short walk to the chevalier field accommodations beside Arkus' pavilion. The guards didn't utter a word as they approached, nor did they protest as they entered the encampment. They passed a slim boy brushing a horse with its nose in a bucket of oats. The next tent over had a lad hastily polishing steel greaves in the light of a dying fire.

They did not find Raymond until they reached the far end of the chevaliers' enclosure. He had no youths attending him. His tent was smaller than the rest and he was setting down a pail of oats for his own nut-brown steed when they reached him.

"Lord Darnuir. Lady Lira," Raymond said, bowing low. "I did not think to expect you."

"I came to tell you I'm sorry," said Darnuir. "It must have been humiliating trying to get my attention. You didn't deserve that."

"You were busy, my lord. One such as yourself need not apologise to the likes of me. I did not acquit myself well during our first encounter, after all."

"I bear no grudge," Darnuir said. "Not to you. Not for that."

"And I the same," said Raymond.

Lira stepped up to Raymond's horse and began petting its mane as it bent over the pail. "What's his name?" she asked.

"Bruce," Raymond said. "'Twas the name of my grandfather before our house had a name. Sanders desired to call him Longshanks. I'm glad I went with my own choice now."

"I haven't seen you ride him on our entire march," Darnuir said. "He isn't injured after the stresses of Inverdorn, I hope?"

"Chevaliers who are banned from wearing their steel cannot ride, my lord,"

Raymond said. "I keep him healthy in case, but alas, I fear I have been reduced to Gellick Esselmont's lackey."

"Is it all my doing?" Darnuir said.

Raymond shook his head. "I returned to Brevia a different man. Sanders' betrayal and your heroics, saving all those people who weren't your own kind, it made me rethink the stories I had been told. The fairies too have surprised me, taking so many humans into their care. You wouldn't think it possible given what is said around the capital."

"I'm glad you don't think of us so poorly, Raymond," said Lira. She scratched Bruce fondly along his neck and shoulder.

"Perhaps not after my display in the throne room and earlier tonight," said Darnuir.

Raymond shrugged. "Your intentions are noble even if your methods are yet unrefined." His eyes widened suddenly. "I am sorry for that outburst. I don't know—"

"It's quite all right," Darnuir said, waving it off. "I want my Praetorians to feel comfortable in telling me when I have erred."

"But I'm not—"

"I'd like you to be," Darnuir said. "If Lira is okay with it." Lira looked as stunned as Raymond. "You're the Praetorian prefect, Lira. You're in charge of recruitment. But I do wish to include all the Three Races in my new Guard. Castallan's infiltration of the hunters has made that difficult, but I can trust you, Raymond. Will you join me?"

"As part of your – *Guard?*" Raymond said, as though the meaning of the word had temporarily left his mind. "What good can a mere human do to help you?"

"It's a sign of what I want to achieve," Darnuir said. "You know honour, you are well trained, and both you and Bruce here would make fine additions, I think. Say yes, Raymond. Say yes and don your steel again."

"I – I accept, Lord Darnuir."

Darnuir shook his hand, careful not to squeeze too hard. "Welcome, Raymond. And please just call me Darnuir from now on."

"And just Lira for me."

"That may take some getting used to, my lor— Darnuir," said Raymond.

Lira smiled. "It gets easier with time."

13

THE BREAKING OF THE BASTION: PART 1

There has been a First War, and a Second. When, I wonder, will the Third War come?

From Tiviar's Histories.

Cassandra – The Bastion

Cassandra was coiled snakelike on her bed when the knock came. Dranus only knew why they bothered to knock. It was tiring that some of those serving in the Bastion still felt the need for niceties. Some didn't, of course. Some seemed to loathe her for being Arkus' daughter.

Her visitor knocked again.

"Come in," she said, scrunching her face into her sheets. The door opened with a faint creak and heeled boots clicked in.

"Good morning, Princess." Whoever he was, he was highborn, for his speech lacked any provincial accent. "The enemy's siege machines are built and they will strike soon. His Majesty will be sure to request your presence in the throne room."

"Just get out." She untangled her face from her sheet and craned her neck. He wore a courtier's purple velvet doublet, pulled in tight about the waist by a belt. Something on that belt caught her eye. Something sharp.

"If it pleases you, I have your breakfast and fresh clothes."

Cassandra didn't answer. Her attention had turned to the bowl on the bedside table, where lay the remnants of her dinner from the night before. It was a sturdy wooden dish. Quite heavy in hand, but would it be enough? Then she looked to the fat volume of Tiviar's *History*.

"Princess?"

"It would please me," she said hastily. "My head is spinning. Perhaps some food will help."

"I don't feel right in the morning until I eat," the man said. He bowed out and Cassandra hopped out of bed. The smell of cold grease from last night's stew made her feel sick as she grabbed Tiviar's tome.

The purple-clad man returned with an oversized tray with folded clothes on one side and breakfast on the other. She gave him a smile to disarm him. Now that she saw him properly, Cassandra could not be sure of his age. He sported only two patches of wispy bristle on his chin and cheeks, which had not lost their youthful chubbiness. He must have been even younger than her.

She had the heavy book in hand, feigning that she was browsing it innocently.

I'll have to be quick.

"I shall give you some time to get ready," he said, turning his back foolishly to her as he set the tray down.

Cassandra stepped towards him, raising the book high.

"Please do not tarry, Princess, as—"

Thunk.

Cassandra felt the blow ricochet up her arm. The boy spun, dazed, his jaw hanging loosely. She struck him again between the eyes and he smacked his head off the bedpost before he crumpled to the cold floor. He lay unmoving with a bloody nose.

A rush of panic came over her. *Is he dead?* She bent down, placed a finger on his neck and found a pulse. She puffed out her cheeks in relief and collected herself.

It's fine. You've done it now.

She deposited the book onto the mattress and began searching at the boy's belt. Hanging amongst coin purses, keys and vials, she found what she was after.

There we go. Thank you, whoever you are.

The knife was stubby but strong. It would serve. She pilfered the belt so that she could strap the weapon to herself. If positioned at her abdomen, she could probably keep it hidden under her clothes. Upon rising, she assessed her situation.

The boy's limp form was still at her feet. It would be prudent to do something about him before anyone else arrived. Cassandra dragged him to the bedside, his leather boots squeaking terribly, and began stuffing him unceremoniously underneath the bed. Another pang of guilt hit her so she placed a pillow under his head.

Before attending to her food, she inspected the clothes. As usual, they were too courtly. There was a clean smock, which Cassandra was grateful for, and she used the knife to cut out the looser bottom half so it became more like a shirt. Then she belted the dagger to her midriff, put on the modified smock, and placed her hunter leathers back on once more, trying to ignore the smell. No one had thought it necessary to clean off the gore from the Charred Vale; it was likely they were trying to force her not to wear them.

The food was next – chewy brown bread with butter to spread, a plump pear, thick wedges of hard tart cheese and crunchy honeycomb. She wolfed it all down. Cassandra wondered whether all Castallan's prisoners ate half so well.

What gruel would Chelos be suffering?

More guilt stabbed at her, and shame. Even as a captive, she could not feel the quiet pride of enduring hardship; of having something active to fight back against. Instead of torture or a cell she had a four-poster bed, fresh clothes daily, food to feed a lord and servants delivering it all. It had always been that way. She was a spoilt prisoner.

Then she saw a smear of blood on her hand. She wiped it away with the ripped remnants of the smock she had no use for. There was some blood on her bed as well, from where she had put Tiviar's book down. She scooped it up like a wounded animal and wiped it clean, making sure it was spotless before returning it carefully back to the library. It was a crime to have used the book in such a manner, yet needs must.

With adrenaline still flowing, Cassandra returned restlessly to the main chamber of her suite. She stood waiting, rocking on the balls of her feet.

Now what, Cass?

Attacking the boy had been impulsive. What she would do with the knife she did not know. Anything she could, she supposed. Someone who searched her might feel it but the leathers were padded and she'd take the risk. Castallan wasn't going to kill her.

But she would kill him if she could.

Chelos was probably dead after all. Cassandra had asked time and again to see him, even just briefly, but she'd never been answered. She hadn't been denied; her requests just fell on deaf ears, as though there was some unspoken agreement to spare her feelings. It hadn't worked. She had thought on it and she'd soaked one pillow with her tears.

Cassandra knew she would fail. It was desperate. Still, she had to try something. She was still standing stupidly in the middle of the foyer when they came to collect her.

"I see you're ready," the huntress Freya said. Her eyes were scarlet. "Come along, then."

. . .

Blaine – Outside the Bastion

Blaine kept low as he crept through the trenches. Lacking his armour and wrapped in a cloak, he prayed he would not be recognised. The digging teams were too busy to notice much beyond the dirt and danger. They had worked day and night, moving ever closer to the outer wall of the Bastion. Shovels rose and fell rhythmically as Blaine passed, the soil piled up on the sides for added defence. Now dawn had passed, archers on the walls resumed taking shots when they could, but the catapults were the greater danger.

"Look out," someone cried, and Blaine whipped around to see a rock impact into the trench behind him. A team of dragons rushed to remove it.

To Blaine's great disappointment, the brave digging teams had not been successful in their main objective. He had hoped to avoid this; hoped the tunnel might be found on its own. It would have been far better that way. Each day he had checked, even nudged the teams in the right direction, but to no avail. And now they were so close to the walls the battle would come soon, perhaps that very day. The ridge of the trench obscured their camps but he could see their lumbering siege towers were complete at last. He had no choice. He couldn't keep quiet about the tunnels and let thousands of dragons die just to safeguard old guardian secrets. Arkus would fume in rage, Darnuir would hate him for it, but he had to reveal what he knew.

I've run out of time.

Cassandra – The Bastion

Castallan's throne room was brimming with armed men and women. Many were hunters of the Dales but many more were regular infantry in padded jerkins. Those more fortunate wore some chainmail. Nearly all had glowing red eyes, save for Castallan and a group of lavishly dressed people crowded around him. He stood in front of his elevated throne.

"It will not be long now," Castallan said. "The great battle for humanity is upon us, friends. Will we be forced to follow the whims of dragons or shall we forge our own future?"

A cheer followed with much clanking of weapons. Cassandra's spirits rose as well.

Soon it will all be over; you will be dead.

Freya manoeuvred Cassandra towards the throne. She was close to the wizard, but couldn't reach him from down here. These red-eyed devotees would easily stop her before she made it anyway.

"Victory today is my burden," Castallan said more solemnly. "All the power of Brevia, of Val'tarra and the dragons, is set against us. I cannot ask you to triumph through strength of arms but through resolve. I ask that you hold the walls, hold the defences and hold together."

Another round of cheering, even louder than the last. So many voices, and this was not even a fraction of Castallan's supporters. Cassandra never had a hope of killing him. But she had to do something. Thousands of dragons, humans and fairies were about to storm the Bastion. She couldn't just sit here helpless.

"You have placed your faith in me," Castallan continued, his voice rising, "and I promise I shall not disappoint when I take hold of the Dragon's Blade and bring humanity into a new age!"

Cassandra covered her ears against the roar that followed this time.

She realised then that these people truly were prepared to fight for him, to die for him too. Did he really stand a chance against Brackendon, Darnuir and Blaine? Surely not. But then, he had all those staffs, grafted and bound to his own. Like each lord's signature on the declaration, each staff added legitimacy to Castallan. Power was persuasive and many had been swayed by it. She looked to the throne, lingered on the gleaming silver staffs, and decided what she must try to do.

The uproar had not died down and Castallan was revelling in it. She'd only have one shot to reach the staffs on her side that were low enough. Realistically, that meant two potential targets.

Her heart quickened and her mouth went dry. The idea was insane.

Out of the corner of her eye, she saw Castallan raise his hands for silence. "Bring in the dragon," he called. Jeers and booing answered him as the great doors of the throne room opened. Cassandra couldn't see through the dense crowd but she knew who it would be. It was another full minute before Castallan raised a hand to bring order. Then he pointed an accusatory finger down the length of the throne room. Cassandra stood on her tiptoes to try and see but it was no good.

"Before you stands an ancient dragon," Castallan said. "One so old he can remember a time before Rectar and the demons, a time when dragon fought against dragon and somehow humanity still bled. Tell me, Chelos, do you still not see the merit in what I do?"

Cassandra started forwards at the name, her fear confirmed, but Freya held her back with an iron grip.

"Never," Chelos said. His voice wavered but there was still strength in it and that spurred Cassandra on.

"No?" Castallan said. "So you do not think I should seek to end the war? I have found the means to defeat our great enemy."

"What you make are abominations," Chelos said. "Are you all fools? How can you follow this man who has set demons upon your own kind?"

There came a piercing, echoing slap.

"Do not harm him," Castallan said lazily. "Let him have his say. Let him rant and preach his old ways, even as they burn around him and a new world begins."

Cassandra renewed her efforts to break free. "Let me see." But her captor wrestled her back. "Let me see him. Let me go. Let m—" Cassandra's breath left her as she was hoisted up onto the platform of the throne.

"Settle down, Princess," Freya snapped. Cassandra could hardly believe her luck. She was standing right beside the staffs. Yet she could not move closer, for Freya held her in place by the ankle. When her red eyes looked up to Cassandra, the message was clear: *not one move*. At least from here Cassandra could see Chelos, forced down on his knees with shackles on his wrists.

"Too much power," Chelos said. "So much you delude yourself into thinking you can kill a god. None will be able to defeat Rectar save those with the grace of Dwna, Dwl'or and N'weer." Chelos met Cassandra's eye then and her heart seized up.

I'm sorry. I'm sorry. I'm sorry. She tried to tell him this through her stare.

Castallan followed Chelos' gaze and his mouth twitched when he saw Cassandra behind him. "She is back, Chelos, and she knows who she is."

Chelos did not break his gaze with Cassandra. He looked to have aged greatly in the time she had been away. The crinkles of his face had deepened and an angry bruise was now spreading across his cheek, but that did not stop him breaking into a smile when he saw her. She saw him mouth out, "Hello, my girl."

"I shall make you a deal, Chelos," Castallan said. "If you, perhaps the eldest of your kind, can admit fault just this once, then I shall be merciful to your people."

"I am not the oldest of my race," Chelos said. "And you will not defeat the Shadow."

"You see," Castallan said. "Even on their knees, dragons will not bend; afraid of change and terrified of losing their power. Even when my intentions have always been for the good of all Tenalp."

A loud mumbling of agreement swept the room once more.

Chelos finally broke his gaze with Cassandra to glare at Castallan. He drew himself up as far as he could, defiant. "Kill me or send me back to my cell. I will await the true king there, and pray you all dare to get in his way. For it will be the last thing you ever do."

The crowd was now close to pandemonium. There were cries for blood, cries of disbelief, taunts, even laughter. Cassandra felt the tight hand on her ankle disappear as Freya moved forwards to add her own insult to the tirade. Chelos received another blow to the face and Cassandra winced, turning away. Her head almost collided with the tip of one of the silver staffs and there she saw a weak point. The wood was thinner near the top of the shaft where Castallan had taken a cutting.

This would be her only chance.

She slipped a hand down underneath her leathers for the dagger. Retrieving it wasn't as easy as she hoped, but she wiggled it free, cutting her chin as her hand jerked upwards.

Everyone else was still occupied. Castallan was forcing his way through the crowd to reach Chelos.

"Leave him," Castallan was saying, amplifying his voice, yet it had no effect on the crowd.

Cassandra took a deep breath, grasped the staff in one hand to brace herself and brought the knife down upon the weakened segment of wood. One blow did little, the second sent up silver splinters. She hacked again, with all the might she possessed, feeling her shoulder pang with the effort. Three, four, five times she swung until, with a crack, the staff gave way. The gnarled head of it crashed to the platform and rolled, bouncing down each step. She watched it go, her heart racing so fast she thought it would burst.

Instantly, the atmosphere in the throne room changed. A deep booming emanated from Castallan, throwing the attendees into silence. The room darkened almost to blackness and the heat dropped to a chill. Desperately, Cassandra raised her arm again, targeting another staff, but she was lifted high into the air before her stroke could fall. She flew, soaring to slam high up against the faraway wall. Steel cuffs appeared to bind her and she looked out across the crowd as a sea of red eyes glared up at her through the dark.

Blaine – Outside the Bastion

Back in his tent, Blaine held the white gem in his palm. The weight of the memories within it threatened to drag him down. He'd got what he needed from it, so placed it back into the hilt of the Guardian's Blade with a satisfying click.

Perhaps that black powder would be enough to win the day, and there would be no need for Blaine to speak up. But he couldn't waste lives for the sake of holding his tongue, nor did he wish for Arkus and Darnuir to feel validated in using it.

Thankfully, he could always rely on hot water being delivered to him each day, and as expected, his tent flap was pushed aside by two young dragons; one carrying a steaming bowl, the other a scrap of parchment.

"Dwna bless you, Lord Guardian," they said.

"Dwna shine upon you both," Blaine said.

"We came earlier but you were not here," said one of the boys. "The water would have been cold."

"Then I am grateful you returned. That will be all."

By the mirror, the water boy looked unsure. "Lord Guardian, I wonder, sir, if I may ask wisdom of you."

"You may," Blaine said, intrigued. "Though I shouldn't tarry. I am already late for Dwna's service."

"It is about the sermons, Lord Guardian," said the boy.

"Oh?"

"You often speak of fighting the Shadow," the boy said, "but here we are fighting humans. Will the gods condone this?"

Blaine rubbed his chin thoughtfully, feeling the rough bristles. "Such questions are difficult to answer. Yet I have done you all a disservice by not addressing it. I shall rectify this shortly."

"Will you fight today, Lord Guardian?" asked the water boy. "Brother Bacchus says the battle will come soon."

"Does he? Well, it likely will."

"We only wish we could do more. My brother and I."

"One day you shall. Do your duty, keep to your training in the Way of Light, and you shall both be Light Bearers one day."

The boys beamed. "Thank you, Lord Guardian," they said together, then left Blaine alone.

He moved to the steaming bowl and examined himself in the mirror.

I look a damned mess.

The hazy dawn through the tent's flap lit the blond dusting across his face. His sunken eyes had not quite recovered from his duel with Darnuir. They looked greyer than usual, the amber less bright

He unwrapped the cloth around the shaving tools and instinctively picked up the razor with the blue pearl handle, even though it no longer brought the joy it once had. He could not help but hear Kasselle's voice each time he held it, with every stroke of the blade. *"I don't think you should come back."*

His fingers felt weak as he placed the razor back down. Thankfully, the hot water was reviving when he splashed his face. He dabbed his face dry then stared at himself again in the mirror.

You are old. Might be you're too old, Blaine. But you must go on.

Once he reached the sermon tent, his spirits rose. His audience had swelled greatly since their time in the Golden Crescent. Though Light Bearers held service across the legions, many dragons chose to make the trip to hear Blaine himself. Fresh banners with the symbols of the gods had been made: the three emanating rays of Dwna; the half-seared sun of Dwl'or; and the three spiralling rays of N'weer.

These banners adorned the space behind the dais, which now shone with a daily polish.

Then his mood darkened in an instant.

Someone was already standing behind the dais.

"My friends, we prepare for battle this day," Bacchus proclaimed. "It is a good omen that the morning light is clear and warm."

"Dwna shines upon us," the congregation said as one. They were answering him; saying the words just like they would with Blaine. He stood dumbfounded. And furious.

"I know some of you question our actions here," Bacchus continued. His voice was different than usual: a smooth, calming, honeyed voice that could convince a queen to marry a beggar. "These are humans we fight today, not the Shadow. Yet as the grace of Dwl'or is always half shrouded, so too is the service that we must make unclear at times. Rarely are matters so clean cut."

Blaine was astounded. He couldn't have put it much better himself. When Bacchus looked at the audience they looked back, locked eyes. And they were listening so closely. Bacchus was addressing concerns that had taken two bold water boys to bring to Blaine's attention.

I've been too distracted lately.

A member of the congregation spoke up. "Dragons lost the Second War. The gods did not shine on us then. What if the same occurs again?"

There was mumbling around the tent.

"Those red-eyed beasts seek to kill us," someone else noted. "Would we need more reason?"

A louder chatter of agreement followed.

"There is a clear difference," said Blaine, finding his voice at last. "Our predecessors wrongly thought humanity to be of the Shadow, as we are of the Light. This is not so. Humanity is neither Light nor Shadow, favoured by no side. We have not lost sight of the real threat."

He made his way to the dais to take his proper place. Bacchus held his ground for a second before stepping aside.

"Dwl'or also shows us that there are two paths in life," Blaine said. "One of Light and one of Shadow. Though every dragon is born under Dwna's blessing, the gods know that some are led astray; taken by the allure of the Shadow. Dranus was one such dragon. He turned his back on the gods and took his Black Dragons down the other path." Blaine paused, noticing that the congregation were looking to Bacchus, as though for a second opinion.

Bacchus looked nervously at Blaine then turned to face them. "I believe we have reached a pivotal moment in our history. N'weer shows us that all things can be restored. Our king was reborn. I foresee our connection to the gods being repaired as well if we can defeat Rectar, and all who stand within the long shadow he has cast across our world. Inside this Bastion hides a wizard and humans corrupted by our enemy. It is our duty to cleanse them."

"Then Dwl'or grant us strength," a call came out.

"Dwl'or grant us strength," the assembled dragons said together.

"Thank you, friends," Blaine said, hoping to regain control. "Prepare yourselves and steel against your fears. Dwna shine upon you all." As the congregation began to rise, Blaine rounded on Bacchus. "What part of 'a one-time thing' didn't you understand?"

"You were late, Lord Guardian," Bacchus said. "And those gathered looked worried. I thought you might be—"

"You thought wrong, didn't you?" said Blaine. "When have I ever missed a sermon?"

"I only thought, with the battle so near, you might be in council with the king."

Blaine scowled. "Do not presume to take my place unless instructed. Is that clear?"

"Quite."

"Good. Now go prepare yourself for battle while I go see our blessed reborn king."

Darnuir – Outside the Bastion – Three Races' Central Command Tent

Darnuir's agitation was reaching new heights. He puffed an angry breath through his nose and saw it steam in the crisp morning air. It seemed the full heat of summer was already passing.

"We are getting nowhere with this," Arkus said, standing safely on the opposite side of the sweeping war table. "This passage may well exist but we should focus our efforts on the assault."

"What say you, Somerled?" Darnuir asked. "This passage is our one best chance at securing victory."

Lord Imar replied with a cold expression. "Well, yer right about that. But for once I agree with my liege lord."

"Your king," Arkus reminded him curtly.

"Hmmm," Somerled said. "Might be king. Though I don't see any other Great Lords here, almost as if they 'av tae obey ye without question. Or they're over the other side of those terribly high walls, I suppose."

"Not for much longer," said Darnuir.

"It's been long enough," said Somerled. "Two weeks it took us tae get here and almost another one preparing. Meanwhile, the demons continue to smash my own people, and are likely to be at Dalridia itself by now. You two kings have argued plenty about how tae storm this place. I agree with Arkus. Nae mer time can be spared."

Off to Darnuir's right, Fidelm's wings buzzed briefly. The general had largely stayed silent on the issue, while Brackendon and Kymethra lingered at the edge of Darnuir's vision, contributing little.

"You are right," Darnuir said, looking to Somerled. "We cannot stay any longer. The Bastion must fall today. Though I shudder at what it will cost us."

"It was not designed to fall," said Arkus. "Even with a dozen trebuchets the outer wall may not give, and then there is a second behind it.

"So we shall use your stores of black powder," said Darnuir. "The Bastion was not designed with such a weapon in mind. Our trenches have at least crept towards the base of the western walls. Sapping teams could begin tunnelling within the day. We could mine down, use the powder, and destabilise the foundations."

Arkus was shaking his head. "The walls are too thick," he said, tapping at the dimensions on the unfurled plans. "We'd need our sapping teams to burn every pig in the kingdom to level those walls."

Darnuir scanned the blueprints again and then it hit him. He cursed himself for a fool not to have thought of it sooner. "We could blow a gate or two open. As mighty as they are, they will be the weakest points along the walls."

"Just the gates, you say," Arkus said, pressing his knuckles down on the table. "We could do that."

Finally, we are getting somewhere.

"We still have a serious consideration," Fidelm said. "Whether the gates are blown open or not, we will likely lose a great deal of troops in the initial waves. Which race is to bear the brunt of the attack?"

Silence reigned.

"I fear there is little either myself or Kymethra can add on this," Brackendon said. "I should like a walk before it begins."

"Of course," Darnuir said. He didn't begrudge Brackendon. Everything would ultimately hinge on his success. "I'll come find you," Darnuir called after them as Brackendon and Kymethra exited the pavilion.

"Well?" asked Fidelm.

"An equal split between the races seems the fairest option, in my eyes," Somerled said. "But as my own people are not part of this army, I feel I too should bow out at this time."

"Very well," Darnuir said. Some minutes passed in awkward silence. Neither Fidelm nor Arkus seemed eager to send their troops first into the jaws of the Bastion's defences.

"Dragons would surely be the most capable of fighting these servants of Castallan," Arkus finally said, a little cautiously. Darnuir sighed, though he wasn't surprised to hear it. Sending humans to scale the walls would only lead to a massacre.

"You are right," Darnuir agreed. Arkus looked at him in shock. "Yet I fear I cannot only use dragons in this battle, else my people may not understand the point in this alliance."

"The old ways are not entirely forgotten," Arkus said. "With packed spear formations and many archers, we will fare well enough given space."

Darnuir knew of these capabilities all too well. He'd watched what had befallen dragons when they did not treat humans seriously. *Caught in the bogs,* he thought, remembering vividly the memory Blaine had shown him. *Caught in the bogs... waist deep in mud and bloody water.*

"If the gates can be taken, then your spears could push in," Darnuir said.

Arkus nodded. "Open the way and humanity will take back what is ours."

"As your people will deserve for their efforts," Darnuir said, finding a smile tugging at this mouth. They were actually agreeing and it didn't seem forced.

"I shall direct my flyers against the catapult crews as a priority," Fidelm said. "But archers on both sides will make our work perilous."

"Enemy archers on the outer wall should thin out once our siege towers gain a footing," Darnuir said. "Then, once the dragons and I have cleared a path, I suggest we bring up hunters to begin thinning out their ranks on the inner wall. Perhaps a company of chevaliers could join the dragons as well at that point?"

"My White Seven are always telling me of their prowess," Arkus said. "I'm sure they will relish the chance to prove it." He ended on a low, satisfied laugh that barely escaped his lips, as though enjoying some private joke. Then Arkus nodded, seeming content. Fidelm nodded as well, cracked his knuckles and stretched his wings as though flexing.

"This will be a hard-earned victory," Darnuir said, heart swelling in anticipation for the coming battle. "But if we use the best of each race, I'm certain we will achieve it."

"I fear many will die in taking this place," said Fidelm.

"There will be no need for any slaughter," Blaine said solemnly, entering the pavilion with a heavy stride.

"And why is that?" Darnuir said. "Your input isn't required here, Blaine."

"Lives will be lost," Blaine said, ignoring Darnuir. "Yet fewer will die if we use the tunnels to infiltrate the fortress."

"We can't," Darnuir said, agitated. "We've dug up half the land near the woods that Cassandra described exiting from to no avail. It was always a long shot. Only Cassandra would have been able to find the entrance."

Blaine didn't seem to hear Darnuir. He drifted over to the table and began shifting amongst the maps and blueprints.

"The tunnels are not shown on those," Arkus said, sounding both confused and concerned.

"I'll need a quill and ink," Blaine said to no one in particular. Darnuir wasn't sure whether to be more annoyed or worried by Blaine. It would be poor timing for Blaine to have lost his wits or taken ill. *But Blaine cannot get ill, can he?*

"What do you need ink for?" Darnuir asked.

"Did you never ask Cassandra how she found out about the passageways?"

"I did," Darnuir said gently. "Her carer told her about them. Chelos, his name was."

"And how do you think Chelos knew of them?" asked Blaine, looking relieved as he spotted what he desired at the other end of the war table and moved to take them. When he returned, he dipped the quill tip into the dark liquid.

"Chelos?" Arkus said. "The name is familiar. You don't mean that old steward of the Royal Tower in Aurisha?"

"The very same," Blaine said, peering intently over the maps again.

"What's he got to do with this?" Arkus asked. "You speak as if you know him."

"I do," Blaine said. "Or I did. It has been such a long time."

"So, you knew him," Darnuir said. "That doesn't explain much."

"Not in itself, but Chelos was once part of my order. He was a Light Bearer."

"Why would a Light Bearer have knowledge of secret passages within a human fortress?" Fidelm asked.

"Why indeed?" said Arkus.

All eyes were fixed on Blaine. Darnuir's instincts screamed at him. Blaine was about to cause another row, a catastrophe. He felt the tension, like a long strained heartbeat before drawing swords. Arkus shouldn't be here. But it was too late.

"Because it was the guardians who built those passages," Blaine said.

And so the hammer falls, Darnuir thought.

"Built them?" Arkus said, his voice suddenly high and rasping. "Built them? The guardians. Built them?" he repeated, as though he had forgotten the meaning of words. "How?" he ended, more coarsely.

"The Bastion was built in the wake of the Second War," Blaine said.

"I know that," Arkus said. "The dragon king himself helped construct it. A measure to guard against future aggression from his own people. Dronithir was ever the greatest of your kind."

"Norbanus felt otherwise," said Blaine.

"Norbanus remained guardian?" asked Darnuir incredulously. "After the disaster of the Battle of the Bogs? After Dronithir defeated him?"

"Yes. The Guardian's Blade must be passed on. Norbanus held on for a time,"

Blaine said. "I told you, Darnuir, that I thought Norbanus to be overzealous. Well, this might be the one thing he actually did right."

"Did right?" Arkus said, turning a shade of red, much like the head on the Dragon's Blade. Fidelm's face was unreadable, as smooth and unyielding as the very walls they were about to assault. His eyes were cast downwards, as though he hoped the earth might offer him some guidance. The only movement he made was a light, nervous fluttering of his wings.

Darnuir wasn't sure what he felt. A part of him, the boy that had grown up the hunter, felt betrayed by the news. The older dragon felt satisfied, as though a very fine meal had just been eaten. His confusion led to a loss for words and Arkus looked at him accusingly, seemingly taking Darnuir's silence as acquiescence to the revelation.

"Norbanus had Light Bearers infiltrate the building," Blaine went on. "Working in secret, placing measures by which the fortress might easily be taken should the need arise. That's why the passages won't show on any plans you possess."

Darnuir closed his eyes, and wanted to cover his ears too.

Stop, Blaine. Just stop. Please. Stop, stop, stop...

"It was a secret kept even from the king," Blaine said. "Darnuir did not know this, Arkus. Only I alone, through memories passed down to me."

Arkus seemed to have lost the capacity to speak as well. He leant his full weight upon the war table, rocking on the balls of his feet, eyes closed, and breathing heavily. He let out a few choked sounds that might have been laughter; an unnerving mixture of hysteria and fury.

"I hoped it wouldn't come to this," said Blaine.

After a dangerously long pause, Arkus found his voice. "I do not feel as shocked as I ought to. Betrayed? No, not quite that, for it was neither of you who did this. It is a surprise, and yet it is inevitable, isn't it? And just when I dared to hope we might be able to work openly together."

"Arkus, please," Darnuir said. "You said it yourself. This crime was not committed by any here. I swear I would never condone such a thing."

"As awful as this news is, it has at least worked out favourably," said Fidelm.

Darnuir cringed.

"Favourably," Arkus repeated. "True. A good thing that humanity never angered the dragons enough again to cause another war. A good thing we had no need to rely on a fortress we thought would help protect us. A good thing, then, that humanity never stepped out of line."

"Arkus—" Darnuir tried to say.

"Enough," Arkus snapped, rising as quickly as he had spat out his words. "I'll still supply the powder to blow through the gates, if that's possible. After we are finished here you can take my fleets to the Splinters and then eastwards to your

Golden City. I want you gone from my lands – all of you. And know this: you will never set foot in my own city again." And with that, Arkus was gone. He did not even stay to see where Blaine had finished marking the tunnels upon the maps.

"Why, Blaine?" Darnuir asked.

"A siege is out of the question," Blaine said, "and I will not waste lives through assaulting the walls alone. The passages are small, though, so we can only pass so many troops through at a time."

Darnuir nodded.

"I did try to speak to you," said Blaine. "Maybe now you will listen to me in the future?"

"Don't use this as some lesson. You've caused irreparable harm."

"Arkus will calm down," said Blaine.

Darnuir couldn't tell whether Blaine truly believed that. "This news changes things," said Darnuir. "If we have access to the citadel tower then Brackendon will have a clear shot at Castallan. I will accompany him, along with my Praetorians."

"Allow me to accompany you with my best warriors," Fidelm said.

"No, General. If only because I require a *trustworthy commander* to watch over the assault," Darnuir said pointedly.

"Must you venture inside, Darnuir?" Blaine droned on. "Let the wizards fight it out. It would not be wise in your current state."

A part of Darnuir yearned to duel Blaine again, then and there. Blaine had just cost him a deal of diplomacy and he was feeling too strained to care what the guardian thought right now.

"I helped to create this mess," said Darnuir. "It seems only right that I help end it. Castallan won't be expecting Brackendon to show up in the midst of battle, and I can help get him there."

"You're not going to listen to me, are you?"

"I'm going," Darnuir said.

Blaine grimaced. "On your head be it. I shall emerge between the walls with the Third. My Light Bearers are ready."

Naturally. You probably told them all of this before you told me, Blaine. No more secrets, I said. No more…

"By nightfall it will be over," Darnuir said, already feeling fatigued. "One way or another."

Darnuir was the first to leave. A darker sky greeted them, the brighter morning having disappeared behind tendrils of ashen clouds, stretching across the sky like grey veins. The wind had picked up from the north, rolling in force from the ocean. It felt unnatural.

Blaine walked off without looking back at Darnuir or Fidelm.

"A shame," Fidelm said, pausing at the tent's entrance. "Not ideal conditions for flyers to do battle in. At least the wind is not blowing from the east against our path." He started to move but Darnuir caught the fairy's arm.

"If I may ask a favour of you?"

"I am listening," said Fidelm.

"Both your eyes will be busy on the battle, but if you can ever spare one, look out for Balack for me, if you can? I'd see him make it through this if I could. I must still make amends."

"I will do what I can," Fidelm said, bowing his head graciously. "We all need the ties of friends in this world. Even kings." And the fairy left Darnuir alone, or as alone as one could be when Praetorians were within a few paces.

Horns began to blow, some sharp, some echoing, some distant; and the drums began to beat. The human army was stirring. At a high price, dragons and fairies would win the walls for them, but Darnuir figured the dragons had a debt to pay, even if most of humanity would never know it.

I have debts to pay as well. To Cassandra, to Balack. I'll need to win back some sorely needed favour with Arkus, if that is even possible.

For all their sakes, a bridge had to be built between the two races. If only Blaine could see that. If only it were not up to Darnuir alone to pursue such a dream. It seemed harder than ever; especially here, as they prepared to spill the blood of the Southern Dales.

A flicker of fear spread through Darnuir that it might be impossible.

14

THE BREAKING OF THE BASTION: PART 2

Dragons won the First War, and the Second was something of a stalemate. Would humanity rise in a Third to become the new world power?

From Tiviar's Histories.

Brackendon – Outside the Bastion

Brackendon heard the horns and the drums, and knew it was time. The defenders of the Bastion answered in kind, roaring the infamous hunter song.

"The wolf may howl, the bear will growl,
   And our arrows shall sing."

The combined army of the Three Races began to stir. Brackendon felt the vibrations pulse underfoot. There was another kind of tremor in the air, though this one felt like the Cascade. It wasn't faint either, but a fierce tide of energy moving unseen towards the Bastion.

"What is it?" Kymethra asked.

"I'm not sure," said Brackendon. "Though it is Castallan's work."

"What is?" asked a battle-ready Balack, armed with a fat quiver, sword, two side knives and swinging his bow over one shoulder.

"Something for me to worry about," Brackendon said. "You keep your keen eyes on those walls."

"Is he making the weather turn as well?" Balack said, pointing upwards to the swirling sky.

For leagues around there was the sun and peace of a fine late summer's morning; however, near the fortress itself the world might have been ending. Ashen clouds coalesced towards the tip of the Bastion's inner tower. Wind buffeted Brackendon. Thunder cracked, and unnatural claws of green light descended towards the citadel tower, lingering for seconds at a time.

"This is the twisted work of the Cascade," said Brackendon. "Though to what end, I do not know." He shared a look with Kymethra. It was the madness of the Conclave tower, magnified and brought to the battlefield.

No one should be capable of this. This must end.

"Well, we have no choice but to face it head-on," said Balack. "This is where Castallan answers for Cold Point, for Grace, for Cosmo and for Eve." He extended an arm. "Thank you for coming to see me."

Brackendon took the proffered arm. "Make sure you live through this."

"You as well," said Balack, moving to give Kymethra a quick hug.

I'm afraid I can't promise that.

The chanting of the defenders grew even louder.

"Still we as men can counter them,
   A dragon dies the same.
   When arrows fly, the wild beasts die,
   A dragon dies the same."

Balack let loose a deep breath then drew in another one. "I'd better go. Looks like you're needed elsewhere," he added, nodding at something behind Brackendon.

Brackendon turned to find Darnuir, Lira and their Praetorians all assembled. Each dragon wore their plate armour, though with pieces strategically removed to make them more agile, like a hunter. They bore two swords each – one regular and one shorter one for shield work – except for Darnuir, who carried only the Dragon's Blade and wore his heavy starium-reinforced armour. Darnuir's expression was akin to that carved dragon draped across his shoulders.

"You have need of me?" Brackendon asked.

"Blaine knows where the tunnels are," Darnuir said.

Brackendon was sure Darnuir threw a glance to Balack as his old friend headed for the assembling army. He wondered whether Darnuir would say anything, call out perhaps, but no, he did not. Instead, the King of Dragons looked back to Brackendon. "Come. Let us take this wizard by surprise for a change."

"Go," Brackendon said. "I shall only be a moment."

Darnuir glanced to Kymethra. "One moment," he said before leaving them.

"So, you'll be out here?" Brackendon asked her, once they were alone.

"I'll be flying high to relay information."

"There's no such thing as high enough," he said, stepping in to hug her. "You hear me? You can't fly high enough." He buried his face in her hair. He did not want to let go. Eventually, she gently pushed him away.

"I'll be fine," she said and kissed him. It was a long kiss, the longest they'd ever shared. But it ended, as it had to.

"I'll find you the moment it's over," Brackendon said. Kymethra nodded, her lower lip struggling to stay still.

"Just don't age too much, all right? The grey hair is enough." She stepped back from him and shifted into her eagle form. She perched briefly upon his arm, skilfully avoiding sinking her talons into him, and nibbled affectionately at his blackened finger before taking off into the dreadful sky. Brackendon watched her soar off; then, tightening his grip upon his staff, he set off after Darnuir.

Brackendon joined them south of the Three Races' army, by the edge of the small forest, which had recently been harvested for siege weapons. The Third Legion was hidden amongst the trees, ready to follow into the tunnel when Blaine gave his signal. The guardian himself was moving across the ground, tapping his feet on various spots as he went.

The assault on the Bastion began. Drums beat louder. Horns blew harder. The bellow of the defenders rose to match the howl of the sea and wind.

With its unique shape, the Bastion was difficult to approach. The sharp angle of the western wall split the advancing army like the bow of a ship cutting a wave. Arrows hailed down from the Bastion. Catapults sent stone crashing against the plated siege towers; some denting them, some smashing sections of the towers clean away, taking golden bodies with them. Angling the towers to align with the Bastion's walls was the most dangerous, leaving them more vulnerable as they tried to turn. On the ground, and in the trenches, dragons made their way towards the base of the walls, shields raised against the arrow storm. But there was no respite. Hunters and longbowmen atop the siege towers let loose their own arrows but their efforts were akin to pushing against a waterfall.

Brackendon ripped his gaze away from the brewing battle. "Remember, Darnuir, you leave—"

"Castallan to you, yes," said Darnuir. "Let us play our part, at least. Are you nervous, Lira?"

"A little," Lira said. "Though I'm glad to finally fight alongside you."

"I'm glad to have you at my side," Darnuir said. "All of you," he added more loudly.

"It is here," Blaine called.

"Open it, then," Darnuir said, running over. The two dragons stamped on the soil until there came a great crack and the ground gave way underfoot. Both fell with the broken door and Light Bearers and Praetorians rushed over to the breach. Brackendon reached the hole first, moving faster than they could hope to.

He savoured the rush down his arm, that oh-so wonderful rush.

He jumped down into the tunnel between Darnuir and Blaine who were still half crouched from the fall. It was pitch black ahead. Only the broken entranceway behind let in dim half-light from the corrupted world outside. The eyes of the dragons flared like cats' in the darkness. Brackendon was about to light his staff when a pale beam was cast from his right. On his left a warmer glow crackled into life as Darnuir set a flame licking up the Dragon's Blade. Brackendon added his own light and they began to run.

Cassandra – The Bastion – Castallan's Throne Room

Cassandra's limbs had never ached more than now as she hung from this wall. Not even when she had spent entire days in the crawlspaces of the Bastion; not even when she had stumbled half-dead into the Boreac Mountains. The bonds at her ankles and wrists were biting and her neck screamed in protest. Somehow, she had gone deaf as well, though she was sure that was due to whatever Castallan had done.

The wizard had ripped a hole in the world. That was the only way she could conceive of it. Thankfully, he had done it far away from her, up near the throne: a gaping tear hanging in the very air. She could see nothing on the other side, only blackness. Yet it seemed more than just darkness. It was as if nothing existed within it. Castallan was standing close by it, his shoulders hunched, and his arms shaking terribly with the effort. She saw his entire right hand begin to darken, a few fingers burning black like Brackendon's. It crept up as far as his neck and then to his ear.

"What are you doing?" she cried, though she could barely hear herself.

Castallan didn't acknowledge her. He stood bent over, frozen in place for perhaps half a minute, his robes fraying at the edges. He started moving towards the chasm he had created, as though it were sucking him in. Even the staffs began to tremble in their holders, and she swore she saw the closest one edge a little out of its grip.

"Stop it," she screamed. It felt like her head was underwater.

Then something wonderful happened. Another one of Castallan's staffs, the closest one, flew out of its bracket, nearly hitting the wizard as it entered the dark tear in the world. A good chunk of the staff remained behind, broken and useless.

Castallan's cry of anger sounded distant until, with a painful pop in her ears, her full hearing returned. Castallan's wail reverberated around the throne room, and a deep blue light shone out from the hole in the world. There was something on the other side now; a bubbling, blue substance hanging in the air. Castallan drew himself back up, his chest heaving. His hair and stubble around his blackened ear was singed.

"What have you done?" Cassandra asked.

"I have created a Cascade Sink," Castallan rasped. "I'm drawing all magic for miles around to it."

"You lost another staff for it," Cassandra said with relish. "That's two gone."

"Be quiet!" He limped away from his creation, groaning and clutching at his side. "Have no fear, Cassandra. The Dragon's Blade will more than make up for the loss. Or the Guardian's Blade. Whichever dragon comes for me first. There will be enough concentrated energy in that Sink to bind the blades to me. Your breaking one of my staffs won't hold me back." Yet from the way that Castallan held himself up, leaning heavily on his own staff for support, Cassandra knew that there was still hope.

Castallan shuffled over to the great doors. "It is done," he called, and the doors swung in. Red-eyed servants swarmed in, carrying baskets of bread and flagons of water. "Any word on Darnuir?" Castallan asked, taking a huge bite out of a steaming roll.

"He and a contingent of other dragons were spotted entering the south-western passage, as expected, Your Majesty," one of the food-bearers said. "Forces have been placed between the walls as instructed. We also believe the other wizard is with them."

"Good," Castallan said thickly, reaching for a second roll. "As expected. But I'd rather deal with one of them at a time. Harry them and separate the group, but ensure Darnuir makes it here. Kill the others if you can."

Darnuir – The tunnels of the Bastion

"Which way?" Darnuir asked as they reached a crossroads within the tunnels.

"Straight ahead takes you under the inner wall towards the tower," said Blaine. "I'll go left and come up between the walls."

"Praetorians, with me," Darnuir said. Brackendon had carried on without him. He didn't want to leave Lira and the others behind so he pounded down the tunnel at an unenhanced pace, following the distant light of Brackendon's staff.

Before long, Brackendon disappeared upwards and his light dimmed. Darnuir tried to intensify the flames on the Dragon's Blade to allow them to see. Yet when he nudged the door to the Cascade, the flow of energy did not increase. Rather than getting hotter and brighter, the flames on his sword guttered out. *No, no, no…*

"Darnuir?" Lira said.

"I can't draw on the Cascade. It feels like nothing is there." He tried throwing the door wide open but it had no effect. Where there should have been a well of power, there was nothing. Not one drop. His armour suddenly weighed double without the constant trickle of magic to help him carry it. His mouth felt dusty and his heart quickened in panic.

"Darnuir?" Lira said again, more concerned. "Are you—"

"Keep moving," Darnuir said, forcing himself to keep the worry from his voice. "I made do without the Cascade for long enough. Stopping is not an option."

When they emerged from the passage, it was into a dank cell. There was a foul-smelling dampness, straw was strewn across the floor, and the grated cell door lay bent and ajar.

"Brackendon?" Darnuir called, offering a hand to Lira to help her up.

"I'm here," Brackendon answered. Darnuir stepped out of the cell to find Brackendon leaning against the corridor wall near a torch bracket.

"I cannot reach out to the Cascade," Darnuir said.

"I can barely feel it," Brackendon said. "It is as though all the Cascade has been taken elsewhere… but it is still here… somewhere." His eyes flicked upwards as though he could see through the stone.

"Wait," Darnuir called, but the wizard had already vanished up a staircase.

"I don't think he wants you to follow," Lira said.

"I know he doesn't, but without the Cascade, what can either of us do?" The rest of the Praetorians began filing out of the cell, clanking loudly in the quiet dungeon.

"You'd never know there was a battle happening outside," Lira said. "Down here we can hear nothing."

"Perhaps we ought to double back and aid Blaine in storming the walls," Darnuir said, thinking aloud.

"Darnuir, over here," Raymond called. He'd done well to keep up and was now standing by a cell, bending low at the bars.

"What is it?"

"A prisoner," Raymond said. "A dragon."

"How can you know that?" Lira asked, moving over. "Oh," was all she added.

Darnuir stepped over, conscious of time slipping by. Inside the cell was a figure slumped to his knees and bound with thick chains on his legs, arms, even neck.

Around his neck was a block of wood, the word 'dragon' painted in dried blood. Whoever he was, he was thin, with wrinkles to mark his age.

An old dragon, here at the Bastion. Darnuir had a mind as to who he was.

"Get him out," Darnuir said softly. Lira pulled at the cell door. It was a touch rusted and came free easily under her strength. Darnuir entered and crouched down. The dragon's eyes were closed and his breath sounded ragged but at least that meant he was alive. "Chelos?" Darnuir said gently. There was no response. "Chelos?" Very carefully, he rocked the dragon. "Chelos?"

"Darnuir, what are you doing?" Lira asked. "We should not linger here."

"Chelos?" Darnuir asked. He knew it was the old dragon. He knew it.

At last, with heavy drooping eyelids, the dragon blinked and looked at Darnuir. "Your eyes aren't red," he said blearily.

"We're here to end Castallan," Darnuir said. "We're dragons too. I am Darnuir."

"And I am Chelos." His words were laboured. "It is... it is... you look so similar. We owe thanks... thanks to N'weer."

"I should thank you," Darnuir said. "For sending Cassandra to me. For warning us all about the invasion from the east."

"She's back here," Chelos mumbled.

"I know," Darnuir said. "That was my fault."

"Throne room," Chelos said. "In the... in the throne room."

"I'll get her out," Darnuir said, but Chelos was already slipping out of consciousness. "Chelos? Chelos, do you hear me?" But he was gone for the time being. Darnuir took hold of the Dragon's Blade and hacked at the chains. Raymond darted in to catch Chelos in his arms.

"Stay with him," Darnuir said. "There are questions I have for him. I think Arkus will have a few as well. Don't try moving him. He's too fragile."

"Raymond can't just stay here if we return to the battle," Lira said.

"We aren't going outside," Darnuir said. He made for the staircase Brackendon had taken.

"No," Lira said. Her tone was defiant, strong. Not her usual self.

"No?" Darnuir said, turning to face her. The rest of the Praetorians hovered uncertainly. Lira hesitated for a moment but soldiered on.

"You said it yourself. We should help the Lord Guardian. There is a war going on out there and you want us to fight through the tower for some girl?"

She's standing up to me. Not the same Lira I first met in Val'tarra.

"You'd be right, Lira. You'd all be right to not follow me if it were just some human girl. But Cassandra is the daughter of Arkus and our relations with him are now at an all-time low. Chelos there is a part of the problem. Cassandra may be part of the solution. If I have any chance of mending relations with Arkus, I need to bring her safely to him. She's too important to risk."

Lira stepped forwards, stopping between Darnuir and the Praetorians. "That's not your only reason." The accusation hung heavy between them.

No, it isn't my only reason.

But he could not admit it to Lira nor his Guard. He'd failed Cassandra twice before, first at Aurisha when she was a baby and again at the Charred Vale. He'd failed her in other ways too, shameful ways. Instinct told him he was right on that. His guilt felt like a heavy stone in his gut. He'd been wrong, but perhaps if he could get her out, perhaps if this time he did not fail, then he could begin to make it right.

"When I said I mean to strengthen the bond between humans and dragons, I meant it. That dream now lies on a knife-edge. This is something I feel I have to do, and I ask that you do it with me."

He could tell Lira wasn't convinced. She pressed her lips together in a thin line, but nodded all the same and drew her sword. Every Praetorian followed her lead and steel rang in the stony dungeon.

Cassandra – Castallan's Throne Room

Cassandra still hung painfully on the far wall from Castallan. He was sitting on his throne, a heap of crumbs on his robes, and shattered glass at his feet from where he had dropped the water jugs. His groaning had only just subsided.

Any moment now someone will come to fight him. Brackendon, Darnuir, Blaine, I don't care who. Soon. Soon...

The doors burst open and her heart raced, but it was only a red-eyed messenger. He bowed before Castallan and relayed word of the battle. Siege towers had made it to the wall. Fairies were targeting the catapults. Dragons had emerged from underground but were bogged down in a fight between the walls. Arkus' soldiers were taking great care to bring up many barrels before one of the outer gates on the western wall.

Castallan shooed him away with a flick of his hand. "I did not expect the walls to hold forever. Just long enough. Leave. Now." The messenger did not need telling twice and scampered out, leaving the doors wide open.

Any moment now.

Were those footsteps she could hear? She was sure she could hear shouting. Was that why Castallan had gotten to his feet and marched down from his throne? The blue light of the Cascade Sink cast a long shadow of the wizard across the floor and picked out the new blackened streaks on his skin.

The messenger returned. Only, he did not return on foot. Through the air he journeyed before disappearing into the blue tear in the world. A red mist puffed up as he entered it. Castallan paid the man no mind. His gaze was fixed on whoever was approaching.

Brackendon entered the throne room.

Cassandra almost cried. The best of the three had come.

His sapphire robes matched the light of the Cascade Sink, and his greying hair was wild. Beads of sweat glistened on his brow and his chest rose and fell rapidly. Had he run here without magic? Darnuir did not follow behind Brackendon. Perhaps Castallan's men had done their job well. She hoped not.

"I know what happened," Brackendon said. There was a strange sense of calm in his voice. "I know about the Inner Circle. What they did. I felt their anger first-hand."

"So, you went back," Castallan said.

"I destroyed the tower."

"Then for that, I thank you."

"I am sorry. For what it's worth."

"It's too late now, isn't it?" Castallan said, lowering his staff at Brackendon. "This fight was inevitable."

"I'm afraid so," Brackendon said, rapping his own staff off the floor and pointing it at Castallan. The jewel-like wood was radiant in the blue glow. "A Cascade Sink. A good thing I can still draw on energy near the well."

"It's not for your benefit," Castallan said. "I never dreamed I would be forced to where I am. For what it's worth, I am sorry too."

Then it began.

Brackendon struck first, pushing himself to the right at speed and sending a ball of fire at the remaining staffs. Castallan sent his own to collide with it in mid-air. Before the cinders reached the floor, Brackendon had already appeared behind Castallan and lashed out with his staff. Castallan spun to counter it, the two staffs failing to hit each other due to some manipulation of the air. They duelled like swordsmen for a time, adding flourishes of fire, or violet and orange arcane energies when they saw an opening.

This seemed a battle of stamina rather than force. Yet Brackendon looked to be increasingly on the defensive, pushing back rather than attacking himself. Castallan had the advantage. He was just that bit faster, his spells always a little stronger.

Brackendon made for the staffs behind the throne again and very nearly destroyed one. He kept pressure on the staffs and Castallan was the one forced to react, barely keeping some strikes from landing. Then the platform of the throne began to shake. From the look of concentration on Brackendon's face, it seemed he was trying to topple the chair. Castallan looked to be countering it, his face twisting in concentration as he spun his staff wildly in both hands. Neither won, but the platform did buckle, the throne jerked forward, and a couple of staffs were thrown from their holders.

"Arrgh," Brackendon cried as a spear of yellow-green energy sent him spinning. He landed close to Cassandra.

"Don't give in," she cried out, not knowing if he would hear her. New white strands were appearing throughout his hair. The magic must already be taking its toll. By the throne, Castallan paused to recover, spitting on the floor.

Brackendon rose. His right arm trembled and his knuckles turned white as he gripped his staff. He looked up to Cassandra. Blood streamed from his nose. Somehow, he still managed one of his chuckling smiles. He too relieved his mouth of a great gob of spittle, then returned to the fight.

Blaine – Between the walls of the Bastion

Blaine missed death through luck alone.

A blue body fell onto his opponent moments before the red-eyed hunter would have gouged at his own face. Gasping for breath, Blaine plunged the Guardian's Blade through the neck of his foe.

He rose laboriously, feeling weaker than he had any memory of.

The Cascade had abandoned him.

No magic was flowing in at his call, even when he flung the door to it open. He had been unable to send up a beam of light to signal the Third Legion. Instead, Blaine and his Light Bearers were caught and surrounded.

A Light Bearer went down beside him and Blaine took revenge at the human's waist. The Guardian's Blade bit through the chainmail with ease. At least his sword offered some advantage.

Arrows clattered off his breastplate. Thwack-thunk.

Sweat ran into his eyes and soaked him under his armour, which was now too heavy. Gods, but he had forgotten what it was to sweat. His muscles protested, his body longed for rest. He didn't feel like the guardian right now, just a dragon. It had been a very long time since he had felt like that.

"Closer together," he called. "Reform with shields. Push to the stairs." Yet Blaine, who had never felt a need for a shield before, suddenly felt very exposed. Forced to huddle within the ranks of his Light Bearers, they edged along, backs to the wall.

They must have expected this. Why else would Castallan divert troops from the walls? There had been no fear in them either, no sweetness. And now there was only the stench of the dying.

Two more bodies fell from the wall above, landing amongst the Light Bearers with bone-crunching thuds. One dragon; one human.

"The Third will arrive soon," Blaine yelled, desperately hoping they would. He clutched a hand over his pounding heart.

Gods, he was old.

And afraid.

Dwna, bless me. Dwl'or, grant me strength.

Their shield wall kept the worst of the arrows off, but fresh defenders on foot were beginning to box them in, red eyes flashing all around, preventing them from reaching the stairs. It wasn't far, either – twenty paces at best. The humans might have been less armoured, but their numbers and compact bodies made it equally hard to find any openings. Blaine tried to thrust his sword out but was blocked each time, swatted away as though his strength was nothing to them.

Then came the bang, and for the third time in recent months Blaine heard the explosive force of black powder, as though a door the size of a mountain had been slammed shut. Screaming followed, from both sides of the wall.

The red-eyed humans nearby began to squirm. A panic took them, eyes darting to the source of the noise, and cries came from among their ranks.

"To the gate!"

"They have broken through!"

"Quickly. Quickly! To the gate."

Suddenly, the crushing weight pressing against Blaine and his Light Bearers lifted. Blaine had never thought he'd be glad that humans were coming to his aid. He now had a chance.

"Break ranks," Blaine cried. "Cut them down." Hacking at an opponent's back had never seemed more appealing than it did now. "Up the stairs. To the wall." It would probably be safer than down here.

Though the explosion at the gate had distracted the humans in the courtyard, those still manning the inner wall were alert. Their arrows continued to fly.

Thwack-thwack-ping.

Only Blaine's exceptional armour kept him alive. He kept his head bent low as he ascended the stairs, praying his gauntlet would stop a shaft from piercing his skull. It meant fighting one handed, another thing he was not used to. A red-eyed huntress nearly knocked him off balance when he blocked her strike. The shame of it alone nearly killed him. Yet in her haste she over-reached and Blaine struck at her knee with an armoured fist while she was wrong-footed. Bones crunched. She toppled off the stairs into the courtyard below.

Blaine climbed upwards, slowing with every step. By the time he reached the top of the outer wall he thought his lungs would explode. Finding his footing amongst the bodies was the trickiest thing. Luckily, the defenders weren't expecting an attack from behind.

Blood sprayed into his face as he waded across the wall. A siege tower lay broken to his left, just short of the wall. Ahead, another tower was being inched into position. At the wall's edge, it paused, then the drawbridges, thickly spiked, crashed onto the parapets. Dragons spilled out of it, even as a thick ballista bolt sailed into the opening.

Blaine locked eyes with his next opponent, some overgrown human with a blood-soaked beard. The man was feet away when a buzzing filled Blaine's ears and a blue blur collided with the human, kicking him in the head. The man stumbled, fell to his knees, and Fidelm finished him with a shove of his double-headed spear.

"You seem breathless, Guardian," Fidelm said. Blaine was so exhausted he could barely think.

"Third," he managed to say. "Where is... Third?"

"The legion? You were to give the signal."

Blaine coughed, hacking away until something in his throat snapped. "Can't," he choked. "Go. In the wood. Tell them to come."

"We'll need the help," Fidelm said. "The powder was set off too soon. Only a segment of the gate was destroyed and there's a crush forming at the opening."

"We won't win like this," Blaine spluttered. "Go."

Fidelm nodded then took off, just as another hunter from the Dales charged across the wall. Blaine raised the Guardian's Blade high and brought it down, cutting through the man's raised wrist and burying the sword into his shoulder. The effort brought Blaine to his knees, unable to resist the momentum of his own swing.

He spent a dazed moment staring at the fresh green pulse wrapping around the citadel. When the Cascade had left him, so too had the sounds of nature. The wind was silent, the ocean still, and every cry of battle sounded thrice as loud because of it.

A hand gripped Blaine by the shoulder but he felt unable to resist it. "Lord Guardian, are you wounded?" Bacchus asked.

That could have been the end of me, right there.

"Only my pride is hurt," he lied. In the courtyard below, Castallan's troops were giving little ground to the humans loyal to Arkus. Hunks of stone continued to be launched by the defenders with very little being repaid in kind. Victory would come at too high a cost. A glance around depressed him further. Even if they took the outer wall, the inner wall remained well guarded. Not far ahead was the gatehouse that stood above the semi-breached gate below. A fierce fight already raged atop it.

"We need to take that gatehouse," Blaine said. "We need it open."

"Are you able to continue?" Bacchus asked. He was looking at Blaine differently than before, with less awe, more concern, and even pity.

"Are you really asking me that?" Blaine said.

"You did not give the signa—"

"I know!" Blaine yelled. Then he was coughing again. Light Bearers were fighting all around him. Their efforts shamed Blaine, enough to force him to stand. "To the gatehouse," he spluttered.

The humans at the gatehouse had prepared a defence, perhaps intending a last stand.

Blaine fell into the brawl clumsily, his arms feeling lethargic. A figure amongst them, a white blur, caught his eye, firing arrows as fast as he moved. The boy was fighting as though the strength of all three gods were at his back.

Is that truly Balack?

Red-eyed humans continued to come up from a staircase leading into the body of the gatehouse below, where the gate mechanism would be. Blaine caught Balack's eye and the boy gave a curt nod before dropping to one knee, hacking at a soldier's shin and allowing Bacchus to finish him. But with every fallen defender, another came.

Blaine could barely lift his arm. He needed the Cascade, but it had abandoned him. *Have the gods abandoned me as well?* Darnuir might be dead. That could be why his powers had diminished.

Another hunter from the Dales locked eyes with him.

I can't do this anymore.

The hunter swung his sword.

I'm just too old.

A screech filled his ears and a tawny eagle dove into the hunter's face, raking at his soft eyes. Kymethra's screeches were painful on the ear.

"Lord Guardian," some deep voice was calling. Fairies flew in to support them on the gatehouse, swarming the defenders briefly. "Blaine," the voice shouted again. "The Third have come." Fidelm was in front of him, bloodied. A chunk of his long hair had been cut away.

"Open the gate," Blaine managed to say. Fidelm strode off, barking orders at some flyers. They disappeared down into the gatehouse proper. Balack was still fighting.

How is he doing this?

Balack took the last kill, ripping out a knife and throwing it into a red eye. The flow of defenders finally ceased. Something stirred within Blaine again. It was far from pity this time – more like pride. *The boy has done well to put his despair behind him.*

Below, on the besieging side, the troops were looking up to them as they stood atop the gatehouse.

"This was your doing, Balack," Blaine said, nodding to Castallan's purple standard. Balack seemed to understand and wordlessly retrieved his knife from the corpse of the red-eyed hunter.

"Lord Guardian, are you sure?" Bacchus said, scowling at Balack's back. "Take the victory for your own."

"He earned it. I can't deny that," Blaine said.

Balack stepped up to the parapet's edge and cut the flag down as the great doors began to open underneath them. A cheer grew across the army of the Three Races. It nearly sparked some life back into Blaine, until he remembered that the inner wall still stood and red-eyed defenders still lined it.

We are far from done.

Another explosion ripped across the battlefield.

Blaine looked up to see a large hole in the face of the citadel tower. The debris blasted outwards, raining onto the battle, crushing those on both sides. And from the wound in the tower came light. It spilled in tiny pinpricks against the ashen sky, as though a thousand shooting stars in a thousand colours were hurtling out from the breach.

You'd better be alive, Darnuir – for both our sakes.

Cassandra – Castallan's throne room

Cassandra thought the heat might cook her alive, but somehow it didn't leave a mark. It had blown half the room apart, though. She looked out onto the carnage below; the armies looked like swarming insects. She couldn't tell who was winning and the fight in the throne room was equally indecisive.

The wizards were circling far apart, whirling their staffs and sending pulses of energy at each other. Countless jets of light in every colour – colours she couldn't name. Brackendon fired energy at Castallan and Castallan batted it back; back and back and back, until the room was blindingly bright. Their attacks seemed to have weight, as the balls of light blew chunks from the floor and walls upon impact. When several had hit the Cascade Sink at once, the explosion had blown half the wall away.

The circling continued. Brackendon was close to the doors when he launched a ball of greenish-purple energy. Castallan, who was closer to Cassandra, deflected it and then sent a silver jet of his own. Something from outside the throne room drew Brackendon's attention for a split second and the silver wave nearly took him. He dropped to the floor, the silver light shattering against the wall behind him. While prone, Brackendon flicked his staff at the open doorway. The doors closed with such force that Cassandra felt the reverberations in her steel cuffs. A muffled bellow came from behind the door.

"Brackendon, don't do this alone."

Darnuir?

"It won't open. Damn it. Lira, hold them off while I try to break through."

"You'd protect him?" Castallan asked, flicking one hand upwards. Brackendon was flipped off the ground and flung towards Castallan. As he passed the crest of his arc, Brackendon righted himself, gripped his staff in both hands like a mace and brought it down on Castallan. They collided with a bang to rival that of the black powder, sending both wizards sprawling.

Thunk, thunk, thunk, came from the doors, as though Darnuir was trying to hack his way through.

Castallan was the first to recover. He looked a mess; his jaw hung loosely, and his left arm was bent backwards at the elbow. Yet he became even more gruesome as he began to heal. As his bones reset, the black lines across his skin slithered further across his neck and up onto his scalp, under a patch of hair whitening to milk then catching fire and smoking.

Brackendon had fared little better. One leg looked crushed and red pools were collecting under his robes.

He wasn't getting up.

"Heal yourself," Cassandra cried out, her throat nearly cracking with the effort. "You can't give in now. Brackendon? Brackendon?"

But Brackendon stayed down. Something rolling across the floor caught her eye. Brackendon's staff, the most powerful staff in the world, was making its way to Castallan's feet.

"No," she sobbed.

Castallan's skin had lost all colour and he looked like a laughing skull as he gently stopped the staff with one foot. Brackendon tried to move, propping himself up on one arm, but it gave way. He slumped down and lay still. Brackendon's power over the throne room doors must have broken for, at that moment, Darnuir stormed in, a bloodied Dragon's Blade in his hand. The sound of a skirmish raged from the corridor beyond.

"And at last, here you are," Castallan said, sounding half dead. "Will you give the sword to me? Or will I be forced to take it?"

Darnuir looked first to Cassandra, then to Brackendon. "Is he—"

"Give me the sword, Darnuir!"

"Never," Darnuir said, taking the Dragon's Blade in both hands. He charged Castallan, who grunted impatiently. Darnuir was halted mid-stride, frozen in place, and the Dragon's Blade was ripped from his grasp. The sword shook in the air, trying to return to Darnuir, but Castallan brought it towards him, an eager arm outstretched.

"And now, the last act I make as a mere man," Castallan said, raising his staff at the Cascade Sink. The blue glow intensified; the substance within it violently bubbled and tossed. The Dragon's Blade started glowing. Heat was rising in it; first a pale yellow, then orange, then red, then white. "Yes," Castallan said, a crazed look in his eye. "Yes. Even this ancient magic can be broken and turned."

Is it really over, then? They can't defeat him. No one could have. Such a thought should have made her weep, but Cassandra felt nothing: just a cold emptiness at the wasted energy. Everything she had gone through, everything they had all gone through; all for nothing.

Then the Dragon's Blade stopped moving.

It hung for a moment in the air between Castallan and Darnuir, close to the wizard. If Castallan only stepped forwards, he might have taken it. But the Dragon's Blade began to move back towards Darnuir, fighting against Castallan's magic. Castallan's eyes popped madly and the glow from the Cascade Sink shone even brighter.

"Come to me," Castallan growled. Darnuir unfroze as the sword drew nearer.

"The Dragon's Blade is mine alone."

"I will save this world," Castallan screamed. "I am the only one who can." And with what appeared to be a final effort, Castallan reached for the sword again. The Cascade Sink produced a near deafening droning, and then, just as the Dragon's Blade was exactly midway between the two, both Castallan and Darnuir began to convulse. Fits came over them. Their eyes rolled up into their skulls. No sane word came from their mouths.

From Darnuir's came something more terrifying – a hint of a forked tongue, and a roar like a true beast. Patches of his skin grew red, hard and shiny. Skin to match the head of his sword.

Cassandra's bonds released and she fell. She managed to roll as she hit the floor, keeping low as the horror unfolded before her. This was no place for an ordinary human.

What do I do? What do I do?

The bestial roar from Darnuir grew louder.

Cassandra forced herself to look anywhere but at him. She whipped her head towards Castallan instead and there, at his feet, she saw it, just lying untouched. Brackendon's staff. She bolted for it, picked it up and tore back to Brackendon. She fell down at his side, shoved the shaft into his hand and closed his fingers around it.

"Brackendon, get up. Fight. Please," she said desperately, shaking the wizard by the shoulders. His eyes were closed. "Brackendon. Please get up. Please. Brackendon." And with a great gasp, as though he had been drowning, Brackendon opened his eyes. He tried to stand but his leg was too badly hurt. Cassandra placed herself under his free arm, and he leaned heavily upon her.

"Thank you," Brackendon said weakly into her ear. "Castallan," he said, raising his staff with an air of finality. "You are just a man."

The Dragon's Blade flew back to Darnuir's grasp as Brackendon broke the bond.

Castallan's eyes rolled back down to face them, one pupil now black. Nearly all his hair had burnt away. It looked like there was no life left in him. Even with all his power, he had failed. It hadn't been enough. The Dragon's Blade had one master.

Castallan did nothing to resist Brackendon's magical push. Perhaps he wanted to die. Cassandra would never know. Brackendon sent him back, right into the Cascade Sink. A puff of red mist, a blinding blue light, and both Castallan and the Sink were gone.

Brackendon became a dead weight, letting out a rattling sigh as he slumped onto her. She couldn't keep him upright so tried to lay him gently down. All his hair had turned white, his right hand entirely black, and a little bubble of blood gathered at the corner of his mouth. He was mumbling, but nothing that made sense.

She pressed the staff more firmly into Brackendon's grip, closing her eyes and feeling hot, salty tears descend. She didn't want to open them again. Every emotion was flaring at once; joy, horror, distress, and despair. Cassandra didn't know what to feel, so she just let herself cry. Brackendon was still breathing, that much she could feel from the shallow rise and fall of his chest. She didn't know how long she knelt beside him. Time simply passed until a soft hand closed over hers.

"There's nothing we can do," Kymethra said. There was no life in her voice.

Cassandra sat back, wiped her running nose on the back of her sleeve, and didn't know what to do. Darnuir looked to be stirring. He'd be fine. So she sat there with Kymethra as the witch lay down beside Brackendon, embracing him in a silent hug and wetting his robes with a downpour of her own tears. It seemed that no sound was fitting for her grief.

Only silence.

15

AFTERMATH

In Val'tarra we bury our dead under the cleansed earth of blackened trees. When the first flower blossoms on that ground, we know our loved ones have found peace.

From Tiviar's Histories.

Darnuir – Castallan's throne room

Darnuir felt like he'd been beaten to death. He never wanted to move again. This floor felt like a feather bed, and the stone was cool on his cheek. It was quite a come-down from the godlike high of only moments before. Every pore of his body had been steeped in magic. It had been so good. But it had been sucked out too soon.

What happened? I shouldn't have had that much Cascade in me. Brackendon won't be pleased... where is he?

Then he remembered where he was, and what he had come here to do.

He slowly opened one eye. A crumpled blue-robed body lay across the room, with two women beside it: one with long black hair, the other brown with white tips. His groggy mind was slow to process it all. A painful rush down his arm towards his sword had started; it felt like bits of gravel were flowing through his veins.

With some effort, he managed to get to his feet. The Dragon's Blade slipped from his limp fingers but flew back when it bounced off the floor. He forced his hand to tighten around the hilt, trying to drain out the poison. A strong wind battered him and he drifted a little closer to the chasm in the wall. A distant cheer was spreading and, even at this height, Darnuir caught a sweet scent in the air.

"Darnuir," Cassandra said. There were cuts on her wrists, her eyes were puffy and had dark circles underneath, but her black hair still fell in thick shining waves. He'd expected his heart to drum when he saw her again; instead, it slowed almost to a halt.

"Darnuir?" Cassandra said.

"Yes." He found it very hard to speak.

"We need to leave," Cassandra said.

"Yes," Darnuir said again. Instinct told him to walk to Brackendon's side, sheathe his sword, and drop to one knee. Brackendon's eyes were milky and blank; his entire right forearm had turned black and scaly. His hair had gone white. Kymethra had her face buried into his robes, one arm clutched like a vice around Brackendon's shoulder.

"Kymethra," Darnuir said, trying to be gentle with his ragged voice. "We have to go." The witch did not move. More footsteps hammered along the hard stone and Lira and the Praetorians came surging into the remnants of the throne room.

"Darnuir, is everything..." Lira trailed off when she saw them.

Cassandra attempted to prise Kymethra off Brackendon. "We need to get out of this tower."

Kymethra resurfaced, her face red and glistening. She wiped at her eyes. "Come on, Darnuir. Use that strength." Darnuir made to pick Brackendon up. "Wait," Kymethra said. "The staffs. Burn them."

Darnuir looked to the toppled throne. The eight remaining staffs were scattered, one lying precariously over the edge of the room where the wall had collapsed. Lira and Cassandra helped collect them, and once heaped together, Darnuir drew out the Dragon's Blade and set them alight. He felt no need to watch them turn to ash.

Darnuir picked Brackendon up in both arms. He felt so light and fragile. They walked in silence down the citadel tower, the Praetorian Guard surrounding Darnuir and Brackendon like a golden shield. Followers of Castallan cowered before them now. Only minutes ago they had rushed Darnuir as he fought up the tower, swords raised and eyes red. Before exiting the tower, Lira sent a few Praetorians down to the dungeons to collect Raymond and Chelos.

Out in the vast inner courtyard of the Bastion, the people parted for them, or ran back into the buildings lined against the inner wall. Darnuir found the sweetness in the air nauseating. Ahead, the western set of gates had been opened. They passed through, past the bodies already being piled and the prisoners already being split up, towards the gates of the outer wall, which were half blown to cinders. Burnt stone, burnt bodies and a trail of embers ran deep into the Brevian army. No one stopped them through all of it, until about a hundred chevaliers marched towards them with a man in billowing black robes at their head.

"It is over, then," Arkus said. His small eyes flitted over Brackendon. "Is he—"

"Broken," Kymethra said shakily.

"Such an outcome was a risk we…" But he froze, having finally noticed Cassandra. Arkus' mouth hung foolishly open and the colour drained from his face. He gulped, opened his mouth as if to speak, then closed it again.

"This is King Arkus," Darnuir said. He wondered if she knew about her parentage. "Arkus, I'd like you to meet—"

"Cassandra, yes?" Arkus said eagerly. "Of course, you look so much like… I — well, I would have hoped to meet under better circumstances." He stepped gingerly towards her, all his regal bearing vanishing. Arkus opened his arms, offering a hug. Cassandra reacted by taking a quick step back, nearly knocking into Lira. Arkus' face fell.

Cassandra steadied herself but crossed her arms. "It's been twenty years. Sorry if I don't rush to embrace you. I need… time."

"Yes – yes, I understand," Arkus said. He let his arms drop to his sides. "I have arranged a private tent for you, and a hot bath and food can be prepared at once. Would that be agreeable for now?"

"That would be welcome," Cassandra said. She didn't give Darnuir a backwards glance as she left with the chevaliers. He watched her go, his heart slowing even further, until he thought it might stop altogether.

The next morning, Darnuir sat at Brackendon's bedside. Tucked under layers of warm blankets, the wizard looked like an oversized and swaddled baby.

"Is there anything that can be done?" Darnuir asked.

"No." Kymethra sniffed, stroking a finger through what remained of Brackendon's white hair.

"Mmbghm," Brackendon mumbled. Kymethra sniffed again and wiped away another tear. Darnuir had never seen someone cry for so long.

"He recovered once," Darnuir said, trying to be hopeful.

"And that took twenty years," said Kymethra. Neither of them spoke for a while. Darnuir took Brackendon's blackened hand in his own, knowing it would be a long time before he saw the wizard again.

"What happened at the Conclave?" Darnuir asked.

"Nothing that matters anymore. If you must know, we discovered that Castallan hadn't set out to destroy the Conclave. He had loyal supporters even then and wanted to help humanity fight Rectar through his magic. But the Inner Circle were worried what the dragons would make of humans enchanting themselves, and things got ugly. Had the Inner Circle not reacted so rashly, perhaps things would have been — would have been…" She choked, hiccupped and took a second to recover. "But it's over now."

"Will you try to rebuild?"

"No," Kymethra said firmly. "Brackendon wanted it to end, whether he made it or not. Look what happens when one wizard gains too much power. You will destroy his staff as well. Promise me."

Darnuir looked to the gleaming silver staff by Brackendon's side. "Will it not help him recover?"

"No. When you break, your body is past the point of flushing the poison out," Kymethra said. "Just burn it. I don't care."

"It's an important artefact of the fairies, Kymethra. I'm not sure if I can simply—"

"Burn the staff," came the reassuring voice of Fidelm. The general stood at the entrance flap of the tent, looking too tall to be there. His hair was chopped unevenly and there was a heavy bandage around one hand. It was hard to tell with transparent wings, but Darnuir thought Fidelm's might have suffered a cut at the edges.

"The Core of the Argent Tree is important to my people. Yet for millennia it lay untouched and unseen, kept where only the queen may visit. No one will miss it, and Kasselle will understand."

"Are you sure?" Darnuir said.

"I'd rather there was another way," said Fidelm. "But my people wish to create, while these staffs are capable of much destruction. This will not go beyond myself or Kasselle back in Val'tarra."

"And when a new queen one day reigns?" Darnuir asked.

"A worry for another time," Fidelm said. "But I didn't come here to talk about staffs. Kymethra, I'd like to give this to Brackendon." From beneath his tunic, Fidelm fished out a piece of silver bark, fashioned into the shape of an acorn and looped around his neck by an old piece of twine.

"I can't let you give your life brooch," Kymethra said.

"What is it?" Darnuir asked.

"A simple thing," Fidelm said, moving to Brackendon's side and tying the bark around his neck. "A cutting from the first tree my mother saved as an arborist. All fairy children are given one by the closest relative who tends the trees. It is said to foster good health."

"But it was from your mother," Kymethra said.

"My mother is long dead," Fidelm said. "And it is only a piece of bark, though I was always a healthy child. Let's see if it has some power. If I ever desire it back, I'll know where to find it."

"That is very kind," Kymethra said.

"We'll give you space," Darnuir said. "Goodbye for now, Kymethra."

"Goodbye," she said, though she only had eyes for Brackendon.

Darnuir took Brackendon's staff and left with Fidelm. When they emerged from Brackendon's tent the daylight near blinded Darnuir. His head still felt like it was made of iron, and no matter how much water he drank, he could not rid himself of the bitterness. What had happened when Castallan had tried to take the Dragon's Blade terrified him. He could only remember flashes, but he remembered the feel of all that Cascade energy, as though his blood had turned to magic. And he remembered the noise that had come from his own throat: that deep, bone-chilling roar.

He rubbed his eyes to stave off the light, his tiredness and his grief.

"He didn't deserve this," Lira said. A green and purple bruise coloured her left temple.

"We all mourn his loss, Lord Darnuir," Raymond said and the handful of other Praetorians with them nodded in a silent vigil.

"This was his fight to win," Darnuir said. "He gave everything. Now the fight is ours. All of ours." He raised Brackendon's staff – taking in its dazzling, diamond-like quality one last time – and then tossed it to the ground.

"I assume your Guard can be trusted not to tell the world what we're about to do?" Fidelm asked.

"I trust each one like I once did my hunter brothers and sisters," Darnuir said, and Fidelm nodded, content. "Is there anything you would like to say, Fidelm?"

"There is little to say, but each fairy is born into a role, and we serve our purpose. This piece of our people was crafted for a role and has served its purpose. It is a fitting end."

Darnuir smiled. "That was quite perfect." Then he drew the Dragon's Blade and set the staff on fire. It resisted the flames from his sword for a while, far longer than wood ever should. But soon enough, it crackled, smoked and hissed, and turned to ash under the intense blaze from the Dragon's Blade. There was perhaps half a minute of silence, as if in respect, then Darnuir sheathed his weapon.

"Fidelm, this seems as opportune a moment as ever to ask if you or some of your fairies might join my Praetorian Guard."

"My role forbids me from such a thing," said Fidelm, suddenly cool. Something about the fairy's bluntness stung at Darnuir.

"You could join ceremonially?" But Fidelm turned away, pretending to be fixated upon something near the Bastion's gates. "Praetorians, give us some space," Darnuir said, and Lira and the others moved away out of earshot. "Is something wrong, General?"

"The Praetorian Guard is for dragons," said Fidelm.

"I'm changing that. Raymond has already joined."

"You never seemed warm to me before," said Fidelm.

"I admit, your attitude towards Ochnic and my Highland expedition annoyed me, but—"

"My attitude has not changed. I don't believe you made the right decision."

"Kasselle herself agreed to help the kazzek," said Darnuir.

"My queen has not always made the wisest choices," Fidelm said. He furrowed his brow in some discomfort. "That was improper of me. My queen is my people."

"Fidelm, I don't see why we can't come to a—"

"How am I to perform my duties and also serve you?"

"I don't need you to serve me," Darnuir said.

"Fairies don't need to be further involved than we already are," said Fidelm. "I couldn't dream of my warriors performing any better than your own. Let dragons guard dragons and let us move on."

"It seems you have resolved to deny me," Darnuir said. He didn't even have the strength to feel angry. "We need to find Blaine and Arkus to discuss our next move."

"Blaine will be in his personal tent," Fidelm said. "I believe he was attending to Chelos."

"Come along then, General," Darnuir said.

They gathered up the Praetorians and marched through the camps, past wagons overflowing with weapons and armour without owners. It would take days to fully strip and bury the dead, but Darnuir intended to set sail with Somerled Imar long before that; today, if possible.

There was still a war to win; the demon invasion had to be repelled and Rectar would need to fall before the end. Like their victory after Cold Point, today was a sombre day. Yet there was cheering coming from somewhere deep within the human camps, although for what, Darnuir did not know.

As Darnuir suspected, there was a crowd gathering at Blaine's tent. A score of Light Bearers stood with shields raised against even more chevaliers. They seemed too preoccupied in their glaring to notice much else. Lira and the Praetorians waited dutifully at the entrance flap as he and Fidelm pushed inside.

"For the last time," said a haggard-looking Blaine, "I will not allow you to question him, Arkus. Chelos has been through enough." They did not notice that Darnuir had arrived. Cassandra was also there, by Chelos' side.

She still won't look at me. At least that answers what that kiss was – a damned mistake.

"If there are any other secrets that would impact on the security of my people, I'd know of them," Arkus said. "Perhaps the guardians dug secret tunnels under the streets of Brevia as well?"

"It was a decision made almost seven hundred years ago," Blaine said. "And you cannot deny that we needed it. Your black powder failed to do its job. Without the passage, we would never have taken the walls."

"And I, Lord Guardian, am informed that without the valiant efforts of the hunter Balack, the gates would never have been taken. I hear you were... less than efficient in the battle." Blaine had no response and Arkus smiled a dangerous little smile, looking very pleased with himself. It was then that he noticed Darnuir. "Ah, there you are. And Fidelm, also. I hope your injuries are not too severe?"

"Not so serious," said Fidelm. "I will not be able to fly for a time, but I'll recover."

No concern to show for me, Arkus?

"Good," Arkus said briskly. "And how is Brackendon?"

"Kymethra says there is nothing that can be done," Darnuir said.

"A great pity," Arkus said. "But perhaps ultimately for the best. Wizards have caused us nothing but hardship."

"For the best?" Darnuir said incredulously. "It's a fate worse than death."

"I sympathise," said Arkus. "And it is no deserving end for another human hero of the Battle of the Bastion. He will not be forgotten and he will receive the best care in Brevia."

"Thank you," Darnuir said. "And, Arkus, I must again profess my sincere apolo—"

"Spare me, I beg you."

"I do not wish to part like this," Darnuir said. "The revelations yesterday were also trying for me. If there is anything I—"

"No, there is nothing," Arkus said. "You intend to leave at once, then?"

"As soon as we can gather the men and supplies," Darnuir said. "Blaine and I will sail with Lord Imar. We'll lift this siege at Dalridia." He looked to Blaine then, and was pleased to see the guardian nodding in agreement.

"Good," said Arkus. "The supplies you shall have. As for troops, you may take as many as there is space for, although I will reserve five thousand soldiers to keep peace in the Dales. The rest will return to Brevia to be sent on with the remainder of my fleet. I feel it is past time that dragons returned to the east."

"That is generous of you," Darnuir said.

"Well, there is nothing more to say," Arkus said. "I shall take my leave. I have a kingdom to attempt to piece back together. Cassandra," he added, far more gently, "you may stay with Chelos for as long as you like. I'll leave a squad of chevaliers to escort you back."

"Thank you," Cassandra said, not looking at her father.

"Hmmm," Arkus grunted, and with that, the King of Humans left them.

When he was certain that Arkus had marched well away, Darnuir said, "I'd feel more comfortable if we had someone we trusted in Brevia to ensure Arkus follows through with sending more troops and supplies on." He looked to Cassandra as he said this, hoping she'd pick up the hint. Hoping she'd look at him at all.

"I will go," Fidelm said. "There aren't enough ships to take my fairies with you." *Yes, Fidelm, don't risk getting 'further' involved.*

"There's barely enough space for the dragons," said Blaine. "I feel we bore the worst of the battle here. Let the humans take back their own islands."

"I would agree," Darnuir said. "Though as you saw, we have little pull with Arkus right now. He wants us gone, and I'm loath to leave any dragons behind when the entire Southern Dales recently declared open hatred for our kind."

"Without Castallan's enchantment, the humans won't dare attack a legion," Blaine said.

"Have you ever considered it is talk like that which infuriates so many?" Cassandra said, though she still looked at none of them. "They wouldn't dare," she said, imitating Blaine. "Keep belittling humans and it's no wonder many push back."

"I'd be more grateful, girl," Blaine said. "It was our strength that rescued you."

"I'm a princess now, Guardian," Cassandra said venomously. "That makes me important as well. And dragons did not 'save' me. Darnuir may well have burned away like Castallan if I hadn't been there to give Brackendon his staff back. What did you do, Blaine?" Blaine sniffed like a bull and Darnuir was prepared for a full row to ensue when Chelos suddenly coughed and sputtered back to consciousness. Blaine bent carefully over his charge, taking Chelos firmly by the hand.

Cassandra took the other. "It is okay, Chelos. You are safe now."

"Cassandra?" Chelos croaked. "Cassandra?"

"He ought to be with the healers," Darnuir said.

"And have Arkus interrogate him?" Blaine said. "No. He'll be coming with us. Back home."

Cassandra looked livid. "You want to take a sick old dragon across the seas with you? What if it kills him?"

"Water," Chelos gasped. Blaine moved to pour a cup and handed it to the wrinkled dragon.

"If we could just have a moment?" Blaine asked fiercely. "Just myself and Chelos."

"But—" Cassandra began.

"Please," Blaine implored.

"Fine," Cassandra said, getting up in clear umbrage. "I'm happy you're safe," she said to Chelos.

"You too… my dear," Chelos croaked.

"I'll walk with you back to your father, Cassandra," Fidelm said. "I must inform him of my plans."

"Very well," Cassandra said, moving swiftly for the exit without a backwards glance at Blaine or Darnuir. His stomach tightened. She was about to leave and he was about to head east to more war.

Do something, you bloody coward.

"I'll expect you on board Lord Imar's ship in time," Darnuir told Blaine hurriedly before darting out of the tent after Cassandra and Fidelm. He half lunged to take her arm, but at the last moment he thought better of it, nearly lost his balance, and only stayed on his feet by drawing on some Cascade energy to snap his muscles into action. Fresh, jagged pain rushed down his arm.

"Cassandra, may I have a word?" She turned and finally looked at him, though it was with deadened eyes. She seemed to consider it for a moment, but came closer.

"I'll give you some space," said Fidelm, moving off. To the side, Lira also took the hint and stayed back, throwing out an arm to stop a chevalier coming any closer.

Cassandra folded her arms tightly. "What?"

What do I say?

"I've been thinking things through," he said. "Thinking about everything that happened. Before Blaine helped to unlock my memories, before I understood what was happening to me, I think being near you helped calm me, because the old me – the memories, that is – maybe thought things were right, you know, because you were the last living thing he had proper contact with, and I think that... that..."

He paused, trying to gauge her reaction. She merely blinked. "Well, I think that it made me think and act in ways I had no good reason to. I'm trying to say sorry. I'm truly sorry." He tentatively extended his arm. Cassandra took some time, looking at his hand as though it were something foul. Then she bit her lip and took it in a very light shake.

"We're fine," she said, even smiling half-heartedly for the first time. Darnuir's heart returned to a more regular rhythm. "Do one thing for me, please. Look after Chelos."

"Of course," Darnuir said. "I hope you find happiness in Brevia."

"We'll see," she said. "I don't know if I want to be Arkus' daughter. I don't know what I want now."

"You'll figure that out," Darnuir said.

"Have you seen Balack yet?"

"I haven't had the chance," said Darnuir, though that was not entirely true. Just then, another resounding set of cheers came from the human section of the camps. "And I have a feeling he is busy right now."

"Well," Cassandra began, withdrawing her hand. "Goodbye for now, Darnuir."

"Goodbye, Cass."

. . .

Later that day, aboard the *Grey Fury*, Somerled Imar's great longship, Darnuir watched the Bastion grow smaller as they cut through the ocean. It wasn't just the Southern Dales he was leaving. He was also leaving the west – the human world he had grown up in. The Boreac Mountains had been his home, but they were now abandoned ruins.

Will I ever return? Will I ever set foot in the cold snow again?

One half of him hoped he would. The other knew the hard truth: he wasn't going back.

The *Grey Fury* sailed at the head of their fleet. Around one hundred and fifty feet long, with three rowers abreast up each side, it was big enough to offer covered shelter at the aft. A square sail of woven wool, fastened with leather straps to keep its shape, stretched overhead, and a wooden warrior wielding a heavy round shield and axe dominated the bow. Lord Imar was still busy seeing to his men and reacquainting himself with news from his lands, leaving Darnuir alone for the first time in recent memory. Blaine interrupted that by appearing at his side.

"I am concerned about Arkus," Darnuir said.

"Do not worry about the rage of one human king," Blaine said. "Humans pass in generations within our lifetime. You may still be the king of our people when Arkus' great grandson inherits the throne in Brevia."

"We may not survive for that long if we cannot work together," Darnuir said.

"He'll work with us," said Blaine. "He just granted us the use of his forces. Defeating the demons works in his favour as well."

"I'm thinking long term," Darnuir said. "After the war, should we win, our people will need ships to ferry them home; we'll need shipments of food until we can begin to regrow our own crops. And I'd rather we were not barred from visiting Brevia."

"That was a throwaway threat."

Darnuir silently hoped that was true. He spent a few seconds picking at a loose chip of wood with a nail before asking Blaine, "What happened to you during the battle?"

"I could not call upon the Cascade."

"Nor could I, but I still fought on."

"Are you suggesting I am no longer capab—"

"I'm suggesting nothing of the sort," Darnuir said.

"Very well," Blaine said. Darnuir didn't fail to notice the slight shake of Blaine's hand. Something about the battle had unnerved him, whether he would admit it or not.

"No more secrets, Blaine," Darnuir sighed. "Do you remember agreeing to that, after the Charred Vale? It wasn't so long ago. No more secrets."

"I remember," said Blaine. He leant over the side of the boat and the chain with the little silver 'A' dangled from his neck.

"What else does Chelos know? Why were you so insistent he come with us?"

"He can help explain me everything to you when he's better."

"If the poor dragon regains his strength," Darnuir said. Chelos looked feeble underneath all the furs. Exposed to the elements, it would only make his recovery more uncertain. "I promised Cassandra I'd take care of him."

"He'll recover," Blaine said.

"He'd better."

16

DA GREAT GLEN

Garon – West of the Great Glen

Garon warmed his hands above the campfire. He rubbed them hard, bringing them up to cover his mouth and nose, and breathed out, trying to warm his nose. The lack of food was starting to make him feel numb and his empty stomach gave him a constant sense of sickening nausea. The only one of his company who did not show weakness to the cold was Ochnic, though the kazzek looked no less despondent as he gazed up at the Principal Mountain looming over them. It dwarfed every other hill and crag, a massive blue and grey barrier against the early evening light. Garon wondered if Ochnic was more worried about reaching his people than relieved.

"It's tae the benefit of our stomachs we'll reach our destination soon," Griswald said as he peered miserably into his ration bag. "Basically all out." He demonstrated by shaking the bag upside down; only a solitary portion of salted beef fell out. "What I wouldn't do tae get ma hands on just one small roast partridge." Griswald hunched over a little more. Garon was pleased to have him there all the same. Being around company was a good sign that Griswald was coming around after Rufus' death. Garon just hoped that Griswald's old spirit would return soon as well.

"Oh, no more meat, I beg you," said Pel. She was staring with equal amounts of despair and disgust at her own preserved beef. Perhaps unhelpfully, Ochnic chose that moment to devour his own portion with great enthusiasm. Pel grimaced.

"Is there anything else Pel might eat, Ochnic?" Garon asked. "Maybe some unheard-of flower of great nutritional quality?"

Ochnic cocked one of his shaggy white eyebrows. "No. Not unless you want to eat da heather." He reached for a bush, ripped off a purple tip and began to chew. He spat it out shortly after. Pel's wings drooped and she hung her head, looking very much a young girl.

"It won't kill you," said Marus. "I know fine well that flyers and warriors are given more meat in their diet."

"Not this much, and it's usually sweeter," said Pel. "I feel unclean, and can smell the stink of it on me. Well, I'm used to the jeers about that." She looked defiantly at each of them, as though hoping to shut down any judgemental set of eyes. Yet, after a scan of the group, her expression softened. "You don't care, do you?"

"D'you think he cares, lass?" Griswald said, waving his shovel of a hand towards Ochnic, who had his head deep in the ration bag.

"Human sense of smell isn't that keen," Garon said. "Marus?"

The legate shrugged. "Won't catch a dragon turning down some meat."

"Oh," Pel said.

"Probably a good thing you've gotten out of that forest, then," said Garon. "Learn how the rest of the world works and such. I never appreciated how much your kind is averse to a good roast chicken. Would you really be treated differently?"

"I *was* treated differently," said Pel. She shivered and edged a little closer to the fire. "It was hard enough trying to speak to the other women in my family without them holding their noses around me. They were all chosen to be healers, or painters, or arborists. Some even served in the Argent Tree. But I was rare and born with wings, so I got handed a spear. No choice about it."

"You would rather be doing a woman's work?" Marus asked.

"I'd rather have friends," Pel said. "I'd rather have my mother understand me and treat me like one of my sisters rather than like a warrior son."

"But you can fight," Marus said, as though that settled the matter.

"Can't do much else, though," said Pel. "We're not taught other useful things in life. 'That's someone else's job,' we get told; it's all we ever get told. And sometimes — sometimes I wish I didn't have wings."

"Oh, Pel," Garon said. "Don't say that. They're a gift." But Pel – Wing Commander Pel – had begun to tear up. She tried to hide it, but she couldn't completely cover up her quick breathing, nor the little sniffs. "I know the food isn't what you want, but you should try to eat it. You'll feel a little better." If this were a young huntress or hunter on patrol, he would have the group console them and make fresh needle brew. Exertion and hunger were usually to blame for breakdowns. Right now, however, he wasn't sure what else to do. Hugging one of his commanding officers seemed entirely inappropriate. As Pel tried to collect herself, Ochnic emerged crestfallen from the empty ration sack.

"I can teach you some ways," Ochnic said. Everyone looked to him, then to Pel, then back to the troll.

"I'm sorry?" she said.

"Teach you," Ochnic said slowly, as though they were all dim-witted. "Ways you don't know. Ways of da plants, da herbs, da wild. Some you can eat and some you use to heal. All kazzek are taught these things."

"You would?" Pel said. "Why?"

Ochnic let out a truly spectacular sigh. "If you are not wanting my help—"

"No, I do," Pel said. "I'm just... surprised. Thank you, Ochnic." The troll growled his approval and thumbed one of his tusks.

Garon beamed. "Well, that's settled then. Now, Pel, will you please eat your— Ochnic?" he said, alarmed as the troll leapt to his hairy feet. "There's no need to start your lessons immediately." But Ochnic wasn't paying him any attention. He was sniffing deeply.

"What's wrong?" Garon asked crisply. He, Griswald and Pel rose as well, while Marus clambered awkwardly up, still favouring one leg.

"Silver Furs," Ochnic hissed.

"What are they?" Marus asked. "Some dangerous animal of the Highlands?"

"Dey are the elite who serve da chieftains," Ochnic said. "Stay here," he added, then dashed off into the heather, low to the ground like a stalking cat.

"It'll be all right," Griswald said. "They wanted us tae come up here, didn't they?"

"Ochnic seems worried," Marus said. He shoved his helmet back on and gripped the hilt of his sword. "His kind have left us out here to half starve already. Better to be safe."

Garon peered in the direction Ochnic had departed but saw no signs of movement. He was considering how hunters could learn an awful lot in the arts of stealth from the kazzek when Pel let out a cry of shock from behind him.

"Back off," Pel said, waving her spear towards two trolls that had appeared near her. Both had silver fur, which was thicker than Ochnic's. Their skin was also grey, but it seemed more vibrant than Ochnic's drabber complexion. Their eyes had a slight glint to them, and even their tusks looked shinier, like marble.

Ochnic emerged from the heather a moment later. "Back off, Silvers," he told the two trolls who had scared Pel.

"Only playin'," said the leftmost of the pair. Ochnic growled deeply again and another five silver-haired trolls emerged from the heather, springing upright to their full heights. The biggest of the lot had foot-long tusks with iron bands around the middle of the bones. Tartan cloth of light reds and greens across blocks of white, covered his upper body. The rest of the Silver Furs bowed their heads and grasped their tusks before him.

"Dis is da Chief of Chiefs," Ochnic said, also bowing his head and taking his tusks in hand. Garon gulped as he looked up at the towering chieftain.

"You look like you might be in charge," Garon said.

"Rohka, I am." The chieftain lightly took hold of his tusks and lowered his head to Garon.

"Well, it's nice to meet you," Garon said. He thought it prudent to bow his own head. "Forgive our dishevelled states. We weren't expecting visitors."

"Got any food there?" Griswald asked.

"Food?" said Rohka. "We struggle ta feed our own."

"So then why are we here?" barked Marus. He clambered upright upon his crutch, no doubt looking distinctly unthreatening to the large kazzek.

"It was not I who convinced da chieftains to send for Lowlanders," said Rohka. He glanced to Ochnic.

"Ochnic promised us we would be provided for," Garon said. "In return for lending aid to your people. We're hungry out here."

"Some of us are starving," Pel muttered darkly.

"You are da pack leader?" said Rohka, looking to Garon.

"I am," Garon said.

"Da chieftains wish to see you," Rohka said. "Come with me."

"Am I to journey alone or can my companions accompany me?"

The Chief of Chiefs and his Silver Furs put their heads together and spoke hurriedly in a language Garon didn't understand. Their native tongue sounded hard on the ear, their low voices flaring in hard rhythmic inflections like a beating drum.

"Da dragon and human may," said Rohka. "Not da fairy."

"Excuse me?" Pel asked.

"Not safe," Rohka said.

"Not safe for who? For me?" said Pel. "I will not be left behind."

"I insist," said Garon. "These fairies have travelled far to help your kind, Rohka."

"She should come, Rohka, Chief of Chiefs," Ochnic said.

As tall as Ochnic was, Rohka looked down on him. "You've brought many warriors Ochnic, Shadow Hunter. But dis is not a matter for you to decide."

"I won't come if Pel can't," Garon said.

Rohka took several tense seconds to think. His lips bulged as he ran his tongue around his teeth. Then he flashed his fangs. "Da fairy can come. Leave your weapons here."

"Very well," Garon said. He unstrapped his belt and set his sword on top of the rest of his gear. "Griswald, you're in charge while we're gone."

The Silver Furs set off immediately. Garon chewed the last bite of his beef, gulped nervously and followed. They skirted the edge of the expedition's camp through the heather, drawing rather close to the fairy tents. As they passed, many fairies stopped what they were doing and stared out at the group of trolls and at Pel in the middle of them, their faces stricken with worry, as though she were marching to her own execution.

"I'll catch up," Pel said, before taking off and flying over to speak with them. They really were a young bunch, probably the greenest fighters that Fidelm could have sent. Garon considered it a cowardly move. Cowardly, and selfish. Fidelm had sat on that council, heard his own queen approve the expedition, and he and Blaine had still tried to sabotage it. The more Garon thought about it, the angrier he got. It wasn't just the trolls they might be sacrificing, but Garon, everyone who had come with him, and the whole of the west. Did their pride and scorn run so deep that they'd rather punish their own people – their own young, in Fidelm's case – to get their own misguided way? And it was definitely misguided, Garon had concluded. Ochnic, on the other hand, had been the pinnacle of a diplomat, even a friend.

I hope you can deal with them, Darnuir. He tapped the scroll by way of solidarity. *Maybe having Cosmo by your side will help.*

Pel rejoined the company as they approached the base of the Principal Mountain. Garon began to wonder where they were being led. There was no obvious route to the Great Glen on the other side. It became especially puzzling when they arrived before a flat face of rock with weeds and moss struggling for life between every small crack.

"Dis is not da way," Ochnic said.

"Oh, der is ways into da Great Glen that few know," Rohka said.

"Special ways through da High Rock," said one of the Silver Furs.

"Da chieftains did not tell me of this," said Ochnic.

"We tell dem who need ta know," Rohka said. "You succeeded in your mission. You may know. Southerners have never been allowed in da glen before. Da chieftains show you a great kindness. Don't go ruining dat."

"We promise," Garon said on behalf of the group.

"Good," said Rohka. "Open da door."

"Door?" Marus said. "What door?" But the trolls had already set about their work. Rohka himself went to pick up an inconspicuous rock, slightly squared at the bottom. It required three of the trolls to lift it. They shimmied themselves up onto a grassy mound and carefully positioned the rock against an indistinct dent in the mountainside. The other kazzek grabbed smaller, longer stones like oversized sausages from around the area with well-practised efficiency. And in a final cat-like display of agility, the remainder of the Silver Furs bounded onto their colleagues' shoulders, or clung to small crevices in the rock, holding up their own pieces to make a giant stone hand.

The mountain groaned in approval and the rock face shimmered as though in a heatwave, intensifying and pulsating until miraculously, even impossibly, an archway appeared; tall enough to fit five Griswalds and wide enough to practice archery in.

They entered the archway, stepping from the fading pink-orange evening into the darkened tunnel. Silver Furs collected some pre-oiled torches and flicked flint against steel to ignite them. An instant later, the light from the outside world vanished. When Garon turned, he saw the archway had silently reformed into smooth rock.

"Onwards," Rohka commanded. They proceeded downwards at first, delving deeper under the mountain. Their steps echoed loudly and the faint light from their torches was not enough to illuminate the cavernous space. They kept close to one wall as they moved, the other well out of sight. Garon placed a hand against the freezing stone to help balance himself as the downward incline became steeper.

"It's rather hard to see," Garon said. "Couldn't we have lit a few more torches?"

"We won't need dem."

"Human eyes aren't so good, y'know," said Garon. But before the troll could say anything further Garon saw light ahead – a dim blue glow, coming from the walls themselves. When he was closer, Garon saw that the stony grains were so fine he could see through them, like a thin shade over a window. A free-flowing blue ooze swam behind the fine rock, lighting the underground world. Each vein through the rock was dim, but combined it was enough to see by and threw relief onto the carved runes upon the walls and floors.

"Raw Cascade energy," Pel said quietly. Garon looked back to her. She was drifting trance-like towards the walls and her sudden change of course nearly caused Marus to crash into her.

"Careful, Wing Commander," said the legate.

"Yesssssss," Pel said dreamily.

"Keep an eye on da fairy," Rohka snarled.

"What?" Pel snapped. "I'm fine."

Other passages peeled off, bending out of sight or leading to giant staircases where each step would require a ladder to reach the top. The air was cool, if stale, and Marus' crutch echoed sharply with each step.

Ochnic seemed the most in awe. "So it is true. Der are tunnels of da golems under our feet."

"And what are they, exactly?" Garon said.

"Living rock," said Ochnic.

"Naturally," said Garon.

"Living rock?" Marus repeated in disbelief.

"You do not have dem in da south?" Ochnic asked.

"Never heard of them," said Garon. "And I used to live in a mountain range similar to this one. There are two Principal Mountains in the Boreacs, but I've never come across such creatures."

"Dey need a lot of da blue poison," said Rohka. "Even here, it is not enough for dem anymore. Dey 'av been dying out for many years and—"

"Pel, no," Marus called. She had wandered closer to the wall again.

"Just one touch," Pel said. Her violet eyes were wide and bloodshot. Some of the Silver Furs tried to shove their way towards her but they were too late. She placed her hand upon one of the thin veils of stone. She screamed wildly, sounding both in pain and ecstasy, and Garon reached for his sword to find only air.

No weapons. Just as well.

Ochnic was the first to reach Pel. His grey hand clamped onto her shoulder but she shrugged him off effortlessly. She tore her hand away from the wall to swat away the other kazzek as they tried to subdue her. Her eyes were completely red now, as though filled with blood from lid to lid.

"Pel, stop this," Garon yelled, but she either could not hear him or ignored him. Marus stood there helplessly, his great strength neutralised by his bad leg. A Silver Fur managed to grab Pel's hands behind her back, but she bent and flipped him over.

There was nothing Garon could do. He was too weak – just a human.

With a cry, he lunged forwards anyway, throwing his weight behind his shoulder and into her legs. He locked his arms around her knees and pulled. She wobbled for a moment and he held on; he held until he felt a blow to his head and his vision spun in a daze. The next thing he knew, Garon was being tossed through the air, landing softly at Marus' feet, but the impact was not as hard as he had feared.

"Da power is draining from her," called Rohka. "Let her settle."

Pel took several more clumsy swipes at the trolls who inched towards her, but her eyes soon began to return to normal. Ochnic brought her down, pinning her flat against the floor with a hand on the back of her neck.

"Calm, Pel," Ochnic said as soothingly as he could. "Calm. Calm…" He kept his eyes locked with hers, and after a few moments of struggle, she finally returned to normal. Tears filled her eyes immediately.

"I'm sorry," she sobbed. "I don't know — I don't know…"

"No harm was done," Ochnic said. "Put dat away," he added to an approaching Silver Fur. "She is not enraged or crazed." The offending kazzek snarled but sheathed his long dagger.

"Let's get you to your feet," Garon said. With Ochnic's help, he got Pel upright and gave her a steadying arm.

"We should hurry," said Rohka. "No more *accidents*." They hurried along after that. With Garon on her left, Ochnic on her right, and the kazzek around them, Pel was at the centre of a wall of bodies ensuring that she could not drift. Yet she did not seem interested as she had before and kept her head low as they passed through the golems' tunnel. As they progressed upwards, the blue light of the raw Cascade faded from the walls and only the torches guided them.

Finally, they reached the end.

The kazzek placed another set of stones against an indent in the wall in the shape of a large hand and an archway to the outside world appeared. The stars were so bright and numerous above the Highlands that Garon could see well enough. Leaves crunched underfoot as he staggered outside and there was a chill in the air.

"Are you okay, Pel?" Garon asked.

"I'm just so hungry," she said weakly. Garon's own stomach rumbled. No matter what came of this meeting, he would have to secure food, first and foremost.

"You might have warned us," Marus said accusingly to Rohka.

"I tried," said Rohka. "Now you know why you might listen to me in de future. Come. Da chieftains await."

The Silver Furs kept them moving at a brisk pace, pushing through the wild growth towards a small ridge directly ahead. As they cleared the top of it, the Great Glen stretched out in its enormity before them. It might have been the starlight, but nearly all of the heather here looked silver; those patches, at least, that were visible amongst the kazzek packed into the valley. Even at this distance, a whiff of smoke reached Garon from countless campfires outside the tightly packed dry-stone-walled homes with high thatched roofs. The Great Glen looked to be more of a permanent settlement, with enough buildings to make a city.

"Like smoking dunghills," Marus said quietly in disgust.

"Marus," Garon warned.

"No wonder we've been left in the cold when dealing with savages," the legate muttered. "I swear we—"

"Stop it," Garon said. "This is just coming from hunger. Don't let your temper unravel weeks of good relations with Ochnic."

"I'll try," Marus said.

"You'll try your hardest," said Garon.

The Silver Furs led them towards the heart of the valley. Kazzek began curiously following them and a muttering grew in tandem with the crowd. Horned cows with shaggy red hair chewed grass methodically and slowly turned their heads to follow Garon as he walked past. He even caught sight of a kazzek child, wrapped in red-green tartan cloth, trying to keep up with the procession – a young girl, judging by the length of her hair. She squealed at the sight of Pel and ran off crying. Pel looked too drained to care. The blue of her skin was dangerously pale.

"How much longer?" Garon asked.

"De First Stones stand in de centre of da glen," Ochnic said. "Not much farther, pack leader."

The First Stones turned out to be an enormous triple-ringed circle of standing stones, erected on the flattest piece of land in the valley. Garon craned his neck to see the top of the stones as they drew closer. The outer ring was the tallest and descended in size towards the middle. Where each of the giant outer rocks stood, there was a large house to accompany it, ten in total. These had the luxury of a second story.

"Homes of da chieftains when in da Great Glen," Ochnic explained.

"Quite the auspicious position," Garon said.

"Da chieftains will have gathered in the stone ring," Rohka announced.

"That's good." Garon yawned. "Any chance they will bring something to eat with them?" Rohka flashed his fangs. "Look, if not for me, can you fetch something for Pel? She'll collapse if she doesn't put something in her stomach soon." The Chief of Chiefs eyed Pel, who was propped up only by Marus, who was propped up himself by his crutch.

"Da fairy touched da blue poison," Rohka said. "She attacked my kazzek."

Ochnic gave a grunt of impatience. "I shall find food."

"I wish you ta be present, Shadow Hunter."

"I won't be long," Ochnic said. He seemed flustered and eager to get away. "Can you eat fish?" he asked Pel. She didn't seem to understand and was unable to make proper eye contact with him.

"Fish is fine in small doses," Marus said. "Better hurry, Ochnic." And he did. Quick as a flash their kazzek guide was pushing his way back into the gathering crowd.

"Be gone now," Rohka shouted to the other kazzek. "Away to your fires. Da chieftains shall converse with da Lowlanders. Der is no need to fear." The crowd seemed unwilling to move and it took the menacing Silver Furs to disperse them. Garon waved an encouraging hand to Marus and Pel, and together they gingerly followed Rohka into the middle of the standing stones. At the centre, eight older kazzek had arranged themselves around a circular stone table. *Eight here, plus Rohka is nine. Nine chiefs and ten houses. Someone is missing.* A noticeable gap had been left for Garon, Marus and Pel, and they moved into it.

No one spoke, not for an uncomfortably long time.

Exhausted and starving, Garon tried to keep his eyes open. He hated feeling so unprepared for this pivotal moment, and yet here he was: as unready as he'd been at seventeen, approaching nineteen-year-old Fiona from Ascent at the station one misguided evening in late autumn. This was an early autumn night, and he was now thirty-six, but he felt like the boy he'd once been. Out of his depth. And probably out of his mind. Still, he'd learned after Miss Fiona that confidence was the key, and so he mustered as much phantom self-assurance as he could and said, "So, is this it?"

"What is dis 'it'?" asked Rohka.

"This," Garon said, flapping his arms to illustrate the situation. "You request help to be sent into the Highlands, we're told the demons are knocking on your doorstep, and then you allow us to walk next to blind through the difficult mountain terrain with no additional food or wildlife to live off. To cap it all, we reach your magnificent glen and you have absolutely nothing to say."

"We have a great deal to say," said Rohka. Garon was about to reply but the chieftain cut him off. "When kazzek receive guests, we always wait for dem to make the first greetings. Your greeting was a strange one."

"Ah," Garon said, feeling foolish. "I suppose it was. Hello, then, great chieftains of the kazzek."

"Hello," the chieftains chanted in unison.

"Allow me to introduce Legate Marus, leader of the dragons on our expedition," Garon said. Marus winced and clutched at his leg. "And Wing Commander Pel, the lead flyer of our fairy forces." On cue, Pel swayed into Marus' shoulder.

"You brought da fairy through da mountain?" one of the chiefs asked in shock. Her colleagues grumbled around the table, audibly grinding their teeth.

"Dey insisted she come," Rohka said.

"I insisted," Garon said. "We three will not be divided on this mission. The Three Races have agreed to help in your fight against the demons, and we will do so together. My orders," he proclaimed, producing Darnuir's scroll and placing it upon the stone table, "from the King of Dragons."

"Lowlanders cannot enter da Great Glen, Rohka," said a chief. This one had tusks that curled upwards, and wore a tartan of yellow and black. Garon whipped his head from side to side and peered exaggeratedly down at his own body, then to Marus and Pel.

"There seems to be some upset, then," Garon said. "For we are 'Lowlanders', as you call us, and we are here."

"Exceptions had to be made," Rohka said slowly.

"Clearly, it is possible for us to enter the glen," Garon said. "What you mean is that you do not allow it, by which you mean you do not wish it."

"Pack leader," Rohka said loudly. He was suddenly stern and drew up to his full and towering height. "Da Great Glen is a refuge in times of crisis. Da kazzek are scared when dey come here. We did not wish to frighten dem further. And our food stores are not as full as you think."

"Then how were you planning to feed us?" Garon asked. All the chieftains exchanged nervous glances.

"We did not expect you to come," Rohka said. "We did not believe Ochnic would succeed."

Garon sighed. "There has been a lot of ill-will towards this mission. But if you would struggle to feed an extra five thousand mouths, then you must be in dire straits indeed."

"We might have made it through da winter," said Rohka. "But now you Lowlanders have arrived…"

Garon's heart sank. "So what are we to do?"

Before Rohka could answer, a familiar voice cried, "Where are dey?" and Ochnic came bounding up to the stone table with a steaming bowl in his hands. "Where are dey? My clan." His voice shook, as did his hands, and a portion of the bowl's contents spilled onto the earth. Marus reached to take the bowl and Ochnic relinquished it without protest.

"Trapped in da east, Shadow Hunter," said Rohka. "Cut off by demons."

"Dey were coming," Ochnic said. "Dey were to leave just after I…"

"Demons came from da Black Rock glens faster than expected," said Rohka. "Too many for us to fight dis time. Even da golems are trapped with your people in da Glen of Bhrath."

"You abandoned them?" Marus asked.

"We left great food stores in da east behind as well," said Rohka. "We had no choice. Until now."

Ochnic turned to Garon and took his arm frantically, squeezing far too hard. "Pack leader. Please. Go we must."

"Ah," Garon grunted in pain. "Loosen that grip there, Ochnic. Of course we'll go. As Marus said, that's why we're here. Regardless of whether anyone in the world cared if we'd succeed, that's why we're here."

"Thhh-ank you," Ochnic said weakly.

"I'll help save your daughter, Ochnic," Pel said. "Even if I have to fly her away myself, I swear." Everyone turned to her, the chieftains in shock and Garon in concern. Spoon in hand, she'd clearly been wolfing down whatever Ochnic had brought her. It looked like a creamy soup with flakes of white fish, leeks, translucent onions and chunks of a golden vegetable that Garon did not recognise. Vigour had already returned to Pel's skin.

"Thank you, too," Ochnic said gratefully.

"Da fairy would swear oaths to a kazzek?" asked the incredulous chieftain in pink and green.

"We've had it rough, but we're learning to look past our differences, for the most part," Garon said. "Maybe you all should as well." He let that settle in the air for a time. "Now, chieftains, if you will kindly resupply our forces, we can move out immediately. With your own warriors and guides as help, we'll stand an even better chance." The ring of chieftains closed together to converse.

"Done," they all said together.

"We shall send one thousand warriors and our Silver Furs," said Rohka. "I will lead dem myself. But I must make clear, de food stores are de priority, for all of us. Without dem we shall starve through da snows."

"Chief of Chiefs, my clan, dey —" Ochnic began.

"Might not be alive," said Rohka. "Dis is hard words, but could be true. If Chief

Orrock and your clan survive, dey will surely be with da store. If not, or if der is a choice to be made, I cannot order our warriors to take any risks. Da food is critical."

"But—"

"Do not overstep your place, Shadow Hunter," Rohka said.

Garon felt like he should say something. He could almost feel Ochnic tense with rage beside him and gently placed a staying hand on the troll's rough hide. It was Marus who spoke first.

"A strong leader knows difficult choices have to be made. My dragons will be at your disposal, great Chief of Chiefs. My king would wish for trust to build between our peoples."

Garon glanced sideways at Marus. *So you'll follow who's strongest, is that it, Marus?*

"We know what to do," Garon said, suppressing his own frustration. He hoped they could leave before anything worse was uttered. "Send along kazzek who know how to make that soup," he said more light-heartedly. "It smells delicious."

When they answered, the chieftains spoke again as one. "Done."

17

WHISKY AND PAINT

The sacking of Brevia was swift and brutal. In 1738 AT, Godred Imar, King of the Splintering Isles, showed his might when he sailed his fleet of longships into the Bay of Brevia and seized the city. At that moment, Godred showed that Dalridia was the true powerhouse of humanity.

From Tiviar's Histories

Cassandra – Brevia – The Throne Room

"Show your love for the hero of the Bastion!"

The crowd in Arkus' throne room roared in approval.

Cassandra watched on surreptitiously from the back of the throne's podium, not wanting to stand front and centre with Arkus and his family.

They are my family too, I ought to remember. Arkus is my father; Thane is my half-brother. Oranna is… well, she's nothing to me, really.

Between his parents, Thane looked rather small. She could see him coughing regularly. Arkus patted his back, but his convulsions could not be heard over the announcer's orations.

"I give you Balack, Hero of the Bastion! A human who took the gates where dragon and fairy failed; a human of the ruined Boreac Mountains who took his revenge; a hunter of the finest quality."

Arkus got to his feet, clapping enthusiastically with the rest. He nudged Balack and the hunter raised an arm to wave at the throng of Brevia's elite. The king let the hall quieten before speaking.

"This is a time of celebration. The tyranny in the south has ended. Castallan has been defeated and his enchantment over the people of the Dales is broken. Their minds are their own once more and we are joined again in a truly united kingdom."

Cassandra yawned deeply as another round of cheering ensued.

"The dragons paid a high price at the Bastion," Arkus went on. "But a price needed to be paid, for it was dragon lords who first pushed Castallan on his path of madness."

What are you doing, Arkus?

"I have sent the dragons east, back to their home, and I shall offer passage to any dragon still in our lands. Let them know they can find that passage from Brevia. It is time to remove the burden of their people from our shoulders." The crowd responded enthusiastically to that. "One final fight must still be won. The Splintering Isles will not fall. No demon will set foot in our lands again. The heroism of humans, of hunters like Balack here, will be what saves our people from destruction." With that, Arkus took Balack's hand and raised it high. "Humanity will stand up for itself. Humanity will not cower!"

Another round of cheering followed.

They'll shred their own throats doing that.

Before it was over, she turned to leave. She'd heard enough bravado for the day. There had not even been a mention of Brackendon, the real hero.

They'll never know, and so he'll never be remembered. The truth of it will die and this rhetoric put in its place.

She wondered then how much had been lost across time. How much of what she had read was true?

I will not forget.

Trumpets blew behind her as she left the throne room. She took the staircase leading directly back to the royal apartments, and had barely emerged onto that floor when four chevaliers blocked her path. They no longer seemed to wear helmets, she had noticed. It made them less intimidating, but their eyes were always visible.

"Move," she said. They stood still. "Move, please."

Still nothing.

"Your father wishes a word with you, Princess," said Gellick lazily. He ran a hand through his mop of blond hair. "We will take you to his council chambers."

"I know the way," Cassandra said. She had been mapping out the palace in her mind since arriving three days ago. After the Bastion, it was easy.

"Your father asks—"

"Fine," Cassandra said, hoping they would lead her there in silence.

She found it uncomfortable when people referred to Arkus as her father. It just didn't feel real yet. Nor did it feel completely true, as if she wasn't the baby girl who Darnuir had left behind in Aurisha. Nor did she feel settled within the palace or the city. She felt as if she might start running at any moment and never look back. Everything was too new. The boundaries of her new life had yet to be drawn and she was on the precipice between this new existence becoming either another prison or, possibly, very distantly, her home.

The trip to Arkus' council chambers had passed her by and the chevaliers led her inside. "The king will be with you shortly," Gellick said as he closed the door.

In the bare room, the painting on the wall behind the desk stood out immediately to her. Cassandra blinked and rubbed at her eyes. For a second she thought she had seen herself in it. The woman in the painting had her hair and eyes; the only difference was the colour of their gowns. The woman's was pale green, Cassandra's white.

She looked happy, this woman in the painting.

"If only you could have met Ilana," Arkus said. Cassandra had not heard him enter, but kept looking at her mother. As though in a trance, she stepped closer to the frame. From here, Cassandra saw Ilana's cheekbones were a little lower than her own, her eyebrows a touch thinner, and her hair parted differently. Ilana's was to the right and Cassandra's to the left. They might be small things, but they were there.

"I would have liked to meet her too," Cassandra said. "But alas..."

"Cassandra, I am so sorry. I've tried to expla—"

"I know. I know... I'm sorry." It had been a cheap dig at the man, and spiteful. She'd heard the full story from Arkus on their journey back to Brevia. He hadn't had much choice. Even so, it still stung.

"This is hard for me too," Arkus said. He removed his crown and let his greying mane fall loosely behind his ears. Placing the crown on his desk, the king moved to sit behind it. "Making time for you is... difficult. I'd like nothing more than to get to know you, but I have a kingdom in tatters. The Cairlav Marshes are more desolate than ever; the Golden Crescent's population is scattered or returning to fields crushed by running dragons; I have thousands of soldiers tied up in the Dales and a war still to wage. To top it all," he added, sounding deathly tired, "Lord Boreac has disappeared."

"One hiding lord seems the least of your worries."

"Boreac's actions show he was clearly involved in the plots against me," Arkus said. "I can't have any ringleaders still at large. He must be brought to justice or I risk it all again."

"But you cannot find him?"

"We'll comb the city for him. He won't last long."

"What makes you think he's still in Brevia, this Lord Boreac?" Cassandra said. It seemed strange to her that, with everything else going on, this one man was on Arkus' mind.

"For one, his regional seat lies abandoned and decimated," said Arkus. "Additionally, it is likely he still has friends and sympathisers in the city. Castallan might be gone, but the networks he built must run deeper than I ever suspected. Then again, I rely so much on information from others who, as far as I know, were part of these plots. I find I am lacking in people I can trust."

"Is that why you are telling me this?"

"No. I have simply been side-tracked," said Arkus, regaining his authoritative air. "You are here on a different matter. One of marriage."

"I think you have more important things to worry about," said Cassandra.

"Were you not of noble birth, it wouldn't matter. But you are. In fact, you're the eldest of my children. You could be my heir if you wanted." Cassandra let out a sound that might have been construed as a laugh, something between a snorting giggle and a choking gag of pain. Arkus' expression remained flat. "It's far from a laughing matter."

"I don't want to be queen."

"Your brother had much the same attitude. Fighting me at every turn." His face paled at that point and he cast his eyes on the floor. Cassandra hadn't considered that Cosmo was her brother; her much older brother, to be sure, but family still. It seemed so wrong, so untrue; and he'd died trying to save her from Scythe's men. That memory suddenly took on a more painful meaning.

"He was a good man," she said.

"So I'm told," said Arkus. "To put your mind at ease, I don't intend you shall ever be queen. Although if both Thane and Cullen died, things would get complicated."

"So why *must* I marry, then?"

"Politics. Thane will remain my heir. Not least because that is how the kingdom has been carefully nurtured these last eight years and because he is promised to the daughter of Lord Esselmont of the Golden Crescent. Doubtless that kept Esselmont loyal throughout the years."

"So, you're going to open up the bidding for me and gain another loyal house?"

"Do not look at me like I'm some monster. This is a time of war and the Assembly must be kept malleable. Your coming has upset the status quo and all will seek to gain from it. However, I do not intend to indulge any of my fine lords."

"Then it is all some ruse?" She was hopeful. Oh, so naively, desperately hopeful.

"I'm taking you out of their sights. I would have you marry Balack."

"Balack?" Cassandra said, aghast. This, she had not been expecting.

"He is the perfect candidate," Arkus explained. "You see, should I grant one lord or rich merchant the honour, then I would face unrest and rebellion. Not openly, of course, not so soon after the Bastion. Yet I would face resistance all the same, particularly from the rivals of whichever family I picked. Choosing one would require me to placate the other in some form and I'd rather avoid playing a continual game of gift-giving; as though all my lords were children, each demanding a sweet treat."

"Surely Balack would offend them all, *Father*." She struggled with the word, as though learning it for the first time.

"Perhaps some will feel snubbed," Arkus said. "However, they cannot complain too loudly. I have arranged for him to visit each district of the city. The people will be singing tales of his bravery before long. My lords might be discontent with the betrothal but they cannot openly object to someone so beloved by the people. And, as no one house will gain anything from it, it will cause no real damage within the Assembly. It's perfect."

"Except for me," Cassandra said. "And Balack," she added. "What does he think about this?"

"I haven't brought it up yet," Arkus said. "I thought you would prefer Balack over some stranger. He tells me that you grew close before you were recaptured."

"Balack is a good friend," Cassandra admitted. "That does not mean I want to marry him."

"How about Grigayne Imar?" Arkus said. "Son of Lord Somerled. The two of you will be of an age – perhaps he's a little older. This is Somerled's idea, of course. I think he feels it would help strengthen Grigayne's position to take the islands to full independence one day."

"Is nobody an option? I'm tired of having no control."

"Cassandra," Arkus said, becoming stern, "do you think any of us have full control of our lives? I am a king, and yet I must do many things I'd rather avoid to maintain stability."

"But—"

"I am a king," Arkus continued, "and yet I must bow my head to a boy dragon. I am a king, and still I could not keep my son from leaving me; I could not bring you home from Aurisha with me; I could not heal your mother's broken heart, nor keep her in this world with me." His voice cracked. "None of us are truly free, Cassandra."

"I have been a prisoner all my life. Am I to swap one jailer for another?"

"You wound me," Arkus said. "If you'd grown up here, you'd understand. But you didn't. So, it will be the hard way. It doesn't matter to me if you love him or hate him. It does not matter to me whether you spend all your days together or merely show up arm in arm when required. But what I do need is the marriage – in ink on parchment."

"You don't care about me at all, do you?" she said.

"I care about our family," Arkus said. "This is the best thing for the family."

"I'm not part of your family," she seethed. She turned away, storming for the door.

"Where are you going?"

"For a very long walk." She ripped the door open.

Arkus was calling after her. "I'll have Gellick accompany—"

"I'd rather go alone."

"Out of the question!" He appeared at the doorway to block her, moving fast for an older man. Furious, she faced him, but his expression had softened. "I just got you back. I won't lose you again."

She shuffled her feet. "Very well. I won't go alone."

"Thank you," Arkus said. He raised a hand as though to pat her shoulder but thought better of it. "He'll be here shortly. I'm expecting him. But if you'll excuse me, I have much work to attend to." He walked back to his desk and Cassandra shut the door behind her. She waited on the comfy bench. When Gellick eventually appeared, he had no fewer than ten chevaliers and a large crate. She eyed it suspiciously, but Gellick's look told her not to ask.

Her hope that a walk through the city might cheer her up was soon dashed. The chevaliers were a sullen lot, walking with their noses up in the air and clanking loudly with every step. She'd rather roam the streets alone and see the city as it truly was, not how a noble was supposed to see it. Little she saw was authentic. The people ducked or bowed their heads as she passed. Anyone who spoke did so with a nervous politeness. Merchants brought out special wares reserved only for the wealthy and some even tried to give her gifts for free if she would tell the others at court where she got this or that.

It was quite tiring.

At a crossroads, which was ripe with the smell of fish, Gellick came to a halt. "Might we venture down to the harbourside now, Princess?" Soldiers in chainmail and holding spears were trudging past.

"It looks busy," Cassandra said. "I'm not sure I'm in the mood for it."

"We also have business there."

Cassandra looked to the sealed crate. "You're very polite to make it seem like it's my decision."

"As you say, Princess."

Down at the harbour proper, Cassandra took in the fullness of the vast horseshoe bay. A forest of ship masts stretched to the colossal white arch that spanned the distant banks. The wind whistled in the space between the ships, seagulls screeched, and she could almost taste the salt in the air. Cassandra followed Gellick's lead as they fought through the crowds. Before long, the rest of the aromas reached her: sweat, horse muck and fish guts. Gellick raised a white silk handkerchief heavily scented with lavender to his nose.

"Put it down over there," he said from beneath the handkerchief, pointing to a group of fairy warriors surrounding two easels. At one easel was Fidelm, brush in hand. Opposite him was another painter, a human in overalls with a long, hanging beard tucked into his belt. The chevaliers carefully placed the crate down before the fairies. "General," Gellick said. "I believe you were expecting this."

Fidelm set his brush down and stretched his arms. "Your timely arrival is most appreciated, Chevalier. My people will take good care of it."

"Take good care of what?" Cassandra asked.

"The scrying orb we recovered from the Bastion," Fidelm said. "Arkus has the one that Blaine recovered. This will grant a method of communication with Aurisha when delivered."

"If Aurisha is retaken," Gellick sniffed.

"That would be a good thing, Chevalier," Fidelm said. "My queen will be sending all the dragons still in our forest on to Brevia soon. The quicker they can be sent home the better, I'd imagine."

"More dragons. Oh, joy," Gellick said. He half-turned to leave, but hesitated. "I hope your wing is on the mend, General?"

"Niceties aren't required," said Fidelm. "You've completed your task."

"Very well," Gellick said. "Come, chevaliers, Princess. Back to the palace."

"I'm not ready to return," Cassandra said. She had no reason to stay other than to be rebellious, and if she couldn't fight Arkus just yet, then Gellick would do.

"I cannot allow you to remain without protection," Gellick said.

"I can have her escorted back," said Fidelm. "My fairies can be trusted. None of them joined Castallan."

"I only accept orders from the royal family," said Gellick.

"I'm the princess."

"Your father outranks even you," Gellick said.

"And he said explicitly that I could not stay at the harbour and keep Fidelm company?"

"The general appears to have a companion already."

The bearded painter nearly dropped his palette at being brought into the discussion.

"Douglas isn't much of a conversationalist when he works," Fidelm said. "A true artist."

"Have it your way," Gellick said. "Bring the princess safely back to the palace or you won't leave this city."

"I'm quaking at the thought," Fidelm said. Gellick muttered something under his breath as he and the chevaliers stalked off. The moment he was out of sight, Cassandra looked quizzically at Fidelm.

"Why help me?"

"Why stay here?" he asked.

"I just wanted to annoy him," Cassandra said.

"Then we were of a mind," said Fidelm.

"So, what are you doing?" she asked.

"I am acquainting myself with the latest Brevian fad," Fidelm said.

"It is no fad," Douglas squawked from behind his easel.

"I like to capture the scene perfectly," Fidelm said. "These broken strokes you've asked me to attempt are making a mess."

"Perfection is not my goal," Douglas said. "I am studying how light affects the scene. The eye does not see everything in detail but focuses on a single point. The rest is blurred. A mere impression of what is there."

"Ah, Douglas, your skills are too great to waste on fleeting fancies. Alas, that is your kind."

"Change can be worthwhile," Cassandra said.

"Why change what does not need to be changed?" Fidelm said.

"But how will you know if things are better or worse without change?" said Douglas, sweeping his brush across the canvas until some yellow flicked off the side and splattered Cassandra's white dress.

Change. Something has to change. Can I really settle into a life here?

"You look troubled, Cassandra," Fidelm said.

"What? No. No. I'm fine—"

"May we have some privacy, Douglas?" Fidelm asked.

"And just when the light was at its best," Douglas said glumly. He got up and shuffled off behind the wall of fairy warriors. Cassandra was left with the ink-skinned fairy, a little unsettled.

What does he want?

She found it hard to judge. His deep blue eyes gave nothing away.

"Well?" Fidelm asked, turning to face her. "Why bite at the chevalier?"

"Why the concern? You don't know me."

"Curiosity," Fidelm said.

"I'm not something to be studied."

"I'm trying to decide whether to feel sympathy for you or not," said Fidelm. "You've been in a foul mood since the Bastion."

"I felt fine until today. Arkus is trying to marry me off."

"So?" Fidelm said.

Cassandra could barely believe her ears. Rage pulsed inside her. She wanted to take his canvas and toss it into the water of the bay.

So? So! How would you like it if Kasselle forced you into something?

Then she remembered that, as a fairy, Fidelm was selected for a role at birth and was stuck there. He likely wouldn't complain.

"It hardly seems right that I should have no say in something like this,"

Cassandra said, forcing herself to remain calm. "It doesn't seem right either that I should work so hard for my freedom only to get stuck in this situation."

"Then do something about it," said Fidelm. "You're resourceful enough."

"It's more a matter of principle," she said. "Of freedom."

Fidelm shrugged. "Freedom to me is having a choice, and you have a choice here."

"No, I don—"

"Yes, you do," Fidelm interrupted. "You can try to act, or you can do nothing and complain. At the Bastion, you could have done nothing, but you chose to act. You escaped, and in doing so helped to bring about Castallan's downfall. Freedom is relative, Cassandra."

"Is that the fairy perspective?"

"I can see why you think that. However, I've lived for a fair time, and in ninety years you see enough to form a broad perspective. Darnuir, for example, might be the most powerful individual amongst the Three Races, and yet he is not utterly free. He cannot do exactly as he pleases. Nor can your father, nor can I, and nor can you. To think otherwise is childish. If you don't want to go down the route Arkus has laid before you, find a way to alter it. As a human, you can."

"I'm just not sure how," Cassandra said. "I've lived my whole life for one thing and that's over now..." She trailed off, lost for words.

Fidelm twisted his canvas around. On it was a half-finished picture of the Bay of Brevia, with a beautiful ship at the centre and an array of dashed strokes around it that helped to give a dream-like quality to it. "Before I started, this sheet was blank. I could make it anything I wanted." He picked up his colour palette. "Look at yourself. You're exactly the same." Then he flicked a little green paint at her. Cassandra hadn't the chance to react. The paint splashed across her dress, crossing paths with the yellow left there by Douglas. Fidelm swirled his brush on the palette then painted a purple stroke along one of her sleeves.

Cassandra found herself laughing. Fidelm handed her the palette and she started smearing paint all over her once-pristine white gown. Red and blue, the brown that Fidelm had mixed for the wood of the ships; her hands rubbed it all over her white satin dress.

Once the paint was gone, she handed the pallet back.

"And people ask why I paint to relax my mind," Fidelm said.

"That was fun. Thank you, General."

"I wish you luck," said Fidelm. "We'll all need it before the end."

Back in her room, Cassandra felt restless. The place was more splendid than her chambers at the Bastion; even the mirror was lined with white gold. But she had nothing to do. Nothing obvious, at any rate. And with little to occupy herself with, Arkus' threat of marriage weighed dangerously on her mind. So she took to the long corridors of the palace, poking her head through every doorway, looking for a distraction, hoping for some inspiration.

What she found was none other than Queen Oranna.

The door had been innocuous; the room on the other side, not so much.

It was lush and packed with more cushions than there would ever be a use for. Most striking was just how much colour was in this one room. Where much of the palace was black with the occasional bit of white, this was a medley of bright yellows, warm oranges, greens, blues and pinks. Frankly, it was unsightly.

Oranna, thin, pale and at odds with her surroundings, was sat in an upright, ornate chair with a purple lining. She held command of the room's majestic easterly view of the bay of Brevia. The queen jumped, startled by Cassandra's arrival, and nearly dropped her teacup. A tray of pots and cakes lay on the table in front of her.

"I'm sorry to have disturbed you," Cassandra said. "I'll just go."

"Oh, no," said Oranna. She got to her feet and faced Cassandra, waving her in. "You might as well come in now if we've already skipped the formal invitation to my parlour, and – well, good gracious, you've dressed to match." She tittered. "How about some tea and cake? My maid just brought a fresh tray."

Praying that this wouldn't be deathly awkward, Cassandra stepped lightly over, like a street dog to a stranger's hand. There were no less than four richly patterned pots on a large tray laden with little cakes, fruit pastries, scones, butter and a bowl filled with what looked like raw sugar. She took her seat, eyeing the raisin scones.

"May I offer you something?" Oranna asked in a voice to match the sugar bowl.

"I'm fine."

"No?" Oranna said, in a pitch slightly too high. "There is shimmer brew and three different varieties of tea. Or perhaps you would like something a little stronger? Some sherry, brandy, or even a touch of whisky. I can have it brought at once. You must be so worn out from your travels and that battle." She gave a little gasp. "A little spirit to lift your own?"

Cassandra wasn't sure what to make of Oranna just yet. She seemed friendly, but perhaps a little too much.

"No," Cassandra said, adding a quick, "Thank you," as an afterthought.

"Well, do help yourself if you change your mind," Oranna said, though she touched none of it herself. She did pour herself some steaming shimmer brew and brought the cup delicately to her lips. Soundlessly, she took a sip. "So, I'm told you were raised in the Bastion—"

"Held captive," Cassandra corrected her.

"Quite so," said Oranna. "I assure you I knew nothing of your imprisonment."

Why is she telling me this? What does it matter now?

"I doubt it was common knowledge," said Cassandra.

"But Arkus knew," Oranna went on, "and I suspect my father knew as well. We women are always the last to know such things – us highborn women, at least. People always bleat about the equality, especially in the lower classes, about how we're so much more civilised than the dragons, but sometimes, I'm not so sure. It could all be an act."

"What about Captain Elsie?" Cassandra said. "She was the very first captain of the Master Station here in Brevia after the hunters were institutionalised following the Battle of the Bogs. Or Lady Margo Foulis, who designed the white arch of Brevia and its defences? Or Queen Flora, who reigned for forty-five years on her own? So many more come to mind."

"But what do they all have in common?" Oranna asked.

"Little that I can think of," said Cassandra.

"Childless," said Oranna. "Yes. All the greats were childless, as though a child shackles a woman. Perhaps it does – children, or the lead up to them. For the lowborn, blood matters little, but for us..." She drew out the word and took another sip of her brew. "I hear Arkus intends for you to marry?" Cassandra thought it a sudden shift in topic but she supposed it was why Oranna had invited her to come in.

Best get this discussion over with.

"I'm sure you know his intentions," Cassandra said.

"Marriage is often a precursor to children," Oranna said rather pointedly.

"He mentioned nothing of that."

"He loves our son very much," Oranna said. "Arkus would do anything for him. I'd do even more."

Oh, so this is what you're worried about?

"I can assure you I want nothing to do with the throne."

Oranna leaned forward. "You know, I think you might be being completely honest with me."

"Why wouldn't I be?" Cassandra asked. "There's nothing I want from you. I'm not playing any game."

"True," Oranna said, before adding in a less sweet voice, "well, you won't mind if I have a whisky, then?"

"Um, not at all," Cassandra said. The words were barely out of her mouth when Oranna produced a small glass seemingly from nowhere and filled it with a golden liquid from one of the pots.

"If anyone ever asks for this one," Oranna said, setting the pot down, "I just tell them it has gone cold and shall taste dreadful." She drank from the cup. "Gracious, that's better." Cassandra stared at the queen, feeling her eyes widen in amazement.

"What?" Oranna said. "You've seen and done more shocking things, I'd wager. Ever tried it?" She proffered the tumbler.

"No," Cassandra said, taking it.

"I'm not surprised," said Oranna. "Southerners tried to make it but failed. The best stuff is from the Splinters because each island has a unique type of peat. That one is from my father's own distillery in the Hinterlands. The hint of Cascade in the Dorain gives it a taste of peach." Cassandra sniffed it. She coughed as something rankled the back of her throat, then took a sip.

"It burns," she said, half-choking.

Have I just been poisoned?

"That's why I love it," Oranna said. "Can hardly taste the peach if I am being honest. I'd tell you I seek the warmth for lack of it from my dear husband, but the truth is I just love it."

"Arkus does not love you?"

"How blunt you are," Oranna said, bringing the cup to her lips again. The queen cocked her head and eyed Cassandra as though she were an exotic animal. "You truly are new to Brevia, aren't you? You don't come with the expectations – the baggage. Take that dress for a start. How wonderfully different. Around most, I must pretend to be the stoic queen." She took another sip from her glass. "Arkus cares for me enough, by the way," she added conspiratorially. "But he's never gotten over your mother. He married me for duty, and for some black stone. I advise you get out of your betrothal if you don't want it."

"I'm not sure how," Cassandra said.

"Find a way," Oranna said. "I'd help you if I could, and not just for my son's sake. I don't imagine you would enjoy putting on the same show that I must. Take these abominable cakes, for example." She looked at the tray as though the pastries had done her great harm. "I am forever being offered them, as though a queen's constitution could be sustained on them alone, and out of politeness I must always try one or two. I used to like such sweets as a child, but now I'm sick of them. It's become a trend in Brevia to even sprinkle extra sugar on top, as if they needed any."

"I'll try one," Cassandra said, and feeling the tension had decreased, reached for a raisin-dotted scone. "Without the sugar."

"Quite right," Oranna said. Their discussion died for a time while Cassandra ate and Oranna topped up her shimmer brew. The hot silver liquid let off its enticing bitterness into the air. It was a pleasant sort of silence. The scone was soft, the raisins chewy, and Cassandra felt quite comfortable. She had the uncanny feeling that she actually liked this bony, pale queen, and very much hoped it wasn't due to the contents of Oranna's glass.

"Do you fight, Cassandra?"

"Sometimes. Only with a sword, though," Cassandra said through her last mouthful of scone. "Do you?"

"Such a dear to ask. Yes, I did a little, in my youth," Oranna said wistfully. "I wanted to be a huntress and roam the rocks and forests of the Hinterlands. But there was a war on, and as my lord father's only child I could not be risked in such a fashion." Oranna sighed then, slumping from her rigid posture. "I'm afraid I wasn't very affectionate towards my father for much of my life. Now I have a son, I can understand his concern. Though I always fancied a daughter." Her eyes fell on Cassandra.

This is getting a little intense.

"But it is too late for me now, and likely too late for us as well," Oranna said. "However, I would like to have one person around here I can talk to without having to pretend to be someone else." The queen wafted a hand around the parlour in demonstration.

"You spoke of helping me, if you could. Does that mean you cannot help me?"

"Arkus has become a stubborn man. Once he sets his mind on something, you can be sure it will be done. I doubt I will ever truly love him, but I do admire him greatly for that. However..." Oranna locked eyes with Cassandra. "He does enjoy cutting a good deal."

"I don't have anything I can offer," Cassandra said. "Nothing that a king couldn't get for himself."

"Ah, there are a great many things Arkus cannot get," Oranna said.

"All I have is myself."

"Then offer him something only you can do."

"But what can I do?" Cassandra said. "I've read a lot, but he has scholars and advisors. I know a lot about the Bastion, but that's useless now. And as you've said, I've just arrived here, so I don't know anyone and no one knows me, so — oh." The realisation struck her.

Oranna beamed. "Go, go. Haste is vital in these matters."

"Thank you for the scones," Cassandra said. She bolted for the door and thought she could hear Oranna call out that they ought to do it again sometime.

Cassandra pelted down the corridors of the palace, ignoring the butlers, and nearly slammed into a chevalier as she rounded a corner. She flew down a set of winding stairs that bypassed a couple of floors and brought her to Arkus' council chambers. She arrived panting.

"Let me through," she commanded the chevaliers. "I must speak to my — my father." They all looked her up and down, hesitated, and then stood aside. She burst into the room, hair tumbling down her face.

Arkus was hunched over a map of the city along with Gellick, tapping the area of the Rotting Hill and muttering darkly. They were both taken aback to see her standing there.

"Well, I see you had an entertaining day out," Arkus said, looking at her ruined dress. "Gellick, please allow me a moment with my daughter. I will call you back to finish our discussion."

"Your Majesty," Gellick said with a bow. Once Gellick was gone, Arkus looked serious again. He withdrew the map under the desk and sat down.

"Have you thought about what we discussed?"

"I have," she said, striding towards him. When she arrived at the desk, she leaned over it. Arkus didn't budge an inch. "There will be no marriage," Cassandra said.

"Oh?"

"I don't expect you to give it up for nothing. What if I deliver Lord Boreac to you?"

Arkus pondered for a while, rapping his fingers across his desk, from pinkie to forefinger, and then back again. "And how do you intend on doing that?"

"I'm not from here," Cassandra said. "Barely anyone knows who I am, which means I can go about the city as a fresh face. I can be a princess when I need the clout, and nobody when I need to blend in. And you can trust that I am not part of any circle that plotted against you. Can you say that of your spies?"

"No," Arkus said. "They are spies, after all."

"Well, then. Do we have a deal?"

Arkus smiled and leaned back. "You realise that, even if you succeed, it won't change your position or who you are? The problems I have would not vanish. Well, other than having Boreac in chains."

"Then keep up the pretence that I will marry Balack until we think of a solution."

"We?"

"Yes, Arkus – I mean… Father," Cassandra said.

"Call me what you want," Arkus said, though he said it with affection. "Very well. *If* you can deliver me Boreac, we'll find an alternative. A nice long show trial for him and Annandale will occupy the Assembly for a time. With their positions vacant, I can dole out their lands and titles. That will keep the vultures at bay." He seemed to drift into his own thoughts for a moment. His mouth twitched and he ran his fingers across the desk again. "There may be some element of risk involved."

"I can handle myself," Cassandra said.

"I wouldn't allow this, but I *need* Boreac," Arkus said, as though nothing else in the world mattered. "Don't do anything rash. If you know where he is, you come to me first. Understand?"

"I'll find him," Cassandra said. Then she left whilst she still felt confident. Outside the council chambers, she allowed herself a smile.

"You can go back in now, Gellick," she said.

18

SHADOWS IN DALRIDIA

The Islanders could be wealthy. Being in the middle of the world, they could have controlled all trade. Instead, they've sought isolation, sometimes even from each other.

From Tiviar's Histories

Dukoona – The Splintering Isles – City of Dalridia

Dukoona withdrew his blade from the islander's stomach and blood gushed. It fell from the man like the rain around him. The constant rain. With the humans nearby dealt with, he turned to help his spectres cleave an opening in the palisade wall. Once a hole was roughly hewn, demons began to scramble through this latest breach – too few demons, in truth. Dukoona saw many slip down high embankments leading up to the walls.

Forward, he commanded to the demons around him. *Do not stop.*

He watched them tear off. *They really are such frail creatures,* he thought. Small and wispy, the shadows of their flesh were more akin to smoke. And even at a distance, he could see their ribs as the dark mist swirled within them. They lacked sense as well, running in every direction within the maze of walls.

The islanders had built their defences to confuse their enemies. Sure enough, a group appeared from a one-way opening in the wall to fall upon the demons in a storm of axes. At least Dukoona knew about that trap now. Dalridia would not fall without a fight.

"Come with me," Dukoona called to the spectres nearby. "We must create more breaches along the wall." They ran off, unable to find any shadows under the heavy clouds. Dukoona took them right, away from the islanders' ambush, searching for a gap in the inner layers of palisade wall.

A group of islanders ahead were blocking a breach with a stout shield wall. Dukoona swung his dark sword at their backs when he reached them, cutting through leather and mail with ease. The spectres ravaged their flank and the humans broke, running back into the labyrinth. Thrilled, the demons chased merrily after them. Dukoona cautiously followed, thinking the islanders might have broken a little too easily. Around a bend, he saw that the humans seemed to have run impossibly far. They stood bashing their shields tauntingly.

Howling, the demons bounded on.

"Wait," Dukoona snarled to his spectres. He let the demons carry on as bait and, midway, the ground dropped, dumping the demons into a pit of spikes.

It was clever of the humans, but only the rain was saving them. Once enough points along the outer walls were breached, they would be overwhelmed. Still, it was a harder fight than he had anticipated. That was all for the better. It granted a chance to relieve his master of thousands of demons. Dukoona just hoped his Trusted were not throwing their lives away.

Stay safe, Kidrian. I need you at my side. I can't do this alone.

Trap after trap, dead end after dead end, and at the cost of many demons, Dukoona pushed his way to the final set of Dalridia's walls. A host of humans gathered to meet him, bloodied, windburnt and covered in mud: the islands' best. To Dukoona's fortune, the clouds finally parted, casting sporadic shadows from shields, bodies, axes and walls.

He reached out to the demons and commanded, *Kill.* They swarmed forwards. The humans pressed their shields together and withstood the impact. Axes arced, spraying smoky blood and chipped demon bone. Demons leapt on top of their brethren to vault over the shields. Just as the first wave was spent, more demons came from behind to join Dukoona. He could always count on having more demons.

Then he felt something twig at the back of his mind. Rectar looked briefly towards him through the bond of master and servant. '*Faster...*' the echoing rumble commanded before he left.

Dukoona froze for a moment, trembling. He rallied quickly and yelled, "Show the humans fear. With me, spectres!" And he dove into the thin shadow under the base of the wall, running along it, judging when best to strike. In the middle of the human shield wall, he half-emerged his torso from the shadow to cut at two of the defenders. He melded again before the humans could react and was already halfway back along the base of the wall when a shield slammed into his path.

Another thud jarred behind him and he knew his path was blocked.

These really are the islands' finest.

He tore from his shadow, his dark blade carving through the soft leather on the legs of the nearest human. Yet now he was surrounded. He had to be careful, weaving within the web of ever-changing shadows in the melee. One false meld and he'd be caught. Done.

An axe sped towards his face. Dukoona sank his legs into a shadow to drop under it. He heard a satisfying squelch as the axe continued into the human behind him. He travelled under the axe wielder's legs, sprang up on the other side, knocking men and women aside, and drove his sword through an exposed throat.

Other spectres had been forced to fight in the open as well, melding as fast as they could so as not to be swarmed. One was caught within his shadow and axe cleaved below the surface of the ground to crack at a head that could not be seen.

"Spread out to fight them," one of the humans roared. Quickly, the flickering shadows on the ground grew further apart. Dukoona spotted the one calling orders and made for him. He seemed young, a little stocky, but was quick and raised his shield against Dukoona's dark blade. Dukoona's swing rebounded off a metal coating. "This one is mine," the boy called.

"Lord Grigayne, stay back!"

Dukoona fell back as the boy lowered his shield and rammed him. He melded into the shadow of the shield, taking Grigayne in the chin as he rose. They were so close. Dukoona's cold tendrils of blue flame lapped at Grigayne's face. He switched from his shadow blade to a dagger instead, the weapon morphing in his hand.

He raised the dagger.

He tried to bring it down.

And felt a ferocious blunt blow at his side. Knocked off balance, the dagger scraped into the meat of the boy's shoulder rather than somewhere more fatal. Grigayne screamed, drawing back the butt of his axe from Dukoona's side. Dukoona melded away under the boy and reappeared behind him. Somehow, the human managed to turn in time to block him.

He was fast and strong, this one; he had to be, to carry that reinforced shield. Yet Grigayne's wound would end him and he raised that shield a little lower with each strike Dukoona sent. And then two spectres emerged, grinning their white smiles.

Dukoona did not recognise the newcomers.

That was odd.

Only the Trusted had been brought to Dalridia; he was certain. It might have been the shock that prevented Dukoona reacting to the dark sword coming towards him. The grinning spectre locked eyes with him under hair of long orange flames. Only a slip on the wet earth saved Dukoona, the spectre's blade slicing his arm instead. The wound smoked.

So, that's what pain is like. I'd nearly forgotten.

The second grinning spectre lunged for him. Dukoona jerked aside then caught the arm of his foe and dragged the spectre onto his dagger. Smoke rose; the grin faded. He threw the body at the first traitor, buying time to switch to his sword. The blade materialised in a whirl of shadows just in time to meet his enemy's weapon. Dukoona pushed with all his might, enough to bend the arms of his foe and impale the spectre upon his own blade.

With the immediate threat over, he looked around. Grigayne and the humans had pulled away from the spectre infighting. The demons themselves had begun to fight each other. Dukoona reached to those nearby and gave the order, *To me.* Many scuttled to his side, yet many also continued killing each other, ignoring the humans entirely.

They're getting conflicting orders.

Spectres were melding in and out of the battle, but they moved so fast he couldn't say if they were friend or foe. Those that leapt for him were clear enough. He knew none of them – they weren't Trusted – but killing them was a blow to him all the same.

Is this how you get rid of us, Rectar? Watching me kill my own kind? Does that please you? But Rectar's power was elsewhere. He wasn't even glancing in Dukoona's direction. Were these traitors acting of their own accord?

A fresh group of spectres emerged from the shadows and Dukoona had never been more thankful to see those guttering purple embers. Kidrian and members of the Trusted came to his aid. Before long, the traitorous spectres were smoking on the ground and the demons ceased fighting each other. Kidrian looked after the retreating humans, ready to give chase.

"Let them go," Dukoona said. "Keep the demons advancing, but all Trusted are to fall back. Now."

Miles to the east, with the Nail Head rising behind them, Dukoona gathered his closest Trusted atop the Shadow Spire they had built upon landing. It was smaller and squatter than the tower back on Eastguard but served well enough. Many galleys sat empty at the coast, their demons either dead, dying or continuing to press Dalridia. Dukoona had ordered the rest to stay on their ships until he got a grip on things. As ever, he needed time to think, but it seemed time had finally run out.

"Who were they?" he asked. No one answered. "I made it clear that I wanted no spectre whom we did not trust to sail with us."

"Perhaps they came from Skelf," Kidrian said. "Longboats landed to the north of the city to reinforce the defenders. Spectres could have travelled on them, melded away out of sight."

"So Kraz is dead?" asked Sonrid, shuffling forward eagerly.

"We have no idea what's happened on Skelf," said Kidrian.

"We need to know," said Dukoona. "If those spectres were only seeking revenge for being sent on a suicide mission with Kraz then so be it. The alternative is… quite unthinkable."

Again, no one answered.

Then, from the bottom of the spire below, came distant growls from the guards. Kidrian peered over the edge, and then looked to Dukoona. He gave a nod and Kidrian melded away to investigate. Dukoona paced, painfully aware that all eyes were on him. They were looking to him to tell them the answers, but he had none.

Has Rectar at last decided to remove me? If so, what do I do? What can I do?

An old haunting memory crept up on him, of when he had first been summoned – a memory of an endless cavern, with demons all around. The demons had charged at him and nothing he had done could stop them. "Know you cannot hope to turn my servants against me," Rectar had told him.

Even the spectres, my own kind, are his servants. Perhaps I could never have turned any against him?

Kidrian emerged from the shadows and Dukoona stopped his pacing. "Trusted have returned to us from the west."

"From the west?" Dukoona said. He had been forced to send spectres to Castallan years ago. "Bring them up." Kidrian disappeared again and returned shortly with a score of spectres. Of the new arrivals, Dukoona recognised the leader with thick, scarlet flames on his head. "Nordin," he said, dragging out the spectre's name in disbelief. "It has been a very long time."

"I regret that we did not leave sooner," said Nordin in a voice like an angry gale of wind. "Less of our brothers might have needlessly died."

"Why are you here now?" Dukoona asked. "Your timing is a pleasant surprise, and yet it is also suspicious." He caught Kidrian's eye and drew a blade from the shadows in case of danger. Other Trusted followed suit.

"We would have come sooner," Nordin said nervously. "We have come because the dragon king slew the human who kept us down, who sent us in for a slaughter at the town of Torridon."

"Slaughter?" Dukoona said. "How many of you remain now?"

"Just over one hundred, my lord."

Just one hundred, out of the three hundred I sent west…

"Then we shall take a moment for the loss of so many spectres," Dukoona said. He closed his eyes, as did all the Trusted. After a minute, he opened them. "Our people are dying; being sent to death or turning on each other. We are too few now, too few to last another war. Who was this human that you allowed to treat our brothers so, Nordin?"

"My lord, forgive me, but there was little any of us could do. Castallan's magic turned them into men and women with glowing red eyes who could match a dragon's strength. The wizard's favoured Commander Zarl was the strongest of them all. There were so few of us, there was nothing we could have done. For years, there was no fighting and it mattered little, but then came Cold Point. And Torridon. And finally, the Charred Vale.

"We did what we could; tried to abandon Zarl and let the demons turn rabid. But each time some of us fled, some of us would pay. At the Charred Vale, Darnuir defeated Zarl, and so we took our chance."

"And the wizard?" Dukoona asked.

"Dead, for all we care," Nordin said. "The Three Races were moving to destroy him."

"Then the dragons will not be far behind," Dukoona said.

"I couldn't say, my lord," said Nordin, and his voice petered out in some deep exhaustion. Not a physical tiredness; spectres did not tire. But something in Nordin and the spectres with him looked worn. Their flaming hair was dim and the shadows of their flesh were thin; more like steam than flesh. He caught Kidrian's eye again and nodded. Kidrian dispersed his weapon with a wave of his fingers and all the weapons among the Trusted began to vanish. "I am glad that you have returned, Nordin. We shall need every spectre – every ounce of cunning. All has not been well in the east and all those gathered here should now know."

Kidrian stepped forwards. "Are you sure, my lord?"

"I am," Dukoona said. "How did you describe these humans, Nordin? That their eyes were red? Another red creature attacked our kind near Kar'drun not so long ago. These things must be linked. The Master does not need us. We've become disposable. Sent to these islands to block his enemies, perhaps to buy him more time."

And even as he spoke, the truth of it dawned on him. He had, after all, been sending Rectar what he had wanted for decades. And what his master had desired was dragons.

"I don't want to give him time," Dukoona said. "We're going back to Aurisha."

"What of the demons?" Kidrian asked.

"Leave those already ashore. Those still on board their ships will come with us. It may pass as a tactical retreat to Rectar if it looks like we are trying to split the Three Races."

"And those on the other islands?" Sonrid asked. "Our brethren at Eastguard, Skelf, Ronra—"

"All the spectres that I care about are here," Dukoona said. "Leave the False to serve the Master a little longer."

. . .

Blaine – The Splintering Isles – Approaching Dalridia

At the bow of the *Grey Fury*, Blaine looked to the swathe of demons upon the shore. They were another sea, black and burning, ebbing and crashing against the battered walls of Dalridia. There was no order to them, but there were thousands, stretching as far as Blaine could see.

One more battle and then I tell Darnuir everything.

It was those memories which, had they not been locked away in his gems, might have haunted him every night. He clutched tightly at the chain around his neck, the terrible evidence of what he suspected. Kroener – the betrayer, the cursed – and Darnuir's father had gone to the Highlands. How else could the trolls have come by the necklace? Two had journeyed northwards but only one had returned. Why that was, he would likely never know. But what happened after, he would never forget.

"Are you ready?" Darnuir said, stepping up behind him. The boy was in full armour and his crimson cloak had been repaired. It fit him well; better even than his father, and far more than Draconess.

Was it all a mistake? Or is this what the gods intended?

"Blaine?" Darnuir said.

"I am ready."

"If you do not wish to fight… if you are still uneasy after the Bast—"

"I'm fine," Blaine said. It was only half a lie. Physically, he was sound.

"You've been quiet of late," said Darnuir. Their ship was now approaching the shore, its shallow hull enabling it to draw right up to the beach.

"The Cascade will not abandon me here," Blaine said. He knew now that was the reason he'd suffered at the Bastion, but it was of small comfort. He'd felt life without magic, without his blade propping up his aged body. What he couldn't be certain of was whether the gods would abandon him.

Perhaps they abandoned me long ago.

"The city stands," Somerled Imar boomed proudly from the portside. "My son has held the demon filth at bay."

"Good," Darnuir said, drawing the Dragon's Blade and spinning it in his hand. "Let's help him kill them."

The *Grey Fury* beached and men and dragons leapt off over the deck rail. The dragons had removed the armour from their lower bodies to better wade through the shallow water. Blaine jumped off with his Light Bearers, Darnuir on the other side with his Praetorians. Hundreds more ships followed in behind them.

The demons didn't seem to know what to do about the landing. Blaine cut through them, the Guardian's Blade fighting the servants of the Shadow once more. It seemed too easy.

Where are the spectres?

"Make safe the city!" Darnuir cried, sweeping westwards and rallying dragons to him.

Blaine scored kill after kill; the demons were numerous and vicious, but lacked any direction. He sensed a trap, a false feeling of security. He kept his Light Bearers close and alert, worried that a huge demon fleet might approach from the rear. But nothing came. The demons were pushed off the beaches, up the land, into the woods, right up against the slope of the Nail Head itself, and were crushed there.

It was good that the victory was so complete. After the Bastion, the men needed a win with less of a toll. Blaine basked in the blow they had dealt to Rectar's forces, yet it was a fleeting feeling. The battle had not been as cathartic as he'd hoped. His mind turned again to the conversation he must have with Darnuir: his king, and his grandson.

19

A DISH HARD TO STOMACH

Out of every major settlement of humans and dragons, I feel most at home in Dalridia. The islanders' earthen halls are closer to nature than anything in Brevia or Aurisha. There may not be trees but the humans of the Splinters show a deep respect and connection to the world. If only it wasn't so wet.

From Tiviar's Histories

Darnuir – East of Dalridia

Darnuir looked up to the top of the strange tower, shielding his eyes against the drizzling rain. It was nothing like he had ever seen before, in this life or his last. He wasn't sure whether to even call it a tower, for it lacked any enclosed space. A multitude of wooden beams criss-crossed upwards to a flat platform under an open sky. The spectres must have built it, yet the spectres had all fled.

They keep on fleeing. Why? Why don't the wretches stand and fight?

He'd enjoyed the battle, enjoyed the feeling of magic in him. The days spent at sea had been dry, for he'd had no excuse to draw upon the Cascade. He needed it now. Needed to feel like he had in Castallan's throne room.

Darnuir feared he was fighting a losing battle with himself.

Each day it was harder to resist. Each day he yearned a little more for magic. And each crucial decision he had to make became harder to focus on, for his mind was often elsewhere. He didn't know who to turn to on the matter. Blaine was acting strangely and would only rebuke him. Brackendon was broken, a terrible sign of what might come to pass.

What can I do? We're in the middle of a war. It can't be delayed just to help me. And if I let them know I'm in this state, they won't follow me.

In this struggle, he could only rely on himself.

Darnuir congratulated himself on his small achievements in this regard. It had been a challenge, for example, to grant Grigayne Imar the honour of destroying the spectres' mysterious tower. It would have made a good excuse to drawn on magic.

To Darnuir's right, Grigayne grunted through the pain in his shoulder and slammed his great war axe down in a two-handed grip. It bit deeply into the wood of a supporting beam. Several hacks later and the beam split with a satisfying crack. His men roared in approval and began attacking the tower as well. A groaning soon followed as the first of the twisting walls came crashing down. Darnuir's golden armour was already filthy so he didn't mind the fresh splatter of mud.

"Foul thing," said Grigayne, jerking a thumb at the wreckage. His reddish hair was pulled back into a knot and the finer hairs of his beard rolled around his face like the froth atop a great wave.

"A foul thing for foul creatures," Darnuir said. "Your defence of your lands has been nothing short of heroic."

"Has it?" Grigayne said, a touch of frost in his tone.

"I'm sorry we did not arrive sooner."

"We've lost Eastguard, Ronra and Skelf after I had to pull my warriors back to defend Dalridia," Grigayne lamented. "The demons sailed right around Ullusay. Took us by surprise here. There are some smaller villages east of the Nail Head – well, there *were*..."

"Demons burned my home," Darnuir said. "There is nothing left in the Boreac Mountains now."

Grigayne nodded wearily. "Rebuilding will be especially hard with winter on the way."

"The demons will be driven back," Darnuir said.

"You dragons never seemed capable of driving them back before," Grigayne said. "Why will this time be any different?"

"Because something is amiss with our enemies," Darnuir said.

"I saw that firsthand," Grigayne said. He frowned in some thought. "While I was fighting one of them – a tough bastard with blue flames – more spectres appeared around me. I thought I was done for. But then they started to fight each other instead."

"What happened next?" Darnuir asked, intrigued by this new development.

"The one with the blue flames was the target. I disengaged due to my injury, and to reform our shield wall. Once one side of the spectres won, they vanished. All of them, though the demons did not descend into madness at that point."

"Something similar happened at the Charred Vale," Darnuir said. "They fled the battle and left the demons rabid. The same thing allowed us an easy victory here."

"Why would they do that?"

"You're asking the wrong person," said Darnuir. "Only their leader could tell us."

"I didn't know they had a leader," Grigayne said.

"A spectre called Dukoona, if memory serves." Cassandra had mentioned it to him. She'd witnessed Dukoona informing Castallan about this very invasion. Things didn't seem to be going Dukoona's way.

"A shame you cannot ask him," said Grigayne.

"A great shame," Darnuir said, although the younger Imar had got him thinking.

Why not go east and find out? Going east with all haste would also mean battle that much sooner. Yes, why not go?

"Actually, I ought to go," said Darnuir. Grigayne looked at him as though he had gone mad. "Not a word of this to the guardian," he added. "Blaine would never approve."

"This could be a ploy of the spectres," said Grigayne.

Darnuir scrambled for some justification. "My gut tells me otherwise. It seems a stretch to think the spectres faked a skirmish in front of you, killing their own in the process, just in the hope you would survive the battle and tell me. If they even knew who you were. If there is infighting among the spectres, then we ought to take advantage of the situation. Strike hard and fast before they have a chance to end whatever strife there is between them."

Grigayne sniffed. "Your army, your decision."

"You are unimpressed, I gather."

"I'm worn," Grigayne said, rolling his shoulders with a deep sigh. He winced and brought a hand up to his injury. "Worn, tired, beaten and in need of rest. And I thought you might be, well…" He trailed off.

"Different?"

"Something like that."

"This is how my people have been for thousands of years."

"I know," said Grigayne. "Yet the way the dragons are spoken of, it made me think you were something more. A boyish imagination that was never corrected."

"May I ask you something personal, Lord Imar?"

"I'm not the lord yet," Grigayne said. "But yes, you may ask."

"You speak differently than your fellow islanders, even your own father. Why?"

"My father wished me to sound more acceptable to the Assembly in Brevia," said Grigayne with a sad smile. "He thought our cause for sovereignty might fare better if

I was able to visit Brevia and not sound so foreign. But isn't there a bitter irony in that? I was to give up the voice of my own people to better argue for their separateness."

"And why does your father feel so strongly about this?"

Grigayne shrugged. "It's the way it's always been. Did my ancestors swear an oath of fealty or merely homage to the old Brevian kings? Who is to say? One way makes us subservient and the other makes us respectful. My father would rather not pay taxes and Arkus would rather he continued. Every generation. On and on it goes. Gives my father a goal in life, if nothing else."

"And what do you make of it?" Darnuir said.

"I don't see why we should break apart. Where would it end? First Dalridia gains freedom from Brevia and then the smaller islands become frustrated with my family. Without Brevia to blame, it will be those ruling in Dalridia who suffer from disgruntlement, from West Hearth to Eastguard, from Southguard to Ronra in the north. How long until Innerwick and Outerwick decide they will fare better if they rule themselves? How long then until even the people of the Wicks begin to disagree with each other?"

"There is strength in unity," said Darnuir. He was pleased by Grigayne's words.

"So long as it is genuine," said Grigayne. "A shield wall is only as strong as the bond of trust between each warrior. What good would a shield wall be if every man and woman bickered with the person on their right and jostled for a better position? That's the kingdom more often than not. There's no single answer."

"That is why I have formed my new Praetorian Guard. I hope to make a force of all the Three Races, built on trust and loyalty. A symbol that we can indeed bring unity. But it has proven... difficult. I'd take you and twenty of your best men and shieldmaidens, if it would please you?"

"I — join your guard?" Grigayne questioned.

"I feel we are of a mind," said Darnuir.

"I'm not so sure," Grigayne said. He took some time. He sniffed again in the misty rain and shuffled his feet a little more firmly into the mud. His chainmail rattled softly with every movement. "It's a noble endeavour, but joining you would anger my father, and how would that favour you? I'm sorry, but I must think of my own people. I cannot abandon them at a time like this."

Darnuir had no answer. *Why do they all resist me on this? Blaine, Fidelm, now the Imars?* This small dream was already slipping away from him. The two halves of his person battled to dominate his emotions: the old dragon snarled in anger at the human's rebuttal, while the younger man felt cowed and foolish. This time, the young man won. *Some king I am. I'm failing more than succeeding and losing more people than I gain.* He'd left a trail of dead or bitter friends in the west. Arkus would shut his gates to him. East was his only road, but he saw nothing on that path but war and hardship. Temptation arose for the Cascade; to draw on it and not feel as powerless for a moment. He clenched his hand into a fist so hard that his nails drew blood, and managed to resist the urge.

Grigayne did not fail to notice this and raised an eyebrow. Darnuir brought his bleeding palm to his mouth and sucked on his self-inflicted wound.

"I should return to the city," Darnuir said. "There is much to do if I am to take my dragons east and chase Dukoona." Grigayne seemed to understand that silence was required. He bowed courteously then took his leave, trudging back to his warriors by the ruin of the tower. The longship sigil on his shield was barely recognisable under all those notches.

Back in Dalridia, Darnuir attended to what Praetorians he did have. Their bow-work was coming along with practice every day, and their stamina had increased considerably. Lira had found an area for them outside one of the enormous long halls that dominated the city. The hall was built of loose stone and topped with earth, allowing daisies and ferns to grow wild on the roof.

"We'll work on our shield wall today," Lira announced. "The islanders impressed me, and we can do better. We must be able to make a bulwark against attack."

"Perhaps I could abstain from this training," Raymond said. "Only I fear I might be crushed."

"Harra, Camen," Lira said, nodding at the Praetorians to either side of the chevalier. "Don't crush Raymond."

"We'll try," Harra said. She slapped Raymond's back plate and he grunted.

Darnuir felt a pang of sympathy for the chevalier. "Play nice, now, or afterwards you can sprint against Raymond while he's mounted." The Praetorians mumbled in mock annoyance and some laughed. Darnuir and Lira set up their drill then stepped back to observe.

"Get your shield up to your chin," Darnuir said.

"Cover the person in front of you, don't hit their heads," Lira said.

"Faster now," said Darnuir. "We may need it at a moment's notice."

"Okay, let's try having half of you form a wall and half push it," said Lira. She divided the Praetorians and set them up. "On the count of three. One. Two. Three." The dragons and an exhausted Raymond charged or raised shields as instructed. The wall formed, held, but a section slid back.

"The ground's too wet," the fallen Praetorian said.

"Wet or dry, grass or snow, we must be ready," Darnuir said. Then, under his breath, "We must be ready, because no one else will join us. No one else will help us…"

"What was that?" Lira said. She stepped even closer to him. He noticed some signs of battle on her. A piece of her ebony hair had been cut away; it was now shorter on her left side, and her blue Hinterland leggings had a fresh tear.

"It was nothing, Lira. Don't trouble yourself with it."

"I'm voicing concern as the Praetorian prefect for my king's well-being."

"Well, I'm fine, thank you."

"If you say so," she said. "Look, I'd like to ask for your pardon for what happened at the Bastion, in the dungeons. I questioned your motivations."

"That's part of your job," Darnuir said.

"Rescuing the princess was important," Lira said. "I only thought you might not be thinking clearly and – well, it does not matter now. Did it help with King Arkus at all?"

"I'm not sure," Darnuir said. "I can only hope that in time he will get over it."

"It's understandable, given what Blaine revealed," said Lira.

"He didn't think," said Darnuir. "He should have told me."

"I think he tried, Darnuir," Lira said cautiously.

"I think I would have listened to him if he —"

"You weren't giving him a chance," Lira said. "You were always wanting to train or fight something. I know he didn't treat the hunters very well, but did you have to shut him out?"

"I was just giving him the cold shoulder," Darnuir said. "With something that important he should have insisted, made more of a fuss..." He trailed off. Lira was looking at him again with a worried face. "What's done is done," he said. "Blaine and I can smooth out our differences when we're safely in Aurisha one day."

"That could be a while off."

"I intend to sail as soon as possible," said Darnuir. "Take the dragons and seize upon this civil war the spectres are in the middle of."

Lira frowned. "Forgive me, Darnuir, but that seems rash."

Darnuir was beginning to feel his temper rise. It came even quicker these days if he couldn't open the door just a little bit; just by a crack. He forced himself to remain calm.

"We could be in Aurisha in a matter of weeks, not months. The spectres are fighting amongst each other. I don't see when we'll have a better opportunity. And what if we miss our chance before winter comes and it becomes difficult to move troops?"

Lira did not answer immediately.

"As you will, Darnuir."

Further conversation was prevented by Raymond's collapse.

"I think Raymond should call the countdowns for a while," Lira said.

"Marvellous," Raymond said. He staggered well out of range of the charging dragons. "By my count, then. One. Two Three."

The Praetorians slammed into each other.

"Ooft, that'll be sore t'morrow," came a rough voice. Darnuir and Lira both whipped around to see a windburnt islander bearing a toothy smile and waving them over with his stump of a hand.

"Do you know who we are?" Darnuir asked.

"What d'you take me for? I 'av one hand, not one eye."

"I'm just used to being formally addressed," said Darnuir.

"Ach, sorry, yer Lordship," the man said. "Lord Imar sent me. Cayn, at yer service." He bowed, though it seemed almost in jest.

"Does Somerled have need of me?" Darnuir said.

"Lord Imar has prepared a special meal and invites you and yer Guard to join him."

"Special, you say?" Lira said. "Good. We have a lot of hungry dragons here."

Cayn led them towards the heart of Dalridia, over the wide waterways that ran through the city like roads in any other. Islanders navigated these channels on scaled-down longships, some rowing, some propelling themselves forward by pushing a stick behind them into the shallow water. Smoke rose from the centre of each earthen hall or home but the light rain drove most of the smell away. Somerled Imar's own long hall was naturally the greatest. It had a second tier and glass windows, complete with a turf roof covered in bluebells.

"Here ye go, milord," said Cayn. "I'm sure ye can find yer way from here. I 'av tae fetch the other one."

"Does he mean Blaine?" Lira asked when he left.

"What a happy gathering that will be," Darnuir said.

He'd expected it to be dark and drab inside the hall. Instead, galleries of bottles of amber liquid lined the walls, reflecting grey light from the windows tenfold in a golden shine. Chunky tables sat before the bottle stacks, gouged with trenches for food. A fire pit at the centre warmed the hall and whole pigs crackled over the flames. The smell of cooking meat and fat filled the air.

"Darnuir!" boomed Somerled from across the hall. "Welcome, all of you. Please follow me." He swept his way into the semi-darkness at the far end of the hall. Darnuir and the Praetorians caught up with him and took their seats as directed. They squeezed around several tables in the shadow of a protrusion of rock which rose high above at a sharp angle. Smoothed steps were inlaid on the side of the rock to climb it.

Somerled clapped his hands and steaming dishes were brought to their table, although the meat was not what Darnuir had expected.

"Not pork?" he asked.

"That's for my men," Somerled said. "I've had my cooks prepare this specially for you."

What's so special about oversized chickens? Darnuir thought, for that was all the meal appeared to be. Enormous fat chickens, roasted perfectly with a golden skin, but that was it. And then the smell of it reached him. A sudden urge came over Darnuir to feed, to rip and tear and gorge. It wasn't a human feeling. His stomach rumbled desperately, and he swore he heard Lira's do the same. His head began to spin and he lunged for the meat with the rest of the dragons. He tore a leg off the bird, biting through the crispy skin, feeling the hot juice run down his chin as he plunged through the soft sweet meat to the bone. He ate so fast he barely tasted it.

Raymond looked disgusted. "May I request a knife and fork?" he asked of Somerled's staff.

"Glad ye all enjoyed that," Somerled told them.

Darnuir felt very satisfied. The sensation had been almost like a Cascade rush only without the side effects. If anything, he felt sleepy. A horrible thought came over him. *Have we been poisoned?* He shook his head and got to his feet to fight the tiredness.

"What did you put in that chicken?" he demanded.

"That isnae chicken," said Somerled. "It's capon."

"Oh…" Lira said in a dreamy fashion.

"Shall I have more brought out?" Somerled said. The Praetorians grinned and nodded slowly. Some started to rub their eyes. Others lay back, a hand on their stomach. Raymond looked at them all, deeply confused, and raised his fork to sniff suspiciously at his piece of capon.

"I'd say help yerself tae the whisky an'all, but you lot cannae handle yer drink."

Darnuir blinked rapidly. "I found that one out the hard way."

"Would make you all a bit less sour-faced if you could." Somerled laughed at his remark.

"Some watered wine isn't so potent," said Darnuir.

"Then you'd better return to Brevia for that," said Somerled. "But 'am glad the meat is tae yer liking. A fine reward for saving my city, I dare say. Once Arkus' fleet arrives we'll relieve all of the Splinters!"

"How long will that be?" Darnuir said.

"Depends on how quickly they made it back to Brevia," said Somerled. "At least two weeks from now, maybe more."

To Darnuir, the thought of two weeks felt abominably long. He almost reached for the door in his mind there and then, but he felt more like having a nap.

"Perhaps I could have a word, Somerled?"

"Aye," Somerled said, a little unsure. Lira attempted to get up but only made it halfway before her tired legs began to wobble.

"You can stay and eat," Darnuir said. Lira smiled stupidly as though drunk and sat back down.

What's come over us? I need to get out of here.

More capon was being served. Darnuir held his breath to try and avoid the smell.

He walked as quickly as he could back outside. Once outside, he began to cough and moved to steady himself on the chest-high wall overlooking the waterway. He gulped in the cool air; it felt fresh and clean, and cleared the haze of capon from his mind.

"Feeling better?" Somerled asked.

"Care to explain how you've incapacitated my Praetorians with poultry?"

Somerled tapped his brow with a single finger. "We islanders hav'nae forgotten everything about yer kind. My father told me, and his father told him, that if dragons ever come visiting, feed 'em capon. Can't get enough of it, he said. Seems to be true."

"I wasn't aware of that," Darnuir said darkly.

"Nothin' sinister about it. Was that yer first time?" he added mockingly.

"It's not exactly a common dish in the Boreac Mountains," Darnuir said.

"Just thought it was something I could offer, seeing as ye don't drink. When you retake all the islands, I'll roast up a whole flock of 'em."

"Ah, about that," Darnuir said. He thought it best to just have it out with him. "I plan to take my dragons east."

Silence.

Darnuir pressed on. "The demons have split their forces and I wish to seize this chance to take back Aurisha before they can regroup in full. Reinforcements will arrive from Brevia soon enough to aid in the retaking of the remaining islands, as you say."

"Soon enough," Imar repeated softly. He slumped over the wall, facing the water below. It rippled under the steady drip of rain.

"I understand your disappointment, Lord Imar, but—"

"Can't yer homeland wait a few mer months? Only, and I hate tae mention it, but doing this might only inflame the opinions of those who think dragons only look out for themselves."

"I did not think you were one of those people," Darnuir said.

"Did I say I was?" said Somerled. "I don't despise yer kind, like some. Yet I don't love you either." One of the little boats passed by then with a family on board; two small girls and a taller lad helping his father propel it along. The two young girls huddled against their mother, shivering in the light rain. The family smiled and waved to Somerled as they passed and he beamed back at them, all trace of disappointment vanishing in an instant from his face. When they passed, his features darkened again.

"They'll be off tae West Hearth, on the island of Nessay," Somerled said gravely. "On that wee boat, out tae our longships waiting for them. We've been sending people west fae months. My own wife is there, along with many of my people. Wondering whether they will return home soon, or whether we'll fail and the carnage will reach them there."

"We won't fail," Darnuir said.

"I lost my father during the last war," Somerled went on, as though Darnuir had been silent.

"As did many," said Darnuir. "As did I." He neglected the fact that he could barely remember Draconess. Only the resentment and anger remained. "Rectar and his demons seek the destruction of us all."

"Seems that way," said Somerled. "And yet, when the dragons vanished, when you disappeared, so did the demons. Poof. Gone. Neither sight nor sound of them fae twenty years until you and yer people come back. Isn't that a coincidence?"

"Rectar was licking his wounds after the Battle of Demons' Folly," Darnuir said.

"So it is just a happy accident?"

"As I do not know the will of Rectar, I cannot give you an answer."

"Perhaps it will be a good thing yer leaving," said Somerled. "Might be we're better aff without ye."

"I am sorry, Somerled."

"You will do as you will, of course. It is yer right."

"I won't be leaving you completely alone," Darnuir said. "Blaine will stay, along with Light Bearers and the Third Legion."

"One whole legion?" Somerled mocked, placing a hand over his heart. "Bless the waves but that is kind."

"We smashed a good deal of the demons' strength here," Darnuir reminded him. "They may have more numbers spread across your islands, but not enough on any single island to hold for long; especially when the reinforcements from Brevia arrive."

"The guardian is pleased with this plan, is he?" Somerled asked.

"I'll make sure of it," said Darnuir, sounding more confident than he felt. Blaine was always quarrelsome, and on this issue, he was sure to put up a fight.

"Looks like now's yer chance," said Somerled. He nodded at something past Darnuir. A group of Light Bearers were approaching Somerled's hall. "I invited them too."

"That's not Blaine," Darnuir said, looking at the dragon that led them. He met Bacchus' eye and they met in person front of the great hall. "Where is Blaine?"

"The Lord Guardian is indisposed," Bacchus said.

"He sent you in his place?"

"He sends no one," said Bacchus. "He talks to no one. He shirks his duties and holes up with that elderly dragon. But the work of the gods does not stop."

"And it's work to come for dinner?"

Bacchus sniffed the air and then his face distorted. He ran a hand through his curly black hair as though lost for words. "They would serve us such unclean food?"

"My roosters are well bred and well kept," Somerled said, puffing up.

"It leaves dragons lax and docile," said Bacchus. "It saps us of our strength and wits. It is unclean."

"I allowed my Praetorians to eat," said Darnuir. "Why not the Light Bearers too? They look hungry. Haven't they earned it?"

"You are not a godly dragon, sire, so I am not surprised. But my Light Bearers do not—"

"*Your* Light Bearers?" Darnuir asked. "Last I heard, you weren't the guardian." He stepped right up to Bacchus and his hand twitched near the hilt at his waist. *Oh, go on. Give me a reason. I beg you.*

"You seem a touch violent, sire," Bacchus said. Annoyingly, he remained so calm a fly would not have budged from his shoulder. "Perhaps an indication that you should not eat unsuitable food."

"Nae drinkin' and nae eating yerselves tae a stupor," Somerled said. "It's nae wonder yer all so cranky."

"Stay out of this, Somerled," Darnuir said. He turned back to the Light Bearer. "Where is he?"

"Over there," Bacchus said, pointing to a smaller earthen hall closer to the sea.

"Then I shall go and see him now," Darnuir said.

"Dwl'or grant you strength, sire," said Bacchus. "Gods know the Lord Guardian needs it." He smiled at Somerled. "Lord Imar, forgive my outburst, but your choice of dish caught me by surprise. I should have made the dietary requirements of the faithful clear upon our arrival." Then he turned to the Light Bearers he'd brought with him. There were quite a lot of them, now that Darnuir considered it. "Let us pay respect to Dwl'or outside of the city. The woodlands of the Nail Head should offer some shelter from the rain." They marched off.

Darnuir found that his hand had taken hold of the Dragon's Blade without him even realising. Magic was lightly flowing down his arm. He let go, wrung his arm, gently closed over the door in his mind, and spat out the bitterness before it grew.

Dukoona had better give me a fight.

"I for one enjoyed the food, Somerled," he said. And with that, Darnuir left the Lord of Isles and made haste towards Blaine's hall.

20

A MURKIER PAST

Schisms in dragon society have frequently centred on their religion. In each case, the orthodox has won, championing the true way since the time of Aurisha. That is how the guardian Nhilus summarises it in his accounts written in 1504 AT. Yet it is clear from the oldest sources available that a formal gathering at dawn was not always practised. The earliest evidence of this behaviour I can find is the year 1362 AT, two years after the quashing of a small subset of worshippers who gathered at the tip of the Tail Peninsula. Was this a new behaviour adopted by the guardians in the aftermath? Perhaps adopted from the very subset they had destroyed? We cannot know, but I am certain of this. Nothing has remained the same across all of time. Not even The Way of Light.

From Tiviar's Histories

Blaine – Dalridia

"He's coming, Lord Guardian," the Light Bearer announced.

"Bacchus?" Blaine said. "I told him to take service today."

"No, it is the king."

Blaine gulped. "Send him through." The Light Bearer disappeared back to the main body of the hall, leaving Blaine and Chelos alone in their enclave. One grubby window let in some light and there was space enough for a bed for Chelos. It was tucked away and quiet, and right now Blaine valued that more than comfort.

"We couldn't keep our secrets forever, Blaine," Chelos said. He coughed and spluttered, struggling to regain his breath. Blaine helped him sit upright.

"It pains me to see you brought low like this," said Blaine. At least the room was warm. All that packed earth the islanders used certainly insulated well.

Chelos shrugged. "I'm old, Blaine."

"I'm older."

"Maybe, but I don't have the advantage of a magical sword and I've suffered much in a short space of time. Even a few years ago, I might have recovered more easily. But now…"

"Do not speak like you are doomed," Blaine said. "N'weer will revive you and you shall stride proudly in the Basilica of Light again."

"Won't that be something," Chelos wheezed.

"Have you lost faith?"

"Once, you would have found the idea impossible. Are you having doubts?"

"About the gods? No. Never."

"But?" Chelos asked.

"Lately, I find myself wondering whether I am the right dragon to carry these burdens."

Chelos grumbled, pulling the bedsheets tighter around himself. "Draconess too had doubts towards the end." His eyes seemed to shrink away, as though lost in his own tortured memories. "Doubts about Darnuir, about himself, even you, though he'd never show them to anyone else. Never about the gods, though, for all the good that did him."

"It sounds like you have lost faith," Blaine said.

"I say my prayers, but I learned that faith won't shield me, nor the ones I love, from harm. I saw what Castallan could do. That was true power. And we know what Rectar is capable of. Perhaps our gods are just weak?"

"The gods do not fail us," said Blaine. "It is only we who fail them."

"Then there's been plenty of failure."

"Blaine?" Darnuir entered their squat little room. His eyes glinted cat-like as he adjusted to the semi-darkness. "This is cosy."

"Get in here," Blaine said. He moved to the doorway as Darnuir shuffled inside. "Everyone is to move to the other end of the hall," he told the Light Bearers outside. "No one is to disturb us." He shut the door firmly. Darnuir had taken up Blaine's place at Chelos' side. "So, Darnuir, you've come to hear it all?"

Darnuir looked a little taken aback. "I came to see why you've shut yourself away and let that Bacchus fellow take charge of things. But yes, that as well."

"You asked me once to tell you everything," Blaine said. "I never intended to keep you in the dark forever. Only, there was so much to tell you, and I wasn't yet ready myself." He closed his eyes and felt his heart beat quicker. "Before we begin, know that everything I tell you is to do with our enemy. It is important. Everything I told you about the Champion's Blade; all of it."

"You said you only had suspicions," Darnuir said.

"The visit from Ochnic gave me fresh reason to believe," Blaine said. He fished out the necklace and briefly stared at the little silver 'A' before taking it off. He tossed it to Darnuir.

Chelos leaned over to stare at the necklace in Darnuir's hand. "It's not possible…"

"Who did this belong to?" Darnuir asked.

"It belonged to your father," Blaine said.

"I have no memory of Draconess wearing such a necklace," Darnuir said, squinting at the jewellery and turning it, as though it would reveal its secrets to him.

"It did not belong to Draconess," Blaine said softly. Darnuir looked at him, perplexed, the faintest shadow of doubt flickering behind his eyes.

And so it begins.

"But you said it belonged to my—"

"Father, yes," Blaine finished. "Draconess, however, was not your father."

So complete was the silence that followed, Blaine thought he heard the worms burrowing within the earth.

"I — I was not expecting that," Darnuir said. "But what has that got to do with anything?" Blaine buried his face in his hands.

Where am I to begin?

Darnuir went on. "Perhaps one of your memories would be useful?"

Blaine shook his head. "Memories must be captured in the gems as fresh after the events as possible. I didn't know that these things would become so important. Had I known, I might have been able to stop it. I shall recall as best I can and Chelos can help confirm it. But, as for the matter at hand, your real father was Drenthir, son of Dalthrak. Draconess was his younger brother: your uncle."

"Uncle…" Darnuir repeated quietly.

"That necklace was given to Drenthir by your mother," Blaine said. His voice was already beginning to falter. "Your mother, Arlandra. She was my daughter."

"So you are — no," Darnuir said, his eyes widening in realisation. He slumped back in his chair, staring dumbstruck at Blaine. For the sake of Kasselle's privacy and dignity, Blaine left her out of it. It occurred to him that perhaps the drop of fairy blood in Darnuir's veins was what drew him to the Cascade so feverishly.

"Did you know of this?" Darnuir asked, rounding on Chelos.

"I did," Chelos said.

"And you kept this from me all of my first life? Why?"

"Because I asked him to," Blaine said. "Chelos is not to blame for any of this."

"We agreed to it, Blaine," said Chelos. "You, Draconess and I. We all agreed."

"You were barely as old as Darnuir is now," Blaine said. "You followed orders and served loyally."

"To what end?" Darnuir asked.

"Let me explain," Blaine said. "It was so long ago, back when the Black Dragons still lived in the lands around Kar'drun and in their own city. It was a brilliant city, in truth – as splendid as Aurisha has ever been. Too splendid and too strong, some said, myself included.

"King Dalthrak, your other grandfather, was ageing, having enjoyed a full reign of peace with the Black Dragons. His line was safe in Drenthir and Draconess. Yet Draconess wanted to be more than merely second in line. I had recently inherited the mantle of guardian and knew the royal family well. I encouraged Draconess to join my Light Bearers and he accepted. Chelos was very young but a faithful ward. You used to fetch the hot water for my morning shave, do you remember?"

"Of course," Chelos said. "I'll never forget how proud I felt. My parents too. Gods, but I'd nearly forgotten I once had parents."

"At the same time," Blaine continued, "there was another dragon showing great promise in the ranks of the faithful. This was Kroener—"

Chelos spat at the mention of this name, narrowly missing Darnuir's boot. "Traitor," he said. "Blasphemer," he managed to add before returning to a fit of coughing.

"Must you do that?" Darnuir asked. "If he is so hated, then why does no one else know of him?"

"Because what happened was kept quiet," Blaine said. "Kroener was just a Light Bearer, after all. Not many knew of him. I was new to the role of guardian, and with an ageing king, many extra burdens fell to me. When the time came for an inspection of the Black Dragons, I passed the responsibility on. Kroener was amongst the Light Bearers who travelled north."

"What do you mean by inspection?" Darnuir asked.

"Officially, they were diplomatic visits," said Blaine. "In reality, we were ensuring the Black Dragons were complying with the treaty that had secured the long stability we were all enjoying. A certain term prohibited our Black Dragon cousins from raising and training soldiers beyond what was needed to keep order in their lands. Anything further would require the express permission of the guardian and king in Aurisha. When Kroener returned from that mission, he informed us that the Black Dragons had violated that term. That they were raising a host and planned to make war on us."

"Was it true?" Darnuir asked.

"We thought it was," said Chelos. "Kroener gave a very convincing speech in the throne room. Do you remember, Blaine?"

"In here," Blaine said, tapping at the white opals on his sword.

Chelos sat straighter, seeming more animated. "I'll remember it always. 'Five days with the wind,' he kept saying. 'Five days with the wind.' And then he held up an oversized fig." Chelos raised both his own hands in imitation. "It took both hands, so large it was. 'Here,' he said, 'is but one result of Black Dragon sorcery. Larger than life and too ripe. Only five days away with the wind.' Then he let it fall to smash upon the floor." There was almost admiration in Chelos' voice.

"And no one else could vouch for these claims?" Darnuir said. "You said it wasn't just Kroener who went."

"Only Kroener returned from that mission," Blaine said.

"A theme that continued with him," said Chelos.

"He claimed the rest of his party had been killed by the Black Dragons and that only he escaped," Blaine said.

"You think he lied?" Darnuir said.

"I do not know," Blaine said. "Either way we were whipped up into a frenzy. By then, Dalthrak was growing ill and his days looked numbered. I stayed in Aurisha while Kroener and your father led the campaign against the Black Dragons. I remember Arlandra begging your father not to leave. She was pregnant with you. She begged him, and then she begged me to tell him to stay. 'You go instead,' she asked of me. 'You go'." The first tears began to distort Blaine's vision. "I — I can see her now, in my mind, in my head, for the first time in years. I hid all the memories away before because it hurt too much. But now I see her again, beseeching me."

The tears fell. He could not remember the last time he had cried. Not even when Kasselle had told him not to return; even then, he had stayed strong. But not for this. He couldn't stand this. His nose twitched, turning visibly redder at the corner of his vision. His breath came in laboured, choked gulps.

"I should have gone," he went on. "I should have gone instead. But I told Arlandra that Drenthir had to go. He would be king soon and he had yet to be blooded in battle; he still had to prove himself a leader... it's all my fault."

He allowed himself this grief. He had ignored it for long enough. Darnuir's face might have been made of stone. His eyes were fixated somewhere on Blaine's chest plate.

"You are not to blame," Chelos said. "You could not have known."

"But my own daughter," Blaine sobbed. "I could never deny her anything except for this. Why? Why did I do it?"

"I agree with Chelos," Darnuir said. "You could not have known."

Blaine breathed deeply, sniffed, and rubbed at his eyes. "Kroener and Drenthir went to war. The first reports were good. The Black Dragons were pushed back mile by mile till their city fell. We all believed the war was over; a swift victory to put the Black Dragons back in line. And then more reports trickled in. Kroener had sown salt into the soil. Kroener had ordered the legions to besiege Kar'drun, where the last Black Dragons had taken refuge.

"Months passed, and Kroener and Drenthir travelled into the Highlands, though to what end we did not know. Each report came with a different story. Then word finally came. Kroener had returned from the Highlands, but not with your father. There was no word of him. I knew then that something was terribly wrong. I think your mother felt it too. Grief struck her despite the happiness of your birth, Darnuir. Perhaps when Drenthir died it echoed across the world to rake at her heart."

"And you think the necklace is proof that my father died in the Highlands," Darnuir said. He ran the silver chain through his fingers. "Do you think the Kazzek were involved?"

"Kazzek?" Chelos asked.

"Frost trolls, friend," Blaine said.

"You encountered them?" Chelos asked. "I wouldn't be surprised if those beasts aided the traitor."

"They aren't beasts," Darnuir said. "No more than humans think dragons to be."

"For all I know, they might have been," said Blaine. "When I asked Ochnic, all he would say was 'Da chieftains know dis, not I'."

"Did you ask nicely? Or did you grunt and call him troll?" Darnuir asked. Blaine narrowed his eyes at the boy but it was Chelos who spoke.

"You should be more respectful," he wheezed. "Blaine is your equal."

"And so I shall speak to him as I will," Darnuir said. "Cassandra loves you dearly, Chelos, and that speaks volumes. Don't give me a reason to find fault with you now. This tale is one of mistake after mistake, of bad assumptions and your order gone wrong. Be on with it. I fear it will only get worse before the end."

Blaine did not have a rebuke this time.

This is not the same Darnuir I met at Torridon. And the more I tell him, the worse it will get. Still, I must go on.

The hardest truth of all for Blaine was that Darnuir might be right. Yet, like a poison, the past had to be drawn out.

"Without news of his son, King Dalthrak feared the worse," Blaine said. "His sickness deepened and Draconess and I began preparations for a regency. You were only a baby and, as you well know, the Dragon's Blade will not pass until you are of age. Even as we were deciding how to proceed, legion upon legion trudged back to Aurisha. Battered and spent, the legates told us that Kroener had demanded they travel with him into the depths of Kar'drun. When many refused, Kroener had called them heretics or Shadow sympathisers. Fighting broke out and those loyal to Kroener remained. Rumours spread that Kroener had an unnatural power since returning from the north."

"You think it was the Champion's Blade?" Darnuir asked.

"I'm sure it was," said Blaine.

"But how?" Darnuir said hoarsely. "How could he have been 'worthy'? And how does Rectar come into this?"

"Something must have happened when Kroener entered Kar'drun," Blaine said. "The Black Dragons always said that when one enters the mountain, someone else comes out."

Blaine's hands were shaking now. He clasped them together, rubbing them to try and ease the tremors.

"Arlandra stayed strong for you but I could tell a part of her had died," Blaine continued. Each word was a knife in him. "No smile could cover it up. I promised her I'd make Kroener pay if he was to blame. Then one night, without warning, he returned. He and his companions kept their faces covered with crimson hoods. When word reached me in the Basilica, he had already entered the Royal Tower. I tore across the plaza but fighting had already broken out. When I arrived in your mother's room, you were gone. And Arlandra was... she was—"

"You don't have to talk about it, Blaine," Darnuir said.

"It's not quite what you think. I mourn still, of course, but the memory of that day is locked in my gem here." He pointed to the topmost white jewel on the hilt of the Guardian's Blade. "Whilst it is in there, I cannot remember the events other than as a vague impression, like the ghost of a dream."

"I remember what you told me," Chelos said from his corner. "How you confronted Kroener in the king's chambers. Darnuir was in his arms, you said. You must have just saved Dalthrak from being murdered."

"That's right, and as I tried to reason with him, he only said, 'The one you see is dead. The child will be mine. I am Rectar. The Shadow will fall over your world'."

"And then you fought him," Chelos said, his voice a strange mix of youthful awe and hardened pain. "I watched you from up high in the Royal Tower."

"Down through the tower and out onto the plaza," Blaine said. "The hardest battle I have ever fought. Near enough killed me, drawing on that much Cascade. I thought I might break."

"Well, you didn't lose," Darnuir said.

"I didn't *win* either."

Darnuir leaned forward and blew out his cheeks. "You think Kroener must have the Champion's Blade because he fought you to a standstill. Seems to me you could look into that memory of yours and see whether it is the right sword."

"I haven't relived it in such a long time," said Blaine. His hand was shaking so violently now that he could barely fumble his fingers on the gemstones.

"Stop," Darnuir said. "There's no need." He got to his feet, moved to Blaine's side and took his hand in a firm grip. "What happened after this duel?"

"I returned to Dalthrak's side. Draconess was there, injured from the battle in the Royal Tower, but not fatally so. I summoned Chelos to attend as well."

"A witness to the King's Will," Chelos said.

"Only it wasn't *exactly* the will of the king, was it?" Darnuir said. He did not break eye contact and Blaine held it. It was a punishing stare with barely room to breathe between them.

"No, it wasn't," Blaine said. "Dalthrak wished for a standard regency. Draconess would have the Dragon's Blade until you came of age and no longer. Whilst Draconess had the sword, its power would naturally dim, as it was not in the hands of the rightful king. Yet, rather than the blade simply passing upon your twentieth year, we altered the wording so that Draconess would hold on to the sword—"

"Until such time as my rightful heir is fit to rule," Chelos recited. "More open to interpretation. Dalthrak sealed it with a drop of his blood."

Blaine sniffed and tried to fight back more tears. "The blades are linked. I hoped that by weakening the Dragon's Blade I would also weaken the Champion's Blade, and thus Rectar. I took the armour of the king with me, for without the full power of a blade, Draconess couldn't wear it. I thought it would buy us some time, and prepare you."

"It might have," said Darnuir, "but it may also have dragged out the war. Why did Draconess not pass the sword along? Why put such a condition on my receiving it?"

"Because we had been wrong about Kroener," Blaine said. "I had, Dalthrak had, Draconess had, and many legions of dragons had. I should have known better than to let one with such a temperament take charge of any army. We had to see whether you would do better."

"Draconess raised you in the Light of Dwna, Dwl'or and N'weer," said Chelos. "But you proved resistant to the teachings. A hot-headed, rebellious young man."

"Was there ever a time when Draconess considered granting me the sword?"

"There was an occasion or two…" Chelos said. "I think he despaired of ever passing the blade along after the incident with Castallan. That is when Draconess gave up, I think."

"You knew about that, did you?" Darnuir asked.

"One of the few," said Chelos. "Draconess confided in me, but even I lost touch with him during those final years. He spent more time in the Basilica than anywhere else, praying day and night."

"And your gods never came," Darnuir said. "And you did not come back," he added, jostling Blaine with his free hand. Blaine lowered his head, utterly drained. He felt more exhausted than after the battle at the Bastion. And yet, a portion of the crushing weight he had carried all these years seemed lifted.

Darnuir was frowning. Blaine assumed the king would scold him, but when Darnuir spoke, there was the softer touch of a grandson in his voice.

"It seems to me you have been punishing yourself for eighty years. Isn't that long enough?" And for the first time, Darnuir embraced him. A true hug, if a little awkward in their armour. "I'll need you before the end. We all will."

Blaine tried to speak but the tears rolled faster and he hiccupped while trying to draw breath.

"I'm taking our legions east," Darnuir said. He pulled away from Blaine but still held his hand firmly. "The spectres have split their forces and the demons with them. I'm going to seize Aurisha while we have the chance and before the wilder winter winds come."

"I will prepare the Light Bearers," Blaine said.

"No," Darnuir said. He was not angry; just firm. "You will stay with the Third to help the humans in retaking the Splintering Isles. Come east when you are done."

"I would fight to retake our city," said Blaine. "Our holy city. I must—"

"Enough," said Darnuir. He raised a hand towards Chelos to prevent him speaking as well. "This time, I don't want to hear it."

"Why are you so insistent I stay?" Blaine said.

Darnuir hesitated. "We owe the humans our help. It will go a long way in showing our continued support if the guardian himself remains to fight."

"That's not the real reason," Blaine said. He'd held back the whole truth for long enough to know when someone else was lying. "Don't go chasing a fight. Don't do what Kroener did."

"You will stay," Darnuir said. As he let go of Blaine's hand, Blaine noticed Darnuir's was shaking. It was only a little, but enough to worry Blaine. His eyes were blinking quickly too.

"You're not well," Blaine said.

"We can't both be absent," Darnuir said. He placed his unsteady hand on the Dragon's Blade and his whole body relaxed. "I'll await you at Aurisha, Grandfather." The king moved to the door and pulled it open. Fresh air reached Blaine's face like a splash of cold water. Before he left, Darnuir looked over his shoulder. "Kasselle is my grandmother, isn't she? That's why you hid there for so long."

"She is," Blaine said.

I don't think you should come back...

"I am sorry, Blaine," Darnuir said. Then he left.

A week after Darnuir left, the first of Arkus' forces along with Fidelm's fairies arrived, having retaken the island of Skelf en route. Blaine found himself attending a celebratory feast in Somerled Imar's great hall.

"Tae retaking our lands!" cried the Lord of the Isles.

"Tae retaking our lands!" the cheering crowd responded. Each islander, man and woman, raised a glass and drained a dram of whisky. Imar himself stood atop the outcrop of rock, nodding happily as he let the furore die down.

The humans were growing wilder with each toast. Many dragons in attendance were slow on capon, slumped forwards with glazed eyes. Somerled had not offered it to Blaine and the Light Bearers. Further down the table, Bacchus held a lively court with some of Blaine's best men. Those closer to Blaine were all taking short shallow breaths to try and avoid the alluring smell of the capon, Blaine included. The heat didn't help. The air was close and so thick with the smell of alcohol it felt strangling. His white linen shirt clung to him with sweat.

The roaring of the humans finally quietened.

"With the help of our neighbours from the mainland, of course," Somerled continued. "And the fairies and the dragons as well. We should make a toast to 'em." He looked towards Blaine. "Lord Guardian, might ye join me?"

The hall burst into a murmuring of agreement at this request. Few of the dragons joined in, being so content with their meal. Nor did the Light Bearers at his table react much, forcing themselves to maintain their composure. Bacchus leaned forward, watching Blaine with a hawkish interest.

I'm still the guardian, boy.

Blaine rose and walked over to the base of the rock. He'd entertain Somerled this novelty, even if he disliked the man. Serving up roasted rooster was a threat in Blaine's eyes; not a treat like some dragons felt. But he'd hold his tongue for the sake of the relationship between their people. Darnuir was right about that much; they needed humanity's help now. More than Blaine cared to let Imar know.

"There's a good sport," Somerled said as Blaine rounded the base of the rock and ascended the carved steps. He gave Imar the benefit of the doubt. He was probably feeling the effects of all that whisky.

Blaine had visited the Splinters only a few times in his past, but he'd never been on top of the rock before. He first noticed that Somerled was barefoot, his feet wedged into two smooth gouges in the stone. It was the ancient coronation site of the Splintering Isles. Barefoot in the rock, it connected their kings to the land and the people.

But there is no King of the Isles anymore. Only a lord who is subject to the rule of another throne.

Somerled was beaming at him.

"The dragons helped save this city and our home," Somerled said. "Now they fight fer their homes, their lands. From body to rock to land to sea, I wish their king the very best o' luck on the battlefield."

The islanders thumped their tankards approvingly.

"But the Lord Guardian remains to help us in our endeavours. His very purpose is tae rid the world of these wee devils. Why, with him and his Light Wielders—"

"Bearers," Blaine muttered.

"We shall drive the demons off our islands. Send them running back tae Kar'-drun. The war shall be over before winter!"

Blaine forced a smile as another round of drinking ensued. The arrival of Fidelm and ten flyers caught Blaine's attention. They looked so small from up here. He leaned in closer to speak quietly to Somerled.

"If I may excuse myself?"

"Be my guest," Somerled said in a hushed voice. Blaine turned and was about to descend the steps when Somerled lightly grabbed his arm. "You will sail as soon as possible, yes?"

"As soon as we have the full contingent of Arkus' fleet," Blaine said. He shrugged his arm free. "Fidelm thinks it another week at most."

"Grand," Somerled said. "Waves be at yer back."

Blaine nodded curtly then took the steps two at a time and swept through the hall. Fidelm met him halfway.

"Enjoying yourself?" Fidelm asked.

"Immensely," said Blaine.

"I hope Somerled realises we aren't ready yet," said Fidelm.

"He does," said Blaine. "He is just eager to capitalise on your victory on Skelf."

"That was barely a fight," said Fidelm. "The demons were fleeing the island as we arrived. Heading east. Oh, look," he said, nodding towards the tables of Light Bearers. "Some of your men are trying to subtly look at you without drawing attention to themselves."

Blaine looked back. Bacchus was on his feet, talking to two whole tables at once.

"I shall deal with this," said Blaine. "Enjoy the feast, Fidelm."

So many Light Bearers were listening to Bacchus that they didn't notice Blaine returning, and he caught the end of the speech. "...doesn't seem capable anymore. We can't afford to lose the Lord Guardian, so perhaps—"

"Don't worry," Blaine said. "You haven't lost me. I'm right here." The Light Bearers' reactions were mixed. Some looked guilty, some looked frightened, and others still bore hard expressions as though bracing themselves for battle. "Bacchus seemed to have you all enthralled there," Blaine added with as much injected confidence as he could muster. Truth was, he was worried by Bacchus' growing appeal.

I might wield the blade, but I no longer wield their hearts.

"Lord Guardian," Bacchus began. "We are your Light Bearers. We look out for the faith and you are the figurehead of our belief. I was only hoping to express my concern that your recent wounds and hardships might have left you fatigued. Your leg at Inverdorn, the strain you endured in bravely storming the Bastion walls, and enduring our faithless king with such patience. And, as I was hoping to convey to my brothers, there will be no need for you to place yourself in harm's way in the coming battles merely out of obligation. You're too important for that."

"Are you insinuating that I am too weak or old?" *How could they do this to me?*

"Certainly not, Lord Guardian," Bacchus said. His tone was impeccable. Unreadable. Undeniably powerful. "You have carried burdens for longer than any of us can dream. I only suggest that you might wish to delegate some more of those duties, such as—"

"Such as entering battle?" Blaine snapped. He glared at each Light Bearer. He didn't have Bacchus' gift of speech, so he drew the Guardian's Blade and enhanced his voice for sheer volume. "I am not as old and done as you think." With a little help from the Cascade, he jumped unnaturally high and landed upon the nearest table. Plates and tankards went flying. The entirety of the great hall was paying attention now.

"That's not what I saw at the Bastion," Bacchus said, his silky voice faltering ever so slightly.

"To lose faith in me is to lose faith in the gods," Blaine said.

He'd neglected a few matters of late, but nothing to deserve this. He was the guardian. He could barely remember life before he had been the guardian. And he had no life beyond it. No family. No lover. Only one old sick friend. Darnuir was his flesh and blood, but he was as much a stranger as anyone in this room.

He raised the Guardian's Blade and lit the metal of the sword until those nearby were forced to cover their eyes. This was what he had. This was all he had.

"Allow me to rekindle your faith in me," Blaine said. "The Third Legion will sail for Eastguard tomorrow. We will break the demons under the light of Dwna, Dwl'or and N'weer. All those who wish to sail with us may do so."

Fidelm was running over, waving his hands in protest. Across the hall, Somerled Imar got on top of his own table and raised another glass.

"Ah ha, there's the fightin' spirit of the dragons. Tae retaking our lands!" His son, Grigayne, threw back his tankard with a grim expression.

Blaine drank in the atmosphere. He only hoped that he was right. He prayed the gods really did favour him.

Dwl'or grant me strength. Every ounce of it you can give.

21

LORD BOREAC'S MANOR

Since the unification of the Kingdom of Brevia with the Splintering Isles, human nobles have continued to compete; not through war but instead through the size of their manor homes. When space ran out in the Velvet Circle, the ornateness of the stonework or design of the garden took over. More recently, size has come back into competition, specifically in how large a lord or lady might make their windows. I theorise this constant need for renovation is also due to picking a permanent place to live, rather than roaming as fairies do. You must keep changing your home or else you'll grow bored with it.

From Tiviar's Histories

Cassandra – Brevia – The Velvet Circle

Cassandra eased her way through the gathering crowds by the water's edge. Balack was making his rounds of the city, Arkus proudly by his side. Today, they were touring along the northern embankment and near the wealthy Velvet Circle. This worked well for Cassandra's needs, for it drew most people to Balack and left the district quiet. Queen Oranna had acquired a set of black leathers worn by Crownland hunters for her to wear. Cassandra was now black from boots to shoulder guards, with only her skin and the delicate white trim on the leather showing any other colour. She felt it suited her. Kymethra, however, was not as pleased.

"This is mighty uncomfortable," the witch whispered as they skimmed around a group of plump nobles. "It's all tight and constricting. How can they sleep in this?"

"I think the idea is you'll be too tired to care," Cassandra said. She smiled broadly at a passing couple that were wrapping scarves around each other against the autumn breeze. Once the couple passed, Cassandra let her smile fall. She had to keep up the pretence of a dutiful peacekeeper, but her cheeks already ached from today's forced grins alone. She was developing real sympathy for Queen Oranna's unique plight.

Her plight might become my own soon enough.

"Did you give Oranna my right measurements?" asked Kymethra.

"I thought you wanted to help me?" Cassandra said.

"I do," said Kymethra. "Doesn't mean I have to wear something that makes me itch in unflattering places."

This can't all be about the leathers.

"Are you sure you're ready to leave him?" Cassandra asked.

"For the last damn time, yes," said Kymethra, though her voice was a touch higher than normal. "There's nothing more that can be done. Brackers is in fine care. All I can add is a bit of soothing magic if he takes a turn, but the fits have calmed now, so... oh, let's just hunt down the bastards who helped cause this." She stopped picking at her leathers and settled into a stride beside Cassandra.

They finally made it through the crowds and into the Velvet Circle proper. Manor after manor rose along the wide paved streets.

A carriage clopped loudly towards them, likely heading down to the hubbub of Balack's rally. The horses dropped their leavings along the way; a stain on an otherwise spotless street. It barely had a chance to smell before a team of boys dashed from the nearest manor armed with spades, sloshing buckets, coarse brushes and thick brown gloves. By the time Cassandra and Kymethra passed them the street was clean once more.

"Remind me again why we are paying Lord Boreac's manor a visit?" Kymethra asked. "Your father already had it picked clean of anything worthwhile."

"That's what he has been told, but we have no real idea of how deep Castallan's networks ran. He needs someone he can trust to hunt Boreac down."

"And you're the best he's got?" Kymethra said. "I mean no offence, but it seems a little desperate."

"You don't think I can manage it?"

"I just think this could be dangerous," said Kymethra. "I didn't think Arkus would want to put you in harm's way having only just gotten you back."

"He didn't. I insisted. I find Boreac for him and he won't push a marriage on me."

"Well, at least you know how to use that sword," Kymethra said.

"I'm not looking for a reason to use it."

Lord Boreac's manor was easy to find, for it was the one with half its contents spilling out onto its now untended gardens.

"I swear that one is snoring," Kymethra said, flicking her eyes towards one of the soldiers posted at the gates. They wore chainmail over simple boiled leather, with short spears that looked fierce enough but would be no match for a sword in close quarters. They weren't asleep, Cassandra saw, but they were far from alert.

"Good day," Cassandra announced loudly.

One snapped his head in bemusement at her. "Who are you?"

"Here to help with the cleanout," Cassandra said. "Captain Horath's orders." She'd learned the names of a few key members of the Crownland hunters, but not much beyond. For these two, she hoped nothing more would be required.

"Horath, was it?" said the other guard, a little dimly. "Didn't he send a message already that we weren't to let anyone else in?"

"I dun' think so, Rob," said the first guard.

"Nat, you can't remember what you ate for breakfast," said Rob.

"Course I can," said Nat. "Bit of watered-down porridge, ain't it? Every bleedin' day. Not got much choice with them dragons piling up outside the city, taking all our food."

"True," grumbled Rob.

"Captain Horath made it clear this job was to be done promptly," Cassandra said. She took a step in between the guards.

"Hold it right—" But Nat's words died in his throat. His face glazed over, as did Rob's. They both looked as though they were supremely contented. "Sure," Nat said, his voice wrapping luxuriously around the word. "Go along in."

"Heh," giggled Rob. "No issue."

Confused but not wanting to question her turn in fortune, Cassandra walked into the estate grounds. About halfway to the front door she turned to check on Kymethra. The witch was right behind her, grimacing and shaking her arm as though she were drying it.

"What did you do to them?" Cassandra asked.

"Soothed them," said Kymethra. "Same as I do to Brackendon when he takes his turns. I hit them with a stronger blast of it to move us along. Dranus, but I'm thirsty now."

"I thought it was for taking away pain?"

"Numbs everything," Kymethra said. "Including thought. Don't go getting ideas, now. It isn't that strong. Just a trick. Those two might not have had a full head put together. I didn't even have to touch their heads like I normally—" Kymethra stopped suddenly and looked past Cassandra. There was a creaking of a hinge and Cassandra turned to see the doorway to the estate open, with a thin woman in a simple pale blue apron looking suspiciously out at them.

"I thought you lot were done?" she said. Her voice gave away that she was a little afraid, trying to cover it up through indignation. "None of us know where he's gone."

"We're sorry to disturb you," Cassandra said. "We just need to ask some more questions. Take a final look around."

"Can't get away from you hunters," the woman mumbled as she pulled back into the manor. Cassandra took that as her cue to follow.

The hallway was bare, although signs of wealth were evident from the lighter patches on the wall where paintings or tapestries had been hung, while scratch marks along the oak floor showed where furniture had been roughly dragged outside.

"Can I take your cloaks?" the woman asked briskly. "I'm still the head of this household, after all. No reason I can't show common courtesy."

Cassandra unfastened her own black cloak and handed it over.

"Thank you, um…"

"Olive, dear," the woman said. "Thought they might have passed along our names at least. Aren't we under investigation and all that?" She took Kymethra's cloak a little gruffly. "Are you okay?"

Cassandra wondered that as well. Kymethra was breathing heavily, her cheeks were flushed, and she held her right arm tightly against her side.

"I wouldn't mind some water," Kymethra said.

"Bit hot under those leathers," Olive said knowingly. "Even in the Boreacs I saw them sweat at times. Come through to the kitchens, then, and may my cooperation show you that the staff and I have nothing to hide."

"Where are the staff?" Cassandra asked. The manor was eerily quiet. Their feet echoed with every step.

"Keeping to themselves mostly," said Olive, leading them down the empty hallway. "Since Lord Boreac took off and armed chevaliers came bursting in looking for him, everyone has been suspicious of each other. No one wants to be marked a traitor."

"King Arkus has offered a general clemency," Cassandra said.

"So I've heard," Olive said. She turned into a narrow corridor winding to the back of the house and into the extensive kitchens. It felt cold. Not an oven was on, not a cook in sight. Copper pots and pans were stacked up in the basin. Cold grease and mould scented the air. Olive sighed. "Such an embarrassment. Twenty staff used to work here day and night. Often Lord Boreac threw parties for hundreds at a time. And now this."

"I'm sorry for your loss," Cassandra said, although she limited her sympathy. This head of the household could be a traitor for all she knew.

"There's a jug of water by the basin there," Olive said to Kymethra. "The mugs are kept—"

"Won't be needing a mug," Kymethra said, darting to the jug and taking great draughts straight from it. Olive looked startled.

"She's a good bet for drinking games at the station," Cassandra said. "Now, I wonder if I might begin."

"Fine, fine," Olive said. She went to sit down at the servants' rather dirty table and waited expectantly. Cassandra sat opposite her and pushed a plate of mouldy cheese away.

"As head of the household, you must have known Lord Boreac well?" Cassandra asked.

"Well enough," Olive said. "Five years of service, after all. I've already gone through this."

"Please, just answer the questions," Cassandra said. "So, was there ever any odd behaviour?"

"Only in hindsight, I suppose," Olive said. "Back in the spring, a messenger came all flustered, talking about some woman named Morwen over and over. Boreac told him to be quiet, ushered him into his study, then dismissed me. He kept everyone out of his study for hours. After that, he was always a little more on edge, but I would never have guessed he was part of some conspiracy against the throne."

"Morwen, you said? Not Captain Morwen of the Golden Crescent hunters?"

"Might be," Olive said. "He got cross when I asked."

That was very interesting news to Cassandra. What was it she had heard one day in Val'tarra? Some burly huntress had claimed that Morwen's body had been found with both human and spectre corpses around it. Morwen had been concerned about a strange black powder being found in shipments that were meant to be fruit from the fairies. Why was Boreac so interested in that?

"Is that the only time you saw him concerned?" Cassandra asked. Olive nodded, looking annoyed already. "How was he behaving while his lands were under attack from Castallan's demons for almost a year?"

"They were — what?" Olive asked, suddenly alert.

"You didn't know?" Cassandra asked.

"None of you lot told me that before," Olive said, sounding frightened. "Tell me. What happened?"

"Why is that such a concern to y—"

"Just tell me."

"Okay," Cassandra said. "The Boreac Mountains are deserted. Its people now are either refugees or dead."

"Dead?" Olive mouthed silently. She ran her bony hands through her thinning hair.

"No one really knew," Kymethra said, coming to join them at the table. "Not up in the capital anyway. Boreac might have been in on it himself if he'd thrown in with Castallan."

"But see this," Olive said, getting a flyer out of her pocket. "This Balack of the Boreac Mountains. This 'Hero of the Bastion', I used to take care of him back when I lived there. It can't be so bad. Or is this all some lie?" She looked desperate as she flung the paper down. It landed upside down and Cassandra reached for it, turning it back up. She had seen these flyers all around the city, proclaiming in large thick print:

Join Balack, the Hero of the Bastion! Come dockside to hear the story of the great battle in the south where humanity triumphed when dragons failed!

Down in the bottom corner was a picture of a black quill dripping ink onto the words: Tarquill Prints.

"It's no lie," Cassandra said. *Though the real hero is lying broken and deranged in the palace.* She placed a hand on Kymethra's arm and caught her eye to prevent her saying anything. *We mustn't seem to know too much.*

"You raised the Hero of the Bastion?" Cassandra said, feigning awe. *She must know the others too. Darnuir, Cosmo, all of them.*

"It was years ago," Olive said, her hardened demeanour crumbling by the second. "I'd doubt he'd remember me. Don't think I'll be able to help you win any favours or gain an introduction. Although it would be good to see someone from the Boreacs again. My sister Grace is still there… or she was still there. If all this has happened — Oh, I should have known something wasn't right when her letters stopped; but then, I knew she had a baby on the way, and I was so busy here…" she rambled.

The mention of Grace caused another look to pass between Cassandra and Kymethra, an unspoken agreement that there would be no need to mention her death to Olive. Not here and now, at any rate.

"This must be distressing for you," Cassandra said, interrupting Olive in full flow.

Olive sniffed. "It's just another thing to worry about."

"I can only imagine," Cassandra said. "Look, if you answer my questions, I'll make enquiries about your sister."

"Would you?" Olive said. "That's very kind, dear. Very well. Go ahead."

"We'll try not to be too long," Cassandra said. She smiled encouragingly at Olive before starting. "We're obviously interested in any close associates he might have had, people who might be harbouring him. Was there any place Lord Boreac might visit frequently? Friends in the city or country who he might have gone to?"

"Lord Boreac preferred to play host rather than be a guest," Olive said. "He rarely left the city. Said his back hurt too much in someone else's bed. Lord Annandale would visit when he came to the capital, but we know why that is now. The only other person who came around regularly was that hunter. Tall, sinewy fellow. Scythe, I think."

"Scythe?" Cassandra and Kymethra said together.

Olive was taken aback. "Is he a bloody traitor too?"

"I'm afraid we can't discuss that," Kymethra said.

"So, he was, then," Olive said. "Curse those men. I built up a reputation, and now no one will hire me. What a waste."

"I understand this is frustrating for you," Cassandra said, hoping to keep Olive focused. "But the quicker we get through this, the quicker we'll leave you be."

"Leave me be all on my own. A big empty house and nothing to do anymore," Olive moaned.

Cassandra pressed on. "When was the last time you saw Scythe?"

"Hmm, oh, would've been when Captain Tael stopped by. About a year ago." The name wasn't familiar to Cassandra, though she assumed this Tael had been the Boreac Captain before Scythe. "Yes, that was it," Olive continued. "Tael was here, asking Boreac for more hunters, and I guess now I know the reason for that too. Actually, something odd did happen that night."

"To whom?" Cassandra asked.

"To me," Olive said. "That Scythe fellow came looking for me, to talk to me. He'd never so much as said more than his food and drink order before."

"Why?" Cassandra said.

"Just to talk," Olive said. "Nothing in particular, just a bit about me, where I came from, my time in the Boreacs. That sort of thing."

"No specifics?" Cassandra asked.

Olive sighed. "Look, it was nearly a year ago, but I suppose he kept trying to worm conversation back to the children I took care of with Grace – the boys in particular, and then the youngest. I didn't know why he was so interested in Balack and Darnuir, but there you go. Well, look what Balack turned out to be, eh?"

Cassandra stared at Olive, trying not to look too incredulous or give anything away.

Lord Boreac really did a fine job of keeping news from you, didn't he?

"Anything more?" Cassandra asked.

"No, that was it. Never saw the man again. Probably dead now, I imagine," Olive added. There was a stilted moment of protracted silence during which faint taps and creaks echoed overhead. Olive looked up. "That'll be Milly, the maid. Pacing around again, poor lamb. She only started here a month before all this horribleness."

"Unfortunate timing," Kymethra said.

"Will you be needing to speak to the staff as well?" Olive asked.

"It may not be necessary," Cassandra said. "I'm sure they have been through enough." Olive pursed her lips and nodded approvingly. "However, there is one last thing. When Lord Boreac fled, was he in a hurry? And what did he take with him?"

"I wouldn't have known he was leaving for good the way he just rushed out the door," Olive said. "He got a letter, I remember. Took it upstairs. Next thing I knew he was bolting out the door. Barely had his evening cloak strapped on. Went without even a goodbye." She sounded hurt at the memory.

Olive had called her time here a waste and Cassandra couldn't help but agree.

At least I have a way out. A way I can make things better. But she won't be able to bring back the dead.

"I think that will be all for now," Cassandra said. She'd gotten enough out of Olive to be going on with. "Perhaps we could inspect Lord Boreac's study?"

"Your lot already took everything away," Olive said, but she got to her feet all the same.

Cassandra shrugged. "Captain's orders." She rose too, as did Kymethra, and they followed Olive out of the kitchen to a servants' staircase hidden away from the main hallway. They climbed to the second floor where the corridor sliced a neat row of rooms in two. It was as bare as the hallway downstairs and a little dusty. As they walked, one of the room's occupants poked his head out from behind the doorframe; an old man, possibly in his sixties, with a white moustache.

"Back in, Perkins," Olive said. "They won't be long." She shooed at him as though he was some unwanted dog. The old man pulled back behind the door and closed it with a click. "The butler," Olive muttered. "Of all of them, I'd trust him the least."

"Mmm," Cassandra hummed but said nothing more. Castallan might be dead, but his legacy of distrust would linger on for years.

"Here you are," Olive announced as they arrived at the end of the corridor. "You can let yourselves out when you're done, I imagine?" She did not wait for an answer before she shuffled off down another bare hallway, around the corner and out of sight.

"Poor thing," Kymethra said. She gave the door a good nudge and it swung open with a thud. They both stepped inside Lord Boreac's office. Drawers lay torn from their desks and cabinets, ink stained the floorboards and blank paper was strewn everywhere. A fireplace lay cold. "Doesn't leave much for us to go on," Kymethra said. "Don't know what you expect to find here."

"Any clue would be useful," Cassandra said. She started feeling along the walls, tapping with her knuckles at intervals. "By the sounds of it, Lord Boreac left in a hurry. That suggests he wasn't planning on leaving. That suggests to me that he felt safely unconnected to Annandale, Castallan and that whole mess by not having some sort of escape plan."

"So what in that letter could have given him such a fright?" Kymethra asked.

"I've no idea," Cassandra said. "Maybe news that Castallan had been defeated? He might have believed that Castallan really would prevail. Enough people seemed to think so." She paused over another likely spot and rapped her knuckles against it. She tutted in annoyance. *Nothing on this side.*

"What are you doing?" Kymethra asked.

"Checking for compartments or other secret openings."

"The hunters and chevaliers picked the place clean. Don't you think they would have already found one?"

"They might not have been looking," Cassandra said. "I used to check every new room of the Bastion I visited." She moved along the next wall, towards the fireplace.

"Boreac likely took anything vital with him," Kymethra said.

"Olive said he bolted with barely his cloak clasped on," Cassandra said.

"All right," Kymethra said. "Boreac can't have been planning on going far, then."

"I do think he is still in the city, perhaps with a nobleman who is hiding him," Cassandra said. "His lands are in ruins. The south is under martial law by thousands of Arkus' soldiers. The Golden Crescent is in disarray, as are the Cairlav Marshes. Maybe he could have travelled north to the Hinterlands, but Oranna's father is too tied in with Arkus to make the region safe for Boreac. That leaves just the Crownlands and the capital, and I'd wager on the capital."

"But who would take him in?" Kymethra said. "A whole city of people. We need to narrow that down."

"We certainly do," Cassandra said. The third wall was an outer one with two windows, so she doubted there would be anything hidden there. She moved to the final wall behind Kymethra. "You could do something, Kymethra."

"Like what?" Kymethra said, lightly kicking an upended chair to one side. "Nothing here, unless you find some secret stash." She began pacing across the study.

This probably isn't distracting her much from her other worries. Please let there be something here.

Cassandra needed a clue to move forwards – one person, one name, one place – anything to point to where Boreac might have fled at the eleventh hour. Halfway along the final wall and her hopes were not high. From the corner of her eye, she saw that Kymethra had settled into a regular patrol of a few square metres.

"When we find him, he'll be sorry," she grumbled. Her steps grew heavier as she paced and the floorboards groaned louder.

Creak, creak, creak, crik.

"Thinks he can get away with it..." Kymethra muttered darkly.

Creak, creak, creak, crik.

The final wall that Cassandra tried proved fruitless. She sighed. She'd have to move onto the floor.

Creak, creak, creak, crik.

"Kymethra, take a step back, will you?" Cassandra asked. The witch did so without question.

Crik.

"There," Cassandra said, pointing under Kymethra's black boot. "You've only gone and found the spot." She got down onto her knees. The floorboard seemed well stuck in place. Determined, Cassandra ran her fingers lightly over its surface and along every grain until, at last, she found a thumb-sized patch that did not conform to the rest of the wood.

This is it.

Her nail caught on the edge of it, digging down a fraction, and then she pulled up the small block, which enabled her to get her hand under the panel and lift it up. Triumphantly, she gazed down and saw a small, bronze strongbox.

"Well, pluck my feathers," Kymethra said.

Cassandra lunged in for it. "It's quite heavy," she said, puffing as she brought it out onto the floor. She dropped it down with a great thud, and the lid rattled loosely. It was already unlocked.

"Looks like Boreac might have had the time to grab something, but not the time to lock it up again," Kymethra said.

Gingerly, Cassandra opened the strongbox fully. It was empty save for a tiny dark grey ball, which had rolled into one corner. There didn't seem to be room for much inside; perhaps a ledger full of illicit notes could have been slotted in. She picked up the little grey ball.

"What is this?"

"Give it here," said Kymethra. Cassandra passed it over and Kymethra rolled it between her fingers, took a closer look at it and then licked it. Cassandra raised one eyebrow.

"What?" Kymethra said. "We had to get to know materials for alchemy back at the Conclave. Not that anything more effective than a cough syrup was ever brewed. This is lead, by the way."

"Lead?" Cassandra said. "Doesn't help me much. I'll hold onto it, though. Whatever it is, Boreac thought it was important enough to store in a strongbox."

"And take with him when he left," Kymethra said. "I suspect there were far more of these in there."

"Agreed," said Cassandra. She got to her feet, stretched her arms above her head and then let them fall limply. She felt thoroughly deflated. Finding Lord Boreac was not going to be a simple thing at all. Her gaze landed on the fireplace. Back in

Chelos' room, it was the bricks of the mantelpiece that opened up the secret passageway. But she was learning that not every large building had such hidden ways. Yet something about the fireplace itself made her linger on it. There was quite a bit of ash, and there were larger white chunks in it. She took a few steps closer.

"He burned some papers," Cassandra said.

"Didn't do a good job of it," Kymethra noted. "He was in a hurry though, I suppose. Likely just ripped the sheets a few times then tossed them in."

"The fire might have already been dying when he did it," Cassandra said. She began rifling through the ashes. She held up a scrap, but all that could be seen on it was a few words, which were meaningless on their own. "Not much to go on. What was so important to burn? And what was so urgent he had to leave without making sure the job was done properly?"

"Cassandra," Kymethra said excitedly, pulling out a much larger strip of soot-stained paper. Her eyes ran animatedly over the short piece. "I think this could be from the letter Olive mentioned."

Cassandra picked it delicately out of Kymethra's hands, hoping it wouldn't crumble away. There was a broken sentence buried under the dirt, the words hastily scrawled.

... I'm unsure about our options. Come to the Station now. R.F.

"R.F.," Cassandra said. It wasn't much, but the initials gave her something to go on. And better still, she had a place, too. "Looks like we'll be paying the Master Station a visit."

22

A FATHER'S PLEA

Garon – The Highlands – West of the Glen of Bhrath

"Feels colder tonight," Garon said, pressing his face into his fur-lined collar to shield his nose. He had reattached the warmer pieces of his leathers.

"Dis is not real cold," Ochnic said. He was crouched amongst the flora and heather, rocking on the tips of his toes and fidgeting with his dagger.

"Aye, yer right on that," said Griswald. "But it's startin' tae get chilly. Feels like home again."

"Da demons will have burned my home."

"We lost our home, Ochnic," Garon said. "Including many people we loved. I do not wish that fate on anyone. We'll get your family to safety."

"Only daughter," Ochnic said. "My life mate, she passed." He said it so plainly, so matter of fact, so indifferently, yet he couldn't meet Garon's eye. It must have caused him all the pain in the world. A silence followed, as though all three were honouring the dead.

The three of them were sat around a collapsed set of smaller standing stones, upon a knoll overlooking the river of this glen. Marus and Rohka were farther out with a vanguard force in case the demons ventured too close in the night. To the east rose another Principal Mountain, the fourth that Garon had seen since entering the Highlands. Its snow-covered slopes rose above the clouds. The cache of food they sought was in that mountain, in some hall of the golems, kept secret from all save the chieftains and their treasured silver-furred guards. A rush of wind sent another chill through Garon and he pulled his cloak closer around himself.

He realised that no one had spoken in quite some time, so he clasped the hunched troll on the shoulder and said, "We'll get her back, Ochnic. We'll save her and your clan. They are still alive."

"I know," said Ochnic. "Da demons be swarming around da Glen of Bhrath for a reason. But Rohka, Chief of Chiefs does not want ta fight through."

"Getting tae yer clan by force would be some task," said Griswald.

"With any luck, we'll only need to fight the demons on this side of the mountain," said Garon. "Rohka says there is another passageway under it, just like there is at the Great Glen. Clearing the demons away from this side of the mountain will allow your clan to use the passages to come to us. Rohka is concerned about the food stores being lost, as he should be, but I don't see how he can object to that plan. We'll have a better grasp on things once Pel and her flyers return from scouting."

"Then we go," Ochnic said.

"Then we'll make plans and go," agreed Garon. "Ochnic, may I ask you something?"

"You ask a lot of questions, pack leader," Ochnic said.

Garon shrugged. "I'm a curious fellow and I wondered about the title Rohka and the Chieftains gave you. They referred to you as 'Shadow Hunter'. Is that what you are?"

"What I was," said Ochnic. "Older now, I am. Those who watch over da borderlands with da Black Rock would stop demons coming through da mountains where we could. I shouldn't have returned, but de younger hunters claimed der were many more demons than dey had eva seen. So I went, and when I saw what was coming I knew de kazzek could not win. My chieftain, Orrock, tried at first. He gave us warriors and called da other chiefs for warriors. Dey came. Many died. Da demons kept coming."

"And that's when they sent you fer help?" asked Griswald.

"No," Garon said, realising. "They didn't send you, did they? At least not right away. I'll bet my share of the food we find that it was your notion, Ochnic."

"Was it, now?" Griswald said.

"It was I," said Ochnic. "Kazzek be needin' help, but Orrock is wary of Lowlanders and said he wouldn't take it to de other chieftains. Dey wouldn't listen at first, but then more bodies came back from da east and da burnings grew so large de clans could see the smoke from glens away. Not all de chieftains wanted me to go. Many said yes to get rid of me, I think. Da eldest, Chieftain Glik, gave me a trinket for da dragon guardian. And de rest you know, pack leader."

"Well, your people owe you a great debt," Garon said. "We Lowlanders included."

"These lands might fall still," Ochnic said darkly. "But no debt is owed. I did dis for Cadha. I cannot understand why de others did not think of der little ones, their future, their world, when we are burned to ash."

"It can be a hard thing tae ask for such change so quickly," Griswald said.

"We must change, or we'll die," Ochnic said. "Maybe those who don't roam da borders with the Black Rock can pretend, but not I; not a Shadow Hunter tired of seeing kazzek fall. We cannot stand alone."

"Many of us in the south have similar issues," Garon said.

Ochnic nodded slowly. "I noticed. I hope dat Lowlanders can settle their grudges."

"You and me both," said Garon. "At least we're trying, eh?" But Ochnic wasn't paying attention. The troll's head suddenly sprung up, sniffing softly at the air.

"Pel is coming," said Ochnic. Sure enough, within half a minute, Wing Commander Pel landed amongst the fallen standing stones with five flyers. In her hand was a giant blue-stemmed, blue-leafed flower with yellow spots.

"There are kazzek on the other side of the mountain," Pel said. "It must be your clan, Ochnic. Something is holding the demons back, though, and they haven't managed to swarm into the glen yet. There's still time." Ochnic sprang to his feet and bounded to Pel as though to hug her, but he halted just short, stubbing a large toe on one of the standing stones.

"Dis is well," Ochnic said through gritted teeth. He bent down to attend to his smarting toe, taking rapid little breaths.

"And I found that plant you spoke of," said Pel.

"Ah, chull weed," Ochnic said. He took it from her. "Dis has a few ways but mostly it clears the head of illness. Place da flower in hot water and place your head over it with a cloth to catch da steam."

"Chull weed," Pel repeated. "Got it."

"Class time's over," Garon said. "We need to take this news to Rohka."

"Yes, we go now," Ochnic said and began running down the hillside towards the river. Pel flew after him.

"Think I'll enjoy the night here for a wee while," Griswald said.

"Very well," Garon said, stretching his arms and legs. "Doubt you'd be able to keep up anyway." Griswald smiled broadly but didn't rise to Garon's bait.

"Right. Off I go, then," Garon said.

He found it a struggle to keep up as he followed Ochnic and Pel along the river-bank. It ran east through the glen, towards where Marus and Rohka would be stationed with the vanguard. Distantly, Ochnic and Pel halted under the shelter of an overhanging crag, where the fire lit the armour of the dragons and Silver Furs nearby. By the time Garon caught up, Ochnic was already prostrating himself before the Chief of Chiefs.

"Please. Please. Leave dem you can't."

"Sorry, I am, Ochnic, Shadow Hunter," Rohka said. "I cannot open de passage to the other side if der is a chance da demons will enter from de Glen of Bhrath."

"Pel, Wing Commander," Ochnic said, looking desperately around for her. Pel stepped forward, a little timid before the towering chieftain. "Tell him," Ochnic said. "Tell him der is time."

"Great chieftain, there is time to act," Pel said. "Something holds the demons at bay. It looked like a storm of earth." All the kazzek turned to each other and began muttering amongst themselves.

"Dat will be da golems," said Rohka slowly. "But even dey cannot hold forever."

"Der are paths, paths on the mountain," Ochnic said. "I know. Long have I roamed these lands. I can take kazzek over and warn—"

"I need my warriors here," Rohka said.

"Pel and da fairies can fly," Ochnic said, more hastily. "She can warn dem and prepare—"

But Rohka shook his great head. "You know dat will not work, Ochnic, Shadow Hunter. Your clan will see fairies as a threat."

"I'm sure Pel and her flyers could carry Ochnic there," Garon said. "Between enough of them, I mean." The Chief of Chiefs eyed Garon. The iron bands around his tusks caught a little glow from the fire.

"I do not condemn his clan, Garon, pack leader," said Rohka. "But we must secure the supplies in full. Else we shall all starve. Your people too. Once dat is done, if we can, we shall rescue da clan. But not before."

Garon looked to Marus. "And what do you think on this?"

"Rohka has a point," Marus said, though he shuffled uneasily on his crutch.

"Marus, don't think with your stomach now," Garon said. "We've come so far. Don't let Ochnic down."

"We came to help the kazzek and save the Highlands from being overrun," Marus said. "Rohka is their leader. How will King Darnuir feel if we ruin our relationship with him? I'm sorry, Garon."

"Please," Ochnic begged again. He was on his knees, shuffling closer to Rohka. "Please, Chief of Chiefs. Don't leave dem to die. Don't leave Cadha to da demons!"

"Dat is close enough, Shadow Hunter," Rohka said. "I have decided. Tomorrow we shall hit da demons on our side of de mountain. We clear dem away and hold dem while we bring out de supplies from da golem halls. If we can still save your clan afterwards, I promise we shall try. But not before." Rohka turned and took his leave.

Garon stood helpless. *This whole mission has slipped out of my control. What should I do? What can I do?* He wished there and then for some power like Darnuir's sword or some title like Cosmo's; something, anything that could make them listen. Before he could do anything, Ochnic had risen and was following Rohka, desperately attempting to turn him around.

"I said dat was close enough," Rohka growled. "Know your place, old Shadow Hunter."

"Please," Ochnic said, utterly desperate. He lunged forwards, as though to grab Rohka by the arm, but his flailing hand grasped a patch of Rohka's silver fur instead and ripped the hair from the chieftain's back. Rohka grunted in pain and spun, smacking Ochnic away. But even then, Ochnic did not give up, scrambling back.

"Take him," Rohka said to his guards. "He needs restrainin'."

"What?" Pel shrieked. She started forwards but several Silver Furs got in her way. Garon looked to Marus again but the legate was staring determinedly at the ground.

"This is how you repay the person who saved your life, Marus?" Garon shouted at him. He whirled to face Rohka's back. The Chief of Chiefs was stalking away, not watching as his guards manhandled Ochnic and gagged him. "Rohka," Garon called. "Don't do this."

Rohka looked over his shoulder. "You have heart, Garon, pack leader. But you are just one human. Accept dis." And with that, the kazzek leader walked away.

23

A SHADOW BELOVED, A LIGHT FADING

Dukoona – The City of Aurisha

The Trusted gathered in the Basilica of Light. One by one, they emerged. Their cold embers were a wash of colour against the surrounding gold stone. Above Dukoona, the dusky orange sky sent pale light through the opening of the domed roof. He stood behind the three plain stone swords in their stone holders at the centre of the chamber. As the last of the Trusted appeared, Dukoona looked to the cut along his own forearm. It had healed over into a black line, but the scar still felt stiff when he twitched his wrist.

All eyes were fixed on him.

"We find ourselves in the greatest of dangers," Dukoona said, elevating his voice to carry throughout the Basilica. "Some of our brothers tried to kill me. Many of you narrowly escaped death as well. Other Trusted did not. We no longer have a choice. To survive, we'll have to work against the Master. We are all bound to Him. If we want to be free, then He must die."

Dukoona was met with silence.

"Our first step will be to weaken His armies," Dukoona said. "The dragons will come to take back Aurisha. We shall let them, but on our terms. We'll bleed the demons slowly until Rectar's army is spent. Only seventy thousand demons remain with us here; the rest are dead or still on the Splintering Isles."

"The Master will not allow this," a raking voice called out. "He'll know."

"He will know in time," Dukoona said. "That is inevitable."

"And then what?" another asked.

"We hope our enemies will kill Him for us," Dukoona said. More silence. "You do not think it can be done? Everything can die, even this God of the Shadows. If He were invincible, He would have no need for demons, nor us. These gods the dragons bow to are not almighty either. Here we stand, servants of the Shadow, in the very temple erected for them."

He pointed to some spiralling pattern upon the wall.

"Where were these gods when we slaughtered dragons and took their home? What did they do when our master came to this world?"

He paced back and turned his attention to the carved swords. They looked so old; so old and so worn. "What did they do?" he asked again. Then, summoning his dark blade into his hand, he struck at the closest stone sword. Its hilt crumbled, breaking into smaller pieces as it hit the floor. The bang of falling stone rang in the Basilica. Dukoona looked up to the hole in the dome, arms stretched wide, waiting for the response from the gods to come.

He waited for a full minute.

"They do nothing," he yelled. He turned on the old stone sword again, hacking at it like a sapling until it was too low for him to reach. Then he kicked the final lump away from its holder towards his spectres.

Little Sonrid was there, at the front, hunched low over the broken stone. He picked it up tentatively and Dukoona gave him a reassuring look. Even with Sonrid's diminished strength, he could crush the stone further in his deformed fist.

"Either they have no power here or they do not care," Dukoona said. "Rectar hides in his mountain, as these gods of the dragons hide from the world. They need us to act for them, to serve them; well, I am tired of servitude."

I hope that His death will free us. It's all I can believe in.

"No one will grant us this," Dukoona told them. "If we want to escape our bonds then we must act."

"I am with you," came Kidrian's voice from nearby. Dukoona spotted his purple embers and, unexpectedly, the spectre stepped in front of the crowd and got down on one knee. "I am with you, my lord, until the end."

"Rise, Kidrian," Dukoona said. "And do not refer to me as lord. None of you will swap one master for another. If you wish to follow me, do so willingly."

"I will follow you, Dukoona," Kidrian said. He spoke loudly so that all could hear.

"As will I," said Sonrid. He opened his hand and let the powdery remains of the stone sword fall.

"As will I," said another.

"I am with you."

More called out. One by one, then in groups, before finally the last of the crowd cried it out.

"Then we prepare," Dukoona said. "We must be careful in allowing the dragons their victory. If they succeed too quickly, the Master will suspect. Beat them too bloody and we might weaken them too much. But be sure of this: no more spectres need risk their lives in this fight. Above all, you live. Let us lure in this Darnuir and his legions. Bring them here. Bring him to me. I mean to speak with their king."

Blaine – The Island of Eastguard

On the island of Eastguard, dragons died. Humans died. Fairies died.

We should not have rushed here so soon. I have failed again.

Blaine spun, sweeping the Guardian's Blade in an arc at the demons around him. More came pouring out of the former town of Errin. Blaine hadn't even managed to set foot in it.

The back of his head throbbed. He reached behind, winced, then drew away a hand slick with blood.

When did that happen?

He lost his footing and stepped in something hot and squelchy. Death reeked in the air and he saw his foot had landed in the torn stomach of a fallen human. Intestines curled around his boot.

Blaine retched, as much from the Cascade as from the corpse.

A spectre rose out of the ground from a crooked shadow cast by their tall spire. Painfully, his arm burning, Blaine blasted it with a beam of strong light from his sword. The spectre collapsed with a smoking hole through its chest.

"Light Bearers," Blaine cried.

No one was near him.

He was alone.

He tried to backtrack across the battlefield but the bodies made it hard to move. There was far more pink and blue among the fallen than black and purple. And lots of red, of course, spilling across the shore to meet the freezing grey ocean, where longships were already leaving.

"Fall back!" Grigayne roared. Blaine couldn't see him. "Back to the ships."

"Retreat!" many cried.

Blaine found himself running for the sea. When he reached the sand, his heavy feet sank and he tripped, falling face-first into the gore. He forced himself to his knees, slimy blood and filth dripping from his face. Heavy clouds that darkened the sky burst and rain lashed down, ticking off his armour.

My hand's empty.

Panicked, he scrambled around for the Guardian's Blade, but was still half-blinded by the mess on one side of his face.

A dragon appeared above him, proffering a hand. "Lord Guardian, let me help yo —" He convulsed, inhaling a sharp rattling breath as he died. Blaine saw the shadowy blade rip through the dragon's waist. The spectre responsible turned on Blaine next. He had spiky yellow flames across his head and moved frantically.

"The Master calls," the spectre said. "He speaks to me. You won't take us."

Blaine's hand finally found his sword.

His fingers gripped the hilt.

The spectre cut.

Blaine raised his sword too slowly. He howled in pain, in horror, in shock. His sword hand flailed and the spectre leapt out of his way. Blaine dropped his sword again.

His smallest finger had been cut clean away. A broken bone jutted from his palm and blood spurted from the wound. His ring finger was badly cut but still intact.

The gods have condemned me.

"Light Bearers," a voice called. "Protect the guardian." The yellow-flamed spectre saw the Light Bearers running over and thought better of it. He melded away, soaring from every small shadow he could back towards the dark tower.

Blaine scanned the ground for his sword, but someone was already handing it to him.

"I believe this is yours, Blaine," Bacchus said. He puffed madly trying to lift the Guardian's Blade, but he managed it, and all those around bore witness. Blaine took it in his left hand. It felt wrong there, clumsy, but he had no need for it right now.

He was running; fleeing to the call of "Retreat!" all around.

24

THE HIGH PRICE PAID

Captain Elsie was not only the first official leader of the hunters; she was the only one to ever win unanimous support. She must have been well loved. Still more impressive is that she achieved this long before the Brevian court started meddling in hunter affairs. Rumours of patronage and rigged elections have grown wilder over the centuries since.

From Tiviar's Histories

Cassandra – Brevia – Arkus' Palace

Cassandra grasped the edge of Cullen's cradle. Pudgy-faced with rosy cheeks, he was sleeping peacefully beneath a white blanket. She was pleased his room wasn't a blackwash like so much of the palace. Around the walls was a painted sequence of a family with a newborn baby, planting a seed and watching it grow alongside the child with a ceiling of rolling clouds and dazzling stars. Cassandra suspected the artistry was fairy rather than human.

Cullen rolled over. He flexed his tiny fingers against his crisp sheets. Cassandra couldn't help but smile. There was something calming about being around him, her nephew. She'd felt it even when she'd held him during the run from Torridon. Perhaps there was some bond there, unspoken, unforced, but there. *If only it were so easy with Arkus.*

There was a soft knock at the door.

"Come in," she said and was surprised when Balack entered. He'd been given a pristine set of custom white leathers because being a mountain boy was good for his story, as well as a black cloak of fine wool. His beard had been trimmed and oiled, and his auburn hair swept in a wave to one side.

"A bit of pampering suits you," Cassandra said.

He pursed his lips and blushed a little, looking at the cradle. "I hope I'm not interrupting?"

"He's asleep. I come to check up on him from time to time."

"I do too, when I can," Balack said. He stepped to the opposite side of the cradle and placed his own hand on it. "King Arkus visits as well, though he is extremely busy."

"You've been busy too. All that touring. All those speeches."

"It's good for the people. Good for morale," Balack said, a little pompously.

"Oh, of course. For the people. And for you?"

He shrugged. "It works, Cass. Recruitment has increased by eight per cent."

"Well, I'm glad," she said. "I imagine the guaranteed meals and clothing are also attractive. The refugee camps are stretching things thin."

"A lot of dragons arrived from Val'tarra," Balack said. "Arkus is worried and the Assembly is terrified."

"Why are they so scared?" Cassandra said. "The dragons are waiting to go home. Arkus even invited them to come get a ship."

"They're dragons, Cass," Balack said, as though it was all obvious. "They might be old, women or children, but that still makes them far stronger than us. It's all the Assembly talks about right now, especially now that the fleet has sailed with the bulk of our army."

"Balack, the dragons are not going to attack us for food."

"Maybe not now, but what about when the food runs scarce? You know fine well what they can be like. They will take what they want," he ended acidly.

Oh, so that is what this is really about.

"Don't let your feelings for Darnuir lead you to blame an entire race," Cassandra said. She felt a surge of anger at him then. "You don't even know what happened. He didn't 'take' anything. As if she—"

Cullen rustled and moaned but stayed asleep. Cassandra hadn't realised her voice had been rising. She let go of the cradle and stalked around to be closer to Balack.

"As if she was yours to have taken from you," Cassandra whispered savagely.

"You don't know," he whispered.

"Actually, I do. Darnuir told me back in Val'tarra." She remembered it vividly; the damp leaves, the confiding conversation, Ochnic descending from the trees. "Eve went after him, not the other way around. He was guilt-ridden, Balack."

"Then why'd he break my ribs? A strange sort of apology, that."

"Maybe he wasn't in his right mind," Cassandra said. "Maybe having memories from your sixty-year-old self forced into your head causes you to act in strange ways."

"And maybe it just shows that dragons aren't worth helping."

She slapped him.

The clap echoed and her palm stung. Balack reacted slowly, his hand rising to touch his cheek only after several seconds.

"He's made mistakes," Cassandra said. "I've decided to forgive him. You should as well. Grow up and get over this."

Hand still pressed against his cheek, he began to nod slowly as though pushing through sand. "You're right," he said, a little choked. "If there is some way I can—"

He was interrupted by a sharp cough at the door. Standing there, seemingly on his own, was Thane. Small for his age and weedy, Thane was bulked out only by his thick black robes. His skin looked even greyer than usual and there were dark lines around his eyes. When he saw Cassandra, he smiled widely then poked his head back around the edge of the doorframe.

"She's here, Mother," Thane called, a little out of breath. "In Cullen's room."

A moment later, Queen Oranna stepped into view behind her son, pulling him in close to her in a one-armed hug. "You shouldn't overexert yourself, sweetling," Oranna said, planting a kiss on Thane's head. In her free hand was a bundle of letters secured with brown string. A flare of excitement shot through Cassandra. She'd been waiting for this, although she'd need to be alone with Oranna to discuss it.

"But I wanted to—" He coughed again and heaved something up into a large handkerchief before pocketing it.

Well-practiced worry lined Oranna's face but she looked to Cassandra. "I hope I am not intruding? It can be difficult to get acquainted with one's betrothed—"

"Balack was just leaving," Cassandra said.

"Yes — I was," Balack said. He bowed to Thane first, then Oranna. "Please excuse me, my prince, my queen. I am scheduled to visit the forges today." As Balack squeezed past the crowded doorway, the queen threw Cassandra a quick wink.

"Mother, may I hold Cullen again?" Thane asked.

"Cullen is sleeping, dear. Perhaps later."

Thane trotted over to the cradle, peering fondly down at his – well, Cassandra was not sure what Cullen was in relation to Thane. *If Thane is my stepbrother, I suppose he is Cullen's step-uncle? I think.*

"I don't see you in the palace much, Cassandra," Thane said. "Would you like to read with me again one day?"

"Cassandra is very busy," Oranna said. "She's the princess now."

"I'm a prince and I'm not busy."

"You will be one day," Oranna said. "Why don't you wait outside, Thane? Mummy won't be long. I need to speak with Cassandra."

Thane seemed unsure.

"I would love to read with you one day," Cassandra said. "We'll sit in your favourite chair and have cake. But I do have business with your mother for now." Thane smiled again, seeming content with this, then obediently shuffled away. Oranna glanced out, making sure he was out of earshot.

"How's he been?" Cassandra asked.

"A little worse," Oranna said. "He had a hard time drifting off last night. Anyway, these are for you." She thrust the letters to Cassandra, who took the bundle eagerly.

"You know who R.F. is, then?" Cassandra asked.

"Ralph Foulis," Oranna said. "It wasn't too hard to narrow it down. The Forsychts have family members in the hunters, but not stationed here in Brevia, and the Finlays only have two sons, one of whom is a chevalier. One of the Feweir daughters is a huntress, but her first name is Maggy so that rules her out."

"Thank you, Oranna," Cassandra said. She took the bundle of letters eagerly and tucked them under one arm. "When have you arranged the gathering?"

"For tomorrow evening."

"That won't seem like too short notice?"

"I am the queen," said Oranna. "The lesser houses can't refuse me, particularly as this is the preliminary meeting to one with my husband. Besides, none of them would miss the chance to have their say in rebuilding and resettling the Boreac Mountains, not to mention the many vacant hunter positions in the Cairlav Marshes, Golden Crescent and the Dales."

"Don't the hunters decide on who gets what position?"

"Ordinarily yes, but the task ahead is such a large one that some formal planning will be required. It's an important matter, one that you can suitably use as an excuse to hand-deliver invitations. A nice gesture from the ruling family. Foulis' invitation to the gathering is in the middle of the pile."

"What if Arkus finds out about the gathering?" Cassandra asked.

"He knows," Oranna said. "I convinced him to let me take the matter off his plate, but I didn't mention our real reason for hosting."

"I don't know how to repay you for this," Cassandra said.

"Repay me?" Oranna said in shock. "You don't owe me anything. Repay me if you must by catching Boreac. I don't think I'll feel Thane is truly safe until this is over."

"I will," Cassandra said and, without thinking things through, hugged the queen. Oranna made a startled little "Oh" but returned the hug, lightly patting Cassandra on the back. Now Cassandra just felt too awkward to even let go. She was saved by Cullen waking up and beginning to cry.

Oranna moved to the cradle. "Was he fed before he fell asleep?"

"I'm not sure," Cassandra said. "The nurse didn't say."

"I think he needs burping," said Oranna, picking Cullen up. She positioned his head on her shoulder and gently rubbed his lower back. "He needs someone who has the time for him."

"There's a woman on Boreac's house staff, Olive," Cassandra said. "Perhaps when this is all cleared up you could bring her on to look after Cullen. If she is cleared of any wrongdoing, that is."

"Why her?" Oranna asked.

"Because she is his aunt," Cassandra said. "His mother's sister." Oranna blinked rapidly, then nodded in agreement.

"You should go," Oranna said. As Cassandra left and passed by Thane, who had his forehead pressed in boredom against the wall, she heard Oranna call out after her, "Be careful."

Cassandra returned to her room and found some suitable clothing. No dress or gown; she wanted to be able to move, just in case. What she really wanted was to take a sword, but that wouldn't do. Cassandra was playing princess today. Yet Kymethra didn't have such restrictions; she could play a Hinterland huntress, perhaps a contact of Oranna's sent for Cassandra's protection. She decided on black dress leggings – the sort that huntress captains might wear to formal occasions – combined with a decorative green silk shirt with frilly sleeves. Once dressed, she rolled up the sleeves to free her hands and strapped on her sword. She would pass it to Kymethra when she found her. Pleased with her attire, Cassandra grabbed the bundle of letters and set off to find the witch.

Her first stop was Brackendon's room and she found the door was already ajar.

"Hush, Brackendon," came Kymethra's voice. She sounded exhausted.

Through the open doorway, Cassandra saw Brackendon sitting upright in bed with Kymethra perched beside him. Brackendon's bedrobe was torn in places and there were scratch marks on his arms and neck.

"Gghhnghhm," Brackendon mumbled. His head suddenly swayed into Kymethra's chest where he sobbed and whined.

"Shhhh, shhh," Kymethra said, barely holding back tears.

"End the magic," Brackendon managed to say. "End the magic, end the—" but he broke down again in incoherent babbling.

"It will be okay," Kymethra said. She placed three fingers carefully just above Brackendon's ear, all the while reassuring him, "It will be okay. You'll be okay." On her last words, her soothing seemed to take effect. Brackendon ceased muttering and his eyes glazed over. Kymethra resettled him back down and he fell asleep. That Kymethra only allowed herself one lone tear was perhaps the bravest thing Cassandra had ever seen.

Cassandra felt like a terrible intruder, walking in on the worst form of intimacy. She thought about turning and walking away but Kymethra saw her then.

"Oh, it's you," Kymethra said. "Oranna set everything up, then?" Her right arm was shaking as she pointed to the letters and a few more strands of her hair had turned white.

"She has," Cassandra said, suddenly unsure about this. "You don't have to come if—"

"I'm bloody coming," Kymethra said with a sniff and a great shake of her head.

"All right," Cassandra said. "If you put on the Hinterland leathers, we can pretend you are the extra protection Oranna has given me, seeing as the chevaliers are spread so thin."

"Bit of a lame excuse," Kymethra muttered. She started rooting around in some drawers, yanking out pieces of blue leather flecked with pale green.

"I need you to put this on as well," Cassandra said, tapping her sword.

"Why? I can't use it."

"A huntress would have a sword," Cass said softly.

Kymethra nodded, taking the weapon from her. The buckle caused Kymethra's shaking fingers some trouble. She started getting angry again, pulling on the leather strap until it tightened like a corset. Cassandra dove to loosen it and fix the buckle in place as Kymethra wheezed above her.

"I can't imagine what you are suffering through," Cassandra said. "And I know you want to help me catch those involved, but you'll hardly help if you're only half-alive."

"I'm fine. Some cold water and fresh bread from the kitchens will set me straight. Let's just go."

After successfully negotiating the winding old streets of Brevia, the Master Station was a bit underwhelming. None of Cassandra's books had ever described the place and she thought she now understood why. Plain and unadorned, the station took up an entire block near the tanneries, which were now part of the larger Trade District. Though simple, there was something stoic about it. Despite the centuries, the station had refused to change.

There was one huntress stationed at the door, looking bored. She questioned them, but was settled by Oranna's royal seal on the letters and the glaring look that Kymethra gave her.

"Captain Horath is out today," the huntress said, her eyes nervously flicking back to Kymethra. "He's giving a speech along with the Hero of the Bastion, trying to beef up our numbers too."

"That's no matter," Cassandra said, relieved she would not have to deal with the captain. "I only need to deliver these invitations."

"Far be it from me to stop you, milady."

Cassandra smiled pleasantly and she and Kymethra walked inside. Even compared to the dim-witted guards outside of Boreac's mansion that had been child's play. *Playing the princess certainly has some perks.*

The station's interior was not as demure. It was decorated with the most impressive kills the hunters had ever made; enormous stuffed dire wolves, great stags with antlers over four feet long and even a silver-furred bear the size of a carriage. Kymethra didn't seem to be paying attention and occasionally passed Cassandra when she paused before a display. Yet Cassandra couldn't help but admire them, even if it was sad to know that such creatures had been hunted from the world, whether for glory or safety. These animals were likely to be extinct now, never to return to Tenalp. The final display was a collection of thick gold-plated armour of varying designs. One suit looked eerily like Blaine's own. A little plaque beneath it read:

The armour of the murderous Norbanus. Gifted to the hunters after the Battle of the Bogs by Dronithir, Humanity's Greatest Friend.

The actual armour of the guardian Norbanus himself? Why isn't this well known? Perhaps it had something to do with the undiplomatic wording on the inscription. The hunters honoured their tradition well. Dragons were their greatest kills, and not all the displays were of extinct species after all.

Not for now, at least.

"Are you coming?" Kymethra asked.

"Yes, sorry," Cassandra said, striding to catch up.

Room after room, fake pleasantries and seemingly endless amounts of small talk were endured before they finally found the office they were looking for. Cassandra knocked lightly at the open doorway.

"Ralph Foulis?"

"That would be me," the man said without looking up from his papers. "You can tell Horath the transfer candidates still aren't drawn up yet."

"I am not a huntress," Cassandra said. Foulis glanced up then and a look of confusion creased his forehead. At a glance, he was not much older than Cassandra, yet his skin was milkier than most hunters, showing he'd probably sat behind that desk for many years. "I have something for you." She entered the office and dropped the letter on top of the documents he was scribbling at.

"The royal seal?" Foulis said, suddenly nervous. "Who are you? Why would Arkus be corresponding with me?"

"That's the queen's seal," Cassandra said. "The king knows nothing about this."

"Does he not?" Foulis said, mincing words as though he'd never spoken under pressure before.

"The king seems to be on your mind," Cassandra said. "Any reason? I could inform the queen herself if it is important."

She'd give him a chance. He looked nervous enough to burst without much pressure.

"If you are so connected to Her Majesty then why have I never seen you before?"

"Because I spent twenty years as Castallan's hostage at the Bastion." Telling half a truth was easier than a full lie, and now she'd dropped another name to make him squirm.

Foulis fidgeted with the letter. "Most unfortunate. Glad that horrible business is all over."

"Is it?" Cassandra asked. "Lord Annandale is to stand trial in the Assembly and Lord Boreac has disappeared. Many seem to think that points to him being involved."

"Well, I wouldn't know anything about all that," Foulis said, without even having the sense to look at her directly. Either that or he found the doorframe very alluring.

"Kymethra," Cassandra said, without taking her own gaze from Foulis. "We'll need some privacy, I think. Go shut the door."

"Hmmph," Kymethra grunted from behind.

Foulis looked alarmed.

It all happened at once. As Kymethra closed the door with a firm click, Foulis' chair screeched out from under him. He jumped to his feet, his slight gut already stretching his uniform, and tried to dart around the side of his desk. A slight limp slowed him, but he had one hand on the sword at his belt. Now half-drawn. Steel visible.

Cassandra lunged across Kymethra's waist and ripped the sword there free. She blocked Foulis with a great clang of metal. He stumbled backwards and she buried an elbow into his soft flab. With both arms he clutched at his stomach, groaning, and leaving himself open. She jabbed the pommel against his wrist and he dropped his weapon.

"Impressive," Kymethra said, stepping up beside her. She was looking down on Foulis with the contemplation she might have given a juicy rabbit in her eagle form.

"He clearly isn't good at this," Cassandra said.

"I won't talk," Foulis said, trying to crawl back to his desk. "My family needs me – the money. I won't—"

Kymethra swooped down upon the man. "Are you in pain?"

"I'm always in pain," he snorted. "My leg. Tendons ripped. Never healed fully. S'why I'm stuck in here."

"That must be a terrible burden," Kymethra said, in a strangely tender voice. "To have to live the rest of your life like that. In pain. Sat there. It's almost understandable, the things you've done. The people you've hurt. The lives you've ruined..." She was on her knees beside him. Something about the glint in her eye made Cassandra uneasy.

"Kymethra..."

"Well, what could I do?" Foulis said. "I won't rise in rank stuck here, and my house needs support. The king's policies don't allow payments to noblemen injured, even when we're flat broke. There are whoresons wounded in the last war getting compensation. But do I? No. Wrecked on my first night of duty in a tavern brawl. The injustice!"

"Oh, so unjust," Kymethra said. She pushed back a bit of his hair, just above the ear. She placed three fingers there.

"Kymethra," Cassandra said, more pressing.

"Do you know where Lord Boreac fled to?" Kymethra asked.

Foulis shook his sweating head.

"No?" Kymethra said. "But we found a scrap of a letter you sent him. It was you, right?" Foulis didn't deny it. "Did Boreac come to see you, as you asked him?"

"He did, but I don't know where he went."

"You don't know, or you won't tell us?" Kymethra asked.

"I can't tell you. If I talk, I won't get the gold to help—"

"Let me help you remember," Kymethra spat. Her fingers seemed to vibrate and Foulis froze, his face suddenly struck with horror.

"No," Cassandra cried. Bringing Kymethra had been a mistake. She was too upset, too unstable.

Foulis' mouth opened in a silent scream. His eyes rolled up, showing only white, and he began to tremble upon the floor. Kymethra grimaced as she worked her magic, looking as if the pain from the poison was as great as the pleasure she was receiving from hurting a man who'd been involved in Brackendon's terrible fate.

Cassandra didn't know what to do, but instinct pushed her to Kymethra's shoulder and she grabbed her, trying to yank her free from Foulis. That was a mistake.

Pain flared throughout Cassandra's body and she fell backwards, colliding with a set of shelves. Paper and scrolls descended on top of her as her vision turned to a revolving blur.

Memories flashed before her. She was nine years old and stuck in one of the Bastion's tunnels with no light or warmth. Trapped. "Chelos," she sobbed. "Chelos, where are you?" She was even younger now, seven and lying on her bed. She was reading stories about children who wanted to run away from home and go on adventures. She didn't understand why they'd want to leave. Everything swirled again, and there was a hand on her shoulder, a scream – and blood was pouring from his chest.

Thud.

Her eyes snapped open. Her head rang in pain. A heavy book lay in front of her; its spine still touched the edge of her nose. With a splitting head, Cassandra got unsteadily to her feet.

Foulis was still writhing and strange foamy saliva trailed from the edge of his mouth. Kymethra's arm shook, yet she held it determinedly in place.

Cassandra looked for her fallen sword and picked it up.

"Kymethra, stop." Kymethra did not. "Stop it now or I swear I'll cut your hand off."

When Kymethra didn't respond, Cassandra raised her sword —

Brought it down —

But she couldn't follow through. *What was I thinking?* She held the cold edge just above Kymethra's wrist, then kicked the witch with all her might.

Kymethra spun away, clipping her head off the desk corner, and Foulis regained himself. His eyes were a web of bloodshot lines. All three of them were gasping for air.

"Right," Cassandra panted, feeling winded. "Now we all have thundering headaches, can we go about this more civilly? Foulis, tell us all you know."

"Why should I?" Foulis moaned. "After that? If this is what Arkus resorts to then what's stopping you from killing me after?"

"Arkus doesn't know we're here," Cassandra said.

"Even more reason I am disposable, then."

Cassandra glanced at Kymethra, who looked thoroughly dazed. A trickle of blood ran down from her temple. *Don't make me regret this, Kymethra.* She tossed her sword well out of reach then raised her empty hands in peace to Foulis.

"All Arkus cares about is Boreac." Foulis still looked unsure. Cassandra slowly crouched down in front of him and he flinched.

What horrors did she make you relive?

"I know a bit about your house," Cassandra said. "I know you once had your time in the sun, that the name Foulis briefly meant something. But that was taken away, wasn't it?"

"What do you know of it?"

"I know an ancestor of yours almost singlehandedly held Brevia from the Islanders when they sacked the city. John Foulis. Just a young man like you; a second son of a third son. A lowly gatekeeper on the city walls. But he rallied his men and barred the doors, and held strong. And when the lords from the Crownlands marched to relieve the city, the gates were open for them."

Foulis nodded along.

"When the White Arch of Brevia was built, its sea defences were entrusted to your family, the defenders of the city. But slowly your house declined once more. Little is written, but I can guess what happened."

"Can you?"

"I don't know if your house was ever rich, but it wasn't when such an important duty was placed upon its shoulders. My guess is that you couldn't maintain the costs of the Arch: its upkeep, the soldiers, the staff. Loans might have been taken, but you couldn't pay them back. You couldn't even lean on patriotism once the Islanders had joined the Assembly and there was no need to defend against the sea anymore. So, while other families rose, yours fell, and I doubt anyone cared.

"Maybe Boreac said he cared. Maybe Castallan promised you wealth and power again. Don't you see why they came to you? Why they used you? They played you for their own ends. And now they've met theirs. Castallan is dead. Boreac is on the run. There's nothing to be gained anymore."

"I need the gold," Foulis groaned. "It's not just for me. My older brothers died in the last war. My parents have worked themselves half to death to keep the estate running. They're good to their tenants, which is far more than I can say for most of the Crownland families. I was their last hope, but I'm injured, stuck behind this desk. I'll never be a captain or rise to anything like this. My sister Ruth is a sweet girl, but homely. She won't marry high in the world. We're done."

Crumpled up, Kymethra finally let loose a groan of her own. Foulis and Cassandra ignored her.

"Boreac promised he'd send word of where he'd stashed some coin for me," Foulis said. "Once he was safe."

"Did he want you to help hide him?" Cassandra asked.

"No. He just wanted some documents I'd kept – letters and such. Secret orders. I thought he would be mad to hear I hadn't burned them, but he was pleased."

"What letters?" Cassandra asked. "What orders?"

Foulis lowered his head. "Look, I'm not talking. My folks need this. I never thought this much bloodshed would happen. Still, it's happened now, and I've made peace with it. So, do your worst."

Cassandra sighed, exasperated. Her knees were beginning to hurt so she sat down cross-legged before Foulis. It was admirable of him, in a way, to risk everything for his parents and sister.

"You must love your family very much," Cassandra said.

"I'd do anything for them," Foulis said. "Wouldn't you?"

"I don't have one," is what Cassandra was about to say. Yet, even as she formed the words in her mind, she knew it wasn't strictly true anymore. Chelos might have been taken from her, but she thought of Oranna and how wonderful and welcoming she had been. She thought of sweet young Thane and even Cullen. Strange as it was to admit, she'd do anything for her nephew. Castallan, Boreac and the rest would probably have killed him if they'd won. That was enough to set a fire in her.

"Yes, I would do anything," is what she said in answer.

"So you understand?" Foulis said.

"I do, but you need to understand that you're caught," Cassandra said. "Your intentions don't excuse what you've done and I need Boreac to fulfil a bargain with my father. Yet he doesn't need to know all the details. So, if you talk to me, tell me it true, then I'll forget all about you."

"You swear?"

"I swear."

Foulis sighed. "Very well. Don't suppose I have many options..." He massaged his head a little before continuing. "Boreac took what evidence I had surrounding the death of Captain Morwen. He was very interested in the cargo Morwen was carrying. He wanted it intercepted; swapped or stolen."

'Cargo' meaning black powder, Cassandra thought.

"But something went wrong," Foulis continued. "Everyone sent on the mission died, including the captain. It was a disaster. I still don't know what really happened. When Boreac asked me for the evidence I thought he wanted to make sure it was destroyed, but he never asked for what I had on that Captain Tael, and that was plain murder."

"What haven't you had your greasy fingers in?" Kymethra said. She was rubbing her head, nursing her arm, and looked too ashamed to face them.

"Things got out of hand sometimes," Foulis said. "Especially when Scythe got involved. I breathed easier when he took Tael's place in the south. Good riddance, I thought. He always made my blood run like ice."

"And in your position, you could arrange for any of Boreac or Scythe's supporters to be placed in any region they wished," said Cassandra.

"That was why they came to me," Foulis said. "I had my uses. Even stuck in here."

"That could be a lot of names to incriminate," Cassandra said.

"You want them?" Foulis asked.

"No," Cassandra said. "Enough blood has spilled, and I suspect many of them died at the Bastion. I'm more interested in why Boreac would want those papers on Morwen."

"He seemed to think it would help him gain sanctuary with the dragons," Foulis said. Then he laughed in a slightly hysterical way. "Maybe he was losing it. I doubt the dragons would be happy to take him in once it comes out he was involved in all this."

"That's where he's going?" Cassandra asked. "He thinks the dragons will keep him safe?"

"He seemed confident enough," Foulis said. "Must be right desperate to avoid Arkus if he's turning to them." He grinned, perhaps enjoying the thought of Boreac turning up outside a legionary camp, begging for mercy.

Cassandra felt this was coming together. "And you don't know where he might be right now?"

"Could be rowing with one paddle across the sea for all I know," Foulis said. A droplet of blood seeped from his eye. He wiped it away and his eyes widened in alarm at the red smear on his fingers. "Not sure how I explain this to the healers."

"One last thing," Cassandra said. She pulled out the little lead sphere from a pouch at her belt. "Do you know what this is?"

Foulis squinted. "Not a clue."

Well, he couldn't know everything. He's been through enough.

"We will take our leave now," Cassandra said. She looked to Kymethra. "Can you manage?"

"I can walk," Kymethra grumbled, getting to her feet. She looked a shadow of her former self. No radiance, no cheeky sparkle in her eye – just a lifeless husk where Kymethra had once been.

Cassandra went to pick up her sword. She demanded the belt from Kymethra, strapped it around her own waist, and then sheathed the blade with a satisfying snap.

"I'm sorry for all you've been through, Ralph Foulis," she said. "I'm sorry the world has left your family behind. If it helps in any way, I do not think we shall ever need to meet again."

"And you'll forget about me, yes?"

"The very moment we leave this room," Cassandra said, giving Kymethra a very hard glare. Then Cassandra turned and took her leave, Kymethra trailing behind her.

25

BLOOD ON THE SAND

Before Dranus led his exiles to settle near Kar'drun, there were no inhabitants of eastern Tenalp. Then came the Third Flight. Forests were felled, cities raised and a great road laid from north to south. The Crucidal Road was meant for trade, but armies have used it more. Some fairies dream of restoring the landscape, but the east has been irreversibly altered, even more so than the west.

From Tiviar's Histories

Darnuir – the shores of the east

Golden sand, teal waters, an autumn breeze; the shoreline might have been a welcoming sight had swarms of demons not marred it. Darnuir squinted against the sunlight reflecting on the water. Demon numbers were impossible to gauge, but the black masses stretched all along the coast. They couldn't know where Darnuir and the legions would land, so had covered as much ground as possible.

Darnuir was glad for the initial advantage that would grant, as it allowed them to press all their forces into one smaller point and punch a hole in the demon lines. However, it would be easy for Dukoona to ensnare the legions once they landed if he wasn't careful.

We'll be harried all the way to the gates of Aurisha and then we'll have to scale the walls of our own city. Unless the spectres just invite us in.

But he didn't want that. Not really.

He needed an excuse to draw on the Cascade. Aside from the mystery of Dukoona's actions, it was why he was here.

He drew a breath, held it, then let it go through his nose. A fresh wave buffeted the ship and sent spray into his face. Wiping away the water, Darnuir turned back to his Praetorians, readying themselves on deck. Lira's eyes looked sunken with tiredness and Raymond's were half closed, blinking rapidly to fend off sleep.

"How are the troops?" Darnuir asked.

"As well as can be," said Lira. "It's not been an easy journey."

"The demons are truly without art," said Raymond, picking at a splinter in his left palm. The ships left behind by the demons near Dalridia were crude, unfinished dragon galleys.

"It's been cramped and hard rowing," Darnuir said. "But comfort and war rarely mix. Time is limited. I want to hit the demons before their spectre overlords have a chance to prepare properly."

"Prepare?" Raymond questioned. "I thought there was some schism amongst them."

"That's what we can glean from Grigayne's testimony," Darnuir said.

Or is this all some ploy, and I've played right into Dukoona's hands?

Lira opened her mouth as if to speak but stopped herself short.

"Speak your mind, Lira," Darnuir said.

"It doesn't matter. We're here now."

"My gut tells me something is amiss with the spectres," Darnuir said, loud enough for all the Praetorians to hear. "Enough to think we might be able to take advantage of the situation, in one way or another."

Lira pointed behind him, out towards the shore. "If Dukoona wants to talk, he's brought quite the welcoming party."

"We have as well," Raymond said. "Seven legions, if I'm not mistaken."

"Seven legions, but not all at full roster," Lira said. "Not after the Bastion and lifting the siege at Dalridia. The legates—"

"The legionary legates have not voiced any concerns," Darnuir said.

"The legates are good dragons who would never talk back to you," Lira said. She hesitated but kept her head held high. "You told me you wanted me to speak my mind."

"And I do."

"You were a hunter once as well," Lira said. "No squad leader would take risks like this. Not without questions from the rest."

"This is different."

"It is?" Lira asked. "Lives are at stake."

"We're an army," Darnuir said, "fighting another army, a much larger army. We're not five hunters in the cold and the dark, stalking a lynx that's strayed too far from its den. It's a risk, but one I'm sure we have to take."

"Can we really take such chances?" Lira said. "So far we've pulled through half on luck and half on the efforts of Brackendon." She was looking Darnuir right in the eye. "Castallan wanted you to run right to him and you did."

"If I hadn't, Castallan would have finished Brackendon off."

"Or he could have taken the Dragon's Blade and killed us all," said Lira. "You didn't think. You went to get that girl."

They think I'm being too reckless.

"I told you the reasons why we had to get Cassandra," Darnuir said. Heat licked at his throat and the door to the Cascade in his mind quivered. How he longed to feel it course through every inch of him.

"The alliance, yes," said Lira. "But you risked everything for it. You didn't consider the bigger threat. Or you did, but just wanted to get her back." She seemed to know she'd taken a step too far then. Maybe it was the look Darnuir was giving her. His vision had turned to two narrow slits.

Raymond took a brave step between them. "Darnuir took a chance taking the humans from Torridon to Val'tarra. That was worth it."

"I'm not questioning every decision," Lira said. "We'd have failed at the Charred Vale had the spectres not fled, and they did so because you killed Scythe."

"It was reckless, I won't deny it," Darnuir said. "But there seemed to be few options."

"You were angry as well," said Lira. "Because Scythe killed Cosmo. He baited you. Like Castallan baited you. Both wanted your sword. This might be the same thing."

"If I may," Raymond began, "it seems to me that it is the enemy who has taken the greater gamble this time. If this is some manoeuvre, we could have ignored it and focused on retaking the Splinters with ease."

"Something is off, that much is certain," Lira said. "The battle at Dalridia went too smoothly."

"I'm taking another gamble," Darnuir said. "An even bigger one. But it's not all about the spectres. By the time we have cleared the Splinters and waited on Arkus' full fleet, winter might make the crossing too difficult for a full invasion."

"Yes, the weather can be frightful," Raymond said, if a little stiffly.

Darnuir understood how pathetic that excuse sounded now. He looked around his Praetorians. Armed to the teeth, they stood silently, mouths pressed into thin lines. They would fight, he knew. Lira too. They would not abandon him. Every dragon in the legions would swim ashore if he ordered it. Yet that was the problem.

Have I chased battle and doomed us all?

"Caution drove us from our homes," Darnuir told them. He had not revealed to the Praetorians yet what Blaine had told him. Some knowledge would be best kept among only a few. "I remember my father, kneeling, praying, and waiting. That time has long passed. Are we to miss this chance to take back Aurisha?"

"Caution also allowed Castallan to spread rot in the Dales," Raymond said.

Lira gave a short sharp sigh. "One day, our luck might run out."

"It won't matter where we are when that happens," Darnuir said. "And it is too late to turn back now. Will you fight?"

"Of course," Lira said, pulling her bow more securely onto her shoulder.

"Good. The legates know the signal?" Darnuir asked.

"Those six who'll be still at sea," said Raymond. "Legate Atilius and the Fifth Legion will be joining us for the landing. They were less than enthusiastic about hearing it from me, however."

"They will learn to deal with you, or I shall find new legates," Darnuir said. "To the boats now."

Once on the sea, Darnuir's boat cut towards the shore. He was crouched at the bow, trying to assess the situation. Closer to land, he saw a series of great wooden columns, far taller than a single tree could be outside of Val'tarra. They were well positioned across the land, heading south towards Aurisha.

Those will cast impressive shadows.

He turned around. Praetorians rowed and looked eager now the battle was close to hand. Lira was on another boat on the starboard side, but Raymond was here, encased from head to toe in his chevalier armour.

"One day I shall see you in action with your horse," Darnuir said.

"Bruce shall be happy to get into the action himself," Raymond said. "I spoiled him with apples and carrots for days after the stress of Inverdorn."

Darnuir laughed. "Do you wish you were back in that velvet waistcoat?"

"Never," Raymond said, slamming his visor shut.

Darnuir returned his attention to the shore, itching for the battle to begin. The first stones from the demon catapults launched at them, crashing into the sea. In the shallows before the shore, they sent up torrents of water. Darnuir shielded his eyes against a salty splash that soaked their boat. He spat a mouthful out and pushed wet hair off his face. From far behind him came screams and the sound of breaking wood.

Black barbed arrows followed once they were almost ashore. Calls for shields rang out. Darnuir brought up his arms to cover his face; the starium-coated armour would provide protection. Yet few arrows came close. As he lowered his arms, keeping his head bowed low and glancing each way, he saw few casualties. Several dark shafts shot into the water between his boat and Lira's.

Are they holding back?

The boat began to slow into the sand. Shrieks met them as demons pelted out from trenches and behind fresh-dug mounds. Darnuir rose from his crouch, drew the

Dragon's Blade and launched it up the beach. It burst through the closest demons in
an explosion of smoke.

"Secure the landing!"

Leaping off the boat, he hit the soft sand: the first dragon to set foot in the east
since the fall of Aurisha. Praetorians flanked him, loosing arrows against the
oncoming demons. The Dragon's Blade returned to his open hand.

Darnuir opened the door to the Cascade and felt a kick at the back of his head; it
cricked his neck and he charged up the beach.

Enhanced with magic, he soon outstripped everyone else with his speed. Rusty
knives and blades scraped uselessly against his armour. Darnuir carved his way
through the demons, letting the Cascade run like a river. But it didn't feel the same.
He did not feel the same high as Castallan had pushed him to. His body wanted
more; needed more.

With a great effort, he resisted throwing the door open wider.

I must hold back. I must try.

There seemed to be no end of the demons. They leapt frog-like from behind their
fellows, flying over Darnuir's head towards where the Fifth Legion would be landing.
Even with his strength and speed, advancing up the banks of the beach was
becoming a crawl. He thought he heard Lira shouting but couldn't tell over the blood
now thumping through his head.

This crush wasn't normal. Demons liked to swarm, spread out, stay mobile, yet
here they were pressing against each other. One of the oversized columns cast its
shadow right into the horde. A spectre appeared in the middle of it all. Grinning, it
motioned for Darnuir to follow before vanishing. The demons descended into a
frenzy.

Darnuir swung the Dragon's Blade around to clear room to breathe.

"For Brevia," chanted Raymond, swishing his sword elegantly yet precisely to
block two demons at once. The din of battle grew louder behind him. The Fifth were
coming in force. Darnuir grunted in shock as a black arrow snapped off the dragon
head on his right shoulder. He wanted to unleash fire upon the demons, but the fight
was becoming so crushed he feared it might burn his allies as well.

More spectres appeared in the fight but did not get close to the action. Darnuir
lunged at them each time, only to watch them flee. One with flaming green hair
gestured for Darnuir to follow before melding off in the blink of an eye.

Eventually, he waded to the end of the beach. A series of wide, deep trenches was
supposed to slow their advance. More rocks fell from the sky. A jagged piece bowled
into the demons' own ranks before continuing into the golden line of dragons. The
sound of crunching bones and metal was stomach-churning.

Or perhaps that was more the effect of the Cascade. Darnuir's arm was shaking
now, for he had not let up, drinking in the euphoria. One of the youngest Praetorians

went down with two arrows in his neck, and the smell of the blood only pushed Darnuir further.

His eyes widened and he no longer blinked. The battle was on him. It was all he could feel.

"Into the trenches," he cried before jumping down. He had no sense of whether anyone was actually following or how far in front he was. In a fury, he tore through this first ditch, coming across a demon catapult. Its crew barely noticed his sword before it ended them. He took his fist to the machine, smashing it with ease.

He was in a trance, drunk on excessive rage. Every spectre that eluded him only made him reach for more magic and more anger. Livid, he jumped six feet from a standing start to chase spectres over the edge of the trench. They had vanished, but a hunk of rock did collide into the ground in front of him.

He couldn't react in time.

The stone shattered against his armour and the impact blew him back. He landed face down in the trench, tasting dirt and rancid demon blood. Hot pain burned in his lower chest.

A hand took him by the shoulder and he reacted quicker than a beat of his thundering heart.

With a fresh draw on the Cascade, he flipped himself around, then up.

He met Lira's grey eyes.

His hand was at her throat.

She struck his head with the hilt of her sword. He spun away, biting his own tongue and tasting blood. She was screaming something at him but he barely heard.

What am I doing?

He dropped the Dragon's Blade and pressed a foot on it to keep it down. Underfoot it wiggled, trying to break free, but he set all his weight onto it. His arm ached as the poison welled up. And, from nearby, a swirl of shadow arose and a spectre took shape. This one had purple embers on its head.

"Come. Dukoona awaits," it croaked. It melded away before anything else could be said or done.

His senses returned, still amplified by the magic pounding in his veins. Darnuir gasped for air as though coming up from underwater. He smelled the very iron of the spilt blood, heard the rattling of demons from far up the beach, saw every hair on his arm shift in the breeze. Turning, his foot still on his sword, he saw Lira gutting one last demon. She mouthed something at him.

Signal. Yes.

Darnuir slid his foot off the Dragon's Blade and it flew back to his hand. Heat rose like a furnace in his throat and he raised the Dragon's Blade, sending a thin stream of fire high into the air. He held it for a good half minute.

When he let go and shut the door, it was all he could do not to be sick.

Lira tossed him a waterskin, which he gulped down too quickly, nearly choking. He swirled another swig around his mouth and spat, but the bitterness stubbornly clung on. His tongue felt drier than dust.

The Dragon's Blade was smoking, as was the dragon's head on his armour. Rusty demon blood dribbled from its teeth, looking like it had spewed a fire of its own. Clutching to the Dragon's Blade to process the poison, he slumped against the edge of the trench, looking out to sea. The water churned under thousands of oars.

Lira stepped cautiously towards him.

"I'm sorry," he said. His voice was like that of a frightened child.

"It's the magic, isn't it?"

He nodded.

"You haven't been right since the Charred Vale," Lira said. "I tried to—"

"I know you did," he said weakly.

She remained standing. Keeping a distance between them.

"I could barely control myself."

"Did the job, though. I think half the demons fell because of you." Despite what he'd almost done to her, she looked concerned for him. She looked him up and down, then turned to check on the demon side of their trench. "They're backing away for now."

Further down the trench, some of the Praetorians let loose a few arrows after them.

"You were right," Darnuir said. "This was too risky. I chased the fight because I was desperate for a reason to use magic."

She crouched down.

"I saw those spectres waving us along. I heard that one tell you to come. The demons threw themselves at us, but like sheep to the slaughter. Whatever the reason, the spectres want you to follow them, badly. We'll just have to keep deaths to a minimum." She stalked off.

Ragged breathing and the sound of clanking plate announced Raymond's arrival. Darnuir watched him limp along and remove his helmet to reveal his face, which was slick with sweat.

"Tired, my Lord of Dragons?"

"Come, take a breather, Chevalier," Darnuir said. He took another long gulp of water as Raymond sat down beside him. "If this keeps up it's going to be a very long road to Aurisha."

26

A SIGN

I wish to know more about the guardians and their Light Bearers. The current incarnation of the order lacks purpose since the end of hostilities with the Black Dragons. Now there is peace, perhaps the guardians can find a more positive role – one that aims to better the whole world, not just dragons. Already there is talk of a promising young Light Bearer. I hear his fellows call him 'Blaine' due to the fire of his zeal. If this Blaine becomes guardian one day, I can only hope he grows to be a wiser dragon than some of his predecessors.

From Tiviar's private notes

Blaine – Dalridia

Somerled's hall was quiet. There was little talk to cover the chewing and grinding of teeth. The fire burned as low as their spirits. The whisky racks lacked their amber glow.

Blaine raised his maimed and trembling hand, trying to feed himself with great effort. He took a small bite from the chicken leg, rolled the cold, dry meat around in his mouth without pleasure, and slowly swallowed. His stomach turned and he felt cold sweat on his scalp. He reached for his water, awkwardly taking the handle of the tankard in a four-fingered grip. It was almost to his lips when he dropped it, spilling water all over the table. What few Light Bearers remained with him tended to the mess while one hastily refilled the tankard.

Across the hall, Grigayne Imar glared at him. He'd suffered a cut across his cheek that had decimated his beard on that side and would surely leave a long scar. When he caught Blaine's eye, he drained his mug and slammed it down so all the hall could see before storming outside. Somerled avoided eye contact altogether. He had not climbed to the top of his rock tonight.

"Lord Guardian, you should eat something more," one of the Light Bearers said.

"I have no appetite," said Blaine. "Leave me." He then realised that only two had remained for any length of time. When they left, Blaine was alone at the table.

He was done, he knew that. He no longer had what it took to be guardian. Perhaps he never had.

"You shouldn't sit alone," came Fidelm's deep tones. "Is that gash under your chin fresh?"

"Cut myself shaving," Blaine mumbled.

The general sat down beside him and Blaine lacked the energy to protest. He let Fidelm take his right hand for inspection. "Are you using your blade to help heal the wound?"

"I don't deserve to use its power," Blaine said. He hadn't touched his sword since sheathing it on the beach on Eastguard.

"Don't be a fool," said Fidelm.

Blaine pulled his hand away and tucked it out of sight under the table.

"At least allow me to apply a paste of silver bark and leaves," Fidelm said.

"No. This is a pain I must endure."

"There is no need to suffer," said Fidelm.

"I was a fool, and — and Bacchus was right about me."

"Look at me." Fidelm grabbed him and forced Blaine to face him. "You should have waited for our full forces. Even so, it's war. Defeats are inevitable as well as victories and we had a lucky string of those behind us."

"I threw lives away. Fairy lives too. Aren't you angry?"

"I'm always angry with you," Fidelm said. "A deep, burning fury that I learned to cope with long ago."

"What on earth do you—"

"One queen, one child, Blaine," Fidelm said. "My race was doomed long ago. The least you can do is not allow this all to be for nothing." He got up and spoke louder. "Most of the remaining Third Legion left an hour ago, heading towards the Nail Head. If you can no longer do this, pass the blade on to someone who can." He stretched his wings, beat them once, then took off, flying through the smoke hole in the centre of the roof.

Blaine stumbled through the dark and misty drizzle back to his tent outside the city. Somerled had not been as inviting this time around. He tried to strip his armour. It was so heavy. The oversized suns felt as if they were crushing his shoulders. His useless hand fumbled and slipped at the knot, jarring the stub of his missing finger against the starium coating. A choking gasp of pain left him, and he almost missed the wheezy cough from the entranceway.

"They've all left with Bacchus for service at the Nail Head," Chelos said. He'd recovered enough to walk freely now. At least that was something amongst all Blaine's misery.

"I know that. I'm not blind," Blaine said, more cruelly than he meant. "Wait," he pleaded. "I am sorry, my friend. Could you give an old dragon a hand with his armour?" With a wrinkled, thin smile, Chelos came to his aid.

"They'll come back, you know," he said, tugging at a strap at Blaine's shoulder.

"Why should they?" said Blaine. He tried to help Chelos by holding the rivets of plate still. Chelos' waxy skin brushed over his own. It felt overly soft, malleable and frail like a silk sheet.

So weak. Yet I am weaker.

Together, they freed Blaine from his metal cage. With the removal of each piece, he sighed in relief as his skin felt the kiss of cold air. He donned a fresh white shirt and washed his face at the basin, though he was unable to cup his right hand properly. Water leaked from the gap of his lost appendage and he reluctantly switched to his left hand. It took far longer than it ought to and foolishly he'd gotten his bandages wet. Changing those would have been impossible without Chelos' help.

"What does he say to them?" Blaine asked.

"You should go and hear for yourself," Chelos said.

"I'm afraid," Blaine said.

"Why? Because you've taken one little knock?" Chelos said. "You faced a god and lived."

"I'm afraid because our gods have deserted me," Blaine said. "How can I face Rectar again if I cannot even win back one small island?"

"And will Bacchus do any better?" Chelos asked. "Darnuir still needs you. You'll face Rectar together."

"I can hardly grip my sword," Blaine said.

"I never dreamed I'd see you like this," Chelos said. "It would break Draconess' heart if he were still alive."

"But he isn't," Blaine said. "He failed. We failed. I failed. It's time I stop pretending I have the grace of the Light. I have nothing left now."

"You'll do what you think is right, of course," Chelos said. "But think hard, Blaine. I'd hate if after all this time, after all this struggle, you just gave up. I'd hate to never see the Basilica in its full glory again." Chelos took a moment to press a fist into his own back. There was a crack and he sighed in relief.

"Chelos, if I give up the blade, I don't know how long—"

"Blaine, don't you dare—"

"Goodbye, old friend. Just in case," Blaine said. He took Chelos by the shoulder and then stepped forward to embrace him. "Thank you for believing in me all these years. You will learn to place faith in another." He took his leave, lacking the strength to look back at Chelos as he left.

The stars and moon were bright enough to see by. He wouldn't draw the Guardian's Blade save for the final time. He was sure he could see where Bacchus was holding his congregation by the fiery glow some way up the lower slope of the Nail Head. Blaine traipsed towards the base of the mountain, glad to reach the woodland of birch trees and inhale the scent of leaves, of moss, of wildness; to hear the warbling song of the night birds and have the time to savour it. A sense of calm had come over him. This at least he could not fail at.

This close to a Principal Mountain, many of the birches had an odd black branch or a silver dusting to their narrow white trunks. In his state of clarity, he could almost sense the Cascade in the air and ground where it had seeped into leaf or insect. A slight swell formed from behind the door in his mind. It almost seemed to call to him, for he heard something, ever so faint, like a distant whisper carried on a light breeze.

Not now, Blaine…

But it was likely just the wind. It was so quiet out here at night. The sea still roared despite being so far away, as though in constant battle with the land. He heard it even as he climbed the Nail Head, heading towards the orange haze. The incline was steeper than he had anticipated, and after a while his calves began to burn. That he felt the exertion only proved his time was over.

Finally, he reached them all. Bacchus had formed his congregation in the shelter of a mini valley between the jagged slopes of the Nail Head. Three large braziers lit the clearing, one of which stood at the head of the crowd. A sole dark silhouette moved beside it. The golden armour of the dragons glittered brightly. Blaine quietly descended to join them, half-sliding on soft earth. As he approached the back of the crowd, Blaine paused for half a heartbeat.

I must do what is right.

Then he took a very deliberate step forward.

And he took another.

Bacchus was projecting his voice well, reaching even Blaine at the back with clarity.

"The Lord Guardian vanished for years and we suffered. He returns; we suffer still. He withdraws from us, shaken from his first real battle in decades, to spend his days with an old dragon none of us know."

"What are you saying, Bacchus?" someone called.

"I'm saying that we deserve a stronger guardian. Dwna, Dwl'or and N'weer deserve a stronger guardian. Light must be brought back into the world. The Shadow has grown dark indeed. It's touched the hearts of wizards and humans; it's lain across our homeland unchecked for twenty years. What I am saying is hard to hear, but I do it out of love for every dragon. It might be time for change."

Blaine hadn't stopped moving. He gently eased his way through the congregation. Soon the dragons were parting for him, creating a road directly to Bacchus. When he made it to the front, he stepped out, turned and faced thousands of twinkling yellow eyes.

"It is the guardian who decides when to pass the blade on," Blaine said. "It has always been this way. Through millennia, long before demons ever crawled into our world."

"None of us can remember such a time," Bacchus said. "All we've known is war and death and endless demons." There was much agreement with this from the crowd.

"The guardian has always decided," Blaine said again. With some difficulty, he took hold of the hilt of the Guardian's Blade. His grip felt weak and clumsy but he drew it out and held it high. He looked to Bacchus and the Light Bearer took a careful step back, perhaps fearing that Blaine would strike him down. Blaine did bring the blade down, with all the might still left to him, and thrust it into the earth at Bacchus' feet.

"But I am no longer fit to be guardian," Blaine said. "If this is your will, then I shall pass the mantle on. Bacchus, you may take the Guardian's Blade. I grant it to you without reservation. Only the gods themselves can object now. And if our Lords Dwna, Dwl'or and N'weer do not wish this, then I ask them for a sign."

He let go of the Guardian's Blade.

He turned his back on it.

The dragons in front of him turned, wide-eyed and fearful.

Light, purest most radiant light, began emanating from behind him. Blaine watched his own silhouette cast forwards in a dark shadow. His arm shook, though he felt no rush down it. Then came a strident cry like a hundred dying owls. He went deaf.

His shadow darkened as the light from behind grew brighter. And his breath caught in his throat. Invisible cords constricted his neck and tightened their control, suffocating him.

Is this how I die?

Something was clogging his mouth and Blaine recovered enough of his wits to spit saliva, thick and blue. The light intensified, growing so bright it removed his shadow altogether.

It is a sign!

Spinning, he faced the source of the blinding light and squeezed his eyes shut against it.

If this is truly a sign, it will not harm me.

He opened his eyes and searing pain did not come. His skin prickled as though bathed in the summer sun and a youthful vitality returned to his muscles and joints; his mind felt clear and alert. In that moment, he forgot what tiredness was. He forgot all memory of hunger. He forgot pain.

Grasping, Blaine's hand found the pommel and slid down to take the handle. He gripped it strongly and pulled the Guardian's Blade free.

His arm seared then, as though dipped in molten steel, and the world darkened. Braziers went out, even the moon and stars, as all light in the world was sucked into the blade. It held for a heartbeat in which Blaine heard a voice.

It is not yet time to give in. Never forget our power, Guardian.

Then, with the boom of a thousand powder barrels, the light radiated out in a single golden wave. Blaine watched it race to the horizon before it passed from sight. Slowly, the moon and stars returned and Blaine looked to the crowded dragons. Many had averted their eyes, crouching down and facing away. Those brave enough to turn back gawked at him, flexing their fingers as if they had felt the same freshening of their bodies. Others looked stark white, as though they'd also heard what he had.

Bacchus traipsed up beside him. "I heard a voice in my mind," he whispered. "It told me, 'It is not your time. It will never be. Never forget our power, Bacchus.'"

"And we never shall," Blaine assured him quietly. His finger was still missing but the gods had made themselves clear. He turned to the dragons assembled there and cried, "Never forget. How could we, now? Never forget!"

When next they landed on Eastguard, things went very differently. The gods favoured them with the weather, driving back the wind and rain if not completely banishing autumn's cold. Despite heavy resistance, the demons folded swiftly under the new fury of the Third legion. On the beach, in the overgrown streets of the town of Errin, at the foot of the great twisted spire, Blaine's dragons were the white-hot knife of the gods.

The humans and fairies were out there somewhere, helping however they could. But he and the Third did not need them.

Even among the shadows of the spectres' mighty construction, the dragons did not falter. This was the reward for faith, for zeal; this was why they, dragons, were the Light's own chosen.

Blaine waded in. He stopped a spectre mid-meld with an intense beam from the Guardian's Blade, obliterating the shadow in which the creature hoped to flee. He kept the light aglow at all times, embracing the burn down his arm, spitting on the face of each spectre he killed to rid the bitterness from his mouth.

Before long they were running up the rickety walkway of the spire. Blaine guessed it was there for regular demons to climb. But it was precarious and weak, cracking under the weight of armoured dragons. Blaine was forced into a Cascade-enhanced jump to hurdle a widening gap. No one else could make it. He saw a Light Bearer try, fall, and descend three storeys to the battle still raging below.

"Return and kill every demon you find," Blaine called to them. "I shall flush out the devils at the top." He continued his charge upwards. From this height, the jagged extensions to the town of Errin looked like a thicket of thorn bushes. Arrows filled the air from the Brevian forces who had finally joined the fight, their spearmen crawling up from the beaches, too far away to make any real difference. The islanders fought better, their axes rising and falling like shiny teeth. They pushed into the town at points where the Third had stormed past.

Blaine climbed higher.

A spectre with shoulder-length orange flames burst from a shadow to his side, howling with the full-blown shrillness of the insane. Blaine spun, quicker than a viper, and caught the spectre by its throat. He squeezed. The orange flames went out. A cloud of smoke puffed up as Blaine dumped the body. Nothing else tried to stop him before he reached the top.

Up here, a fierce cold wind bit at him. He waited for his foes to reveal themselves. When they did not, he flashed the Guardian's Blade brightly and cried, "Out, demons. Out, foul servants of Rectar. Out, and meet your end." From a sliver of a shadow across the platform emerged a wounded spectre. It clutched at its side, smoke rising between its fingers, and stumbled to face Blaine. It had peculiar flaming hair; short spikes, lemon yellow in colour. Blaine recognised it as the one who'd taken his finger.

"Struggling, scum?" Blaine spat.

"The Master lied to me," it said in a high, scraping voice. "Lied," it repeated, in some pain. "'I shall watch over you, Kraz. Always,' he said. I remember. You can't forget a voice like that. Not one in your mind." He grinned madly. A few teeth at the front had been chipped or knocked clean out. Blaine looked around warily, wondering if this was some trap. The spectre babbled on and Blaine doubted there was any semblance of control left to even prepare an ambush. He stepped forward, blade raised, and was within reach of the spectre when he spoke again.

"Everything's a lie," Kraz cried. "The old one lied to me as well. Curse Dukoona.

Master, curse him." Blaine halted. That name was familiar. Kraz wouldn't stop his wailing. "He tried to have me killed. Curse him for abandoning us. Lies. You lied."

"Silence!" Blaine's voice brought the spectre back to reality. Kraz focused his black eyes on him and gasped. "I will give you a quick death, wretch," Blaine went on, "if you tell me about this one you call Dukoona." He prayed that the gods would not be angry at him for talking with this spawn of the Shadow, but he had to know.

"Dukoona?" Kraz said, eyes popping. "Dukoona. The old one. He led us, led us all for years."

"And then what?"

"I know," Kraz said, unhelpfully.

"Know what?"

"Why he left," Kraz said. "Clear now. So, clear. We tried to stop him. We failed."

Blaine seized Kraz with his free hand. "Tell me why he left," he demanded, shaking the spectre. Kraz's wound smoked more profusely, smelling of rust and death.

"He hates the Master," Kraz said. "The Master told me so."

"Your own leader? Dukoona works against Rectar?" Blaine asked. This was surely some lie, something to distract or disarm him. But if it was true, then Darnuir might—

"Why?" Kraz shrieked. He stumbled back from Blaine, dripping blood. "Why, Master, have you left us to die? Did I displease you? Do you not need us?" He was stepping unwittingly close to the edge of the platform.

"Wait," Blaine said, lunging for him.

"No," Kraz screamed, swiping wildly with a conjured dark dagger. He did not stop creeping backwards. "The Master only spoke when he needed us. To use us."

Then he fell.

Blaine moved carefully to the ledge and peered over. Kraz was falling, a black speck soon lost against the writhing mass of demons and dragons below. If that was their leader, or one of them, then this battle would be over soon.

Blaine pulled back from the edge and extinguished the light on his blade. Within seconds he felt nauseous from the magic he'd used. Lack of sleep hit hard as well now there wasn't a burn of Cascade energy fuelling him. Phantom pain from his lost finger flared. Days away from that transcendent moment upon the Nail Head and his grip had begun to feel lax again. He'd have to train, or learn to switch hands; not something easily done.

For now, he stole a precious half-minute to collect his breath and let the poison drain down his arm. All the while his thoughts were fixated on Kraz's troubling words. This spectre lord, Dukoona, had gone rogue and fled east. Would he seek to cut some deal with Darnuir? His sympathetic grandson, so concerned about alliances, might very well listen. The gods would not tolerate that. He'd known

Darnuir was in no fit state to lead either, but he'd not stopped him. Another failure, but one Blaine would rectify.

I should not have let him go alone. We shall forgo rest and sail east to Aurisha with all speed.

For the idea of Darnuir meeting this Dukoona worried Blaine.

It worried him more than anything.

27

JUST ONE MAN

Garon – West of the Glen of Bhrath

Garon had not wasted his time before dawn. He sharpened his sword and dagger, brought out his bow from storage, re-strung it, checked the fletching of his arrows, trimmed them where necessary, filled his quiver, tied on his harder leather shoulder guards – making him appear about three inches broader – and splashed his face with freezing river water to awaken him and calm his nerves. The river ran in a clear ice blue down from the mountains. Its water tickled his skin in a gentle burn that washed away the dirt of his travels and left his face feeling supple and fresh. Then morning came.

A layer of mist rose to meet the soft light and reddening leaves fell in pairs from the trees of the glen. He closed his eyes and listened to the sound of lapping water. He breathed in deeply and exhaled slowly through his nose.

What should I do?

Ochnic was being restrained by the Silver Fur trolls. Marus seemed decided on appeasing Rohka, and without the dragons behind him, Garon had little sway on his own. He tapped the scroll still at his waist. *What would you do, Darnuir? What would you do, Cosmo? What's the right thing?*

Ahead, at the eastern edge of this glen, Garon saw the first waves of dragons and kazzek warriors begin to move, heading to engage the demons under cover of the morning mist. Pel had kept her fairies back; the hunters remained as well, waiting for Garon to decide. They'd need their full strength against the demons if they were to succeed. But if the demons were pushed back, they were likely to turn their full attention on the Glen of Bhrath. Ochnic's clan would be lost. His daughter killed. Garon had to decide.

'On patrol, you never leave a squad mate behind,' Cosmo's voice reminded him. 'Dead or dying, you bring them home, just as you would want to be.'

"That's well and good, Cosmo," Garon muttered to himself, "but Marus has a point. Rohka is the kazzek leader and Darnuir wants unity. It's not down to me to jeopardise that."

He paced through the heather, torn. Then he remembered it was Darnuir who had risked all to bring the humans safely from Torridon to Val'tarra. He wouldn't have been able to live with so many deaths on his hands.

'You never leave a squad mate behind.'

Ochnic is my friend, Garon thought. *He's the best of us.* And Garon made up his mind.

Half an hour later, Garon had made his plans and was approaching the Silver Fur guarding Ochnic with as much confidence as he could muster. The Silver Furs had camped by the edge of the treeline that ran towards the peak of the nearest hill. Distant sounds of battle from the east reached Garon. Marus had engaged the demons. There wasn't much time. The Silver Fur didn't seem to notice him coming. He was too busy looking in the direction of the battle, though nothing could be seen from here. He rustled around and kicked the nearby heather.

Ochnic was sitting cross-legged on the ground. His arms were tied behind a stake planted in the earth and he was still gagged.

"Why, hello there," Garon announced loudly.

The Silver Fur snorted and whipped around. "Der is no need to be here, pack leader. Der is a battle to be fightin'."

"Wouldn't you rather be out there?" Garon asked.

"My Chief of Chiefs gives me this task," said the Silver Fur. "Watch over Ochnic, Shadow Hunter, I must."

"Ochnic is no threat," Garon said. "He's just worried for his family. Let him go. Who will fight the demons harder than him?" The Silver Fur furrowed his brow in thought and Garon took the moment to check the treeline behind the kazzek.

Ochnic moaned incoherently through his gag.

Garon snapped back to the Silver Fur. "You see? He's very eager."

The Silver Fur curled his lip up to reveal his fangs. "He stays here. Rohka commands it."

"Well, I didn't expect anything different." Garon sighed. He drew out his skinning knife. "I'll just let Ochnic go myself, then."

The Silver Fur laughed, a low, guttural sort of laugh. "No further, pack leader. You Lowlanders without the golden clothes are not so strong. I don't wish to hurt you."

"You're right," Garon said. "We aren't *that* strong. But we're quite good with a bow." He looked to the treeline again and whistled loudly, a sharp, oscillating signal of the hunters: three short blasts to call an ambush. Griswald and a score of hunters materialised from behind the nearest trunks, their bows raised. Fairies flew out in a torrent of leaves from the trees as well. Pel led them down to surround Ochnic and keep him safe.

The Silver Fur was aghast. "Der's no need," he said. He grasped his tusks, crouched and bowed his head to Garon.

"No need at all," Garon said. He nodded to Pel and she cut Ochnic free. They replaced him with the Silver Fur guard.

"Rohka will be angered by dis, pack leader," Ochnic said as he nursed his wrists.

"He can't push the demons back without us," Garon said as he sheathed his skinning knife. "He'll deal with it. Now, we have to move quickly. You mentioned mountain paths into the Glen of Bhrath. Can you lead us to them?"

"I can," Ochnic said.

"What of the demons?" asked Griswald. "Paths like that in the Boreacs were steep-slanting treks with sheer drops. I don't much fancy having tae fight up there."

"We will walk high," said Ochnic. "Da demons should not notice us if dragon legate is fighting dem."

"Marus is fighting already," Garon said. He hesitated for a moment. "You must try and forgive him, Och. He is only doing what he thinks is best for everyone."

"As is Rohka, Chief of Chiefs," Ochnic said. "But not you, pack leader?"

"I couldn't bear to let you down," Garon said. "Not after we've come this far. I'm not sure I was ever cut out to lead armies and play nice in negotiations."

"But Darnuir, Dragon King, chose you," Ochnic said. Pel giggled.

"What?" Garon asked in mock indignation. "Think I was a bad choice?"

"A hunter with no experience of large-scale command?" Pel asked. "You were the perfect choice."

"I'm thinking you might have been more agreeable when you were hungry and cowed, Wing Commander," Garon said. Pel flapped her wings playfully. "Look, Darnuir is expected to lead large armies, and he never even got around to leading patrols first."

"Aye, but that's different, innit," Griswald said. "Magic sword, a wizard companion, long-lost ancient mentor figure and all that."

"Yes, a different set of rules," said Garon. "I, however, am a hunter, not a commander of armies. My experience is in hit-and-run, in quiet ambushes and toiling across hard terrain. And after coming this far you'd have to think me mad not to see this through to the end with you, Ochnic. You're our friend and we're going to save your daughter."

The troll broke into that toothy smile of his. "Glad for de help, pack leader."

"All right, then," Garon said. "Let's go join Marus. There are demons to kill."

They gathered the full might of the fairies and hunters and sped to the battle-front. As they came into view, Garon saw that Marus and Rohka had already cleared enough of a space to begin entering the mountain passageway. To the right, dragons stood in tight ranks with shields raised, holding back the demon horde in the narrowest corridor between the mountain slopes. Behind the dragons, the kazzek warriors dealt with stray demons that managed to worm their way over or around the Ninth Legion. To the left, a great archway was already materialising in the mountainside. Silver Furs were disappearing into the dark passage.

This will be our chance.

"What's the plan?" Pel asked, drawing up beside him.

"We'll need to hold the bulk of the demons here and secure this side of the mountain. I'll take around a hundred hunters with Ochnic to warn his clan. The remaining seven hundred will stay here to fight."

"What about the doorway on the other side?" Pel asked.

"Chieftain Orrock will know," Ochnic said. At the battlefront, Marus' line of dragons took a very visible step back.

"We need to move now," Garon said. "Pel, help Marus. The moment things look stable here, you fly to us and let us know it's safe for the clan to leave."

"Stay safe," Pel said, then she took off. All her flyers followed her into the sky and hovered high over the demons, waiting for the hunters to send their arrows first. The dragons took another step back.

"Hunters!" Garon cried. "Into position behind the dragons. Three volleys, then let the fairies descend." Word spread around the hunter forces and their arrows cleared some ground, enabling the dragons to inch forwards again. Garon kept close to Ochnic as they weaved through the back ranks of the battle, towards the beginnings of the mountain path. Ochnic was already leading the splinter force of hunters up it when Garon heard his name over the carnage.

"Garon. Garon, turn around." It was Marus, breathing hard as he limped to catch up. He had perhaps two score dragons with him.

"You don't look bloodied yet," Garon shouted to him.

Marus scowled. "I can hardly fight directly." He looked up towards where Ochnic was climbing. "He shouldn't be free."

"I had to do it," Garon said. He pulled out the scroll from Darnuir and threw it at Marus' feet. "Orders are to help Ochnic and *his* people in any way we can. His people are trapped on the other side of his mountain."

"That's interpreting my king's words very loosely," Marus said. "You know what he really meant. I won't be the one to cause discord between us and the kazzek. Now come back or I'll have my men take you."

"Rohka can take any anger out on me," Garon said. "Ochnic saved your life, Marus. He saved both our lives from that red-eyed huntress. We both owe him."

"I hate being reminded of that," Marus grunted.

"Let us go, and the debt's repaid," Garon said. "Give us the chance to save his only child."

Marus pressed his lips together, ruffled his brow, and ground the heel of his crutch into the damp grass. "Go," he said. Garon smiled and turned. He was about ten paces away when Marus called, "Wait!"

Garon halted. Revolved slowly on the spot. And saw Marus shuffling towards him.

"Yes?" Garon asked.

"Take care out there, human," Marus said. He grasped Garon's forearm. "Don't die on us."

Garon took the legate's arm in return. "Why, thank you, Marus. You stay alive too. Don't get any more limbs sliced open." Marus gave a stilted laugh and Garon took it to be his equivalent of a delighted roar from Griswald.

On a narrow ledge, high above the battle raging below, Garon tried not to look down. He inched carefully along the ledge on his heels, his back to the mountainside, arms pressed against it for dear life. He tried not to peer down and see where he would splatter onto the rocks, but he couldn't help a glance or two. Their combined forces had gouged a chunk from the black mass of demons now, but their advance was slowing somewhat as they spread out. Mercifully, the demons had not noticed Garon and his company's progress on the mountainside. Garon was even more grateful when the ledge widened out at a sharp turn, taking him out of sight of the battle.

Hours passed before Ochnic announced he was in sight of the Glen of Bhrath.

"Cannot waste time," he called. "Da golems work without rest."

"Golems?" Garon said under his breath. And then he saw their work. At the southern pass into the glen the earth churned. Boulders broke off the mountainsides and crashed down to form blockages or crush demons. The golems themselves stood just below the height of the surrounding trees upon limbs of dark stone webbed with blue lines like veins. Three in total, their silver eyes were the size of arched windows and they leaned forward, pressing giant hands glowing with silver-blue light into the ground.

"And I thought I'd seen all the extraordinary things the world had to offer this year," Garon said.

"Bloody hell," Griswald commented.

"Dey cannot keep dat up forever," Ochnic said. "Let us hurry."

On their descent, Garon saw the golems weren't enough to hold all the demons at bay. Many made it through the tossing earth and were met with grey-skinned warriors of the kazzek, moving sluggishly compared to others of their kind.

How long have they been fighting for? It's a wonder they can even stand up at this point.

Ochnic's own energy seemed to redouble as they entered the valley, and he started running off to where smoke was rising.

"Ochnic," Garon called, but it was no use. "Come on then," he said resignedly to Griswald and the other hunters. They followed the troll up the glen. When Garon first saw the camp, his stomach sank.

Old trolls with thinning tusks and wrinkled hide lay unmoving under the sky without shelter. The children looked thin and shivered against the cold. Their blankets were worn and damp. One group was segregated from the rest. They were paler, with patches of fur missing, and Garon feared a sickness had begun to spread.

"Now that's a sorry sight," Griswald said.

"That it is," said Garon. "I'm glad we came. Seeing this – it's what it's all about. What hunters should be all about: helping people. And I've never seen a group more in need, not even us when we were fleeing the Boreacs." Sadness and anger flared within him. He felt like crying and hitting something all at once. He looked away from the emaciated trolls and felt cowardly for doing so.

It was just so hard to see.

Ochnic was busy scanning the area, his eyes darting madly left and right, up, down, until his ears visibly pricked up.

"Papa!" a high-pitched voice squealed from amongst the refugees. "Papa."

"Cadha!" Ochnic cried. He spun madly to find her.

"Papa," came the voice for a third time and a small kazzek with short tusks like baby teeth came running into view.

"Cadha," Ochnic said, half-weeping, falling to his knees as his daughter jumped into his open arms.

"Papa," Cadha sobbed into his fur. "Miss you. Miss you, I did."

"We were needin' help," Ochnic said between planting kisses on her head. "But I back now, Cadha. I will never leave you again."

Garon felt a tremor underfoot and saw another great golem plodding through the camp towards them.

"Garon," Ochnic was calling. "Come here. Cadha, my sweet, this is Garon. He is a human who has brought many Lowlanders to help us fight da demons." Cadha looked up apprehensively to Garon, her wide, wet eyes as cold in colour as her father's. He thought she looked terrified at seeing flesh that was not hard and grey. She clung to a hairy, three-legged toy as though it would defend her from this foreign creature.

"Where's his fur?" Cadha asked.

"Same place as your papa's," Garon said. "Just not so much of it on me. I wear clothes to stay warm, see?" He tugged at his leathers. A moment passed in which the girl contemplated him, then she giggled.

"Cadha," Ochnic began, "what has happened?"

"You left," Cadha accused.

"Cadha, I had to go," Ochnic said. His daughter looked no more appeased. "Cadha, tell Papa—"

"You left," she said again, "and Chief Orrock died—"

"Orrock is dead?" Ochnic asked.

"And demons chased us, and I nearly lost dolly, and…" Her words were muffled as Ochnic hugged her close. Garon suddenly felt sorry for any delay he might have caused on their journey.

She is far too young to have been left alone. Ochnic must have believed in his mission like Blaine believes in his gods.

"I will never leave you again, sweetling," Ochnic was telling her. Father and daughter remained embraced when the golem reached them. Its enormous eyes had no pupils but it swivelled its head and tilted it downward, seeming to gaze upon Garon. It extended its boulder-sized hand, palm up. Instinct told Garon to do the same and he placed his hand upon the golem's own. His view of the world began to change: rock and stone became brighter, more colourful, more than just black and grey, and yet he could not comprehend it. He saw faint blue lines run through the hillsides, through the earth, and felt pulses from underfoot like many slow beating hearts. After a moment, a voice spoke in his mind. It sounded older than the mountains and tired in a way beyond his own comprehension.

'It has been an age since I have seen your kind, human.'

What is happening to me?

'Do not be alarmed. Our senses have joined to form this connection. What is your name?'

I am Garon. What can I call you?

'These kazzek call me the Stone Father. That will suffice. You bring warriors, young Garon?'

A hundred or so. Not many, but we'll fight hard.

'My brothers and sisters hold the southern pass but will not last.'

My hunters and I shall aid them. Can you open the mountain passage on this side and let the clan through?

'I can open it now, if the way is clear?'

No, not yet. I await word on that. Ochnic will prepare the clan to move. Ochnic? Ochnic? Oh, right, I'm talking in my mind…

Garon pulled his hand away from the Stone Father, feeling dizzy. His vision cleared, returning to a human's again, and the golem lumbered off.

"Uh, that's disorientating. Ochnic, you need to get your clan ready to move."

Ochnic, at last, looked up from hugging his daughter. "Dis I will do, pack leader."

"Right, then." He turned to Griswald and the rest of the hunters. They were a mix of Cairlav hunters, of Crescent hunters, of Boreac hunters, some of the last of his white-leathered friends. Each looked determined, likely masking fear, just as he was.

"Hunters, this is why we're here. We've got a clan of kazzek to save and a southern pass to hold. Fight harder than you've ever fought in your lives. Aim true and earn your leathers. With me!" He bolted south and they followed. No one challenged the need to help these poor creatures who were trapped, hungry, despairing and no different at heart from any human or dragon or fairy.

Amongst the woodland at the southern end of the valley they came across kazzek from Ochnic's clan, wounded and exhausted. Garon thought their defeated eyes regained a small spark when they saw the hunters coming. They didn't even question humans showing up. They just rejoiced at the arrival of aid. One ran off to inform the golems. Groans of exertion from the golems carried through the very ground. Garon felt it more than he heard it and saw trees pushed aside as two of the three golems began to fall back.

"The demons will take advantage of this," Garon called. "Into the woods. Let's set a surprise for them." He was one of the first in. Those kazzek who could still fight joined the hunters, climbing tree trunks into the canopy with all the speed of squirrels.

Drawing his sword, Garon wedged himself between two trunks and peered through the narrow gap between them. His heart pounded, his breathing increased, his fingers twitched with a nervous energy. He could just make out the final golem ahead, still maintaining a churning stretch of earth which blocked much of the pass. Yet, with two of the golems gone, a portion of the ground had become still and demons were spilling in over it.

Normally, before a fight, Garon would turn to Cosmo for a reassuring nod, just like he'd had done since he was fifteen. This time, it was hunters who caught his eye and he nodded to them, grinning in a way that only the insane or the patrol leader ever did. He could not seem downcast. He smiled just like he had to Darnuir, Balack and Eve the first time they had come across a fully grown and angry wolf; the same smile he'd seen from Cosmo, and the same one he'd seen old Captain Tael give Cosmo many years ago.

The demons drew closer.

They crossed from tossed soil to the red and yellow leaves of the woodland floor. Closer still.

A few ran past the trees Garon was pressed against.

He let another heartbeat pass. "Now," he roared.

"Get stuck in," bellowed Griswald.

Garon picked his target and came out hacking. He caught the demon and smoke spiralled upwards from the wound. He kept moving, shouldering into another. He stamped on its small foot and smashed the pommel of his sword into its howling face.

As the second wave of whooping demons reached the hunters, the kazzek descended from the trees, crashing to the earth in a blaze of knives and orange leaves. Garon felt a burst of newfound energy and battled on, rushing at the nearest demon, thrusting his sword at its neck. The demon's dying body stumbled backwards, stepping in front of a running kazzek who flipped over the demon, landed, and continued to run.

Demons kept coming and the day wore on. As the light began to fade, the death toll of the hunters steadily rose. Garon stumbled on a red-leathered body and the act of balancing himself took him out of his tempo. Suddenly, his exhaustion hit him and he found it hard to breathe in air now thick with smoke. He fell to one knee, panting. *We cannot last much longer like this.* Even as he thought it, a kazzek fell from above with two black arrows in his chest.

More demons were coming.

There were always more coming, but strangely no spectres yet.

Garon clenched his fist amongst the wet leaves and blood squelched between his fingers. He rose to meet the demons and saw he was not alone. A fairy landed and struck at two of their backs with her spear. Garon cried out from the exertion of blocking the third demon. He held it in place and the very tip of a spearhead punched through its stomach.

"Pel," Garon gasped.

"It's done," she said. "The western exit is secure. The demons are falling back."

"Fly up the glen. Tell Ochnic." She took off at once and Garon summoned what strength remained in his voice. "Back! Back now. We're getting out of here. Hey," he yelled at a passing kazzek, grabbing him by his arm. "Tell those golems we're going."

"Dey will know," the troll insisted, nodding vigorously. Garon ducked to avoid being shredded by his long tusks. Sure enough, the ground began to shake, signalling the golems were on the move.

Garon joined the stream of hunters and kazzek fleeing the area. He could no longer feel his legs, but he ran. Closer to the camp, Ochnic ran out to meet them, his daughter sitting on his shoulders.

"Lead da demons away. Da clan are still moving into de passageway."

Garon nearly collapsed at Ochnic's feet. Doubled over, he was helped up by an enormous set of hands.

"Up ye get, lad," Griswald said. Even his beard looked drenched in sweat.

"You're older than me," Garon said. "How am I the one struggling?"

"Who said I wis'nae struggling?" wheezed Griswald.

"How many of us made it?" Garon asked.

"About half," Griswald replied.

Garon supposed it could have been far worse. "We need to give the kazzek more time."

"Come," Ochnic said, bounding off towards the mountain pathways he had led them on. "We distract da demons dis way, draw dem off."

"Ochnic, what about Cadha?" Garon cried.

"I won't leave her."

"But—" Garon tried.

"Don't bother," said Griswald. "We hav'nae the time."

"No, we don't," Garon said. "I'm surprised they haven't caught up to us already." The sound of demons cackling was certainly louder than before, but not as close as it ought to have been. Garon looked back to the southern pass and realised then that only two golems were retreating with them. "Where is the third?"

"Must have stayed behind to buy us time," said Griswald.

"If only we had half its courage," Garon said.

"If only we were that big and made of rock," said Griswald. "Let's follow Ochnic. C'mon."

They did. The remaining kazzek warriors and hunters dashed up the mountain path. The last golem was doubled down at the southern pass, its feet and hands dug deeply into the earth, drawing up raw Cascade energy in luminescent pools. The blue liquid steamed and smoked, turning the grass and trees silver or burning them black in a slowly growing radius. In what seemed a final effort, the golem pressed deeper into the earth. Deep cracks appeared in its stone body. It wasn't in vain, for the ground quaked and broke in an arc before the golem, swallowing demons whole or crushing them beneath a flood of soil. Some demons still made it through, swarming over the hunched form of the golem. Garon had no idea how long the golem might last like that. Already the smoke and steam of the raw Cascade was blocking it from view.

Garon reached over his shoulder and was pleased his bow was still intact.

"Hit the demons in the flank," Garon yelled. "Draw them away from the clan."

Bowstrings twanged as quickly as the hunters could draw and release. It worked a little too well. The demons changed course to chase them.

"Move!" Garon called. "As fast as you can. Move!"

It was precarious trying to run along the narrow path with a sheer drop on the left. A full moon and starlight helped but not by much. The kazzeks' natural agility served them better than the humans. One hunter ahead stumbled and fell, tumbling out of sight.

At some point, wings buzzed overhead. "The clan is safely in the tunnel along with three golems," Pel shouted down. "The doorway is sealed behind them." The battered kazzek warriors running with Garon and the hunters rejoiced, throwing their fists into the air. "Move fast. The demons are finding their way onto these trails and we've seen spectres popping out of shadows cast by moonlight." The celebrating stopped at once.

"Thanks for the encouragement," Garon said. Pel descended to Garon's level, fluttering beside him, an arm's length off the safety of the path.

"You're welcome," said Pel quietly, not catching the sarcasm. "I'll bring more flyers back with me." Then she was off, and in his delirious exhaustion Garon had a nightmarish image of spectres emerging all along the narrow path, their dark razor-sharp swords cleaving at their ankles.

He slapped himself in the face and carried on.

An hour passed, then two. Their progress heading back was far quicker than it had been on the approach. Pressure from demons at the rear kept Garon's legs working. He could still hear the tumult of the demons. It never grew louder, but nor did it fade away, a constant reminder of what hunted them. His vision was blurring and shifting as though he were drunk. He kept focused on Cadha in front of him. She was on Ochnic's back, her little arms and legs wrapped tightly around her father.

Then something appeared below at the base of the mountain. It seemed to be a new shimmering river. No, that couldn't be right. He tried to focus on it but the golden glint stung his sore eyes. *Golden.* His mind worked slowly. *Golden — that's no river… Dragons! It's the dragons.*

"We've made it back to the other side," Garon blurted out.

"Just a little further, pack leader," Ochnic shouted back.

The path began to descend. When they were about thirty feet from ground level, Garon could make out the Ninth Legion more clearly and the fairies alongside them. Ranks of dragons ran right up to the base of the cliff face below. Many were pointing up at Garon and the others. Yet even as he looked over their allies, the glint of the dragons' armour vanished. A jagged cloud had cut across the moon and shadows spread along the mountainside. And like a drunkard suddenly forced to cope with some harsh reality or danger, Garon felt alert in an instant.

"Spectres!" came the cry.

They came up from the path underfoot just as he'd feared. They came with axes, swords and maces, swirling in purple shadows. They came like smoke caught in the wind. And they came screaming.

"Kill, kill, kill," the spectre closest to Garon screeched. "The Master calls. He caallllsss—"

Garon silenced him with a sword in the gut. More spectres were emerging from the steep slope of the mountain, sliding down towards them, shouting incoherently.

"The voice, it calls."

"In our minds."

"Killll," they screamed.

"Kill us!" one roared and even attacked another spectre.

What precious space there was on the mountain path quickly disappeared. Garon swung his exhausted arm and his sword caught on a spectre's heavy axe. Griswald boxed the spectre off the ledge but more came. The tendril of cloud blocking the moon seemed unwilling to move on.

"We are sorry," the spectres cried. "Sorry to disobey you, Master."

"Master, Master, Master," others pleaded.

"PLEASE," said another, even as it tried to skewer both Ochnic and Garon. Ochnic slashed at its throat and Garon steadied the troll with a helping hand. Cadha clung bravely to her father, not uttering a word. A spectre rose in the sliver of a shadow between them. Garon and Ochnic were shoved aside as it sprang upwards. The force of it knocked Cadha from Ochnic's back and Garon stumbled, lost his balance, and fell from the edge of the ledge.

Below, the dragons were still battling with the demons. Garon fell towards them for a second, and then a rough hand caught his forearm.

Ochnic grunted. The troll had fallen flat on his belly and was being pulled closer to the edge of the path by Garon's weight. Garon tried to swing his free hand up to grab the ledge. His fingers brushed the dirt but he couldn't gain a grip.

"Papa," Cadha yelled. Ochnic held onto them both, one in each hand, but the battle with the spectres was not over. A kazzek body fell past Garon as he tried for the ledge again.

He missed.

Ochnic wouldn't be able to hold onto them both forever, nevermind pull them both up. One of them had to fall. Garon didn't need to think it through.

"I can't make it. Let go of me."

It was the only choice he could make. And he meant it.

"Don't say dat," Ochnic said in evident pain as his chest scraped a little further over the ridge. Cadha was sobbing.

"Ochnic, don't be a damned fool. She's your daughter. She's why you did all this. Let. Me. Go."

Ochnic moaned from the effort.

Garon felt his hand slip.

"Papa, I can't hold you," Cadha wailed.

"Let me go," Garon said. "If she falls, this has all been for nothing. We came to save your people. We weren't all going to make it."

"Be quiet," Ochnic said. "Cadha, sweetling, hold me. Hold on, you must." He began pulling Cadha up, every muscle fibre on his sinewy arm shaking under the strain. Garon felt himself slip a little more and Cadha dropped her doll to grab onto her father's arm with both hands. But she wasn't strong enough to cling on and she slid down Ochnic's arm.

Garon met the troll's eyes, and his fear was plain. Ochnic's lip trembled but he unfurled his hand from Garon's arm.

"Bye, Och."

Garon let go too.

There was a great sense of freedom just falling through the night. He saw Ochnic grab Cadha with his unfettered hand. Saw him pull her up. Saw the flash of a spectre swing its sword above Ochnic, down into his back.

No!

Ochnic's hands unclenched and Cadha fell.

No. This isn't right. Only Cadha's silhouette falling after him remained visible. And the thing that caught her.

A blue streak blew by so fast Garon almost missed it. It caught Cadha, swerved wildly around and headed west, away from the fight.

That's better. That's right.

The rush of wind blocked out all other sound.

He closed his eyes.

Crunch.

Pain. There was definite pain. Lots and lots of pain. But if there was pain, he could not be dead. Not yet, at least. He was on top of something metallic and solid, and decided it was best to roll off it. His face landed on cool grass and he sighed. Even sighing hurt. Slowly, as slowly as he could, he opened one eye.

"Marus?" Garon couldn't believe it.

"Not a word, human," Marus groaned. He too was lying on the earth, spread-eagled with pieces of his crutch by his side. "Saw you lot up there. Couldn't let you die."

"I might have preferred it to this," Garon said. "I think everything is broken."

"You'll mend," Marus said.

Both of them lay there, taking laboured breaths, enjoying something close to a respite. Before long there were dragons and fairies all over them like a hot rash. Garon felt himself being lifted and carried away. Marus had fared a little better and could at least be pulled to his feet. It was a pleasant weightless feeling being carried like this. A pleasantness sorely interrupted by the appearance of Rohka. The Chief of Chiefs loomed over him as his carriers continued to bear him away from the battle.

"You went against my wishes, Garon, pack leader."

"You got your food and we saved the clan as well," Garon said. "Are my people up on the ridge? Is Ochnic —"

"I sent my Silver Furs up to aid dem," said Rohka. "As for da demons below, they're going mad. Wild. So are de spectres. Dey are dying quickly."

"Everyone wins, then," Garon said.

"Everyone but you," Rohka said.

"Well, I don't matter much," Garon said. "After all, I'm just one human. Aren't I?"

"Rest, you should," Rohka said. Starlight flashed against the metal on his tusks and he left. Garon moaned softly, though the pain wasn't so intense when his body didn't have to carry its own weight.

He closed his eyes. He did not intend to open them for a long time.

28

A SHEEP AMONGST DRAGONS

The First War between humans and dragons began at the Rump Coast, to the east of Deas. Enough sources confirm that a dragon trading galley was shipwrecked there late one autumn. Dragons claim the humans refused to feed the survivors. The humans claimed their harvest had been poor and so they had little to share with ravenous dragons. Tensions mounted and sadly, blood was spilt. A human child was supposedly the first victim. Those shipwrecked dragons were all cornered and killed in revenge, save for one who managed to flee. When he reached Aurisha with the news, war was inevitable.

From Tiviar's Histories

Cassandra – Brevia – Arkus' Palace

I know where Lord Boreac is.

Cassandra tossed and turned in bed, kicking off her sheets despite the cold night. The howling wind and lashing rain might have been blamed for disturbing her, had her mind not been racing.

I know where Lord Boreac is.

She had repeated that to herself and Oranna for days now. The words echoed in her mind as she drifted from sleep to near-sleep. In her broken dreams, the thought floated above her like a butterfly she couldn't catch. Then her hands caught it, crushed it, and its wings turned to ash.

She woke in a start.

Sitting up in bed, she rubbed her eyes, grinding the crust of her disturbed sleep away. She reached for the half-drained cup of wine at her bedside, hoping the heavy red would weigh her mind down and let her dream in peace. The windows rattled in their lattice frames. Then a more unsettling sound reached her – a baying of pain. Brackendon was not sleeping well either.

Cassandra finished off the rest of the wine. She hadn't been allowed much at the Bastion, but here she was offered it daily. She could even make demands here, have things brought to her, done for her. She'd gotten used to it quicker than she cared to admit. She'd got more used to wine as well, and after some weeks of wincing at the taste, she was enjoying it. Already, she felt more settled.

I know where Boreac is.

The words came song-like as her head hit the pillow.

She was sure; in her gut, she was sure. The trouble would be finding him amongst all the dragons. Tomorrow was her chance. There might not be another. She just had to trust that Balack would come through.

At last, she slept.

In the morning, Cassandra threw on black leathers again and pulled back her hair in a ponytail. She ate breakfast with Oranna in her colourful parlour. It was becoming a habit of theirs. Even the clash of colours had become welcoming; a burst of brightness within a gloomy palace. Thane would sometimes join them when he had slept well enough to rise early with the rest of the palace. Today was just such a morning.

"Mother," Thane said, pushing his scrambled eggs around his plate. "Will Father join us?"

"Father is busy meeting the lower houses, darling," Oranna said. "Come along. Eat up." Thane pushed a forkful of glistening egg into his mouth and chewed slowly.

"You know my stomach feels wriggly in the mornings," Thane said.

"Just have what you can manage," Oranna said.

"Arkus will be busy all day, then?" Cassandra asked.

"All day," Oranna said, her voice full of knowing. "I doubt he'll have time for anything else. Especially the dragon refugee camp."

Cassandra smiled and helped herself to another strip of bacon. The fat was perfectly seared. Arkus being kept out of the way was one part of the plan. Cassandra had been tempted to go to him and tell him everything, but thought better of it. He would not want her to go alone, and would insist on sending the hunters in force while she stayed safe in the palace. Cassandra had weighed those options but flooding the refugee camp with hunters to look for Boreac would only increase tensions there. Worse still, it might spook Boreac into fleeing further afield. The missing lord might not even be there, of course, and so a lot of effort might go to waste. Better to catch Boreac and come to Arkus bearing the fruit of her investigation all at once.

"Your talks with the houses went well, I take it?" Cassandra asked.

"Well enough," Oranna said. "The MacKenzies and the MacKinnons both think they should take the lion's share of Boreac's lands. The Erskines have agreed to bring their extensive construction assets to help rebuild the worst affected areas – for a pretty price, I will add. It's tricky, but we might be able to come to an amicable arrangement in time. Everyone feels reconciliatory and polite right now, the scoundrels."

"Mother!" Thane exclaimed. "Father says we are to be nice."

"I am," Oranna said. "But some of them must have been tangled up in the plots against us. Forgive them, Thane, but do not be so foolish as to forget." She turned to Cassandra. "More shimmer brew?"

"Please," said Cassandra. She'd need the energy. "Thane, could you pas—" But Thane had already taken up the pot and was at Cassandra's side in an instant. He began to pour, filling the cup dangerously close to the brim.

"Is that enough, Cassandra?" Thane asked brightly.

"Perfect," Cassandra lied, cautiously taking a sip to lessen the chance of a spillage. Thane beamed then returned to his breakfast, attacking it with a little more gusto than before. Cassandra couldn't help but feel a pang for him whenever he took ill – a protectiveness she had never felt before.

"I should take my leave," Cassandra said. "Thank you again, Oranna."

"For the breakfast? Nary a thought, child. Don't mention it. Go on now and be safe."

"For all your help, as well," Cassandra said. "Goodbye, Thane." The prince waved at her with a slice of toast dangling from his mouth.

The parlour door opened just as she was reaching for it. Gellick's tall frame loomed on the other side of the doorway. He pulled himself back in a great show of humility, bowing his head and saying, "Princess," ever so solemnly as she walked by. She heard him step inside the parlour after she left.

Down in the palace courtyard, Cassandra waited for Kymethra, but after twenty minutes of feigning interest in the artful work of the hedge trimmers, she moved on. She slunk casually out of the palace grounds without anyone paying her a passing notice. Brevia was quiet now that the troops had sailed. Many soldiers were still in the Dales, leaving only the hunters to keep watch on the dragon refugee camp. As the camps sprawled, the nerves of those inside the city strained. The people of Brevia had drawn a collective breath. Waiting.

The quicker the war is over and the dragons can go home, the better. For everyone.

To her relief, Balack was already waiting at the southern gates, surrounded by a baggage train to support a small army and an eclectic entourage – hunters and huntresses, merchants and giggling admirers. Balack stood a little apart from them all, looking nervous.

"Quite the retinue you have these days," Cassandra said.

"The extra hunters are to help keep order," Balack said. "And many of the city's traders were interested in helping me in this endeavour."

Cass thought them sycophants hoping to absorb a splash of the honour and prestige now associated with Balack. At least they were helping, she supposed. A beefy man with a red face in a red doublet smiled hungrily beside a stacked cart.

"If nothing else, the poor dragons will eat a little better today," Cassandra said.

"Humans need to eat as well," Balack said. "If this keeps up for long, even the palace will have to start rationing."

"Well, I'll live. It's not the dragons' fault they're stuck here like this."

"It might not be so drastic if Arkus hadn't issued an open invitation for them to sail home." Balack stepped closer to her then and glanced quickly around before continuing. "Arkus may well have made a mistake. He's trying to appease the Assembly, but such a huge migration to Brevia is putting the city under pressure. Lord Esselmont says that his harvest in the Crescent will fall short with all the damage and disruption."

"Yes, the kingdom is a wreck," Cassandra said. "We'll just have to pull through it. Complaining won't help, nor will blaming it all on the dragons."

"I know, but it's easy for people to blame others, as it was for me." He turned to look at the city gates, staring intensely, as though seeing through the iron and wood to the refugee camps. "Arkus won't be pleased when he finds out what I've done. But I want to help. I find myself without my home as well. The Boreac Mountains are deserted, the people I knew dead or scattered. I won't claim to have it as hard as the dragons out there, but I can sympathise with them, I think. I should have done so sooner."

Cassandra looked at him when he turned back to face her; really looked. Under all the pampering, Balack was hurting. His eyes gave it away. They lacked their full colour and he seemed distant within them, as though still tethered to the sorrow and pain of his recent heartbreaks.

"You're doing the right thing now," Cassandra said. "And don't worry about Arkus. If I find Boreac, he won't care."

Balack nodded. "I hope you're right. You should have told me sooner. We need to get that ridiculous engagement cancelled."

Cassandra gasped in mock anger. "You'd reject your princess in such a manner?"

"I know how hard you can slap a man," Balack said. "I just wouldn't feel safe,

Your Highness. Besides, you wouldn't want me. Too many damned issues of my own to sort out." He smiled, then stepped back, put two fingers between his teeth and whistled loudly. The cogs above, twice the size of cartwheels, began to grind with the effort of moving the enormous gates.

An hour later, they were at the centre of the refugee camp. A podium had been hastily thrown up at Balack's request. Grim-faced dragon after grim-faced dragon had gathered with an eerie stillness. Most were female, with children following dutifully at their heels. The few men were the old or wounded, scowling from their loss of dignity. Cassandra felt a tension here as well. It wasn't the quietly brewing fear inside of Brevia, but a grief at fallen pride.

They were bitter, these dragons, and it only intensified each day. They'd been sent from Val'tarra by Kasselle or travelled of their own volition, all under the promise of going home. Instead, they'd been penned in. The number of hunters out in force for Balack couldn't be helping. It gave an impression of herding animals. At least this stunt was having the desired effect. The city-sized camp was pooling in the centre with the promise of food, dragging even the most distant dragons in. After the night's storm, the chill morning and freshly sodden ground, some thought of relief would be welcome. If Boreac was indeed here, she reckoned he would stay well away. There were too many hunters, who, as far as he knew, could be chasing him down.

Balack took to his stage, not as confidently as he had been doing for human audiences. There was no Arkus to back him now, no resplendent chevaliers to add glamour. The eyes of the dragons looked not to him but to the sacks, carts and barrels collected behind him.

"I have been called the 'Hero of the Bastion'," Balack began. He'd grown skilled in projecting his voice and it carried towards the back where Cassandra was lurking. "But I did not storm the walls alone. How could I? It was dragons who took the walls, who fought on them, bled on them, bled for us all."

Arkus would not like this at all. Cassandra wondered whether the hunters cared, whether they would trip over each other to report it to the king or his chevaliers. *I'd better find Boreac after all this or I'll find a white gown and veil in my room at the first opening in Arkus' schedule.*

Something sharp nudged at her ankle.

Cassandra felt relief at seeing Kymethra behind her. The witch would be invaluable in covering the camp quickly. Cassandra held out her arm and Kymethra settled there, delicately placing her talons into the thick leather vambrace. The weight made Cassandra's knees buckle before she gained her balance. Kymethra's big bird eyes looked imploring at her.

"I'm glad you came," Cassandra told her. Kymethra opened her beak and tilted her head playfully. It sufficed for a smile. "Are you feeling up to it?" Kymethra nodded. It was singularly strange to see a bird make such a movement. The witch lifted a wing and stretched it to its impressive length behind and around Cassandra's head. *Is this a hug?* There were equal white feathers to brown now, but they were soft, comforting, like the taste of butter on hot bread.

"I forgive you," Cassandra said through a mouthful of feathers. She ran a finger down the back of Kymethra's head and the witch closed her eyes in some pleasure. Afterwards, Kymethra pulled her wing back, snapped her beak happily, and turned with those penetrating eyes to stare across the camp.

"Look for any man on his own," Cassandra said. "He'll be older and likely staying as far away from the hunters as he can."

Kymethra took off in a flurry of beating wings and Cassandra began her search the only way she could. One tent at a time. One row at a time.

Most of them were empty, but some were occupied by women with infants or newborns at their breasts. Cassandra hoped someone would bring them some of the food. One growled, low and threatening like a mother wolf when Cassandra peeped behind the tent flap. Cassandra ducked out immediately, hardly wishing to come to blows with a dragon. Two children passed her looking especially dishevelled, their clothes ragged with neglect and dirt, and their bodies were little better. Thin, with wild hair and sharp long nails, the children looked feral, staring at her as though sizing up a meal.

Poor half-starved things. Are their parents even here? Are they even alive?

"Haven't seen an older human wandering around, have you?" she said. They just gazed blankly at her. *I guess not, then.* "You should follow the crowds," Cassandra told them. "There will be food. Here," she added, tossing them the oat biscuits from her ration pouch. The children descended greedily upon them. Within seconds the biscuits had been devoured.

"There." One of them pointed through the camp to the south-east. "A white-haired man. He doesn't run so fast when the food comes."

"And he stumbles in the dark," said the other. Then they scampered off. Cassandra looked to the sky and waved her arms around. Kymethra eventually saw her and she descended, blowing a rush of air over Cassandra's head before landing in front of her.

"Try the south-east portion," Cassandra said. "If those children were right there is at least one human there." Kymethra cocked her head at her. "What? We don't have many other leads." The witch snapped her beak and took off again.

Cassandra wove her way towards where Kymethra was flying. Already there were dragons returning from the rally, looking disgruntled, perhaps at a failure to secure more food or let down that the announcement was not for ships to take them home.

She didn't think Balack would have finished so soon but neither could he keep them all interested for long.

Come on, Kymethra. Find him.

As though hearing her plea, Kymethra let loose a shrill squawk and dove downwards. Cassandra's brisk pace turned into a jog and then a sprint as Kymethra's cries grew louder. She covered herself in wet mud as she splashed through dirty pools. She leapt over tent pegs and cookpots, over ash-grey dead fires and bedrolls exposed to the elements. Kymethra rose out of the sea of mismatched cloth and hovered over one spot. Breathing hard, Cassandra arrived beside Kymethra, now in her human form.

"I got a bit overexcited," the witch said. "He got a fright and ran inside." The tent before them looked thoroughly dishevelled. It was greyed with time, patched and no longer taut; the very worst of the old ruined stock the hunters were handing out.

"I'm certain it was a human," Kymethra said. "He was slow and weighed down carrying a sack, as though his whole life was inside it."

"Might well be," Cassandra said, puffing slightly, "if it is him, of course. That, or you've just scared some poor old dragon half to death."

"Shall we?" Kymethra said.

"You keep watch," Cassandra said. *We don't need a repeat of last time.* Kymethra nodded slowly and did not protest. "If anyone seems to be heading this way, give three sharp screeches," Cassandra added. Kymethra morphed back into the eagle and took flight.

Carefully, Cassandra approached the tent at a crouch, then lay down at the edge of the material. She gently lifted a section of the tent wall. It was empty save for the brown sack near the back. Boreac might be a smart man, but he couldn't have been used to anything physical like this, not least because she was sure she could hear his panicked breathing from the corner to her left.

Waiting with something heavy or sharp to strike me with?

She inched silently along the ground and lifted the tent wall just enough to glimpse the soles of some bare feet. Then she heard a foolishly loud sigh of relief from the owner of the feet. Cassandra sat back up in a crouch, drew out her sword, and then struck hard with the flat of her blade at where she thought the knees would be.

There was a heavy grunt of pain and Cassandra doubled back and barged in the tent's entrance. She was on him then, pinning him with pressure to the small of his back and twisting an arm up behind him. He had white hair as the children had described. It was thick, but matted and filthy. Entire tufts had fallen away. His face was cleanly shaven although she spotted several small bristles under his jawline.

"Lord Boreac?" Cassandra whispered into his ear.

"If you're here to kill me, then be done with it," Boreac muttered. At least, that was what Cassandra thought he said. His speech was muffled with his mouth half full of grass.

"Oh, no. The king wants you for trial."

"Dranus' hide he does."

"He was quite insistent on finding you." She took both his hands and bound them together with a strand of strong silver silk. She moved to do the same to his feet.

"I'm not going to run," Boreac said. "I'm too old to try and outpace you and I have no weapons to speak of. Wouldn't have gotten into the camp otherwise."

That's true enough. "What's in the sack?" she asked, eyeing it up.

"The last scrounged-up possessions of a fleeing man," said Boreac. "Some clothes, some trinkets of my ancestors—"

"Some papers on the suspicious death of a hunter captain?"

"Found Foulis, did you? Look, why don't you let me sit upright and you can fling accusations at me in a more civilised manner?"

Cassandra increased the pressure on his back. "Don't try anything."

"I assure you I am too old, too tired and too weak to attempt much."

"No sudden moves," Cassandra said, keeping a hand on the hilt of her sword just in case. She stood up and allowed Boreac to rustle himself upright. With the entrance flap shut, the tent was dim inside, but the material was worn so thin that a gloomy light seeped through. Aside from the brown sack, there was only an aged bedroll, another handout from the Master Station.

On the ground, Boreac groaned again. His dirtied tunic was torn in places and vibrant purple-blue bruises were visible on his shoulder. Every muscle was defined due to his emaciated flesh and the smell was quite potent, like vomit outside a tavern on a hot morning. He tilted his neck to one side and there was a crack like breaking stone.

"Gahh," he gasped. "It's crick after crick sleeping this rough."

"How long have you been out here?"

"When did the Bastion fall?"

"Just over two months ago."

"Then that long," Boreac rasped. Cassandra unclipped the waterskin at her belt and threw him it. "Thank you," he said, taking two long gulps and dribbling some of it down his chin. "That's a kindness."

"We're being civilised," said Cassandra. He chuckled and took another sip of water. "The sooner you come with me, the sooner you can regain some of your dignity with a bath and clothes."

"Give an old man a moment." He stretched out his legs lethargically, seeming utterly disinterested in the idea of movement. "I didn't think I'd be found here. Reckoned the camp would be a blind spot for Arkus."

"Arkus doesn't know," Cassandra said. "Not yet, anyway. I might never have guessed you were here had you not told Foulis you intended to go to the dragons. That was your biggest mistake."

"I was in a rush," Boreac said. "And how did you find Foulis? We were careful about him."

"There was a scrap of a letter in your fireplace."

"Hmmm," Boreac mused. "This is my first grand escape. I was bound to slip up."

"You didn't have a plan in place to flee?"

"All our plans were ruined the minute Castallan died," Boreac said. "And you know, I'm glad he's dead. I planned to stop one man gaining too much power and instead helped one far worse – one far less predictable. What poor choices I have made."

"You haven't asked me who I am."

"Does it matter?"

"I might be able to have you treated better. If you're cooperative." Boreac looked at her properly for the first time, squinting in the gloom of the tent.

"Ah," he sighed, realising. "There is much of Ilana in you. We were close once, your mother and I. Once I would even have named Arkus a friend. How times change. Here I am, defeated, and here you are, looking so much like her. Yet I feel there is more Arkus in you than your appearance would suggest. You're clearly cunning and resourceful, just like him."

"Is that an insult?"

"Far from it," Boreac said. "Although it depends on whom you ask these days. Once, your father was a good man, if not a great prince or king."

"Or so you say," Cassandra said.

"Believe what you wish. He changed when Ilana died."

"Are you a good man, Lord Boreac?"

"No more or less than most, I'd wager," Boreac said. "What did you do with poor Foulis in the end?"

"I agreed to forget all about him," Cassandra said. "He can go on living a normal life. You're the real prize."

"I assume there's no way to persuade you to just forget about me as well?"

"Wouldn't count on it."

"Such loyalty to a man you barely know."

"I didn't do it for Arkus. I did it for me. That would have been enough. But I've seen the trail of broken people that your failed revolution has left and I was there at the heart of the Bastion. So many died because of you. So many lives ruined."

"Arkus has ruined lives as well," Boreac said.

"Not in the same way."

"More slowly, perhaps. Less obviously," Boreac said with an exaggerated shrug.

"Still, he has been just as ruthless. Houses rise and fall on his whim. Forgive me if I wanted to be on the right side of a power shift."

"The Assembly holds much power," Cassandra said. "We aren't like the dragons."

Boreac raised his eyebrows. "I forgot you were an expert, having arrived in the city two months ago. You may not believe me, but it's true. Each year Arkus takes more control – subtly, of course. Oh, he's very good, but taking power and influence still; a little here, a little there. There's no use in an Assembly that is under the king's thumb and I'm afraid our failure has only accelerated that. What?" he added, smiling at Cassandra's confusion. "You don't think I'm right?"

"You're all just power grabbers," Cassandra said. "Are you trying to say that Castallan would have shared power equally?"

"You make a fine point," Boreac said. "Getting caught up with the wizard was a mistake as well, but Scythe and Annandale got more radical as the years went by. They began listening to Castallan and blamed the dragons more and more. They were an easy scapegoat, I suppose. It worked so well because there is a grain of truth to it. But Dranus take them for their bloodshed. I never wanted it to come to that. I wanted to fight Arkus at his own game, stop him upending our world to forge his new one. He's won now, though."

"Unless you get to the dragons," Cassandra said. "That's why you're here. Do you really think Darnuir will listen to this tale you're weaving for me?"

"There is always a chance the dragons will see how far they can kick my head from Aurisha's plateau. My actions have condemned me, but what I have to tell them should save me. I'm confident of that."

"Which has got something to do with Captain Morwen, black powder, and this," Cassandra said, pulling out the little lead sphere. It left a trail of dark grey on her skin where she rolled it between her fingers.

"From my lockbox?" Boreac said.

"You must have dropped one. Why would Darnuir care about this?"

"Because it could mean a change in power across this world like we've never seen before," Boreac said. "And with the dragons already weakened, it could mean—"

A sharp screech came from outside. Cassandra turned to face the tent entrance and heard Kymethra's piercing cry two more times.

She rounded on Boreac. "Help coming for you?" Her stomach sank. Boreac might have been keeping her talking on purpose.

"No one knows I'm here, I swear it."

"Get back, then," she ordered and Boreac hobbled to his feet and stepped back, closer to his precious sack of goods. Cassandra resisted drawing her sword. If it were hunters on patrol, they might just pass by.

She tried to calm herself. *That's all it will be, surely?*

Voices were muttering outside now. They weren't moving on.

Stay calm.

"Definitely the witch," a man's voice said.

"Stay out here in case she lands," said another. "We'll go in."

Cassandra drew her sword as five hooded figures entered the tent. Black cloaks hid their bodies, but links of chainmail slithered out from their sleeves and a glint of dark steel was visible at their collars.

"Not with you?" Boreac asked.

"Not with me," Cassandra said.

"Put your sword down, Princess," the lead man said coolly. "You aren't going to die for him."

He was right. She couldn't win this fight. A scuffle came from outside and then the last hooded man joined them, Kymethra in tow. Her hands were bound behind her, a cloth gag had been shoved into her mouth and a long dagger pressed lightly at her back. Kymethra looked to Cassandra, her eyes pleading. She could almost hear the witch's thoughts of *"Magic! Let me use my magic."*

But it wouldn't help.

Cassandra might take one, maybe two, and Kymethra another, but there were six opponents in this cramped space. No room to move. They wore armour and she did not. And Boreac's life wasn't worth her own. She'd caught him. The deal with Arkus was done.

Cassandra dropped her sword on the grass.

"Wise move," said the lead man. He drew back his hood to reveal his dark blond hair and pristine skin. Gellick smiled at her. "You've done very well, Cassandra. Your father will be pleased."

"Gellick Esselmont," Lord Boreac said with disdain. "Unsurprising to see you padding alongside Arkus like a good pup. Quite young to be positioned so close to the king."

"He needs men he can trust," Gellick said. "You've proven false, Geoff Boreac. A pity. I always enjoyed attending your feasts as a boy. Your cooks had a way with guinea fowl."

"You've been following me?" Cassandra asked.

"Dranus' hide, no," Gellick said. "Someone like me would have drawn too much attention. You said it yourself. You could do this because you aren't known yet. We only knew where you were today because Queen Oranna came to me in confidence. She was worried for your safety, Princess. Asked us to keep an eye on you. We nearly lost you in this dragon cesspit but Kymethra conveniently flew overhead for us. And, well, this will make matters cleaner than back at the palace."

"Cleaner how?" Cass said.

Gellick smirked. "I must ask you not to scream. Do you promise, Princess?" But he didn't give her time to answer. "Do it," Gellick barked. One of the chevaliers pulled out a slender knife, stepped up to Lord Boreac and stabbed him in the gut. Boreac's wheeze of surprise faded as he fell into the fabric of his killer's cloak. The knife plunged wetly for a second time.

Cassandra stepped forwards. "No!" She looked to her sword, bent to pick it up, but Gellick's steel-encased foot weighed it down. He hoisted her up by the leathers at the nape of her neck and flicked out his own dagger, pointing it at her.

"I said no screaming."

29

RETURN TO AURISHA

For those not fortunate enough to have journeyed to the dragon capital, allow me a moment to describe its splendour. Everything gleams there, from the stone at night to the eyes of dragon children, so comfortable and assured in the most powerful city of the most powerful people in the world. Contentment is high and life is stable. Lemons, plums, figs, quinces, melons from the peninsula, and every sort of nut and grain overflow in their markets. Smells of cooking meat are often on the air, though that does not please my tastes as much. Every home and street is spotless.

From Tiviar's Histories

Darnuir – West of Aurisha

Every mile to Aurisha had been with plagued with demons. They put up little resistance, but they were still in the way. Each time Darnuir thought to deviate their direct southern route the demons would harry them, just enough to get them to move onwards, closer to the city. It seemed Dukoona wanted them to reach Aurisha in good time. He wanted it badly.

Darnuir thought his heart would swell when he laid eyes upon Aurisha, but he was disappointed. He didn't feel anything. He just saw a city he had to take. It didn't feel like it could be or should be home. The plateau still commanded the landscape, and the walls were still high and thick, fanning protectively around the northern edge of the city from shore to shore. But it was the demons that stirred emotion in him. Their host sat idly outside the walls, uncharacteristically still.

I must be wary. I must try to think clearly. One false move and twenty thousand lives will be on my hands. His head throbbed with want of the Cascade. His fingers twitched, longing for his sword, to enter battle, to let the power flow. With a great effort, he shoved the impulse down and took a drink from his waterskin to cool his urges. Something of his struggle must have shown on his face for Raymond looked down in concern from atop his horse, Bruce.

"Are you not exhilarated to gaze upon your ancestral home?"

"Brevia might be the black city," Darnuir said, "but Aurisha looks dead."

"Your people will return Aurisha to her former glory," Raymond announced, clenching his fist dramatically. "Why, look, the demons have been gracious enough to leave the gates open."

"Not open but broken," Damien said. The outrunner was sitting down, rubbing his bare feet. He had been tireless in scouting ahead on their march south.

"Broken suits us fine," Darnuir said. "We can walk straight in."

"There are a lot of demons barring our way," Lira said.

"Sixty thousand at a rough gauge," Damien said. His thumb reached a particularly tender spot under the arch of his foot and he sucked through his teeth in pain.

Lira looked to him. "Are you all right?"

"I'll get back up, Prefect Lira." Despite his smile of assurance, he sounded strained. "We're so close to home now. Then I can rest."

"Outnumbered three to one, however," Raymond mused.

"We faced those odds at the Charred Vale," Darnuir said. "But there we had no choice. One lucky chance cannot stand as the basis for our plans. I've driven us on into this, but that does not mean we should hastily press further." He glanced to Lira for confirmation but she did not acknowledge him.

"The demons have offered precious little fight so far," said Raymond. "Practically asking to be slain."

"That does not negate the possibility of some ruse or feint," said Lira. "Lure us here, let us drop our guard or our senses, then crush us."

"I agree," Darnuir said. "Although it is likely such a move has cost them the Splinters. If it's all to try and reel me in, then it would be a foolish move. As foolish, I dare say, as chasing an army triple your size on a hunch alone."

"Some would call it bold, sire," said Damien. "The men respect your audacity. Your father lost too much of that in his later years."

"And gained too much caution. I'm aware," said Darnuir. "My former self certainly thought so, but then he got himself killed in the end. Following my old self's example would not be wise." But he'd like it. He'd rather have the fight there and then, of course, as his thumping head reminded him. His right arm began to shake and he tried to hide it by tucking it close to his body under his cloak. Lira met his eye then but held something back through flattened lips. He pretended as though nothing untoward had occurred. "A part of me wants to believe that we could walk up to the gates and be welcomed in, but if Dukoona truly wished to meet with me then he could have come himself already."

"What is to be done, then?" asked Raymond.

"Nothing for now," Darnuir said. "I need time to think."

Dukoona – Aurisha

"I cannot see them from here," Sonrid said. "Forgive my poor eyes, my lord."

"Neither Kidrian nor I can see them," Dukoona said. "It is just nice to get out of the Royal Tower on occasion. A change of view."

"They are out that way, I assure you," Kidrian said. "Less than a day westwards, still close to the sea." Sonrid gripped the edge of the balcony and gingerly hoisted himself up on his toes to peer out west. The bottom tier of the city was hundreds of feet below, a sheer drop from this terrace, which protruded from the face of the plateau. Many of Aurisha's fine homes had such balconies. This one had a table and a set of chairs, beaten roughly by years of wind and rain. Dukoona imagined dragons sitting here, eating supper, peeling a grape or picking at olives, and watching day fade to night. Now he watched to see if Darnuir would come.

"We did not manage to kill enough demons," said Dukoona. "More should have died to tempt Darnuir to seize the city."

"They've been crawling along since their landing," Kidrian said. "It's been rather vexing."

"I imagine it seems to them too good to be true," Dukoona said. "I'd move our forces well away, but that would look even more suspicious, and not only to the dragons." Rectar's vast presence had paid fleeting glances in Dukoona's direction. They had usually been harassing the dragon army during those times, so it had always looked good. However, were Rectar to glimpse the dragons inside Aurisha while sixty thousand demons ran merrily in the opposite direction, a passing glance would quickly become a fixation.

"Why not just send the demons to attack?" Sonrid asked. "Get it over with. Let them die."

"My dear little Sonrid," Dukoona said. "You cannot control our mindless cousins at the best of times so you won't understand how hard it is when they are whipped up into a battle frenzy."

"Especially that many," Kidrian said.

"Many more dragons would die than we now wish," Dukoona said.

"So all we can do is send smaller groups?" Sonrid asked. "Like we have been doing?"

"For now, that will have to suffice," said Dukoona. "Kidrian, send one hundred demons every hour towards their camp and empty the city of every demon. Make a big show of it. Let's see if we can provoke them into an attack."

"Yes, my lord," Kidrian said. He placed a hand into a nearby shadow, submerging most of his forearm, but hesitated. The purple fires on his head had dimmed.

"What troubles you?" Dukoona asked.

"Even if we manage this and Darnuir comes, and takes the city, what then?" Kidrian said. "He might simply kill you."

"I'll ensure there are plenty of shadows. He'll find me hard to kill."

"The Master, then," said Kidrian hurriedly. "One day he'll find out. And then what?"

"I'd have it so Rectar does not find out until it is too late," Dukoona said. "But should the worst happen, then I hope the punishment does not last for eternity." He took Kidrian by his shoulder, squeezing hard, and the shadows of his flesh swirled energetically underneath. "We will be free."

Kidrian nodded then melded fully into the shadow on the balcony.

Darnuir – West of Aurisha

Darnuir scooped up the last fistful of silver alderberries from the deep copper bowl and rammed them into his mouth. He chewed frantically and swallowed. His armour had felt suffocating, so he'd taken it off, but his white shirt clung to him with cold sweat. He paced in his tent. Up then down, up then down, to his bed, back to the table. He needed an answer to their plight but he couldn't think. He needed the Cascade. Just one drop. In a nervous fidget, he reached for the empty bowl.

"No," he wailed. "No, no, no..." Unabashed, he licked the bowl, covering every inch with his tongue, tasting nothing but the tang of metal. In a rage, he bent the bowl out of shape and hurled it. The crumpled copper hit his armour stand with a clatter.

Sucking in choked breaths, he surrendered. He could barely keep his hands still, yet he forced one onto the hilt of the Dragon's Blade. He nudged the door open in his mind. And he sighed. During one, long, luxurious exhale through his nose, he closed his eyes to enjoy the relief. His throbbing head ebbed away. All his troubles seemed to—

"Darnuir," Lira said. Her voice was like needles in his ears. "Stop."

"I can't," he whispered. Then he felt her hand fall bravely upon his own. He opened his eyes and looked at her. She wasn't afraid.

"You must," she told him. The memory of standing over her during their landing, a stroke away from killing her, brought a wave of shame. It was strong enough to out-burn his need for magic. Each finger suddenly felt made of rock and protested as he unfurled his grip. With a great effort, Darnuir released his hand, drawing on a last quick stream of power before his pinkie left the hilt.

"Can I at least get more silver alderb—"

"You've eaten them all," Lira said. "They aren't easy to find, you know."

"I'm sorry. I know I keep having to say that lately, but I am. I'm not so stubborn that I can't admit fault."

"Our people need a king with a clear head."

"I know. But there is little I can do about it right now. I can't cleanse myself of it before the war is over, before we are on the other side of Aurisha's walls." He breathed heavily again.

"The demons came again," Lira said after a few moments. "On the hour, just like the last five."

"Think we could kill them all if we waited long enough?"

"Do you think you could wait that long before offering battle?" Lira asked. He didn't have to answer. "He's baiting us. It reminds me of tracking this huge silver dire wolf back in the Hinterlands. We were used to setting traps for white wolves from the Highlands that strayed too far when hunting. White wolves can be large, but this silver one was something else entirely. We stalked it, laid out meat to lure it away from the villages and quarries, but it didn't run back north. Once a civilian lost their life, we had no choice. But killing it wasn't easy. I think it enjoyed the sport. It was fast enough to grab the carcasses and bolt before we could take clean shots. Some of us were brave enough to wear extra padding and plate armour and stand near our offerings to catch it that way. Obviously, it didn't come close then.

"Eventually, we took down all the game in the area. The wolf started to grow hungry. And as it grew hungrier it dared to come closer, a little more each day. Finally, it couldn't wait anymore and came for its food. Even with the iron traps in its hind legs, more than twenty arrows and two spears, it still killed those brave men in the armour. Its teeth could bite through the steel. But it got hungry and it came at us and it died."

"Are we the wolf in this scenario?" he asked hoarsely, abruptly aware of how dry his throat was. He looked to his jugs but he'd drunk all the water as well.

"You're the wolf," she said. "You said it yourself. You're craving the fight to draw on magic. How long until you grow too hungry?"

"Not long at all. I can't think straight. I don't trust myself to make decisions anymore."

"I've always thought that had the wolf run away, we would have chased it," Lira said. "If you're the wolf then the demons will follow."

His head was pounding again. "We should run from Aurisha?"

"Not all of us," Lira said. "We'll do something the silver beast could not. We'll split in two."

Dukoona – Aurisha – The Royal Tower

Dukoona was lounging on the throne of the dragon king, his head dangling over one stone armrest, and his legs stretched out across the other. Many of the Trusted were with him, waiting. Sonrid crouched at the base of the stairs to the throne.

Most spectres were out with the demons, trying to keep them in line. They were growing restless; Dukoona could feel their agitation even atop the plateau. He wondered if Rectar would be able to feel it soon, all the way over at Kar'drun. If his master checked in now things would not look good at all, but Dukoona tried to keep his fears to himself and not worry his spectres.

"Have any of you ever wondered what it would be like to eat?" Dukoona asked the room at large. The two dozen or more spectres in the room all looked taken aback.

"It is an advantage not to require regular provisions," one spectre said. "We do not need to stop or rest."

"An advantage to whom, though?" Dukoona asked. "It makes us better killers, better soldiers, but does it make our existence any better?" No one answered. "I feel we're missing out on the ability to taste. Humans, fairies and dragons gain some pleasure from it."

"A temporary pleasure," another spectre said.

"I once found killing to be a temporary pleasure," Dukoona said. "A brief glimmer of satisfaction. Do you think it is the same feeling?" Again, no one answered. "I'm not seeking a definite answer, I merely—"

"My lord," came the croak of Kidrian. He sprang from a shadow upon the wall, landing in a kneeling position. "The dragons are moving."

Dukoona flicked his legs around and jumped to his feet. "Do they approach the city?"

"They stole a march in the night when our melding is hindered," Kidrian said. "Heading north, my lord." All the spectres present growled low at the news, a mixture of excitement and disapproval.

"North," Dukoona repeated quietly. "How many?"

"Seven dragon standards were seen," Kidrian said. "It could be all of them."

"To what end, I wonder?" Dukoona said. "Send our army in purs—"

He felt it then – a burning at the back of his mind; the feeling of being watched, magnified a thousandfold. Rectar was glancing his way.

"My lord?" Sonrid said in concern.

"Send our army in pursuit of the dragons," Dukoona said, forcing confidence into his voice. He could not let them know. "And reserve five thousand demons inside the city in case of any trickery on the dragons' part," he added, looking right at Kidrian as he gave the order, willing him silently to understand, to not ask questions. For a nervous second, Dukoona thought Kidrian would not realise what was happening. Rectar's gaze was lingering.

"At once, my lord," Kidrian said, bowing his head deeply, overly so. He had understood.

"Go," Dukoona told them. As the spectres melded away, Rectar's piercing presence left him as well. They had made it through another passing glance. Dukoona hoped it would be enough.

Darnuir – West of Aurisha

Half a morning's march north from camp, Darnuir awaited news on the demons. He stood with Raymond and five Praetorians, armed with sword and bow, neither in sight of Aurisha nor the sea, under the shading of a small collection of stone pines. These trees were the sad remains of a larger area the demons had likely cut down for their ships. With clear skies, the land was free of shadows cast by clouds, meaning the fear of spectre attacks was minimal. Still, the wait was dragging on and Bruce flicked a hoof impatiently, sending up a muddy-red dust cloud.

I know how you feel.

Raymond comforted his steed by gently scratching his great neck.

Darnuir was still itching for magic, and he absentmindedly ground his foot into the dirt as a poor means of release. More reddish, dusty earth puffed up. Beneath the grass, much of the land was cracked, like dry lips. The closer they were to Aurisha, the more the land appeared in that condition.

"There," Raymond announced, pointing and elevating himself on his stirrups. "I do believe it is Damien." Sure enough, the outrunner materialised within the minute, pelting at a great pace from the north.

"Take a moment to find your breath," Darnuir said.

Damien groaned. "No need, sire." His feet were swollen.

"Damien, I do not require you to run yourself to death."

"It's just my time approaching, sire," Damien said. "Runners don't last forever, and there's fewer of us now, so we're each doing more."

"Soon we'll have our city and you can rest," Darnuir said. "You've earned far more."

Damien smiled painfully. "Once we've won back our home, I hope to start a farm down on the peninsula."

"You would choose the life of labour?" Raymond said.

"Better than my feet becoming bloody stumps."

"You shall have your farm," Darnuir said. "Now, as for the demons?"

"It's working. The host chases Prefect Lira. They are now well removed from the city."

"A fine plan," Raymond said. "I just hope holding back an extra legion's worth of dragons does not cause Lira any more danger."

"She just has to take the demons as far from the city as she can," said Darnuir. "After two days, they are to wheel about and return to the city with every ounce of speed and strength left to them. As for our extra men, I thought it a prudent measure."

"Well, I shall not complain to have more dragons around me," Raymond said. "It will be a victory to savour."

"I hope so," said Darnuir. "Back to camp for now. We move at nightfall."

When the sun set and darkness fell, Darnuir and his two legions set out as quietly as they could towards Aurisha. Stars appeared and the city shone faintly despite its state of disrepair. Darnuir's starium-lined armour began to sparkle as well. They headed for the main gate, a large gaping hole in the otherwise indomitable walls. Chunks of the old gate lay broken and untouched in the courtyard beyond.

Darnuir was the first to cross the threshold. It was dark and bleak, lifeless and soundless. Even the sea was calm and could barely be heard. He turned his attention to the plateau and there he saw a sole red glow, high above the plaza. It could only be coming from the Royal Tower. Praetorians formed up around him and followed his gaze, staring up at the sinister light like a beacon calling to them.

"If this Dukoona is here then he is unlikely to be alone," Darnuir said. "Stay vigilant."

They encountered no demons as they advanced along the northern thoroughfare. The Great Lift would have made the trip to the plateau painless, but it looked hoisted and tied up and, in any case, it would be too risky. It would be the long walk for them, first south to the harbourside and then up the switchback streets of the sloping side of the plateau. Darnuir had met his end running down that way, caught by demons and stabbed in the gut. He would not let that happen again.

"Stay close," he ordered. "Shields up."

All was quiet as the masts of the demons' ships came into view and they drew closer to the harbour.

And then they came.

Shrieking demons fell on them, from above, from the side streets and alleys, from every doorway and window like black ghosts. But the dragons had their shields raised and the demons did not work in a swarm. They fought alone and died alone, each one falling quickly to a sword or a crushing fist. More demons sprang on them a hundred yards down the road and again they were soundly beaten.

"Small waves," Darnuir noted to those around him. "He's trying to kill them off." He couldn't keep the hint of anger and frustration from his voice. This was no real fight and he had no need of the Cascade. Just easy kill after easy kill, a laborious grind. So few demons came that sometimes he was robbed of even that satisfaction.

Ahead, spectres began to appear. Hundreds lined the streets, stood out on rooftops and half-emerged from moonlight shadows, midway up walls or the rock of the plateau. The array of coloured fires was a sickening rainbow, and Darnuir had the unnerving sense that they were all looking to him.

"Come," many raspy voices called.

"Come, Darnuir."

"Come, Dragon King."

"Come, come, come," they chanted. Praetorians took shots at them but the spectres vanished only to reappear after more waves of demons. At the harbour, they began to scream at him, some clinging to the masts of their ships.

"Come. Come. Come."

Their calling didn't cease, not when Darnuir reached the incline of the plateau, not even as they cut their way through the demons on the switchback roads. And as the night wore on, so did Darnuir's patience. He fought against the impulse to throw open the door to the Cascade and tear off after the spectres. It was harder with each turn in the road, with each cautious but safe step that the dragons took, leaving a smoking trail in their wake.

At the summit, the demons finally abated. The final hunched creature, all swirling flame and dark mist, leapt towards Darnuir. It cackled, entirely happy to fight alone. Darnuir killed it with a well-timed lunge. Across the plaza, the spectres gathered. They smiled and their perfect white teeth appeared to float in the darkness.

"Come, Darnuir," they said. "Come alone."

When Darnuir stepped forward they vanished into one shadow or another cast by the moon. All that lay before him was an empty plaza and the red glow from the Royal Tower.

No more games, Dukoona. Blaine gave me answers and so will you.

"Form up," he called to his dragons. "Take count and take rest. And rejoice, for today we have won back our city." There were no cheers or celebrations. After more than twenty years, it was too simple to just walk in the front gates; to have it politely handed over. Perhaps the slow march through their dead city had sapped their spirits. Darnuir wished he knew what was going on. He didn't even raise his hand to tell them to stay because it was shaking again. "Wait for me," he said. "And do not follow."

The marble archway at the entrance to the tower was fractured at elbow height. It felt cold inside and Darnuir lit a fire on his sword. His grateful body sucked up the magic as he let light and heat flow from the Dragon's Blade. He moved up the grand staircase, one echoing step after another, and reached the spiralling stairs. They wove upwards for a long time. It was all vaguely familiar. Impressions from the memories left to him began to surface as he passed hallways, statues and rooms he used to see every day but could barely remember.

Eventually, the red glow indicated he'd reached the right place. The doors were opened and inviting. To his surprise, he discovered he was sweating. It ran from his brow and stung at his eyes. He wiped it away, even as the bitterness grew in his mouth, and entered.

This was the war room, he remembered, with the great crescent moon table and carved seats for the king and guardian. Candles were everywhere, on the tabletop, on the floor and hanging from lanterns, along with a dozen torches lashed onto the balcony outside. Shadows crossed everywhere in a black mesh.

"I've been waiting," a sly voice spoke.

"Show yourself, spectre."

"I think not. What advantage would I have if I were to step out of my shadow?"

"Then I shall set this room ablaze to find you," Darnuir said.

"But I only wish to talk," Dukoona said.

"Is that so?" Darnuir said. "How can I be sure of that?" He took a few measured steps deeper into the war room.

"Because if I wanted you dead—"

An ice-cold hand gripped his throat and a razor-edged knife materialised under his nose.

"You already would be," Dukoona said gently in his ear. Darnuir wrestled forward but Dukoona tightened his hold on him, keeping Darnuir's arms down. "I am strong myself."

Let's see how strong, then.

Darnuir shoved the door in his mind open and pushed his arms outwards against Dukoona's locking hold.

"Gah," the spectre cried as he was knocked back. Darnuir spun, poison shuddering down his arm, but Dukoona was already gone.

"Melded away again?" Darnuir taunted, though it was nearly a gasp. He slammed the door to the Cascade shut. "You've made your point, Dukoona. If you want to speak with me, then speak." Still there was no answer. "I know you've been holding back. Your spectres fled the Charred Vale after I killed Castallan's commander. You abandoned your siege of Dalridia and I've seen spectres vanish in the midst of battle since landing in the east, leaving their demons exposed."

There was still no answer.

"Why?" Darnuir yelled.

"Where is your other half?" Dukoona asked from some unknown place.

"Blaine would call it blasphemy to even hesitate in killing you," Darnuir said. "But I'll hear you out."

There came a sound like wind blowing, and Dukoona appeared in the chair of the king. The carved dragon atop the chair looked down on the spectre menacingly. Dukoona rested his feet lazily up on the war table and held his blade of shadow across his lap.

"Come, take a seat," said Dukoona.

"You're in my chair."

"Oh," Dukoona said, looking up as though to check. "Force of habit." He melded into the shadow cast by the snout of the carved dragon and rematerialised on the chair of the guardian. "Does this suit better?"

Darnuir couldn't help but smirk. "And your weapon?"

"I'll keep it ready, I think," Dukoona said. "I imagine you shall do the same." The spectre pointed his sword towards one of the dusty chairs across from the great stone seats. Darnuir drew up behind it but did not sit down.

"You seem to have put yourself in a difficult position," Darnuir said.

"You cannot begin to comprehend."

Darnuir frowned. "Why this ruse?"

"I want my people to survive, as many as can be saved. Too many have fallen already."

"Those still on the Splintering Isles?"

"They are nothing to me now. Only those I trust most dearly are with me."

"Seems callous," said Darnuir.

"Loyalty is worth more than anything when you live forever," Dukoona said. "So far as I am aware, I shall not decay. I will only die in battle, by my master's wishes, or by a traitor's knife. I very nearly did."

"You were ambushed at Dalridia," said Darnuir, remembering Grigayne's words of a blue-flamed spectre being attacked by several others.

"I was, and so I left those whom I cannot trust to rot on those islands."

"The guardian will see to them," said Darnuir. "And with the help you have provided we have made incredible gains with minimum losses. The end will come soon."

"Yes, but likely not in the manner you intend," said Dukoona. "I do not know when, but my master is almost ready."

"Ready for what?"

"To release his new servants," Dukoona said. "I believe my kind are no longer as valuable to him as we once were. There have been deaths, disappearances, strange red creatures with incredible strength leaving Kar'drun."

"What new servants do you speak of? New demons?"

"That is the frightening question," Dukoona said. "I only have a theory, though I am certain there is no other explanation. Especially since reuniting with those spectres who were long under Castallan's tyranny."

"Why are you telling me this?"

"To warn you, for one," Dukoona said. "And to offer you my help in killing him."

"Your help?" Darnuir said, quite taken aback. "Why should I believe you?"

"Sonrid, come here," Dukoona called. A twisted, hunched-over creature hobbled out of a dark corner of the war room.

"What is that?" Darnuir said.

"This is Sonrid," Dukoona said. "A Broken spectre, the result of my master's lack of power following the taking of this city."

"Does it speak?" Darnuir asked.

"Yes, I speak," Sonrid said, trying to pull himself up another few inches. "I also think and feel."

"I can hardly believe I'm even having this conversation," Darnuir said. "So, Rectar failed to summon more spectres properly. Forgive me if I do not grieve."

"He treats us like tools to be worn into disuse," said Dukoona. "Sonrid's suffering is uniquely painful, but all spectres suffer. We are slaves, not servants. And we want to be free."

Silence reigned for a few moments.

"What is coming?" Darnuir asked. "What are you afraid of?"

"Castallan experimented on humans with his magic, making them stronger," Dukoona said. "He was successful, I am told."

"Too successful," Darnuir said.

"Strong, were they?"

"As tough as a dragon. Some, such as Scythe, he made even stronger."

"Hard to fight?"

"Hard enough," Darnuir said. "Get to the point, spectre."

"For years Rectar commanded me to capture dragons, not kill them." Dukoona seemed to weigh up his next words. "They were sent to Kar'drun as prisoners. What he did with them, I never knew..."

Darnuir gripped the chair more tightly, crushing through it even without reaching for the Cascade. "No," was all he could say. It was unthinkable. To face such enemies would be impossible. Fighting Scythe had been difficult enough.

"What can we do?" Darnuir asked softly.

"I'll do what I can from Kar'drun," Dukoona said. "But their army will be your trouble."

"As will killing your master," said Darnuir. "I'm not seeing what I gain from this truce."

"Kar'drun is a labyrinth," Dukoona said. "You could spend a lifetime and never find your way. But I know, and if you can make it to the mountain, then I will take you and the guardian straight to Him."

"That's it?"

"I am a demon and he is my master," said Dukoona. "There is little I can do in truth. But I want him dead. I do not see a place for my kind once Rectar's new servants are ready." Dukoona spoke more urgently, all pretence at intimidation gone. It was almost a plea. "I do not see a... a—" The spectre stuttered and then paused, as if he had been struck dumb. "No!" Dukoona wailed, then vanished again, reappearing moments later by the balcony facing north. He clutched at his fiery head with one hand as he stumbled out to the balcony's edge.

"What is going on?" Darnuir said, rushing over to him.

"He's retaking control," Dukoona said, the agony evident in his broken speech. "The forces I sent away from the city—"

"They're coming back," Darnuir finished for him. "You must stop them."

"I can't stop Him," Dukoona said. "Not when he—" Dukoona burst into a scream. It was a sound Darnuir had never heard before, chilling him beyond all the cold of the Boreac Mountains; a sound not of this world. Darnuir bent and took hold of Dukoona, thinking he might help, but not knowing how, nor why he should truly trust him.

"Fight him," was all Darnuir could think to say.

"We must go to the mountain," Dukoona said meekly. The dense shadow of his body began to swirl, unravelling a little, revealing glimpses of pristine white bones underneath. "I cannot resist..."

"You must!" Darnuir implored. "How else will you fight him?"

"Do you trust me now, Dragon King? Do you trust me?"

Darnuir did not answer. He could not answer. He could not be sure.

Dukoona pulled him in closer with one of his dark purple hands, the other groping for a nearby shadow. "We do not have to be enemies," he whispered before his finger found a shadow and he was gone.

30

UNTO THE DAWN

Humans and fairies will rarely settle in Aurisha. For the fairies, there is precious space to attempt cultivating a silver tree, while humans feel they have no place. Military service lies at the heart of dragon culture but a human could never hope to join a legion. Intermarriage is scarce and children of such unions are considered unfit for service. And how can the new human baker or tanner or shoemaker compete with the established businesses that have been running since before they were born and will continue after they die? It is a wondrous city, something all should see. Yet the future of our alliance won't be served in such an environment. However, I am merely a chronicler. I do not have the solution.

From Tiviar's Histories

Darnuir – Aurisha – war room of the Royal Tower

Darnuir remained on his knees after Dukoona left. When he got up, his muscles felt stiff and tired. He went to the balcony's edge and leaned forward, as if he might see across countless leagues to the demon horde heading back to Aurisha. He'd been killed in this city once before. A second death now looked possible. *I've gambled too much. I've caused this.* Darnuir could only hope that Lira would discover what had happened and return in time.

He wrenched himself away from the ledge and strode back into the war room to be greeted by the sight of the little spectre.

"Why are you still here?"

"The master did not call me," Sonrid rasped. "He never calls the Broken."

Darnuir contemplated killing the half-formed spectre. He looked in pain, after all. *Wouldn't it be a kindness to put him out of his misery?* He drew the Dragon's Blade just enough to show an inch of golden metal.

"I do not wish to die," Sonrid said.

"Oh? Why is that?"

"I asked Dukoona once to end my suffering," Sonrid said. "He refused. He said it would be better to live and seek revenge on the Master. Dukoona has shown me I have worth to him. I've aided him and he has given me hope. I wish to do what I can."

With a loud snap, Darnuir sheathed his sword. "You have a lot of respect for Dukoona."

"He looks out for the Broken; the Master does not."

"I've never seen your kind before."

"Most of us cannot escape from labour in Kar'drun or the Forsaken City," said Sonrid. "I only got away because of the red creature I witnessed. Dukoona's closest, those he calls the Trusted, brought me here to tell my tale."

"Trusted..." Darnuir said. "This rebellion sounds like it has some weight behind it."

"Dukoona has gathered spectres to him for many years," said Sonrid. "He means what he says, Dragon King. He wants the Master dead."

"Then we share that goal." He crouched down to Sonrid's level and looked into his small twitching eyes. He held out a hand, palm upwards, and after a moment of confusion, Sonrid placed his own crooked hand upon it. "Your body is freezing. I never knew that before."

"And I never understood how warm your kind is," Sonrid said.

"I suppose I never stopped to think much about spectres," Darnuir said. "When I was young, I had a sword thrust in my hand and was told to kill demons."

"We are spectres," said Sonrid. "Our lesser brethren are beyond help."

"It's a curious thing. I've been trying to bring the Three Races together to stand strong against Rectar. I've not enjoyed a lot of success. Everyone has a grudge or wants something in return. Dukoona asks for nothing. He offers help instead."

"We want to be free," said Sonrid.

"One day, I hope you are," said Darnuir. He withdrew his hand and rose. "Will you meld and travel back to Kar'drun as well?"

"Melding causes me great pain," Sonrid said. "The Broken struggle with it. I will return to Kar'drun, though. I have nowhere else to go and Dukoona might have need of me."

"I'll escort you to the city gates."

Sonrid dismissed the notion with a wave, as high as his tightened shoulder would allow his arm to rise. "You will have much to prepare. I will meld my way to beyond the walls then make my journey from there."

"Then I wish you luck, Sonrid," said Darnuir. "If we ever meet again, may it be over Rectar's corpse."

Sonrid sniggered, unable to form a full laugh. He shuffled over to the balcony and staggered towards a shadow on the ledge. When he melded, it was slowly done. Spectres normally zipped into their shadows in an instant but for poor Sonrid it appeared to be a lengthy process. He groaned and winced as his hand vaporised, then his arm, then a leg and torso. After about five full seconds he had finally melded and Darnuir was alone in the war room.

He stood frozen for a moment in the grip of fear.

Over fifty thousand demons. Six thousand dragons.

This time there was no Scythe to kill. No head of the beast.

Darnuir sat down in the king's chair. The pressure of his armour as he sat instantly made him uncomfortable. The stone chair as a whole was rather uncomfortable. He was just a little out of reach of the crescent moon table, meaning he couldn't even lean on it. So he slumped back, tired, craving magic, bitterness building up again in his mouth. This moment should have been triumphant, but instead he was alone amongst the candles and flickering shadows. Darnuir placed his head in his hands and sighed, feeling his hot breath on his skin, and tugged at his hair.

He sat there for a long time.

In the daylight, Aurisha looked even worse for wear. Most haunting of all was the plaza. The stone was charred black from some great fire, and there was a red tinge to it that was too close to blood to be anything else.

"Something terrible happened here," Raymond said. He rubbed his eyes furiously, revealing dark lines when he withdrew his hands.

"And it could happen again," Darnuir said. He felt as energetic as Raymond looked. Small bursts of the Cascade had fuelled him through the night while they gathered their supplies, equipment and, of course, Bruce. Morning came in the middle of their toils and a fatigue had settled over the legions. Darnuir couldn't sleep in his current state, but did not wish to be alone. Raymond kept him company by the pulley of the Great Lift, taking in the view and soon-to-be battlefield.

"I assume we will be defending the plaza in lieu of the walls," Raymond said. He gestured to the six working catapults they had managed to salvage from the demon warships.

"That is my intention," said Darnuir.

"A necessary step," Raymond said. "Blocking the gate would prevent Lira from entering as much as the demons."

"And if we're stuck inside, we can't help Lira in turn. Fleeing on the ships left by the demons is not an option either. Lira and her legions would be caught in the open. No, we make a stand here. Bring the demons into the narrower streets, break up the horde, and with some luck Lira might be able to smash those caught outside against the city walls." He felt the bite in his own voice and his pulse quicken just thinking about it. "We've been tiptoeing around avoiding battle for weeks. It's time to fight. I ache for it. I need—" He stopped himself.

"Lira told us about your… condition," Raymond said. "Sickness is not your fault."

Darnuir sniffed and looked to his boots. "I'm not entirely innocent. The consequences of my actions could lose us the war. And I've caused enough pain to those I care about already."

Raymond straightened his back and stood tall. "If it helps at all, Darnuir, I'm glad I joined you. You are still in need of some refinement, but your intentions are right. I'm used to refinement, but from those who are selfish and manipulative. It took you to show me what honour really is."

"Me? I've not been so honourable of late."

"Dalridia would not stand were it not for you," Raymond said. "I would still be Gellick's whipping boy. Lira might not be with us at all. And then there was Torridon, where I grew to admire you more than any chevalier who's ever reigned above me. You do improve the lives of those you meet. You have done good. Don't forget that. Right now, you're sick, but you'll get better. And we'll be there for you."

Darnuir allowed himself a half-smile. He felt some of the tension unwind from his back and shoulders and he actually sagged from the relief. "Thank you, Raymond. I didn't know how much I needed to hear that. Go get some rest."

Raymond yawned. "You will not sleep?"

"I'll sleep when this is over."

Raymond bowed and took his leave. Darnuir turned to stare out across the city and the Crucidal Road running straight to the north.

He had omitted to tell Raymond that his decision to forgo sleep was also due to fear. He doubted his body would rise in time for the battle, if he rose at all. Only the Cascade sustained him and he dreaded going without it for any length of time. Withdrawal would cripple him. Of course, breaking would be worse. The image of Brackendon wrapped tightly in blankets like a baby reminded him of the consequences. Despite this, his shaking hand could not help but find the Dragon's Blade for another reassuring drag.

Run, Lira. Run faster than you ever have before.

The demons appeared at twilight, kicking up a cloud of dust as they trampled onwards. Darnuir forced life back into his stiff limbs, stretching and rolling his shoulders. He'd never gone so long without sleep, not even before the battle at Cold Point. He could hardly believe that had only been earlier this very year. Now here he was, a king atop his hill, preparing to face an equally dismal fight.

I wish you were here, Cosmo. Brackendon and Balack too. I wish you were all here to help me again.

He wanted to turn back time and save Eve, to not act so foolishly with Cassandra, to get to Cosmo's side in time and never have to see his dying body pinned against that tree. More than anything else, right this instant, he just wanted to rest.

Seven hundred feet below, the demon army began to converge, forming into a thinner stream at the city gates like water flowing to the path of least resistance.

It was time.

He stepped forward to address his six thousand dragons. The two legates were at the front, the red plumage of their helmets ripped or frayed in places, and they called the men to attention. Flanked by tall colonnades, the dragons barely filled a third of the plaza and seemed small beside the Basilica of Light.

"This will be the longest night of our lives," Darnuir cried. "But if we can hold until the dawn, then we few will have held where our whole race once fled. This is not our grave. This is our city, our home; and Rectar and his demons have held onto it long enough." He raised the Dragon's Blade and let a jet of fire pour forth. "Unto the dawn!"

Unto the dawn? I'm beginning to sound like Blaine.

The response was comforting; each dragon roared their ascent to fight.

"Rain stone upon them," he said to a group of outrunners. They dashed off to inform the catapult crews. Four had been placed on the western edge of the plateau while the other two were stationed upon flat roofs facing south over the switchback road, down which the legions were already marching.

Darnuir dashed to the head of the column, leading them into position. Halfway down the first road, he heard the clunk and whoosh as the catapults let loose their first loads. With the steepness of the plateau's slope and the buildings all around him, Darnuir didn't see the rocks land. But he did hear the demons' death shrieks, and their hissing, howling and shrill, chilling cries as they grew closer.

"Shield wall," he ordered and the front ranks held their barriers with strong arms. The second row moved forward and raised their shields to cover the heads and shoulders of those at the front. All had short swords in hand for the crushing melee and stood ready as the first demons came scuttling into view at the bottom of the road.

If the creatures felt tiredness, they did not show it, running uphill with the enthusiasm of a routing army. Many tried to jump at the golden shields, failing and tumbling back. But on they came and the battle was quickly upon the dragons.

Weapons scraped like talons against shields, screeching with each strike and prickling the hairs on the back of Darnuir's neck. Beyond the front wall of dragons, the demons piled up as they found their path blocked. They began leaping upon one another without concern until the tottering demons looked likely to hop over the shield wall.

Darnuir twisted his torso then threw the Dragon's Blade towards the boldest demons. Before he even saw the bloody results, he looked to the red-slated roofs above and cried, "Javelins."

His order was repeated throughout the legions. Dragons appeared with steel-tipped shafts in hand. In unison, they pulled back, held, and threw. Javelins ripped into the demons, spraying smoke and chipped bone. More followed, raining down like oversized arrows. But still the demons stacked upon each other, caring little about trampling their comrades underfoot. They seemed driven to overcome the shield wall at all costs.

And many did.

Darnuir met the first one with fist alone, cracking its chin to ruin with an upward blow. The second to land near him was killed by the hilt of the Dragon's Blade caving in its skull as it returned to Darnuir's hand. Yet more came. Darnuir gutted one, snapped the weak rusted sword of another, but soon their numbers were overwhelming. Without resistance, they began savaging the shield bearers from behind. Bile rose in Darnuir's throat as he saw his dragons fall within a swarm of hacking knives. Amidst the agonies of the dying dragons and the delight of the demons, calls for, "Next line forward," were bellowed, and Darnuir found himself surrounded by a new shield wall.

It will just keep happening.

Through the gaps between the shields, he saw the demons scrambling up their extra few feet of hard-won road to begin the construction of a new body pile to climb. Crunches and cracks cut across the battle as those at the bottom of the heap were weighed down.

Rectar must be forcing them on. Even the spectres would not do this.

Darnuir shoved the Dragon's Blade through a gap in the shield wall, skewering the already dead demons on the other side, and threw the door to the Cascade open. His head cleared, his arm tensed with the flow of energy and searing flames gushed from the blade. He swept the immediate area in a wave of red fire. His exhausted body protested quickly under the strain of it. He closed the door over, leaving it open by a crack.

He stumbled back from the shield wall, his vision a golden blur. The shredding, zipping sound of arrows passed by in both directions. One unfortunate dragon was taken in his left eye and Darnuir felt a flash of pain from the side of his neck as an arrow ripped his skin. Another two arrows rebounded off the thinner plate around his forearm and he groaned from the bludgeoning.

Even as his senses refocused, the second shield wall was being enveloped by the horde.

Something had to be done.

"Third wall," he cried and a new line was dutifully formed. "Hold and step back on my order. Stay strong. Ready — Step. Step. Step." The third wall took careful but sure steps backwards, maintaining their defence. Demons scrambling up from the carnage of the second wall were caught off guard. Some tried to make the jump, fell, and rolled backwards, tripping others, and caught more in a gathering crush.

The blockage granted Darnuir precious time.

He tore back through his own ranks, praetorians hurrying to keep up as he made for the top of the final road before the summit. Somehow, the sun had set without him realising. Night had fallen and the city had begun to radiate its dim glow under the stars. The legate of the first legion met him.

"My king," he shouted, slamming a fist over his heart.

"We'll need to try our plan sooner than expected."

"Sir," the legate yelled in understanding and moved with intent towards the buildings lining the edge of the road overlooking the assaulting demons. On top, the javelin throwers were still launching their attacks while the third shield wall began to falter.

"Fall back," Darnuir called. "Fall back to the plaza." As word spread, the dragons began an orderly retreat. Those keeping the brunt of the demons at bay bravely held their shields high. If a gap appeared, another dragon hastened to take his place. Step by step, they pulled back to Darnuir. "Hold," he bellowed.

And hold they did.

The line steadied against the onslaught and the demons pressed forwards with a single-mindedness no free-thinking creature could have, creating a new build-up of demons before the wall began in earnest.

Darnuir held for long as he dared.

The stack of demons grew.

He held a little longer.

A couple of demon heads appeared above the shields.

"Now," he roared with the enhanced power of the Cascade. His voice boomed loud enough to make the demons flinch. And from the building at the bottom of the incline, where the curve of the road turned down a level of the switchback road, dragons charged into the flanks of the demons. They formed fresh walls, three men deep, facing both towards the bulk of the horde and back towards Darnuir, trapping the demons stuck in between. A second wave of dragons emerged from buildings all the way up the road. A full three-hundred-man cohort slammed into the demons like golden spikes.

"Forward!" Darnuir cried, his voice cracking under the strain of the Cascade. He kept the magic flowing as he leapt over the wall of his men, crushing both demon and paved stone as he hit the ground. He cut down every demon within reach, embracing the blood pounding between his ears as the Dragon's Blade burned white-hot. The smoke from his flames and the demons' blood grew so thick it was almost blinding, yet through the haze the dragons pushed down the road.

Darnuir left them well behind, working himself up into a bloodlust he hadn't felt since their landing weeks ago. He half-slid his way towards his men at the bottom of the road, facing the entirety of the demon army. With a mad draw on the Cascade, he sprang over the new shield wall with the power of an unloading catapult.

He sent the Dragon's Blade flying on another murderous journey when he landed, letting fire lash freely from it. With his empowered muscles, he swept his arms and bowled demons over. One he missed, but the demon was close enough for him to headbutt. Its skull exploded in a shower of rusty bubbling blood. A splash entered Darnuir's mouth and it was honey compared to the rancorous Cascade residue.

He stood alone in front of the shield wall, awaiting the Dragon's Blade. As the sword sliced its way back through the demons to his hand, the draining of the poison continued. Unrelenting, the demons swarmed forwards again. Darnuir blew out his cheeks at them like a snorting bull. He raised his arm.

But found he couldn't lift it past his shoulder.

Something in him finally gave out.

He froze. His legs were leaden and he couldn't move. Dragons were around him immediately. Praetorians had fought their way out to his side, forming a defence around him. Some began pulling at his waist. Pulling him back. He let them and they hastened back behind their shield wall.

Darnuir dragged himself back up the road. At the summit, he collapsed, panting. Praetorians closed in and someone handed him a waterskin. Even Raymond was amongst them.

"Our rocks bombard them," Raymond said, "but it doesn't disrupt their ranks. Shall we continue?"

Darnuir swirled, gargled and spat. He sat up but remained bent over for a second, fighting back the urge to retch. "Nothing else we can do," he said to the ground. His head was making a strong argument for detaching itself and dying peacefully elsewhere.

"They aren't going to flee this time, are they?" a Praetorian asked. He was one of the youngest and blood dripped from his left arm, which hung wounded and limp.

"If that didn't encourage them to back off, nothing will," Darnuir said. "It must have always been the spectres who felt the fear. Rectar controls them directly now. He won't stop until all his demons are dead or we are."

The shield wall took another cautious step backwards, javelin throwers warned of dwindling supplies, and the demon army began to laugh hauntingly as one; as if Rectar were relishing his victory through more than fifty thousand cackling creatures. Their laughter filled the night, filled the city and filled Darnuir's ears.

Survival seemed a distant thing.

Lira – North of Aurisha

Lira ran.

Her legs screamed, her muscles burned, but she ran. She'd been running for so long she'd almost forgotten what it was to walk. Behind her, fourteen thousand dragons stampeded through the night.

When the outrunners had reported that the demons had wheeled around, Lira had gathered the legates, hastily got their bearings and tore after them. It had been almost impossible to tell where they were in the dark, but since finding the Crucidal Road, they had followed it south. It would lead them back to Aurisha.

How long ago had that been? A few hours? It had all vanished into the grind.

We should break soon or we'll all collapse before even sighting Aurisha.

But stopping a run like this would be tricky; if she suddenly stopped, she'd only get trampled. So she slowed her pace, very carefully, gradually, and the Praetorians near her slowed too, as did the legates, and eventually their speed was close to a human's jog. She called a halt and, exhausted, the dragons wound down.

"We should remove pieces of our armour," she suggested to the legates assembling around her.

"Lady Lira," Quintin, Legate of the Fourth, began, "we cannot weaken ourselves just to make the run easier."

"We'll still have our shields and our strength, or what's left of it," Lira said. Quintin was a hulking figure and she craned her neck to speak to him.

Another beefy legate spoke up. "We understand this is your first command, but—"

"But nothing," Lira said. "Legate Quintin, you will defer to me as Praetorian prefect. I outrank you and I say we strip our armour. This is a chase, not a lumbering march. If we don't reach Aurisha quickly we'll lose the king. Keep your breastplates if you feel the need but have the men strip their greaves, vambraces, gauntlets, anything unessential. With any luck, the spectres will turn tail if we smash their army in the rear. Well?" she added when no one moved. "Go. Now."

The legates exchanged looks before leaving to spread her orders. They did so grudgingly, Lira knew. This had been her idea and it might have backfired. But there was no time to waste on worrying or pandering to the egos of old legates. She'd hit Darnuir across the face. The legates were nothing on him.

She hadn't expected this, of course, when she had left her mother behind to go join their people gathering in Val'tarra. Lira hadn't thought she'd be made the head of Darnuir's guard. She never thought she'd be shouting down dragons three times or more her age. Yet here she was, the Praetorian prefect, whether she could believe it or not, and Darnuir was in sore need of protection. She'd bring him his five legions, weakened as they were. She would do her job.

Lira returned to the few Praetorians she had brought with her. It was a relief to sit and she unpacked her rations. The mutton was cold and chewy with fat, the bread hard. She'd never tasted anything half so good. A Praetorian nearby, Sabina, removed her boots to inspect the growing blisters, releasing a rancid smell of feet baked in days of sweat.

"Don't touch them," Lira told her. "It's tempting, but you'll only risk infection if you break the skin." Sabina gritted her teeth miserably. "Eat," Lira implored, "and elevate your feet if you want while we rest. It won't make getting up again any easier, though." Sabina took the advice, propping her legs on top of her ration pack and shield whilst she lay flat on her back, exhausted. Wrinkled and swollen, her feet almost throbbed with bulbous green-yellow pus-balls on her heels. Lira turned away, not daring to inspect her own feet. She wanted to keep her food down.

I'll have to remember to be more in awe of Damien in the future.

After devouring every morsel, Lira began removing her armour and the Praetorians followed her lead. The pieces clunked one by one to the ground. She hesitated with her breastplate but took it off and breathed easier. All she wore was basic leather padding, britches and a white shirt; no protection at all. Hunter leathers would have been preferable. But this would get her to Aurisha with some energy left to fight, and that was all that mattered.

She rubbed her eyes, fighting back a yawn.

And mother used to worry I wouldn't get tired enough during training and reveal I was a dragon. If you could see me now…. I'm going back. I'll find our old home.

Lira rose with determination and within half an hour the legions were running again, less encumbered by armour and provisions. They had their shields, their swords and, for now at least, their will.

When they reached Aurisha the demon army was pressing towards the bottleneck at the gates. It was impossible to say for sure whether they even noticed the legions approaching from behind. Some did, slowly. Fiery eyes began to turn to face Lira and move in her direction as the legions manoeuvred into a giant wedge formation.

Distant sounds of a battle indicated Darnuir's men were still alive. There was a slim chance. They had to take it.

As the number of demons turning grew from a trickle to a substantial wave, Lira called for the charge.

Sword out, shield raised, throat ragged from shouting, Lira was the first forward. Her legs wanted to buckle, her shoulders ached deeply at the joints, but she ran. With the last scrap of her strength, she ran. This was it: the last great battle. And the ground shook, and the demons came on, and the dragons roared with such might as to be beasts of old once more.

Lira hit the first demon so hard it burst. She hit the second just as hard, and the third harder. She careened into the meat of the demon host and none held under the fury of the legions' thunderous boots. No demon withstood her until the momentum of the charge died. Lira felt herself slow as the press of the demons became thick and unyielding. Somehow, she found herself standing still and blocking attacks from angry shrieking demons.

They haven't broken. The realisation almost killed her.

Dragons closed in around her, but they were now bogged down. Before long the dragons were falling and they were all taking a step or two back.

It didn't seem right.

She scanned for shadows, anticipating spectres, but none came. Only now she realised she hadn't seen any spectres. None. Only demons, howling, laughing, squealing like frightened pigs but swarming like a nest of hornets. The dragons hadn't even made it close to the walls. Lira assumed she and all around her were doomed. But she kept fighting.

In the east, a red dawn broke to usher in a bloody day.

Darnuir – the plaza of Aurisha

Darnuir slipped in blood pooling underfoot. Fresh red rivers flowed down the switchback roads, filling the air with a coppery stench. He watched demons enter each building on the final road, overwhelming the dragons there. His trick of feigning retreat to the plaza had worked a second time. It had not worked a third.

Now he really had pulled back, but they could only retreat so far before the width of the plaza would stretch their formation too thin. And this was it. They could give no more ground.

Darnuir remained at the front, all his focus directed on the next demon; the next demon; the one after. Time vanished. Nothing else mattered. Just the next foe. He'd heard his men cheering from far behind at some point but he didn't know why.

When it became too much, he stumbled back through the legions to catch his breath. He'd drawn on as little magic as he could, but the culmination of it hit him hard as he closed the door. He lurched towards a marble column, steadied himself with one hand, and then vomited behind it. He gasped as the acrid taste lingered. He peered worriedly at the back of his right hand. His skin had turned white but not yet black.

Looking up, he found Praetorians close about him, fewer now than when the sun had set. Dawn had come without his noticing and towards the north he saw Lira's legions surrounded, like a golden coin on a black field.

Darnuir pointed to them. "When did they arrive?"

"Just before daybreak," Raymond said. "Yet they have the same problem as ourselves. Without the demons breaking—"

"They'll be swallowed up," Darnuir said. The cruel fact was that Rectar did not need to keep his demons. Their final task would be to weaken the dragons if not outright kill them, softening them for this new threat warned of by Dukoona. He stared blankly out at Lira's forces. The golden circle contracted with each heartbeat.

"We're out of ammunition for the catapults," Raymond said. "Darnuir?"

"Yes," Darnuir said, snapping back to the situation. "Out of stones, yes." He paused again, looking from the Royal Tower to the Basilica. They could try setting a defence within one of those stout buildings, but eventually they would die.

That is not the way I will go. That is not the way we will go.

"Sire!" The call came from behind. Darnuir whirled to see a member of a catapult crew waving him up. "Flyers," the dragon called with childish glee. "Flyers in the air."

"It can't be," Darnuir whispered. He sprang towards the announcer with fresh spirit, leaping in a Cascade-enriched jump to the roof of the villa. What he saw from the south pulled his lips into a broad grin.

Fairies were indeed approaching, their wings invisible blurs, and further beyond, so small in the distance but unmistakable, the black and white sails of Brevia were making for the harbour.

"We might survive this," Darnuir said. The catapult crew were smiling too, looking half-mad from sleep deprivation. "Join us below," said Darnuir. He turned and hopped back to the ground. "We will survive this," he told the Praetorians and those dragons in the back ranks nearby. "Raymond, fetch your horse. We push back."

"With pleasure," Raymond said.

Darnuir felt life return to him; his aches seemed to dull and he felt the blood rush to his cheeks, so jubilant was he at this moment. Dragon's Blade in hand, he opened the door and pulled on magic to enhance his voice.

"Dragons," he bellowed, moving back to the front. "Unto the dawn, I told you. Well, the dawn has come, and with it comes your guardian with all our allies from the west. I say we venture down and meet them. What say you?" His men bellowed their assent; a chorus of song-like joy at their salvation. The demons didn't comprehend their change in fortune. Perhaps Rectar did not know. They kept up their attack but found their way blocked more aggressively. The dragons took steps forwards rather than back.

Across the plaza, Raymond came cantering upon his great steed. Darnuir called, "Let him through," and the chevalier drew up by his side. "Today we take back our city alongside humanity," Darnuir told them. "Today we win this fight as we should have years past, united and stronger together. Let us usher in that future. For dragons, for humanity, for fairies, for the Three Races!"

And so, they charged.

The demons were unprepared. They were knocked aside or trampled as the dragons ran. The natural descent of the sloping roads made leaping over the body piles of the fallen shield walls easier. Darnuir and Raymond spearheaded the counter-attack, Bruce the horse scoring as many kills as his master. Halfway to the docks, the first of the fairy flyers dove down into the fray, helping to clear the way. Darnuir spotted Fidelm's inky skin whiz above, twirling his double-ended spear in smoky spins. He met the general when they reached the harbour's edge.

"Blaine landed with the Third Legion and the islanders while we sailed around the peninsula," Fidelm informed him.

The demons were hit with precision by the mangonels of the human fleet. Soon, their own spearmen and archers were disembarking, and the demons could not hope to withstand an assault from three sides.

Darnuir led the push through the city, scouring every street and alley. The demons refused to flee. At the city walls, he ran up to judge the battle beyond.

Blaine was coming. A new golden formation – small, but compact, and driving on with purpose – approached the remaining demon flank. A dazzling light issued from the figure leading them.

When Darnuir rejoined the slaughter, he forgot to check how much Cascade he was relying on. The door in his mind pulled free of its hinges and when he tried to spit out the bitterness it was more like dry retching. His stomach was empty. The heaving brought on muscle spasms. And as the last demon fell dead on the dry earth, he thought he saw Blaine stepping cautiously towards him. He thought but could not be sure.

Then he blacked out.

31

REVELATIONS

The Champion's Blade is an enigma. Dronithir is the only person to wield it. Many have tried to theorise why he was 'worthy'. Did he give up Elsha, the woman he loved, for the greater cause? On and on it goes. In the end, it is naïve to place our own conceptions about 'worthiness' onto Dronithir's story. With each generation, the theory shifts as values change. And even then, the story that the blade shall appear to 'those who are worthy' comes from a time little better than legend. If we take a leap, and believe it all, then the gods of the dragons blessed the creation of the blades. Who is to say how they would judge who is worthy? It could not be for us mere mortals to know. I've said it before, but it could all be a myth; a story invented to give hope in the darkest of times. I'd prefer that. Hope saves us from despair. It saves lives. I've never known a sword to cause anything but pain.

From Tiviar's Histories

Garon – the Great Glen

Rain drizzled upon the Great Glen. Garon struggled through the thick mud at his boots and his waterlogged cloak weighed uncomfortably on his smarting body. The splint rubbed roughly on his forearm, his sling pulled painfully at his neck, his shoulder throbbed, a rib or three were bruised and he'd suffered a concussion, but otherwise he was fine. And so, while the weather wasn't the most fitting return for the victorious, it didn't dampen his spirits much. He was alive, walking, and, given the circumstances, very, very grateful.

A little rain didn't stop the kazzek from celebrating either. Music filled the glen from kazzek blowing into long pipes attached to swelling bags under one arm, sending out high-pitched blasts at a thunderous pace.

"Daa-daa-dee-da," Ochnic hummed.

"Know this one?" Garon asked.

"De song? It is familiar," Ochnic said. He winced loudly, sucking air through his large teeth. Tenderly, he placed a hand at his back.

"The wound hasn't opened," Garon remarked as he checked the linens for signs of fresh blood.

"I will mend," Ochnic said. Then he returned to humming. "Daa-daa-dee-da."

"Papa, you're not keeping in time," Cadha said. Ochnic's response was to hum louder and even more offbeat. Cadha laughed and thumped his leg with her tiny fist. She hadn't mourned the loss of her doll.

"Foul water," grunted Marus. "Your people know how to cope though, Ochnic."

"We hadn't had da rains yet," Ochnic said nonchalantly. "So now we get dem all at once."

"Look at us three now," Garon said. "The walking wounded. Ochnic bent at odd angles with his back, I'm favouring my right side so much I might tip over, and Marus limps along as usual."

"Just means we've done our duty," Marus said.

"And then some," said Garon. "Where has Pel gotten to? Has she acquired any debilitating injuries since the battle? She can't be flying in this rain, surely?"

"She isn't." Pel came sloshing up in between Garon and Ochnic.

Cadha jumped for joy at her arrival. "Can we fly again, Pel?"

"Later, I promise," Pel said. "If the rain ever stops. Could we hurry up and get out of it?"

"We can only go so fast as our broken bodies will carry us," said Garon. "You're young, though, and mostly unscathed. Run ahead if you like."

"And sit in a room with those chieftains alone? No, thank you."

"I don't blame you," Garon said. "Rohka hasn't seemed too angry, though. Am I right, Ochnic?"

Ochnic gave a rather large and rather unhelpful shrug.

"We'll face them together," Marus said.

"Marus," Garon said in mock exclamation. "Are you telling me that you will stand by us? Are you saying we're one solid tea—"

"I should have let you fall," Marus muttered darkly. He smirked and Garon returned the gesture. Then he grunted from fresh jolts of pain as they began to descend farther into the valley.

The ancient set of standing stones looked even larger than Garon remembered, dwarfing even the Stone Father standing sentinel at their front. The blue lines on his rocky body pulsated lightly. When Garon reached him, the golem proffered a vast hand, palm up, and Garon placed his own upon it. His senses morphed as they had done back in the Glen of Bhrath. He saw all rock and stone in great clarity, saw the presence of magic lining the mountains and felt the strange heartbeats from deep within the earth.

'We owe thanks to you, Lowlander. You and all those who came with you.'

We failed one of your golems. I'm sorry for your own loss.

The Stone Father sighed deeply. It echoed around every crevice of Garon's mind.

'My kind has accepted our fate. The day the Dark One came to the Black Rock the blue of our halls began to fade. There is no point in clinging on when other creatures might live and carve out their own path in earth or stone. Your coming made my sister's sacrifice mean something. For that, I thank you.'

Sister? Garon thought, but the Stone Father's presence was already retracting from him. The golem withdrew his hand and took his leave, heading for the eastern mountainside and leaving large muddy pools in his wake.

"You don't look well, Garon," Marus said.

"It leaves you disorientated for a moment," said Garon. But it was more than just discomfort from the strange sensory experience. The Stone Father's words had left him disheartened. A golem had died for them, and there were so few left. He took a moment of silence and listened to the pitter-patter of rain on Marus' armour. The arrival of the Chief of Chiefs forced him to smile.

"Da kazzek owe you thanks," Rohka said, a little stiffly. "Our food stores are filled and a clan was saved, even if you risked much." Although Rohka was intimidating, Garon held his gaze. "Da chieftains insist da you come now and eat with us." He led them towards one of the more lavish homes surrounding the ancient stones, the one with smoke rising from four chimneys. Stepping across its threshold was a relief Garon hadn't realised he needed. Crackling fires and the smell of roasting beef warmed him to the marrow, and a portion of tension in his back unknotted. A young kazzek in black tartan took their cloaks, paused, seeming unsure what to do with them, then tossed them roughly in a pile by the doorway. Garon couldn't help but laugh. The young troll looked confused but Garon gave him a wink and carried on.

How will I ever return to stodgy civilisation after this?

It seemed this floor of the house was one large gathering area. A feast was arrayed haphazardly in stone dishes upon the floor. Kazzek were merrily helping themselves, using their hands to place food on their boards of wood which they used for plates, and using no cutlery to tear or mash their meals. Many stood but some were on stools fashioned from thick blocks of wood, cut in whole cylinders from tree trunks.

Garon picked a stool and helped himself to one of the small round golden vegetables he'd seen before in Pel's soup. He bit at it tentatively and blew fiercely as steam rose from inside it. Its skin was crisped and coated lightly in salt and garlic, yet its inner flesh was light and fluffy.

"What are these little wonders?" Garon asked.

"You don't have dem in da south?" Cadha gasped.

"Potatoes," Ochnic said. "Dey grow well up here."

"I'll have to bring some back with me," said Garon. "After we see out the winter."

"Hmmm," Ochnic mused.

As Garon went to examine some more of the fare, he saw a kazzek presenting Pel with a separate deep wooden dish, which looked filled to the brim with a mashed gloop of carrot, neeps and cauliflower, glistening with butter. Pel accepted it happily.

"Mmmmm," she said, taking a second bite. The kazzek looked even happier and bowed his head. He walked away with pride on his face.

Their fellow guests consisted of the chieftains and some assorted staff or higher-ranking clan members. Occasionally, they stared at Garon, Marus and Pel, and put their heads together to talk more quietly. Even Ochnic received a few looks. After sufficient time was granted for everyone to eat their fill, the Chief of Chiefs called for silence and moved to address them.

"Today, we remember those kazzek lost to us. Orrock was a chief like us, and he is no more. Many more kazzek have gone unburned and I hope da blue poison will let dem rest."

"Let dem rest," muttered the rest of the kazzek, including Ochnic and Cadha.

"Now der is a decision ta make," Rohka said solemnly. "Will da Lowlanders stay?"

Silence reigned.

"Where else would you like us to go?" Garon asked. He felt a bit bold, perhaps due to the first proper hot meal he'd eaten in months. "Winter approaches and the demons may yet return. You'd really send us marching off in the cold?"

Rohka's nose twitched. "You have great spirit, Garon pack leader. But you were also reckless, and dis decision cannot be made lightly."

"Lowlanders should not be in da Great Glen," said the chieftain in the pink and green tartan.

"Dey have earned a place," Ochnic said. He did not bow his head or hold his tusks this time. "My clan would be dead if it weren't for dem. Da Stone Father too. Chieftain Rohka would not have helped us."

"I took a risk, yes," Garon said, "but I did it because I felt it to be right. Now, I know the kazzek have bad history with the fairies—"

"And da dragons," someone called out.

"Dat was da work of one mad dragon," said Rohka. "It was agreed. The Wise Ones declared dis long ago."

"Dragons?" Marus said. "What have we ever done to your kind?"

"Dey do not even know," bemoaned the chief in yellow and black.

"What is this all about?" Garon said.

Ochnic set Cadha down from his lap and got to his feet. "Dey have earned der place. Dey have righted da wrongs of da past. Let it go."

"Who was this dragon?" Marus said. "I know nothing of dragons in the Highlands."

"It was before even your birth," came a wizened voice. "Before even da demons came." A very old troll stepped forward from between two concerned bodyguards. Her tusks were worn down to the roots, her white hair was cut closely to her scalp, and she was wrapped in an extra layer of tartan.

"Chieftain Glik, der is no need to trouble yourself," said Rohka. "Please sit."

"It is no trouble," said Glik. "I fear da truth is forgotten. De years will have worn at the tale despite my trying." She was shaking a little in the effort to stand, so one of her guards produced a chair. He slid the cut tree trunk underneath her and she sat down. "It was over eighty years ago. I had only seen my tenth summer when dey came."

"Who came?" Garon asked.

"Drenthir, Dragon Prince, and Kroener, Cursed One," said Glik. The kazzek chieftains responded to the last name in their own choice way. Some spat on the floor, some gnashed their teeth, some growled low in their throats. Others simply seethed in silence, pressing their lips into thin lines.

"Wait one moment," said Marus. "Eighty years ago, the then-prince was surely Draconess."

"Der was no Draconess," said Glik.

"You are mistaken," said Marus.

"Chieftain Glik never forgets," said the Chief of Chiefs.

"Never," Glik repeated. "It was Drenthir and Kroener, Cursed One. Dey came in search of da Black Dragons, those who had fled their homes after Kroener slaughtered the rest of der people."

"Slaughtered?" Marus said. The colour was rising in his face. "The Black Dragons were our sworn enemy. Agents of the Shadow, they—"

"Marus," Garon snapped. He grabbed the dragon and pulled him closer. "What happened to you not truly believing in all that religious stuff?"

"This — this is different," Marus said.

"I'm not so sure it is," said Garon. Then, for the room to hear, he said, "Let Chieftain Glik tell her tale."

Glik carried on without even a momentary pause. "As I was tellin', Black Dragons were fleeing north into our lands. We took many in. I remember helping a young boy who was sick and underfed. Each day I mashed up potato and fed him spoonfuls until his strength returned. But Kroener came for dem, and that little boy, the one I had helped, was rounded up and slain like a beast.

"Dark days followed and Kroener came down hard on us kazzek who had tried to help da Black Dragons. My mother and I were taken by da dragons, chained and held for questioning. Kroener marched as far as da Glen of Bhrath, though it had another name in those days. Der was only one who spoke against Kroener, as I remember, and that was Drenthir, Dragon Prince."

Glik paused then and signalled for a drink of water. As she drained her mug, Garon chanced a glance at Marus. The legate's cheeks were ablaze and growing hotter with each second. To Garon, the whole story seemed well rehearsed. Doubtless the old troll had told it hundreds of times. Glik passed her mug back, wiped her mouth and continued.

"Kroener found out about de roads of da Stone Men and thought he could enter Kar'drun through dem. Black Dragons eluded him in its depths. Drenthir tried to change his mind. I remember, one night in my pen, the two of dem were close by, hoping to talk away from der men. Drenthir told Kroener he was wrong, that having fought the Black Dragons he saw dey weren't different. Dey were not the enemy, and nor were da kazzek. Drenthir spoke of dark creatures from Kar'drun, which the Black Dragons had been trying to keep in check. Now dat the Black Dragons were all gone, what was to stop these new creatures? Drenthir told da Cursed One dat he thought dey had made a great mistake. Kroener disagreed.

"Two nights later, Drenthir came around da holding pens. He broke our chains and set us free. He told us dat a mighty weapon had been granted to him, a sword of great power. He said a guiding voice had spoken to him whilst on da mountainside, telling him he was right. He told us not to fear da Cursed One anymore. But I was scared and did not move even as my mother called me to follow her. I sat curled in my pen, not trusting dat Drenthir could stop Kroener. As de others fled, Drenthir walked over to me and knelt by my side. He pulled out a chain of silver from around his neck and told me it had been given to him by da woman he loved. She was the daughter of a powerful dragon. Da dragon guardian. Drenthir said da guardian would listen to him because of this and not Kroener. He said dat together they would stop Kroener. And so I got up and ran with my mother to safety.

"Da dragons did leave in da end. Once we were sure dey had gone, my clan went back to check for more prisoners, or see what the dragons had left behind. What we found were dead dragons. Many of dem. Drenthir was one of them. He was lying on a sleeping roll, with ruins of da camp all around him. His throat was cut open. When I saw da necklace, I thought it too precious a thing to throw away. I picked it up and it remained with my clan until I gave it you, Ochnic, Shadow Hunter."

"You remember all that?" Garon asked incredulously.

"We told you, pack leader," said Rohka. "Glik does not forget."

"If that is all true…" Marus began, but he didn't seem able to finish his thought.

"All of it," said Glik.

"But this — this," Marus said. "I may need a moment."

"You see why we are distrustful of Lowlanders," said the chieftain in yellow tartan.

"And what of my people?" asked Pel.

"I think you already know," said Rohka.

"Fairies are told that frost trolls – the kazzek, that is – used to hunt and kill our kind if we ever ventured north," Pel said.

"And why did da fairies come to our lands?" asked Rohka. "To seek da blue poison, and—"

"And those who found it snapped like I did," said Pel. She seemed to ponder for a moment. Her wings fidgeted, buzzing in short bursts. "You could have warned me, or at least explained. Instead, you decided to hate me." She spoke to Rohka but it was old Glik who answered.

"Not hate, young one, but fear. Fear of what fairies will become when dey touch da raw blue. In times past, our people tried to warn you, tried to stop your kind reaching it, but you would not listen. We defended ourselves and then we tried to prevent you reaching it. Perhaps we were wrong. It was long ago. I say," Glik added with sudden volume, "I say we forgive da Lowlanders. Ochnic, Shadow Hunter, is right."

Marus stood up suddenly. He wobbled on his bad leg and placed a hand on Garon's last good shoulder to steady himself. "For what it's worth, I am sorry for any crimes my people have caused. One day I hope King Darnuir will make amends on behalf of all dragons."

"I believe he will," Garon said.

"What do you know of da dragon king?" asked Rohka.

"I know more than most," Garon said. "I was there when he was a baby born again. I was there when he learned to walk, learned to talk and learned to hold a sword. He's a little rough on the outside but I know he has a good heart. He is a good man. A good dragon, despite what may be happening to him. Could anyone alive claim to understand what it is like to have lived two lives? No, of course not. But I do know this. He is trying to make a better world, one where all the races can work together. And if he is trying in the south, then we should be trying in the far north."

The chieftains and their attendants descended into muttering again, whispering in their earthy tongue. This would be it. Garon's mission would hinge on the next few moments. He wondered if there was anything more he could say, anything more he could do, and then his shoulder, arm and chest throbbed to remind him of what he'd already done. It was enough, surely. Yet even if it wasn't, he felt proud. He'd hauled his grumbling force northwards and saved the family of a friend. Val'tarra and all human lands were safer for it. Even if no one ever thanked him. Even if no one ever knew or cared; they'd done it.

It was Ochnic who made the first move. He stood by Pel, swelling up his hairy chest, and announced, "Da pack leader is right. From now on, I call Pel fairy friend."

"Me too," squeaked Cadha. She took Pel's arm and hugged it tightly.

"Well, I for one am touched," Garon said. "While we're all sentimental, I guess I should say, Marus, that you're not as grouchy as when we first met."

"Thanks," Marus said coolly.

"And I suppose I owe you my life now," Garon said. "I should probably stick around until I repay that debt. Friends?"

"It is one's duty to save one's commanding officer," said Marus. Garon frowned at him. "Very well," Marus said. "Friends it is, human."

"Thank you, Marus," Garon said. Something about the dragon's moment of humanity touched him, and then he realised that very word was wrong. Marus hadn't become more human, because really he and the others weren't so very different in the end. Garon addressed the room himself now. "You kazzek refer to me as pack leader, and that's flattering, I think. But that makes me sound superior or special, and I'm not. None of us are. Not Marus, not Pel, not Ochnic; we're actually mostly the same. We care about our loved ones and families. We'll do ridiculous things to help those we care about and even set aside our pride and duty in some circumstances." He looked to Marus at that. "What I'm trying to say is we're all really much the same. I know the thought of thousands of outsiders coming into your homes is frightening, but know we've been just as frightened. So what do you say, Rohka? Can we stay?"

All eyes began to turn to Rohka. "You can," said the Chief of Chiefs. "For now," he added. "We do owe you much." That seemed to settle the matter. One by one all the chieftains gave their consent and a drink was called for.

Mugs were brought out on oversized trays. Garon lunged for the closest one, looked at its contents, and found not beer, nor ale, nor harder spirit, but something white. *Is that milk?*

"To new friends," roared Rohka. He raised his own mug and some of the milky drink sloshed over the side.

"To new friends," repeated everyone; the chiefs, the guards, the servants, Marus, Pel, Ochnic, Cadha and Garon too. He tilted his head and threw back the mug. The drink was ice cold and tasted of creamy milk sweetened with honey. It was delightful. It felt clean. And then the kick came in the aftertaste, a bitterness that plunged down his throat and set a fire in his stomach.

"Phwoa," Garon said, shaking his head, enjoying the immediate tingling around his body. Pel gasped; Marus already looked drunk and hooted loudly. The kazzek chuckled at their intolerance.

"More," Rohka called. Their mugs were refilled with the hazardous milk and a pair of kazzek took up instruments that looked like long curving fiddles. A soaring wave of music filled the common room and Garon felt his aches and pains lessen.

He had not felt this good in years.

32

THE WAR IS WON, THE WAR IS JUST BEGINNING

There is a simple saying among my people: 'rotten to the roots'. Arborists use it when a tree is beyond saving and should be cut down, burned, its very roots dug away. The poison runs so deep, even the roots must go to give the best chance for new life to grow. As I investigate the history between the Aurishan dragons and the descendants of Dranus, I am inclined to say it. Rotten to the roots. With humans, it is only marginally better.

From Tiviar's Histories

Darnuir – Aurisha – The Royal Tower

Darnuir was running through the snow. It was freshly fallen, soft on top, and crunched pleasantly underfoot. He came across a golden stone table, perfectly round, with chairs set at equal intervals. Instinct made him place a hand on it, then sit down slowly in one of the chairs.

"What are you doing?" Cosmo asked. He was leaning on the table, whole and healthy, looking down at Darnuir.

"I asked them to come join me," he found himself saying. "Arkus, Somerled, Blaine, Fidelm and Kasselle. But they're not here yet. I'm waiting for them."

"I'm hardly surprised," Cosmo said. "Better you than me."

"Will they come?" Darnuir asked.

"Hopefully," said Cosmo. "You invited them, and you are the dragon king. Don't they have to?"

"I think so," Darnuir said, looking down at his knees. "Cosmo, what if I can't do it? What if I—" But Cosmo was not there. He'd vanished.

The falling snow thickened and Darnuir felt a chill run from his ears to his toes. He wrapped his arms about himself, rubbing his chest and puffing out steamy breaths.

"Well, this won't do," said Brackendon, appearing from nowhere in the place Cosmo had been. With a thud of his silver staff, a ball of warming fire materialised, bobbing in the air between them.

"Can you help me?" Darnuir asked.

"Castallan must pay first," Brackendon said.

"He's dead. You killed him. Don't you remember?"

Brackendon's eyebrows shot upwards. "Gracious, really? Well, then, we should be moving on."

"On?" Darnuir said. "But I have to wait here."

"Oh, no," said Brackendon. "There's worse out there. Who do you think is causing all this snow? Come along now, my tamed dragon." Darnuir stood and everything started to spin. When the world righted itself, he was at the base of a huge mountain, the rock of which was burned black. "He's in there, Darnuir."

"Rectar?" Darnuir said. He reached for the Dragon's Blade at his waist but the sword was stuck fast in its scabbard. "Brackendon, help me."

"I can't help you in there. Not anymore. You burned my staff." And as he spoke the silver wood in his grip turned to ashes.

"I thought you wanted me to," Darnuir said. "Kymethra told me."

"I did," said Brackendon.

"It is I who should break and not you."

"A generous offer, Darnuir, but we'd all be better off without magic."

Darnuir craned his neck looking up at the black mountain. His heart quickened in fear. His palms felt sweaty. "How can I fight Him without magic? Without you?"

But like Cosmo, Brackendon had disappeared as well.

A doorway opened from the mountainside and Darnuir walked towards it. Over the threshold he fell, into utter darkness. He saw nothing. He felt nothing. Not even a rush of wind against his skin. He hit cold stone with a wet thud. And he lay there, flat on the ground, unable to move. Someone shook him and he rolled over, got up. He couldn't see his saviour's face for they were looking downwards, half veiled in shadow. A red glow came from where their eyes should be. The person, whoever they were, drew something from their waist, bringing it up to Darnuir's chest, and—

Bang.

Darnuir's eyes flew open.

"Careful, human," Blaine said in his most condescending tone.

"I did not intend it, Lord Guardian," came Raymond's voice. "Those doors are rather heavily designed."

"I think he's awake," Grigayne said. Darnuir blinked painfully; the sleepy crust felt like cement on his eyelids.

"Yes. He yet lives," intoned Fidelm.

"Darnuir?" Blaine said. "Darnuir, can you hear me?"

He tried to speak but only croaked something incoherent. He was parched. His throat felt like he'd swallowed sand and his eyes seemed determined to squeeze out from his skull, as though trying to escape the pain in there. His head hurt so much he considered yanking his mind out through his nose and letting it writhe in pain elsewhere. He was lying on a hard, unforgiving bed. The sheets were clingy and damp, and he wished dearly to die there.

"He needs water, surely," Raymond said.

"He needs magic," Blaine said. "Darnuir. You haven't broken, but you came very close." He seized Darnuir's hand and pressed it against the hilt of the Dragon's Blade. "Your body depends on the Cascade. Draw on a little, quickly."

Darnuir fumbled at the door in his mind.

"Do it now, Darnuir," Blaine said, squeezing Darnuir's hand to the sword. Darnuir felt the door give and the magic pour in. For a moment, it rushed through him, thrumming towards the Dragon's Blade. Just as he wished to rip the door apart and drown in the ocean beyond, Blaine yanked his hand away.

"What?" Darnuir gasped, feeling a modicum of his strength return.

"That's enough for now," Blaine said. "You'll need to be weaned down from this overindulgence."

"Overindulgence? Blaine, I didn't mean for this to happen. At the Bastion, I —" What was the point in making excuses? He bowed his head, feeling too ashamed to meet Blaine's eyes. "How long was I out for?"

"Just over two full days," Raymond said.

"Then I should see the city," Darnuir said. He managed to rise painfully to a sitting position.

"Take rest, Darnuir," Fidelm said. "The war is won and your city will still be here when you are better." Darnuir's thoughts turned to Dukoona's warnings.

"No," he grunted. "There is much to be done." Shakily, he stepped out of his sodden bed, the same one he slept in when camped. A larger bed was next to him, with a frame of carved starium and a dragon looming above a ripped old mattress. "Where is Lira?" He asked. Then the horror struck. "She isn't—"

"She's alive, and unharmed for the most part," Raymond said. "Cuts, some deep, some not. Remarkable, considering she had no protection."

"Foolish girl," Blaine said.

Raymond ignored him. "I believe she is taking care of some personal business in the Lower City."

"Very well," Darnuir said. "I shall need to thank her. All of you, as well. I owe more thanks than I can possibly convey in words. For standing by me, Raymond; for your timely arrivals, Blaine, Fidelm; for bringing your own people to my aid, Grigayne, even after they have endured so much."

"Yes, we have endured much, haven't we, Guardian?" Grigayne said bitterly. Darnuir noted the animosity Grigayne shot Blaine, knowing he'd need to ask about that later. Grigayne looked back to Darnuir more kindly. "There is no need to thank me, Darnuir. You rescued me and my city; I've helped secure yours."

"I may have to ask even more of you before the end," Darnuir said, "of all of you."

"The demons are defeated," said Fidelm.

"But not their master," said Darnuir. He looked to Blaine for support.

"This will not truly be over until the Shadow of Rectar is banished from the world," Blaine said. "But Fidelm is right in a sense. With his armies destroyed, Rectar will fall soon."

"His armies are not gone," Darnuir groaned. Fresh pain stabbed at his stomach, chest and kidneys at once, as though several fists with ragged nails were clenching his organs.

Blaine's brow creased. "I believe we saw to the demons, and the spectres for that matter. I saw none in the battle."

"Ah," Raymond said, raising a finger. "The spectres vanished, Lord Guardian."

"They fled again?" Blaine said.

"Not exactly," said Darnuir.

"And how would you know?" Blaine said. He narrowed his eyes at Darnuir, searching for the cover-up, the lie. Darnuir stared right back, quite willing to have it out.

"Because I had words with Dukoona," said Darnuir. The colour of Blaine's face grew closer to beetroot.

"But Darnuir, many of the Brevian forces are already setting sail for home," Fidelm said.

"What?" Darnuir snapped. "No. They can't. I need them to stay here."

"Arkus will require the ships to send your people across the sea," Fidelm said. "He won't take kindly to his troops staying here while dragons —"

"We can negotiate with Arkus later," Darnuir said. "For now, I need those troops to remain. Fly, Fidelm. Prevent more ships from sailing."

"What shall I tell the admiral?"

"Tell him he has to stay," Darnuir said, clutching his head. "Tell him the war is not over. Tell him anything…" He trailed off into another headache, squinting down against the array of colour assaulting his vision. He gently massaged the side of his eye to little effect and did not see Fidelm leave.

"I must consult with my father," Grigayne said. "I'll send a message to Dalridia, but our warriors and shieldmaidens will remain for the time being." More footsteps and the loud closing door signalled he too had left. Darnuir had his eyes fully shut now.

"Might I have some privacy with my king?" Blaine asked.

"I leave only if Darnuir commands it, Guardian," Raymond said with more defiance than his usual bearing.

"Thank you, Raymond," Darnuir said. "But I shall speak to Blaine alone." A quiet scrape of metal meant Raymond had bowed.

"Careful with the door," said Blaine. No bang followed this time. Darnuir risked opening his eyes again but kept massaging his skull.

"What's gotten into you?" he demanded of Blaine, albeit weakly. "You seem back to your old self and I don't know if that's for the better." It was then he noticed Blaine's maimed hand. "Dranus' scales, Blaine. What happened to you?"

"Did you want to see the city?" Blaine said.

Back to avoiding questions again too, I see.

"I'd like one last walk while I still feel capable," Darnuir said.

"You'll have to enter a period of rehabilitation," Blaine said.

Darnuir sighed. "How long?"

"It can take ninety days," said Blaine. Darnuir winced. "But," Blaine continued, "as we've caught it early on, and the Dragon's Blade is second to none at processing, you may recover faster..."

"And if we forced the issue?" Darnuir asked. "Cut me off for longer stretches and really hastened things?"

"It could kill you."

"I know you won't let that happen."

"Let's go for that walk," Blaine said, placing a gentle guiding hand on Darnuir's shoulder, and they went in silence down through the Royal Tower. Passing the war room, Darnuir saw the half-melted candles left by Dukoona had been cleared.

"We found another scrying orb in the throne room but it was smashed," said Blaine. "Luckily, Fidelm brought us the spare from the Bastion. Arkus has the orb I found among Scythe's camp."

"Good," said Darnuir. "You'll be able to communicate with Arkus in my absence." They continued their descent, still in the grip of silent discord. After a while, Darnuir felt compelled to speak. "You might start with a full apology regarding the Bastion. You might then inquire about the rest of our people back west. See they are treated well and get as many home as you can. It's a task I don't envy. Arkus is sure to want his own men home for late harvests and for sowing in the spring, but Rectar does not work to the seasons. Well? Nothing to add, Grandfather?"

"I shall make these demands, if you wish."

"Not demands," Darnuir said.

"Would you accept an alternative?" Blaine asked.

"Within reason, but, broadly speaking, no. We need their soldiers."

"Then you are demanding," Blaine said.

Darnuir wanted to shout, to scream at him, but his head was spinning again. He lost his footing on the stairs and scraped his arm to a pink flaky ruin against the coarse stone railing.

"Draw on a little more magic," Blaine said curtly. "Just half a second." Darnuir did and steadied himself. For now, he focused on making it down the stairs. The pain from his arm barely registered amongst everything else.

One step at a time. Just one step at a time.

"You should not have conversed with a spectre," Blaine said. "They are full of madness and lies."

"Not this one. I won't apologise for speaking with Dukoona. I'll apologise for the recklessness, for my addiction, for a lot of things, but not that. It was worth it. We'd never have found out about this new threat otherwise."

"And what threat is that?"

"The very thought frightens me."

"You need not be afraid, Darnuir," Blaine said, pausing to face him. That momentary stop made Darnuir lose his hard-won rhythm in tackling the stairs. He began to feel dizzy. "Come to the Basilica with me," Blaine urged. "I'll show you why you ought to start believing."

Gingerly, Darnuir began moving again.

One step at a time. Just one ste—

His hand slipped and his feet gave way under him. A solid edge of rock dug into his hip when he went down.

"Ugh," he moaned, but the greatest pain of all was the yearning to open the door. "I can't do this, Blaine. I need more magic. Please," he begged, spittle spraying from his cracked lips. "Please. Just let me draw on more. I can't — I can't go on like this." Blaine stared down at him, lying spread-eagled and pathetic. He bent down to Darnuir's side and reached out a hand to cup his face. Blaine's eyes widened, and for a moment, he was a concerned grandfather. Then the guardian returned.

"Back to your chambers."

Lira – Aurisha – the Lower City

. . .

Lira picked her way through the streets at the foot of the Great Lift. This had been the poorer part of town, this cramped, tight maze of wooden extensions upon ancient stone homes. The wind was prevented from freshening the air and it was often in the shadow of the plateau. Aurisha had been constructed thousands of years ago, so Lira supposed there had been more than enough space for the dragons at the time. But not as the city grew. Those extensions rose six storeys in places and many now looked tilted and unsafe. Yet she could ignore those. Her old home would be at street level, the one home with the green door. A bit of green to liven the city, her mother had said.

She found it on a narrow street four doors down from the base of the plateau. Her mother hadn't exaggerated. Every other doorway was a pale yellow, but not hers. It didn't even look damaged. Lira pushed it in, crossed the threshold and half-choked on the stale air.

A feeling of being unwelcome came over her, as though the abandoned rooms had grown accustomed to their solitude and wished her gone. A layer of dust covered everything, from the ceramic pots on the low-built shelves to the still-set table at the centre. Three plates were laid out: one for Lira; one for her mother; and one —

She looked away, feeling foolish at grieving for a father she never knew. An urge to leave washed over her. She'd just find that damned doll her mother always talked about and get out. A last memento of her father. He'd made it for Lira, apparently. Not that she could remember. She found it flung unceremoniously on the child-sized bed in the tiny room off the kitchen. Its limbs were bent at bone-snapping angles, the wooden joints frozen in time like the rest of the place. She picked it up, admired the carved detail of the woman's face: the broad smile and the happy blue eyes. Something gave inside her and an unwanted tear splashed on the wood.

Doll in hand, she left the house with the green door. She glanced back once then retraced her steps towards the Great Lift. When she arrived, the lift had just finished a downward journey and dragons pulling carts of dead bodies from the plaza trundled out. They marched, stern-faced, towards the broken city gates, taking the corpses out for burial. The dead had been stripped of anything useful and left virtually bare, their skin exposed to the elements. Already, an awful smell of rotting meat followed them.

Lira felt more tears well in her eyes, and she knew it wasn't all for some doll or a promise made to her mother. It was this, being paraded right before her. Nothing but death, death and more death. Out of the heat of battle, it was sickening, terrifying. How much blood had been spent taking back the city? How much had been spent since the first demon crawled out from Kar'drun, and how many tens of thousands before that in every war ever fought by every king or guardian?

She was exhausted. She had been exhausted even before she had run for a full day to crash into a horde of demons that didn't break. Everyone around her was tired as well – just no one would admit it. Tired of fighting. Tired of death. At least for now they might rest, and, with the demons defeated, begin to dream of peace.

She looked up to the plateau where all the greatest of her kind used to dwell. Up there, amongst all the marble and the finery. Yet, while Darnuir recovered and Blaine droned on about his divine experience, the Great Lift brought more bodies down.

Two waves of carts passed Lira before she finally moved on.

Darnuir – the Royal Tower

Darnuir sat shaking in a starium chair. The Dragon's Blade lay sheathed across his lap, the hilt just a little out of reach. His hands, arms, shoulders, waist, thighs, calves and feet were all bound.

"I'll likely rip out of these bonds," Darnuir said.

"I'll have stronger steel chains brought soon," Blaine said.

Darnuir nodded, breathing hard. He'd been allowed one final draw before the real recovery began. Already, he felt desperate to feel the Cascade in his veins again. Failing that, he just wanted to scream.

"Before this begins," he said, practically panting, "what's made you so sure of yourself? What happened on the Splinters to bring you back?"

"I asked our gods for a sign and they answered," Blaine said. His expression did not betray any twitch of a lie or coercion or anything except the plain truth. Blaine believed every word he said.

"And your trouble with Bacchus?" Darnuir asked.

"Gone. He has returned as a devout Light Bearer and follower."

"A follower of your religion or of you?"

"When you have recovered, ask any of the Third who were there at the Nail Head. It was a holy event. Why else do you imagine the demons have crumbled before us now?"

"Because the spectres let them die," Darnuir said. "Because Rectar didn't care for them any longer. Because something worse is coming."

"Don't trust a spectre's word."

In his frustration, Darnuir bit on his lip and tasted blood. He could move nothing else. "Damn it, Blaine. Dukoona wants to *help* us. He's warned us. Rectar has dragons, enchanted like Castallan's red-eyed humans. You must prepare. You cannot ignore this."

Blaine wrinkled his nose. "How can dragons fall to such a thing? We are the Light's chosen race. We shall prevail."

"Of course we can fall," Darnuir said. "One of your own did. Have you forgotten?"

Blaine leaned in, right up to his face. "I am nothing like Kroener."

"Of course. You only have nine fingers," Darnuir said. "Did your gods give you comfort when you lost it?"

"I'll forgive that based on your current condition," Blaine said. "If only you believed."

"It's not that I don't accept there is something powerful out there," Darnuir said. "Rectar has power. He reaches out to the minds of his minions. He summons them to this world from somewhere — somewhere else. Kroener alone, one dragon, even with a blade, could not have this much power. There is something we don't understand, but I don't think we'll have any help in this fight. We're on our own, Blaine, but we don't need to be. Let the humans in. Let the bickering and the hate end. Look at what we've achieved in one year together. Let your prejudice go. Please. There's no point in it. Please…" He hung his head and licked his lips, attempting to regain control of his breathing. Muscles in his back twitched, threatening seizure.

"N'weer watch over you, Darnuir," Blaine said, taking his leave and slamming the door behind him.

33

LIFTING THE VEIL

The First War between humanity and dragons was bravely fought, but bloody. Humans hoped to match the dragons by breeding warhorses of immense power and size, even larger than the destriers used by present chevaliers. Mighty they may have been, but when the humans charged at the Battle of Deas the dragons stood there, allowing it. Some say they even laughed as the first ranks dodged the steeds with ease, cleaving into their legs and knocking them down with plated fists. In response, the earliest hunters were formed. Humans set aside the notion they could beat the dragons with brute force. Leathers and mail replaced armour, bows would kill from afar and dense spear formations absorbed the brunt of a dragon charge. Where dragons have been content to rely on their physical prowess, humans have sought other means to fight and I suspect they always will.

From Tiviar's Histories

Cassandra – Brevia – dragon refugee camps

Cassandra had not anticipated feeling this distressed by Boreac's death. For what seemed an aeon, she stared at his corpse. His blank, terrified, still-open eyes looked up at her in shock.

Gellick remained before her, waving his fine dagger in a vaguely threatening manner. He didn't mean her harm, but he would not allow her to act either. There was nothing she could do.

Does it matter? What's one more killing when the whole city, the whole kingdom, has been backstabbing, plotting, scrambling over the top of one another? And all for what? For this? A dead old man running half-starved from his home. It's over. I shouldn't care. She looked again to Boreac's body. *No. It's wrong. He was caught, cornered. He would have come quietly.*

Gellick's crisp voice snapped her back to reality. "Search him. We'll take these possessions he deemed most dear back to the palace. I dare say a reward will be in order, gentlemen." His voice was fat with triumph. The other cloaked chevaliers murmured their agreement. Kymethra had stopped trying to break free from her captor. Boreac's murder had left her just as still and confused as Cassandra.

This is wrong…

"This isn't right," she finally said aloud and was pleased to hear she sounded calm and still together, though the opposite was true.

"Nor is plotting to overthrow the king to whom one is pledged," Gellick said.

"You can't," Cassandra began. She stepped towards him with no real plan. She tried to gently push his knife aside but he whipped a leather-gloved hand across her face, leaving a stinging scrape on her cheek.

"It's done. Take it up with your father, Cassandra. We're leaving. Now."

"What about the body?" asked the man who had done the stabbing. His face was still hidden beneath his hood.

"Leave it. King's orders. Now, let us depart. *Quietly*," he added with a fresh flourish of his dagger at Cassandra and Kymethra.

Back at the palace, their small company moved without a word to each other. Kymethra was escorted off to her quarters, still gagged. Cassandra was forced to follow Gellick towards Arkus' council chambers. The chevalier had a bounce in his step and his blond hair flopped with each rise and fall. He had Boreac's worn sack over one shoulder and something in it clanked against his armour. There were no guards outside the council chamber.

"Arkus will be meeting with the minor houses," Cassandra said. Gellick didn't acknowledge her. He sniffed and began leading her upstairs to the doors outside Oranna's parlour. There were five chevaliers there, all with their visors up. They saluted Gellick as he approached.

"You're dismissed," he told them and the men marched off without dispute. He knocked once, twice, still no answer. "My king," he called. "I have urgent news of—" But from the other side of the door came laughter, a mixture of low voices and high tenors. Gellick pushed on the door, revealing a scene of Arkus and Thane guffawing at some private joke. Arkus was kneeling by Oranna's regular tray of overly sweet cakes with purple frosting spread across his nose. Thane stood in front of him, with pink icing and crumbs in his hair, wielding a purple-covered sponge in one hand like a mace.

Their laughter took Cassandra by surprise. It was a happy, joyful, songful noise, the sort of laughter that might have forced a smile across the most dour-faced dragon. Neither father nor son noticed Cassandra and Gellick's arrival.

"My king," Gellick said again. This took Thane by surprise and he half choked in turning to face the chevalier. His caught breath sent him into a fit of coughs, hacking loudly into a white doily cloth that Arkus snatched up from the tray. The king rubbed the prince's back and gave Gellick a look as though he wished the chevalier to boil inside his steel. Cassandra dashed forward and poured a cup of water from the jug beside the cake tray, ready for when Thane surfaced from his episode. After half a minute, Thane calmed, and yellow-green mucus clung like tar to the now ruined white doily. Cassandra offered him the water and Thane sipped it, sighing heavily between gulps as he sought to steady his breathing. A lone tear left Thane's eye from the exertion and Arkus pulled him in for a tight hug.

"Go on and find your mother now."

Thane nodded and left. Cassandra thought she saw Gellick flare a nostril in disgust before arranging his expression into one of deep concern. The moment Thane was out of the parlour and the door closed behind him, Arkus rounded on Gellick.

"Is it done?" he asked brusquely.

"It is," Gellick said. He dumped the sack at Arkus' feet.

"This is all of it?"

Gellick nodded.

Arkus bent down and rummaged frantically in Boreac's last possessions before pulling out an object that Cassandra had never seen before. It looked like a hollow wooden tube with a slanted handle and some mechanism fashioned from metal pieces just above where Arkus held it. He let loose a shivering sigh as though over-coming some powerful trepidation.

"Hiding in the refugee camp…" Arkus said, more to himself. "Nearly had me there, Geoff. Nearly got away with it." He turned to Cassandra. "You cannot know how much of a relief this is. You've done so well, Cassandra."

"You never said Boreac was to die. What about the trial?"

"Annandale will suffice for a trial," Arkus said. "And you have no idea the danger Boreac might have placed us all in. We're not yet ready. We're—" He had seen the cut on Cassandra's cheek. "Did Boreac do that?"

"Ask the young Lord Esselmont here," Cassandra said.

Arkus whirled, rose and asked, "You did this?" Each word was a bite as if chewing wood.

"Just to move things along, sire," Gellick said, his aura of pomposity suddenly shaken. "The princess and the witch were—"

Arkus struck Gellick's face with the bronze butt of the handle. Gellick snorted in pain but had the grace not to clutch his bleeding and swelling face. He took his punishment well.

"Never harm my daughter again."

"Never, my king," Gellick said, a little thickly.

"Leave us, before I rethink your approval to the White Seven." Gellick did not need to be told twice and was careful to shut the door gently behind him. Arkus turned the strange weapon over in his hand, inspecting it and a tiny chamber which opened at the ridge of the handle.

Cassandra shifted her weight between her feet, looking from Arkus to the thing in his grasp. Boreac had believed that Darnuir would be so grateful to hear about the weapon's power, he would keep him safe from Arkus. And Arkus had been desperate for Darnuir not to find out. Desperate enough to hunt Boreac down. The old lord had died for this thing.

The parlour seemed dull and lifeless now, the colours less vibrant without the early morning sun. Brevia itself looked grey under the overcast sky, half shrouded as though veiled in some secrecy.

Brevia, the palace, the queen, Kymethra, Thane; it had started to feel comfortable. She'd dared to hope she'd found a home. Had this changed anything? *No, this is all Arkus. I might be caught up in his games, but the others are genuine. Right?*

"Your betrothed caused quite an upset with his speech to the dragons," Arkus said, still inspecting the weapon. "Or should I say, your former betrothed?" He glanced over to her. "We made a deal, after all."

"And you'll honour it?"

"Of course," Arkus said. "I do not think you need to be bartered off. My grip on the kingdom is firm now. The minor houses have been easy to appease with so much to be divided up; lands, titles, positions. You've helped, of course."

"Me? All I did was find Boreac."

"And ended my fears of the dragons catching wind of my activities. Annandale broke quickly. He thought information about his fellow schemers would make me more lenient. He was wrong. But he did go on about Boreac's obsession with a secret project of mine here in the city."

"Were you always going to kill him?"

Arkus tapped his fingers over the ridge of the device. "Yes. Does that bother you?"

"That's why you wanted me to come straight to you, because—"

"Because I didn't want you to come to harm."

"How do I know that's not another lie?"

"I like to think of it as omission," said Arkus.

"So what happened today with Gellick? He said Oranna spoke to him. Does that mean she—" This time her voice broke. She didn't want to ask. She didn't want to risk knowing Oranna had been lying to her as well. Arkus' expression softened, his lower lip rose and he cocked his head by the smallest tilt.

"Oranna was worried about you. Like me, she understood there might be some danger in hunting down a wanted man. She acted out of affection, and then Gellick came to me."

"But she knew I was looking for Boreac."

"Yes, but like you, she didn't know the full reason why," Arkus said. "Just as she knows nothing of the weapons I have been producing here in the city. And even though I recruited hunters from the Hinterlands to be retrained, Lord Clachonn never let Romalla know their purpose. I have found it is... safer that no one person knows everything. Easier to track betrayals."

"You seem to trust Gellick," Cassandra said.

Arkus shrugged. "Gellick's one of the best at what he does."

"Which is?"

"Serving me," Arkus said in his most kingly tone. "Keeping our family alive."

Cassandra lightly touched her stinging cheek. "I wouldn't trust him. If he's an Esselmont, then the only thing making him less fickle than others is his sister's betrothal to Thane."

"I'm more than aware of that," Arkus said. "I am under no illusion whatsoever. Gellick and his father will be loyal so long as they have a stake in power. This can be carefully handled. Dangerous rivals are those who have nothing to lose and everything to gain by changing the balance of things. Boreac, old and childless, was one of them. Humans I can deal with, but the dragons..." He trailed off ominously.

"The dragons are our allies," Cassandra said. "They destroyed your enemies for you. And now they're outside your walls, cold and hungry. Feed them, shelter them, and what will they have to hold against you?"

Arkus took a moment to think. He strode to the windows with the whole city in view and tapped the wooden tube lightly against the glass.

"Pride," Arkus said, as though addressing all of Brevia. "Dragons will be accommodating and grateful whilst they need humanity. Yet, if the dragons regain their former strength, they'll dominate us again. You have a mind for the past, Cassandra. You of all people should know. The dragons have either made war upon us or dragged us into them. That guardian, Blaine, is of the old ways, and he is a walking warning. The tunnels of the Bastion prove we have never been safe. I cannot tell you how many contingency plans against dragon invasions relied on the Bastion holding strong.

"And I remember the old Darnuir as well. I could never have felt secure around him. He seems to have changed, I grant you, but it may be an act. Even if it isn't, even if Darnuir is sincere, and all the good things a fellow ruler could be, he won't live forever. So how long, Cassandra; how long until another fanatical dragon decides humanity must be purged? My predecessors were foolish in keeping to the status quo. They voluntarily remained weak, a second-rate race. Castallan would have made us stronger, I have no doubt, but then we would have been reliant on him, and not even Castallan could have lived forever.

"I have secured our future through craft and intelligence, through ingenuity and creativity. Humanity will no longer have to fear the dragons. That is the only way a true alliance can ever be formed." Arkus ended his speech a touch breathless. There was spittle against the window.

Cassandra had taken several small steps back without being conscious of it. Her calves pressed up against one of the plush sofas and she was sorely tempted to fall into it. This was the real Arkus. Stripped of any need to perform. This was the man – a cunning, careful planner who worked in decades, not mere years. And he had everyone either fooled or under his thumb.

"Is that thing your grand solution?" Cassandra asked. She pointed to the wooden tube.

"This is just one small piece," Arkus said. He let the weapon fall into the sack. "If you come with me, I'll show you everything."

Night had almost fallen and so, under the cover of darkness, Arkus and a guard of chevaliers headed by Gellick spirited them through the palace to the back courtyard, where there was a postern gate in the perimeter wall. Heavy vines hid the door in the wall but it only led out to a nondescript segment of the city.

Cassandra wondered where on earth they were heading. Before long, the back alleys began to reek of urine and vomit. A tavern rumbled far to their right and lanterns covered in a red film winked at passersby. These were the outskirts of the Rotting Hill, only now there was no tower to guide one's way. Arkus and the chevaliers made their way without discussion. They had clearly walked it many times before.

Deeper they went into the run-down borough until no citizens could be seen or heard. And still they walked on. Cassandra felt the land begin to rise as they approached the hill where the Conclave tower had recently stood. For a wild moment, she thought they might be taking her to the ruins of the site. Perhaps this wasn't a trip of trust after all.

She felt exposed, foolish, unarmed and unable to run. Boreac lay dead and the dragons were neatly set up to take the fall for his murder. Her own body could disappear here without incident.

"Cassandra," Arkus gently called. He had taken down his hood and was standing in the doorway of a crumbling building. "Are you coming?"

She looked to the hooded chevaliers around him and then to the ruined frame of the building. "Will I come back out?"

Even in the weak starlight Arkus looked hurt. "I would never harm you." He stepped a little closer. Cassandra responded with a step back and drew an inch of steel. Arkus raised his hands and said, "You are my daughter. I'm so proud of how strong you are, despite all you've gone through. I lost you once, Cassandra. Never again." He didn't come any closer or move to embrace her but she could see into his eyes from here. Small and narrow though they might be, they swam with an honesty that no one could feign. She'd only seen that before in Chelos when she was frightened or injured or upset, and he'd hold her and tell her, "I'm here for you, my girl. I'm here."

And Cassandra believed him.

She sheathed her sword, along with her fear. She was safe, even if others weren't. Yes, Arkus was a killer, yet half the world were killers, for one reason or another. Arkus strove for power but also for survival and to defend his family. And they were her family now too: Thane and Oranna. She would fight for them, if she had to. Many who fought gave the same reasons as Arkus and were called heroes. Was there really such a difference? He was flawed, but he hadn't done anything irredeemable. Not yet, anyway.

Arkus was beaming. "Not long now." Together they returned to the chevaliers and filed into the wrecked building. Two great ovens, cold and lifeless, indicated this had been a bakery. The wood was wet, parts were rotting away, and yet the door above the cellar looked new. Heavy iron locks held it in place. Gellick took out a set of keys and opened it.

"Come," Arkus beckoned. "Gellick and his men will guard the entrance."

They descended deep into the earth, for how long Cassandra was not sure. It was surprisingly well lit and clean and soon a faint rumbling sound came drumming from the end of a long corridor. Arkus led her towards it.

As she walked beside her father, Cassandra realised the true extent of what Tiviar had meant when he said that most of what people read about the past is a lie, a trick, or a condensed and simple narrative. Arkus had proved frighteningly good at retelling events already. He'd become a butcher, cutting away all the sinew and mess from events at the Bastion to leave an easier tale to swallow. One of human triumph and dragon failure. Boreac was growing as cold as his namesake; his story would not be told. As for Annandale, Cassandra guessed his word would be twisted beyond recognition, and who would stop it? Arkus had won. He had control, and he had Lord Tarquill to print and spread any story he liked.

Another round of loud cracks came, like breaking rocks echoing in a valley. She could make out many individual ones now, coming close together, but not at the exact same moment. They reached what she hoped was the final door and Arkus pushed it open.

If there could be such a thing as a horizon underground, then the space before her reached out to it. A vast cavern, supported by pillars and beams, not roughly constructed but laid with a stone floor. There were even carpets, desks, chairs, and beds stretching off. It might have been a hunters' lodge. Men and women sat working, scratching at pages furiously as though they had no concept that night had fallen and the day was over. Two soldiers in black uniform sprang up when they saw the king.

"Your Majesty," the female of the pair said. "We were not expecting you."

"No matter," Arkus said. "Take me to General Adolphus. I can hear he is at drill."

"You have soldiers living down here?" Cassandra asked. "Shouldn't they be fighting in the war?"

"They will be soon."

In another equally vast chamber, columns of soldiers paraded around, carrying weapons like the one Arkus had shown her only far longer, which they propped up on one shoulder. Others cleaned theirs; others still practised some art with the latches on the ridge of the weapons while blindfolded. More soldiers were placing those little lead spheres into black pouches.

Ahead, some of those who were marching stopped to raise their weapons straight with rigid shoulders. Deafening bangs followed. Smoke rose from between their hands, rising towards a series of shafts that must have led up to the borough above.

Behind the marching troops, a light-haired fellow with an oversized moustache and wispy goatee was yelling orders. When he saw the king, he approached them briskly with long strides, arms swinging like pendulums at his side. "My king," he barked in greeting, snapping his feet together.

"General." Arkus nodded. "Circumstances have contrived that my daughter must be shown our work here."

"Very good," Adolphus said, without so much as a glance at her. "I shall continue with the drill." The general returned to his troops and resumed his flurry of orders. A fresh round of the weapons went off. A hundred yards opposite them, stuffed targets exploded with straw. The targets were replaced and armour placed over the top of them. "Fire," cried Adolphus and the metal plates gave way under the force of the projectiles. More straw spewed to the floor.

"What's causing that?" Cassandra asked. "You're using black powder to propel something. But—" She realised what it was. She reached into her leathers and pulled out the little lead ball. It rolled in the dip of her palm.

"You found a musket ball as well, did you?" Arkus said.

"Muskets," Cassandra said slowly. She was taking everything in.

BOOK 2 - VEILED INTENTIONS

"Igniting the powder proved more complex than we originally thought," Arkus said. "The first designs required a match cord to be lit, fastened into a spring catch, which used to be above the trigger – where the soldiers are pulling their fingers back," he added for clarification. His eyes were alight. She had only seen him more animated when playing with Thane. He continued. "But that was cumbersome and too dangerous. Now there are pieces of flint secured to the hammer you can see them cocking back. When the trigger is pulled, down it comes, sparks, and—"

Bang. Another round of the weapons fired. The musket balls punched holes into the thick metal plates over the targets, ripping the metal like sharpened steel through leather. It was only now she paid attention to the plate that she realised the armour was golden; of dragon make and design.

Who do you intend to be aiming at, Arkus?

"Why use that armour?" she asked.

"Strongest in the world," Arkus said offhandedly. "Why test on anything less? I'd like to see how it fares against starium stone, but our testing with granite would suggest the weapons have little impact. At least, not our hand-held muskets. Larger units are being finalised for that."

"Larger?"

She thought she saw one of these larger muskets. A team of four was slowly pushing around a long thick bronze tube on wheels. Fear and awe took her as she imagined the damage that thing might do.

Cassandra's apprehension only grew as she scanned the rest of the compound. She saw an armoury, stockpiled with weapons. Row upon row of muskets glinted in the depths, their polished wood barrels catching the orange lantern light. Mountains of black ammunition pouches must have carried enough shot to block out the sun a thousand times over.

Drill sergeants and Adolphus each shouted their orders in rhythm but the men and women were a fraction ahead, already confident units firing, marching, loading, and firing again.

Those at the front took their shot, turned, marched to the rear of their five-man columns and began to reload. They bit at white rolls of paper, poured black powder into the weapon, closed the hatch, sank the remainder of the powder down the muzzle, loaded a ball, stuffed the paper in after it and, from the side of the barrel, pulled out a thin rod to ram it all down. This whole process flashed by, the soldiers ready to fire again by the time they reached the front, keeping up a steady barrage. Within one rotation, the targets were nothing but shreds of metal.

"So this is your alternative to Castallan's magic?" she asked. "This is how you will make humanity strong?"

"Yes," Arkus said, as though there was a great weight to his voice. "This is how I'll keep our family safe."

"Fire," Adolphus called.

And bang went the muskets.

Bang.

Bang.

Bang.

EPILOGUE

Dukoona – in the depths of Kar'drun

Pain. Had such pain ever been felt?

Dukoona howled into the crevice of rock he had been plunged into. Or was it an endless cavern? Nothing had made sense. There had only been darkness. And the flames. There had been the flames.

He slipped in and out of consciousness. One moment had felt like a lifetime, and cognizant moments between hallucinations were precious. Yet, when they stopped, there was only darkness.

And the flames. He could not forget the flames.

Mercifully, he closed his eyes.

"Awaken," the voice rumbled around him, through him, in his very mind. Dukoona felt his eyes wrench open to a blue light. It came from a great shimmering something in the distance. Its size was hard to gauge. He felt like he could be worlds away from it. Whatever it was, it was oval in shape and a bubbling blue substance boiled within it.

Against the blue glow, the outline of a body began to form. Its darkness was utter and complete. It seemed to suck light into it because the cavern dimmed further as the figure took shape. Floating, the dark form drifted towards Dukoona. It looked down upon him with a faceless head.

Pain seared within him, but he no longer had the energy to scream. His thrashing limbs were locked in place by some unseen force.

There came a loud crack and before him stood a spectre. Dukoona thought he recognised this one; a member of the Trusted, with curling green flames upon his head. The spectre spun wildly until he caught Dukoona's eye. There was no point in reassuring him. Dukoona could do nothing, say nothing that would save him.

I have failed them all.

The dark figure descended gently down behind the spectre and placed a hand upon his shoulder. In a cry of anguish that might have split the earth, the spectre smoked inch by inch from existence. First his hands and feet, then his arms and legs, then only his torso was left fizzling out of the world. As his throat smoked away, his last scream echoed on until he and it were gone.

Dukoona watched it all.

"Kill us and be done with it."

"Your service has been lacking," droned Rectar's voice. Slowly, the dark figure began to solidify. When it finished, there was little to see, as a shredded crimson cloak wrapped its entire body. Its head was shrouded by a hood, though a few blond strands of hair poked down at the neck. Just visible through one of the tears in the cloak was a pale hand, gripping the steel hilt of a sword covered in fine black and gold cloth.

"We should never have granted your kind such freedoms and powers," Rectar said. "We should have chosen our servants more wisely. The Others should have chosen more wisely as well. Dragons were strong. And now they are mine."

"I have been your slave," Dukoona said.

"I am the Shadow," Rectar said. That seemed to be his answer.

"And I have destroyed your armies," Dukoona said. It was his one victory. His best act of defiance.

He fell back into agony again. A hundred small cuts suddenly appeared on his body, the dense purple shadow ripping apart to ooze his smoking blood. Beneath the flaps of his torn flesh, he could glimpse his pristine white bones.

"You have caused me a great setback," Rectar said. "But you have not destroyed my armies. Not all of them."

Dukoona's pain ceased. His cuts healed over and he hung his head, exhausted. Done. Defeated.

There was another terrible crack and all light was taken from the cavern. A moment later, heavy footsteps crunched towards him and even heavier breathing came from above. Dukoona brought his hanging head up, looking for whatever it was. He could barely see anything, but he was sure it was there. The breathing sounded heavier still. He craned his neck to look upon the thing. A long red-scaled face snarled at him with fire-bright eyes.

Rectar's voice rung through his mind; a fierce, amorous whisper.
'The end is nigh for all.'

MICHAEL R. MILLER

THE
DRAGON'S
BLADE

THE LAST GUARDIAN

PROLOGUE

Eighty-One Years Ago
Kroener – The Depths of Kar'drun

Beneath the burned mountain, he walked alone. One heart beating in the darkness. How far had he descended? He'd lost all sense of time.

Within his mind, Kroener pushed on the ethereal door and reached for magic. It kept him going down here, even if the Cascade felt ragged and weak.

He'd assumed the Black Dragons were drawn to Kar'drun for its well of energy, so where was it? Had he been wrong? If recent months had taught him anything, it was how little he had truly understood before.

How little they all had understood.

Of the people he'd helped to eradicate, he'd known even less. He realised this now as he walked their endless corridors in search of this God of the Shadow.

Being tall and leaner than most of his Light Bearer peers, they'd called Kroener thin in his youth, scrawny even. Drawn cheeks accentuated the sharp angles of his face, which did little to alleviate such insults. But he was strong. Always had been. That was why Blaine had chosen him. And that was why he would be guardian next.

Once he returned. Once he had conquered their great enemy.

He reached another fork. One way led directly ahead; the other was a set of stairs leading to a deeper darkness.

'*Descend*,' the voice rang in his mind. It was far stronger here, under the mountain, and he was grateful for the guidance of the gods in this final hour.

He raised the Champion's Blade higher, to be ready at a moment's notice, and took the stairs as instructed. The way ahead was lit in the usual manner; by light that came from shelves cut into the rock. Light from lanterns, he had first thought. Each shelf contained a floating ball of fire – flames of all colours. Yet they were far from cheering. Something made the light dirty, impure; the yellows were more akin to piss than the sun; the greens closer to bile.

But he could not turn back.

He had no choice. His only hope of justifying his actions and proving that he was the true chosen Champion of the Gods lay at the end of this dim underground journey.

'You are close now, Kroener. The Enemy is close. Rectar must be slain.'

I will do this, Lords.

He wasn't sure whether mighty Dwl'or, Dwna and N'weer could hear his reply. They'd never given any sign that they did, but he answered all the same. He reckoned they only spoke when necessary, allowing him to forge his own path.

At the bottom of the staircase, there was something on the edge of the Champion's Blade that caught his eye. Blood. Dripping, luminous blood. His thoughts began to spin. He saw Drenthir look up at him in horror, heard a gargled choke, and felt warm blood upon his hand as the prince's life gushed from his slit throat. But he'd had to do it. He'd had to.

Kroener blinked, shook his head, and realised there was no blood on the blade at all. The metal had caught the glow of a red flame from an alcove, shining like raw meat.

Breathing hard, Kroener paused in his march. His heart was racing. He drew in the foul air deeply three times, coughed once, and then fought to steady his breath.

He'd suffered these mild panic attacks each time he thought about what he had done. Killing the Black Dragons had been easy. They were the ancient enemies of Aurisha and the Gods of Light, or at least they *had* been. From the looks of the bodies he'd passed under the mountain, the Black Dragons had been fighting and dying long before Kroener had brought the might of the Aurishan legions to bear.

Perhaps Drenthir had been right? But no. The gods had confirmed Kroener was doing their work in the Highlands. Persecuting the trolls may have been a waste of energy in the end. Likely that was why the gods had come to him, to place him back on the righteous path.

There was only one small doubt that still plagued him, one thing he could not quite make sense of: his new weapon.

He looked again at the Champion's Blade. Such a plain-looking thing; the black and gold cloth around the hilt was even a little frayed. A simple steel knob made the pommel. Only the grainy gold of the blade marked it as special, and a sibling to the

Dragon's Blade held by old King Dalthrak and the Guardian's Blade possessed so proudly by Blaine.

Now Kroener was their equal. He may even surpass Blaine, because the gods had chosen Kroener to receive it. They had urged him to take it – that was undeniable. And yet, if it had been meant for him, why grant it first to Drenthir? It was a test, he had concluded. One last test to prove that he was willing to do anything to serve.

It is not up to me to question the gods. I am but their champion, their sword against the Shadow.

'Yes...' came the voice, smooth as satin. *'You are our Chosen. Go deeper into the mountain. You are close.'*

Kroener puffed out a breath and straightened, feeling bolstered. The gods had answered him.

Lords of Light, I thank you for my chance to prove myself. But I find I am afraid. If you are with me in this fight, please grant me a sign.

Nothing happened.

A simple sign, Lords. I am but mortal, after all.

Nothing came.

Kroener's pulse quickened again. "I've done so much in your service; will you do nothing to raise my spirits?"

This time something happened. All the ghostly fires around him went out and the door in his mind groaned with the sudden swell of the Cascade.

Unprepared for it, the energy overwhelmed him and he fell to one knee, staggered by it like a freezing tide.

Then came euphoria.

Yes, he could do this. He could do anything. In that moment, he was a beacon of the gods on this world; far more than smug old Blaine could ever be.

As quickly as the feeling came, it went.

Magic retreated from him until the well of power behind the door felt empty. A painful rush swept down his arm towards the Champion's Blade. His mouth went dry and a bitterness lay upon his tongue. An odd sign, but it was enough to go on. The gods had granted him what he needed. When he battled this Rectar, they would fill him with their power.

'Forward, Kroener.'

Kroener rose, bidden by the voice, and he stalked down the rocky corridors of Kar'drun. Soon, the hallways widened and the ceilings rose. The sickly flames were replaced by blue lines in the walls, running like veins towards the heart of the mountain.

He continued on until he entered a vast cavern, so large that a full-sized dragon of bygone eras might have flown there. And at its centre hovered a shimmering blue oval.

Kroener felt the door in his mind quake. This thing before him must be a Cascade Sink. He'd heard some wizards from the Conclave in Brevia mention such things in hushed tones. The wizards thought it a dangerous thing but the God of Shadows evidently did not. Rectar had gathered a great deal of power.

'You have arrived.'

"Show yourself, Rectar, enemy of the Light." He braced himself for battle, feet apart, his hands tight upon the hilt of his blade.

Against the blue glow of the Cascade Sink, an outline appeared. It was humanoid in shape but featureless and blacker than night. It wasn't merely darkness; it drew light into it to be destroyed.

This was Rectar. This was why he was here, yet how was he to fight something like this? Could the Champion's Blade cut through this force floating high above him?

As the figure floated down, Kroener took an unconscious step back. He felt something press upon his mind; not the door to the Cascade, but something entirely new. An unwelcome probing feeling, like a brusque surgeon prodding to find where it hurt.

The figure dropped through the air towards him, a dark hand outstretched. Kroener winced at a stabbing pain in his head but he rallied, fighting against this attempt of his enemy. Finding his courage, he yelled, "You shall not have this world, foul Shadow. I am a servant of the Light. I am your end."

He stepped forward with purpose, putting all the power he could behind his swing, and aimed for Rectar's exposed arm. His blade met only air. The faceless figure had faded away. Feeling it must have retreated closer to the well of energy, Kroener gave chase, his blood up, all nerves taut for the fight to come.

As he neared the centre of the cavern, his shadow grew longer. Then he saw it at the corner of his vision, mirroring his movements, but not at all where it should have been, given the direction of the light.

Kroener halted. Had he imagined it? His own shadow then lurched in front of him, raising its dark sword, independent of his own movement. Impossibly, his shadow rose off the ground. No, not his shadow. He had no shadow anymore. Yet in that moment of hesitation he froze, and Rectar charged him. A shrill rush of wind echoed in his wake.

Kroener almost failed to block the strike. He managed only by drawing on some magic. Rectar attacked again, placing a compelling strength behind his incorporeal blade. Kroener staggered, found his footing, whirled around in an arcing blow and fought the shadow in the blue glow.

The fight was like nothing he had experienced before. His whole life, everything that had ever happened in the world, had led to this day, this confrontation under the charred mountain.

And he was losing.

Even with the Champion's Blade, he was still made of flesh, blood and bone. This shadow he fought never slowed, never showed weakness. Rectar moved in ways that a living thing could not, bending his arms at bone-breaking angles; his movements rapid and precise. All the while, Kroener felt the probing against his mind increase with fresh vigour.

"Help me, Lords," Kroener cried.

'Let us in. Let us fill you with our power.'

The shadow was slicing towards him, filling the air with a shrill squeal like scraping steel. Kroener let the gods enter his mind.

And froze.

The intrusion entered his consciousness like a lance of ice. His body went numb. Unable to move, he could only watch as the dark blade pierced his armour and slid into his heart. But he did not die. He felt tendrils of hate coil around his being. His thoughts grew smaller and smaller. His very soul dimmed. He saw the shadow press itself right up against him, until it was all he could see. It pushed further, pressing into him, merging with him, even as all his thoughts and memories continued to wilt under its wroth.

'Thank you, Kroener, for letting me in. Drenthir was too much a tool of the Others.'

This cannot be. I am the Light's champion.

'You killed the Light's champion. You slit his throat under my suggestion.'

Under your—

'And you did it so willingly. You always had ambition in your heart, didn't you? I thank you for bringing me one of the blades, and a host to wield it. I can complete my work here.'

So it had been a lie. All of it.

Drenthir had been in the right, and he, Kroener, in the wrong. Gods, he had been wrong. Oh, gods, what had he done? What had he allowed to happen? Rectar wanted his body for the Champion's Blade. What worse things would occur if Rectar took hold of such extra power?

No!

Kroener summoned what pieces of himself remained and lashed out against his enemy. With every effort, he sought to take control of his sword arm. He'd die before he let the Shadow take him. He almost managed it. Cold metal kissed his throat before Rectar reacted. In the ensuing battle for control, Kroener's body began to spasm. His crimson cloak billowed around him and was shredded by his flailing sword arm.

No, he thought again. Though if thoughts had volume, his would have been the whispers of the meekest creature. His body stopped thrashing. His will had no power left.

'Know that you have helped in the downfall of your gods. Die now, Kroener.'

His last thought was not of guilt or regret, or even shame, but fear. Terrible, terrible fear. N'weer would not accept his spirit now. Where would he go? He had no time to consider. Rectar squeezed the last resistance from him and Kroener let go. Forever.

1

THE SLAVE

Present Day
Dukoona – The Depths of Kar'drun

It had been nearly a full day since Rectar had tortured him, though it was hard to tell for sure. There was no rising sun down here. No stars. Not even the luxury of movement remained to while away the time. As a spectre, Dukoona never slept. Suspended by invisible bonds, he hung, rigid, six feet off the ground, limbs stretched to their limits; bound by Rectar's will.

Whether a day or an hour later, Rectar would return. It was inevitable.

"Awake again?" Rectar's voice hissed. Somehow, his voice never seemed too close, nor too far away.

Dukoona shuddered at the words. It took longer each time for his wits to return, as though his conscious mind had retreated further into a quiet recess of his being, burrowing deeper in the hope that even Rectar could not reach him there. Perhaps he would eventually retreat forever. And that might be a blessing. When he could think clearly, he was haunted by his failure. He'd failed to keep his spectres safe. He'd failed to protect his Trusted, but worst of all was knowing that he could never have succeeded. Rectar always had the power to reel his servants back in.

"Get it over with," Dukoona whispered. And somehow, no matter how quietly he spoke, Rectar always heard him.

"Why don't you ask for death?"

Dukoona had his answer ready. It was the reason he'd given to little Sonrid for not granting his own request for death.

"I want revenge. I want to die free."

"Then your wait shall never end."

A great crack rent the air. He lowered his head in distress, not wanting to look, knowing what usually followed those sounds. Rectar would have summoned one of his spectres to be tortured in front of him. Dukoona mustered the strength to raise his head, yet lost all spirit when he saw the spectre before him.

It was Kidrian. The guttering purple embers upon his head were unmistakable. He met Dukoona's eye, and his courage showed in his tightly pressed lips.

I'm sorry, Dukoona mouthed silently.

Behind Kidrian, Rectar landed softly and began to take on his earthly appearance, though his body was shrouded by a ripped crimson cloak and a drawn hood hid his face. A pale hand slipped out from under the cloak and gently brushed down Kidrian's embers. Kidrian writhed at the touch, winced and ground his teeth. But he did not scream.

Rectar seemed displeased at this. Red eyes flashed from beneath his hood. He looked to Dukoona, and then Dukoona felt his master forcibly enter his mind. It felt like Rectar was squeezing on his consciousness with a plated fist drawn from a fire. An unbreakable grip that was just as strong as it had been back at Aurisha, when Rectar had torn Dukoona away from the city and from Darnuir. And then Rectar's voice was in his head.

'I'd like you to kill him.'

You'll have to make me.

'KILL.' Rectar's command dominated him. Dukoona's mind emptied. Now, all he desired was Kidrian dead on the stone floor, to see smoking blood rising from a dozen wounds.

Dukoona found his bonds were broken. He fell to the ground, rose, enjoying the freedom of his limbs. He stepped towards Kidrian and began summoning his sword. Shadows swirled and the blade formed in his hand.

Kidrian did not break eye contact as his executioner approached. "I do not blame you," he said. "It was an honour to fight; to try. And better by your hand, Lord, than His."

A distant part of Dukoona, the minute part that Rectar had not grasped, looked on in horror as his body drew up before Kidrian. This was no fitting end for his most loyal spectre, the leader of his Trusted. Dukoona felt his sword arm rise, readying the killing blow.

No, he thought. He had to fight. He must resist until the bitter end.

Dukoona pushed against Rectar's will with everything he had. It was enough to nudge his arm off course as it descended, slicing through Kidrian's arm instead of cutting across his chest.

Kidrian shrieked as his limb fell wetly to the floor. Smoke billowed from the wound. Dukoona himself felt both grief for his friend and frustration at not fulfilling the burning command that Rectar had placed in his mind. Yet no matter how much he fought it, his arm rose again for the kill. He ought not to have tried to stop the inevitable. Kidrian would die now in agony. He deserved better. Hating himself, Dukoona gave up.

At that moment, Rectar turned sharply around. From the darkness, a distant roaring reached Dukoona's ears. As it increased in volume, the grip Rectar had on Dukoona's mind lessened. Rectar took a step towards the noise, and Dukoona felt a great deal of his master's presence leave him. Without pausing to consider the matter, Dukoona attempted to retake control of his body. The feeling was like nothing he'd felt before. He strained, his mind searing in pain as he fought against Rectar, but his arm slowed and stopped, just above Kidrian's exposed neck.

He hardly believed it. Rectar's presence was still very much in his mind, a vast mountain to overcome. And Rectar himself was standing only feet away. It was the closest Dukoona had ever been to his master. Could he kill him? The wild thought might be futile, but it gave him a burst of hope. Even if he failed, so what? What could happen now? How could things possibly get any worse?

The roars persisted and Rectar's grip loosened further.

Dukoona had to try.

He gathered the last remnants of his strength and pushed back against the lingering presence of his master. His body lunged forwards and he swiped at Rectar's back. The dark blade swished and would have caught the crimson cloak, but Rectar had vanished. In the same moment, his master's presence left him entirely. Dukoona regained full control.

He darted to Kidrian's side, though there was nothing he could do to heal such a wound. He knelt, cradling Kidrian in his arms.

"I am ashamed," he said.

"Never give in," Kidrian said. "If we die, we die free, yes?" The shadows on his flesh were thinning and parting, fleeing like steam through an open window, leaving his bones bare.

"We'll die free," Dukoona said. He didn't know what else to say.

Kidrian smiled weakly, and just as the light in his eyes looked to flicker and die, he gasped and sprung up from Dukoona's cradling arms. Kidrian's shadows thickened and formed, the wound by his shoulder closed though his arm remained missing. Yet before Dukoona could react, another great crack sounded and Kidrian vanished as quickly as he'd appeared.

"Kidrian?" Dukoona called. "Kidrian?"

But it was no use shouting. No use in hoping. He sank back down, letting his blade turn to wisps of shadow, and held his head in both hands. It was times like these that he wished he could weep like the other races could; wished for some way to release the fear, and guilt, and pain welling inside of him. Nonetheless, he gave it a go, resulting in shortened, painful, dry sobs. His hands shook so badly that he feared he'd lost all control of them.

He regained himself after a time, and found it strange that Rectar had left him for so long. What had happened? What would cause Rectar to lose his grip? To Dukoona's knowledge, nothing could. And he was under no illusion. He'd only gained back partial control because Rectar's hold over him had weakened. Something else must have taken his power. Yet the only living things down here were his master's new servants. Could they require such an exertion of Rectar to control? The thought of that was frightening.

The distant roaring still sounded, although fainter than before. Dukoona looked through the gloom in the direction that it came from. Ahead, a great oval-shaped pool shimmered, like a towering window onto an ocean of bubbling blue blood. Black silhouettes moved against the blue tear in the world, with pairs of red eyes bobbing like fat angry fireflies.

When at last the roaring ceased, the light in the cavern shifted. The blue pool in the distance vanished, the red eyes snuffed out. Flames encircled Dukoona, but he'd grown accustomed to this frequent trick. Even Rectar had his routine. So it came as no surprise when the crimson-cloaked figure returned.

'Kneel,' Rectar commanded, but there was no need. Dukoona remained on his knees, but the command compelled him to straighten his back and face his master directly. Rectar stepped through the ring of fire, which extinguished at his touch, drew out his sword and pointed it down. Its blade reminded Dukoona of the starium stone of Aurisha, dull and grainy and gold.

"I'll ask again. Do you wish for death?"

I won't say it. I won't ask you for it.

The crimson hood tilted to one side. "Well?"

Dukoona hesitated, confused. *Can he not hear my thoughts? If he is in my mind, he can; but until that time, I am free. Free to think, at least.* Dukoona had always assumed his master's power over him was complete. But then, he had not been in such close proximity to Rectar since the time when he had been summoned to this world. Perhaps he had assumed wrong.

"My answer remains the same," Dukoona said.

Beneath the hood, Rectar's red eyes flashed. "Your endurance is pleasing. Looking back, I ought to have stripped some of your free will when I brought you and your kind to this world. A mistake I shall not repeat."

"Who are you, Rectar?" Dukoona had asked that question many times when he'd first been summoned. This time he desired more than a name.

"I am Rectar, God of the Shadow. One of three." And to Dukoona's surprise, Rectar lowered his hood. His face was both ordinary and distinctly alien. His skin was too smooth to be natural; his cheeks pinched too tightly; the irises on his eyes widened and closed hastily, as though adjusting to an ever-changing light. Dark-blond hair fell past his shoulders, a mark of the race he belonged to.

"This vessel had the strength to contain me," Rectar said. He raised a stark white hand as though to examine it and his eyes narrowed in disappointment.

"Who was he? The dragon whose body you use."

"Kroener was his name. Unlike you, he was a good listener."

'He obeyed my voice.'

Dukoona winced as Rectar's voice burned in his mind. Thankfully, as quickly as Rectar entered his mind, he was gone.

"I would have preferred the other one," Rectar said. "Had I taken his body, I would have had access to two blades. Yet the young prince was strong in will and strong with the Others. Kroener was the more malleable. My deception was upsetting for him, at the end. What's left of him whimpers still, even to this day." There was no pity in Rectar's life. No emotion at all. Not even a sick pleasure. "Power in this world is crude but potent when channelled correctly. The Others helped their servants craft such fine weapons to harness it. I wonder if they regret it?"

"What do you speak of?"

Rectar cocked his head, ignoring the question. His shifting red eyes looked Dukoona up and down. "Such a shame. You could have been so much more. Alas, it is always the way with lesser beings. You lack the focus, the patience, the foresight. Lesser beings count time in years, whereas I and my kind count it in millennia. I wonder if the dragons have disappointed the Others as you have done me. But they are mine now. I have made the perfect servants. And all worlds will fall to them." To Dukoona's shock, Rectar knelt to face him. He cupped Dukoona's chin in one of his freezing white hands. "Your strength is admirable nonetheless."

"Admirable?" Dukoona struggled to speak with his master's hand around his jaw. "I destroyed your armies."

"You did, though the demons were measly creatures. All I could summon and control once the power of this blade had diminished. The guardian delayed me. He played for as much time as he could. If I had been able to kill their infant king—" Rectar trailed off in a throaty growl. For once, he seemed frustrated.

Dukoona took heart at these words. His master had failed before, then. Perhaps there was hope?

"The guardian has their king by his side now," he said. "If you could not kill Darnuir as a child, how will you face them both? Darnuir will stop you."

"Will he?" Rectar said, locking eyes with him. "Let's discover why you feel so strongly about that." And then followed the lancing pain as Rectar pierced his mind. Dukoona had no strength to even flee as his master raked through his memories, each one replayed at speed across his mind's eye. It wasn't long before he was reliving that night when he'd met Darnuir atop the Royal Tower. He relived the nerves, the excitement, the fear that Rectar would surely see; and the faint relief, the desperate hope that this young dragon might have listened to him. As he lay writhing on the terrace from Rectar's summons, he looked up at Darnuir. 'Do you trust me?' he asked. The king's face was struck with worry, but he did not answer. Dukoona reached up and pulled Darnuir closer. 'We don't have to be enemies,' he said.

His free hand had found a shadow and he melded away, and as he did so, so did the memory, and the presence of Rectar from his mind. Dukoona returned to the present with a gasp, back in control of himself.

Rectar withdrew his hand and got to his feet, his hood drawing up of its own accord.

"You may still have a use before the end."

Dukoona didn't wish to know what use that would be. For now, he was lifted back off his feet and bound by invisible cords. Fresh roaring echoed from the blackness and Rectar moved off to deal with it, morphing into his shapeless form once more. Dukoona was left hanging helpless in the dark of Kar'drun, with only the cries of Rectar's new servants to break his thoughts.

2

THE ADDICTED KING

"Mind addled, soul torn. Body aged, blackened and worn. Resist, resist, resist the blue, else horrors and woe will find you."

Ancient fairy verse

Darnuir – Aurisha – The Royal Tower

Steel chains bit at his arms. Hot blood ran from the chafing points, and he heard the tap, tap, tap as droplets hit the floor. He shouldn't squirm, but his hands couldn't help but struggle to reach his sword. People were approaching, yet his vision was so clouded it was hard to tell how many. At least three people, he thought. Maybe four. One brought a cloth to dab at his brow and he felt cold water run down his face. His eyes closed against the water and, sighing at the momentary relief, he drifted away from the world.

Sleep enveloped him like a hot bath. He was safe, and whole, and calm; not in pain from his hunger. He was at peace.

Then the steel chains turned into snakes.

Their white fangs flensed his flesh. When he screamed his defiance, the snakes only turned their baleful eyes upon him and hissed. Red tongues and scarlet eyes; they mocked Darnuir. Him, of all people. Did they plan to make a meal out of the dragon king? Darnuir began to laugh instead. These snakes were worms compared to him.

As he laughed, the room around him came into focus. It was Castallan's throne room. He was sure of it because a segment of the wall had been blasted away, and blue light shone from the Cascade Sink. Magic welled up behind the door in his mind. Powerful, delicious magic.

No, no, I mustn't use it.

The red snakes began to drink his blood, their scaly bellies swelling fit to burst. So Darnuir relented; he had no choice.

He let the door burst open, filling him from head to toe with Cascade energy. He felt unstoppable and his laughter at the snakes turned to a roar. Deep, guttural, bestial. He saw what remained of his skin turn scaly and red, felt the heat rise in his throat, and saw the fear engulf the little snakes as they tried to slither away.

He crushed them all under his claw, leaving a mess of blood and cracked stone. The throne room became constricting as his growing wings scraped against the ceiling. Just as he thought about making for the broken wall to escape, the Cascade Sink turned from blue to yellow and shone brighter than the sun. Darnuir groaned, worried that the light would blind him. But it didn't. Somehow it burned brighter and still his eyes remained unharmed. Yellow deepened to gold and amber, and Darnuir heard a voice in his mind. Such a quiet voice. An echo of a whisper uttered long ago.

'Three blades were given.'

Darnuir dug his talons into the stone beneath and dragged himself towards the light. Just before he reached it, pain seared his eyes. He rammed them shut. Something burned them and he was desperate to rub them, tear them out. But his arms were held in place.

"Hold him. Prefect Lira is on her way."

Red snakes, red eyes. What was it Dukoona told me? Darnuir's mind raced for the answer.

His eyes opened and he saw he was back in his chambers. There were no snakes. No light. Only two young Praetorians and Lira before him, holding a solitary candle. She stood taller than he recalled, her grey eyes hard and cold. Her mouth moved as she spoke to the Praetorians, but Darnuir couldn't make out her words. The Praetorian handed her another cloth and she brought it over his face, dabbing gently at his burning brow.

His thoughts kept spinning. Red snakes, red eyes. Dukoona warned him. Dragons taken to Kar'drun.

Lira finished her work and stepped away. Darnuir wanted to hear what she was saying but couldn't. His ears rang, and he shook his head repeatedly, as though water was trapped between them.

Dragons twisted like Castallan's men. So many. Coming. We must prepare.

Lira was at the door now, but this time he caught a smattering of words.

"His turns don't last nearly as long, Prefect."

"Then we must hope he'll return to us soon," she said. "Dranus be damned, but I can't make Blaine do a thing on my own." She looked to Darnuir again. "You better feed him today," she added.

Darnuir tried to say her name but the word died in his dusty throat.

"He hates it when we use the tube, Prefect."

"It's all we can do," said Lira. "And give him as much water as you can. We need him back." She turned away. She was about to leave.

"Lira," he gasped. In an instant, she was back at his side, her face silhouetted in the weak candlelight. "Lira," he wheezed again. She took his hand; her own was warm against his cold, clammy skin.

"What is it?"

"They are coming," Darnuir said. "Dukoona warned. Dragons. Stronger than us. Must prepare... must prepare."

She smiled weakly. "Thank you, Darnuir. I shall try my best. You must rest now, if you can."

Darnuir nodded, unable to say anything more. Lira patted his hand before leaving with the other Praetorians. The door closed. He was left alone, head drooping to one side. Drool dangled from his mouth, and he hadn't the wit to spit it away. Then his eyes closed again, this time to a merciful, dreamless sleep.

3

THE PREFECT

"I'm going to write it down. Everything that happened."

Author Unknown

Lira – Aurisha – The Royal Tower

Lira closed the door to the king's bedchambers, shut her eyes, and blew out her cheeks with a heavy breath. She allowed herself this moment before straightening. The muscles in her back and shoulders somehow tightened further and fought her attempts to move them. Her eye fell upon the open crate nearby. Feeding tubes. Such a horrible act they'd been forced to adopt. And fresh steel chains should Darnuir break another set. The Praetorians who had attended Darnuir with her took up positions on either side of the door. They would all be needed to contain him if he took a turn for the worse. Three more awaited her by the stairs.

"The king improves," she told them. The Praetorians nodded silently. Lira wondered whether any of them ever believed her. "We must keep working hard for him. There is still much to do if we are to face this new threat." The Praetorians continued to nod. She resisted biting her lip. She wasn't the most rousing speechmaker. She'd opted for a no-nonsense, blunt and to-the-point approach in dealing with matters these last two months. A nagging part of her knew that if she had even half the charisma of Bacchus, she'd have gotten more done.

A young boy emerged from the stairs, carrying a fresh jug of water for Darnuir. Seeing the very young dragons always knotted her stomach. It wasn't fair to bring them on campaigns with the legions. They were children still. The boy brought the water to the guards by the door, then saluted Lira. She looked him up and down, from his fraying breeches to his overgrown, unkempt hair. Who even looked after these young boys? Their mothers weren't here with them. They were all stuck in the camps outside Brevia, she supposed, perhaps with her own mother as well.

Lira offered the boy a smile in return. "You're not even breathless. You could make a fine outrunner one day. Make sure the king drinks plenty," she added to the Praetorians by the door. "And fetch more if needed. I'll return at nightfall." She made for the stairs leading down the Royal Tower, the boy and her three attending Praetorians following in her wake.

Near the bottom of the tower, Lira entered the throne room. She and the Praetorians had taken it as their main base of operations, the better to represent Darnuir in his absence. The blocky starium throne lay unoccupied, its steps leading down to the largest tables they had found intact within the upper levels of the city. Stacks of parchment sat beside open maps of eastern Tenalp, and more detailed sketches of Aurisha and its immediate environment. In the middle of the room was an iron plinth, holding up the scrying orb that had been salvaged and brought from the Bastion. Despite going to the trouble of bringing the communications device, it had barely been used. Presently, the orb's misty innards were white and calm.

Lira spotted Raymond conversing quietly with the outrunner Damien, their heads together at the base of the throne's steps. She made directly for them and Raymond greeted her with a warm smile. Lira found she could always rely on him for a smile.

"How is he?" Raymond asked.

"He's not screaming as much, and his turns don't last as long," Lira said quietly, so that only she, Raymond and Damien could hear. "Yet again he reminded me of our impending doom." She sighed and chanced a look towards the scrying orb. "Has Arkus—"

"I'm afraid not, Prefect," Damien said.

The tension in Lira's shoulders twanged again. "Very well. Then has Blaine—" She stopped herself this time, seeing Raymond's shaking head. "Why must he drag things out? If he doesn't wish to speak to Arkus then so be it. I only need him to operate the damned thing with his magic." She pinched hard between her eyes.

Raymond closed what small gap remained between them, placing his hand on the small of her back. "Perhaps you should take some rest? Real rest. Even for a dragon, you haven't slept in a long time." She gave him a weak smile. He was trying to be kind, of course, but he'd been working just as hard as her, relatively speaking. Well, he'd done what he could. For a human.

"I'll sleep when Darnuir returns to us or when we're ready to face this attack. Whichever comes first."

She moved to lean her weight upon the table, poring over the map of the city. Countless scribbled notes detailed the damage that had been done while the city was occupied by the demons, highlighting the weak spots in case of a frontal assault by land and possible choke points within the streets should the walls fall. The harbour at the southern end of the city was Aurisha's soft underbelly, made more vulnerable by Blaine sending most of the human fleet back to Brevia, ostensibly to collect the dragons that were stuck there. No ship had yet returned. Still, Rectar wouldn't risk battling on the open sea. Any advantage these twisted dragons would have would be best exploited on land, so it had been to the northern defences that Lira had focused her efforts.

"Do we have a progress report on the gate repairs?"

An older dragon shuffled forward seemingly out of nowhere. He must have been waiting for an audience, but in her haste and half-exhausted state, she had not even noticed him. Indeed, her tiredness was beginning to seriously alarm her. She knew she recognised the dragon but temporarily couldn't place him. He was short and squat, and his crooked smile revealed he had a missing tooth.

"I can update you on the city gate, Lady Prefect," he said. His speech contained a light whistle.

Lira's embarrassment at not remembering this man's name all but evaporated. Only the old dragons felt the need to preface her title with 'lady'. In giving him a cold stare, she forgot to say anything at all.

Raymond stepped in. "Vitrus, what is your assessment as master engineer?"

Vitrus gave no acknowledgment that he could even see Raymond, let alone hear him.

"Lady Prefect, I have used the Eighth Legion to clear the debris and make what easy repairs can be made to the city walls with what resources are available to us."

"That sounds like good news," Lira said. "Truly, we are grateful that you journeyed east with us."

Vitrus wrinkled his nose. "The legate of the Eighth recruited me from the camps at Brevia. He considered my talents would be useful."

"Well, I'm glad some of those in charge of our legions have sense," she said, forgetting that it wasn't only the Praetorians who were around her. Maybe she did need sleep.

Vitrus met her remark with barely contained disapproval. "Our legionary legates have been leading men and defending our people for twice as long as you've been alive, Lady Prefect. They've been fighting longer than any of this *guard*." His sharp conveyance of the word brought his whistle to a high pitch. "I lost this damned tooth when we fled Aurisha twenty years ago. Some of you were barely walking then. Little better than hatchlings, the lot of you, but my king chooses you, so…"

Raymond and Damien shifted uneasily, as did some of the guard unused to blunt words such as these. Lira, however, was more used to hearing this line of late. She held her composure.

"Yes, he chose me."

"Don't mistake yourselves for him," Vitrus said.

So, this was what it had come to, was it? The legates voicing their concerns through any dragon that was sent to the throne room?

Lira sniffed. "I could never mistake myself for the wielder of the Dragon's Blade." Vitrus had all the beginnings of a smug smile, but she raised a finger and met him with a fierce stare. "And yet, I won't have it so easily forgotten that it was I who brought the legions back in time to save the king when fifty thousand demons cornered him atop the city's plateau. I trust also that your opinions have not hindered your trade?"

Vitrus folded his arms. "I take pride in my work, Lady Prefect. As a matter of fact, I was inspired by the gate mechanisms at Brevia. Far more sophisticated than the ancient doors that were in place before the fall of Aurisha. I have designed a way to adapt these elements on a scale and strength worthy of our race."

"An impressive claim, if true."

"However, I regret that it cannot be done. To build such a gate would require a great deal of wood, time, and fresh custom-forged components. Wood we could manage, though the nearest abundant source is north and east, closer to Kar'drun as the bird flies from here. Time is for the gods to decide. As for the metal, we have no ore. There is no trade. I can't build on air and necessity alone."

Lira looked down and lightly rocked her knuckles across the tabletop. The parchment of the maps felt dry and rough. "So, are you telling me we are to have no working gate?"

"Not without a sudden influx of supplies from the west," Vitrus said, and looked to Raymond. "Any chance of that, human?"

"I am hardly in a position to say."

"Something must be done to block the gap," Lira said.

"Whatever for?" Vitrus said. "Then we can't get out."

Lira rolled her knuckles more vigorously. "I do not mean for us to be blocked in at once. I merely need the option."

"In case of what?"

"In case we are attacked, Vitrus."

"Lady Prefect, the war is over. The demon armies are destroyed."

Lira inwardly cursed. She exchanged nervous glances with Raymond and Damien.

Their ability to maintain order was tenuous without Darnuir, and most attempts to explain that a new threat was on the way had been met with scepticism. If the legates ever decided that the mad young Praetorians ought to be pushed aside for the time being, there would be nothing Lira could do about it. She doubted Blaine would rush out from the Basilica to intervene.

Their brief silence caused Vitrus to frown and Lira hastened to say calmly, "It was our Lord Darnuir's wish that the city be made as secure as possible. I fear a gate-sized hole in our walls fails to meet those orders."

"Quite," Vitrus said. He made a sucking sound as he considered and then said, "Much of the debris we cleared has been taken outside the city for disposal. I could arrange for it to be brought to the breach and there lie in wait should we have need to block the gateway."

"That's something, at least," Lira said. "Thank you, Vitrus. You should begin at once." The older dragon stepped back two paces before he turned his back to Lira and headed out of the throne room. She thought she heard some mutterings of 'wasted time'.

"Please tell me that's all there is to deal with this morning." Raymond and Damien exchanged looks and she knew it wasn't so. She sighed. "Out with it, then."

"Another human officer arrived just after dawn," Raymond said.

"Spare us," Lira said. A throbbing grew behind her eyes. "Not more shouting matches in the streets again? I told them. We can't investigate on nought but speculation."

"It was more than words this time, I'm afraid," Raymond said. "He claims there was a fight."

"A fight?"

"I imagine it was more of a scuffle," Raymond said.

"Don't downplay it. What happened?"

"The usual nonsense was shouted, apparently. 'Dragons are superior. Dragons are blessed. Humans should leave our city at once.' Only this time, the humans didn't sit idly by. Seems they had had enough of talking. Although it was five on one, the dragon who was shouting beat the others soundly. He evaded capture, outrunning the humans with ease. It seems we can no longer pretend dragons are not involved."

Lira nodded slowly. "My hopes that humans were winding up their own was always a faint dream. Is there still nothing that obviously links these incidents to Blaine's followers?"

"Nothing beyond the words they reportedly use," Raymond said.

"Well, that's not enough to accuse them," Lira said in frustration. Not that she would know what to do if a bunch of Blaine's Light Bearers really did start beating up humans. How would she be able to stand up to Blaine if it came to blows? How could any of them? They sorely needed Darnuir back for this sort of thing.

"I admit I'd find it strange that Blaine would be so…" Raymond searched for the word. "Careless."

"Well, they've all gone a bit cracked since the Nail Head," Lira said. She made a swirling loop of her finger above her ear but ceased when she caught Damien's eye. "Still. We should follow up with him again, just to make sure. So many have joined his flock lately I'm sure there are some that are acting beyond his direct control."

Damien cleared his throat loudly. "If I may make a suggestion, Prefect?"

"What do you have in mind?"

"If restlessness is leading to bad blood, perhaps we should find more work to do. Taking more humans out of the city might appease whatever group this is and make use of idle labour. The fertile land of the Tail Peninsula was once a great source of our people's food. Much work will be needed if we are to sow our own seeds this year and mark our new beginning."

"As a human, I can guarantee that will not go down well," said Raymond. "I fear such a move would only aggravate matters to dangerous levels. We cannot ask humans to prepare dragon fields while their own back home go wanting for labour."

"We could ask only for volunteers," Damien said. "Dragons too. I could go with them myself. We need to begin the work, and Lord Darnuir promised I could retire to the Tail."

Lira considered him. An outrunner's feet showed how fit they were. She glanced down at Damien's and her first thought was to marvel at how his bare feet had not turned into blocks of ice over winter. They were looking rough, to be sure; the skin was more like hide and covered in blotchy purple-blue bruises that were unwilling to fade.

Damien caught her looking. "Already my heels cause me pain." He said it with such stoicism. He could be fighting back tears; she'd never know. And he would never admit it. Perhaps it would be kindest to allow him to rest.

"It would be a great shame to lose you," Lira said. "Darnuir values your abilities and I your insights."

"There are other outrunners still," Damien said. "Will you think on my proposal?"

"I will, but I cannot make any promises."

"Lord Darnuir may not regain his strength for another month," Damien said. "You may have to make hard decisions."

Lira frowned and felt her shoulders sag. "I fear I may push the patience of the legates if I do…" She trailed off. Anger and frustration and exhaustion made a poor mix. She felt light-headed.

"Darnuir will return soon," Raymond said. "He grows stronger each day, as you say."

"Let's hope so," she said.

Lira pulled herself together and rubbed again at her tired eyes. "I'll go and see Blaine about this human-baiting. Might as well get it over with."

She was already halfway to the throne room doors when Raymond called out, "I shall come with you."

Lira halted and turned. "No," she replied. It sounded far harsher than she had intended. Raymond recoiled mid-stride, looking wounded. She'd hurt his pride, but Lira only wished to see him spared from the Light Bearers' scornful stares; their cutting words.

"You know what they're like," she said, "but you hardly need me to tell you that. If you want to come, it's not right that I should stop you."

He smiled that warm smile of his, and she felt bolstered. He stood at her side as she summoned another half-dozen Praetorians. Together they made their way out of the Royal Tower and across the plaza towards the entrance of the Basilica of Light.

A crisp wind swept across the plateau, but the day was clear, and a pale sun attempted to warm the world at winter's end. Cold blue light tinged the entire plaza. Marble columns sparkled like pillars of ice. Yet no light could soften the reddened, charred grounds at its centre. Lira could only guess as to what had happened here, and it was the sort of thoughts that were best left for nightmares.

The Basilica itself dominated the south side of the plaza, its great dome rising like a half-sun of golden stone. A colonnaded entrance sat atop an imposing set of marble stairs, and Light Bearers stood between each column to guard the eerie, candlelit hall within. Each of Blaine's men faced their shields outwards to the world, displaying the painted yellow emblem of a sword cutting through a sun of spiralling lines.

Lira approached with purpose. She was the Praetorian prefect, whether these older dragons liked it or not. She had authority over the king's elite guard. Besides, she would not be interrupting a sermon this time. However, as she walked past, the Light Bearers didn't so much as glance at her. That irked her more. She also deserved respect.

Within the Basilica, there were only three other Light Bearers present, looking like wooden miniatures by the stone sword-holders under the dome. A beam of that cold winter light shone through the opening in the dome above.

Her footsteps rang loudly but the figures by the stone swords did not stir. Drawing closer, she saw the dragon in the middle of the trio was none other than Bacchus. His olive skin was smooth as worked alabaster, and his expression was entirely passive as she approached. Only when they were ten paces away did Bacchus throw out his hand.

"Halt there, young Lira."

She deliberately walked another three paces before stopping. When nothing more was said, she tutted loudly and glanced towards the alcove that led down to the Guardian's Sanctum.

"You know I am here to speak with Blaine. His second won't do."

Bacchus tilted his head, as though observing a precocious child. "I remind you to refer to him as *Lord Guardian*. And why not converse with me? I might be a second, but so are you." His voice was smoother than silk, richer than sweetened cream, and yet never sickly. Lira understood why Blaine valued Bacchus as a speaker to his faithful, even if the man had attempted a coup of sorts only months before. He was keeping his enemy close, she supposed.

"I would also remind you, Bacchus, to address me by my title: Praetorian Prefect. My age is irrelevant. And while I might be a second, the king is currently indisposed, while the Lord Guardian is merely down in his chambers."

"The Lord Guardian is out among his people."

Lira shook her head. "Don't bother. He rarely leaves this temple. That much I know. If he left more often, perhaps I would not need to be here. Fetch him for me. Now." She was as stern as she dared and held Bacchus' eye.

Without breaking that eye contact, Bacchus took a few steps closer and said more quietly, "Remember, Lady Prefect, that our Lord Guardian has been touched by the divine. He is chosen by our gods to lead us in the fight against the Shadow. Thousands bore witness to the event. Darnuir may be our king, but he is only that." He took a final step forwards, lightly so, even a little threatening. Raymond stepped lithely forward too, throwing up an arm towards Bacchus.

"That's close enough, Light Bearer."

Bacchus smirked. "But of course, human. I certainly wouldn't want you to hurt yourself in defence of your superior. Such loyalty." He flicked his perfect olive-green eyes between Raymond and Lira, his smirk unwavering. "As you clearly won't leave, I shall adjourn and request the Lord Guardian to grant you his time."

Once Bacchus had entered the alcove and descended the stairs out of sight, Lira rounded on Raymond and thumped him squarely on his breastplate. "What was that about?" she hissed. "Goading Bacchus – are you mad? He'd crush you."

Flushed with embarrassment, Raymond stepped back. "You're right, Lira. I'm not sure what came over me."

Lira pinched between her eyes again. She hadn't meant to snap quite so severely. She was just so tired. Lira endured another round of rapid blinking during which dark blots flashed across her vision. Holding her eyes shut a moment longer seemed to ease the symptoms, and her moment of flared temper cooled as well. "Raymond, I—"

"There's no need," he said, looking anywhere but at her. "I think I hear them coming."

Sure enough, Blaine and Bacchus emerged from the alcove. Blaine drew up before Lira and the Praetorians, while Bacchus lurked farther back by the stone swords.

It had been over a week since Lira had last seen Blaine. His skin appeared lighter than before, likely because he was spending so much time in the Basilica. In his heavy guardian's armour, he still looked larger than life; his feet shoulder-width apart, hands cupped behind his back. That was something he had tended to do lately. Lira thought it was to hide the missing finger on his right hand. Injury aside, Blaine was the picture of health. Lira still found it hard to believe he was one hundred and fifty years old. The only place she could see his age was in his eyes. Their blue was deeper than any she had ever seen, as though each year of his life had added a layer of colour, each one darker than the last. She didn't like to hold his gaze for very long, however. Doing so reminded her of how she'd felt the first time they'd met in Val'-tarra; her nerves, and her disappointment. She'd only wanted to lend her sword to the war effort and Blaine had scorned her for it. Privately, Lira relished the triumph of standing before him, forcing him to acknowledge her.

"How gracious of you to step up from your chambers," she said.

Blaine's face was impassive. "Unless Arkus has finally reneged and is sending our people who are stuck in those wretched camps home, I don't see what we have left to discuss."

"How about members of your flock abusing our human allies?" Blaine merely raised an eyebrow. Lira pushed on. "Earlier today we received a complaint from a human officer. I'm not blaming you, Blaine—"

"Lord Guardian," Bacchus snapped, sounding just like that legate had back in Val'tarra.

"Lord Guardian," she said bitingly. "Though I only have to say it once, isn't that right, Blaine?"

"It is." Blaine offered nothing more. This was how it had been since Darnuir had taken ill; like trying to wring shimmer brew out from blackened leaves.

"So you claim to know nothing of dragons harassing humans?"

"Do you have proof that these dragons have something to do with my followers?"

"Who else calls dragons a blessed people?"

"Perhaps this officer misinterpreted events," said Bacchus. "Or overreacted. Humans can be soft at heart."

"I would have hoped that we had proven ourselves to you by now," Raymond said.

"Not all our kind can be so easily won over by combed hair and a smile, Cheva-lier," Bacchus said. His eyes flicked very deliberately to Lira.

Blaine glanced over his shoulder. "Quiet now, Bacchus. Let the young Praetorians speak."

Lira stepped forwards. "Blaine, if your people are harassing the humans in any way, it must stop. Darnuir would not abide it and neither can I. We need their support. You know of the threat we face."

"A threat conveyed to our king, a self-confessed Cascade addict, by a spectre who is unreliable at best and still working for the enemy at worst. It's been nearly two months. What is Rectar doing if he has a powerful new force to use against us?"

"Do you not believe Darnuir?" Lira said. "Is that why you do so little to prepare our defences?"

Blaine narrowed his eyes. "Careful, Prefect. My patience will not stretch to such questioning. It is not my fault that our king chose to blunder on quicker than he had sense for. I did not leave us stranded in this city over winter. And as for our defence, I have been sending faithful followers from the Third Legion to secure and repair our abandoned northern forts along the Crucidal Road."

Lira could hardly believe what she was hearing. "And you didn't think it prudent to inform me?"

"You'll also recall," Blaine continued as though he had not heard her, "that I sent ships from the Brevian fleet west, and requested that Arkus send our people home. This I did at Darnuir's behest. That Arkus has not complied is no fault of mine."

"You could ask more than once. You've barely spoken to Arkus and I can't work the orb without your magic."

"And," Blaine went on, "I am even now preparing to repair our city's gate. Plans have been drawn but it may take some time for materials to—"

"Stop," Lira said. She balled her hands into shaking fists. "I've been preparing to repair the gate as well. Why didn't you tell me? Why haven't you communicated with me?"

Blaine withstood her anger, perfectly cool. He barely moved. "Lira, I do admire the way in which you led the legions hurriedly to battle. But do not overstep your position, nor place responsibilities upon your rank that are not yours. You're the head of Darnuir's personal bodyguard; not his replacement, not his regent, and certainly not my equal. The guardian exists for times just such as these: to lead our people if our king is indisposed. That is what I am doing, and I do not need to consult with dozens of younger, less experience dragons and a former chevalier. I have entrusted you with Darnuir's care. Let that be enough."

A lengthy silence followed. Lira opened and clenched her fist several times, all the while staring at Blaine's implacable face. Her fury found its way through a shuddering whisper.

"If that is your role, Blaine, then where were you for decades while our people were at war and then in exile? Where was our great guardian then?"

"I do not have time to explain," said Blaine. "I'll let Darnuir answer your questions, if he sees fit." Blaine appeared to turn to leave, but hesitated. "How is he?"

"Come visit him yourself if you wish to know," Lira said.

"That at least is a fair remark," Blaine said. "I ought to do more for him. Now, if you'll excuse me…" He really did begin to walk away this time. To Lira's horror, she saw Raymond step forward too, moving as though to intercept Blaine.

Before she could draw breath to stop him, Raymond called out, "Lord Guardian, I do not believe you answered Prefect Lira satisfactorily."

Blaine stopped walking but did not turn around.

"Raymond, get back," she urged, but he continued.

"Will you make inquiries into these accusations?" Raymond took another step closer and Bacchus moved between him and Blaine, grasping the hilt of his sword.

"No further, human. You are not worthy to be so close to our gods' chosen champion."

Lira's heart felt like it would punch through her chest. She rushed to Raymond's side, her hand upon her own sword. "Back off, right now. Both of you."

"Bacchus," Blaine called airily, without turning. "Step away from the Praetorians. There will be no fighting in this sacred place." Bacchus scurried back to Blaine like a dog to heel.

"And will anything be done about what we have discussed?" Lira said.

"I shall inform you if so," said Blaine. And, with that, he descended into the alcove, Bacchus trailing in his wake. Lira found herself short of breath. Once again, she rounded on Raymond.

"What's gotten into you?"

"They're just so difficult," he muttered.

"Yes, and I don't need you making it harder," she said, exasperated. Raymond shuffled his feet, eyes rigidly fixed on the doorway.

"Shall we leave?"

"Yes, but not back to the tower." She spoke to the group of Praetorians at large now. "We'll go to the Lower City and see what we can uncover for ourselves. Come on."

4

THE DOUBTFUL CHOSEN

"With sanction from both gods and dragons, I thought daily tribulations would ease. I thought I would feel rapture, yet I felt as I always had done. And I struggled on just the same."

Records of the Guardian Nhilus, 1507 AT

Blaine – The Guardian's Sanctum

Blaine descended beneath the Basilica with Bacchus, heading towards his inner sanctum. They passed barracks and quarters for Light Bearers, the space now much needed for their swelling ranks.

Blaine entered the sanctum and admired, as he had of late, the two great hearths and ornate pulpit upon the dais, all cut from marble. A wide balcony overlooked the switchback streets that led down to the harbour. A chill breeze swept in and Blaine shivered, his breath rising in steamy clouds. Yet, ever watchful of his health, the Guardian's Blade warmed him without the need for fire. Bacchus was not so fortunate. Blaine allowed a moment to pass, letting Bacchus try to mask his own shivering; letting him see again the difference between them.

"You wished to speak to me?" Bacchus said.

"What was that about with the girl? I thought my instructions to the Light Bearers were quite clear."

"Your order was disseminated among the faithful," Bacchus said. "Her reports must be false."

Blaine studied him, searching for any sign of a lie. However, even through the slight tremors from the cold, Bacchus' expression was as impenetrable as ever.

"Are you aware of who the perpetrators were on previous occasions?"

"I am," Bacchus said.

"And did you reprimand them, as discussed?"

Bacchus broke eye contact and looked just past Blaine's shoulder. "No. I did not."

"Why?"

"I did not feel such minor acts warranted the removal of shields," Bacchus said. "I did, however, make it clear that you wished their behaviour to cease."

"But you do not wish it?"

"I followed your word to the letter, Lord Guardian. Even if—" He hesitated.

Blaine raised his eyebrows. Was Bacchus' slick demeanour at last showing cracks? "Go on."

"Even if I do not see why the humans ought to be coddled," said Bacchus. "They ought to stay outside the city walls. This is a holy site, after all, and we've just earned favour with the gods. Why put that in jeopardy? Some of the men are concerned."

Blaine shook his head. "If the men are concerned about the presence of humans then they have little grasp of the true threat we face."

"The situation is far from ideal."

"We must all, at times, endure situations that are not favourable. I recently endured your own thinly veiled attempts to usurp me."

Bacchus' nose twitched. "As I have explained, Blaine, I only sought to—"

"We shall speak no more of it. What happened on the slopes of the Nail Head has united us all in our faith."

"It has, Lord Guardian. It has. Faith in our gods. Faith in you."

"Indeed. Now, gather the rest of the Light Bearers and bring them here. I wish to address them on this matter." Bacchus bowed and took his leave. Blaine watched him go, wondering whether he had done the right thing in forgiving him. Either way, the decision had been made now. He couldn't change his mind after months, and it would be better to keep Bacchus close where he could ensure his loyalty.

Such assurances would be prudent. For all he went along with the title of the 'Gods' Chosen Champion' or 'The Champion of the Light', Blaine himself had never once said it. Yes, the gods had spoken to him at the Nail Head; they had whispered to everyone assembled there and had confirmed him as guardian; still, their exact words caused a flicker of doubt in Blaine.

'It is not yet time to give in.'

That had been what he'd heard. Not 'you are guardian forever more', not 'never give in, Blaine'. Their words had been both invigorating and agonising. Gods would not be careless with their words. Yet they had not been clear, either.

Absentmindedly, almost from habit, he brought his right hand around from behind his back and unfurled the fingers he still had. A fleshy bump of stretched skin protruded where his little finger used to be. He flexed, grasped the hilt of his sword with his injured hand and squeezed. No matter how hard he clenched, his grip couldn't match its old strength. That made him nervous. Was that why the gods had been reserved in their wording? Blaine had no doubt he could overpower every warrior Tenalp had to offer. He still had his blade, but could he face the true enemy like this?

He'd faced Rectar before, of course, when he was whole and half his age. And he'd barely walked away from it even then.

He ought to take out the opal he'd stored the memory in and relive that fight, study it for any potential weakness in Rectar. Yet he thought he'd be wasting his time on that account. There had been no weakness. No sign of frailty. Moreover, he'd rather face their enemy a hundred times than relive that terrible night.

Everything changed after that day. Nothing had been the same.

His hand left the cold grip of his sword and fumbled instead for the chain around his neck. Fishing it out, the silver 'A' felt warm to the touch. Arlandra had given this gift to Darnuir's father long ago; a token to ensure that a part of her would be with him on his travels. Kasselle had helped her make it, infusing it with some magic of her own. She'd done too good a job. Pressing tight on the necklace, Blaine swore he could sense his daughter still. A song-like laugh, the gleam of silver hair, the citrus scent of water lilies which were her favourite. Yet all of it was distant. An echo.

A blessing and a curse.

He tucked the chain away, feeling suffocated, and moved to the balcony for air. Outside, with the sun on his face, his thoughts drifted again to the life he might have had. Kasselle breakfasting with him out on this terrace. Wrapped up in bed with her on a cold winter's day. His hand curled in, searching for what he had lost. Try as he might, he hadn't been able to rid her entirely from his thoughts, whilst awake or asleep. And he knew, given the choice, he would have that love back rather than his missing finger. Even if that meant he wasn't capable of fighting the Shadow – he'd take the happiness again, even for just one day. Some Champion of the Light he was.

Baying seagulls jarred him from his reverie. Footsteps approached from the hallway beyond and so Blaine made his way over to the pulpit to await the Light Bearers. He needn't have hastened. It was only Chelos. His lifelong follower shuffled into the sanctum, wizened and slightly hunched.

"Grim news this morning, I hear?"

"A nuisance, more like," said Blaine. Hidden under many layers of warm clothing, Chelos moved slowly. A sole seat was arranged to the side for him and Blaine moved to lend a hand in reaching it.

"Don't make a fuss," Chelos said, waving him down. "I can manage. Still made it here before the rest of them, didn't I?"

"Yes, you did. How did I ever earn such loyalty?"

Chelos offered him a crinkly smile. "Childhood heroes are ingrained in each of us, I think."

"You're too kind."

"For the gods' chosen champion, I fear I don't offer enough praise." Having shuffled to his destination, Chelos sat down with a groaning sigh. He then looked to Blaine intensely. "What will you do about these attacks?"

"Nothing, I hope."

"Nothing?"

"I'd rather it is contained," Blaine said. "So, I shall address the men again and see if I cannot convince those responsible that their actions are folly."

Chelos sucked in a breath through his teeth. "You tried that before."

"Clearly I wasn't forceful enough. I've kept Bacchus close, but I can't trust him completely. Still, an odd word from him here or there might be... mistakenly interpreted by some of the new recruits." He eyed Chelos. "You haven't noticed anything untoward within your own batch of recruits?"

"Not at all," Chelos said proudly. "I think they see me as wise, gods help them. No, my boys do as I tell them."

Blaine nodded, his thoughts wandering again. "I should spend more time with them all. Get to know them."

Chelos shrugged. "That is not your place. I will do what I can to uncover any unsavoury attitudes from Bacchus' circle."

"Thank you, friend," Blaine said.

"However," Chelos added slowly, "Should we be unable to reach the root of the rot, perhaps you ought to consider tackling the cause."

"Sending Bacchus away would be more dangerous."

"I do not mean him," Chelos said. "I'm talking about the humans."

"You'd have me send them away? Appease the crazed notions of a minority?"

Chelos grumbled. "I'd see you do something, Blaine. You do not act."

"There is little to be done until Darnuir awakens." He set off back towards the pulpit.

"Our gods chose you," Chelos said. "Everyone there bore witness to it. Why do you still hesitate?"

Blaine stopped dead. Did he dare reveal the words he had heard? Matters were already fraught. How terrible might they become if he pulled that safe blanket of certainty from them?

Blaine answered without turning. "What would you have me do? Storm Kar'drun single-handed and strike our enemy down?"

"Don't treat me like a child," Chelos said. Blaine turned and found a real severity in the gaze that met him. "Draconess had similar excuses as he despaired; as he languished. But he did not have the divine touch upon him as you have. Our gods are real and with us. So why this wait? Go, Darnuir or no, and finish this fight as we planned long ago."

Jaw clenched, Blaine moved to kneel before Chelos and hold his waxy hands.

"Chelos. Old friend. Loyal, faithful, Chelos. Do you trust me?"

"Yes."

"Then please, keep your faith a while longer. Before I march on Kar'drun I need one more sign from the gods. One last answer on what I should do."

Chelos' eyebrows flew upwards. "An answer on what?"

"You will know it when it comes."

More footsteps tapped along the hallway.

"For now, I beg you to trust me," Blaine said. He let Chelos go and moved swiftly to the pulpit to stand above the Light Bearers as they filed into the sanctum. As the first attendees nodded his way, he realised his maimed hand was resting on the dais. Quickly, he tucked it behind his back, out of sight, and straightened to his full height to better command the room. It was easier to speak to the Light Bearers en masse down here where he didn't have to call upon the Cascade to be heard. Yet there were well over one hundred of them now, not including those he'd sent north. The sanctum soon became claustrophobic. Perhaps recruitment should cease. Growing their numbers might only invite more troubling incidents and Blaine was fast losing track of them as it was.

Bacchus was the last to join the group. He wove his way towards the front, the men parting for him in some reverence, but never taking their eyes from Blaine. He was the Champion of the Light, after all. Bacchus, for all his charisma, remained merely Bacchus. Chelos, sitting low behind a wall of fresh new faces, was lost from sight.

Blaine cleared his throat, then addressed the crowd. "Dwna bless you, my friends."

"Dwna shine upon us," they recited back.

"I have gathered you to speak about a growing issue among our numbers. This issue is, simply put, human-baiting. Let me be clear: I do not condone it. It is also a waste of valuable time on your behalf to be engaged in it." He swept his gaze across the Light Bearers, looking many in the eye as he did so. "Directing your energies elsewhere will be a far better way to serve the gods. Our northern outposts require more men. A strong garrison at the Nest will be vital to our long-term—" He stopped speaking, hearing a murmuring among the Light Bearers. "I am accustomed to silence when addressing the faithful."

"Why should the humans remain?" someone said. They had spoken just loudly enough to be heard and no more. No heads turned to face the speaker and mark him out from the crowd.

"The war is over," another remarked.

"The war is not over," Blaine said. "Rectar lives. So long as he exists, the war will never be over."

"It's been months, Lord Guardian."

"Rectar would have attacked by now if he had the strength to do so."

"Never make assumptions about our enemy. The Shadow works best in confusion and darkness. Until this city is made strong again, the humans are here to shore up our defences."

"They should not tarnish our holy city."

Blaine gripped the edge of the pulpit box, and the reminder of his weakened grip only flared his anger. "The humans are beneath our gods' attention and so they should not consume yours. It was false belief in the relevance of humans that led the guardian Norbanus into a disastrous war and a bloody battle in the swamps. Yes, this city of ours is a holy site. We stand beneath the very spot Dranus reached out and touched the minds of the gods. Yet none of you suggested removing the islanders from their homes after the Awakening on the Nail Head. If our Lords Dwna, Dwl'or and N'weer are troubled by the human presence in this city, they would say so."

"You asked the gods for a sign upon that mountain." This had been Bacchus. Blaine faced him slowly, fighting to keep his composure. Bacchus looked at him earnestly. This wasn't some ploy; he really thought he was on to something. "You asked our gods for a sign and they answered." Bacchus stepped closer to Blaine, his voice rising. He looked out across the assembled Light Bearers. "We all remember."

A great deal of muttering and nodding followed.

Blaine pressed his lips into a thin line. He'd never expected an answer. The truth was that he believed he was giving up the Guardian's Blade the moment he'd thrust it into the ground by Bacchus' feet. To call for a sign again and receive none would only shatter their confidence and faith in him. It wasn't worth the risk.

"The gods are not nursemaids, nor tutors at our beck and call," Blaine said. "We cannot request guidance on every matter. Where would that end? The gods chose to lift us all up at our lowest point. Let that be enough."

Let that be enough, he thought to himself. He'd said the same words to Lira this very morning. *Let that be enough.* Why were they always looking to him for more? Always more than he could give.

"Perhaps a sign could be sought in some other way?" suggested a Light Bearer by the door. An excitable buzz grew this time.

"Listen to me," Blaine said. "The Shadow of Rectar is the more pressing issue. Humans are, for better or worse, our allies in this fight. They have been instrumental in this war; I cannot deny it. Yes, we fought against some of them at the Bastion – a rogue group twisted and tainted by the darkest magic. Dragons suffered such a splinter in our race with the Black Dragons millennia ago. Do we condemn ourselves for this? No. If you seek to please the gods, then help prepare for the next great fight to come. I sense we draw to a final confrontation. One in which the Shadow will be cast over this world forever or new Light will rain down from Dwna above. Let the humans go from your minds. Brother Bacchus," Blaine added, extending an open palm to him. "What say you?"

Bacchus' mouth twitched. Few would have seen it, only those Light Bearers at the front if they had been paying attention. Blaine knew Bacchus' feelings on the matter but decided that a test of loyalty was due. His word still carried weight with many of the faithful. If he united with Blaine there should be no further problems.

Bacchus smiled serenely and spoke to the crowd. "The Lord Guardian has the right of it. Let us focus our energies towards rebuilding our northern defences, this city, and the lands of our people. It is a shame that the purity of our city lies in question, yet it must be borne. Were it so that there was a way to rid ourselves of this vexation. Alas, there is none." He faced Blaine, arms outstretched, and dramatically dropped to one knee. "Heed Blaine's words, for he is the Light's Chosen." The Light Bearers stomped their feet in approval. Those with shields bashed them loudly and Blaine rose a hand for silence.

"I hope this is the last I speak on this issue. Go now and carry out your duties. Those who wish to volunteer for the northern assignments should see Brother Bacchus."

The Light Bearers slowly exited the Inner Sanctum. About ten lingered back to speak to Bacchus, hopefully putting themselves forward to join those Light Bearers and members of the Third Legion that were already stationed at the Nest. The more the better. The old fort at the fork of the Crucidal Road was in a sorry state, or so the initial reports had said, and supplies and tools were in short enough supply, never mind the manpower.

Blaine eyed the group huddled around Bacchus for a time before slinking down from the pulpit. He brought his maimed hand in front of him this time, so those left in the sanctum would not see it as he made again for the freedom of the balcony.

"I shall see you at this evening's sermon, Lord Guardian," Chelos said from behind.

Blaine jumped. He'd forgotten Chelos was even there.

"Very good," he said. Chelos left without another word. Voices from the sanctum faded. Feet tapped, the door thudded shut, and Blaine was left alone with his thoughts.

So often, he was alone.

5

THE PRINCESS AND THE SHOW TRIAL

"To date, the longest span of time without an Assembly is fifteen years. A time of peace, prosperity and frustratingly little intrigue. It is not worth my ink to recount."

From *A Lengthy History of Brevia* by Maddock the Scribe

Cassandra – Brevia – The Assembly Hall

From her advantage point in the Royal Box, Cassandra held a commanding view. Eight triple-tiered platforms rose like stumpy trees, running four abreast down either side of the hall. Each tier was for a Great Lord and his retinue, in full pomp and ceremony. Two of the eight were empty, however, what with Lord Boreac dead and Lord Annandale about to go on trial. To cap it all, she was to give testimony as part of the proceedings.

Restless from waiting and nervous about speaking before all these people, she repeatedly smoothed the green silk of her huntress dress-shirt.

"Take a swig of this, dear," Oranna said. She gave her hipflask a shake.

Cassandra accepted it gratefully, inhaling the smell of smoked oak that wafted from the canister. She gulped too eagerly and felt the whisky burn down her throat, but managed to avoid spluttering.

"I think you're starting to like the taste," Oranna said.

"Well, if I am, it's your fault." She winked and gave the queen a nudge for good measure. She raised the flask again for another calming swig, but Oranna pried it from her grasp.

"I reckon one's enough," Oranna said with a wry smile. "You do have to be coherent and stand of your own accord down there."

Cassandra grumbled and leaned forward, resting her hands on the back of the bench before her. Then she sat back and fidgeted with her fingers to channel some of the leftover nerves.

"How long until it starts?" Cassandra asked.

"Once all the representatives are in their seats," Oranna said. "We're still waiting on the islanders."

Down on the central stage, Arkus himself was pacing in long strides. He wore his customary black robes trimmed in white, and even had his crown on today. Pausing, he looked to his wife and daughter, offering a wave, perhaps looking for a smile of support. Cassandra smiled politely and waved back, then sat upright so as not to look weak to him. Oranna, however, pressed her lips into a thin, distasteful line and folded her arms across her white gown. Her smile might have been more genuine if it had been carved from stone.

Cassandra leaned in. "We're in public, Oranna."

"I'm aware, dear," Oranna grumbled. Yet only then did a radiant smile break out across her face. She waved to Arkus, who, once satisfied, went back to his pacing. Oranna's jaw stiffened and she turned to Cassandra. "Are you sure you want to do this?"

"Annandale was part of Castallan's inner circle. Why wouldn't I want to give testimony?"

"Because *he* suggested it," Oranna said, nodding towards Arkus.

"No... I definitely offered."

Oranna raised an eyebrow. "Are you quite sure about that? I remember that dinner. He did lay it on thick how hard it was to find witnesses, how important it was to be seen dealing justly with Annandale, even if we all know how the last lord turned ou—"

"Oranna," Cassandra said sharply. She glanced around to check no one had overheard. The hubbub of the hall would drown out most conversations, but a keen-eared listener on the benches behind might overhear. Finding no eavesdroppers, she whispered fiercely, "Some things are best left unsaid."

Oranna arched an eyebrow. "They may well be, but don't turn into him now, dear."

Cassandra took Oranna's hand. "I don't intend to. I understand why you're angry at him, believe me. I didn't appreciate being lied to and used. Still, everything he did, he did for you, for Thane." *For me,* she thought, but didn't wish to say it aloud.

That might make it more excusable. Murder, however done, was a hard thing to excuse.

"For the family," Oranna ended, echoing Arkus' well-worn reasoning. She gave a disdainful sniff and lowered her voice further, so Cassandra could barely hear her. "I think a large part of what Arkus does, he does for himself."

"I don't think you're wrong," Cassandra said. "But things have been better, right? And after this Annandale business is sorted out, he'll calm down."

"I admire your optimism," Oranna said. "Let's just get through today first and see."

Cassandra nodded and turned her attention back to the Assembly Hall at large, taking interest in the arrival of the delegation from the Golden Crescent. Lord Esselmont himself climbed the short flight to take his seat atop the Crescent's allotted tier. It was hard to tell at this distance, but he seemed a trim man with the same blond hair as his son, Gellick. He was down at the bottom of his father's tier, helping their entourage arrange the wheat stalks and baskets of grain they had brought as decoration.

"They usually scatter the grain willy-nilly," Oranna said. "This seems a rather pointed way of saying how the war has affected the harvest."

"As if Arkus is responsible for demons stamping all over the Crescent," Cassandra said. "I thought Esselmont was in Father's pocket?"

"He's just taking what little dig he can," Oranna said. "I note that the merchants haven't reduced their piles of coins."

Cassandra looked to the far end of the hall where representatives in purple velvet waistcoats busily stacked coins atop sheets of gold cloth.

"It's a good thing you're here to keep me right," Cassandra said. "Nothing I've read mentioned all this decoration."

"Well, they've been doing this since I was a girl at least," Oranna said. She pointed animatedly towards a central tier that belonged to the Hinterlands today. "And as you can see, unlike the penny-pinchers amongst us, my father does not stint on his adornments."

Oranna's father, Lord Clachonn, was already in his seat, peering around at his colleagues. Cassandra couldn't make out his finer features at this distance, but couldn't fail to notice a theme of grey, from his well-combed hair to the well-fitted waistcoat and trousers. To adorn his tier, he had brought statues of bears, wolves, mountain goats and other animals from the northern fringes of the kingdom; each one a rare coloured rock, shining from a lacquer coating.

"In fairness, we can hardly compare rocks to crops," Cassandra said. She faced the queen again, concerned. This mood wasn't like her. "Is everything all right? How is Thane?"

Oranna squirmed. She fished out her hipflask and took a drink of her own.

Cassandra gently stopped her taking another. "One's enough, right?"

Oranna nodded and placed the flask away.

"I thought he was doing better," Cassandra said. "I haven't heard him cough during the night for nearly a week."

"I thought so too. But he had a rough morning. Threw up his breakfast after a fit of coughs over not being allowed to come to the Assembly with us. I had Gellick take him out to the gardens for a walk and fresh air." Cassandra tutted and looked back across the hall towards the jailer's box, folding her arms tightly. Oranna sighed. "I know you don't care for Gellick, but—"

"He's a lickspittle who is quick to reach for threats and violence," Cassandra said. She could almost feel the stinging pain where he'd struck her with the back of his rough gloved hand.

"I had no idea he was going to – oh, let's not drag ourselves into this again," Oranna said.

"I told you, I don't blame you," Cassandra said. It was true. Oranna had only been looking out for her and that was hardly a crime. "I understand why Arkus ordered it, and I understand why Gellick followed it. But I'll never forget it. You said something similar to Thane once, as I recall."

"I meant that to be in the context of our enemies. It saddens me it must apply to those around us as well."

"Well, you have me," Cassandra said. "I can take care of Thane next time. I'd be happy to. I don't get to see him as much as I'd like, and I bet Gellick isn't much fun. Probably too worried about dirtying his armour or handkerchiefs to play on the grass."

"I thought you'd like time to prepare for today. Next time for sure. Thane enjoys being with you, though I'm afraid to report he likes Gellick just as much. Young boys have a habit of looking up to knights in steel with awe, and Gellick is nothing if not the idol of that. Still," Oranna added slyly, "I fear Gellick doesn't quite have your wits. Nor is he as proficient in a game of hide-and-seek, clanking and shining with every move."

Cassandra's chuckle developed into a hiccup, which set Oranna off laughing harder. The queen composed herself in a rush, taking a deep breath through her nose.

"I think no drink for you next time," Oranna said. "One must compose oneself at these ghastly public occasions, but I'm glad of it today all the same."

An announcement from behind them signalled the arrival of the final delegates, those from the Splintering Isles. They carried a long ship's mast upon their shoulders and propped it up behind their designated tier. They fastened it in place and pulled the white sail out until it was taut, securing everything with thick, weathered rope. Cassandra leaned forward over the edge of the Royal Box to observe the proceedings, wondering if she was to finally get a glimpse of this Lord Somerled. When it was announced that Lord Somerled had sent an ambassador in his stead, Cassandra looked to Oranna to see if this was normal.

Oranna shrugged. "It's not unusual for Somerled. He likes to show minor defiance in this way. Often he'll send his son instead, but I imagine Grigayne is preoccupied by the war." She glanced around the hall. "That looks like everyone now."

As though in sync with the queen's thoughts, the royal announcer boomed in his ringing voice, "All will stand for the *King's Lament*."

All rose and the two court minstrels took centre stage beside Arkus. The minstrel in white produced his flute and struck up the now-familiar song while the minstrel in black began to sing.

"There once was a black-haired beauty, with starlight in her eyes..."

"Every time," Oranna whispered.

Cassandra held her tongue. She understood why Oranna was upset, yet didn't feel that Arkus needed to come under attack for it. The tribute to her mother did not hold the same place in Cassandra's heart as it did for him, but there was something comforting in hearing it all the same. And as the singer sang his final sad words, and the flute rang its last sombre note, she could, for a moment, feel her father's pain for that loss.

With the song over, the minstrels departed and the lords and ladies took their seats. Arkus wasted no time in facing them all in turn, smiling broadly, his arms open.

"You all know why you're here today, so I shall not waste your time on preamble. These are hard times, and our task is a stark reminder of that. We've faced fractious rebellion, terrible infighting and a war costly in blood and gold. But here marks the end of that discord. Whatever the verdict, we will move forward together stronger than before." He allowed a moment for his words to be absorbed before sweeping dramatically towards the merchants' tier. "I call upon the honorary Lord Jasper, Head of the House of Tarquill, to conduct these proceedings as a fair and impartial observer."

Oranna snorted at that claim. Cassandra couldn't help but agree. It was well known that the Tarquill's printing press was Arkus' preferred service. If anyone else felt that, they held their tongues. Silence reigned as Jasper Tarquill struggled down the merchants' tier, then huffed his way up the short flight of steps to meet Arkus on the podium.

To say Jasper was a fat man would be an insult; he had the sort of bulk that was rewarded only through dedication at the dinner table. He was a keg on legs, with arms to match, and supported himself on a sturdy black cane. His doublet was a rich purple with silver buttons, and his moustache thick enough to offer warmth during winter. He bowed before Arkus as far as his size allowed .

"I am humbled to undertake the position of arbiter today." Though breathless from his climb, he spoke with a confidence earned from having wild success in life. "I have no lands damaged by the war, and no reason of birth or rank to seek the accused's demise in advancement of myself. If any would oppose my arbitration, speak now."

No one did.

Cassandra wondered why they bothered with all of this. Most of the real discussions had already happened behind closed doors. Lands granted here, titles there, chevalier positions offered for spare sons. All of it owed to Arkus.

Jasper thumped his cane once in satisfaction. "Very well. We shall begin. Bring forth the prisoner!"

A distant door crashed open and four chevaliers marched in, surrounding a man with a wildly overgrown beard. They marched Annandale into the jailer's box and attached his chains to two iron posts. He was not given a chair.

Jasper crossed the podium to address Annandale, his great buttocks quivering behind him.

"Robert Annandale, former Great Lord of the Southern Dales, you stand accused of high treason against your king and the kingdom."

Annandale raised his cuffed hands, shaking his chains. "Former Great Lord?" he said in a hoarse, weakened voice. "Have you already condemned me? What sort of justice is this?"

"You will have your say," Jasper said. "But you have been accused, I repeat, of high treason. You stand accused of conspiring with the wizard Castallan to raise an armed rebellion and seize this kingdom for your own."

"It was Castallan who wanted to seize the kingdom," said Annandale. He looked imploringly at his colleagues around the hall. "You see what they have done to me? I am one of you! And Arkus chains me like a dog before my trial begins, tries to force me into admittance of a crime I was not responsible for."

A short, completely bald man stood up from the top seat of the Cairlav Marshes tier.

"So, you deny you were involved? We all saw your proclamation to make Castallan the king. What do you take us for?"

"Lord Reed," Jasper barked, as though snapping at a servant. "Please do not make uninvited exclamations in this hall." Lord Reed sat back down looking quite disgruntled. Jasper continued: "Yet despite being raised early, the point is valid and stands. Lord Annandale, the document in question was signed by your hand. The signature has been recognised by many members of this assembly. Hunters and troops from the Dales fought against our united forces at the Bastion. Do you have a defence?"

Annandale was shaking his head gently, as though in disbelief. "He was a wizard, you fools. You must have seen what he did during that battle. He could make anyone do anything he wanted."

There was some murmuring at this.

Jasper rapped his cane to call order and then brandished it at Annandale like a lance.

"Are you claiming you were not in your right mind? That you were hoodwinked or enchanted in some fashion?"

"So soon, Robert?" Arkus muttered. Cassandra started, not having noticed Arkus return to sit beside her in the Royal Box. Her father's hands were held up to his face, fingers meeting in a steeple. He was smiling, though why, Cassandra wasn't sure. If Jasper wasn't careful, he might lead Annandale by the hand towards a lenient sentence or possibly an acquittal. She'd been there at the Bastion. None of those men had been magically brainwashed. Castallan had charmed them through promises and words, and they had followed.

"Precisely right," Annandale said. "I was enchanted; placed into a dream-like state. I signed what he asked, did what he asked."

She resisted a sudden urge to jump to her feet. Perhaps Arkus sensed her frustration for he tilted his head towards her and whispered, "You'll get your chance. As discussed."

Upon the podium Jasper had begun to pace, his heavy steps sending out creaks from the platform.

"Many might call that an easy excuse."

"I call it the truth," Annandale said.

"Hmmm," Jasper blustered. "A truth that, conveniently for you, nobody can prove or disprove. You were granted a chance to name any witnesses who might corroborate your story. Have you anyone to call upon?"

"No," Annandale croaked. There was an edge of defeatism to his voice. "Many of my closest friends, family, advisors, were killed at the Bastion or are suffering from your occupation forces."

Lord Esselmont rose this time. "Our peacekeeping soldiers would rather be at home with their families. Those who still have families, after your accomplice sent demons ravaging across our lands."

"Precisely," Lord Reed cried, leaping to his feet once more. "My friends, let us dispense with this farce. We know where this is heading. Annandale must pay for his atrocities against us all." The Assembly broke out into murmuring. Lord Reed smiled cruelly, tasting Annandale's blood in the air. Jasper Tarquill brought down his cane so hard, Cassandra was surprised it did not break.

"Lord Reed, you have been asked already to refrain from outbursts. One more and you shall be ejected from this hall."

Cassandra glanced at Arkus, but his face was unmoved. She noted that no reprimand had been made to Lord Esselmont, the far more powerful lord who was closer to Arkus than the lowly Reed. She felt a little pity for the Lord of the Cairlav Marshes. Brevia couldn't be an easy place for a noble when common merchants outstripped you in real power.

Jasper continued. "By all the conventions of this Assembly, Lord Annandale will be given a right to be heard. Although it seems he doesn't wish to exercise that right fully."

Annandale was busy picking at his teeth with a fingernail. "I agree with the Lord of the Bogs. I'm likely to be condemned no matter what I say. However, even you must admit that in order to sentence me, it must be proven beyond common doubt I was *not* under the wizard's spell."

"The Crown would like to call a witness for that," Arkus said. "Princess Cassandra."

The Assembly collectively turned to face her with much grunting and scuffling of chairs. She felt hundreds of eyes examine every inch of her, drinking in the princess who had returned from the dead.

She made her way out of the Royal Box towards Jasper upon the stage. The hall had gone deathly silent. A solitary, quiet cough echoed loudly. Jasper was a huge man in every sense of the word, towering over Cassandra despite her wearing her heeled black boots.

"You have evidence that you wish to present to the Assembly?"

"I do." She kept her focus entirely on Annandale. Time in the palace dungeons had left its marks upon him. Deep lines framed his eyes, his skin was grey and his face was thin, almost feral. Yet she had no doubts about this. Annandale deserved to be punished. Anyone who supported Castallan did.

"Princess," Jasper began, "it is said that you were held hostage at the Bastion for most of your life. Is this correct?"

"It is."

"And during all those years, did you ever have cause to think that Castallan used his powers to brainwash those who supported him?"

"No. I believe those who joined Castallan did so willingly. They willingly killed in his name."

"Well, case closed, then," Annandale said. "I notice nobody questions her loyalty after spending so long in the wizard's company."

"Castallan was my jailer," Cassandra said. "Watching him die was a relief I'll likely never feel again." That had come out colder than she'd intended. She supposed it would take more than mere months for her to begin getting over her hatred.

Jasper cleared his throat. "A relief we all felt, Princess. Please continue."

"The day your proclamation was signed, Castallan brought me to his throne room. I saw the remnants of a feast, thrown in celebration because of the alliance you had just made with him. He told me you had signed the document and mentioned nothing of using magic to brainwash you."

"So he lied," Annandale said offhandedly.

"Why throw a feast if he was controlling you by magic?" Cassandra said. She smirked at him. "I was also in Castallan's throne room prior to the beginning of the battle. Castallan made an impassioned speech to hunters and soldiers from the Southern Dales. Why would he bother with such a thing if he held you all under his thumb? He would not fake all of this for my sake."

The muttering from the lords confirmed they too thought as she did.

Annandale shrugged. "Castallan had a taste for the dramatic. Think what you will. Your mind is made up."

"Is there anything else, Princess?" Jasper asked.

Something sprang to her mind then and she felt a pang of guilt for not thinking of him sooner. Adjusting to her new life had been so all-consuming that she'd nearly forgotten about Chelos. That had been selfish of her.

"Yes, I do. While I'm here, I should add torture to Annandale's list of offences." Annandale looked taken aback but she pressed on. "There was an old man who cared for me while I was a prisoner at the Bastion. His name was Chelos, and he was tortured for sport when I fled. He suffered because of me and I owe him justice as well."

"Chelos?" Annandale said, his face a picture of confusion. He furrowed his brow, lost in thought for a moment before wide-eyed realisation hit him. "That dragon?" And then he did the most despicable thing of all. He laughed. He laughed high and he laughed hard, ending on a spluttering cough when his breath caught in his throat. "Not for sport, Princess. No, not merely for the sake of it... don't you know?"

"That is enough testimony from the princess." Arkus' voice rang with all the authority of his position. But Annandale seized his moment. He rattled his chains as loudly as he could, drawing attention back to him.

"No, Arkus. You promised to let me have my say. Then I'll say this, and may you regret it, old friend." He turned to speak directly to Cassandra, though his voice remained loud enough to carry. "Do not throw all of Castallan's crimes at my feet, Princess. I am not him. As for this dragon you wish to defend, I think my fellow lords deserve to know why Castallan had to forcibly extract information from him."

"I said enough."

Yet no one was paying attention to Arkus now. The whole hall was enthralled by Annandale. Cassandra was also transfixed, but with fear. Fear of the information that Chelos had given to Castallan. About the passageways around the Bastion; passageways that had been built in secret by the—

"Dragons," Annandale boomed. "How they have always spat on us. In the Dales, we remember the First War well, and the Second for that matter. These wars were why the Bastion was built in the first place, was it not? Our new dragon friends aided in that construction; a sign of peace and assurance… or so we thought." He let the implication settle on the room for a moment.

Cassandra's insides squirmed. What had she done? She hadn't thought before of mentioning Chelos; it had just spilled out of her in her anger. She looked around the hall and saw only grave expressions.

Annandale smiled and carried on. "The dragons constructed secret ways beneath and within the walls of the Bastion – the very fortress that was supposed to be a deterrent against their aggression. They always had an easy way to breach it."

The reaction from the hall was predictable.

Many jumped to their feet, shaking their fists or banging them upon the pews in a storm of protest. The calls for order went unheard.

Cassandra fell into a trance, frozen by guilt and astonishment at her own blundering. A hand fell upon her shoulder, but it was only Arkus. He said something that was lost to the din, but she read, 'Back to your seat,' from his lips. She tried to say she was sorry, but he shook his head and gently pushed her in the direction of the Royal Box. She hurried away as the noise swelled.

Annandale had the room now. All eyes were upon him, and a persistent shaking of his chains eventually brought the volume of the hall down.

"And who has brought tens of thousands of dragons to live outside your very city?" he cried. "Why, King Arkus has." He pointed an accusatory finger, leaning as far forward as his restraints would allow. "He's let that traitorous race camp outside your very doorstep. What happens when the next betrayal comes?"

"The only betrayal that matters today is yours, Robert," Arkus said. He opened his hands, his palms facing upwards in an appealing fashion. "Noble lords, ladies, dear friends, these past months have been hard. They have pushed many of us to the brink, both in resources and in will. But when it comes to loyalty, my will shall never be broken. This man, this former friend, betrayed not only myself, but all of you. Sons and daughters from your lands bled because of him. And while his accusations about the dragons are true – oh, yes, I am all too aware of that – his actions cannot be redeemed. Before you stands a man who attempted to seize power from us all. He failed. He and his partner in the matter, Lord Geoff Boreac. And, my friends, if you fear the dragons now, be thankful that Boreac failed on his side of their scheming."

"What trumped-up charge is this now?" Annandale said, sounding genuinely aggrieved. Cassandra understood why. There had been no joint scheme of theirs. Boreac had told her so when she'd found him and he had no reason to lie by then.

"No further words from you, traitor," Arkus called. "Your words are poison." He turned his back on Annandale and faced the Assembly. "I did not want to reveal this delicate information to you all in such a heated and public manner. Yet I feel I must. For the truth must be known. Boreac and Annandale conspired to develop a dangerous new weapon, one they planned to use against our armies, but the rebellion began before they were ready. Such was Boreac's wroth at our victory, he intended to seek his final revenge by delivering this new weapon into the hands of the dragons. Sadly for him, the dragons were not accepting of him. Whether he angered them or not is unclear, but Lord Boreac's body was found in the dragon camps some weeks ago." Gasps of shock issued from throughout the Assembly. Arkus raised his hands to keep the quiet. "We are investigating what we can of his death. This new weaponry, thankfully, never made it across the sea. Chevaliers secured it and I have sought to understand it; to turn it to the advantage of our race."

Cassandra shuffled in her seat. The Assembly were buying this story. And why shouldn't they? It all sounded plausible, and goodness knew there was enough anti-dragon sentiment over the camps alone for people to latch onto this version of the story. She caught Gellick Esselmont's eye and Boreac's killer had the temerity to wink.

Annandale was yelling now, his chevalier guards closing in on him, swords threateningly in hand. "He lies, he lies, he lies, I tell you. You must believe me, he lies."

"Coming from the mouth of a traitor?" Arkus said.

"He's seizing power away from you all, don't you see? He's an oppressor!"

But the lords did not want to hear him. Their booing drowned out Annandale's last desperate pleas. The chevaliers grabbed Annandale and held him still.

"Now seems a good time to deliver the verdict," Arkus said, looking to Jasper Tarquill. Poor Jasper appeared lost for words, his jaw hanging slack. But at Arkus' words, he rescued his composure, shook his great mass and thumped his cane.

"Indeed, my king. The Lords' Assembly shall now pass judgement on this man. All those in favour of his innocence?" The crowd went silent. "And all those who find him guilty of treason?"

Lord Annandale's fate was sealed with a thunderous cry and a storm of raised hands, except for Oranna's father. Lord Clachonn kept his hands clasped in his lap even though most members of his entourage threw theirs into the air.

But the verdict was clear.

Annandale howled as the chevaliers dragged him away. "So much for childhood bonds, Arkus. So much for a kingdom bound in brotherhood. Ilana would hate to see what you've become; do you hear me? She'd be sick at the man you are now."

"Speak of her again and you'll die in your cell!" Arkus' composure was ruined. The king turned away, trying to calm himself. Annandale was hauled away, all the while yelling further insults from times long past.

Arkus only called for order again once the former Lord of the Dales had gone. He thanked Jasper for his time and then opened up the floor to questions. All three of the remaining Great Lords sprang to their feet, but it was Esselmont who spoke first.

"My good king, might you tell us more about these weapons you have been, erm, investigating?" Cassandra saw something like hunger in his eyes.

Arkus breathed out slowly, anger visibly draining from his face. "I am aware that you will all want to know as much as possible about this matter. I wasn't sure whether I was yet ready to unveil my achievements so far, but under the circumstances, it will be easiest to simply… show you. Gellick, will you fetch our closest squad of sharpshooters for your father?"

Gellick slunk off, heading for the guardroom behind the Royal Box. He returned a short time later, too short a time to have ventured all the way to the compound beneath the streets of the Rotting Hill. The troop of sharpshooters marched to join Arkus on the central podium. The Assembly collectively gawked at the soldiers, many members scrambling with each other to get a better view, leaning over the railings of their tier and jostling for position.

"My friends," Arkus began exuberantly, "I give you the next stage in humanity's development. With these weapons, we shall never again have to rely on oversized fortresses or the temperaments of wizards."

"What do they do?" someone called out.

Arkus smiled. "Why don't I show you? Company, destroy the jailer's box." In unison, the soldiers turned, heels snapping into place. The front row dropped to one knee. All raised their muskets to chest height. They must already have been loaded, for they fired immediately. The great bang of the guns was followed by the crunch and crack of wood; one musket ball hit the iron posts with a clang that sent a shiver through Cassandra's bones. Within seconds, the jailer's box was left a ruin.

A tense silence followed.

No one was gawking now.

Cassandra wondered if they would allow Arkus to hold this new power for himself. Would they question why he had not shared it sooner, or how he could possibly have developed it so quickly? Or would fear stay their tongues? It seemed that he would get away with years of secret planning.

Arkus himself beamed. Down on the podium, he was in his element; all pomp and dazzle, with a crown, new weapons, and an audience to show it all to.

"As you can see, friends; powerful indeed. And as a sign of my personal gratitude to those of you who have shown me loyalty through these trying times, I make a gift to each of my lords. Each shall be granted a full company of trained musketmen and women as a sign of good faith in the relationship that exists between the Crown and the Lords of the Kingdom." This went down well with the Assembly. A buzz of excitement rose, with only Lord Clachonn as the sedate exception.

He got to his feet again and waited for a chance to speak. "May I be the first to thank our king for this most generous gift. Truly, we will all be safer for it. I wonder, however, if I may broach the topic of what will happen to the lands of the traitors

Boreac and Annandale? The entire south of the kingdom lies in disarray or ruin, and Your Highness has raised so many new companies of soldiers that our healthy labourers have been drained to dangerous levels."

"Indeed, Lord Clachonn, the kingdom is in such a sorry state," Arkus said. "It will take a strong, guiding hand to set things right. The Crown shall absorb the territories of the fallen and take on that burden, until such time as new regional courts can be established." This announcement was met with less enthusiasm than the gift of soldiers, but no one made any open objection. Clachonn flexed his fingers but sat down without further incident.

"You need to try harder than that, Father," Oranna said quietly.

"As for the raising of new companies," Arkus continued, "I realise this has strained our manpower almost to breaking point. However, the mighty king of our dragon allies demanded I send his people east while he kept our troops for his own. I did not find that transaction a fair one, my lords, and so we were in a deadlock. Yet these refugees further drain our resources and humanity once again comes off worse. I wished to bring our soldiers home so they may be retrained with these incredible new weapons, but alas, I was denied. I did not wish to tell Darnuir my true reasons, and I hope you will understand why. I did not know how he would react, nor did I wish to play our hand before knowing if we could harness the power fully. It turns out that we can. Quick to produce, quick to train in, our new weapons shall make a swift end to this conflict that the dragons seem incapable of winning." He ended by shaking a closed fist. "That is enough for one day, I think. You are welcome, as always, to petition me in private if you wish to discuss matters away from the public forum. Good day to you all."

"All rise," the announcer's voice cracked like one of the muskets.

Cassandra lingered as the hall emptied, unsettled by what had just occurred. Those soldiers had been brought from the compound in advance; there was no other reason for them to be there. Had Arkus planned it all? She couldn't say. He had lied about his acquisition of the muskets, that was for certain. And now every lord was to be given a company of their own – companies of soldiers who were loyal to Arkus first and foremost. He'd just placed both spies and enforcers in every household in the land, and they had applauded it. Had it all been another plot, another game, and she a mere pawn in it?

Annandale's parting words had also intrigued her. They had been friends once, by the sounds of it. Boreac had said much the same thing. What had gone so wrong? Oranna was turning sour towards him now; had he pushed others away as well?

She decided she would find out, and made a vow to herself never to be used blindly again by him. Once was forgivable. Twice made her a fool.

There would not be a third.

6

ESCALATION

"They never envisioned where it all would lead."

Author Unknown

Lira – The Royal Tower

After weeks of fruitless investigation, things had only gotten worse. There had been more fights, more accusations, more foul words from human officers groaning under the stress of it all. And still no dragon had been apprehended, if it was indeed dragons causing it. Lira suspected the only thing that was keeping the humans in the city was the lack of any ships left to spirit them away. They were all stranded together in this cold, crumbling city.

Tonight, the weather was especially bitter. Even in her hunter gear, built to fend against Highland ice caves, she could still feel it biting. She breathed onto numb hands and blinked, trying to focus on the report that she'd been handed earlier. Numbers lost from sickness over the worst of winter. It was hardly pleasant reading. She felt slow and groggy besides. Her bed lay unmade; when had she last slept?

The candle's flame was particularly hypnotic. A flickering orange hillock. A rhythmic flick of fire. She was so very tired. So very, very—

With a jerk she snapped awake, elbow flailing sideways. Her empty tankard descended to the floor with a clatter. Sluggishly, she collected it and thought she ought to get it refilled with hot water. Shimmer brew was to be reserved, but just the heat of the water alone would be comfort enough. Firewood was another commodity not to be used with abandon.

She sat back down, as close to the tiny flame as she could, and put her hands over it. Life slowly returned to them. Refocusing on the report proved futile. These days her mind revolved around these attacks, but no solution would present itself. Perhaps Damien's idea of sending soldiers to the Tail to sow crops was the only way. It would be good for those sent there to do something constructive and ease matters within the city. But would any humans be interested? Raymond had thought not. Yet if the situation deteriorated, the officers might see the benefit of the scheme.

Her mind was racing now, grasping at the edge of an answer just out of reach.

She needed someone to speak to.

Before she knew it, she'd reached her door and pulled it open. "Ah, Camen. Good."

Camen, a hard-faced, serious young Praetorian, stepped away from his guard position, turned and saluted. "Prefect?"

"Go fetch Raymond for me, please."

Camen's eyes betrayed his surprise. "At this hour, Prefect?"

"I need him." She turned and shut the door, her mind already circling back over the question of how she might quell the rising feud between the races. Blaine's people were involved. It had to be them.

She paced from the hearth to her bedside.

How had it come to this? How had all this come to weigh upon her shoulders? Darnuir, still sick as ever. Blaine, aloof and unsupportive, leaving her to deal with their allies while he whispered words in dark rooms. The Praetorians looked up to her but precious few others did, despite her role in the battle for the city. Blaine had received most of that glory for showing up at the end to save them.

A knock came at the door. Raymond entered, his eyes half-shut and his hair all on end. She sniggered. Rather than his knightly attire, his body was hidden beneath his bedspread, which he clutched together awkwardly in his fist.

"What are you doing?" she asked.

Raymond stifled a yawn. "Do you have any idea what time it is?"

Lira fought a yawn in return. "Night-time."

"It's the middle of the night."

"I've had things to do," she said irritably. Why had she wanted him to come again? "Go back to bed if it's too much trouble."

"No – that's not what I meant." He shook his head to wake himself. "I'm here now. Happy to help." He smiled and looked so ridiculous, with that bed hair and the sheets, her irritation soon dispelled.

"I'm sorry for summoning you at this hour. I must have lost track of time. And I've got used to having you around."

His smile faded into a frown. He straightened. "You are the prefect. It is well within your rights. What's the matter?"

"I've been thinking again on Damien's suggestion for the Tail Peninsula. I don't see any other alternatives."

"We might find a way to catch the culprits."

"I'd like a backup plan."

"In case we don't apprehend the perpetrators?"

"In case we don't catch them quickly enough." She turned and began pacing again. "I doubt it's a small group anymore. Four fights broke out at once the other night."

"Lira," he said, though his voice sounded shaky. "It will be a hard sell to get humans to go with Damien. Aside from the work, many will see it as giving in to this violence." His voice shook again. She turned and found him shivering.

"You're freezing."

"You're not?"

She shrugged. "Sometimes I wonder if I have too much on my mind to feel... anything." She considered the little fireplace.

"We should set an example," he said through chattering teeth.

Lira moved to the fireplace and picked a dried log off the meagre pile.

"I'm fine, really."

She ignored him. After creating her fire, she returned to her desk, snatched up her tankard and called for Camen. He duly arrived.

"Go fetch another cup of hot water," she instructed. "And get one for yourself. Grab an extra ration too, if you fancy. If anyone gives you lip, you can tell them to come and see me. Got it?"

"Yes, Prefect," Camen said. He stared wistfully at the burgeoning fire but moved off without further question.

Raymond looked quite put out. "I could have managed. And we ought not to spend precious resources when we tell others to refrain."

"I haven't lit a fire in over a week. Besides, you were freezing to death no matter what you say. You've never been on a hunter patrol, but taking care of your squad is the most important objective."

"We're not on a mere patrol. There are bigger things at stake than my comfort."

She was fast losing patience. "Why do you always act like this?

"Like what?

"Trying to be tough. Trying to play the hero."

"I'm trying to be honourable."

"And freezing to death will do that, will it?"

He opened his mouth but stopped himself, swallowing whatever words he was about to utter. "No. It won't. You're right, of course. I just don't like the idea of us living in comfort while those out there are huddled together like cattle to stay warm."

"Didn't you grow up in nothing but comfort?"

"Exactly, and what good did I ever do for anyone? I had a chance here to give my life some meaning. Some purpose."

"Had?" Lira said. "What do you mean *had*? You're still here, aren't you?"

Raymond grumbled and looked to his toes. "A slip of the tongue."

Lira folded her arms. "You came here to help Darnuir."

"And what use have I been to him? I can barely keep up with the rest of you. I'm just a human in the end."

Lira bit her lip. She wasn't sure what he needed to hear, but some reflex kicked in from her hunter days; something that Captain Romalla often did to the recruits who were flagging. She grabbed Raymond by both shoulders, looked him square in the eyes and told him, "You help me a great deal. I wouldn't have made it through these last months without you. Do you think I'd have asked you to come tonight if you didn't?" The words just tumbled out of her, though they were not exactly what Romalla used to say. Actually, they were nothing like it.

Raymond grimaced.

"What now?" she demanded.

"You're crushing me."

"Oh." Lira released him and took two embarrassed steps back.

Raymond rolled his shoulders and grunted. "Thank you."

"For crushing you?"

"No, for what you said. It was... good to hear it. I'm happy to help you."

"Well, I'm grateful."

She was left unsure of what to say next.

Raymond smiled awkwardly and fumbled on, "About Damien's plan—"

"It was a foolish hope."

"Taking back this city was a foolish hope," he said. "Fighting Castallan seemed like a fool's errand too. But we did it."

"A moment ago, you said it wouldn't work."

"A moment ago, I was feeling sorry for myself. Let me try. I am the human representative on the Guard, after all. This should be my burden. We'll gather the legates and human officers together. Who knows, a joint enterprise and fresh ideas might invigorate them."

"Great," she said. It wasn't much. Not much at all. But it felt like progress. She became horribly aware that he was waiting for her to say more. Her hands began fidgeting of their own accord. "Well," she began, "I suppose... that's all for now, then."

"I suppose so," Raymond said. "We can start working on the finer points in the morning."

"In the morning, yes."

"Or now?"

She felt suddenly off balance. "Err—" she started, unsure why this strange departure was dragging out, nor why her cheeks felt so hot. A knock at the door saved her. Once again, Camen was there, only he held two steaming tankards rather than one.

"Harra was doing the rounds for those on night duty," Camen explained. "So I thought I'd get one for both of you."

"Right," Lira said, a little dazed. "Thank you, Camen. You should still grab that extra ration, if you want."

"Oh, I want it." He licked his lips and hastened to leave.

Lira turned and stood stupidly for a moment holding both cups. "You might as well stay and have this. I wouldn't say no to the company." Raymond shuffled forward and took one. "Why don't you sit down," she added, directing him to the bedside. "There's no need to stand on ceremony."

"Not while I'm dressed like a pillowcase." He shuffled again to the bedside, and carefully sat down on the straw mattress. Cradling her drink, Lira sat herself down beside him. A pleasant moment passed wherein the only sounds were the crackle and spit of the fire and their attempts to blow the worst of the heat from their water. She could still feel him shivering, but after a few sips, it began to ease. After a while, he sighed in relief.

"That's better. I can feel my fingers again." He took another drink, looking towards her desk. "Ah, so is that the doll?"

Lira followed his eyes. It was indeed the doll she'd recovered from her family's home in the Lower City, and even that felt like a lifetime ago already. It had sat here in her room ever since, the perfect smile of the girl forever painted onto the wood, impervious to the woes around her.

"That's the doll."

"I thought you were going to throw it away?"

She'd planned to, once. Well, she'd said she'd planned to.

"I couldn't do it."

"Good," Raymond said. "You'd have regretted it. It's only right to have something left to remember him by."

Lira felt the sudden twitch of her cheek as her eyes began to well. "It's the only memory I have of him."

"Tell me."

"There's not much to tell. I just have a faint memory of running in through the front door, and he was already at the table. I can't even make out his face. All I see is how tall he is, how he's smiling, and then I look only at the doll. That's it. All too focused on a block of wood." She wasn't sure why she was telling him this, but it didn't feel wrong or embarrassing.

He placed a gentle hand on her shoulder. "You must have been so young. It's hardly your fault."

She sniffed and pre-emptively wiped her eyes. "It's scary how quickly it upsets me. But you're right. Mum was always happy I had at least one thing to remember him by. I promised I'd check the house to see if it was there... I never expected to actually find it."

"She'll be glad to see it again too, I'm sure."

"She will." Lira wiped at her eyes again and took a reassuring gulp of hot water. "I hope she stayed at home and hasn't ended up in those camps."

"The Hinterlands avoided the war," Raymond said. "I'm sure she stayed."

Lira nodded quickly and drank again to excuse her lack of reply. She didn't want to break down completely. Damn, what she wouldn't do for a proper shimmer brew right now. Heck, a flagon of ale.

"Sorry," she sniffed. "I'm sobbing on about a father I never knew when you've gone through much worse. You must think me pathetic."

His hand squeezed her shoulder. "I think you're one of the strongest, bravest people I've ever met. Dragon or human. Or fairy," he added. "We're both a little out of our depth, but I never would have coped this well if I were in your position. And don't be afraid of telling me when you're not okay, either. Naturally, you miss your mother. It was just the two of you for years. As for your father, I hope you don't mind me saying it, but I envy your memories in a way. You have this pure and good thing to cling on to to. Knowing Sanders turned into what he did... well, it's horrible all in its own way."

"Do you miss him?"

"I miss the younger brother he once was, but he hadn't been that for many years." He considered his own drink then, looking long and hard into the rising steam. "I've wondered whether it was my own fault. Other children at court used to pick on us, you see; blue-bloods who looked down on our family. Sanders looked to me to defend us, but I wasn't capable of standing up to the others. Not back then. Sanders developed his own armour, to act like he didn't care at all. Or worse, to become one of those who, in turn, pick on more impoverished nobles; those with better blood but less gold. It was a vicious, spiteful little cycle. Father always took more of an interest in me as the first-born. Sanders had ample reason to resent me, to resent the status quo. We didn't get along so well in the end."

Lira faced him directly. This time it was she who placed the comforting hand on him. "You too were just a child."

He nodded. "I hate what happened to him. I hate what he became. Thinking about how he hacked down that hunter in Torridon makes my blood run cold. Still, I'm glad I didn't see Blaine actually kill him."

Oh, real nice, she thought. *Good one, bringing Blaine back into the discussion. So smart, thoughtful.* Alas, she hadn't known that detail.

"I'll tell you who I grieve for," he said, in an oddly cheerful voice. "My first horse, Sorcha. I was seven and she was three, so we learned together. She was quite a social creature, always sidling up to annoy my mother's mare in the stables. She was very protective of me and could be fierce, but I was never scared of her. I'd sneak carrots from the kitchens to give her while out on longer country rides when no one else was watching. Cruelly, the years sapped her strength while mine increased. I was nineteen when she passed. I ran from the chevalier barracks all the way to the stables, gaining all manner of blisters from my boots. I think she'd been holding on for me to get there before letting go. I brought a carrot for old times' sake. I swear, if horses could smile—" He choked. "Damn it, but I loved that horse."

Lira's hand fell from his shoulder, landing upon his own. "Well, Bruce is a very lucky horse to have you now."

She became very aware of where her hand was. In the warm glow of the fire, she was conscious of how pale she really was, how sickly looking. She hadn't been a beauty before this stress, and hadn't dared to find a mirror to observe the toll.

Yet when he met her eye, she rather felt that, for a moment, she was the only person in the world worth looking at.

"Lira," Raymond began, "I know these last months have been hard, but I—"

A voice rang from the stairs beyond.

"Prefect. Prefect Lira."

Footsteps pounded down the corridor and within seconds there was banging at the door. Lira growled and jumped to her feet. *This had better be important.* She braced herself, because of course it would be.

"Perhaps Darnuir has woken?" she said aloud. "Come in."

Several Praetorians tumbled inside the room, all breathless. The matter was urgent indeed.

"General Fidelm has arrived with grave news, Prefect."

"He begs you come at once."

"Of course," Lira said. "Raymond, will you join—"

"I think I will change first." Sheepishly, he pulled the bedspread even tighter around his person.

"That would be wise," she said, already turning to leave. "We'll see you down there." If the other Praetorians had anything to say about Raymond's dress or presence, they kept it to themselves, both in speech and expression. And she was quite thankful for that.

Down in the throne room, Fidelm, flanked by four of his fellow winged fairies, awaited her. His usual serene bearing was marked with distress, his dark skin further deepened under the dim, hastily arranged candlelight.

"General," she said, reaching him.

He gave a curt nod. "Lira, can you trust your men implicitly?"

"Yes," she said without any hesitation. "Whatever is the matter, Fidelm?"

The general gave her a grave look, then stepped aside. Behind him on the ground, between the fairies, was an elongated sack that could only be one thing.

She gulped. "Who is it?"

"I don't know," Fidelm said. "It is, however, a dragon."

"You're sure?"

Fidelm clicked his fingers and one of his warriors unveiled a large rectangular shield. The emblem of the guardian was painted on it. Lira took hold of it, running her hand over the grain as though to check it was real. She was left dumbstruck.

"We have had some luck," Fidelm said. "It was one of my flyers who spotted the body being dragged through the streets. She descended to inspect it once the coast was clear."

"Where was he found?"

"On the outskirts of the human quarters in the Lower City. Specifically, at the narrow neck of streets between the plateau's base and the western wall."

"I assume those carrying the body were masked or hooded," she said.

"All that could be discerned was that there were several of them, suggesting they needed the extra strength to dispose of the body quickly, suggesting they were—"

"Humans," Lira finished. Her throat felt chalk dry. "Who else knows?"

"So far, only my most trusted flyers, you, these Praetorians here. And Raymond also, it would seem."

Raymond then joined them, now dressed in a shirt, jerkin and trousers, the chill of the night perhaps forgotten in the heat of the situation.

"Surely we are at the point of confronting Blaine," he said.

"We can't," Lira said. "Do you think he'll sit idly by if he discovers humans have killed one of his own?"

Fidelm's wings buzzed gently. "He will surely find out sooner rather than later. If one of his men turns up missing—"

"He has so many these days I doubt he'll even notice."

"Someone will notice," Raymond said. "If not Blaine himself then Bacchus or the older one, Chelos."

Lira looked to Fidelm for support, but he seemed eager for action. His fingers twitched, anticipating drawing his double-bladed spear. Was this what they'd come to? So cooped up, so mistrustful and resentful and lacking in leadership that they were ready to tear at each other's throats?

"No," she said flatly. "I won't have revenge killings. I won't have the city going to war with itself. I won't have Darnuir awaken to an insurmountable mess. Fidelm," she rounded on him with what little energy she had left, "I'm grateful you brought this directly to me but I'm surprised at how quickly you wish to come to blows. Darnuir would not be pleased."

"Darnuir is not present," Fidelm said quietly. "And with all due respect, do you believe that he, of all people, would hold back on this?"

"You're right. He wouldn't hold back," Lira said. "He'd go thundering off, sword in hand and temper flared. But where did that get him before? Chained to a chair, leaving us to deal with this. And with all due respect, General, I command the Praetorians, and I will not draw my own sword just yet. You won't take on Blaine alone. We'd need to bring the legates in as well."

Fidelm's wings twitched again. "I wouldn't be so certain of whose side the legates would pick, Prefect. I do not think we want to risk finding out. If we are to act, it must be hard and swift."

Fists clenched, she turned to Raymond next.

"Striking by surprise in the dead of night is not an honourable move," Raymond said. She smiled, thankful for his support, but Fidelm rolled his eyes.

"There is honour and then there is necessity. I have given my council, but the decision is, as you point out, yours. I cannot move without you."

"We keep this quiet," she said. "And we make haste with what I hope will be a peaceful solution." She explained to Fidelm their plan for the peninsula.

"It won't work," he said.

"We will try regardless," she said through gritted teeth.

"You will," Fidelm said. "You have clearly decided. There seems nothing more to discuss for now. We shall take our leave." He clicked his fingers again and his fairies formed into a single rank to march from the throne room. Fidelm followed them.

"Thank you," Lira called after him. But he did not respond.

"What's his problem?" Raymond said. "Not exactly serene and fairy-like."

"It's this horrible restlessness we all find ourselves in," Lira said. She glared down at the body bag. Why? Why had whoever he'd been ventured into the human streets and provoked them?

She needed Darnuir back now more than ever. They all needed him back, or there might be little left for him to return to.

7

CONDEMNED RESEARCH

"A story gives delight to read though it be fabulous indeed. Why must we know the fact from fae? It tells the truth in its own way."

From Jon Barbor's *Scorching of the Dales*

Cassandra – Her Private Chambers

A candle burned to keep the night at bay. The palace was quiet beyond her room, the inkwell was drained to its last drops, and the stack of letters barely dwindled. For every two she signed, it felt like another three were added to the pile.

A soft grunt came from the nearby crib, and Cassandra glanced up from her work to check on her nephew. Still asleep. A small mercy. Cullen had taken ages to settle this time, and had left her with a nice headache as a present. But she was more than happy to watch him when Olive took her well-earned days off or went outside the palace.

Cullen was a pudgy little bundle of innocence amidst a life of intrigue, suspicion and word games here in the palace. She felt the same about Thane, doubly so because he could even talk, and run, and joke and laugh with her. Thane and Cullen gave her the first chance that she'd had of knowing family members for life, and she planned on making the most of it.

Cullen began whistling lightly from his nose, then gargled, then mewled. Just as Cassandra thought she ought to do something, he snorted loudly, then rolled his head to the side to get comfortable. She couldn't help but giggle at the whole affair. Whoever said that babies slept peacefully clearly hadn't been around one very much. His little chest rose and fell in a gentle rhythm, and she was satisfied all was well.

She returned her attention to the tottering stacks of letters, moving Cullen's empty milk horn aside to give herself more room. Five letters later, a pain shot through her wrist.

I really am a proper princess now, she thought, rubbing gently at her ailing joint. *Getting a sore hand from writing too many letters. I'd better slow it down before the legends of my ferocity grow too wild.*

With a sense of guilt, she picked the top template off the nearest stack to continue. In neat black print, this letter began the same as all the rest:

Dearest member of the Kingdom of Brevia,
It is with a heavy heart that the Crown must inform you of the loss of

This was where Cassandra wrote by hand the name of the soldier. At the appropriate points, she would insert the battle or location of their death, where they were buried, and what of their possessions had been recovered. But other than her additions, each was identical. In times past, the royal who wrote the letter would have done it all by hand; given it a certain personal touch. Such things were over. Times had changed, and Arkus had ordered Tarquill to print thousands of copies. At least Jasper had foregone sticking his seal on them all.

She checked the duplicate of the military log that she'd been given and filled out the details of the next name on the list. This man had been a weaver's son, from the western coast of the Golden Crescent. He'd died on Eastguard, a long way from home. A single gold coin would be handed over with the letter to his mother, the first payment of a monthly stipend that would last for one year.

Though she tried not to admit it, she'd gotten bored enough during one session to flick through a dry tome on the history of the city by Maddock the Scribe. According to him, until the Second War it had been five gold pieces each month for ten years, but after this conflict, the hunters were formed into an official arm of the kingdom under the eye of Elsie the Green. Because of this commitment from the Crown, the stipend dropped to three pieces each month for only three years. In the here and now, Arkus had almost wiped it out entirely.

She wondered how the writings of this time would consider his actions. Would they condemn Arkus for removing this insurance for his subjects? Or would they praise him endlessly for doing what was necessary to save the kingdom, even the world, when the formidable dragons could not? It would all depend on whether they survived the coming years, or, moreover, who survived to tell the tale.

Already Arkus had spun so many tales. Few would know the truth. Fewer still would ever bother to discover it. And the years would tick by.

What had happened to turn so many against him? Boreac said they'd once been friends, and Annandale had shouted much the same as they'd dragged him away. Perhaps he could shed more light on it.

A knock at the door interrupted her thoughts.

"Come in," Cassandra said, placing her quill back in the inkwell.

A thin, middle-aged, severe-looking woman poked her head around the frame. It was Olive, the woman she'd interrogated at Lord Boreac's manor. Thankfully, it had gone unspoken that the trickery Cassandra had employed to get information about Boreac would never need to be discussed.

"Get anything nice?" Cassandra asked. Olive had mentioned a trip to the shops near the Velvet Circle.

"I needed some fresh stockings," Olive said crisply. She peered hawkishly over at the crib. "How has he been?"

"Well, he got a lot quieter when he fell asleep."

"Mmm," Olive mused. "He likes to know he's got your attention. His mother was a bit like that, going in a huff until you did what she wanted. How Cosmo put up with her—" She stopped herself and smiled weakly instead. "I shouldn't drone on. They were good for each other."

"You must miss her?" Cassandra said.

"Missed her since the day I left the Boreacs, but that was many long years before... well, before all of this." She sniffed lightly, her brusque demeanour faltering. "I'll take him off your hands now, Princess. Let you get on with your work."

"All right," Cassandra said, somewhat wistfully as Olive carefully picked Cullen up. The woman was indeed experienced. Cassandra almost always woke Cullen whenever she had to move him. "Bye bye," she said, giving a small wave, although he would not see it.

"Good night, Princess," Olive said. She took her leave.

Cassandra returned to the letter she'd been filling in about the weaver's son from the Golden Crescent. She'd almost finished. Each one ended with the same words: 'With our sincere condolences'. She was to sign her name below. Cassandra decided to add a little extra to this one and wrote: 'I'm so sorry.' These words weren't enough, but they were written by hand, and that might make it look like somebody else cared.

She sealed it, placed it within the half-full sack at her feet, brushed her hair off her face and looked to the others. The remaining piles now felt crushing. She'd signed away too many lives. Guilt bit at her as she got to her feet. She ought to get through them all, but she couldn't get her mind away from Arkus and Annandale. She yearned for answers and sitting in her room wasn't going to get her any. And if she was going to have a chance of speaking with Annandale before his execution, she knew just who could help her with that.

Mere minutes later, having torn through the palace to find him, she received her answer.

"Absolutely not," Balack said, turning green at the very thought.

"And why not?"

"Because – because if Arkus finds out you went down there—"

"But he won't find out. Will he, Balack?"

The so-called Hero of the Bastion opened his mouth, hung it like a fish, then closed it without a word. He too had been given a private room within the palace, the better for Arkus to summon him when required. She'd found him there, bent like an archivist over his own correspondence. A pile of unopened letters sat to one side of a heap of ripped paper and broken seals, though unlike her letters, these were ones he had received.

Cassandra placed her hands on her hips, awaiting an answer. Balack growled and placed his head in his hands.

"Are you asking as a friend or ordering me as a princess?"

"I'd hope as a friend."

"Why do you want to speak with him, anyway? The man's a traitor. Unless… unless you look to take more direct revenge?"

"Of course I don't," Cassandra said sharply.

"Good," Balack said, pushing his chair back with a screech.

"So we can go now," Cassandra said, half-turning towards the door.

"I didn't say I was going to help."

"Did I mention how good you're looking these days?"

Standing to his full height, his shoulders looked broader than ever; his neck was thicker and his forearms rippled beneath the white brace of his rolled-up sleeves. Arkus' desire for Balack to look the part had gone beyond just the cared-for hair, the surgically trimmed beard, and even, when times demanded it, the brush of red powder on his cheeks.

"Flattery won't help you either. Why is this so important to you?"

"It's hard to explain," she said. And it was. She barely understood the compulsion herself, only that she needed to hear the other side to all of this. Annandale was one of the few people left who still had their own opinion intact. Whether she'd get the honest truth was another question entirely.

"You could try?" Balack said. He stepped closer and spoke quietly. "I owe a lot to Arkus, Cass. I know this hero façade is a sham, but I've got a role, I'm comfortable, and I'm safe from the front of the war. Truthfully, I think many would kill to have the latter, even if their pride won't admit it. I'd rather not jeopardise that."

"It's not a complete sham," she said. "You were instrumental at the Bastion. Kymethra said so."

"What did I say about flattery? Now, taking Kymethra to the dungeons seems like a solid alternative. She could wiggle her fingers and put the guards to sleep or something."

Cassandra's mind turned inexorably to the magical horrors she'd endured. The tight corridors. Screaming steel. And that had been by accident. Poor Foulis had taken the brunt of it.

"I'd rather not have to resort to that. Besides, she's very busy taking care of Brackendon and watching over the scrying orb. All you're doing is answering mail from sycophants and lustful noblewomen."

"Lustful," he laughed, then shrugged and nodded. "All right, suppose we do go down there, I don't know what you expect to hear or what you think it will achieve. At the end of the day, he sided with Castallan, and countless people are dead because of it." His eyes fell to the satchel she carried. "What's in there?"

"Some paper and ink." Balack raised an eyebrow. "In case he says something… useful, interesting; something worth not forgetting," she added.

"Sure," Balack said. He reached for his white leather jacket, the signature piece in his lowly Boreac hunter image. It was more ornate than a regular-issue version and had been fitted to Balack exactly, hugging his chest and tightening at his waist. Next, he found his bow, a small quiver, and slung them over his shoulder.

"No pistol?" Cassandra teased.

"I can fire arrows quicker than loading those monstrosities," he said, opening the door. "Wait here until I have the keys."

It didn't take him as long as she feared, and after the jailer had been convinced to take his leave early, they descended into the palace dungeons. Though dark, it eventually became clear to her that full brick walls stood in place of bars. The cells, for want of a better name, were more accommodating than the common dungeons of the Bastion's dark underbelly. But they were silent. Cassandra couldn't hear a thing; not a scurrying mouse, nor the patter of pacing feet. There were no voices or sounds from the palace above, and no sign as to what the weather was like outside. A storm might rip Brevia to timber and rubble, and down here you would never know. Only the light jingle of the keys in Balack's hand stopped her fearing that she'd gone deaf.

"Is anyone else down here?" Cassandra said.

"Not that I know of," said Balack. "The place hardly gets used. It's a hangover from the days before the kingdom was united. But Annandale is a special circumstance." He suddenly stopped before a door and placed the torch in the sconce beside it. "This one's his."

Cassandra gazed upon the plain door. Even its handle lacked any shine. Despite what Annandale had done, Cassandra felt a wave of sympathy for the man. She imagined the room beyond to be pitch black and freezing.

"Last chance to turn back," Balack said.

"No. I'm going in."

"I hope you find what you're looking for," he said. Then he placed the key into the lock and turned it with a snap.

Light hit her eyes like dirt blown in the wind, sore and stinging. She raised an arm to shield herself until her eyes adjusted to the violent change. It turned out to be the combined glow of five lanterns, magnifying candle flames behind latticed glass covers. The cell was not the full horror she had imagined, although a wicked stench was heavy in the stale air. There was a comfortable-looking bed, a clean rug on the floor, and, bizarrely, piles of books taking up the bulk of one corner.

Robert Annandale, former Great Lord of the Southern Dales, lay on his back with a book propped open on his chest. His tangled beard now obscured his neck. He lowered the book as Cassandra and Balack entered, a glint in his eye.

"My, my," Annandale croaked, his voice scratching at the air like nails on rock. "You two look positively angelic compared to my usual guests." He closed his book with a thump and jumped to his bare feet. He tried to move to them but was restrained by the iron girdle around his waist, attached by a chain to the wall. Grunting and baring his teeth, he looked even more wolfish than he had in the Assembly Hall. He stumbled backwards and sat cross-legged upon the edge of his bed, pointing a dirty finger at Cassandra.

"You're the princess. I remember you. And you," he redirected his finger towards Balack and frowned. "I don't have the faintest idea who you are."

"That's oddly refreshing," Balack said.

Annandale ignored him, being far more interested in Cassandra. "Are you to be my executioner?"

"That will be one of these new firing squads. With Arkus present."

"Good. Good. I want to look him in the eye when he gives the order. I want to see if he's as dead inside as I fear. And I want my face to haunt his dreams, if he still has those."

"Did you hate my father this much before you tried to take his crown?"

"It was Castallan who wanted to be king, Princess, not me. Hate is also a strong word, and too often thrown around Brevia to still hold its meaning. I never hated Arkus. Neither did Boreac for that matter."

Cassandra mentally noted that. It tied together with what Boreac had told her at least, and as it had come from Annandale without prompting, she considered it genuine. He made a sucking sound with his tongue, then ran it along his teeth, puffing out his lips. His eyes shifted to Balack, specifically to his bow.

"Neither of us is going to harm you," said Cassandra.

"As long as you give us no reason to," Balack said, stepping lightly past Cassandra.

"I wanted to ask you some questions," Cassandra said.

Annandale rocked on the edge of the bed. "Questions, you say?"

"Yes," Cassandra said, sounding unsure. Perhaps he was ill. Annandale didn't seem quite all there.

"Ugh, blasted head," Annandale said. He rubbed at his eyes. "I fear my solitude is rotting my mind. I try to read to keep myself sharp, but..." He trailed off, tapping the book he'd been reading. "But even that is getting harder."

"You have a lot of material here," Balack noted from the corner where the books were stacked.

"I was allowed one request," Annandale said. "I asked for something to read, and they brought me these."

"Looks like the guards were generous," Cassandra said.

"They brought two chamber pots as well, but I don't think that was born from generosity."

Cassandra tried not to breathe through her nose as the nature of the smell took on fresh meaning.

"The lanterns, too?" Balack asked. "These cells are supposed to be dark."

"A small bonus," said Annandale. "I pointed out that I couldn't read without light, so they provided me with a few more. Arkus might not torture, but his tactic of starving you of your senses or distraction does more harm, I think."

"At least they gave you plenty to read," Cassandra said.

"It's mostly history tomes."

Cassandra perked up at that. "Can I see?" she said, stepping forward and looking at the book beside Annandale.

"Cass, don't," Balack said sharply. But Annandale picked up the book and passed it to her without protest.

"Likely they thought it would be dreary and add to my torment," he said. "As it happens, I have my own library of these texts back home... or I *had* a collection."

Cassandra glanced over her shoulder at Balack. "Don't be so worried." She began to thumb through the book, the dry pages feeling coarse against her skin. The print had been transcribed by hand, and the words hard to discern by modern standards. Even the editions of Tiviar's work that she'd read had been printed via an early press. Cassandra checked for the author and tutted. "Barbor was a poet, not a scholar."

"And his version of the First War is a lot nicer to read because of it."

"It is, if you like storytelling over truth."

"Let me guess, you're some sort of Tiviar purist," Annandale said. He didn't give her time to answer. "You're right, Princess. Barbor is biased. But his words stir something in the reader, especially if you are from the Dales."

"Is it books like these that turned you against the dragons as well?"

"The dragons earned my scorn for dragging us through a century of devastating war," Annandale said. "There's a truth for you, if that's what you want. And this book resonates with me and others because it prods at that sore spot. Yes, Barbor exaggerates the dragon numbers and the human deaths; yes, more towns burn in his telling than there were in existence back then, but so long as you're aware of what it is, what's the harm? The Dales suffered in that war. That cannot be denied."

Cassandra set the book down like she might a glass of soured milk. "If it prompted you to listen to Castallan's madness about surpassing the dragons and join him in rebellion, then I think it is very harmful."

"I didn't rebel against dragons, did I, girl?" he groaned. "I've been judged enough. If you only came here to lecture me, then leave."

Cassandra sat herself down at the end of the bed. "I wanted to ask you about what happened. Why you joined Castallan. Why you rebelled in the first place. Everything, really."

"To what end?" Annandale asked suspiciously.

"I'd like to know your side of events. Wouldn't you also want that heard? You weren't exactly given a chance in the Assembly."

"True, though I wasn't expecting anything less than a well-rehearsed performance."

"Is that why you tried to disturb matters by yelling about the dragons?"

Annandale nodded sombrely. "I tried. You gave me a nice opening too, but it didn't work. Arkus is slippery. Any time you think you have him trapped, he greases his way out of it." His eyes drooped, looking exhausted and done. "Ask away, girl. I've got nothing left to lose."

Cassandra rummaged in her satchel for her paper, short quill and inkwell. She poured ink into the well from a glass vial and carefully replaced the cork. Annandale watched her in bemusement.

"Just in case," she said. "Right, then—"

She froze, unsure of where to begin and what to ask. She had despised this man from afar, but now she'd met him…

"Let's start with Boreac. When did the pair of you decide to work together to undermine Arkus?"

Annandale tugged at his beard. "Might be five years ago. There wasn't some official signing of illicit documents. We'd known each other forever, of course. We all had."

"Who is 'we'?"

"All the sons of the Great Lords, including Arkus. It was your grandfather's idea, old King Malcolm, he brought us together as lads and had us live like brothers."

"That's news to me," Cassandra said, trying to hide her intrigue as best she could. If it were true, then Arkus had been close to all of them, and his ruthlessness chilled her all the more. She scribbled a note. Hopefully, Balack was listening as intently as he was staring at Annandale.

"I imagine many things come as news to you," Annandale said. "I do not mean that as insult. You were cooped up in the Bastion for a very long time."

"Arkus knew I was alive, but could do little about it. Or so he says."

"Castallan made sure that Arkus knew what would happen to you if any armies were seen heading towards the Bastion." He began counting on his fingers. "Then Arkus told myself, Geoff – er, that was Boreac's first name—"

"I know."

Annandale raised a fourth finger. "And Esselmont too. We few knew. Enough to help keep the peace and save any stirring from our own vassals with regard to the lack of an heir. Things got easier when Thane was born. But then, things also got worse. Far worse."

"Just the four of you?" Cassandra asked.

"Just us," said Annandale. "We'd grown up together, we'd worked to bring the kingdom together and make it stronger, even during the war. You might remember little Lord Reed from the Assembly Hall? He was younger than us and his family poor; well, naturally, they own swamps. Your grandfather didn't see fit to include him in our group. I'd say it was a mistake, but it matters little. And before you ask, Oranna's father is a good nine years our senior. So, it was us four. We were to be the backbone of the kingdom."

"What changed?"

Annandale screwed up his face in thought. "It's hard to point to one event. I suppose it was a lot of smaller things that built up."

"I'll need more than that," Cassandra said.

"For your notes?" Annandale jeered.

"You've had a lot of time to reflect, I'm sure."

He scoffed. "Too much. Far too much." He let out a long sigh and his eyes glazed over. "If I had to pick one thing that cut to the heart of the matter, it would be this: I think Arkus grew to resent those of us who still had what he'd lost. You can't fail to notice that he keeps Esselmont's boy close. He understands full well the sort of power that gives him. Geoff, on the other hand, never started a family; perhaps that was why Arkus let him remain in the capital while the rest of us were pushed out to our regional seats. I never noticed it at the time, but looking back, yes, yes, I think it might be the reason. My family's time in Brevia grew shorter. Then he asked us to move. Then the invitations became less frequent and finally, I alone was asked to come; just for business. Then I could be on my way, and with each year the Assembly Hall grew dustier between meetings. The idea of a kingdom these days is a sham. Has been for a long time."

Boreac had said similar things. Cassandra noticed she'd barely written anything, caught up in the pain that wavered in Annandale's voice. She gulped, remembering what this man had helped cause.

"Your rebellion cost thousands of lives," she said. "Maybe tens of thousands by the time this is all over. Can you really sit there and justify it because Arkus stopped being your friend?"

Annandale's expression turned. He looked to her, his eyes bloodshot and jaw clenched. "What were we to do, Princess? We hoped that Oranna might change things, and we looked to Thane's birth like a promise in a prophecy. If anything, things got worse. Arkus became more focused on Brevia than anywhere else; busy building the chevaliers into a personal army, rebuilding and strengthening the city walls, and secretly funding these new weapons of his, it seems. This all cost, and he drained our lands to do it."

Cassandra's thoughts flicked again to the pitiful sums to be paid to the families who had lost children, fathers, or even mothers.

"Our people suffered for it, and the Dales had suffered the hardest in the war already," Annandale continued. "The south always suffers the most somehow. And then there was Castallan, always there, always looming over us. We didn't just decide to act upon a whim, Princess. We saw the direction Arkus was taking us all in. We tried to dissuade him, tried to reach out to him like the old days, Geoff even more than I, but in the end, we were ignored."

"You would have let Castallan be your king?"

"Arkus promised us nothing. He took as much as he could from us; perhaps because he was trying to fill the void in his life. I'm trying to be kind, rather than say he's become paranoid and a despot. But in the end, he gave nothing back. Castallan may well have done the same, but there was the chance of a change. We took it."

"Do you regret it?"

Annandale's lips began to tremble. "I regret how things have ended between us, all of us. And I cannot think for a second about what will happen to my family without me; to Finnon, my boy, and his own girl, little Isolde. Because if I do – if I do..." His words were choked and thick. "She's just a baby," was all he managed.

Cassandra watched the old man descend into quiet grief, his eyes watery but lacking the strength for real tears to fall. She thought of faceless soldiers coming to drag Cullen away from her and her stomach clenched.

How many was this now? She'd met three men who'd been driven to despair by Arkus – Annandale, Boreac, and even the lesser figure of Ralph Foulis, whom she'd let go. How many hundreds more felt the same as them? How many thousands? Maybe there came a point where that much discontent was a sign in itself.

"Will you help them?" Annandale asked. "My family. Will you help them?"

"I... I..." She didn't know what to say.

Annandale took her by the shoulders with a catlike agility, the movement knocking her inkwell over to soak the paper and bedsheets.

"Please," he begged.

A bowstring was pulled back with a sharp creak.

"Let her go or I'll pin your arms together with this arrow."

"Loyal, this one," Annandale rasped.

"No need, Balack," Cassandra said. She clasped her hands together then swung her arms up, knocking Annandale at his elbows and breaking his grip. She followed through to her feet and took a prudent step back.

Balack was between them before she could even blink. "We're done here."

"I'm not finished," Cassandra hissed.

He scooped up her things in a single sweep of his arms and said again, "We're done." He'd already heaved the door open by the time she'd drawn breath to argue.

"Balack, you can't just—"

But he had. He was out the door and out of sight. "Leave the traitor."

She hesitated, wondering whether she ought to stand her ground. But Annandale was sobbing now, and he'd returned to swaying like a grotesque rocking horse. His eyes were a watery red mess from lid to lid and they stared blankly upwards, as though no one were in the room with him. Her hand was shaking, half from what she'd heard and half from fury at Balack. Of the two, anger rose to the top and she stormed out after him.

Momentarily lost in the darkness of the hall, she didn't see him. The door slammed shut and locks crunched as several keys turned.

"Come on," Balack said. He picked the torch back up off the sconce and his face became a dance of orange and black. Cassandra followed him, keeping her rage in check long enough for them to make it up to the black-carpeted halls of the palace, where she grabbed him roughly by the arm and yanked him to a stop. Balack gasped as she hauled him back, dropping her satchel and items to the floor, whereupon the inkwell shattered.

"What was that about?" she said, breathing hard

"He's half mad, Cass."

"He's been penned down there like an animal for months. You'd go mad too."

"Probably," Balack said. "But I'm not planning to start a war in order to scrape back a little power."

"It didn't sound like that's why he did it," Cassandra said. "Weren't you listening?"

"Yeah, and d'you know what I heard? I heard the man who is responsible for thousands of deaths – tens of thousands, as you said so yourself – all I heard was him looking for some sympathy."

"He broke down thinking of his family." She stepped away from Balack in disgust, looking at him in a new light. All the pomp and pampering made him look false now, a gloss that hid the man he'd been. "Why are you so ready to defend Arkus?"

Balack puffed his chest, opened his mouth, closed it. That minor hesitation sent her mind racing.

"What's he promised you?"

He averted his eyes.

"Tell me."

"Arkus has mentioned I could become the next Lord of the Boreac Mountains."

Cassandra's stomach entered a feeling of freefall. "He's bribing you." It was a statement, not a question.

"It makes sense," Balack said fiercely. "All the mountainfolk Kasselle was sheltering in Val'tarra have been sent on their way. The people from the Golden Crescent at least had homes to return to, but not those from the Boreacs. They came here, desperate. I'm from the region, Arkus needs a new lord, and my standing is enough that it won't seem bizarre. I'll do a good job for them. I want to. This isn't amoral. Arkus is our king, and he's your damned father. Why are you so keen to find any story, however wild, however discreditable a source, to use as – I don't know exactly – evidence against him in some wild vendetta?"

"Arkus is a murderer," she whispered. He didn't know the full story of what had happened with Boreac but she was certain he knew enough. Her words cut through Balack's anger all the same.

He stared at her in disbelief. "Arkus has killed. So what? Annandale has killed, even if indirectly. Boreac too. I've killed, Cass, and so have you."

"That's diff—"

"Why? Because it was self-defence? Because it was war? Annandale thought he was defending himself. Arkus was defending himself. It was war, Cass; people die. Every day they die. I know as well as anyone. I lost people back in the mountains, friends and loved ones – I've lost Grace and Cosmo and Ev—" He stopped mid flow, balling his hands into fists so hard that his knuckles turned white. "Darnuir, too. I don't know which one hurts more."

"I think you're getting wound up because you know I have a point."

"I'm wound up because I'm worried you're creating something out of nothing. There are bigger issues, more pressing ones. The dragon camps, for a start; when was the last time you walked those mud fields?"

She shook with anger but couldn't answer him. She'd only been once, and it had been harrowing enough.

"Arkus has me out there every week," Balack went on. "They're starving, they're freezing. That's the real problem. Whatever your issues with Arkus are, that's for you to sort out. Don't dump your shit on me, *Princess*."

Cassandra had half a mind to punch him and rattle that perfect hair of his when a whistle cut across the hallway.

Gellick Esselmont was strolling towards them in full harness with a pistol at his side, despite the lateness of the hour. He grinned like a fat cat with a bowl of cream.

"What have we here? The Hero of the Bastion and Princess Cassandra out late at night? Perhaps a lover's quarrel?"

"Hold your tongue, Gellick, or I'll rip it out myself," Cassandra said. Remnants of her feigned engagement to Balack still cropped up at the worst moments. The chevalier raised his hands in mock surrender. "Haven't you got something better to do?" she snarled.

"I am tasked with overseeing the movement of our equipment out of the Rotting Hill compound," Gellick said. "The king has requested that I be there at his side," he added pointedly to Balack.

Balack's face had reddened. "Well, it is late, as you say. And I'm tired," he added through gritted teeth. "Good night."

Gellick didn't bother to step aside for him. "Perhaps you should retire as well, Princess."

Cassandra gave him a strained, twisted smile. She stepped delicately towards him, using every fibre of control to contain her fuming, seething mood. Her heart hammered, and blood pounded behind her eyes. She glared at Gellick, desperate to just hit him; oh, she wanted to hit something. His otherwise marble skin was marred by the broken nose that Arkus had given him; that was satisfying.

"One day," she said, "I'm going to take that pistol and smash it across your smug face."

Gellick sniffed lightly but didn't rise to her threat. "Sleep well, Cassandra."

He left her standing there, alone in the quiet and empty hallway.

8

TIPPING POINT

"So long as humans have the west and dragons the east, I see no reason for further conflict. The world can be shared."

From Tiviar's Histories

Lira – Harbour of Aurisha

Dusk settled over the city. The world was still and the sky dimmed to a burnt orange as it met the ocean. At the waterfront, Lira drank in the beauty of the night, glad to be away from that arduous meeting.

"It's nice to know not everything is so bleak," Raymond said.

"We did our best," she said. "They may yet come around."

Raymond hung his head. "I failed."

"It was always going to be difficult. Perhaps we shouldn't have invited the fairies too; there were too many voices."

"I shouldn't have expected to do better," Raymond continued, as though he had not heard her. "The officers of noble birth look down on me, while those of lesser station see only the gold and the privilege. The rest narrow their eyes to see me serving dragons. I can't help you to convince them, because they do not trust me. I don't belong to any group."

"You belong with us," Lira said.

"You're a dragon. This *is* where you belong. And you deserve better."

He stared down into the sea as though he was contemplating descending into its darkest depths. Lira wanted to ask what he meant by such talk, but noticed Grigayne Imar breaking away from the milling crowds.

She nudged Raymond. "Grigayne is coming."

At once, Raymond rolled his shoulders back and stood tall. The Praetorians parted ranks, and the heir apparent to the Splintering Isles joined them. Grigayne's red hair had grown wilder during his time in Aurisha, with the knot he used to secure it growing ever more elaborate.

"Don't look so miserable," Grigayne said to Raymond. "It could have gone far worse." It always amazed Lira at how levelled and neutral his accent was compared to the other islanders.

Raymond inclined his head. "I must offer my thanks, Lord Imar. You at least behaved as a friend and spoke with decency."

"I'm not the Lord of the Isles yet," Grigayne said. "And there is no need to thank me. I could see the merit in your scheme, but I also understand why the others weren't in favour. Something has to give, though. This city is a boiling pot with the lid welded on."

Lira wondered how much he knew. She glanced to Raymond and he met her gaze with an equally concerned expression.

"Lots of rumours down here in the Lower City," Grigayne said. "I'd ask you which ones are true, if I thought you'd give honest answers."

"We're trying to diffuse things," Lira said. "Not inflame them."

"Understandable," said Grigayne. "But perhaps a little more..." He searched for the word. "Conviction is required. Before things get out of hand."

"What are you suggesting?" said Raymond.

"Look, I'm on your side. But this unrest is reaching even my people. I've ordered that the islanders be off the streets after dark but a few are still slipping away to listen to this jumped-up Brevian inciting all sorts of things. Not least of which involves stealing our longships and sailing home." Grigayne looked between them, searching for some sign of recognition. "You haven't heard of this man?"

"No. We haven't," Lira said. The pounding returned behind her eyes. "Does he have a name?"

"My people are calling him The Preacher. His true name I am yet to discover."

Preacher? Was it some assault on the Light Bearers? Lira's pulse quickened as thoughts of Blaine's reaction beat through her mind.

"Why are you only coming to us with this now?" she asked.

"Because it only recently came to my attention as well," Grigayne said. "I can't say how long it's been happening for. The Preacher might be the cause of these street

fights for all I know." He glanced behind to the dispersing mob of legates and officers. "Without Darnuir, there are too many hands on the oar. Either we find a solution to this or I will withdraw my islanders for their own safety. I won't have them
being stirred up into foolish action and getting themselves killed."

"No one is talking about violence," Lira said.

"Small comfort to the man already dead," Grigayne said. Lira couldn't help but
look alarmed. "So it's true," Grigayne said sombrely.

"I hope we can count on your discretion," Raymond said.

"You can, but any more human deaths and—"

"It was a dragon," Lira said. "A dragon was killed. By humans."

Grigayne's sighed hard. "I'm not sure what to believe anymore. Look," he
dropped his voice, "my people who brought this Preacher to my attention are going
to take me to him tonight. Why don't you come too? See for yourselves."

"I'm not sure that's wise," Raymond said.

"We may have to," Lira said.

Raymond ran a hand through his hair. "If you're caught there—" But he stopped,
the answer apparently too awful to say aloud.

Grigayne looked her up and down. "Change of clothes, a helmet, and no one will
know."

Lira knew she didn't have a choice. She'd have to investigate the depths of this
and frankly didn't trust the Brevian officers to cooperate on the matter. At best,
they'd fear telling her of the true extent of the issue. At worst, they'd actively cover
it up.

"We'll come with you."

An hour later, Lira, Raymond, Damien, and some select Praetorians were still at
the water's edge, only now they were dressed as islanders. Hard-boiled leather over
mail, round shields upon their backs, and axes rather than swords. Lira had also
donned a simple bowl helmet with a nose guard to further hide her features. Night
had fallen, which would further help with their disguises.

"This is... ill-fitting," Raymond said

"I'm sure you'll live without a tailored shirt for a few hours," Grigayne said. Stepping back, he examined his work. "It's the lack of beards that could be a problem."
He scratched his own fuzzy cheeks thoughtfully. "I'll bring some of my warriors
along to help balance things out."

"You're being very helpful," Lira said, a sense of suspicion rising in her.

Grigayne shrugged. "Despite Blaine's blunderings, I owe your kind. Far more
islanders would have died if Darnuir hadn't landed at Dalridia to break the siege
when he did. While he's out, I figure you need all the help you can get. Besides,
we're all on the same side, are we not?"

Lira nodded. "We are. There is just one thing left to do. Harra, Camen, take our gear and return to the Royal Tower."

"We should stay with you," Camen said. "What if something goes wrong?"

Let's hope not, Lira thought. "Grigayne will be with me. The Brevians aren't going to attack us with the heir to the Splintering Isles among our number."

"Damien isn't even a Praetorian," Camen protested. The outrunner had said little, looking more brooding than ever. He was disappointed in their failure to convince the humans about the peninsula scheme, Lira knew, and the boots made his feet ache worse than ever.

"It's standard procedure to have an outrunner at all times," Lira said.

Harra stepped up next, hands on hips. "If it comes to a fight, we'd be more useful."

Raymond shuffled awkwardly; not agreeing, but not protesting either.

"He stays," Lira said, sharper than she'd intended. "He'll have insight into the humans."

Harra raised an eyebrow. "More than you? More than Grigayne? I really think—"

"Harra, please," Lira snapped. "I don't want to bring more of you than I have to, and I've got enough on my mind. I've made my decision." Deflated, Harra silently nodded in agreement. Lira felt worse for her brusqueness. "I'm sorry. I know you're only telling me what you think is best; it's no more than I tried to do with Darnuir. I'm just… under a lot of strain." She looked to Raymond then, hoping to see a reassuring smile of thanks and support; he was smiling, but weakly, and a light flush coloured his cheeks.

"We know," Harra said. "Come on, then." She whacked Camen on the arm and the pair of them returned to the dock buildings where they had changed.

"Let's get moving," Lira said.

Grigayne rounded up some of his men to flesh out their party, and they began their journey north, following the western cliff face of the plateau away from the harbour and towards the city gates. Grigayne led their company, while Lira, Raymond and Damien followed at the rear. There was a silence she found uncomfortable. She drifted to Raymond's side and saw that he was more preoccupied with his feet than looking ahead to where they were going.

"Is everything all right?" she asked quietly.

He appeared to wake as though from sleepwalking.

"Yes, of course." He smiled more warmly this time, but Lira wasn't fooled.

"What's troubling you? You aren't letting what Harra said bother you?"

"Not what Harra said. No."

"Something I said?"

"Of course not," he said, a bit hastily. He glanced over to Damien, perhaps checking whether the outrunner could hear him or not. "I'm finding it hard to express what I'm feeling," he said in an undertone. "It might just be the fatigue. We're all worn, you most of all. And that meeting – the legates may as well not have been there. How is it that all of them together cannot make decisions? It's intolerable. Dragons seem like lost children without their king." His cheeks turned scarlet this time. "Sorry. I didn't mean to—"

"Don't be," Lira said. "You're not wrong. It reminds me of back before Darnuir returned. Mother knew where many other dragons were; a network of sorts existed, ready to mobilise quickly, as they did when news of Darnuir spread. Yet none of them thought to take charge while he was gone. They look at what I'm trying to do now and are confused by it. My whole race shuts down like bees in winter if their king isn't in perfect health."

Raymond laughed, a low and throaty chuckle. She hadn't been expecting that.

"I'm glad it seems as alien to you as it does to me."

Lira shrugged. "A consequence of growing up among humans. Though I'd also call it common sense."

Ahead, Grigayne took a right turn off the main thoroughfare and led them into a series of smaller alleyways running east along the northern base of the plateau.

"Your mother must be a sensible woman, to allow you to grow up without poisoning your mind against humans."

"She's tough," Lira said. "It wasn't easy for her as a dragon, but she managed. I think she took heart from seeing huntresses sticking up for themselves."

"With any luck, she'll be able to return from the west soon, along with all the dragons stuck outside of Brevia."

"With more luck than I dare dream of."

She could have used a hug from her mother right then.

Grigayne paused at a seven-way crossroads in the narrowing streets and consulted with his guides. They were entering deep into the Lower City's most crammed and labyrinthine streets. Despite the late hour, many humans were still milling about. Perhaps boredom due to a lack of activity had made sleep elusive. Was this Preacher turning their restlessness into action?

"The Preacher doesn't use the same spot every night," Grigayne said. "But if we're right on tonight's location, we should be getting close – ah, in fact, I might be hearing it now."

Lira heard it too, a guttural cheering and laughing. After a final turning, they discovered a wider street which cut between two tall and teetering housing blocks. Here, the wooden frames towered to six storeys, with a great mass of soldiers gathered between them. The crowd stretched right down to meet the base of the eastern segment of the city's wall.

Lira gently pushed through until she gained a view of what everyone was looking at: a pile of crates before the wall and the man who stood atop it. The Preacher. He was tall and wiry, in a plain Brevian uniform over mail. Unremarkable in truth, although the audience was enraptured. With sweeping arms, he held court with as much ease as Bacchus might.

"More of our lads getting beaten up every night, but we can give back just as good, can't we?"

A few ayes and grunts of agreement sounded.

"Safety in numbers. Move in groups of ten or more. These Light-spouting dragons is cowards in the end, and won't try it if they think they'll have a real fight on their hands. They want us outta the city, tossed out inna' the cold. If I recall, we helped take this city back, didn't we, boys?"

"Aye," came another appreciative rumble.

"And ladies," the Preacher added, offering a blown kiss to a woman near the front of the crowd. "Fairies too, though I don't see any o' them here." He raised his hand as though blocking the sun and peered mockingly around. "Lots of folks took part, is me point on all this. So why are we to bugger off into the cold and danger while they stay behind nice big walls?"

It was then he caught sight of Lira and smiled broadly like a contented cat.

Her heart hammered, and her hand flew to her sword.

"Annnnd would ya look right here. Islanders have come ta see me humble show." The man gave an exaggerated bow. "Well, they'll know a thing or two about seeing light shining in unusual places. Tell me, sir," he directed his appeal to Grigayne, "when the dragons came back down from that mystical, magical, better-than-your-first-time mountain, did you too feel a godly finger tickling yer arsehole?" The crowd bellowed. Some turned to await Grigayne's answer but many were too consumed in mirth to do anything more than maintain their breathing.

The Preacher signalled for silence. "Friends, I jest, but the matter is entirely serious. Now, there has been talk of stealing our friends' ships and buggering off ourselves. But I think that's ill-mannered talk. Humans is humans. Be welcoming to our salty cousins and we'll be better off for it. Strength in numbers, I says. Gotta show we ain't afraid."

He clapped his hands and, a moment later, a shield was passed up to him from below. A large, rectangular shield with the painted emblem of the guardians on it.

Lira tensed. Was it the shield of the very dragon who'd turned up dead?

"Ooo, it's heavy," the Preacher said. "Quite pretty, I s'ppose. Might look quite nice up on the wall. Me dashing assistant here is going to help me paint it."

A broom was handed to the Preacher, followed by the thud of a bucket. The Preacher lowered the broom down, dipping into whatever the contents were below. Lira doubted it was paint. As the Preacher began to work, it became all too clear what it was. Taking shape upon the wall was a larger imitation of the sword cutting through a spiralling sun, smeared in a soft brown gloop. Bits of it slid down the wall and the front rows recoiled.

Lira spun, grabbed Raymond and Damien both by the arms and edged back through the throng of soldiers. She'd seen enough.

Just as they got free of the crowd, a roar of laughter erupted. The Preacher must have finished his art. She closed her eyes and buried her face into her hands. This would surely get back to Blaine; there was no way something on this scale could be kept from him.

"What are we going to do?" Raymond asked.

She had no answer.

Grigayne and his men emerged from the crowds too, looking grim-faced.

"It's like he's asking for a sword through the guts," Grigayne said.

Another bout of raucous laughter filled the air.

"Though he's little more than a comic. Maybe Blaine will ignore it," Grigayne said.

Damien was frowning so hard his brows had become one. "He might be a fool, but he's a fool that provokes. The Light Bearers will hear of this, Prefect."

"So we'll deliver it first," Lira told him. "It's all we can do to get ahead of this. Go to Blaine at once, Damien. Tell him that I wish to meet tonight and never mind the lateness of the hour. Keep the details to yourself if you can. I'd rather he didn't turn up already in a fury. We have to come to some solution on this."

"At once," Damien said. He bent to unstrap his boots, the better to run, but she threw out a hand.

"Wait. If you run barefoot through the streets, they'll know you're a dragon."

Damien pursed his lips but retied the straps he'd just loosened.

"I'm sorry, Damien. I know you're in pain."

"No more than I can handle." He spoke proudly but she saw him wince and clench his jaw as he took off at a gentle pace to mimic a human.

Upon returning to the Royal Tower, Lira decided out of habit to check upon Darnuir. Muscle memory brought her to his room before her overtired body had registered the trip. There she stood, fixated on the door. Darnuir was on the other side, still recovering. Maybe she had been too critical of him before. From the outside in, the job looked easy. But that was because he was Darnuir, with the right blood and the blade. She'd had to fight for every ounce of respect and had barely earned any. It wasn't right. Still, he had to deal with Blaine, with Arkus, with all of it; it was little wonder he'd turned to magic. She understood that better now. What other release did he have?

"Are you well, Prefect?" It was Harra, her face full of concern.

"I'm fine…"

"Do you wish to see the king?"

"Is he awake?"

"He's sleeping for now," Harra said. "Has been since I took over the watch."

"I'll sit with him for a time," Lira said. She wasn't sure why. Solidarity, perhaps. Harra gave her another concerned look then stepped aside.

Lira entered and found two Praetorians tending to Darnuir, gently mopping his brow and some of the fresh cuts along his arms. She waved a hand by way of telling them to continue and leaned back against the wall, watching the Praetorians as they worked. Darnuir did not so much as move. This was one of his deep sleeps, and she doubted the arrival of Rectar himself could wake him. Once, he had been out for nearly three days and they'd all feared he would never wake again.

The Praetorians finished their work and looked to Lira, clearly expecting instruction. "Bring two extra blankets," she said. "The night is cold."

Left alone with Darnuir, Lira slumped again to the floor. Back against the wall, with all the weight taken off her body, she had no intention of moving. Her legs wouldn't move in any event. They'd gone numb. It was fitting, really. Two battered dragons in need of their rest. But she'd have to move to meet Blaine. He must have come by now. She had to move.

Her eyelids fluttered. She couldn't stop them from closing.

9

WAKING NIGHTMARES

"Better green than silver with a charred tomorrow."

Old Fairy Proverb

Darnuir – The Royal Tower

A panicked voice reached him.

"Prefect Lira, you must come."

More voices, high and fearful this time, but muffled by the door and his own swimming head. He tried to focus on them, grasping at this small piece of lucidity. Lira had to go. Why? Had Rectar's army come?

"I'll need my gear." It was definitely her voice, but stronger, sounding more assured. That was good. He needed her to be strong. "Assemble in the throne room. Every Praetorian save three to watch over Darnuir. Now."

Desperately, he tried to waken; to see her, to ask what was happening. With an effort, he raised heavy eyelids and saw Lira's back as she darted out of room.

"Lira," he said faintly. "Lira," he tried again, croaking her name this time. His head lolled, chin bashing against his chest, causing him to bite his tongue. Blood swirled in his mouth. Fresh sweat ran down his face. He found it hard to keep his eyes open and blinked so rapidly that everything became a blur.

"Water," he whispered, begging that someone would hear him.

Someone did.

Freezing metal touched his lips, the rim of some jug. The pourer tried to gently tip the water into his mouth but a fresh desire for the Cascade overcame him. Muscles spasmed, causing his head to jerk upwards and scrape his cheek against the rim of the jug. Clanking metal and a loud splash followed.

"Get another," someone said, "and bring the tube too."

"No. Not that," Darnuir murmured.

"My king, you must have water."

A Praetorian gingerly approached, holding a tough tube, the sort that healers might use to drain poison. A cone-shaped funnel had been fashioned at one end. Darnuir hated this thing. He hated it when strong hands held his jaw open; hated it when he half-choked as it was edged down his throat; hated the overwhelming desire to retch as the slop or water plunged into his stomach. Worst of all, he hated how powerless it rendered him.

The Praetorian with the tube now stood over him.

"No," Darnuir said. "I can manage. Please. Try it normally. I will keep control this time." The Praetorians looked to each other for confirmation. The girl who held the jug visibly gulped. Harra, that was her name. She'd fought alongside him to defend the plateau of Aurisha. "Harra, you've faced worse than me being irritable. Please, try again. If I don't manage. Then... then you may use the tube. I won't fight you."

Harra smiled, looking a little nervous, but it was a smile. Carefully, she stepped up to Darnuir's side, brought this new jug to his lips and slowly tipped it.

The water was cold and clean. It swept away the bitterness of magic and the tang of blood. It soothed his raw throat and dampened the fire in his stomach. Darnuir drank greedily, nearly choking in his haste to satisfy his dreadful thirst. He took in too much, dribbled, then spat the rest out. Harra mopped the blood and water from his chin, as though he were an infant, and what little pride remained in him died.

"Thank you. I shall rest now."

"It's nice to hear you speak again, sire," Harra said. She and the other Praetorians then trooped out and shut the door.

Sleep eluded Darnuir for a time; he was caught in that semi-delirious state between waking and rest, where his body was numb but his mind raced. Desire for the Cascade flared, though not as fiercely as it had before. The last embers of a great bonfire. Yet it was still there, and so long as it compelled him to reach for his sword for no other reason than to draw on that sweet energy, he could not risk it. Waves of pain crashed in his head, urging him to reach for relief. He struggled against his bonds, all the while hoping for sleep to take him...

. . .

"So, you think you are ready?" Draconess said. His darkened eyes met Darnuir's disapprovingly. Darnuir looked to the Dragon's Blade hanging at Draconess' waist and deeply desired it. They were alone in a dazzling white room. Or was it merely bright light? Was this memory, or his own imagining?

"You can't even take your eyes from it," Draconess said.

Darnuir shifted his gaze. "I wasn't—" he began stupidly.

Draconess held up a hand. "I understand your frustration. We're dragons and we're strong, and yet we cannot fight this foe. I have the blade that is the essence of our people distilled, our people's power placed into a single weapon, and yet I alone can do little."

"You don't even try, Father," Darnuir said. Wait, that wasn't right. Not father, but uncle. He'd never known his real father. Blaine had explained it all. Whatever the case, the disdain towards Draconess in his voice was visceral. It at least, was real.

"I'm out there, neck-deep in the blood of demons and our own people. And you're, well, you're scribbling at parchment, taking meetings – nothing helpful."

"Nothing helpful?" Draconess said. He shook his head sombrely. "You will never be ready for the blade."

"And why is that?"

"Because you do not understand, even when I speak plainly to you. I cannot change the tide alone. You could not change the tide alone. One person, no matter their power, cannot win a war on their own, nor keep an alliance together. We need the humans and the fairies."

"The fairy flyers have their uses," Darnuir admitted. "But I find the humans often get in the way."

Draconess began to pace. "How long do you think we would survive without food shipments from Brevia? Hmm? Or Val'tarra, for that matter? Do you think we could feed or clothe our people when almost half of our lands have been scoured by demons?"

"Fine, so we need their labour."

"Will you ever understand? I used to think like you. Most of our kind still think like you; gods, it was far worse when I was a young hatchling. But I've spent decades trying to hold this all together, and I'm afraid it's beginning to crack. Three human kings I've dealt with. This youngest one, Arkus, he begins to question why he is doing what I ask of him. 'What am I getting in return?' he asks, and frankly, I'm not sure."

"Were it not for our legions, the world would be crawling with demons. We are the bulwark against this Shadow, Father. Our warriors will be the ones to push to Kar'drun and end it."

"And when exactly will that be?" Draconess said.

"When you take some fucking action."

"And on and on it goes," Draconess said. "I say I cannot make a difference alone. And nor will you."

"Does the blade have no power?" Darnuir asked. His voice had risen higher, into something like a plea. "Is that why you do nothing? Is it all just a lie? When you pray, too, is that a lie? When you tell me of the gods and a guardian, are you lying to me?"

Draconess closed his eyes. "The gods will favour those who earn it. They will smile and shine upon us when we do all we can to help ourselves. Hmm? Running and hiding and burying our past will not aid us..." He trailed off, sounding bitter.

Darnuir was lost. What was Draconess talking about now? Had he gone mad?

"Tomorrow," Draconess continued, "you will take our newest legions north. I implore you again to devise a joint strategy. Become one army, not three."

'*Three blades were given,*' a voice whispered in his mind.

"How did you do that?" Darnuir said.

"Do what?" Draconess eyed Darnuir suspiciously.

'*Three blades shall be returned...*'

"Talk in my head – how?" He backed away from Draconess, a little unsteady on his feet.

"You look pale, Darnuir. Pale and sickly." Draconess stepped cautiously towards him and, as he did so, he began to morph slowly into Blaine. Soon the guardian was standing over him, looking down in disgust.

Darnuir was on his knees, licking desperately at a bowl full of mushed silver alderberries. He needed every drop of the juice.

"Such a disgrace," Blaine muttered.

"Help me?" Darnuir moaned.

"Help you?" a deep voice called. Blaine was gone, replaced by Dukoona amidst a fog of purple mist and dancing shadows. Dukoona took Darnuir by the scruff of his neck and hoisted him upright. The blue flames of the spectre's hair flew wildly about his face.

"I've done all I dare to help you. It is up to you now, Dragon King. The red dragons come!"

And then Dukoona threw him backwards, and Darnuir was falling freely through white light: falling and falling and falling, until he smashed against dry, red earth. A mountain of burnt rock loomed above him, stretching well above the clouds.

"Help me," Dukoona's echoing voice came from the mountain.

Despite his great fall, Darnuir felt no pain. He got to his feet and walked towards it, trying to steady his shaking hand, which held the Dragon's Blade. A passage opened in the mountain and he entered it. The tunnel walls began to whip past him, although he walked no faster. *Rectar will be at the end of it*, he thought, *ready to strike me down.*

Yet all he found was a Cascade Sink. It shone like a blue sun, and then he saw it: a black figure outlined against the light. Before Darnuir could steel his courage, an invisible force yanked him inexorably forwards. Clumsily, he raised the Dragon's Blade, ill-prepared, knowing death would come. Yet, before he reached it, the Cascade Sink changed. The light turned to ambers and golds, and a voice rang out from it: "Three blades were given."

Darnuir hit the golden light and woke.

Panting, he looked fearfully around. He was only in his bedroom atop the Royal Tower. The same made but unused bed sat to his left, and moonlight glinted off the steel chains holding him in place. How long had he been out for? As his breathing calmed, he noticed that his head was clear for the first time in recent memory. His heart beat regularly, not threatening to burst through his ribs, though pain reached him from his legs and arms, as if reminding him that he ought to be suffering. The chains had made fresh cuts and abrasions, likely during his last intense fever dream. Had some of it been real? The part with Draconess, perhaps? That had seemed more real. There had been a voice telling him something, but the details of it were slipping away.

He looked to his abused forearms. Blood and pus oozed from half-healed wounds beneath the steel. Despite the pain, he was in control for the first time in months. And that felt very good indeed.

"Hello? Is anyone there?" He had to call twice more before the Praetorians entered. They looked tense and approached him cautiously, as though he was a mother wolf defending her den. "I think it's over. Will you release me?"

Perhaps it was the calmness of his manner and voice that made the Praetorians feel at ease. He imagined he had asked to be set loose before now, though not so nicely. Whatever led them to believe him, they began to loosen his chains. Each bond they removed brought the relief of stepping into a hot bath. He winced as some segments pulled at sticky, still-healing flesh. The wounds stung fiercely and would need proper attention. He wouldn't dare use magic to speed his recovery.

When the chains were removed, Darnuir tried to stand. His initial attempt was faltering. His muscles ached, his joints cracked as he stretched. He had to steady himself with a hand on the chair, and remained hunched for a time, worried he would fall. The Praetorians came to his aid, placing caring hands under his arms and upon his back, pressing his sweat-drenched shirt unpleasantly against his skin. Harra was there again and took his hand.

"Thank you," Darnuir said. He had never felt more humbled, nor more grateful. "I owe you all a debt I fear I can never repay." They walked for several steps together, but he couldn't emerge into public like this.

"Let go for a moment. I must try to stand."

Dutifully, the Praetorians withdrew, and Darnuir took his first clumsy steps.

Thankfully, his body began to remember how this was done. After a circuit of the room, he made his way towards the balcony, although he didn't step out onto it. He leaned against a pillar there and took in what he could of Aurisha.

The starium of the city twinkled under the silver moonlight, and in a moment of true daring, Darnuir pushed away from the pillar to force his legs to cope with his own weight.

He swayed once, twice, then stood. He straightened and breathed deeply, accentuating the rise and fall of his wasted chest. Under his damp shirt, he could see the outline of his ribs. Yet for all his setbacks, he was here, high above the ancient dragon city. He'd brought his people home.

And Darnuir, King of Dragons, was on his feet once more.

10

HONOUR AND NECESSITY

"What happened that night is lost to us now."

Author Unknown

Earlier that same evening
   Lira – The Royal Tower – The King's Chambers

Voices reached her as if through water. Short, sharp, blasting voices that sounded closer with every second. *I should wake up,* she thought. *I should wake up. I need to know what's going on.* But she couldn't quite manage—

A great bang rent the air. Lira awoke with a start, sitting bolt upright, reaching for a sword she wasn't wearing, and breathing hard. Praetorians swarmed into the room, fully armoured. Several began speaking at once.

"Prefect Lira, you must come."

"The Light Bearers, they've—"

"Attacks on humans—"

"In the Lower City."

For a second, Lira sat still as panic took over her. She desperately wished this to be a nightmare, but the aches from her sleep-deprived limbs were too real. And if the worst had happened, if it had come to violence, at least that was simple. She jumped to her feet, her heart pumping fresh energy through her.

"Assemble in the throne room. Every Praetorian save three to watch over Darnuir. Now." They bolted and Lira followed, sparing a last glance for Darnuir as she left him behind.

Please wake soon, Darnuir. I need you.

Down in the throne room, all the Praetorians were gathering as she'd ordered, helping each other secure pieces of their plate armour. Raymond was there as well. A pang struck her: fresh, raw, unexplainable horror. An image flashed before her of Raymond crushed by a Light Bearer's fist. She couldn't let him go. Yet she could say nothing for now, for General Fidelm and a contingent of fairy flyers approached her.

"Lira, this must be contained," Fidelm said. His wings crackled, and he gripped his double-bladed spear tightly. A fury lit his eyes like she'd never seen before and she was very glad he was on her side.

"That's my intention," Lira said, holding steady while Camen tightened her breastplate together at the shoulders. "What's going on exactly?"

"Light Bearers have struck at groups of humans. I'm not certain how many, or who. If you're heading out soon, I will go now and do what I can."

"Go first to Grigayne," Lira said. "Tell him what's happening. The islanders need to stay out of the way. Grigayne will understand, but we have to be clear these attackers are not under any orders."

"That we know of," Fidelm said darkly.

Lira felt another great weight plummet down through her stomach. She looked hard at Fidelm. "You don't seriously think that Blaine—"

"I'm not sure anymore," Fidelm snapped. "He and his followers have become possessed since the Nail Head. We'll know by morning."

Camen secured the final fastenings of her armour. Lira rolled her shoulders and shook her arms, her legs, trying to expel her nerves. This was madness. Pure, simple madness. What if Blaine was leading them? How were they supposed to fight him?

"Go, Fidelm," she said. "We'll see you down there."

The general gave a curt nod and flew from the throne room. Once he left, Lira noticed that a tense silence had fallen over the Praetorians. Most were ready now and looked to her. Something jingled softly. Camen had thrust her sword and belt towards her, the metal buckles slapping together. Lira clenched her jaw then took the sword from him. She strapped it on and picked up a shield.

"There will be no more deaths," she said. Her voice reflected her strain, but she steadied herself and slowed the pace of her speech. "No deaths so far as we can help it. Enough dragons have died. Enough humans have died. We'll take these Light Bearers and they will answer for what they've done. We'll show the humans and the fairies and our own people that this is not our way. This is not Darnuir's vision.

When he wakes, it will not be to our alliance burning around us. No more deaths," she added again. "Fight together, Praetorians. With me."

The Praetorians thumped their shields twice in approval and then darted from the throne room. Lira hung back and caught Raymond at the door, putting a hand on his chest. He tried to push through but could make no headway against her strength.

"Stay, Raymond."

He looked defiant and hurt, as she'd known he would.

"What honour will there be left for a disgraced chevalier if I stay while people are in need? What use can I be to you here?"

"What use will you be with a broken body? If you get hurt, I'd never forgive myself." He screwed up his face in determination and tried to push forwards again. Lira's arm relaxed a fraction, but then she pushed him back. He stumbled, nearly lost his balance, and a grudging acceptance entered his eyes.

"Stay," she said again, and then she ran.

She caught up with the Praetorians halfway across the plaza. The night seemed peaceful up here, with no sign of trouble other than fifty Praetorians tearing towards the switchback roads. As they passed the Basilica, she considered securing it first. The usual guards between the columns were gone. But no; they had to protect the humans. Yet there were dragons emerging from the temple: non-armoured Light Bearers by the looks of them, and they were running to intercept Lira.

"Form south," she called. As one, the Praetorians halted, turned to face the Basilica, closed ranks and locked their shields. The Light Bearers hesitated, then came to her regardless. Closer up she saw they weren't even armed, so she kept her sword in its scabbard. For now.

"Lady Prefect," one wearily said. "What is happening?"

"You tell me. General Fidelm brings word that Light Bearers are attacking humans in the Lower City." She marched towards them. "Where is Blaine? Did he order this?"

"We don't know," said the Light Bearer. "We only came because the guards on duty didn't wake us for our rotation. We feared we'd overslept. We had no idea that—"

"I advise you to go back to your beds," Lira snarled. "Now." They gave her and the Praetorians one last, wide-eyed look, then dashed back to the Basilica. Lira turned away in disgust. "We move on."

Running down the streets of the plateau's slope was at least easy. Momentum spurred her on to keep that pace as the streets levelled out, then emerged at ground level by the harbour.

Ahead, near the city gates, human troops were now forming ranks, spearmen and archers readying. Confusion streaked every face and Lira and her dragons blazed past without resistance. She wove through the narrower streets, retracing her steps from earlier in the night, hoping to reach these Light Bearers before the human troops could march in.

She neared the eastern wall. Distant cries could be heard. A small battle was occurring, but a battle nonetheless. A man was screaming. His howl gave her some direction and she chased it, growing closer and closer, until she saw the backs of human soldiers ahead, near the bend in the road. Their archers were firing at something out of sight.

"Out of the way," Lira cried.

Seeing more dragons hurtling towards them, the humans scattered. Without slowing, the Praetorians charged on, rounding the corner to find Light Bearers in a small shield formation. Outnumbered, the Light Bearers broke and ran. Lira gave chase. She did not fail to notice the bodies that lay strewn on the ground. There weren't many, thankfully, but they were all human. Looks of shock were etched forever in their unclosed eyes.

Soon the chase led Lira to a familiar sight: the wide lane between two tottering stacks of housing. Only now there was something hanging in the air between the buildings. A man, his limbs spread-eagled and stretched. She couldn't yet be certain, but she knew it would be the Preacher.

A wound at his waist was still dripping blood. Droplets fell to the street and shone in the firelight. As she advanced, she saw the blood had been drawn into the symbol of the guardians on the ground beneath him. Lira nearly threw up there and then.

The bulk of the Light Bearers were at the far end of the street, close to the city wall. Their backs were against it. They had nowhere else to run. But they didn't seem to care. They didn't even bother to form a shield wall.

"Looks like a hundred of them, Prefect," Camen said.

"They'll need the advantage of numbers," Lira called. "We are Praetorians. We can handle these old men."

The Guard bashed their shields and cried out their agreement. This was still going to be a brutal fight, even if they won. Blaine did not let just anyone join his ranks. All of them were grizzled veterans. Two to one wasn't good odds, but the true loss lay in how many had come to commit these crimes.

Could it be true? Could they have all lost their minds?

She drew her Praetorians to a halt, her chest rising and falling lightly from the run. It had been a good warm-up. The Light Bearers were not moving, so she had time to survey the situation. The street itself would mean their numbers would count for less. One small win for her. Still they had not formed a defence, so that must mean they intended to bring the fight to her. Again, this was a small advantage. If Bacchus had gotten them trapped here then he would make them fight until the last. At least she had their leadership clear in her head. The idea of Blaine leading them was too horrifying. If not Blaine, then Bacchus had done this.

And she'd bring him in herself.

"Bacchus, end this now!"

No answer.

"Put your weapons down, all of you. This is pointless. The king will never forgive you for it. If you fight, the humans will swarm in here and kill you all."

Still, there came no answer.

"What in the world has possessed you?"

"Only the love of our gods, girl," a voice called. She didn't recognise it.

"They're your gods too. You should not work against them."

"These humans anger the gods. We have asked for a sign. This man will face Dwna as the light rises and be judged."

"We are the Light's chosen. You hatchlings should learn this."

The last of the Light Bearers' voices dimmed and they took a deliberate step forward.

"One. Last. Chance," Lira boomed, knowing full well that her threat meant little with only half their numbers. "Put your weapons down."

Above, she saw fairies landing on the rooftops. Fidelm had arrived. Yet the Light Bearers took no notice. And in their assuredness, they charged. Lira locked her own shield firmly in place.

"No more deaths," she reminded them.

Crazed and screaming, the Light Bearers came on, shields tossed aside, swords raised. Lira felt the force of the impact through her entire body, blow after blow. They ricocheted up her shield arm, threatening to shake her shoulder from its joint. They weren't holding back. These were strikes intended to kill.

"Hold," she screamed. Time to see whether all their training had paid off. "Hold," she cried again. Two rapid, powerful strikes hit her shield and she nearly staggered. She felt pressure from the enemy increase, heard their feet scurry and slip as they lost any sense of cohesion. Now was the moment.

"Push!"

And, as one, the Praetorians stepped forwards. One pace, two paces, three. They stopped. The Light Bearers were thrown off balance. Lira took the lead in breaking from the wall, driving her shield onto the first lightly armoured foot she saw. Bones cracked. Howling, the Light Bearer fell.

Their shield wall barely reformed before the next assault came. This fighting, back and forth, lasted for a time. Lira dared not risk pushing too far when she was stepping, not least because wounded Light Bearers started getting in the way.

"Prefect!" The shriek came from the back of their own ranks. Lira risked a glance behind and saw Light Bearers amongst them. They were jumping down from the upper storeys of the buildings. Praetorians raised their useless shields against the impact of their falling enemies. One Light Bearer cut at two fairies on his descent, slicing flesh and wing alike.

Blood had been spilled.

A sword struck past her shield, missing her face by a hair's breadth and catching the Praetorian behind her in the shoulder. More blood. No more death, she had said. She'd meant it. Hatred for these Light Bearers burned within her; these old, bigoted fools.

The ranks on both sides broke down. Light Bearers diving from above was not something the Praetorians had trained for, and their shield wall broke down. A melee ensued; a free-for-all in which orders were drowned out in the confined street.

Lira scanned for Bacchus, hoping that if he fell, the others would give up. But the crush of fighters made it difficult. A downward slash forced her to raise her shield and the Light Bearer behind the strike rammed into her. She fell to her knees and took the chance to cut at his shins. He collapsed, shrieking, but would live. More than he deserved.

Another came at her, leaping over a limp Praetorian, and she gave no ground this time, striking quickly and forcing him to parry, block, step back. Two fairies descended upon him before Lira could catch up and began lifting the Light Bearer into the air.

"Don't kill him."

She had no idea whether the fairies had heard her, but they veered left and threw the dragon against the side of the building three storeys up. The Light Bearer fell from view and she found the combatants on the street had thinned. Light Bearers were moving into the houses, clearing the street to avoid the fairies.

Blood beat between her ears; her heart raced from more than just battle. Again, she searched for Bacchus, but there was no sign of him. He might have retreated inside, or he could be one of the bodies. So many, so quickly. How had it come to this?

Light Bearers and Praetorians were both groaning in pain, some crawling along the ground. She saw dead humans, dead dragons, and dead fairies, without one demon to be found.

"Enough!" The voice was deafening.

Blaine strode towards the battlefield, clearly just out of bed, wearing only a white shirt and leggings. The Guardian's Blade shone brightly in his grasp.

Lira had never been more grateful to see him. He hadn't condoned this. There was hope, and the look on his face made her feel like a child. Chin lowered, jaw set, his features unnaturally darkened. What sadness had been in his old eyes was burned away, and a century's worth of rage now pulsed behind them. For the first time, she understood why he was the guardian of the world.

"Come out. Now," Blaine said, his voice magnified by magic.

"Praetorians, to me," Lira said. They trooped to her side, bloodied and bruised. Each looked in shock, their eyes wide and mouths slack, as though unable to believe what had happened. When few Light Bearers emerged, Blaine entered the closest building himself.

Fidelm fluttered down. He didn't so much as look at Blaine. "That was hard, but necessary, Lira."

She looked to the general and saw his knuckles were scraped and bloody, but the blade upon his spear was clean. He too had held back from the kill where he could, and her respect for the fairy swelled.

Lira pointed up. "Bring that human down before their officers see him." Fidelm took off just as a Light Bearer flew from the doorway Blaine had entered moments before. The dragon crumpled on the opposite side of the street and did not stir. After that, the remaining Light Bearers began filing out like children. Some tried begging their case,; on their knees, hands clasped and pleading, shocked at Blaine's anger. He silenced them with one look.

"You did not heed my words? You have brought shame upon us."

Lira moved to his side. "Where is Bacchus?"

"Bacchus is not here," Blaine said through gritted teeth.

Lira was lost for words.

Fidelm returned, carrying the human like a baby in his arms. It was the Preacher, now pale and glassy-eyed. Fidelm closed the man's eyes.

"I saw the human troops closing in," he announced.

"I know," Blaine growled. "I passed them on the way here."

Fidelm sniffed. "I'll send flyers ahead to try and calm them. Tell them it's over." He shook his head. "Blaine... I... I can't find the words." He looked down at the human he cradled. "I'll leave this one among the rest of the bodies. The true horror doesn't need to be known."

"Very well," said Blaine.

Once Fidelm and his fairies were gone, Blaine turned to Lira. His rage had died down now; the age was showing again. He opened his mouth but Lira interrupted him.

"I have nothing to say to you." Her body quaked. "Praetorians, help the wounded. We do what we can for them here, then run them to the healers as fast as we can."

"All the wounded, Lira?" Camen said. Blood ran from his temple but otherwise he seemed unhurt. He was eyeing a Light Bearer at his feet in disgust.

"All the wounded," she said as evenly as she could. "I'm sure the guardian has to take his men back to the Basilica."

. . .

After what seemed an age later, Lira stepped off the Great Lift as dawn broke. A smoky red light burst from the horizon, a mark of the night before. Her body felt beaten, her mind empty, her emotions flogged. She walked slowly with her Praetorians across the plaza, not even fully lifting her feet at times. Halfway back to the Royal Tower, she stopped completely, sparing a dread-filled glance at the Basilica. Guards had returned between the columns. Many of them. They didn't move but the message was clear. Blaine did not want anyone coming near for now.

"Are we not returning?" Camen asked her. She didn't respond. She felt lost and afraid, and she felt a failure. She didn't know what she was going to do.

A figure emerged from the base of the Royal Tower and was hurrying towards them. It was Raymond. Lira found herself drawn to him, silently, without giving orders to the others. She collapsed into his arms and he held her tightly.

"I said you should stay," she said weakly. The fact it was all over didn't cross her mind.

"I know, Lira, but I had to find you."

"Why?"

"It's Darnuir. He's back."

11

RHUBARB PUDDING

"Make your choice. Own it, even if it's hard. A man lives at ease, who freely lives."

From Jon Barbor's *Scorching of the Dales*

Cassandra – The Palace Grounds

There was something sad and pitiful about seeing Annandale standing before the musket squad. Maybe if he had kept the blindfold on, it wouldn't be so painful to watch. She sensed the unease of the nobility, too. There had not been an execution like this in living memory. Certainly not of one of their own.

A section of the palace gardens had been appropriated for the grisly task, whole hedges ripped out to make room for stands and chairs. The Assembly of Brevia sat and watched as though it were a show. The king made it theatre, giving an oratory before them on the merits of loyalty and the price of dishonesty.

Oranna stood at his side this time, the better to be seen agreeing with her husband, yet Cassandra didn't fail to notice the glances she made to her father in the stands. Lord Clachonn was enraptured by Arkus, never taking his eyes off him, his jaw tight.

Even Thane was forced to sit and watch. She leaned in to whisper to him.

"You don't have to look when they do it."

"Father says I ought to."

"I won't tell."

"No, I need to be a strong prince. Father says they must all see that I'm str-strong —" With cruel fate he started to cough, a high-pitched squeak that rattled high in his throat. Cassandra dove beneath her seat and poured a goblet of water, which had been set there for this very reason, and emerged to find Thane still in convulsions. She hadn't the faintest clue what to do. She never did. Rubbing his back made it worse if anything, so these were moments he just had to work through. Yet it was horrible watching him struggle. He was such a frail thing, she half expected to hear his ribs crack. At least the surrounding nobles had also learned not to make a fuss, allowing Thane to hit his own little fist on his chest until he had regained himself. Red faced, he slumped back in his chair, tugging at the collar of his heavy robes as sweat glistened on his brow. Cassandra handed him the goblet, but he avoided her eye, trying to stay focused on his father; trying to be strong.

Arkus himself only had eyes for his prisoner. "You would not wear a blindfold, but you will not be forced to watch, should you prefer. I grant you a final chance to turn away."

Annandale was unmoving. "I want to look you in the eye as you do it, old friend. But it's clear there is nothing of you left. Only a husk wearing a crown."

"Do not call me friend," Arkus said. "I am your king."

"You ceased being a real king years ago. Do what you will." He didn't even close his eyes.

The crowd tensed. The wind itself dropped. One corner of Arkus' mouth tugged upwards, then he brought his arm down. A sergeant roared, muskets blasted, and at the last possible moment, Cassandra looked away. Thane buried his face against her chest. She wrapped an arm around him, waiting for the crack of the guns to subside.

"Don't tell," Thane said quietly.

"I won't," Cassandra said. She kissed the top of his soft hair.

Around them, the nobles began to stir. Unsure of the procedure, some even got to their feet, eager to leave. Oranna was nowhere to be seen but Arkus still stood by his soldiers, staring at Annandale's body, as though making sure he was dead. A patch of blood ran down the red-brick wall.

"Come on," Cassandra said. "Let's get going. I think you've earned yourself something nice from the kitchens."

Thane pulled back from her and flashed a hopeful smile.

"Like iced rhubarb pudding?"

She winked at him. "I asked chef to prepare some specially."

Thane beamed, and with a sudden burst of energy, he was on his feet and pulling her by the hand through the press of bodies, heading towards the servants' entrance of the kitchens.

Rounding a hedgerow into a cooling space by a fountain, they came across none other than Oranna and Lord Clachonn in a whispered conversation. All froze as the pair turned sharply to see who was intruding; all except Thane, who continued to heave at Cassandra's arm, pulling himself free in doing so and stumbling forwards to thump into a hug at his mother's waist.

In response to the commotion, heavy boots clunked from the other side of the hedge. A chevalier rounded the corner. Cassandra did not recognise him. His square jaw and elevated chin put her in mind of Gellick, and that set off an immediate dislike in her; yet his hair was a weaker strawberry-blond, curled in a way that softened his appearance. A warm, genuine smile helped as well, although he had one hand upon the hilt of his sword and no less than two pistols at his hips.

Clachonn rounded on the knight, signalling that he should stand down.

"It's all right, Merrick. It's Her Highness, Princess Cassandra."

Merrick's jaw dropped. "I'm so sorry to have borne my steel against you, Princess."

Cassandra too was taken aback, unused to such humility. "Do not fret, Chevalier. You were only guarding your lord. There is no grievance to bear. And please, Lord Clachonn, call me by my name. I am not merely a title." Clachonn inclined his head to her but his jaw remained stiff.

"Thane," Oranna began, "why don't you go splash some water on your face? You look too hot. Here, let me take those silly robes off." She grabbed the robes by the shoulders and Thane wiggled out. He skipped happily over to the fountain and scooped some water up to his face.

With one eye on Thane, Oranna said, "Relax, Father. It's only Cassandra. We can trust her."

"Doesn't seem we have a choice, now you've made it sound like we've got something to hide. Be more careful, sweetheart."

He turned his attention to Cassandra next, running a piercing gaze up and down her. The Lord of the Hinterlands wore what she now assumed was his customary grey attire, broken only by black buttons on his well-fitted waistcoat and black dress shoes. Up close, even his eyes were grey, though intelligent, and despite being Arkus' senior, he didn't look as damaged.

"You really are Ilana's daughter," he said.

"You're too kind." It was the easiest response to make to this frequent comment. "And there is no need to stop your conversation. I was just taking Thane to the kitchens."

"No, no, no, that won't do," Clachonn said. "It's not a Crown secret, and better you know than go off wondering whether it's worse. Wouldn't want a repeat of today's demonstration."

Oranna whacked him. "I've told you, Cass isn't her father."

"He'll find out soon enough, I suppose."

Cassandra couldn't help but look from Clachonn to the chevalier standing right there and happily overhearing everything.

"I trust Merrick implicitly," Clachonn said, answering her unvoiced concern. "Arkus has his lapdog whom he's bought through marriage alliances, whereas I have cultivated close family friends over the years. Merrick's father guarded me before him."

"You flatter me, Lord," Merrick said. "But I shall step aside in any case. It is not my place to hear more than you wish to tell me." He moved off to join Thane by the fountain.

Clachonn brought his hands together. "So, the business at hand. The great conspiracy," he chortled. "Oranna and I were just discussing her returning home for a while."

"You're leaving?" Cassandra said. Her voice rang out much higher than she expected. Suddenly, Cassandra too felt overly hot, and she didn't think it was entirely due to the unusually warm day. "What about Thane? You can't leave him."

Oranna gave her a confused smile, as though wondering whether she was joking. "I'll be taking Thane with me, of course." They all looked to the prince then, who had progressed to dunking his entire head into the water. "Oh, don't do that," Oranna said tersely. "Pull him out, Merrick."

Thane resurfaced, hair and face sopping wet, and looking entirely pleased with himself.

Cassandra tried to imagine life in the palace without him: endless stacks of soulless letters to sign, the forced pleasantries, the even more forced tea parties that she would have to host with Oranna gone; Balack, grumpy and very soon leaving himself. All this without Thane to spare her from it.

"You can't just go," she said.

Oranna raised an eyebrow. "And why not?"

"You have duties. You're the queen. You have to be here."

"I'm sure the kingdom will survive. I haven't been home in years. Thane hasn't even seen that part of the world. I think it would be good for him to stretch his legs; get some clean mountain air in him."

"Don't use him as an excuse," Cassandra said, taking a step forward and lowering her voice so that Thane would not hear.

"Truly, you are Arkus' daughter as well," Clachonn said. "What does it matter if my own daughter and grandson, who I *hardly see*, come to visit me?"

"It doesn't," Cassandra said defensively. "I just... I just would rather not see you go."

Oranna smiled weakly. "It's not an indefinite move. But I do feel the need to get away from the palace, from the city—"

"From Arkus?" Cassandra added.

"Yes," Oranna said, with a touch of frost to her tone. "From my beloved husband as well. This horrible business with Geoff and Robert has made me feel sick. He gets that look in his eye more often lately and I can't stand to see it."

"Oranna," Clachonn said forebodingly, squeezing her arm.

"No, it's fine, I understand," Cassandra said. "I've seen it too." She'd seen it that night he'd led her down into the compound beneath the Rotting Hill; as he'd explained everything about flintlocks and powder charges, about formations and fire-power, all while musket balls tore through every type of armour in the known world as if it were parchment. "Maybe the worst is over now, with Annandale dead." She found it harder to say aloud than she thought. Balack may have been right. Maybe she should never have gone to see him.

"You'll be fine, dear," Oranna said. "And we'll be back before you know it."

Thane came wandering back over then, still dripping, and started pulling on Cassandra's arm again. "Excuse us, Mother. Cassandra was taking me to the kitchens for rhubarb pudding."

Oranna snorted a laugh. "Well, the mystery of why he loves you so much is solved." She leaned in, ensuring only Cassandra heard. "Don't tell Arkus yet. Not until I'm sure." Cassandra wanted to protest again, to tell her that she didn't want the people she cared about most to leave her stranded. But Oranna didn't give her the chance. "Right, off you two go, then. But mind he doesn't eat so much that dinner is spoilt." Still a little dazed, Cassandra nodded and allowed Thane to drag her off like a bloodhound on the trail.

"And dry him off," Oranna called.

Together, they finished their short journey to the servants' entrance and Thane slammed the door knocker loudly until a hassled looking pot boy opened it. The smell of sizzling onions, roasting meats and simmering broth made Cassandra's stomach squirm in delight. Stepping inside, the clank of pots and pans, the thump of chopping and the calls of instruction fought for dominance. One voice won out above all.

"I've explained it a thousand times already," Kymethra said to a flustered chef. "The fresher the bread, the more chilled the water, the better. It all helps to soak up the magic in him. Seeing as the delivery has gone awry, I'll be doing it myself from now on, all right?"

"As you say, as you say," the chef said. "A new batch will be ready soon. You're welcome to stay until then. Ah, Princess," he added, looking thankful to have an excuse to escape the witch. "Do come in. I shall fetch your order for His Highness as requested." He bustled off.

Kymethra huffed and sat on a stool by the closest workbench, ignoring the mound of carrot peelings that lay before her. She gave Thane and Cassandra a half-hearted wave, almost as an afterthought.

Seeing the witch warded off some of the dark clouds that had just gathered over Cassandra's mood. At least Kymethra would remain in the palace, even if it was difficult to see her between princess duties and Kymethra's own, which consisted of watching over the scrying orb for activity and caring for Brackendon. The latter was far more taxing. New white strands of hair had appeared since they'd last spoken.

Cassandra mouthed that they'd be over soon, then dragged Thane over to the hearth to dry off his hair with a clean dishcloth. It did the job well enough and the kitchen heat had done most of the work already.

By the time they joined Kymethra, the head chef was already heading back their way, carrying a worryingly large bowl before him. Kitchen staff appeared from nowhere with extra stools and spoons, and the chef placed the dessert between the three of them. Kymethra gave the smallest shake of her head and politely handed her spoon back. Cassandra contemplated the contents of the bowl.

Apparently, it had been an accidental creation. A porridge gone awry. Yet Thane had loved it so much it was now a staple of the palace cookbook. A mixture of oats gently cooked in milk, sugar, cream, and rhubarb juice, then left to soften and chill. Even as Thane reached in for his first spoonful, the chef rounded it off with cubes of sweetened rhubarb on the top. With Oranna's words about ruining Thane's dinner ringing in her mind, Cassandra pushed the bowl towards him, intending to stop him before he devoured the entire thing. With the prince happily tucking into his treat, Cassandra playfully flicked one of the wayward peelings at Kymethra.

"Been a while."

Kymethra eyed the peeling, which had fallen into her lap, then picked it up between finger and thumb and burned it to ashes in a tiny, brief ball of fire.

Cassandra fidgeted and cleared her throat. "Bad day? I couldn't help but overhear you just there. If the staff aren't bringing Brackendon what he needs, I can have a word with—"

"They are, they are," Kymethra said. She slouched into the peelings with one elbow and rested her head in her hand. Sighing, she said, "It's just not enough and they don't understand it; but then, nothing will be enough. I'm sorry. It's not your fault."

"Are you sure there's nothing I can do? I want to help."

"It's fine, really," Kymethra said. "Besides, I'll probably be taking Brackers to Val'-tarra soon, now the worst of his breaking is past."

Cassandra blinked. "You're... you're leaving?"

"Once he's able to get through the day without needing to be soothed then he'll be better off with the fairies. They know how to handle people in his condition better than anyone."

"Would you come back once he's settled?" She regretted it the moment she said it. How selfish must she sound to Kymethra, a woman who had given everything for those around her? Had she ever once made a demand for herself?

Kymethra became very interested in an apprentice cook stirring the contents of a black pot over the fire. "I don't know, Cass. I've not felt comfortable here for a long time. Brackendon's care hasn't been easy. Mostly the chevaliers stomp by to check that he hasn't done any damage rather than ask how he is, not to mention the day and night I spent gagged and bound."

"That was Gellick."

"On—" Kymethra seemed to change words mid-speech with a quick glance to Thane. "On *his* orders."

"I know, I know." Cassandra buried her face into her hands.

"I like Gellick," Thane said happily, though he didn't turn away from his food. "He lets me sit on his horse sometimes. He says he'll teach me how to use a sword when Father approves." He shoved another generous spoonful of sweet oats into his mouth.

"People aren't always what they appear to be, little prince," Kymethra said.

"That's right," Thane said thickly. "You can turn into an eagle and fly and scratch people's eyes out."

Kymethra chuckled. "Yes, well, that is true."

"I wish I could fly," Thane said. He manoeuvred his spoon through the air like a bird in flight, before descending again into the bowl. Cassandra noticed an alarming amount of it had already been eaten.

"I think that's enough for you," she said. Thane groaned but continued to play with the mixture, pushing it around the bowl.

An oven door creaked open somewhere behind them and the soul-warming smell of fresh bread filled the kitchens. Kymethra rose to collect her order and Cassandra felt compelled to not leave things in such an uncertain state. She caught the witch's arm.

"Please consider coming back. Who else can work the scrying orb but you? I'll talk to Arkus. Things will be better." She hesitated, then just said it. "I'd miss you."

Kymethra smiled and bent to give her a one-armed hug. "You can get up to no good without me. Besides, I won't just up and leave without telling you, nor is Brackers ready yet. But it's something I'll have to do, Cass."

Cassandra held on a little too tightly as Kymethra pulled back then turned to meet the head chef coming towards her with a basket of steaming loaves.

She returned her attention to Thane and caught him red-handed sneaking another spoonful. He pushed the bowl away without much of a fight and followed her back through the palace to the royal apartments.

Cassandra's thoughts were heavy with the news of the day. Everyone seemed to be leaving. The root of the problem was Arkus. He seemed to be at the heart of every problem; rebellions and dysfunctional marriages alike. Perhaps he didn't realise what his behaviour was doing to people. Maybe she could get him to change course? She resolved to try, at the very least.

12

THE UNLIKELY SOLDIER

"I have observed adversity to be the true driving force amongst all races."

From Tiviar's Histories

Sonrid – The Outskirts of Kar'drun

Out here, the days turned from sun to stars in silence. No birds chirruped their songs. No wind blew. No precious water ever fell across the cracked plains surrounding the mountain. The only sound came from Sonrid himself. His breathy grunts of pain, the soft drag of his bad leg across the earth. There were no clouds today, so he could not meld into their shadows. He was secretly glad for it. Unlike his fully formed spectre brethren, melding was painful for him, so he preferred to hobble. Yet guilt jarred at him every step of the way.

Dukoona and the Trusted had been summoned back to Kar'drun. They would be suffering at their master's hand, likely far worse than even Sonrid had. He had to reach them; had to do something, and time would be of the essence. But there was only so much agony a creature could endure, even a Broken so used to it like himself. A shadow meld across the continent, even with the aid of moving clouds, would have killed him.

After weeks and weeks, his march was drawing to an end. Kar'drun dominated the landscape; a burnt and hulking mountain flanked by the easternmost edge of the Highland range. All the smaller mountains had snow-capped peaks, but not Kar'-drun. It looked like a lump of charcoal amongst cooler ashes.

He let out a fresh groan. It felt like his leg was on fire, though aside from a slight bend at his knee, there was nothing visibly wrong. He raised himself up as tall as his hunched body would allow and pressed on, dragging himself a few more steps, and then a few more. He'd shuffled like this since leaving Aurisha, taking the occasional shadow when he had felt strong enough. Rest helped to ease the agony, but he was so close now. He ought not to stop for long.

Yet when a shuddering pain ran throughout his body, he was forced to a halt. The shadows of his poor leg, already wispier than a normal spectre, parted and swirled madly. Bones were visible. Not good at all. Reluctantly, he decided to rest.

I'll be even more useless if I can't walk.

He imagined what Dukoona might say if he heard Sonrid call himself useless. Dukoona would tell Sonrid that he had a part to play against their master. Sonrid wasn't so sure, but Dukoona had been the first spectre to show him kindness of any kind. Before that fateful day when he had seen the red creature emerge from Kar'-drun, spectres had largely ignored him, like Rectar did. Sonrid's existence until that point had been as close to pointless as he could comprehend.

He remembered other broken spectres seeking their end, walking into the dark ocean to never return, or limping off some high ruin in the Forsaken City and ending their miserable lives. Sonrid too had contemplated such acts, but cowardice had kept him alive.

His leg eased up. The shadows there reformed into a denser purple and he squinted again at the mountain of Kar'drun. What purpose he now had in his life lay within its endless caverns. Slowly, he began to walk forwards.

He noticed that the chalky red earth extended even further from Kar'drun than before, as though Rectar's malice emanated outwards to spoil the world. There had been life here before. Sonrid used to notice it on the rare occasions he had dared venture this far from Kar'drun. Green grass, flowers with white and yellow petals he did not know the names of; birds in the sky and insects that thrived low in the soil.

On he struggled, until the sun had risen directly above him and his pain increased to crippling levels. This time, he collapsed. Every joint flared and his whole body became a furnace of pain. His head hit the earth, his vision spiralled and darkened. He wondered whether he would die, if he'd somehow pushed his broken body beyond what it could handle. Spectres did not sleep, so he did not pass out. Instead, he lay where he had fallen with incoherent vision and nothing but anguish and the desperate hope that it would pass.

. . .

When he regained himself, the light in the sky was pale and shimmering. He had no idea how long he'd lain there. His mind worked sluggishly, but after a time he was forced to accept the fact he was still alive. The thought of standing was intolerable. Perhaps if he lay here for long enough a cloud might pass and he could meld with it. Which would be harder to manage? Which was the lesser torture?

He saw movement from the corner of his eye. A large beetle was scuttling towards him. It had a moss-green chitinous shell, ill-suited to blending in against the red earth. As its antennae probed the world ahead, the beetle slowed as it drew closer to Sonrid's face. Uncertain in its course, the beetle halted. Both he and the beetle remained motionless. Perhaps it was stubborn and thought he ought to move out of its way.

"You'll be waiting for a rather long time." His voice was even weaker than usual.

The beetle's antennae wiggled at the sound of his voice, but otherwise the creature seemed unconcerned. He wondered if it felt pain like he did. He had wondered that about every creature he'd come across. Singing birds could not be in pain or they would not fill the air with their music. Yet there was no longer any birdsong. Were they suffering too? All life might just be one of pain. He just felt it worst of all.

Unmoving, like the distant mountains, the beetle remained.

"If you are to wait it out with me, you shall die and rot, while I shall remain. I will—" He stopped himself. Whatever pitiable thing he said, this beetle would not care. He could just lie here, but he'd remain forever unless some dragon, human or fairy found him and killed him. To actively find an end of any sort meant moving forwards. Only under Kar'drun would he find peace. He'd either die in the attempt, or aid Dukoona and the Trusted, witness their vengeance against Rectar and then, once he had some meaning to his suffering, ask Dukoona to kill him. Dukoona would not refuse him then.

This hope of death dulled the pain from his joints.

Unsteadily, he rose.

Once upright, Sonrid saw the beetle continue along its resolute course. *What a defiant little thing*, he thought, smirking at the green bug that had bested him. He turned to face Kar'drun in the distance and his smile morphed into a determined frown.

Groaning, he limped on.

13

DEATH TO THE DRAGON

"Common is the dragon willing to fight and die. Rare is the one who can sit with patience and lead."

An old dragon maxim

Darnuir – The Royal Tower

It had been the worst morning of Darnuir's life. His first day emerging from recovery had been one of perpetual bad news. Conflicting witnesses gave hastily-made accounts and he had received nothing but silence from Blaine. It all sank into him slowly, like a thick poison passing through his veins. He'd even wondered hopefully for a time whether he was still hallucinating.

But it was not a nightmare. It was all real. As night fell, a deathly quiet choked the city of Aurisha, and Darnuir walked the hallways of the Royal Tower alone. Though weary from the day, he felt no need for sleep. He'd slept for long enough. And while his body still ached, his mind felt clearer than he could ever remember it being. So, while half the Praetorians kept watch on the Basilica and the others slept, Darnuir stalked the darkened corridors of his ancestors, allowing his mind to work on his myriad problems.

He entered a moonlit hallway, curved like all the rest in the tower. Life-sized statues lined the walls, disappearing around the bend. They'd been cut from starium, but the grainy quality of the stone had been smoothed away to leave unblemished faces. Each dragon held a carved version of the Dragon's Blade and struck a similar pose, thrusting their sword high and forwards to create a tunnel of swords under which Darnuir now walked. Had their faces not been different, Darnuir might have thought them all to be exact copies. These must have been the kings, though their names and when they had reigned had not been deemed important enough to remember. The uniformity of the kings, while unnerving, was not surprising.

We are a stubborn race. We are a violent race. We are a crude, unthinking people.

No king was depicted as a scholar; not one sat in contemplation. No dragon king stood here with friends. None held a tool, only their deadliest weapon. Now the Dragon's Blade hung at his hip, the source of his strength, his kingship. And his disgrace. Just looking at its blood-red hilt sent a shiver up his spine. He flinched as though the sword had bitten him. He hated it as much as he loved it, and a flood of empathy for Brackendon filled him. At last, he understood the wizard's struggle.

One statue caught his eye. Darnuir recognised Dronithir's face – the great hero of the Second War. He had stood alongside humanity as a prince and defeated the guardian Norbanus in single combat in the marshes. Blaine had shown him that old memory within the Guardian's Blade. Blaine had also said that he could see events repeating, if he looked back far enough. Darnuir examined Dronithir's lifeless eyes.

Am I you, but in the here and now? Must I defeat another guardian?

Although, Darnuir thought, *Dronithir didn't truly win in the end.*

He might have won the battle, but he failed to win Norbanus' heart. Seven hundred years later, Darnuir faced the repercussions of it. Secret tunnels in the Bastion. A betrayal that was centuries in the making.

As he drew away from the statue, he vowed to do better. Unlike Dronithir, Darnuir would not heedlessly charge in, roaring with a blade in hand. He was too tired for that. The hot anger that had flared in him since receiving the Dragon's Blade had lost its fuel. It might return, of course; he couldn't be sure. Yet he didn't think so. The Darnuir pre-Cascade cleansing would have stormed into the Basilica, Praetorians by his side, seeking retribution for the human killings; seeking answers; seeking action to vent his own fear and anger. But not now. Oh, he would have answers, but not at swordpoint. Not unless there was absolutely no other way.

At the end of the hallway, he found Draconess' statue. It was rougher, the stone not yet smoothed to a shine like the others. Yet, to Darnuir, it seemed the only one worth looking at. Here, at last, was some sign of frailty. Here, whether it had been intended or not, was the truth: that dragons draped themselves in gold but there was nothing precious underneath. Just creatures, struggling in life like any human or fairy. As Darnuir exited the passage, he decided he would not add to this strange collection.

Let the world have something worth remembering me by that isn't holding a sword.

He ended his night-time excursion in the throne room, sitting upon the steps leading to his throne. No compulsion filled him to sit on that cold stone chair. He hadn't earned the right to look down on anyone. And as the early dawn light broke the darkness, Darnuir had decided what he would have to do.

Later that morning, Darnuir perched on the same step beneath his throne. He ate a small breakfast and drank three flagons of water. His appetite was there but his throat still ached from the use of that hard, unforgiving tube. Once he was finished, two Praetorians brought the scrying orb to the foot of the stairs so that it stood at eye level with him.

"Is there anything else, sire?"

"No, that will be all for now. Fetch Raymond and Grigayne Imar as instructed. Grigayne is to be at the front. His position demands the courtesy." The Praetorians bowed and left him with only the orb for company. It was his duty to tell Arkus. His alone.

From what little he had gathered, activating the orb wasn't hard. It took one who had been touched by the Cascade to work, and so he reached out to it and spread his hand wide over its glassy surface. If there were many orbs in the world, he would have had to direct the connection, but there was only one other now.

The misty innards of the orb rippled then parted, revealing a hazy version of Arkus' private council chamber. As the image sharpened, he could see a lone chevalier gawking back at him.

"This is Darnuir, King of Dragons. I would speak with Arkus."

Slack-jawed, the chevalier nodded then disappeared from view. Darnuir withdrew his hand, and when the connection seemed to hold, he relaxed a little upon the steps. Resting his elbows upon his knees, his chin upon his hands, he patiently watched the empty room.

Arkus had not redecorated since Darnuir had visited. It was still largely bare, with little to suggest it belonged to a king. Perhaps it was in service to that portrait of his departed wife hanging behind his desk. Ilana's smile, her grass-green eyes and wavy black hair, were rendered more beautiful with the flecks of colour and light that only a painter's brush could add.

It had maybe been half a year since he'd stood in Arkus' room with that painting, but it felt far longer. It felt like years.

Lost in thought, Darnuir heard something from the orb and lifted his head. Arkus stepped into view and the chevalier Gellick followed a moment later.

"Greetings, Darnuir," Arkus said. He had his crown on and this time did not remove it. "I see you have, erm, recovered?"

"I have overcome my addiction to Cascade energy, yes."

Arkus smiled. "My congratulations. Now, let's get our business out of the way, shall we? It's rather late at my end."

"My thanks, Arkus, and very well. Let's begin, though I will need to be brought up to speed on a couple of matters. From what I gather, you and Blaine have not had regular contact. Did he speak with you regarding the position of our people camped outside of Brevia?"

"We spoke, but dear old Blaine offered me no exchange. The guardian's generosity knows no bounds, as does his arrogance."

Darnuir sighed into his hands so that Arkus could not hear. He'd known the pair of them would not see eye to eye. It had been one of his fears in withdrawing from the world to heal, but by the time he had resigned himself to the chains and the chair, he could barely stand upright, never mind negotiate.

Arkus's eyes shifted from side to side. "Where is he, anyway?"

"Blaine is... busy. I am sorry if he offended you. I'm sorry that I've been absent and that your soldiers have remained here for so long without obvious cause. But of every thing I am sorry about over both my lives, this news might be the worst. I have something I must tell you, but perhaps I could tell you privately?" He looked to Gellick. The chevalier cocked his head, as though amused.

"Gellick is my right hand in all matters," Arkus said. "Much the same as that huntress is to you. Though I note with interest that she is not with you either."

"Lira is resting. She's been through a lot."

Arkus stood straighter at those words. "Has Aurisha been attacked? Has this vague new threat materialised?"

"No, and the threat is real. Rectar has taken dragons over the decades of war and enchanted them the same way that Castallan enchanted humans. They will be the deadliest foe we've ever fought. Rectar has simply not unleashed them yet."

Arkus leaned closer to whisper to Gellick. After a brief exchange, Arkus returned his attention to Darnuir. "Why not? Why would the enemy hold back?"

"I do not know."

Arkus frowned. "Well, what's your plan exactly? Why keep my soldiers? What good will humans be in a fight like that?"

"Long spears, dense formations, hails of arrows; your troops can do a lot that mine cannot. I have high walls I can defend should it come to it. This gives us some advantage, but—" Darnuir took a moment, struggling to tell Arkus of the tragedy which had occurred. The scrying orb was a miraculous device, but he couldn't read much in Arkus' eyes. From here they simply looked black and small, lacking the shrewd glint that existed in the flesh. Would Arkus remove his troops because of what had happened? And could he, Darnuir, refuse him now?

"But what?" Arkus said, suspicion creeping into his voice.

"Please, Arkus, believe me when I say you'd rather hear this in private."

"Speak now, Darnuir, or don't. Whatever you tell me, I'll relay to Gellick in due course."

Darnuir sighed wearily again. An ache ran through him, but he was sure to look Arkus directly in the eye as he spoke, as one king to another.

"It is with a heavy heart I tell you of this. The day before yesterday, a group of radical, zealous dragons took violent action against members of the Fifth Regiment, men of the Crownlands, I believe. Lira and General Fidelm did everything in their power to end the hostilities and bring those dragons to justice. A small battle ensued, with deaths on both sides from all races. So far, there have been eighty-seven confirmed human deaths. Dozens more may die from injuries, though the fairy healers are doing everything they can for them."

Gellick's mouth disappeared into a razor-thin line. Arkus had raised a hand to his mouth, half covering it as though he might be sick. He slumped back again, looking as worn and tired as Darnuir felt. This was not the reaction that Darnuir had expected. It was somehow worse, this quiet shock. Outrage, he'd been expecting; anger, he could understand.

"Arkus, if there is anything I can—" But Arkus raised a hand and Darnuir, respectfully, did not press on. The time it took Arkus to compose himself felt like an eternity.

"What were you doing during this?"

"I had not yet recovered. By the time I awoke it was already over."

"Have you completely lost control over there? Who were these dragons?"

"Some were Light Bearers. Others were regulars from the Third Legion. We're still piecing it together."

"And what will be done to punish them?"

"There is need for dangerous hard labour to repair our northern fortifications. I shall send them there and see they repay their debt. I shall not be dealing out death for death."

"That is your right," Arkus said, wrapping his voice around each word as though trying to strangle them. "Blaine. I want him stripped of his rank, stripped of his power, whatever you have to do. This is the second grave insult he has dealt me and my people."

This was it. The promise Darnuir could not make.

"I'm told Blaine was the one who ended the attacks. He didn't orchestrate this."

"Then he no longer has control over his own followers," Arkus spat. "He's caused nothing but harm. I want him gone."

"I understand why you ask this, Arkus. Believe me, I do—"

"Yet you don't seem angered by it?"

"Oh, I am angry, so very angry. I think a part of me is always angry. I'm just not letting it take over me, as it once did." He leaned forward, closer to the scrying orb until its bright swirling edges became painful to his eye. "I cannot promise how this will play out, but I can promise you this, with every fibre of my being, with every drop of blood in my heart: I will do whatever it takes to make things right between our peoples. I will bend, and I will gift, and I will draw up new treaties, and work with you and your Assembly until all the wrongs of the past are wiped clean. This I promise to do, once the war is won. Until Rectar is defeated, I cannot, will not sacrifice all the gains that we have made. I need Blaine to help me win this fight.

"I know I ask for a lot. I want my dragons to come home. I want to reunite their families. I want to begin settling our lands and building anew. Most of all, I want to take the pressure off your city. I know you will want your own soldiers in return for this, especially now, but until the war is over, I cannot do that. Surely you can understand that? As a sign of good faith, I will send back the survivors of the aggrieved Fifth Regiment and one other regiment chosen at random, unless you have a preference?"

Arkus ran a hand through his greying hair and he too stepped closer to the orb, until the painting of Ilana, the room and even Gellick were gone, and only Arkus' lined face remained.

"You have asked me to understand a lot of things, Darnuir, both in this life and your last. The Assembly found out about the Bastion tunnels, I'm afraid. My lords and wealthy merchants aren't looking favourably upon your kind. You wish to rebuild your home, and they wish to rebuild their kingdom, to plant their own crops and return to some sense of normality. I fear if I give in to your demands now, they will think me weak, and I have just suffered one rebellion. I cannot release your people."

"They aren't prisoners, are they?"

"Poor phrasing on my part," Arkus said impatiently. "Your decision to send some of my soldiers home is a welcome one and may help your case with the Assembly, but I can make no guarantees. You ask much of me. And your people are already draining my resources."

"Then send them home—"

But Arkus whipped back from the scrying orb at his end, his black robe billowing around him like a tempest.

"We are at an impasse, Darnuir. Until next time."

He and Gellick stormed away, leaving only the bare room and the painting upon the wall. Darnuir lingered upon Ilana's portrait a while longer, wondering about Cassandra and how she was faring in Brevia. He'd forgotten to ask. Perhaps next time.

Groaning, the pains in his joints and muscles still very real, Darnuir got to his feet and placed a hand upon the orb. The scene within it spun as the white mist expanded to engulf the space once more.

Well, it could have gone worse. Though how much worse he didn't wish to contemplate. For all he willed that the animosity between dragons and humans might end, things had only frayed further. A part of him wished to send the humans back to Brevia before things got worse. Perhaps some time apart would cool the emotions between the races, as quarrelling lovers needed their space. Yet the fear of red eyes on black silhouettes haunted him from his fever dreams. Just dreams, he knew, but the fear was real. Despite reclaiming Aurisha, his people were weaker than ever; he was weaker than ever. And they needed humanity more than any dragon would ever admit.

"What would the wise ruler do?" he asked of the throne room.

He thought upon the last broken dream he'd had during his recovery. He was sure it had been a memory, mostly. Draconess had been careful and cautious to a fault, but he had held the alliance together. He reached out for help when needed and made Arkus and Kasselle feel a part of decisions. That would be something worth learning, but right now, Darnuir didn't have the luxury of time. He would stick to the plan he'd concocted.

He rose and called, "Praetorians," and two entered the throne room, a boy and girl, both only eighteen. He thought of them as far younger than himself, though he was only a few years their senior. Had it been right to recruit ones so young? They shared his vision – they too had grown up among humans – but he'd dragged them through horror and ill-conceived battles because he was their king; because he had thirsted for magic. He'd have to do better by them as well. They looked to him expectantly, and he asked, "Have they arrived?"

"Yes, Darnuir," said the girl, Arabel.

"Good. Send in Grigayne, please. I will speak to them one at a time."

Arabel moved to the door while the boy scurried up to haul the scrying orb out of the way. His name escaped Darnuir. *I shall have to take the time to know them better too.*

The heavy throne room doors swung open again and in stepped Grigayne. A group of islanders followed in his wake, all with axes at their waists or greater ones upon their backs. Grigayne looked casually around the hall, a little perplexed.

"I noticed many of your Praetorians are outside the Basilica."

"They are a Guard, and so they are guarding. I don't need protection."

"No, you don't," Grigayne said. "I admire your Praetorians for quelling those Light Bearers. Lira performed admirably in your absence, but—" He moved his weight from foot to foot, clearly working up to something. "But she is not you. She could not command Blaine's attention, nor that of any of his kind. This is no fault of hers; it is his attitude and that of his followers. Back on the Splinters, Blaine and his men caused great harm as well. And so, before you say anything further, I fear I must make my position clear, as regrettable as that may be. In light of recent events, I doubt I can force my people to remain while Blaine and his fanatics are still at large."

Darnuir's heart sank. He should have expected this, but he'd barely got to grips with the events that had occurred on the Splinters. And now two powerful human lords demanded Blaine's removal. But what could he do? They were equals, he and Blaine; and they would need to stand side by side to fight Rectar.

What would the wise ruler do?

"You wish to leave?" Darnuir asked.

"Give me a reason to stay. Is this new threat we've been warned of real?"

"I am certain it is real, although I have no proof to offer. To have trust in a spectre seems wild, but I don't believe Dukoona lied to me, nor do I think he had lost his mind. If you wish to sail, that is your choice. But if you will stay, then I assure you that Blaine and his followers will be dealt with. They've gone too far. I cannot tolerate it."

"Good," Grigayne said. "I'd rather we didn't leave before the end. I won't have it said that the islanders didn't play their part in the war for Tenalp. Brevia also needs reminding that we are strong."

"I thought you were against independence for the Splinters?"

"What I am against is Brevia believing it owns us when it does not. We're not just another region of the kingdom, no matter what Arkus might think. They combine their armies into one, while we stand on our own. It's important. It matters."

"Then I must thank you for staying," Darnuir said. "I am sending the rest of the Fifth Brevian Regiment home and another company as a sign of goodwill. It would be only fair that the islanders have the same option—"

Grigayne scoffed and waved his hand. "We're not so soft as the Brevians. Isn't that right, Captain Cayn?" he appealed to a gruff member of his company. Darnuir thought he recognised the one-handed man.

"Aye, right enough, lad," said Cayn. "Not enough salt in their water, that's what."

Darnuir smirked and Cayn grinned widely. Grigayne looked pleased and visibly relaxed. He even took to scratching his beard.

"I must apologise, Darnuir. It was you who requested my presence."

Darnuir nodded, hoping the friendliness he'd fostered would not be squandered. "I would like to ask a favour. We'll need fresh supplies if we are to survive here. Food, armaments, clothing and armour, cloth for bandages, anything and everything. I do not think Arkus can be relied upon any time soon."

Grigayne broke eye contact with him to stare at the floor instead, but Darnuir pressed on.

"The Splinters have already given so much, but if they would give more, such generosity would not be forgotten. I, at the very least, would personally owe you a debt."

"I am not the one you must convince," Grigayne said. "I'm afraid my father was less than amicable towards you after your hurried departure. Yet we did not understand the full picture then... I'm sure I could convince him. If he understood more fully how this debt might be repaid."

Darnuir wasn't sure if this was the wisest move, but it was the only one he could make. One that he had to make.

"I think the autonomy of the Splintering Isles would be well secured for the future with my backing."

Grigayne's nod was the most delicate of movements, but still a nod. "I would be hesitant to make guarantees. And I would need to remove a large portion of my fleet to accommodate a resupply, though I will take as little crew as I can. With spring fast approaching, the weather won't be as gruelling."

Feeling more relieved than he dared show, Darnuir stepped towards Grigayne, hand proffered for a shake. The heir to the Splinters shook it firmly, bowed courteously, and then made his way out.

Raymond entered as the last islanders left, looking downcast and dishevelled. He hadn't shaved yet and was not in his steel. It made him look far smaller than usual, far from the haughty noble who'd looked down on Darnuir from atop his horse in Torridon. Now that truly felt like an age ago.

"Come, sit with me," Darnuir said, gesturing towards the steps to the throne. "I'll cut right to it. I need you to travel to Brevia."

"You're sending me away?" Raymond's voice was thick with a sort of grim inevitability.

"For a purpose."

Raymond sighed. "I understand. There is little I can do here. When it happened, I felt... so useless."

"And where was I, exactly?"

"You know that's different."

"You're human, Raymond. That isn't a weakness. I'm sending you to Brevia because no one else will be better for this task. Not even myself. It's not something that requires brute strength, but knowledge, tact, and, I admit, connections."

Raymond looked up, his brow furrowed. "What can I do?"

"Arkus and I are having difficulties finding common ground. It's understandable in light of recent events."

"You told him? So soon?"

"Of course. Long-held secrets have only damaged the relationship between humanity and dragons, and in any case, this will hardly be kept quiet. At some point, word will reach Brevia about it, and I'd rather it came from me, king to king. I hope his anger is temporary, but I do need my dragons brought here. I must think in the long term. I know there will be more fights to come, but it has already been months.

Who knows when Rectar's next attack will come? And we cannot survive by begging for rations. The Tail Peninsula needs to be repopulated, crops sown, old lives pieced back together."

Raymond winced. "We tried to send humans to the peninsula with equal numbers of legionaries to do just the same. It didn't end well."

"Hence I need my people to return. They're our lands, and it's our task."

Raymond nodded. "How can I help you in this?"

"You know the Lords of the Assembly, and you will have a far better chance of success than any dragon, including me. Tell them the truth: that the older dragons resist change, but the young are ready to embrace it; that you, a human, have stood alongside the king of dragons in battle and given valued counsel. No, in fact, tell them more. Darnuir the king of dragons sees Raymond of House Tarquill as a friend."

"There's no need for false flattery, Darnuir." His voice was stiff. "And I cannot guarantee success in the Assembly. However, if duty requires it, I shall go."

"Duty? Raymond, you are a free man. You owe me nothing more than you've already given. If you like, you could step off your ship in the Bay of Brevia and never look back. But I truly hope you don't. I thought you wanted to join our cause?"

"I did, and I do," Raymond hastened to say. "But partly it was because I had no place in the chevaliers when you asked, and I have worried that your invitation was born out of guilt or pity."

"Lira and I do not make invitations to the Praetorians lightly. In many ways, Raymond, you are my most valuable Praetorian. It's one thing to want closer unity, but another entirely to take steps towards it. It's been a hard fight, that one, and I think I might be losing it. But I shall keep trying. Cosmo shared that vision too, and he died for it. I wonder if things would have been easier if he were still alive. Perhaps Arkus wouldn't be so cold; perhaps he would have gotten through to me about my addiction before it had deepened. Perhaps our outlook wouldn't be so bleak. Yet I have you. If you can convince the Assembly that there is no need for fear or bitterness, if you can bring my people home, then you'll have done something a thousand dragon Praetorians could never do. This is the mission I give you. But, as I say, your path is yours to choose."

"I shall try," Raymond said. He smiled. "May I say, Darnuir, that you seem... different."

"I think that's for the best. Make what preparations you need. I intend for you to sail as soon as poss—"

"Bruce," Raymond exclaimed. Darnuir blinked, unsure for a moment about who Raymond was referring to. "I doubt I can take him with me. Will you ensure he's cared for? I shall leave instructions."

His horse, Darnuir realised. "He'll be kept as well as can be."

He considered telling Raymond that he'd send Bruce back west too, should he decide not to return. Yet withholding it may give Raymond more reason to come back. He loved that great beast. Darnuir would never hold the creature hostage, but he desperately did not want Raymond to stay in Brevia. He'd failed to build the multi-race Guard that he'd dreamed of and Raymond was the one glimmer of hope Darnuir held onto.

"Thank you, Raymond. That will be all for now."

Raymond bowed, left, and was replaced by Damien. Where Raymond was dishevelled and grim-faced, the outrunner was nervous. His eyes were bloodshot, and he walked with the distinctive shuffle of the guilty.

"What is the matter?"

"My Lord Darnuir, I— I—" He choked on his words, in too much distress to get them out.

"Come sit with me." He indicated the spot that Raymond had just vacated. Damien sat upon the step but averted his eyes from Darnuir, hanging his head low.

"Are you going to speak?"

"I think it might be my fault. I think I should have said something sooner. I never saw Blaine," Damien said rather quickly. "I might have stopped it from happening."

Darnuir was taken aback by his earnestness. It was not like a dragon, especially one like Damien who was older than the Praetorians. "How could you have stopped it? Those Light Bearers and legionnaires were mad. Who did you speak to if not Bla—"

"Bacchus, sire. I spoke to Bacchus. The Lord Guardian was asleep at the time, he told me. He didn't let me take the stairs down to the Guardian's Sanctum. He was quite forceful. I should have protested more, but, well, I had no idea he would – oh, forgive me."

Darnuir grasped Damien by the shoulder. "Whatever those dragons did is on them. There is nothing you could have done."

But Damien shook his head. "I should have notified Prefect Lira immediately. Only I knew how exhausted Prefect Lira was, so I didn't want to disturb her when I found her asleep." The pace of his speech was rapidly increasing again. "Bacchus said only the faithful could enter the sanctum and he would take the message straight to Blaine. Another lie, it seems."

"We don't know exactly what happened," Darnuir said. "Bacchus wasn't among the zealots attacking the humans. It's a mess right now, but I will find the answers. Don't suffer like this. It's not your fault."

"An outrunner takes his message to the recipient and them alone," Damien said. "I failed. And it *may* have led to deaths. That's something that will haunt me." He finally faced Darnuir again. "Send me on another run. Let me repent through service."

"What about starting a farm? I fear I'll need more farmers than soldiers before long."

"If I leave now, I'll carry this with me."

Darnuir hesitated. To have guilt eat away at Damien was unfair, but Darnuir did have need of intelligence on their northern outposts, especially on the Nest. And he needed to send someone that he could trust. With Blaine in seclusion, no one else seemed to know what was happening in that area. Yet was it fair to ask Damien to go? One look at his feet was alarming. They were swollen, the veins visible beneath the skin, his heels akin to sandpaper.

"Are you sure you can manage a run?" Darnuir said.

"I wouldn't ask you if I couldn't, and I won't need to run so hard when it's just light reconnaissance."

Darnuir explained what he needed and Damien accepted.

"Take a small team with you. Share the burden."

"I'll work faster alone," said Damien. "Besides, we have too few outrunners left as it is. None are being trained and two died during the battle for the city."

This time it was Darnuir who cast his gaze to the ground. "Another thing that's been neglected. I shall try to remember it. Thank you, Damien. You have no idea how much I rely upon all of you. And please, do not let the actions of the Light Bearers weigh upon you. I look forward to your return." Damien smiled weakly, then he too left.

Once again, Darnuir found himself alone in his throne room. His neck now throbbed with a fresh ache, and he tried to rub some of the tenderness out of it. Miraculously, he hadn't craved magic. Not once. Not even a drop. As worn as he was, he felt liberated. His mind was free and fully his own; no longer in thrall to the Cascade.

He risked a glance at his sword. The rubies of the dragon's eyes twinkled up at him and a fleeting panic took hold. What if it happened again? When the inevitable battle came, would he succumb to magic's alluring strength? Only time would tell.

He decided some fresh air was in order and set out for the plaza. Stepping out of the Royal Tower, he had to press his eyes shut against the sunlight, as he was no longer used to it. It felt good upon his skin, though; warm and clean, like life being massaged into him. He moved slowly between the towering columns that lined the plaza, keeping the Basilica and the Praetorians surrounding it at the edge of his vision. The sight of the domed temple sickened him, so he turned down a street between two crumbling villas. It led him to an open viewing point where he could freely see the lower city, the walls, and the tint of gold from the Crucidal Road stretching to the horizon.

And he was not alone.

Fidelm sat upon an ancient stone bench with an easel and a half-worked canvas propped up before him. The general's spear lay discarded to one side, but the way that he wielded his paintbrush so dextrously, so finely, one would not think of him as a hardened fighter. He registered Darnuir's arrival with a curt flick of his eyes before returning to his art.

"This is a side of you I haven't seen," Darnuir said.

"Hmm," Fidelm intoned. He made a particularly delicate stroke with his brush then sat back, examining its effect.

"I'm sorry for disturbing you," Darnuir said. "While I'm here, I should give my thanks for aiding Lira during the crisis. I know you lost fairies that night. I'm sorry."

Fidelm offered nothing.

"I'll leave you, then," Darnuir said. He turned and entered the street leading back to the plaza.

"Ironic, isn't it?" Fidelm called out. "The guardian. What has he guarded? He's left only misery in his wake."

Darnuir returned to his side. "Blaine stopped the attacks."

"Would they have ever occurred if he and his *flock* weren't trying to convince so many of powerful gods who favour dragons above all else?"

"We'll never know," said Darnuir. "Many of my kind look down on humans; that's sadly a fact. But if Blaine had not rallied what support he could when he did, and come to rescue me, I might have perished in the Cairlav Marshes and the west would have fallen under Castallan's rule."

Fidelm sighed. "It's only natural to defend your grandfather."

Darnuir's mouth fell open. "How did you—"

"I know much more than I think even Blaine wants to admit," Fidelm said. "I am my queen's general, but also her confidant. Someone who isn't merely stuck to the Argent Tree and can offer insight from a life lived beyond its branches. Besides, the fact that Blaine stayed as a guest in secrecy for so long was enough of a sign that their relationship ran deeper, even if that had been long ago; even if it was broken by the time I discovered it." He pondered his piece again, scrunched up his lips in thought, then swirled more brown paint into the golden colour he had mixed for the city's stone. He dabbed the darker shade onto the canvas.

Darnuir stepped around to get a look at the scene. Fidelm had accentuated the decay of the city; where the stone was crumbling or worn, he had brought out the detail while blurring the areas best preserved. It gave Aurisha an ancient look without any grandeur; age lacking in wisdom; the sickly yellow of illness creeping across skin. It shook what optimism Darnuir had left.

"You have talent."

"I've had many years of practice. I've always found it a release to paint after blood is shed. It's good to stay sane. I've noticed that my whole race has become more obsessed with art and creation in recent decades. The arborists work tirelessly with their budding nurseries, the carpenters create masterpieces in half the time, and the paint often runs dry before more can be made."

"Why the change?"

"I do not know. It is in our nature to create and nurture but perhaps, as a whole, we feel compelled to work harder because we are decaying."

"What do you mean?" The fairies weren't in any real danger. Not like the dragons were, bearing the brunt of nearly a century of war.

Fidelm put his brush and palette down, and finally met Darnuir's eye. "One queen, one child. That is how it's always been."

"I see," said Darnuir, not sure if he wished to probe further. How much bad news would it take before the weight became crushing?

"Many have long suspected something is wrong," Fidelm went on. "A queen should raise and train her daughter to replace her. Kasselle's lack of an heir wasn't unexpected during the initial turbulence of the war but, as time has slipped away, whispers have begun."

"Can't a new queen be found, when... when the time comes?" He'd meant to say 'when she dies' but thought it might be harsh to speak of her in such a way. After all, as surreal as it seemed, she was his grandmother.

Fidelm was staring blankly off into the distance. "I don't think we've ever been without a queen."

"Your people can adapt, I'm sure."

"As the dragons did when you died?"

"That's different," Darnuir said, though he immediately felt foolish for saying it. It wasn't different. Not truly. "Well, if I die now, what will the dragons do? Will they all drop dead on the spot? I think my people would learn to live without me if I were gone. Put some more hope in your own kind as well."

Fidelm's expression darkened. "I've never seen any real hope for change. And I'm part of it. I was wrong, you know. Oh, yes." He nodded along to his own words. "I was wrong to treat the troll so poorly. Wrong to judge you for trusting him. For wanting to work with him. I took the anger simmering within me because of Blaine and directed it down the easiest path."

"Is this why you turned down my offer to join the Praetorian Guard?"

"I refused to join you because I think I've lost hope, and that makes me angry too."

Darnuir sniffed and straightened. Was there anyone left who wasn't old or exhausted or done with it all?

"Kasselle is far from dead, and so am I. When we defeat Rectar we'll either figure out a way to help her or work out how a new queen might be chosen. But until then, we need to remain focused. Don't worry over something that hasn't yet happened."

"I fear it is too late," Fidelm said. "Kasselle is the heart of my race and her heart has been broken for too long. I told her she should have sent Blaine away, but she couldn't do it. She couldn't send him away, but having him near hurt her just as much. She was trapped. And so are we. I feel like I can sense her pain even across the world."

Darnuir breathed in deeply. He took a moment to regard the city, the lifeless place it had become. Was it all merely war-weariness, or something more?

Back in the Boreac Mountains, when he was still just a hunter, when they'd retreated inch by inch with no end in sight; even then, things had not seemed so bleak.

Maybe it had been Cosmo who had radiated hope because he had known about Darnuir, and that Brackendon would one day return to them. Right now, they could all use a little hope, only Darnuir was struggling to find it. His thoughts darkened and then he remembered that all had seemed lost before when the demons came to Cold Point. Everyone had assumed the battle would be a last stand. And then Brackendon had come, and Danuir had been given a sword which turned the tide. A year later, he now stood overlooking the city of Aurisha with Rectar's demon hordes vanquished.

I'll cling on to that, even if no one else will.

He'd placed hope in Raymond and Grigayne's missions. He had to have hope to move forwards.

"Do you think you can ever forgive Blaine?"

"No," Fidelm rasped. "Deep down, I only wish to create, and I'm forced to kill instead. Those dragons wanted to destroy needlessly. I despise that."

"I'll leave you to your painting, General."

Darnuir ambled back to the plaza. Slowly and without fuss, he joined the Praetorians outside the Basilica and simply watched it for a time. No one stirred in its dark doorway. Darnuir approached the Basilica and climbed the stairs halfway before stopping.

A part of him still wanted to yell out for Blaine, to demand that he show himself and answer for what happened. But that part of him was small now, and not even a flutter rose in his throat. Screaming would earn him nothing. It had earned him only disrespect and error so far. Yet he stood there for a while, wondering whether Blaine might come of his own accord. He wondered desperately what he would do if that happened.

14

DOWN IN THE GUTS

"Despite months of effort, no converts have emerged from the cells beneath the Basilica. The guardian assures me they will break soon, yet I wonder if pain is the best reinforcer of dogma."

King Darklin, writing in 856 AT

Blaine – The Basilica of Light

"He's still outside, Lord Guardian," Chelos said.

Blaine didn't register the words at first. He was too busy staring at the stone swords, in particular at the dusty empty holder. The demons must have destroyed the sword and the gods had done nothing.

"Blaine? The king stands there. What will you do?"

But Blaine did not hear.

Demons took this city and the gods did nothing. Rectar came to this world and the gods did nothing. "What is he doing here?" Chelos asked.

There was a scuffle, sounds of a struggle.

"He insisted upon seeing the Lord Guardian."

Blaine brushed the dusty remains aside with a finger, feeling a grooved edge in the stone. *Will I also do nothing?*

"Let me explain, I beg you," Bacchus pleaded.

Something snapped within Blaine. He shook his head, turned from the stone swords and found Bacchus on his knees, his eyes dark and bloodshot. Charm had all but abandoned him. Behind Bacchus were two loyal Light Bearers with a hand each upon his shoulders.

Chelos stood uncomfortably to the side, looking between Bacchus and Blaine, a worried look in his eye. He had a right to be worried, for Blaine's hand curled inward, though not for Kasselle's sake this time. This was a fist he dearly wished to swing at Bacchus.

"I told you to remain in your quarters."

Bacchus gulped. "I know, Lord Guardian. I just—"

"I've been lenient so far. Your involvement with the murderers is—"

"Please," Bacchus said. He clasped his hands. "I told you, I had nothing to do with it. Nothing. I'd never condone mindless killings. Blai— Lord Guardian, please."

"You tried to take my place. Do you think you were ready for that?"

"No, Lord, I was not. You are the Light's Chosen. We all saw. We all heard." He looked desperately around; to Chelos, to the remaining Light Bearers. They all averted their eyes, as though merely looking at Bacchus would infect them with his disgrace.

"How far you've fallen," Blaine said. "How far we've all fallen to repeat the mistakes of the past."

Bacchus nearly wept. "I had no idea that my words would lead to this. I did not mean it. I did not wish it."

"You'll have your chance to speak," Blaine said, looking to the entrance of the Basilica. "The Praetorians are mobilised in force out there. Perhaps I ought to throw you to them."

Bacchus' eyes widened. "But the king." His voice was laced with fear.

Blaine thought he caught a whiff of sweetness from him. Blaine even felt a twitch of fear himself. For a moment, he'd forgotten Darnuir was standing outside.

"Yes, the king is out there. Waiting for me, I dare say, but I'm certain he'd like to hear from you. I imagine he isn't pleased with what has happened in his absence." Bacchus didn't respond. His chest rose and fell quickly as his breath came in ragged puffs.

The satisfaction of seeing Bacchus so cowed wasn't enough to alleviate his own misgivings. His grandson had a fierce temper and was lukewarm at best to the Way of Light. Why had he gathered his Praetorians outside? Did he intend to strike at them? If so, why wait? Blaine had been prepared for swifter action, but Darnuir's more subdued reaction was unnerving.

Bacchus sucked in a wet breath. "Hear me out, Lord. Hear me out and speak to the king first on my behalf."

"If you had remained in your quarters as ordered, you might have earned some small favour with me. As it stands—"

"Hear me, please. Do not let your prejudice against me cloud your judgement."

Blaine bit his lip. What did Bacchus hope to achieve? Did he think he think he could talk his way out of this one?

"Be quick and true, and I'll make my decision," Blaine said. "And once you've told me your story, you shall return to your quarters, and there you shall stay. Leave again without permission and I'll presume your guilt."

Bacchus took a deep breath to steady himself, and then he began. "I was on night duty while you slept, Lord, as you know. The outrunner Damien came to deliver a message to you from the girl – from Prefect Lira. Damien said he would only speak with you, Lord. I told him you were not to be disturbed. He tried to move past me, down into the sanctum below, but I stopped him. I may have used a little too much force in blocking him – that was wrong of me, I know, a foolish misstep." He rattled through his last words, embellishing his remorse. It wouldn't help.

"Go on."

"In the end, I managed to get him to tell me the message and assured him that I would pass it on to you."

"Why didn't you let him through?"

Bacchus gulped again. "I didn't think it—"

"You didn't think it important enough?" Blaine finished for him.

Bacchus grimaced. "You've rarely responded to Prefect Lira's requests to meet before now. I assumed it could wait."

Blaine clenched his jaw. Bacchus wasn't wrong. "I have always been the one to judge that."

"You're right. Forgive me," Bacchus said.

"Get on with it."

"Yes, of course. The outrunner spoke of trivial matters, Lord. Well, ones I thought to be trivial. Just some fool human amusing his fellows down in the Lower City. Why you would have to be disturbed for that, I don't know, but yes, you are right. Naturally, I should have brought it to you."

"And then?"

"Well, my duty ended at the end of that hour. As the whole shift changed, I debriefed the men on what had happened. You had received a message, but I would tell you in the morning."

"And did you explain the contents of this message to the Light Bearers taking over from you?"

"I did, but as briefly as I just told you. I knew few details myself, after all."

It was a lie. If not an outright lie, then a poor half-truth. Blaine could read it plainly on Bacchus' face. In his panic, he'd lost his silver tongue.

"So," Blaine began, "these Light Bearers and legionnaires just happened to take it upon themselves to, what, seek vengeance for the insult offered by this human?"

"If you worry that I told them to, Lord—"

"I am not worried by you anymore," Blaine said coldly. "Did you or did you not give the order for the atrocity?"

Bacchus finally lowered his hands, his expression resolute. "I did no such thing."

There was a certain air of honesty about that. Blaine stepped closer to him, sniffing lightly, trying to discern if he could truly smell fear on him. Alas, he could not. Such sweetness was only reserved for humanity, after all.

"Perhaps, and perhaps not. The prisoners have already crowed your name, Bacchus. I will get to the truth of it."

"If I ordered this thing, why wouldn't I go myself?" Bacchus said.

"To have a chance to deny it?" Blaine said. "I don't claim to understand the workings of your mind. You work subtly when you want to. But enough for now. Take him away." With that, the Light Bearers hoisted Bacchus up.

"I know I've given you ample reason to mistrust me. But please, how can I convince you of my innocence?"

"You cannot," Blaine said. "Stand on guard, you two," he added to the Light Bearers holding him. Bacchus hung his head and said no more, allowing himself to be escorted away.

The Basilica fell deathly silent.

Those Light Bearers left in the hall stood tense, alert, their eyes fixed towards the single entry point from the plaza. Each cough, each rattle of a sword hilt could be heard reverberating off the hard marble floor. How long would this last? Blaine felt under siege and overwhelmed. As quickly as life had sparked back into the old religion, it teetered now upon the verge of collapse. Dragons who had approached innocently for morning service had been turned away by the Praetorians.

Whatever was going to happen, it would happen soon. It wasn't in Darnuir's nature to be patient. For Blaine, the real question was if Darnuir chose to fight, would he fight back? He gripped the hilt of the Guardian's Blade and let a shuddering sigh out through his nose at the weakness of his grip.

He looked around at the three reliefs of Dwna, Dwl'or and N'weer depicted on the walls in stone. Light cut down from the dome, landing to the side of the seared sun of Dwl'or. He gazed at the crisscross gouges in the stone, at the detail of the sun's rays; trying, without success, to discern some understanding from it. Little made sense. Little had ever made sense, yet the one-sided nature of his relationship with the gods had always stayed a constant. Gods did not speak to their worshippers, he had learnt as a very young dragon. The guardian of his youth had told him that one morning, when Blaine had brought him his water to shave.

The memory came vividly now.

'And why not?' Blaine had asked.

'Because if they answer us once, we'd come to them with every trivial issue. Why should the gods stoop to hold our hands?'

'I would not trouble them on trifles,' Blaine had said. 'I'd only seek assistance when the need was great.'

His mentor had scoffed. 'I think you'd find that you'd turn to them more often. Sometimes, I wish someone was here to hold my hand through life. One day, if you take my place, you'll wish the same.'

Gods, but I do now, Blaine thought. He'd been fortunate enough to have answers given once. He couldn't expect it during every crisis from now on.

"The king has left, Lord Guardian," Chelos told him. As before, it took Blaine a while to register the news.

"And the Praetorians?" he asked, turning away from Dwl'or's image.

"They are still assembled."

"So be it. They won't act without Darnuir, so we can stand down for now. Take some food and rest," he added to the Light Bearers at large. "Say your prayers to Dwl'or for strength."

"I shall make arrangements," Chelos said.

"No, friend. I'd like you to come with me to see the prisoners."

Chelos inclined his head and followed.

Those responsible for the attacks were being held in the old cells once reserved for Black Dragon prisoners. They were several floors deep inside the plateau, and the damp darkness of the place had earned them the name of the Gut Cells, not least because of the smell. The last time Blaine had walked these halls, he had been eight years old. Yet, despite his age, the same feelings resurfaced in him as he marched into the chill heart of the plateau.

A shiver ran through him, but not entirely from the cold.

For a moment he was that child again. Screams rang across more than a century of time to fill his ears. He smelled the blood, the sweat, the filth and decay. He was a boy observing the last horrors of a long-forgotten war. And he was horrified.

"You are too young to have walked these halls before, Chelos."

"I fear that is a privilege."

Blaine placed a hand on the wall to steady himself. "I did not relish my duties here as a hatchling." He breathed out, regained himself. "Forgive me. Let's go on."

Long-forgotten memories trickled to the surface as he walked. A peace accord with the Black Dragons was signed shortly after his last visit here. Everyone rejoiced, happy to sheathe their swords in favour of prayer and prosperity, though many had hoped for war to begin again, and to do glory in the name of the Light. And the occupants of the Gut Cells had not been freed.

Blaine had sworn to the narrative of peace ever since. For so long, in fact, he'd have gone on swearing blind for years to come. Perhaps he should rethink how Kroener had rallied so many for another war. Perhaps he placed too much blame on him, when so many had thirsted for it. Blaine had bent his memories to suit him, to mask his fears and the dirty truth.

What a dangerous thing it was, to live forever.

He blinked and rubbed at his eyes, digging in well with his knuckles. The hallway loomed and twisted as his vision refocused. He found he was breathing hard, shocked from his own dark recollections.

"I made a mistake in using this place."

"Must doubts plague your every thought?" Chelos asked, his tone harder than usual.

Blaine had no answer. He was spared giving one by their arrival at the strip of cells that held the prisoners. The loyal Light Bearers on duty seemed on edge as well, even though none of them would have been alive to see this place in its heyday. None of them would have been a distant fantasy in their grandparents' dreams back then, and these dragons were far older than the ones who followed Darnuir. Blaine's age struck him again, like being woken with cold water from a deep sleep.

He couldn't shake the feeling of being trapped in a vicious cycle. For all their reverence of the gods, for all the work the dragons had done in their name, where had it gotten them? As he closed the distance to the nearest cell, as he watched a Light Bearer pull open the rusting grate for him and saw the puffy, bruised face of the prisoner inside, another image of his youth flashed by.

A Black Dragon sitting naked, bleeding and whimpering. All these years later, Blaine was here again.

Darnuir had a point, he decided. Dragons had to change.

"Are those injuries from the battle or from the guards?" Blaine asked.

The prisoner squinted at Blaine. "Both."

Blaine eyed the guardsman, who shrugged. "They didn't come quietly."

The prisoner spat. "We'll be the ones singing when the gods reward us."

Blaine regarded the gob of spittle by his boot and twitched his nose distastefully. "What do you imagine they will thank you for?"

"For starting to make things as they once were," said the prisoner. "Dragons with strong faith without the nuisance of other races. We were strongest when we stood alone. The humans will go now, you'll see. They won't stay after that."

"And this is helpful to us, it is?" Blaine said. The prisoner opened his mouth to reply but Blaine cut him off. "No. Hold your tongue for now." He stepped back out into the corridor. "Bring them all out."

"All of them?" a guard said nervously.

"All of them, if you please." Despite his bad hand, Blaine was confident he could handle these unarmed, weakened dragons if the need arose. The prisoners were ushered out of their cells and shoved into a kneeling congregation before Blaine. It wasn't reverent stares they gave him but deadened, unyielding eyes.

Blaine kept his head held high. "I'm not here to hear your reasons, for there are none that will acquit you. I am not here to pass judgement either, for your king must also have a hand in your fate. I am only here to find out how this started." He did not go so far as to include Bacchus' name. He didn't want to lead them by the hand.

"Well?"

No one answered.

Blaine narrowed his eyes. "Are you all such cowards that you would attack humans at night but not answer a simple question?"

One near the front spoke first. "Tulio's the one who led us down there, but he's dead. The girl wounded him badly."

"Lira bested you all," Blaine said. "Make no mistake, you were losing that fight even before I arrived. So, Tulio was your leader?"

"Not so much a leader," said another. "More the first one to charge out the door. We all went as one, Lord Guardian." The others shuffled uncomfortably and shied away from him, as though hoping Blaine would heap punishment upon him alone.

"But why? What drove you that night?"

"The scum were mocking the gods, Lord." This voice came from further back in the group.

"They had to be stopped," said another.

"They shouldn't be in our city."

More outbursts followed. Blaine wondered where this had come from. Had he instilled this belief in them? Had Bacchus?

"Enough," Blaine called. "How did you know about that particular human's little show?"

Silence reigned again. None of them wished to be the one to turn on their leader.

"Remember to whom you swore your oaths," Chelos said. The prisoners looked to Chelos, then back to Blaine.

The dragon at the front cleared his throat then said, "Bacchus, sir. It was Bacchus."

"Bacchus," Blaine said, his voice dropping like a dead weight.

"He laughed about it as we changed guard duty," the prisoner continued. "Said he'd love to teach that human true respect for the gods."

Blaine clenched his jaw, forcing down a sudden urge to be sick. "Is that all?"

"We thought he was suggesting something should be done, Lord," another said.

"After I explicitly told you to leave the humans alone?"

"We think you are wrong, Lord," said a brave soul from the back of the group. "We have the backing of the gods and yet you do not act. You wait for the king to recover when his desires run against what's best for our people."

"We did it all for our people. We did what we felt was right."

Blaine puffed a hard sigh. That miracle upon the Nail Head seemed more and more like a curse. He looked over the prisoners again. None met his eye. Death wouldn't be beyond the scope of punishment but, in truth, Blaine didn't have the heart to kill any dragons while their people were so few. If it came to it, he'd let Darnuir take his anger out on them. Let him bloody his hands if he wanted. Blaine had had enough.

"You'll all remain under heavy guard, but not here. You'll be confined to one of the empty barracks and await the king's judgement." With that, he swept out of the Gut Cells without a backwards glance.

Chelos hurried up behind him, panting. "Shall the prisoners be moved immediately?"

"Without delay. See to it yourself, Chelos. Use as many loyal men as you see fit. And when you close the door to these corridors behind you, lock it up and throw the damned key into the bay. I never want to walk these halls again." Chelos nodded. "Thank you, old friend," Blaine added. "If you don't mind, I will hurry from here. Ill memories and all."

"As you will," said Chelos.

Blaine smiled then placed a hand upon his sword and drew on some magic to bring him speedily away. Once back in his Inner Sanctum, he rushed to the balcony and gulped in the fresh air. He gripped the rail, as well as he could with his maimed hand, and the tension eased out of him.

He reflected on what the prisoner had said. How Bacchus had made jokes; perhaps crossing a line into suggestion, perhaps not. That human they strung up had been making jokes too. How had laughter led to such ruin?

Blaine felt like he was watching some perverse show unfold, unable to interfere or change its course. He was supposed to be at the centre of things, and yet he barely had control. At the Nail Head, the gods had told him, 'It is not yet time to give in.' He thought that time might now have come.

15

ALL TALK

"Words have no power should they fall on deaf ears."

Author Unknown

Cassandra – The Palace

She'd been standing outside Arkus' door for a minute already. There were no guards to hurry her along, as every chevalier had been sent to patrol the dragon camps. Breathing low, she tried to summon the extra nerve to step inside and say what was on her mind. She'd already worked up the courage to make it this far, so why not this last step? It wasn't like Cassandra was afraid of him. But she was afraid of what might happen if things continued as they were.

Everyone was leaving, or planning to, and all because of her father in one way or another. She couldn't let that happen. She couldn't be stuck alone in this place, not when she'd just found somewhere she might call home. Without Oranna, Kymethra, Thane and even Balack, there would be no buffer between her and Arkus. And yet it was perhaps just as well that this was happening. It was pushing her towards making her larger concerns heard.

Try as she might, she could not fool herself any longer. In order to distance herself from her father and his actions, she'd simply avoided serious matters with him, opting instead to play the princess and the happy daughter. After everything with Boreac, never mind events at the Bastion or before, she'd only wanted a chance to live as normal a life as she could.

Yet, who was she kidding? A lost princess trapped in a fortress by a megalomaniac wizard; normal wasn't to be her lot. With a swell of daring, Cassandra knocked on the door and entered before Arkus had finished granting permission.

He was at his desk, scratching away at some long document, with all the usual piles of parchment, paper and maps around him. A pot of shimmer brew sat beside a steaming cup, its enticing bitterness heavy in the air. All was as it should be. Except for the crown itself. Usually, she'd seen it lying uncared for on the desk, sometimes under a pile of papers as though it meant nothing to him. Now, however, Arkus wore his crown. Even here, where no one else could see him.

"What a pleasant surprise," he said, setting down his quill. "And just when I needed a lift today. Tell you what," he said, leaning forward with a childish grin. "What do you say to taking a stroll to the Velvet Circle this afternoon? You can pick out whatever you like."

"No, not today. I'd rather—"

"How about a little voyage out of the bay, then? A brisk sea breeze and the open water might be nice." He slumped back in his chair, seeing her expression. "Well, you pick, then. There's been so much... so much to think on lately. Yes, I don't care what we do, so long as I can spend some time with my daughter."

With a heavy heart, she firmly shut the door. She didn't want to upset him, not really, so she approached him with her arms open as apologetically as possible.

"That's not why I'm here."

Arkus looked crestfallen. Up close, the many late nights and missed dinners were taking their toll on him. His eyes were puffy and dark, and new lines had etched onto his temple. And he wasn't exactly a young man.

"Well," he said, "what is it? I've got plenty to be getting on with."

"Such as?" Cassandra said, nodding vaguely to the paperwork before him. It would be better to warm him up rather than dive straight in to the tough part of the conversation. "I'd have thought with Annandale out the way, a few things would be off your plate."

Arkus raised an eyebrow. "Oh, you did, did you? Well, Cassandra, you'll find that, in ruling, the moment you pull up one weed, another has grown behind your back. Or even worse, a whole thorn bush."

"What are you talking about?"

His gaze unmistakably flicked to the scrying orb then back to her. "Nothing you need to concern yourself with." A great yawn suddenly took control of him and he rubbed his eyes.

"You know, if you're looking for somebody to relax with, you should find Oranna."

"Oranna?" Arkus said, a little sharply. "Why? Is she a weed I ought to be worried about?"

"No, of course not. She's just feeling upset and neglected, I think."

"She's spending an awful lot of time with Clachonn."

"Must you see an enemy in everyone? Isn't losing two friends enough?"

"They weren't my friends."

"They were once."

Arkus sniffed fiercely, rapping his fingers across the undried ink he'd recently written, turning his fingertips black. "Whatever Geoff and Robert told you, you shouldn't believe it. They were traitors, Cassandra. Oh, don't look so surprised," he added. "Did you think Gellick wouldn't be able to piece it together? A fight in the corridors of the palace near the entrance to the dungeons; he overheard enough."

Cassandra played out smacking Gellick a few times over in her head. She balled one hand into a fist to ease that feeling.

"Look," Arkus began, his tone now conciliatory, "I don't think I have to be wary of my own wife. I know she's upset with me, though I'll be damned if I can figure out exactly why."

"Well, you haven't made much time for her."

"She's my queen first and then my wife," Arkus grumbled. "Must I stretch myself even further to pretend to be a normal man and husband when I'm clearly under so much strain? She's not a starry-eyed girl. She should know better."

"She's an intelligent woman, a brilliant mother to Thane, and a great friend," Cassandra said. She'd been unable to hold that back. "Do you really only see her as a queen? As a title?"

Arkus pursed his lips but said nothing. It seemed that was to be the end of it. He returned to his work.

Cassandra carefully leaned forwards, hands upon the desk. "Oranna isn't the only reason I'm here."

"Oh?" Arkus sniffed again without looking up at her.

"Listen to me. I'm trying to help you, but you won't hear it. Step away from the desk and the throne for a moment before—"

"Before what?"

"Before you go too far. Killing Annandale unnerved most of the Assembly. I could feel it. I saw it in their eyes."

Arkus glanced up then, his lip curling up. "That was sort of the point, Cass."

"Father, look at what you're doing. Placing armed soldiers into the household of all your lords and ladies? I fear it's a step too far. You never discussed it with us beforehand."

"Oh, and I should have sought your expertise, should I?" he said. She had his full attention now. "I wouldn't be so quick to throw that one in my face. I wasn't the one who blundered into bleating about Chelos and leading Annandale straight to the dragons and their secret tunnels. That knowledge would have been best kept between the few of us who knew. Now the whole world knows. Bringing in our new soldiers seemed like the best way I could make them feel safe and secure at short notice. I admit, gifting a small company to each of them was something I had only been considering until then, but I was inspired to act in the moment. It's a move that shows the Crown supports them."

"It's holding a knife to their throats and you know it."

Arkus grinned and chuckled. "Good. You're learning. And so will they. You're right, I do benefit from it too. But I capitalised on your mistake."

Cassandra backed away from the desk. "My mistake?" Her voice wavered.

"Don't worry about it," Arkus said. "It worked out well for us in the end. You'll learn to control your emotions in public better with practice."

Cassandra swallowed her pride. "I'm more worried that another rebellion might be caused by this. I'm worried things will be upended."

"You needn't be worried. I have everything very much under control; everything on this side of the world, at least." He nodded to one of the extra chairs sat by the wall. "Why don't you bring that over and I'll tell you everything. I've tried not to burden you and Oranna with these matters, but it seems that was a mistake."

Biting her lip, anxious and intrigued all at once, she grabbed herself a seat and dragged it over. The chair's back was rather stiff and uncomfortable, made to make even high-ranking chevaliers and nobles understand their place before the king.

"This is very sensitive information, Cassandra, and if you blunder this out in public, we could have far worse than an Assembly with ruffled feathers. Swear to it that you will tell no one else without express permission."

"I swear." And she meant it.

Arkus clasped his hands together as a healer might who has ill news to bear.

"Darnuir reached out to me via the scrying orb a few days ago."

Cassandra sat bolt upright. The last they had heard, Darnuir had been stuck in some magical fever and Blaine was in charge. A hundred thoughts and questions raced through her mind – what was happening? Had they marched on Kar'drun? Who was still alive? Was it over? – but she restrained herself, and merely nodded instead.

"It was not with good news," Arkus said. "Although he has now recovered from his illness, he was too late to prevent the deaths of many humans at the hands of a mad group of dragons." He went on to explain in full, as best he understood it, the tragedy that had occurred in Aurisha. It left her throat dry.

"That's terrible," was all she found she could say. She dug her nails into the arms of her chair for want of something more helpful to do. "You're right, this can't get out. Who else knows?"

"For now, only Gellick. He was present when Darnuir contacted me. Others will have to know soon; Oranna for one, and the White Seven. We'll have to keep a closer eye on the camps and remain vigilant. I'm sure many of the dragons out there hold the same beliefs as Blaine." He rubbed at his eyes. "Damn, but I'll be thankful when we ship them all home. Bringing them here so soon was a mistake."

"When will you go?" Cassandra asked.

"We'll sail as soon as the weather becomes more predictable, which should not be long with spring here. We're still replacing or repairing ships lost during the storm that hit the fleet on its return journey. Blaine and Darnuir might risk human lives in a winter voyage, but I won't. In the meantime, I'll be putting more musket-bearing companies on the streets and in the camps to show our strength."

"Balack says the dragons are starving."

"We give them all we can spare," Arkus said. "Food is scarce. You know this."

"Our kitchens aren't."

Arkus frowned. "If you want to live off hard bread and water for the next few months, be my guest. Even if I sent all of our personal supplies out to the camp it wouldn't make a dent in the problem. Less than a hundred people are fed and watered each day in the palace while there are thousands upon thousands of dragons out there. Our priority is to stockpile enough for the army to go and win this war. I'd have thought the dragons of all people would understand that. We must put our people first, Cassandra. Don't ever forget that. And on that note..."

He raised a finger indicating she should wait, then leaned back and turned a key in a desk drawer. He pulled out an ornately patterned sheet of parchment, the stuff of official royal business, and set it before her so she could read it. For a moment she thought it was the declaration that Annandale had made proclaiming Castallan as king, but it lacked the colourful seals of the families of the Dales, though there was space left at the bottom to indicate where seals would be added.

"A royal charter?" she said aloud. "The Renewal of the Unity of the Kingdom."

"Read it," Arkus said with a wry smile.

She did, and by the time she'd finished she was more certain than ever that Arkus was going too far too fast. She dropped the charter as though it were poisonous.

"I don't think you should do this."

"In practice, little would change."

"Except all the nobles would technically owe their lands and powers to you. Meaning you would hold it over their heads."

"Which hopefully I'll never have to do."

"Father," Cassandra said, trying to implore him, trying to make him understand, "I know you think your friends turned against you, and maybe they did, but they said it was because of things like this; and not even anything as extreme as this. You cut them out, took too much power for yourself."

Arkus leaned back, bringing his fingers together in a steeple. "And rather than talk to me about it, they started plotting."

"Well, I'm here, talking to you right now." Her voice wavered a little, her nerves creeping to the surface as she trod closer to dangerous ground. "I'm telling you I think you've gone far enough. You'll only make it worse if you force people to sign this charter."

"It is for your benefit as well."

"I don't see how, if it causes distress amongst the Assembly."

"You don't see?" He closed his eyes, as though in deep thought. "People rarely see as I do. They're frightened by change, scared by progress, terrified that the status quo might shift. Robert and Geoff were such men."

"Annandale said you shut them both out."

Arkus' eyes flashed. "They tried to hold us back. Not just me, but all of humanity. They would rather our capital city was left with inadequate defences, even though the dragons were defeated and a demon host had landed not far from the city's doorstep. Had we lost the battle of Demons' Folly, Brevia wouldn't have lasted a day. And they bleated about taxes and conscriptions. It was war. It has been war ever since we were born. No one had a plan on how to end it, not my father, and certainly not any so-called *Great Lords*. I, Cassandra, I alone had the vision. We would not have the navy we do now, we would not have our new weapons, and if I have to start being more aggressive in order to make them all fall into line, then so be it. I will end this war, I will do what those before me could not, and I will make our family safe. And if a few lazy lords in their manors are upset that their purses are lighter or some dragons go hungry a while longer, then I think that's a small price to pay. So," he added in something akin to a growl. "Do you still have any issues you'd like to raise?"

She searched his shrewd eyes, trying to decide whether he genuinely believed what he said or if it was more of his theatre. The trouble was, with Arkus, she found it hard to tell. You couldn't read him like other people. He was too guarded.

Whatever his beliefs, she still thought the charter was dangerous. He'd already gotten all he needed to achieve his goals and this was overreaching. She was sure of it. Yet it was clear he had no intention of changing his attitude; Oranna would still leave, Kymethra wouldn't come back. She'd failed.

Finally, she said the only thing that she could. "No. I have nothing more to raise."

"I'm glad," Arkus said. "Now, if you don't mind, I must finish these orders recalling the bulk of our troops stationed in the Dales. We'll need them retrained with muskets quickly if they are to join the expedition east."

Cassandra got to her feet and walked slowly to the door.

Before she left, Arkus called out, "I'll arrange a special ride into the country with Oranna. Just her, myself and Thane. Having it be just us again might help to recall simpler times. She's always been fond of wilder lands, and besides, you can't ride. You won't mind, will you?"

She kept her back to him. "No, Father. I won't mind at all."

With that, she stepped out of his council chamber and closed the door. A hot tear ran down her cheek. She'd lied, of course. She did mind. Oranna wasn't upset with Arkus for bringing Cassandra into the palace; quite the opposite. She knew Oranna valued her company and being able to have someone she could speak freely to. To insinuate that Oranna would rather have a family trip without her was not true. Did he not understand? Had he even listened to what she'd just said? Did he not believe he could be the one at fault? Would he ever see?

No, don't be foolish, she told herself. Arkus was the one causing strife and he was only going to get worse. Yet for now, she was unsure of what her next move would be. Swinging a sword in the chevalier training room might help clear her head. It had been a while, and it would be empty right now.

She trudged down the black-carpeted halls in a foul mood and found the grand doors of the chevalier hall already ajar. Soft echoing thuds rang from within. Cassandra slipped inside to find Balack standing in the centre of the arena, feet wedged into the sand underfoot and taking aim with his bow. Even Balack's arrows were tailored to him these days. Black paint covered the shafts, and pristine white feathers made up the fletching.

She made it all the way down to the combat pit without him noticing and entered through the swing door behind him. The creak of the hinge gave her away and Balack spun around, his latest arrow still drawn back and ready to fire.

"Oh, it's you."

"Hello," Cassandra said curtly.

They hadn't spoken since their spat outside the dungeons and she certainly hadn't forgiven him yet. She tied her hair back and nodded towards the rack of swords.

"You don't mind, do you?"

"Not at all, Princess," he said, all too formally. "Shall I withdraw to give you privacy?"

Cassandra considered sending him away. If he was going to act obtuse, she'd let him. In the end, she said, "No, you can stay, Hero." She bit down on his so-called title. He grimaced, inclined his head, then returned to his target practice.

Chevalier blades were made of the finest steel that Brevian smiths could provide, though it had been so long since she'd last gripped a sword that her shoulder and forearm struggled with the weight. Without a sparring partner, she had two options.

Practice her positions and footwork, or whack a stationary target dummy to no real avail. Balack cleared his throat in a manner crafted for annoyance. She chose the latter option.

Steadying the weight with her free hand, she assaulted her target with unnecessarily brutal swings. Chips of wood ripped free as she struck at its bulky chest, her own laboured breath punctured only by the whistle and thunk of Balack's arrows. She swung again, and again, and again, not training at all, only throwing all of her frustration and fear behind each blow. Her vision narrowed as she homed in on the arm of the dummy, which she hacked clean away. All breath left her as she screamed with her next strike against its shield. The impact against the metal boss rent a deafening clang and sent a painful kickback up her arms. Hands numb and sore, she staggered back, and only then heard her name.

"Cass!"

Breathing hard, she turned slowly to face him. Balack had lowered his bow, and was staring at her with a mixture of concern and disgust.

"What's wrong now?" He threw up a hand. "If it's Arkus again, I'll—"

"You'll what?" she spat.

He struggled for a moment to keep his own composure. "I'll ask you what's really going on. You were fine for months. What's changed?"

Cassandra stared back at Balack and pictured him not being there at all. When the only person left who'd care how she felt would be Arkus, and only then when it suited him. She saw the training pit truly empty, saw herself walking the palace grounds alone or escorted into Brevia by guards she barely knew. She saw herself back in her chamber atop the Bastion, during the longest portion of the day when Chelos could not be there with her, and she remembered how quiet it had been.

She dropped the sword onto the sand. "Everyone's leaving!"

Balack's expression softened and he made his way over to her.

Unable to fight the tears, feeling stupid and ashamed, she planted her face into the rough leather over his shoulder.

"I'm sorry for before," he said. "About Annandale and what I said; I shouldn't have said it. You should feel able to confide in me."

Cassandra sobbed a choked sob. "It was selfish of me to drag you down there with me and risk your favour with Arkus. You've earned it."

"Why do you think you're going to be alone?"

"Because he's being stubborn and dangerous. Oranna isn't comfortable around him anymore, and after seeing what happened to Annandale, who could blame her? Who could blame any of them? She's going away soon, and she'll take Thane with her."

"But she's the queen. She has to come back."

"Maybe, but there's precedent for royal children to tour the kingdom at a certain age. If she prefers to stay away, she might use that as an excuse to move around for years."

"I'll still be here."

"You'll be here until Arkus sends you south to your new lordship."

"I suppose," Balack said solemnly.

She pulled herself away from him, feeling she had calmed down. "It's not just about me. What he's doing, it's not right. I thought that if I could convince him to change, then it would be all right. But he won't." And in a painful moment of realisation, it dawned on her what she had to do. "So, we'll have to make him change."

Balack's eyes popped. "That sounds dangerously close to—"

"Nothing violent," Cassandra hastened to add, shocked he'd even think that was what she meant. "We just need to get a majority of the Assembly to oppose his new measure. In fact..." She started to ramble, unsure of whether Balack was even aware of the proposed Charter of Unity that would ruin what semblance of contentment was left amongst the powerful families.

"That's not what I meant," he said, cutting over her. "I meant you came dangerously close to involving me in all of this."

She frowned. "You won't help at all? This would affect your future too."

"You'll do what you must. Just don't tell me anything, okay? I can't report facts that I do not know."

"And would you?

"If I knew there was going to be a threat on my king's life or a threat to the ruling of the kingdom, yes. The war isn't even over yet. Stability at home is critical. So, don't tell me anything and I won't be able to hinder your efforts."

"But you won't help me either."

"Not in this, Cass," he said, and was quite firm on it. "Even if I wanted to, I couldn't. I have my hands full with the camps. You want my opinion, you should be trying to improve things there. Try to get more food and clothes sent. It's painful to see."

She nodded dimly. Truthfully, she hadn't thought much about the camps of late. Her experience there – seeing all that suffering, and then what happened to Boreac – she'd tried to put it out of her mind. But nothing would change if she couldn't get through to Arkus in the first place.

"I'll try," she said.

He smiled and nodded. "Very well. Then we each have our tasks. Remember, don't tell me a thing." He then took his leave, heading up to the exit which led directly into the chevalier barracks.

Cassandra replaced her fallen sword upon the rack and left the training hall through the door on the opposite side, back the way she'd come. Of all the matters that lay before her, the most difficult would be gathering all those she had to convince together in secret without Arkus knowing. No small task in itself. And she wasn't sure where to even begin.

16

TROUBLE IN THE STABLES

"You will imbue honour and strength; your presence will bring fear and admiration. Yet always remember, you are nothing without your horse."

From *Nobles & Their Steeds: A Chevalier's Compendium*

Lira – The Royal Tower

The bustling of the throne room cut through Lira's fatigue like a hot knife. Despite nearly two days of sleep, a tiredness had sunk into her very bones. Pressure, stress and ultimate failure had done this to her. She shouldn't have been made prefect. She was just a huntress who had been given a command beyond her experience. It surprised her that Praetorians still saluted and smiled as she passed them. Harra was among those most eager, running to her side, all wide-eyed.

"Prefect, it is good to see you on your feet again. Are you rested?"

Lira blinked, unsure what she should tell her. "As much as I can be, though I've slept for too long already."

"Darnuir said you were to have all the time that you need. If you'd like to return to your chambers—"

"No," Lira said, harsher than she intended. Did Darnuir think her weak, then? Did he regret leaving her in such an important position? Either way, it wasn't Harra's fault. "I'd rather be doing something useful. The skirmish was hard on us all and no one else will have slept for this long."

Harra looked downcast and averted her eyes. "I wish I had been there to help you. What you did was amazing, taking on all those Light Bearers."

"We had help," Lira said.

"But they're all older, more experienced warriors," Harra said. "Camen told me how you stood up to them."

Lira felt her throat tighten. "You would have liked to fight our own kind?"

Harra looked sheepish. "Well, no. Of course not. I just mean, I'd have liked to have been there with you. Supporting you. I didn't mean—"

"I know," Lira said, patting her on the shoulder. "And thank you. It means a lot to hear you say that. I for one just wish it hadn't happened at all." She scanned the room for Darnuir but couldn't locate him among the activity. He wasn't on his throne.

"Where is the king?"

"He's in council with the humans," Harra said. She pointed towards the throne.

A circular table had been placed at the base of the steps. Despite knowing where to look, Lira almost missed him again. Darnuir wasn't wearing his armour, nor his crimson cape; he sat in a plain shirt. The Dragon's Blade was hidden from view under the table. Compared to the regalia of the human officers around him, he looked quite ordinary. A few days ago, the thought of having Darnuir back would have thrilled her. Yet now she had seen him, no sense of relief filled her, no hope burst within her chest. Just another disappointment, she supposed.

She must have lingered on him for too long, for Darnuir turned his attention from the humans and caught her eye. He got to his feet and her heart skipped a beat. Would he dismiss her here in front of everyone?

Darnuir waved her over and she found herself walking trance-like to his side. Here, she got a better look at the humans. Some were from the navy, others were high-ranking hunters in black leathers, and the rest were army officers in their white and black uniforms. Their expressions weren't as foreboding as they might have been, which was some comfort.

Darnuir beckoned her closer. "Prefect Lira, we're all glad to see you. We owe you our thanks."

Lira was taken aback. "Thanks?"

"Were it not for you, matters the other night would have been far worse," Darnuir said.

One of the human officers stood up. Lira vaguely recognised her from the many fruitless meetings over the past weeks. She had a stern face with sharp eyes and a slightly hooked nose.

"You did well, Prefect. We are in your debt."

"I didn't stop it from happening."

"You can't stop madness," the female officer said briskly. "You saved more of my regiment from being slaughtered, and saved the rest of our forces from a brutal fight in the streets."

"The Fifth Regiment will return to Brevia," Darnuir said, more for Lira's benefit it seemed. "As will the Eighth, we have just decided." The commander of that regiment barely suppressed a smile of relief.

One of the navy officers leaned forwards, a high-ranking man judging from the silver trim on his uniform. "It's a kind gesture, but it will be hard to avoid the reality of what happened when reports reach the Assembly in full. If we could be sure of what will be done to the perpetrators, it would go a long way towards showing justice being done."

"I have told you of my intentions for the Light Bearers in question."

"And yet nothing has been done." The officer attempted to be bold, but something about Darnuir's look seemed to hold him back and his voice faltered. It wasn't a menacing stare; far from it; but there was a firmness in it, a calm confidence that Lira had never seen in Darnuir before.

"I believe you have ships to prepare," Darnuir said. "Rest assured that when you return, the situation will be fully dealt with."

The officer grumbled but voiced no further objections. "Tell your dragons and your chevalier to report to me at nightfall. We'll leave at dawn."

"Raymond?" Lira said, confused. A knot formed in her stomach. Something in her expression must have given away this discomfort for Darnuir looked at her in concern.

"I think that will be all for today," he said to the officers. "Thank you all for hearing me out. I hope to work more closely with you all over the coming weeks."

Once the humans had departed, Darnuir sighed heavily and rubbed at his eyes. Lira noticed then how sickly he still looked. His eyes were dark, his skin sallow, and he was thin. Not quite wasted, but more veins were visible in a more striking blue than was natural. She wondered if that was due to the Cascade.

"Come, sit with me, Lira." He sat down on the steps behind them and let out another sigh of relief. A little hesitant, Lira sat beside him, feeling strange to be so inactive while the rest of the Praetorians carried out their tasks. Darnuir stretched his arms behind himself and she heard his back pop.

"That's better," he said.

"How are you?" she asked. It seemed a foolish thing to ask, but she didn't know how else to phrase it.

"My body might be worn but my mind is clear," Darnuir said. "I'll be fine. I'd rather know how you are holding up. It can't have been easy while I was... gone."

"I wasn't prepared for it."

"Yet you did admirably."

"I did what I could, but it wasn't enough. Dragons need a king."

"A weakness in our people I'd like to change," Darnuir said. "We can't fall apart simply because one individual is out of action. But that's something for the future. For now, I simply want to thank you for all that you did, and for taking such swift action the other night. It's awful that it happened, but you're not to blame – no, don't even think of taking on that burden," he added, placing a hand on her shoulder. "I remember you watching over me during my recovery. On top of everything, you still made time for that. It's much more than I deserved. The Praetorians admire you, love you even. I couldn't ask for a better Prefect – nor, I hope, a friend."

Lira gulped away the lump that had formed in her throat. Was this really Darnuir?

"Thank you." It was all she could think to say.

"Do you still wish to remain prefect?"

Lira half-opened her mouth, then closed it. She wasn't entirely sure. Being made prefect had been sudden and an honour, but she wondered if she was really the best person for it. She had been able to keep Darnuir in check, to some degree, but he seemed different now. Would she be needed for that any longer?

"I hope you do, but I'll understand if you don't," Darnuir added. "Having had to handle me before cannot have been pleasant."

"A challenge is more how I'd describe it," Lira said, chancing a smile. Thankfully, he smirked in return. "Can I think about it?" she said.

"Of course you can. But not for too long. Raymond is debating on whether he will return from Brevia. I'd hate to lose you both."

The knot in her stomach tightened. "Why is he going?"

"I am sending Raymond on a goodwill mission. I hope he can make headway in bringing the rest of our people home and relieve the pressure on Brevia."

"But—" She stopped herself, not sure what she was going to say, and not even sure why she was trying to say anything at all. It was Darnuir's choice, not hers. She settled on saying, "Why might he not return?"

"That's for him to decide. Maybe you should speak to him yourself if you're concerned. Give him a reason to stay."

"What reason?" she snapped.

Darnuir chuckled and leant his chin upon his hands. "That's also for you to figure out. But I know that look."

Lira frowned, her ire flaring "What look?"

"The same look I used to see one dear friend give another…" He trailed off, his voice betraying a pain that she wasn't aware he carried. He pressed his face fully into his palms, groaned, then got to his feet. "If you're going to see him, you'd better go soon. He'll leave for the ship tonight."

"Right," she said, feeling dazed. This had been an unusual experience with Darnuir, but it felt better than it had before. Hopefully, it was a sign of things to come. She stood a little hastily, felt the blood rush from her head, and thought longingly again of bed. Fighting the feeling, she took her first steps towards the throne room doors.

Darnuir called after her. "If you're looking for Raymond, he'll be—"

"I know where he'll be."

As expected, she found him in the makeshift stable they had constructed for Bruce in one of the ruined villas near the Royal Tower. She lingered in the doorway, not wishing to interrupt what looked like a tender moment between horse and rider as Raymond brushed Bruce's long mane. Lira was also nervous, although she felt foolish for feeling it. Yet the more she thought on it, the more she got mad at him. Thinking of leaving, was he? After all of this, he was going to pack it in and crawl back home to his comfortable mansion? Well, she was going to call him out on that.

"All packed, are we?"

Raymond whipped around, fumbled with his brush and dropped it in the process.

"Lira? How are you feeling?"

"Fine."

"You look more human than the other night – I mean, well, you know what I mean."

"Hmmm," she said, slinking into the so-called stables. Bruce blew out his cheeks at her and bobbed his head enthusiastically. "I don't have any apples for you today," she told the great beast. Bruce eyed her empty hands then snorted his displeasure.

"Is something wrong?"

"No," she said. "I just heard you were leaving."

"Darnuir sends me to plea with the Assembly. It won't be an easy task."

"He also said you might not come back."

"He granted me that option."

"And you're considering it?"

"I am."

"Even if it means leaving someone behind?"

His eyes popped. "What?"

Lira frowned and waved a hand pointedly towards Bruce.

"Oh," he said. "Yes, I've considered that." His face gave nothing away, but his tone was quite firm.

Lira froze, rooted to the spot a few steps away from him. He was serious; really, truly serious. He loved that horse. And if he was this serious about it, how could she persuade him otherwise? Something of her anxiety must have shown on her face, for Raymond frowned at her.

"What does it matter?"

"What does it—" Lira hissed. She shuffled awkwardly, pursed her lips, then looked around the battered ruins of the villa, anywhere but at Raymond. The words she sought eluded her.

"It's not like I'm a huge help here," Raymond said. "You even told me to stay behind the other night."

"Not this 'being a hero' stuff again?" she said, finding her voice.

He rolled his eyes and turned away. "Easy for you to say. You're a dragon." He seemed to vent some of his own anger on Bruce, giving the horse a tougher scratch along the neck than normal. Bruce snorted again and twisted his head away. Raymond stepped back, lost his footing on a chunk of carrot underfoot and fell.

Lira dropped to his side. "Are you hurt?"

"I'm fine," he groaned. "I'm not as fragile as you think."

"I never said you were." She withdrew her proffered hand and folded her arms. "I didn't tell you to stay because I think you're weak."

"It's not just that," he muttered.

"Then what?" Lira said. She felt lost; bewildered. What was going on?

"Even before, over the last few weeks, I couldn't put in the shifts you or the others could. I always got tired or couldn't keep up."

"No one expected you to."

Raymond grimaced. "That doesn't make it better." He sighed. "It's... difficult to explain."

"Darnuir didn't bring you into the Guard to be more muscle."

Raymond's eyes finally met hers. "I was to be some sort of symbol... well, look how that turned out. I've done no good as an ornament."

"And you think you could have done more standing on ceremony back home?"

"Home?" he said, his voice a touch high. "Home feels like a distant memory here. This city is a cold and dying place."

"We all feel homesick, Raymond. Me too. This is all so new, and my mother—"

"Is still in the west. I know. I was going to come find you to say—"

"Yes?"

"To say that I'd enquire as to her whereabouts. Find out if she's in these camps and, if so, let her know you're well."

"That would mean coming back to tell me?"

Raymond pushed around some straw on the floor, not looking at her. "I could write."

Lira huffed. "I don't believe you'd ever abandon us while there is still a fight ahead."

"I'm just not sure what I have to offer; really offer," he said quietly. He swept his now dishevelled hair off his face to look at her more intently. "What can a human offer a dragon?"

His phrasing was odd, but Lira brushed it aside. "You offer hope; hope to Darnuir's cause, which we all claim to believe in." Raymond looked dejected, his gaze falling to the floor. Lira was lost. Raymond had heard this reasoning a hundred times, but he didn't believe it.

What does he want to hear? And what do I want to say?

She tried to remember why she'd come in the first place and it all seemed a blur; a mixture of fear, anger, nerves and habit. She didn't want him to go. Using Darnuir was just an excuse. And if she could admit that to herself, she could admit it to him.

"Look, you gave me someone to lean on. You're a good listener, and it helps more than you might think. I didn't need just another dragon carrying heavy crates around. It was nice to have something... more."

Raymond smiled, but it was a soft, sad sort of smile. "You speak as though I've already left."

"Then don't."

He sat up to face her properly. "I wondered if you'd rise before I left for Brevia. I wanted to say goodbye – just in case," he added, a little stiffly.

"Well, I'm awake."

Raymond gulped. "Goodbye, Lira."

Her nose prickled from oncoming tears. She forced them down, quite embarrassed that she'd even come close to it. She got up quickly, turning her face away to hide the signs of them and shook her head in an attempt to clear her thoughts.

Raymond was clambering to his feet. She grabbed his hand and yanked him up as though he were a child. At his full height, she had to tilt her head to look up at him.

"You'll take care of Bruce, won't you?" he asked.

"Yes," she said, exasperated.

"Bring him apples when you visit; he'll need the treats." Raymond spoke as though the warhorse was a mewling puppy.

"Yes," she said, more mechanically.

"And take care of yourself, too. You deserve better than this."

She realised she hadn't let go of his hand. "Come back, okay?" The words had left her mouth before she could register them. Before she'd even considered them.

She let go of him, gingerly retreated as though he were suddenly poisonous, then pivoted on her heel and strode off. On her way out of the villa, she flexed her hand and kept her focus determinedly forwards, not quite sure what had just happened.

17

INTRUSION

"Behind burned rock and mistrust, a veil has hidden the goings-on in Kar'drun for thousands of years."

From Tiviar's Histories

Dukoona – The Depths of Kar'drun

Arms quivering, shoulders aching so much he thought they would tear away, Dukoona pushed downwards. Pale blue light from the Cascade Sink was barely enough to see by as he struggled to break his restraints. Weak though he was, he strained his body in a desperate bid for freedom. The bonds began to shake and hope kindled in him; he would not give in, he would not relent, he would suffer whatever pain was necessary. His hands pushed down to his stomach, the furthest he'd reached yet.

The bonds tightened, about to give. He was close.

A cry of pain burst from his throat.

"I can hear you," Rectar said. The crimson-robed figure appeared, hood up. "If you are attempting to escape, do so silently."

The bonds heaved Dukoona upwards, rendering his efforts useless. He gasped as his body was stretched, joints popping loudly; then the bonds began to undulate, thrashing him around like a strip of cloth caught in the wind. When it was over, he hung limply, in no mood to try again.

"I will stand over your body and laugh one day," he muttered.

'I heard that as well,' Rectar announced in his mind. *'I hear all. I see all. You are in my domain.'* Rectar had taken control of him again, forcing Dukoona to retreat to the smallest crevice of his consciousness.

Distantly, he became aware of one of his arms falling, then slapping against his side. Rectar had removed the bond at his wrist but Dukoona was in no position to take advantage of it. The same hand then started tearing at his own face. Dukoona watched on from afar, powerless to stop the clawing sweeps across his vision. Smoke fumed from the wounds, but cowering in this cramped corner of his mind, he didn't feel it.

'I am the Shadow,' Rectar said. *'I am your creator and I will—'* His master went silent and Dukoona's hand froze mid-scrape.

Rectar left his mind, and Dukoona hurtled to take back control of his body. Every sense returned in full at once: the searing, sharp stings from the many cuts on his face, the utter silence of his prison, the pressure of the bonds on his limbs. But not on *all* of his limbs. Not now.

Dukoona raised his hand with a mixture of delight and horror. Rectar had not replaced the bond there. He flexed his fingers, wondering whether this was all some cruel new ploy. Yet he didn't waste time thinking on it.

Quickly, he summoned his blade from the shadows. It gathered in his hand, rippling like dark water. He hacked at the bond on his other wrist. Forgetting his feet remained bound, he lurched forwards and now dangled upside down. Curling his body up, he slashed in a broad stroke and both his feet were set free. He fell to a heap upon the stone underneath and groaned.

What now? he asked himself.

He should search for his fellow spectres, but he doubted he'd find them before Rectar returned. *He sees all, he hears all. What could I possibly do?*

The first thing would be to stand.

As he stood, a red cloak fluttered in the half-light.

Dukoona ran. He got a whole twenty paces before his body stopped accepting his instructions. His legs and arms locked in place and he toppled, striking his head hard as he hit the floor.

"Why do you even try?" Rectar said aloud. A foot covered in gold armour stepped in line with Dukoona's eyes. Though dazed, he heard roaring in the distance.

"Are your new servants troubling you?"

More snarling reached Dukoona. It sounded close.

"They are strong creatures, despite my adjustments," Rectar said. "I learned my mistake from you and have stripped them of all will. They are more akin to how their race existed before the Others intervened."

"If they are so powerful, why haven't you unleashed them?"

"Because of you," Rectar said. He knelt over Dukoona, taking his bleeding face in a pale hand. "Your betrayals forced me to relinquish control of my better servants while I dealt with your kind. Setbacks occurred. But soon it will be ti—" Rectar was silenced again.

He vanished, leaving Dukoona alone, but unable to move.

Thunderous footsteps followed, heavy beats thrumming through the cavern floor.

A red dragon careened into view, enormous, scaly, long-faced, with a thick tail trailing heavily behind. It lashed at the air with its forked tongue and sniffed loudly as it traced whatever scent it searched for. Despite himself, fear gripped Dukoona. There was nothing this creature could do that would be worse than what Rectar was capable of, yet the dragon was terrifying to behold. It locked eyes with Dukoona and regarded him as an oddity, something it had not seen before. He thought it would attack him, but then it returned to sniffing the air, crouching low to the ground. Its hands were less bestial, remaining capable of holding swords or other tools, yet they were still covered in scales. The creature crawled forward on them, eerily swift and smooth for something so large.

The beast paused and whipped its head to one side. In the same moment, a second red dragon leapt from the darkness. A savage fight ensued, one in which the only weapons were teeth and talon-like fingernails. The second creature held one advantage. It wore sheets of dull grainy gold over some of its body; not full armour, but strategically placed on its forearms and shoulders, where it might make use of them in battle. The noise of the skirmish was incredible; the roaring and howling as they ripped and bit at each other was unlike anything Dukoona had heard before. One of their tails slammed into the cavern floor so hard it cracked the stone.

Rectar reappeared, this time in his shadow form. The black figure hovered above the battling dragons, radiating power. Dukoona felt it crashing into him in hot waves. Rectar extended a hand and the red dragons stopped fighting, falling uncannily quiet. In that moment, Dukoona felt control of his body return to him. Unfrozen, he rolled over and then staggered upright. His shadow blade was still in his grip and Rectar was hovering right there.

Without considering the madness of it, Dukoona surged forward.

Rectar raised a dark hand towards him. The force of his master's will felt weaker than before, strong enough to slow Dukoona down, as though his legs were made of lead, but not enough to stop him completely. With a growl, the two red dragons began fighting again, their movements sluggish like Dukoona's. He fought on, exerting every bit of inner strength he had to keep Rectar from his mind. He managed to take two steps forwards like this, and then Rectar's will snapped away. Dukoona staggered mid-stride but kept on running.

The reds became immobilised again. Above them, Rectar shifted into his physical form and dove down, driving his blade into one and pummelling the other with his fist. Dark, sludge-like blood gushed from the creatures, and when their writhing ceased, Rectar moved to meet Dukoona, his face still hidden beneath the hood.

Dukoona knew it was foolish but raised his sword anyway. He had nothing else to lose and it would be better to die fighting rather than in chains.

Dukoona's blade struck his master's and he was blown backwards. Rolling, his body crashed against stone with each bump before he came to a scraping halt which sheared yet more flesh from him. He'd poured everything he had into that desperate attack and it had made no difference. Well, he hadn't expected it to. Not truly.

In silence, Rectar approached him. He raised Dukoona's bleeding body to hang by fresh bonds like a slaughtered pig and left without further torture. Dukoona's blood smoked gently around him.

Sonrid – The Entrance to Kar'drun

With a grunt of pain, Sonrid dragged his leg the final stretch and crossed into the shadow beneath the shelf of rock. There were many entrances to Kar'drun, which was just as well, as the main one would be watched. Sonrid would take a lesser-used spectre doorway. It was far above him, however, and would require a shadow meld to reach.

Better get it over with, he thought, and began the slow process of melding. He sank into the shadow and travelled along it, up to the ledge above the rock shelf, where he struggled to emerge as though he'd actually climbed the distance. Once fully formed out of the shadow, Sonrid lay face down, his eyes shut, willing his pain to leave him by making timely and satisfying groans.

A hoarse voice spoke. "Sonrid, what are you doing?"

Panic took hold of him, but there was little he could do in his present condition. He thought he recognised the voice, though.

"Zax? Is that you?"

"It is. You've been gone for a long time, brother."

Spluttering, gasping, Sonrid picked himself up and looked at Zax. His fellow broken spectre suffered too from a hunched and crippled body, though where Sonrid's leg was malformed, both of Zax's were fine. Instead, his right arm had failed to form and lay shrivelled against his side, making him look like a bird with a clipped wing.

"I'm back now," Sonrid said. "But what are you doing out here?" Sudden thoughts of Zax being a watchman for the Master jolted him.

"I enjoy the sunlight upon my face," said Zax. He glanced to the sky and nodded knowingly. "The weather is fine today, and soon the sun will be overhead."

Sonrid cocked his head. "What nonsense are you speaking of? We can't *feel* the sun like other races."

Zax shrugged as much as one can shrug when their arms are locked in place. "It does something, friend. I don't feel in as much pain after a day under the sun."

Sonrid had never experienced this himself, but he wouldn't begrudge Zax of something that helped him. Broken spectres had little enough relief. He too needed to wait for the sun to reach midday and so looked up to check its position. Yes; it would be time soon.

He returned his attention to Zax, narrowing his eyes. "So, you aren't guarding the passageway?"

"Guarding it from whom?" Zax said. "All the spectres are locked up and the Master doesn't care what we do. Should I be preventing your entry?"

Sonrid laughed, a sound like rusty nails on rock. "That would be a fight to behold. Shall we bash heads until one of our skulls cracks?"

Zax did not join in. He looked serious. "Where have you been?"

"I've been helping Lord Dukoona."

"You?" Zax said, incredulously. "What can a Broken do?"

"Whatever we can," Sonrid said. It was a strange feeling to be so defensive over this. Only months ago, he too would have assumed he had nothing to offer. "Dukoona finds value in all his spectres, Zax. We must help him, if... if he's still alive?"

"He's down in the utter depths. In the central chamber, chained up by the Master."

A little tension eased from Sonrid. Dukoona's fate had been the greatest unknown in returning to Kar'drun. Without Dukoona, any resistance would fall apart.

Zax was looking at him suspiciously. "What does it matter? Whatever the spectres have done to anger the Master is their business."

"Dukoona and his Trusted are different," Sonrid said. He wanted to say more, but a fresh wave of seizing pain pulsed from his spine. He gasped when it ended, a small part of him wishing to leap off this ledge of rock to his fate, but he didn't listen to it. He had work to do.

"Help me, Zax. The Master fails to notice us. We could rally the Broken, free the spectres, and—"

"And what?" Zax said. "The Master will bind them again and kill us."

"Is that such a terrible thought?"

Zax regarded his shrunken arms. "No. No, it would be welcome."

"Then why not try? Come with me."

Zax sighed. "I just... I just want to feel the sunlight, Sonrid. You can't show up here and drag me back down there. Not back into the dark."

Sonrid huffed and shuffled forward. He lacked the time and energy to convince Zax, and the sun was almost at its optimum position. Zax hobbled to block him.

"Move," Sonrid said.

"Don't be a fool. You look even worse than we usually do. Your shadows are wafer-thin and I can see your bones. You're exhausted. Rest first; sit with me for a day or two and think it over."

Sonrid considered this. He was deathly tired, and he could feel every scrape of his joints when he moved. But what good would waiting do? He raised his arm, as high as his shoulder would allow, and patted Zax on his misshapen arm.

"No amount of sunlight will help you with this. We're not of this world, Zax. Rectar summoned us here, and yes, I will use his name," he added in response to Zax's look of horror. "Rectar is his name. He has a name, like us, and so he can be killed. Rectar summoned us here and we are bound to him. Perhaps, if we are free of him, we can return to where we belong and be whole again." He'd expected Zax to think him mad and step back, to flinch and shake his head and say it wasn't possible. Instead, Zax pursed his lips, looking sombre and a little sad. The golden rays of the sun lit his face on one side, leaving the other side darker than the rock of Kar'drun.

"Other than our own death, there is only one way we can be free of him," Zax said.

"I know."

"If even Dukoona can't defeat him—"

"The dragon king might," Sonrid said. "Dukoona spoke to him. And so did I. Darnuir will be the one to kill Rectar."

"Are you sure you haven't gone quite mad?" Zax said. "That wouldn't be a problem, you know. You can tell me. There's no need for a healthy mind at Kar'drun."

"This is real," Sonrid said. "Will you help me or not?"

Zax stared down between his toes. "What can we Broken do?"

Sonrid smiled. "Anything we can."

Zax looked up, smiling weakly himself and nodding slowly. Then he stepped aside with a glance to the sky. "You'd better move quickly. The light is perfect now."

"I've always hated doing this," Sonrid moaned, but he made his way to the crevice in the rock face which was the entrance to the passageway.

It was small, no wider than a clenched fist, and only accessible by a shadow meld; a long and narrowing tunnel with small jagged rocks like rows of sharpened teeth.

Only when the sun was at a precise point in the sky, and the day was clear, did light hit the tunnel in such a way that shadows were cast all the way to the end. It required precise jumps during the meld, from one speck of shadow to another, and to miss the mark would be fatal. If he didn't land properly, he would begin to reform in the too-cramped space, be crushed long before his body truly formed, and end up as dust coating the stone.

"Better to be cautious than fast," Zax said. "Good luck, brother."

Sonrid rallied what courage he could, then reached out with a finger to touch the sliver of shadow at the entry point. He melded slowly and painfully as ever, and then began to flow down the shadow. The small, teeth-like rocks loomed like world-breaking mountains when you were condensed down to the size of a grain of sand.

The first jump came quickly. He landed on the edge of his next shadow with precious space to spare, and wove around the gouges in the rock, which seemed like canyons to him. Two jumps later and he found himself flying by chips of bone; white, pristine bone, scattered like snow all around. A graveyard of spectres who had not made their jumps correctly.

As the passage narrowed further, what little light there was became more ragged, leaving the last shadows of the tunnel razor thin and fading. Sonrid fast approached the last, most dangerous section of the meld. He jumped again, this time directly upwards to where the shadow ran along the top of the tunnel. It was almost impossible to distinguish true shadows from the general darkness at this stage and he landed a little off target.

At once, he began to grow, expanding to the size of a pinhead, then an ant.

He was going to grow until he was crushed in this darkness and never know what it was like to be whole and pain-free.

The shadow moved.

It was a movement he wouldn't have seen as a formed spectre, but down here he noticed it shift. The sun's rays must have begun moving away from their optimum position, changing the shadow's position by a hair's breadth. It connected with Sonrid just as he was expanding to the size of a small pebble, and he re-melded with it. Relief blazed in him and he felt a rare sense of glee as he flew along the shadow's surface.

A pale glow ahead showed the end was in sight. Sonrid reached the end of the shadow and bounded from it into the dimly lit room. He landed awkwardly, lost his balance and fell, but he was whole, and that was all he could ask for.

Never again, he thought, picking himself up and getting his bearings.

Like most of Kar'drun, this room was lit by an ethereal floating flame, this one a muddy brown. Having spent some time in Aurisha, Sonrid noticed how the shape of the room resembled the designs of the hallways and homes carved out of the plateau itself; all severe and straight-edged. Sonrid trudged onwards, hoping he could remember his way down here.

Dukoona – The Depths of Kar'drun

He awoke to the sound of roaring. The red dragons must have been causing trouble for Rectar again. *Let them kill each other. Let them be too much for even a god to handle.*

The Cascade Sink appeared smaller than before. Rectar must have moved him further back. Only his own flaming hair granted him light to see by. Still, he had some hope to keep him going. He'd broken free of Rectar's will, if briefly, back when Rectar had been preoccupied by the reds. But he had done it. Not that it would be much use if simply meeting his master's blade with his own sent him reeling.

Darnuir had a blade of power, so he would surely be able to meet Rectar on an even footing. Where was that dragon? One moment he'd been rushing halfway across the world, the next he'd sat in Aurisha for who knew how long. Such accusations might not be fair. Dukoona still wasn't sure how long he'd been down here for. A day? A year? However long, it must have been long enough for Darnuir to rally his forces. It had to have been.

Doubt. That all too familiar feeling gnawed at him. Perhaps Darnuir wasn't coming. Perhaps he'd listened to Dukoona's pleas and decided he couldn't trust a spectre after all. They had been enemies of the dragons from the first. Would one brief conversation be enough to change all of that?

A tapping sound came from nearby. It was light. It couldn't be one of the red dragons. Whatever it was grew closer. A small, dark figure shambled into view, obscured by the lack of light.

"My Lord Dukoona," it said. Its voice was strained and hoarse. He knew that voice. He wanted to cry out in relief to Sonrid but stopped himself at the last moment. Rectar could hear and see all he did. If he spoke to Sonrid, Rectar would know.

"Dukoona? Lord, I have come to aid you."

How can I speak to him without speaking?

"I could try to break your bonds. I can manage to summon a small dagger if I concentrate." Sonrid's hunched form limped a little closer.

No, no, stop, Dukoona thought. If Sonrid cut him down, Rectar would surely know. But how could he communicate this to Sonrid? If only Sonrid could hear his thoughts, then he wouldn't have to speak directly. Rectar was able to speak in Dukoona's head when possessing him. That was because Dukoona was Rectar's minion, and yet Dukoona had been able to issue orders to demons before through thought alone. Sonrid wasn't a regular demon, but he wasn't a full spectre either. He was broken: trapped somewhere between lowly demon and mighty spectre.

Tentatively, Dukoona crested forth with his thoughts as he would to command a demon. What he found was Sonrid's mind; not wide open like the demons, but not completely sealed either. Dukoona pushed harder.

'Sonrid, stop. Don't come any closer.'

It didn't work. Sonrid continued to creep forwards until Dukoona saw him clearly below. The poor wretch looked a mess, little better than a puff of smoke in the air, his bones visible under parting shadows. He must have worked himself hard to make it here. Sonrid's loyalty warmed Dukoona in a way that he hadn't felt in a very long time, not since Kidrian had saved him in battle decades ago.

Oh, poor Kidrian. What have I done?

A fresh pang of guilt hit him, and he let out an involuntary, shuddering sigh.

Sonrid looked up. Dukoona cursed himself for the outburst but caught Sonrid's eye and tried desperately to convey in a look that Sonrid should stop. He didn't dare mouth any words nor move his head in any way that would signal he was communicating with someone. Sonrid seemed to take his stare as a plea for freedom. He raised his crooked arm and grunted as a dagger formed in his hand, the shadows gathering slowly like tar. Knife in hand, he brought his arm back, aiming for the knot of shadows that tethered Dukoona's right foot.

'No,' Dukoona screamed in thought, reaching out as before. The urgency had removed his reservations and the force was a bellow in the space between them. The little spectre staggered and looked to Dukoona again, less sure this time.

'Sonrid, listen to me.'

Whatever protection was around Sonrid's mind now buckled; not cracking entirely, but for a moment Dukoona was through. He was behind Sonrid's eyes and his own all at once. It was the most singularly confusing and sickening feeling that Dukoona had ever experienced. Was this what Rectar felt when taking control of him?

He sensed Sonrid cowering somewhere out of harm's way, and Dukoona hated himself for it.

'Dukoona?' Sonrid said meekly.

'Sonrid, don't cut the bo—' But he was ripped out of Sonrid's mind, unable to hold the connection. Sonrid remained still. He'd lowered his dagger but looked afraid. Dukoona closed his eyes, and told himself it was the only way to speak with Sonrid. He'd have to learn to live with it later.

The next thought Dukoona cast took every bit of his inner strength. He smashed through Sonrid's shielding and took hold of his mind. There was no subtlety to it. Dukoona was a battering ram at the enemy's gates. Sonrid's fleeing consciousness backed away from him and Dukoona could feel the fear as if he too were afraid. It didn't matter that Sonrid trusted him; this invasion went beyond anything decent. It was the realm of their cruel, uncaring master. Regret swelled in him for all the demons he'd ever ordered around on a whim. Had they all been this afraid every time? In his own way, Dukoona had been his master. He'd been a hypocrite. A fiend. The very thing he despised.

'Sonrid? Sonrid, I am so sorry for this.'

'What are you doing? I'm trying to help you.'

'I know, and I'm grateful,' Dukoona said. 'But Rectar will hear anything I say or see anything I do. He overlooks you, but if you cut me down, he'll know.'

'What should I do, then? Shall I free the Trusted?'

'No. We cannot escape Rectar, even if we flee the mountain. And I won't have any more spectres suffer because of me.'

His guilt and pain flared again.

'That was not your fault,' Sonrid said.

'You felt that?' Dukoona asked.

'I did. I am sorry about what He made you do. Kidrian will know you had no choice. He will understand.'

'I asked you all to place so much trust in me. If I hadn't led you all along my path, we wouldn't be in this position. More of us would still live. We wouldn't be prisoners.'

'We have always been prisoners. You showed me that. Without you, we would always have been slaves.'

A warmth rose in Dukoona. 'Do you mean that?'

'I didn't hobble all the way from Aurisha for nothing.' Sonrid sounded bolstered, perhaps from the shared affection of their mingled emotions. It was pushing back his fear. But he'd invaded Sonrid's mind for long enough.

'Right now, I am at a loss as to what we can do,' Dukoona said. 'I told Darnuir I would guide him through Kar'drun. Speaking to him was my last, desperate act. Yet he has not come.'

'I am here,' Sonrid said. 'Darnuir let me go in peace after you were summoned. I think he listened to what you had to say.'

'Yes, you are here, aren't you? I hope you're right. For now, we must wait and—' Pain seared into Dukoona. Sonrid flinched away. The source of it was from Dukoona's own body. He looked up, through Sonrid's eyes, and saw the telltale hundred cuts ripping at his body.

'Sonrid, He's coming. Hide. Don't act before it is time. When Darnuir comes, you must bring him to me. Trust no one else.'

He left Sonrid's mind and was sucked back into his own. Sonrid scuttled off into the darkness just in time to miss the crimson cloak swishing into view. Rectar intensified the pain of the cuts on Dukoona's flesh, deepening each wound, leaving Dukoona screaming amidst another wall of rising smoke. It ended mercifully quickly. His shadows reknitted in an instant.

"You have proven a distraction," Rectar said. He brought his hands together slowly in a soft, barely audible clap. When his hands met, the world spun. When things settled again Dukoona was dizzy, but could no longer see the Cascade Sink. He couldn't see anything at all.

"Here, you shall not be a temptation," Rectar announced from some place unseen, his voice echoing into nothingness.

18

CRUMBLING THE PAST

"Yet on these things, do not dwell. The man gazing into the past turns his back upon the future."

From Jon Barbor's *Scorching of the Dales*

Darnuir – The Plaza

Darnuir passed through the crowds, towards the Praetorian foothold. Word of the stand-off between the king and guardian had spread. The stillness of the crowd was a pressure upon him, the air thick with tension. Darnuir noted with relief that few of the onlookers had come armed. He wasn't sure how the crowds would react if things got heated inside the Basilica. The legates were still firmly in control, so far as he was aware, and all legions bar the Third were loyal to himself first and foremost. In theory, at least. There was a marked difference between the threat of violence and it actually happening.

If Darnuir was forced to draw weapons, would his people accept such a move?

He stopped just shy of the Basilica stairs. Lira awaited him, fully armoured, a grim look on her face.

"We'll be with you no matter what happens," she said.

"Blaine's devout, but not insane," Darnuir said. "All I want is justice, and for him to come out of his shell. We're going in with the intention of talking. Nothing more."

Lira bit her lip. He understood her feelings completely. He meant what he said, but he was not taking any chances either. Whatever happened, Blaine's power and influence had to be quelled. First, there was the Bastion, then the acts of terror caused by his men; not to mention the old secrets of Kroener, of Rectar, of placing Draconess upon the throne for longer than he had any right to. No, Darnuir was certain of this. Blaine had caused more harm than good.

It ended here.

"Praetorians," Darnuir called. In the eerie quiet of the plaza, his voice sounded like a thundercrack. His Guard fell in and clanked their swords once upon their shields. Darnuir drew a deep breath, closed his eyes, and held that breath for ten heartbeats. His pulse slowed. His nerves cooled. He let the breath out steadily and found nothing more he could do to delay this.

"Forward," he said, slamming his foot upon the first step.

The Basilica loomed larger than ever as he ascended, the arched entranceway foreboding like the images of Kar'drun he'd suffered in his fever dreams. Lira marched beside him, and her conviction to join him was reassuring. This had to be done. When Darnuir crossed the threshold of the temple it felt like he was stepping over the line of no return. There was no turning back.

Light Bearers stood ready inside, and all was gloomy save for the beam of light entering from the gap in the dome, bathing the image of Dwna in the morning sun. Further back, Blaine stood among the stone swords, facing the relief of Dwna, as though drawing strength from it.

Instinct directed Darnuir's hand to grasp his sword, but he stopped himself at the last moment.

Not unless I have no choice.

He marched forwards, determined but not aggressive. Boots rapped off the marble floor as Praetorians flanked him. The Light Bearers locked their shields together, tightly enough that their faces disappeared behind the wood and yellow paint. Whether they were afraid or full of hate, Darnuir could not say. He kept his focus upon his grandfather, but Blaine didn't deign to look at him; not even when he drew within striking distance of the Light Bearers.

"You must have known I would come," Darnuir said. "Why delay this, Blaine? Why hole up in here?"

Blaine turned his head sombrely, finally looking Darnuir in the eye. "It is sacrilege to spill blood upon these hallowed floors."

"Then don't fight me," Darnuir said. "I've come for the murderers you are harbouring. They must answer for their crimes."

"You can have them."

Darnuir had already opened his mouth to argue but quickly closed it, taken aback. That had been easy.

"If you have no issue with this, why the shield wall?"

"If you're only here for the prisoners, why your full Guard?"

He's afraid, Darnuir thought. *He doesn't want a battle any more than I do.*

"I'm prepared to send my men away, if you will do the same," Darnuir said.

He took a careful step forward. The Light Bearers didn't move. Darnuir risked another. The shield wall bristled but remained in place. Darnuir raised his hands to calm them.

"I don't want to spill more dragon blood. Can't we just talk?"

Blaine's expression was a mixture of jubilation, disbelief, and suspicion all at once.

"You want to talk?"

"Yes," Darnuir said in as steady a voice as he could. "If you thought I'd come tearing in here, flames lashing from my blade, then I understand. I probably would have before, when I had more anger than sense. But I've changed, Blaine. The last thing I want is to come to blows." With his hands still raised he took another cautious step forward. From behind the Light Bearer wall, he thought he could hear the scrape of swords from scabbards. His heart stopped.

"Stand down," Blaine called. "Sheathe your weapons and let the king through."

Darnuir breathed easy. He heard Lira sigh in relief as he turned to see her removing her hand from her own hilt. Darnuir walked on through the opening in the Light Bearer lines and Blaine moved to meet him. They met midway.

"You look thinner," Blaine said.

Darnuir smiled. "You look rough too."

"I've not slept. I've worried about this."

"I don't want to fight, Blaine."

"You mean it?"

"There's only one enemy and we have to face Him united."

"I don't want to fight either," Blaine said. "You've been right. I've been a stubborn old fool." He looked Darnuir up and down again. "Your stance, your bearing... is different."

"I told you, I've—"

"Changed, yes." Blaine gulped. "I'm glad you pulled through."

"Don't worry. The power of the blades isn't lost yet."

"What?" Blaine said. "You think that's it? No, boy. I care because you're the only family I have left." And before Darnuir could react, Blaine pulled him into a firm embrace; as close as one could while wearing heavy starium-lined plate. A little shocked, Darnuir laughed and returned the hug.

"I'm still here," he said quietly into Blaine's ear. "Somehow, I'm still here." He pulled back from Blaine but kept a hand upon his shoulder. "Did you really think I was going to fight you?"

"I could ask you the same."

"Well, I earned that," Darnuir said. He turned around. The Praetorians and Light Bearers were gawking, their faces a mixture of relief and bewilderment. All except Lira. She was smiling – the first smile Darnuir had seen on her since his recovery.

"There will be no need for swords today," Darnuir told them. "I hope there will never be a time again when dragons draw swords against each other, or any other race for that matter." He withheld his fear about Rectar's enchanted dragons for now. It was better to let this optimism settle in for once. "Blaine, will you accompany me outside? I think the crowds would benefit from seeing us together."

"It would be my pleasure."

And together, as one, the Praetorians, Light Bearers, Blaine, and Darnuir exited the Basilica.

The gathered thousands seemed to draw a collective breath at the sight of them, and their relief was palpable. Darnuir sensed a change in the air; it lightened and freshened, as though a heavy cloud had lifted. Blaine even had the good grace not to try and make a sermon of it. He made no mention of his gods; only a remark that there would still be no service that day, for he had much to discuss with the king. Dwna was to shine on them all, apparently. Darnuir looked to the sky at that, where the sun did shine, and indeed upon them all. Whether a god directed it or not, he couldn't say.

In the end, the crowd cheered them. Darnuir took Blaine's wounded hand and raised it high; a final seal on the hopefulness that swept the plaza of Aurisha.

Later, with the crowds dispersed and the guards given new duties, Blaine and Darnuir found time to be alone. They sat by the stone swords under the dome, disturbed only by the occasional Light Bearer or Praetorian entering or leaving the sanctum below.

"We should get this business with the prisoners out of the way," Blaine said darkly. "What do you think should be done?"

"Did they at least have remorse?"

Blaine pursed his lips, considering the matter. "In truth, no. None that I could see."

"The humans want blood."

"It is not for Arkus to decide."

"No, it's not. But with the Bastion and now this? Wars have been started over less."

Blaine sighed. "I know. It is with blind arrogance we've walked for far too long."

Darnuir raised his eyebrows at that. Blaine frowned and leaned in. "We both have, in our own way."

"On that I quite agree," Darnuir said. "Once it's all over, and assuming we're still alive, we can begin to make things right."

"But what will we do in the here and now?"

"With regard to the murderous zealots? I say send them north. Exile them from the city to repair and garrison old outposts along the Crucidal Road. Something you were already doing, I hear."

"You should keep your enemies close," Blaine said quietly.

"Like you did with Bacchus?" Darnuir said. Blaine's cheek twitched and Darnuir felt petty. "I'm sorry. That was a cheap dig. What he did is not your fault."

"It's more mine than yours," Blaine groaned. "He at least among them seems to have guilt."

Darnuir had wondered about that. "True guilt, or is he just scared for his own life?"

"Both, I imagine."

"Yet he did not take part in it himself?"

"Bacchus' most dangerous weapon is his tongue. With it, he very nearly became guardian. I do not think he'd feel it necessary to dirty his hands himself."

"Send him north as well," Darnuir said, resigned. "I've already sent Damien to scout the region. If Bacchus stirs up any trouble, he'll let us know. My priority is to remove them from the city, away from the humans."

"The Nest at the crossroads should be in better shape by now," Blaine mused. "I ordered work to begin there weeks ago, though supplies are short."

"Everything is limited. Our numbers, our food, our time, and most of all our goodwill with our allies. We're in a great deal of debt on that front."

Blaine clenched his jaw. "I agree that recent events have been harmful, but we did drive Rectar's armies back."

"Not without help," Darnuir said. "And not without some mistakes. Even the islanders have grievances against us both."

"You don't win every battle in a war," said Blaine. "I won back Eastguard in the end."

"You shouldn't make dangerous landings before you're at full strength."

Blaine tutted. "Look who's talking?"

"I know. And I nearly got us all killed. If you hadn't shown up in time we'd have died here. Luck and chance won't be with us now. Dukoona helped us more than you know. But I fear he can aid us no longer."

Blaine shifted his eyes.

"He wants to destroy Rectar as much as we do," Darnuir said.

"We'll see," Blaine said, barely moving his lips.

"Are you afraid the gods will be angry at you if you don't discount Dukoona's word?"

"I'm not a child," Blaine said. "I distrust Dukoona because he is a spectre. Their behaviour over the past year was unusual, I grant you. But it would be foolish to trust blindly. Just like it is foolish to have blind faith."

Darnuir shook his head, not sure if he had heard correctly. "Are you saying you no longer believe—"

"All I'm saying is, I will think for myself now. If the gods feel strongly about something, they can let me know. Otherwise, I'll do what I think is right and won't wait until they deem to intervene."

"I find that very reasonable, Grandfather."

Blaine scowled. "I don't expect you to believe as I do."

"It would be stubborn of me to insist that there is nothing out there. What it is, or they are, I do not know. But Rectar is a force beyond us. He summons demons not of our world. His power makes Castallan seem a novice, and look how much Cascade energy he could process. No, Rectar must be something more. And despite my personal feelings towards your faithful, I can hardly deny it when thousands report the same event upon the Nail Head."

"That too seems reasonable," Blaine said.

Darnuir took the chance to stretch, leaning back until he felt a good burn through his shoulder blades. His eye fell upon the carving of Dwna upon the wall, in which the god was represented through three emanating rays.

He took a moment to consider the other carvings; the three spiralling rays of N'weer and the half-seared sun of Dwl'or. One stone holder aligned perfectly with each relief. Three stone swords and three gods. One for each.

Yet when did the third sword get destroyed? Darnuir searched what memories of his past life remained to him. There weren't many of the Basilica; he'd barely entered the place even back then. Vividly, one recollection rose to the surface.

"I argued with Draconess here, shortly before we both died." He spoke without having meant to.

"What about?" Blaine asked.

"About everything. About how he did little other than pray upon his knees."

It came back to him then, as clearly as though he had stepped into a memory trapped within the rubies of the Dragon's Blade. He remembered the seething frustration he'd felt, and the blood rushing hotly to his face and throat. His resentment had been raw, and Draconess knew it. He'd given up hope of Darnuir being able to take possession of the blade, and he'd been right to withhold it. Darnuir knew that now.

"I'm surprised he didn't despair sooner, given how I used to be." To his surprise, Darnuir found a lump in his throat. "He asked when I began to hate him; asked it so calmly, as if he'd long accepted it. He said he prayed for answers, but they never came."

"I prayed too much as well," Blaine said. "It wasn't right that I left you and Draconess alone. It wasn't fair."

Darnuir wasn't sure what else to say. Recalling that memory with Draconess had shaken him. It was so similar, so eerily like where he was now. Once again, he found this old religion troubling him and an old dragon sitting low between the stone swords. What, if anything, had truly changed?

His people were hardly in a better position than they had been back then. One bad loss away from annihilation. He was king now, and he had the Dragon's Blade. At a terrible cost, he'd gotten what he'd always desired.

But I don't desire it. Not anymore.

He had no thirst for the power, not like back then. He was no longer the foul-tempered prince but a king who'd had sense beaten into him.

Darnuir got to his feet and extended a hand to Blaine. "You're here now. I can't fight Rectar without you and frankly I don't want to."

Blaine looked to the proffered hand, hesitant to accept it. "I shouldn't fool myself or you. I don't know if I can stand at your side." He raised his hand with the missing finger. "Having a second blade in our fight against Rectar would level the field, but this injury drags me back down."

Darnuir gave him a hard stare. "Are you Draconess? Are you giving up too?"

"I'm only thinking of what is best—"

"Look at me, Blaine. I'm half-wasted away here. We need to train. We'll train and grow stronger together, rather than lock horns as we used to. We'll teach you how to use your left hand if needs be. What do you say?"

Blaine's fingers twitched, a moment more of hesitation, then he grasped Darnuir's hand and rose. "We'll train."

Darnuir grinned. "I'm glad to hear it." He looked to the stone sword on his right, the one opposite N'weer. And once again, the empty holder caught his eye. "That third stone sword must have been destroyed by the demons."

Blaine eyed the spot sadly. "I think you're right. If you're sure it wasn't already destroyed?"

Darnuir dredged the memory with Draconess back up. "Yes. There were three there before I died." He drifted over to the sword before N'weer and ran a thumb over the worn stone, grainy and rough to the touch. "The demons suffered no repercussions for doing it."

He instinctively wrapped his fingers around the sword's hilt as though he were about to draw it. He felt the stone give a little, even though the pressure he applied was minimal. The stone was starium and ought to have been stronger. Then again, it was wafer thin, as thin indeed as a real blade might be. A new thought came to him.

"Let's break them."

Blaine's eyes widened. "What?"

"We're doing things our way now, aren't we? Not relying on signs from gods that clearly don't care enough to help us. If a spectre or demon broke the other sword and the gods did nothing, why should they act if we do? It may even jolt them awake."

"I... I..." Blaine's face was a picture of torment. A century and a half's worth of belief and ingrained values battled his desire for change, his features passing from shock, to outrage, to fear, to determination in the blink of an eye.

"I'll go first."

"That's the spirit," Darnuir said as Blaine strode to the sword in front of Dwna. The guardian took a deep breath, widened his stance as though for battle, then drew his blade. He raised his arm, held it, and for a moment Darnuir thought he was having doubts. But Blaine struck hard, and the crack rang throughout the Basilica. He kicked next, sending the bottom half of the free-standing stone crashing against the wall.

Darnuir followed, gripping the final stone hilt with all his might, and ripped the top half away. A back-handed blow finished the rest. Within seconds there was nothing left; just three empty holders before three silent gods. He looked to the dome above and casually raised his hands as though preparing to catch a sack of turnips. Nothing happened.

"I don't think they care, Blaine."

"I wonder now if they ever cared," Blaine said. "And I fear that I have wasted my life and the lives of those I love on them."

"We look to the future now," Darnuir said. "No more lingering and reflecting. We've gone through fire and back, Blaine, and we've still got worse to come. Whatever's happened has happened, and we'll do all we can to right it." He smiled again and puffed out his chest. It felt good, this; feeling vaguely in control for once.

"Come on, Grandfather. Let's work on that grip of yours."

19

THE RAG RUN

"The oldest parts of Brevia clustered behind early walls. With unification came security and peace. Immediately, the rich fled across the bay to create their boulevards, estates, and promenades along the shore."

From *A Lengthy History of Brevia* by Maddock the Scribe

Cassandra – Brevia – The Rag Run

The buildings leaned like crooked trees, trapping the air and noise together in a hot, grating storm against the senses. The Rag Run was one of the oldest sections of the city. From what she had gathered, it had always been cramped and downtrodden, but at least it was cheap. The war had done the area no favours. A dearth in trade, plus the requisitioning of soldiers and supplies, had turned the down-on-their-luck to the poor, and the poor to destitute. Each queue that led to chevaliers handing out coins and bread had swollen over the day, until they now seemed one single mass. Despite her sympathy for the people here, Cassandra felt anxious.

For her benefit, Arkus had ordered the chevaliers to double their numbers for the day's alms, but Cassandra couldn't fail to notice that she and her guards were now an island amidst a sea of the desperate. And the angry. Should the crowd turn against them, there would be nothing they could do. Guns or no guns.

A young woman no older than Cassandra in dirtied grey overalls held a baby's bundle in her arms. She caught Cassandra's eye and wailed.

"Won't you help us, Princess?" Shaking, she extended an open palm. "Oh, please, Princess. You are so fair and lovely and kind."

Cassandra's breath caught in her throat. That could have been her, save for the royal blood in her veins. She gulped and opened her mouth to say something, anything reassuring, if only she could think of what words could alleviate the girl's fear. A wall of steel formed between them before Cassandra had a chance. She forced herself to turn away before she risked doing something foolish.

She couldn't show favour to one over the others, no matter how much her heart ached.

Withdrawing to the centre of the chevaliers, she took a moment to collect herself. Behind the sacks of bread, several knights protected heavy chests secured with thick iron locks. At great resistance from the Merchant Lords, Arkus had managed to increase the donations from the Assembly. It was far more than he was obligated to give, and that generosity had lightened the dark thoughts she'd held towards her father, at least for today.

Everything came at a cost, however. Rations to the dragons had to be cut back to afford this. She wasn't sure she could have made such a choice.

As she picked up another coin pouch to distribute, she wondered if it had been wise to use this as a cover for her real intentions. Yet she had to steel her resolve. The need of the people was great, but temporary. When the war was over, things would return to the way they had been, given time. However, should another full-blown rebellion rise against Arkus, then conditions such as these might return. Arkus might be able to bully individual nobles into signing his new charter, but if she could get a powerful enough bloc to oppose him, he'd have to back down. She clung to that thought, telling herself it was all for the best.

Returning to the front of the crowds, she found Merrick, Lord Clachonn's right-hand chevalier, straining his voice so as to be heard.

"One at a time," he called, swatting at a bony hand near his waist. "One at a damned time. You'll get your fair share, but not if there isn't some order."

"A fair share of nuthin' ain't sumin' worth waiting for," said a shrunken man at the front of the line. "You give plenty to them dragons, I wager." He screwed up his crinkled face in defiance as Merrick towered over him. She felt desperately sorry for the old man. Even above the stench of the crowds, he reeked of a sewer in high summer.

"It's just words," she said. "Give him his share and let him go."

"Just making sure things don't get out of hand, Princess," Merrick said. He snatched a black loaf out of the hands of the squire tending the sack and shoved it gruffly into the old man's arms. "Go on. Away with you."

The man's eyes popped. "What about 'em coins? I seen others with coins." His voice rose to an indignant screech. "Not even coppers for old veterans and hard workers. You'll be showering gold on the dragons, I wager—"

"Here," Cassandra said, placing his share of three egg-shaped copper coins into his hand. He looked at her, hungry for more. "That's all," she said sternly above the racket of the crowd. She was now very aware of all the extra pairs of eyes following her; well, following her hand back to the bag of coins. Suddenly, all desire for the bread had been momentarily forgotten.

"King Arkus gives all he can spare. Wars are expensive things."

A bold youth spat at Merrick's feet. "Gold enough for this lot's horses and armour."

"Gold and blood to buy dragons back their homes while ours burn," another cried.

"And them is murderers!"

A quick glance around the crowd showed that many had Arkus' latest pamphlets clutched in their fists, distributed to give information regarding today's alms and also to stress caution in regard to dragons. It seemed a prudent enough measure given the events in Aurisha, but rumours had begun to spread. How, she wasn't sure. Perhaps that was why Gellick had been assigned to the less glamorous duty of the camps. Perhaps he'd told the wrong people, those with loose tongues.

A woman at the front of the crowd pushed herself forwards. Her hair was grimy, her cheeks hollow.

"Still got money for some fine silks, don't you? Lovely green shirt, Yer Highness." She reached out a long-nailed hand and missed taking hold of Cassandra's arm by a hair's breadth. Glinting steel sprang between Cassandra and the woman, who shrieked as they grabbed her.

"Don't hurt her," Cassandra ordered, not knowing if her command could even be heard. "Let her go."

Crack.

The gunshot was deafening at close quarters; the sulphuric tang of powder quickly infused the air. Cassandra covered her ears uselessly against the painful ring and turned wildly for the source of the shot. Merrick stood with his pistol raised, a thin trail of smoke billowing from the flint.

"You," he said, pointing to the old man clutching his bread, "move along. Next person forward. Nice and orderly, now,"

The wall of bodies backed away as best they could, budging against those behind them, feet scuffling loudly in the silence that still reigned.

Cassandra watched the old man fight his way back through the throng, biting greedily at his bread and evading groping hands that tried to take it from him. She glanced to her left and right, and saw the masses begin to press forwards again. It was all the chevaliers could do to prevent a full-blown stampede.

For a time, there was a semblance of order, but the memory of the gunshot soon faded. The clamouring swelled anew as the hungry saw those with their baked prizes retreat to feast in private.

Merrick appeared by her side, sweat glistening on his face. He gently took her arm and pulled her back to the relative safety by the coin chests. He looked concerned and unclipped his water flask, handing it to her.

"Are you feeling ill?"

She took the water gratefully. "I'm fine. Just the foul air, I think."

"If you are feeling capable, now would be a good time to slip away." He stepped closer. "The crowd will only grow more desperate as the day wears on, and above all else, I am to ensure your safety. We might wait a little longer but I'd rather not risk it."

Cassandra briefly checked on the other knots of knights. The plan seemed good enough on paper, but she hadn't considered how tightly packed they would be.

"Won't someone notice us leaving?"

"Most of these chevaliers are from the Hinterlands. The queen and Lord Clachonn have gone to great pains to arrange this. Those men are trustworthy, but I cannot speak for the others. If we are to go, I would rather feign you are being taken back to the palace. It's unlikely there will be another opportunity like this. There is a wider space along the base of the outer walls, a channel created unintentionally around the uneven old districts of the city. That was the intended escape route and sticking to that plan should dispel suspicion."

Her thoughts turned again to that girl in rags with her child and she felt a pang of guilt again, but securing a better future would be better in the long run. She had to keep telling herself that.

"Let's get moving then."

Merrick smiled. "Good. I shall set things in motion."

When he returned, his expression was grim, as though he was only now realising the potential repercussions if things went awry.

"Grab the 'special' chest, Julian," he said to a particularly young-looking chevalier who had joined them. Despite his baby-faced youth, Julian quickly unstacked the laden chests with commendable strength and speed, grabbing the smallest one at the back. With this in tow, their small company hastened away, slipping away into the shelter of a dilapidated alehouse the chevaliers had earlier claimed as a base of operations.

The men inside nodded in quiet acknowledgement of Merrick and Cassandra, clearly in on the plan.

Behind the bar, a ladder led down into a basement full of rows of old kegs. Many were leaking, and the smell of stale beer was thick in the air. A group of rats licked at a brown puddle. Merrick led their company to a service entrance at the back of the establishment.

Emerging back into open air, the din of the crowd was still great, even with several walls between them. In the shade of the tavern and the sharp, sheer rise of the black city walls, it was at least far cooler.

With pre-rehearsed precision, Julian set down the chest and unlocked it. Inside were tunics usually worn by the common man. To her surprise, Merrick and his four comrades stripped off their armour, right down to unadorned leggings beneath, and replaced their fine shirts with the plain tunics. The garments were strategically dirtied or torn. To finish the look, they ran their hands through the dirt underfoot, applying it to their nobly clean hair and faces. They even unstrapped their swords, placing them down beside their discarded armour. Julian, who had moved quickest of all, presented Cassandra with a light cloak. She put it on, presuming it was to hide her face. She'd have smeared the street onto herself as well, although whether she'd get the chance to clean herself before seeing Arkus that evening made her pause.

In barely a minute, the chevaliers were unrecognisable.

"Ready?" Merrick asked the group.

"You're leaving your weapons and armour behind?" Cassandra asked.

"Our men in the tavern will collect them," Merrick said. "At any rate, we're not expecting any trouble. But should it come, Julian can handle things with fists alone." He nodded to the young chevalier, who grinned.

It clicked for Cassandra. "You're a dragon, aren't you?"

Julian winked but said nothing.

"Come now," Merrick said. "There isn't a moment to spare if you are to return to the palace when expected."

The chevaliers led Cassandra east, further east in the city than she'd been before. They followed the outer walls until the rim of the basin began to naturally descend to the narrow inlet of the bay. Here, the city barracks brimmed with new inhabitants, for the armies guarding the Southern Dales had returned for retraining. Soon they would be joining their fellows out east.

For now, the roads were quiet; unnervingly quiet after the crush of the Rag Run. In fact, so quiet that Cassandra was worried the size of their company would draw attention from the few souls still out. Cassandra kept her head low and her hood up, staying close to Merrick as he led them on a winding route north towards the White Arch itself. Cassandra marvelled at its size. Its cresting bridge was a high white wave above the water, held aloft by strong chains from four towers that rose like twisting snow-covered mountains upon the banks of the bay. The sun was westward now, casting a deep shadow on the eastern side of the great arch. Merrick took them down into the depths of that shadow, to an old guardhouse at the base of one of the conical towers.

Before the final approach, the dragon, Julian, made a hasty sweep of the vicinity. Only when he returned and curtly nodded did Merrick seem satisfied they had not been followed.

An exchange of knocks was made at the doorway.

A bird cawed above and Cassandra jumped as though a musket had gone off. Perched on the roof was a fierce eagle with white feathers. Cassandra mouthed 'thank you' to Kymethra. It was good of the witch to come.

Merrick ended his tapping and the door swung inwards to a black beyond.

"Inside. Quickly," a gruff voice encouraged. Merrick bade her enter and Cassandra slipped inside ahead of the group.

"Upstairs," the doorman said.

Light from under a doorway flickered at the top of the stairs and low voices filtered through from the other side. Steeling herself and clamping down on her nerves, she pushed on the door and marched confidently inside.

Voices hushed. Heads turned.

"You weren't followed?" Clachonn asked.

"Not to my knowledge, Lord," Merrick said, striding in past her. His men filed in behind him.

Clachonn clicked his tongue. "It was still a great risk."

"Greater than the risk we are taking already?" Cassandra said. She cast around to assess the extent of their activity. Their conspiracy looked a dull affair so far – a lot of papers, ledgers, and long calculations written in small numbers. There were few of them, too. Oranna and her father were the only ones Cassandra recognised. Besides them there was a short-haired huntress, unsurprisingly wearing the blue-green leather of the Hinterlands, the chevaliers who had travelled with Cassandra, and a few nervous looking merchants. Those men were of the higher tier of their trade and wore the purple cloth to prove it. Kymethra would keep watch outside.

The windows were closed, their shutters drawn, and dim lanterns cast pale shadows on every face, while a fusty smell of damp wood lay in the air.

"So," Cassandra finally said, striding forwards and placing her hands on her hips. Her mind betrayed her at the last moment, going blank. "Thank you all for coming."

Clachonn snorted. "I hope you have more to say than that, Princess."

"Well, you know the purpose of our meeting," Cassandra said. "I'll get straight to the point. This charter marks a turning point in the kingdom, one I doubt you wish to sign. If you want to stop Arkus, we'll need to take action. Sooner rather than later."

"It might be too late for that," Clachonn said. "Esselmont has already signed it, of course. Lord Reed has little choice. The lesser lords will fall one by one in time. Somerled will even have received a copy by now. He may hold off, but unless he wants to risk more serious repercussions—"

"It sounds like you've already given in," Cassandra said. "Surely this will only cause more harm in the years to come."

"I agree," Clachonn said through gritted teeth. "Maybe not with Arkus, but one day some royal will overstep the mark with their new power. Yet we are hardly able to take direct action now."

Cassandra looked to Oranna for support.

The queen shrugged. "What do you want us to do, exactly?"

"Gather support," Cassandra urged. "You're in the best place possible to do so. Build a bloc of nobles and powerful merchants," she added, waving to those men at the back of the room. "And fight him in the Assembly Hall."

"You think he'd listen to reason?" Clachonn said.

"I have to hope so," Cassandra said. "He won't listen to me alone. He thinks he's doing the right thing, after all, but if enough of you stand together—"

"When Arkus sets his mind on something, it usually happens," said Clachonn. "I agree something should be done. My own father would turn in his grave if he thought our lands were being handed freely over to the Crown."

One of the merchants spoke up. "Such measures also concern us, Princess. If Arkus has control over which lands he returns to his peers, he will gain unprecedented power over trade routes and borders. He could keep the most profitable avenues for himself."

"It is well that the merchant guilds join the cause," Clachonn said. "Though the old and newer families of the kingdom have locked horns over the years, this is a chance to unite for a change. We'll need them on side if we hope to take control of the capital, even if our chances of doing so in the first place are slim."

"Oh, I don't know." The short-haired huntress finally spoke up, pushing herself off the wall she had been leaning on. "The king intends to sail east as soon as he can. If the bulk of the army goes with him, that makes things possible. And I know of another army in the Highlands that might be called upon. A whole legion of dragons and fairy flyers. If it came to a coup—"

"Absolutely not." Clachonn's tone offered no rebuke. "Using dragons and fairies would look like a foreign takeover, never mind placing Queen Kasselle and King Darnuir in untenable positions."

Cassandra was still in a daze from the huntress's words. The army she described sounded like the task force that Darnuir had sent to aid Ochnic and his people.

"How do you know this?" Cassandra asked.

"Because Garon led that bizarre host of his through my territory on their way north," she said. "Name's Romalla, Princess."

"Captain Romalla was due in Brevia for a gathering at the Master Station," Clachonn explained. "I thought her input would be of value."

"Let's be clear," Oranna began. "We're not planning military action. Are we?"

"No, of course not," Cassandra said. "Why would I? He is my father, after all. I don't want him cast down, just reined in."

Clachonn bit his lip, and Merrick shuffled uneasily.

Both Cassandra and Oranna said together, "What is it?"

Clachonn's eyes darted between his daughter and Cassandra, unsure who to address first. He landed on Cassandra.

"Princess," he began, speaking slowly in his search for the right words, "once we start down a difficult path such as this, I'm afraid there is no telling where it might end. Your father is a stubborn and proud man. Both Boreac and Annandale tried to use their words at first too, I remember. And look where they ended up."

"Then we do nothing," Oranna snapped. "I don't know why I agreed to this meeting in the first place, Cass. It's ludicrous. The father of my son, my own father, you, or countless others could be harmed. This is the exact reason why I want to get away from the city. There's so much bad blood as it is." She looked imploringly at Clachonn. "You agree with me, don't you, Father?"

Clachonn faltered again, licking his lips and fiddling with a button on his waistcoat.

"I'm afraid you both have valid points. Truthfully, I'd rather return home as well, but this charter is an insult, and a dangerous start on a far more slippery slope. While there is no need to envision rash action, we should start to build our alliances and take full advantage of Arkus' absence in the east to create a barrier against him."

Cassandra's heart skipped a beat.

"This does mean we'll have to remain in the capital for some time," Clachonn said.

Her heart soared. He'd said what she'd hoped he'd say. She couldn't help but grin.

"That's such good news," Cassandra blurted out. Oranna's attention turned on her like a bird of prey, eyes narrowing darkly. "I'm so relieved we can agree upon this, Lord Clachonn," she added, trying to recover. She added a little curtsy but Oranna's glare did not abate.

Clachonn, however, was waving his merchant friends over. "Alastair, Owen, I'll need your help in reaching out to the Guild at large. Those with the most to lose will be a good start, and make sure that mountainous glut Tarquill doesn't catch wind of any of this. Merrick." He spun to find his right-hand man. "We'll need to know of any other chevaliers we might rely on. Avoid those with connections to the Golden Crescent. Esselmont's grip there is too firm. Also—"

Oranna seized Cassandra by the arm, pulling her attention away from Clachonn.

"Can we talk privately for a moment?" Her tone implied it was not a question.

Taken aback, Cassandra nodded and allowed Oranna to drag her out to the darkened stairwell, where the fading light of day cast hysterical shadows upon the queen's face. Oranna's hands were shaking and she drew on a small hipflask with a sigh.

"It smells extra strong today," Cassandra said, attempting a friendly tone.

"Oh, spare me, girl. I'll be carrying a bottle before long if you and Father keep driving me to distraction with this madness."

"Nothing bad will come of it," Cassandra said. "If enough people stand opposed to Arkus, he'll have to bend."

"I know fine well why you're doing this," Oranna said. "You've been acting strangely ever since I told you I was planning on leaving the city."

Her stomach knotted in a ball of shame, like a child caught red-handed at some mischief.

"I — I—" She stumbled over her words. It was condemning enough.

"Well, I hope you're happy."

Cass stood her ground. "Do you know what? I am. How awful of me to not want to see you and Thane go. Admit it, you'd have spun out your trip into years."

"If I had, it would have been my right to do so. It's my life. He's my son."

"He's my little brother."

"Half-brother," Oranna corrected. "And don't you think it would have been good for him to see more of the world? Learn of the kingdom? Meet others his own age? No. I imagine you didn't." She looked Cassandra up and down with eyes alight with indignation. "Father was right. Truly, you are Arkus' daughter. You know what you want and you'll make damn sure you get it. Screw the consequences."

Those words cut Cassandra to the bone. The last thing she wanted was Oranna to think less of her.

"Oranna, please—"

"No, I've had enough for one day," she said. Her eyes darted to the window and the darkening world beyond. "You'd better get back for dinner or he'll get suspicious."

"Aren't you coming too?"

"I'll remain with my father this evening, I think. I need to make what few decisions about my life and whereabouts that I still can." And with another swig from her hipflask, Oranna stormed back inside the conspirators' room.

Cassandra stood frozen as all the elation she had felt just minutes ago was sapped away.

Merrick emerged onto the stairs with her, looking sheepish. "The queen has instructed we escort you back to the palace."

She forced a strained smile and nodded. She'd done the right thing. She had to remember that. Even if Oranna hated her right now, she'd thank her in the years ahead when Thane's reign was more secure, more peaceful. She had to keep telling herself that.

"Thank you, Merrick," she said softly. "Let's not delay. Night is already falling."

20

DINNER WITH ARKUS

"Break bread, not bones."

A fairy saying

Cassandra – Oranna's Parlour

It was well after dark when she arrived at the palace. Fresh clothes and a wash of her face wouldn't have gone amiss. Spending half a day in the heat trap of the Rag Run had done her few favours, but time was short. And the door to Oranna's parlour was already open when she arrived.

A candelabra with a white marble base sat at the centre of the dinner table. Arkus and Thane awaited her, dressed in their finest black robes, looking like two dark rain clouds against the rainbow of Oranna's coloured walls.

"Cassandra, you're late," Thane accused in mock anger, beaming all the same. "Come sit next to me."

"Your sister should sit opposite you, Thane, as is custom."

Thane huffed. "Must we sit so neatly? Let Cassandra move her chair, Father, please."

Arkus eyed Cassandra for a moment, taking in her heavy breathing, the sweat across her reddened face, her less than formal attire. A tense second followed.

Cassandra was sure his gaze pierced right to her heart and saw all her secrets laid bare. Then it passed with a chuckle from the king.

"By all means. We can forego formalities amongst ourselves. If Cassandra does not mind?"

"Not at all," Cassandra said, dragging her intended chair around to sit beside Thane.

"Good. And Mother can sit beside you," Thane said.

"I fear Mother will be late as well," Arkus said. He raised his full glass of red and took a measured sip. "Perhaps she is spending the evening with grandpa Clachonn?"

Cassandra's heart thumped painfully. "I'm sorry I'm late," she said in a rush. "There was such a gathering in the Rag Run, it took ages to gain some semblance of order before we could ensure everyone got their equal share. The people, Father, they were frightened and desp—"

Arkus threw up his free hand. "It's no matter. You were performing your duty and you're here now." He set his glass down carefully, pondering for a moment. Then he rose. "I think I shall move as well. I'd like to sit across from my children." He picked up his chair and brought it silently around the table to sit opposite Thane and Cassandra, leaving his plate and cutlery forgotten. Arkus looked upon them with a strange intensity, as though he was seeing them again after a long absence. Then he clasped his hands.

"I'm starving. Who's ready to eat?"

"Meeee," Thane cried.

Cassandra's stomach rumbled now she thought about it. "Me too."

"Well, let's begin. And if the queen doesn't join us until later, all the more food for us." He winked for good measure. "Thane, would you like to do the honours?"

He passed Thane a little brass bell. Thane took it with glee, ringing it with surprising restraint. It echoed like hailstones against a window, and a concealed servant's door opened to reveal two footmen in black velvet waistcoats. They glided in, carrying fat silver dishes and crystal decanters of water. Without instruction or question, they rearranged the plates and cutlery to suit the new arrangement and set their burdens down.

The final piece was a gleaming boat of dark green sauce, the smell of mint rising strongly from it. Yet it was nothing compared to the smells released as the lids of the dishes were raised. Racks of lamb, speared with garlic and dripping in their sweet roasting juices. The second dish was revealed to be piled vegetables, glistening in butter; the third, fresh-baked rosemary bread.

The mix was so intoxicating, it alighted some primal need to feast.

More guilt stabbed at her. Cassandra had spent the morning giving little better than scraps out as royal charity. And this was her reward.

Arkus helped Thane load his plate before piling food onto his own and taking his first bite, all while Cassandra sat in a dilemma.

"Isn't there a shortage of food?"

Arkus slowed in his chewing. "Let's not worry over that tonight. The kingdom won't be doomed because we have one fine meal together."

"But—"

"Cassandra," Arkus said, a low flash of anger in his eye. "Every day I deal with these matters. I had hoped not to hear it tonight as well."

Cassandra withheld her response, forcing a smile before taking some of the lamb. She gave herself a smaller portion in protest.

Arkus finished his mouthful and took another sip of wine. "So, Thane, I've not heard you awake at nights as often lately. You're looking much stronger these days."

"Uh-huh," Thane said, attacking his meat. "Nanny Olive reckons I am growing too. She says I shall need bigger robes soon."

"Indeed," Arkus said. "Well, I shall speak to Ms Olive about it. And while we're at it, maybe we should measure you for your first set of mail as well?" He raised his eyebrows expectantly.

Thane's grin did not disappoint. "Really, Father? Mail and my own swo – swo—" In his excitement he descended into coughs and splutters. Arkus hastened to pour some water and Cassandra passed the goblet to the prince. Thane resurfaced, drank some water, and carried on as though nothing had happened.

"Do you mean it?"

"I do," Arkus said, though his tone was more cautious now. "A light set of mail, mind. Just enough to help build your strength while you train. An hour each day with Gellick, and we'll see how you do. I'll try to come watch you, when I can."

"Will you, truly?" Thane said.

"As much as I can," Arkus said. "I've been an absent father of late. But some things are important. It's necessary to remember who your family are, and to be there for them. Not to let them down."

Cassandra had the painful feeling that Arkus had deliberately looked at her on his final words. She tried to ignore it, returning to her meal, and accidentally scraped her knife loudly against her plate. Thane shuddered at the noise but Arkus didn't flinch. A few seconds seemed to stretch out to an eternity. Then Arkus picked up his knife and fork like nothing was amiss.

Luckily, Thane had much more to say on the topic of his first weapon. Eyes alight with thoughts of swords and armour, he told them all about his hopes and dreams in entering the world of knights and heroes, as he saw it.

"One day, I'll be as tall as Gellick," he said. "One day, I'll hit more marks than Balack. I'll slay all the demons and I'll take the black powder to Kar'drun and blow it up!"

Arkus laughed. "That's not a bad idea, really." Downing the last of his wine, he set the glass down beside his equally cleaned plate. Cassandra still played with her meal. With little food in her, the wine had hit her head and made her nauseous.

Thane yawned. "Is there anything sweet to come?"

"I have arranged for a pear tart," Arkus said.

Thane pouted.

"It's your sister's favourite." He looked to Cassandra, anticipating some reaction from her. She looked up eventually as if from a dream.

"Oh," she said. "Oh, good." It was, sort of. She'd made a big deal over how delicious one had been once. It must have stuck in his mind. Arkus smiled warmly and she knew it was genuine. Despite her strained feelings, despite all the things she wanted to say to him, she didn't have the heart to correct him and wipe that smile away.

"Yuck," Thane said, sticking out his tongue.

"You don't want it?" Arkus said.

"Nope."

Cassandra gave him a gentle poke in the stomach. "I saw you scoffing two slices last time we had it. Don't act up for Father."

Thane gave her a withering look, a fine imitation of his mother to be sure. Cassandra followed up by tickling him. He squirmed, giggled, and clamped his hands upon hers to stop her.

"I just like rhubarb pudding so much better," he said.

Arkus considered it. "Well, as we've had such a nice evening, why not indulge a little more? I'll send word to have it made."

Thane threw his fists triumphantly into the air and a knock came at the door.

Arkus frowned, turning in his chair.

"My will was clear. No disturbances."

The door opened anyway.

Olive stood straight-backed like a soldier between the frame, seemingly unfazed by the king's ire.

"Begging your pardon, my lord, but I've come with Prince Thane's medicine."

Thane's fists fell, and he made another face of disgust.

"Ah, yes," Arkus said. "I'd forgotten the time, I admit. Do come in," he beckoned with an inviting wave.

Now bidden, Olive bustled in with purpose, holding a vial of green-grey liquid and a tablespoon thrust forth like a cudgel.

Thane groaned but accepted the strange liquid with weary resignation. He winced as he swallowed it.

"Good boy," Arkus said. "Olive here can take you down to the kitchens and the chef will make you whatever you like."

Thane's face lit up. "Thank you, Father." He hopped off his chair in excitement and was halfway to the door before he returned to give Cassandra a breathy farewell hug. He hugged Arkus too, and the king kissed him on the head. They all smiled at Thane's cheerfulness, even Olive, yet once the door clicked shut, and Cassandra sat alone with Arkus, those smiles morphed. He pressed his lips together in a thin stern line, while she pursed hers in defiance.

Arkus rapped his fingers on the table in a manner that foreshadowed his temper: pinkie to thumb and back again. He picked up the wine jug, poured what would be his third cup, but proffered it to Cassandra.

"No, thank you."

Arkus accepted this silently, placed the jug down, leaned back, swirled the wine and sighed.

"What have I done now?"

Cassandra didn't answer. She didn't know if she dared speak and risk everyone else.

"I've left you well enough alone," Arkus said. "No more fake engagements, no dangerous assignments. Well, perhaps today was a touch risky, but there were plenty of guards."

Cassandra was at a loss. Did he really think she was upset about that?

"It's not how you treat me, but others."

Arkus' nostrils flared. "Not this again?"

"I can't begin to imagine the strain that ruling has had on you, Father, especially these recent years as Castallan grew more powerful while the dragons and fairies stood and did little. I know they aren't perfect. You must have felt alone against insurmountable odds. It made sense to gather strength, to build high walls, to make new weapons, to try to gain the power you needed to face those threats."

Cassandra couldn't stop herself now. Nor could she quite rationalise it. Seeing Arkus sitting a little slumped, tired, not wearing his crown, which was both a burden and the mask he hid behind, she thought she might reach out to him: the man behind it all. Arkus thumbed the rim of his glass, saying nothing. Yet despite all her reservations, despite all her flickers of fear and wariness, he was the only direct blood relation left to her and she didn't want to see him cast down.

If she could make him listen, then there would be no need for secret plots.

She gulped before pursuing her final course. "Father, let the kingdom know you mean to rule justly. Don't print pamphlets that make people afraid of dragons, but let them know about the troubles we all face. Speak in truths, not half lies. Don't send armed men as knives to the throats of your lords. Don't force them all to sign a charter they'll hate you for. Don't push Oranna away because she isn't your first love—"

"Stop," Arkus said. He spoke softly but it halted Cassandra mid flow, the breath catching in her throat. Arkus stared blankly at the tablecloth, his upper lip curling back on one side, trembling in grief or fury.

"Just stop. You can attack me on whichever front you wish, but don't drag your mother into this. It's not for her that... no. No, that would be a lie." He threw back the contents of his glass, seeming to work himself up to something. He looked his age right now, the grey hair a sign of years rather than dignity.

"Arkus," Cassandra said. "Father. I say these things to... well, I only mean to help you. I —"

"Does Oranna resent me so much?"

Cassandra had walked into dangerous territory now. How far should she go? A moment's hesitation would give it away anyway.

"The last year has been hard on her as well."

"Answer me," Arkus said. "Does she resent me enough that she has you trained to mouth the opinion she herself won't give?"

Cassandra felt cornered now. "She hasn't been happy. But I think you've known that for a long time."

"Hmm," Arkus mused. He poured another glass of red, the remnants of the wine sloshing against the sides of the emptying jug. "Do you know what today is?" he asked. "Of course you wouldn't," he said, not giving her time to answer. "I'll give Oranna the benefit of the doubt and assume she's simply forgotten as well. Today marks the date of your mother's passing." His fingers shook, wine spilling over onto the pristine cloth as he took another drink. "Each and every year since, this day has been cursed for me. A black mood comes over me. This year, I thought I might spend an evening with my family. My whole family," he added. "That means Oranna as well. Yet she spends her time with her father and I cannot begrudge that. Who am I to rob a father of time with his daughter, when I was robbed of mine?"

Cassandra found herself at a loss. Where was this going? And did she want him to take them there, sinking into feelings which had barely surfaced for her yet might drown her if she fell right into them?

"You couldn't even let me have one night free of my burdens?"

"I didn't know," Cassandra said. "I'm sorry if I hurt you. That wasn't my intention."

"D'you know how fragile this is?" His words bore a hint of the wine, but his eyes were as sharp as ever. He cast a hand around the room, then between them. "Not the palace or the power, but us. You, me, Thane and Oranna. It wasn't fair, not fair at all that Thane should be born so frail. Was it so wrong of me to try and strengthen what I could? To protect what little I had scraped back from the world?"

"And now you have it all figured out," Cassandra said. "You've won."

Arkus got to his feet, knocking the table as he rose. "And because of that, I have it all to lose all over again." He raised his glass, but thought better of it as it touched his lips. Carefully, he set it down, withdrew his hand and pressed a fist into the table, knuckles turning white.

Cassandra maintained a steady breath. Now was not the time for sudden outbursts. Arkus was laying himself raw before her. She might steer him in the right direction, but anything too aggressive would put his back up stronger than ever.

"I fear, Father, that in seeking to strengthen yourself you only made enemies you otherwise wouldn't have."

She expected him to deny it, to shout her down, tell her that she didn't understand.

Yet Arkus frowned and nodded. "It might be you're right. I may have gone too far. Though it was only ever in defence of the family I couldn't bear to lose a second time. But," he said, his voice lowering, "I have blamed the dragons also, and not entirely unfairly. For it is their war and their enemy and their failure that brought us to the brink of defeat. Yet I am not so deluded as to not realise that much of that anger comes from frustration, even jealousy. Yes, jealousy," he said, in answer to Cassandra's surprise. "Their king has the unwavering loyalty of his subjects. Always Draconess spoke, and his will was followed. Always Draconess had respect, and love, and never had to employ an ounce of fear, nor more generosity than he saw fit. And I saw his arrogant son, so full of pride it reeked, and I had to accept that one day he would be their king; that Darnuir would inherit that sword and rule effortlessly without a care for those under him or sitting across the table from him. I was jealous of them both. I nursed a quiet hatred. And in my darkest days, I turned to that for some comfort.

"I sought power for myself because I said it would make all of humanity stronger. But it was really for me. All so that I'd have something when everything else had been taken from me. Even now I am jealous of the boy king, for he has all the experience of a child and still his word alone is law. You ask me to give it up, the power I have gathered. Would it sicken you to hear that I do not wish to?"

Cassandra felt sick enough already. What little food she'd eaten wasn't sitting well and she hadn't a clue of how she should proceed.

Something in her made her stand and lean across the table to match Arkus. "It would sadden me greatly, if you became the very thing that your former friends feared."

"Say it."

"Tyrant."

The word cut through the short space between them like a knife in the dark, unseen but piercing.

"Oranna says this?" Arkus said, menace in his eye.

"I say it," Cassandra said. "I say it. Oranna has nothing to do with this. It is I you must satisfy, Father. I say it. Tyrant."

Arkus seemed unbalanced, both in mind and body. His mouth opened in a stunned gape, his hand slipped upon the table and sent the wine glass flying so that the dark red liquid seeped into the cloth and carpet. He slumped back into his chair, hands grasping the armrests.

Cassandra remained standing, leering over him. Her hair framed her face like a black cloak, and her chest rose and fell with short breaths. She'd abandoned caution. Perhaps Arkus would only listen to threats.

"You need to start to make things right. It can be step by step, but you must. If you don't, then one day the kingdom will rise against you again – or Thane, if he is king – and the cycle will run forever on."

"What have you done?"

"Enough to set things in motion."

Arkus collected himself and sat straighter, staring at Cassandra in new wonderment.

"And you're just telling me boldly that you're working against me?"

"You won't hurt me, Father. So listen to what I'm saying."

She braced herself, ready for the fallout of her folly. She'd gotten worked up and had acted too soon. Fear that she'd misjudged Arkus' feelings for her blazed white hot, and an image of a soundless dark cell below the palace flashed before her.

The crystal decanter of water was shaking powerfully. She only now realised it had been her trembling hand upon the table.

Then Arkus barked a laugh. "I don't think I've ever been more proud." He laughed again, almost madly.

Cassandra breathed a little easier. "I said it before. I know you have suffered a lot over the years. But it's all over. Now is the time to make a change."

Arkus reached for the jug of wine and drank straight from it. Some beads ran down his chin as he gulped. When he reappeared, much of the tension had passed from him. He was even smiling.

"Never before have I had an enemy I did not wish to fight." He considered for another long moment. Cassandra tapped her fingers, much like her father. Finally, he met her eye and said, "I'll send word to Jasper to halt production of the Charter. I'll even order them to be recalled."

She heard the words but almost couldn't believe he'd said them. But he had. And something about the way he looked at her left her stunned. She'd never been able to read his eyes before, but now they were wide and open and honest. He really meant it. He really had changed his mind.

"Hopefully, it's not too late," Cassandra said, but in the spirit of conciliation, she hastened to add, "but it's a start." She slumped back down as well, feeling fatigued.

The pair of them were breathing hard, as though a battle had been fought.

Neither had anything else to say.

Another knock came at the butler's door and their heads snapped in unison towards it. The butler entered, nose up, face made of stone, ignoring the mess and the dishevelment of his king and princess. Between his arms he held a tray that he brought to the table. A smell of pastry and caramelised sugar burst forth as the pear tart was revealed. The butler's underling brought the serving slice, the bowls, the spoons, and cleared the remnants of the lamb away. Without a word, they left.

After a time, Arkus stirred. He cut a slice of the tart, slid it into a bowl with a grunt, as though even this small effort was exhausting, and pushed the bowl across the table to Cassandra. He dropped down a spoon beside it with a clatter.

Cassandra blinked. Her fingers felt numb as she picked up the spoon, not really registering the cold metal.

As she began to eat, Arkus cut himself a slice and quietly joined her.

When she had finished, Cassandra reached for another slice. Arkus did the same.

The only sounds were the chink of spoon on bowl, the soft squish of pear being mushed or cut, the crunch and churning of their chewing.

Slice by slice, in charged silence, they ate the entire tart.

21

THE LOYAL SON

"Of the old island kings, it is said that when a storm approached, a true Imar would smile."

From Tiviar's Histories

Grigayne – Dalridia – Hall of Somerled Imar

In his father's hall, Grigayne rubbed his hands together over the central fire. The smell of woodsmoke was a fine companion to the warmth, as was the rich amber glow from racks of whisky lining the walls. The heat, light and smoke were comforting senses of home he'd not known he'd missed. Yet the hall was dull today, the servants keeping their heads low as they went about their tasks. The whole city had been subdued now that he reflected on it, and he'd been escorted in, not by islanders, but by Brevian soldiers.

That had not been so comforting. He'd brushed it aside, however, thinking them to be Arkus' fresh troops who had been sent to the east and were merely stopping in Dalridia along the way. Even as he considered more disturbing possibilities, Somerled emerged from his rooms behind the King's Rock. And he was not alone.

Five Brevian soldiers flanked him. Only their uniforms differed from Arkus' regular footmen. They lacked any mail, or even heavy padding, wearing black coats with white buttons and trim. Propped up on their shoulders were – well, they were the strangest looking weapons that Grigayne had ever seen. At least, he assumed they were weapons, for they seemed like short spears to him with the blade removed – basically clubs, and not a lot of use if so.

The soldiers hung back as Grigayne greeted his father in a strong embrace.

"Ye look knackered, son," Somerled said. His voice was deadened, not its usual high sharp bite. Between the two of them, Grigayne thought his father looked the more haggard. His face was grey, and his hair looked thinner.

"I'm just tired from my journey," Grigayne said. "But why do you look so worn?" He eyed the soldiers suspiciously before continuing. "Listen, I know it is a tough thing to ask, but I return seeking more warriors and supplies to return to Aurisha with. Every man, woman, turnip and flank of mutton you can spare."

Somerled scrunched up his lips, then gestured with an open palm to the long wooden table underneath the King's Rock.

"Let's sit and eat first."

A little puzzled, Grigayne sat. The King's Rock rose sharply above their heads. Lord Somerled often made his speeches while standing upon it, placing his bare feet into the carved footprints like the island kings of old. Somerled continued that tradition, even if the line of Imar had long ceased being royal.

Grigayne checked on the Brevian soldiers. They'd sat down at a long table not so far away, throwing them an occasional glance. He then wondered when his father had last stood upon the King's Rock.

Servants appeared carrying their meal; a heavy black pot of barley broth for two, cold slices of pink beef, hot bread, and soft butter. Grigayne was most thankful for the mug of ale placed before him and drained half of it in one long gulp.

"Missed that, did ye?" Somerled asked.

Grigayne gave a satisfied sigh. "One grows tired of water in prolonged dragon company."

"Aye," Somerled added. He half opened his mouth as if to say more but stuffed in a chunk of bread instead. They ate in silence a little longer. It was most unlike his father and a sense of foreboding grew in Grigayne.

"Mother is safe and well?"

"What? Oh, yer mother? Aye, she's fine – fine and well, o' course. The demons never made it tae West Hearth." He smiled then returned to his broth.

Grigayne glanced again to the soldiers. Each had a mug of ale, sipping it quietly and talking in low voices. They weren't watching him and Somerled now, but their presence was like a bulbous red welt upon the nose.

"Perhaps we should move elsewhere?" Grigayne said. "To a more private setting?"

"Not right now."

Grigayne leaned in. "Father, what is going on here? Who are those men?"

"They are our guests," Somerled said in an equally hushed voice. "Our very *honoured* guests."

"You've never let Brevian troops enter armed into your hall before."

"Times change," said Somerled. "Old things wane and new ways rise. Look at the dragons. They're failing."

"Hardly," Grigayne said. "They'll rebuild in time. And you still haven't answered my question. Why let these soldiers in?"

"What makes ye think they're soldiers?"

"It's clearly weapons they carry. They treat them like our warriors treat their shields and axes. Though what they do I don't know."

"That's a rare glimmer of innocence, that is," Somerled said. "I wish I didnae know what they did."

Grigayne felt the corners of his mouth pull and twitch. Never had he seen his father so cowed, so lifeless. He jumped to his feet, knocking his half-empty ale mug over in the process. His sudden move drew the attention of the soldiers. A couple of them fingered their weapons carefully but did not hasten to rise themselves.

It was Somerled who did that. "Grigayne grieves at the suffering our people have endured in the war. It's eaten right away at his sensibilities, and his *sense*." He turned to stare hard at Grigayne, urging him with his eyes to sit back down.

Grigayne had wanted to shout at the Brevian soldiers, but his father's fear had finally gotten to him. "My father speaks true," he began, faking a teary, half-choked voice. "I find myself on the verge of tears. So much death. So many innocents. I've seen children dead upon the ground, their faces blue and cold—" He found he no longer needed to fake it. He'd seen some horrors over the last year. The body piles outside the town of Errin would haunt him forever. "And I would shed these tears were it not for the strict custom among my people not to show weakness before guests." He spoke imploring now to the soldiers. "Please, might you briefly step outside, so I may release my feelings and maintain my honour as an islander?"

The Brevians rolled their eyes but rose and trooped outside of the hall, disappearing from the whisky light and to the grey world beyond.

Grigayne smirked, delighted. "Do they know so little of us that they believed that?"

Somerled scowled. "Wit' was the need in that?" He sounded far more like his usual self.

"Speak freely, Father. Why do these soldiers frighten you?"

"Because 'av never felt so powerless." Somerled sagged and sat back down. He placed his elbows on the table and planted his head in his hands. He rubbed at his face, then spoke again. "Arkus has informed me that the burden of war on the kingdom has been great."

"On our people most of all," Grigayne said.

"Ach, there's been plenty of devastation everywhere."

"You never saw the war here," Grigayne said. He wanted to say, 'You never saw our people massacred, burned, their homes ruined,' but he held back. It wasn't Somerled's place to witness these things firsthand. He sighed heavily and said, "Sorry, Father. Please go on."

"To begin recuperating the losses of the war and fund reconstruction in the Boreac Mountains, the Cairlav Marshes and the Golden Crescent, there's tae be more tax on produce high in alcohol." He spoke in a mock pompous accent that was quite close to Grigayne's own in truth. The very accent that he'd ensured Grigayne would have.

"Is that all?" Grigayne said.

"Of course not. A bit o' bloody tax I can handle." He growled and closed his eyes, apparently having to dig deep to find some inner strength to carry on. "King Arkus has also proclaimed that the powers o' the kingdom should be brought closer together, tae avoid a repeat of Castallan's rebellion. As such, Arkus has *encouraged* all remaining nobles to sign a Charter of Unity." Somerled's voice was rising to a dangerously high pitch now. "A fine thing in theory to do. Another thing entirely to have us sign it."

"What does it say?" Grigayne asked.

"As a sign of faith in the Kingdom of Brevia, all lords will sacrifice any legal or inherited claim to the lands they possess. Instead, all land of the realm is now under the sole domain of the Crown of Brevia. In practice, we will all receive our lands and entitlements back as gifts. In practice, very little is likely to change. But... but..." Somerled was truly struggling now. Fury and shock were making him shake. Grigayne thought he knew what was coming. Only one thing could have stripped his father of all his former bearing.

"But you would give up all claim of sovereignty over the Splintering Isles," Grigayne said. "Any chance for independence would be—"

"Over."

Grigayne swallowed hard. "Father, have you signed this thing?"

"Aye," Somerled shuddered.

Grigayne bit down on his fist, then thumped it on the table. "It's only words. So, you've signed one piece of parchment. Another can undo it. This doesn't destroy your dream."

"Is it not also your dream?" Somerled said. He looked very intently at Grigayne.

"You know I've been torn on the matter," Grigayne said. "I have thought it a strange battle to be fighting when there were greater problems in the world. But this underhanded ploy does not sit well with me. Not at all." Grigayne felt a hot anger flourish in him like never before. Arkus' document was little better than a back-handed slap, a slight against his father, his family and his people. Arkus overstepped himself. Surely the other lords were just as furious? He was taking advantage of their weak position in the middle of a brutal war.

Grigayne pictured Arkus sitting on a plump cushion, his fingers coming together in a steeple, a smile curling up his face.

"When the war is over, I promise to aid in whatever way I can to undo this. I'll put the voice you have given me to good use in the Assembly. I'm a proud islander, father, and I won't have us treated like Lord Bog of the damned marshes."

"I fear I've taken an irreversible step," Somerled said. "Without a claim, what do we have now? Just desire or will. But how to assert that will?"

Grigayne pondered for a moment, then drew out his smaller axe from his belt and slammed it into the table. It quivered there for a moment, the steel lodged deeply into the wood.

"That's how we can assert our will. The Splinters are far larger than any one region of the rest of the kingdom. We sacked Brevia once before. Our numbers have always been one of our bargaining chips. No king in Brevia has tried to push the boundary of their power here because of it."

"You'd threaten him?"

"I'd make it clear that Brevia would have a hard time taking what it wants by force," Grigayne said. "I've seen their so-called *warriors* in action. Our women would make them wet themselves. Besides, no one would stand for it if Arkus started killing lords who didn't bend the knee to his whims."

Somerled shook his head. "Not anymore. Annandale's been executed. By these new weapons, no less. People are frightened. I'm frightened. Son, I'm afraid we're beat."

"Why? How?"

"The weapons are called muskets and will cut through any shield wall as if it wasnae' there. They're fuelled by that black powder I saw at the Bastion. Arkus must have been developing them for years... all in secret. All fer him."

Grigayne struggled for words. This was indeed troubling news but there was a more pressing problem.

"Our immediate danger still lies in Rectar. To that end, I'd like to take back as many warriors and resources—"

"Naw, that's no happenin'," Somerled said. "That boy king ran off east with his armies right when we needed him most. He did us nae favours leaving that bleedin' guardian behind. You can't have forgotten that?"

"I'll never forget the disaster at Eastguard," Grigayne said. He turned his face to show the scarred tissue where a spectre had gouged at his cheek. "Never, Father. But

Darnuir was not wholly in his right mind at the time; an addiction to magic, I'm told. He's better now and his head seems sewn on correctly this time. He's calmer, more considered. In any case, it is he who will deliver us Rectar's defeat, if such a thing is possible. I would help him do that. It's in all of our interests, after all."

Somerled shook his head more forcefully. "I forbid it. No more islanders will die on account o' dragons. You say Darnuir wasn't in his right mind before? Well, I see that as a good reason not tae trust his judgement, whether he's better now or no. What's to stop that happenin' again? He made demands of us while his mind was addled. No. No more of our blood shall be spent."

"We have thousands of warriors in Aurisha already."

"Then retrieve them."

Grigayne stepped away from the table. Dismayed, he placed his hands behind his head and pulled his elbows in towards his face.

"I cannot do that. I won't have us abandon the fight. That *would* hurt my honour as an islander."

Somerled got back on his feet. "Am I not the Lord of the Isles still? You will heed my orders."

"I thought we weren't lords of anything anymore," Grigayne said bitterly. "Don't let your anger at Arkus lead you to forsake the dragons just because it's the one bit of authority you can cling to. That is true madness. And pettiness. I thought we were above that."

Somerled stepped away from the table too. Grigayne was taller than him, he had been for years, but the look his father gave him made him feel eight years old. Grigayne had touched a nerve.

"Are you still capable of commanding our ships, or do I need to give the honour to an islander more loyal to their lord's will?"

Grigayne snorted, but when he spoke, he restrained himself. "I am quite capable, Father."

"Good. Then you'll scurry back to Aurisha and you'll bring all our warriors and shieldmaidens home. Let the mighty Arkus handle this war on behalf of humanity. We've played our part." Somerled skulked off and did not look back.

Grigayne remained rooted to the spot. What had just happened? His father had lost all backbone. And so quickly. Things were unravelling fast. What careful stability had existed for most of his life was being dismantled in a matter of months. Three islands of the Splinters lay in ruin; the traitor Castallan was dead, Lord Annandale was dead, Brevia was more powerful than ever, and the King of Dragons said he was relying on extra help from him, Grigayne. What could he do?

He could move, for a start. Standing in Somerled's empty hall, in the shadow of the ancient King's Rock, only added to his sense of dismay. He pulled his axe free from the table and marched outside with it still in hand. Perhaps that was why the Brevian soldiers raised their muskets when they saw him.

"You can return to your babysitting," he spat. In a moment of daring, he twirled the axe in his hand, and the soldiers took more exacting aim at him. Staring down a black barrel, Grigayne placed the axe back at his belt and strode past.

Half-drunk on anger and confusion, his feet guided him instinctively through Dalridia. Spring had brought bluebells and daffodils to life on the earthen rooftops of the city, which blurred into a green-blue-yellow haze as he strode over the waterways.

At the eastern gate of Dalridia he stopped to examine the gouges in the wood and the broken sections of the palisade maze; the city's own scars of the war. The sight brought back the vivid memory of lashing rain, fighting on an empty belly, the manic cackling of demons and the cruel white smiles of the spectres. As he thought about the wound he'd received from that spectre with the flaming blue hair, a twinge of pain shot through his shoulder.

It had been Grigayne's own account of the strange behaviour of the spectres that had prompted Darnuir to head east more quickly. Perhaps if he hadn't told Darnuir what had happened, he would have stayed; Eastguard would have been liberated on the first attempt. Instead, Blaine had hastily sailed there simply to prove something to his own men, and the islanders had paid another high price. Grigayne thought on this deeply as he descended the slope towards the beaches.

Maybe his father was right. Maybe their people owed Darnuir nothing more. Yet that was unfair. Dalridia would have fallen were it not for Darnuir landing upon these very beaches and smashing the demon host.

He had made it to the edge of the shoreline now. The tide had retreated, leaving seaweed and stranded jellyfish in its wake. The day was warm enough to start baking this debris of the ocean, filling the air with a distasteful eggy smell.

Before boarding the *Grey Fury*, his family's massive longship, Grigayne scooped up a handful of pebbles and began tossing them into the sea. A well-rounded stone fell into the water with a satisfying plop. With the tide heading out, he'd have plenty of time to stew over his predicament.

He had most of the fleet of the Splintering Isles; more than enough, he had thought, to bring extra men and supplies back to Aurisha. They weren't fully crewed. He'd left as many warriors in Aurisha as he dared while still being able to cross the sea. He supposed it had all been for nothing. He'd return empty-handed to Darnuir; worse, he'd have to tell the king that he was to take his islanders away. The mere thought of it flushed his cheeks with shame.

He respected Darnuir, especially his handling of the murderous Light Bearers. Would he even be considering following his father's orders if he'd accepted Darnuir's invitation to join the Praetorian Guard? He didn't know. He was just grateful not to be trapped in that position.

Another fine splash sounded as the last of his stones hit the water. It didn't have the calming effect that he'd hoped for.

"Ye willnae catch fish like that, lad." Grigayne knew that coarse voice well. He turned to face its source and smiled. Cayn was approaching him with a resilient bearing. Though windburnt and leathery, Cayn still had the energy of a far younger man, if not the nervous nature of someone speaking so openly to his lord. His missing hand prevented him from handling an oar, but his experience of the waters of the Splinters made him invaluable.

"Sumin' troubling ye?"

"As ever, Captain Cayn. As ever." Grigayne huffed, sniffed and regretted it immediately on account of the seaweed, then thought of asking for Cayn's opinion. "Would you ever run from a fight?"

"We ran from Eastguard."

"That's different. We were retreating, not running with the intention of never coming back."

Cayn shrugged. "S'not up to me mostly. I've rowed where a've been told. Fought when a've been told tae fight."

"All right, a different question," said Grigayne. "You're from the island of Baltyre, right? What would you have done if the demons had been poised to attack, but I told you we were pulling out all support. Would you be able to follow through?"

Cayn cocked his head and gave his scalp a good scratch. "Dun't seem like something you'd do, lad. Nae point worrying over something you won't ever do, I say."

Grigayne gave a breathy laugh. "No, I suppose you're right. But sometimes we are forced to do things we otherwise wouldn't, aren't we?" He thought heavily on his father and the disgraceful charter he'd been made to sign.

"Nah, I think that's just excuses," Cayn said. "Gotta live with yerself first and foremost. If ye cannae dae that, there'll be no livin' wae others."

Grigayne wanted to think that was true, yet he suspected his conundrum was so far removed from the trials of daily life it was at odds with sailor wisdom. As he said nothing more, Cayn took the chance to spit onto the still-damp sand.

"So, what's ol' Somerled wanting ye tae dae, then?"

"Something I fear I'll have to do, whether I can live with it or not." He resigned himself. "We'll be heading back to Aurisha tomorrow."

"By which way?" Cayn asked.

Grigayne smiled, bemused. As if there was a choice. He wanted to say, 'East, naturally,' and chide Cayn about losing his senses, but then they could row south between Guffarne and the two Wicks, approach Aurisha from further south than before. They could pick up some food or other supplies that way at least, and by the time Somerled found out it would be too late.

Or – and Grigayne froze at the sudden thought – or, they could go west to Brevia first. His father hadn't said to go immediately to Aurisha. He hadn't specified a way. It was a poor excuse and perverse logic, but it lit a fire in him. Yes, he could take his fleet to Brevia and bring Darnuir back something even more valuable than island warriors.

"West, Captain Cayn. We'll go west."

22

THEY ARE AFRAID

"Fear is really just a fear of death. If I die, I know my gods shall take me in. This I know. So why am I still afraid? Afraid of my king's wroth, afraid of the Shadow returning. I cannot reconcile it, and I cannot let the world know."

Personal writings of the guardian Norbanus

Blaine – The Inner Sanctum

"Step back from that ledge, Chelos."

Chelos turned from the precipice of the veranda and threw him a dark look. "I'm old, not senile." He observed Blaine struggle with the fastenings of his armour for a while before making his way back inside.

"Don't," Blaine said. "I can manage."

"It doesn't seem that way."

"I've lost a pinkie, not a thumb."

Chelos sighed heavily and paused by the balcony's opening. Guilt hit Blaine for his snappy remark. Helping Blaine with his amour gave Chelos some extra purpose, so he feigned losing his grip on the knot.

"Damn," he said. "But it does make matters more aggravating. Could you lend a hand?"

Chelos smiled, a brief tug at the corners of his mouth. If he suspected what Blaine had done, he didn't show it.

"You seem in better spirits today."

"We've languished for too long. Training will do us all a world of good."

Chelos twisted the straps into an expert knot in seconds. "The men have been restless. Better they get their blood moving before it turns to sludge in their legs." He bustled off to clear away the foamy remnants of Blaine's morning shave.

"Why don't you come watch?" Blaine said. "Even pick up a sword yourself if you feel up to it."

"Hah," Chelos barked, his back still turned. "A year ago, I'd have done anything to hold a sword by your side again. Had more energy back then, too. Trained Cassandra as best I could, mind, but after what that wizard did to me…"

"I understan—"

"And old age and whatnot," Chelos said, not hearing Blaine. He began to tidy away the razor blades laid out by the basin. When he reached the silver razor with the blue pearl handle, he paused to admire it.

"D'you know, I've only just realised who this must be from."

"I'll thank you not to mention her name," Blaine said.

"I considered throwing it away not long ago. You never use it anymore." Chelos' tone was musing but something in his eye suggested a knowing that Blaine did not appreciate.

Blaine picked the silver razor from Chelos' fingers. "I'll thank you not to do that either." He spent a foolish second lingering upon her gift, feeling his insides turn to stone. Not without effort, he tossed it to join the others with a clank and clatter. Blaine pinched between his eyes then drifted back over to the veranda for some fresh air.

"You would do well to forget her," Chelos called after him.

"Excuse me?"

"You heard me fine. That blade keeps your ears healthy."

Blaine turned, slowly. "What do you think gives you the right to say it, though?"

"The right of a friend, or so you call me," Chelos said. He pursed his lips, resisting further words. Then the dam broke. "Do you know why those dragons acted as they did?"

"I sense I am about to be told."

"Because you did not act. Even after the Nail Head, you did not act. Draconess at least had reasons for shutting down; lingering here and managing a kingdom under siege for all those years. But you… you just had a broken heart."

"How dare you," Blaine said, pointing an accusatory finger. "You've never gone through it. You haven't felt loss like that – you don't understand."

"And why is that? Because I've spent my entire life serving the pair of you."

Chelos' voice wavered with well repressed resentment. He almost said more but cut himself short, pressing his lips shut and rubbing his shaking hands together.

Blaine's own anger cooled at seeing this. Chelos had served loyally his whole life and Blaine had rarely stopped to give that a second thought.

"You have sacrificed everything," Blaine said. "It was callous of me to suggest otherwise. I am sorry too that you have not had the chance to live a... well, a normal life."

There were tears in the old man's eyes. "I did it all to serve our faith, and our people. I did it willingly and I'd do it again." He began to break down. "Forgive me, Blaine?"

Blaine rushed to him and pulled him into a firm embrace. How long had Chelos been suppressing these feelings?

"There is nothing to forgive," Blaine said. "You aren't wrong. I let myself wallow for too long. I should have done better by everyone, but you as well." Chelos sniffed and hugged him back. For a moment they held, then Blaine stepped back, kept an arm around Chelos' shoulders and walked him outside to the air and view.

"I was so relieved when I heard you lived. I thought you'd died along with Draconess. Had I known that the wizard had you prisoner, I might have—" But it wouldn't do to make claims he wouldn't have fulfilled. "I might have slept easier during those first years after Aurisha's fall."

They made it to the veranda's edge and Chelos placed a frail hand upon the railing. Together they drank in the view, listening to the gulls in the bay far below, enjoying the gentle heat of the spring sun.

At last, Chelos spoke. "After all this time, it finally feels like we've come to the end of a very long journey."

"Things are far from done."

"A matter of time," said Chelos. "With both you and Darnuir working together, we'll pull through. I'm only saddened that Draconess isn't standing with us."

"Me too," Blaine said. A great weight suddenly formed at his waist, the memories in the white jewels of the Guardian's Blade reminding him of all that had occurred.

"It was his dream for so long," Chelos said. "To see you back here."

Blaine bit his lip then pressed against the top white gem, popping it out into his hand. It dragged his arm down, buckling his knee as he fought against its weight. Beautiful, sparkling light hid the horrors within the opal. Blaine's terror. His nightmares, captured and made everlasting. He handed the gem to Chelos.

"Oh, my," Chelos said, bringing his free hand up to support it.

"I've hidden most of my pain inside it," Blaine said. "There are some memories of Draconess, and you as well, in your youth. Most of them are from the night when Rectar attacked—" He stopped himself. It would always be a hard thing to speak of;

the night when their enemy had murdered his daughter, beat Blaine half to death, and set everything that had happened since in motion.

With an unspoken look of knowing, Chelos told him it was okay. He understood after all.

"But there are some earlier memories too," Blaine said. "Happier ones. Those that I couldn't let dissolve away with time. You're free to delve in, if you want."

"I might just do that," Chelos said. He beamed at Blaine, the strain on his face unearthing new wrinkles.

"Time I got moving," Blaine said. "I'll see you in the evening for pray—" No. No, he wouldn't. They'd forgone formal worship for weeks now and absolutely nothing had happened. No signs. And no voices.

Blaine believed. He'd believe until his dying day after what he'd seen and heard. But after so many of his Light Bearers, and Bacchus, had been sent away in exile, he hadn't the heart to continue the façade. For that was what he thought it now.

The gods were real.

That was certain.

And they would know of his faith, with or without ceremony.

"I'll see you in the evening," he said to Chelos, leaving the sanctum to meet Darnuir along with the remnant of his Light Bearers.

The soldiers of the Three Races had already gathered on the plains outside Aurisha by the time Blaine arrived. For many, it was the first time they had left the city boundaries in weeks, maybe months. They stretched their legs and entered strange new formations. Darnuir had worked tirelessly with Fidelm and the human officers to devise strategies for mixed units and the drills to practice them.

Blaine walked wide-eyed through gathered troops, watching as human, fairy and dragon learned to move together.

It wasn't easy.

There were accidents, collisions, but spirits were high. Activity and fresh purpose were wondrous things.

Blaine watched one formation, which seemed to have a better grasp of their orders. Dragons stood in a wedge at the front. Behind them were humans carrying their long spears, with three clear channels leading through their ranks to archers at the back. The archers were in two groups, one group carrying short composite bows near the spearmen, while longbowmen stood considerably further back.

A legionary legate marched to the head of the formation, the plume of his helmet flapping in the wind. He inspected the dragons at the front, then bellowed, "Begin."

The dragons raised their shields with trained alacrity, fending off imaginary foes while the longbowmen nocked invisible arrows, pretending to aim high. Blaine supposed they didn't have the spare arrows to practice for real. The dragons feigned a fight for a time then stepped back carefully before breaking rank and bolting down the three channels in the human lines. Spears fell forwards at this, presenting a steel fence to the pretend foes, and the humans closed into tight-packed ranks as the dragons retreated. Those archers with composite bows, more impactful at short range, pretended to nock and loose arrows, while the dragons, still running, came bursting out from the sides of the spearmen to attack any enemies that may have slipped down the formation's flanks.

It could use refinement, but Blaine thought it a bold starting point.

At the head of the training grounds, he saw Darnuir. The king was gesturing animatedly to Fidelm as the young Praetorians trained in swordplay with the largest and most brutal fairy warriors; wingless fairies who had packed on muscle to compensate.

Blaine approached with the remainder of his Light Bearers and suffered a grim look from Fidelm. Such was the general's stare that Darnuir turned to see what was causing it. Blaine had an inkling why Fidelm scorned him so; he'd suspected this for a very long time, and knew that he'd have to have it out with the fairy. Perhaps not here on the plains, in front of all their men. Fidelm made the decision for them both and took flight before Blaine could reach him.

Darnuir watched Fidelm fly away, a vexed look creasing his face. "Will you two sort out your issues?"

"He isn't able to feel angry at his queen, so I get it all."

Darnuir flicked his gaze from the sky to Blaine, his eyes piercing. "Is it true what he says? That Kasselle cannot have more children."

"Is this really the time to discuss it?" Blaine said. A pain seared in his chest and he felt sick at the thought of it. "It can't be changed. It can't be fixed."

"No, not now," said Darnuir. He nodded towards the new formations at their drill. "What do you think?"

Blaine frowned. "I think it's impressive. It may need refining but I can see what you're trying to do."

Darnuir raised an eyebrow. "Which is?"

"Slow the enemy down or pin them in place as best you can while arrows are showered upon them. Useful, if the enemy has superior strength."

"You believe me about these enhanced dragons, then?"

Blaine shrugged. "I'm opening my mind to the idea of them. Best to devise some countermeasures either way. If all we end up facing are regular demons and spectres, then we can go back to what we know."

"The spectres are done," Darnuir said. "Rectar may have killed them all. Dukoona wanted our help in killing him and I doubt he got off lightly for that. No, I'm sure we face a deadlier enemy. I just wish I knew more. How much stronger will they be?

Castallan made humans to be our equal. If a similar increase in strength is possible…" He trailed off. "Well, it might not matter what tactics we try."

"Yet try we must," said Blaine. "What of the fairies? I don't see them involved in these formations."

"We haven't factored their ground forces in yet," Darnuir said. "But I have managed to convince Fidelm to experiment with flying our best marksmen around the battlefield." He turned and pointed.

"What the—" Blaine's shock left him speechless. Fairy flyers were hovering in the air, carrying hunters on their backs like pack mules.

"They can't fly as fast like this, of course," Darnuir said. "I'm hoping enough of them working in unison will help to punch a hole through the enemy, shore up weak points, or cover a retreat. Unless Rectar has also made these dragons of his fly, they likely won't have a countermeasure."

A cry of victory split the air, coming from the duelling Praetorians and fairies. Blaine looked over to find Lira standing over four yielding fairies, their weapons thrown out of reach. The fairies were panting; Lira breathed more easily, though her brow glistened with sweat. She grinned and said something that Blaine could not hear. The Praetorians laughed. The fairies were sporting and laughed too as they clambered to their feet.

"You did well keeping her close," Blaine said.

"I don't deserve such a loyal prefect," Darnuir said without taking his eyes off Lira and the fairies. "And she deserved far better treatment than you gave her."

"She did."

Two of the fairies grasped Lira, trying to pin her arms in place. She fought them, her face turning purple from the strain, then lunged forwards, throwing the fairies onto their backs. More appreciative laughter and clapping erupted from the onlookers.

Blaine inspected his own Light Bearers. They stood silent. Unmoving. A little lifeless, truth be told. With them, Blaine had nothing like the brotherhood Darnuir and Lira had with their own men.

Inspiration came to him.

"You know, as the soldiers are beginning to work together more cohesively, perhaps it is no longer… necessary… for us to have separate guards." He'd not intended to sound so sheepish, but he couldn't stand the thought of asking directly. It would be too close to admitting yet another failure, and he'd had plenty of that already.

"Blaine, are you suggesting that we combine our elite forces?"

"I am," Blaine said, if a little stiffly.

Darnuir smirked. "I'm all for it. But it won't be me you'll have to convince." He nodded towards Lira, engaged once more in wild fighting with the fairies.

Blaine swallowed what remained of his pride. "So be it," he said and made his way over. "Prefect Lira," he called over the clangour of steel. She didn't stop and instead knocked a fairy to the ground with a thrust of her forearm. "Prefect Lira," Blaine called again, "A moment of your time, if you'll indulge me?" Still Lira fought, not giving any sign that she'd even heard him. The Praetorians nearby watched nervously, their eyes darting between Lira and himself.

"Prefect Lira," Blaine called again, louder still. "I'm sorry."

Lira stopped dead where she'd parried a blow, a screech of metal ringing.

"I'm sorry for all of it," Blaine said. "Every missed council, every cold remark, every belittling look and every prejudiced thought an old dragon like me has ever held. As for that night... there is only one thing I regret more than that in my long life."

Lira drove her sword into the earth and turned. "And what could you possibly regret more?"

Blaine's answer sprang from his lips before he'd considered it. "Sending another in my stead to war eighty years ago; the dragon who became Rectar."

The world turned still.

Dragon and fairy alike gawked or gasped.

Blaine found he didn't care what they thought. He even felt a little liberated by it. It was gratifying to know he could still have that effect on people, even if their stunned silence was not brought on by admiration.

Lira, however, was different. She did not drop her jaw like a fool nor inhale sharply. She approached Blaine slowly, as though to either kiss him or slit his throat.

"Is that the truth?"

"A shortened version of a very long tale, but yes. It is the truth."

"That must have taken a lot of courage to admit so openly."

"Half a lifetime's worth."

Lira extended her hand. "Let's put it behind us," she said. Blaine shook her hand. She squeezed firmly, though not as aggressively as he'd expected.

"I have something to ask you."

Lira blinked. "Looking for favours already?"

"I feel it's high time we abandoned the barriers between the Light Bearers and the Praetorian Guard." He looked around, trying to gauge the reaction from the Praetorians nearby. "Darnuir and I have vowed to work together, with no further pettiness. I'd like it if my older dragons could train with the young. I'd like us to learn from you, and perhaps we too can offer something in return."

Lira shuffled her feet then widened her stance, hand on her sword. "Would we need a new name for a new guard?"

"That can be for you to decide," Blaine said. "Although, as I am taking Darnuir's lead now in matters, it makes sense if we are all his men. All Praetorians."

Finally, she smiled. "I like that idea." She walked a few paces then doubled back. "I wouldn't have fought Darnuir on it, if he'd wanted it. You know that, right?" She saved him the trouble of answering. "How about a sparring match? No magic. See how you fare?"

Darnuir arrived by Blaine's side at those words. "I'm afraid the pleasure of duelling Blaine belongs to me. We're here to train, after all. And we with the blades only have each other to test ourselves against."

"Suit yourself," Lira said. She returned to the four fairies, drawing her sword.

Blaine felt pre-fight nerves tingle in his muscles and joints. A duel would do him good.

"The last time we clashed blades, Brackendon had to break us apart."

"I'd like to think we have more control than that now," Darnuir said. He unsheathed the Dragon's Blade, its hilt shining like fresh blood under the sun.

"Agreed," said Blaine. He drew the Guardian's Blade. Light rippled off the opals like cresting waves on a golden sea.

And so they duelled.

Not the bitter clashes they had fought before or to test who was the stronger, but to teach one another. Neither the master, neither the student. They started slow, some basic steps, a few flourishes. A little more, a little harder. Slowly building, until Blaine felt his pulse struggle to keep pace with the swing of his arms, the twists of his torso, the drive of his legs.

Through unspoken words they tested each other, pushed each other. To the onlookers their fight must have seemed a blur, and yet Blaine could not shake a feeling at the back of his mind.

We're both weaker than before.

Phantom pain burned from his lost finger. His grip felt lax. He'd feared this, had spent weeks coaxing his left hand to work as well as his right, but being in the moment of that weakness was mortifying. Surely Darnuir was aware. His blows weren't hitting with the force the boy was capable of. He was giving Blaine a chance. A kindness the Darnuir of old would not have granted, but one which Blaine could not reasonably allow.

Blaine noticed other telling signs. Darnuir was not ridding his mouth of the bitter taste of magic nor forcibly gulping it down in painful lumps. His sword arm was steady as a master archer's – too steady for one drawing on the Cascade.

Blaine opened the door in his mind further and power billowed into his body, taking his pain away, dispelling his tiredness, rushing through shoulder to hand to blade in a wonderful burn. Darnuir's movements became sluggish by comparison. Blaine outstepped him and struck Darnuir with the flat of his sword. There was a crack like exploding black powder and Darnuir landed some thirty feet away, leaving a gouged trail of earth in his wake.

The king lay still.

Blaine closed the door and walked to Darnuir's side. "You're not using magic."

Darnuir sat up with a groan. "I am. You just... caught me off guard."

"I thought we were being honest with each other," Blaine said, helping Darnuir get to his feet.

"I'm not lying. I was drawing on the Cascade. How else would I be keeping up with you?"

"Were you drawing on as much as you could?"

"As much as I felt was necessary."

"And when we fight Rectar, how much will be necessary then?"

Darnuir massaged the back of his neck, stealing a moment in which he did not need to answer.

"We cannot hold back," Blaine said.

"How's your grip?"

Blaine twitched his remaining fingers. "It's as strong as I can make it."

"And will that be enough?" Darnuir said. They exchanged a hard, knowing look. "You haven't tried switching hands."

Blaine huffed, then tossed the Guardian's Blade between hands, catching it in his left.

"You're right. I'll try my untrained hand and you won't hold back on me – agreed?"

Darnuir nodded, not meeting Blaine's eye.

They trained again, only this time Blaine cursed himself for not maintaining his off-hand training. He drew on increasing volumes of Cascade energy to fuel his inexpert muscles, while Darnuir rained punishment down upon him.

Blaine widened the doorway in his mind until a torrent of energy poured freely, too much to maintain for long. And still he could barely match Darnuir. A sinking feeling took hold of him, even in the midst of battle. No matter what he did, how much power he drew upon, it would not be enough.

Blaine fought until the taste of bile on his tongue grew unbearable, until chewing sawdust would have been refreshing to his parched mouth. Bellowing from the effort, he blocked Darnuir's sweeping blow, dropped to his knees, and drove the Guardian's Blade into the soil.

"I yield," he said. His left arm quivered violently from the poison welling up in it. Desperately, he gripped the hilt of his blade, the veins on his hand and wrist swelling from the magic in them.

Darnuir spat the residue from his own mouth, though he looked far from worn.

"Why aren't you pushing yourself further?" Blaine gasped.

"You don't train someone by beating them senseless," Darnuir said. "If we're going to get your off hand up to scratch, I can't go all out."

Blaine was still on his knees, breathing hard. "We might not have the time for that."

"Then we train," Darnuir said. He too knelt to Blaine's level. "We train every morning, and every night. Every moment we can spare. Until you're able to beat me as soundly as you did back in Val'tarra."

"I doubt I'll ever manage that again."

"Aim high, Grandfather," Darnuir said. "Now get up. People are beginning to stare."

His arm still shaking, Blaine rose. "Don't hold back either. Not even one bit. Rectar won't."

"Blaine, what part of training do you—"

"Don't use me as an excuse. You're holding back because you don't want to draw on magic. It's understandable, but you need to move past it."

Darnuir suddenly became very interested in his fingernails. He looked at them, picked at them, and admired them at different angles. Blaine grasped him by the shoulder, weak hand and all.

"You cannot let what happened drag you down. I mean it when I say Rectar does not hold back. I fought him, remember? I fought him and it damned near killed me just keeping up."

But Darnuir, for all he'd aged of late, briefly became a boy again. His mouth hung ajar, his shoulders hunched and the king's whole presence seemed to shrink away, no longer filling the great armour he wore.

"I'm afraid."

"Don't be," was all Blaine thought to say. What more could he say? That he was afraid as well? Terrified even to face this God of the Shadow again, so much so that a part of him didn't even wish to go on.

Darnuir's arm began to shake. "It's not as simple as that. I broke, Blaine, or I came as close as anyone has ever come to that abyss without falling over it."

"I can only imagine it," Blaine began. "But this isn't the time for—"

"You can't imagine this," Darnuir said. He shrugged Blaine off and staggered backwards. "I am afraid," he wailed. "I clung on to my sanity by a thread. I heard voices, I suffered waking nightmares; all day, every day. I couldn't tell reality from dream. I woke up as a bag of bones in a sack of skin. All of that because I couldn't control the Cascade. All because I didn't listen to the warnings you gave me, that Brackendon gave me. I liked how good it felt. I overindulged. And it can never happen again." He ended on a hoarse note, staring blankly off, as though the wicked horrors from his fever-dreams had spawned into the world.

"I'm afraid, Blaine."

Blaine couldn't help but notice the guard members staring at them now. As before, he found he didn't care.

Let them look, he thought. *Let them see we are flesh and blood like them. Let them see we can suffer as they do.*

"I'm afraid," Blaine said, and he said it loudly. He said it again, louder this time, letting his voice carry to all the Praetorian Guard. "I am afraid." Saying it was a relief. Saying it broke shackles on his spirit that he never knew chained him. "I am the Guardian of Tenalp, and I am afraid!"

He knew that the last one would carry far, as far as the mixed groups of training soldiers of all the Three Races, who were all here at last, together, in a way no one from Blaine's generation had ever dreamed.

Darnuir was laughing. A nervous laugh, a touch high, but a laugh nonetheless, and it came with a grin.

"All right, I believe you. But it doesn't change the fact that we're both terrified."

"I have little left to be hopeful for," Blaine said. "Being honest, we might not stand a chance, even together. Yet I feel much better facing Him again knowing you'll be there with me."

Darnuir nodded. "Me too, old man." He drew the Dragon's Blade in one fluid motion and spun it playfully around in his hand. "We'd better make ourselves ready, though we may not have much time."

Blaine too twirled the Guardian's Blade, trying out his maimed hand and then his left. It would take a lot more work yet.

"One day, one month or one year. We'll do what we can, while we can."

Darnuir widened his stance, bent his knees. "We'll train."

23

THE DISILLUSIONED HERO

"Surely it could have been avoided? Yet such questions are moot now. Only for those who care to speculate. Or for the guilty who survived it."

Author Unknown

Balack – Brevia – Dragon Refugee Camps

Balack rubbed at his eyes and stifled a yawn. It had been another long day in the camps, for human and dragon alike. Rain drizzled, dampening the world and their spirits.

For Balack, the constant vigilance against the crowds was the real strain. Handling a mob would be hard enough, but these were dragons. Women, children, their oldest men and the wounded, yet dragons nonetheless. At least Arkus' musketmen helped to keep order. All were fearful of these new weapons.

He stood upon a command deck constructed at the heart of the camps, a semi-fortified area raised above the ruined mud fields below. Here, the hunters and chevaliers could keep watch and organise the dispersion of rations.

He swept his eyes over the remaining meagre supplies. There wasn't much left. Not enough to feed those still waiting today. These were mostly the older men, wrinkled and grim, veterans of a life of war but either their age or wounds had finally caught up with them. They always let the children go first, then the women. And so, they were often the ones left starving.

Balack considered that most dangerous of all.

Old warriors who knew how to use a sword and work together. Might be they had their old equipment still. With sunken eyes and cheeks, they stood as still as statues. They were quiet too, in a way that the less seasoned young hunters of Brevia found foreboding.

Balack eyed one young hunter now, clad in the black leather of the city though he looked barely over the age of joining. The lad still had some growing to do, and his eyes shifted nervously over the assembled dragons, his jaw clenched.

"You feeling all right there?" Balack asked.

The boy blinked and nodded. "Fine, sir." He clenched his fist, crunching up one of those Tarquill flyers in his fist.

Balack studied the hate in the boy's eyes. "Sure about that? It's been a tough day. You've worked hard. Why don't you head home?"

That only seemed to make the boy worse. "Don't want to go home."

"Why's that?"

"Mam's too scared and angry. It's... it's better to go home near the end of the day when she's too tired to be anxious. Don't know what to do when she's upset."

Balack hadn't failed to notice the pistol at the boy's hip. Training properly with a bow took too long, so they'd shoved one of these into his hands. Neither did he fail to notice that the kid was thumbing the butt of the gun, not taking his eyes off the dragons.

"They aren't going to hurt you, lad."

"Really?" The boy was shaking now. "You've got to have heard what happened in their city. Out east."

"Yeah, I heard," said Balack. The rumours and whispers were everywhere. "But you shouldn't take hearsay for fact. We don't know the details."

"They say the Fifth Regiment was hit hardest," the boy rambled on, not paying attention to Balack. "Me brother was in that company."

Some of the dragons had noticed the boy's fixated stare, a few holding his eyes in some wordless challenge. Balack spun the lad to face him instead.

"Only thing you know about your brother for sure is he's out east. That's all." The boy nodded. "What's your name?"

"Mikle."

"All right, Mikle. Listen to me. Really listen now. Hey." He snapped his fingers. "I know what's it's like to wait on news you're dreading. Each moment you go from joy to terror as you turn it in over in your mind. But you can't—"

"Lord Balack," a crisp voice cut him off. Gellick. He'd appeared on the other side of the platform's rail, mounted atop his great white stallion. He called him 'Lord' in public, though he wasn't officially titled yet, and Gellick always said it with a hint of derision. "The southern and western quadrants have been patrolled and supplies distributed. With your leave, I'll take my companies back to barracks."

Balack considered this. Gellick needed his permission in theory since Arkus had made him the de facto head of camp relief. Again, he imagined Gellick only did it when other people were in earshot.

Balack straightened and adjusted his bow upon his back. "You have my leave. Return to your company and bring them this way to give Mikle here a lift back to the city." He regarded the boy, sizing him up again. He still looked jittery and on edge. Best to keep him close. "In the meantime, you can help me with the handouts." He thumped Mikle on the arm. "And drop that flyer. Don't think you want the dragons reading that."

Down below, in the quagmire of mud that rose past their calves in places, Balack passed soft apples and heels of bread to leathery dragon hands. Mostly the dragons grunted. A show of thanks might have made them less intimidating, but Balack couldn't blame them for their bitterness either.

The latest dragon was aggrieved enough to say something. "Used to be full loaves, enough for three days," he said, looking discouraged by his portion of stale bread.

"Times are tough for all," Balack said.

The old dragon looked him up and down and curled his lip. Balack kept his face resolute, knowing full well that his healthy skin, fine clothes and clean hair made his words sound hollow. He thought of the smells of the palace kitchens and knew his words *were* hollow.

"My mam didn't eat yesterday," Mikle said, his voice quavering a little. "Gave all the food to me. We aren't feastin' either."

Balack placed a hand on the boy's shoulder again but spoke to the dragon. "If I had more to give you, I would. Please move along and let the next man through."

The dragon narrowed his eyes and stood his ground.

A comrade of his stepped up. "Least you and your mother have a roof, child. Care to languish out under the stars, in the rain and the muck and the cold?"

"Leave the lad alone," Balack said. He tried to push Mikle back behind him, but the boy resisted.

"I ain't afraid of yous," Mickle said. He slipped under Balack's arm.

"Mickle. Get back."

But the boy didn't listen. He stood before the dragons, and what had possessed him to try and defy them Balack couldn't say.

The dragons began to laugh. Not cruelly, but they evidently found him quite amusing. A few more gathered in about Mickle, finding a bit of light entertainment in their dreary lives.

"What yous laughing at?"

"You, child. You're a funny little human with a high squeak." The dragon glanced from side to side and seemed to notice what Balack had just realised himself – that he and Mickle were now hemmed in against the platform. Other hunters and chevaliers were a way off, dealing with their own queues.

Balack's heart beat faster, his tongue went dry. He'd let this kid and his own tiredness throw him off. He should never have allowed them to become separated from the larger group.

The dragon smirked. "Go on, child, hand us more of what's in that sack."

Balack took a bold step forward. "Only one portion each. You know the ru—"

"I don't want just one portion," said the dragon. The creases on his forehead made one large frown. "I fancy a little more today."

Balack's heart skipped too many beats. A sharp pain gripped his chest and for a moment he could barely breathe. Perhaps it would be better to let them have it, just this once. In future, he'd make sure to bring even more hunters to—

"You heard the Hero," Mikle said, his voice reaching a whole new pitch. "One. Portion. Each."

The dragons all laughed again. More pressed in, tightening the ensnarement. One sharp-nosed, gaunt-faced dragon even looked to Mikle with hungry eyes.

"Bet you'd taste good, child."

Balack moved in front of Mikle. "You can have it all and fight amongst yourselves to share it. All I ask is that you part and let us pass."

They did not part.

One began sniffing the air. "Afraid, are we, human? The air smells like honey."

"Oh, gods," another dragon said, "don't mention honey."

"Nice bit of honey on bread."

"With cheese."

"And some meat," said the sharp-nosed dragon. He flashed teeth that looked too pointed, a wild gleam in his eye. "Haven't had a bit meat in ages, have we?"

He took a step forward.

The first dragon, the eldest, blocked him. "Calm yourself. You're not some animal." The advancing dragon brought his pointed teeth together in a clapping bite. An argument ensued.

Balack hadn't realised he'd moved until his back hit the underside of the platform. He looked for the boy. Mikle had frozen near the sack of food.

"Come here," Balack whispered fiercely.

The arguing dragons came to blows, the elder with the apple turning the fruit to pulp on the other's face. Friends of the victim jumped forth, and friends of the instigator followed.

A smaller dragon, a youngster just like Mikle, all skin and bone, darted out from the brawl, his eyes on the food sack.

Balack watched as though in slow motion as Mikle brought out his pistol with shaking hands. He yelled something, but the young dragon carried on.

Mikle pulled the trigger.

The shot silenced all noise and sent a ringing through Balack's ears.

The younger dragon lay spread-eagled on the ground, blood mixing with muddy water.

"That's for my brother," Mikle cried. He turned the pistol towards the rest of the dragons. "Back off. Back off now—" But the dragons were leaping towards him. The boy was lost and more shots fired wildly.

Knowing he had only moments, Balack spun around and jumped, grasping onto the rough, wooden support beams of the platform, splinters digging into his skin. He began to climb.

A final shot from below, then screaming. It ended with the sound of tearing flesh, cracking bones, the great pop of a joint ripped from a socket.

Balack felt bile rise in his throat, and it was all he could do not to retch.

He wasn't out of danger.

Not by a long shot.

With a yell of exertion, he heaved himself over the last portion of the wall and onto the platform, rolling on his back across it, seeing the sky above whirl into dark wood and back again.

Bows twanged. Guns fired.

Voices bellowed. Death screams dominated.

"You all right, sir?" a huntress said, helping him upright.

"Dranus' arse, no, I'm not fine," Balack said. "None of us are fine." All around he saw dragons running, storming towards their position at the centre of the camp. Most of them were too busy fighting amongst themselves for the remaining food, but some were making straight for the hunters or chevaliers left on the ground.

Battle had come, and instinct brought his bow into one hand and three arrows into the other. He nocked one, drew, found a target. The torn arm of Mikle arced up and over the writhing dragons, with red tears in the muscle. Nothing Balack did could convince himself that those weren't bite marks.

He hesitated, unable to loose his arrow. It was all too much. Too sudden.

"Sir?" The huntress looked for orders.

He was meant to be the Hero of the Bastion. What kind of hero was he now?

Hooves beat into the slush, thundering above all else. Gellick was approaching from the south, riding at the head of his company, sword drawn.

"For Brevia!" he cried before slamming into the knot of dragons. Scores of pistols cracked. Horses whinnied angrily. Swords screeched from scabbards and thunked wetly into the surprised, unarmoured dragons.

Yet the horror was spreading fast.

In every direction, dragons were stirring, and given a chance, they'd have cleaved through the humans, cavalry or no. Even those who were left after the impact of the horses pulled some of the knights from their mounts, tossing them like rag dolls before a blade or musketball could end their rampage.

Balack lowered his bow, running to the stairs. "Back now," he called at the top of his lungs. "Back to the city."

"Balack," Gellick shouted, cutting his way through. "Get on."

Balack scrambled atop the horse, holding the chevalier around the waist. He saw other chevaliers make room for passengers, even though the fighting was drawing close in around them.

"Ride now! To the city," Gellick bellowed. A horn blasted from behind and with a lurch they were off, charging up the mud tracks towards the main gates.

Balack knew he was in some form of shock. His mind inexorably turned to those humans still out there in the camps, those who would not make it to the walls before the bloodlust had spread.

Long, cumbersome wagon trails clogged the road leading to the gates, which had been left wide open.

"Abandon your carts," Gellick cried as they rode past. "To the gate. Flee to the gate." All the chevaliers took up the call of retreat and flight without explanation. Balack only hoped that nobody would tarry.

As the company rode through the gate, hooves clopping onto firm stones, there came a moment of relief.

Balack swung himself down, fighting to keep control of his breath as the full horror began to reveal itself to him.

With the gate half blocked by lumbering wagons, they couldn't shut it quickly. And if they couldn't bar entrance to the city—

A distant roaring rent the air – thousands of howling, snarling beasts. No, not beasts. It was the dragons, only he had never heard them sound less human.

Gellick looked stricken. "Not even in my worst dreams did I truly fear this."

Balack rounded on him. "Maybe you ought to have—" He wanted to say more but caught himself. Now was not the time. "Back to your barracks with you. We'll need every mounted chevalier you have."

Gellick nodded, turning his steed northwards. "Company, heed the orders of the Hero. I shall return." He galloped off as the roaring from the camps grew louder.

Balack craned his neck to try and spot the deck of the gatehouse guards. A pudgy-faced man was looking fearfully down at him.

"What are you waiting for?" Balack yelled. "Ring the fucking alarms. Every bell and trumpet. We need the garrison. And start closing the damned gate. Chevaliers, bring your horses. We need these carts moved."

The perilous process began, though not as hastily as need demanded.

"Make a corridor first for those fleeing," Balack said. With a route freed of obstacles, streams of hunters, soldiers and some remaining chevaliers crossed the threshold of the city. Most bent over double, panting, or vomiting against the base of the city walls.

"Don't just stand there. Move. Let others through or help clear the way."

He pulled back and tried to form some semblance of defence upon the road: upturned wagons forming hasty palisades, for all the good they would do. Something twigged in his mind and he turned towards the Rag Run, the closest populated area to the gates.

"Get the civilians out," he commanded a group of young hunters who were shaking half to death. "Get them out, further east or across the river if you can."

One side of the looming doors had shut fully, but the other was only halfway there, a stream of humans still desperately trying to make it in before the storm hit. The roaring grew louder with each passing second. Through the gap left in the closing gate, just over the downward dip of the road, Balack saw the dragons moving like the rush of a swollen river.

The gap in the gateway narrowed, but he feared the dragons would close the distance first.

And even as that gap shrunk to a sliver, as the humans on the other side screamed at being trapped beyond, Balack saw the dragons charge up behind them, running the stragglers down like bulls trampling upon grass.

The cruellest part was that the gate had very nearly closed when the dragons threw their weight against it. Gears creaked, groaned and the gap began to widen. The dragons' starvation and weakness were Balack's only source of hope to make it through this.

He nocked an arrow, glancing at the hunters and soldiers by his side, who were all too few.

Bells rang loud and hard across the city.

Hands emerged from behind the slowly closing gate, gouging into the wood.

Balack found the strength to let his arrow fly this time. A true shot. Its head buried into one of those distant hands. Each shaft he sent felt like a betrayal, and yet everything had changed in mere minutes. All the world was crashing down.

With a deafening crack the gate was at last pushed inwards, the hinges breaking. The dragons were in. There was something almost demonic about the way they swarmed forwards.

A hundred pitiful defenders raised muskets and bows, while a cannonball thudded down a long barrel.

Balack swallowed his last hope. "Fire!"

24

GARDENS OF BLOOD

"After the islanders sacked the city, people found it hard to return to the shores. They called it the Bay of Blood, where the worst killings occurred."

From Tiviar's Histories

Cassandra – The Palace – Brackendon's Chambers

Bells rang.

Kymethra furrowed her brow and darted to the window, cracking it open. The clanging grew louder, emanating from all around the city. Footsteps scurried on the floor above. Panicked voices called from the hallway and the grounds outside. Cassandra's mind raced. A city-wide alarm meant an attack.

"But it can't be demons," she said, as though working it through aloud. "We'd have heard. There's no way—"

A series of distant cracks rang, a light yet unmistakable patter of musketfire.

Kymethra unlatched the window fully and threw it wide open. "I'll go see what's happening." She jumped outside, morphed into her eagle form and swooped over the trimmed hedges of the palace gardens before veering out of sight.

Cold sweat gathered on Cassandra's neck and palms. Her first instinct was to find Oranna and Thane. Her sword was a total afterthought.

Wailing snapped her back to reality. Brackendon had woken up, his hands clasped tightly over his ears against the pitched bells, his face screwed up. She ran to the window, intending to close it. Then she thought of Kymethra. The witch would need it open to enter again should Cassandra leave before she returned. Yet the ringing only intensified and Brackendon sobbed harder. Pity welled up in Cassandra. She left the window open and was by his side in a heartbeat, trying to take his hand.

"Naaoooooo." Brackendon batted her away. Snot bubbled from his nose, pooling with saliva at the corner of his mouth.

"Brackendon, Brackendon," Cassandra said in a panic, unsure what she should do to help him; if she could even help him.

He opened his eyes. The silver irises remained pure as ever, yet the whites were bloodshot – if blood were black, that was. Brackendon stared at her, trying to work out this face before him.

"I don't – I don't—" he began before descending into incoherent babbling.

He didn't recognise her. Cassandra felt crushed by that. They hadn't been close, but she'd have liked them to be. She had hoped to sit with him for hours, as they'd done in that cart speeding to Val'tarra, letting him fill the many gaps in her knowledge or spar with him over which writer had argued best. That would never be now.

Brackendon entered a fresh spasm. He flailed with his hands, struggling to decide where he should place them.

"Here," Cassandra said, falling to her knees by his pillows and closing her own hands over his ears. "That better?"

He quietened down, gripping his bony chest in one spot and then the next. Then he settled. The bells were still clanging, so Cassandra took extra care in adjusting her position, so as not to lift her hands away. With some wriggling, she managed to sit upright, leaning her back against the headboard, and allowed Brackendon to loll his head into her lap. With one hand, she kept his left ear protected, and with her free hand she lightly patted his remaining white tufts of hair as though he were a sick kitten.

It seemed demeaning to treat him so, but his whimpers slowly lessened. So she kept it up, all the while keeping her own ears pricked for any sign of —

A blast sounded, short but powerful, its echo long and deep. A cannon. That had to be cannon fire. Brevia was under attack, but from whom? Where?

Brackendon moaned again.

"It's okay," Cassandra said. "It's okay. Whatever it is won't get us here."

The wizard craned his neck to look at her, staring up with inquisitive eyes. A silver sparkle twinkled within them and for a moment he looked every bit the man he'd been: calm but fierce when pressed, wise but not a preacher, softly spoken yet passionate in his words.

The twinkle died, and he closed his eyes, breathing lightly.

Cassandra didn't move. She didn't want to risk waking Brackendon and, in any case, she was afraid. The gunshots became more frequent and louder. The fighting was drawing closer to the palace itself. Demons couldn't move that quickly. Which meant only one thing.

The dragons were attacking them.

And they were heading right for Arkus.

There came a tap at the window and the hinge creaked as Kymethra returned, morphing back to herself in the space of a breath. Her look confirmed Cassandra's fears.

"Why?" Cassandra croaked.

"No clue," Kymethra said. She looked shaken, staring off into the middle distance. "The Rag Run is on fire. The city gates are broken. Dragons are pouring into the southern city. Cass—" she said, as though only just noticing another person in the room. "They're coming for the palace."

"What can we do? Inside the palace is surely safer than outside it."

Kymethra didn't answer. She was looking at Brackendon. "What happened?"

"He didn't like the bells – he was in pain, I wasn't sure what to do so I—" She was rambling, trying not to listen to the crack and patter outside the window. She thought she could even smell the gunpowder now, but that could have been her imagination pulling a cruel trick.

"It seems to have worked," Kymethra said. She joined Cassandra, sitting on the other side of Brackendon. Cassandra let go, passing him over as though he were a baby, and he winced as the bells briefly refilled his ears. Kymethra positioned three fingers above his ear and he calmed while she groaned from the effort.

"I'd go out and help in some way, if I could. But I can't risk him losing control."

Cassandra rolled off the bed. "I should go. Arkus will want us all togeth—"

Steel screeched and men cried from the very corridor outside their room. Soldiers hurried in one direction while heavier, faster footsteps pounded further down the hall. Musket balls zipped by the open doorway as Cassandra scrambled to slam it shut. She locked it out of instinct and backed away, scanning for anything she might use as a weapon.

Perhaps the dragons would simply pass on without trying to enter, or the soldiers would push them back.

The heavy footsteps drew closer and closer, until, almost right outside the door, they crashed into whatever lay in their path. Fresh screams, breaking bones and squelching sounds mixed into one horrible note.

The proximity of the violence upset Brackendon more than the bells. He thrashed, knocking Kymethra's elbow up into her own face. Then he got to his knees upon the bed, swaying and mewling.

"What's that?" someone growled from outside.

"In there."

The dragons didn't even try the handle.

Cassandra dove out of the way as the door came hurtling inwards, kicked with the brute force of two tall dragons; older men by the looks of them, but with a maddened glint in their eyes. Their feet and legs were caked in mud, their torsos in blood. Sticky, dark gore dripped from the hands of one of them.

Brackendon pointed and howled.

"What's this?" one asked, stepping inside. Several others followed him. They sized up Cassandra, a small woman; Kymethra, another small woman; and Brackendon, a crazy old man, and shrugged. Not a threat in their eyes.

"Any food?" the dragon barked.

"Awayyyyy," Brackendon said, pointing a long finger at the dragon.

"Shut up, old man."

Another dragon bounded forwards, the one with blood on his hands. "Snapping his neck should do that." He took a stride forwards before a comrade stopped him.

"Leave it be. There's been enough killing. We came for food."

The bloodied dragon snorted. "We've found none so far. And it doesn't help that the air stinks with their fear." He scanned the room again, his eyes landing upon Cassandra. "Wait. I recognise that one. That's their little princess."

The older dragon looked to Cassandra with widened eyes. "Are you sure?"

"Yeah. Take her."

Cassandra scrabbled to her feet, but the dragons were on her quickly. She shrieked and kicked to no avail, but managed to sink her teeth into the arm of one of the dragons, biting hard enough to break the sweaty skin and taste warm blood.

The dragon yelped, dropping her. But Brackendon yelled loudest of all.

"Gooooo. Leeeave." He faced a palm towards the bloodied dragon, sending him hurtling against the wall. There was a snap and the dragon's neck bent at an angle.

Enraged, the remaining dragons started towards Brackendon.

"Stop," Cassandra screamed. "Leave him. I'll come with you. Just leave them."

The older dragon nodded to this. "Let the old man be, boys." He glanced to the dragon with the broken neck. "That one had gone savage. Better he got a quick death."

With that, he took Cassandra by the arm and manhandled her out of the room. Bodies were strewn up and down the corridor, humans and dragons both. The humans had fared worse. Where the dragons had neat bullet wounds or cuts, the humans had been torn apart, smashed with sheer force, bone and flesh pounded into the black carpet which now oozed blood with every step they took.

"Naaaooooooo," Brackendon cried behind them and an invisible force blocked the dragons' path.

Cassandra turned to look back up the corridor, as best she could in her captor's embrace, and found Brackendon standing outside his room, legs wide apart, his quivering arms outstretched. Kymethra sprang from the doorway, trying to pull him back inside, but whatever magic he wielded kept her at arm's reach.

The dragons growled, but the look on Brackendon's face made them hesitate. His eyes had turned pure silver with thin black slits, and the skin on his face withdrew closer to his bones, casting his features into menacing shadows. His hair was all on end and his robes billowed behind him, though there was no wind to speak of.

"Leave her," he said in a cruel voice which was not his own.

The hands on Cassandra's arms released their grip. She stumbled forwards, trying not to look Brackendon directly in his terrifying eyes.

"She's the only thing that will get us out of here," a dragon said.

The part of the hallway between the dragons and the wizard began to shake. Paintings fell from the wall, their heavy frames cracking on the floor.

"C'mon," the lead dragon grunted. "We'll take our chances."

"No. She's all we've got." Another hand caught Cassandra's wrist, and then the sound of more running footsteps came from behind.

"Get back," the lead dragon called. "All of you, get back—" But his voice was lost in the roaring of the new arrivals. This lot sounded as bestial as the one Brackendon had killed. Did he even know he'd done it?

Cassandra reckoned there was no conscious thought in him right now. He was all instinct and wrapped magic. When he saw the new dragons running up the hall, his face darkened further and every crease and fold deepened into blue-black hollows.

"Leeeaave!"

The walls shook harder than ever. Dust, chips of stone and then whole fragments of the ceiling began to break away. Cassandra raised her arms desperately as a whole sofa crashed down, its spongy innards spewing forth from a tear in the lining. Humans and dragons both tumbled from the floors above, shrieking as they fell.

Cassandra tried to make a dash for Brackendon, for beyond him all was normal. Yet the floor was already splitting beneath her. In a last bid for survival, Cassandra leapt, her hands outstretched, fingers craning for the last solid edge.

She missed.

Screaming, arms flapping wildly, she fell. A sloping piece of a broken hallway rushed to meet her. She hit it hard, then rolled, thudding off debris and people as the destruction plunged into the depths of the palace.

Another deafening bang pierced her ears.

Her world shook, blood pounded in her head, and her whole body exploded in pain.

With a sudden slam her descent ended, and her world went dark. What part of her that could still think panicked that she'd gone blind. Dust clogged her throat and she began coughing, fighting for breath. That fight brought her back onto her hands and knees, and her vision refocused with each convulsion. She winced as the agony from her shoulder finally filtered through. Her left arm hung limp, numbed of all feeling, and warm blood trickled down to her fingers.

She didn't know how far she'd fallen. She closed her eyes, counting out thirty painful seconds to adjust her vision, even as her heart hammered at thrice that rate. Forcing herself to breathe deeply, she reopened them.

There had been lanterns on the walls. Some lay broken on the floor, wax creeping forth to join the dust and blood. Others were still intact, but their candles were extinguished. No natural light came from windows, but it definitely wasn't the dungeons. A smell of roasted meats, chicken and pork, grew in the air. Brackendon had sent them crashing down as far as the kitchens.

A great sloping slab of stone made a barrier between herself and anything behind. In her vicinity lay the bodies of those who'd fallen with her, humans and dragons. Most were still, either dead or out cold. Some were stirring, but just as slowly as she was. If she moved fast, she might get away.

Pushing herself up, wobbling like an infant taking their first steps, she began stumbling through the gloom, fighting against a dizziness that threatened to overwhelm her.

Following the smells, it wasn't long before she came upon a crowd of aproned kitchen staff. Some held cleavers and vegetable knives in trembling hands, terror in their eyes.

"Princess," a few exclaimed when they saw her and dashed to her aid. She welcomed their supporting hands, taking the weight off her own battered body.

"Thank you," she said hoarsely.

"What will we do?" a girl moaned. "Two royals down here now."

"Two?" Cassandra said, still dazed. She searched around.

"Cassandra, you're hurt." Little arms suddenly wrapped around her waist.

"Thane?" Cassandra's heart burst into a series of rapid, fearful beats. Thane was here. He was still here. He shouldn't have been. He should have been up north with his mother, far away. Not here. It was because of her that he wasn't safe. She shook her head, trying to clear it.

"Why are you down here?"

"No reason," he said sheepishly.

"Little prince wanted his favourite treat," a young cook said. "Been coming down quite a bit lately, haven't you?"

"Yes," Thane admitted.

"That doesn't matter now," she said. "The dragons are looking for food. They're bound to end up here eventually, we have to—" But even as she said it, the sound of a skirmish on the stairs reached them.

Cassandra seized Thane's hand. "Come on." She dragged him into the kitchens. "We have to get out."

In her current state, the goods entrance at the back of the kitchens felt like a league away. Roaring fires made the air stiflingly hot. Sweat clung to her face. Thane panted as he struggled to keep up. Coughing and spluttering, he worked his legs furiously. She didn't dare slow down.

At the doors, she let go of his hand to turn the handle.

It was locked.

"Who has a key?" She rounded on the staff, who were all in various states of breathlessness. Those closest looked confused, then their jaws dropped in horror.

"The chevaliers will have barred it as part of the lockdown. Must have done it when the bells started."

"Bloody chevaliers," Cassandra fumed. She stomped and kicked at the door, only to receive a throbbing foot for her efforts.

"Where will we go?" Thane asked.

"I don't know," she said. She felt defeated.

Gunshots sounded from the other side of the door.

"The fighting has reached the palace gardens, so the chance of escape out there may be little better than waiting in here," Cassandra admitted

Dragons began entering the kitchens at the far end then, sniffing and drooling like wild animals, throwing themselves upon any piece of food they could find.

"Group together," Cassandra said. "Stay packed in here and don't provoke them." At least if they stood together they would look like less appealing targets for the furious dragons.

Yet the dragons were too preoccupied with looting to care. Many were fighting each other now, beating one another senseless over access to vats of soup or doughy, half-baked bread. One dragon seized a chicken still burning hot on its spit from the fire and tore into it, oblivious to the searing heat.

Despite the carnage, Cassandra's plan seemed to be working. Some dragons drew close but avoided their large group. The chefs, pot boys and washer girls threw out any food within reach, sending the dragons running like dogs chasing sticks.

Cassandra pushed to the back of the human crowd and pulled Thane close. She caught him wiping a fearful tear from his eye, though he was fighting to keep a straight face, trying to be brave.

"What will happen?" he asked.

Cassandra leaned in close to his ear. "We'll be okay. The dragons will leave when they've eaten. We'll be okay." She hugged him closer and kissed him on his soft cheek. She wasn't entirely convinced by her own words, but what else could she tell him?

Her injured arm felt cold now. She tried to twitch a finger, but they wouldn't obey her. She inspected the cut. Dark blood bubbled from it, staining her clothes and dripping down her arm. Feeling dizzy again, she swayed where she stood. Only then did someone have the sense to tend to her, tying a cloth into a tight knot above her wound.

It didn't take long for the dragons to pick the kitchens clean. A few sat with swollen stomachs and satisfied grins. Others still fought for the last morsels when some new arrivals stormed into the already crowded space.

Brevian troops cut their way inside. Chevaliers, normally so composed, looked livid and fearsome, having fought the most brutal battle of their lives. Their steel had dents now and was no longer pristine. All were covered in blood. And there was no mercy in their eyes.

The dragons sensed this too. Perhaps they smelled no fear on the soldiers, or perhaps they read the signs as well, but most of them chose to run instead of fight. They shoved past Cassandra's group, tossing aside those in their way, and kicked at the locked doors. After a few concentrated blows the doors gave way and the dragons fled.

Yet not all the dragons went so easily. Some had the notion to grab the kitchen staff as human shields. The cooks nearest Cassandra were carried off like trophies, slung over the shoulders of two grey-haired dragons.

Then two younger dragons, a boy and a girl, appeared above Cassandra and Thane. Hand in hand, the pair looked to each other, a silent conversation passing between their eyes. It took Cassandra a second to register their intent.

"You'll be quicker without us," she pleaded.

The young couple looked over their shoulders, to the chevaliers with death in their eyes. They bent down and dragged Thane and Cassandra up.

"We're sorry," the girl said as her companion picked Thane up. He kicked and screamed and tried to fight, but it was no good and he sent himself into a fit of coughs, enough to turn his face beetroot red. Cassandra didn't resist. She didn't have the energy. She let the girl guide her with one overly strong arm to the door and they emerged into the open air.

Away from the heat of the kitchens, Cassandra felt a little better. But it seemed they had entered a battlefield.

Dragons ran, clashing with soldiers or trying to escape from the palace grounds with no sense of order. The sky had grown dark, threatening heavier rain. Gunsmoke rose in thin, tall clouds all around and crows circled above, cawing with delight.

The young dragons moved quickly, following the edge of the palace walls for some time before the net of Brevian soldiers began to ensnare them. It seemed to happen quite suddenly. One moment they were running, half-dragged across the palace grounds, the next they were slowing, caught up in a knot of fleeing dragons, and then they stopped entirely.

Younger dragons threw their hands up or prostrated themselves. Older ones looked resigned, closing their eyes as though they were ready to embrace death. Whoever commanded the troops had some sense about them, calling out not to fire for they had hostages.

Negotiations began, but Cassandra couldn't hear all that was said. Her captor was shaking and, despite her obvious strength, seemed unable to hold onto Cassandra any longer. Her mate's chest rose and fell heavily, and he put Thane down, trusting he wouldn't move. Thane remained where he was, as fearful as the rest of them.

Cassandra felt very weak now. With her good hand, she searched for Thane's, as much for her own comfort as his. When her finger brushed the back of his hand, he pulled back in alarm.

"Thane," she whispered. He looked up at Cassandra, his eyes still wet from fright, but he was smiling at her. Cassandra felt a rush of warmth for him. He was such a brave little boy. He shouldn't have been here. This time he placed his hand in hers and squeezed it tight. She squeezed back and made sure he was looking her in the eye when she said, "I love you, Thane. We'll be okay."

She realised that was the first time she'd ever said that to anyone. Not even to Chelos, at least not since she was a little girl. She'd always thought it went without saying. Well, that had been short-sighted of her. She'd been a stubborn, spoilt fool. She should have said it every day to the old dragon. Now she may never have the chance again.

"All right," barked the chevalier heading proceedings. "No sudden movements. Hand over the hostages slowly, one by one, and you can leave, one by one. Nice and fucking orderly now. Any sudden movements and you'll get a bullet in your back."

The process began. One by one, the human hostages were sent walking over to the soldiers and the dragons were allowed on their way. All of them were sick of killing for today. A kitchen girl near Cassandra kept glancing back at her as she walked to the safety of the Brevian line. Cassandra saw her beg the chevalier to speak to her. Then as they spoke, she kept pointing back to Cassandra and Thane. The chevalier's whole body snapped to face them, his eyes popping.

"Those two," he called, pointing their way. "They are to come to the front. Now."

Dragons and hostages called out in confusion. "What?"

"Why?"

"I was next."

The chevalier primed his pistol. "Do as I say and do it quietly. You beasts are lucky that we've made terms at all. Now, bring them to the front and we can continue as we were. One at a time, starting with the boy."

The young dragon holding Thane turned. "Celia, you go first. Take my place."

"No – I won't go withou—"

"Go," he said. The boy had a sense that Thane was important enough to warrant some demands of his own. "Celia and her human go first," he called to the chevalier.

The chevalier's cheek twitched as he weighed up the situation. "Very well, very well. Come here." He beckoned to Cassandra, though his eyes remained on Thane.

Cassandra found herself shoved forwards. She made it halfway then stopped, wanting to turn and make Thane go first, but her head felt so light she could barely stand. She swayed again. Her arm was so cold.

"Princess, please come," the chevalier said.

The young female dragon was gone but her partner still had a hand on Thane's shoulder. The prince wasn't crying anymore. He stood with his chest puffed out. Cassandra wanted him to come with her, but the world started to spin. She fell to the grass.

High above, there came a sound of smashing glass.

A dragon landed with a wet thud on the damp earth, took one look around him, and made a break for it. Seeing a chance to run, other dragons made a mad dash for freedom too, some still carrying their prisoners.

The boy with Thane remained rooted to the spot.

Muskets cracked all around.

The chevalier bellowed for them to cease.

But it was too late.

It took a moment for Cassandra to realise what had happened.

The dragons lay dead. Every single one. A small knoll of bodies and amongst them must have been—

"Thane," she whispered to herself. A fresh energy rose in her, blasting away her fatigue. She scrambled along the ground towards the slaughter. "Thane," she screamed. She'd never screamed so hard in all her life.

Sound vanished but she could still feel her throat working, her body straining as she cried out all the air in her lungs and all the grief in her heart.

She found him before anyone else got near. His eyes were still open, his little mouth agape. Cassandra wiped at her face and noticed her hands were covered in blood: Thane's blood.

The sky above finally broke, drenching her and washing some of the gore away. Cassandra threw back her head, her streaming tears lost within the falling rain.

25

THE TORN SON

"Let your heart shine as bright as your steel. Always do what is right."

From *Nobles & Their Steeds: A Chevalier's Compendium*

Raymond – The Bay of Brevia

Raymond steadied himself against the wall of his cabin. He closed his eyes and breathed slowly, trying to fight back the nausea. The voyage had been turbulent. Spring was not entering the world quietly. Raymond had never stepped on board a ship until he had sailed to Dalridia with Darnuir. He'd now sailed three times in half a year and was thoroughly sure that he was not bred for a life at sea.

There came a knock at the door. "We're entering the Bay of Brevia now."

Raymond sighed. *Thank goodness for that.*

"One moment, Harra," Raymond said. He gulped, staving off the feeling of bringing his breakfast back up, before carefully making his way to the door.

Harra awaited him on the other side. A full head shorter than Raymond, she appeared slight even in her Praetorian armour. Her blond hair was tied up in a small bun and her youthful eyes looked him up and down.

"Shall I fetch the bucket?"

"No need," he said. Yet even as he waved her off, he felt a nauseous bubble rise from his stomach and placed a precautionary hand over his mouth.

"I'll get a bucket," Harra said. She started to climb the stairs leading to the top deck.

Raymond cursed himself. Must he always appear weak to his fellow Praetorians?

"Please, I'm really quite all right."

Harra paused midway up the flight and faced him with a knowing smile. "I won't tell Prefect Lira, if that's what worries you?"

Raymond's stomach clenched at this, his sickness replaced by chagrin. "My only worries are for the mission at hand."

Harra shook her head and carried on up the stairs. Not that he could blame her. He wouldn't have believed him either.

Following Harra, he emerged onto the open top deck. It was a cool morning with a bracing breeze, and their ship had just entered the Bay of Brevia. It was the busiest port in the world, yet no other ships sailed its waters today. Moreover, the city felt eerie and still. Even the water barely moved. A grey sky hung low, and Brevia's buildings rose like tombstones towards the city's enveloping black walls.

Raymond followed Harra to the bow of the ship, where Camen was looking out to the southern bank of the city. He was frowning, his mouth pressed into the thinnest of lines.

"What's the matter?" Raymond asked.

"I do not recall the southern districts of the city being blackened before. Those look like scorch marks."

Worried, Raymond looked to the south. Camen was right. The older districts of the city had suffered some terrible fire. The areas most affected were those closest to the Master Station and, worst of all, the Rag Run itself.

"It does not seem dry enough for a fire to burn so wildly through the streets," Harra said.

"No, it does not," said Raymond. A chill ran through him. "Let's focus on our mission. We can enquire as to what happened in due course."

The lack of activity began to prove a problem for the ship's captain and helmsman as they debated which dock they ought to make for. Eventually, the man in the crow's nest reported torches being waved ahead and they assumed this was to be their destination. As the crew brought the ship into position, Raymond saw that a large welcoming party was assembling.

Black-clad hunters multiplied in number, until over thirty of them stood in wait. Raymond's sense of foreboding deepened. Darnuir might have messaged ahead to Arkus to inform him that Raymond was being sent to the city, but Arkus could surely have no way of knowing the exact time of his arrival, or the vessel for that matter. And would so many hunters be necessary to greet them?

When at last the gangway was lowered, Raymond informed the captain that he would deal with the hunters and walked with confidence from the ship, flanked by Harra and Camen. He reminded himself that he had nothing to fear: he was a human, a former chevalier. His family were of the highest tier of merchants. This was merely Arkus' way of making a show of strength.

Ten of the hunters stepped forward to meet him; men and women armed with a full quiver, two knives and a sword. Each also bore a strange-looking instrument that Raymond was not familiar with: a wooden tube with a curved handle hanging at their hips. Leading the group was a hunter with auburn hair who Raymond thought he recognised, yet couldn't quite place. The black eye didn't make it any easier. His leathers were white and grey, so he was of the Boreacs, but what had he just been through? Were those rips made by a hand or a claw? Now he looked at the hunters more closely, Raymond saw they all bore signs of a recent struggle; small wounds, a hardened look in their eyes.

"A chevalier amongst dragons," the lead hunter said. "You must be Raymond."

"Raymond of House Tarquill, at your service. Though you seem to have me at a loss," he added, stepping forward with a hand outstretched.

The hunter eyed his hand but did not take it. "I do not believe we ever formally met. I'm Balack. Just Balack."

"What has happened here?" Raymond asked, but the looks the hunters were giving Harra and Camen gave him an idea.

"Best avoid that topic," Balack said. "Why are you here?"

"Did Darnuir send word of our coming?"

"Not that I am aware of."

Raymond glanced over towards the heavily armed men and women. "Quite the welcoming party nonetheless."

"Let's hope they remain welcoming," Balack said. He sighed, then hung his head. "We're all a bit on edge. And exhausted. Please don't make this take longer than it needs to. Why are you here, Raymond?"

"Darnuir has sent me to speak to the Lords' Assembly on his behalf. Specifically, to—" He paused, unsure how much he should say in front of random hunters. Did they know of events in Aurisha?

"To what?" Balack encouraged.

"To open up more direct communication with the Assembly, and to escort two Brevian regiments home as a sign of good faith in our alliance." He felt that being vague yet positive was best in the current atmosphere.

"And two whole regiments fit onto that one ship, do they?" Balack said.

"The rest of our flotilla is anchored out to sea. At your leave, my ship will return to them and signal they may enter the bay."

The hunters fidgeted restlessly at this, some gripping their weapons. Balack turned sharply around, indicating they stand down.

"He said human regiments. Calm yourselves and learn some sense. Darnuir has not sent legions to attack the city, nor would he ever give such an order." He rounded on Raymond. "You may come ashore, Raymond, but I'm afraid your companions cannot."

"And why is that?" Harra asked.

"A matter best discussed quietly," Balack said. "Away from loaded pistols," he added, casting a wary glance to the hunters he led.

Camen, ever stern, said, "We come on behalf of our king. To deny us is to deny him." He pushed past Raymond and was immediately met with a dozen drawn weapons.

Balack raised a hand. "Stop. Don't move another inch or I will be forced to let them kill you. Dragons are no longer welcome in Brevia, I'm afraid."

"And why's that?" Camen snarled.

"Because the day before yesterday, the dragons encamped outside the city rioted. We're still counting the dead. They even attacked the palace itself. The place is on lockdown and the black flag of mourning flies. It is rumoured a member of the royal family was harmed." He spoke these last words with some difficulty.

Raymond's mouth went dry. "What? How?"

"Poor judgement, worse decisions, hearts inflamed by false words and stomachs left empty for far too long," Balack said. "The fault lies on both sides as far as I'm concerned, but I'm afraid there can be no dragons in the city. Praetorians included."

"The issue of the refugees is why we are here," Raymond said. "If you will allow us to entreat with—" He choked on his own breath. A terrible smell forced itself upon him with the change of the wind. A fierce breeze from the south brought a ripe foulness, of death, of burnt flesh and wood. Raymond pulled out his handkerchief and held it to his nose. Some of the hunters pinched their noses but Balack fought through it.

"Whatever your mission was, you're too late."

Raymond removed his handkerchief to speak freely. "I'm afraid I must try."

Balack looked resigned. "I cannot stop you entering, Raymond. Yet I cannot take you to the Assembly Hall or the palace. There is too much confusion and fear. You said you were of House Tarquill? From the Velvet Circle? Perhaps you should seek out home for now until matters cool down. I will take you there now, if you must insist upon continuing."

"I fear I must," said Raymond. Gingerly, he addressed his companions. "Harra, Camen, will you remain aboard as requested?"

Harra didn't pay him any mind. She was staring intently at one of the strange new weapons being pointed at her.

"What will that thing do?"

"If I fire, it will blow your skull apart," the hunter said.

"You would dare draw blood? Camen said.

"Your kind did so quickly enough." There was a hardness in the man's eyes that showed Raymond he would do it. He almost looked eager. Camen boldly met the hunter's stare in a moment of challenge. Thankfully, it passed.

Camen puffed out his cheeks. "I grieve for all who died in this disaster. Human and dragon both." He turned and walked back up the gangway with heavy footsteps.

Harra slumped her shoulders. "We had family in those camps." She couldn't say any more, so followed Carmen.

The hunters eased their stances and lowered their weapons. Raymond looked over his shoulder at his companions, feeling guilty. Harra had hoped for a chance to hold her young sister. Was she even still alive? Camen would sit restless, unable to serve his king. Though it wasn't Raymond's fault, he felt responsible for their lack of entry.

Steeling himself for the task ahead, he said, "If there is nothing else, then let us be on our way." Balack fell in beside him and they made their way along the promenade, heading to the northern half of the city.

The harbour was no longer the bustling hub of the kingdom that Raymond remembered. Mostly, it was hunters or soldiers, with few civilians to be seen. Other armed escorts were moving in close-knit groups like packs of fearful dogs. Not speaking, not stopping. Steep, winding stairs offered a shortcut to the Velvet Circle and Raymond took them out of habit, throwing off Balack who was veering towards the main roads. At the top of the stairs, before turning into narrower streets, Raymond looked back across the bay. His ship had become small in the distance, but thankfully, there were no signs of a struggle.

Balack cleared his throat. "Your friends won't be harmed so long as they stay on board."

"You'll forgive me if I'm not entirely reassured," Raymond said. "Your fellow hunters looked positively passionate for a kill."

"You wouldn't blame them if you'd been here when it happened," Balack said. He rubbed his hands anxiously, cracking the odd knuckle. "I barely survived myself. I thought I'd burn alive in the Rag Run."

"Somehow you pulled through," Raymond said, impressed that anyone had lived after fighting the dragons. "Your skills must be prodigious."

Balack shook his head. "They were starving, weakened; they had no weapons or armour, while we had plenty of both. Yet still it was terrible." He stared off, lost in some painful memory. "Now we are away from prying ears, do you want to tell me the real reason you're here?"

Raymond decided it best to do so. This must be why Balack had asked to escort him alone.

"Darnuir wants his people brought home. Yet now..." He trailed off. How on earth would this be resolved? Could it be? He began to walk again, hoping the movement would offer a stroke of inspiration. Balack hurried after him.

Raymond said no more for a time, his mind reeling with the weight of this knowledge. It was the tragedy of Aurisha wrought a thousand times over. Could words possibly be enough to settle this disaster?

After navigating the streets on the edge of the Royal Exchange, he stepped out onto the familiar boulevard leading to the heart of the Velvet Circle. No damage had been caused here at all. The rich had been spared. New leaves tentatively grew upon the trees that lined the wide, smooth-paved road upon which five mounted chevaliers lay in wait. Breath rose from their great steeds in white clouds, and the sight of them sent a pang through Raymond.

He missed his own horse. He'd never been so long apart from Bruce, and yearned for the quiet, peaceful hours that he spent grooming and tending to him. In leaving him behind in Aurisha, Raymond felt he'd broken an unspoken bond they shared. The dragons didn't even have a proper stable to keep him in, leaving Bruce housed like a common gelding in that ruinous villa. Lira would keep him company, though the thought of her gave him a sinking feeling as well.

Should he have run after her as she'd walked away? Was he mad to think there might be something there? And why was the fear of being wrong in this matter more terrifying than facing down a horde of demons at Aurisha?

The chevaliers noticed him staring and lightly kicked their horses into a trot. They wore their steel, and even their mounts wore a portion of their barding. Raymond recognised the closest rider: a recent recruit by the name of Crispin, remarkable for his height and skinniness. He drew up his horse and looked down the length of his long nose.

Raymond stared right back. "Your steel fits you well."

Crispin pursed his lips. "I thought you served the dragons now?"

"I was invited to the personal guard of their king, and I am here on his behalf."

"We're just passing through, Chevalier," Balack said. "It would be best if we did not tarry."

Crispin threw Balack a dirty look but relaxed his shoulders. "You were a chevalier once, Raymond, and by my measure that still counts for something." A smidgen of the younger man's reverence for older knights crept into his tone. "You may pass, of course, but understand that your new masters are no longer welcome here. If I were you, I would seek clemency from the White Seven and remain in the west before you become... tainted."

Raymond clenched his fist. Brats like Crispin made him regret his time as a chevalier, yet he could hardly deny that his words bore truth. His choice to return to Aurisha would mean much more than it already did.

"My thanks for the advice," Raymond said. "I shall rest easy battling our foes in the east knowing that the boulevard of the Velvet Circle is so well protected." Before Crispin could react, Raymond raised his hands and indicated he wished to stroke Crispin's horse. "May I?"

Crispin was caught off guard, disarmed by the change in topic. He tilted his head to better gauge the mood of his steed. Seeming satisfied, he nodded. Raymond smiled and checked the horse's mood for himself. It turned its head to face Raymond and its ears were pricked forwards towards him. A good sign. He reached out with both hands, lightly patting the horse on the shoulder. He gave it a good scratch up its neck and back down its mane, pushing lightly again at the shoulder to tell the horse he was leaving.

Above, Crispin pulled gently on the reins. "If only one could deal with dragons so easily. Farewell for now, Raymond. I hope you make the right decision." With that, the chevaliers moved off. Raymond watched them go, feeling longing and resentment all at once.

"I hope I never sounded that condescending," he said.

"Oh, you were pretty damn condescending at Torridon," Balack said.

Raymond scowled. "You were there?"

Balack hesitated. "I trained with Darnuir when we were young."

"You're a friend of his?"

"Something like that."

"Well," Raymond said, turning sharply away, "I'll ask you not to mention that dreadful day." He began walking at pace up the boulevard. The hunter persisted.

"I have a lot weighing on my mind," Raymond said. "And I know the way to my own home, sir. So, unless you can somehow sway the Assembly for me, I'd rather be left alone."

Balack grabbed him by the arm, forcing him to halt. "I've already helped you," he said in a hushed tone. "Any chevalier or other senior hunter would have killed your friends on sight."

"So now thanks must be given for sparing innocent lives?" Raymond said. "What have we come to?"

"We have come to a dangerous crossroads," Balack said. "I fear this is the end of the alliance between dragons and humans. Arkus was never in favour of it, and few now will object to his way of thinking."

"All the more reason why the dragons should go home," Raymond said.

"Look. Arkus has the Assembly dancing to his tune for the most part, yet there are those who are not happy about it. There are forces in the city that are readying to oppose him."

"Are you one of those forces?" Raymond asked.

Balack leaned in, though it was only the two of them upon the road. "I am torn, Raymond. I've seen children ripped apart and their bodies fought over. Things that turned my blood to ice. All I wanted to do was curl up into a corner and weep.

"I do not know who I will stand with should the hammer fall, but I do know that the only hope we have of preventing further death is to send the dragons home. I didn't act before when I should have. I ought to have tried to persuade the king to ship the dragons east long ago. I didn't want to stir up trouble for myself. I acted as a coward would. But I'd rather fight for others again, as a hunter should. I won't be idle anymore. If there is anything I may do to be of service, send for me at the Station."

Something in Balack's eyes left Raymond stricken. "I thank you for your offer. I may well have need of you, for it seems the world is set against my success here. My training was to uphold honour and help those in need. This I intend to do, even if my order has abandoned those values."

Balack smiled softly. "Do not be so hasty to dismiss your brothers. The chevaliers fought valiantly during the riots, Gellick Esselmont most of all. I saw him run into a burning building to save a child. Had he not led his company into the thickest fighting in the Rag Run, I fear few civilians would have lived."

Despite himself, pride rose in Raymond. "I am glad to hear my former brothers acted with honour. More than I thought them capable of. Thank you, Balack."

"I shall take my leave now. I've said my piece, and I wish you well at home. Your father is well in bed with the king these days, but I suspect you know that better than most. Tread with caution and remember my offer."

"I shall," Raymond said. They shook hands, firmly this time, and Balack departed.

Raymond arrived at the gates to the estate shortly after. A venerable arched wooden doorway stood next to a drawing room extension built of black stone and sharp angles. Coupled with the brutal acquisition of the place, the modern extensions that Jasper Tarquill had imposed on the property had earned the Tarquills no favours amongst the blue-blooded of Brevia. Raymond secretly agreed with the whispers on at least one front; the manor clashed and looked appalling.

At the door, he rapped the brass knocker. Gyles, the family's aging butler, answered it; a willowy fellow in a spotless velvet waistcoat, whose pale skin mirrored the grainy texture of the very door he was holding.

"Master Raymond," Gyles said without showing a hint of surprise. Raymond stepped over the threshold and sighed in relief at the warmth of the vestibule. He cupped his palms, breathed, and rubbed fresh life into his hands. It was then that he noticed he and Gyles were not alone in the hallway. There were perhaps half a dozen soldiers carrying larger versions of the new weapons he'd seen down at the docks.

Raymond was shaken from his thoughts by Gyles, who coughed lightly.

"Master Raymond, your boots are—"

"They were cleaned yesterday."

"I'm certain, sir. Though I was intending to raise concern for the floor panelling. Her Ladyship only recently had new oak laid. Not that one more pair of boots will matter now..." His steely gaze turned to the soldiers.

"What are they doing here?" Raymond asked in an undertone.

"A measure from the king to protect members of the Assembly from further dragon uprisings," Gyles began through gritted teeth. "Not that a handful would help, and not that your father couldn't hire his own protection if he deemed it prudent."

"Is my mother home?"

"Lady Fenella is raising donations to help repair the damage dealt to the Rag Run."

"And my father?"

Gyles didn't answer. He'd returned to narrowing his eyes at the soldiers.

"Gyles?"

"My apologies, sir. Lord Jasper is in the solar."

For Gyles to come close to losing his demeanour was telling. Raymond thought it best to throw the old man a bone.

"I would hate to scuff Mother's new floor. Removing my steel would make me a good deal more comfortable."

Gyles' mouth curled into what counted as joy. "Very good, sir."

Stripping off his armour and weapons gave him the feeling of being naked. He'd barely been out of his steel in months, always prepared. But it was more comfortable, and he was home now, after all. Gyles kindly fetched him a more fashionable leather jerkin to cover the mundane padding that he wore, as well as soft slippers for traversing his mother's prized flooring. As his feet met the cushioned soles, a tension unwound from him. He'd forgotten what it was not to be on high alert at every moment.

"Shall I escort you, sir?" Gyles asked.

"I know my way," Raymond said. He placed a hand on the butler's shoulder. "Thank you, Gyles. It's good to see you doing well."

Gyles gave a throaty hum of disagreement then bustled into the manor proper, muttering darkly as he passed the soldiers. When Raymond reached the troops, they parted wordlessly for him. He navigated the corridors of the manor on muscle memory, his feet taking him to the solar while his mind tried to focus on what he might say.

Hello, Father. I know the city has just been ravaged by a dragon mob, but I'm here to speak to the Assembly about offering safe passage for the refugees back east. What's that? Oh, no, our troops are to remain defending the dragon homeland while we turn the other cheek....' Even in his head he could not imagine this going well. What a terrible mess.

He gasped in pain, his toe throbbing from having just been stubbed against a heavy door. He had arrived at the solar without realising it.

"Come in."

Raymond took a deep breath, then entered. Unlike much of the house, the solar had survived the renovations. The only new addition was the family sigil of a black quill dripping a blob of ink, chiselled into the brickwork above the mantel of the fireplace. A fire crackled in the hearth, radiating heat and the smell of scorched wood.

Jasper Tarquill was sitting in the largest armchair by the fire, sipping at a glass of brandy. Though well over six feet tall, his domination of a room was due largely to his girth. Brevian nobles who were lacking in originality often said he must stash his piles of gold in the lining of his vest and braies. His quilted cream doublet stretched tight around his waist. A moustache thick enough to scrub boots capped his upper lip, even bushier than the last time Raymond had seen it. Presently, Jasper finished sipping at a glass of brandy, placing it down beside the crystal decanter alongside a half-eaten wheel of cheese and a stack of oatcakes.

"What is it, Gyles?" Jasper said without looking to see who was approaching him.

"It's me, Father."

Jasper dropped his brandy glass. When he saw it really was Raymond, his beefy face broke into a wide grin.

"Raymond, my boy. Where? How? Why?" He clambered to his feet, supporting his bulk with a strong walking cane – a black rod of hard wood topped with a white gold handle. Jasper's excitement turned his usual limp to a near bounce as he embraced Raymond in a bear hug.

"It's good to be home," Raymond wheezed.

Jasper held onto Raymond's shoulders as though fearful he would run away. "We were so worried about you. Oh come, come, and sit down by the fire with me."

Raymond did so, sinking into the adjacent armchair with a distinct weariness. Goodness, but it was nice to be in a truly comfortable chair again, not some stone-carved slab. The warmth from the fire cradled him, making him sleepy.

Jasper struggled to retrieve his fallen glass, and unable to bend over sufficiently, he resorted to lifting it up with the end of his cane, bristling at the waste of good drink. He poured himself another and cut a new wedge of cheese.

"You must be exhausted," Jasper said.

Raymond rubbed at his eyes, aware again of the tension in his back and neck. "You can't imagine."

"Brandy?" Jasper offered.

Raymond nodded. It felt like an age since he'd had a drink. The alcohol lit a warm fire inside his body and he very nearly drifted off to sleep then and there. Maybe he would remain in Brevia, whether he failed or succeeded in this task. What life was there back in Aurisha? A cold one, a hard one, certainly not suitable for long-term health.

Jasper placed a cheese-loaded biscuit into his mouth, looking rather satisfied. His face darkened upon looking at Raymond and he frowned.

"Something troubling you?"

Raymond rubbed at his eyes. "I worry whether I will be able to complete my task."

"Task? Hmm? What's this, then?"

"To take the dragons back to their homeland."

Jasper nearly choked. Pieces of half-chewed oats and cheese were jettisoned from his mouth as he fought for control, punching a fist against his meaty chest.

"Father?" Raymond said, getting to his feet to help.

Jasper flapped an arm for him to sit down. With a cough, a gasp, then a wheeze, he recovered, face purple from the effort.

"Seems you have about the same hope as I do," Raymond said.

"What in blazes has possessed you to do this?"

"I'm on a mission from Darnuir."

"Well, you can forget it," Jasper said. "You're home now. You're safe. Your mother and I were speechless when we heard you'd run off with the dragons. What would a dragon king want with a human in his service?"

Raymond slumped further into the cushions.

"How can one help guard a person who needs no protection?" Jasper rambled on. "Completely preposterous."

"He wanted to make a guard of all the races..." But he trailed off. Saying it aloud felt flimsy, and even his father had cut to the heart of the matter. What did Raymond really contribute?

"And ruddy dangerous to boot," Jasper continued. "I'd say you should return to the chevaliers, but that won't do either, now they're at the front lines themselves. No. You've done your bit. Besides, it's high time you learned the family trade."

Raymond closed his eyes. The same time-worn argument.

"I do not want—"

"Want has nothing to do with it. The family needs you here, not as some ornament for the dragon king."

"I was reduced to little better by the chevaliers in the end. I was stripped of any real role or respect, and worst of all my steel. Darnuir felt it was unjust."

"Sounds to me like he felt sorry for you."

A heat rose in Raymond's cheeks. Another invitation to a fighting elite not earned from merit, though this time through pity, not gold. Maybe his father was right. Maybe it would be best if he didn't return.

Jasper smiled warmly, his many chins aquiver in anticipation of Raymond's resigned answer. Raymond made up his mind. He opened his mouth, drew breath, and then stopped himself. The image of Lira walking away burned itself across his mind's eye and he felt truly cowardly for the first time in his life. He had to return. He had to know. But there was no way he was telling Jasper that.

"Honour demands I return," he said. "I swore an oath. I cannot abandon Darnuir and the others. I have a duty."

Jasper took a while to respond. When he finally did, he leaned forwards and spoke too calmly.

"You swore an oath to Arkus and to the White Seven. You broke it happily enough."

"You're a man of business, Father. What happens when someone breaks their contract with you? You're no longer obligated to them. Honour and oaths work much the same to my mind. The White Seven and Arkus broke their bonds to me. I had no duty left to them."

"You had a duty to this family," Jasper said. "You're now my only son and heir. Your place is here. And by Dranus, it was the dragons who put you in that position by killing your brother."

"Sanders was a traitor. I... I did try to explain it to you."

"What does it matter? He's dead either way. They killed him."

"It matters a great deal, Father. One way makes it seem like murder, the other justified."

Jasper rose to his feet, moustache bristling dangerously now. "They killed him."

"Yes, they killed him."

"Ah ha, so you admit to i—"

"I tried to kill him too. My own brother," Raymond said. He was shaking now. What ill thoughts had Jasper concocted in his grief? What false stories had he invented to make it all better and shift the blame from his own son? "He'd gone twisted and evil, Father. An agent of Castallan."

Jasper let out a cry and thumped his cane off the floor. "Damned if I'm not sick of hearing about Castallan as well." He blustered, then straightened and attempted to collect himself, smoothing down the rumples on his doublet as though to iron out his rage. "The main thing is you're home now. You're safe. I won't let you blindly throw that away."

"The only thing I throw away is any shred of dignity I've got left," Raymond said. "Darnuir gave me the choice, but I don't think there ever was one. Even if I can only do a little, I cannot run from the fight. I have to return."

"If honour is what you seek, then return to the chevaliers, if you must. I'm sure I can persuade the king—"

"Arkus hardly needs more guards. And I found little honour there before."

"Oh, for goodness' sake," Jasper said, exasperated. "I didn't get the pair of you into the order for honour. I did it for the family, for money, for power, for influence; the same reasons any decision is made in this damned city."

"For money? But you bought our places—"

"I paid by offering Arkus deep discounts," Jasper said. "And who has he turned to ever since for all those flyers, pamphlets, and posters nailed around the capital? Overnight, I stole the trade. For honour," he added with a bark of a laugh.

"I see," Raymond said. "So Sanders and I were simply assets in a negotiation."

Jasper gasped, breathless from his outburst. His jowls sagged, and he slumped down into the armchair again.

"It was an excellent move for you both. Training, prestige, connections. I hoped you might manoeuvre into strong marriages, be seen differently in the eyes of this two-faced city. I wanted a better life for the both of you." His voice broke. "But somewhere along the line, some old knight must have put foolish notions of honour into both of your heads. And Sanders ran off to join a romantic rebellion and died for it. I blame myself."

"Father, no."

"Perhaps if he had more to do, more of a stake in the family, he wouldn't have been swayed away so easily."

Raymond moved to his father's side, taking his trembling hand. "You are not to blame. Do you hear me? You are not to blame for any of it."

"Don't... don't you follow him. Don't fight in a hopeless cause, for a master you admit will let you leave. Honour be damned. He doesn't want you. He doesn't need you. Stay home."

Raymond's heart nearly broke right there. He was torn in two between Brevia and Aurisha, between family and friends. Between the right thing and the easy thing.

"You're right," Raymond began, and found his own voice quavering. "You're right about everything except the last. Darnuir does want me there. He might not *need* me, but he'd rather I returned, as does, I hope, well... that isn't so important."

He screwed up his courage.

"I am going back, Father, and just because the nobles of this city aren't worthy of praise does not mean we shouldn't try. We should be better than them. You can do better than them. Be the better man."

Jasper gave a final great heave. He reached shakily towards the crystal decanter and Raymond hastened to pour a brandy for him. Jasper muttered his thanks, swigged the drink, then seemed to settle.

"It seems I cannot convince you otherwise," he said. "Yet, will you permit me one last try? I do not think it wise to attempt your mission. Wouldn't failure ruin your standing?"

Raymond considered this, pacing slowly before the fire. If he returned empty-handed then he'd truly have done nothing to help the cause nor earn his place in the Guard. What would Lira think of him then? No, best not think about that. Returning to Aurisha with nothing to show for the trip would be no good. He might as well stay.

"I do not wish to return with nothing to show for it. I believe you're right that approaching the Assembly or Arkus myself would not bode well. But if someone more influential was to do so..." He paused, gauging his father's reaction. Jasper suddenly became very absorbed with the cheeseboard again. Raymond braced himself for another row. "I wouldn't ask this if I had any other choice."

"It's not that I don't want to help you," Jasper said. "You, mind, not this Darnuir. But I admit, I am more fearful of our own king than theirs."

"But you said it yourself. You have a relationship with Arkus."

"Don't exaggerate my connections. They are mainly business." He dropped his voice to an undertone. "Look, things have gotten tense in recent months. Annandale's execution was particularly disturbing. To actually kill a Great Lord..." He sucked in breath through gritted teeth. "And I imagine you saw our, erm... guests, on your way in?"

"I did."

"They weren't exactly invited," Jasper said.

"I see," Raymond said, fearing he did not wish to hear more. "These new weapons—"

"Will change everything," said Jasper.

"You're sure?"

Jasper's mouth twitched again. "You won't ask me that once you see for yourself."

Raymond was sceptical. He'd seen Darnuir in full fury at Aurisha, and doubted anything could be more powerful than that. Yet, if the refugees were now beyond his reach, perhaps he could bring something else in their stead. The city needed supplies, and not just food; bandages, kindling, whetstones, fresh-forged weapons and, perhaps, new ones.

"So, speaking to the Assembly is out of the question. Very well. What of these weapons, then? If they are so powerful, then they would be better served out east than in Brevia."

"I'm not sure I like this line of thought."

Raymond huffed in frustration. "What would you like? For us to lose the war? It won't be Arkus you'll have to worry about if Darnuir fails."

"You think he can win?" Jasper said. "I'm not one to make an investment without a guarantee."

"He'll win or we'll all lose. Help me to help him. Forget Arkus, forget Brevia. Think of me, Father, as I stand on the battlefield—"

"All right! Enough. I relent. There's just one thing."

Raymond clenched his jaw. He should have been expecting this. "What?"

"If I do this, then you must do something for me in return. You must come back. After this is all over," he hastened to add. "Just – just promise to come home?"

Raymond hesitated. Lira wouldn't leave her position. He couldn't ask her to do that either, could he? He clenched a fist – why was he even letting her influence him? What if it was all in his head? He was a mere human. Good to talk to, it seemed, but she wouldn't want him. Yet there was always a chance.

"I won't make a promise I may not keep," Raymond said.

Jasper sighed, then raised an eyebrow. "What's her name?"

"What?"

Jasper smirked. "What's her name?"

"What are you talking about?"

"Come now, boy," Jasper said. "Other than precious honour, there's only one thing that makes young men act like fools."

Raymond's cheeks were hot with embarrassment. "It could be nothing." He tried to read his father's face. "Are you mad?"

"That she is a dragon is... ill-timed," Jasper said. "But no, I'm not mad. On the contrary, I'm rather pleased. Better to think your defiance isn't in the name of insufferable honour. I'm glad to hear there's some blood in your veins."

"You'll help me, then?"

"I'll see you are sent with as many muskets and as much ammunition as I can afford, and every soldier I can bribe with an advancement in arrears. An artillery crew might be possible, but the cannons themselves are the hard part. Several were sent to the Master Station and, so far as I know, the hunters haven't even unboxed them yet. However, I'm afraid my contacts there aren't what they used to be."

Raymond smiled. "Well, it just so happens that I know someone who might help us."

26

THE FIFTH FLIGHT

"Brevian by decree, an islander by birth. Kept alive by the whims of the sea."

Proverb from the Splintering Isles

Grigayne – South of Brevia

The *Grey Fury* beached just within sight of Brevia's black walls. Grigayne gripped the edge of his father's flagship, wondering for a moment whether he ought to turn back. As more of the fleet reached land, and islanders sprang onto the shore, he knew it was too late for that. The time for second thoughts had passed.

Grigayne jumped ashore himself, sinking a little into the wet sand. His islanders were already gathering, the faint dawn light glinting off the bosses of their shields like so many candles. With luck, most of Brevia would still be asleep, and they could make their getaway quickly. Should all go well.

He was going to spirit the dragons east and stick it to Arkus and his well-crafted schemes. The king had brazenly overstepped his position. It was only right that someone showed him there was will left to resist, and if this would help fulfil his sworn promise to aid Darnuir and his people, all the better.

He felt a thump on his back. Cayn walked by and Grigayne followed the grizzled captain towards the crowd. Before addressing them, he looked out to the camps arrayed between them and the city. It looked more of a bog than anything, a great grey-brown sore under the rising sun.

Grigayne drew his axe and banged his shield. "Men of the Splinters, shieldmaidens, sons and daughters of the seas. Today, we repay our debt to the dragons, who saved our lands from conquest."

There were a few rumbles of agreement, though not yet a chorus.

"Aye, I understand you have reservations. I felt them too. Anger held me for a time, but the dragons stayed and fought and bled with us. They led the charge at Eastguard, tore the Shadow Spire to the ground. And where were the Brevians?"

"Takin' a leisurely stroll up the beaches," someone answered.

"Weighed down by all that fancy armour."

Grigayne smiled and bashed his shield again. "The dragons gave lives for our people. What did Arkus and Brevia give?"

"Sweet fuck all," Cayn said, sharp and high. Laughter rippled through the crowd.

Grigayne let it settle, finding himself laughing too. His fury with Arkus, mixed with frustration at his father, had granted him a clarity he'd rarely felt.

"The dragons saved our families. Our loved ones, our elders, our children. Look how their own loved ones suffer." He pointed his axe towards the camps. "You all know why we're here. I say we save them."

A resounding, "Aye," was declared, followed by waves of shield-banging.

Grigayne brought a finger to his lips and the noise reduced to a low thrum. "Wouldn't want to wake up our lords and ladies from their sweet dreams, would we?" He earned another rumbling chuckle. "All right, quickly as we can. Let's take these dragons home."

Cassandra – Oranna's Parlour

Oranna stroked Thane's hair for the thousandth time.

"I want him taken north, to my lands." Her voice hovered above a whisper. "He deserves to be buried in the mountain soil. Amongst the scent of pines and clear waters."

Sitting on the edge of the sofa, as dead and grey as a walking corpse, Arkus finally met her eye.

"I already have one son buried in the middle of nowhere. You would take another from me?"

Oranna's lips trembled. "I won't have him laid to rest in this place. In this graveyard of a city."

The argument carried on.

Cassandra only half listened. She was in one of the plush chairs opposite Arkus, her body sunk deep into the soft cushions. A terrible voice kept telling her she was partly to blame. If only she hadn't been so selfish. If only she'd let Oranna take Thane and go. What had all her trouble gotten in the end? It had all been too little, too late. Perhaps the chair would continue to swallow her, so she wouldn't have to think; wouldn't have to hear.

Thane's casket lay on a bed of flowers. What remained of the palace gardens had been stripped to form it. Their scent caressed Cassandra, and she felt disgusted with herself for finding it pleasant. She shouldn't have found them pleasing. Not with her brother lying cold upon them.

The argument escalated and Arkus sprang to his feet. "How dare you. How dare you say I don't care." He looked to Thane, his eyes entirely bloodshot. "I'll see justice for this."

"Justice?" Oranna said, her voice shrill. She rounded Thane's casket and stomped towards her husband. "And who will you punish?"

"The drago—"

"There are bullet holes in his chest," Oranna screamed. "That's how he died."

"You'd blame my men, our men, our soldiers?"

"Your men. Your weapons. You're giving them to any boy who can carry one." She drew up right before the king.

Arkus stood his ground. "Are you really blaming me for—"

"I hate you."

Oranna clawed at Arkus' face, a bear-like swipe from ear to nose. He barely tried to avoid it, accepting the punishment. Blood seeped from five ragged lines. Tears rolled from his eyes.

Oranna beat him with bony fists. "I hate you. I hate you. I – hate – you."

Her fury died as she descended into uncontrollable crying. Arkus found some strength and pushed her away, and Oranna collapsed into a sobbing heap upon the floor.

Cassandra dove silently to her side, wrapped her arms tight around her. Oranna howled and buried her face in Cassandra's shoulder.

Cassandra looked to her father. There was no emotion in him. The blood dripped steadily down his face and onto his robes. After a time, he pulled out a white handkerchief, much like the chevaliers bore, and gently dabbed at his face.

"Guards," he said softly. He coughed, then tried again. "Guards."

Gellick entered with five chevaliers. He looked from Cassandra and Oranna rocking in a ball upon the floor to Arkus' wounded face, alarmed.

"My king?"

"Please escort the queen to her chambers. She is overcome with grief." His words came out abrupt and stilted. She wondered if he was in pain. The gouges on his face seemed to barely register with him. Blood still seeped from the wounds. "Something to help her sleep would be a kindness," Arkus added.

"And for you, Lord?" Gellick said uncertainly.

"I require nothing. Please. Do as I say."

Gellick bowed. He looked to Thane then quickly averted his eyes.

Out of all of them, Cassandra had to wonder whether Gellick cared at all. She couldn't quite decide before he lifted Oranna to her feet and left Cassandra sitting alone, legs sprawled awkwardly. It took a great deal of coaxing to get Oranna past Thane, but she relented in the end, too exhausted to fight anymore.

When the door closed behind them, Arkus stepped to Cassandra's side and proffered a hand. Choking back her own fresh tears, Cassandra took it and rose. She caught sight of Thane's pale face, and that set her off again.

"I do not need to hear 'I told you so'," Arkus said.

Cassandra shook her head. "What would be the point?"

"It's all right," Arkus said. "No one opinion will matter anymore. What's happened is too much."

"What does that mean?" Cassandra said hoarsely.

"They've attacked us in the east and now they've attacked us at home."

"We're still piecing together what happened," Cassandra said. She was desperate not to let him run on to some terrible conclusion, whatever that might be.

"You blame me as well."

"I think you blame yourself."

A tense silence followed, broken by a great knock at the door.

"Come in," Cassandra called.

Gellick returned, this time breathless.

"Have the dragons stirred again?" Arkus said.

"They have, my lord," Gellick said. He threw up a hand. "But not like before. They are running south, boarding longships—"

"Ships?" barked Arkus, suddenly alert. "Where the... oh, Somerled, I will ruin you for this." He spoke low, more to himself.

"I've called the chevaliers," said Gellick.

"Call up every damned man," Arkus said. "Every boy, every girl who can level a musket. The dragons are not to escape without judgement." He was shouting now, spittle flying. "They shall not get away with murder."

Gellick looked stricken and, for the first time, looked pityingly upon his king. "We'll never stop them all. Many have already left—"

"Then ride and stop those you can," Arkus said. "Then summon every able-bodied person we have left, all the cannons, all the guns and all the powder. Prepare to sail east afterwards. It's time this war was over."

· · ·

Grigayne – South of Brevia

The gates of Brevia were opening. Well, they were opening further, having already been damaged by recent events.

Talk from the dragons had been disturbing. There had been killings and maiming. Rioting and death. And now, it looked like every chevalier still with a warhorse was galloping out of the city, cutting a straight line south towards the longships.

Grigayne ran his fingers through his scraggly beard, his mind racing. Dragons were stumbling past him; old and sick, young and fearful, lost orphans, and thin mothers clutching babes to their breast. Not all the dragons had agreed to come. Many of them were too scared to move, he reckoned, but those who were fleeing might not all make it. The riders from the city were fast gaining ground.

"Back to the ships," he called, and the message spread from islander to islander. The dragons picked up their pace as best they could, but the chevaliers only rode harder. Would they really ride him and his warriors down as well? Would they start a war with the Splintering Isles just like that?

A tremor ran through the earth at their approach and Grigayne felt it best to run now, think later.

After a minute of flat-out sprinting, he risked a glance behind. It was no use. They'd be upon them before the last ships could depart. Worse still, beyond the riders, marching down from the city gates, Grigayne could see soldiers and hunters emerging in force. It seemed they were about to start a war.

"Have the Brevians lost all sense?" he said to Cayn, who'd stuck close during the evacuation.

"Nae point dwelling on it now," Cayn said. "We cannae take back what we've done, just as the dragons can't. Or them," he added, pointing to the gleaming chevaliers. Cayn hawked and spat in their direction for good measure.

Grigayne gulped. "What happened here must have been horrific. Worse than we can imagine."

"I dunno. I can picture a lot of bleak things, m'lord," Cayn said. "Like getting caught out by them horses."

"Horses aren't known to be swimmers," Grigayne said. He unslung his war axe and shield, and cricked a sore spot in his neck. "See the last of our ships are ready to sail, Captain Cayn. I'll do what I can to hold back this storm."

Cayn flashed a toothy smile of encouragement then slapped a hand on Grigayne's back. "Don't let this wash you away. I don't fancy tellin' ol' Somerled how you died."

They both looked out to the riders again, then to each other.

The chevaliers were close enough to begin a charge.

Hooves hammered. Trumpets blared.

"I'll see you on the *Fury*," Grigayne said. Cayn was gone in a flash and Grigayne faced the onslaught, clanging the head of his axe against the iron boss of his shield, making as much noise as he could to draw attention.

"Shield wall," Grigayne ordered. His warriors and shieldmaidens came running. "We hold them here."

The islanders still close to the camps fell to the chevaliers, knocked aside or sliced to ribbons.

"We hold the line," Grigayne shouted.

The chevaliers drew out smaller versions of their muskets and fired at a hundred paces out. Wood cracked followed by the meaty thud of punctured flesh. Yet the wall held.

"We are free," Grigayne roared. "We do not bow to Brevia."

The roar of the islanders temporarily drowned out the charge of the chevaliers.

Then the crash came.

One young noble tried to break the line. His steed did damage but the line absorbed it, bringing the horse down. The boy flew from his saddle, landing within reach of Grigayne. Puppy fat clung to the boy's cheeks and his eyes were swollen with dreams of glory. Grigayne brought his axe down hard, extinguishing those dreams.

He'd never killed another human before. It wasn't like killing a demon. This was thorns passing through his guts. This made him sick.

Most chevaliers broke against the shield wall like water on rock, splitting their formation and riding left and right in a flanking manoeuvre. Some carried on past, hunting down the dragons as though they were escaped cattle.

"South face," Grigayne bellowed, trying to keep the wall well-formed against the next assault.

"East face."

"North face."

On it went, with little ground given, but with less hope of making a last mad dash to the ships. The chevaliers had them penned in and the foot soldiers would arrive shortly to finish them off. Grigayne tried to have his fighters take what steps to the shore they could before the next charge came. He just hoped that Cayn and the other captains would have the sense to flee once the dragons were aboard.

He could feel the resolve of his people weakening, saw their shields lower with each turning. A wedge of chevaliers, older-looking, experienced, set spurs to beast with lances lowered.

"Hold," Grigayne tried, but his voice was hoarse now and he too felt the fear. They hit the line. Grigayne was thrown back and hit his head on a heavy boss as he met the ground. Colour and light exploded in his vision. By the time he staggered to his feet the wall had fragmented. The last charge had lodged like an arrow in a shield and the chevaliers were entering the breach.

Grigayne knew it to be over.

He cried for his people to fall back, his throat burning from the strain.

Terrible memories of Eastguard flashed before him as he sprinted for the *Grey Fury*. The carved axeman on its prow looked comforting and strong. Then its face blew apart. Grigayne saw dozens of dragons and islanders fall to projectiles unseen, though the bangs rang clearly.

His warriors were by their ships now, fighting desperately in small units. The chevaliers had mostly backed off, letting the infantry march on. Yet a great bulk of the Brevians were not advancing. They remained out of reach of the battle, led by a white-clad figure with a bow held aloft. Was the man telling the regiments to stay? There wasn't time to consider.

A dozen Brevians were running towards the *Grey Fury* armed with muskets, a chevalier leading their small charge.

Grigayne looked about him, saw the last of the stragglers still climbing onto the deck of the *Fury* and found that he alone was left ashore to face the threat.

Waves be at my back, he thought.

Then he ran.

He hadn't felt so wonderfully mad in all his life. He'd always been the voice of caution to his father, but now his blood ran like hot whisky. His father had been right about Arkus, about this disgusting city, and now the Brevians had shown their colours.

The soldiers saw him burst from the back of the refugees and halted. They raised their weapons. Took aim. Grigayne dove to the earth, heard bullets zip above. He rolled, body crunching on his own shield, but momentum brought him to his feet.

The fools had fired all at once.

Grigayne reached them as they scrambled for powder. He swung his axe up, down, and whirled it overhead in a twisting blow, screaming out all the breath he possessed. Four men fell. He leapt over a body, thrust his shield into one soldier's neck and cleaved at another's stomach.

He gasped, half-laughing as the remaining cowards began to flee.

Something hard hit the back of his head. He crumpled. The world spun, and a chevalier loomed above him like a steel mountain. Grigayne cursed that this man would be his doom. He was a perfect stereotype of the city: a blond-haired, high-nosed prick, though it looked as though that nose may have been broken once. His horse reared, front hooves snapping in the air like pincers. Grigayne rolled again, missing being crushed by inches. He hit a fallen dragon and stopped dead. All hope fled from him as the blond fop drew one of those little muskets.

An arrow with black shaft and white feathers thwacked into the chevalier's shoulder. He cried, his shot went wild, and he fell from his horse.

Grigayne didn't stop to think why an arrow came from the chevalier's own side. He just knew it was high time he was gone. There was nothing more to do here.

Dizzy, he staggered to the water's edge and fell again. Heavy salt water washed into his mouth. He choked. Spluttered. Couldn't open his eyes. Yet hands seized him roughly under his arms and dragged him up.

"C'mon, lad." Cayn's coarse voice sounded melodic compared to the carnage. "This ain't the day you return to the sea."

27

LITTLE MASTERS

"Serving oneself may keep you alive but a life of service is to have lived."

Dragon Proverb

Sonrid – Kar'drun

After many days of searching, this passageway held potential. In truth, it was more a great crack in the side of the mountain, but natural light ahead held the promise of a larger opening. Sonrid shuffled towards the light. The space might be a touch tight for a human or dragon, but it seemed passable and he didn't remember Darnuir as being unusually large. With any luck, it would serve.

Before long he emerged to fresh air and screwed up his eyes against the sun. Within the mountain it was easy to forget a world of warmth and light lay beyond it. He'd grown accustomed to the sinister flames, the howls of the red dragons, and the lonely corridors.

He risked opening his eyes and found there was a small outcrop on which he might sit, though it was a long way down from here with a sheer drop. Yet his bones ached worse than ever from his tireless wandering, and so, carefully, he sat down to rest.

Crack, crunch, went his lower back and he grunted in both pain and relief. With a rasping sigh, he settled himself, legs dangling over the edge. The distant world beyond the immediate lands of Kar'drun had turned a richer green since he'd last seen it. Near the charred mountain, however, seasons came and went without change. The trees that still stood were as black as the rock, with no birds to fill the air with song, nor flowers springing up to display their colours. Sonrid had seen and heard such things even at the Forsaken City, the old ruined capital of the Black Dragons. But not here. Not so close to the Master.

After admiring the view for a while, Sonrid peered again over the edge, down to the chalky red earth far below, and withheld from congratulating himself on a job well done. The passageway might be large enough but it was terribly high up. Darnuir would surely be unable to reach it. Not without a deal of help. Perhaps fairies with wings could carry him up, if he wasn't too heavy for them.

A scrape and a grunt interrupted his thoughts. "You might have slowed down," Zax complained. Sonrid felt a weight upon his shoulders as Zax steadied himself.

"Careful," Sonrid croaked.

"Budge up," Zax said. He sat down too, so that his shrivelled arm was beside Sonrid, allowing for a little more room. Zax inspected the area. "Nope. This place won't do. Can't even lie down here."

"I'm not looking for a spot to soak in the sun," Sonrid said.

"You're not, but I am. That all right?"

Sonrid grumbled. "Why must you insist on following me around?"

"Something to do, isn't it?"

"And what is it you think I'm doing?"

"Something doomed to failure, most like," said Zax.

"Most probably," Sonrid said bitterly. "Well, the fewer who know, the better."

Zax gave a rattling laugh. "You're worried I might run to the Master? As if he'd notice or care if I started howling as loud as my torn throat will allow."

"Not the Master," Sonrid said, losing patience. "Red dragons, or perhaps a spectre the Master has deemed loyal to him. Any might catch you."

"I ain't seen a free spectre since they were all brought back. And I wouldn't tell them, even if I did," he added, clearly hurt by the implication.

"They might torture you and make you."

Zax laughed again. "I'm in enough pain already. Would be a challenge for them to add any more."

"There's always more pain," Sonrid said, remembering how Dukoona forced his way inside his mind. "Not all of it from our shadows or bones."

Zax grunted and began swinging his legs, gently kicking the mountainside. "Fine, don't tell. I'll go on assuming that you're looking for a nice spot to sit and watch the world go by. Or end, as the case may be."

"I think you want to believe something can be done," Sonrid said. "I think that's why you're pretending to be my shadow. Why not just admit it?"

"Or I just want to have a good spot when everything comes crashing down."

Sonrid faced his Broken brother. "What do the others say about me?"

Zax remained silent, deliberately avoiding eye contact.

"They think me mad, don't they?"

Zax's continued silence amounted to a yes.

"I thought as much."

"I think you've got spirit, though," Zax said. "More than all the others put together. Some are beginning to... well... not dismiss you out of hand."

Sonrid shook his head. "Perhaps it's just as well. On my own, I am likely to fail. But I do not trust so many to hold their silence, even if the Master ignores us normally. On this, he might just listen."

"They're afraid," Zax said. "Afraid and in pain and beaten down. Your coming back to the Mountain was shock enough without your talk of overthrowing the Master. Us, take action? The Broken? What good can we do?"

"All we can," Sonrid said.

"You say that a lot but it's no use if you won't even tell me what you're up to."

Sonrid ground what teeth he had. Zax wouldn't go to Rectar, he knew that. He held his tongue because Dukoona had told him to trust no one else. A simple instruction. Not one he ought to break.

And yet Dukoona himself had built his Trusted spectres for many long years before the resistance was discovered. Even Dukoona accepted that he could not work alone. If Sonrid was caught and killed, there would be no one left to fulfil the mission. Without debating any further, it all came tumbling out of him.

"I am trying to find a suitable entrance by which to bring Darnuir, the dragon king, into Kar'drun with ease. Once in, I will lead him to Dukoona. If Dukoona is already dead by that point, I'll lead him straight to the Master."

It did sound alarmingly wild to say it aloud.

Zax's small eyes popped in amazement. After a moment of stunned silence, he doubled over in his rattling laugh, a sound like broken glass being swept up by a steel broom. Sonrid lowered his head even further than the hunch of his shoulders, muttering darkly to himself. Zax ended his fit with an almighty cough and a number of deep, scratchy breaths.

"You are mad, Sonrid. But by the Shadows, you might have said so sooner. I know these strange entrances better than most."

"You know of a place?" Sonrid said eagerly. "Somewhere on the ground?"

"Not at ground level. Don't be foolish. The red dragons prowl there too often, we'd be caught. But there is a spot, still some ways up the mountainside but far lower than this." He ended by pointing a crooked finger downwards, as if Sonrid wasn't aware of the drop.

"Then what are we waiting for?" Sonrid got back to his feet as quickly as he dared, steadying himself against the rock face before slipping into the narrow chasm leading back inside.

Something in the dark stopped him dead in his tracks. Eyes. Many pairs of eyes were fixed on him from the gloom of the ancient hallway. Demon eyes, with whites as pristine as their bones. Sonrid struggled to see much more, having just come in from a bright day, and the ghostly green fire set into the wall did little to lift the murkiness.

He froze in place, unsure whether they would attack or not. He'd have no way of preventing them if they did.

There came a scuffle from behind. "You could have lent me a hand, Sonrid, you ungrateful—" Zax fell silent upon seeing what lay before them.

Things remained like that for a tense minute.

Sonrid's mind raced. He hadn't encountered any demons since returning to Kar'-drun and had assumed them all dead, wiped out at Aurisha. Clearly, he was wrong. Yet it wasn't normal for demons to sit so quietly. They were restless, mindless, aimless, or so he had always believed. In many ways, he'd envied them. Better to have no sense of what was going on than to live in constant torture.

His eyes grew reacquainted with the dark and the demons took shape slowly, as though drawn in black ink. Swirling shadows and flames of their flesh followed. They were thin and wiry, yet a few stood taller than himself, hunched over as he was.

If they came at him and Zax, it would be over for them. Broken spectres could summon a small dirk from the shadows if they strained and concentrated for long enough, but that wouldn't help here.

And still the demons stood where they were, in their pack, in the dark.

It was Zax who found his voice. "What should we do?"

"Let's carry on. Hopefully they were just roaming and happened to hear us."

One of the larger demons took a step forward, and to Sonrid's utter shock, it spoke.

"Zzee-grou-Ghaster."

"What was that?" Zax said, sounding as alarmed as Sonrid felt. Demons did not speak. Howl, yes. Shriek, yes. Scream in delight when blood was in the air, certainly. But they did not speak.

"Zzee-grou-Ghaster?" the demon said again.

When Sonrid and Zax did not respond, the demon repeated himself, this time sounding urgent. Something twinged in the back of Sonrid's mind. For a wild moment, he thought he understood the demon. That understanding flitted in and out of him like a familiar sound from long ago, distant and yet distinctly recognisable.

"I think it's asking us something," Sonrid said.

"Impossible," said Zax.

The demon crept closer. "Zzee-grou-Ghaster?"

Sonrid clutched at his forehead but this time thought he could make something out in the demon's words.

"Master. It's saying something about Master."

"They mean to kill us, then," Zax said. "They've been sent by Him. If we retreat outside, and are lucky, we might lose them in a shadow."

Another demon asked the same question of them. "Ze-rou-Mhaster?" Sonrid thought the demon's speech was less gargled and confused than its companion's had been.

"How are you understanding this?" Zax asked.

"I... I don't know," Sonrid said. Delicately, he moved towards the first demon.

Zax threw out his one good arm. "Don't get too close to it."

Sonrid paused and frowned. "Why do we call them 'it'? They are related to us, after all."

"But they aren't like *us*."

"And what are we? Broken. Neither full spectres nor lowly demons. Stuck somewhere in the middle..." He trailed off, remembering again how Dukoona had taken a grip on his mind just as a spectre might do to a demon. Dukoona had managed it because he, Sonrid, was closer to being a demon than a spectre.

"They've never done this before," Zax said. "And that's suspicious in itself."

"We've never stopped to think or try before," Sonrid said. "The spectres were always the ones to issue commands. We had no need to hear the demons speak and they had no need to seek orders. That's it," he cried, and the demons startled at his outburst. "They aren't here by the Master's will. They are looking for a master, or masters."

Zax groaned, waving his hand as though to shoo the idea away. "You really are mad, Sonrid. Maybe the pain has finally cracked your mind."

Sonrid ignored him. "Demon," he began, unsure where to go after that. "Demon. Are you looking for a new master?"

The demon cocked its head and spoke, and this time Sonrid closed his eyes, concentrating hard on the words. "Be our master?" He was sure that was what was said.

The effort to translate was dizzying. Sonrid opened his eyes, the hallway spun, and he swayed for a moment before he got a grip on himself.

"We are Broken," he told the demons. "We cannot command you."

"Mhhhaster," the demons called eagerly.

Zax began to back away. "Sonrid, how can you understand them?"

"You'll be able to as well. Listen carefully when they speak. You'll feel it in your mind, that part of you that is closer to them. It's not easy, I'll grant you."

Zax screwed up his already tight face, eyes shut in concentration as the demons began barking delightful cries of, "Masters. Masters. Masters."

"Gahh." Zax spat in dismay. "I can sense... something. It's infuriating. As though just out of reach."

"Perhaps I'm just more open to the idea," said Sonrid.

"Well, if they think you're a spectre and they wish for instruction, give them some."

"How, exactly?"

"Just be open to it, Sonrid," Zax said mockingly. "Go on. Try reaching out to their minds like the spectres do. And don't say it's impossible. You couldn't understand their speech until a minute ago."

Sonrid looked deep into the demon's stark eyes. It cocked its head the other way, as though inviting him to do just what Zax had suggested. Sonrid attempted it. Not since his first days in this world had he tried to mimic the spectres' abilities. He reached out with his thoughts, and the pain did come, as it did when melding, but he could feel the demons around him. It took every ounce of his will to keep expanding towards them, like wading through thick, sticky mud. He reached the nearest demon, taking many seconds to achieve what a full spectre could do reflexively, and broke through its weak defences.

"No," he said aloud, his body shaking from the effort. "No. I won't do this, Zax."

"They want you to," said Zax.

"Do they?" Sonrid said.

Even then, with the connection still fresh and raw, the demon collapsed to its knees. It howled in a chilling shrill cry, then curled up on the floor.

Not 'it', Sonrid thought. *I must stop calling them it.*

"You're hurting it," Zax said.

"Invading his mind is what's hurting him," Sonrid said. As the demon started to whimper, Sonrid pulled back. With a great gasp his thoughts retreated to his own mind and the pain of the exertion began to ease. "Dukoona spoke to me this way, to avoid the Master hearing," he explained, though he heaved as though winded. "It was the most unpleasant experience of my wretched existence. I won't do it to them. Look." The demon's whining subsided but it lay where it had fallen.

"Masssssster?" the other demons asked as one.

"I will not be your master," Sonrid said. "The only master we've ever known has been cruel. I despise him. I deny him. I will not become that simply because I can. Now, if you will not stop us, my friend and I have business down below." He hobbled with force through the demon ranks. They parted for him and Zax, who shuffled sheepishly behind.

"Perhaps I should lead the way," Zax said. "As I'm the one who knows where we're going."

"Yes, yes," Sonrid puffed, and as he turned to answer Zax, he saw the demons were scuttling along after them, their bulging eyes watching him eagerly.

"Leave," Sonrid said. "Go back to whatever forgotten part of the mountain you've been hiding in. I can't help you."

Yet they did not listen.

They followed Sonrid and Zax through endless hallways, down countless stairs, not even attempting to hide themselves. With frequent bursts of, "Master. Master. Master," the demons hounded their every step.

"Master," they called again as Zax led them round a sharp corner.

"Can't you at least shut them up?" Zax said. "As if my aching bones weren't enough ailment in life. Must we hear this nattering forever more?"

"Master," the demons yapped unhelpfully.

Sonrid groaned, feeling a hot burn in his own legs. His poor twisted knee flared worst of all, the joint scraping as though between two blunt knives.

"Are we close?" he asked.

"Just a little farther," Zax said. "At the end of this hallway. By the twin yellow flames."

"Master!"

"Oh, will you do something, Sonrid? If they keep up this clamour, we'll have the red dragons on us."

Sonrid stopped, if only to give his legs a break. Sometimes, he wished he had one less limb like Zax, so long as the others worked better. He rounded on the demons, his pain manifesting into an angrier glare than intended. The demons halted before him in a packed semi-circle.

Sonrid raised a finger. "You mustn't make any more noise. I will be your master for now if you keep silent." Their wide, gawking eyes followed the movement of his finger as he wagged it. He took their lack of reply for understanding. "Good. Well, if you must follow me, come along quietly." He made to catch up with Zax, heading for the twin yellow flames ahead. Their fires burned like two pale watery suns on a winter's day.

Zax stood waiting. "Out there," he croaked with a nod. "I'll remain to keep watch."

"Stay," Sonrid told the demons. "Wait with Zax." They stopped as instructed. Some even took to sitting down. Zax slid further away from them, muttering darkly.

Sonrid forced his malformed body onwards and was distressed to find a small staircase. Why did it have to be stairs? Every step felt like scaling the whole of Kar'-

drun. Mercifully, the flight was short. Daylight shone upon him and he came upon the ruins of a once-fine terrace.

It must have been built by the Black Dragons long ago, though not from tough starium stone, as the supports had crumbled through time and neglect, leaving only a fraction of the standing space behind.

There was barely room to step out beyond the boundary of the mountainside, which was probably why he hadn't seen it from above. Yet otherwise, it would be perfect – a wide-open doorway straight into Kar'drun. And though many levels from the ground, it didn't feel as unassailable as before.

Yes, this would do. Now they had to simply avoid death and capture until Darnuir arrived. If he arrived. For now, however, his task was complete. He'd have to find Dukoona again and make sure he knew the way—

A boom emanated from deep within Kar'drun. It drew out into a low rumble that grew with each passing second. Pieces of rubble vibrated near his feet. It continued, loud as thunder with a crack to match it. Only the great gates to the mountain made such a sound.

Something appeared by his side and made him jump, but it was only Zax.

"What's happening?" Zax said. "Is it the gates?"

"I fear so," Sonrid said, risking a step out onto the ruins to get a clearer view. Roaring answered their question, even before they saw the wave of red dragons come hurtling out of the mountain.

He heard shrieks of fright and found some demons had followed Zax. Sonrid tried to calm them, telling them it was all right, that they were safe up here. Those claims felt feeble as the world shook. Soon, the army stretched from mountain to horizon, already a crimson wound upon the world.

Sonrid's pain was swept away, caught up in witnessing the beginning of the end of all things, one way or another. The time for freedom or death was drawing close.

Rectar's new servants had been unleashed.

28

THE SPENT RUNNER

"Fairies value the tending of crops. Many ask, so I shall explain. Some days you need a healer, some days you need a warrior. But each and every day, you need a farmer."

From Tiviar's Histories

Damien – The Nest

The old watchtower stood at the centre of the outpost, protected on all sides by a thirty-foot wall. Elevated upon a knoll, the Nest was a solid advance garrison at the fork in the Crucidal Road, or at least it had once been.

Damien stood on the observation deck of the watchtower. The fading light of twilight hid some of the Nest's decay. Repairs had been ongoing, even before he had arrived with the banished Light Bearers, but it was far from secure. Ancient stones crumbled and wood rotted unchecked. A new roof over the tower was something to be grateful for.

A biting pain ran from his toes to his ankle and he shifted his weight again, leaning on the railing of the decking to spare his aching feet. He'd run so much lately to assess the conditions of their old fortifications that he planned on walking most of the way back to Aurisha. Darnuir could wait a few extra days for him to return.

Unsurprisingly, his report would not be favourable. North of the Nest lay Kar'-

drun, perhaps a four-day march as dragons moved. At the edge of Damien's considerable sight was another watchtower, though this one was solitary and abandoned – a
blue outline in the gathering darkness. They'd be better served to have every tower
repaired, with outrunners ready at each to relay news. They were fortunate to have
the Nest in decent order, he supposed.

A cold breeze brushed against his bare feet and he decided to retire into the
warmth. Light Bearers knelt on cushions inside and prayed silently. Damien tiptoed
past them towards the ladder. He might be a sceptic, but he wasn't rude, and this
group had been part of the original garrison force, not those that had been sent more
recently. Those zealots were housed in the barracks, so they were kept away and out
of sight.

Quietly he descended, though each rung of the ladder pressed against the arches
of his tender feet. Thankfully, ground level was only four floors down. Regular
soldiers from the Third Legion were attending to their modest dinner and Damien
joined them, finding a spare stool among the men.

He ate his meagre portion of hard cheese and some bread that had been left from
the day before. He even managed to get a hold of their pot of alderberry preserve and
spooned a little onto his last bite. It was one of the few remaining luxuries brought
from the west. The smell of sweet fruit was a brief relief against the aroma of the
many bodies huddled inside against the still-cold spring nights. Damien couldn't
imagine being penned up for so long. He was used to running through wild country,
feeling the wind against his face and soft grass underfoot. His meal was over all too
soon, and feeling unsatisfied, he fidgeted with his hands.

"Done with that?" a solider asked him, nodding towards the preserve.

Damien picked it up, then held it close to his chest. "I have half a mind to take it
back to Aurisha with me."

"Over our cold corpses, outrunner," the soldier said, though he smiled in jest. He
extended his hand expectantly and Damien handed over the pot with a sigh.

"Does anyone wish me to take anything back to Aurisha? A message for a loved
one, perhaps?" He was answered by a few low coughs. The soldier with the jam carefully spooned out a portion, holding the ceramic jar delicately, as though it were a
newborn babe. Damien caught his eye again.

"Do you have nothing at all for me to deliver?"

"You have my best wishes," the soldier said. He wolfed down his dinner in three
bites.

Another soldier spoke up. "You said yourself, outrunner, the humans have not
sent our people over the sea. Who are we to write to?"

"Brothers? Fathers? Friends?"

No one answered. As it dawned on Damien, he felt his chest tighten. These men
here had only each other now. Through battle or time, they had no one left. Their

whole race was dying, and more fell with every battle. Not even a bucket of jam could sweeten that thought.

"Letters could be stored for those still across the sea," he said, hoping someone might salvage his mood.

"I'm afraid we can't spare the ink." The voice had come from near the ladder and Damien turned to see Grakon, the Light Bearer in charge of the garrison. "Or did you think I asked you to memorise your report out of malice?"

"I just thought it would be a kindness, that's all. Some may have wished for it."

"What we wish for is more food," Grakon said, "More equipment, more volunteers, rather than forced labourers. And we wish for the blessing of the gods."

"I shall inform the king of your needs. The gods I cannot guarantee."

"Do you mock us?" Grakon asked.

"I meant no offence," Damien said. He cursed himself inwardly and tapped his feet on the ground. He often did that when he was nervous, perhaps from some born instinct to run. He collected himself. "I only meant that I have the king's ear, not the Lord Guardian's."

"I take my orders directly from the guardian and have remained faithful, unlike others." Grakon's steely gaze wandered to the doorway, as though Bacchus and the rest were lingering there. "Have no fear about my connection to the Light. I was at the Nail Head. I felt the touch of N'weer upon my flesh, heard his voice encourage me."

Damien glanced around. The soldiers of the Third Legion watched him closely. "Truly, you and all who were there were blessed. I only wish I'd experienced it as well." He meant the last part. To have felt what they had, to believe so strongly; it must be wondrous. He looked imploringly to those around him, hoping his words had appeased them.

What little fire was left in Grakon's eyes diminished. His shoulders sagged and he raised his hands apologetically.

"I am sorry, outrunner. My tone was unwarranted. I've been on edge since the exiles arrived. We all have."

Damien then noticed that the soldiers staring at him weren't doing so in anger but in jealousy; that he should get to return to Aurisha when they did not.

The mix of Light Bearers and soldiers did not seem to have anything more to add. Damien rose, stretched, and thought a walk along the walls might help to settle him before bed.

"I shall leave at daybreak and not miss an hour of light."

"You will be eager to return to the city, of course." Grakon extended a hand. "Run fast, Damien." They shook hands and Damien took his leave.

Outside, the crisp air was now a welcome relief from the stuffiness. After a circuit of the Nest, he climbed to the top of the northern wall and rested there awhile, enjoying the peaceful silence under the stars. It was comforting to think that he might get to enjoy endless nights such as these. Spring would bloom in earnest soon, and new crops had to be sown fast if they were to be sown at all. With luck, the Tail Peninsula would groan under the weight of produce come harvest and he would have found a place by the sea to let his feet rest in warm sand. There were still other outrunners. What more could Damien do? What better service could he give than help provide for their people?

Before the fall of Aurisha, Damien's mother used to take him through the markets of the city. On the hotter days, she'd buy watermelon for him to eat. He still remembered the taste of the juice bursting in his mouth, the sweet water dribbling down his chin. He'd grow watermelons on his farm by the sea, far away from it all. He'd even grow berries to make his own preserve, perhaps raspberries, blackberries, and alderberries too, if he could find a fruiting bush to gather seeds.

His ears pricked up at the sound of footsteps on the stairs.

From out of the shadows skulked none other than Bacchus himself. He was even thinner than when Damien had last seen him, his skin dry and cracked, his hair overgrown and unkempt. He bore no weapon, for the banished had been stripped of those upon arrival.

"I saw you walking around the fort," Bacchus said. "You are to leave tomorrow, yes?" Whatever strings had produced his mystical voice were frayed now; a fitting end, Damien thought, for a charming tongue that had brought nothing but strife in its quest for influence. Despite the obvious loss in charm, Damien braced himself to remain firm.

"Grakon has warned me of your attempts to make a plea," Damien said. "I fear it would go unheeded, even if I should wish to take it to the king."

"Please," Bacchus said, bringing his hands together as though praying. "I cannot sleep, I cannot eat; even the others neglect me now. I am utterly alone. I never wanted it – never—" His voice snapped and he made a few hacking coughs to right himself. When he recovered, his words came as whimpers. "Please. Please. I only ask you to hear me out. It could be weeks before another outrunner returns."

Damien almost felt sorry for him. "Do not drive yourself to your own grave. What good would that serve? As for the rest of the exiles, well, they held no loyalty to the Lord Guardian. It seems fitting that they should also abandon you."

"I did not lead them," Bacchus said, and he was quite firm and steady now, some of his old bearing having returned.

"They named you."

"Yes," Bacchus hissed, "and I believed them at first. It drove me half to madness to think that my words had caused it. So, I had to know. I had to know what I did to drive them to such action, but they turned me away with cold looks and blank stares.

I might even have taken it as their blaming me for their circumstances, were it not for the fear in my heart. I do not think they spoke the truth."

Damien considered his response carefully. It was clear that Bacchus felt guilt, and that was something; more than the others, for that matter. Perhaps he really hadn't meant it, or had convinced himself that he hadn't. Either way, a few words of comfort might save him from self-destruction and spare one more precious dragon life.

"I too feel guilt for what happened," Damien said. "Not as much, I grant you, but enough to seek to wipe it from me before I end my service. If you serve our king and guardian well from now, forgiveness may come. But to dissuade blame, I do not think that is the best path, Bacchus. It is done."

"I can accept the consequences for my actions, outrunner. But I tell you, something is not right. I say I did not lead them, and that is the truth. Answer this: did I take part in the slaughter myself?"

"No, you did not. But a leader does not have to lead from the front."

"So you accuse me of cowardice too?" Bacchus said. "If I had wanted such a thing, I wouldn't have been so meek as to let others draw blood while I slept."

"Then who else? No other senior Light Bearer was with them, and you would have known them best."

"Would I? I did not recruit most of those men. That was the old man."

Damien took a step back. "That is a very serious accusation."

A wild energy rose in Bacchus' eyes, catching in the moonlight. "Yes. You believe me? You will take my warning back with you?"

"I—" Damien began, unsure.

It was then that something caught his eye to the north. A glint of moonlight on something far away. Something moving.

"Did you see that?" Damien asked.

"What?" Bacchus said, near breathless with excitement. "I see nothing. Damien, will you take—"

"Quiet," Damien said. He focused on where the outline of the closest northern watchtower had been, now lost to darkness. Even among outrunners, his keen eyes stood him apart, but perhaps he was being jumpy.

A lookout had appeared by his side. "You saw it too?"

"I think so," Damien said.

It happened again; a quick flash, like a spark.

The watchman gulped.

Two more flashes came, so distant and so quick most would have missed them.

"Return to the tower," Damien said. "Ready the men."

"What's happening?" Bacchus asked.

"I'm not sure, but better safe than sorry."

Damien peered into the night. Nothing happened for a while and he worried he'd raised the alarm for nothing. Then three more flashes came. And then a light, which grew, devouring upwards. The northern tower was on fire.

Enemies were out there, but would they come to the Nest? Did they even know about the garrison? It was likely; spectres could go unseen if they wished to and learn all they needed. If this was an attack, Damien couldn't stay. None of them could. Their numbers were too few. With unrivalled timing, his feet throbbed in pain and he closed his eyes at the thought of running on them. By the time he reopened his eyes the fire was blazing.

Grakon and the garrison arrived upon the walls in haste. The commander of the Nest turned to Bacchus and gruffly handed him a sword. Another soldier handed over a shield.

"Don't look so shocked," Grakon said. "Against our true foes we are still allies."

For once, Bacchus had nothing to say.

Beyond the wall, the enemy advanced at tremendous speed. Flames from the burning tower lit up a glistening red mass. Hideous roars of battle reached the walls over the swiftly closing distance. A gentle rumble ran through the earth. Demons were not heavy enough to cause that, even thousands and thousands of them. The garrison fell silent and dread filled Damien. He couldn't tear his eyes away from the burning tower.

"We should go," Damien said.

"Abandon our post?" Grakon said without looking at him.

"No one would blame you."

"We have the favour of the gods."

"Your Lord Guardian retreated on the first attempt to retake Eastguard. If he can admit defeat, then so can you." He forced himself to look away from the fire and face Grakon. All those with him were in full armour, with shield and sword. "You'd better take all that off if you're going to run."

"We're not leaving, outrunner," Grakon said.

"The Lord Guardian will not be angry."

"What's left for us to return to?"

"So you're just going to throw your lives away?"

"You're young still, Damien. Most of us are not. Dranus be damned, I'm eighty-three. My wife died during the sack of Aurisha, my only son was killed in battle before that. I'm not fit enough to run like you can, and I'd rather go out fighting. We all would."

"But your gods," Damien said. "You were all at the Nail Head. Doesn't that give you hope?"

"More than anything," Grakon said. "It gives me hope that there is a life beyond this world. Hope that I might find my wife and child again. I certainly won't find them here. All of us have lost so many. Let us go and join them." His gaze and those of the garrison were fixed collectively north.

Only Bacchus seemed unsure, looking between his sword and shield as though it were the first time he'd ever held such things.

Damien gulped. "Very well, if that is your decision. I'll need to get water before I—"

"Here," Grakon said, thrusting a heavy waterskin against his chest. Damien took it gratefully. Others passed him their skins and someone had the foresight to unstrap their belt and hand that over too. Damien threaded the skins along it and strapped it all over one shoulder. With some luck, it might see him back to Aurisha.

"Go, now," Grakon said. The old Light Bearer drew his sword and the rest followed.

Damien looked at them all again, imploringly, but their faces were resolute.

They had made their decision.

And Damien had a job to do. He had hope for a life beyond the war.

He'd made it to the stairs when Bacchus took his arm and spoke fiercely. "It seems the gods deem this to be my fate. But I would not have my legacy be one of disgrace. Please, tell Blaine what I said. Tell him that I'm sorry I failed to notice what was going on within our ranks. Tell him I'm sorry for everything."

"I shall," Damien said, and he meant it. Bacchus nodded curtly; his expression hardened, and then he turned his back on Damien and rejoined the ranks upon the wall.

Damien too turned his back upon it all as he descended the stairs. He jumped the last six steps and pain exploded up his legs – hardly a good omen. This was going to be a hard run. The hardest he'd ever done. So he gritted his teeth, breathed deeply, and kept going.

Within seconds, he'd crossed the ruins of the Nest to the eastern gate. Two remaining guards there hauled the door open for him, and he passed the threshold without a word. He heard the metal hinges of the gate screech as it slammed shut.

The Crucidal Road lay a few hundred yards ahead. Hard stone would be excruciating so he kept to the grass by the edge of the straight-cut slabs. A short while later, the fading sounds of distant battle reached him, only to disappear as he ran on. Just as well. He didn't want to hear the screaming, and the rushing air soon rang between his ears.

Heat from his driving limbs kept any chill of the night well at bay. The smell of the grass, of wild flowers and earth, was heavy in the air. After a time, his feet went numb and that made things easier. He'd feel the pain once he stopped. If he stopped. Whatever those creatures were, they were fast, and Damien would need to beat them home with time to spare if he was to warn Darnuir.

No; not home. Aurisha isn't home. I've still got to build mine. This is it. One more run. My last run.

He lost track of time, slowing only when thirst overcame him. During one water break, he risked looking back. Far off now, the Nest burned like the flame of a candle across the hall of the Basilica. He spared a thought for the dragons who'd stayed and died there, Bacchus included. He hoped they would find their loved ones, and their peace. Perhaps they had bought him some time, which he should not waste by watching their distant pyre burn.

He turned south and powered on. He did not stop, did not look back.

He just kept running.

29

BEFORE THE STORM

"Mountains, dey can be scaled. Paths can be found in da forests. Yet der is no runnin' from a black sky. Some things can only be endured."

Kazzek wisdom

Darnuir – Harbour of Aurisha

"They don't look very threatening," Darnuir said, peering into the open crate. Inside, neatly packed, were the muskets that Raymond had been speaking endlessly of.

They'd secluded Raymond's cargo into one of the ancient dry docks. Blaine said that whole galleys used to be constructed here within three days, and it was certainly spacious enough. Each clank of a crate lid rang under the high roof. Blaine was here too, as was Lira and their new combined Guard, all inspecting these new weapons more closely for themselves.

"Perhaps they do not look as mighty as your blade," Raymond said. "But they are powerful. Terrifying even, given that anyone may wield one." He had a smaller version hanging at his hip right now.

Darnuir considered the weapons again. "And how many does Arkus have?"

"An entire arsenal, from what I gather."

Darnuir looked to the full company of troops that Raymond had brought back with him. The carefree way in which they rested their muskets upon their shoulders showed that carrying these weapons was already second nature to them. This was no sudden development. Arkus must have kept this from him.

Darnuir let the anger wash over him, embracing caution instead. Until he knew Arkus' true intentions, he'd give the man the benefit of the doubt. Raymond's other news – the riots, the killings – that was the more pressing concern.

Blaine scoffed loudly. "And it was Arkus' first move to turn these weapons on our own people?"

The human company shuffled nervously.

"I cannot say what events in Brevia led to atrocities being committed on *both sides*," Raymond said.

Blaine wrinkled his nose.

"We've had our share of failure and horror here in Aurisha too," Darnuir said, his voice as steady as he could force it. His hands, however, were clenched. "All the more reason why we must seek an end to the war. Sooner rather than later."

Blaine considered the muskets again, as though someone had just served him a lump of rotting meat. "And these *things* will help us to do that?"

Lira bounded up, her youthful energy back since Raymond's return. She had a musket in one hand.

"Black powder is used to power them. They must have a real kick."

Darnuir thought there was one way to find out. "Raymond, may I borrow that?" He gestured to the gun at Raymond's waist.

Raymond handed it over. "They call these pistols."

Darnuir bobbed it in his hand like weighing up any sword or bow. He enjoyed the balance. *Well crafted*, he thought, pointing it towards the faraway wall.

"So, I squeeze this part with my finger," he said, flexing his forefinger in the space beneath the barrel. He didn't wait for a reply. He pulled; the hammer fell; a spark flicked; the bang took him by surprise. Smoke trailed upwards from the pistol and a tiny mark could be seen on the wall.

"I didn't feel anything," Darnuir said.

"Your strength must negate the recoil," said Raymond.

Darnuir pulled the trigger again. Nothing.

"It must be reloaded, much like another arrow to a bowstring," Raymond explained. He demonstrated the cumbersome process.

Lira watched intently, a mixture of curiosity and nerves battling it out on her face.

"What's the rate of fire?" She directed her question to Raymond, but it was the slick-haired human captain who answered.

"Trained soldiers may unleash three shots a minute."

Darnuir frowned. "Experienced hunters can loose twenty or more arrows in the same time."

"That is why we employ the volley, my Lord of Dragons," the captain said. He spoke quite plainly but licked his lips before and after his words. Darnuir sniffed at the air. A little sweet. The humans were afraid, not overly so, but still wary. And he supposed that made sense, given what had happened in Brevia. Darnuir scanned the company again, seeing a few soldiers gripping their muskets hard enough to turn their knuckles white. *Might be best to have them unload some of that tension.*

"Could you demonstrate?" Darnuir said.

"What, here?" Blaine said.

"We have the space," said Darnuir. "I'm eager to see what Arkus has created in aid of our alliance." He nodded to the captain. The human licked his lips again, straightened his black coat, and then stepped to the side of his soldiers.

The company was arrayed ten deep, with space between each person. They began what looked to be an intricate process, though they performed it quickly. First, powder went into the chamber. Padding was then placed into the barrel, followed by ammunition and some more padding, the soldiers shoving it all down with a long, thin stick. Weapons primed, the front row raised their muskets at the ready. They really were highly trained. A legion of dragons could hardly have performed their drills faster.

When the captain called to fire, it sounded like a storm unfurling within the dock. Fragments of starium stone exploded off the opposite wall. More orders were called, though Darnuir reckoned the soldiers were acting on ingrained muscle memory. The first row moved off, the second stepped forward, then fired, and marched back to the end of the line. On it went until the first man was back again.

"Cease fire," the captain called, though he made a broad cutting signal with his arm as well.

As the cacophony rang out, Darnuir stood transfixed by the power of these weapons. It wasn't quite the continuous hail that trained archers could unleash, but arrows could not make marks like that on starium. He looked to Blaine, who was staring at the damage to the wall as well. Judging from his sudden paleness, he was thinking much the same.

"Er, how was that?" the captain asked.

"Excellent, Captain. Most excellent."

"We could demonstrate the cannons next," he said, sounding more eager now that he'd earned some praise. "Firing into the sea, of course."

Darnuir eyed the long barrels set on heavy wheels. The balls used in them were the size of his head.

"No need," Darnuir said. "I feel I have a sense of it." Realising he still held the pistol, Darnuir thrust it back to Raymond like an incriminating, blood-soaked cloth. "A full demonstration can be arranged for later. You're free to go and report to whichever of your generals you see fit."

"Begging your pardon, my lord," the captain said, "but we've been instructed to report to Raymond or you. Those were the orders from Lord Tarquill and from the Hero."

"The Hero?" Darnuir wondered aloud.

"Your old friend, Balack," Raymond said. "I had the pleasure of his company in Brevia. He's gained quite the reputation, both from the Bastion and from, well, more *recent* events."

Darnuir's throat tightened. "I see."

"He was instrumental in supplying these troops and helping us to depart Brevia without incident."

A smile tugged at the corners of Darnuir's lips. So Balack was doing well for himself, and more importantly, he lived. There was still some hope for a reunion, even if faint.

"Very well, Captain," Darnuir said. "You shall report directly to Raymond for the time being. Go and settle into the quarters we have assigned to you. They're not far from here. One of the Guard will guide you. Raymond, please stay for now."

As the humans marched out, Blaine stepped lightly to Darnuir's side. "What are we to make of this?"

Darnuir didn't answer right away. There was too much to consider. Too many moving parts at play.

"I think we're in a very precarious position, Blaine."

"I agree."

"I want to give Arkus the benefit of the doubt," Darnuir said. "I want to believe he simply didn't mention these weapons because they weren't ready. But to have trained regiments and created such stockpiles as Raymond claims in this short a time—"

"I know," Blaine said coldly. "We have been lied to."

Darnuir's heart thumped as panic tightened his chest. He hadn't felt anxiety like this since he'd been on his first night patrol as a hunter, hearing wolf howls close by their camp.

"Perhaps his secrecy was merely pragmatism," Darnuir said. "Perhaps..." But he trailed off. He couldn't work around it. The fact was that Arkus could have told Kasselle at any point over the years. He could have – should have – told Darnuir during their time together last year. But he had refrained.

"At least we have powerful new weapons," Blaine said. "Even if I do think them crude."

Darnuir furrowed his brow. "Our priority must be taking the fight to Rectar."

"We're not ready. Not our armies, nor us."

They'd been training hard, but Blaine was right. They had a long way to go before the thought of fighting a god became a step down from insanity.

"I know, Blaine, but soon it won't matter. Either our food will run out – these fresh supplies from Raymond's family are welcome, but limited – or Arkus will retaliate in response to the... *troubles* back in Brevia. Our people may be left to starve, or he may pull all his troops home, and then we'll have no chance at all."

"We won't let the humans go, then."

"Is that so?" said Darnuir. "No hope lies down that road. None. I fear we will need to march before month's end to prevent that possibility."

Blaine took Darnuir by the shoulder, pulling him close. "I'm not ready."

"We'll have to try."

"And what if we do succeed? How will we handle Arkus? Whatever happened, he has slain dragons now, many more in cold blood for all we know. That cannot stand."

Darnuir met Blaine's hard stare and spoke in just as fierce a whisper. "You're right, Blaine. It cannot stand. It should not stand. But it must. War against the humans is unthinkable."

"Our people won't understand—"

"Our people will be grateful that the fighting is over," Darnuir said. "As will we. As will the humans. Nothing may come of it, but rest assured, for as long as I am king, I shall never forget it. For now, let it go." And he let go of Blaine, stepping away and pretending to observe the last of Raymond's company departing.

Lira had gone to help Raymond with some of the weapon crates, stacking them up one by one as easily as bed pillows, and earning sideways glances from the humans. The pair of them shuffled awkwardly around each other, raising hands and jumping back overly politely if they drew too close, faces noticeably blushing all the while.

How wonderfully innocent, and naïve, and sweet, Darnuir thought. He'd never been like that. Something of the dragon in him had always made him too serious, always training or trailing behind Cosmo rather than mingling at the station with the others. He ought to have relaxed more, yet those days felt several lifetimes in the past. And as he watched Raymond and Lira give each other foolish glances, Darnuir had a yearning to return to calmer days, before the weight of the world had been thrust upon him. To sit by the fire in the tavern at Cold Point with Balack and Eve; to run out into fresh snow, build a plump snowman from it and search for a carrot for its nose; to sleep and not dread waking.

His reflection was interrupted by an outrunner, who came pelting into the dry dock, feet slapping loudly, artfully dodging the humans in his way.

"There is news," Blaine said unnecessarily, striding forward to meet the messenger. Darnuir followed, catching Raymond and Lira's eye, indicating that the two should join them.

"It is Damien, sire," the outrunner reported.

"He's returned?" Darnuir said eagerly. News on the northern outposts had plagued his mind. "Why hasn't he come to me at once?"

The outrunner hesitated. "He's... he's trying, sire."

"What do you mean?"

"He's injured. Very badly. He had a hard run but insists on coming to you. I thought it kinder to find you and—"

"Say no more. Where is he?"

"Limping up the northern road."

Without another thought, Darnuir started to run; out to the harbourside, along the banks and towards the switchback stairs, wind buffeting his every step. He became aware that he'd outstripped even Blaine. Lira and Raymond were well behind, but he didn't stop. The suddenness of his fear for Damien had taken him by surprise.

Something inexplicable drove him on and, as Darnuir emerged onto the northern road, he saw a sight that made his stomach fall further. Upon the golden road many had gathered as though watching a parade. Yet they were hushed and cowed, for the procession was made by one. A single dragon, who stumbled on, one step at a time. Blood trailed brightly in his wake.

Darnuir ran to him.

Cascade-fuelled, he was by Damien's side in seconds. Residue rushed down his arm, but he ignored the burn, all his fears about magic temporarily washed away.

Damien looked a mess. He might have run through a mile of gorse thicket and come out cleaner. His eyes were almost two dark holes, his skin dry, flaked and reddened from exposure. His legs bulged with throbbing, torn muscles, and his feet were in ruins; marbled bloody from splits in his skin. It was a miracle he stood at all.

Having found Darnuir, Damien collapsed into his arms.

"Why have you done this to yourself?"

Damien blinked blearily, his parched lips attempting to sound out words.

"Water," Darnuir yelled. "He needs water." None magically appeared in his hand. The gods were cruel indeed.

"Sire," Damien managed.

"You're not to die," Darnuir said. "That's an order. You're not to die." It was a futile effort but Darnuir found himself saying every foolish thing he'd ever heard Cosmo say to wounded hunters. *Where is that damned water?*

"Had to... warn you," Damien gasped. He coughed and more blood left his body. "They are coming."

Darnuir understood what he meant.

"Had to run. They're so fast. Barely stayed... ahead."

"How long do we—"

"A day... maybe less. Bacchus, the others, they held for a time." He motioned feebly for Darnuir to come closer. He spoke of the exiles, of a final conversation upon the walls of the Nest and a warning he'd sworn to give. With his final words, it was clear he was letting go. He'd given his last message. "Forgive him, sire. Forgive... him."

"I do, Damien. I do." He didn't hesitate in saying it, though he pressed this new knowledge down, so as to remain in the moment. With one hand he clasped Damien's own, and with the other he cradled his head. "Hold on. You have a farm to tend and things to grow. Your life will not only be of war."

Damien smiled through the pain. "I fear that was always to be our way."

Darnuir tried to say more but he choked. He was vaguely aware of people gathering around them, but he didn't acknowledge them. Here lay one of the younger of his kind, one who might have helped lead the way in the better world Darnuir had dreamed. And it was now that he allowed all the grief for his slaughtered people in the west to surface. The deaths of so many he had failed to protect, and, perhaps, the death of that dream.

"I'll see your body is taken to the peninsula," Darnuir said thickly. "I'll see it done. You deserve more. Damien?" But now only unmoving eyes stared back at him. Lifeless. He closed Damien's eyes and sat peacefully out of respect. Sometime later, Lira's shadow cast over him.

"I hate to burden you further," she began.

Darnuir sniffed, then looked up at her in silent question.

She squatted. "There are longships coming from the south. It must be Grigayne. You should meet him. We'll take care of Damien."

Darnuir nodded. Without fully processing it, he got to his feet, still carrying Damien's body. He passed him to Harra and Camen to carry. "See he's given every honour. Wash his worn body. Without him we would not have had warning of the battle to come."

All eyes widened at his words.

"They're coming?" Lira said.

"We must prepare immediately," Darnuir said, his mind sharpening again. "A good thing Grigayne has come now. We'll be in need of every spare warrior from the Splinters that he has mustered."

30

THE BEGINNING OF THE END

"How many dragons fell before the end? How many died to save us?"

Author Unknown

Darnuir – On the Walls of Aurisha

The city was braced. A hush fell over the defenders. Even Darnuir stopped his pacing, taking a central position above the battered gatehouse and peering out across the open land to the north.

They'd done all they could in the time they had. Now would come the test of their training. In the end, it may not have mattered. This new enemy might sweep across them as easily as locusts turned to feast upon flesh. His thoughts were interrupted by the arrival of Grigayne, stepping up beside him on the battlements.

"You wished to see me?"

Darnuir peeled himself away from the parapet. "I did." He looked Grigayne over once. He had no obvious injuries, save the scar he'd gained from the failed assault on Eastguard. "I see you made it through your latest ordeals intact."

Grigayne swallowed. "Many didn't. Many of both our peoples."

Darnuir nodded heavily. "I still don't think the full implications have hit me yet.

This impending battle is a distraction. A good thing, or we might all be at each other's throats."

"You're not angry with me?"

Darnuir raised his eyebrows. Truthfully, he wasn't sure how he felt. "I appreciate what you have risked and done for me. Truly, I am. Whatever the outcome may be, you did it with the best of intentions. And if the Brevians attacked you... then you had no choice but to defend yourself. That you arrived at this hour... well, you cannot be blamed for bad timing. It was the task I laid before Raymond, even knowing the danger posed to my people here as I did."

Grigayne relaxed a little, his hands resting more easily upon the wall.

"But," Darnuir continued, "if I may ask, and please be honest, would you have helped my dragons if you'd known beforehand about the riots?" The question had troubled Darnuir too. For while the dragon in him raged at his people's treatment, the human, and now the king, deplored the violence, no matter the provocation. Dragons always prided themselves on being a better race, yet they had acted like beasts and would have to carry that knowledge forever more.

Grigayne scratched what remained of his scraggly beard. "Honestly, I think I would have stayed away, not knowing what to do."

"That feeling I understand," Darnuir said. "A battle is one thing. But all this bad blood? I don't know how to fight that. It goes beyond any weapon and will need more time and patience than I fear we have."

Grigayne hung his head. "I worry I made a terrible mistake. I—"

"Stop," Darnuir said, raising his hand. "This talk will do us no good. Not now. You and your islanders have a mission. See it is done."

"Are you sure we cannot be of more... military assistance?" Grigayne said. He fingered his axe.

"I'd be sending your people to their deaths if I asked them to fight. This enemy will be the deadliest we have ever faced, and even my dragons will be hard pressed. Keep my people secure atop the plateau and I will hold the ground. Or die trying."

Grigayne bowed his head and took his leave.

Lira – The Plaza

Gingerly, Lira picked her way between the islanders and the famished members of her race. Every voice from an older woman made her snap around. Each time, she was let down, and a little relieved all at once.

She didn't much want to think on what might have happened to her mother in the camps. Then again, she didn't even know if her mother had left the Hinterlands, so all this worry could be for nought. It was the not knowing that was killing her.

Another voice reached her, a cool, discerning tone that she'd grown up with. Lira spun. Sighed. Not her mother either. The poor woman looked old beyond her days, wasted away; her scalp prominent beneath thinning hair, her shape all but gone. She was clutching at the hand of a frightened young boy.

"What you looking at?" she demanded.

Lira blinked, startled. She hadn't realised she'd been staring. "I'm sorry. To both of you. For everything," she said, somewhat foolishly. The woman narrowed her eyes and had half-turned when Lira called after her, "Wait. I'm searching for my mother. Her name is Bellona. Have you seen…" Her voice trailed off as the woman shook her head. "Oh. Well, take care up here." The woman squinted at her then hurried away, son in tow.

Lira groaned at her useless remarks. Any promise of safety must seem empty now. From one hellish existence to an impending battle.

"Lira," someone was calling.

She spun wildly again, looking for the source. "Mother?"

"Lira, come here," the woman called again, and a young girl came running to her own mother's summons, before melting into open arms.

Lira closed her open mouth, then tightened her jaw as she fought a fresh wave of embarrassment. This was no good. It was a churning sea of people up here, all yelling, moaning, weeping, or trudging in defeat.

She ought to be down on the walls, helping lift those heavy cannons into position. Raymond would be down there. He'd be doing his duty. And she was the Praetorian prefect. She ought to be showing an example, rallying the troops, being seen at the front and thick of things.

Her feet betrayed her thoughts, taking her deeper into the throng of the plaza. Sharp hunter training allowed her to notice every swish of bright blond hair, and every time to no avail. She must have seemed half mad, wandering around, asking for a woman no one seemed to know. Crazed and lost would only make her fit in.

Apartments inside the upper plateau were being used to house the refugees from Brevia; perhaps her mother had already descended to them. She might have been one of the first off the longships. Then again, Bellona had lived down in the narrow ground levels of the city. She wouldn't know her way up among the villas.

She might also be dead.

The thought brought Lira to a halt. A couple of islanders bumped into her, grumbled and pressed on. For a time, she stared at her toes, suppressing the urge to hyperventilate. Once again, they were on the verge of a battle they had no great hope of winning and it wasn't right that her last goodbye with her only family had happened over a year ago.

She drifted for a time, another lost soul amidst the swirl of fear and suspicion. A terrible combination. All were alert like abused animals, dark eyes darting quickly, legs braced and ready to run at a moment's notice. Not an ounce of trust remained. Dragons must have been as awful to each other as any human had. Round and round she went, calling uselessly for her mother, her voice lost in the crowd.

"Lira," a voice called. Lira twisted her neck so fast it cricked, but it was clearly a man's voice on the second calling. "Lira." It was Raymond's voice. "Lira, there you are."

Mounted on his towering horse, he cut a pathway through the crowd to her. Even allowing for the fact he was atop Bruce, Raymond looked taller somehow, his hair and steel glittering in the hazy sunset.

He dismounted when he reached her, looking deeply concerned. "You're crying," he said softly. Lira blushed so fiercely she thought her cheeks would catch fire. She made a fist and was about to rub at her eyes when Raymond raised a silent finger as though telling her to say nothing. Then he produced one of his white handkerchiefs.

Lira couldn't help but laugh, a half-choked laugh, the kind of small laugh that could battle tears. Raymond looked unsure what this meant as he handed her the cloth, but she smiled at him as she accepted it. He was as heavily armoured as any Praetorian, with the stiff upper lip of Brevian blue-bloods, and rode a war horse so large it might bite a man's arm off, but he still kept these dainty fancies on his person.

"Thank you," she said, dabbing at her eyes. "What are you doing up here?"

Raymond looked sheepish. "I assumed you'd be looking for your mother, and as I failed on that front before, I thought it only proper I should offer assistance. I'd like to," he added.

Lira shook her head. "We don't have the time to spare. I shouldn't even be here."

"I'm so sorry, Lira. This must be torture for you."

"Yes, it is. I don't feel grounded without knowing she's okay. Does that make sense?"

Raymond took a step closer, then hesitated and drew up short. "For what it's worth, if she has even half your tenacity, then I know she'll be just fine."

Lira felt a hug wouldn't have gone amiss, but at the same time, she didn't want to collapse into a bubbling heap in front of him. A cluster of beleaguered dragons squeezed by, forcing the pair of them to step very close together to avoid a collision. Lavender carried gently from him, light and pleasant. Damn it, what was wrong with her? She'd spent the weeks he'd been away rehearsing her speech if he ever returned, and when he did, she'd panicked. Said nothing. They were about to face a horrific enemy and probably wouldn't survive it. So why was saying a few words to Raymond still so terrifying?

'Why did you come back?' she'd planned to say. It sounded casual enough. 'Was it duty? Was it me? Was it Bruce?' It sounded clever in her head, a nice bit of humour to end on. Though if it was for the horse, she'd look a right idiot.

She opened her mouth, then hastily closed it. No, no, no, she couldn't ask it.

He smiled awkwardly at her.

She smiled even more awkwardly; the most awkward smile, in her opinion, that had ever disgraced the face of dragon or human alike.

Also, she was painfully aware of his hand hanging close to her own. Her fingers felt numb, as though plunged into a bucket of ice.

Some courage surged within her and she opened her mouth to speak, but Bruce had another mind. The great horse nuzzled his nose in between them, his big sad eyes looking at her. Lira rubbed at his neck, just the way she'd learned he liked it.

"He really loves you now," Raymond said.

Lira gulped. "Does he?" Her voice was high and traitorous.

"He's never taken to anyone else so quickly." Raymond sighed and gave Bruce a scratch too. "This battle will be no place for him. Shall we put him in his stable, then head for the wall? The company awaits us there."

Lira tried not to show her disappointment and annoyance. It was the bloody horse, wasn't it?

"Yes, that sounds good. I should get away from here. Work on the walls will take my mind off... off everything."

Darnuir – The City Walls

The sun was beginning to set when the red dragons came. Darnuir saw the crimson line appear on the lip of the horizon like the crack of dawn. They came on quickly, too quickly, so fast he could hardly believe what he was seeing. How had poor Damien outrun these things? It was no wonder it had killed him to do so.

Rectar's new servants flooded the land, a wild sea of blood.

And they did not slow down.

It was evident they had no siege equipment; no towers, no ladders; and it seemed they were in no mind to construct any. Some of the troops nearby were pointing this out to each other, exclaiming at their fortune.

"Rectar will not have released his armies without the means to destroy us," Darnuir said. "We are in for the worst fight of our lives."

He gripped the handle of the Dragon's Blade, looking down at his weapon in trepidation. The head of the dragon was a dark blood red. It always had been. Was this what his people truly were when stripped to purely the dragon?

Ahead, with the sun rapidly falling, the red dragons advanced even faster, seeming to gain fresh energy as they neared their goal.

Darnuir filled his lungs, tightened his grip on the blade and unsheathed it, cutting skywards. He gulped, fear of magic piercing his courage more so than these creatures. But if they were to have any hope, both he and Blaine would need to find their strength.

He reached for the handle to the door in his mind; pulled it open.

The kick at the back of his head was the firm embrace of an old friend. His eyes widened, his body grew taut with power, and the burn down his arm felt reassuringly warm. Carefully, he steadied the doorway until only a gentle flow of Cascade ran into him. He'd have to pace himself if he was to last the night.

The red dragons continued to advance across the plain, their roaring now reaching the city walls.

Darnuir channelled the magic into his voice. "This night, we fight as one. All the Three Races. And we will stand together, hold together, or die together." He turned to face the city, looking along the walls and down into the packed streets below, to the mixed formations of soldiers looking up to him. He felt something more was needed, so he set the Dragon's Blade alight with a stream of flames. "You've trained together, bled together, grieved together. Put aside lingering fears and fresh anger. Tonight, you do not fight for dragon lands or a dragon city. Tonight, you fight for your world. Our world. I would see us save it. Would you?"

The defenders of Aurisha cheered, clashing weapons and stamping their feet; a moment which drowned out all the enemy's noise.

Darnuir returned his gaze northwards as the first of the reds passed the line at which the human cannons could reach. Lira and Raymond did not need an order.

The blasts stole Darnuir's breath away. Dark balls hurtled out to meet the enemy, crashing into their swarming mass, throwing up soil and bodies as they pounded into the earth. Rectar's minions did not pause, but the weapons proved to be effective. Too effective. In that moment, Darnuir had nothing but hatred for Arkus for withholding this from him.

They might have stood a chance of survival if all of Brevia's new army had been here to face Rectar's own.

Closer now, Darnuir could make out the beasts wearing spiked armour along their forearms, shins and feet. They each bore an enormous black broadsword, crudely cut, more like a giant razor blade than a balanced weapon.

Musket balls penetrated their hide, but Raymond's company were too few in number, and so the majority of the enemy drew close to the walls. Yet there was no point in holding back. On the rooftops behind him was every hunter, bowman, and catapult crew they had spare. He pulled back the Dragon's Blade, magnified his voice again and cried, "Hit them with everything."

Darnuir lit the Dragon's Blade and launched it as well.

The impact of the arrows was not as it should have been. The enemy ran through the storm as though each steel tip was nought but rain. Some fell, but it seemed there were few vulnerable spots on their scaly bodies. Rocks still crushed them, and the Dragon's Blade skewered two like meat.

As Darnuir caught his returning blade, the first red dragons made it to the wall. They leapt, eight feet, ten feet, maybe higher off the ground, driving their spiked armour into the stone of the wall, cutting deep and holding firm. Only starium could so easily cut into itself. Rectar had gone to great lengths to equip his dragons.

They scurried up the walls like fat bloated spiders. Their taut tails maintained their balance and forked tongues lashed from long snouts. Arrows pinged off hard scales. Muskets cracked, cannons boomed, rocks thudded into flesh and earth.

Darnuir had never been less sure of victory. But he couldn't show it.

"Make them pay for every inch," he bellowed. He turned to one of his closer Praetorians. "Release the oil."

"It's not hot yet, sire."

"I'll make it so."

He strode to the vat, tipped it over the wall himself, and sent a blazing cone of fire from his sword. Magical residue built disgustingly in his mouth and he spat the thick gob over the edge for good measure.

A smell like rotting meat being roasted churned his stomach.

Taking his cue, the defenders tipped all the oil barrels over. He hadn't meant for that, but he couldn't let it go to waste. He pulled on more magic, sending tendrils of flames licking left and right far along the walls, setting the spills alight.

Sweat dripped into his eyes as the inferno raged. The trick had decimated much of the first wave but more of the enemy now jumped through or over the fires to begin their climb up the city walls. Darnuir pulled back as the first creatures crested the battlements.

A towering monster near seven feet tall swept savagely with bulging arms and thick tail, shredding soldiers with the spikes of its armour.

Darnuir charged. The beast sensed he was the real threat and roared at him, its putrid spittle flying into his face. Darnuir's Cascade-enhanced block shattered the beast's weapon. That caused it alarm. It panicked, roared again, but Darnuir ran it through, the Dragon's Blade cutting right through its armoured hide. A Praetorian tried his regular sword on it next, and it took a few hard shoves to break the scales.

Along the walls, red dragons clashed with the defenders. Their shields helped, but the dragons had never faced a foe who could outmuscle them.

"Work as one! These are not demons to be taken on singlehandedly."

He stamped on a long nose as it poked above the parapet. He sent another crashing to the ground amidst the reds who were working to clear the rubble that was blocking their entry at the gate. He ought to have stayed on the gatehouse to observe the whole battle and delay their breaking in below, but the fight for the walls already looked desperate.

"Stay here," he told the Praetorians. "I'll be back as often as I can." And he was on the move, dashing to every weak spot, Cascade thrumming though his veins. He was the one person who might fight these things directly. He alone was stronger, faster, fiercer, even louder, as he called orders and encouragement with the power of a hundred horn blasts.

"Fight them," he heralded, running from west to east, knowing in his heart that he could not keep this up forever.

31

THE LAST GUARDIAN

"There has always been a guardian and a king. An eternal balance, neither stronger than the other."

From Tiviar's Histories

Blaine – The Lower City

A third round of Rectar's monstrosities joined the battle upon the walls. Their red eyes burned brightly, as large as eggs upon their beastly faces. Rectar had corrupted his people beyond all recognition. And he'd been allowed to do so.

Blaine looked to the stars and scowled. If the gods had let this happen to his people, to their chosen people, then what kind of protectors were they? Darnuir was right. Down here, in this world, they were alone.

He refocused on the battle. Blaine was five hundred paces from the broken city gates, where only heaps of starium rubble blocked the enemy's entry. A great formation of dragons and human spearmen stood prepared as the first line of defence for when the reds inevitably broke through. Bows twanged from above as the hunters unleashed their stores, for all the good it seemed to do.

The first gap in the mound of debris appeared. Red claws began sweeping great chunks of rock away as easily as digging through dirt.

Blaine tightened his grip as best he could upon the Guardian's Blade. Before the night was over, he'd stand side by side with his grandson and prove to Rectar how strong they were. Or might have been, at any rate.

Should it come to it, Blaine still had one last option he could employ. It would break all the tradition, laws and understanding of his race. It might break the very rules of the gods.

That thought caused him to smile.

More holes appeared in the gateway rubble, with more scaled hands scraping in. Snouts poked in after, puffing hot breath, desperate to join the battle.

Above, on the wall, the number of red dragons looked dangerous. Blaine saw half a dozen arrows splinter harmlessly off one. Their archers simply weren't causing enough damage. Once, Blaine would have scorned fighting from afar, but with these monsters it would be foolish to engage head-on. Their necks appeared to be weak points, but surely there were others?

The flames of Darnuir's oil trap created a flaming haze to see by. Red dragons jostled for position, as aggressive with each other as they were in taking the walls. Blaine watched eagle-eyed as arrows flew at them. He saw the arrow from one hunter's bow more easily pierce the back of an enemy when it was turned around in the crush. The creature's limbs jerked, froze at angles, then it fell from the wall to the streets below.

So that was it. They had to hit them from behind.

Blaine empowered his voice. "Fidelm. I need you."

The fairy general was by his side surprisingly quickly, his expression eager.

"Guardian?"

"Time to make use of our flying archers," Blaine said. "The enemy's scales are weaker on their backs. Take hunters and hit them as they climb the wall. We must thin their numbers or we'll barely hold another hour."

Fidelm took off just as the barrier at the city gate was breached and the first of the enemy hurtled through.

"Hold fast," Blaine called.

Their shield wall held better than it had any right to, yet the agile reds were soon jumping or slipping around the defences. Surviving dragons fell back through the channels in the human ranks and row upon row of spears thwarted the enemy advance.

For now, the northern road was held. Yet the enemy were fast swarming into the city, finding every available path and alleyway like running water, scrambling along buildings with their spiked armour and falling upon the weaker flanks of their formations.

Blaine rushed to meet them, leaving the relative safety of the back of his formation. What good was shouting for bravery if he showed none himself?

He needed the Cascade to meet every twist and turn of the creatures, yet while they were powerful, Rectar's new minions were crude in style. Spectres were skilled fighters. These reds relied solely on their size and strength, and Blaine could beat that, if barely.

The Guardian's Blade itself proved to be his greatest asset, cutting into their hard exteriors without effort. He blinded one with a burst of light from the blade. The red howled, clawing at its own eyes, and Blaine ran it through. As its great body slumped from his sword, the first of Fidelm's flyers buzzed overhead. He would have said a prayer for them if he thought it would help. He lost sight of the flyers behind the curtain of smoke beyond the wall but swore the red dragon numbers had begun to abate.

With fresh hope Blaine spurred himself on, a river of Cascade running through him, desperately keeping the brunt of the attack at bay.

Darnuir – The City Walls

Darnuir slid along the blood-slickened wall, leaping over body piles. He spun in mid-air, kicking a red off the wall. He landed, skidded again, keeping his balance through magic alone, then smashed into a clump of reds, cutting or knocking them down. A group of defenders shouted their thanks, but he was already moving.

Squinting, it was clear that red scales far outweighed golden armour upon the wall. Fidelm's flying archers might be the only thing preventing them from being overrun.

Ahead was the section protected by Raymond's company. Darnuir reached them and relieved the beleaguered defenders by cutting down the enemy. He looked for Raymond and Lira. The chevalier was directing the fire of his men, wisely keeping back from the melee. Panic took him when he couldn't find Lira, but someone took his arm. He turned and groaned with relief.

"Thank goodness you're all right."

Lira was breathing hard, her hair slick with sweat. "We can't hold here."

"The gate has been breached," Darnuir said. "I fear we'll have to take all fighting to the streets sooner than I would—"

"Look out," Lira cried, pointing with her sword.

Red dragons landed amidst the musket company and more were leaping over the dragon defenders, making for the softer humans.

Darnuir called upon more magic, determined not to lose their one precious advantage. He moved so fast it was instinctive, taking down four reds in the space of an eyeblink. His arm ached. Bile rose in his throat. The Dragon's Blade seared with heat, cauterising wounds even as it inflicted them.

He thinned their numbers, and Praetorians fought the rest, fighting solo, unable to form any formation in the crush. Lira's sword arm was knocked aside, leaving her exposed. Darnuir rushed to her side as the howling red brought its spiked arm towards her face.

Darnuir thrust his sword through the beast's tail, pinning it to the stone. It tugged the red back, ripping its tail into bloody ribbons, but its talon-like nails caught Lira. She screamed, doubling over, and Darnuir, enraged, grabbed the fleshy ruins of the red's tail and launched it off the wall.

The Dragon's Blade wiggled in the stone before pulling itself free. He caught it and paid the price for drawing on such force. Venomous residue pulsed down his arm, bulging his veins bright blue. He pushed past the pain, remembering Lira was hurt. Raymond was already there.

"I'm okay," she said.

"Is that what you call bleeding like this?" Raymond said, pressing a swiftly reddening handkerchief to Lira's forehead. He pulled away for Darnuir to see. The cut was deep but had narrowly missed her eye.

"I should've gotten to you faster," Darnuir said. "Can you go on?"

"Of course," she said and gently pushed Raymond away.

Darnuir took stock. The balance of crimson and gold on the wall had moved even further towards the red.

"Fall back," he said grimly. "Take the cannons to the secondary positions and get your company down to help stem the tide on the northern road."

As they burst into action, he continued along the walls, calling the retreat with his enhanced voice.

Blaine – The Northern Road

Darnuir's bellows to abandon the walls felt like an age ago. Each encounter sapped at his strength and there was no respite.

The dense spear formations held well enough, but Blaine could see the faltering signs. He and the dragons couldn't block every red dragon descending from freshly conquered rooftops.

Blaine saw that happen now but was unable to break away from his current adversary. He dove down, sprang up under its sweeping arms, and drove the Guardian's Blade through the red's chin. By the time Blaine reached the humans, a score of them had fallen. A nauseating sweetness laced the air, more powerful than the smoke and blood and sweat. The humans were terrified.

And Blaine shared their fear.

Perhaps their enemies could smell it too; they were dragons, after all. Their slithering tongues licked the air, spewing their own foul breath. Blaine took pleasure in severing one before roundly striking the beast clean through the face.

He fought on, seeing every kill as a victory in this last stand against the Shadow. For this would surely be their last battle. He and Darnuir could help to stem the tide in places. But all around their troops were dying. And where was the king? Blaine no longer spotted the fiery trail of the Dragon's Blade upon the walls.

"Make way."

The call came from a street to his right. Blaine turned, shocked to see Praetorians running at full tilt, carrying those black iron cannons between them. The walls were lost, then. They would be heading to the harbourside to set up the cannons as planned.

He saw Lira at their head and met her eye. She nodded wildly, lacking the breath to speak. More of her Praetorians came running, carrying the human soldiers either in their arms or on their backs, all the while stalked by reds leaping from wall to wall.

"With me," Blaine cried.

He charged down the street, meaning to cut off Lira's pursuers. Those human weapons were their only advantage. He would not let them fall.

In the confines of the street he lost the light of the stars. He lit the Guardian's Blade against the crushing darkness and saw the reds perched or hanging above, their eyes turning to him. They dropped to the ground, sending tremors upon impact. He felt it from all around, with no sound of a skirmish behind him.

Blaine realised then that he was alone.

He had called, and there was no one left to follow.

He'd sent so many of his Light Bearers away. He would join them soon.

Red dragons surrounded him, moving slowly, wary of him but knowing he was theirs. Deep within the web of streets under the plateau, no one else would be coming. His grip felt weaker than ever, but he doubted even that would save him here. Still, he wouldn't go down without a fight. He had one choice.

He raised his blade.

Every red pounced.

Blaine swung. His strike glanced off a starium vambrace, and a huge red fist smashed into his torso. He felt hammering blows on his back, then on his entire body. Claws scraped at his armour. Starium-lined plate was all that kept him alive. A tail took out his legs, and another body blow sent him hurtling backwards, hitting solid brick. Pain exploded along his spine. He crumpled. With his vision swimming, he was only vaguely aware of the red eyes dashing close to finish him.

No muscle moved for him. Nothing. He had to risk healing.

But his hand was empty.

The Guardian's Blade lay out of reach, its glow already dimming. It lay there, as he lay here. Unmoving. This was how Norbanus had been defeated. Disarmed in a bog. Blaine had been disarmed in an alley. Both inglorious ends.

A long red snout loomed over him. Blaine feared this would be the last thing he felt; the hot breath of this monster and its gloopy saliva, dropping in thick gobs onto his face. Blaine looked defiantly into its burning eyes, ready for death.

A crack sounded. One. Two. Three – a whole volley of them.

The head of the dragon blew apart. Blaine's world went scarlet before he had the sense to close his eyes. More firing sounded, more death screams of the enemy. It ended. Lighter human footsteps patted over, and the corpse of the red was pushed off him. Raymond proffered a hand.

"I can't move," Blaine said. "Need. Sword."

Raymond scanned around. "There. Bring it quickly," he commanded his men.

Five humans groaning with effort managed to move the blade. They dropped it into Blaine's numb hand and, slowly, he felt life return to his body. He drew on the Cascade, sending it to his back, wincing as the muscle and bones reknitted. His spine crunched back together, and he sprang upright, gasping from the toll.

The Guardian's Blade was built for health, but that had been a hard task. A few of his fingernails turned black and hairs were falling clean from his scalp. His left arm still hung uselessly, blood dripping from his fingers, but he didn't dare heal anymore.

"That was too close," Raymond said. "Can you move?"

"Enough to get away."

"We'll take you to the northern road. We're heading —"

"To the harbour, I know. Lira passed this way."

Blaine struggled to his feet and began to stagger southwards.

"Blaine?" Raymond called. "Let us assist you."

"One was never going to be enough," Blaine muttered to himself. He was done. He had one working arm and knew in his heart that something drastic was needed if they were to see the morning.

"Blaine?"

He glanced around. "Get word to Darnuir to meet me in the sanctum. There is something I must give him."

Lira – The Lower City

. . .

The cannon was heavy and cumbersome, but with the help of Harra, Lira hauled it all the way up the northern road. Near the harbourside, she thudded it down by a collection of ammunition and powder they'd set up for this eventuality. This inevitability.

Now the huge guns aimed directly up the northern road, as though the ancient boulevard had become a great shooting gallery. Nearby, Harra doubled over, huffing and trying to catch her breath. Lira felt no better; her side was a spasm of pain, her legs burned, her head throbbed. Blood ran into her mouth from the cut, and dizzily she joined Harra in doubling over. Perhaps she'd just leave the cannons on the next retreat. They'd have to fall back towards the switchback road next, where these long-barrelled machines would be ineffective anyway.

Artillery crews – or what was left of them – arrived half a minute later, carried by dragons from the front.

"Thank ye kindly," their commander said as he was placed down like a toddler.

Lira couldn't help showing her surprise at the courtesy. "You're welcome," she managed through a wince.

The commander was already in action. "Fast to it now, gents. Prefect, do we have permission to fire?"

Lira turned her attention northwards to the horror of the battlefront. The walls were lost, fire had entered the city, red dragons were crawling along the buildings and running unchecked over rooftops. Stronger formations held on the main roads, but beyond a certain point, all was lost.

Her jaw clenched. No matter how far back they aimed, friendly fire would be a high risk to those potentially trapped near the walls. But she couldn't just let the enemy run amok.

"Hit them as hard as you can."

Something heavy seemed to sink through her as she made her decision, pressing down on her gut. She took her dragons and fled the scene as though it could exonerate her.

As they tore back up the northern road, she saw Darnuir running towards them, blazing a trail through the night. He was drawing on a lot of magic. It was necessary, but she still couldn't help feeling wary about it. Even more worrying was why Darnuir was leaving the battle.

"Blaine needs me," Darnuir growled, as though sensing her question. "Raymond says he's injured. Take the rest of the Guard." He waved towards the dragons who were struggling to keep up with him. "And do what you can to slow the enemy's advance. Fall back as you see fit."

"But you can't—" Lira began, but he was already on the move and quickly out of sight.

The crack and splutter of musketfire cut above the rest of the battle. Lira's thoughts abandoned Darnuir and turned back to Raymond. He and his company were still in the thick of it. He needed her.

She ran back towards the hell of the front lines without another word, the wearied Praetorians following in her wake.

Darnuir – The Basilica of Light

Darnuir skidded towards the stairs leading down to the depths of the sanctum below, jumping whole flights at a time in a Cascade-induced sprint. He arrived in Blaine's Inner Sanctum, breathing heavily, arm searing, his tongue dry and heavy from magic.

His hammering heart froze when he saw Blaine.

Chelos was carefully removing his breastplate while bloodstained linens sat over a limp arm.

"How bad is it?" Darnuir said, rushing to his side.

Blaine waved him off. "Injuries occur in battle. Do not worry about me."

"Won't the healing powers of the Guardian's Blade help you?" Darnuir said, not caring whether panic had seeped into his voice. Blaine looked a mess. His hair seemed to be falling out, and there were black blotches on his skin.

"I've healed enough already," Blaine said. He sat up, placing his good arm around Chelos to steady himself. "Were it our only option, I'd take the risk and heal. But I fear I'm too old for such bravery."

"What other option do we have?" Darnuir said, fists clenched. He could not tarry here. But without Blaine, what were they to do? What was he to do?

"I can't do this alone," Darnuir said.

"Yes, you can," Blaine said, biting through the pain.

"I have one blade."

"You might have two."

Darnuir staggered backwards, the implication hitting him like a gale of wind.

"You cannot mean—"

"I do."

"Blaine," Chelos said, aghast. "You cannot. The balance. The system of the gods—"

"Has not helped us enough," Blaine said.

Darnuir's mind raced. He was already gripping the Dragon's Blade so hard his knuckles were stark white, his veins pulsing silver-blue as he drained the poison already in him. Would two blades process the power quick enough so that he wouldn't break from it? Or would he find himself chained again, wailing in a cold sweat and slipping into a nightmarish sleep forever more?

Darnuir shook. "No one should have that much power."

"Rectar does," said Blaine. "Look at his foul sorcery. He is a god who has upped the stakes yet again. We must do the same. This was the way it always had to be. I should have known that. I cannot wield the blade of the king. I do not have the blood. But nothing says I cannot pass the Guardian's Blade on to you."

"But Chelos is right. The balance. We'd shatter it."

"This is no time for delicacy. No guardian has dared dream of it, for it could be the ruin of our race. But if we don't do something, there won't be a dragon race left. It isn't lightly I do this." He stood, took the few uneasy steps to Darnuir. "If you had asked me to do this the day I met you in Torridon, or in Val'tarra, I would never have entertained the thought. I believed I would be the one to lead our race to salvation. I was wrong. You're a better man than I, and you'll be a far better ruler if we make it through this." He drew out the Guardian's Blade, looked upon it with both old fondness and grief, yet passed the hilt towards Darnuir without hesitation.

Darnuir took another step back. "It cannot be this easy."

"We are in their temple. There is ceremony and flattery for the gods that usually accompanies it, but I do not intend to ask for their blessing. 'It is not yet time,' the gods said to me. I think they foresaw this." He pushed the blade closer to Darnuir. "I know you are afraid of magic, and rightly so. And if it breaks you to kill Rectar, it will at least be a worthy end. Finish this long war and try to right my sins. Our sins."

Darnuir contemplated the sword being freely handed to him. The Guardian's Blade was as beautiful as his own weapon, the otherworldly metal of the blade flowing like molten gold, the white opals bright as stars.

Had this been his secret fear all along? Had he sought to reinvigorate Blaine not out of loyalty or an attempt at familial bonds, but from fear that this might happen? And a fear that he could never hope to be a normal dragon again, never mind a normal man?

Darnuir reached his free hand towards it, hesitating just above the hilt.

"Do you, Darnuir, accept the mantle of guardian? There are many duties I could list but only one that matters. Will you take the Guardian's Blade and rid this world of the Shadow?"

"I shall."

Behind Blaine, Chelos made a shuddering sigh and sat down, clutching at his heart. Darnuir shared his shock. He couldn't tell how fast his own heart was beating, and could barely manoeuvre his numb fingers onto the Guardian's Blade. But he did. His free hand grasped the hilt and he squeezed to be sure it was really there; feeling how perfect it was in his hand, as though it had been made for him. A second doorway appeared in his mind, already open.

Power thundered into him.

. . .

Lira – The Lower City

Watching the spearmen break was grim. The reds waded into the humans, chopping and cleaving at will. Lira faced away, unable to witness the butchery. It would come for them all soon enough, she supposed.

She redoubled her efforts to hold down the flanks of Raymond's company as they began their rotating fire. With her shield raised, she took blow after blow, fearing her arm would snap under the strain. Each chance she got, she stabbed downwards, looking for the softer feet between the joins of their spiked armour.

One grabbed her shield and hauled her with it, sending her spinning in the air. Her back hit a wall with nowhere else to go.

Three reds lay between her and the rest of the Guard.

A treacherous, exhausted part of her didn't want to resist the inevitable.

Then she saw Raymond breaking out of the formation, running her way.

"What are you doing?" he cried. "We must save her."

One of the three red dragons turned and swatted him, knocking him to the ground with a clang.

"No!" cried Lira, emptying her lungs, all thoughts of giving up now gone.

She kicked off the wall, leaping for the creature looming over Raymond, and cut into its softer back. Pivoting, she faced the second; blocked once, blocked twice, and then she struck so madly her swing nearly took her off balance. She managed to snap the red dragon's shard of a sword near the hilt and it didn't raise its armoured arms in time to save itself from her next attack.

The third red, however, would get her. That, she understood.

A pistol fired and the last enemy stumbled, its leg gone. Lira staggered up and ran her sword through its roaring mouth.

She didn't bother to watch it fall, but ran to Raymond. He'd managed to roll over, a smoking pistol shaking in his hand. As Lira pulled him to his feet, she suddenly felt overwhelmed with anger.

"You idiot."

"You're welcome."

"Why? Why must you always act the bloody hero?"

"Because I came back for you," he said, almost exasperated. She met his eye and her fury snapped into delirious relief. She yanked his head to her own and kissed him.

Now her heart really did feel like it would explode. His hand found her hair, he kissed her back, and for a blissful moment the whole world stopped.

Then she remembered they were in the middle of a war.

They pulled apart, but she resisted looking upon the horror of the battle for a moment, trying to savour the last good thing she was likely to know. When she did, there was fresh yelling from their troops.

"The king," they cried. "It must be the king."

About time, Lira thought, looking everywhere for Darnuir. But she couldn't see him.

"Look up," Raymond said, pointing wildly.

Lira did, unsure of what to expect. But there he was. Darnuir soared overhead from what must have been the most powerful Cascade jump she'd seen him make. He'd most certainly break from this much magic. Yet something was different. At this distance it was hard to say, but that needle of fire must have been the Dragon's Blade, and the luminous strip of light, well, that must be—

No, she thought. *It cannot be.*

Darnuir soared past and she lost sight of him. Then something hit the bulk of the red horde with more force than a dozen cannonballs. Red dragons parted, dead or fleeing before two radiant pillars of swirling fire and golden light.

32

AFTER THE STORM

"How does it feel to wield that much power? We'll never know."

Author Unknown

Darnuir – The Plaza

Darnuir walked under the purple pre-dawn clouds. He'd driven the red dragons off, sending them in a furious retreat north to their master. One final confrontation remained.

His blades were sheathed; the Dragon's Blade at his waist, and the Guardian's upon his back like a quiver. With each step he took, he felt as though he might launch into the sky. Flesh and bone caged him, his body now a hindrance, unable to react the way the power within him desired. It was well he was restricted. No one was meant to hold two blades. In other hands, this would be the end of them. Of everything.

Rectar could not be allowed to take a second blade. Darnuir understood that now; truly understood it, beyond the notion that the enemy had to be thwarted. It was a good thing Castallan never got his heart's desire to control the Dragon's Blade, and a better thing still that he – Darnuir – had only received his second in dire straits when need demanded it. And that was with Blaine's insistence, rather than from pride or greed.

Knowing now what it was like, he would never have been prepared for this in his first life. He spared a thought for Draconess, and whether he would be pleased with the man he'd become. Even if it had taken far too long to get here.

Out on the plaza, he found himself inexorably drawn towards the Basilica. A force, light yet unassailable, made him drift towards it like liquid in a groove. The feeling reminded him of old memories in the Dragon's Blade pulling on his mind, only this power was drawing him forwards rather than back. And perhaps it was merely that his senses had gained new strength, but it seemed the dome radiated a glow it never had before; dim as a low-burning candle, and yet still there. Song notes drifted from the doorway to the temple, faintly as a lullaby from the earliest of memories.

It wasn't long before a lone figure exited the Basilica, carefully taking the stairs down. Yet Chelos could still move briskly enough, coming to meet Darnuir as bidden. The old steward had wrapped himself in a thick grey cloak against the morning cold, something Darnuir could no longer feel.

"Blaine still sleeps," Chelos said. "He took rest the moment he heard the city had been made safe, and he sleeps so deeply I'd ask you not to disturb him."

Darnuir nodded, taking in Chelos as a whole. The old dragon; Blaine and Draconess' confidant in their plans; Cassandra's carer and tutor. He'd never seemed so small. Perhaps because he was hidden beneath that cloak, or because his skin now matched the colour of his hair, leaving only puffy eyes apart from the grey, and that was a telling sign in itself.

"I have no desire to wake Blaine," Darnuir said. "Let him sleep, and may he have pleasant dreams for once. It is no longer his duty to bear the burdens of our people. I dare say you too could do with more rest?"

Chelos grimaced. "I have not slept well of late."

Darnuir was not surprised. "These last months have been harrowing. I find a walk can help clear the head. Will you walk with me, Chelos?"

"Of course, my king."

Darnuir did not lead the old man far. He made for the vantage point where he had first met Fidelm after waking, and insisted there that Chelos sit on the ancient stone bench with him. Darnuir joined him in suffering small jolts of pain for his efforts. All his senses were heightened, every nerve on edge. Even sitting felt uncomfortable. He heard Chelos' slow breaths as if they were the heaves of great struggle. He even heard the low beat of his heart. Blood and the sweetness of human fear hung in the air, as did the seaweed from the ocean and the sourness of spent powder. He smelled it all, heard it all, could see beyond the sight of hawks and swore that he saw the outline of a great mountain far away. This ought to have overwhelmed him, but it didn't. His mind felt expanded, wider, and yet more collected all at once.

There they sat, overlooking the smouldering city, and spoke for a while on small matters; on the bravery of those refugees still huddled within the plateau itself, of the remaining victuals, and how the city might be remade. When Darnuir asked him what he thought of the humans' new weapons, Chelos admitted quite plainly that he was afraid. When Darnuir did not respond immediately, the old dragon asked if that would be all.

"No," Darnuir said with a heavy heart. "That will not be all."

He made sure he faced Chelos, to meet his eye and attempt to read his true feelings there. The twitch of Chelos' cheek, the way his gaze darted away and back, told Darnuir he was right.

"I know what you did. I know it was you."

A gulp of choked fear bulged in Chelos' throat, but his jaw was set.

"I never meant for them to kill."

"That does not make it right."

Chelos sniffed. "What made you suspect?"

"Honestly, I found it odd that Bacchus would have been so brazen, yet with all that was happening I let my doubt slide. When Damien returned to warn of the red dragons, he also brought another message – a plea from Bacchus to consider more carefully what had happened. How you were the one who recruited those men. You even had him convinced that he'd accidentally wrought those crimes. It makes me sick just to think of it. How could you?"

Chelos' face had turned to stone, a dozen new lines chiselled into his brow.

"Because I felt it to be right. You've never seen our people strong, Darnuir, but if you had, as I have, as Blaine has, then perhaps you wouldn't have ignored our faith so easily. I remember when our people were great, when our belief was strong, and we stood above all, not begging for scraps nor stooping to placate others. You also won't remember watching Draconess fall, and back then I think you were happy to see him diminish, pushing you one step closer to your prize."

"A feeling that disgusts me now," Darnuir said. "I think Draconess was right to change as he did. I thought – well, I hoped – that you would have felt the same."

Chelos shook a little, though more from anger than fear. "You have not spent your life in servitude to them and their failed plans. All failures. Again, and again, and again. Every time, I held faith in them, but that may have been misplaced. All my faith, all my loyalty should have always been with the gods. Not in Blaine. Not in Draconess. Even after the Nail Head, even after Blaine heard their voices as so many did, he still doubted, he still stressed caution. And he did not act." His last words were spat through gritted teeth. "I wasn't even there to bask in the gods' presence. I was stuck as I've always been: in Blaine's shadow, tending to his trivial matters back at camp."

"It sounds like you are jealous."

"Jealous?" Chelos barked. "Yes," he growled. "Perhaps I am. A lifetime of service, Darnuir, all to those I was told knew better. But they didn't. A lifetime of faith and I was not granted their blessing that night."

"So you thought killing some humans might earn that?" Darnuir asked. "Have Blaine's warnings about the folly of Norbanus taught you nothing?"

"I told you, I never desired deaths," Chelos said. "I only thought to drive the humans and fairies out of the city. You cannot understand," he added, in a tone as though speaking to a young child asking tough questions. "Our race was at its finest before these alliances. I only sought to take us back to those days. The gods are on our side, Darnuir – why is that so hard to comprehend anymore?"

"I think because people like you act as you do," Darnuir said. "I do not think you are right, but even if you were, I still would not change my mind. If our so-called gods are pleased by what you did, by what Norbanus tried to do, then they are no gods of mine. Real or no. As it stands, they seem to have no opinion on it, and so I reserve my judgement on them."

"I never expected you to understand."

"I doubt I ever will. It saddens me that you chose this path right at the end. I think Draconess would be heartbroken to know it."

"I don't care what Draconess would think."

"You're lying," Darnuir said, his tone firm. Chelos lifted his head. Whether he was feigning indifference or not Darnuir wasn't certain, but if Chelos did not react to the next question, then he was truly lost. "Cassandra would be horrified. I know you care about what she thinks."

Whatever defences the old man had raised shattered. He slumped further into his cloak, hanging his head to his chest.

"Well, she isn't here," Chelos said to his toes. "So luckily I did not have to think about her much in this." He gave another choked gulp and turned his attention towards the precipice of the plateau, as though contemplating the drop. "Will you tell Blaine?"

"I haven't decided."

"Will you kill me?"

Darnuir considered, bringing his fingers together in a steeple. "That would be a greater waste. Bacchus already died in your stead, and I see no way to fully right that injustice. Nor do I wish to be the one to explain to Cassandra why you are dead, and that it was by my hand. She has suffered enough. No, you will not die for this, Chelos, but you are done. Blaine is no longer the guardian and I have no use for you. Should we survive the coming weeks, you will leave to the west in exile. The excuse will be that you wish to return to Cassandra, whom you dearly miss, and who I'm sure misses you, and frankly it's far more than you deserve."

He reached behind his head, drew the Guardian's Blade free and placed it on his lap. He pressed on the top opal on the hilt and it fell into his hand, weighing more than any stone had a right to, and yet it was a feather compared to the ruby he'd held in Val'tarra; before he had unlocked the memories within. Perhaps this was because these memories were not his own, not his failures or troubles or woes, and so they could never feel as heavy to him as they did to their owners. In time he might explore all the memories of the guardians, but for now, he had a task at hand.

"In time, I may tell Blaine," Darnuir said. "But, if I may venture, I think you still care how he thinks of you, more so than even your gods. I wonder whether it was their approval you were seeking, or his? Whatever the case, I shall store this memory of your confession as evidence should the need arise. Stay well-behaved in your exile or I shall tell Blaine, and he will no longer think of you as a lifelong ally, follower and friend, but only as another failure."

Chelos looked upon the gemstone in fear. "Blaine gave me that stone so that I may relive parts of his past. It was strange to see myself through his eyes. To see the absolute reverence I once had. The follies of youth."

"Youth did not cause these tragedies. Youth is not to blame."

Chelos grumbled. "I also found the memory of the night that Kroener – well, Rectar – returned to the city. You might study it to find a weakness in him."

Darnuir lifted the opal higher, feeling its weight grow as he imagined that fateful night. The familiar tugging sensation on his mind grew as the memories sought to reveal themselves, but for the moment he resisted them.

"I may well do that," he said. "Now, return to the sanctum and do not give me cause to call upon you again."

"Yes, my king."

Chelos shuffled away so painfully slowly that Darnuir almost felt ashamed of himself. The truth truly was worse than the lie this time, to know Chelos had fallen so very far.

Darnuir remained on the bench, playing with the opal between his fingers. He had forgotten that Blaine had hidden many memories away in the gems that weren't purely about his duty as guardian. He'd even buried happier thoughts away in them as well, so they would not rise to haunt him nor decay over time. A notion came over Darnuir to find one of those first.

The tapping on his mind grew like an eager guest at the door and Darnuir let it in. His vision abandoned reality, whirling instead through blinding colours as he sought for the feeling he desired. It didn't take long before joy burst all around him, the wheel of colours blooming in orange and yellow, and so he let that memory of Blaine's form.

Yet, for a few seconds, he wondered if something was wrong. He felt the warmth of a fire but could not see it, heard the laughter of a woman but could not see her.

"Can I open them now?" Blaine asked.

"Not yet," came the high voice of a very young girl. "Mummy is still painting me."

"And if you sat still it wouldn't be so difficult."

Darnuir swore it was Kasselle's voice, though far lighter and happier than he had ever heard it in this life or his last.

The girl squealed with laughter. "But it tickles."

"Arlandra, hold still for your mother," Blaine said, repressing a giggle in his own voice. Darnuir had never heard such a sound come from Blaine before. He also felt a desperation he'd never felt before; that was his mother, albeit young, but still that was her voice. He wanted to see her.

"Almost there," Kasselle said. "Just this last one." A few moments passed, and then: "There, all done. Go show Daddy."

"Open your eyes now," Arlandra said in a sing-song voice.

At last Darnuir was able to see. Painted patterns on silver bark walls showed they were in the Argent Tree, with only the canopy between them and the night sky. Starlight shone between the leaves, giving an illusion of a diamond-studded roof. A small fire crackled in the middle of their group, as though they had made camp. Kasselle sat on her knees with her legs tucked underneath her, beaming brightly at him. Well, beaming at Blaine. Other than her mood, she didn't appear any different than she was in the present.

But Blaine only had eyes for Arlandra. He must have been sitting on the floor as well for she stood at eye level with him, grinning so widely he could see every one of her baby white teeth. Her skin was not as deep a blue as a normal fairy's, but a faint tinge of colour caught in the firelight. She had fully inherited her mother's silver hair and it hung down her front in a long ornate braid. One half of her face was hidden behind finely painted lines in greens and blues.

Arlandra raised a hand and shoved it towards him, palm first. "This one means you."

"Why, yes it does," Blaine said. "You even used gold," he added to Kasselle. The queen shrugged as though it meant nothing, but smiled at some private joke. Darnuir recognised the symbol of the guardian all too well.

"And this," Arlandra said, raising her other palm aloft, "is for Mummy." It was the Argent Tree wrought miniature in paint, a masterwork all on its own. Blaine beckoned her to come closer and Arlandra happily obliged, falling into a hug upon his lap. She looked up to him with those big eyes flecked with amber – his eyes.

"I missed you," she said.

"I missed you more," said Blaine.

"Why do you have to be away for so long?"

"My duties lie in Aurisha, and it's very far away from here."

Arlandra pouted. "Can't you stay longer this time?"

"We talked about this, sweetheart," Kasselle said.

Arlandra gave an exasperated sigh. "I know."

"Maybe it's time for your presents," Blaine said. Arlandra perked up, looking between her parents expectantly. Kasselle moved first, opening a jewellery box, yet what she retrieved from it was neither gem nor precious metal. Rather, it was a leaf made of varnished silver wood with a simple string of twine looped through it.

Arlandra's gasp was of excitement this time. "My life brooch?"

"It's time I gave you this," Kasselle said. She came over to their daughter's side, knelt again, and placed the brooch around Arlandra's neck. "That piece of bark is from the very first tree I helped to save when I was a young princess. The sapling was almost completely blackened from magic's poison, but my mother taught me how to save it. She also said to keep a piece of its bark for my own daughter one day, and so I did."

"It's pretty," Arlandra said.

"It will bring you good health while you're away," Kasselle said.

"While I'm awa– what?" Arlandra looked between her parents again, for a moment unsure. Yet Kasselle was smiling and Blaine turned his daughter's cheek gently to face him.

"Now it's time for my present," he said. "This time, you'll come back to Aurisha with me for a while. You'll get to see the Golden City."

"Thank you, thank you, thank you..." Arlandra's words became muffled as she buried her face against his chest in a fierce hug. Blaine squeezed her back, and started to tickle her, evidently unable to resist.

"You're very welcome," he said. "I'm so looking forward to showing it to you. Happy birthday."

And with that, the memory began to dim, darkening as though Blaine had closed his eyes. The sound of happy laughter faded into silence and Darnuir entered a world devoid of all sensation, white and empty, until the colours began to spin once more, and soon a howling wind could be heard as he materialised into another memory; the one he was supposed to be here to see.

Rain lashed upon the plaza of Aurisha, but not a drop touched the crimson-cloaked figure before him. Blaine raised the Guardian's Blade, a dazzling light against this starless, moonless night. Rectar's eyes flashed red beneath his hood. Their blades clashed with an ear-splitting screech. Then they battled upon the very steps of the Basilica, as though Blaine were barring his way.

Darnuir couldn't help but dwell on what must just have happened prior to this. Blaine must have found Arlandra dead, and run to save the king and rescue Darnuir from Rectar's clutches. Darnuir was glad he didn't have to watch that. Like Blaine, he'd rather think of Arlandra as someone who lit up the world, and not as a cold body. How Blaine had found the strength to stand, never mind fight a god, after finding her dead spoke volumes of his will.

Yet while Blaine wasn't exactly losing this duel, he was far from winning. Rectar's strikes seemed effortless, while Blaine's slowed or lost their power. Eventually, the enemy took his chance to speed away inside the temple itself, something Blaine had not mentioned when telling this tale before. Without the memory fresh in his mind, he must have lost some of the details. Without the courage to relive it, he'd forgotten.

Blaine caught up soon enough. With the storm raging outside and not a lantern in sight, the Basilica felt ice-cold and foreboding. Lurid shadows crept from all directions. Rectar had brought his poison into the very heart of Blaine's faith. Their enemy was within the circle of stone swords, crouched low, muttering something in a harsh tongue and touching each stone blade in turn.

Blaine raised the Guardian's Blade and, breathless, managed to bellow, "Be gone from this place." And then shone such a light as Darnuir had never seen.

But did it come from Blaine's sword or down from the dome itself?

Darnuir could not be certain. It all happened too quickly, yet when the light died, Rectar was gone. Blaine collapsed onto the marble floor and Darnuir found himself being yanked away from the memory, flying without a body once more as he returned to himself.

He awoke in the present, leaning a little on the bench but still seated. The opal's weight had lessened greatly, yet it gained some more once he'd added in the memory of Chelos' confession.

The sun was higher in the sky now. Darnuir stood, stretched, aware that every muscle in his body was latent with energy, poised for anything. Even the fight he knew had to come. He took another walk instead.

As before, he strayed towards the Basilica. It was gentle, though, this strange pull he felt; like drawing close to home after a long journey. The temple looked peaceful under the morning sun, not the menacing nightmare as in that memory.

Someone sat alone upon the stairs and for a moment he thought it was Chelos. However, it was Blaine who caught his eye. The former guardian looked older already. Darnuir hadn't realised before how much of Blaine's vigour was due to the healthy, golden glow of his skin; a shine that was now extinguished. The bloody sling which supported his arm hardly helped, nor did the black nails or the bald patches.

Darnuir met his eye, and in that moment, they shared an understanding.

Blaine was done.

Darnuir joined his grandfather and for a while they sat together, saying nothing. The few dragons, humans and fairies who passed by gave them peace, too weary to do more than stand on their own feet. For his part, Darnuir felt a little guilty for having pried into Blaine's past without his permission. On the other hand, having seen him face Rectar and survive it, Darnuir also felt a swell of pride for the aged dragon.

He decided to be bold and broke the silence. "So, what now, Blaine?"

"You'll go and fight our enemy. With luck, you'll succeed."

"I meant for you."

"For me?" Blaine said, a tired sort of surprise in his voice. "I have absolutely no idea. Only the gods know how long I may live without the blade, and they aren't likely to tell me."

"Have you asked?" Darnuir said, unable to suppress a laugh.

"Once politely and twice not so. I've yet to hear an answer."

"I hope you have many good years left," Darnuir said. "I'll need you. I can't do everything on my own."

Blaine hung his head. "I hardly have anywhere else to go."

In the semi-distance a company of fairies flew past, moving so artfully they might have been dancing with each other in the air. It was hard to believe that he, Darnuir, had some fairy blood in him. He'd never been half so elegant. If he made it through the war, he'd have to revisit his grandmother. Perhaps Blaine could come with him?

"Quite the sight, aren't they?" Darnuir said.

Blaine took a second to understand. "Oh, yes – yes, they are. A beautiful people with kinder hearts than ours."

Darnuir smiled and placed a gentle hand on Blaine's good shoulder.

"She loved you. I'm sorry to have intruded on your past but I've seen it now with my own eyes. She loved you both. And she's still out there, Blaine. What's an ocean if you still love her?"

Blaine breathed deeply. "All the distance I need to stop fooling myself. To prevent old wounds reopening. She told me not to return; it wasn't an invitation to try harder, to fight for her. Even if she hadn't said the words, her voice said it all. I cannot go back, no matter how much I may yearn for it. What once was is gone forever. All things end."

Darnuir sniffed, unsure why Blaine's words struck at him so. Did two blades heighten his emotions as well?

"I should like to see you happy again," he said. "If I can."

"I do feel happiness," Blaine said. "Happiness in seeing the dragon you have become. I hope to see the new age you'll bring. The old ways of our people have ended too. They did many years ago. I just fought against it."

"I'm sorry for the loss of your men at the Nest. It must be taking its toll on top of everything."

"I mourn more for the innocent who were there. Sent by me."

"They gave us precious time, without which we would have surely crumbled. Even those who caused us strife bled their last for us in the end. I say they fought to redeem themselves, Bacchus and all the rest. And that is a noble thing."

Blaine mused and nodded in agreement. Darnuir stretched, sighed from the relief, then slapped his hands upon his knees.

"So, one last fight, and then we can rest?"

"One last fight," said Blaine.

"Why do I feel like we've said that before?"

Blaine smiled. "We? I wouldn't say something so naïve, boy. Now, help an old man to his feet."

33

WORDS ARE NOT ENOUGH

"And when the dragons finally sailed back east, there was not a soul in the Dales who could rejoice. All that was left was silence."

From Jon Barbor's *Scorching of the Dales*

Darnuir – Harbour of Aurisha

Three days after the battle, the full extent of the casualties was known. Two legions, the Second and the Sixth, were so diminished they were folded. Their surviving members replenished the ranks of the others. Blaine's Third was gravely shaken, given the loss of many of their comrades at the Nest. The Brevians had taken heavy losses as well, with several regiments entirely wiped out. The fairies had fared best, if it could be called such, as their flyers largely stayed away from the thick of the fighting. Still, many were injured or incapacitated, and what hope Darnuir had of striking out against Rectar at his stronghold relied entirely on Arkus. On that front, he'd find out soon enough.

For more ships were coming, ships with the black and white flags of Brevia. It must have been the entire fleet that Blaine had sent back months ago. Enough to carry reinforcements, if Arkus willed it. Darnuir would know today; the outrunners and flyers had reported so. His gut told him that Arkus himself was coming east.

Nobody had answered his attempts at contact via the scrying orb, and he took the lack of communication as a very dangerous sign.

Arkus' fleet entered the harbour under heavy grey-blue clouds. Any intrigue regarding how much military might Arkus would bring was swiftly laid to rest. Men and women in crisp uniforms with flintlock muskets on their shoulders marched ashore in long columns. Cannons were wheeled over the stone roads, over thirty of them.

Darnuir watched this grand procession with a wary eye. Arkus came last, ensuring his many soldiers were seen by Darnuir and those who stood at his side: Blaine, Lira, Raymond, Fidelm, and Grigayne.

The King of Humanity brought a guard as well, no fewer than fifty seasoned troops. Judging from their shoulder width, they must have been hunters once in their life, who had been retrained with even deadlier weapons. Yet it was the man on Arkus' left who drew Darnuir's attention.

It was Balack – a more regal, older-looking Balack – but his friend was visible beneath it all. *My former friend*, Darnuir corrected himself. He chanced a smile at Balack, who responded with a thin-lipped grimace. Hardly encouraging.

"Do you find something amusing, Darnuir?" Arkus said, his voice higher and colder than the tallest peaks of the Boreacs.

Darnuir continued his smile, determined not to meet Arkus' anger. It would do no good, and his people had inflicted two severe blows against humans now. Godly madness and starvation might be excuses, but they could not undo the harm.

"I am joyed, Arkus, to see you bring so much strength to bear against *our* great enemy. It is also pleasing to have you here in person. After our last parting, I feared we might—"

"Spare me, Darnuir. Spare me your words, your lies, your false modesty. I haven't the patience left to mince words with the ruler of beasts and butchers. Do you mock me with your smile? Hmm? Do you think it sporting to see which members of my family you can rob me of next?"

"Rob you of?" Darnuir said. His mind clicked the pieces into place. Arkus had lost another family member, a dear one. "Cassandra?" he blurted out. "Is she—"

"She is fine." It was Balack who spoke. Darnuir sagged in relief and nodded his thanks. Balack said no more, withdrawing a step behind his king.

Arkus sniffed. "I see where your priorities still lie, Darnuir. I lost my second son, in fact. Dead because of your kind."

"Thane," Raymond gasped. He stepped forward, jerked back a little by Lira's firm grip on his hand. "We had no idea."

"Indeed," Arkus scoffed. "I understand you visited Brevia briefly, stealing a company of good soldiers and some of my cannons. I must have a word with your father when I return."

Balack opened his mouth again, but Raymond beat him to it.

"It was all my doing. Take your anger out on me."

"You've grown bold," Arkus said. "Could it be the dragon clinging onto you?" He shot Lira a venomous look. "Be careful, Raymond. If she hungers in the night you might find a piece of yourself missing in the morning."

Arkus rounded on Grigayne next. "And you, young Imar. Know that you and your family will regret your errant decision."

Grigayne rolled his shoulders and cracked his knuckles. "Is that a threat, my king?"

"It is," Arkus said without an ounce of humour. He raised a hand. "The islanders attacked my city like the days of old and retribution will come."

"We did no such thing," Grigayne growled. "You attacked us first."

Arkus was unmoving. "Deny me on this or insist I make peace, and I shall put my muskets and artillery back on my ships and sail away."

Darnuir stiffened but said nothing. He couldn't risk Arkus leaving.

Grigayne stepped forward. "You put a gun to my father's head and are angered when I disagree with that," he spat. "Reap what ye sow, Arkus," and he sounded like a fierce, true-born islander for the first time. "You are no king of ours." The young Lord of the Isles turned about and strode off without another word.

Darnuir clenched his jaw. For all the power he now possessed, he could not draw his blades and cut the very past away.

"What of Cullen?" Darnuir asked, hoping to steer the conversation again.

"The babe is fine," Arkus said, though he did not seem moved either way. "He's in the care of the sister of the harlot who married Brallor. Does that please you, Darnuir?"

Darnuir bit his tongue. This was just raw emotion. Arkus meant nothing by it.

"I'm pleased to hear Olive is safe and well. She was family to me once, as was Grace. Mothers to me, in many ways. Your son loved Grace dearly; he wouldn't appreciate your words."

"Rub salt in the old wound, will you?" Arkus said. "Does it please you, knowing Brallor loved you more than me?"

"I take no pleasure in it," Darnuir said, feeling his lingering grief for Cosmo, for Grace, and for all those lost from the Boreac Mountains come flooding back to the surface. "A loss such as Thane is beyond words. I am so sorry, Arkus. So deeply, painfully sorry."

"Are you?"

"He is," Blaine said, standing shoulder to shoulder with Darnuir. "We all are. I too lost my child, my joy, and though it was long ago, it still aches."

Brow furrowed, Arkus pinched between his eyes as though fending off a fierce headache. "Do not speak, Guardian. Your voice is ragged nails to my ears."

"I only mean to say that I understand your suffering," Blaine said kindly. "Yet unfounded accusations and blaming will not aid you. Darnuir did not cause either of your sons' deaths."

Arkus' hand reached for the butt of a pistol at his waist. He toyed with the idea of grasping it, before curling his fingers into a fist. Darnuir sighed in relief while Arkus rounded on Blaine.

"I said I do not wish to hear your voice, you treacherous, lying worm. You and all your followers. Murderers now, too. How dare you speak to me of false accusations and blame. You hold more blame than any of us, mighty Guardian. Or what are you now?" He nodded up and down Blaine's battered body. "Injured and without your weapon, I see."

"You're right," Blaine said, without a trace of anger. "I hold the most blame of any here for all that has occurred. I am no longer the guardian. I have passed that power to Darnuir, so he may end the threat against us."

Arkus raised his eyebrows. "Both blades, Darnuir? Do you even need my men to finish this war?"

"All will be needed before the end," Darnuir said. "With your leave, we will march to Kar'drun as soon as possible."

"How soon?"

"Tomorrow, if we can."

"Done," Arkus said. "I'll leave General Adolphus here to consult with you all. I already tire of your company and there is nothing more to say." Arkus kicked his horse and trotted away, the fifty guards and even Balack following in his wake. A tall, stiff-looking man with a blond moustache marched imperiously to Darnuir, yet offered no salute.

"Just tell me how to work around your legions, and my companies will decimate the enemy," Adolphus said.

Darnuir didn't answer, still watching Arkus' back and then Balack's. Was it just his imagination, or did Balack seem less hostile towards him? Was there hope, then?

Adolphus cleared his throat.

"Of course, General," Darnuir said, leading him over to Fidelm and Lira. "We saw what just one company could achieve during the recent battle. Having many may well tip the balance in our favour."

"I have no doubt," Adolphus said.

Darnuir hoped his confidence was well earned. He looked out again to the north, over the ruins of the lower city, over the walls, to the faint outline of the hulking mountain he swore he could see. Perhaps it was only a figment of his fear, but whether real or imagined, it loomed over him, through both wakefulness and sleep, all along that long road north.

34

A FINAL PROMISE

"I came here to prepare the hunters against future dragon wars. Doing so almost wills conflict to happen, yet to do nothing is to leave our loved ones vulnerable. Doomed one way and doomed the other."

Elsie the Green, First Captain of the Master Station

Sonrid – Kar'drun

Sonrid sat at the edge of his secret entrance to the mountain with his back against the wall. Zax lay against a curved groove in the rock, looking quite relaxed.

"You should take a break," Zax said. "Move around a little."

Sonrid eyed him. "I must be here the moment the Three Races arrive."

"It's been nearly two weeks since the red dragons returned," Zax said. "Perhaps they killed all the Master's enemies."

"No," Sonrid mused. "Something would have changed if that were so. There were fewer than before. I think they were falling back."

"Doesn't mean the Three Races will come marching here right away. Go stretch your malformed legs for a while."

"Won't you get lonely?" Sonrid jibed.

"Got plenty of company these days, haven't I?" Zax said. He faced towards the stairway that led down to the tunnel lit by the twin yellow flames. "Isn't that right, demons? Come here."

A few small demons scurried out of the gloom. "Little masters," they said together.

One came over to Sonrid's side, while two visited Zax.

"See, they like me best now," Zax said. "Go for a stroll, Sonrid. Dukoona's mission is not your burden alone."

Zax was being kind, yet Sonrid couldn't help but feel responsible for the matter. He turned to the demon beside him. It was a touch too close for his liking, perched with its hands on the ground and knees out wide like a frog about to leap. It cocked its head and blinked at him.

"Have you found more spectres than yesterday?" Sonrid asked. You had to keep the questions and tasks simple. The demon nodded. This could mean they'd found precisely one extra spectre prison or that they'd found a hundred. Either way, more was better. Sonrid couldn't be picky.

Zax looked to him. "And you're certain Dukoona has not been moved?"

"Last I checked he was in the same place," Sonrid said. Locating Dukoona would have been impossible were it not for the demons. They were unrivalled at skulking unseen through Kar'drun, and having their help had been invaluable.

"Maybe you ought to go for a walk and make sure?" Zax said.

Sonrid frowned. "Why are you being so insistent?"

"You know full well that inactivity only makes it worse for us."

Sonrid shrugged and turned to look out over the dusty landscape again.

"And it would be a shame if you grew so sore you couldn't make it to Darnuir – or, worse still, make a mistake in melding to him and one of his soldiers crushes you like a bug."

"I won't allow my melding to fail. This is too important."

"I want you to come back, y'know," Zax said.

Sonrid croaked a laugh. "I'm touched."

Zax fidgeted with his hands. "Been nice having you around, is all. Rather not have to go back to sitting around all day by myself."

Sonrid smiled. "I'll come back. Maybe on our next world, if there is one, we'll have a better time of it."

"Can't get much worse," Zax said. He glanced towards the horizon. "Shadows take me, I think that might be them."

Sonrid scrambled to his crooked feet, groaning at the terrible stiffness. Zax had been right, damn him. He'd also been correct about the approaching army. Unless Sonrid's eyes deceived him, those blots against the sky were fairies and below were ranks of dragons and humans.

"I'll wait until they have stopped," Sonrid said. "A camp will grant more shadows. Guard this entrance as best you can."

Zax struggled to his feet as well, stepping closer to the ledge. "I'll round up some more demons. Not sure what good they'll do but it's better than me guarding alone." He placed his one good arm on Sonrid's back. "Take care out there." He left, and the demons scampered after him.

Sonrid watched the armies of the Three Races trudge towards Kar'drun, trying to rally his protesting body for the efforts to come. This would be it. The end of the Master or the end of all else.

Darnuir – The King's Pavilion

Darnuir, Blaine, Fidelm, Lira and Raymond stood in council before the forward command tent.

Kar'drun rose beyond sight, swallowed by dark clouds. The ground underfoot was dry, cracked and mud-red; a lifeless, barren land. For Darnuir it was lifeless in more ways than one. The Cascade was weak here, or at least it was weak this far from the mountain. It reminded him of events at the Bastion, when the Cascade had vanished, sucked into a great pool of energy by Castallan. As Rectar must surely have need of the Cascade, Darnuir assumed the same had occurred here.

Tapping into the well of power would mean getting as close to Kar'drun as possible, a feat easier to theorise than achieve.

"I only know of one entrance," said Blaine, pointing vaguely to the base of Kar'-drun. "The Black Dragons constructed their gates to be invisible to the naked eye. Some even say it wasn't the Black Dragons who made it, but some ancient race of sentient stone." Blaine's tone implied he thought this unlikely. "Whatever the truth, I doubt we shall see the entry point until Rectar sends his army forth."

Fidelm's wings buzzed in anticipation. "And when exactly will that be? What is Rectar waiting for?"

"Perhaps he knows of Arkus' anger and hopes we'll turn on each other first," Lira said.

Darnuir sighed and kicked at the ground. "You say that lightly, but—" He bit his lip, the thought of it unbearable. "If Rectar will not make the first move then we shall. The reds are terribly strong, but if we close the distance between us and the mountain, there will be less space for them to move in. With their backs to the mountainside, they'll be at a disadvantage."

"We'll box them in and shoot them," Raymond said. He shrugged with a half-smile. "As good a plan as any."

"I feared marching north before," Darnuir said. "Meeting such an enemy in the field seemed suicidal. It still might be, but Arkus' new weapons have done more to tip the balance than months of training in new formations ever could."

"Whatever happens out here, this battle will be decided by your duel," Blaine said. "All we can achieve in fighting the reds is allowing you to enter the mountain."

Lira ran her hands through her hair. "The entrance will be the most heavily guarded section. We'll have to utterly defeat the red dragons in order to break in."

"And we don't even know what lies beyond," Darnuir said.

A cloud passed overhead, casting some much welcome shade over their small company.

Darnuir's heightened senses suddenly twinged – a sense he hadn't known he had. It was the feeling of being watched made tangible, and as real as smell or sight or sound. Something had moved unseen, heading behind him into the pavilion proper.

Darnuir looked to his feet and followed the line of the shadow to the flapping entrance of the tent.

"Excuse me for one moment," he said.

Fidelm was striking up further points as Darnuir entered the pavilion. Inside was the usual grand war table, strewn with old maps of the area and of the Forsaken City to the east, as well as wooden figurines, stacks of notes, half-eaten rations. There was no one else in the tent, at least not in their full form.

"Dukoona?" Darnuir said quietly.

There came a crash. The table shook and plates fell off the far side with a clatter. A groan followed. Darnuir drew one sword and stepped lightly around to see who was there.

"Oh, hello there, Sonrid."

Dukoona – In the Depths of Kar'drun

Rectar floated in the air before him, in his crimson-cloaked form. "They have come." He sounded happy; playful, even.

Dukoona blinked, straining to look up. His neck had been hunched over for so long it didn't care for movement.

"About time," Dukoona said.

"Fear may have kept them at bay. Yet they have a great power in their midst. Darnuir now wields two blades. I can feel him like a hot sun in the cosmos. It's a surprise they did not do this sooner; then again, the guardian was always stubborn. My host's memories tell me that much."

Was that a touch of nerves in Rectar's voice? Anything that gave Him pause was a good thing.

"Does that concern you, Master? Would you prefer I go outside and check for you while you rot down here like you've alwa—"

And then came the pain. Dukoona screamed, as loudly as he possibly could. He'd found that screaming helped, channelling his focus into something else.

"I have been patient," Rectar said. "Time has never been a concern for me. Even after Darnuir falls today, I may wait another century if I must, millennia if needed. My army, my true army, must be perfected first before I assault the Others with their own creations." He vanished, then Dukoona felt a soft breath on his ear. "Pray it does not take me that long. For as long as we remain on this world, you and your people will suffer every day."

"Let them go," Dukoona said. He'd asked so many times, asking again would do no harm. "Let my people go. It was all my scheming. All my decisions. Punish me for eternity if you must but let them leave. Have I not earned at least one favour for sending you so many dragons over the years?"

His master reappeared before him, so close that the blond hair tickled his nose. Dukoona's head was roughly grabbed and bent backwards, forcing him to meet Rectar's molten eyes.

"I think the time to put you to use has come. I shall grant you one last chance at favour. I shall let your people go, if you do something for me."

"Name it."

Rectar smiled. "Should Darnuir enter the mountain, he may come for you, thinking you're his ally. I'd like you to keep up this pretence. Then kill him."

"How can I possibly do that if he has two blades?"

"Surprise him," Rectar said, as though it were obvious.

Dukoona pondered, then felt revolted that he'd even considered it for a moment. But his will had been grated away by punishment. He wanted it to end. If there was any chance to save his people, he'd have to take it. And two blades or no, Darnuir's chances of success were not guaranteed.

"How can I be sure you'll keep your word?" Dukoona asked.

"I shall make this oath under the bond of master and servant," said Rectar. He placed a pale hand on Dukoona's fiery head. "Such bonds cannot be broken. Kill Darnuir and I shall release your people from my service."

Dukoona gasped as Rectar worked some magic and the oath that he'd sworn manifested in his mind; solid and immovable. Dukoona had never been more certain about anything. If he fulfilled this task, then Rectar would do as he promised. It could not be broken.

Rectar shook him. "Do you understand?"

"I do."

"Very well." He waved his hand and a deafening roar from unseen red dragons filled the dark cavern. "It shall begin."

He vanished.

If spectres could weep, Dukoona might have done so. He felt dishonourable, unclean, unworthy. He wouldn't have agreed to such a thing months ago before all this pain had chipped away at his resolve.

Dukoona hung his head. "What have I done?"

35

THE LAST BATTLE: PART 1

"The gods are on the side of the mighty."

Dragon Proverb

Darnuir – The Front Lines

The red dragons advanced more slowly than they had at Aurisha, letting their mighty feet and tails send quakes through the earth. All legions and companies were ready and in position. Darnuir, however, was off to one side by the artillery.

"Comfortable, Sonrid?"

"No worse than usual," Sonrid said. He was on Darnuir's back, his arms and legs half merged into the slivers of shadows under plates of his armour. Darnuir noticed the aghast stares he got from nearby soldiers for having a demon on his back, but while he twirled two blades in his hands, no one openly objected.

"Adolphus," Darnuir called, looking for the general.

"Lord?" Adolphus said, turning away from his terrified officers.

"I'd like you to concentrate all your cannon fire down this line," Darnuir said, pointing to what he hoped was a clear path to where Sonrid's secret entrance lay.

Adolphus coughed. "May I enquire as to why?"

"I need to reach the mountainside quickly and with as little resistance as possible. I'll send a pillar of flames as a signal when you can cease firing and shift your focus back to the battle at large."

If Adolphus was surprised at these commands, he did not show it. "Won't we be risking your life through friendly fire?"

"Don't worry about me. Just focus on clearing me a path and await my signal."

"It shall be done." Adolphus bristled his great moustache once, clapped his hands together, then strode off, barking orders with a great energy. The cannon crews began adjusting their positions.

"You're certain you can make this climb?" Sonrid asked.

Darnuir twisted his head so that Sonrid was on the edge of his vision. "Sonrid, a climb will be the least of our worries. I'm more concerned about what happens once I'm inside."

"Good. Good. I would hate for my efforts to be wasted."

Darnuir laughed, probably too loudly, drawing yet more stares from the humans.

"All right. Let's go free Dukoona and kill a god."

He opened the doors in his mind, though sadly only a trickle of Cascade came through. The closer he got to Rectar's well of energy, the more he'd be able to draw upon. Thankfully for now, energy spent on movement was cheap, or else he'd be in real trouble.

"Fire at will, Adolphus."

And then he ran.

Charging the red dragon line reminded him very much of charging the demon line at the Charred Vale. He'd run fast then. He ran faster now. Even in full armour, he tore across the plains of Kar'drun. At the Charred Vale he'd also leapt into the demon ranks, so he'd do that again too. He fed what magic he could gather into his legs, propelling him on.

Ahead, lead shot hammered into the enemy, spraying up earth, as though giant moles were bursting from the ground.

As the second round of artillery boomed, Darnuir leapt. Sonrid wailed as they flew, clearly thinking that Darnuir had overestimated his own power. He hit the earth with as much force as any cannonball, knocking aside nearby reds and cutting down stragglers. He sucked in a breath and felt for more magic – it was still only a trickle – and ran on with what reserves he had.

The bombardment began to have effect as the red dragons moved aside to avoid it.

Bolder ones didn't. They tried to step in his way.

Darnuir swiped left to right with both blades, spinning around in full turns to cleave most of them from his path. Those he couldn't reach he side-stepped, determined not to get bogged down in any fighting. To slow down for a second could mean a cannonball in the back.

More shot hummed through the air, but he could sense their approach, letting him pivot and dive aside as needed. Sonrid screamed with each narrow miss but Darnuir pounded on, legs pumping like a drummer's sticks.

It got easier as he approached the mountain. More magic trickled in the closer he got, until he found a slow but steady current, pushing him on to greater heights.

Before long he was at the sheer black rock face. Learning from the red dragons' assault on the walls of Aurisha, he jumped and dug both blades deep into the rock to brace himself. He made the climb this way, cutting his way up one strike at a time.

Cascade energy flowed more easily now. The kick came unexpectedly, and in that moment of joy he almost missed his next cut with the Dragon's Blade. Arm still flailing, a cannonball hit perilously close overhead, blowing a chunk from the mountain. Chips of rock fell against his eyes, and the impact knocked the Dragon's Blade from his hand.

Sonrid offered fresh screams.

"It's fine," Darnuir called, as the Dragon's Blade flew back to his grip.

"Are they trying to hit you?" Sonrid shouted.

Darnuir hesitated. Sonrid hadn't been serious, but he'd touched a nerve there. Darnuir shook his head and forced himself on, bringing the Dragon's Blade up to continue the climb.

He carried on, enjoying the warm burn down both arms as the Cascade began to process. Higher and higher he went, using the blades as picks in the rock. He kept going, entering a rhythm and not truly paying attention.

"Back down there," Sonrid cried.

Darnuir paused, his blades cutting through the rock like butter until they caught fast.

"What? Where?"

"To your left."

Darnuir looked and saw a small lip of an old platform below. He drew the Guardian's Blade out of the rock, and leaned back as though rappelling, keeping himself upright by holding on to the Dragon's Blade that was still stuck fast in the mountain. For a second he hung over the reds below, like a piece of meat over a pit of rabid dogs.

He looked down and regretted it immediately.

Fresh tremors ran from the impacting cannon shot and he waited for the moment to pass, feeling the Dragon's Blade edging slowly out of the rock. It was now or never. Darnuir took what few steps back he could, then ran parallel to the mountainside, kicking off on his last step with a burst of Cascade.

He caught the edge of the ancient balcony with the Guardian's Blade and only breathed easy when his free hand made purchase.

Sonrid moaned as though he was being sick.

Darnuir made the final leg of the climb and hauled himself over the edge. He lay on his back for a moment, never more thankful to have solid stone beneath him.

Sonrid melded away from him. The little spectre staggered forward, spitting and cursing under this breath. Then he stopped, going suddenly silent.

"No," Sonrid whined.

Darnuir rolled over. "What's the matter?" All he could see were demon corpses, though that had never been a bad thing.

"They were discovered," Sonrid said. "Come, Darnuir. Come." He was shuffling as quickly as his stubby legs allowed, down a set of stairs and out of sight. Darnuir picked himself up and almost forgot about sending out the signal to Adolphus.

He thrust his hand forth, concentrating on the Dragon's Blade until it pulled free from the mountain and returned to him. With it, he aimed high and launched a swirling cone of flames, so large it could not be missed. The cannons fell silent.

He turned, and with a burst of speed caught up with Sonrid.

At the bottom of the stairs, under a ghostly yellow glow, were the bodies of two red dragons, still bleeding from many wounds. Around them were dozens of demon corpses and another small spectre, like Sonrid, slumped against the wall.

Sonrid was by the spectre's side. "Zax? He's still alive, Darnuir."

Darnuir picked his way over and knelt beside them. The other spectre had a shrivelled arm, as though a baby's arm had been attached to a child.

Zax coughed wetly. A wisp of smoke trailed up from his mouth.

"What happened?" Sonrid asked.

"What does it look like?" Zax whispered. "The demons were fierce things. Swarmed all over the reds. Got 'em with my dirk too," he added, raising his good hand with evident effort. The dagger spun out of existence, turning back into swirling shadow.

Sonrid sighed, took his friend's hand and bowed his head. "I am so sorry."

Darnuir was unsure what to say. They were demons, but they too suffered at Rectar's hands. They'd probably been affected more than anyone in the Three Races. Out of the gloom came a regular demon, the flames under its shadowy flesh flickering lightly in the darkness. It sat by Zax with wide eyes.

The demon started speaking. Darnuir couldn't understand its words, but he could recognise sad tones. Sonrid responded to it in a language oddly soft upon the ear.

Darnuir was at a loss. Was anything as simple as it had first appeared? He placed a hand on Sonrid's hunched back and marvelled again at how cold his body was.

"I'm sorry for your loss, Sonrid. But we must move on." He looked to Zax next. "I could ease your passing, spectre. I owe you something for the help you've given Sonrid and myself."

"Leave me," Zax croaked. "I do not feel anything right now. Let me live a little while not in pain. Kill our master, Dragon King, and I'll consider us even."

"That I shall try with all my strength."

Sonrid let go of Zax's hand. "Goodbye, my friend. Perhaps we'll meet on another world."

"I'd like that," Zax said. Another puff of smoke billowed from his mouth. "Go now."

Darnuir didn't need any more reason. He was about to pick Sonrid back up, but the spectre was already moving, nattering something to the demon in a hurried voice. Some way up the corridor more demons were tentatively emerging. Sonrid spoke to them. As Darnuir's eyes adjusted to the darkness, he saw many heads with fiery eyes nodding excitedly. Some let loose their usual howling. They scattered soon afterwards in all directions.

"What did you say to them?"

A smile crept up Sonrid's face. "I told them to free the spectres and rally the other Broken for aid. The time has come to fight the Master."

"Not in my wildest dreams did I think I'd be calling a spectre a friend," Darnuir said. "But here I am. Come along now, we have to find Dukoona." He scooped Sonrid up like a kitten, ignoring the protests. "Be quick with the directions. Every second is precious."

He charged off down the dank, eerie corridor, past grey light, and brown, sickly light, and through no light at all.

At a fork in the tunnels, a red dragon came bounding towards them, roaring mightily, forked tongue lolling madly. In the confined space the creature looked monstrously large. Darnuir met it coolly, letting the red swing its weapon to clang against the ceiling while he jumped, pushed off the nearby wall, twisted under its arms and thrust the Dragon's Blade neatly through its skull, before landing in tune with the red corpse as it thudded to the floor.

"Perhaps you can do this after all," Sonrid snickered.

"Let's hope so." He pointed his sword towards the fork in the road. "Which way now?"

Sonrid kept up a running stream of directions as they descended deeper into the heart of Kar'drun. It all led to a cavernous hall with only the light of the Guardian's Blade to see by. The Cascade felt stronger the deeper into the mountain they went. He amplified the golden glow, bathing the place to find Dukoona. The space truly was vast. Several Basilicas would have sat comfortably within it.

"Above us," Sonrid said.

Sure enough, high overhead, strung up by thick ropes of coiling shadows, the Lord of the Spectres hung. Darnuir recognised those long tendrils of blue flame.

He glanced about, as though Rectar might jump at him from a shadow, then placed Sonrid down and went to the first bond. He drew the Dragon's Blade and, with both blades ready, paused.

Would this be wise? He'd come all this way, and he didn't think it all a ruse. That performance from Sonrid at the alcove couldn't have been fake, could it? In a horrible moment of doubt, he wondered whether his trust of Dukoona had been born of real gut instinct or whether his attempts to rebel against Blaine months before had led him to trust for the wrong reasons.

Darnuir decided to trust himself.

With both blades he severed each dark bond and Dukoona fell silently, landing with a seamless meld into the shadow cast by Sonrid's body. Dukoona bounded back out at once, unfazed by the fall. He looked no different than when Darnuir had last seen him, with no visible signs of pain or torture, yet there was something in his eyes. The whites were clouded and grey, perhaps the only outward sign of suffering that spectres could show.

"You've done better than I dared hope, Sonrid," Dukoona said. "And you, Darnuir, I am grateful you have come at last." He sounded pleased, though he did not quite meet Darnuir's eye.

"Are you fit to fight?"

Dukoona hesitated, flexing his fingers. A blade swirled into his hand from the purple shadows, flickered as though about to fail, then fully formed.

"I am."

Darnuir nodded. "Good. Your people are being released to join the battle outside. The sooner we find Rectar and kill him—"

"The spectres are fighting?" Dukoona said, sounding alarmed.

"I have sent demons that remain to free them," Sonrid said.

"But they would be safe here," Dukoona said.

"Wouldn't they rather fight?" Darnuir asked.

"They've suffered enough."

"So have my people," Darnuir said. "We all have. Now is not the time to falter."

Dukoona groaned. "How strong are you now? Can you defeat Him?"

"I wish I could tell you yes."

Dukoona at last met his eye and Darnuir saw some struggle in him, though what, he couldn't say. Rectar would have punished Dukoona for his attempted rebellion. It probably made his own time in the chair seem relaxing. He just needed some encouragement.

"Fight with me," Darnuir said. "Together, we stand a better chance. That's not changed."

"He is my master," Dukoona said. "There is only so—"

"Much you can do," Darnuir finished for him. "You said before. Can you fight at all? I know he can possess you or force you to do things against your will."

"He has to focus on us to do so," Dukoona said. "With his mind bent on the battle outside, and you, I do not think he will have the will spare to control me. But I cannot make guarantees."

"I understand," Darnuir said. "Let's start with finding him. Where is he hiding?"

Dukoona's eyes widened. "He does not hide. He comes for you, if he deems it." Dukoona opened his arms wide and looked up as though to the sky. "Master, I will fulfil my promise."

"Promise?" Darnuir began.

But before any more could be said, a sharp crack rent the stale cavern.

A distant blue light pulsed into life, beating gently, growing, until Darnuir could see a great oval of boiling blue. He'd been right in his assumption, then. Rectar did have a Cascade Sink, just like Castallan, though many times larger. A cloaked figure was outlined against it, so far away it seemed tiny.

The figure landed and started walking towards them.

Darnuir looked to his companions. Sonrid had retreated. Dukoona's sword arm trembled.

"We can do this," Darnuir said. "We have to."

"We will do what we must," Dukoona said.

Darnuir nodded, hoping Dukoona would find that formidable part of himself soon. He lit the Guardian's Blade, bright as a summer's day, and blazed life onto the Dragon's Blade. Magic was no issue here, not so close to that well of energy.

Rectar fast approached them. His steps were regular and small, though he covered the space as though running, leaving a blurring trail of himself in his wake. The cloak he wore was in shreds from the waist down, yet the hood shrouded his face. Was that Kroener's face he could see underneath or something else entirely?

Darnuir steadied himself, trying to maintain a level head when everything in him urged him to charge. Why wait? This was why he was here, and for every second he wasted more dragons, fairies and humans would die outside. Arkus' anger would grow, and hope would fade. So why was it so hard to move? So hard to breathe?

He had two blades. No one had ever held two blades before. Even Rectar only held one, which he was now unsheathing slowly, as if savouring the moment. Darnuir caught sight of the plain handle, unadorned save for a grip of black and gold cloth. The Champion's Blade. The same blade he'd witnessed Dronithir use to defeat Norbanus in that memory. The blade supposedly borne only by 'those who were worthy'. Either these gods had told a pack of lies or ancient dragons had been inept in interpreting them. At worst, the gods were uncaring to have let this happen.

Rectar ran a deathly white hand lovingly from the tip of the Champion's Blade to its hilt, leaving a purple-blue shine to the metal like a bruise forged in light.

"You are far stronger than he was," Rectar said. "In every way you are greater. But you will die."

Darnuir's heart pumped madly, and his caution of a moment before burned away.

Everything, everything had led to this. Every death, every loss, every moment of despair and fragile hope. Cosmo, Eve, Grace, even Damien, and poor Brackendon; they'd fallen to get him here, or he'd failed to save them. But not now. Not with the whole world resting on the outcome of this duel.

"I will not fail," Darnuir roared, magnifying his voice, refusing to be thrown off by Rectar's confidence. Darnuir found a use for his old anger again and embraced it.

He kicked in both doorways in his mind.

And he charged this God of the Shadows.

36

THE LAST BATTLE: PART 2

"It has been two thousand years since a true dragon soared across the sky."

From Tiviar's Histories

Dukoona

He watched Darnuir run at his master. The pair quickly became a blur of motion and colour, tinged blue from the light of the Cascade Sink.

He was grateful that Darnuir had torn off without warning. It gave Dukoona an excuse for his lack of action. This wasn't like him. He normally knew what he had to do, even if it was hard. Even if it meant sacrifice. Could he risk his people entering an endless nightmare? Riveted by the fight, he merely looked on, trying to decide.

Darnuir was unleashing a fury upon Rectar. They slowed down briefly enough for Dukoona to see the King of Dragons swing a blow, a kick, another blow, another spinning kick, and end on a hammer strike. Rectar evaded or parried his blows but not without some exertion. Ribbons of crimson cloth fell away from Rectar's cloak as Darnuir scored near misses.

Was Rectar truly on the back foot or was he just toying with Darnuir?

Or was it all for his, Dukoona's, benefit? Some last terrible test after decades of servitude? Rectar could force Dukoona to do his bidding if he committed his will to it; this was just another form of torture. To make him choose.

"Dukoona, help me," Darnuir bellowed over the clashing swords.

'Dukoona,' Rectar said in his mind. *'Don't forget my promise. Don't let your people down.'*

He was just so weary, so stiff, so sore in a way that no spectre should have been.

'I'm waiting, Dukoona. Do not fail your peo—'

Rectar's voice hissed out of his mind as Darnuir locked swords with him, pressing so hard that the dark god slid back across the cavern floor. Dukoona perked up, hope now kindling inside him. Fighting Darnuir clearly took a great deal of Rectar's power. Maybe they could defeat Rectar together.

The tremble refused to leave his arm. He'd called out to Rectar that he would follow through, yet now it came to it…

Damn it. Why couldn't he just decide and be done with it either way?

Ahead, Darnuir attempted to break the stalemate by dousing Rectar in fire. A cocoon of orange-white flames spiralled around Rectar, tightening like a noose. Dukoona started forwards. Had he managed it?

No. Such thoughts were folly.

The fires began to swirl away as a wall of shadows beat back Darnuir's flames. Then a screaming rose, a shrill bone-piercing cry that Dukoona had not heard since he'd been summoned to this world. It seemed to come from the shadows that Rectar commanded, as though each one was a tortured soul he'd savaged and kept as a plaything. Thinking of the red dragons, he might have done just that.

Darnuir's flames burned brighter; Rectar's shadows screamed louder, until fire and shadow burst in a wave of heat and smoke. Both combatants were swept off their feet, Rectar towards the Cascade Sink, Darnuir towards Dukoona.

Darnuir skidded, slowing himself down by digging his swords into the cavern floor, then halted on one knee nearby. Panting, he looked pleadingly at Dukoona.

"What are you doing? Help me."

"I—" Dukoona started, but his two sides were warring within himself. He wanted to explain, to run away, to not have to do this cowardly act. The other voice told him that Darnuir was so close; unsuspecting, weakened, on his knees. He raised his sword.

"Darnuir. I'm sorry, I—"

Rectar interrupted, trying to take Darnuir by surprise. The King of Dragons was knocked over on his back. He crossed his blades, catching Rectar's own weapon between them. The tip of the corrupted Champion's Blade hovered an inch from Darnuir's throat. Rectar was going to win, and if he made the killing strike then the spectres would never be free.

Dukoona had no need to consider. He hurled himself forwards, adding what strength he could to aid Darnuir. Together, bit by bit, they pushed Rectar back, until Darnuir found the strength to stand and their duel resumed.

Dukoona's head exploded in pain as Rectar entered his mind.

'Next time you'll take your chance. You could have finished him. I've directed my dragons to kill your kind first. You're running out of time.'

Dukoona gasped as his master left him and he knew that he was right. He'd saved Darnuir when he could have killed him. And now more spectres had perished. He tightened his grip on his sword, collecting himself. The tremor in his limbs ceased.

He'd have to kill Darnuir.

Dukoona tried to intervene in the fight, but they were both so powerful he could barely keep up watching them, never mind join the fray. He was nothing on either of them.

Rectar's figure dissolved, reappearing far away from Darnuir, near the Cascade Sink. He entered Dukoona's mind again.

'Come on, Dukoona,' he raged. *'Your people die outside. One by one they fall. There goes another. And another. And ano—'*

"Stop it," Dukoona cried aloud, falling to his knees. "I will do it, Master. I will do it. But I need the chance."

Rectar may have been distracted by the brief exchange, for he seemed sluggish in deflecting the Dragon's Blade as it hurtled towards him. Rectar knocked it off course, sending it spinning towards the Cascade Sink. Darnuir had covered half the distance when his sword hit the well of energy and the blast sent him clean off his feet. A spike of raw Cascade lashed forth from the Sink like lightning, hit the edge of the cavern and exploded.

The whole mountain shook. Dukoona lost his footing and fell. He rolled and spun and sought shadow after shadow as great hunks of stone crashed down. Everything was deafening bangs of breaking rock and painful vibrations. There seemed no end to it. Was all of Kar'drun crumbling around them?

When it finally ceased, Dukoona blinked against the daylight that had been made hazy by the dust clogging the air. A gaping hole loomed in the mountainside, large enough that a cloud might have floated through it

Darnuir was face down and covered by debris. Rectar was already on his feet, moving back to the Cascade Sink with a slight limp.

The sounds of battle drifted in, notably regular booming blasts that Dukoona had never heard before.

"Those humans are ingenious with their craft," Rectar declared. "I shall deal with them while you recover, Darnuir. Or not, as the case may be."

'Do it now,' Rectar's voice burned in his mind.

Dukoona looked to Darnuir, who was slowly stirring. His hand emerged first from the rubble and Dukoona saw the Dragon's Blade zooming back across the cavern, seemingly unscathed from the explosion.

Rectar reached the glowing well and extended the Champion's Blade slowly towards it, as though hoping to tame a wild animal. Blue streaks of raw Cascade sparked towards the tip of the sword, then wrapped themselves around it, flowing up and entwining themselves around Rectar. The Sink itself started to shrink, as though the stored energy was being drained into Rectar, burning away like wood in a fire.

And Rectar began to change.

His arms stretched and arced as he grew leathery sinew and hardened bone spikes. His body swelled, his skin turned to red-black scales, his neck lengthened, his face became a snout with a pit of razor teeth. His talons raked at the cavern floor as he landed, roaring in a way that snuffed out the courage in the hearts of mortals.

He had become a full dragon; a beast from times this world had long forgotten.

Rectar flapped his great wings and took off, flying out of the hole in Kar'drun to wreak terror on those outside.

Any thought of resistance was shattered. It had always been a distant dream.

Darnuir was on his feet now, bent over and coughing up thick scarlet blood.

Dukoona melded across the numerous new shadows to his side. "I am sorry. I never understood the extent of his power. I thought there was a chance."

Darnuir groaned, blood dribbling down his chin. "I was close. I can beat him. I know it." He groaned more as he tried to step forward.

"How can you?" Dukoona said. "What possible way is there?"

Darnuir pointed towards the Sink.

"That is a risk," Dukoona said.

"What choice is there?" Darnuir said. "We'll all die otherwise. Your people and mine."

No, Dukoona thought. *Not my people.*

He gazed again at the well of energy, bubbling away in the semi-distance. Darnuir took one small step towards it and Dukoona found himself behind the dragon king.

"You'd do anything to save your people from further harm?" Dukoona said.

"Anything I could," Darnuir said.

Dukoona formed a dagger in his hand. "So would I." He plunged it through Darnuir's exposed neck. He drew it back and thrust it through the weaker join at Darnuir's waist.

Darnuir jolted, his body jerked around in a fit of shock. Dukoona had never seen such hurt and rage blaze across a face. Before Dukoona could make another assault, light and fire burst around Darnuir. Dukoona howled from the pain, barely escaping into a shadow with his life.

He fled desperately from shadow to shadow, leaping from one to another, trying to outrun the light and fire hounding him. He wanted a dark hole in the earth in which to hide. He hated himself. Hated his cowardly act. But the choice had been clear. The spectres would be free if Darnuir died. If he failed, then he'd failed them all, especially himself.

Darnuir

All the breath left his body as he fell to his knees. Fire and light died around him. Very distantly, he could hear a terrible roar. Blinking, his vision darkening, hands numb and cold, he dropped the Guardian's Blade. Hot blood gushed down his back and chest, soaking under his armour and padding. He couldn't breathe. Everything went numb as he scrambled half-blind for the Guardian's Blade. He collapsed onto his stomach, hand still questing for the hilt.

He found it.

But he was dying, if not already dead. He couldn't feel the Cascade, let alone reach out for the doorways. Death's hand was ice cold, and only the warmth of his own blood let him know he could still feel.

'It is not your time,' a voice told him; the same voice he'd heard in his Cascade dreams, and his nightmares. A voice like many in one, and as soft as a whisper.

Why say something now? If he was to die, he wanted to know.

'*Death breaks the walls between us; that, or great power. Here there is such power, and yet even it is not enough.*'

I am dead, then? I have failed.

'*Rise again. You have done so before.*'

Darnuir tried, yet his grasp upon the doors was so weak. *I can't,* he told the voice.

'*Reach out,*' it said, though it too sounded faint. And Darnuir swore he felt another hand upon his within his mind, guiding him, helping him to turn the handle on one door.

With a shuddering gasp he began to heal. The Cascade ran unchecked within him. Both his hands seared as the draining poison swelled in his veins. The blades hummed from the efforts to process it and Darnuir winced as his body knitted back together.

When he had finished, he felt more exhausted than he'd ever been in all his life; even worse than after he'd recovered from his addiction. After this, he'd be lucky to avoid it again.

He forced himself to sit, arms shaking horribly as the residue raced towards the blades. The veins on his hands had turned worryingly black. He tried to lick his cracked lips but there was no moisture left in his mouth. And through the throbbing head pain he had but one agonising thought, worse than all the pain.

Dukoona had betrayed him; literally stabbed him in the back.

What a fool he'd been to think they could have worked together. Hadn't his childish hopes of bringing dragon and human together been naïve enough? To think that he had relied on a spectre.

His anger was abated by a fresh wave of bone-aching agony from the magic. The battle lust was already fading from him, letting his more rational mind return, sluggish as it was.

Dukoona had deceived him. Then again, Dukoona probably thought he had no choice. He'd mentioned something about a promise he'd fulfil for Rectar. That must have been it. Dukoona loved his people fiercely, that was plain. It was for them that he'd abandoned all honour. Darnuir hated it, but he could understand it.

Jamming the Dragon's Blade into the ground, he rose, placing his weight upon it like a walking stick. Though every step jarred his battered body, he went as quickly as he could to the diminished Cascade Sink. The closer he got, the more he felt a familiar tugging sensation in his mind, the same one he'd felt draw him towards the Basilica.

Rectar's echoing growls chilled his blood. How much damage would he be wreaking outside? Darnuir had to fight. Had to try. Everyone, everything relied upon him.

And as he stood before the still-towering well of energy, he heard the voice again.

'We rely on you too...'

Flexing his stiff fingers around the grips of the blades granted him a precious second of delay. Rectar's roaring reached him again. *Just do it,* he told himself.

The Guardian's Blade and Dragon's Blade raised as he approached the Sink, just as he'd seen Rectar do. And the well answered. Raw magic coiled around his swords, and then him. The doors in his mind were ripped from their hinges, and he was drowning in power; yet it was sweet, not bitter; soothing, not painful. The feeling that his body was confining melted away as he grew, larger and larger, his muscles booming with strength, his neck and head reaching high towards the cavern's roof; hot fire, a true fire, burning deep within his throat.

Blaine – The Plains of Kar'drun

The battle had been faring well enough; not badly, but not brilliantly either. Human muskets and cannons kept the brunt of the reds at bay, yet the enemy were quick to close distances and all too often dragons were needed to prevent the humans being routed. The arrival of the spectres had been – and he cursed himself for thinking it – welcome. They had moved at speed throughout the red dragons, able to cut many down unseen from their shadows. They had even drawn the attention of the enemy onto them. Blaine did not complain.

It was a fragile balance, but it would suffice, so long as Darnuir succeeded.

From the back of the legions he watched the battle unfold, directing events where he could. Then a chunk of Kar'drun blasted outwards.

Blaine watched in astonishment as rocks the size of buildings flew. The explosion was on the eastern slope, far away from their own armies. A mercy, which he thanked the gods for.

Then the roar came.

All on the battlefield paused when they heard it; dragon, human, spectre, fairy and red dragon alike. The muskets and cannons fell silent. The world stopped.

Something in Blaine recognised the sound. Some ancient part of his very being, deep in his blood, knew that sound.

A dragon of black and red scales hurtled from Kar'drun like an arrow. It shot high above the clouds, out of sight, roaring all the while, then descended, soaring down to their armies. Everyone panicked. They looked to Blaine for orders, but he was utterly speechless.

Rectar, for it must have been him, swooped over the battlefield. His wings cast a great shadow, his jaws snapped at fairy flyers, his tail pounded into dragon shield walls. He turned, gliding over the humans next and bathing them in molten flame, igniting all the powder and flesh in his line of attack.

Burning flesh and acrid, sour smoke blew across to Blaine as he watched Rectar plunge into the Brevian ranks and begin a slaughter the likes of which he'd never seen. Hails of bullets rebounded from him. Cannonballs bludgeoned him but caused no harm.

Like any dreadful horror, Blaine found himself transfixed, unable to turn away. Rectar roared anew and his red dragons followed suit. Assured of their victory, they redoubled their attack on the legion lines, jumping over shield walls without a second thought.

In the midst of it all, Lira appeared by his side, blood running from her nose. "If it's over, Blaine, we should go out fighting." She offered her hand to him.

Blaine nodded. He drew out the regular sword he'd acquired; such a plain and simple thing, so light both in weight and in burden. It felt flimsy. Then again, he felt flimsy too.

He ran with Lira to the front, and his presence seemed to lift the spirits of those he passed, if only by a fraction. The Praetorians still fought the fiercest, with all the spirit of fighting a hopeless cause that youth is cursed with.

Blaine joined them, landing a lucky stroke against a red that had stuck its neck too far forward to taste the blood of its last kill. Legionaries began to rally to them for one last stand.

"This is the end," Blaine called to them. "The end of all things. But I would have us make a worthy end. Stand with me. Take as many down as you can. To the death."

"To the death," many chanted.

Blaine felt a great sense of relief knowing it was over. There was something darkly comforting about knowing that this was where he would die. In the end, he'd done all he could. Any grief he felt for Darnuir's loss was no longer felt, kept at bay by the rush of battle.

A good clean death. That was what he desired now.

A fresh roar sounded from closer to the mountain. Rectar must have finished with the humans, perhaps flying around to make a pass at the dragons next.

An answering roar came, this one from the west and south, where Rectar had last been seen. Soon the roaring was all Blaine could hear, drowning out even the enemies right before him. The roars were distinct, the second lighter, higher, younger; it bolstered the spirit rather than sapped it.

Could it be?

Blaine backtracked through the Praetorians and legionaries, nearly falling in his haste. He looked up in time to see a golden-scaled dragon soar overhead, homing in on the great red-black beast.

Tears welled in Blaine's eyes as Darnuir, in dragon form, crashed into Rectar talons-first, driving their enemy to the ground.

Arkus

"You must fall back, sire," a chevalier cried, tugging at his arm.

Arkus shrugged him off. "No. I will see this."

Balack came next, bow in hand and quiver near empty. "It's too dangerous. You should not be here." He spoke with a confidence far above his station. Well, that was his own fault for engendering it in the boy.

Arkus opened his mouth, but his half-formed words were drowned out by the two true dragons. One of them, the black one, had the other's tail between its teeth. Arkus tried again.

"When I say I shall stay, I shall stay. Think yourself fortunate, Balack, that you still walk free after aiding Raymond in his thievery and sticking an arrow in the back of my closest chevalier. Go and fight, for that is all you're good for now."

Balack scowled and ran off.

Arkus returned his attention to the battle. Still a fair distance away from the thick of things, he was close enough to have felt the slaughter by the black dragon deep in his heart. All those people, burnt to cinders or blown to pieces from exploding powder. All in a second. If this was Rectar, their so-called great enemy, then he'd earned that title. The golden dragon was Darnuir, Arkus assumed, but how he'd managed to transform into such a creature was beyond him.

Magic. All his woes came back to magic, and those who wielded it.

The two dragons took off, flew high, scrambled at each other in the air, then began to fall back down, still scratching and biting while spiralling towards the earth. A second before impact, Darnuir twisted up and away, beating his powerful wings and leading Rectar away from the battlefield.

Arkus scanned over the rest of the dragon army. So many thousands of them still, and if they were all capable of turning into such beasts – if Darnuir had found the way to transform back again – then, well, humanity was doomed.

How he hated them.

The human lines faltered in the wake of the destruction wrought by Rectar. Artillery fire was still helping to cover the dragon front lines. *Not for much longer*, he decided.

"Send word to Adolphus. All cannon fire is to assist human companies only."

"That will concentrate the enemy directly onto the legions," a chevalier said.

"What of it?" Arkus spat. The chevalier gave him a grim look then got up on his mount and rode off without further question.

The man was right enough. Before long, with the artillery focused solely upon supporting the humans, the red dragons turned their attention entirely towards the legions. Golden armour shimmered and flashed, and shrank in number with each heartbeat.

Blaine would be amongst them. Perhaps he was already dead. Arkus smirked, the closest he'd come to a smile in weeks.

Every fallen dragon was a blessing. For how could humanity ever live in safety while powers such as Darnuir and Rectar walked freely? What good could men and women do against such vast power? Nothing. They would die. As easily as so many had at Brevia. And wasn't it his duty to do all he could to keep humanity safe? A cruel joke, for he'd never been able to keep his own family from harm.

Thane's cold body, already turning blue, flashed before him. The grief, still too near, threatened to choke, deafen, and blind him. He didn't know why he wrestled with his desires anymore. Before him was his justification. The dragons were too dangerous.

As more fell, Arkus' smirk crept further up his face. It gave him more pleasure than he'd felt in years.

Darnuir

. . .

Above the clouds the air was chill, the sun searing. He climbed higher, as high as he dared to fly. Each stretch and beat of his wings grew harder and his tail became a dead weight behind him.

He barely thought. All was instinct and some ancient primal knowing. He simply knew how to fly, to turn, how to dredge fire from the depths of his belly.

He could still feel, at least; the euphoria of flight, the panic of the battle. Fear shook him for a moment too. What if he could not turn back?

Rectar's roars signalled he was still in pursuit. Darnuir pressed on, but when the air thinned and the sky darkened, he felt he could climb no more. He swooped around, hoping to catch Rectar by surprise.

Rectar pivoted, a breath of black fire billowing from his mouth. Darnuir spun, like an arrow spinning through the air, missing the flaming breath as it whooshed past him. Rectar's tail clubbed him, cracking into the bulk of his body. Darnuir roared, slashing at the tail with talons that were as thick as ship masts. He cut into the meat of Rectar's tail and black, smoking gore poured forth like bile.

Locked again, neither could beat their wings, and once again they fell through the air, all the while biting and tearing at each other; trying to get purchase with tooth or claw. Turning all the time, Darnuir only saw the ground rush to meet them in flashes.

Far away. Still far. Closer now. Too close.

He kicked away from Rectar, stretched his wings to their full length and glided above the warring armies. He sensed Rectar was not following and turned. Rectar hovered over the legions, preparing to spew his own fire onto them. Darnuir beat upwards, then dove, tucking his wings to his side, slicing through the air faster than a musket ball.

He felt the heat scorch his underbelly as he took the brunt of Rectar's attack, sparing those below. Fighting through the pain, he hovered, looked Rectar in his jagged red eyes and cursed as his enemy took flight, heading back towards Kar'drun. Darnuir pursued him towards the hole from whence they had come.

He pumped his wings with all his newfound might, meaning to prevent Rectar from reaching his goal. If Rectar sought it, it could only mean ill for him.

He rammed Rectar into the mountainside and they fought there upon the black slope, rearing on their hind legs to strike at each other like warring horses. It was a battle of sound as much as muscle, each one trying to deafen the other.

Darnuir's head hit rock and pain exploded behind his eyes. His world spun in a haze of colour. When he righted himself, he saw Rectar had taken off again, this time climbing high as he'd done before, perhaps trying to lose him in the clouds. Darnuir gave chase, but lost track of Rectar's swishing tail, until he vanished for good in the gathering clouds.

Beating his wings to remain in place, Darnuir turned, sniffing the air, hoping to find the trail of his quarry. Rectar had stopped roaring. Everything felt still.

He saw the movement from the corner of his eye, but too late. Rectar swooped upon him silently and the pair were locked brutally together once more. This time, Rectar seemed to have no intention of letting go. His jaw clamped around the joint of Darnuir's left wing. Darnuir howled as he was pinned in place. They hurtled towards the solid rock face of Kar'drun. He'd be taking the full impact of it.

Darnuir struggled, kicking and flailing with his talons, but to no avail. Rectar had him and sank his teeth in deeper for good measure. Through the dizzying pain, Darnuir saw Rectar raise his wings to help angle their descent. Darnuir took his chance. He heaved up a blast of bright orange fire, concentrating on the softer tissue of Rectar's wings.

His fire burned a hole and Darnuir began to bite, tearing sinew away in vile-tasting chunks, biting on the bone of the wing until it snapped.

Rectar released Darnuir to roar in his own agony.

Darnuir flipped them mid-flight and sent a taut, powerful stream of fire at Rectar; a mixture of flames and light. Rectar met it with his own, the jets clashing into a hellfire between them.

They held for a time, each trying to outdo the other, neither quite succeeding, yet always falling. Blinded by the inferno, Darnuir lost sight of Rectar, but not the sound of him. He heard Rectar crashing into the mountainside, the dark fires extinguishing soon after.

Darnuir had no time to react.

The hole in the mountain rushed to meet him.

He crumpled against the breach, then followed Rectar down through it.

Back into the cavern he fell, semi-conscious, hearing only a vague rumble of screams and cannonfire. The blue light of the Cascade Sink was fainter now, the oval of bubbling blue far smaller. The Cascade Sink was greatly diminished, as though an ocean had been drained to a pond. If there was battle left, it would be through raw strength, raw determination.

Rectar hit the cavern floor with a heavy thud, sending dust and rubble out like a tidal wave.

Darnuir hit the ground seconds later. All went black.

His fingers tightened desperately around the hilts of both blades. So, he had arms and hands again, and a throbbing from his legs confirmed they too were back. Cascade residue flowed down his arms like shards of glass. Even with two blades, even with all his exceptional new power, he sensed that his body was reaching a new breaking point.

Perhaps it was for the best that he sensed less energy behind the doors in his mind. Fighting against every protesting muscle, Darnuir rose.

He spat blue-tinged residue and scanned the area for Rectar. Amidst a ring of rubble, he spotted the crimson cloak now. Rectar got to his feet and the shredded cloak shifted from his shoulders. Darnuir saw the wiry body beneath. Kroener had not been as bulky as most dragons. His arm hung by a sickeningly exposed tendon, the result of Darnuir's focused efforts on the wing. As Rectar began to heal, the Cascade Sink shrank further, until its light was but a gloomy lantern in the still-dark segment of the cavern. Rectar's arm snapped back into position and he threw back his head in ecstasy at the relief. His crimson hood fell back, at last revealing the face of Kroener in its entirety.

It was a face of sharp angles, with a brutally edged jaw and brow. Looking at his whole person was to look upon a knife-edge made flesh. He met Darnuir's gaze with vacant, glacial blue eyes. In that moment, Darnuir felt pity for the dragon he'd once been. Was a piece of him in there still? Had Kroener been forced to watch all Rectar had done, or had he embraced Rectar willingly? Blaine believed that Kroener had murdered Darnuir's father, and if this was true, then Darnuir ought to feel no sympathy at all. But the only father Darnuir really had, the one who'd raised him, had died at the Charred Vale. For Kroener, he held no anger. A terrible fate it must be to be possessed by a force such as Rectar. If the so-called betrayer had deserved punishment, he'd received it.

The moment passed. Rectar repositioned the hood and Kroener's narrowed eyes were lost beneath it, glowing red once more. Rectar strode towards Darnuir, dragging the Champion's Blade across the ground in a skin-crawling scrape. The God of the Shadows seemed to move slowly, in a more considered approach. Clearly, he was weakened, though Darnuir hardly felt better.

He raised both blades and staggered forwards to meet his foe.

Dukoona

He heard the almighty crash, but did not investigate. Rather, he kept to his dark corner, awaiting Rectar's punishment for his failure. But it wasn't from his master that he hid. His fear was of another spectre coming across him; of having to look them in the eye and explain how he'd let them down.

So when he heard footsteps tapping lightly nearby, he ducked away, unwilling to face judgement.

"Dukoona, what did you do?" Sonrid's voice was weak, as though in shock.

"What I thought I had to," Dukoona said, not looking at Sonrid. The little spectre had been so brave. Sonrid might be one of the Broken, but it was he, Dukoona, who was truly broken now. Rectar had ground all resistance from him.

"Darnuir is our best hope," Sonrid said.

"And even he cannot do this. It is impossible."

Sonrid groaned as he hauled himself closer. "That's not what you used to say."

"The pain... You cannot possibly..." But he trailed off. *Look who I'm speaking to.* "You must understand."

"I believed in you," Sonrid said. His words hurt Dukoona more than Rectar ever could.

"I'm sorry. I failed us all."

"It's not over," Sonrid insisted. "Darnuir fights still. For how long, I don't know, but he's there and his blades still have light and fire to them. He has not given in. Nor should you."

Dukoona stirred, finally looking at Sonrid. "The Master promised to free you all if I killed Darnuir."

"Kill the Master and we'll be free regardless."

"There's no guarantee—"

"There never was," Sonrid said. "Dukoona. I did not suffer the walk from Aurisha for you to reduce yourself to this. I once asked you to kill me, so I'd be free of my pain. But you refused. You said it would be better to live, to suffer, but fight. And if we died, we would die free, of our own choices, not under the Master's neglect. All the Trusted followed you because they felt the same. You fail them by surrendering to Rectar, not by dying in battle. They are prepared to die to give you the chance. So, what are you waiting for?"

Dukoona's resolve stiffened. He rose, summoning his shadow blade into his hand.

Darnuir

If ancient gnarled trees could pick up roots and fight each other, it might look like this. At least, that was how Darnuir felt. Most likely they were moving quicker than any normal dragon and far beyond a human, yet to him, to what he'd recently experienced, this felt like a slog. He spat out another gob of gloopy blue residue, barely noticing the bitterness anymore.

Finesse was gone. It was heavy swings and thrusts, followed by punches, shoulder barging, or stamping kicks.

Darnuir cut upwards, grunting like an old man clambering out of bed. Rectar met his strike silently, still with a good deal of force behind it. As the fight wore on, Darnuir began to accept that his own strength was fading, while Rectar's rallied.

With ragged breath and his pulse hammering, Darnuir tried to regain the upper hand. He brought his swords across from one side, then the other, back again; up and across, then spun and back the other way.

Rectar's last block sent him reeling.

Darnuir fell, crushing small stones under his armour. He had enough wits left to roll away, and the momentum brought him up in time to face Rectar's overhead strike.

Darnuir brought both blades up in a cross guard, catching the Champion's Blade between them. There he held, but he knew it would be his last move. His arms trembled from the strain and the dregs of magic still thrumming through them. Rectar pressed his advantage. Darnuir took a step back.

"You have the power and will to go on," Rectar said. "But you are flesh, and blood, and bone. Like he who came before you, you will tire. Your body will wane and break, magic or no. I will not waver. I am restless. Endless."

Darnuir stepped back again and felt his knees buckle. Under the crushing force of Rectar, he dropped to one knee entirely, and through the gap in the blades, he saw Rectar's eyes shift to his chest.

Still holding the twisted Champion's Blade in one hand, he reached forwards with the other, his milk-white fingers turning into their true shadows as they moved towards Darnuir's heart. Unable to move, unable to resist, the shadowy fingers plunged unopposed even through the starium-lined armour.

Shards of ice entered Darnuir's heart. Breath abandoned him. Hope left him. When next he heard Rectar's voice, it was inside his mind.

'I will take you, as I took him. You could never have wo—'

The chill in Darnuir's heart disappeared as Rectar's fingers withdrew. The pressure on his crossed blades melted away. Blue light from the Cascade Sink burst like the rising sun, the well rapidly expanding. And in that brighter light, a shimmering blade of dark purple glinted right above where Rectar's wrist had been.

Rectar gasped as the Champion's Blade hit the cavern floor with a clang.

Bladeless, Rectar froze, eyes wide in horror. Darnuir didn't catch Dukoona before he melded away, reappearing behind Rectar. The Lord of the Spectres spoke quietly into his ear.

"Die now, Master."

He shoved his sword through Rectar's chest. The shadowy blade burst through like an arrow shaft, though no blood spilled.

Rectar began to flicker and fade between Kroener's possessed body and his true dark form, blurring until, with an almighty crack, the crimson-cloaked body was left behind, and the shadow split apart from it.

Rectar's dark form moved sluggishly through the air, an elongated body with limbs stretching further with every second. It made for the Cascade Sink, arms outstretched, but dissolved into nothingness before managing to touch the well of magic. A final shrill scream rang, echoed, and died.

Rectar, God of the Shadows, was gone.

Darnuir stood upright, fighting to control his breath. Jubilation, exhaustion, apprehension – he didn't know what to feel first. He hadn't forgotten Dukoona's recent transgression and so raised the Dragon's Blade pointedly towards him.

Dukoona already had his hands raised. "I was afraid, and made a mistake."

"You tried to kill me."

"I thought it would be the only way to save my people. We had a bargain, you see. And I did not think you could do it."

"I would have lost, if you hadn't come."

"And I would never have been able to avoid his possession had you not distracted him so well." Dukoona offered a smile, but it didn't make him any less foreboding.

Darnuir wasn't sure what to do. Dukoona had tried to kill him; he'd come damn close, in fact. Yet the spectre's bearing was wildly different than it had been earlier in the battle. The confidence Darnuir had sensed when they'd met at Aurisha had returned. He stood taller, straighter, his blue flaming hair thicker and livelier. Dukoona had done right in the end.

Darnuir lowered his sword. "Why did you return?"

Dukoona looked about as though searching for something. "Because I was reminded about the value of resistance. Even if the odds are slim."

"Thank you," Darnuir said, if a little stiffly. "Though as you put a dagger in me, I hope this is a parting of the ways."

Dukoona's eyes rolled upwards and he tilted back his head as though looking to something high above them. "Do not fear, Dragon King. Leaving this world is something my people dearly wish, something I think is already starting." And before Darnuir's very eyes, Dukoona's body began to disperse into smoke; his feet and legs first, working slowly up.

Darnuir stepped forward as though to help him. "Does it hurt?"

Dukoona smiled. "Not at all."

"Where are you going? What will you do?"

"I hope somewhere far away, to do whatever we like."

"Farewell then, Dukoona. And good luck."

"Farewell, Darnuir."

Dukoona's final words became a whisper as the smoking dispersion reached his head. The spectre too was gone, leaving Darnuir alone in the depths of Kar'drun with only his aches for company.

37

THE SCARLET FIELDS

"Even here, we could have taken another path."

Author Unknown

Darnuir

The dust fell gently, caught by the light spilling in from the chasm in the mountainside. In the vastness of Rectar's lair, Darnuir stood alone, embracing the peace in this moment of calm. Rumblings reached him from the world beyond, but not enough to disturb this strange tranquillity. The Cascade Sink slowly swirled away as the energy returned to the surrounding world but Darnuir ensured the doors were firmly shut inside his mind.

He supposed he should be on his way. The job was done. The world was saved.

So why did he feel so... so empty?

Just the tiredness, he assumed. Once the blades churned through the magic, and the victory had a chance to sink in, he was sure he'd feel it. Whatever it would be.

He was just about to leave when he remembered the Champion's Blade. It must have fallen close by. Darnuir bent down amongst the rubble to search. It couldn't have gotten far; Rectar hadn't thrown it, yet there was no sign of it. Frustrated, he allowed a smidgen of magic back in to light the Guardian's Blade and illuminate his surroundings. He sighed. Nought but dust and rock.

Darnuir craned his neck, gazing through the crack in the mountain, trying to see past the sky, the sun, to whatever lay beyond.

"Did you take it back?"

No answer.

"If you have, I wouldn't give it away again."

When still the gods said nothing, he turned away from the breach, dimmed the light on the Guardian's Blade and began his journey out of Kar'drun.

Out upon the red fields before the burned mountain, the armies of the Three Races had separated. Dragons stood farthest south of Kar'drun in their shimmering golden armour, where the battle had drawn them into thin lines. Fairies hovered in the skies or else stood behind the legions. Human companies had drawn to a halt between the mountain and the dragons.

As Darnuir picked his way across the battlefield over the thousands of dead red dragons, he got a sense of what had occurred. The humans had forced a push on the enemy flank, cutting through to the mountainside, then turned east and blasted their way through the rest of the reds.

Perhaps things had gotten easier when Rectar had died. The enemy may have lost all their senses, or given in. Darnuir did not know. All that was certain was not a single red dragon was left alive.

Black-uniformed humans parted for him as he walked, looks of awe upon their faces and a touch of fear in their hearts. The sweetness in the air was light, but it was there. He supposed he would be wary of himself if he were them. He'd turned into a true dragon of old and flown above their heads. Although it was so recent, it somehow felt long ago and distant, as though it hadn't really been him that had transformed.

In time, Darnuir emerged into the gulf between the human and dragon armies. A knot tightened in his stomach. This should have been a time of rejoicing, yet all was stilted, silent, grim and still. The hundred paces he had left to reach the dragons seemed to stretch out like a second horizon.

A few steps forward, his sensitive ears pricked. Hooves were thundering from the west and Darnuir turned to find King Arkus and a guard of chevaliers cantering his way. Oddly, they stayed within the ranks of their soldiers, not coming out to greet him man to man.

"You succeeded then, Darnuir," Arkus called out.

Darnuir nodded slowly. "Somehow, I have. We have," he added, gesturing to Arkus and the humans at large. "We can begin to rebuild again. It's over."

"Yes," Arkus said, a bite in his voice. "Yes, it is over. Your kind's domination and abuse of this world is also at an end."

Darnuir's heart stopped. "We make no claim to the world. It belongs to us all. Human, fairy, dragon, troll, and anyone who comes after."

Arkus' face was unreadable, his features, and perhaps his will, set in stone. "Fine words, Darnuir. Fine words. But centuries from now, what is to stop this madness occurring again?"

"I have the Guardian's Blade. If I do not pass it on, I might live forever. I could be your guarantee."

"So I am to let a wielder of not just one but two of these mighty blades walk freely? I am to put all my faith and trust in you?"

"I want what's best for all of us. Please, Arkus, put your hatred for my kind aside. You must. We've all lost so much—"

"Don't you dare, Darnuir," Arkus cried. "I warned you before. And as for your offer to maintain the peace singlehanded, I'd rather not place the future of my people solely in your hands. You have more power than I can possibly fathom, but you have a mind like any other, and a mind can change."

"I will give up my positions," Darnuir said. "Dragons will find a new way to select their rulers if it comes to it. I shall claim no control over any man or woman from any race; no armies and no lands."

Arkus shook his head. "Even if it could be done, could you truly be neutral in affairs? You are a dragon – we've all seen the extent of that now – and you will always be a dragon."

Darnuir took a step towards the humans, his hands outstretched, unarmed. "What do you want from me? You think me some god, but I cannot bring back the dead, no matter how much I too may wish it. I'm sorry Thane died. I'm sorry Cosmo died. I'm sorry for every death caused in the long wars we've faced, but it's over now. Let go of your anger and weep instead. Weep, and we'll all weep with you."

He extended a hand, begging Arkus to come down from his horse, walk out and take it.

Arkus' small black eyes narrowed further, then his whole body sagged. But he did not come down from his mount.

"I must do what I think is right," he said. "Companies, prepare to fire."

A dead weight plunged from Darnuir's throat through his stomach as thousands of muskets clicked into place. Dull thuds in the earth spoke of legionaries bashing shields and forming ranks, as if it would do any good.

"Stop this," a new voice cried. "Stop this now." And soldiers near Arkus were shoved aside as Balack emerged into the empty field to stand beside Darnuir.

"Balack," Darnuir said, his voice suddenly hoarse. "You don't have to—"

"I do," Balack said, waving Darnuir down.

Darnuir lunged for his arm. "I'm sorry, Balack."

Balack looked taken aback, but returned the gesture, grasping Darnuir by the forearm in a brotherly shake. "Me too," he said, then he faced the guns. "Lower your damned weapons."

Some did; others hesitated, pointing their barrels to the ground but not fully lowering. Many stayed in place, either through discipline, loyalty, or from sharing Arkus' beliefs. Ripples flowed along the whole front line as human troops either wavered or held their nerve.

Arkus looked livid. "Balack, you might think you're being noble, but you are not. You of all people understand the damage their kind can cause. Return to my side."

"I won't. Darnuir is right. It's over. It's all over. How can you think of spilling more blood now?"

Arkus played with his sleeve, apparently buying time to think. When he looked up, his face held no emotion. He might as well have been dead.

"You're right. So much blood has been shed already. A little more won't hurt."

Arkus raised his arm high.

But he didn't bring it down.

He held it in place, a single finger trembling as his muscles began to strain.

Darnuir sniffed at the growing sweetness upon the air. Whether fearful of a battle with the dragons or simply fearful of being given the command to fire, the humans weren't all as strong in their conviction as their king. More muskets began pointing towards the ground. And Arkus had not yet dropped his arm.

Perhaps, Darnuir thought, just maybe, they could yet get out of this—

A lone crack sounded, some ways down the line.

Darnuir near enough snapped his neck turning towards the noise. He saw the tiny smoke trail rising from the fired musket. His heart stopped beating again. A few more cracks sounded, first sporadic, then growing in number, though haphazardly so; individuals firing rather than whole companies.

Balack cried again for all near him to put their weapons down. Darnuir caught Arkus' eye, looked imploringly at him, and poured magic into his voice.

"You do not have to do this." His words rang across the plains. "Throw down your guns, all of you, and return to Aurisha as friends."

But the avalanche had already begun.

There was no turning back.

"FIRE!" Arkus bellowed.

To Darnuir, the horror unfolded slowly. Flashes from the triggers heralded the doom, stretching a mile to east and west. The deafening bang seemed to come a long time after that.

Darnuir dropped to the ground, pulling Balack with him as a hail of lead cut overhead, slamming with sickening crunches into the dragon lines.

The next row of humans stepped forward, angling their muskets down at him. Darnuir drew the Guardian's Blade and cast a light forwards, strong enough to truly blind those who looked upon it. The screams of the blinded were drowned by cannon fire. Darnuir twisted around, only to see his people falling in droves.

"Run," he ordered, powering his throat with enough Cascade to yell above all else. "Flee to Aurisha. Do not fight." Hoping Blaine and the others would do as he said, he turned to check on Balack.

His friend was lying face down and unmoving. Dreading what he'd find, Darnuir rolled Balack over, and was met with a vacant stare, a half-formed cry caught in his open mouth. Darnuir only noticed then that his own hand was slick with blood. A couple of entry wounds oozed from Balack's chest, soaking those brilliant white leathers.

Tears welled and fell before the impact of the death fully hit. His blood-covered hand found and cupped Balack's head as though it might bring him back.

Above, the humans were rearranging their lines, bringing non-blinded troops to the fore. Through the chaos, Darnuir saw Arkus still sitting there upon his horse.

He could kill him. It wouldn't be hard. If he threw open the doors in his mind, he could gouge a bloody hole through half of humanity before he was finally brought down. He did throw open the doors and let the Cascade wash in, but he did not start forward for revenge. Doing so would only prove that black-hearted bastard right. And he had to save his remaining dragons, if he could. He couldn't do that as a corpse.

So Darnuir grabbed Balack's body and ran. He ran faster than the wind could blow and caught up with the fleeing dragons in seconds. He tore past them, meaning to reach Aurisha first and relay news of Arkus' treachery. That was about as far as his plan went. What they did next, only these gods could know. If they would deem to tell him.

38

ROTTEN TO THE ROOTS

"When arrows fly, the wild beasts die. A dragon dies the same."

The Way Of The Beast, a hunter's song

Cassandra – Oranna's Parlour

Cullen guffawed merrily, flashing his big babyish smile and windmilling his arms in fat little circles. He'd been set off by Cassandra sneezing, of all things. He laughed at most stuff; someone entering the room, someone leaving the room, and getting his hands on absolutely anything was a cause for great joy.

Cassandra blinked, fighting back fatigue, and bounced Cullen on her knees. He giggled again, and she couldn't help but smile back at him, despite everything. What a blessed little existence he led, no thought nor worry beyond what he would next put in his mouth to bite on. Arkus had left no instruction where Cullen was concerned, but he would be the next heir, she supposed.

Or I might be.

"Do you want to be king, Cullen?"

He made a gooey 'ohhh' sound in response.

"I thought not," Cassandra said. "It's no fun, I can tell you."

Sometimes, she felt guilty for enjoying her time with Cullen. A mean little part of her raised its eyebrow, as if to say, 'How can you enjoy this when Thane has so recently left us?' She forced herself to ignore that guilt, at least while she was with her nephew. To do otherwise would be to drown in grief, and she'd rubbed her eyes raw plenty of times.

Oranna did not have such an escape. The queen spent most of her time alone in her chambers, seeing few visitors and taking on fewer matters of state. Those tasks, such as they were – mostly painful decisions dealing with the consequences of the riots – had fallen to Cassandra.

Cullen burped and laughed at the noise, looking around for the source of it.

"You silly thing," she said affectionately.

A knock came at the parlour door and Cassandra called to enter, expecting Olive with Cullen's milk horn. Olive did enter with Cullen's refilled milk, but Kymethra too followed in behind, looking flushed. The witch had a fresh crease of worry on her brow, which left Cassandra's throat dry. What else had happened?

Cullen accepted the horn greedily and began to suck. He'd gulped through his first of the day in no time at all. Cassandra reckoned a royal cow might be needed to maintain a steady source at the rate he was going. She moved him off her lap on to the plush sofa. Contented, his eyes rolled upwards as he continued to drain the horn.

"I had this batch warmed," Olive said. "He was up so early this morning, so I'm hoping he'll nod off and get some… get some sleep," she yawned. It triggered a reaction in Cassandra, who couldn't hold back a yawn herself, followed by Kymethra, whose eyes were darkest of all.

"Is something wrong with Brackendon?" Cassandra asked.

Kymethra shook her head. "No change there. It's the scrying orb, I'm afraid. It's activated."

"What's wrong?"

"I'm not sure of the details," Kymethra said hastily.

"Is it my father?"

"It's Darnuir," Kymethra said. "You need to hear him out for yourself." The witch shuffled awkwardly. "But after hearing what he said… I… well, I've decided I'm going. Today. Straight away, in fact. I need to get Brackendon away from here – to Val'tarra. I should have gone long before—" She caught herself before bringing up that day. Cassandra wanted nothing more than to leap to her feet and hug the witch, but word of her departing left her numb. Kymethra always had to go, at least for a time.

What she had to ask was, "Will you come back?"

Kymethra's lower lip trembled. "Not now, Cass."

"What's happened?"

"That's for Darnuir to tell you. It's not my place." She sat herself down by Cassandra, perhaps sensing her inability to move. Gingerly, Kymethra moved closer and wrapped an arm around her as though she were a wounded animal. "Take care of yourself, okay?"

A lump had formed in Cassandra's throat. She could barely speak. "You too."

Kymethra turned one last time before leaving, giving the smallest of waves. Then she was gone. Even Olive, always so stern, seemed moved. Were those tears in her eyes?

"I think he's settling down," Olive sniffed, ruffling Cullen's tuft of sandy hair. He was still sucking dreamily at his milk, his eyelids beginning to droop. "I'll take him to his chambers, Princess."

Cassandra handed him over mechanically and came back to her senses some time later, when she was very much alone in the parlour. Taking a deep breath, she found the strength to stand and started on her journey to speak with Darnuir.

Before departing Brevia for the east, Arkus had ordered that the scrying orb be moved from his council chambers into the throne room. This was to enable him to announce victory and the end of war to the whole court, the Assembly and as many people as they could cram into the hall. He was never one to miss a chance at pageantry.

Right now, Cassandra entered the throne room alone and the creak of the old door rang terribly under the high vaulted ceiling. With the shutters over the closed windows the place was dark and cool. What slivers of light did creep in reflected off the white marbled floor, glistening as though it were a still lake under moonlight.

She took the steps to the throne's platform. Front and centre before the throne stood the scrying orb atop its black iron plinth. Its misty contents were drawn to the edges, revealing the unmistakable face of Darnuir at its centre. Yet, though it clearly was Darnuir looking out at her, he was not the same man. He looked older, though his skin was somehow brighter, lacking any blemishes. His hair had white streaks running all throughout it, even more than Kymethra's, yet the most changed of all were his eyes. Magnified in the orb, she couldn't help but notice the flecks of silver, but it was more than that: she saw a deeper weariness she'd only seen before in Blaine. And was that the hilt of a different sword poking out from behind his head?

"Cassandra —" The King of Dragons hesitated. "Thank you for coming."

"Why wouldn't I?"

Darnuir nodded behind her. "You won't sit down?"

Cassandra glanced to the tall black throne. "It doesn't suit me."

A silence followed. It seemed Darnuir did not wish to say whatever he had to, and he avoided meeting her eye.

"What's happened?" she asked nervously.

"I'm not sure how to say this, but Arkus has – has—"

"He's been killed?"

"No," Darnuir said sharply. "If only." He grimaced, trying to recollect his features. "I'm sorry. I know he's your father—"

She waved him off, bracing herself for the worst. "Just tell me."

"Arkus has betrayed us. We marched on Kar'drun and were victorious. Afterwards, Arkus ordered his army to open fire upon my people. I believe he intends to wipe us out."

Cassandra had surely misheard. That could not be true. Never, never had she thought – not even in her darkest dreams. It couldn't be.

"What?" she said like a frightened child.

"I assure you it's true," Darnuir said. "I ran ahead to Aurisha at great speed. The remainder of my own forces should return within the next few days. Arkus and the humans will take longer, but if he presses his troops—" He hung his head, lost for further words.

"I'm sorry," Cassandra said. What could she say? What did you say when you heard that your father and king was exterminating a whole race? "Won't you fight back?"

"No. My people here are starved and terrified. My soldiers are worn beyond words."

"Are the islanders still there?" Cassandra said. "Perhaps they could take them away like they di—"

But Darnuir shook his head. "I won't have Grigayne risk his people's lives more than they already have. I fear Arkus has some retribution in store for them already. But I do have a plan, of sorts. A last, mad plan. More of a feeling, really. It may work. But if it doesn't, well, we're doomed as it is."

"But you defeated Rectar? You must have?" Cassandra said, unable to keep the awe from her voice. "You actually did it?"

"I did."

"How?"

Darnuir reached behind his head and drew out the sword there. Now she could see the Guardian's Blade clearly, she gasped.

"Blaine is still alive," Darnuir said. "He granted me the blade in our darkest hour. With two blades, I defeated Rectar, with some help from Dukoona – do you remember telling me of him?"

She nodded; the memory of that spectre would never leave her. A lot had happened out east that she'd never know about. That nobody would know, if Darnuir and the dragons—

No. The thought was utterly unbearable. She felt ill as her mind considered the pathetic excuses Arkus would bleat to the Assembly and their people, and how they would applaud it.

"I turned into a dragon, Cass," Darnuir said, sounding much younger again, far more like the anxious boy her own age she'd met in the Boreac Mountains. "I flew, and breathed fire, and felt unstoppable. I was also completely terrified that I wouldn't turn back." He met her eye, then became suddenly solemn. "I am afraid I have more bad news."

Cassandra braced herself again. "Go on."

"Balack fell."

The punch to her stomach was just shy of Thane.

"He died trying to get Arkus to reconsider," Darnuir went on. "He stood by my side and told those fools to put their weapons down. He said he forgave me." His voice cracked. "I'm sorry, Cassandra. I'm sorry I couldn't stop this. All this strength, yet I was powerless."

She reached out instinctively, as if to rub his shoulder, but met only hard crystal.

"It's not your fault. I'm sorry too. I tried to get Arkus to change and I think I nearly did manage it, but then things unravelled too quickly. But it's not over yet," she said, her voice hardening. "Oranna and I had started putting contingency plans in place. We could overthrow Arkus even before he returns and—"

Darnuir was smiling weakly. "I know you could overthrow him if you set your mind to it. But I doubt Arkus would accept a change bloodlessly. He's too far gone. Spare yourself from further harm." He looked away, as though something on his side was drawing his attention. "Cass, I don't have much time. If I can ask one thing, if I've earned it, please do what you can for my dragons still in the west. Send them to Val'tarra for safety, if that's possible. Anything you can."

Cassandra opened her mouth but caught herself. What dragons remained had been herded into the empty city barracks with the army gone. Getting them out wouldn't be easy, but Darnuir didn't need to know that.

"I'll do everything I can."

"Thank you," Darnuir said. He'd half turned to leave when he paused and turned back. "It's not right that this is how things end. I wanted to make a better world. Perhaps if I knew then what I do now... perhaps if I'd just been better the first time... I hope something good can still rise from this. Though it may be down to you who are left to do it."

"What does that mean?" Cassandra said.

Darnuir smiled. "Goodbye, Cass."

Before she could say anything more, the orb began to swirl, Darnuir's face dissolved and only white mist remained.

Alone in the throne room, Cassandra considered her options. There weren't many, in truth. Do nothing and await Arkus, or leave. And of the two, there was only one choice she could reasonably make. Arkus had gone beyond the point of redemption; he'd gone beyond her very worst fears. Brevia had always felt a little cold, but her budding family had been warm. Now the city and its people chilled her bones. She would leave Brevia, and she'd take the dragons with her.

She paced along the platform, thinking on the matter. Had it been her alone, it would be a simple affair. Taking thousands of weakened dragons with her was quite another. Getting through one of the city gates would be nearly impossible without meeting firm resistance. She needed Oranna, and Clachonn, and she needed their plans put into action to secure the city gates.

These thoughts propelled her to the queen's chambers and powered her knocks upon the door.

"Oranna? Oranna, please let me in. We have to speak."

The door swung inwards, but it was not the queen who greeted her.

"This isn't a good time," Clachonn said.

Cassandra stormed in regardless. "I have news from the east. Terrible news. We have to go. We have to pa—" The word died in her throat. Four great trunks already lay opened and half filled; wardrobe doors were flung open, their contents gutted. Oranna herself was clumsily folding a blue satin dress, not even registering Cassandra was there. Her eyes were webbed in bloodshot lines.

"What's this?" Cassandra said sharply, though it was clear what was going on.

"Keep your tone civil," Clachonn said. "Oranna is still your queen."

"A queen that's running away."

Oranna at last rounded on her. "And had you let me run before, when I wanted to, my son would still be alive." Her voice was hoarse and hard. "There's nothing left for me in this wretched city. You were just about to suggest we all run now that it's convenient for you, so I won't apologise for it." She glared for a moment, then softened. "I'm sorry. I've tried being angry at everyone, but it doesn't help. Not really. I was going to tell you, I swear."

Cassandra wanted to believe her, so decided to put aside any doubt for now. "We just need to get moving."

"We?" Clachonn said, as though he'd never heard of the word. "And why are you so desperate to leave?"

She told them. Told them everything that Darnuir had said, and what she suspected he was holding back in order to spare them. There wasn't much to say in the end and it only ignited the fire in Oranna to move faster.

"Father, we can have Merrick and his men take control of the city gates as planned. We could leave tonight."

"And the dragons?" Cassandra said.

Clachonn hesitated, rocking on the balls of his feet. "Very well, they can come. I can't in good conscious let them all get slaughtered like cattle. But Arkus will surely know where they've gone."

"We just have to make it harder for him to track them down," Cassandra said. "It's all we can do."

"Agreed," said Clachonn.

"Then I'll meet you both later tonight," Cassandra said. The Lord of the Hinterlands frowned, then opened his mouth to speak, but Oranna cut across him.

"Of course we will. Tonight. We're *all* leaving tonight."

39

THREE BLADES

"One blade for the king to watch over their bodies. One blade for the guardian to watch over their souls. One blade for a champion for when his brothers have lost their way."

From *Tiviar's Histories*

Blaine – Aurisha – The Basilica of Light

It was unmistakable. Under the dome, stuck fast into the stone holder before the seared sun of Dwl'or, was the Champion's Blade.

Blaine couldn't help but stare in amazement at it. Why was it here? It had never simply sat in the Basilica before. It had always been a myth, a legend; yet here it was. Had Darnuir freed it from Rectar's grasp and returned it here, or had it been placed?

What could it mean?

Gingerly, he reached a hand towards it. He half expected it not to be real, perhaps some apparition of his ancient mind. It came as something of a shock when his finger touched the cold metal of the pommel, so much so that he flinched as though burned. It was real, then. The metal, the cloth on the grip, the bone-metal-starium fusion of the blade itself, glittering under a strip of light from the dome above. It was only the light that seemed unreal. The thin beam hadn't moved with the passing of the day. The night before, when Blaine had arrived, there had been a pale sliver of moonlight illuminating it. He'd thought it just fortuitous timing then, but now, he was not certain.

"What do you have in store for us?" he said aloud, then faced each relief of the gods in turn. No answer came, as ever.

"Blaine, are you coming?" Fidelm's voice rang through the temple.

He turned to see the fairy waiting for him in the middle of the hall. Darnuir had called a meeting, and Blaine had gotten distracted by the blade. And yet, it was just as well he had this chance to speak with Fidelm alone. Perhaps the gods would give him this much.

"The others will be waiting," Fidelm called.

"A moment or two will not hurt," Blaine said. "You've avoided me for so long. I know you resent me for what I've done to her, but would you do one last service in her name?"

Fidelm's wings flickered.

"Please?"

Fidelm flew up the hall to Blaine's side, landing hard. "Pick your words carefully. You are no longer the guardian, and all that shields you is her will."

"Would you really kill me?"

"If you gave me cause."

"Such as wishing to journey back to the Argent Tree?"

Fidelm drew his war spear, each end whistling as it cut the air. "Is that your wish?"

"No. Kasselle made it clear I should not return, and I would be a fool to think things have changed. I do not intend to return." Fidelm narrowed his eyes and Blaine saw the hate in them. "Will you kill me anyway, General?"

"And what would that achieve? I know she loved you, Blaine. I understand that better than anyone." For the first time, Blaine saw Fidelm's outward demeanour falter. His hands shook, but he lowered his weapon. "What is this task you would ask of me?"

Blaine inclined his head in thanks, then pulled up the silver chain which had hung for many months around his neck.

"Please take this back to her," Blaine said. "It was Kasselle's idea, if I recall. She had it forged with the skill of your people, and it was supposed to let a piece of Arlandra be with her own beloved while he was away at war. I think its magic may have been all too real, and why Arlandra all but died when Drenthir did. But there is a small piece of her left in it. I can feel it. Take it back to her mother and let her feel it too."

His hand still shaking, Fidelm opened his palm to receive it. Blaine struggled for a moment, squeezing the necklace in his fist, hearing Arlandra's song-like laugh again, seeing the swish of her silver hair in his mind, smelling the citrus scent of water lilies in her room.

In the end, he let go. The last of his memories fell from his grasp into the hand of another, and he felt free.

Fidelm placed the chain around his own neck. "I will do this for you, Blaine, and for my queen."

"Thank you. I shall remain here by Darnuir's side until whatever end comes for us." And feeling no more words were required, Blaine swept past, heading for the plaza and then the Royal Tower, with Fidelm following silently in his wake.

Once they ascended the tower, they joined Lira, Grigayne and Darnuir himself in the war room to sit for the grimmest of all their councils. They all sat on one side of the crescent moon table; Darnuir was on the other. Not wanting to favour either of his roles by choosing a chair, Darnuir had employed his incredible new strength and lifted both the solid rock chairs of the king and the guardian, moving them both aside, choosing to stand before them instead.

"I do not mean for this council to be lengthy," Darnuir said. "There is precious little time and even fewer options open to us. I hope you don't mind my lack of debate, but I've made my mind up and I feel it's the best course we can take. How like Draconess I sound now." He paused, staring off vacantly into the past for a moment before continuing. "I have spoken with Grigayne, and his fleet will sail as soon as it's ready."

"We'll stand with you if you wish it," Grigayne said, thumping his fist upon the table.

"I'm grateful for it," Darnuir said. "But I don't want to see either the islanders or the fairies caught up in this vendetta."

"We would have stood by you too, until the end," said Fidelm. "This treachery runs deeper than the blackest roots."

Darnuir shook his head. "If I wanted to, I could kill my way to Arkus and slay him. Then I could kill and kill and kill, but what would that achieve? What fragile friendship existed between our races was fraying these past months. Now it's utterly severed. More war won't solve it."

"So we are to flee?" Lira asked.

"In a manner of speaking," said Darnuir.

All the attendees exchanged looks.

Blaine leant forward on the table. "Wherever we flee to, Arkus will only follow in time. The world is not so large."

"It's dragons he wants," Darnuir said. "And I don't intend he'll take any more of our people, not those I can help at least. We will leave, to somewhere Arkus cannot reach. You must trust me on this."

Blaine exchanged further glances with those along his side of the table. They all nodded, Blaine included. The boy had done it after all. He'd killed a god. The power he held now must grant him sight beyond what any mere mortal – dragon, human, or otherwise – could see.

Blaine rose. "My faith has wavered of late, and for good reason. Yet now I do believe again. I believe in you, Darnuir."

Darnuir's soft smile conveyed thanks in a way that words could not.

"The fairies are welcome aboard my ships," said Grigayne. "We'll sail first to Dalridia, then a smaller fleet will travel west with your people. They'll take you down past the southern cape and up to Val'tarra. Fewer ships should easily outspeed anything Arkus sends, though I may need to ask that your people house and feed my own until they are ready to return. It will be a long journey for them through unfamiliar waters."

"It will be done," Fidelm said. "I fear our peoples will rely on each other in the years ahead against Arkus."

Grigayne sucked in his breath. "Let's hope we do have years ahead left, and many of them."

"What of the dragons?" Blaine asked.

"For now, let them take what rest they can," said Darnuir. "If I'm right, we'll need to be able to bring them all through the plaza and quickly. Lira, can I leave this task with you?"

Lira agreed.

"Then it is settled," Darnuir said.

"If I may remain behind?" Blaine said. "I have something to ask you. Privately."

"Very well."

The others trooped out, Fidelm opting to take flight from the balcony instead. Once they were alone, Darnuir was the first to speak.

"I know what you're about to ask me. The Champion's Blade."

"Do you know why it's in the Basilica?"

"I have a... feeling as to why," Darnuir said. "I'm afraid I cannot give you certainty. It's hard to explain." He made a move towards the balcony as well, and beckoned Blaine to follow.

Outside, the world seemed so harmonious, with a crystal-clear sky and just the right strength of breeze. Blaine took a moment to glance down at the Lower City. The destruction looked even worse from up here, seeing it all at once.

"Terrible, isn't it?" Darnuir said, following Blaine's line of vision. "A shame we must leave Aurisha in such a sorry state. A gem reduced to rough-hewn rock and rubble."

"We'll restore it one day," Blaine said. "I always believed that as well."

Darnuir sniffed, then snapped his gaze northwards as though he could see the human army beyond the horizon.

"We won't be coming back, Blaine. Not to fix the city. Not ever."

Blaine uttered stutters of ill-conceived thoughts, but the right words were lost to him. Darnuir could not be being literal.

The king groaned, gripped the balcony with both hands, and sighed. "I never wanted to abandon Aurisha again. The memory of the meeting in which Draconess ordered we evacuate the city comes back to me so plainly. It's why we stood when the red dragons came. But this... this is different. Same city, same overwhelming odds, same decision; but a different king, a different council and a different means of escape. Strange, isn't it?"

Blaine still didn't understand what Darnuir intended, but he trusted him, and right now his grandson needed encouragement, not derision or pointless questions.

"Do you remember our time in the Hall of Memories?"

"Of course."

"I mentioned that events often repeat themselves. Once you look far enough back, you can see it. This is something like that, I suppose. This city is our home, and so long as we have enemies, we will be threatened here."

"It won't be our home for much longer."

"I'd fight to the end."

"I know you would," Darnuir said. "I know you all would. But I don't want to fight anymore. Deep down, I don't think you do either."

Blaine smiled, a weak, old smile. "Not so deep down, I must admit."

"Every day I respect Draconess more," Darnuir said. "I wanted to defend the city against impossible odds back then and he decided otherwise. I hated him for it. But he was right. Well, now I learn from his example. We're leaving, Blaine."

A flicker of worry crept up Blaine's spine. Just what was Darnuir planning to do without Grigayne's ships? Yet, as though he could read Blaine's thoughts, Darnuir took him by the arm and said, "Come. We'll discover soon if my feelings are correct. Let's pay a visit to the Basilica."

Darnuir – The Basilica of Light

He'd been worried that he'd merely imagined the sensations he'd felt in the Basilica when he had arrived back in the city. As he and Blaine climbed the stairs to the cavernous temple, those worries were thankfully laid to rest. His mind was once again filled with a warmth and an understanding that he could not explain in words. There was a tug on his mind pulling him towards the stone holders and the Champion's Blade, but he knew he shouldn't try to pull it free.

A curious beam of light still fell upon the Champion's Blade, exactly as it had when Darnuir had first arrived back. The sense of knowing without truly understanding grew in him; a melody played lightly over and over in his mind.

Darnuir drew up between the two empty stone holders, smiling as the warmth inside him let him know that all would be well; this was what he was meant to do.

Blaine's mouth fell open as realisation dawned on him. "Why are you so sure?"

"Because I believe the gods are guiding me."

"They never have before," Blaine said, with hurt in his voice. They never guided him before, he meant.

"I'm not sure that was out of neglect," Darnuir said. "Since gaining the Guardian's Blade, I've felt their presence more. At Kar'drun it was greatest, but the Cascade is also strongest at Kar'drun. It's the largest of the great mountains, after all. That's why Rectar chose there in the first place, perhaps because it was the only place where magic was strong enough to fuel him and his plans. Aurisha sits on the ruins of a Principal Mountain and so its magic is far weaker. At Kar'drun I heard the voices of the gods, as you must have on the Nail Head. Yet now I hear nothing. But they can reach out to me in other ways because of the blades; because I am, like Brackendon was in Brevia, a conduit in an otherwise barren land."

"You worked this out alone?" Blaine asked.

Darnuir gently shook his head. "I just know." He took hold of both blades and drew them in a single combined flourish, holding them over the stone holders. "You may want to step away. I have no idea what will happen."

Once Blaine was safely away, Darnuir drew in a breath. He held it and let the music in his mind reassure him. Then he plunged the Dragon's Blade and the Guardian's Blade down into the empty stone holders; the former before Dwna and the latter before N'weer.

For a while, nothing happened.

Then he began to feel it. The Cascade in its full glory, magic beyond comprehension, a world's worth of power flowing in great currents towards Aurisha. A third door appeared in his mind, but he could not touch it. Nor could he reach for the other two. Instead, all three paths to the Cascade merged into one grand gateway, its opulent door covered in a language he did not understand. He could not touch this doorway either, yet it opened all the same, and beyond it the Cascade was not bubbling blue, but as smooth and golden as honey.

In the physical world, Darnuir's body went taut, his hands held fast onto the blades as though welded on by a smith. Golden strands wove around his hands, then his arms, and soon his whole body. Orange strands followed, yellow, amber, and every shade of autumn leaves, bands of light moving like quicksilver to form at a point just beyond the Champion's Blade.

Where the light and power met, a pool began to form. It swirled and spiralled, like a Cascade Sink but far more beautiful, and golden as a wheat field on a summer's eve. Once formed it rose to twice the height of a man, extended wide enough that three could stand shoulder to shoulder inside it, and seemed to stretch forth like a well-lit road offering safety through the darkness.

Out of the corner of his eye, Darnuir saw Blaine tentatively edge forwards. "What is this?"

"A portal."

"To where?"

"Beyond," Darnuir said simply.

The song that had filled his mind began to fill the real world, amplifying under the dome of the Basilica. Its sound was so pure that no mortal mind could have crafted it, no living throat could have sung it or plucked it on a crude string.

"Now's the time to find your faith again, Blaine."

Blaine looked upon the portal, his face struck with concern. "What about you?"

Darnuir glanced to the blades on either side of him. "I fear if I let go, the portal will collapse. I must stay until the end. No, Blaine," he said, cutting the old dragon off before he could protest. "This is how it must be. Go now, summon our people. They must leave, and we have precious time."

40

A KNIGHT AT HEART

"Rise above the politics of the realm. You are the arm, you are the sword, you are the shield. Let other sons become the poisoned knives."

From *Nobles & Their Steeds: A Chevalier's Compendium*

Cassandra – The Gates of Brevia

The night was warm, the city quiet, the ranks of dragons shuffling out through the city gates quieter still. Ironically, their plan to secure the city was also useful in escaping from it. Lord Clachonn's loyal chevaliers and hunters had little trouble in taking control of the gatehouse late at night, and all without a drop of blood being shed. Julian the dragon had been sent to gather his people from the city barracks, and what few soldiers there were had not felt like resisting. How Julian had been able to communicate what he was up to was still a mystery to her, but here the dragons were, marching meekly past them out of the city gates. She wondered if they knew where they were going. Or if they even cared. She pulled the hood of her cloak up, not to fight off a chill, but to try and avoid their hollow stares as they walked by.

Another hooded figure approached her, though she knew this was the queen.

"All has gone as well as we could have hoped for," Oranna said. "Time to go, then?"

"Has Olive arrived?" Cassandra glanced about, even though it would be futile with so many people around. Olive was to bring Cullen down, though she had been late in meeting them in the palace grounds.

"I assume so," Oranna said.

"You assume? We can't just assume on this."

"We also can't tarry," Oranna said. She grabbed Cassandra's hand.

Cassandra wrested free of the grip. "I'm not leaving without them."

"Not everyone wants to anger their king," Oranna said. "Perhaps she's had cold feet."

"But Cullen—"

"Is not your responsibility."

Cassandra scowled and Oranna seemed to sense she wasn't going to convince her.

"We have to go." She made another attempt to pull Cassandra away, but she resisted.

"I'm going back for him. You go on. I'll catch up." She ignored Oranna's pleas as she began to run. There was no way she was leaving Cullen in Arkus' hands to grow up as twisted as he'd become. With her nerves on edge, she barely noticed the journey back, nor the stairs up to the royal chambers. Cullen's door lay open.

"Olive?" Cassandra called before even rounding the doorframe. "Olive, come on. We're going now, and—" Her breath stuck in her throat. Gellick Esselmont was standing behind the crib and was pointing a pistol right at her.

"Hello, Princess," he said in a hushed voice. He raised a finger to his mouth. "Quiet now, the little prince is sleeping."

Olive lay spread-eagled on the floor at his feet, her face covered with a wild tangle of her hair.

"Is she—"

"She's alive. I only knocked her out."

Cassandra stifled a snort of anger. He'd gone too far this time, the pompous prick. Furious, she reached for a sword she didn't have. That angered her more, and she stifled a squeal of annoyance.

"What do you think you're doing?"

Gellick was breathing hard, sweat gathering at his hairline. His injured shoulder still caused him an imbalance, forcing him to lean on the crib. Perhaps he wasn't in his right mind? As well as the sling on one arm, he looked a mess, his eyes two sleepless chasms.

"All I can do in service to my king," he said. "I cannot stop you all from leaving the city. I'd be a fool to try it. We have too few men left here and Clachonn had more in his service than we anticipated. But I can stop you taking the baby." Both he and Cassandra looked momentarily to Cullen. He continued to sleep peacefully, unaware of the instrument of death pointing at his aunt.

"Why are you doing this?"

"My sister could still marry Cullen instead; she'd just have to wait a while longer, that's all. Father would be happy enough with that."

"You're not seriously going to shoot me to achieve that, are you?" She fought to keep her voice calm, her tone confident, but inside she was a fearful wreck. She didn't think Gellick, Arkus' most loyal man, would shoot his king's daughter. But his finger might slip. Or he might have snapped enough to do it anyway. The world had turned mad enough for such things to happen.

"Not unless you force me to," Gellick said. His arm shook and he winced in pain. That didn't fill Cassandra with confidence.

"Put the gun down, Gellick." She took a tentative step forward.

"Stop right there," he said. He cocked the hammer of the pistol. "You shouldn't be so sure of yourself. Killing you would give Arkus no choice but to name Cullen his heir, so it would work out better for my family were I to do it."

"And when Arkus finds out it was you who killed me?"

"There are no witnesses."

"So go on then," Cassandra spat. "What's stopping you?"

Gellick's lip curled up into a sneer. "I know you think I'm some brute, carrying out your father's orders, but that doesn't mean I relish death. Oh, don't give me that look," he said in answer to Cassandra's scowl. "If you're referring to Boreac, then he was a self-confessed traitor. And the dragons? They attacked the city. Ravaged the Rag Run. I was there. I saw it. I couldn't just let them escape afterwards. No," he said sharply. "No, I did what was right."

Cassandra took a bold step forward. She wasn't leaving the only blood relation that didn't make her feel sick behind. A dozen insults sprang to mind but she held her tongue. There was no point in provoking him.

"Did you ever question any of it?"

"Never."

She raised an eyebrow. "And what if he ordered you to murder in cold blood? Kill the innocent? Even children?"

"He's never given such an order."

"You won't have heard what's happened in the east. Arkus is killing the dragons. All of them. He's going to wipe them off the face of the world." She let the news hang in the air for a moment. "What do you make of that?"

Gellick did his best to remain stony-faced, but she saw it; a moment of torment flashed in his eyes. "I'm sure those beasts deserved it."

"Darnuir, their king, defeated Rectar, at great cost I suspect, only to have Arkus betray him. Is that deserved?"

"They ate humans during the riots, Cassandra."

"They saved the world."

"I told you to stop," Gellick said. "Don't come any closer. I mean it."

Cassandra had crept towards the side of Cullen's crib, close enough that she might make it to Gellick in a few lunges if she dared. He kept the pistol trained on her, the barrel a black eye of death following her every movement.

She swallowed fresh nerves and risked pressing him further. "Do you wish you were out there now? Helping?"

Gellick's cheek twitched. "I told you, I don't relish it. Their legionnaires would be one thing, but their children too?" He glanced down at Cullen. Cassandra chanced another inch forward. "Thane was bad enough," he said, not looking up. "And there were so many Thanes in the streets that day. I never want to see a dead child again. No, stop," he snapped, registering Cassandra's movements. He fully extended his arm, thrusting the pistol out as far as he could reach. "Damn it, Princess. Don't force me."

"No one forces you to do anything."

"Maybe he doesn't make you do things," Gellick said. "You don't see the side of him that I do."

"I do, Gellick. I do," Cassandra said. As she spoke, she took two more steps, emerging around the crib on the same side as him. "Arkus is a broken man. I've seen that. Felt that. Does he threaten you?"

"No," Gellick said, sounding shaken. "Not directly. But my family is the last to stand unharmed. All the others have fallen. Only the Clachonns are safe because of the queen."

"You think getting your sister betrothed to Cullen will spare your family?"

"It worked while she was betrothed to Thane," Gellick said. He took a step forward to close the gap between them. The barrel touched her brow.

Cassandra froze. Shut her eyes. Her breath came in heavily through her nose, her fists clenched, her whole body tightened. Her heart was about to explode. Yet, through it all, a defiant part of her rose and she rose with it, straightening to her full height, pressing back against the gun.

She forced her jaw to work. "Do it, then."

Gellick did nothing. Said nothing. A tremble ran from her forehead as the pistol began to shake.

"Put it down," Cassandra said. Her voice was high, close to tears. "Too many horrible things have happened already. Wouldn't you want a chance to escape all of this? Don't condemn a baby to live with a monster. Let me go. Let me take him away."

Gellick made a choked sound but still nothing more. The pistol pushed harder against her and she felt a tear roll down her cheek, into her mouth. It was warm and salty, and it might be the last thing she ever tasted.

"You're right," Gellick said.

The pressure on her brow lifted. Her muscles unwound, and she sighed in relief.

When Cassandra opened her eyes, she saw Gellick was handing the gun to her. "I have no right to ask a favour of you, but if it looked like there was a struggle, and I at least tried to stop you, it might help."

Cassandra took the pistol, holding it by the barrel like a hammer. The weight in her hand felt good. She'd always pictured a moment like this, yet now it came it didn't feel anything like she'd imagined. It wasn't the same when you were on the same side.

"You've done the right thing, Gellick. I won't forget it." Then she cracked him across the face with the butt of the gun. He spun away, hit his head on the nearby wall and crumpled to the floor. He was still breathing but he did not stir.

A smear of blood, like a red rain, streaked across the painting of the sweet fairy family and their baby acorn.

Her shoulder rang from the impact of the blow. She dropped the gun, and her breath came in shuddering heaves. If it hadn't been for Cullen, she wouldn't have risked that.

The commotion had finally woken Cullen up and he announced his displeasure to the world. Cassandra dove for her nephew, trying to calm him, but to no avail. The sight of the two bodies on the ground distressed him; a new experience he did not greet with laughter.

Cassandra waited until he was settled before she contemplated moving. She didn't want to wake up any more of the palace if she could help it. She looked about for Cullen's bag, which Olive should have had with her. It lay across the room from Olive, perhaps tossed wildly in some struggle. Cassandra bent delicately for it with one arm, keeping Cullen upright in the other, though he was getting heavy for that now.

With the baby's bag strapped over one shoulder, she guessed she should go. But what about Olive? She couldn't just leave her.

A muffled sound of heavy greaves on carpet came from the corridor.

Cass ducked low for the pistol. There was still a loaded shot in it if need be.

The boots clunked into the room and Cassandra sprang up, pointing the gun at the doorway.

"Merrick," she gasped, relieved to see him. Julian bounced in behind, his jovial smile vanishing when his eyes fell upon the bodies.

"Oranna wanted to wait for you," Merrick said, "But Lord Clachonn insisted they had to go. We volunteered to come back." He looked to Gellick apprehensively.

"I just knocked him out," Cassandra said.

Merrick stepped to Gellick's side, placed two fingers on his neck. He stood back up and gave the body a firm kick.

"Just to check," he said.

Julian sniggered.

"Let's just go," Cassandra said. "Julian, can you carry Olive?"

Julian gave a nod and a mock salute then scooped Olive up as easily as a bundle of rags.

They got on their way, and with every barrier they passed Cassandra felt like more weight had been lifted from her; through the palace gates, ushered quickly through the broken city gates, past the boundaries of the former dragon camps, until they joined the slow-moving train of people beating a path northwards through dark country.

She had no intention of ever returning to Brevia.

41

ALL THINGS END

"My body wanes and soon I shall leave for N'weer's embrace. My king feigns sorrow, my successor toes the line. No matter. I have left behind the means to reinstate our might. Dragons will prevail. The Shadow shall fade."

Personal writings of the Guardian Norbanus

Darnuir – The Basilica of Light

Out of fear of losing the connection, Darnuir had stood firmly in place for two days. This pure form of magic was more than enough to sustain him. How it would affect him once he let go... well, it didn't matter.

Lira and Blaine stood ahead near the portal's entrance, directing and observing their people through it. Dragon after dragon traipsed into the spiralling light, vanishing as though they were sinking beneath an impenetrable ocean. Outrunners had entered the portal carrying Damien's body, and Darnuir hoped a more fitting resting place awaited him on the other side. The dragons marched in twos, nice and orderly; he had commanded there to be no rush that would risk trampling the elderly or weak. There was still time until Arkus would arrive, or at least there had been when they began.

Lira suddenly frowned at something behind Darnuir. Not able to turn around and face the long nave of the Basilica, he was unable to see who was approaching, though from the speed of their feet, it must be an outrunner.

"Bring your message to me," Darnuir called.

The outrunner arrived, looking shaken. "The humans are on the horizon. They will be here before day's end."

Darnuir nodded, glad that he hadn't let the outrunner proclaim his message to all and cause a panic. He caught Blaine's eye and his grandfather came quietly over.

"Arkus will arrive by the end of the day," Darnuir told him. "I don't want a stampede, but we must pick up the pace." Blaine nodded and moved off to spread the word around the former Light Bearers and Praetorians. It was only a temporary solution. Once the humans marched into sight from the plateau, there would be little he could do to prevent fear from rising. He just hoped enough of his people would make it through before then.

He didn't want this strange peace to end so soon, either. Having this purer magic beat through him, as if it came from his own heart, was more soothing than anything he'd felt before. As the melody infused him, he felt as though no wrong could be done.

Before long, Grigayne Imar appeared before him, red faced and breathless. "Arkus will be upon the city soon. The last of my ships must leave now. Anyone else who wishes to come is welcome." He looked around expectantly. No one moved. "So be it. I await Raymond and then we'll g—"

A clatter of hooves announced Raymond's arrival up the hall. He appeared in seconds within Darnuir's line of sight, Bruce neighing appreciatively at being in service again. Grigayne opened his mouth to greet Raymond, yet the chevalier rode right on past, reining his horse in before Lira and almost tripping himself up in his haste to dismount

Raymond dropped to one knee before Lira, a nervous look in his eye. He presented her with a wooden doll that Darnuir had never seen before.

Lira gasped, taking it and holding it close to her chest. "I'd nearly forgotten. Thank you."

Raymond struggled for words. He gulped, then took her hand. "Stay in this world. Do not leave, I beg it."

"I—" Lira began but Raymond was rambling on.

"I know Darnuir is your king and you must all do as he insists, but please, deny him this one thing. The world will be darker without your race and my own world will be darker should you go. Stay here. If not for me," and his voice trembled now, "If not for me, stay for your mother. She's still west somewhere, I'm sure of it. We can find her together. You're young. You still have a life you can lead and a reason to—"

Lira threw up a hand, biting her lip. She looked at him intently, as though he were the only person in the world. Darnuir could imagine the battle waging behind her eyes: to stay behind with those she loved, or walk into the unknown? Put that way, it didn't seem like much of a choice, and from the smile now spreading across her face, Lira agreed.

"Yes," she said.

Raymond nearly fell over again as he scrambled to his feet. "Yes?" he croaked. "You will?"

Lira kissed him.

"Yes, I'll stay."

"Sorry to interrupt," Grigayne said. "But we really must go." Then in a softer tone he added, "Captain Cayn can officiate things for you on the voyage west, if you like?" Raymond and Lira's cheeks turned so red they might have been branded. Grigayne threw Darnuir a wink.

Darnuir watched Raymond and Lira standing hand in hand, grinning stupidly at each other, and his own heart soared. Here was a glimmer of hope that he had not been mad to dream, that he had not utterly failed. It was all Arkus. He'd turned down a path without thought of returning, and that was all on him. It could have been so different. Perhaps it still could be.

"You'd better go," Darnuir said. "And anyone else who desires to remain in this world may do so. I give you free rein." Some dragons did join Lira, mostly the younger Praetorians who might have had family in the west like her, or who did not feel the need to pass beyond, unlike the older dragons, worn and weary of a battle-scarred life.

Raymond got back upon Bruce and the great warhorse whinnied, rearing onto its hind legs as though saluting the dragons marching past. Lira and those leaving with her gathered beside Raymond, and then, with a final encouraging nod from Darnuir, they set off. Grigayne swept away too, giving a bow as he did so.

Blaine appeared to be taking the distraction as an opportunity to say farewell to Chelos, and Darnuir jerked his head to bring the wizened dragon over. He'd almost forgotten.

"Am I to leave with the humans?" Chelos asked quietly.

"No," Darnuir said. "Sending you west will likely be your death, and I meant it when I said I wished no more of that for dragons. You may join our people through the portal, though you do not deserve it."

Chelos visibly fought back tears. He gulped and found his voice. "Thank you, my king."

"It isn't fair that you should escape some justice," Darnuir said. "But who knows what awaits us on the other side? Perhaps these gods will judge you for themselves."

Chelos shuffled off, and with a final hug from Blaine, the old steward of the Royal Tower stepped into the golden light and disappeared.

And so it was just Darnuir and Blaine left to watch over the last of the dragons in Aurisha. And as the day turned to a crimson sunset, and distant cannons began to boom, Darnuir stood his ground. At some point Blaine had moved to be by his side, though he could not say when that had occurred. They'd stood in silence too, for what more was there to say?

His heightened senses picked up humans shouting from the lower city, then the switchback road; thousands of feet pounding the city streets, reverberating through the plateau. Thankfully, the last dragons were entering the portal.

"You should go too," Darnuir said to Blaine. "You've earned rest."

"Is that what we'll find?"

"I dearly hope so."

"And you'll follow?" Blaine said.

Darnuir nodded, yet doubt spiked inside him, cutting even through the satisfying haze brought on by the perfect processing of the Cascade. There might still be dragons in the Highlands, those he had sent with Garon and Ochnic on their mission. Could he abandon them? They did not have the choice to leave or stay, and what sort of world was he giving them? As guardian, his duty was over. As king, he arguably had work to do.

Blaine seemed to sense his dilemma. "I think you have earned rest as well." He stepped closer and embraced Darnuir. "Whatever you choose, it will be the right choice. And I will have been privileged to have known you. Thank you, Darnuir, for helping me find peace after I'd despaired for more than a lifetime."

Darnuir had no words. He felt like Blaine could be right.

Not so distantly, he heard humans entering the plaza.

Blaine took a few good breaths to stir himself, then finally turned and walked towards the spiralling light, his head held high.

And Darnuir was left alone.

His heart beat in rhythm with the boots of human soldiers. He had a choice to make, but really, he'd made it already, hadn't he? He didn't want to fight, and staying behind would mean more fighting. Blood was bound to spill whatever he did. As guardian he'd banished the Shadow, yet as king he'd failed to lead his people to a better future. Perhaps, for those who had stepped beyond, things would be better now. He'd like a respite as well, and if he could, find out who he was under all the deaths and memories and burdens.

The humans were running now, heading straight for the Basilica.

Quite steady, Darnuir released his grip first from the Guardian's Blade, and then the Dragon's Blade.

A clank reached him. A hundred flintlocks being primed.

The spiralling portal was already ebbing.

Darnuir closed his eyes, and without seeing, without knowing what would happen, he leapt through the air towards it.

42

ALWAYS, DER IS HOPE

"At the end of every era we find the seeds of the next."

From Tiviar's Histories

Cassandra – The Hinterlands – Tuath

Purple outlines of Highland mountains sat against a blazing northern sky, every cloud reflecting the dying embers of a warm spring day. Cassandra stopped to drink in the view, huffing from their strenuous march. Already the smell of pine drifted down from the Highlands. It was fresh and clean, and precisely what she desired from this part of the world.

Another new beginning.

A keen-eyed dragon at the head of their ragged column came back with reports of hunters coming down the road ahead. Cassandra and Oranna calmed him, sure that it would be Romalla's men.

For once, their hopes were not dashed. Romalla met them on the road with some supplies and fifty hunters to help lighten their loads and escort them to the edge of the town of Tuath.

That night, the dragons, nearly dead on their feet, gained some much-needed rest. Cassandra walked among them, doling out what food there was, her spirits lifted by the sparks of life that had returned to many of the young children's eyes. Their hope was infectious.

As she finished her loop of the new camp, baskets empty, Romalla beckoned her to join her. The Hinterland captain brought her to a private meeting on the banks of the River Dorain. A single table sat under a canvas cover, with half-drunk goblets of shimmer brew. Romalla mentioned she would return shortly and dashed off.

Lord Clachonn was already present, comforting Oranna, who was still not old enough to be beyond crying onto her father's shoulder.

As it transpired, the tears were not all shed for past events.

"I'm sorry," Lord Clachonn told Cassandra. "I simply can't shelter you or your nephew. Having my daughter flee back home in a state of grief is one thing; hiding dragons amongst my towns, my private guards, my keep, is doable; yet I cannot foster the heirs to the human throne without repercussions."

Cassandra's throat went dry. "No one need know who we are." Even as she said it, she knew it was no good.

To his credit, Clachonn looked downcast. "Cullen could perhaps grow up in secret. Possibly. But too many people know you now. If you could be parted from him, then we could take that course."

Cassandra stared at her toes, the fresh buoyancy she'd been feeling of late deflating in a moment. So, she was to abandon what family she had. And she would, if pressed. She'd rather not be parted with either Oranna or Cullen, but if it was the difference for him between a good life or the risk of death on some open road, then it was no choice at all.

"Father," Oranna said hoarsely, emerging from her sobbing. "You promised Cass could stay with us. She left Brevia under that impression."

Clachonn's expression hardened. "I did it in the hope it would spur you to leave. I would have had us leave quietly had she not come to us that day. But I knew you wouldn't go without her then. You are my life, Oranna, and if my honour and word is besmirched in securing your safety from that lunatic then so be it."

"Don't force me to part with something else," Oranna urged.

Clachonn gulped, clearly struggling. "I'm sure... I'm sure Cassandra understands."

Cassandra nodded, fighting hard to rein in her panic and sorrow. Clachonn smiled weakly and took his leave.

Oranna gave a great sniff. "I'm so sorry. We'll figure out what to do for you. Do not worry – do you hear me?" She sounded desperate. Cassandra nodded again, and the queen hugged her tightly. "I'll keep at him," she said, then she too left.

Cassandra stood in a daze. The slap and trickling churn of the river was soothing. If she focused on it and nothing else, then it didn't feel so bad. Whether a minute passed or ten, she didn't know, but tingling pins and needles in her feet compelled her to move.

She drifted to the table, checking if there was still fresh brew available. There was none. She considered the half-drunk goblets then poured the remains into a single cup and threw it back. Cassandra had never drunk cold brew before and understood now why no one else did. Wincing, she felt the little kick hit her and it temporarily blotted out her darkening mood.

Atop the pile of parchment was a sheet of scrawled notes, just a line or two about the numbers of those fleeing from Brevia. The rest of the sheet was blank. The quill sat on the top right corner, dripping ink. It looked remarkably like the Tarquill symbol. With any luck, she'd never have to see one of those pamphlets again. How many would Arkus print off to justify what he'd done? Would he even need to bother justifying it? Would anyone know the truth?

A sudden compulsion came over her. She picked up the quill, dipped it into the inkwell, and wrote:

I'm going to write it down. Everything that's happened.

She knew she didn't know the whole story, but as fairly, as accurately as possible, she'd try her best. Arkus certainly wouldn't tell the truth, so someone ought to. Before she knew it, Cassandra had covered nearly all of the parchment in her rambling thoughts, each word a small release of her anxiety.

She was so enthralled, she had not noticed anyone approaching her, and only looked up when she heard a thud on the damp grass beneath the nearest tree.

"Ochnic?" she gasped. "What are you doing here?" She was sure it was the troll she'd met back in Val'tarra. He had the same white fur jerkin across his torso, the same ice-blue eyes that seemed to pierce right through her, and a leather satchel thrown over his shoulder, although this one was clean and new. The greater difference was the strip of dark red and green tartan, wound from shoulder to waist and pinned at the top with a clump of heather and thistle.

"It is I, Cassandra. Though it is Chieftain Ochnic now. Much has changed."

A thousand questions raced through Cassandra's mind, but all she asked was, "What are you doing here?"

"Romalla, hunter captain, told me der was a meetin'. I ran ahead."

Just then, a squawk came from above and Cassandra found an eagle with white-tipped feathers perched on a thick branch. It flapped its wings enthusiastically and snapped its beak. Relief surged through Cassandra as Kymethra landed and transformed a few paces from Ochnic.

Ochnic jumped back. "A true shifter of shapes. These things have not been seen in da north for many lifetimes."

Kymethra squinted at him. "Ah, it's you. You were at that war council in Val'tarra. Erm..."

"Chieftain Ochnic, of de—"

"Yes, that's it," Kymethra said, turning away from the bowing troll to face Cassandra. "What? You look shocked to see me."

"You came back," Cassandra said. She could hardly believe it.

"The fairies will take good care of Brackers. Besides, this Pel wouldn't stop badgering me; half-dragged me out the Argent Tree." Kymethra smirked then winked at Cassandra's reaction. Cassandra laughed in relief and moved to hug her. Kymethra was taken aback but returned it warmly.

Moments later, a young fairy flyer landed in their little group. She was all lean muscle and energy, with a double-bladed spear upon her back and violet eyes popping in excitement. She held what appeared to be a dirty, silver strip of wood up to Ochnic.

"A silver root," Ochnic said in awe. "Pel, fairy friend, where did you find dis treasure?"

"Val'tarra's full of silver trees, Och. I thought you'd like it."

Ochnic reached out for the root as though it were an injured lamb. "Dey say such roots will take again in the thinnest soil and bear fruit all year."

Pel nodded sagely. "We'll plant it the moment we get back. And with the extra magic in the Highlands, just think of how big it will grow." Pel only then noticed Cassandra was there. "Oh, hello there. Who are you exactly?"

Cassandra was spared answering by yet another arrival. Garon, for she recognised him, emerged at a run from the woods to join them. Upon reaching the group, he bent over double and fought for breath. Ochnic made as though to aid him but Garon raised a finger to ward him off.

"Just... just a moment."

"You push yourself too hard, Garon, Kazzek Friend."

Garon righted himself, though his face was purple as a beetroot. His black beard was thicker now but otherwise he looked much the same. "You know I feel left out when you run off like that, Och. Besides, can't get soft and let Marus beat me when we return."

Pel rolled her eyes. "He's got a maimed leg."

"And he's also a dragon, so that makes it even," Garon said. He too now noticed Cassandra. "Nice to see you again. I hear you're a princess now?"

"Technically," Cassandra said. "But I'm trying to get away from all of that."

"Cosmo's little sister," Garon said. "Who would have thought? Where is he these days, anyway? Out east with Darnuir, I reckon. Guess I have a lot to catch up on?"

Cassandra hesitated. She didn't relish the idea of breaking his heart. "There is much to discuss, yes."

"Well, we'll have plenty of time for that," Garon said.

"We will?" Cassandra asked, now thoroughly dazed by the company she was in. For a moment there she'd forgotten her plight, but she hardly had time for idle chatter if she was to find Cullen and herself a new home.

Garon nudged Ochnic. "Go on, tell her."

Ochnic puffed his furry chest. "We come bearin' news. News from Rohka Chief of Chiefs. Da kazzek will no longer hide from de world. We owe our lives ta others and all are now welcome ta join us in da north."

"Really?" she exclaimed. The Highlands were as far away from Brevia as she could get.

"Really, really," Garon said. "Mission accomplished, I dare say." He raised an eyebrow at what must have seemed her overenthusiasm and looked to Pel and Kymethra as if enquiring about her state of mind.

Cassandra didn't care. Grinning wildly, her cheeks felt flushed and she was nearly in tears from the joy. She had been so afraid of being alone again, but felt foolish to think that Kymethra would leave or Oranna would be so cold. There was hope. There was a lot more hope in her life now.

Ochnic cocked his head quizzically. "Dis pleases you?"

"Yes, Ochnic," she said. "It pleases me very, very much."

43

REGRETS

"The king is the realm. His health is the realm's health; his stability, the people's peace. Guard his body with your sword and guard his mind with your counsel."

From *Nobles & Their Steeds: A Chevalier's Compendium*

Two Months Later
Arkus – Brevia – The Throne Room

The chevaliers had been silent the entire time. Arkus loomed over them, standing on the platform of the throne and they on the marble floor beneath him. Exasperated, tired, Arkus dismissed them. They had their orders.

"Not you, Gellick," he said pointedly.

Gellick took a second before turning back. He didn't make eye contact as he approached the platform again. Once, he'd been the king's close confidant and finest chevalier; now, Arkus glared upon him.

"You have need of me?" Gellick asked.

"Your father has not come to the city as I asked," Arkus said. He pulled out the brief letter he'd received that morning, one which bore the insignia of the Golden

Crescent. "He regrets to inform me that the harvest requires his full attention and has granted you powers as his proxy."

"Lord," Gellick intoned. He bowed and brought a fist over his heart. His movement was stilted and awkward. As he tapped the plate mail covering his chest he winced, then his arm quickly fell back to his side.

"I see your injury still causes you pain," Arkus noted without emotion.

"It improves a little each day."

"Balack is dead. Did anyone tell you that?"

Gellick shook his head.

"Does it please you?"

There it was. The moment of hesitation, the flicker of fear.

"Traitors get what they deserve," Gellick said.

"Traitors..." Arkus hissed the word. His gaze fell upon Gellick's other injury, a scar running from above his left eye to his temple. "You've suffered many ills at the hands of traitors, haven't you?"

Gellick stiffened. "A chevalier knows he may be injured in the line of du—"

"How did it happen?"

"I've already explained it you, Lor—"

"Remind me."

It wouldn't do any good to catch Gellick in the lie. Nothing would be changed by it. Arkus needed the Esselmonts on side. Especially now. Still, there was little advantage in letting Gellick think he'd got away with it completely.

"I was guarding Cullen, as you instructed." Gellick's voice turned wooden as he recited pre-learned lines. "The princess arrived with several men, one of whom must have been a dragon, judging by how hard he hit me. He moved so fast I couldn't get a shot off."

There was a grain of truth in the tale and that was why it was a good one. Were it not for Gellick's change in demeanour and Lord Esselmont's clear snub, Arkus might have believed it.

I know you let them go. I know it in my bones.

"I shall have to ensure your bravery is *rewarded*," Arkus said. Now it was his turn to spin words. "One day we shall retrieve Cullen, and your sister may be betrothed to him as she was to Thane. Things may return to how they were."

It was a lie. Things would never be as they were. Never.

He clung on to the notion of retrieving Cullen, he said the words and outwardly made the plans, but deep down he didn't have the stomach for it.

What's the point anymore?

"May that day come soon," Gellick said. "Reports are still coming in. The princess was certainly with the queen in the Hinterlands but has since vanished. There are no signs of a new infant arriving on any of Clachonn's estates. The princess likely took Cullen with her."

"Do we know where?"

Gellick shook his head. "Those hunters in the region more loyal to the Crown than Clachonn are giving mixed stories. Some say she went to Val'tarra. Some say north. Some say to the Splinters. Some say they do not know."

He prattled on. Arkus only half listened. His mind was starting to spin again, as it had done on and off since he'd returned to the city and learned Cassandra was gone.

She abandoned me.

"—likely we're being fed misinformation—"

He'd known Oranna would go. She'd turned cold long ago, just as Boreac and Annandale had.

They all turned on me. They all left me.

"—Romalla can be replaced as captain but it will take time for the Master Station—"

Tyrant, that's what Cassandra had called him. He'd listened well that night. He had been on the cusp of repealing the Charter as she'd wanted... then everything fell apart.

Thane's blue-grey body haunted him even when he was awake. Oranna's shriek of hatred still rang in his ears; his cheeks stung from the gouges she'd wrought across his face. He could still feel her nails digging into his skin; warm blood running down his cheek.

The dragons had done it. Without their riot it would never have happened.

He could have done better. Should have done better.

He hated the dragons. He hated himself.

His mind spun.

I did what was needed for humanity, he thought.

'You did it for the power,' another part of him thought.

I did it for the family.

'You drove them away. First Brallor, now Cassandra.'

And deep down, that was what tore at him. He knew it was his fault they'd left him.

Gellick was still droning on. Arkus raised a hand. "That's enough... that's enough. We haven't the resources to hunt for her and Cullen for the foreseeable future. The treasury is drained from the war and development of the guns. The garrisons in Aurisha, the divisions we left at Dalridia and those still maintaining a presence in the Dales might break us as it is."

"We are all war-weary," Gellick said. "There is no appetite for fresh conflict. Not now."

"Not now..." Arkus trailed off.

Not now, but someday. One day, they'll come for me. Or I shall strike first. That's how it is now, ever since Geoff and Robert turned their backs on me.

"Might we force Clachonn's hand?" Gellick suggested.

"What?" Arkus said. He shook his head and tried to focus.

"If we demand Lord Clachonn raise fresh levies to aid garrisoning the Splinters and the Dales, some of my father's troops could be freed up to aid in the harvest."

"It's too soon," Arkus said. "Everything teeters on a knife-edge."

Things were precarious; one wrong move and his crown would tumble. He had no heir; at least, no heir under his sway. If Clachonn refused openly it would only embolden others. Somerled was cowed for now, but his son was still at large. Not every island could be manned in force and unless Grigayne was turned in there would be trouble soon. Perhaps he could count on Kasselle to remain at peace; she would not want to risk the damage to her forest he would sow with cannon and powder.

Arkus realised he'd been quiet for a second too long and cleared his throat to excuse the silence. "What plunder we took from Aurisha will be dispersed to the people of Brevia, the Crownlands, the Marshes and the Crescent. Soon we'll grant lands in the east to loyal citizens. It should keep them firmly on side. Tarquill owes me, too. He'll ensure the people hear our side of the story or I'll have his estates seized. Is there no word on his treacherous son yet?"

"No sign of Raymond anywhere," Gellick said. "We are stretched very thin."

"Spare a pair of eyes for the Tarquills regardless," Arkus said.

Gellick inclined his head. He seemed like he wanted nothing more than to leave the throne room and never return, yet he remained, lips twitching in a sign of inner debate over whether to speak.

"Spit it out," Arkus said.

Gellick finally looked him directly in the eye. "What is the story you'll have Tarquill print?"

Arkus narrowed his eyes. "That after the battle was won, Darnuir demanded I cede all human lands to him; that humans would serve as farmhands to fill dragon bellies while we starved. All that magic clearly corrupted his head. Turned him mad. Every soldier there can attest to the true dragons that took to the field – no bullet or shot could penetrate their scales. We would have become slaves. So, I had no choice."

Gellick took a deep breath. "And what really happened?"

So, we are dropping all pretence, are we?

When Arkus next spoke, he was slow. Deliberate.

"I did what was best. For humanity."

Gellick's mouth became a thin line.

"You think me a monster for it?"

"I saw what they did during the riot," Gellick said. "Better than any. I have no love for them, but—"

"But?"

"Their women and children too…" Gellick worked himself up to the crucial question. "Was that necessary?"

Arkus had considered this every day since the Scarlet Fields. Would he have followed through to such a degree?

"As it happened, Gellick, by the time I reached Aurisha, they were all gone."

"Gone?" He sounded as confused as Arkus had been at the time.

"Vanished like smoke in the wind," Arkus said. "Where and how, who knows? Some magic at work. But they were all gone."

Gellick breathed easier, then seemed to remember he still required an answer to his question. His face and voice grew stern again.

"If they had been there, would you have done it?"

Would I have done it?

He remembered the moment on the Scarlet Fields well, the one order he'd never forget giving. His hand had been held high for a long time; his shoulder had begun to ache, his finger to tremble. Very nearly, he hadn't given the signal to fire. Once the shots started, and the barrage began haphazardly, it had seemed too late to turn back.

Weakness had almost stayed his hand, but his rage had driven him through it.

So, in the heat of the moment, yes, he would have hounded them all to the ends of the world. By the time he'd marched his army to Aurisha, he couldn't say; and he'd never know for sure. Faced with the choice now…

"We'll never know, will we?" Arkus said in answer to Gellick. "And as far as the story goes, Tarquill will print that the cowardly dragons fled before me and abandoned their city. As revenge for the crimes committed in Brevia, I levelled their Basilica and Royal Tower."

He had tried to destroy the blades as well. Yet no matter how much powder used, or cannon shot fired, the cursed swords remained steadfast in their stone holders, even as the rock around them was blown asunder. Arkus had buried the swords under the rubble instead, hoping that would be the end of them.

"Leave me now," Arkus said. "I wish to be alone."

Gellick stiffened. "You ought to have guards. Allow me to send—"

"I said leave me!"

Gellick inclined his head without another word. He snapped to attention and then left the hall. As the closing doors echoed, Arkus turned slowly to face his throne.

Though only a few steps away, the journey to it felt like a mile. He'd fought his whole life to keep that throne, to strengthen the meaning of the crown upon his head. A lifetime of toil – and for what?

He stood before the high black seat, feeling his age as he reached out an unsteady hand for the armrest. Slowly, he sat, facing out to no one and nothing but the dark.

Victory was his. Victory.

Tears fell, those he denied others witness to and which carried him to sleep each night.

King Arkus remained upon the throne for some time. Yet the chair was cold. His hall and his heart were empty.

44

A PLACE TO REST

Darnuir - Beyond

It could have been a dream. Darnuir found himself in a glade upon a mountaintop, far too pristine for reality. Despite the altitude, there was no snow up here. The air was warm and calm, the grass thick and green, and alderberry bushes bore clumps of ripe silver fruit. Not a single cloud roamed the sky.

He still wore the armour and clothes he'd jumped through the portal with; only the blades were missing.

And he was not alone.

Standing across the glade was Draconess. Darnuir blinked, but Draconess didn't disappear. This was no apparition. Draconess, if it was truly him, was smiling and standing patiently with his hands behind his back.

Darnuir approached. "Is this real?"

"It is real, although not in a way you could comprehend with mortal senses."

"And where am I?"

"A representation of the great mountain that crumbled into the sea."

Darnuir understood. Aurisha had been built upon the ruins of that mountain. He hesitated before asking his next question. "Are you really—"

"Draconess died long ago. Those who pass the veil of death go on their own journey. We have merely taken his form to speak with you."

"We? You are one of the gods? Or all of them?"

"In a manner of speaking."

Darnuir nodded but was unsure what he wanted to say next. For a moment there, he'd thought this a chance to make amends with his uncle.

"You have wondered whether Draconess would have been happy to know who you have become," the spirit said. "Know that he would have been. You've grown to be everything he prayed for."

The spirit's words conveyed a truth and certainty no mortal could. Upon hearing them, an old, bitter and broken part of Darnuir mended. A final weight lifted from his soul and the regrets of his former life were at last healed.

"What of my dragons?" he asked. "Where are they? Are they safe?"

"Do not worry for them. They have passed beyond already."

"And where is that, exactly?"

"A place for you and your people to rest."

As before, the truth of the spirit's words could not be doubted. Darnuir's heart lightened. He'd been sure the golden portal was the right choice for them, but it was a relief to have it confirmed all the same.

"Why have I remained here in this... place between?"

"We wanted to meet you," Draconess said. "As you are now, before moving on. And to thank you."

Darnuir hung his head. "Spare your thanks. I don't feel so triumphant. Our 'victory' at Kar'drun proved more bitter than sweet."

Draconess raised an eyebrow. "If that is so, why then did you not stay? You could have destroyed Arkus, found the rest of your people, and begun again."

Darnuir narrowed his eyes at the spirit. It was a final test of sorts, it had to be. But one thinly veiled. "I didn't relish the reality of it, but leaving was the lesser of two evils. To stay would have been to slaughter thousands to reach Arkus."

Draconess stood aside, waved one hand, and the air before them swirled and parted to reveal an old man sitting on a high-backed chair. As the vision focused, he saw it was Arkus sitting on his black throne. The hall was empty and Arkus sat like a statue, eyes bloodshot and tears streaming. His skin was grey and drawn, his face closer to a skull than a living soul.

"What if you could return to this very spot you see before you?" Draconess said, alluding to the throne room of Brevia. "No others need die."

"What would that solve?" Darnuir said. "I'd only prove Arkus right. I had to leave. I don't regret it. Raw strength cannot solve every problem, nor should it. The rift between humans and dragons would not end if I toppled one man, not after all that's happened. Such deep sickness cannot be lanced as a cure. I have learned that much from both my lives."

In the vision of the throne room, Arkus hadn't moved a muscle. Fresh tears fell and kept falling; his dead eyes were more phantom-like than the spirit Darnuir now spoke to.

"Consumed by grief and rage," Draconess noted. "We are not without sympathy. It is a hard task to rise above such pain and mend a heart torn asunder. The hardest of all. Yet necessary."

Darnuir tore his gaze away. "Please, no more. My guilt for leaving those dragons behind is already great. I can only imagine they have a terrible road ahead."

"Not as terrible as you might think," Draconess said. "Look again."

Hesitantly, Darnuir did so. The image of Arkus melted away, replaced by a great valley in the mountains, and swiftly descending to ground level. There Darnuir saw people from every race – human, dragon, fairy, even troll – all together. He saw Garon again and his heart leapt at seeing him still alive.

"This is real?" Darnuir asked.

"Of course," said Draconess.

Darnuir watched eagerly. Within Garon's group he recognised the troll Ochnic, although he wore a tartan garment now. A smaller troll – a girl, judging by the length of its hair – came running to Ochnic's arms. A dragon, a legionary legate, limped behind the girl. And then Darnuir saw her. Cassandra. He almost missed her face among the circle surrounding Garon. She held a baby in her arms.

"Cullen?"

"It is," said Draconess.

Darnuir gulped. An old pang for Cosmo echoed through him.

"Your hopes did not burn out at Aurisha or upon the plains before Kar'drun," Draconess said. "That dream is alive and thriving. It was you who planted the seed in their hearts. Garon never forgot it."

"Do you know what will happen to them?"

Draconess shook his head. "Even we cannot see all ends."

Darnuir nodded, unsure how he felt about it. *So much hurt has been done. Can the world truly move on from it?*

"Would you like to return to them?" Draconess asked.

Darnuir gazed at the scene before him. They seemed happy, despite it all. At least for now, the woes of recent times had shifted. He very nearly answered 'yes' but restrained himself.

He wanted rest. The world was no longer his to fight for. It was theirs.

"I'd made up my mind when I took the leap."

Draconess inclined his head again. The swirling air revealing the world below them evaporated, leaving only the glade behind.

"What happens now?" Darnuir asked.

"Your world shall be left to move on alone. You cut the connection of the Shadow yourself, and after this, our own ties shall sever."

Given the endless cycle that had plagued the world until now, Darnuir thought cutting ties with these higher powers could only be a good thing. Yet by the spirit's own admittance, there had been a connection, and they had some influence while it existed.

"You've taken on Draconess' form. Did you not hear his pleas over the years? You never answered his nor Blaine's prayers. Why? Why did you ignore those who believed in you most?"

Draconess frowned. "Do you think we ought to have—" he snapped his fingers "—and done everything Blaine or others like him asked?"

"You allowed suffering to occur. If you could have prevented it—"

Draconess shook his head. "Without suffering, there is no joy. And how could it be possible for us to answer every prayer? Those who pray speak in wishes, desires and dreams, the consequences of which are as open and endless as the number of requests. If every prayer was answered, chaos would reign. What sort of world would that be?"

Darnuir hadn't thought of it that way before. He supposed it wasn't so very different from being a king, having all parties making demands of you; and if you acted it had to be wisely, if you acted at all.

"Perhaps guidance, then?" Darnuir asked. "Advice could have been offered in the darkest of times."

"It was," Draconess said. "We reached out to you as you fought Him under the charred mountain. And when Blaine risked placing the Guardian's Blade into dangerous hands, we reached out to him at the Nail Head. He asked for a sign then, and we provided one."

"I remember the aid you gave me," Darnuir said. "But there were so many other times… it would have been a comfort—"

"It would only have coddled you and all the others. If we guided you every time you were in need, we'd be no better than the parent who will not allow their child to fall and learn to stand back up. As it was, our connection to the world was ever weakening. Reaching out cost us dearly."

"And only through places of great magical power," Darnuir said, hoping to have his theory confirmed. "At the Principal Mountains."

Draconess inclined his head.

So far, so good, although Darnuir couldn't help but wonder if their lack of direct action was merely due to a weak connection rather than some higher moral.

"You doubt us," Draconess said. "You always have."

"I just… find it hard to accept you wouldn't have intervened to stop Rectar. If you could."

Draconess frowned again, and this time he lowered his head. "It was our greatest test not to. He could have ended us."

"Have I earned the right to know what it was all about?" Darnuir asked. "I fought for you, even without knowing it. My people died by the thousands for you. Tell me why."

"You have earned that right." Draconess considered for a moment, looking off into the semi-distance, and then met Darnuir's eye. "Walk with us. The glade is beautiful."

Darnuir walked by Draconess' side, eager to hear the answers.

"There has always been a war between the Shadow and the Light," Draconess said. "The Shadow has often been stronger. Its nature is to dominate, bind, use, and discard. It seeks to corrupt enough worlds to tip the balance in its favour. On your world, we arrived first and charged the dragons to safeguard it. Our great enemy thought to make your world the final battleground. To win there, to spoil your race and assault our realm with our strongest defenders would have been the end. Your victory, Darnuir, not only saved your world but helped to balance the powers of Shadow and Light. All worlds are safer for your deeds."

At these words, Darnuir drew to a halt. It was a lot to take in.

"You placed a lot of hope in me, and in dragons. We very nearly failed."

"Nearly. But you did not."

"I wonder whether too much is placed into 'hope' and 'faith'," Darnuir said. "Good did not always come of it. Blaine and his followers often spoke in chilling words. Faith in you led to terrible action. You must know of Norbanus, of Kroener, and what more recently occurred with Chelos."

He had to know the truth of this. He'd told Chelos he would reserve judgement on these gods without knowing how they felt about his crimes.

Darnuir continued. "These were your most loyal servants, who claimed to follow your teachings. Are you happy with them?"

"Certainly not."

Darnuir was taken aback by the bluntness of the reply.

"Let me guess. To have intervened would have made you no better than the Shadow that seeks to control?"

"Indeed. And it was our own actions which were almost our undoing."

"The Champion's Blade," Darnuir said. "My father found it, and Kroener took it from him. Had you never revealed it to my father... well, who knows what might have happened."

For the first time, a sadness entered Draconess' eyes. "We thought your father would be able to correct Kroener's downfall. The blade worked as intended when we offered it to Dronithir in his fight against Norbanus. However, we were not aware of how much sway Rectar held over him."

"He might have thought himself doing your will," Darnuir said, "if Rectar was whispering to him."

"His mind became unclear to us once Rectar took hold of it. Although to commit murder in our name should have made him realise he was being deceived. To fall so far so easily speaks volumes of who he truly was."

"One of the dragons who passed through the portal committed terrible actions in your name. An old dragon."

"We know of Chelos."

"His actions led to needless deaths."

"And what would you have us do?"

Darnuir considered the matter. He hadn't pronounced death on Chelos; he'd decided upon exile. But the conversation had come to a head now. Darnuir had to push these gods, had to know what they thought upon the matter.

As before, Draconess answered Darnuir's unspoken question. "Chelos requires no more judgement than you gave him. No more than he has given himself. He lost the inner struggle and fell into the Shadow. He carries that shame beyond and will feel it eternally. That is punishment enough – if punishment is truly what you seek."

"I don't want to punish," Darnuir said. And he meant it. "I just had to know if you condoned his actions or not."

"Are you satisfied that we do not?"

Darnuir nodded.

"We are glad to hear it," Draconess said. He inclined his head again, this time with more reverence. "Your opinion matters to us."

"Mine?" Darnuir laughed. "You're the gods."

"We are eternally as we already are and always have been. We cannot be otherwise. You had a choice; you had many choices, and you chose to become the dragon you are now. It could so easily have been otherwise. That is why you are remarkable."

"I'm not so remarkable," Darnuir said quietly. "All my power and I couldn't even save my friend—" He choked thinking on Balack; on Brackendon. On everyone.

Draconess cocked his head to one side, as if examining Darnuir in a new light. "To stand against the Shadow is a battle on all fronts, but the most important fight lies within. This is what we taught your kind when we first came to your world. Regrettably, over time, our teachings were twisted, morphed, and nearly ruined altogether. Dranus, Norbanus, Kroener and Chelos; they were all victims of this forgetfulness. We have found it is the fate of mortals to tarry in this way. Mortals care too much for the external. They forget that the greatest battles lie within. Or perhaps they avoid fighting them because they are the hardest. To lose the inner war is to lose everything."

Draconess stepped closer and grasped Darnuir by the shoulders. Power radiated from this being, more power than Darnuir had felt even while channelling the magic of all three blades.

"This is your victory, Darnuir. You won your inner battle. You became a better man. In doing so you struck a great blow against the Shadow and even freed those enslaved by the enemy. Chelos fell. Norbanus fell long ago. Arkus falls further with each passing day. Even now, here, at the edge of life and the beyond, with the temptation to return laid before you, you made the right choice."

Close up, Darnuir now better studied Draconess' eyes. They mimicked the real Draconess so well, yet Darnuir felt himself being pulled towards them, drawn through an expanse of knowing and time unlike anything in the mortal plane. Blaine's eyes had seemed deep with age. The eyes of Draconess – of this spirit – were timeless.

"What now?" Darnuir asked.

There was nothing else left for him to ask. Nothing left to say, or to do.

Draconess stepped back and held out a hand. "If you're ready, take our hand and join us."

Darnuir flexed his fingers, then took Draconess' hand. At once the glade around them flattened into a sapphire-blue sea. Its glassy surface ran to meet the horizon before it too fell away into an endless nothingness and all became white.

Darnuir closed his eyes as all worldly feeling left him; all pain, all ill, all toil. He felt weightless, free, and heard that beautiful music. A harmony, ever changing yet ever perfect.

At last, here, wherever here was, he could rest. Forever.

EPILOGUE

Green light. There was so much of it. Dukoona wondered what it was, and where he was. He seemed to be moving, though he did not feel air against him. There was no resistance. He just flew along through this blinding green, as he had done before Rectar summoned him.

But this time, he was not alone.

Other spectres appeared beside him, under him, over him; he looked behind and saw that more were following. There was Kidrian to his right, laughing merrily as he flew, his lost limb now restored. To his left, Dukoona saw a spectre both familiar and yet new. It had Sonrid's features, though complete and whole, as they should have been, with a mane of orange flames and a full body, neither hunched nor broken. Sonrid, for that was who it must be, beamed at him as well.

After a time, though how long Dukoona could not reckon, the green light abated. He entered a darkness, deeper and more complete than the caverns of Kar'drun. Was this to be the end of his kind? An eternal blackness for fighting against their creator?

More time passed. It might have been a second, a year, a month, or forever, but light began to flicker again. Tiny specks, like stars against a clouded sky. He thought it might really be stars, thousands of them, growing ever brighter, and between them, smaller lumps that looked like rock, some green, some blue, and some both.

He pivoted and found he swung around weightlessly. Behind him was the deep darkness, the edge of which grew more distant. He swivelled again and saw a pulsing pure light, a strand of its golden brilliance recoiling from the closest blue-green rock. A writhing part of the utter darkness was pulling away as well, leaving it stranded in the middle between the shadow and the light.

He noticed there were many things between the borders of those two forces.

He and his spectres included.

There was no commanding voice this time, no master tethering him or controlling him.

And so, in this void between worlds, where time had no meaning, Dukoona soared: finally, he was free.

The End

AFTERWORD

Thank you, reader, for making it to the end of my trilogy. And yes, this is indeed the end.

There's a story to tell in the ending of this trilogy. After *The Last Guardian* released in March 2018, I received messages from readers asking if there would be a fourth book. Some felt the series was incomplete with too many things left open. At first, this irked me. Not the question, but the idea that I'd messed up. I think any creator would be annoyed to find a portion of their audience dissatisfied. The question is how to deal with that dissatisfaction and those demands.

For a long time, I simply ignored it. I felt the books ended the way I'd always intended and that was that. Yet time apart from the series, much more experience as a writer and watching franchises I love fall victim to inconsistent writing or rushed endings made me stop and self-reflect. A small voice at the back of my mind grew louder and it said the ending to Dragon's Blade could be clarified. This could be done without 'altering' the intention of the ending. As such I returned in 2019 to add two additional chapters onto the ending of book 3.

Hindsight is 20/20 and now those chapters have been written and added to the story, I think they should have always been there. My defence is... well... at the time of finishing book 3 in 2017, the idea that these scenes were required never even crossed my mind, but good writers should always learn and improve on their craft. Being independent I am free to make updates to the story at any time, which has proven a blessing in the case of the final chapters of *The Dragon's Blade*.

The question of a fourth 'Dragon's Blade' book is more complicated to answer. I will never say definitively 'never' as I can't tell what the future holds for my career or what ideas may come to me. However, it has never been a serious consideration to write another book in this world and I shall briefly explain why.

This trilogy was always the story of Darnuir and the dragons. An original blurb idea from when I was much younger read something along the lines of: "This is the story of the dragon kings. The people they loved, the wars they fought and how it led to their ruin." To me, that story, of Darnuir and his dragons; of redemption from a dark past is complete.

Darnuir's departure from the world signaled a choice he made at the end of his character arc. Rather than stay and fight - and win as he surely would with his new power - he chooses to quietly fade instead. To rest. He could have defeated Arkus easily at the end, but it would have been a bloody end, and in doing so he'd only be proving all the worst fears of Arkus and those who fear dragons like him believe. Had this happened, in what way would Darnuir have changed from the hot-blooded man he used to be?

Arkus for his part did not 'win' - far from it in my eyes. He lost everything that mattered to him. And when he returns home, he finds what few bonds he had left severed. All he has is his throne and it's a cold chair with no love. He fell where Darnuir grew.

As for the other characters, I wanted to give strong hints as to the directions they'd head in. Short of giving everyone a happily ever after or death, it's hard to wrap absolutely everything up. I also intended the ending to be bittersweet from the outset, although I hope in the final analysis it feels more sweet than bitter overall.

If I were to return to continue some of these secondary/tertiary threads it would be a very different sort of story with less magic and fantasy than the series previously had. Magic has been pushed out of the world. I don't think fans of *The Dragon's Blade* would enjoy a story like that, not least because I would not enjoy returning to tie up all 'loose ends' when I do not necessarily see them as loose.

As I said above, I'll never say never. But a fourth book is extremely unlikely. I'm sorry if that is disappointing to anyone out there yet I feel it's better to be upfront rather than vaguely promising something that never materializes.

The Dragon's Blade was my very first series. I learned a lot in writing it, and thanks to readers like you giving it and me a chance, I've been able to make being an author my full-time job. That's a true privilege. Now it's over I want to pursue other series, other ideas; build even greater worlds and stories using the experience from this one.

Thank you for following this story and making it all worthwhile. I hope you have enjoyed it. And I hope to see you back again soon for another tall tale, in whatever new world I have to share.

Dwna shine upon you all,
   Michael

Enjoyed Dragon's Blade? Please Leave A Review!

If you enjoyed *The Dragon's Blade*, I'd appreciate it if you took two minutes to write a brief, honest review of the book. Reviews help other people to find my stories and lets Amazon know it's a book worth showing to other readers.

If you'd like just a little more from this world, you can grab The Huntress, a FREE novelette set 700 years prior to the events of the main series. Explore the Second War between dragons and humans through the eyes of Elsie, a lowly huntress from the Cairlav Marshes.

As well as The Huntress, you'll receive another FREE story set in my new *Songs of Chaos* series called *The Last Stand of The Stone Fist*. Just enter your email and join my mailing list here!

https://www.michaelrmiller.co.uk/signup

You can also chat to me and other like minded readers by joining my Discord server here https://discord.gg/C7zEJXgFSc

ALSO BY MICHAEL R. MILLER

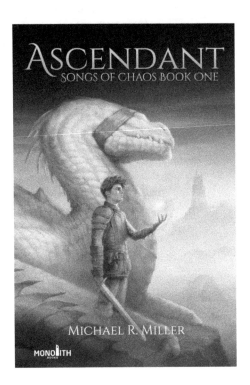

In the mood for a brand new dragon rider epic? I've got you covered with my newest book, *Ascendant (Songs of Chaos Book One)*!

The start of a new dragon rider epic combining the best of Eragon and Pern with the hard magic of Brandon Sanderson and Will Wight.

Holt Cook was never meant to be a dragon rider. He has always served the Order Hall of the Crag dutifully, keeping their kitchen pots clean.

Until he discovers a dark secret: dragons do not tolerate weakness among their kin, killing the young they deem flawed. Moved by pity, Holt defies the Order, rescues a doomed egg and vows to protect the blind dragon within.

But the Scourge is rising. Undead hordes roam the land, spreading the blight and leaving destruction in their wake. The dragon riders are being slaughtered and betrayal lurks in the shadows.

Holt has one chance to survive. He must cultivate the mysterious power of his dragon's magical core. A unique energy which may tip the balance in the battles to come, and prove to the world that a servant is worthy after all.

You can find Ascendant on Amazon in ebook, on Kindle Unlimited, in paperback and on Audible narrated by Peter Kenny.

Book 2, *Unbound*, and book 3, *Defiant*, are out as of summer of 2023 and there will be two more books in the series.

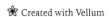